Unintended Consequences

John Ross

Unintended Consequences

Accurate Press
St. Louis, Missouri

Library of Congress Cataloguing in Publication Data
Ross, John, 1957-
　　　Unintended Consequences / John Ross.
　　　　　p.　cm.
　　　ISBN 1-888118-04-0
　　　I.　Title.
PS3568.O84348U55　1995
813 ' .54--dc20　　　　　　　　　　　　　　　95-41174
　　　　　　　　　　　　　　　　　　　　　　　　　　　　CIP

Fifth Printing

0 9 8 7 6 5

Printed in the United States of America

Dedication

This book is dedicated to the three women in my life:

My mother, Lucianna Ross, who taught me by her example that you have to spend on your talent and do what you believe is right;

My wife, Caroline Ross, who urged me to start this project and who believed this book needed to be written;

and

My daughter Lucy, who I hope will have more individual freedom when she becomes an adult than her parents did.

Acknowledgments

I am indebted to a number of people for the help they gave me with this book. Much more than anyone else, Tim Mullin was a constant source of inspiration, not only for his friendship, encouragement, and advice, but also his encyclopedic knowledge of political history.

Dr. Martin Fackler, Greg Jeffery, Neal Knox, James Pate, Joe Tartaro, and Aaron Zelman were invaluable in helping me flesh out the details of several of the real-life events portrayed herein. If any technical errors have crept in, the fault is mine, not theirs.

In alphabetical order, Joe Adams, Colonel Rex Applegate, Dale Blaylock, Dave Cumberland, Richard Davis, Art Freund, John Holmes, John Huffer (Chief AJ), Lee Jurras, Richard Kayser, Arnaldo LaScala, Bob Landies, Kent Lomont, Bruce McArthur, Stokely Meier, Tim Mullin, David Scott-Donelan, Paul Reed, Britt Robinson, Dan Shea, Charlie Steen, Joe Tapscott, Piers Taylor, and Leroy Thompson all provided technical expertise in the areas of shooting competition, aerial shooting, small arms design, close quarter combat, accuracy gunsmithing, load development, body armor, explosives and demolition, investigative techniques, field interrogation, live pigeon competition, African hunting, and desktop publishing. Frank Y. Gladney at the University of Illinois, Urbana, was a great help with appropriate Slavic names.

I would also like to thank the agents of the Bureau of Alcohol, Tobacco, and Firearms, the Federal Bureau of Investigation, and the Secret Service who helped me with sensitive background material but who wish to remain anonymous.

I am indebted to the Olin Corporation for the photos of Ad Topperwein and Herb Parsons on pages 18 and 120, to the American Rifleman for the photo of Ed McGivern on page 123, to Gilbert Early for the photograph of the cape buffalo shot with a 4-bore on page 392, and to Caroline VanStavern Ross for use of the lyrics to "Poopy Diaper Baby." Passages quoted from the *Guinness Book of World Records* and *Gun Week* are used with permission.

Most writers have had a mentor at one time or another. In my case it is Robert Stone that I owe for giving me much-needed criticism when my writing skills were first developing, and Stuart Kaminsky for doing the same thing more recently. Albert Zuckerman at Writer's House, out of sheer kindness, also took time from his hectic schedule to counsel someone he barely knew on how to tackle this ambitious project. Last of all, I would like to thank my publisher, Greg Pugh at Accurate Press, for believing in this book and publishing it.

This is a work of fiction with a story line based on political history and historic precedent. The real-life events that comprise much of the book have been re-created to the best of my ability using as many sources as I could locate. Court documents, news footage, recordings of phone conversations and police radio transmissions, medical records, coroner's reports, FBI reenactment tapes, and sworn testimony of impartial eyewitnesses were all used. In some real-life events described herein, there are conflicting accounts as to what actually happened. In these cases, I have chosen to describe the version that is consistent with the physical evidence and the various laws of nature. To help tell the story, I have at times invented specific thoughts and dialogue and ascribed them to real people. I did this where specific facts were nonexistent or unobtainable, as in the case of people now dead, or where the subjects were not available to be interviewed. The reader should remember that this is a work of fiction.

Alex Neumann, who first appears as a minor figure in one real-life event, is a product of my imagination. So are all members of the Bowman, Mann, Collins, Bedderson,

Caswell, and Johnson families, and virtually everyone in the 'Present Day' section of the book. Real-life figures in this story are used fictitiously.

Finally, for those readers who have no experience with the shooting sports: All of the shooting feats described in this novel are achievable. The more difficult would require roughly the same amount of talent as you would expect of a ten-year-old who was serious about mastering a musical instrument and who had been playing for two or three years. The most difficult accomplishments, in this author's opinion, are some of those achieved by the late Ed McGivern. Anyone interested in accurate speed shooting would do well to read his book *Fast and Fancy Revolver Shooting*, which is once again in print.

Author's Note—A Warning and Disclaimer

A friend in law enforcement told me that because of this book's content, I should not let it be published under my own name. Violent events happen in this story, and our country's current situation is such that these events could indeed come to pass. My friend's fear was that this book might precipitate such violence. He told me to expect to have drugs planted in my car during routine traffic stops, or have other similar miseries befall me and my family. He advised that if I did have this work published, I should use a pseudonym, employ an intermediary for all publisher contact, and in general prevent myself from being linked to the finished work, to avoid reprisals.

I didn't do that, not only because of free speech considerations, but because I disagree with my friend's hypothesis. I believe that if the instigators glimpse what may lie ahead, they will alter their behavior before wholesale violence becomes unavoidable. It is my hope that this book will reduce the likelihood of armed conflict in this country.

History has shown us that government leaders often ignore the fundamental fact that people demand both dignity and freedom. Because of this disregard, these decision-makers then initiate acts that are ultimately self-destructive. To illustrate this point I will remind the reader of the origin of two of modern history's most destructive events, and of all the warning flags that were frantically waving while the instigators rushed headlong towards the abyss.

In the late 19th and very early 20th centuries, European leaders formed two major alliances. Germany, Austria, and Italy comprised one coalition, and Britain, France, and Russia the other. Belgium remained neutral per an 1839 treaty signed by all of these nations except Italy. The smaller European countries became indirectly involved in the two aforementioned alliances. One such example was Serbia, a country Russia had pledged to aid in the event of war between Serbia and Austria. Despite Russia's presence, Austria annexed a large part of Serbia, a province called Bosnia, in 1908.

Few people remain emotionally indifferent when their culture and country are taken over by an aggressor, and the Bosnian Serbs were no exception. Many Bosnians despised the government that had chilled their independence. In spite of this obvious fact, the Austrian leaders sent an archduke to the capital of Bosnia to survey the people Austria now ruled. This archduke was resplendent in full military ceremonial dress, festooned with medals and other military decorations, and accompanied by his elegantly-dressed wife. An objective observer might at this point have said, *"Stripping motivated people of their dignity and rubbing their noses in it is a very bad idea."*

Archduke Ferdinand and his wife arrived in Sarajevo in an open vehicle, and the only protection either of them had was their chauffeur. This man was expected to drive the car and at the same time protect the Archduke and his wife with only a six-shot revolver he carried in an enclosed holster, and no spare ammunition. Our theoretical observer might here have said, *"This is a recipe for disaster."*

Almost as soon as the Archduke and his wife arrived in Sarajevo, a Serbian National tossed a bomb under their car. Its fuse was defective and the bomb did not explode. Here, our observer might have advised, *"A miracle happened. Go home. Now. Immediately."*

Despite this obvious wake-up call, the Royal Couple shrugged off the assassination attempt and continued their tour of the Bosnian capital. Later that same day, a second Serbian National shot them with his .32, killing them both. The Austrian leaders blamed the Serbian government for the assassination and demanded a virtual protectorate over Serbia, issuing Serbia a list of demands. Serbia acceded to all but one of Austria's stipulations. Here, our observer might have said to Austria's leaders, *"Russia has pledged to aid*

Serbia in any war with you, and Russia has both powerful allies and powerful adversaries. Serbia has agreed to almost everything you demanded. Settle, and avoid a world war." Instead, Austria shelled Serbia's capital with artillery fire.

Our observer might here have told Russia's leaders, *"Serbia is not worth starting a world war over,"* but Russia honored its commitment to Serbia and mobilized its army, sending troops to the Russian-Austrian border. Since this left Russia vulnerable to attack from Austria's ally Germany, the Russian Army mobilized against Germany as well.

This forced the German Army to mobilize. Since France was allied with Russia, the Germans feared an attack by France in the west while German troops went east. So Germany decided to invade France immediately, VIA Belgium. Here, our observer might have said, *"Saying this is your 'destiny' is not going to be good enough, Germany. When you invade a neutral country and rape their women and slaughter their livestock and burn their houses, Britain is not going to just look the other way."*

When the Germans invaded Belgium, Britain honored its commitment to defend Belgian neutrality, and declared war on Germany. Every major country in Europe was now at war.

Four years later, over thirty million people were dead, half of them killed directly in the war itself, and the rest so weakened through shortage of food and medicines that they succumbed to the influenza epidemic. In addition to the lives lost, the war's monetary cost in 1918 was almost three hundred billion dollars.

No sooner had the war ended than the victors demanded their pound of flesh at the Treaty of Versailles. The treaty required Germany to accept sole responsibility for causing the war. It dictated that German military leaders were to be tried as war criminals. It prohibited the German army from possessing heavy artillery. It abolished the General Staff and the German air force, and prohibited Germany from producing military aircraft. As in 1914, our observer might have said, *"Stripping motivated people of their dignity and rubbing their noses in it is a very bad idea."* But if such words were in fact uttered, they fell on deaf ears. A humiliated Germany was ripe for the nationalist message of Adolf Hitler, and in this fertile soil were planted the seeds of the Second World War.

Today in America, honest, successful, talented, productive, motivated people are once again being stripped of their freedom and dignity and having their noses rubbed in it. The conflict has been building for over half a century, and once again warning flags are frantically waving while the instigators rush headlong towards the abyss, and their doom.

It is my hope that these people will stop and reverse their course before they reach the point where such reversal is no longer possible.

John Ross
September 1995

Foreword by Timothy Mullin

For those of you who pause to read this introduction before plunging into this book I would like to say a few brief words, perhaps to help you better appreciate the work.

The voyage on which you are about to embark will be an enjoyable one, yet one which is an important trip. This book chronicles an attempt to destroy a culture, and it also gives at least one view of a possible resolution of the issue. I was present when John Ross first started writing this story, and I spent many enjoyable hours reading the initial draft of the material and discussing the story line. I predict you will feel good just reading of the characters and their experiences. Many of them will seem like old friends that you once knew, now perhaps long gone.

This novel tells the tale of a young man growing up with classic American values and living immersed totally in the 'gun culture'. His story is much like that of a Native American who grows up in a society where the rules were simple: 'To ride, shoot straight, and speak the truth', to quote a well-known advertisement. You will find much that is familiar in all of the characters herein and you will no doubt feel at home with them. Others who seek to stamp out this 'gun culture' will be appalled at the valor portrayed here of free men who seek to live their lives unfettered by government chains. So much the worse for them.

Guns are an important element in any truly free society, for a society that does not trust its citizens with individually owned weapons really does not trust its citizens. However, words are also important, and in this book many will no doubt be encouraged to continue the good fight to protect a cultural value that is worth defending vigorously. By making it clear that the attack is not on guns but rather on a cultural group, this story may provide much inspiration to the millions of people who are in that group.

In recent years we have witnessed violent attacks on people in the gun culture. These attacks amount to genocide. It is my hope that this book will cause those who blindly seek to destroy the gun culture to pause for a moment and recognize that their random actions are in error, and to reconsider their evil ways. This could come from an intellectual conversion and a new appreciation of the culture's values. It could also result from a pragmatic concern for the inevitable consequences of continuously attacking a cultural group who wishes to be left alone and whose overriding philosophy is one of freedom. Either way, it doesn't matter. The goal is to stop the attacks and prevent a violent confrontation which could prove harmful for all parties concerned.

Enjoy the book, follow the characters' action, and think of old friends. As you find yourself drawn into the story, remember that to the anti-gun zealots of HCI et al, this book will be like a nightmare penned by Stephen King!

T.J. Mullin is a former Captain in the U.S. Army who has taught police weapons training for more than twenty years. He is the author of Training the Gunfighter, which Elmer Keith said was one of the ten best books ever written on the subject, and the 'Testing the War Weapons' series. The first volume, The 100 Greatest Combat Pistols, is now available from Paladin Press. Mr. Mullin currently practices law in St. Louis, Missouri.

Present Day

It was late afternoon when he finally heard them coming to kill him. The wind was blowing gently towards him, and it carried the sound well. *Two choppers*, he judged from the pitch of the engines, *possibly three*. Henry realized that his first emotion upon hearing the sound of rotor blades approaching was an overwhelming sense of relief. The waiting was over.

His next thought concerned the relatives of the men that were about to die. *The widows will never understand that their husbands died because the government got a little too heavy-handed after June of 1968.* He scanned the sky until he spotted the aircraft approaching from the north.

That isn't quite right. The Kennedy and King killings weren't the first links in the chain that dragged us here. No, the death sentence was handed down before World War II. Henry settled in behind the big Solothurn and checked his field of view through the weapon's optical sight. The gleaming example of Swiss craftsmanship had been manufactured in 1939. The irony was not lost on Henry Bowman.

In March of that year, the U.S. Supreme Court had heard a case involving a moonshiner who had been arrested in 1938. A Federal District Court had thrown out the charges as being unconstitutional, and the government had appealed. At the hearing, something very unusual had happened. Neither the moonshiner nor his lawyer had seen fit to appear before the Court to argue the case. They didn't even bother to file a brief on the moonshiner's behalf. The Court ruled for the government, judicial precedent was set, and the issue was never again heard by the Supreme Court. The 1939 ruling became the foundation on which many additional laws were constructed.

Supreme Court's been ducking that issue ever since Henry thought as he strained to hear a change in the approaching noise. *Well, guys, the tide has turned. It's time you thugs had a little history lesson. I don't suppose you're familiar with what happened in the Warsaw Ghetto in 1943.* A small smile appeared on his lips, as Henry remembered something. *It's just like the story Uncle Max told me when I was a kid. About Billy Dell, pulling a Paul Bunyan.*

Henry Bowman's right hand tightened around the walnut grip of the Solothurn S18-1000. The weapon had been a present from his father, given to him on his fourteenth birthday in 1967. *Cost $189.50 back in the sixties* Henry thought irrelevantly. *I thought that was a steal. Dad's friends thought it was astronomical. Wonder what they'd think now.*

As he followed the progress of the helicopters through the binoculars, Henry Bowman reflected that the 1930's era weapon would now likely cost over ten thousand current dollars to manufacture. It had been made in a time when production methods and philosophies were much different. Fewer than 500 of the obsolete Swiss guns had been imported over a ten-year period in the '50s and '60s, before the law change.

Pay attention here, guy Henry chided himself as he focused on the problem at hand. *You don't get any practice runs with this one.* Henry twisted his head methodically and arched his back as he lay there on his stomach, working the stiffness from his body. He had lain prone for over an hour with his face pressed against a pair of binoculars, and he needed to be loose for what he was going to have to do.

The helicopters appeared over a ridge that Bowman had previously determined was a little more than two miles distant. They were following a heading that would take them to the spot that he had selected, next to the water-filled quarry pit. He steadied the binoculars by resting his right wrist on the top of the Solothurn's receiver and cranked the zoom control from ten power all the way up to twenty. The binoculars amplified the heat waves in the air that are invisible to the naked eye, and called 'mirage' by competition shooters who use high magnification optical sights.

The boiling, shimmering image in the glasses gave a surrealistic appearance to the approaching choppers, but Henry could make them out well enough. *Three of them. Bell turbine model, Jet Ranger or its descendant. A door gunner with a belt-fed machine gun poking out of the right side of each one. Possibly the Belgian MAG-58, but more likely M60s*, he thought with derision.

They should have brought armored Apaches carrying napalm, he thought. *Or nukes*. A grin split his face.

Oh, those poor bastards.

Part One

SEEDS

The sun no longer shows his face, and treason
sows his secret seeds that no man can detect.
Fathers by their children are undone.
Might is right, and justice there is none.

—Walther von der Vogelweide

December 11, 1906

The 2 1/4" pine cube spun in the air, and a cheer went up from the crowd as the wood block bounced in the dirt. There was a grey-ringed hole through the center of it.

"That's the last one, Topp," one of the men said unnecessarily. "Fifty thousand with only four misses. I wouldn't have believed it if I hadn't been here."

The lean, mustachioed rifleman with the broad-brimmed black hat lowered his gun to waist level. It was a Winchester Model 1903, a semiautomatic rifle introduced three years before. It held ten rounds of .22 Auto, a new rimfire cartridge loaded with the recently developed smokeless powder. Ammunition loaded with black powder, such as many existing stocks of .22 Long, would foul autoloading weapons in short order.

The man withdrew the magazine tube from the rifle's buttstock and dumped the five remaining rounds into his hand, then worked the action and ejected the round that was in the chamber. He handed the empty rifle to one of his loaders, who was already holding a second Model 1903.

Adolph Topperwein held the world's long-run record for percentage shooting of aerial targets with a rifle. The rules regarding this sport had been laid out by the exhibition shooter Doc Carver three decades before: Targets were to be wooden cubes or clay balls not more than 2 1/2" across, and were to be thrown vertically twenty to thirty feet in the air by a person standing not less than twenty-five feet from the shooter. Other long-run shooters had shot at 50,000 targets, but they all had missed more often. The previous record-holder had missed 280 targets out of 60,000.

The young thrower bent over and picked up the final block. Instead of tossing it onto the pile with the others, he walked over to Topperwein and handed it to him. Topp reached out gingerly and took it from the boy. His arm and back muscles were screaming in protest from being made to throw rifle to his shoulder once every four seconds, eight straight hours a day, for a full week. It was an effort for him just to remain standing.

Ad Topperwein examined the piece of wood, noting that he had hit it almost dead center, then looked over at the mound of blocks he had shot in the past week. The pile was eight feet high and over thirty feet in diameter. He tried to massage his arm muscles, but his own fingers had no strength.

"Ready for a hot bath and a soft bed?" Ad's wife Plinky asked. "Or can I get you some lunch first?" Plinky Topperwein was also an exhibition shooter for Winchester. The company had hired her after she had set a world trapshooting record in 1904 at the St. Louis World's Fair.

"Not just yet, hon," he said to his wife.

"If it's not too hard for you, Mr. Topperwein, we'd like you to sit on top of the pile of blocks for a picture." This was the San Antonio State Fair's photographer speaking.

Topperwein gave a slight grin. "Sure, I can climb up there. It may take a little longer than normal, that's all." He turned to one of his loaders. "We've got use of the fairgrounds and the assistants paid for another three and a half days, Ed. Seems a shame to waste it." He narrowed his eyes. "Cap Bartlett shot 60,000 back in '89." Topp nodded at the huge pile of wood cubes. "Have the kids go through and pull out the ones that aren't split in two. I want to keep going." His loader's jaw dropped in astonishment.

"And get hold of the Winchester rep. Tell him we're going to need more ammo by tomorrow afternoon. Six cases, just to be on the safe side." He pitched the 50,000th block underhanded onto the pile where it disappeared among the others. "I'm going to take about twenty minutes to cool off these arms and get a sandwich. Let's get going again about one-thirty." He turned to the photographer. "Just before I start shooting again, I'll climb up there for your picture. Pile isn't going to get any bigger. But no awards or any of that stuff. I got a few more good shots in me. Let's see where we end up." He turned and started back towards his trailer, leaving the knot of helpers and spectators standing there speechless.

When the San Antonio fairgrounds closed on December 15, 1906, Ad Topperwein, using three semiauto Winchester 1903 rifles, had shot at 72,500 wooden blocks thrown in the air. He had missed nine. More than a half-century later, another man, employed by Remington, would hit over 100,000. His throwers, however, would stand by his left shoulder and gently toss the blocks straight out along the same path that the bullet would take.

Topp's record, shot under the rules laid out by another man in the 19th century, would never be broken.

In 1906, skilled riflemen were universally admired, and people like Ad and Plinky Topperwein spent much of their time urging young boys and girls to learn gun safety and hone their shooting skills.

The phrase did not exist in 1906 when Topp set his record, for a special term was unnecessary, but years later the fact would be evident: Ad Topperwein and his wife Plinky were part of the gun culture.

May 10, 1918

"Matt, I know I've been dealing with these government people for thirty years, but I tell you I will never get used to it. I had the water-cooled gun finished almost twenty years ago, and offered it to them for next to nothing. They didn't show a lick of interest until *after* our country joined the war. It's not as if they didn't have any advance warning. Germany has a quarter *million* eight millimeter Maxims up and running." A gust of wind threatened to blow John Browning's hat off. He pushed it farther down on his head, then went on.

"What did we have when we entered this war? Less than two hundred of my old air-cooled '95 Colts, a few hundred of those French things, and less than three hundred Colt 1904 Maxim guns. Every one of those weapons is an entirely different design, and not one was originally designed to use the current issue .30 caliber round!"

John Browning knew he was repeating himself, but he couldn't help it. He also knew his brother would let him go on as long as he liked. *I had the Model 1901 water-cooled medium machine gun ready to go almost two decades ago* he thought. *The government showed a complete lack of interest in it.*

What was particularly maddening to John Browning was that he was not some stranger the government had never heard of. Browning was the man who had made the country's first gas-operated machine gun in 1889, had demonstrated for the Navy in 1891 a machine gun which fired 1800 rounds in 3 minutes without a single stoppage, and who had designed the first machine gun ever used by the U.S. military, the Model 1895 Colt 'potato digger' machine gun adopted by the U.S. Army in that year. In 1900, three-quarters of the sporting arms made in the U.S. were Browning designs. With sidearms, it was Browning's Model 1911 .45 automatic that the government had adopted when .38 caliber army revolvers had failed to stop the crazed Moro warriors during the Philippine insurrections in 1898.

"So last year," John went on, "with the country on the brink of war, the War Department finally realizes that U.S. soldiers armed with handguns and bolt action rifles are going to face hundreds of thousands of Maxim machine guns already in use by the German army." John Browning shook his head. He did not say it, but he was thinking of the great irony of this.

Hiram Maxim, an inventive genius the equal of John Browning, was an American. Maxim, however, had no prior designs which had been adopted by the U.S. Armed forces, and he had taken his inventions to Europe, where their value had been immediately appreciated. Now hundreds of thousands of American soldiers would face these lethally efficient weapons, designed by an American but manufactured by seven German arsenals and issued to German troops.

"I have serious doubts about this idea of 'walking fire'," John said to his brother, "but my gun will do it all right."

"You got it done faster than you said you would, too," Matt said. The U.S. Government had implored John Browning to design an automatic rifle that could be carried by one man and fired with full control 'from the hip' on full automatic. It was the experts' theory that a line of soldiers equipped with such weapons could sweep an area clean. Browning had obliged with the 17-pound Browning Automatic Rifle whose design had been finalized three short months after the government's initial request.

John and his brother Matt were now on their way from New Haven to the

Winchester firing facility on the waterfront bordering Long Island Sound. The Browning Automatic Rifle, or BAR, was just now going into production, and the inventor had been asked to be present at an official demonstration for military observers. As the two men walked towards the firing range, John Browning continued the largely one-sided conversation with his brother.

"Now that they've finally got the gun into production, just about in time for the end of the war, they want us up here to watch them shoot it. What use *that's* going to do, I have *no* idea."

Despite his grousing, John Browning loved military demonstrations of his designs, and was secretly glad to be going to another one. His weapons always delivered more than the authorities expected. At the official demonstration of the Browning Model 1917 watercooled belt-fed machine gun in May of that year, the weapon had digested 40,000 rounds of ammunition without missing a beat. It had finally succumbed to the malfunction most common to John Browning's designs: it ran out of ammo.

"I wish to heaven the BAR could have been in our soldiers' hands this time last year. I looked at that French Chauchat they've been trying to make do with. It's a disaster. I'd be afraid to fire it."

"Val says in the 79th, they plug the bore and fire them with a string to blow them up, so no one will use them in combat." Matt Browning was referring to his nephew, John's son, who was currently stationed in France. The family received letters from him regularly.

"Let's hope Uncle Sam sends the first batch of BARs to his division."

"They ought to, with the deal you agreed to." John Browning had sold the rights to the BAR for $750,000 outright. Under standard military contract terms, Browning would have ultimately received twenty times that amount in royalties. The first shipment of BARs would, however, go to Val Browning's division, the 79th, in July of 1918.

"Don't begrudge them our agreement, Matt. I'm sixty-two years old. I wouldn't live long enough to see much more in royalties than they already gave me. And as for the family, the royalties for the auto shotgun will pull more from the civilian market than my children could spend in a dozen lifetimes."

"I think you're right about that." Matt Browning smiled at the memory of his brother's refusal to sell the patent for the Auto-5 outright. Up until 1902, every Browning design had been sold for cash to either Winchester or the U.S. Government. Because of John Browning, Winchester had a lock on the sporting arms market.

With the auto shotgun, John had demanded a royalty contract, and Winchester had refused. It was one of the costliest mistakes that company would ever make. Fabrique Nationale in Belgium had agreed to Browning's terms, starting a mutually profitable relationship that would endure until the designer's death in 1926 at the age of seventy-one. In 1918, FN was producing the Auto-5 shotgun and several Browning-designed automatic pocket pistols. The firm would come to manufacture John Browning's Superposed shotgun, his 14-shot 9mm P35 Hi-Power pistol, a fine pump action .22 rifle, and eventually several refinements of the BAR that the inventor and his brother were about to see demonstrated.

"So what do they have planned for this little get-together?" Matt asked his older sibling.

"Undoubtedly the standard routine. Reliability demonstration, show of controllability, ease of handling." John said these words without rancor. Although such events had become commonplace, it still pleased the inventor a great deal to see in operation the weapons he had designed. "I'd also be amazed if they don't have some guy who's been practicing blindfolded stripping and reassembling the thing. Ever since I showed them that trick they've been talking about it. I think the Army's apt to make it part of their training with all their weapons."

John Browning was right about the blindfold demonstration and about the coming decision to make it a part of basic training. He was right about reliability and controllability being the standard elements of the exhibition. Browning was asked to be part of the demonstration, as had been his custom with earlier sessions involving other Browning designs. This, as always, pleased the inventor.

What John Browning did not know was that the people in charge had prepared an additional element as part of the afternoon's coming activities.

***

"Gentlemen," the Winchester representative said to the spectators assembled near the shore of the Atlantic Ocean, "you have all seen the reliability, power, and controllability of the new Browning Automatic Rifle. It gives the infantryman effectiveness he has heretofore only dreamed about. Production is underway, and in a matter of weeks the first shipments of these guns will be in the hands of some of our troops." He paused to let this information sink in before continuing.

"Many of you may assume that this weapon is of necessity much more cumbersome to handle than the Krag or Springfield, and that as a machine rifle, is of little use firing single shots. That is not true, as you will now see." As the Winchester rep said the words, John Browning watched a slender man of about forty-five with a mustache step up to the firing line. Strong gusts of wind were blowing in from offshore, and the man removed his hat and laid it on the table, weighting down the brim with two loaded magazines.

"This is Ad Topperwein, who works for us. He's going to give a little demonstration of just how manageable this rifle is on single fire. I'll let him tell you what he's going to do." The factory rep stepped aside and took a seat. Topperwein held up some steel discs for the audience to see, and then addressed the crowd.

"It's very windy today, and we need a target that won't blow around so much. The fellows in the machine shop had some inch-and-a-half steel rod, and I asked them to chuck it up in the lathe and cut off some quarter-inch thick sections." He held one of the steel discs edgewise for the audience to view. "They shouldn't move around too much in the wind," he explained.

"What's this fellow think he's going to do with them?" John Browning whispered to his brother. "Shoot them out of the air with a seventeen-pound machine rifle that fires from an open bolt?"

It soon became apparent that that was *exactly* what Ad Topperwein intended to do. The audience watched with rapt attention as an assistant took a stack of the heavy steel discs and stepped seven or eight paces away from Topperwein towards the ocean. Topp picked up one of the BARs that had just been used in the endurance demonstration, pulled back the bolt, and inserted a loaded twenty-round magazine. He held the weapon at waist level.

"All twenty face-on. Throw the next one as soon as you hear the shot," Topperwein instructed his thrower. The man nodded and tossed the first disc twenty feet into the air, spinning it like a phonograph record so that it did not tumble. Topp threw the BAR to his shoulder and the gun fired as the disc neared the apex of its ascent. Immediately the thrower sent another disc aloft.

In less than thirty seconds Topp had fired twenty shots. The audience had strained to watch the discs move or to hear the impact of the bullets on them. It appeared that some of them had wobbled, but the muzzle blast of the weapon drowned out any noise of bullet impacting steel.

"I think he hit a couple of them," Browning said to his brother with genuine admiration in his voice. At sixty-two, John Browning averaged over ninety-five percent at trap, and he could not imagine hitting a single one of the steel discs using a machine rifle firing from an open bolt.

The audience watched the thrower walk around and pick up the twenty steel discs that lay on the ground. When he brought them over to the group for their inspection, John Browning drew his breath in abruptly.

All twenty discs had 3/8" holes in them, very near the center in each case. The metal had flowed back in a lip around the circumference of each hole, as is typical when a high velocity bullet meets mild steel, and each hole was washed with silvery metal from the cupro-nickel jacket of the .30 caliber bullet.

"The current issue round is a 172-grain bullet, but I'm shooting up some old stock with the 150-grain slug. What the soldiers are getting now is much better at long range, but the 150 is faster up close, and it's a lot faster than the old Krag load," Topp explained. "It goes through quarter-inch mild steel without giving much notice." He removed the empty magazine from the gun and replaced it with a full one. "Put 'em all up again, same way, only edgewise this time," he instructed his thrower. "Stand a couple steps closer—this gets a little harder."

The man scaled the first disc upwards with its edge to Topperwein and the crowd, and Topp threw the BAR to his shoulder. This time when the gun fired, the blast was followed by a howling noise as the disc was driven spinning far out over the ocean. The thrower immediately scaled the next one into the air with identical results. In a short time, eighteen of the steel discs had been sent screaming out over the water, hit on the edge by a one-third ounce bullet traveling at over twice the speed of sound. Topp had missed two of the targets. He put the BAR back on the table and went to pick up the two discs he had missed. Ad Topperwein examined them, then turned to the awestruck crowd.

"I don't have much experience with machine guns," he allowed, "but the BAR is one of the smoothest-operating rifles I've ever fired. I think all of us should thank Mr. Browning here, not only for this superb rifle, but for all of the fine weapons he's put in the hands of our servicemen."

John Browning said nothing. He was still thinking about what he had just witnessed. John Browning was also part of the gun culture.

April 18, 1919

Back home at last the twenty-year-old soldier thought with a smile as he stretched his arms and legs. Lieutenant Cameron Wilcox Bowman listened as the brakes squealed and the train slowed to a crawl. A blast of steam was released from the boiler, and the locomotive slowly pulled the railroad cars into the station in Kansas City.

"Cam!" his brother Michael yelled in greeting from the platform.

"Hey, I didn't even recognize you! Lord, is that grey hair you're getting?" the soldier said as he stepped onto the platform and looked his brother over. "Now how did that happen?" Mike was ten years older than his brother Cam. He was *not* getting grey hair.

"How's the baby?" was the next thing Cameron asked. Mike's wife had given birth to a son just before the United States had entered the war. Cam suddenly looked horrified. "Flu didn't get him, did it?"

"No, we missed *that,* thank God. But he's not much of a baby any more—he's almost two years old and running around everywhere. Wait 'til you see him. You're going to just die."

***

"What on earth do you have in here?" Michael Bowman demanded. They had located Cam's bags and were muscling them out of the freight section.

"Oh, I brought you back a few things," the lieutenant said.

"Like what?—the anchor from your troop ship? This thing weighs a ton."

"Picked up some guns and brought 'em back with me. Jerries didn't need 'em any more. Brought you a Luger. Also got a .45 auto I'd like you to have. Not many of the troops got 'em in time, but my unit was led by the son of the guy designed it, so I got one. Got a BAR, too, if you can believe that. Thought maybe they'd squawk when I stuck it in my bag, 'cause they're so new. Figured I'd give it up if anyone asked. Nobody said a word, though."

"Lord, they better not have," Michael said immediately. "You earned it, I'd say. Now what's in here?" He judged that the bag must have weighed a hundred pounds.

"Got a Maxim and a Schwarzlose in that one," Cam answered. He glanced around the station platform. "Let's see if we can find a wagon, or a cart, or something."

Michael Bowman grinned and shook his head. "It's not too far to the truck. C'mon, we got lots of time."

At train stations all across the country, similar scenes were being played out as servicemen happily returned home. Most of them, like Cam Bowman, brought both domestic and foreign ordnance back with them in their belongings.

U.S. service weapons were technically considered government property, but at the end of the war, many soldiers felt they had earned the right to keep the arms they had carried through the mud while bullets flew around them. Few combat veterans in positions of authority disagreed with this attitude.

In addition to issue arms, virtually every soldier who had served overseas had, like Cam Bowman, brought home captured foreign weapons. Mauser and Luger semiautomatic pistols were universally admired for their workmanship, accuracy, and rapid delivery of shots. They also had detachable shoulder stocks the German craftsmen had designed for them so that they could be converted into short, light, medium-range carbines. It was a rare doughboy who had returned to the States without at least one of these handsome weapons in his duffel bag.

The stock for the Mauser pistol doubled as the weapon's holster. The one Bowman had liberated had been peppered with the same shrapnel that had killed its former owner. The stock was perforated in three places, and the magazine well of the gun itself had a dime-sized gouge in it. Looking at the gun was a reminder of what often happened to soldiers in combat.

Mauser bolt action rifles were quite common war trophies, and a few soldiers even brought back the huge 45-pound .56-caliber Mauser antitank rifle to impress the folks back home. Cam Bowman had had one of the massive weapons, but had lost it in a shipboard poker game on the voyage home.

Most highly prized of all (though sometimes awkward to transport) were the fully automatic machine guns brought back from France and Germany. The little nine-pound German MP-18 Schmeisser that was wrapped in Cam Bowman's trousers inside his duffel bag fired the same 9mm pistol cartridge as the UZI and Heckler & Koch submachine guns that would be used by the U.S. Secret Service half a century later. These later arms, however, would be made of steel stampings and molded plastic, and would not exhibit the fine finish or machining of the 1918 weapon.

The German Maxim and Austrian Schwarzlose that Cam Bowman had liberated were large belt-fed watercooled machine guns fired from bipod and tripod, respectively. The Maxim was the better of the two, and this was evidenced by the fact that Hiram Maxim's basic 1884 design would still be in use by major world powers such as Great Britain up until 1962.

As the Bowman brothers lugged the heavy cases out to their vehicle, other soldiers from the train poked through the piles of baggage to find their own belongings. Almost every serviceman's bag contained at least one war trophy that the young man intended to hang over the mantle, shoot on weekends, or give to a friend.

Of the hundreds of thousands of soldiers returning home, not one of them could have imagined that in the future, citizens like themselves would be judged unfit to possess the very arms they had used to defend their country.

July 16, 1932

"Take it from me, this is the greatest demonstration of Americanism we've ever had. Pure Americanism—willing to take this beating as you've taken it, stand right steady...you keep every law! And why in the hell shouldn't you? Who in the hell has done all the bleeding for this country, and this law, and this Constitution anyhow, but you fellows?"

General Smedley Butler, United States Marine Corps (retired) ripped his fist through the air to emphasize his last point and paused to take a breath before continuing. A roar of applause from several thousand men split the hot summer afternoon, and Cam Bowman felt the hair on his arms stand up. General Butler's words were lifting Bowman's spirits in a way he would not have thought possible twelve hours earlier.

The slender, sinewy, retired officer stared out at the fourteen thousand veterans of the Great War and prepared to continue. He had an angular, hawklike face and everyone except those in the very back could see the burning intensity in the man's eyes as he spoke. Butler wore rumpled civilian clothing: twill trousers with suspenders, a colorful tie, and a white dress shirt with the sleeves halfway rolled up. His bushy eyebrows danced as he went on with his speech.

"But don't, *don't* take a step back! Remember that as soon as you haul down your camp flag here and clear out of this thing—every one of you clears out—this evaporates in thin air. And all this struggle will have been no good."

All around him, Cam Bowman could see veterans nodding at the General's words. He found he was standing straight, as if at attention. *I've come a thousand miles and camped here on the mud flats for over almost two months* he told himself. *I'm not going to give up yet.*

Cameron Wilcox Bowman was a veteran, and like all U.S. veterans of the Great War, he had been promised a bonus by the U.S. Government. The bonus was one dollar for every day of active service in the U.S. during the war, and $1.50 for every day of service overseas, payable in 1945. The total payment due in that year was over three billion dollars.

1932 had been the worst year yet of the Great Depression, and many veterans realized they might well be dead by 1945. The situation was especially grim for those from farming communities. The typical farm in the first part of the century was 160 acres, which, not coincidentally, was the amount of land allotted by the Homestead Act of 1862. These farms, for the most part, were self-sufficient and produced a modest surplus that their owners sold.

In the late 1920's, however, many farmers began assuming large amounts of debt from ill-advised expansion, and the disastrous Smoot-Hawley Tariff Act of 1930 brought U.S. tariffs to an all-time high. Soaring debt and plummeting demand for what they produced was a devastating combination for farmers, and the situation was exacerbated by the drought that swept the midwest. Thousands of farms were driven into bankruptcy, and starvation loomed for many families.

In the spring, a young veteran from Oregon, Walter H. Waters, had led a group of 300 veterans across the country to peacefully assemble in Washington. There, the 'Bonus Expeditionary Force', as they called themselves, hoped to persuade Congress to authorize immediate payment of the bonus money that they so desperately needed.

Cam Bowman had lost his farm in Missouri the previous year. He had joined

Waters' group and been among the first two thousand veterans to arrive in the Nation's capital. The veterans had set up living quarters in several abandoned buildings on Pennsylvania Avenue, but as hundreds of World War veterans poured into the capital daily, much more space was needed.

In response, Washington police cleared a patch of ground on the mud flats near the town of Anacostia, on the other side of the Anacostia River from the city of Washington. The location suited the Administration, for the veterans were separated from the city by the river, and any who wanted to assemble in the city had to cross the bridge and complete a substantial march first.

It was here that Cam Bowman and other veterans camped in makeshift dwellings made of cardboard, sheet tin, and scrap lumber. By mid-June, over ten thousand veterans were living on the flats in what would become the nation's largest and most famous 'Hooverville'. In addition to these men were several hundred wives and children that had come with them.

On June 15, 1932, the House of Representatives voted to authorize early payment of the veterans' bonus. Two days later the Senate took up the bill and overwhelmingly killed it. The Bonus Marchers were stunned.

In the weeks that ensued, veterans continued to pour in from around the country and the ranks of the Bonus Marchers swelled to over 20,000 veterans. Legislators left the capitol and otherwise ducked the issue. Senator Connally's proposal to pay the veterans the present value of their 1945 bonus lost 11-4. Senator Thomas (of Oklahoma, whose constituents were especially destitute) proposed that monies be paid early to those veterans who could present proof of 'absolute want'. Thomas' motion met with a similar fate. In mid-July, Congress adjourned without any further action on the issue. The Bonus Army stayed, hoping for a miracle.

There were three remarkable things about the Bonus Army's 20,000-person assembly on the Anacostia flats. The first was that while Washington, D.C. and each branch of the Armed Forces were themselves strictly segregated, the Bonus Army was not. White and Negro veterans and their families lived side-by-side in makeshift hovels on the flats, and *The New York Times* published an article entitled 'The Bonuseers Ban Jim Crow'.

The second remarkable thing was that the veterans in the Bonus Army, by universal agreement, were completely unarmed. No member of the Bonus Expeditionary Force had brought anything more lethal than a penknife to Washington. This was not for lack of ability. Virtually every veteran, after the end of the war, owned at least one military-issue firearm, and most, like Cam Bowman, owned several, including machine guns. Some had sold their guns, but war trophies were worth next to nothing when people needed every dollar for food. Most of the veterans' weapons sat in attics of friends and relatives who were still able to make mortgage payments, and the array of armament that the veterans did not bring to D.C. was startling.

The third remarkable thing was that no legislator had proposed the obvious solution, which would have solved the problem without increasing the government's financial obligation by a single dollar or altering its schedule of payments in any way.

Now, in spite of the adjournment, General Butler was urging the veterans to keep the faith and stay camped on the flats. Cam Bowman looked at the other men around him. *I guess Butler thinks maybe a miracle will happen* he thought. *I've come this far. I'll see it through to the end.*

Cam Bowman did not know that the government had its own agenda concerning the Bonus Army. Cam Bowman had less than three weeks left to live.

July 28, 1932

Jesus Christ, they're coming to kill us all thought Cam Bowman as shouts of alarm rose throughout the group. The veterans had been silently shuffling around the Capitol in what had come to be known as the 'Death March'. It was an eerie thing to watch.

Earlier, soldiers had thrown tear gas canisters at the bonus marchers. The veterans, who were destitute but had not forgotten their training, easily tossed them back. Tear gas was nothing for a soldier to get excited about. What was coming next was another matter. When the veterans saw what was approaching them now, many were wrenched back into the horror they had experienced fifteen years before.

Advancing towards the unarmed marchers were scores of soldiers equipped with gas masks, and carrying rifles at port arms with bayonets fixed. Behind the foot soldiers rode cavalry soldiers with sabers drawn. Behind the horse soldiers rolled a number of Whippet tanks.

It was the tanks that did it. Some of the Bonus Marchers who had been inspired by General Butler's words, and who had stood firm even after Congress had adjourned, now turned and ran. They ran out of the Capital, heading for the bridge that crossed the Anacostia River and the safety of the camp.

Lieutenant Cameron Wilcox Bowman stood his ground and waited as the cavalry approached. A mounted soldier singled him out, and Bowman stared him straight in the eye as the soldier, ten years his junior, drew back his saber. Bowman refused to believe that this man, a fellow officer in the United States Army, was going to kill him. He was determined not to flinch, no matter what the horse soldier did. As the blade of the saber sliced through the air, however, Lieutenant Bowman's instincts overrode his brain, and he reflexively threw his left arm up to prevent the blade from decapitating him.

The soldiers had been instructed by their commander to clear the Bonus Marchers out of the area by striking them with the flats of their sabers' blades, not the cutting edge, and this is what the cavalryman did. It was like being struck by a three-foot steel bar, and Lieutenant Cameron Bowman's left wrist was shattered like kindling. He did not cry out or fall down, but when Bowman saw the soldier prepare to deliver a second blow, he finally accepted his fate and gave ground.

As he made his way towards the bridge, his ruined wrist beginning to scream in agony, Bowman saw three men leading the Army troops, and he was stunned by what he saw. He did not recognize the two Army Majors who would both later come to prominence. The man in charge of leading the infantrymen, cavalry, and tank division, however, was impossible to miss.

The lesser-ranked officers were Major George S. Patton and Major Dwight D. Eisenhower. The senior officer was the Chief of Staff of the United States Armed Forces: General Douglas MacArthur.

***

Cam Bowman huddled on his filthy blanket. His body was drenched in sweat. He had wrapped a dirty scrap of cloth around his damaged wrist, but one of the bones was poking through the skin, and the rag was soaked with blood. All around him people were running, and he wasn't always sure if the screams he was hearing were those of others, or if they were his own.

It was almost midnight, and though he knew he was delirious, the screaming intensified and there was a distinct smell. *It isn't my imagination. Tear gas, of course, but also...oh, no. Wood smoke.* He squeezed his eyes shut and willed it to be May again, willed it to be a dream, willed this all to be anything but the true horror that he knew was coming.

"Oh, Sweet Jesus," Lieutenant Cameron Bowman softly said aloud. His voice was a cracked whisper of utter despair. "General MacArthur's burning us out."

May 10, 1936

"Are you sure this is *really* what you want, Zofia?" The middle-aged woman's eyes showed great sadness as she looked at her middle daughter. "An American? I am sure he is a fine man, but you cannot speak a word of English! And to go live in New York..." Her voice trailed off and she squeezed her hands together, ignoring the arthritis in her fingers.

"You had no such fears when I went to London, Mother. English is the language of that country as well, and I will learn it in time. I was fine in London. Does it surprise you so that I would meet my future husband there?"

"But an *American,* Zofia," her mother pleaded. "And he is four years younger than you. To live in New York, where there are so many other..." she searched for the gentlest phrase, and finally said "...American women..." and trailed off without elaborating further. The sound of defeat was plain in her voice.

Her daughter jumped to her feet. "You think I won't be good enough for him? You think he must be crazy to want to marry an old Polish woman, and in a little while he will come to his senses and run off with an American girl who deserves him? Is *that* what you think?"

Zofia Szczupak's nostrils were flared and her voice shook with outrage. She was practically screaming, and it was because her mother had touched on the one thing that absolutely terrified the young woman. Why had Maxwell Collins asked her to marry him? Was it on impulse? Would he soon regret it? These questions had kept her awake for long hours every night since his proposal three weeks before.

Zofia was twenty-seven, which was hardly dried up, but she was definitely older than most single women she knew. When Max had noticed her and asked her to dance that first night in the London nightclub, she realized he was the most exciting man she had ever seen in her entire life. His presence was absolutely overwhelming to both men and women. She had made him understand that she did not speak English. He had nodded, then through her friend Kirsten who was fluent in both languages, he had told her that in one week he would be able to speak Polish. And he had! From the moment he had said 'Is this good enough, or should I go back to the book before I ask you out again?' in her native tongue, she had been smitten.

And she knew, though she tried not to think about it, that she was not the first woman who had ever been smitten by this man, and would not be the last. She was, however, the one he had asked to marry him. She was not going to turn that chance down. She took a deep breath before she spoke again. When she did, her tone was soft and understanding.

"I know you are worried, Mother. I understand that. I am sorry that you fear what may happen to us. But I think you know that my mind is made up. Will you not give both of us your love and blessing, and wish us well?"

The older woman's eyes filled with tears. "Of course I will, *Kochanie.* How could I do anything else?" She embraced her daughter and pulled the girl's face close to her own. "Go with God."

Magda Szczupak had been sitting quietly in the corner of the room as her older sister and her mother talked of the pending marriage. At seventeen, Magda was the baby of the family, and she was absolutely thrilled at her mother's final acceptance of her older sister's romance with the American.

The teenager's excitement was not because of a special bond she shared with her older sibling, for the ten-year age difference had prevented them from being together to any great extent as Magda had grown up. Her excitement was also not because of any romantic ideas she might have conjured up about a man she had never met. Magda Szczupak had something much larger at stake here, and of considerably more personal interest. Magda Szczupak had a boyfriend, and she had not yet told her mother about him. He was not Polish, he was German, and she had met him two months before in Danzig.

Irwin Mann, at nineteen, was the handsomest, kindest, most thrilling young man that Magda had ever met, and she was sure that she would marry him. Magda jumped up and ran over to kiss her sister. Zofia thought it was in congratulation of her coming wedding. In reality, it was the little sister thanking Zofia for breaking the ground for her own startling news than would arrive in due time.

In several weeks, Zofia Szczupak would sail for New York, and would soon be living in a small apartment with her new husband. She would spend the rest of her long life in the United States. Her own fears, and those of her mother, would prove to be well-founded. Max Collins was a decent man, and the fact that his wife was Polish and would never speak English terribly well would not be the cause of Zofia's heartache. The problem, as Zofia had feared, was that people were drawn to Max Collins, and when those people happened to be women, he responded to them, and his getting married did not change that fact.

Magda Szczupak would marry Irwin Mann the following year, and help him operate a small grocery store in Danzig. Irwin would remain utterly devoted to his wife, and she to him. Throughout her life, Zofia Szczupak would always wish that her own marriage could have been more like she envisioned her little sister's. Yet in later years, Zofia Szczupak would also never forget that Maxwell Collins gave her something that ultimately was worth more than everything else that the rest of her family possessed: Max had brought her to America.

Zofia Szczupak would be living in comfort in the United States, well-nourished and with a sharp mind, when every one of her blood relatives had been dead for over fifty years. For the boy that her sister Magda had met and would marry that fall was not only a German.

Irwin Mann was also a Jew.

ze! Federal Agents! You're under arrest!" Anderson bellowed as he broke into

g.

men with the sacks on their shoulders stopped dead and waited. Anderson fteen feet from them with his gun held out in front of him in his right hand. nd slowly. Don't move your hands or I'll put a big hole right in the middle of u." The men turned slowly to face their captors.

e you Jack Miller?" Agent Anderson demanded of the man who had been dri- ruck. The man nodded silently. "Put that sack down slowly and keep your hands an see them." Miller did as he was told. "Now you," he said to the second man, complied. "What's your name?"

rank Layton," he said sullenly.

gent Turner was moving away from his partner, over to where the still was hid- ind the clump of trees. He dreaded what he thought he would find there. hat's in the sack?" Agent Anderson demanded. Turner closed his eyes with dis- e knew what Miller's answer would be.

ugar," Miller said simply, as the younger Treasury agent had known he would. he young Treasury agent stood staring at what had once been an operating still. pper condensing coil was still intact, but the boiler had been destroyed years ago, evidenced by the collection of rust on the big gashes that made it inoperable. Next ruined relic were some heavy tarpaulins. One of them was folded back to reveal l neatly stacked hundred-pound bags of sugar.

There's no still here."

"What?" Anderson yelled, forgetting his training and turning his head to look at e Turner was standing.

Agent Turner walked over to his partner. "The still that's there hasn't been in oper- for years. All they've got is some sugar stored under a tarp. Looks like our boy did- ive us the location of Miller's real still after all." Turner walked slowly over to er's battered truck while keeping a careful eye on its owner.

Jack Miller's eyes narrowed and Anderson saw a tight, humorless smile cross his for a brief moment. Miller stayed where he was and said nothing to the city men in s. Agent Anderson walked over to the ruined still. His face showed undisguised dis- t and hatred. He shook his head in disbelief as he pulled back the tarp in the vain hope t there might be something illegal under it. *More sacks of sugar. That's all.*

"Fuck." Anderson spat out the word. "It's no crime to have a shitload of sugar, even ll four of us know exactly what you two're going to do with it. Get your miserable es out of here." Jack Miller and his companion turned towards the truck, but Agent rner blocked their way. Turner was holding the shotgun that had been on the truck's ssenger seat. "Where did you fellows come from?" the agent asked.

Miller and Frank Layton stared at each other. Finally Miller said, "Oklahoma."

The agent held up the double-barreled shotgun.

Miller licked his lips as realization set in. The man was going to kill them with Miller's own gun and leave them here, and there wasn't a thing they could do about it. Then the agent smiled, opened the action to remove the two shells, and looked at Anderson.

"Partner, we've got our collar. We're not going home empty-handed after all."

Anderson shook his head. "It's no crime to have a shotgun in your truck, and I'll be damned if I'm going to lie and say these stupid hillbillies threatened me with it. I don't have the stomach for that kind of thing."

June 22, 1938

The Treasury agent did not like being in the woods. Anderson always thought of an Indian moving silently among the twigs, leaves, and other natural detritus, and his own clumsy efforts at stealth came up woefully short of this imagined standard. The agent much preferred to enforce the law back in Little Rock, where there were paved streets to drive on with real maps and road signs to tell you where you were, warehouses with real addresses when you had to bust in somewhere, and snitches to let you know what to expect when you got to where the bad guys were. That had been the environment in which he had operated for nine years, and it had suited him well. He had racked up an extensive arrest record, and he had been quite proud of it.

All that had changed five years ago. No more following midnight deliveries made by drab vehicles with bogus furniture company lettering on the sides. Now the drivers for Anheuser-Busch drove big red trucks with the company logo on them, and they smiled at him when they pulled in town to make their delivery runs from St. Louis.

He didn't disagree with the reasons for repeal. Anderson had seen from his very first day on the job that as long as there were people who wanted to drink liquor, there would always be other people to see to it that they could buy whatever booze they wanted. If buying liquor was illegal, that meant that the people providing it would not be mere busi- nessmen, but businessmen that were willing to break the law as a basic, necessary matter of business policy. And sometimes, that meant killing people. Since repeal five years before, he had yet to hear of a licensed beer or liquor distributor getting into a gun battle with a competitor.

Anderson's displeasure with the repeal of Prohibition was purely selfish in nature, and he did not try to tell himself otherwise. *I had it good for nine years. I could blend in when I went out on a case, I knew what was waiting for me when I went through a door, I knew who would pay off and who had to go down, and the guys we were after were mak- ing so much dough that they knew it was a minor setback and that their lawyers would get them sprung. Just part of the cost of doing business.*

The man squinted and looked over to where his partner was standing behind a tree, studying a topographical map. *Now I'm stuck here, God knows where, chasing after illit- erate hillbillies so dirt-poor that the only way they can get by is to cook up this stuff and sell it to people who can't afford the real thing because the government puts a big tax on it. And when one of them goes down, it may mean that his family is going to starve to death, so he might as well back-shoot me from behind a tree before I can make the col- lar.*

The Treasury agent took a few deep breaths. He did not like this at all. *I'm banking only a third of what I was five years ago, with ten times the risk of ending up in an unmarked grave out here in the middle of nowhere. Maybe I can get transferred to coun- terfeiting detail* he thought for perhaps the hundredth time. He uttered an oath under his breath.

"Have you figured out where we are?" the man asked his partner. Agent Turner glanced up from the map. He was new to the Department and some fifteen years younger than his companion. Since he had arrived at Treasury well after the repeal of Prohibition, Agent Turner did not have the basis for comparison that his partner did, and so did not view this job with the same loathing. Agent Turner had also not yet felt the lure of bribes, payoffs, and untraceable money that are always present wherever lucrative criminal enterprises exist. Agent Turner, at that moment, was concentrating on the job at hand.

"We need to go up that valley about four hundred yards," Turner said quietly, nodding his head to indicate the direction, "and climb the hill on the right. It's flat on top, and there's supposed to be a small clearing where he's got his still." Anderson grunted in acknowledgment. He had heard the briefing about how the equipment was hidden on top of the hill. The Department had leaned on some other wretched hillbilly, and he had ratted out his friend in the hopes of getting a reduced sentence. "The road he uses comes up from the other side," Turner continued, "and we should be out of sight until we're almost on top of him. If he's there," Turner added as an afterthought.

"If he's not there, then we'll damn well wait for the sorry bastard," Agent Anderson asserted. "I'm not going to come out here and play Daniel Boone 'less we go back with a collar."

"I'll lead," Turner offered as he started to walk methodically towards the valley. *Kid knows I hate going first in the woods* Anderson thought with mild irritation.

Agent Anderson said nothing as he fell in behind the younger man. He found his partner's upbeat attitude vaguely irritating, but he was happy to let Turner lead the way. *Let the kid get his ass shot at first*, Anderson thought sourly. *That'll give me a chance to hear where this hillbilly is hiding in this fucking jungle.* He instinctively ran his hand over the butt of his service revolver, a .38 caliber Smith & Wesson Military & Police model with six inch barrel, that he carried under his coat. The older man looked bleakly at his partner's back. Agent Turner seemed to be covering ground without making much noise at all.

Agent Anderson grimaced as his next step caused a twig to snap with an audible crack. He wished there were more than just the two of them. He wished he were sitting in the car they had left two miles away, smoking a cigarette. Most of all, Agent Anderson wished he were back in his office in Little Rock, pouring himself a stiff jolt of Irish whiskey so he could forget about ever looking for ignorant, inbred, white-trash moonshiners.

It took the two Treasury Agents the better part of an hour to traverse the valley and climb the hill. They stopped regularly to get their bearings and try to spot any signs of human life, but there were none. The only other creatures around them were the mosquitoes that they slapped away, and the unidentified insects that did not bother them but provided a constant backdrop of buzzing and chirping noises which helped a little to muffle the sounds of their progress.

At Agent Turner's insistence, they crawled the last hundred yards to the top of the hill. Squirming on his belly though dead leaves did nothing to improve Agent Anderson's outlook on the assignment.

As they finally reached the last few yards before the summit, the two Treasury agents slowed their progress to where they were only moving an inch or two at a time. Suddenly Turner shoved his hand back towards his partner, silently commanding him to stop moving and be still. He turned his head around slowly and whispered.

"I can see the top of it. It's about thirty yards away. It's hidden in some trees, but I can see the cooling coils. Wait here." Turner crawled a few feet farther, to a spot where he could peer over a fallen log at the top of the hill. He turned to Anderson. "I don't see any sign of anybody," he whispered softly. "Come on up."

Agent Anderson grunted and heaved himself to his feet. His partner tried to silently protest, but Anderson ignored him and walked up to where Agent Turner lay behind the log. He squatted next to the younger man and nodded. "Well, Daniel Boone, looks like

you got us to the right place." Agent Turner smiled at th

"What do we do now? Go look over the setup?"

The older man shook his head. "I don't want to leav boy off when he comes here. For all I know, every son-of can tell at a glance if a mouse has walked by. Also, he ma

Turner nodded his agreement. The risk of being kill versally accepted, but it was every agent's nightmare to be inal's efforts to protect his property. It didn't happen often men knew it.

"Let's find us a good spot to watch from, and sit our sick of crawling around like a damned lizard." Agent Anders pants and looked around for a suitable spot to begin their vigi

"Over there," Turner said, looking at a large oak tree w base of its trunk. "We can sit behind that log and still see whe Anderson considered the suggestion and nodded. The two me oak tree and the log and sat down. Without discussion, they face other to afford themselves the ability to survey a wider area. Sile wait.

***

Anderson was in a foul mood from the many mosquito bite the fact that after two hours his bowels had demanded relief. Ther tive but to walk down the hill, find a log, and use leaves in place of t neglected to bring. He had caught Turner grinning when he retur helped his attitude at all. He was about to say something when the y his hand.

"Listen."

The two men heard the unmistakable sound of a vehicle laboring ly making its way up the opposite side of the hill. Both agents were fu ing completely still and waiting for their quarry to come into sight.

The old truck suddenly came into view about seventy yards aw Turner followed its progress as it vanished and reappeared several time of vision through the patchy foliage. There were two occupants. The tru to the group of trees that concealed the illegal still, twenty yards in front o The driver backed the vehicle around until it was facing away from them see the bed of the truck. It was empty.

The door opened and a tired-looking man got out of the cab. He absentmindedly and trudged towards the clump of trees. He wore torn, fade had several day's growth of beard on his lined face. He was joined by the who was a bit younger. Anderson and Turner heard rustling noises, then gru In a few moments the men emerged from behind the trees. They each carr sack, and each man's body was bent under the burden. The first man was ca ping over a fallen log on his way to the truck when Anderson stood up. His b his partner, and he did not see the worried look on the younger man's face. Ag had just realized that something was wrong with what he was seeing. Turner r to stop his partner, but it was too late. Agent Anderson was already running afte with his gun drawn.

"No, you're missing it. National Firearms Act. Federal violation. Passed in '34. Illegal possession and interstate transport of an unregistered shotgun with a barrel less than eighteen inches long."

Jack Miller, who normally knew enough not to speak to law enforcement agents, could not contain himself. "Illegal possession, Hell! That's *my* gun! Can't nobody say different! I've never stolen a thing in my life!" This last was not entirely accurate, but it was true that Mr. Miller had indeed acquired the gun legally.

Agent Anderson was looking even more bewildered than Jack Miller, though less outraged. "What the hell are you talking about?"

"The National Firearms Act of 1934. Passed in June of that year." He was grinning broadly now, playing to his audience.

"What we have here is the illegal possession and interstate transportation of an unregistered shotgun with a barrel less than eighteen inches in length or an overall length of less than twenty-six inches." He held up the shotgun. The barrel was about sixteen inches long, maybe a bit more. "Registration of said weapon must be made with the U.S. Treasury and a two hundred dollar tax paid to the Treasury. After registration, subsequent sale of said weapon must be first approved by the Department of the Treasury and will be subject to a two hundred dollar tax payable to the Treasury by the seller each time the weapon changes hands." Agent Turner was grinning like a Cheshire cat. "So unless either Mr. Miller or Mr. Layton here can produce registration papers for this weapon, I'd say we've got ourselves a couple of federal criminals."

Miller, a poor man with little formal education, had jerked as if jolted with electricity at the mention of the dollar figure. "You mean I got to pay two hundred dollars to you federal men if'n I decide to sell that five-dollar shotgun to my friend here?" The concept was beyond his comprehension.

Agent Turner smiled patiently. "That would be true, Mr. Miller, if you or your friend had already paid two hundred dollars to the Treasury in 1934 when the law was passed, and registered this gun with us at that time. Since you did not, you and Mr. Layton are guilty of illegal possession and interstate transport of an unregistered weapon controlled by the National Firearms Act of 1934, and you are each therefore subject to a fine of five thousand dollars and a prison sentence of five years. Now turn around and cross your wrists behind your back."

Miller's jaw dropped in disbelief, but he did as he was told. Agent Turner took the chromed steel handcuffs from the case on his belt and locked them around Jack Miller's wrists. "Go get in the front of the truck," he commanded. Miller obeyed. "You going to cuff the other one?" he asked his partner.

Agent Anderson cuffed Layton and pushed him towards the truck. Then he stared at his young partner and grabbed him by the shoulder.

"What the fuck kind of crazy, made up, horseshit story did you just tell those peckerheads? You expect them to believe that they're going to prison for five years because the barrel on a shotgun is an inch-and-a-half shorter'n you say it should be?" Anderson spoke in a coarse whisper, his mouth only inches from his partner's ear. "The chief will have our balls for making a false arrest!"

Special Agent Turner continued to smile as he shook his head patiently. "Not what I say it should be. What the Federal Government says it should be. No horseshit at all. It's Federal law. And now we've got our collar. Come on," he said soothingly. "Let's see if this old rattletrap can make it back to our car." He started walking towards the vehicle. The older agent followed him slowly, shaking his head in disbelief and disgust.

Prohibition had been crazy enough, but this? Five years in prison because a piece of steel *was two inches too short?* He hated this job now more than ever.

Anderson's final words were lost as Turner ground the starter and the tired engine coughed to life.

"I'd've sooner gut-shot the fuckers and left 'em for the buzzards."

September 8, 1938

"Bud! Bud, come here! Come in right now! I don't believe this! You've got to see it!" The woman's face was a mixture of amazement and delight. Her husband, a lean, strong man of thirty-two, heard the urgency in her voice immediately and came trotting over from the barn, wiping grease from his hands with a rag. He started to speak, but as he reached the doorway, he saw what had so astonished his wife.

He was walking! Only eight months old and Raymond was walking!

Bud put his arm around his wife's waist and hugged her to him. His smile was as broad as it had been when he had seen his son for the first time twenty-eight weeks before.

"I don't believe it," he whispered, shaking his head slowly. Raymond was taking small, careful steps. His arms were held out for balance and he was looking towards the floor. He was oblivious to the presence of his parents. All of a sudden, he lost his balance and his knees buckled. The baby sat down abruptly on the thin carpet. His mother gasped and started towards him, but her husband held her back. "Wait. Let's see what he does."

The child inhaled, and for a moment his parents thought he was going to cry. But Raymond's eyes were alert, and he looked at his immediate surroundings. He focused on the overstuffed armchair two feet from him, and crawled to it. With awkward but purposeful movements, the little boy clutched the fabric of the chair in his fingers and used it to steady himself as he pushed himself to a standing position again. Slowly, one hand at a time, he let go of the chair and took two wobbling steps. He stopped, holding his arms out like a tightrope walker, and stayed on his feet. He turned his head and saw his father, and an enormous grin filled his face. He made a loud, happy noise, and started to lose his balance again.

Emmett (Bud) Johnson could not help himself. He grabbed his little boy under the arms as he started to fall, threw him up in the air, caught him, and hugged the small body to his chest. "Look who can walk! Look who got tired of crawling already! Is it time to get you a little pair of boots? Is it time to give you a little pitchfork so you can help with the horses? Are you going to help us out at rodeo time?" He tossed the little boy in the air again, and Raymond's smile got even bigger.

Louise always felt her heart in her chest when Bud did that, but she had long ago given up on trying to get her husband to stop throwing his son in the air. Raymond obviously loved it, and Bud had insisted with a straight face that it would help their child have better balance and prevent him from 'being afraid of things that he shouldn't be afraid of,' as her husband had explained it. Maybe he had been right. She was still marveling at the fact of her little boy taking his first steps.

Bud and Louise Johnson had been married for nine years, and they had been trying to have a child ever since their wedding night. Louise had suffered three miscarriages in that time, and her doctor had told her that her body was not built for having children. He told her that childbirth, if she were able to carry a pregnancy to term, might well kill her. She had been adamant, and had forbidden the doctor to tell her husband of his fears.

When Raymond was born, there had been severe complications, and the doctor had had to perform a cesarean section. Bud had been frightened out of his mind that his wife would die. Raymond had been healthy, if small, but Louise could not have any more children. That reality had ground on her for the last seven months. She had come from a large family and always expected to have one herself.

Bud put Raymond down next to the armchair where the little boy could hold onto it for balance. He turned to his wife and hugged her to him. "Honey, I know we wanted a girl, too, but I'm beginning to think that this little fellow might be about all that just the two of us can handle." Louise's eyes brimmed with tears. For seven months she had feared that Bud was unhappy with the prospect of always having only one child. "I have a feeling this one's going to amount to a lot more than just a cowpuncher."

Louise looked up at her husband in amazement. She had never heard him run himself down before. He saw her expression, and smiled before explaining.

"I don't mean anything bad. There isn't a place I'd rather live or a life I'd rather lead, and you know that. I'm just lucky our kind of life suits me as well as it does, because you and I both know it was a stretch for me to get through high school. This one here," he said, nodding at Raymond, "you can see it in his face. He's *smart*. He wants to *do* things. I could see that as soon as you got home from the hospital. And that's not just a proud daddy puffing up his chest. I've seen enough other babies. Raymond got a double helping of something pretty strong. He's going to have the chance to be things we've never even dreamed of." There was obvious pride in his voice.

Louise nodded. She had seen it, too, but she had assumed that every new mother felt that way about her firstborn. She glanced at her husband, who had a pensive look on his face.

"Better get used to the idea of not getting to see him grow up all the way."

"What?" She turned to face her husband, a horrified look on her face. He saw her alarm and quickly explained.

"I just mean that I think our Pitkin County schools are going to take him only so far. I think he's going to outgrow them, and if I'm right, we're going to make sure he goes someplace where the teachers are smarter than he is."

"But he's only eight months old!" Louise protested, laughing. Yet even as she said the words, Louise found herself inwardly agreeing with Bud's surprising declaration.

"He'll be fifteen before you know it. Hell, woman, it seems like yesterday I was trying to put my hand up your dress for the first time." Louise flushed scarlet.

"Emmett Johnson!" she squealed. She always used his given name whenever he said something shocking that nonetheless pleased her. His fingers went to the buttons of her blouse.

"Raymond's got himself occupied learning how to walk. Let's us go practice something on our own."

"But, just this morning, we already..." Her voice trailed off at the touch of his fingertips.

"That's right, darling, and I want to make damn sure I don't forget how. Like I told you, I never was much for brains. It would be a real shame if I went a little too long and all the things that you like me to do just kind of slipped my mind. We'd best get some practice in so's your thick-headed husband doesn't disappoint you, some night when you're feeling frisky." He scooped her up easily and carried her over to the big couch.

"Mmmmmm...." she breathed. "You're right. We don't want that to happen." She glanced over at the little boy. Raymond was using the chair again so that he could stand up. Louise closed her eyes and moaned softly. Her husband Bud was accomplishing something entirely different.

November 9, 1938

There was no warning at all. One moment the watch repair shop on Bergerstrasse was quiet and peaceful, occupied only by its owner. An instant later, the storefront window vanished, imploding inward in a shower of glass shards under the force of three expertly-wielded truncheons.

Before the jagged pieces had all come to rest on the drab but immaculate shop floor, the watchmaker *knew.* He knew that the whispers he had been pretending didn't exist were true. He knew that the hope he had held out had been utter self-deception. He knew that however bad things were going to be tonight, they would get much worse in the days and months to come. He had talked—*oh, how endlessly he had talked!*—to the other Munich shopkeepers and merchants in the area. They had all agreed that it was nothing to worry about. The sentiments that were building were nothing new. Hadn't they always been resented for their business skills? Hadn't they always succeeded in commerce, and part of that success meant accepting hostility? They had agreed to do nothing, for taking action might bring them harm.

That was what they had all agreed, and the watchmaker now saw, with absolute clarity, the fate to which they had consigned themselves.

"Schnell!" came the harsh voices of the three uniformed men stepping over the windowsill into his shop. "Filthy Jewish swine! Get over here! You are under arrest!"

The man did not protest. He knew it would only enrage these animals further. He knew that any resistance would be an excuse to use their truncheons on his old bones, and he doubted that his body would hold up any better than his storefront window had. He knew that the only thing to do was go along, and pray for the best.

He thought of his favorite nephew, Irwin Mann, who lived in Danzig and sold produce and tinned goods. He had always hoped Irwin would prosper as he had. *Now look who's the prosperous one* he thought bitterly. He did not know that in four years his nephew would be 'relocated' to Warsaw, and soon find himself faced with a similar problem. Young Irwin Mann, however, would respond in a very different manner than had his uncle.

The future of his nephew and the role that the young man would play in history was only one of the many things that the watchmaker did not know. He did not know that in addition to being arrested that night, he would also be fined for damage to his own shop. He did not know that there would be twenty thousand others like him arrested in the next forty-eight hours. He did not know that he would never again be a free man.

He most certainly did not know that within a year, he would weigh less than half his current sixty-eight kilos, that most of his fingers and toes would have been lost to frostbite and gangrene, and that when he finally died of internal bleeding, he would have lived the last seven weeks of his life as a blind man.

He did not know, but would come to learn, that he would soon spend the rest of his life, (all sixteen months of it) in a facility not twenty kilometers northwest of his Munich watch repair shop, just outside a town on the Amper River. The town was a small one, over five hundred years old, whose previously innocuous name had recently taken on a sinister air whenever Germans spoke of it.

The watchmaker shared a fate with almost a quarter-million of his countrymen and every single one of his relatives who was still in Germany as of November 9, 1938.

He was going to Dachau.

January 3, 1939

"All rise. District Court, Western District of Arkansas, Fort Smith Division, is now in session, Judge Heartsill Ragon presiding."

"You may be seated. First case, UNITED STATES v. MILLER et al. Mr. Gutensohn?"

"Right here, your Honor." The defense lawyer from Fort Smith stood up. Paul Gutensohn was a smallish man with thinning black hair who wore round, wire-rimmed spectacles. His quick movements and his sharp, prominent nose gave him a slight hawk-like appearance.

"Your Honor, if it please the Court, my clients, Mr. Miller and Mr. Layton, are guilty of no crime whatsoever. Their arrest under Section 11, 48 statute 1239, is clearly in violation of their Constitutional rights for two obvious reasons. First, the so-called National Firearms Act, though presented as a revenue measure, is clearly a Federal attempt to usurp power reserved to the States. This should be obvious as the so-called 'tax' of two hundred dollars is greatly in excess of the value of the arms on which it is levied. Second, the National Firearms Act of 1934 is completely in conflict with the second article to our Constitution's Bill of Rights. To wit, 'A well regulated militia, being necessary to the security of a free state, the right of the people to keep and bear arms shall not be infringed.'

"Inasmuch as both Mr. Miller and Mr. Layton are able-bodied and between the ages of sixteen and forty-five, they are clearly members of the Militia of which the framers of our Constitution spoke. Further, unlike the Fourth Amendment against 'unreasonable' search and seizure, the Second Amendment makes no mention of 'reasonable' infringements on the people's right to keep and bear arms. The article states that this right shall not be infringed, period. There is no way to interpret our government's attempts to levy a tax of two hundred dollars on any weapon which can be used to defend oneself and one's freedoms as anything other than a gross and willful infringement on the people's right to keep and bear arms.

"Mr. Miller and Mr. Layton are guilty of nothing more than exercising their Second Amendment rights. Indeed, the arresting agents reported that both my clients obeyed all orders given by the agents, and that at no time did either of the defendants threaten either agent in any way, with or without the weapon in question. In fact, the agents both admit that the shotgun in question was found by one of the agents on the seat of Mr. Miller's unoccupied vehicle when the arrest was made.

"Accordingly, I have filed a demurrer challenging the sufficiency of the facts stated in the indictment to constitute a crime, and further challenging the sections under which said indictment was returned as being in contravention of the Second Amendment to the Constitution of the United States, U.S.C.A You have the demurrer before you, your Honor." Gutensohn sat down.

District Judge Heartsill Ragon looked at the slender man and his two clients. He had read the demurrer already, and it had been a rare experience for him. He could not recall the last time that he had felt so strongly in this particular way about a case presented before him. He had seen numerous cases where the arresting officers had lied, made up charges, manufactured evidence, and beaten suspects into confessing.

This case was not like that. The Treasury agents who had arrested the two men had behaved properly in every possible way. Their arrest procedures had been straight out of the textbook. The problem with this case was why the two men had been arrested in the first place. Judge Ragon knew that the reason the Treasury agents had followed the defendants was to catch them making liquor without a license. He also knew that due to bad luck, there hadn't been any moonshine to be found when the agents had sprung their trap.

But the agents hadn't let the men go. No, the agents had acted in a reasonable and prudent manner when they had arrested Miller and Layton for being in clear violation of a Federal statute.

The problem with this case was that defense counsel was exactly right. The Federal statute, the National Firearms Act of 1934, was absolutely and unquestionably in violation of the Second Amendment to the United States Constitution.

Judge Heartsill Ragon paused a moment to reflect on the men in the Federal legislature who had created this piece of legal garbage. *What kind of person would propose that a man be put in prison for five years based on the length of the weapon he carried to protect himself? What kind of person would expect the man to pay* twenty times *the value of the weapon to the Treasury for* each *such weapon he owned to avoid going to prison, and then pay the $200 again when he sold the gun? What kind of legislature had agreed to this insanity?*

The law was even worse than this case would indicate, the judge reflected. He had taken the time to read all the provisions of the 1934 statute, and Judge Ragon had been amazed at what he had seen. In addition to throwing people in prison if they didn't pay $200 taxes on ten-dollar guns, the National Firearms Act put people in prison if they failed to pay $200 taxes on three-dollar sound mufflers. This was a cruel addition to an already terrible law.

Judge Ragon had spent his adult life studying the law and had not fired a gun since his service in the war with Spain in 1898, but that was not the case with his three brothers. All three of the now middle-aged men had fired guns their whole lives. And all three were now almost completely deaf, and there was nothing that any doctor could do about it. *What was next?* wondered the judge. *$200 taxes on knives?*

Judge Ragon took a deep breath and looked at the U.S. District Attorney, C.R. Barry.

"Mr. District Attorney?"

"Your Honor, the National Firearms Act of 1934 is not in any way in contravention with our United States Constitution. The defendants were found transporting a sawed-off shotgun in interstate commerce. Neither defendant disputes this fact. Nowhere in the United States is a sawed-off shotgun of the type transported by Mr. Miller and Mr. Layton issued to members of the military. Accordingly, it is entirely reasonable that the Treasury enforce the National Firearms Act as a revenue-raising measure, and demand that those who are in violation of it be sent to prison, just as we tax liquor producers and expect those people who make illegal alcohol products to be sent to prison."

The judge smiled at the D.A., but it was entirely without humor. "Mr. Barry," he said in a resonant voice, "there is *no* mention made in the Constitution about making whiskey. There is a very *clear* mention made of the right to keep and bear arms. You may be entirely right that our government does not issue our soldiers shotguns of the exact type that Mr. Miller had in his truck. However, you are forgetting everything you were taught in grade school civics class." The District Attorney turned crimson at this barb.

The judge went on. "A militia, by definition, is a group of citizens who use their own weapons for defense of themselves and their freedoms. We cannot throw them in prison or fine them five thousand dollars for failing to have exactly the same type arms as are carried by the National Guard or any other branch of our standing army, or expect them to pay two hundred dollar taxes at the whim of the Treasury merely to exercise their Constitutional rights."

"But, your Honor..."

"Mister Barry, I have carefully reviewed this 'National Firearms Act' of yours, and it imposes the same five year prison sentence and $5000 fine on interstate transport of automatic weapons as well." The District Attorney got a sick look on his face. He knew where this was going. "Tell me, Mr. Barry. Are you familiar with the Browning Automatic Rifle, the model 1918 BAR?"

"Yes, your Honor."

"So am I. In fact, my son carried one in France at the very end of the Great War. A marvelous weapon, and one he could well have used at the *beginning* of the war and not just the end. In fact, the BAR is a weapon which I wish *I* had had when I fought in the war with Spain in 1898. And, Mr. District Attorney, the Browning Automatic Rifle is, I believe, currently issued to U.S. soldiers and members of the Arkansas National Guard, *is it not?"*

"I believe so, your Honor."

"Mr. Barry, if the Treasury agents had found a BAR and not a shotgun in Mr. Miller's truck, would they have arrested him for violating the National Firearms Act?"

"I can't say what the agents would or wouldn't have done, your Honor."

"I'll rephrase the question, Mr. Barry. If the agents had arrested Miller and Layton for possessing a Browning Automatic Rifle without having paid a $200 tax and without possessing the stamp-affixed federal order form as per this National Firearms Act, would you be prosecuting them under the National Firearms Act as you are now doing?"

The District Attorney licked his lips. *How the hell do I answer this one?*

"Well, Mr. Barry?"

"They would be in violation of the Act, so yes, I would prosecute them, your Honor."

"And if I happened to have a Browning Automatic Rifle at home in my bedroom, the very same type weapon that my son carried proudly defending our country in 1918, and if this weapon in my bedroom was not stolen from a government arsenal, but rather one that I had bought with my own money from the Colt factory in 1920 so that I would be prepared to act as a member of the militia, or to defend myself from an abusive government should the need arise, and if I had brought this BAR here to my Arkansas bedroom from my former residence outside the state, would you prosecute *me* for violating the National Firearms Act and recommend that I be thrown in prison for five years, Mr. District Attorney?"

The D.A. was sweating despite the cool air in the courtroom. "Your Honor, I would never prosecute someone who has not been arrested."

"And if I *were* arrested, Mr. District Attorney? Should I then go to prison for five years, pay a $5000 fine, and be disbarred, according to you and your National Firearms Act?"

"Your Honor," he said, holding his hands palms up and pleading with the judge, "the Treasury agents would never arrest *you."*

"Why not?" thundered Judge Ragon. Because I'm a *judge?* Because I'm not a *moonshiner?* Mr. District Attorney, I see no exemptions in this National Firearms Act for judges or any other categories of 'the people', to which our Bill of Rights refers. Do you?"

"No, your Honor," Barry said softly.

"I didn't think so. I believe you understand my position, Mr. District Attorney. Mr. Gutensohn," he said, addressing the defense lawyer, "the demurrer you filed is accordingly sustained. The National Firearms Act of 1934 violates the Second Amendment to the Constitution of the United States." He banged his gavel once upon the bench. "Case dismissed. Mr. Miller and Mr. Layton, you are free to go."

Paul Gutensohn stood up. His heart was racing. There was no feeling like this one. Winning a case on a technicality or insufficient evidence was one thing. This was so much better. He, Paul Gutensohn, had seen that the law which had been applied to his clients was in fundamental violation of their rights, and he had made it stick. A piece of illegal Federal legislation had been struck down because of his efforts, and his efforts alone. This was better than money. *Hell,* he thought recklessly, *it's better than sex.*

Jack Miller and Frank Layton stood in front of him. They were wearing their best clothes, which was to say they each looked a little more shabby than the people in the back of the courtroom. Miller twisted his hat in his callused hands. He was obviously relieved at the decision, but also anxious about what he wanted to tell his lawyer.

"We made it, didn't we?" Gutensohn said, clapping Miller on the back with a broad grin. Jack Miller looked slightly embarrassed.

"Mr. Gutensohn," Miller began awkwardly, "I never did feel right about you agreein' to do all this work on your own just 'cause you thought what them Fed'ral men done wa'n't right. I didn't have no money when we first talked, and you said no matter. Well, that ain't the way I ever done things. Here," he said, thrusting his hand out to the lawyer. "It pro'ly ain't what you got comin' to you, but it's all I got. It ain't been stole."

Paul Gutensohn took the handful of bills. He had seen this happen before. Sometimes it was five or ten dollars in ones, sometimes a side of beef, a slab of bacon, or fresh vegetables from a client's garden. The lawyer looked at the money, and was startled to see it was six twenty-dollar bills. *This is probably the most money this man has ever had in his hand at one time in his entire life* Gutensohn thought. He looked up uncertainly at Miller.

Jack Miller gave an embarrassed smile. "I figure it's a sight better'n goin' to prison, 'n' havin' my family left with no way to get by. An' it's less than what them Fed'ral men said I was s'posed to give 'em back in '34 to keep my gun."

Gutensohn smiled and nodded once. Miller looked relieved, and quickly put on his hat. "We got to go," he said quickly, and he and Frank Layton walked out of the courtroom.

Paul Gutensohn picked up his valise and looked around the courtroom with satisfaction. His step was light and his pace even quicker than usual as he walked out of the building and into the chill January air. Normally he hated cold weather, but for some reason it felt invigorating today. He looked up into the clear blue sky and fingered the bills in the pants pocket of his grey suit. *It's great to be alive* he thought happily.

March 6, 1939

"'Morning, Paul. Welcome back to our wonderful Arkansas weather."

"Right. I was thinking I should have stayed in Mississippi. What did I miss while I was off being the dutiful son? Did you sell our practice?"

"I wish. No, it's been pretty quiet around here. Got one lover's quarrel late last week. Guy belted his lady friend, cracked her jaw. Her dad's making her press charges. I'm representing Romeo, if it ever gets to court."

"What's your defense?"

"You know, typical shouting match that went a little too far, 'this is the first time it's ever happened, your Honor, don't throw my client in the jug, he has a steady job and will of course make restitution, blah, blah' the usual drill. Oh, I almost forgot. Just after you left—that case you nailed just after New Year's on Constitutional grounds? The Feds have appealed it to the Supreme Court. I tried for almost a week to track down your buddy Jack Miller, but the guy's vanished, and no one has a clue where to find him. Same with that Frank Layton. The notice is right there, on top of your pile of mail."

Paul Gutensohn sighed as he picked up the Notice of Appeal. This was the last thing he wanted to hear first thing on Monday after being out of the office for two weeks. He looked at the court date for the case: Thursday, March 30. *Three weeks*. He folded the document and put it back in the envelope.

"So what are you going to do?"

"I don't know—try to find out where Miller is, I guess. Although I doubt he'll be up for another round in court, especially a thousand miles from here in Washington, D.C. I can't say as I have any burning desire to hop on a train and pay for a hotel room for Lord knows how long. Whatever Mr. Miller's desires might be, providing I can find him, I don't think paying my expenses are within his budget, to say nothing of the actual legal fees."

"You going to file a brief on his behalf? Mail it to 'em?"

Paul Gutensohn sighed again. This was starting to give him a headache. "I don't know. I ought to, but you know the rules. The U.S. Supreme Court won't accept typed briefs. They're above all that. For them, you have to get your briefs *printed*. I'm not eager to pay for that out of my own pocket, either. I think we're at the point where we're not going to do these charity cases any more." He thought for a moment before continuing. "I'll try to get hold of Miller or Layton. Maybe I can convince one of them that paying for a little more of my time and effort is good insurance against having their case over-turned."

"You think the Feds have much of a shot?"

Gutensohn shrugged. "I don't think so. Ragon laid it out pretty plainly in his Western District ruling. That National Firearms Act is garbage. Completely unconstitutional. You know, I think maybe they passed it because with Prohibition gone, all those Treasury agents needed something to enforce." He chuckled to himself. "You ever hear of our government laying a bunch of their own people off?" His partner laughed out loud.

"Ever since our current president seized power, I haven't been able to keep up with the alphabet soup of three-letter government programs. And you know, that Socialist bastard would never have managed to get any of his schemes passed into law without packing the Supreme Court first. What's that they're saying now—something like, 'Become a Roosevelt Democrat—it beats having to find a real job'?"

The partner's tone became more serious. "To answer your question, Paul, no, I can't imagine the Treasury Department laying off three-fourths of its agents just because there isn't the Volstead Act to enforce any more. They have to have a bogeyman to go after. I looked at your case, though. It was ironclad. I don't see how the Supreme Court could reverse, even if King George himself were Chief Justice."

Paul Gutensohn's partner did not know it, but he had just delivered what would prove to be the worst legal opinion of his entire career.

March 30, 1939

"The Supreme court of the United States is now in session, Chief Justice McReynolds presiding."

"UNITED STATES v. MILLER et al. Mr. Gordon Dean for the United States. For the appellees...?" Chief Justice McReynolds looked around the courtroom. No one volunteered to speak for Jack Miller or Frank Layton, because no one was there on their behalf. "Well, then. Mr. Dean?"

Gordon Dean took a deep breath. He had prayed that no opposing legal counsel would show up, and when he had learned that no brief had been filed, he realized that his prayers had been answered. An opponent to challenge what he was about to say would have doomed his argument. Without opposition, there was a chance he could squeak by. All it would take was some creative manipulation of the facts, and some monumental omissions.

"Yes, your Honor. If it please the Court, the District Court's prior dismissal of this case and ruling that the National Firearms Act is in contravention to our Constitution has no rational basis in the law. The National Firearms Act levies a tax on the interstate commerce in sawed-off shotguns, and affixes a Federal stamp to the order as proof that the tax has been paid. Mr. Miller and Mr. Layton transported in interstate commerce a sawed-off shotgun without having in their possession a stamp-affixed written order for the firearm. That fact is not in dispute.

"The weapon that Messrs. Miller and Layton transported in interstate commerce, a double-barrel Stevens 12-gauge shotgun having a barrel less than 18 inches in length and bearing serial number 76230, is not issued to any military entity anywhere in our country. To say that this weapon is part of any well-regulated militia is utter nonsense."

Gordon Dean knew he had just stretched the truth about as far as he ever had in his professional life. Short-barreled shotguns had been used in every military engagement in the last fifty years, but what Dean had actually said was that *serial number 76230* was not government issue, so it wasn't a lie. That's what the lawyer told himself, at any rate.

The U.S. lawyer looked into the eyes of each of the Supreme Court Justices and felt a trickle of sweat run down his spine. He was searching for any sign that one of these men had seen military service, and had used a shotgun with a barrel shorter than eighteen inches. *If any one of them has, he's going to skin me alive* Dean thought. He pressed on.

"The National Firearms Act is, once again, a *revenue*-raising measure. It raises monies for the Treasury by levying a tax on certain weapons. Mr. Miller's right to keep and bear arms was in no way infringed. He was merely required to pay a tax on a weapon that has no relationship whatsoever to a militia. Mr. Miller could have paid this tax, and he would have committed no crime. He also could have chosen to transport a *different* weapon across state lines, such as a military rifle, and again, he would have committed no crime. He failed to pay this tax, and then transported the NFA-controlled weapon in interstate commerce. This is a crime, pure and simple. You have the Government's brief, your Honor."

Gordon Dean held his breath. He was dreading the inevitable question about the National Firearms Act also restricting interstate commerce in *automatic* military arms. He also dreaded the question of how a $200 tax on a $10 gun could be anything but an infringement on the right to keep the weapon. As he stood there in front of the U.S. Supreme Court, he could not help but think about the purpose of the Second Article in the

Bill of Rights.

The Second Amendment is a recognition of the danger of standing armies. Its purpose is to recognize that every citizen has the right to keep and bear the same type of basic arms as a soldier in a modern military. A militia embodies all able-bodied men over the age of sixteen. Therefore, a militia will always outnumber a standing army by at least twenty to one. If this militia is armed with weapons similar to those used by the individuals comprising the standing army, it will be impossible for that standing army to inflict the will of a tyrannical government upon the people. The Second Amendment is the guarantee behind all the other articles in the Bill of Rights. It is the ultimate guarantee that citizens in the United States will remain free.

Gordon Dean waited for the Justices to look at the wording of the National Firearms Act and ask him, based on his own arguments, how the Act could restrict private commerce in not only Stevens shotgun serial number 76230, but also the exact weapons currently issued to infantrymen in our military.

I'm not cut out for lying to the Supreme Court. This isn't what I had in mind when I went to law school he thought. *Thank God there's no opposing counsel to bring out the truth.* He was beginning to feel physically ill.

The question from the Justices never came.

May 15, 1939

World events were coming to a head. The Munich Conference had been held eight months earlier, and British Prime Minister Neville Chamberlain had made his famous claim of having secured 'Peace in our time' by acceding to Hitler's demand to occupy western Czechoslovakia with German troops. Although most Americans did not even know how to spell Czechoslovakia, let alone care what happened between it and Germany, in three and a half months the little man with the toothbrush mustache would start the invasion of Poland. America would soon agree with Winston Churchill's assessment of the seriousness of the Axis threat.

Those national sentiments were months in the future on this Monday in May, however. On this spring morning, the Supreme Court would issue a ruling that virtually no one at the time would notice. Further, the ultimate results of the decision would not fully be felt by U.S. citizens for many decades.

The Court had spent considerable time reviewing the government's brief in the case. It was not often that a district court ruled that a federal law was unconstitutional. It was even rarer that one of the participants not even show up to argue its side of a Supreme Court case, or file a brief on behalf of the client.

Still, the court considered the government's position in the fairest way that it could, without assuming any facts or statements not presented.

The decision, unlike most Supreme Court decisions that would come in future years, was only four pages long. The reasoning behind the Court's decision was contained in the second paragraph:

"In the absence of any evidence tending to show that possession or use of a 'shotgun having a barrel less than eighteen inches in length' at this time has some reasonable relationship to the preservation or efficiency of a well-regulated militia, we cannot say that the Second Amendment guarantees the right to keep and bear such an instrument. Certainly it is not within judicial notice that this weapon is any part of the ordinary military equipment or that its use could contribute to the common defense."

Gordon Dean's straw man argument had worked. Without opposing counsel, the Court was never told that shotguns with barrels of less than eighteen inches *were* used in the military. The Court was never informed that the National Firearms Act applied to automatic weapons that were obviously military issue, which would have killed the government's own argument right there. Finally, no one had pointed out, as had District Court Judge Heartsill Ragon, that militia weapons were, by definition, the personal arms of the private citizenry, and therefore whether or not a particular weapon was issued to army troops was completely irrelevant.

The language of the decision would ultimately cause the government much trouble, however. The wording clearly showed that the Supreme Court viewed all military-issue small arms as being Constitutionally protected. Since the National Firearms Act infringed upon the citizens' right to keep and bear many obviously military-issue small arms, the Court should have found the Act unconstitutional. But the Court did not know about this element of the Act, and so the National Firearms Act remained on the books as part of federal law.

Jack Miller and Frank Layton, innocent men the day before, were once again guilty of a federal crime. They had no known address, however, and in 1939, tracking down a couple of poor Arkansas hillbillies because a year earlier they had had a piece of steel shorter than a certain length was not top priority for Treasury agents. Jack Miller and Frank Layton were never seen again by law enforcement authorities.

In 1939, few if any people complained about the National Firearms Act, just as few people complained about the much more obvious 'Jim Crow' laws that existed throughout the country. Just like the doctrine of 'separate but equal,' the National Firearms Act would remain an embarrassing stain on the nation's fabric for over half a century. Just as with that other civil rights violation, the National Firearms Act would spawn other, more outrageous infringements, like a tumor that slowly metastases into ever-widening and ever more aggressive forms of cancer. Finally, as was true of civil rights violations everywhere in the world, the choice would come down to eradicating the cancer or letting it kill the patient.

That decision, however, would not happen for more than fifty years. When it did, it would be precipitated by several people who on that May afternoon in 1939 had not yet been born, and one who was then only a year old.

Part Two

GROWTH

May 12, 1942

"Listen, Goddamnit, I told you I was going to enlist, and this is the least you could do for me, for Christ's sake!"

"But Max," Zofia pleaded, pronouncing his name 'Mecks', "you have a child. You are almost thirty years old. Your family needs you here. If you must leave us, do it. But please don't send this letter. It is a...a lie."

"I'm not going to get stuck on some base in Texas while there's a war going on in Europe! You have to sign this letter. It's the only way I'll get in the Airborne. The kid will be fine with you, and you can live with Father in St. Louis. You've been bitching about New York for two years now." He looked her in the eye. *Jesus, I hope this stunt works* he thought. *This woman is driving me crazy here.* "I would have thought you'd be more supportive. After all, it's your relatives that are being slaughtered over there by the krauts."

His final words did it. Zofia Collins hung her head in shame and signed her name to the letter her husband had typed to the War Department.

"Collins, this has to be you. Jesus, man! You must have *really* wanted to get away from that wife of yours. I guess nobody will call you a liar any more." Private Hemmings had just run into the barracks, and now stood by Max Collins' bunk, holding out a folded section of the New York Times. Everyone in basic training had heard the story of how the oldest new recruit on the base had made his wife sign a letter to the War Department demanding they accept her husband for combat duty.

Max looked down at the newspaper and laughed out loud. "In the goddamn *New York Times*! I'll be a son-of-a-bitch!" He took the paper from the younger man and read the news item

Wife Wants Father Of Her Child In Combat
Begs War Dept. to Put Him in Airborne
N.Y. Times Staff Report

Most women weep at the thought of their husbands going into combat. A Polish-born woman in St. Louis, Missouri, however, has urged the War Department to make sure that her husband gets in the Airborne, even though he is twenty-nine and they have a young daughter. The letter was sent to one of the husband's relatives who is connected with the present Administration. There, it was forwarded to the appropriate department. In part, it reads:

...my husband is strong man, and going nuts with war in Europe and nothing can do here. You must take him or not good for me live with here more. My husband must go jump in where fight, not stay at Texas waste of time...

The letter goes on to state that the writer's American-born husband is very concerned for her family in Poland. The couple has not heard from any of them for almost two years

It is not often that a wife insists that her husband be accepted into the Airborne during wartime. Our prayers are that such demands will soon be unnecessary.

"Well, I guess I'm not a liar after all," he said with a smile.

Some of the other men looked at Max with dubious expressions. All of them were single, and few could imagine wanting to leave wife and child to join the 82nd Airborne.

That was just one of the things that differentiated Max Collins from other men.

June 9, 1942

Buell 'Anvil' Jenkins was a short, barrel-chested man with a look of perpetual disgust on his face. At forty-one, he was old enough to be the father of most of the other enlisted men on the Pensacola Naval Air Station, and a few of the officers. A year earlier, he had been the hard-drinking crew chief of an Ohio dirt-track team that had aspirations for a shot at the Indianapolis '500'. His nickname came from the fact that he built durable cars. "My rides don't break," he had often said. "They ain't the lightest ones on the track, but they'll be there at the finish if the damn drivers do their part."

One day a new mechanic had made a mistake when working on the steering of the team's sprint car, and the driver had crashed into the wall during practice. When Jenkins had discovered the cause of the accident, he had hit the mechanic hard enough to detach his retina, leaving him blind in the left eye. The judge had given Anvil Jenkins the choice of five-to-ten in Marion, or the opportunity to serve his country in the war that the judge felt the United States was sure to join. Despite his age and lack of prior service, the Navy needed men with Jenkins' exceptional mechanical skills. The mechanic had chosen the second option, but not without considerable deliberation.

Jenkins, with his uncommon talent, had quickly become a qualified airframe and powerplant mechanic in the Navy, but he hated it. He had the best tools and equipment to work with he had ever seen, but it was wasted. The airplanes, especially the clunky old Stearman biplanes, had engines that were antiquated by race car standards, and the planes themselves were boring. The young fliers were worse prima donnas than the most irritating race car driver he had ever met, and they treated him like he was the garbage man instead of the one who made sure they didn't fall out of the sky. The officers were the worst of all. It was more than he could stand to have to call these young punks 'sir', and he had gained a reputation for never speaking unless he absolutely had to.

One of them was walking towards him now.

"Mind if I help with that damaged wingtip, Chief Jenkins? I'm a fair hand with wood. I know it wasn't my student that groundlooped it, but I like these planes, and I'm not doing anything else. Can you use some help?"

Jenkins was surprised by the request, and curious, so he grunted his agreement. *Never seen a college boy yet could use his hands* he thought.

"Lieutenant Walter Bowman," said the young man, extending his right hand with a smile. The older man shook Bowman's hand without expression and was surprised to feel calluses on it.

"Folks call me 'Anvil', sir," Jenkins replied without explaining.

In the next two hours they worked quietly together, with the mechanic occasionally giving a brief suggestion to the superior officer. Anvil Jenkins immediately learned that the young pilot had great woodworking skill. His own experience had always been with metal, but Jenkins could see craftsmanship in any area, and the young man obviously had talent.

"Why do you like these old Stearmans so much, sir?" the older man finally asked. "I figured you'd much rather be in a fighter." Bowman shrugged and gave an answer the mechanic had never expected.

"Fighters are fast, all right, and they're getting better all the time, but there's maneuvers I'd be afraid to try in every one I've ever flown. You can't break a Stearman without flying it into the ground." Anvil Jenkins looked up and Bowman misinterpreted his look of surprise. "Don't believe me? What's the redline speed on a Stearman? It doesn't have one. What's the maneuvering speed? It doesn't have one of those either. You can put a Stearman in a vertical dive with full power from ten thousand feet until it won't go any faster, and then haul back on the stick as hard as you can, and you might black out but you won't break anything. Most planes will have the tail come off in the dive, and the ones that stay together there will have the wings come off in the pullout. I honestly don't believe you can hurt one of these 'yellow perils' while it's still in the air. That's why I like these old yellow, open-cockpit biplanes," he said with finality.

So this is the guy who bet one of the other instructors that a Stearman wouldn't lose its wings in a maximum-G pullout Jenkins thought. "That was you, huh? Pretty relaxed about the taxpayer's money, ain't you, sir?" The mechanic expected a reprimand for his tone of voice, but the young lieutenant was smiling.

Bowman shook his head. "I knew they'd stay on. I even offered to try it without a 'chute." He winked to let the mechanic know his last statement was a joke.

Anvil Jenkins looked at his own powerful arms and then at Bowman's thinner ones. The words that came out of his mouth startled him. "Lieutenant, what if you'd had another 200 pounds in the plane and two more arms hauling back on the other stick to pull out faster?"

Walter Bowman was already heading for the door. "One way to find out, Anvil."

***

The Stearman's 220-HP Continental engine fired up on the second revolution. As he watched from the front cockpit, Anvil Jenkins could not believe what he was doing. He didn't much like flying straight and level in airplanes, let alone trying to make them disintegrate in midair. His stomach was churning, and they were still on the ground.

Walter Bowman gave the engine full power and shoved the stick forward while stepping on the brakes. The tailwheel lifted off the ground, although the plane was stationary. He pulled back slightly on the stick, keeping the biplane balanced on the mains only, and released the brakes. Through judicious use of power, stick, and brakes, Bowman taxied the Stearman out to the end of the runway without ever letting the tailwheel touch the ground. *Damn* thought Jenkins. *I heard about this, but I never saw it. Like a good driver, steering with the throttle. Guy's having fun with his favorite airplane.*

There wasn't another pilot on the base who could taxi a Stearman on the mains without putting a prop tip into the asphalt. For a few minutes, Anvil Jenkins began to feel a little better about the whole endeavor. His comfort was short-lived.

***

It seemed to take forever to get the biplane to altitude, and as it climbed slowly, Anvil Jenkins' wish to be on the ground grew stronger. *What kind of idiot goes up in an airplane trying to tear it apart? We don't even know if these chutes'll work. Hell, we don't even know if there's really chutes in these backpacks.* The plan was looking more and more like insanity with every additional foot of altitude.

At ten thousand feet, Walter Bowman pounded on the fuselage with his fist and the mechanic turned in his seat to see Bowman nod his head. Anvil Jenkins turned forward, took a deep breath, clamped his left hand on the back of his neck, and began to count to twenty. Immediately, Bowman shoved the control stick all the way forward. The engine was already at full throttle. The Stearman nosed over sharply, and the two occupants were forced upwards against their harnesses. *Oh, Jesus* Jenkins thought. The mechanic's stomach felt as if it had relocated itself to a spot underneath his breastbone. When they were looking straight at the ground, Walter Bowman eased off on the forward pressure, and the plane stabilized in an attitude that was slightly past vertical. He had explained to the mechanic during the preflight that if you aimed the plane straight down, the shape of the wings' airfoil would cause the plane to move forward slightly. To get a true no-lift dive and the absolute maximum speed, the aircraft had to be positioned slightly past vertical, so that it would fly straight down. *No wonder fighter planes have their tails flutter and disintegrate* Jenkins thought dismally as the shriek of the wind flowing over the flying wires increased in pitch. Anvil Jenkins had never felt such pure terror in his life.

The young pilot had told him that it would take sixteen seconds for the plane to reach a speed where wind resistance would let it go no faster. *Kid must have timed it with a stopwatch Jenkins thought. Crazy fucker does this shit for fun. Guy said to count to twenty 'cause I'd probably be excited and count fast.*

The mechanic reached a count of twenty but the pitch of the screaming wires was still changing. *No way this college boy is going to tell me I jumped the gun* he thought grimly. He stopped counting but kept his hand behind his head. When the tremendous noise in his ears stopped changing in pitch, he raised his left elbow slightly to signal the young man in back, and pulled his arm down into the cockpit where his left hand joined his right one on the control stick. Anvil Jenkins pulled the control stick towards his gut with all his might. His upper body was thick and powerful, and at the moment he was charged with more adrenaline than he had ever been in his life.

Walter Bowman's hands were already on his own control stick. When he saw Anvil's hand drop from behind his neck, he tensed his stomach muscles as hard as he could and then hauled back on the controls with all his strength. Just as he started, he felt the older man's efforts join his own, and the stick moved backwards more quickly than he had ever experienced. The elevator was forced against the stops, a feat Bowman had only accomplished at lower speeds before, and the controls would move no farther. New sounds emanated from the screaming aircraft as the atmosphere was forced in a new path over the tail's control surfaces. Bowman had experienced high G-forces before, but none like this. His body pressed into the seat as if it weighed over eighteen hundred pounds.

The aircraft was almost level and passing through four thousand feet. Walter Bowman noticed that his own peripheral vision was diminishing but Jenkins was still helping hold the controls against the stops. Bowman smiled into the horrendous wind blast. The G-forces were dragging the flesh of his cheeks and lips downwards, making the young man's face look like something out of a carnival funhouse.

Suddenly the controls got much heavier in Walter Bowman's hands. Anvil Jenkins had released his pull on the stick, and Bowman knew that Jenkins had either lost his nerve or blacked out. Positive G-forces drove the blood out of the brain, and could cause unconsciousness at modest levels if the passenger was a neophyte, or in anyone if the forces were high enough. It was a lesson Walter demonstrated to each new cadet on his first flight by pulling enough Gs to put the new student out. It taught respect for the dangers of flight. It also caused the young lieutenant to be referred to as 'Blackout' Bowman by his contemporaries on the base.

Walter Bowman relaxed backpressure, reduced power, and was prepared to let the biplane fly itself into level equilibrium when suddenly the stick jerked forward in his hand and the airplane nosed over again into a dive. Bowman pulled back as hard as he could, but the stick wouldn't budge.

He immediately realized what had happened. The unconscious man had slumped forward onto his own control stick. The G-forces had caused Jenkins' heavy body to compress the seatpack emergency 'chute enough to make the harness loose. Bowman's 'chute pack, after daily high-G maneuvers, had already been as solid as a rock.

The pilot knew that he couldn't possibly budge the other man by pulling on the stick, so he did the only logical thing. Bowman pushed the controls forward to steepen the descent. As negative Gs raised the unconscious man's body off of the stick, Walter pushed his own control hard against his left knee. The biplane started to roll, and when it was inverted, Bowman leveled the wings. The airplane was now flying upside down at a speed of about a hundred seventy knots, descending in a steep dive at a rate of over three thousand feet per minute.

Walter pushed the stick forward, raising the nose, until the biplane was flying straight and level. The pilot and the mechanic were suspended in their harnesses, blood rushing to their heads. The unconscious mechanic's arms flailed over his head in the windstream. Walter flew the plane upside down on a heading towards the airfield and waited for the older man to regain consciousness.

When Anvil Jenkins came to, he immediately realized he was about to die. *I'm falling out of the plane* he screamed silently to himself. *It's upside down and about to crash!* The mechanic frantically grabbed the edges of the cockpit to hold himself in. *I'm strapped in! Got to unbuckle the harness to bail out. Oh Christ, the ground's right there, and where's the release? I didn't practice this—where's the fucking harness quick relea-*

Before he could get a grip on the quick-release mechanism, the plane miraculously righted itself and flew normally. Jenkins held onto the sides of the open cockpit with a death grip, hyperventilating and waiting for the plane to try to kill him again, when he remembered where he was and who he was with. He turned in his seat to look behind him and saw the smiling young face of Lieutenant Bowman, who was giving him the 'thumbs up' signal. Waves of relief swept over him, coupled with stark horror that he was the one who had suggested this adventure.

The trip back to the base was uneventful, if you ignored the snap roll that Walter Bowman executed on final approach at an altitude of three hundred feet. When the plane finally rolled to a stop on the flight line, Anvil Jenkins climbed down out of it on shaking legs. The mechanic resisted the overpowering impulse to lie down on the asphalt and hug the earth. He could feel his heart rate slowly returning to normal.

Bowman was smiling at him. "You've got a hell of a set of arms, mister. We bottomed out the elevator with the airspeed indicator pegged."

Guy actually looks happy Jenkins realized with astonishment. *Better get my sorry ass together, 'fore he thinks I should be wearing diapers.*

"Uh, what'd we pull, sir?" Jenkins asked. The mechanic noticed that it didn't bother him so much to address the young officer properly.

"Anybody's guess. My peripheral vision was closing in, so I was getting close to a blackout, even with this damn thing on the last notch." Lieutenant Bowman unzipped his flight suit to expose a thick leather harness that compressed his abdomen like a corset, which he then began to unbuckle. The mechanic looked at him quizzically.

"Had it made. Holds your guts in on high-G maneuvers. Keeps you from blacking out as soon. I've pulled eight with it before, in a plane with a meter, and didn't feel anything like what we got today. I'd say we saw at least ten."

The mechanic shook his head in amazement and reached over to pluck at one of the flying wires, expecting it to have lost some tension. It thrummed like the string on a bass guitar. Bowman tied the plane down and the two men headed back to the hangar. The mechanic was thinking.

"Awful strong airframe, but a little shy on power, ain't it, sir?" the man ventured, remembering how long it had taken the 220-horsepower Continental to get them to 10,000 feet.

"No need to buy expensive engines and burn twice the fuel just to train cadets," Bowman replied realistically.

"I might could do something about that...sir," the older man found himself saying. He was starting to feel eager about something for the first time since joining the Navy. Bowman turned towards him and brightened visibly.

"That's right! You build race car engines!" He frowned and shook his head. "I think the brass would come down hard if they found out you modified an engine in a trainer. It wouldn't be worth it for a few more horsepower."

Anvil Jenkins let out the first laugh anyone on the base had ever heard him utter. "A *few* more horsepower? Hell, I ain't talking about tryin' to soup up one a them worthless Continental stem-winders! That thing was out a date the day the first crankcase came out a the foundry. This ain't the race track, with some damn rule book to get around. I got me a wrecked SNJ sitting back of the hangar. Think you could fly that plane of yours with a *real* engine in front of you?—uh, *sir?*"

Walter Bowman was not a man who was easily surprised, but his jaw dropped. The SNJ was a heavy, all-metal trainer. It was powered by a Pratt & Whitney Wasp nine cylinder radial that produced six hundred horsepower.

"You want to put a *Wasp* in a *Stearman?*" Bowman was incredulous, but thrilled at the same time. "What about the CG?" He was referring to the change in the center-of-gravity the heavier engine would make, but already he was thinking of the solution. "The plane's got such big control surfaces, moving the CG forward would probably make it more stable. And we could probably relocate some components aft, section the front of the fuselage..." He was imagining his airplane with almost triple the power. "Damn, Jenkins, the thing would climb like a rocket."

"What else would you want to change, sir?" Jenkins had his head cocked, and was eyeing the young man speculatively.

"A wish list? Well...ailerons on all four wings, first of all, for better roll. Maybe aileron spades, too, to reduce control pressure. Shorten the wings, even. Shorter throw on the stick, too, if we don't need as much leverage any more, lighter gear if cadets aren't going to fly it..." His voice trailed off. "Hell, what am I saying? We'd both face court-martial if you start sawing on one of the trainers on the flight line."

Anvil Jenkins looked at the young man with an evil grin, and for a moment he forgot who he was talking to.

"Those college boys may run most a this base, but I run the maintenance shop. I got me a Stearman in the back with a cracked block and some gear damage, and if I say it ain't fit to return to service with students, then it ain't, and that's that. And I got me that wrecked SNJ, and before you tell me the base might need it for parts, let me tell you that we got another wrecked one behind the south hangar, and if these kay-dets keep slammin' 'em into the runway like they been doin', we're gonna have *another* wrecked one pretty soon, and the one spare part we *don't* seem to need is engines, 'cause that Pratt & Whitney is a pure-D anvil. Unless I start drainin' all the oil out of 'em before puttin' 'em out on the flight line, we're likely to end up with nothin' but busted airframes with hundred-percent engines by the time this damn war is over.

"Now, you got you a ride what won't bust 'less you run it into something, and I reckon you ain't gonna do *that,* but it's got no steam." He spat on the tarmac. "Well, if you want to put together a Stearman that'd make a Boeing engineer's hair stand on end, and you want to do most of your own woodwork, 'cause I'm a hammer man myself, I got me a machine shop Wilbur Shaw would kill for, and I'm sick of seein' it used on nothin' but these airyplanes what look like they was taken to a dee-molition derby by drunk kids in short pants."

Lieutenant Bowman was astonished. He did not know it, but he had just heard the longest continuous utterance Anvil Jenkins had issued since his forced enlistment in the Navy the previous year. He was at a loss for words, so he looked at his watch absent-mindedly. "I've...got to check in. When can I look at that Stearman?"

"I'll be in the shop all night, sir. Come by after dinner if you want."

"I will," the young lieutenant said, nodding slowly as he turned to leave. He was still shaking his head when one of the other instructors hailed him near the Officer's Club.

"Didn't I see you with Jenkins by the hangar? What were you doing with that sour old prick?"

"I'm not sure," Bowman said with a puzzled look on his face. "I think I may have created a monster."

August 6, 1942

"Both of you—on your feet. You will come with us." The four men in uniform looked terrifying to the young couple.

"But—"

"No talking." The soldier in charge looked at Irwin. "You have one minute to pack a bag. You," he said, addressing Irwin Mann's twenty-three-year-old wife Magda, "will not need anything else. *Now!*" he commanded.

At least they won't be detaining her overnight Irwin thought. As if in a daze, the young grocer retrieved a battered case from under their bed and hastily put some clothes and toiletries in it. He wanted to find out where they were taking him, but the four soldiers with submachine guns did not look as though they would be agreeable to questions right now.

As they left the small shop, Irwin took out his keys to lock up. One of the soldiers snatched them from his hand. "We will take care of your shop for you," he said in a tone that invited no argument.

Irwin and Magda, flanked by the four soldiers, walked down Bahnhofstrasse. As they came up to the edge of the railway station, Irwin Mann's heart sank. There were scores of Jews being herded along towards a freight train. All of them were men.

"I believe your husband has a ticket for this one, *Frau* Mann," said one of the soldiers, and his three companions broke out into raucous laughter. Two of them started to lead the girl away.

"Wait! You can't—" The rifle butt hit him squarely in the solar plexus, and Irwin Mann was immediately doubled over in agony. He could neither talk nor breathe.

"Don't worry, *Herr* Mann," one of the two departing soldiers said over his shoulder. "I assure you that your wife will not be bored. I am sure that our fine officers will keep your little Polish cunt occupied in ways you have never imagined." The others laughed as they picked Irwin up and threw him bodily through the open door of the freight car.

"Irwin!" Magda screamed as the freight car door clanged shut.

They would never see each other again.

August 8, 1942

Irwin Mann could still not believe it. *The day before yesterday I was working in my produce and grocery shop in Danzig* he thought. *Now I'm packed like a piece of livestock into a vile-smelling railway car.* The train had made several stops to pick up more citizens, but no one had been permitted to get off. There were now so many of them in such a small space that if anyone fainted from fatigue, he would be held erect by the closeness of the others around him. The passengers' requests to be allowed to relieve themselves had been ignored. The oppressive heat generated by so many human bodies packed together made the inevitable result all the more nauseating.

Irwin knew they were being taken to Warsaw. The men in the freight car had talked freely at first. Then, as their confinement in the darkness of their current prison had continued, Irwin had seen their spirit disintegrate. *Now, no one is speaking* Irwin thought. *Many of these men have much more education than I, and are in well-respected professions.* Their demoralization was overwhelming. Irwin, too, felt the crushing reality of what was happening to him build on itself, but he was younger than most of those around him, and he had not yet lost his young man's unerring faith in what the future held in store for him.

The train finally arrived at its ultimate destination. The air brakes filled the cars with a cacophony of hisses, squeals, and sounds of creaking metal as they gradually dragged over 1200 tons of freight train to a halt. Immediately, the passengers heard the sounds of soldiers pounding on the latches to open the freight doors on the sides of the cars.

When the doors swung open, all the people inside squinted in the bright sunlight as they stumbled and fell out of the cars. Irwin was stronger and quicker than most of the others, and he escaped the wrath of the soldiers who stood to the sides of each freight car door, urging the captives out.

"Move! You are delaying the others!" A soldier was prodding a man of about sixty with the bayonet attached to the muzzle of his rifle. The man had fallen from the freight car to the gravel and wrenched his ankle. The soldier kicked him in the thigh. "Jewish filth—you have soiled yourself. Animals!" He spat on the fallen figure and turned to vent his anger on another captive.

When Irwin Mann's eyes adjusted to the bright daylight, he was amazed at what he saw. The railroad yard appeared to be at the edge of a city. A high wall extended as far as he could see between where he stood and the city itself. At an opening in the wall, Nazi soldiers armed with submachine guns stood guard. *Can this wall extend all the way around the city?* he asked himself in disbelief. *They have transformed all of Warsaw into a prison camp!*

"Your things are being unloaded now. Take them and get moving!" Irwin looked in the direction of the soldier's gaze and saw some shabby-looking Jews haphazardly throwing suitcases and duffel bags off of one of the freight cars. "Get going!" the soldier commanded, and to emphasize his point he jabbed at the people nearest him with his bayonet, eliciting two screams.

Irwin followed the others towards the pile of baggage. He noticed a few women among the group. *None of them are under thirty-five.* A feeling of dread ran through him as he located his bag and followed some of the others towards the gap in the wall. When they passed though it, Irwin Mann saw that his suspicions had been accurate. They were in the city of Warsaw, and the wall extended around all of it that he could see. There were other drab-looking people off in the distance. The entire tableau before him was one of utter despair.

"Now what?" asked an elderly man standing near Irwin Mann. He was addressing no one in particular.

"I think we're on our own," Mann said as he started walking into the city.

August 10, 1942

"More right rudder! More *right* rudder!" Lieutenant Walter Bowman yelled into the funnel. *Hell*, Bowman thought, *he can't hear me any better than any of the others could.* The instructor looked at the back of his student's head and felt foolish for even trying to use the ridiculous 'intercom'.

The Stearman biplane, in Walter Bowman's very biased view, was one of the finest creations on earth, but the funnel-and-tube communication system was a joke. Bowman unbuckled his harness and prepared to effect the cure that had unintentionally become one of his trademarks.

Grabbing the edge of the cockpit with his left hand and the semicircular cutout in the trailing edge of the upper wing with his right, Bowman lifted himself to a crouched position in the hole in the fuselage in which he had been sitting a second before. With a fluid movement that was the result of having performed this particular maneuver many times in the past, he swung his right leg over the edge of the cockpit and planted his foot on the wing root of the right lower wing. It took serious effort to combat the strong wind blast provided by both the plane's 80-knot forward speed and the prop wash of the big propeller.

Using the bracing wires and the wing strut for handholds, Walter Bowman put all his weight on his right foot, pulled his left leg out of the rear cockpit, and took two more steps into the wind blast until he stood on the part of the wing next to the front cockpit hole in the fuselage.

The student snapped his head to the right and his eyes grew wide inside his flight goggles. He had been rendered unconscious on his first flight with this insane man, and he had been told by his fellow cadets to expect this current atrocity, but it still had not prepared him for the sight of his instructor standing on the wing of the airplane that he, and he alone, was now flying.

Bowman held the edge of the front cockpit with his left hand and a bracing wire with his right. He leaned over and put his mouth next to the cadet's right ear.

"You've got the nose too high. We're still in a climb, and that's why we don't have any speed," he yelled. He let go of the edge of the cockpit and reached in to tap the face of the altimeter for emphasis. "I told you on the ground to level off at five thousand. Look." The student, momentarily horrified that his instructor had let go one of his handholds, looked at the altimeter. The clock-like hands showed that they were at 5200 feet.

Bowman grabbed the control stick and said "I've got it. Keep your feet on the rudders." He pushed the stick forward until the plane was flying straight and level. His position on the side was an awkward one from which to try to exert force on the controls, and it took considerable effort. The airspeed indicator started to climb gradually. He pushed harder, lowering the nose further, and the big Stearman began a slight descent. Keeping and eye on the altimeter, he leveled the plane at five thousand feet.

"Hold it there," he commanded. He released his grip on the stick when he saw that his student had control of it. "Do you see the position of the horizon?" The student nodded his assent. "That's what straight and level looks like. Try to remember it. Now," he shouted, tapping the face of another gauge on the panel, "look at your slip-and-skid indicator." The device he was pointing to was a curved, fluid-filled tube, aligned like a frown. A black ball floated in the clear liquid, somewhat closer to the right end of the tube than the left. "You need more right rudder. Step on the ball, remember?" The student nodded vigorously as he increased pressure on the right rudder pedal. The black ball drifted a bit left of center as the cadet pushed a little too hard with his right leg, then settled in the proper center position when he relaxed pressure slightly.

"That's good," Bowman yelled. "After I get back in, I want you to show me a three-sixty to the left, and then one to the right, staying at five thousand feet." The student nodded, his eyes looking at the relationship of the horizon with the leading edge of the top wing. Bowman tapped the slip-and-skid indicator once more for emphasis. "Make sure your turns stay coordinated while you're in your bank. Then head for home." He patted the cadet on the shoulder, climbed back into his own cockpit, buckled his safety harness, and flexed the muscles in his feet and calves to relax them.

The student looked over his shoulder and saw his instructor nod his head. He rolled the biplane into a thirty-degree bank to the left and held it there. *The nose is a little low and we're going to lose a little altitude,* Bowman thought. *His rudder control is spot-on, though.*

Walter didn't need to look at his own instrument panel to judge the young man's efforts. When a turn and bank was properly coordinated, the people in the plane didn't feel their bodies pushed to the outside or falling to the inside of the turn. Walter's favorite demonstration of proper control coordination, when he was in an enclosed airplane, was to set a water glass on the top of the instrument panel and fill it from a pitcher without spilling a drop. This would be no great feat, except that Walter Bowman did it while making the airplane perform a barrel roll. It was a demonstration that had won him not only the respect of the other instructors on the base, but also quite a bit of their pocket money as well.

As the student rolled out of the left-hand 360-degree turn, he saw that he had lost almost 100 feet of altitude. Pushing the stick to the right to roll into his right-hand turn, he increased back pressure on it to raise the nose slightly. His instructor smiled. *This kid's going to be one of the better ones.* Walter Bowman never lost sight of the fact that in an all too short time, his pupils were going to be using their new skills in a much more hostile environment than clear skies over the coast of the Florida panhandle.

When Ensign Taylor Lowell rolled the wings level on his original heading, he looked at his altimeter. It read a fraction over 4900 feet. His second 360 had been made holding a constant altitude. Ensign Lowell felt a surge of pride that surprised him with its intensity. The fear of not measuring up that accompanied the excitement of flying dropped down a notch.

With a sixth sense about such matters, Lieutenant Bowman felt the difference in the young man's attitude. When they turned back towards the base, he elected to let his student fly it all the way into the landing pattern before taking over the controls for the landing itself. On the way back to the airfield, the big biplane felt a little more steady, its heading a little more consistent, and the thrum of its engine just a little more smooth.

***

"How'd the babes in the woods do today, Blackout?" Lieutenant Homer Tapscott was grinning at his friend and fellow flight instructor. "I can see you're going to have to requisition another flight suit. The Navy doesn't tolerate shoddy uniforms." Bowman looked down and saw that the bottom of his right pants leg had finally become frayed from high-speed flapping in the wind. *The right ones always seem to wear through first* he thought. *The supply clerk must be getting used to seeing me every ten days or so.*

"Any day that ends with the bird still airworthy and free from vomit is a success," Bowman said pleasantly. Walter Bowman was the only instructor at Pensacola whose students had never damaged an airplane, but he had not been able to prevent a few of them from throwing up. "The kids they're sending us seem to get younger and greener every month."

"We're just getting old." Lieutenants Tapscott and Bowman were each twenty-six. "I'm done for the day. Join me at the O.C. for a bit? Grab a Coke?" Tapscott knew his friend never drank alcohol.

Walter Bowman's smile was small, but it showed excited anticipation. "No, I heard Anvil had some good news for me. I think I'll go take a look at his welds." He turned his back and started to walk towards the hangars. He could guess what Tapscott's reaction would be.

"He got the mount finished? The hell with the officer's club—I gotta see this!" Homer Tapscott broke into a trot to catch up with his friend.

***

The big Stearman looked considerably different than it had several months before. The wings were twenty-one inches shorter on each side, and the upper ones had ailerons just like the lowers. The wing struts, handholds, and step had all been reshaped to make them more streamlined. Everywhere that the biplane had been square and angular, it was now more rounded. The landing gear was lighter and slightly taller to compensate for the larger prop that the craft would be using, and the main wheels were covered with beautiful, hand-formed aluminum wheel pants with flawless welds. 'Just like making little bitty sprint car bodies,' Anvil Jenkins had proclaimed.

The biggest change, however, was in front of the firewall. Where once had been a six-cylinder Continental engine displacing 540 cubic inches now sat a nine-cylinder Pratt & Whitney radial with 1320 inches of displacement. Jenkins saw the two men looking at the engine and walked over to them.

"Got it back further than we thought, Lieutenant. Relocated a couple things on the firewall that were in the way"—Walter Bowman saw that this was a gross understatement—"and got her snugged all in tight. Be stronger that way, too, engine won't have as much leverage with a mount a couple inches shorter'n the one came off it."

Bowman examined the handmade engine mount. It was a beautifully formed piece made of myriad short sections of steel tubing expertly welded together. Every part of it had been triangulated. There was not a single bend in any section of tubing. It did not look heavy, but Bowman knew he would have to crash the plane to make the engine mount flex.

"Been thinkin' about what kind of prop to use. I figure you want her to climb like a bandit, sir, so we need one with a flat pitch if you're going to spin her up 500 RPM more than what you're turning now. Maybe have to have one ma–"

"*What?*" exclaimed Lieutenant Tapscott in disbelief. "Turn a Wasp five hundred over redline? You'll blow it up!"

Walter Bowman smiled. "I told Anvil I didn't want to exceed factory stress levels. He lightened all the reciprocating parts and cut down the counterweights on the crank to balance it. We got three of the slide-rule geniuses in Artillery to give us a new redline based on the new recip weights. They all three came up with the same number independently. Should run all day at the new setting." Tapscott was speechless.

"Shaved the heads, too, along with cleanin' up the ports. I think the engineers at Pratt were maybe plannin' to sell these engines to some Meskins who'd run 'em on creosote. Got to drink grape juice now, but hell, Lieutenant, we got plenty of that." Anvil Jenkins was explaining how he had raised the engine's compression ratio and increased its ability to consume the air/fuel mixture that fed it. Aviation fuels were color-coded by grade, with the highest-octane, 115/145, having a purple tint that earned it the nickname 'grape juice'.

"What about torque factor?" It had been some time since Homer Tapscott had ventured into the hangar, and he was awed by what had taken shape there.

Jenkins smiled. "We been wonderin' about that, sir. Made the rudder 'bout twenty percent bigger, but I figure that old Pratt's going to be kickin' out at least eight hundred, maybe eight-fifty. Don't think Lieutenant Bowman's going to want to use full throttle on takeoff, or he might end up on his back. And I suggest nobody get in a ass-kickin' contest with him in a few months. If he flies this bird as much as I expect, he's going to have the strongest fuckin' right leg on this air base. sir." The mechanic was referring to a phenomenon called 'P-Factor' where, in a climb, the right side of an airplane's propeller had more thrust than its left, necessitating the pilot's use of additional right rudder. The effect was increasingly pronounced with more powerful engines.

"It's going to be airworthy that soon?" Tapscott was amazed.

"Seems like the green ones are bangin' up the trainers less often these days, sir, and, uh, the kids in the shop here are kind of itchy to see if this thing will fly. They got kind of a different attitude 'bout their job since they seen that ass-over-teakettle thing the Lieutenant here did last week."

"We better get back, Homer. I've got ground school to teach. It's looking great, Jenkins."

"It's an anvil, sir," the mechanic said with a grin. The two officers returned smiles and departed the hangar.

Anvil Jenkins' comment about the junior mechanics referred to the fact that Walter Bowman, in his endless quest to find out what a Stearman could do, had discovered a flight maneuver no one on the base had ever seen, and had performed it for the base on July 4th.

In virtually all maneuvers by aerobatic aircraft, although the airplane might be pointed straight up, straight down, on its side, or upside down, it is still flying. That is to say, the plane is still responding to control inputs because at least one of the movable control surfaces still has air flowing smoothly over it.

In a stall, the wings quit flying but the rudder and elevator are still effective, and can be used to get the wings providing lift again. In a spin, one wing is not flying, so the plane corkscrews down, but the rudder and elevator are again still effective and can break the plane out of the spin. A snap roll is merely a horizontal spin while flying straight and level. It is performed by forcing one wing to quit flying by abrupt use of elevator and rudder, then reversing the process so that both wings provide lift again after the aircraft has made one revolution. Even in a tailslide, where the plane is flown straight up and allowed to fall back, air is flowing backwards over the elevator and rudder, and moving either of these controls will flip the plane over to where it is flying forward again.

Walter Bowman had discovered that it was difficult, but possible, to make a Stearman quit flying altogether. With little fuel, and with some lead weights firmly bolted to the inside of the plane's fuselage behind the rear cockpit, the aircraft's center of gravity was past its aft safe limit as determined by Boeing engineers. In this configuration, Bowman found that if he initiated a climbing inverted snap roll at a higher-than-average rate of speed and held the controls in that position rather than reversing them to end the maneuver, the Stearman would tumble.

To an observer on the ground, the maneuver looked the same as if a toy metal airplane, designed only to sit on the mantle, had been grabbed by the back end and thrown like a tomahawk across the sky. No two performances of this maneuver were quite the same. The plane tumbled randomly. After two or three somersaults, the huge amount of drag produced by the large wing and fuselage surfaces slowed the Stearman to where it started to fall out of the sky. When it did, it would enter a spin, either an upright one or inverted. These are both standard aerobatic maneuvers (though horrifying to the uninitiated) from which any accomplished aerobatic pilot can recover. The tumble that preceded them, however, was a new one to everyone on the base.

The pilots at Pensacola had taken to calling the maneuver a 'B-Squared,' math notation for BB, which stood for 'Blackout' Bowman. The young lieutenant did not think he had invented something no one else had ever done before; he just couldn't find anyone who had ever heard of such a maneuver, let alone seen it.

Thirty years later the maneuver would be common at air shows around the country. It would be called a *Lomcevak*, a Czechoslovakian term given the maneuver by a Czech pilot who had mastered it in the early '70s in a Zlin. The word has no literal English translation. Loosely interpreted, it means 'I have drunk too much wine and my head feels awful'. Aerobatic pilots after 1972 would often refer to it as 'The Hunky Headache'.

The airshow circuit pilots who would employ the Lomcevak in their repertoire in future decades would perform it in purpose-built competition aerobatic machines such as the Zlin, Pitts Special, Christen Eagle, and the Laser. None would use a Stearman, which became a staple of airshows but would be generally relegated to wingwalking acts. Few pilots fifty years after WWII would trust the structural integrity of a plane originally built for $1500 in 1929 to endure the stresses created by a Lomcevak. Fewer still would bolt lead to a plane built in 1929 and move the CG aft of its design limit just to see how much caution the original engineers had exercised.

And not a single one of them would have Walter Bowman's absolute certainty that a Stearman could do anything, if only you were good enough.

September 12, 1942

Okay, feet together, hands up on the risers, knees bent slightly, get ready to drop and roll... Max Collins ran through everything he had been taught and had practiced in jump training. There was one thing Collins could not do, however, and that was change the fact that he was 6'3" tall and weighed 203 pounds in his underwear. The jumpmaster had warned Collins time and again that he was going to hit hard under a 24-foot canopy while carrying forty pounds of gear.

The other men in his unit were a good forty to fifty pounds lighter, and for the first time in his life, Max Collins wished he were smaller. He had made thirty-one jumps, and had felt every one of them. This was his thirty-second.

Wind moving me back and right, okay, twist a little and... Max Collins' feet hit the ground just a little sooner than he had anticipated, and he had not yet tensed his ankles as he had been taught to do. As he slammed into the hardpacked earth, there was a pop that he felt all the way up to his knee.

Shit! Broken ankle he thought instantly, and cursed himself for failing to remain vigilant. He rolled on the ground and came up on his one good leg, hopping towards the canopy to keep the lines slack so the 'chute wouldn't drag him.

Damn thought Collins, for what would not be the last time. Then another thought filled his mind, and he focused on it: *I am going to heal, and I am not going to let this put me on the sidelines. By God, I'm not.*

April 17, 1943

Irwin Mann stared at Stern, waiting for him to speak. The older man's eyes were fixed on four handguns which lay on a dilapidated table in front of him. *He doesn't look happy* Irwin thought. *And little wonder. Four well-worn pistols in several calibers, with only a handful of ammunition that may not even fire. Not much to bet our lives on, after his speech last night.* Irwin Mann looked around at the others. The faces of many of the men showed unmistakable signs of defeat. Fear was there also. It hung like a noxious fog in the crowded room. The penalty for having a gun was death, and each man there knew it. None of these men had been soldiers. None had been policemen. Not one had ever himself owned a firearm. *I doubt any of us know how to use them, even if they do work* Irwin thought grimly. *No surprise Stern doesn't know what to say.*

"We are doomed," came a voice from the group. The older man looked up, but could not tell who had spoken.

"We are certainly doomed if we do nothing," Stern said. "The Nazis have been shipping our people away by the trainload. I can scarcely believe that we were so blind as to think it could have been to someplace better."

"But maybe it *is* someplace better. They say it is because of the overcrowding here." The speaker's voice had a desperate sound. Stern fixed him with a penetrating stare, and Irwin saw that Stern was acting as a leader should, defusing the feeling of hopelessness that threatened to kill their resistance movement before it had made even a symbolic gesture.

"Are you volunteering to go on the next train? Or are you eager to promise the Nazis you will help them fill the train with others headed for this 'better place', if they let you stay here?"

The man turned his face away in shame at Stern's question.

The reality the men in the group faced was so overwhelming, no one dared speak of it. The decision to implement the 'Final Solution' had been made by the German High Command in early 1942. The residents of the Ghetto did not know that, exactly, but they were well aware that railroad cars were leaving Warsaw every few days with hundreds of their people. It was impossible for them not to piece together what was happening. Nazi soldiers hinted broadly at the fitting end their leaders had devised for the sub-human creatures whose existence they had been forced to endure for so long.

At the Battle of Stalingrad in late 1942, Germany's advance to the east had been stopped in its tracks. Almost a million German troops had perished in that battle alone. Everyone knew that it was just a matter of time before the Nazis were defeated, so some residents of the Ghetto were doing their best to get along with their captors, trying to stay alive long enough for the liberating forces to arrive. The problem was that keeping oneself alive meant helping the Nazis round up others for shipment out of the city, and the shipments were getting larger and more frequent. Some of the Jews had decided that they now had to fight, regardless of the odds.

A young man named Mordecai Anielewicz had called upon others in the Ghetto to mount a resistance effort. Several men with influence in the Ghetto had taken his idea to heart, and had assembled their own groups. Stern was one such person, and he was the reason Irwin Mann and the others were gathered that evening in the small room.

Stern looked away from the man he had reprimanded and returned to the subject of their meager arsenal. "We have done well to amass these weapons," he said, indicating the guns that lay on the table, "And with them, we have a chance. You are forgetting, my good friends, that we have many, many more weapons available to us now, all with plenty of the proper ammunition, and all in good condition." *Exactly right* Irwin Mann thought as he looked around at the skeptical, tired, faces, all but devoid of hope. And Irwin Mann smiled.

It was a genuine smile, full of comprehension and expectation, and Stern saw it instantly.

"Let me have the revolver," Irwin said when he saw Stern looking at him. "It is least likely to malfunction. I will get more weapons for us." All heads swiveled to look at the one who had spoken.

"Your name, young man?" Stern asked softly. Irwin Mann's smile disappeared, and a pained look of shame replaced it.

"I am here in Warsaw because my name was known to those who wish to exterminate us. My wife was taken from me. I pray that she is dead." This brought a gasp from some in the group. "I fear that if she is not," he went on, "she may be in a place where she wishes that she were. I am not known here. I have no friends, and I will make none. But if you will give me that revolver, I will bring you more weapons."

"You believe that one of us might somehow betray you by knowing your name?" One of the older men in the group was speaking. His eyes were narrow slits and his seething anger was quite obvious.

"I believe that many things will happen which we cannot now imagine," Mann said levelly. "I know that I can scarcely believe what I have already seen with my own eyes. There is no benefit in any of us having information about each other that we do not need." He looked at Stern. The old man nodded, and handed him the revolver.

"I asked the Lord to send us a sign. He has done so," Stern said, nodding at Irwin.

No one spoke. All eyes were on Irwin Mann as he slid the gun into the side pocket of his tattered, filthy overcoat and briskly walked away from the group. In a few moments he had vanished up one of the alleys and was gone.

Irwin Mann's heart was racing. The bravado he had shown in front of the others had been utter fabrication. He had been terrified that his voice would crack with the fear that was churning in his guts. He knew nothing about guns. He recalled that he had once heard that revolvers were more reliable and easier to use than the other kind of gun, and had suddenly found himself blurting out his demand for the weapon. In truth, he was not sure he knew how to make the gun fire at all.

The young grocer from Danzig had one tremendous asset, however, and it was what had given him the courage to seize the opportunity to control his destiny. Irwin Mann was a very analytical person who had an innate understanding of machinery. He let this fact give him comfort as he stepped through the doorway of an abandoned building and walked over to a broken window.

With shuffling motions of his feet, Irwin used his ragged boots to sweep the glass and debris away from beneath the window and clear a spot so that he could lie down. He wanted both privacy and decent light. He needed to be able to examine the gun and figure out exactly how it worked before taking any action. He had a plan in mind, but it did not allow for hesitation or uncertainty.

The young Jew took the revolver out of his coat pocket. He knew enough to keep the barrel pointed away from any part of his body and his fingers away from the trigger. He did not know how hard you needed to press on the trigger to make the gun fire. He did not think it logical that a slight touch would discharge the weapon, but he had no intention of doing anything rash to find out.

Irwin turned the weapon in his hands. He knew the fat bulge in the center was the cylinder. It held the ammunition—six shots. He could see the cartridges even though the gun was closed up and ready to fire. The back edges of the brass cartridge cases could be seen through the space between the back of the cylinder and the chassis of the gun. *Was chassis the right word?* He wasn't sure.

Irwin looked at the front of the gun, not letting the barrel point straight at his head but rather angling away from it. His heart jumped when he saw the dull white-grey of oxidized lead visible in the four chambers of the cylinder that were not in the top or bottom position, and he was struck with a thrilling thought: *If a gun like this is pointed at you, and you are close to it, you can tell if it's loaded or not!* He was determined to figure out how to take the ammunition out so that he could better understand how the gun worked.

His attention was drawn to the gun's hammer. It stuck up on the back, and had grooves machined or filed into it. They looked like they were there to provide a non-slip grip for a finger or thumb. He started to pull the hammer back, and as he did so, he saw the cylinder start to turn. He realized he was starting to cock the weapon, and that was something he did not want to do. He slowly lowered the hammer to its original position. The cylinder stopped turning. He saw that there was no longer a chamber lined up with the barrel of the gun. Irwin touched the cylinder and realized that it now would turn freely. He rotated it with his finger, and when one of the chambers in it containing a cartridge was lined up with the barrel, the cylinder locked into position with an audible click. Mann realized he could no longer turn the cylinder with his hand.

I have to unload this weapon, he thought. He looked at what he had believed was the gun's safety catch. It was a serrated, rectangular button on the left side of the gun. He pushed on it. Nothing happened. It was under spring tension and returned to its original rearward position. Irwin pushed it again, with the same result. *It doesn't feel like anything is broken. Why won't it stay in the new setting?* He held the gun up close to his face, looking in all the gaps and spaces between parts as he pressed the button on the left side forward once more.

Irwin saw minute movement of two of the internal parts. They were both on the centerline axis of the gun's cylinder. He held the button forward and gripped the gun firmly with his free hand, being careful not to touch the trigger. The cylinder, which had been locked rigidly in place, moved slightly. He pushed on it, first to the right, then the left. It swung out of the gun's frame on a pivoting metal arm. All six cartridges were plainly visible. *It's not the safety* he thought triumphantly. *It's a latch to open the gun and load or unload it!*

The young man held the gun with the muzzle pointed towards the ceiling of the ruined building and shook it gently. Three of the six cartridges dropped out of the cylinder into his left hand. The other three stayed where they were. Irwin started to look for a stick or a nail to push the remaining ones out from the front. *That can't be right* he thought. *There must be another way.*

A slender rod extended from the center of the cylinder. Irwin grabbed it and tried to pull it out, thinking that it was there for the shooter to poke the cartridges out one at a time. It would not move. On an impulse, he pushed on the rod. It immediately slid into the front of the cylinder. At the cylinder's back, a flower-shaped piece of metal underneath the rims of the cartridges extended rearward an equal amount, extracting the remaining rounds of ammunition all at the same time. The cartridges fell to the floor, and when Irwin let go of the rod, it snapped back under spring tension and the six-pointed piece of metal attached to its back end was once again seated in the rear of the cylinder. Mann smiled.

He looked the empty gun over carefully. He held it up to the light and peered down the bore. Irwin saw five spiral grooves evenly spaced, twisting down the barrel's interior. In a sudden flash of inspiration, he realized they were there to make the bullet spin and fly straight, like a football thrown by an American he had seen on a newsreel ten years before. As the gun gave up its secrets and revealed the unerring logic of its design, Irwin Mann felt his anxiety replaced with exhilaration, hope, and an overwhelming sense of purpose.

In the next hour, by practicing with the empty weapon, Irwin learned that there were two ways to make the gun fire. First, as he had seen earlier, if he pulled the hammer back until it caught, the cylinder turned into position and the trigger only took a slight pull to make the hammer fall and fire the gun. If he pulled the trigger without first cocking the hammer, it took a lot more effort and it made the cylinder rotate and the hammer retract before falling on the new chamber at the end of the stroke. *There is no safety on a revolver* he realized. *The effort and distance required to pull the trigger when the hammer is not cocked makes it impossible for it to happen by accident.* He was also aware of another truth: *If the ammunition is bad and doesn't go off, I can try the next cartridge just by pulling the trigger again. That's why I have heard that revolvers are easier to use and more reliable.* Irwin Mann's confidence continued to increase.

For the next hour the young Jew practiced pulling the empty gun out of the pocket of his overcoat, pointing it at an imagined enemy, and pulling the trigger. He realized that an alert adversary might react to a sudden movement, and he tried holding his left arm bent and in front of his body to ward off defensive maneuvers, keeping his gun hand at his side where it touched his waist just above the hipbone.

Got to find a soldier in the area who is alone Irwin thought. *The patrols invariably travel at least in pairs, and usually in groups of three.* Irwin Mann had no illusions that he would be able to prevail against anything more than a single, unsuspecting enemy. *But a soldier will go out alone when he's doing something he doesn't want seen by his companions* Irwin reminded himself. This was not unusual. Extortion was common. So was bartering military issue foodstuffs and medicine for the gold and gems that some of the Jews had brought in to Warsaw with them. Rape was also a fact of life. The Germans soldiers would almost never touch the Jewish women in the area—they were seen as subhuman. Lithuanians and Poles had no such qualms. *Maybe I can find one on a solo outing with rape in mind* Irwin told himself. His thoughts went to the last time he had seen his wife. *I will take great pleasure in changing the man's plans.*

Most of the soldiers patrolling the Ghetto were in fact not Germans. It was considered light duty, and much of the work was performed by Lithuanian militiamen and Polish police who were viewed with scorn by Nazi soldiers. The benefit of this fact was that if a Lithuanian or Pole went missing, he would be assumed to have skipped out. *No one will think he has been the victim of an ambush* Irwin reassured himself. *Not the first one, at least.*

There is also the matter of noise Irwin reminded himself. *Even when I find a lone soldier, I must be sure that others do not rush in too soon at the sound of a shot.* Risky though it might be, he decided that his best chance would be to shove the barrel of the gun into the fabric of the thick uniform coat that the soldiers wore, before pulling the trigger. It would mean rushing up to the intended victim instead of shooting him from a position of concealment, but Irwin decided it still offered the best probability of success. *It will also be a lot less likely that I'll miss.*

He carefully reloaded the revolver and put it back in the right pocket of his coat. From the left pocket he withdrew the other weapon that he intended to use. It was a well-worn but serviceable pair of small Zeiss folding binoculars. He had managed to acquire them several weeks before from a young woman who had also been relocated to the Warsaw Ghetto. Irwin Mann had not been sure how he would use them, but he had never doubted that they would become a great asset.

Using the glasses, Irwin looked out the broken window and up and down the street. He saw only other Jews trudging beside the buildings. *Only one thing to do, then* he decided. *It's time to go hunting.* Mann went back out the doorway and walked into the street. His head was bowed as he took on the defeated, hopeless air of the other residents of the city, but his spirits were soaring. For the first time in months, he felt truly alive.

It did not take long. In a few blocks, he came upon a German soldier who had just finished using the butt of his rifle on a man who appeared to be about sixty-five years old but who was actually fifty-one.

"Filthy cur! You will not again waste my time when you have nothing to trade. Or perhaps you will be on Friday's train and there will not *be* a next time, eh?" The soldier had just finished reslinging his rifle over his shoulder when Irwin Mann acted. The young Jew thrust the barrel of the .38 revolver against the soldier's spine between his shoulder blades, pushing it into the man with both his hands. He was driving forward just as he would if he had no gun and were trying to shove the soldier across the street. As he felt the man's body start to give under the unexpected force, Irwin pulled the trigger.

He had expected the technique to somewhat muffle the report of the gun, and he was not disappointed. As with any revolver, some high-pressure gases escaped between the thin gap between the cylinder and barrel, so the sound of the shot was still there, but all the burning powder that normally would have blasted out the muzzle was trapped.

That caused a result that Irwin Mann had *not* expected. With the muzzle of the gun pressed firmly against the Nazi's back, not only had the bullet entered his flesh, but the entire explosive force of the burning powder and high-pressure gases behind the bullet in the barrel of the gun had been directed into the man's body as well. The net effect was the same as if a small explosive charge had been detonated inside the soldier's body. One vertebra, the ends of two ribs, part of one lung, and the edge of the man's heart were destroyed in a millisecond. A slurry of these ruined parts sloshed down onto the dead man's diaphragm, leaving a cavity the size of a cantaloupe where the organs had been just a moment before.

As this happened, the barrel of the gun slid into the entrance hole in the soldier's back and the jagged bottom of the upper section of his ruined spine snagged the gun's front sight. Irwin Mann, who was holding the revolver with an adrenaline-charged grip, was pulled down on top of the falling body. The force of his own weight landing on the dead Nazi drove the air out of the remaining lung and made a retching sound that startled the young man. In the instant before his mind realized what had happened, he thought the man might still be alive

Irwin immediately leaped to his feet, withdrawing the gun from the soldier's back. He was vaguely aware of the gore which dripped from it as he thrust it into his coat pocket and grabbed the corpse by the ankles. Irwin turned his head so that if the old man that the soldier had clubbed was looking, he would not see Irwin's face. His heart was racing, and with the strength that fear and excitement can bring, he quickly dragged the body into the alley.

The Jew had half expected to feel nausea after the killing, but the fear of discovery and the fact that his job was far from over combined to fully occupy his senses. He would not feel the magnitude of what he had just done until much later.

Irwin's first surprise was that it was harder to remove an overcoat from a dead body than he had ever imagined. After the coat was off, the former grocer wrapped the rifle in it so that it would be a little less conspicuous. He also took the spare ammunition for the rifle, the 9mm Luger autoloading pistol from the man's belt holster, the spare loaded pistol magazines, and a handful of paper currency. He pulled off the man's boots and socks, and cut off his shirt and pants with a pair of tailor's shears he had carried in his pocket. He then covered the body with debris from the alley. Irwin hoped that to a casual glance from another soldier, it would look like just another Jew who had died of starvation or exposure. The discovery of a slain German soldier would be big news indeed, and elicit a response he could not afford.

Using a different route, Irwin returned to a building he knew was unoccupied. He knew it was vacant because one of the weaker inhabitants of the Warsaw Ghetto had died in the basement six days earlier, and the corpse was still there. The stench was terrible, but it discouraged others from using either the basement or the ground floor. Irwin stayed long enough to study the rifle to make sure he understood how it worked.

The rifle was a Mauser 8mm Model 98, a bolt action weapon whose method of function was immediately obvious even to someone with no previous experience. Lifting the round end of the bolt handle rotated the bolt and unlocked it so that it could be drawn to the rear. Pushing the bolt forward from that position placed a cartridge in the chamber, and pushing the handle back down again locked the breech and rendered the gun ready to fire.

Irwin drew back the rifle's bolt and saw a full load of ammunition in the magazine. The top round slipped under the extractor as the bolt reached its rearward limit. He pushed the bolt forward and the top cartridge slid into the chamber. Irwin retracted the bolt once more and the cartridge was thrown out onto the floor. The young man practiced the maneuver until all the cartridges lay at his feet. He was satisfied that he understood the weapon's basic functioning. It did not register on Irwin Mann that the rifle had had no round in the chamber when the soldier had been carrying it.

Irwin wrapped the rifle, the Luger, and the ammunition in the soldier's coat and stowed them under the stairs. He left the overpowering smell of the basement and went outside. It was time to look for more prey.

In the next three hours, using much the same technique, Irwin Mann killed two more armed enemies. The first was a sallow-looking Lithuanian. The other was a conscript of indeterminate origin. The young grocer's efforts netted him two more 8mm Mauser rifles, a 7.62mm Polish Nagant revolver, a Walther P38 9mm pistol, seventy-two cartridges, three packs of cigarettes, a gravity knife, more deutschmarks, and some Polish zlotys. Both soldiers had been carrying their rifles with empty chambers. The handguns had loaded chambers and had been ready to fire, but they had been carried in flap holsters with thongs tying the flaps shut. It would have taken the soldiers less time to load their rifles than to get their pistols free from their holsters. Irwin Mann was too excited to notice this fact.

The fourth soldier Irwin chose was a Lithuanian carrying an MP28 submachine gun. He had spotted him just before dusk by using the binoculars, and decided that he had to get the gun. His people would need such a weapon for when they were attacked by a group of Nazis coming to take them away. Irwin knew it would not be a matter of *if*, but *when*. Bunches of Jews were being herded out of the overcrowded ghetto and into railroad cars every day. None, of course, had ever returned, but the crude comments of the storm troopers could not be discounted. The Jews were being sent to mass executions.

Irwin used the same technique that had worked successfully thrice before. The soldier had just started to turn when the muzzle of the revolver, backed by 70 kilos of charging 25-year-old, hit him just below the right shoulder blade and knocked him off balance as Irwin Mann pulled the trigger.

Click.

Whether the round of ammunition had gone bad or whether the gun's mainspring was just a little too weak to always fire the cartridges reliably, Irwin Mann would never know. What he *did* realize in the instant that he landed on top of the startled soldier was that he was going to have to use his bare hands to kill a man with a machine gun.

The soldier was young and in good physical condition, and his reflexes were quick. He had been taken completely by surprise, however, and this was the first time he had actually fought for his life at close quarters. As he landed on his left side with the young Jew tumbling on top of him, he made the common error of trying to get his weapon into play rather than react with a quicker though less lethal response.

Irwin Mann instinctively pounded at the soldier's face with his right fist, which was still holding the revolver. The barrel punched into Private Mueller's right eye socket just as Irwin Mann did another instinctive thing, and pulled the trigger.

The gun did not misfire this time.

The explosion of the cartridge was again contained, but this time within a much smaller and less elastic space than the chest cavity of a grown man. This time the pressure was released inside a small chamber made of thick bone. Fluid dynamics dictated that the soldier's brain matter be driven out of his skull through the paths of least resistance, and it was. The bullet severed the left optic nerve, and Private Mueller's left eyeball was blown out of his head. It came to rest almost ten meters down the street, where it was soon eaten by one of the many scavenging creatures that fed on corpses before work details hauled them away. Brain matter followed the eyeball, and a small amount also came out the dead man's ears and nostrils. The balance of the grey tissue followed the bullet out the hole it made in the occipital region at the back of the soldier's head.

The soft lead bullet was stopped by Private Mueller's helmet, and it left a visible dent, which gave the steel headpiece the incongruous appearance of a large, green, woman's breast. The helmet also prevented the bullet from shattering Irwin Mann's left hand, which it would have done if the young private had been bareheaded.

Irwin Mann scrambled to his feet. This time the sight of the dead man had a definite effect on him. The soldier's face had been barely a foot from his own, and seeing the man's brains spilling out of the eye socket and clinging to the back of Irwin's hand had suddenly made the young grocer feel lightheaded and faint.

Mann realized he could not afford to indulge in revulsion. He wiped his right hand, which still clutched the revolver, on the soldier's tunic. For a final time that day he dragged the dead weight out of sight where it would not immediately be discovered. The sling of the MP-28 submachine gun slid off the dead man's shoulder, and Irwin ran quickly back to the middle of the street to retrieve the weapon.

This time he did not strip the corpse. Irwin removed his own coat and slung the short weapon over his neck after removing its magazine. When he put the coat back on and fastened the two buttons it still retained, the gun was not visible. The man had carried no sidearm or other weapon, and Irwin soon learned why. To his great pleasure he discovered that the soldier had been carrying six spare loaded magazines for his MP-28,

76

in addition to the one that had been in the gun.

Irwin would not know exactly that he had another one hundred seventy-five rounds of ammunition until he unloaded the magazines and counted the cartridges, but he knew it was a lot. *Fine work for my first day on the new job.* He put the seven magazines into the left side pocket of his coat. They were too long and protruded several inches out the top. Irwin cut a section from the dead soldier's shirt and tied it around the exposed ends of the magazines. Dusk had come, and the makeshift cover would be adequate for the journey back to where he had hidden the other weapons.

Irwin Mann walked briskly out of the alley and down the street. His discomfort at the sight of the man's ruined face was completely forgotten.

April 18, 1943

The people in the crowded room stared silently at Irwin Mann. Their expressions showed admiration, respect, and horror. Lying on the blanket in front of them were the weapons, ammunition, money, and other assets he had acquired the day before. It was Stern who finally spoke.

"You have done what others would not, young man. I am proud of you. Proud, and thankful."

"He has murdered in cold blood! He is no better than the Nazis themselves! Look at him! He has their blood on his hands and clothing even as he stands here before us!" said a man of about 40 at the side of the room. Stern fixed the speaker with a penetrating stare.

"You have forgotten your Talmud, sir. 'He who comes to kill you, arise and kill him.' Sanhedrin 72a; Berachos 58a and 62b; Makkos 85b; and Midrash Tanchumah, Pinchas:3." His gaze softened slightly. "Leviticus 19:16 is worth remembering, as well: 'Thou shalt not stand idly by the blood of your brother.' I am afraid we have all stood idly by for far too long." He turned to Irwin Mann. "Perhaps it would be best if you were to advise us on the proper use of these tools." Stern nodded to Irwin, transferring his authority to the younger man.

"We have three rifles, three pistols, and a small machine gun," he started. "The three rifles all use the same ammunition, and we have thirty-one of those cartridges. Two of the pistols and the machine gun all use another kind of ammunition, and we have two hundred twenty-one of that type. The revolver here," he said, pointing to the Nagant, "uses a third type of ammunition. We have twelve shots for it." The group looked on silently, waiting for him to continue.

"Our armament is minuscule compared to that of the Nazis. For this reason, we must not waste a single one of these bullets. If we make each one count, we can continue to replenish our stocks." He saw nods of agreement among several of the assembled men, and he went on.

"This is the way the rifles work," he said, picking up a Mauser and manipulating the bolt. "They hold five cartridges in here." He pointed to the magazine well. "This lever prevents the gun from firing." Mann flipped on the safety and made a show of pulling the trigger. Nothing happened. He flicked the safety to its previous position and pulled the trigger again. The striker made a loud click as it fell.

"How do you aim it precisely?" a man asked him. "If you want to shoot...something that is not so close to you?" Everyone knew what 'something' was going to be.

Irwin took a deep breath. He was rapidly approaching the limit of his knowledge of firearms. "You line up the notch in this piece of steel here," he said, pointing to the blade of the rear sight, "with this thin piece here," pointing to the front sight, "and then put the two of them both in line with the Nazi you intend to shoot."

"Let me try it." Irwin handed him the empty rifle. The man put it up to his shoulder and squinted. "Hard to hold it steady." He stepped over to the wall and pushed his left hand, which held the stock's forend, against the door frame. "That's a lot better. Is the front sight supposed to stick up over the notch in the piece at the back? Is it supposed to cover up the spot where you want the bullet to hit?" Irwin started to say he wasn't sure, when another man spoke up.

"Let me look at it, please." He took the rifle and examined the rear sight carefully, noting the numbered markings on it, how it moved up and down, and how it clicked into different settings when he manipulated it. Then he sighted along the barrel as the other man had done.

"The rear piece adjusts, and is marked for different ranges. By moving this piece to a higher numbered position," he demonstrated by raising the rear sight to a new setting, "the rifle will be aimed upwards to a slightly greater degree, and the bullet will strike a more distant target. Here. I will illustrate." He reached for a stone to scratch with in the dirt on the floor.

"You are familiar with weapons?" Irwin asked in surprise. The man paused and shook his head.

"No, but I have a degree in mathematics, and I am well-versed in the physics of moving objects. Though I have no experience with guns or bullets, I am absolutely certain they must obey every one of Newton's laws."

He scratched a curve of decreasing radius on the floor, and lay a small stick in line with it, touching the start of the curve. "This stick is the rifle. The bullet will describe a parabola through the air, like this scratch. Up close, the path will curve so slightly as to appear to be a straight line." He held his hands on each side of the first six inches of the curve. The section did indeed appear to be straight. "At greater distances, the curvature will be much more apparent, and errors in aiming or in range estimation will be more pronounced." He moved his left hand farther away from the right, and the curvature of the scratch was obvious.

The mathematician laid a straight piece of wood above the small stick, parallel with the start of the curve. "The edge of this wood represents a straight path from the eyeball to the target. That is the shooter's line of sight. Suppose we raise the rear sight, like so." He lifted the back of the piece of wood, and then picked up the rifle and held it level. His finger touched the weapon's rear sight, and he made a motion for the group to imagine that it stood up much higher. He angled the gun so that the imagined new rear sight and the sight on the muzzle were once again level with the floor. "If we line the sights up with the spot we wish to hit, you see that the barrel of the gun is angled upwards slightly. The path of the bullet will rise at first as the bullet approaches the target, because the gun is angled upwards. As gravity continues to exert its relentless pull, the bullet will curve back towards the ground." He ran his finger along the curve to illustrate his point. "If the shooter has estimated the distance to the target correctly, and placed the rear sight in the appropriate setting, the path of the bullet will intersect the line of sight *at the target*." He paused to make sure everyone was with him. There were only a few puzzled looks, so he went on with his explanation.

"You see that if the rear sight is raised higher than it should be," he said as he tipped the rifle's muzzle up farther, "you will shoot *over* the target. If the rear sight is set too low..." Here he held his finger against the barrel to indicate a lowered rear sight, and leveled the gun once more, "and the target is far away, the bullet will strike too low, because gravity is pulling it down as it flies towards the target."

The mathematician looked at the group and saw nods of understanding and a few tentative smiles. "As to exactly how the two sights should be aligned, I am not certain, but I suspect the gun should be positioned so that the top of the front sight is level with the sides of the rear sight."

A short, balding man cleared his throat and spoke for the first time. "I do not know for certain, either, as I know nothing of guns, but I am an optometrist. I can say with conviction that the eye and the brain are very good at detecting whether or not two identical shapes standing side-by-side are level or if one is slightly above the other. The eye and brain are not so good at recognizing whether or not a difference in alignment is exactly the same as a previous misalignment. It would be easiest for the person using the weapon to duplicate his results if he aligned the sights in the manner you have described." Further nods followed this explanation. Irwin Mann felt a surge of hope. The men in the group were applying themselves to the problems at hand, and working together. Confidence and sense of purpose were building.

"How critical is distance estimation?" asked another member of the group, directing his question to the mathematician.

The scholar nodded. "A good question. It becomes more critical with either increased distance or smaller target size. Or both." He examined the rifle's rear sight again. "From these markings, it appears that at any distance under one hundred meters, the path of the bullet will be near enough to straight that no adjustment is needed."

He held the rifle up, bracing it against the door frame and aligning the front and rear sights with a distant point visible through the broken window. He raised the rear sight to the 200 meter setting while continuing to stare at the distant mark. "Even at two hundred meters the change is slight—less than ten centimeters difference." He was thinking quickly as he analyzed the unfamiliar weapon using the comforting logic of mathematics. "That should not be critical on a target the size of a man's chest. The most important requirement will be careful alignment of the sights, holding the rifle steady, and squeezing the trigger carefully so as not to move the gun before it fires. Whoever uses these rifles should also have excellent vision." He smiled ruefully. "A steady hand, good muscle control, and calm actions may be difficult to achieve when the natural tendency is to panic."

"Who among us is a surgeon?" The question startled the group with its seeming incongruity, then everyone saw the logic of it. It was no accident that Stern was a leader.

"I am," two men said, very nearly in unison. They were both gaunt, like almost everyone else in the group. One appeared to be in his late fifties, the other was almost completely bald and therefore looked older. Stern looked at both the men.

"If both of you are capable of delicate surgery in the face of complications, I suspect your eyes and coordination are good, you have steady hands, and are not likely to panic." He paused a moment and continued. "Your knowledge of anatomy would also be a definite asset," he added without elaborating further. "Shooting carefully at a distance should not require the energy and stamina of a young man. Will the two of you accept this task for us?"

The two doctors looked at each other, and nodded. "You brought us these weapons," Stern said to Irwin Mann. "Do you concur with my suggestion?"

Mann nodded his immediate agreement. "We must make the best possible use of the individual talents we possess. There is a third rifle," Irwin pointed out. "This man," he said, indicating the mathematician, "does not strike me as someone prone to panic, and his inherent understanding of the flight paths of bullets is probably far superior to that of anyone else here. I think he should be our third marksman." The mathematician was startled by the term used to describe him, and felt a surge of pride as he saw the entire assembly nod agreement to Irwin's suggestion.

"Is anyone here especially good at estimating distances? Each of these three men will need someone to help determine how far away the targets are." It was a new participant speaking. Everyone in the group looked around, but no one had a vocation which required an ability to accurately judge unknown distances.

"Perhaps I have an answer." A man of about forty was now speaking. "My training is as an architect. Distances can be determined mathematically by the simple method of proportionality, if the size of an object at the unknown distance is known. Since most soldiers are about 1.8 meters tall, I think that with this gentleman's help," he said, indicating the mathematician, "we should be able to construct a simple rangefinder out of a ruler and perhaps a piece of string or thread, to hold the ruler a known distance from the eye."

"An obvious answer," said the mathematician with mild embarrassment. "I don't know where my mind is." He did not say that he had been preoccupied with how Irwin Mann had referred to him as a marksman.

"Are all of you *insane?* What you are describing is utter suicide! We have no chance at all against the forces that will surely be massed against us if we persist in this madness!" The speaker was the man who had earlier accused Irwin of being no different from the Nazis, and had been rebuked by Stern. A few voices murmured agreement. Anyone who stopped to think about what they were planning could not avoid being overwhelmed by the enormity of the task they faced.

"Perhaps I can convince you otherwise." All heads turned towards the newest speaker.

"I am not a Jew, I am from Warsaw originally. My wife is a Jew, and I am a teacher. A teacher of history, who has some knowledge of warfare and battles." He paused, framing his explanation in his mind before speaking. "In every war, but particularly those wars that have been fought in the last 150 years, there have been many examples of superior attacking forces being repelled by defenders with woefully smaller manpower and weaponry. Many scholars wrongly assume that this is the result of embellishment, because of our natural tendency to wish that the weak prevail through sheer bravery, just as David smote Goliath." He shook his head slowly. "That is not at all the correct explanation." His audience waited for him to continue.

"The nature of warfare changed forever with the development of weapons which could be carried by a single soldier and yet were capable of dealing a lethal blow at a distance." He paused to let those words sink in.

"With the advent of such weapons, the determining factor in any single ground conflict was altered for all time." The man's nervousness vanished as he fell into the familiar role of teacher lecturing his class. It had been two years since he had been a free man, but the rhythm and method came back immediately.

"With swords and shields, all conflicts were out in the open, and the combatants had to be close enough to touch each other for any fighting to happen at all. Sheer numbers were by far the most important factor in determining the outcome of a battle.

"When the bow and arrow came into use, this was changed somewhat, but arrows fly slowly enough to be visible, and are effective only at short distances. A shield easily stops them, and the bow is unwieldy when the enemy is close at hand and charging with his sword and shield."

Irwin Mann could see where the scholar was leading, and the hairs on his back stood up. The speaker continued his explanation.

"The crossbow was powerful enough to penetrate shields and armor, and could be used at greater distances. A man who concealed himself behind obstacles could make life very unpleasant for six strong men who were trying to kill him, if that man had a crossbow and could use it well.

"The advantage shifted much further in favor of the defending side as more accurate and compact weapons were invented that were usable at greater distances. We are all familiar with how an American band of farmers defeated the finest army in the world during their War of Independence.

"I am perhaps more familiar than the rest of you with the events of that war, not only because of my former profession, but also because Casimir Pulaski and Tadeusz Kosciuszko, two Poles who fought with the Americans, are national heroes here. Perhaps a history lesson about that war will be helpful to our own plans." He saw that he had their attention, and launched into his lecture. The old habits of teaching a group came back instantly.

"In 1775, with the exception of Switzerland, every single country on earth, if it was ruled at all, was ruled by kings—kings that had the divine authority to do anything that they pleased by virtue of their birth." He paused to let that sink in before adding, "Men who often behaved much like Adolf Hitler.

"France was ruled by King Louis XVI. What we now call Germany was ruled by King Frederick II of Prussia. Russia was ruled by the Tsar Peter III's widow, Catherine the Great. China was ruled by Emperor Ch'ien Lung. Japan was ruled by Emperor Tokugawa. All of Latin America was ruled by King Charles III of Spain, except for Brazil, which was ruled by King Joseph of Portugal. Scandinavia was under the power of the King Gustav III of Sweden. Africa was a vast continent of warring tribes, each with its own tribal king. That continent had small coastal pockets of organized civilization. Every one of those was ruled by the king of the European country that had colonized it, like King George, who ruled England and all its colonies." He stopped to take a breath, and saw that the group's attention was total. "That included the colonies in America."

Lecturing transformed the Pole into a different man. There was unmistakable steel in his voice as he continued the history lesson, and the men in the group were transfixed by his words. He was a powerful instructor.

"In 1775, King George sent his armies to America to make the Colonists give up their weapons. At Lexington, British Major Pitcairn said 'Drop your weapons and disperse, rebels.' The Colonists said no, and fired on the British soldiers." There was no sound in the crowded room except for soft breathing.

"We must never forget just who these people were. The British soldiers' uniforms of the day were bright red, and it is far too easy to think of them as amusing, costumed characters in a children's play. Perhaps you have recently noticed some ornate uniforms which by themselves might be seen as amusing." This brought nods of understanding from his audience. "The British Army was one of the largest, strongest, best trained, and best equipped armies in the entire world. In 1775, *they* were the SS. *They* were the Gestapo!"

"A bunch of farmers said no to that army. They said they would not be ruled by a king. They said they were going to determine their own destiny. Those farmers fought that world-class army, and they drove it all the way back into Boston. The men in that world-class army who were still alive hid in Boston and were afraid to come out because those farmers would kill them as soon as they did." He paused again and tried to make eye contact with every man in the room.

"And that is why a famous American poet called it 'The Shot Heard 'Round the World'. It took a long time for the sound of that shot to reach France, and Germany, and Italy, and Asia, but reach them it did. Do you think there would have been a French Revolution if the Americans had not shown that it could be done?" Most of the men in the room shook their heads involuntarily.

"In some countries, the people have not yet been able to wrest control of their destiny from tyrants. That is why America has become the adopted home of many of the world's oppressed people.

"Bravery and heroism are absolutely necessary, make no mistake about that. We will certainly fail if we are unwilling to take the risks required. But those American farmers had an advantage in addition to their bravery. They had weapons which could be used from positions of concealment, and were skilled at using them. That is how they protected themselves from the attacking forces. It is how we will do it as well."

"But the Nazis have many more of these same weapons, and are much more skilled at using them!" blurted out one of the group. The former history teacher smiled and addressed his pupil.

"That does not matter to nearly the degree that you believe, my friend. As defenders, we possess a great advantage. In order for the Nazis to do us harm, they must come search us out. Look for us. Smash in doors and break windows, never knowing what they will find. They cannot do these things without regularly exposing themselves. From our positions of concealment, we can kill them, take their weapons, and return to different hiding places." The men in the group looked at one another, further sobered by the speaker's words.

"In modern ground warfare, when an attacking force intends to overpower an entrenched adversary, the attacking force must be vastly superior in number, and must be willing to pay a very high price of heavy losses of its own soldiers. I am not at all convinced that the soldiers assigned to guard Warsaw will be eager to pay such a price."

"The Storm Troopers had no trouble before, when they broke our windows and smashed our doors to send us here like sheep for slaughter," a voice said from the back of the room. An older man standing next to Irwin spoke up in reply.

"The Nazis were not stupid. In fact, they were very logical. They knew that in order to accomplish what they intended, we had to pose no threat. We had to be stripped of the ability to defend ourselves. Do you not remember the law passed five years ago prohibiting us from having guns without government permission?"

The history teacher nodded. "The Americans wrote that very issue into their list of fundamental citizens' rights, a part of their Constitution, so that such tragedy could *never again* occur in their country." He paused, a sudden realization coming to him. "Does it not seem odd to you that the Nazi leader has avoided any effort to send his troops to invade tiny, rich Switzerland? That instead he should concentrate on a larger country far more distant, and requiring a crossing of the English Channel?"

Another man spoke up quickly. "I have been to Switzerland several times, and England twice. Each Swiss home I have seen contains a machine gun." At this statement, the group erupted with protests of disbelief.

"No, it is true," said another over the hushed arguing. "I have seen it myself."

"When I was in England," said a man who was speaking for the first time, "A few of the wealthy had shotguns for shooting game birds." Murmurs of disapproval coursed though the assembled men. Killing animals for sport was contrary to Jewish law. "I saw no weapons such as we have here, that would be most suitable for repelling invaders."

"The English expect the Americans to rescue them," said a new voice. The history teacher replied to this.

"Is that not ironic, given that it was the English who attempted to disarm the Colonists a century and a half ago?" Puzzled looks greeted his question. The teacher looked startled. "Have you never heard of one of their favorite stories? Of Paul Revere?" A few heads nodded. "Paul Revere is an American hero because he warned the Colonists that the British were on their way to seize their weapons, and the Colonists said *no*."

"If the Colonists had said *yes,* and stacked their arms for confiscation as we did five years ago, the Colonists would have been executed, and every country ruled by a king in 1775 would probably still be ruled by a king today."

"You cannot be serious! We are, what? Thirty in number?" Once again, it was the man who had pointed out the blood on Irwin's clothing. Now Irwin spoke up.

"I was only one, and I am still healthy. *You,* sir, I do not trust. I do not trust you to help us, and I do not trust you to resist betraying us." He reached into his coat pocket, withdrew the revolver with which he had killed the four soldiers, and handed it to one of the men he knew well.

"Take him to another building where he cannot hear the rest of what we have to say. Give us half an hour. Then give him the gun and let him go." Irwin turned to face the protester.

"There is one cartridge left in the gun. If you return with a German military weapon, it shall be yours, and I shall apologize in full for my lack of trust in you. Now go." Several in the group began to protest, but Stern raised his hand.

"He is asking only what he himself volunteered to do for all of us." The others fell silent, and Irwin's friend pushed the protester out of the room. No one there ever saw him again.

After the pair had left, Irwin held his hand out to the Polish history teacher. "My name is Irwin Mann." The teacher nodded.

"Piotyr Halek."

"Piotyr Halek, you have given us all much wisdom and hope. Somehow I feel that there is another shoe you have not let drop." Halek nodded at Irwin's intuition.

"With the weapons we possess, we can effectively counter Nazi attempts to search us out. But there are methods they can use which are equally effective at dealing with entrenched adversaries."

"Yes?" Irwin said, waiting for Halek to continue.

"Methods which are much older that the weapons in this room. Ones that the Nazis have already been using against our people."

He took a deep breath. "Starvation, for one. That will be a very real threat, more than it has been so far. Poison gas, for another. The Nazis are experts at confining large groups of us to small spaces and killing us in that way. But neither starvation nor poison gas should worry our group of resistance fighters as much as another method of destruction." He waited to see if any of his pupils would realize what that weapon was. Suddenly, Irwin Mann's eyes widened.

"*Fire,*" he breathed softly. Several men in the room gasped. Halek nodded at his student and smiled without pleasure.

"Exactly so. We are confined to a prison here in this section of Warsaw. Fire is our biggest enemy."

"Is there nothing we can do?" asked Irwin. The Pole's smile became more genuine.

"There is *always* a counterstrategy."

Irwin Mann took a deep breath. "Then, Piotyr, let's talk about fire."

The strategy session began in earnest.

May 14, 1943

"Give me your hand." The boy refused. "Give me your hand and climb down. They'll kill you if you stay up here!" Sporadic gunfire crackled in the distance.

The boy looked at the open sewer cover and shook his head violently. "They are flooding the sewers, and filling them with gas, which they then ignite! We'll be burned alive!"

What the boy said was true. In 1940, the German conquerors of Poland had confined almost a half-million Jews in the Warsaw Ghetto. By April of 1943, barely a tenth that number remained. Over 300,000 of them had been sent to death camps, and the rest had died of starvation and disease. The remaining 60,000 prisoners had realized they were doomed, and had fought back, despite the fact that they had only a handful of weapons.

Since April 19, the Warsaw Ghetto had been under attack by over 2,000 heavily armed German troops, in addition to many more Lithuanian militiamen, Polish police, and Polish fire fighters. After almost four weeks, only a few of the inhabitants remained alive. The Germans had systematically set the Ghetto on fire block by block, just as Piotyr Halek had predicted.

As Irwin and his few remaining compatriots had watched each potential refuge become an inferno, they realized that escape was their only hope, and that the sewers offered the only chance of that. The Germans had seen this as well, and were pumping the underground tunnels full of water and flammable poison gas.

Irwin Mann was running out of patience with the boy. "If you won't come with me, then take this," he said finally, thrusting the Luger into the boy's hand. "You have eight shots. Use them carefully. This is the safety," he said, pointing. "Push it down before you want to fi—" The boy ran off while he was still explaining, and Irwin watched with dismay as he saw him cast the weapon aside, letting it clatter on the stones.

Irwin Mann retrieved the pistol and thrust it into his pocket. *He'll walk right into their arms* he thought with disgust. He climbed into the sewer and pulled the cover back into place.

Blackness enveloped him. He had a few precious matches, but he did not intend to use them until he absolutely had to, and was sure he was not in the presence of flammable gas. Feeling around blindly, Irwin climbed down the iron steps set into the concrete and reached the bottom of the sewer. He heard the sound of a rat scurrying away from him, and he felt waves of both nausea and relief.

Rats made his skin crawl. For months he had seen them feeding on the corpses of those who had succumbed to the starvation conditions of the Warsaw Ghetto. The noises they made in the darkness here, however, gave him hope. The passageway was probably not choked with sewage, and that had been his far greatest fear.

The floor of the sewer was relatively clear, even dry in spots. *We have had so little to dispose of* he thought with black humor as he felt his way on hands and knees down the pipe. The utter darkness gave a surrealistic feeling to the entire process, and Irwin found that if he closed his eyes it was less disorienting than if he left them open. Breathing the dank air was unpleasant, but not as foul as he had expected. His spirits lifted slightly. *Maybe I really am going to make it.* As he slowly moved along in the blackness, his hands and knees protected with rags he had tied around them, Irwin asked himself once again if he had done the right thing.

They had always known they could not prevail, not ultimately, unless the Americans rescued them. After three weeks, the Warsaw inhabitants knew that was not going to happen in time. Their tiny armed resistance had surprised and astonished the Nazis at first, but the Germans came with more and more soldiers every day. The Jews had had less than twenty guns in all, and not a single skilled marksman among them. *That surgeon did all right, though* Irwin remembered with satisfaction. *Killed at least twenty before the heavy machinegun fire demolished his final hiding place.*

Irwin himself had used his earlier technique of killing at close range in the first few days of the resistance. After that, the troops had come in much greater numbers and never alone, so he had shot them at longer range from positions of concealment.

The young fighter was bone-tired, but he continued to make his way down the dank passage in total darkness. After a period of time that Irwin couldn't judge, he came to a larger space. There was a bit of light filtering in from a grating above, and he realized he was at a junction of several sewer tunnels. He lay still on his stomach and held his breath, listening. Irwin believed that he wanted to angle off towards his right, but in his exhausted state, he had a sudden fear that he had become disoriented. He tried to ignore the beating of his heart, and listened for noises.

The distant sounds of battle came through the grating above, but down in the sewer it was impossible to judge the direction from which they came. A pair of rats scurried out of a tunnel to Irwin's left and ran across the larger space into a tunnel on the right. *That settles it* Irwin thought with relief. *Rats don't run towards trouble.* Irwin Mann heaved himself to his hands and knees and followed after the vermin.

The tunnel Irwin was in sloped upwards, and that was why the rodents had chosen it. The rats had run when they had first heard the sound of water, and their primal instincts drove them towards higher territory. It was the creatures' innate ability to survive that saved Irwin Mann's life along with their own. The water that the Germans were pumping in flowed to the lowest part of the sewer lines. As it did, it formed a barrier between the higher end where Irwin was, and the opposite end where the German soldiers were dropping their poison smoke candles. By the time the Germans had discovered that the sewers at the edge of the Ghetto were still clear and took steps to change that, Irwin Mann had passed under the walled boundary and had escaped into the Polish section of Warsaw.

***

"Keep pumping!" the Nazi officer commanded when he saw water bubbling out of a sewer grate onto the street sixty meters away. "The sewers are almost full." He imagined the wretched Jews underneath his feet, unable to breathe.

Suddenly he saw fingers push through the bars of the grating, and he stood near the opening, waiting to see if the man could raise the heavy cover. The soldier aimed his pistol at the sewer grate, ready to shoot if the man lifted it off. The drowning man slowly released his grip on the bars, and his fingers disappeared under the water. The German holstered his pistol and smiled with satisfaction. It was not as satisfying as watching them burn, but very good nonetheless.

"Shut off the water! No air remains!" the Nazi yelled to his men. He was walking back to them when the bullet struck the edge of his spinal cord just below the base of his neck. The shot did not kill him, but he was now paralyzed from the neck down. For the rest of his life, he would be fed, bathed, and clothed by others.

Isaac Epstein, former math teacher, gave a sigh of contentment and lay down his rifle. He did not bother to work the Mauser's bolt, for the gun was now empty and he had no more cartridges. Neither did he attempt to leave his place of hiding. His right ankle was broken, and he had inhaled enough burning gas that he knew he did not have long to live even if no soldiers came for him. Isaac Epstein lay back among the rubble and closed his eyes, waiting for the Germans to find him. *Marksman* he thought with pride. *That's what that young man called me.* A smile of satisfaction came across his tired face.

A few moments later, his heart stopped beating. The smile remained.

May 16, 1943

The Nazi general surveyed the smoking ruins of what had been the Warsaw Ghetto. A bitter smile curled the corner of his mouth. He took the proffered field telephone from his aide and spoke into it.

"The former Jewish quarter of Warsaw is no longer in existence," he said succinctly. "I shall have a casualty total by tomorrow morning, and you can expect my full report within forty-eight hours. Heil Hitler." He handed the instrument back to his aide and returned to his staff car.

***

Two kilometers to the east, Irwin Mann crouched in an alley. He had slept fitfully, always frightened of being discovered. His fears, while justified, were exaggerated. Huddled amongst refuse in the dim Warsaw morning, he was just another undernourished Pole with nowhere better to sleep. No one who saw him would have suspected he was a Jew who had escaped from the Ghetto, for that was unheard of.

Irwin assessed his situation. His clothes were in tatters and unspeakably dirty. They would have to be replaced. He himself was filthy, and he had not eaten for almost three days. On the positive side of the ledger, he still had a few zlotys in his pocket, as well as the Luger and a full magazine of cartridges. His body, though weak, was undamaged. *I have come this far* he thought with grim determination. *I will not be defeated now.* He stood up and stretched, working some of the stiffness out of his aching muscles. The air was thick with the smell of smoke, and Irwin turned to look at the blackened sky in the distance. Some ideas were coming to him. *I am going to get through this* he decided, and began planning his next move.

***

"We have found no survivors, *Herr General,* and but a handful of weapons," said the young soldier as he clicked his heels together and saluted. The General acknowledged the soldier and nodded.

"These swine had no chance against us. It is appalling that they even resisted." He did not say what was actually on his mind. A ragged band of Jews with a few guns and no military training whatsoever had managed to hold off the best efforts of the German Army. This fact went counter to everything the General had ever known about Jews. He briefly wondered how they had accomplished this feat and who had been leading them, then pushed the disturbing thoughts out of his mind and returned to more immediate tasks.

The general's unease was well-founded, and the Warsaw ghetto resistance would be a valuable history lesson for anyone who studied it. With less than twenty weapons, a starving band of resisters had held off the German Army for twenty-seven days and nights before being defeated.

When the German Army had conquered the entire country of Poland in 1939, it had taken them sixteen days.

June 6, 1944

Max Collins fixed his eyes on the small, distant square. He turned his head slightly to the right and spat into the dust in the corner. *They'll be there soon.* Collins saw a slight movement in the distance. He reached into his breast pocket and withdraw the small monocular he carried. After a long look and a quick breath, he put it away. *They're here.* Now he had his job to do.

The glider descent had gone seriously awry. The pilot had tried to center the fuselage between the two trees to clip both wings off and slow the craft down, but he had been too far to one side. The glider had spun to the left and overturned. Collins had come to in the grass, wet with his own vomit and another's blood. Not until he had seen the tattered wings had he remembered where he was. He hadn't been able to determine how long he had been unconscious, but it was long enough that there seemed to be no reason for great haste. The wreckage had been extensive. The jeep had broken its moorings and caused most of the damage. Impact with the ground had done the rest. Max had found no other survivors. The green, padded canvas case had made it safely, though. He had found it cushioned between two still-warm corpses, and had gently retrieved it. It, too, was stained with blood.

At least the landing went undetected, Sergeant Collins had thought as he had trudged off in the darkness towards the town with the case under his arm.

He had immediately realized that the bell tower was the best choice. It surveyed most of the town, but was well away from the heart of the village. Max Collins had quickly found the proper entrance at the back of the church and settled himself in a corner of the elevated, open-sided structure. Then, as always, he had slept. There was nothing more sensible to do before sunrise.

Dawn had broken, and now it was time. Max gently slid the rifle from its drop case and slowly surveyed it for damage. None was visible. The rifle was mute testimony to the Army's willingness to bend the rules to further its own interests. It was a Springfield, and it had been issued, but there ended its likeness to the standard weapon. Collins had spent hours of his time, while the others played poker, removing the barreled action from the stock, coating it with a mix of lampblack and oil, replacing it, and removing it again. From the black marks on the bare wood, he had seen the high spots where metal rested on wood. Through tedious scraping and repetition of the entire process, he had achieved near-complete contact of the action with the stock. The wood under the barrel was relieved to let the barrel vibrate when the gun was fired, in accordance to its natural frequency. The rifle, as Max was fond of saying, shot like it had eyes.

His efforts, however, had not stopped there. The outside of the stock had been treated to twelve coats of marine spar varnish, insuring that it would not warp when the humidity changed. A change of a thousandth of an inch could move the bullet's point of impact half a foot at a hundred yards, and it was not possible to sight the gun in anew every time the weather changed. The rifle's most flagrant departure from regulations was the 2 1/2 power Lyman Alaskan scope, anchored to a bridge mount Max had persuaded a machinist to make for him. The magnification it offered was less important than the fact that sights and target were now in the same plane of vision, and therefore always both in focus.

General Gavin himself had seen Max shooting this rig for group at three hundred yards, as he did every few days when circumstances permitted. The general had taken time to examine the group—five shots in four and an eighth inches, about average for the gun—looked at the headstamp on the fired brass, which said 'National Match', meaning it was authorized for use only by military marksmanship teams, and had said, "Carry on, Sergeant." After that, Max Collins had quit worrying about what officers might do if they saw his rifle.

Max folded the blood-stained case and laid it on the ledge as a rest. He was risking being seen with the forend and barrel of his rifle exposed, but in the early dawn he'd take the gamble. Through the telescope he saw the two sentries. Collins was using a three-dot reticle, and the smallest dot, the one lowest on the vertical crosshair, covered two minutes-of-angle. Two inches at one hundred yards. With that fact, you could use the reticle to calculate range if you knew the dimensions of the object you were looking at. He centered the dot on the German's face. The man's face was more than covered by the spot. He moved the rifle slightly, so that the dot reticle was next to the man's head. He decided that the dot was twice the width of the soldier's face. *One minute-of-angle to cover his head.*

Max Collins let out a long breath. His pale eyes narrowed as he laid the rifle and case back on the floor of the tower. Before he had enlisted, Max had been an illustrator, and like any decent artist, he knew anatomy well enough to teach it. *Cheekbone to cheekbone, the widest spot on the head, on an average man was five and three-quarter inches. Five hundred seventy-five yards.*

He didn't like it at all. Trying to get closer would be risking discovery as well as eliminating his already-slim chances for escape. He picked up a small chunk of concrete and started to scratch in the dust.

At five hundred seventy-five yards, the rifle would put five shots into an eight-inch circle under ideal conditions. *About the size of a man's head,* he thought. *At five hundred yards, point of impact is thirty-one inches low, and at six hundred yards, sixty inches low. Fifty-five inches low then. The air is cool and misty; denser than usual. More resistance. More drop.* His gut said two percent more air resistance. That translated to an additional four percent drop below line of sight. *Another two inches. Hold fifty-seven inches high, then.* The problem of windage remained.

Max looked down at the crude diagram he had scratched on the stones. It was an oval with a vertical line bisecting it. There was another line perpendicular to the vertical about three feet above the oval, and below this he had scratched '57'.

He turned and spat more dust out of his mouth. He felt not even a whisper of wind on his cheek from where he sat in the high, open tower. *Two hundred yards out, though, something's making that smoke from the chimney drift to the left and away.* Over almost six hundred yards, the wind could easily be blowing in more than one direction. He closed his eyes and sat motionless for a few moments. *Too many variables.*

Max opened his eyes and looked for more smoke. He found another chimney in operation this early in the morning. It was in line with the target area, but quite a bit past it. As close as he could tell, its smoke was drifting in the same direction as the other's. *Well, that's something.* He looked again at the smoke. *A drift of about ten miles per hour. No, a bit less than that. More than five, though. Call it seven.* But it was not a seven-mile-per-hour crosswind. He looked again, resisting the natural impulse to squint. *Damn near forty-five degrees. Another break. Crosswind component seventy-one percent, times seven miles per hour and we're back to a five mile per hour breeze drifting the bullet left. With the 172 grain military match boattail, at 2800 feet per second at the muzzle, ten inches drift at 500 yards. Fifteen inches at 600.*

A private had once asked him what the trick was to figuring out the various drops and wind drifts in different winds, when a ballistics table was not at hand.

"Ever hear of those guys can take two three-digit numbers and give you the product straight off?" Max had replied.

"Yes, sir, I believe I have. But I don't know how *they* do it, either."

"Same simple trick I use. Pure rote memorization." Like Ad Topperwein and John Browning, Max Collins was part of the gun culture.

Max lifted the stone again, cushioning it against his callused fingers. Along the horizontal scratch, about ten inches to the right of the vertical mark, he made an "x". Between this mark and the vertical line he scratched the number 14. Now, as long as the conditions remained the same, there was just the waiting. He pulled the monocular out of his pocket once more and put it to his eye, watching the square.

Max looked down at his drawing. *Not much else to do now but wait, and watch the conditions.*

Bingo! Max said silently when a figure appeared in the monocular. *No I.D. training needed to pick this one out he told himself.* The way the German moved and the way the others reacted to him was all the proof Max needed. *How many stars would he have if he'd been born a few thousand miles farther west? No matter. They can give him a hero's funeral.*

Max folded the canvas case in half and laid it on the ledge. He put the rifle on top of it, pointing towards the distant square. Through the scope he could see the man standing in perfect profile, giving orders. The American centered the crosshairs on the general's head, and then released the rifle. It rocked on its canvas rest and pointed ten yards left of where he wanted to hit. He cradled the rifle once more until it pointed where he wanted, this time pressing the weapon firmly into the rest before releasing it. The crosshairs shifted only a few feet, and in a vertical direction. When the rest was trying to hold the gun in a different spot than the shooter was, the gun would never shoot where it was supposed to.

He put his shoulder to the flat steel buttplate and grasped the smooth grip with his right hand. The left thumb and forefinger pressed the sides of the buttstock, urging it to the exact spot. Collins placed the officer's throat equidistant between the man's heel and the center dot of the reticle. Then he moved the dot over two head-widths. *Too far. Ease it back some. Fourteen inches?* Collins willed his head closer to the eyepiece, straining for that last bit of definition with which to measure the fourteen inch space. He was glad that he never failed to fire a fouling shot with commercial, non-corrosive ammo after cleaning his rifle. The first shot from a clean, dry bore never went into the same place as subsequent ones. *Let's stick this one in his ear.*

Urged on by the gradually increasing pressure of his index finger, the sear released and the rifle bucked, taking him just a little by surprise. *A good letoff* he instantly realized as the steel eyepiece at the back of the scope met his forehead and left a crescent-shaped gash on top of a half-dozen tiny white scars of the same shape. *Crowded it too close again* he thought with the small part of his brain that wasn't filled with more important issues.

As the blast rang off the ceiling of the bell tower, Max Collins' flushed all the concerns of the last three hours from his mind, and replaced them with an entirely new set. He had fired the only shot he was going to get. He had to get down and away immediately. And for one absurd, sickening moment, he had the irrational fear that he had found the wrong town, and the rest of the 82nd Airborne was miles away, about to storm the *real* Ste. Mere Eglise. He dismissed this nightmarish thought and scrambled down the ladder.

The barometric pressure had been a bit higher than Max had estimated, and the range thirty yards farther. The bullet struck several inches lower than Collins' calculations had predicted. The general had been standing in profile at attention addressing his men, and the bullet struck him on the point of his shoulder. It deflected off the underlying bone and assumed a banana shape, as engineers a generation before had designed it to do. Yawing slightly, the slug ranged upwards, exited out the trapezius muscle, and immediately slammed sideways into the German's neck. The tumbling bullet severed the General's spine, leaving his head attached only by a few muscles in the left front of his neck, before burying itself in a door frame thirty meters beyond.

The quick commands stopped in mid-sentence with a noise that sounded like a leather bag bursting. Several enlisted men were sprayed with the dead officer's blood as he fell on his chest, struck down as if by a thunderbolt. His face bounced off the granite cobblestones with a sickening sound, breaking off both the front teeth. The force of the impact twisted the head around so that the corpse's face stared sightlessly to the side. One-and-a-quarter seconds later came the distant roar of the rifle.

By the time the German soldiers realized what had happened, Max Collins was at ground level, exiting the church. By the time the shocked Major realized that he was now the senior officer and began issuing commands, Max was halfway to the relative safety of the woods. There, he knew he stood a chance of holding his own by silently removing his pursuers one at a time. *I can stay alive at least for a day or two, and by that time it will all be decided, one way or the other.*

As he continued his methodical-frantic escape, the Sergeant's thoughts returned to that one fact which might comfort a gentler man in civilian life, but which stuck in his mind infuriatingly now:

I may never know for sure.

May 16, 1945

"At ease, Lieutenant. You're being sent home, and there are a few things I've been wanting to say to you before you leave the base." The Colonel shuffled through some papers that were in front of him and selected a set of onionskin sheets that were stapled together.

"Your flight training methods have been...unorthodox. And they have been unorthodox, I'm told, since the day you started teaching here."

Walter Bowman said nothing. *It's never wise to answer a ranking officer's question until after he's actually asked it,* Walter silently reminded himself.

"I gather that you have felt cheated that you ended up here nursemaiding cadets through flight training for the duration of the entire war." The Colonel was staring at him with intense scrutiny. "It must grate on you that you'll likely never find out whether or not you really have what it takes to be a fighter pilot when the targets are shooting back with live ammo."

You got that one right Bowman thought. His lips compressed at the stinging words, but he remained silent. The Colonel had accurately assessed the inner frustration he had felt for much of the past two years.

"I don't know how you would have done overseas. My inclination is that a man who doesn't think an inverted spin five hundred feet from the ground is anything too hard to handle would probably be able to keep his wits about him in the face of tracer fire and flak. But maybe not, and not knowing is something that every soldier who never sees combat has to live with." He looked at the paper in his hand. "I had my adjutant look into a few things for me. Things that involve you," he said pointedly. "Would you care to tell me, Lieutenant, how many cadets you have trained on this air base?"

Lieutenant Bowman spoke for the first time. "I don't know exactly, Colonel. I've been here three years. I'd say it must be over a hundred, sir."

The colonel stared at the stapled pieces of paper. "You have trained four hundred thirty-seven airmen, Lieutenant. That is slightly more than twice as many as the next busiest flight instructor on this base. I suspect you have a better estimate of the number of your students who have been injured or killed on this facility?"

"None, sir."

"That's right. And the number of your students who have washed out of the flight program?"

"David Hearnes and Paul Warner," Bowman said without hesitation.

"Correct," replied the Colonel, although he had not known the two cadets names and was startled that the Lieutenant remembered them. "And the number of aircraft your students have damaged?"

"Three, sir."

"Three aircraft that, according to my records, were each repaired and returned to service within forty-eight hours. Not totally demolished. Not like..." he scanned the pages until he found what he was looking for. "...*six* of Lieutenant Harrison's eighty-three students managed to do." He put the sheets back on his desk and once again looked the young man in the eye.

"Lieutenant Bowman, after reviewing these figures, I did some more research. Or, more accurately, I told my adjutant to go do some more research for me. I asked him to find out how many of the airmen who have been trained on our base have seen combat, who their instructors were, and which of them have been shot down or killed while in their airplanes. The information I asked for is incomplete, but two facts have clearly emerged. Lieutenant, the percentage of your students who have seen air combat is higher than that of any other instructor at Pensacola. The percentage of your students who have been shot down is the lowest of any instructor here." He let his words sink in for a few moments before continuing.

"There is another thing that I think you should know. When Chief Jenkins, arrived on this base as our oldest seaman, I did not want him. He had been given the choice of prison or the Navy, and I damn well thought prison would have been much more suitable. I was wrong. And I was wrong, I now believe, because of you, Lieutenant." Bowman raised an eyebrow reflexively, but said nothing. The Colonel inhaled and chose his next words carefully.

"You have an ability, Lieutenant, to cause others to put forth their best possible work. To inspire them to levels of achievement neither they nor their superiors would have thought them capable. Our greatest military leaders exhibit that ability on the battlefield. I believe you have it as a teacher.

"I am telling you this for two reasons. First, although it is none of my business, I think you should give serious thought to pursuing a teaching career as a civilian. I frankly doubt that there will be the need for your flight instruction skills in a postwar setting; as we'll likely have more than enough trained pilots for all the aviation jobs available. I also think you would be rather bored ferrying cargo for some commercial venture. But your ability with students is not limited to future aviators, and I hope you'll continue to use your teaching gifts with others.

"Secondly, I'd like to make you Pensacola's new chief flight instructor and director of flight training, if you're interested in staying on for a while. I don't know if any of your methods can be implemented on a base-wide basis, but I'm willing to listen to your suggestions. If you do decide to stay here, I want a written proposal as to how you would recommend flight training here be improved." The colonel saw that Bowman did not know if he was supposed to reply. "Take a few days to think it over. Come by my office on Monday morning.

"Oh, and that reminds me. I'm authorizing a four-day leave for you, effective immediately. It has come to my attention that there is an aircraft on this base which meets none of the Navy's stringent regulations for training aircraft. You are familiar with the plane I am talking about?"

Bowman's heart sank. Whatever was coming would not be good. "Yes, sir, I am."

"This plane, I understand, is totally unsuitable for student use, is it not?"

"That's correct, sir."

"It is, in fact, so overpowered as to pose a safety risk to all but expert pilots, and it has no suitability whatsoever for air combat."

"No, sir."

"In that case, Lieutenant, I am placing you in charge of disposing of this aircraft in such a way that it can no longer endanger the lives of anyone on this base. Report back here Monday morning when you have completed that task."

"Dispose of it, sir? In exactly what manner do you want me to do that, Colonel?"

The man ignored the question. "Chief Jenkins has been making sure that the craft is airworthy. Go talk to him. You've got four days. That should be sufficient time to do the job. Dismissed, Lieutenant."

Walter Bowman left the colonel's office feeling miserable. He walked the half-mile to the maintenance hangar where his plane was usually stored. It wasn't there. Bowman caught one of the mechanics and asked him where Anvil Jenkins was.

"He said if you came looking for him, sir, to check hangar six."

"Thanks, Ensign." *Why'd they move it to the paint shop?* he wondered. He was still in a daze about the meeting with the base commander.

He met Jenkins as the mechanic was coming out of hangar six. "Where's my bird, Anvil? Colonel says you've been getting it ready for me to 'dispose' of it."

The older man's face betrayed no emotion whatsoever. "Figured it needed a few things if its days here were over, sir. Come on in and you can see for yourself." He held the door for the lieutenant. As Walter stepped through the doorway Jenkins flipped a row of switches and the inside of the hangar was lit up by a dozen floodlights. Lieutenant Bowman drew his breath in. Whatever he had imagined, he had never expected this.

There stood his Stearman, but he hardly could believe it was the same airplane he had flown only a week before. The prop hub was no longer exposed. It was now covered with an aluminum spinner polished to a mirror finish. The big radial engine was also covered with a beautiful cowling to further streamline the front of the airplane and duct cooling air over the cylinders. The entire aircraft gleamed as he had never seen before.

It was also no longer yellow. The clipped-wing Stearman had been thoroughly wet-sanded and repainted entirely. It was now white, with dark green sunburst stripes on the wings and two thick longitudinal stripes of the same color on each side of the fuselage. On the side of the fuselage behind the cowling was a rendition of a nude, voluptuous woman. She was contorted into an impossible position, with a startled look on her face. Beneath her figure was the caption *Every Which Way!*

Below the aft cockpit were the words *Lieutenant Commander Walter Bowman*, painted in black with a gold shadow line. On the engine cowling, and in much smaller lettering, was written *Tuned by Jenkins Engineering*.

"Had a harder time than I expected getting an exact match on the green," the mechanic said, deadpan. He had painted the biplane in the school colors of Bowman's alma mater, Dartmouth College in Hanover, New Hampshire. Bowman was speechless. Finally he found his voice.

"The cowling..." he said, his voice trailing off.

"Now *that* took a while. Told you I was a hammer man, though. Took me a day or two to think it through, and my aluminum welding is a sight better now than it was when I cut the material for it. Those blister bumps over each knuckle on the rocker covers, made them by buildin' a fixture and a steel die I made on the mill, then rigged up a rubber diaphragm and forced grease into it under pressure. Pressure-formed 'em in that soft aluminum pretty as you please. The spinner, Jones made that for you. Told me he knew a girl back home with titties just the right shape, and almost as big, and he said he'd copy one from memory. He got so excited when he was done I half 'spected him to knock out another one so's he could have a pair. Harrison did the artwork and lettering. Seems he's a mite tired of using nothing but stencils, like on everything else around here, so I give him a free hand, sir. Hope you ain't offended."

Bowman just shook his head. "All that work..." Bowman was thinking of the tremendous effort the men in the maintenance shop had gone to just to let him fly the Stearman to some Navy boneyard for dismantling.

"Lieutenant, every man in the shop knows about the numbers the Colonel was askin' for. Hell, Colonel's aide got some of 'em from us. We did our own figurin', and come up with the fact that you saved this shop one major shitload a work with all the planes them kids had sideways an' you managed to get back on the ground with nothin' bent. This here extra work, weren't as much time as fixin' the mess made by just one groundloop."

The mechanic motioned Bowman over to the side of the Stearman and moved on to a different subject. "Now take a look at this, Lieutenant. You got a temporary ferry tank I rigged up in the front hole, should be good for two extra hours if you don't goose the throttle too often. And back here," he said, with a voice tinged with pride, "is a couple things this bird has needed ever since we got her finished. Did a little horse-trading to get 'em." He led the officer to the aft cockpit and pointed to the instrument panel. A new airspeed indicator had been installed, one which read all the way to three hundred knots. "I gave it the best calibration I could. When Anderson follows you in the SNJ, you can double-check it. Three hundred's a pipe dream, but let me know how fast my motor can pull this thing."

Next to the airspeed indicator was an instrument that was entirely new. It was a G-meter, and it was calibrated to +12 and -8. "Knowing you, you might peg this one, Lieutenant," Jenkins said, tapping its glass face, "but they won't make one that goes any higher. Probably don't have any equipment strong enough to calibrate it."

"A *ferry* tank?...and a *G*-meter?...What the hell *for,* Anvil?" Walter Bowman's voice showed his absolute bewilderment. Jenkins finally realized what the young man had been thinking, and an exaggerated look of outrage came over his weathered face.

"Jesus fuckin' *Christ,* Lieutenant! You think you're going to take this screamer to some scrapyard out on the palmetto flats and let a bunch of friggin' lop-eared kids cut her apart with a Mexican speedwrench? Whole maintenance shop would *mutiny,* but not 'fore they cut your heart out an' took turns pissin' in the hole...uh, *sir,*" he finished, his voice slightly more subdued.

"Then.....?" Bowman said, distracted by the older man's creative outburst.

"Sir, Anderson's all set to follow you up to St. Louis and play taxicab."

"WHAT?"

"Damn right, sir. This bad girl was built just for you. You're taking her home."

January 1, 1951

Raymond Johnson stopped and listened to the wind in the Aspen trees. He liked using snowshoes. He had discovered that he could actually make slightly better time on snowshoes after a snowfall than he could in hiking boots on dry ground. The second semester of Eighth grade started in four days, and he intended to get in a lot of small game hunting before then.

Ray saw the unmistakable tracks leading to the base of a lodgepole pine, where needles and bits of bark darkened the snow around the trunk. He grinned involuntarily as he looked up and saw the fat porcupine thirty feet up the tree, munching contentedly on the side of the trunk. Ray never shot porcupines. They weren't any good to eat and there was no challenge to stalking them, but he loved to look at their spiky round bodies. He watched the porcupine for a few more minutes and then continued his trek up the south side of Aspen Mountain.

Aspen had been a booming mining town sixty years earlier, but the demonetization of silver in 1893 caused silver prices to collapse. Pitkin County's central industry became unprofitable overnight. For fifty years, the town had been quiet. Then, in the decade after the Second World War, a new business had emerged.

The Tenth Mountain Division had trained in Leadville, Colorado since 1936, and many of the troops had made the 82-mile trip to Aspen on weekends. After the war, several men from the Tenth returned to Aspen, determined to make it a world-class ski area.

In 1947, the Aspen Skiing Corporation had cleared trails and installed three lifts on the north face of the mountain that had once been worked by the Ajax Mining Company. In the four years since, the Johnson family had watched with interest as more people each winter came great distances to ski on Aspen Mountain. Some of them liked the area enough to return in the summer, and a percentage of those, usually the older and more affluent ones, ended up moving to Aspen permanently.

Ray's father Bud had seen his own business increase, and Bud and his brother Carl were getting to the point where they were going to have to hire more help and build new stables. There were more and more people who wanted to ride, and some of the new residents were buying horses and having them trained. The income from boarding fees had risen every year in the past five, and the Johnson brothers knew the market was far from saturated. They were in the fortunate position of having the largest tract of land in Pitkin County, and it was only two miles from the center of the town of Aspen. The brothers had resisted offers to sell off any of their property, recognizing early on that they were witnessing the beginning of a fundamental change in the area.

Ray continued up the snow-covered fire road on the back of the mountain, wondering if the skiers on the opposite side were having as good a time as he was. He judged that he was about two-thirds of the way to the top of the mountain, which had a vertical rise of about 3300 feet. The boy saw a fallen pine tree that lay at the proper height, and he clumped over and sat down on it. It was a little after noon, and he was hungry from his climb. Ray shrugged off his day pack and unbuckled it. He took out a ham and cheese sandwich wrapped in waxed paper and a quart Thermos bottle of hot tea. He unwrapped the sandwich and eagerly bit into it. *They taste so much better when you make them with toast instead of bread* he thought with satisfaction.

Ray and his father both liked their sandwiches made with toast. Louise usually let the two of them fix their own lunches, but whenever she threw together a sandwich or fixed hamburgers for either of them, she made sure to toast the bread.

As he finished the last bite of the sandwich and started to unscrew the top of the vacuum bottle, he saw movement ten yards away in a clump of Aspen trees. A rabbit stared at him from behind one of the slender trees. Ray carefully set down the tea and reached into his coat. His hand closed around the grip of the Smith & Wesson .22 revolver carried in the crossdraw holster he wore in front of his left hip. It had been a Christmas present from his father, who had said Ray deserved it for getting yet another semester of straight 'A' grades. He had wasted no time becoming proficient with it. In the past week, Raymond had fired almost two full cartons of 500 rounds each through the gun.

He cocked the hammer while the revolver was still under his coat to muffle the metallic click and slowly withdrew the gun from the holster. Taking careful aim at a spot just behind the rabbit's left eye, he let half the air out of his lungs and gently squeezed the trigger. He had loaded the gun with .22 Short cartridges, which were less powerful than the normal .22 Long Rifle ammo he used on inanimate targets. The weaker round would damage less meat if his shot struck the rabbit's body instead of its brain.

Ray's precaution was unnecessary. The revolver cracked and the bullet struck the rabbit a quarter inch from where he had intended. The animal collapsed in the snow, killed instantly. The boy holstered the gun, took a long drink of tea from the Thermos as he stood up, and walked over to where the animal lay. He reached into his pocket as he clumped through the thick snow, and withdrew a small, two-bladed pocket knife. Unfolding the smaller blade, he picked up the rabbit and slit open its belly. In less than a minute the carcass was gutted and lying on top of an identical one in the game pouch belted around the boy's waist. His mother made a delicious rabbit stew, and he was already imagining how good it would taste after an entire day of snowshoeing.

Ray put his daypack back on and continued up the fire road. The cold air felt invigorating in his lungs, and he started whistling a song his father sometimes sang when he was shoeing the horses, 'Foggy, Foggy Dew'. Nineteen-fifty-one was shaping up to be another good year.

March 10, 1951

Harold Gaines looked at his newborn son and knew he should feel happy. He knew he should be grateful that both his wife and the baby were healthy, and there had been no complications. All he could see, though, as he stared at the tiny, wailing infant, was a mounting stack of bills. This was Harold and Linda's third child, and they had been pinched even before the eldest, Harold junior, had been conceived. Harold's latest job, as a shoe salesman, was not working out as well as he had hoped. St. Louis was known for its shoe industry, but that fact did not do entry-level salesmen like Harold much good.

Linda Gaines looked at the child lying on her chest, and her eyes brimmed over. "He's *beautiful,* Harold. Look, he has your jaw." Her husband smiled a smile he did not feel, and hoped his wife didn't see that it was forced.

He needn't have worried. Linda Gaines was exhausted from the ordeal of childbirth, and the part of her that remained alert was entirely focused on the tiny child that she was holding. They had agreed that if the baby was a boy, they would name him Richard, after Linda's late father. "Richard, do you see your Daddy?" Linda said softly.

The baby continued to wail.

October 14, 1951

"Four hundred thirty-six Trinity Street in University City," Irwin Mann said in clear though accented English. The cab driver nodded once at his lean, somber passenger and pulled away from the airport taxi stand. Irwin collapsed into the back seat of the taxi. His quest was coming to an end, and now he wondered for the hundredth time if he was making a mistake.

It had taken Irwin Mann a long time to decide to come to America. For four dismal years after the war had ended, he had searched for some clue as to what had become of his wife Magda. Not only was Irwin unable to find anyone who knew a single thing about what had happened to her, he could not find out anything about any of the rest of the Szczupak family, or any of his own blood relatives. It was as if none of them had ever existed.

Finally, he had decided to come to America to find the only other known living member of his or his wife's family, her older sister Zofia. Irwin's attempts to locate Zofia and her husband Max Collins in New York had been fruitless while Irwin was still in Europe. Three weeks ago, he had finally decided to make the journey to the United States.

New York City had been an education for Irwin Mann. He had never seen a place with such vitality. The buildings had been bigger than he ever would have believed. Everywhere you looked there were people with a purpose, working, traveling, getting something done. The level of energy was greater than he had ever seen. The hotels were clean and it seemed that anything a person could ever possibly imagine wanting was available at any number of stores. It was so different from the shortages and restrictions that had been a part of his life for as long as he could remember.

Most impressive to Irwin was the seemingly universal attitude Americans had that anything was possible. He had often found himself wishing, in his first days in America, that there had been more people like this with him in Warsaw eight years before.

It had taken two days of blundering about, running into dead ends, and feeling ineffectual before Irwin Mann explained his entire story to a young man in the city records division who was about to go on lunch break. The man had immediately decided it was a matter of pride to track down Irwin's sister-in-law's husband. It had taken the young city clerk less than two hours to find the firm for which Max Collins had worked before joining the Army.

After that, it had taken another day before Irwin had found a former co-worker in New York who knew that when Max had joined the Army, his wife and children had moved to St. Louis to live with Max's family while her husband was overseas.

His phone call to the Collins house in St. Louis County had brought about immediate insistence that he come there immediately. And so, Irwin had taken a flight from New York to Lambert Field in St. Louis, and now he sat in the back of the cab, wondering if this had been a good idea after all. *They may insist I stay with them, but the husband may not truly wish it. I hope this does not end up a disaster.*

The cab pulled into the driveway of a small two-story house in the middle-class neighborhood of University City, a suburb of St. Louis. Almost all the streets there were named after colleges, which explained the area's name. Irwin paid the driver and lifted his suitcase out of the back of the taxi.

Before Irwin Mann had even started up the steps to the brick residence, the front door opened and Max and Zofia Collins stood in the doorway. Irwin's first impression of his sister-in-law as he climbed the steps was that she was excited and embarrassed at the same time. Zofia was a trim woman in her mid-forties, with light brown hair just starting to show traces of grey. She wore a pale blue cotton dress that showed the effects of many washings, and Irwin could see a resemblance to his dead wife. Her husband stood with his arm around her shoulders, grinning broadly.

As Irwin climbed the steps, he could not help but smile. Before he was close enough to shake Max's hand, he felt the man's overwhelming presence. His sister-in-law's husband was a big man, almost two meters tall, and he radiated good cheer and genuine welcome. He liked the man instantly, and just as quickly realized that the effect would be even more pronounced on women. Max reached out to take Irwin's hand in both of his.

"*Cześć*," he said, greeting Irwin in perfect Polish. "Or perhaps I should say, "*Guten Tag*." Zofia beamed.

"My English improves since the few days in this country. I am very glad to meet you also. I am ashamed it has taken so long."

"Not at all. I'm the one who snatched Zofia away from her family and took her to the other side of the world. Here, give me that suitcase." He ushered his guest into the house, and his wife followed Irwin closely. Having him come was the most exciting thing that had happened in her life for a very long time.

The woman fussed over him and took his coat, and Irwin felt awkward for a moment. *She's not at all like Magda was* he thought. *I'm the one who should be nervous.* Suddenly she started talking to him in rapid Polish.

"When you telephoned it was like a thunderbolt out of the sky. We had no idea that my sister's husband might still be alive. The rest of the family, as you know..." she trailed off and then brushed her hands together as if to wipe away the memory. "Come, come! You must be tired and thirsty. I have iced tea, hot coffee, juice, soft drinks, beer, liquor... What will you have?"

"Iced tea, please," Irwin replied in English. Max caught his look and realized what was worrying his guest.

"Please feel free to use Polish," Max said in his wife's native tongue. "Zofia has been jumping up and down waiting for you to get here. She's been dying to have someone else to talk to." Irwin smiled and nodded. The two men sat down in the living room while Zofia went to the kitchen to get refreshments.

"Your call was a very pleasant surprise," Max said easily. "Zofia has talked of little else since you phoned. We both thought that all of her family and relatives had been lost."

"I spent several years searching in Poland and Germany after the war. I am afraid her blood relatives were all killed. As were my own. It took a long time before I was able to believe...no, that is not the right word...*accept* that."

Zofia Collins returned with a tray. On it were two tall glasses of tea and a short glass with bourbon on ice. She served their guest first, then her husband, and then sat down next to Irwin on the couch. Her face was alive, and her eyes brimmed over with tears. Abruptly, she took Irwin's glass from him, put it down with her own on the coffee table, and threw her arms around her dead sister's husband.

"You cannot know what this means to me," she said as she hugged her brother-in-law to her. What came next was an impassioned outpouring in Polish of love and despair about the fate of her sister, and guilt that she had been safe and happy in the United States with two wonderful children, while Magda was left to the barbaric Nazis.

Irwin was stunned. He had feared that Zofia would blame him for her family's fate. If Magda had not married a Jew, she and the rest of the Szczupaks might still be alive. He stammered a reply, but it came out as gibberish.

"Did you think it was your fault, what they did?" Max was speaking softly. Irwin nodded, almost imperceptibly. "No, son," Max said heavily, and Irwin Mann was struck with how right the term felt in the present setting, even though he was only seven years younger than the American.

"You weren't the reason," Max continued, "You were the excuse. If they hadn't used you for the excuse, they would have come up with another one. Those kind always have an excuse for what they do."

Zofia excused herself to go to the washroom and compose herself. The guest felt relieved but awkward, and knew that his host could see his discomfort. Max Collins sat back in his armchair with the glass of whiskey held loosely in his large hands. "There's no need to talk about it right now, not unless you want to. There's all kinds of time for that."

Irwin nodded and looked absentmindedly around the room. The house, while modest by American standards, was finer than any Irwin had ever lived in himself. The floors were oak and covered with handsome rugs. On the walls were a number of oil paintings. Some were portraits and others were landscapes, but there was a similarity to the brush strokes, and they appeared to have been created with the same hand.

As Irwin looked across the living room, he saw an open doorway to what he realized had to be Max Collins' study. The wall that he could see was dark wood, and the chair visible was heavy leather. Above the chair was a painting of a man in a bell tower. He had a look of concentration on his face, was smoking a cigarette, and cradled a rifle that carried a telescopic sight. Irwin rose from his chair and walked to the door to the study. Max was saying something to him, but he did not hear him.

A heavy mahogany desk filled the corner of the room. Next to it was a gun cabinet with glass doors which held eight or ten rifles and shotguns. The walls of the study were covered with more paintings. All of them depicted scenes of graphic violence, and Irwin was at once repulsed and fascinated. There was a scene of a lynching in the old west, and another of a shapely young woman in tight '30s garb tied to a chair and about to be tortured, while a man dressed in black hid behind a bookcase, evidently prepared to rescue her.

When Irwin noticed the signature in the corner of this second work, he realized with a start that all of them had been painted by his host. Then he chastised himself for forgetting the reason Max and Zofia had been in New York. Max had been a cover artist for Street and Smith, the publishing house Irwin had tracked down in New York City. They published pulp fiction and other short stories, mostly aimed at a male audience. He continued to look around the study.

Irwin Mann's eyes fell on a painting of a scene that commanded his attention. It showed a dirty, thuggish-looking man with an ugly grin on his face who was pressing a large revolver into the back of a uniformed policeman. The policeman was slender, with a slight potbelly that looked inappropriate. He was off-balance, his knees were buckling, and there was a slackness to the officer's features. He looked as if he had been overwhelmed by having this criminal gain the advantage on him. The detail in the painting was exceptional.

Then Irwin looked at the gun in the criminal's hand. The hammer of the revolver was in the forward position, but the thug's finger was holding the trigger to the rear. Looking closely, he could see that there was a dull orange glow around the back of the barrel. Irwin felt the hair on his back stand on end as he realized the painting depicted the gun being fired and the policeman dying.

"That's one of my favorite ones that got rejected." Max Collins stood next to his guest and slightly behind him, holding his drink in his hand and gazing at the canvas. Irwin had not heard him come into the room. "The lead story that month was about a crooked cop who got greedy with the rackets boys he was shaking down." Max saw his guest's puzzled reaction to the slang and explained. "The policeman in the story was demanding money from the criminals. He was sharing in their illegal business. He wanted more and more of their money, and finally they killed him."

"Your publishers did not like the quality of your work?" Irwin asked in amazement.

Max Collins laughed softly but with genuine amusement. "Quite the opposite, I believe. Selling a magazine with a story about a cop getting killed is apparently acceptable, but putting a picture of it happening on the cover is not. They wanted me to redo it to make it look like the cop might kill the other guy. That was never in the story—the whole point of the cover was to show the cop getting killed."

"The bulging stomach on the policeman..." Irwin Mann had an idea what Max was about to say, and he felt slightly queasy.

"They bitched about that, too. Thought my eye for perspective was off." He snorted. "I told old man Curtiss that when you put the muzzle of a gun against somebody and pull the trigger, all those expanding gases go into the body right behind the bullet. I said I had wanted to show the guy's guts all being blown out the front of his body by that big .45 slug, but that might be a little too vivid for the editors, so instead I captured the instant before the bullet exited his body. Curtiss just about had a stroke when I told him that."

Irwin Mann felt lightheaded. "Could not the bullet have remained inside the man's body?" he said finally. *This is quite an amazing conversation* he found himself thinking.

"Sure, if he'd been shot with a .32 or a .38. Not with a forty-five. I wasn't about to paint a cover that didn't jibe with the story inside, and the author had the crook using a 1917 Smith from the First World War. Anyway, even without the bulged abdomen, they weren't going to run a cover of a cop getting blasted like that. I said screw it and painted a new one of a gangster's babe with big tits, looking like she wanted to fuck. That's always a sure thing."

Irwin gave a wan smile, and chose his English words carefully. "I believe your second effort would please many readers, but this painting here," he said, indicating the one on the wall, "has much meaning for me." He took a deep breath. "You see, I was in the Warsaw ghetto in the Spring of 1943."

"You were part of the uprising?" Max Collins' eyebrows went up as he stared at his guest, who nodded in reply. "I think you need a drink," the host said. He handed Irwin his glass and motioned to the leather armchair.

Irwin Mann took a long swallow of the bourbon as he sat down. He had never spoken of his experiences during the war with anyone who had not been imprisoned with him. He now began to tell the American, whom he had known less than an hour, exactly what had happened in Warsaw during the months of April and May of 1943.

Zofia Collins returned from the washroom and found the men in the study. She started to speak, but Max held up his hand. "No arguing, Soph. Irwin is staying here with us. He's leaving when he gets sick of us both. Not before."

Zofia Collins threw her arms around her husband's neck. She had not been as happy since the day of her wedding.

January 10, 1953

"So, do you want to see your son, or are you going to sit out here all night?" Walter Bowman leaped out of the chair in the waiting room and stood facing the doctor.

"Son? I have a son? Is he healthy? Is my wife all right? How is she? Is she conscious?" The doctor chuckled at the string of questions the anxious man fired at him like a burst of machine gun fire.

"Your wife is in fine shape and awake, if tired. Your son is healthy and strong, and weighs eight pounds, two ounces. I think both of them would like to see you. Come on in." The obstetrician turned and went back through the doorway, followed by a very excited Walter Bowman.

Catherine Bowman held the baby on her chest. His little legs were bent and his hands made grasping motions. He had a surprising amount of hair. "Henry, here's your Dad," Catherine said with a tired smile. Walter gently picked up his son and held him up at eye level. Henry opened his eyes and seemed to look at his father.

"He's just *wonderful*," Walter Bowman said without thinking. "We did good, didn't we, sweetheart?" Catherine hummed her agreement. "Look at how he's looking at us, honey."

"I bet he inherited your vision." The last time he had been to an eye doctor, Walter Bowman's eyes had checked out at 20-13. Little Henry closed his eyes and brought his hands together. He opened his eyes and reached out towards his father.

"That's unusual," said the doctor, narrowing his eyes. "We seldom see motor skills so soon after birth." He shrugged. "Probably just a coincidence." After staring at the baby for a moment, he turned to the parents and nodded. "I'll leave you two alone now." He left the room.

Walter Bowman beamed and looked over at his wife, shaking his head at the doctor's comment. "Coincidence, my foot! Great coordination from the word go." He looked back at the newborn. "Are you going to be ready for a checkout in the Stearman soon? Are you going to show up your old man and make his maneuvers look sloppy? Are you going to complain that you need more power?" He stroked the baby's wispy hair and laid him back down on top of his wife.

"The baby's less than an hour old, and already you've decided he's got exceptional coordination," Catherine laughed. "The thing is, I bet you're right." She cradled little Henry in her arms and smiled. Walter sat down in a chair and looked at his wife and son. He didn't say anything for quite a while. It felt good just to watch over the two of them.

Whether it was a coincidence or not, in the coming decades Henry Bowman would prove that he did indeed have exceptional coordination, and as he grew up it would be obvious that his vision was even better than his father's. Henry would also become an accomplished pilot whose aerobatic flying abilities would be a source of great pride for Walter Bowman.

The younger Bowman would never be quite as skilled in the air as his father, though this would upset neither of them. For although Henry had inherited his father's great passion for excellence, he would come to channel it into another area. It was an area which, like aerobatic flying, demanded superior coordination and eyesight.

Walter Bowman's passion for flying had helped save the lives of many good Navy men and had contributed to the death of a number of enemy pilots during the war.

His son's passion would ultimately bring about similar results. Henry's effect, however, would be on the entire United States.

July 19, 1955

"Eleven for the gentleman," said the croupier as he stacked a large number of chips and slid them across the table. Max handed him one of them and collected the rest.

"I'm out. When you triple your stake, it's time to go and leave some of the luck for the next fellow." The croupier smiled. Max Collins had surprised him a week ago by offering to pay a hundred dollars an hour for advice at the tables. Max had told him at the end of the afternoon that it was the best money he had ever spent. 'Leave after you've tripled your money' was one of the rules the pro had impressed upon his eccentric client. Max gave a brief salute to the man and headed towards the cashier.

The man behind the barred window looked mildly bored as he counted out seventy-one $100 bills. Max put the money in his pocket and smiled. His bag was packed, his trap guns were stowed in the trunk of his car, and he had already checked out. It was time to head home.

Max walked out into the parking lot and breathed the cool night air blowing in off the desert. He slid in behind the wheel of his new Chrysler 300 coupe and twisted the key in the starter. The big high-compression V-8 with its hemispherical combustion chambers, long duration cam, and high-flowing ports rumbled to life. He dropped the lever into Drive and accelerated smoothly out onto the strip.

Second place at the trap shoot wasn't bad he reflected, *and more than doubling the purse at the tables made it even better.* He rolled down his window to let the wind blast blow through the car. *I love this state. Big-money trap shoots, high-stakes craps, more puss than you have time to even look at, and no open-road speed limits day or night. Best goddamned use for a desert I've ever seen.*

He flicked on his high beams and the pair of aircraft landing lights he had had installed the day after he'd bought the car. The needle on the speedometer was passing through 110 miles per hour and the engine was getting into the RPM range where it was happiest as he cruised east on Highway 50. Max liked driving at night. *It's too late to give Zofia a call. I'll get a room when I hit Wendover at the other side of the state, and call her in the morning* he decided. *Make sure everything's all right at home.*

The lights of the town of Wendover came into view less than three hours later.

June 16, 1956

"Cath, honey," seventy-eight-year-old Charles Collins pleaded to his daughter Catherine Bowman, "he's going to hurt himself." Henry glanced up at his grandfather. *I am not* the little boy thought willfully, then went back to concentrating on what he was doing.

The two adults were sitting in the back yard of Charles Collins' summer residence in Jefferson County, Missouri. Walter, Catherine, and Henry lived there with Catherine's father during the summer months.

"Father, we just have to take that chance." They both watched carefully as three-year-old Henry Bowman industriously tapped the hammer on the broad head of the six-penny nail he pinched between the small thumb and forefinger of his left hand.

Henry had watched his father do woodworking projects for more than a year, and the day before, Walter had shown him how to use a hammer. A thick section of tree trunk stood on end at the edge of the driveway near the back porch, and for several years people had used it for a seat. Under Walter's supervision, Henry had hammered a handful of nails into the end grain of the log.

Henry had hammered for over an hour before dinner, and had bent over only two nails. The next morning, before Henry woke up, Walter had thoughtfully pulled the bent nails from the stump. Now the youngest Bowman was back at it, diligently hammering away. He had not yet hit his fingers.

The old man shook his head. "I still don't think he should be doing that. He's too little." Henry didn't hear his grandfather say this, for his concentration on his last swing was total. The nail head lay flush with the wood, and the little boy stopped to rest.

"Father, I don't think we're going to be able to keep him from hammering nails now that he knows he can do it." Henry heard this comment clearly, and he smiled gaily at his mother.

"Hm," her father said, trying to be irritated but failing in the face of his happy grandson. He looked up as he heard the sound of his son-in-law's Oldsmobile pull into the drive.

Henry put down his hammer and ran to meet his father. "Daddy! Look at how many I did!" Walter Bowman opened the driver's door and stepped out. He was carrying a paper sack in his right hand. With his free arm, Walter picked up Henry and carried him over by the log.

"Well!" he said with feigned surprise. "Every single one is hammered in perfectly!" Henry beamed at the compliment. "But there's something wrong. You're using a damaged tool that has been misused and neglected." Henry had been using a rusty hammer he had found while he was playing in the pole barn. "A good craftsman should always use good tools and take good care of them." He handed his son the paper sack. Henry looked inside.

"Is it mine?" he squealed. *This is the best present I ever got* he thought gaily.

"It's your very own. It's an Estwing, just like your old man's." Walter grinned as his son held up the hammer. Unlike most hammers, which were wooden-handled, the Estwing was forged from a single piece of steel, with a grip made of leather rings shrunk around the steel shaft and polished. Walter had found one that was used for cabinet work and was several ounces lighter than the standard model. "Here. I picked up some different sizes of nails, too." He handed Henry several small packets. "Make sure to throw the papers in the trash can."

Henry quickly went back over to the log with his new prize. Catherine was shaking her head and grinning. "His own cabinet maker's hammer at three years old."

"Good tools last more than a lifetime and instill pride. And pride makes you do better work and get more satisfaction out of it."

"He seems to be getting plenty of satisfaction out of hammering nails into that old log," said Charles Collins dryly.

In four summers, the section of the oak tree would have its entire top surface covered with overlapping nail heads, so that none of the end grain was visible. There would be over four thousand nails embedded, every one except the first few driven home by Henry's Estwing cabinet maker's hammer. 'Henry's nail log,' as it came to be known, would elicit an interested comment from every person who saw it for the first time.

He never did hit his finger, despite his grandfather's fears.

***

Standing on the bank of the Roaring Fork river with his fly rod made of split bamboo, Ray Johnson reflected on his Junior year in high school, which had ended the day before. Once again, he had maintained his 4.0 average, even though he had been taking Senior-level math and science courses as a Junior. The rest of his classmates were going to be together in Pitkin County for another year, but he would not be with them.

Eastern schools were always on the lookout for talented applicants from parts of the country that were not normally drawn to New England. Ivy League universities felt that diversity of the student body was very important, provided that each member of the incoming class had the ability to do the work. The admissions officer at Brown, after reviewing Ray's academic and athletic record, had been extremely impressed. He had not seen this kind of applicant from a rural area in a state like Colorado before. He had offered to take Raymond a year early, if he would make a firm commitment to Brown.

I wish Mom didn't seem so sad about it he thought. *Dad was as excited as I was. Maybe I can get a moose permit in Maine during the winter. I'd like to get a chance to hunt in a different part of the country.* What Raymond had learned of the Brown campus and its academics had excited him, but school was out now, he was standing on a riverbank in Colorado, and outdoor pursuits occupied his mind much more than calculus and chemistry.

Raymond felt the faintest of twitches, and then the hand-laminated fly rod bent into the shape of an inverted 'J' as he flicked it, setting the hook in the trout's mouth. He played out the 4-weight line, giving the fish room to run, so as not to snap the lightweight tackle. Musings about college receded from his mind.

Not as good as hunting he thought with a grin as he played the fish. *But it'll do.*

June 5, 1959

Six-year-old Henry Bowman was terribly excited, and just a little scared. The feeling, he decided, was a good one. He turned as far around as he could in the front cockpit so he could look at his father. A homemade seat raised Henry up high enough to look through the short windscreen in front of him. The little boy wore a pair of goggles that dwarfed his head and gave him a bug-like appearance. He had a huge smile on his face.

"After the engine's running, you won't be able to hear me. Remember, don't touch the stick at all until I give you this sign." Walter made an exaggerated 'thumbs up' gesture. "Hold onto the sides of the cockpit like I showed you, so I can see where your hands are. If you start to feel bad or you want me to come back to the airport here and land, just turn around and point at the ground like this." He made a pumping motion of his right arm towards the ground with his index finger extended. "It will be a little hard to see out the front when we're still on the ground, but once we're in the air it should be easy. All set?" Henry nodded enthusiastically.

Walter Bowman clicked his harness into place and lit up the big Pratt & Whitney radial. As the noise and the prop blast enveloped him, Henry realized he had never been so excited in his life. His father taxied the plane out to the runway, but he did not lift the tailwheel off the ground. The throttle response on the overpowered plane had always been instantaneous, and the prop was longer than a standard one. He had never been willing to risk putting a tip into the asphalt and damaging the crankshaft with a technique that worked well on a standard engine.

After the runup and all pre-takeoff checks, Walter Bowman pulled out onto the runway, straddled the center line, shoved the stick forward, and gave the big radial two-thirds throttle. The Stearman leaped forward and the right wingtip raised slightly from the torque of the engine. Walter countered with right rudder and aileron, and in a few seconds fed in full throttle, holding the biplane straight and level a few feet off the runway, building speed. At the mid-field mark they were indicating 140 knots. At the far end of the runway, Walter pulled the stick back in his lap and released backpressure when the airplane was flying straight up.

Oh boy Henry thought. *This is like what those rocket plane pilots do.* He gripped the sides of the fuselage as hard as he could. When the airspeed indicator had wound down to 70 knots indicated, Walter kicked in full left rudder and rolled the wings level, flying at a right angle to the runway at an altitude of 1000 feet above the ground. *Wow!* Henry thought, as he saw where the ground was. His head swiveled left and right like a spectator at a tennis match. Walter laughed into the wind blast. Henry was having even more fun than he was.

They headed out across the Mississippi river and over Illinois, climbing at 3000 feet per minute. At 5500 feet, Walter leveled the wings and held a steady 140 knots airspeed. At that altitude, the temperature was eighteen degrees cooler than on the ground, which made it a very pleasant sixty-eight. When they were over the open soybean fields in Illinois where he could easily land if there was an engine failure, Walter began the standard maneuvers he had previously explained to his son.

He rolled the plane left into a thirty-degree bank and made a complete circle, ending up on the same heading. *It hardly feels like we're moving, now* Henry marveled. *It's just real loud and windy.* The stick between his legs tipped to the right as Walter reversed the controls and began a circle in the opposite direction. *It's just like Dad said* Henry thought as the stick returned to the vertical position and the plane stopped rolling but stayed in the bank.

Henry was thinking about this when Walter lowered the nose, put the biplane into a modest dive, and increased the throttle setting. At 160 knots, he pulled back on the stick and held it there. *Ooooh* Henry thought as his insides were dragged downwards from the G-forces. They were well past vertical before the pressure subsided. *I'm floating* Henry thought as Walter eased off on the backpressure. *Floating upside down.* The Stearman flew itself over the top of the loop and into an inverted descent. When they were aimed straight at the ground, Walter once again pulled back on the stick, jamming Henry into his seat once more and finishing the maneuver with the plane straight and level. Henry twisted around in his seat and gave his father a huge grin.

Walter gave his son the 'thumbs up' sign, and Henry took his hands off the sides of the cockpit. He pushed the stick to the left and the airplane rolled into a bank, somewhat shallower than the one his father had used. The nose dropped slightly as the plane continued on its circular path. Henry saw the river appear again after the plane had traveled 180 degrees. A dark green field appeared in the distance that Henry remembered had been in front of him before he started the turn. When he saw it, he rolled the wings back to level. His father looked at the compass. Henry was off of his original heading by only ten degrees. The boy hesitated for a few moments, then rolled the airplane into a right turn just as his father had done. This time he pulled back on the stick a little bit to keep the nose up in the turn. Once again, he rolled the wings level when the green field appeared in front of him. Henry twisted in his seat and saw his father smiling and nodding at him. He needed no further urging.

The young boy pushed the stick forward and put the biplane in a slight dive as his father had done. Then he hauled back on the stick with all his strength. Walter Bowman saw that Henry was not strong enough to exert the required amount of pressure, so he hooked his index finger around his own control and gave a little assistance. He also judiciously used the rudder pedals to keep the aircraft stable on its yaw axis.

Henry Bowman was so excited and amazed he felt as if he would burst. *I'm making this airplane fly straight up! It's doing whatever I make it do!* As the Stearman passed through vertical he remembered to relax backpressure as his father had instructed him, and he let the plane continue climbing inverted until gravity and the airfoil of the wings pulled it over into an inverted dive. When he saw they were aimed at the ground, with the wind noise increasing in his ears, for the first time that day six-year-old Henry Bowman was genuinely scared. *Dad can save us if I don't do it right* he reminded himself, and with that as his mantra, the little boy concentrated on completing the maneuver. He pulled back on the stick as hard as he could to finish off the loop, and he felt a knot in his stomach as the noise continued to increase. Walter was helping with the effort required to hold the stick back, and in ten seconds the biplane was once again flying straight and level. The boy let go of the stick and gripped the sides of the cockpit where his father could see his hands. His heart was pounding and blood roared in his ears. He had never had a feeling like this one before.

Three feet behind him, his father was laughing into the wind blast. The sight of his son's little head peering over the windscreen in front of him with his hands gripping the edge of the cockpit pleased the father no end. He flew the plane straight and level for a while before continuing with any other maneuvers. He didn't want to do too much too soon on his son's first time up.

After a while Walter saw that their fuel was getting low, so he turned back towards the airport. He put the airplane in a steep dive over the river and leveled it at 300 feet of altitude and 200 knots airspeed. At that height, the speed that they were traveling was very apparent. *Boy,* Henry thought, *we're really moving now. This is lots faster than a car.*

Walter raised the nose as they approached Missouri and traded the airspeed for more altitude as they got over land again. He headed back to the airport at an altitude of 1000 feet above the ground, entered the pattern, and made a flawless landing.

Walter taxied to the hangar and stopped the engine, then climbed out of the rear seat and went to help his son out of the front. Henry's face was streaked with oil and dirt, and he kept licking his teeth and swallowing.

"You'll have to learn to keep your mouth closed in open cockpits, kiddo. The wind blast will dry you out in a hurry. You might end up swallowing a bug or two, also."

"That was the most fun I've ever had! Can I go with you again next time, Dad?"

"Of course. But right now we've got to get the plane tied down in the hangar, and then get back home in time for lunch. Here, let me help you out of there." He grabbed his son under the arms and lifted the laughing boy out of the cockpit and onto the lower wing.

When the two arrived back at the house, Henry couldn't remember anything about the drive home. He was still reliving his first flight.

***

"Can't you do anything right?" Harold Gaines demanded as he looked at his son's report card. The highest grade on it was a 'C', in Social Studies. Richard Gaines hung his head but did not reply. He had not seen his father this angry over grades before, and he decided to stay quiet until the situation was clearer.

Harold Gaines was not specifically upset about his son's low grades. They were, in fact, very similar to what the father's own grades had been when he had been that age, and this report card was no worse than the others that his son had brought home that year. What made the elder Gaines so angry was the note that Richard's teacher had printed at the bottom of the official document:

> I am recommending that Richard repeat the Second Grade. It is obvious that he is not ready to progress with the rest of his class. Please contact the school at your earliest convenience to discuss this matter.

Harold Gaines put the report card back in the envelope and shook his head in disgust. "The boss won't get off my back at work, and now you surprise me with this crap! We'll talk about it later. Tell your mother I'm going out for a while. Don't expect me for lunch." He put on his hat and walked out the door of the cramped south side apartment. He fingered the two crumpled dollar bills in his pocket. His friend Jerry tended bar in the mornings. Harold thought he might be good for a free one, or at least a little credit.

Richard Gaines snuffled miserably as his father headed out the door.

***

"Raymond Emmett Johnson, Summa Cum Laude, Phi Beta Kappa Society," called out the administrator. The young man in black robe and mortarboard stood up and walked to the stage, accepted the proffered diploma, and shook the hand of the Brown University President. He smiled and nodded at the older man amid cheers and applause from the audience. He felt a slight fatigue that was somehow very pleasant. *Not bad* he thought with mild pleasure. *Not bad at all.* Ray made his way back to his seat as the administrator's sonorous voice announced Arthur Johnstone, the next Brown University graduate on the list.

After the Commencement exercises were over, the students broke up and mingled with the friends and family members who had come to see them graduate. Bud and Louise stood under an oak tree, with Bud's brother Carl a few feet to the side. All three were beaming.

"Wasn't sure you really did it, not until he'd handed you that sheepskin and then gone on to call the next boy's name." Louise Johnson rolled her eyes at her husband's attempt at humor and gave her son an enormous hug.

"You probably want to go be with your friends. Don't mind us." Louise Johnson was not at all used to New England, and she was unaccountably nervous being at a large university. Raymond was the first person in her family that had gone to college, and it showed.

"I've been with them for four years, Mom. I'd rather spend this time with you." His Uncle Carl laid a gnarled hand on Raymond's shoulder and drew him aside.

"Four years in college and you still haven't figured a damned thing out about women. Your mother is trying to tell you that she's about to bust out in tears because nothing like this has ever happened in her life before, and you need to understand that and make yourself scarce for a few minutes, so she don't embarrass herself in front of her only son. Now, Raymond, things have been better'n we had any right to expect out at the ranch, an' I don't know what Bud and your Ma have in mind for you, but this here is a present from me. Don't you give me no lip, now, 'cause I'm older than you and you ought to respect that. I also got no family of my own, and I'm just as proud of you as Bud an' Louise. Don't let on I give it to you, and please spend it on something you really want, like a party with a bunch of them coeds or whatnot. That's all I'm going t'say, now. Congratulations." He thrust a tightly folded envelope into his nephew's hand and turned away. Raymond put it in his pocket and stepped over to his parents.

"Give me a few minutes. There's a few people I'd like to talk to before they leave with their parents." He walked purposefully towards a group of graduates he knew vaguely, but all Raymond hoped to accomplish was to give his mother the time his Uncle Carl had said she needed. He engaged a young man he barely knew in congratulations and small talk for a few minutes, then moved on to another cluster of classmates and their families. When he was well away from his own family, he pulled the envelope from his pocket and opened it. It contained one thousand dollars in cash.

For a brief instant, Raymond tried to imagine what kind of party with coeds could possibly cost a thousand dollars, and he grinned at his uncle's admonition. He knew exactly what he was going to spend the money on, and it was not women.

***

"I think your father has something else for you." Catherine Bowman had been listening to her six-year-old son talk endlessly of the morning's experience flying the Stearman.

"Honey, after this morning, I don't think it will be very interesting," Walter told her.

"What is it, Dad? Can I see it? What's Mom talking about?" Like virtually all six-year-olds, Henry Bowman loved presents and surprises.

"You've become such a good reader, so I got you a book that every young man should have. To know what to aim for," he added. "Here." Walter handed his son a hard-cover book about an inch and a quarter thick. Henry took the book from his father and looked at the cover. There were several pictures printed on it. One was of ten men all pedaling a very long bicycle. Another was of an enormous flag hanging on the side of a building. A third photo showed a huge diamond set into an ornate staff.

Henry looked at the title. The large first word was unfamiliar to him, but the others were easy to read. **GUINNESS BOOK OF WORLD RECORDS** the title said. Underneath was the explanation

which is HIGHEST LOWEST BIGGEST SMALLEST FASTEST SLOWEST OLDEST NEWEST LOUDEST GREATEST HOTTEST COLDEST STRONGEST

As his father had known he would be, Henry was fascinated. He had never heard of such a book. "Thanks, Dad!" He gave his father as forceful a hug as he could.

"A little on the dry side, don't you think?" A listing of unrelated facts was not Catherine Bowman's idea of the ideal book to curl up with at night in a comfortable chair.

"We'll see if it bores him," her husband said with a laugh. Both of them knew their son well enough to know that was the last thing that was likely to happen.

"Can I go to my room now?" Henry asked. His parents both nodded. He ran up the stairs clutching his new treasure.

Henry Bowman spent most of the afternoon poring over the Guinness Book. The Table of Contents listed various categories such as The Natural World, Human Achievements, Man-Made Objects, and the Animal Kingdom, which made it easy to find interesting areas to explore. It was also the first time Henry had ever used an index, and he was delighted at his discovery that he could dream up something and then find it immediately.

He was thrilled when he saw that what his father had told him was confirmed by this book: The tallest known man in the world had lived just across the river from them in Alton, Illinois. His name was Robert Wadlow, and he had grown to a height of 8'10" before he died. Walter had met him, as the two men had shared the same doctor. Henry learned that other people had claimed to be much taller, some insisting they were over ten feet, but would always be proven wrong when they were measured. When he read this, he got goose bumps as a revelation struck him. *Teddy Block at school tells lies, but some grownups do it too! If you don't know someone really well, you need to get the proof, no matter how old they are!*

As Henry continued searching, he saw that many people had made claims that they could not back up, but the Guinness Book only accepted records that were proven.

As he was looking through the section on sports records, his mind began to wander. The listed times for running and swimming various distances didn't mean anything to him, and he was about to go back to the section about thinnest and heaviest people when the word Shooting caught his eye. *My Uncle Max shoots clay pigeons, and rifles and pistols too* he thought excitedly. *I'll look up the best shooter and next time he comes over I'll ask if he's ever met him.*

Henry examined the information listed but it was in the form of a table, and the types of competition were confusing. *Free pistol? Running deer? What kind of contests were these?* Further, all of the record-holders were from other countries. It was not near-ly as compelling as the photos of weight lifters or the descriptions of men who had sur-vived falling from airplanes without a parachute. He continued to look through the sec-tion about guns and shooting when another item grabbed his attention.

Block-Tossing. The world record for shooting a rifle at 2" wooden blocks thrown into the air is 72,491 (nine misses out of 72,500 thrown) by Adolph Topperwein (U.S.), accomplished over a 12-day period at the San Antonio, Texas fairgrounds in 1906.

Revolver. The greatest rapid fire feat was that of Ed. McGivern (U.S.), who, on August 20th, 1932, at the Lead Club Range, S.D., twice fired five shots in .45 seconds at 15 feet which could be covered by a silver half-dollar.

Henry completely forgot about the world's biggest ship or fastest airplane. *Five shots from a revolver in less than a half second. A man who used a rifle to shoot over 72,000 wooden blocks, and only missed nine. And it took a week and a half to do it! Ordinary people did these things.* Henry felt shivers run down his spine. *I wonder if my Uncle Max has heard of these men.* He continued looking through the section on guns and shooting when he came upon another interesting item:

Highest Caliber. The largest guns made were 2-bores. Less than a dozen of these were made by two English wildfowl gunmakers about 1885. Normally the largest guns made are double-barreled 4-bore rifles weighing up to 26 lbs., which can be handled only by men of exceptional physique.

Henry read the words over and over. He knew that wildfowl meant birds, and that the 2-bores described were shotguns. But a 26-pound rifle! *...can be handled only by men of exceptional physique.* The words gave a powerful jolt to his imagination. Henry thought of his father lifting their new refrigerator on his back and putting it in the kitchen. *Dad could shoot one of those. So could Uncle Max. Maybe Uncle Max even has one!*

Henry Bowman closed his eyes. *He was grown up, holding the enormous double-barreled rifle to his shoulder. The corded muscles in his arms stood out under tension as he held the rifle firmly in position, both eyes open. As he pulled the trigger, a deafening roar filled the air and he was rocked backwards by the recoil. Smoke and flame belched out of the gun's muzzle, and a hole he could stick his thumb into with room to spare appeared in the dead tree. Chunks of dead wood exploded out the back side of the tree as the huge bullet exited. He brought the rifle back down out of recoil, leaned forward, and pulled the trigger a second time. Once again the huge rifle thundered, and the hole in the tree enlarged slightly as the second bullet went in almost right on top of the first. He low-ered the rifle and smiled with satisfaction.*

Henry opened his eyes, stood up, and walked downstairs to ask his parents when Uncle Max was going to visit. The six-year-old had no way of knowing that double rifles like the 4-bores mentioned in the Guinness Book had dual triggers, not the single trigger he had imagined. Apart from that minor error, Henry had accurately seen into the future. Something else had happened, as well.

Henry Bowman had just become a member of the gun culture.

"Going to miss hunting with you, Ray." The owner of East Bay Sports smiled as he spoke to his younger friend. "Never had a customer before or since that knew as much as you about reading sign or where the likeliest spot was to find game." East Bay Sports was Gene's attempt to give sportsmen in the Boston area an emporium similar to Abercrombie & Fitch in New York City. He had come pretty close, and Raymond dropped in often when he was free. He liked Gene a lot.

"When I came here from Colorado in '55, I was afraid that everything would be so built up there wouldn't be any good hunting at all." Ray grinned at his friend.

"You're as bad as these folks around here that think everything west of Pennsylvania is a vast wasteland." Gene was originally from New Mexico. He changed the subject. "Listen, as a kind of graduation present, if you want anything before you leave, I'll give you twenty percent off anything in the store, ten off any guns here on consignment. I got to make a little something on you," he added with a chuckle. It was well known that the fee for all consignment sales was twenty percent.

"That's very generous of you, Gene. You sure you want to do that? Your prices have always been very reasonable, to my way of thinking." Ray did not like the idea of taking advantage of their friendship.

The owner shrugged and leaned on the glass-topped display case filled with fly-fishing paraphernalia. "You taught me a few things these past four years about tracking. Anything you buy, I can replace."

"Not the stuff on consignment."

"Hell, that doesn't matter. If it's still in the rack it's obviously not a real hot item. You got something particular in mind?" The older man looked at Raymond with keen interest.

Raymond nodded and gave a small smile. "I got a little money as a graduation present from my uncle yesterday. I'll take the Holland."

A broad smile creased the face of the store owner. "Now why did I have an idea you were going to say that?" He walked away from the gun case and over to the picture window in the front of the store. Cradled in a horizontal rack in the center of the display was a Holland & Holland side-by-side double rifle in caliber .600 Nitro. The gun was ornately engraved and weighed 14 1/2 pounds. Above it was a sign that Gene had made. He had hoped it would help sell the gun. The rifle had been owned by an elderly man who had commissioned it from the famous London gunmaker prior to World War I. He had died five months ago, and neither his widow nor his daughter had any attachment to the beautiful rifle. It had been on consignment for three months and had failed to attract a buyer. Raymond looked at the large sign.

Largest Rifle Ever Made
Holland & Holland .600 Nitro Express
With Fitted Leather Trunk case And
250 Rounds Of Ammunition
$800

Gene lifted the rifle out of its stand and handed it to Ray for perhaps the fifth time in three months. Raymond threw it up to his shoulder with a fluid motion. His face laid easily on the stock's cheekpiece and the sights lined up instantly with his right eye. "Whoever had this built years ago must have been my size. The stock fits just right. It would be really frustrating if it had too much drop, or some other fault that would be hard to change."

"Think you'll make it to Africa?"

Ray shrugged. "Some day. Law school comes first. Then I've got to get established. But I think that before I'm thirty-five I should be able to afford a decent safari." He swung the big rifle up to his shoulder once more, imagining that an angry cape buffalo was fifteen yards in front of the muzzle. Another customer walked over and joined the two men. He was in his fifties, and had come in to pick up some twenty-gauge shotgun shells.

"A little too much gun, don't you think?" Ray and Gene turned to look at the man.

"No such thing as too much gun when the game weighs six tons and is likely to decide to kill you," Ray said. "Gene's sign in the window isn't quite accurate, though. This .600 is the largest modern, smokeless powder rifle ever made. Back in the late 1800s before cordite was invented, the Brits built some much larger black powder rifles. I saw a picture of an 8-bore double rifle once that must have weighed eighteen pounds," Ray said easily. The newcomer snorted.

"You an African hunter, son?" the man asked with more than a little scorn. Raymond paused to look the man straight in the eye before replying.

"Not yet." The man looked slightly chastened and took a different tack.

"Well, that thing's awfully expensive and heavy. Winchester makes their Model 70 in .458 Magnum now, and it holds four shots and probably only weighs half of what that English gun does, if you're really serious about hunting big game. And a bolt action will take a lot more pressure than that side-by-side there." The man's confidence level was returning as he continued to talk. Raymond smiled benignly.

"That's one opinion. The other side to that argument is that high pressure bolt-action loads can also mean sticky case extraction in an African climate. No big deal if you're shooting a deer a hundred yards away. Not the same thing if it's something dangerous at twenty feet.

"The .458 does duplicate the power of some of the medium-sized English double rifles such as the .450 Nitro, just like you said. No bolt action that I know of, though, will throw a sixty-two caliber bullet like this rifle will. It has been my experience, on large American game at least, that big, heavy bullets kill more reliably and cleanly than smaller ones.

"I also like the fact that with a double rifle, you essentially have two complete rifles that are already loaded. You have a second shot as soon as you can pull the gun down out of recoil, and if something breaks, like a firing pin, you can continue to reload and shoot the remaining good barrel. A broken firing pin in a bolt action in Africa will get you killed.

"Last of all, and the Winchester rep would shoot me if he was here, the Model 70 is mass produced for American hunting. Ninety-nine percent of them are thirty caliber or smaller. If they occasionally balk when you work the bolt quickly, which I have had them do, or if they sometimes fail to extract, which I have also had them do, it's a minor irritation for someone on a deer or elk hunt. In Africa, it's a disaster.

"Winchester went and put a .458 barrel on the same action and the same stock as their .270 and they call it an African rifle. In the four years that I've known Gene, he's sent back three Model 70s in .375 caliber that split their stocks from recoil. I suspect their new .458 is going to be an even worse warranty problem for Winchester if any customers actually shoot it very much, as anyone serious about hunting Africa would." He hefted the Holland again and stared at it.

"This rifle was designed and built by a company that has supplied professional market hunters in Africa for over a century. I'd feel a lot more confident with it in my hands than a tarted-up deer rifle."

Raymond handed the gun to Gene and reached in his pocket for his money clip. He peeled off $800 and handed the bills to his friend. After a moment's deliberation, he turned back to the other customer.

"Gene's too polite to say it, but if this was my store and some loudmouth came in and tried to kill a sale on a rifle that cost half as much as a decent car, I'd tell him to go buy his shotgun shells at the local hardware store and never come back." The older man's jaw dropped. Then he turned on his heel without a word and went to the clothing section of the shop.

"Hey, I'm sorry, Gene. For four years I've listened to fools like that give advice when it wasn't wanted, and I'm going home in tomorrow, and I just couldn't help myself."

The owner laughed softly. He was biting his lip so that the distant customer couldn't hear. "You only said what I wanted to. You got to realize, though, a lot of people operate on envy. Guy like that," he said, nodding towards the back of the store, "he would never spend the money to buy a rifle like this, let alone the cost of a safari, no matter how much he has in the bank. Even if someone gave it all to him, he wouldn't have the nerve to go. Guy like that gets very uncomfortable at the notion of a young fellow like you who intends to make it happen. Makes him feel like going out with his box of skeet shells isn't any fun any more." Gene's face took on a sad expression.

"Problem is," he went on, "people like him, they get half a chance, they'll do their level best to screw it up for anyone else. You got to watch out for them *all the time*. Envy and resentment are terrible things." He took the bills to the cash register, rang up $720, added sales tax, and gave Raymond his change. "You want all the ammo now, or should I keep it here until you're about to leave?"

"Keep it and the rifle, too. I'm moving out of my room tomorrow and won't have anyplace to store it before I go. I'll be by around noon day after tomorrow, if that's okay."

"I'll be here all day Monday."

Raymond looked pensive. He chose his next words carefully. "I shouldn't have unloaded on that poor guy. He was just talking. I doubt he cares one way or another what I or anyone else does with his money."

"I hope you're right. But there's a lot of envy out there. Just hope you never find yourself under the authority of someone with a big dose of it."

Raymond Johnson left East Bay Sports and walked to his car. In a few minutes, thoughts of seeing Colorado again would push what Gene had said from his mind. Over thirty years later, he would remember his friend's words as clearly as if they had been tattooed on his flesh.

June 18, 1959

It was moments like this that made him wish he had become a dermatologist in California instead of an obstetrician in New York City. He looked down at the pitiful thing to which the Gutierrez woman had just given birth. The baby girl's head was unusually small, and only smooth skin was visible where her eyes should have been. He pinched off the umbilical cord and slapped the baby on the back to get her breathing. She made a faint sound, but her lungs did start working.

The doctor realized immediately that the baby girl was blind and brain damaged, and it filled him with great sadness. He wished her respiratory system were equally defective, to save the family some long-term heartbreak. He'd seen enough babies to know that this one would almost certainly live, if that was indeed the proper term for a body without benefit of a spirit.

He looked down at the barely-conscious woman on the delivery table, and made a quick decision. "Take over for me here," he instructed the attending nurse. "I need to tell the father." He pulled his mask down and walked out of the delivery room.

The young intern watched the tired, hopeful face of Pedro Gutierrez collapse when the maintenance man saw the look in his eyes.

That day was one of the few that the young doctor truly hated his job.

June 20, 1959

The big man and the little boy walked into the showroom on Olive Street, and Henry's jaw dropped. *Wow! I've never seen so many guns in one place before—not even at Uncle Max's.* In addition to rack upon rack of rifles and rows of glass cases displaying pistols, there was a full size mounted polar bear standing midway between the front door and the far wall. The walls that did not have gun racks on them were covered with framed photos of men and women. Some were shooting, and others were smiling at the camera, kneeling next to game animals. A very pleasant aroma was faintly present also. It reminded Henry of a workshop .

"Welcome to Goodman's," said the man behind the counter. He was short and rather pear-shaped, with round glasses, a prominent nose, and curly black hair that was starting to turn grey.

"Al, this is my nephew Henry Bowman. He's my sister Catherine's son, he's six years old, and his summer vacation just started. Henry, this is Al Goodman. He and his brother Harold own this place." Henry stepped up and shook the man's hand once, using a firm grip as his father had taught him. Al Goodman's handshake felt as if the man were unconscious.

"Pleased to meet you," Henry said politely. He could not help looking away from the mild-looking owner and staring at the wealth of fascinating sights throughout the store. Al Goodman had a knowing look on his face. He had seen this happen before.

"Is Henry here to get his first rifle?" Al asked mildly. His voice had a nasal quality, but it was not unpleasant. *A rifle?* Henry thought with a start. *That can't be right.*

"Not just yet," Max answered. "But we'll be back for that before too many more years go by. I thought I'd introduce Henry to this place, and you and Harold, and maybe see if there isn't a pocketknife or two he'd like to have. He also wants to look at a gun he read about, if you've got one in the store."

"Well, the knives are over here." Al walked to the glass display case at the end of the row, nearest the front window of the store. Henry walked over and peered into it. There were more than a hundred different knives, ranging from small folding penknives to large hunting blades. Henry's eyes were drawn to a massive Bowie knife that was the center of the display. Its blade gleamed like a mirror.

"This is one that every boy should have," said Al in a monotone, pulling a box out of the case and laying it on the glass top. Henry felt mild disappointment at the small size of the box, but he opened it and pulled out a medium-sized folding knife with red sides bearing a white cross. He turned it over in his small hands, examining it. It had several blades folded into it on one side, and a spiral device folded into the other.

"Swiss Army Knife," Al Goodman explained, taking the knife from Henry and opening the main blade and then the smaller blade. "Has two sizes of knife blades, one for general cutting and the other for delicate work." He folded them back and opened another blade with his thumbnail. "This is a standard-size screwdriver, and this part," he said, pointing to the curved cutout on the side of the screwdriver blade, "is a bottle opener." Henry immediately recognized that it was exactly the right shape to open soft drink bottles, and a huge smile came over his face. Al closed the blade and opened another. "This one is a small screwdriver," he said, touching the blade's tip, "and this part is a can opener." Al continued with his presentation. "Here you have a Phillips screwdriver, this is a leather punch, and this curly thing here is a corkscrew, for opening wine bottles. You can lend it to your Uncle Max when he gets thirsty," Al added, deadpan.

The Bowie was forgotten. Henry was enthralled. *It will fit in my pocket, and I can take it anywhere! Whenever we have sodas outside, people are always looking for the opener. And Dad has to go to the basement whenever he needs a screwdriver upstairs to fix something.* Henry imagined reaching into his pocket and pulling out his knife when his father needed to open a soda bottle or tighten the thing on the screen door that made it close slowly instead of slamming.

Henry didn't see Max Collins roll his eyes. "Don't you want a real knife, like this one here?" the big man asked. He pointed to a large, stag-handled folding knife with two blades half-opened for display and nickel-silver bolsters on each end. The word CASE was etched on the larger blade. Al Goodman reached in and withdrew it. He placed it on the glass next to the multifunction tool.

Henry stared at the knife. It was very impressive. He licked his lips and looked back at the red pocketknife. "Maybe you'd like a larger Swiss Army Knife," Al droned, pretending not to notice Max Collins' pained expression.

"*Larger?*" Henry said reflexively. The store owner withdrew another cardboard box from the case and opened it. He handed Henry a knife similar to the first one, but twice as thick.

"This is our biggest. It has all the blades I showed you before, and also some others." He opened one and since it was obviously a tiny pair of scissors, he did not bother to explain. "This one here," he continued, opening a new blade, "is for scaling fish." Henry had never been fishing. He remained silent. "This one," Al went on, "is a wood saw, and this one is both a metal file and a metal saw that will cut though steel if you keep at it." His tone of voice was the same as if he was reading the telephone directory.

Henry was transfixed. *A saw that will cut through wood, and another for steel!* Henry realized Al was explaining again. "...is a toothpick, which is kind of pointless I think, but the thing that slides out of *this* side is a small pair of tweezers, and they can come in handy when you get a splinter."

Henry Bowman's eyes were wide as he stared at the amazing knife. "Which one do you like best?" Al asked finally. Henry's gaze went back to the beautiful two-bladed CASE knife, and he bit his lip. He knew he would not use it or carry it as much, but he would love to own it.

"What the hell are you giving the kid a hard time for, Al?" Max demanded. "He obviously likes both of them, or have your eyes really gotten that bad? Maybe you should let Harold run the sales floor from now on."

Al Goodman looked up and saw the big man grinning at him. The storeowner had never pushed a sale on Max Collins in the twelve years they had known each other. Max, in turn, had accounted for more business than any other individual customer. The Goodman brothers kept very meticulous records of things like that.

"I'll put both of these aside for you," Al told Henry, "over here by the register, so that you and your Uncle Max can look around the rest of the store." He scooped up the bigger Swiss Army Knife and the two-bladed CASE and walked over to the cash register. Max walked over to a display case in front of a rack of fine shotguns. Henry followed his uncle, but his mind was elsewhere. He was having a hard time believing the good fortune which had just befallen him.

"Al, let me see that Model Twelve pigeon gun." The short man handed Max Collins the pump shotgun. Its receiver was ornately engraved. Max opened the action to make sure the chamber was empty and threw the gun up to his shoulder. "Decent rib pitch, and the comb's about right," he pronounced. "Been using a double, but the patterns aren't exactly matching. After watching Herb, I think a pump may be even faster since your left hand will pull it out of recoil." He laid the shotgun down on a rectangular pad on top of the display case and squatted down next to his nephew.

"You see that picture there," Max said, pointing across the room. Henry nodded. "That's Herb Parsons. He's an exhibition shooter who works for Winchester. He can hit seven clay birds with seven shots before they hit the ground, all thrown in the air at the same time, using a gun just like this one. He's doing it right there."

Henry examined the photo. A man with his back to the camera had a shotgun pressed to his shoulder. There were five black puffs of smoke hanging in the sky and two clay birds about to be hit. "A Model Twelve will fire as soon as the action closes, if you've got the trigger held down," Max explained. "Not all pump shotguns will do that, 'cause most of them use a disconnector. If a man practices enough, he can shoot a Model 12 accurately even faster than an automatic. Herb'll be at the range next month. We'll go

June 20, 1959

shooting out there and you can meet him." Max stood up and turned to Al Goodman.

"We'll take this one, too. I'm going to see if I can learn to shoot it the way he does. If not, I'll trade it back for something else." Henry stared at the photo for a few moments longer, then remembered the thing he had intended to ask.

"Do you have a 4-bore here?" he asked the older man. Al Goodman was startled at the six-year-old's question, but he answered immediately in his trademark nasal monotone.

"It's illegal to hunt birds in the United States with any shotgun larger than a ten-gauge. Has been for fifty years or so. I'm afraid you hardly ever see those big old wild-fowl guns any more, except in museums and once in a while in a private collection." He turned to Henry's uncle. "Does he understand the way the gauge system works?"

"As a matter of fact, he does," Max answered, nodding.

The day that Walter had given Henry the Guinness Book, he had explained to his son that shotgun bores were sized based on how many pure lead balls exactly the diameter of the bore would equal one pound. Thus, a twenty gauge had a bore the diameter of a pure lead ball that weighed 1/20th of a pound, (about .610"), and a 12-gauge gun had a bore the size of a pure lead ball that weighed 1/12th of a pound, which measured .722". The smaller the number of the gauge, the bigger the gun. Max had been surprised on the drive over to the store that the boy understood this system of measurement.

"Not a shotgun," Henry broke in. "A 4-bore *rifle*. A double barrel. Really heavy—about 25 pounds."

Al Goodman opened his mouth and was about to tell the six-year-old that such a rifle did not exist, but he paused before speaking. Gun shops tended to attract people who possessed tremendous amounts of misinformation about firearms, and Al and Harold both put up with ridiculous questions each business day. They had an ironclad rule never to embarrass or shame a customer no matter how stupid his claim, and Al was not going to break that rule just because the customer was six years old. Furthermore, to Al Goodman's knowledge, Max Collins had never uttered a single wrong statement about firearms, and he noticed Max wasn't correcting his nephew now. Al closed his mouth and revised what he was about to say.

"I have never seen a 4-gauge rifle, Henry, either single or double barrel. Did you see a picture of one somewhere?" Henry shook his head.

"I just read about it." Al Goodman nodded. He was imagining a piece of fiction in a 'Real Guts' type magazines, but what Max said next caused him to revise his thinking once again.

"Saw an eight-bore double rifle once, out in Vegas," Max said. "Underlever hammer gun with nice engraving. Huge goddamn thing, must have weighed over sixteen pounds. Took a big brass case about three-and-a-half, four inches long, with a cast lead bullet in the end as big as your thumb. Guy from California had it. Wasn't looking to sell, he'd taken it to Africa and killed a buffalo with it and I think he wanted to show it off. Said it was made about 1890."

Al Goodman looked at the boy with new respect. "Where did you read about this 4-bore rifle, Henry?"

"In the Guinness Book of World Records," he replied immediately.

Al nodded again. "Always learn something new from my customers." Henry felt flattered at the comment. "I'm afraid we don't have either a 4-bore or an 8-bore rifle here right now, but we get a lot of guns in every week. I'll tell Harold to keep his eyes out, and we'll call your Uncle Max if one comes in. Wouldn't surprise me if he bought it on the spot," Al added in his monotone.

Goodman's for Guns was arguably the finest gun store in the midwest. Its owners, ironically, had no interest whatsoever in either shooting, hunting, or owning fine firearms. They had a very keen interest in making money, however, and it was their insight in attracting and pleasing good customers who did love fine arms that was the foundation of their success.

As it turned out, though, the Goodman brothers never would see a 4-bore rifle come into their store. None of the three there that day knew it, but there were fewer than fifteen of the massive guns in existence in the entire country.

"Henry's learned a lot from the Guinness Book," Max explained to Al. "His father gave it to him a couple of weeks ago, and I think he's read it cover-to-cover by now."

"If Henry likes to read, maybe he'd like this year's *Gun Digest*. It's got a lot of interesting articles in it." The way Al said it he might as well have been reciting a recipe for meat loaf. He reached up to a shelf and took down a large softcover book about an inch thick. The *Gun Digest* came out annually. Al Goodman had himself never read a single article in it, but customers bought a lot of them, and were forever quoting from it. He handed the book to the boy.

Henry looked at the cover. It was a color drawing of the strangest-looking pistol Henry had ever seen, lying on top of a wooden bench with five paper targets standing in the distance. He opened the cover and found the table of contents. He was looking at the articles listed in the left-hand column when two-thirds of the way down a title leaped out at him:

"*Ed McGivern!*" Henry exclaimed, turning quickly to page 80.

"You know who Ed McGivern was?" his uncle asked in surprise. Henry nodded. "He died a year ago last December," Max added. Al Goodman knitted his eyebrows together. He had never heard of the man.

"He could fire a revolver five times in less than a half a second," Henry said with confidence. Al opened his mouth to comment on this obvious exaggeration when Max Collins spoke again.

"Damn right he could. I saw him do it at the Montana State Fair almost thirty years ago. I think it may have been even faster than that. Sounded like one quick roar—faster than the Tommy guns I shot in the Army. But *Jesus,* you should have seen him shoot things in the air—marbles, washers with paper pasted over the hole, clay birds, two guns at once—I never would have believed it if I hadn't seen him do it."

"Like this?" Henry held the book open. On the left-hand page was a photo very similar to the one on the wall of Herb Parsons, except the man doing the shooting was holding a revolver instead of a shotgun, and there were five black puffs of smoke in the air instead of seven.

"I'll be dipped in shit! I saw him do that! There it is—Central Montana State Fair in 1931. Had a job on a cattle ranch the summer after high school, and we went to the fair one weekend and damned if Ed McGivern wasn't there. Never saw anything like it." He looked at his nephew with interest. "You really *do* like to read, don't you?" he asked the little boy. Henry nodded.

"I've got Ed McGivern's book at home. Tells all about how he trained himself to do all the things he did." He looked at the store owner. "Al, do you have a copy of *Fast and Fancy Revolver Shooting* here?" The owner shook his head. "Hell, kid, I'll let you have mine." He turned to Al Goodman. "Put the *Gun Digest* on my tab, too." The big man turned to his nephew. "Ready to go?" Henry glanced over to his right. Max Collins had a knowing smile on his face when he asked the next question. "Want to go over and look at the bear, while I see if Al's got anything else for me to take home?"

A huge grin appeared on Henry's face and he ran over to where the mounted polar bear stood. As he did so, the door to the store opened and in walked a slender man of about thirty-five. He was carrying a long gun under his arm. It had two shotgun barrels side-by-side, with a rifle barrel underneath. The owner looked up and acknowledged him as he walked over.

"Good morning, Major."

"Morning, Al. Thought I'd see what you'd give me for this German drilling," the man said, using the correct term for the hybrid sporting arm. Al Goodman took the gun from the young man and opened it, looking down the bore of the rifle barrel. The newcomer continued. "Picked it up during the war. Hardly been shot at all. Tightest action you've ever seen. Sixteen gauge over 8x57 Mauser. Balances beautifully, and can take any kind of game on the continent. Gorgeous engraving, and look at that wood!"

Al examined the Teutonic engraving on the metal and the deep-relief carving on the wood. He had never liked carving, and much preferred standard checkering, to the extent that he cared at all. He was evaluating the gun, trying to decide what a customer might pay for it. He knew that Max Collins thought combination guns were for fools. Before he could say anything, the young man finished his sales pitch with what he believed to be the clincher.

"And what's more, this was the *personal* weapon of Hermann Goering." Al Goodman looked up at his customer, who was grinning broadly.

"Well, of course that would endear it to me."

Al's face and voice, as always, were both entirely devoid of emotion or inflection. Al was wearing an open-necked shirt, and a mezuzah hung around his neck. The Army

Major either did not see it or did not care.

"I can't give you a price until Harold sees it, and he doesn't usually work on Saturdays. You can leave it here and I'll call you Monday, or you can bring it back any time during the week."

"Hang on to it," the man said airily. "I'm going to see what you've gotten in lately in your pistol case." He moved away from Al and Max towards the far end of the store.

Max Collins reached in his pocket and leaned over to whisper to the smaller man. "Al, I'll give you a hundred bucks right now if you call that guy back over and say 'Sir, I've considered this very carefully, and I'll give you twenty dollars for this gun'."

For the first time that day, Al Goodman smiled. Even if Max Collins had not been Goodman's best customer, he would still have been Al's favorite customer. The store owner had no doubt whatsoever that Max Collins would carry through on his offer, and be glad to do so.

"I'd do it for nothing, Max, but he's a good customer. Just a little slow, that's all."

Max Collins shook his head and clenched his teeth to keep himself from breaking out laughing. He laid three hundred-dollar bills next to the cash register and Al Goodman rang up his sale. "All set, kid?" He called out as Al handed him his change and the shotgun. Henry came running over, and Al held out a sack containing the boy's *Gun Digest* and his two pocket knives.

"Thank you, sir," Henry said solemnly.

"Let's get you home so you can fool with that pocket tool kit of yours and read up on Ed McGivern." The big man and the little boy walked towards the door. As he was about to exit the gun shop, Henry Bowman looked over his shoulder and called out to the owner.

"I really like your store."

"Well, thank you, Henry," replied the proprietor.

Al Goodman smiled for the second time that day. It was a record for him.

January 6, 1961

"Hey!" the man yelled out across the office, his hand covering the mouthpiece of the telephone he held. "Wagner just had a heart attack. DOA at Barnes. We've got to move fast—the vultures will be circling."

His partner sat bolt upright. His mind was racing, and he was already thinking several steps ahead to the necessary special election that would be held to replace the dead legislator. "Shit! On the first week of the session, for Christ's sake!"

"If Holmes and Armitage get into it, they'll be at each other's throats the whole time. They hate each other, and the last thing we need is a mudbath between those two, fighting for Wagner's seat. It might even throw it to the Republicans," the first man warned.

The second man grimaced with distaste at this last thought. There had never been a Republican state rep in his district during his lifetime. He intended to do his part to see that it stayed that way. "Can't have that," he said, shaking his head.

"What we need is someone everyone can live with. "Belson?"

"Too young. Need someone older, that the unions can go for."

"Andrews?"

He shook his head. "A lot of people see him as mean-spirited. You won't get Holmes or Armitage to step aside for that guy." His friend nodded in agreement.

"How about Joe Hammond?"

"Joe Hammond..." He said the name slowly as he mulled it over in his mind. He hadn't thought of Joe, but the suggestion had a certain logic to it. His friend held up his left fist and started to enumerate points by raising fingers one at a time.

"He's sixty, or thereabouts. Made a pile in construction, and always used only union labor. I never heard of him screwing anyone on a deal, and the only people who don't like him are the ones who resent him for being a success when they weren't. He's given a lot of dough to the Party over the years, and I think he's ready to get out of his business."

"We might sell that..." His wheels were turning. "Think he'd want it?"

The other man shrugged. "Can't tell 'til we ask him. Decent chance, though, if you ask me. Political power can be pretty attractive, particularly if getting it's painless. You know anyone who'd turn it down?"

"Not many. Particularly if they're already about to get out of what they're doing. Let's run it by Harris and Fields, and then let's meet with Joe Hammond."

The State House representative for the 92nd District of Missouri in south St. Louis had just been decided.

January 14, 1961

Henry Bowman was as excited as he could ever remember being. This was even better than the last time he had been to Goodman's, a year and a half before. As he and his father walked through the door, he smelled the faint aroma of Hoppe's #9 solvent. It was very pleasant, and it brought the memory of his first visit to the store into brilliant focus in his mind.

"Mr. Goodman, Walter Bowman. I understand you've already met my son, although it was a couple of years ago. The tenth was his eighth birthday, and we're here to get his first rifle." He held out his hand to the older man, who took it in a lifeless grip.

"Please, it's 'Al'. Your son made quite an impression on us when he and his uncle came in last. He's quite a reader, as I recall, and I learned a few things from him. Tell me, Henry, are you still looking for a 4-bore rifle?"

"Do you have one *here*?" Henry asked immediately with unconcealable excitement.

"No," replied Al Goodman, shaking his head and putting a sad expression on his face, "we've never had one come in. I found out that they're terribly rare, and the few that do exist are mostly in Europe. But I did find a book by a man that used a 4-bore in Africa, and I also have a photo of one." He walked over to a shelf and took down a copy of *Wild Beasts and Their Ways* by Sir Samuel White Baker.

"This man hunted all over Africa with some very large rifles about a hundred years ago. You're welcome to borrow this book and read about him." Al Goodman opened the cover and withdrew a photograph. "This is a photograph from a store in England that sells fine guns." He handed the photo to the boy.

Henry stared down at the picture. Two guns were lying on a tabletop. The first was of normal size, and appeared to be a double-barreled shotgun with fine engraving. The gun below it was slightly shorter in length, but massive in its construction. The barrels were twice as thick, and the huge receiver had a pair of exposed hammers above the breech. The engraving was of even higher quality than that of the smaller weapon.

"I promised to return the picture, but I told the owner I had a friend who would like to look at it, and he let me keep it until you had a chance to come in." Walter Bowman smiled at the older man's characterization of eight-year-old Henry as his friend. "He told me the 4-bore weighs 24 pounds empty, and 25 1/2 pounds loaded." Al turned to Henry's father. "I've been in this business for thirty years, and your son told me about a rifle I had never heard of. It wasn't until last month that I even saw a picture of one."

Walter Bowman looked with great pride at his son, who was staring intently at the photograph. "Henry is very good at learning all there is to know about subjects that interest him."

"Has he told you what kind of rifle he wants?"

"As a matter of fact, no, he hasn't. I thought we'd get your suggestions, and then maybe Henry will be able to pick one out."

Al Goodman nodded, but he wasn't learning what he really needed to know, which was how much Walter Bowman was willing to pay for his son's first .22. A Marlin single shot bolt action .22 with birch stock retailed for $17.25. A Browning autoloading .22 with a beautifully figured French walnut stock and Grade III factory engraving retailed for $159.50. The recently discontinued Winchester 52 sporter bolt action was the same size and quality as their Model 70 centerfire, and had sold for $200.

Al Goodman would have been amazed if Walter Bowman intended to buy either of the last two rifles for his son. Most fathers bought the cheapest single shot available for their sons' first rifle, for children were not always good at taking care of valuable equipment. The same was true of some adults, and Al recalled the condition of some of the used guns that people brought in the store. Assuming that a customer was going to want the least expensive choice, however, was not how Goodman's had become such a great success. Walter Bowman's next comments clarified things considerably for the store owner.

"He probably needs a repeater. I think it's a foregone conclusion that Henry's going to do a lot of shooting. We spend each summer in the country on the Mississippi River, and he can shoot every day there if he wants to. I don't think we want a rifle for formal competition shooting at paper targets. It's my understanding that they are rather heavy, and I think Henry's more interested in shooting sticks floating in the river right now." He looked over at his son, who was nodding agreement.

"Also, I'd like him to have something of good quality. I don't know much about guns, but I believe in good tools that will last a lifetime. Henry's Uncle Max shoots guns that his father gave him almost forty years ago. I think Henry's first rifle should be something that he'd still be proud to own even after he's grown."

Al Goodman nodded sagely. "I can show you a few choices. Is it fair to say that if they're all in about the same price range, the one that feels the best to Henry is probably going to be the one you want?"

"Yes, I think so." Walter Bowman suppressed a grin as he watched the least enthusiastic sales technique he had ever seen.

"In that case, if you want a repeater for doing a lot of shooting, one with a tubular magazine is easiest to load and holds the most cartridges. You won't have a separate clip that can be misplaced or get separated from the gun. Some rifles have their tubular magazines under the barrel, and some have them in the buttstock, but they both work the same way. Do you know if you are interested in a bolt action, a lever action, a pump, or a semiauto?" The two men looked at Henry.

"If it's okay, Dad, I'm pretty sure I want a pump or an autoloader." Henry did not say so, but he knew exactly what he wanted. He wanted either a Winchester Model 61 pump, or if he could really have any rifle at all, a Winchester Model 63 semiauto.

Henry had seen Herb Parsons use both of these guns 18 months before at the Olin range in Alton, Illinois with his Uncle Max. With the pump gun, Parsons had turned the rifle on its side and held it at chest level. He worked the action briskly to eject the fired case vertically into the air. Then he had snapped the rifle up to his shoulder and hit the airborne empty with the next shot. He had repeated this procedure until the gun was empty. With the Model 63, he had hit three eggs thrown in the air at the same time with three shots. Henry did not think he would ever be able to hit fired .22 cases in the air, but he thought he might learn to hit a tossed hen's egg. Herb Parsons had also told him that each of the two guns had over 100,000 rounds fired through it, and that if they ever broke just from shooting, Winchester would fix them for free. Henry had been impressed.

When Henry had done research in his 1959 *Gun Digest,* he had discovered that the Winchester 63 was the most expensive .22 made, not counting special target rifles and guns that were engraved. It sold for a few cents under eighty dollars. Other pumps and semiautos sold for less than half that amount. *And the price on the Winchester has probably gone up in the last two years* he thought dismally.

"Remington and Winchester both make good pumps and autos, and Browning makes a nice auto but no pump." The short man gently lifted two rifles from the rack. "For customers interested in guns of lasting value, we suggest sticking to those three makes, at least as far as twenty-twos are concerned." He laid the two rifles on the padded counter. "In the slide action, Remington makes the 572 and Winchester makes the 61. The Remington comes in two versions, either a steel receiver, or an aluminum one for a bit more money. The aluminum-receivered gun is lighter, has a chrome plated magazine tube, and an aluminum cover on the barrel. Some people like the lighter weight but neither gun is very heavy. The one here is steel, but I can show you the aluminum model also. It comes in different colors." Al Goodman did not think Mr. Bowman would think much of an anodized aluminum rifle.

"I can imagine what my brother-in-law would say if we brought home something like that: 'I thought you were going to Goodman's, not a goddamn whorehouse!'" Al Goodman laughed at Walter's startlingly accurate impression of Max Collins.

Henry looked at the two men, and they both motioned for him to pick up one of the rifles.

"Press this small lever with your trigger finger, and work the slide with your opposite hand to make sure the gun is empty," Al instructed. Henry did so, and then closed the action and threw the rifle up to his shoulder, aiming at a spot on the wall well away from any people in the store. The stock was large for him, as almost any stock would be for an eight-year-old, but his position was right and the sights lined up with his right eye.

"Try the Winchester." Henry repeated the procedure, and realized that the second gun's stock and forend were slightly smaller and were easier for his hands to grip comfortably.

"This one feels better. Especially in my left hand."

"Winchester makes their stocks a little slimmer, and they groove the forend deeply to give a good grip when you work the action. Remington made their gun look like one of their centerfires, but it doesn't seem to handle as nicely for most people as the Winchester." Al put the Remington back in the rack and withdrew two more rifles, laying them next to the Winchester pump.

"In semiautos, you have more choices," Al went on in his expressionless voice. "Remington makes three. These two, the Model 550 and 552, are somewhat similar. The 552 is newer, and is designed to look like one of their deer rifles. It has a few aluminum parts, and weighs a few ounces less than the 550. This one," he continued, lifting a third rifle from the rack, "is their newest model. It's called the Nylon 66. The entire one-piece stock is made of DuPont Nylon, and that's what all the pins ride on. It's not very pretty, but it works well. Remington advertises you can drive a truck over it and it will still work." Al looked up at Walter Bowman. "I'm not aware that any of *our* customers make a habit of driving over their guns, but perhaps Remington has found an untapped segment of the market." Walter smiled at Al's deadpan humor.

Henry looked at the rifle. The brown plastic stock was exceedingly ugly. He had read of how a shooter named Tom Frye had been hired by Remington and had used two of the guns in late 1959, soon after they first were introduced. He had hit 100,000 wooden blocks thrown in the air, missing only six. Frye had broken Ad Topperwein's fifty-year-old record, but it was not an exact comparison. Topperwein had adhered to the old rules where the targets were thrown twenty or more feet vertically by a person standing at least twenty-five feet in front of the shooter. Frye had his throwers stand right by his shoulder, and throw the wood blocks along the intended path of the bullet.

Henry picked up the rifle, checked the chamber, and threw it to his shoulder. It was light and balanced well, but he hated the feel of the cold plastic. He tried the other two Remingtons and although the wood felt better in his hands, the guns did not seem to fall

128

into place as had the Winchester pump gun. He laid each rifle back on the counter and looked at his father.

"Dad, I'd rather not have a rifle with a plastic stock. I don't care how strong it is."

"I guess all that time spent with me in the shop rubbed off on you. Al, put that nylon one away. Anything else we should look at?"

"Yes, the Winchester 77, and the Browning. The Winchester doesn't have a tubular magazine, but if you don't mind loading a clip, it's a fine rifle. Here, let me show you one." Al Goodman carried the Nylon 66 back to the rack and returned with the Winchester in his left hand and the Browning in his right. He handed the Winchester to the boy. Henry looked at it carefully and opened the action, then threw it up to his shoulder. He laid it down next to the other three rifles. He had a look of concentration on his face as he stared at the four guns. Then he looked back at the store owner, who handed him the Browning autoloader. It was the most finely finished of all the rifles there, and the grain of the wood was very handsome. The very slender receiver necessitated a swelled shape for the forend, which Henry thought was vaguely strange looking. It handled beautifully. Henry was well aware that it was the most expensive rifle in the group, and he had hoped he would not like it as much. He didn't want his father to think he wanted it based on its price.

"What do you think, son?"

"Let me try them again." Henry Bowman snapped each rifle into position quickly, one after the other. When he had laid the fifth one down, he looked at his father, and then at Al Goodman. He felt awkward with what he was about to say. He didn't know if it would sound stupid. "The sights on the Winchester pump line up the quickest with my eye, and the Browning auto is almost as good. The other three, it seems like I have to squash my face down on the stock a little to line up the sights."

"Your son is exactly right," Al Goodman said to Walter Bowman. "The Winchester and the Browning are the oldest designs here. The others you've seen were brought out in more recent years, since scope sights became affordable and more people wanted them, even on twenty-twos. Their stocks are shaped to hold your head higher up, in line with where a scope would be. You see these grooves here?" Al asked, indicating two parallel channels milled in the top of the Remington. "They are for mounting a lightweight .22 scope. The Winchester pump doesn't have them. The Browning does, but the factory has only recently started putting them on, and they didn't change the stock dimensions from the original." He looked Henry's father in the eye. "Is your son this observant about everything?"

"About things that interest him, yes. Always."

"Are you planning to use a scope with your rifle, Henry?" The way Al said it, Walter Bowman imagined he was hearing a recording on the telephone.

"No, sir. I want to hit targets in the air like Herb Parsons and Ed McGivern." Walter Bowman was momentarily embarrassed and started to say something, but Al was talking again.

"If you're serious about trick shooting, either of the two guns would work, but with a low-recoil gun like a .22, the semiauto will be better." He looked at Walter Bowman. "You should know that all the other rifles are between fifty and fifty-five dollars. The Browning is seventy."

Walter Bowman was no stranger to fine craftsmanship, and he waved his hand in dismissal. "It looks well worth an extra fifteen dollars." He turned to his son. "Shall we take it home?"

Henry smiled, but he had an anxious look on his face. He turned to the mild-looking owner of the gun store. "Do you have a Winchester Model 63?"

Al Goodman shook his head. "Winchester stopped making the 63 last year. It wasn't selling well, because it was a more expensive gun to make than their competition's." Al squinted, and continued. "Now, I do have a used one that was part of an estate collection, but it's about twenty-five years old."

"Could I see it?" Henry asked immediately. He did not know what an estate was, but he did not particularly care.

"Of course." Al Goodman walked twenty feet over to the used gun section of the store and withdrew a rifle from the back row of the case. He brought it over and handed it to the boy. It had a tubular magazine which was filled through an oval port in the right side of the stock, just like the Browning. Unlike the Belgian gun, however, the Winchester had a taller receiver and the contours of the wooden forend blended smoothly into it. The bluing was worn from all the sharp corners of the receiver, and bare metal shone through. The same was true of the muzzle. The gun was well oiled, and no hint of rust or corrosion was evident anywhere on it. The grip section of the stock and the center of the forend had a different sheen to them than did the rest of the wood. Walter Bowman recognized instantly the signs of wood that had been long exposed to the polishing effects of human hands.

Henry threw the rifle up to his shoulder and a huge smile split his face. The sights fell in line the instant his cheek hit the stock. The rifle felt like it was a part of him. "This is my favorite, Dad," he said immediately, and handed the gun to his father.

"It looks like it's been well cared-for by someone who used it quite a lot," Walter Bowman said to the older man as he examined the rifle. "Is the bore in good shape?" He was no firearms expert, but he knew enough to ask about that.

"Twenty-twos will never wear out a bore from shooting, but any obstruction can ruin the barrel if a shot is fired through it, and unlike a centerfire, you usually can't see the damage from the outside. Twenty-twos get shot so much, that's a real risk with a used one, and we see our share of jugged barrels. We won't accept those, either in trade or on consignment. You're right about the owner. He shot this gun quite a lot in the last twenty-five years, but he never shot bad ammo that left a bullet in the bore, or accidentally poked the muzzle in the dirt. You may have known him—name of Hamilton. Passed away last month. His widow brought in his entire collection." Al Goodman remembered Walter's question about the rifle and added, "I'll be glad to get you a bore scope and let you examine it yourself, if you'd like, but we both know Henry's uncle would skin me alive if I sold you a rifle with a bum barrel."

"Do you think a semiauto is a good choice for an eight-year-old?"

"Another good question. Ordinarily, we recommend a single shot as a first rifle for young boys, because you have to manually operate the action and insert a new cartridge between shots. Most people think any manually operated repeater is safer than a semiauto for first-time shooters. But the fact is that anyone who shoots much gets into the habit of working the action immediately after firing a shot, so that the gun is ready to fire again. That's true for a bolt action, lever action, or pump. Your son has demonstrated impeccable safety habits here today. I think he will be equally safe with any of the rifles we've looked at, if you or his uncle gets him started with his new rifle."

Walter Bowman looked at his son, and held out the Winchester. "This the one you want, kiddo?" Henry nodded, and Walter turned to the older man. "We'll take it, Mr. Goodman."

Al Goodman liked customers who didn't haggle over prices, but he wasn't used to ones who didn't even look at the tag. The Goodman brothers had enough finances that they could buy large collections outright from heirs eager to get cash. They always tried to buy estate collections for less than a third of what the guns cost new. Used guns had more profit margin in them than new ones, and thus more room for negotiation. The Goodmans also liked to have a new customer eager to return. Al looked at the price tag on the rifle and mentally subtracted five dollars.

"That gun is twenty-five years old, and the finish is worn. The last list price on a Model 63 was eighty dollars. I can let you have that rifle, along with a soft case so it won't get scratched, for forty-five dollars. How does that sound?"

"It sounds like we'll be able to afford quite a bit of ammo. Any recommendations?"

"Winchester Super-Speed is good. The bullets are copper plated so they won't leave lead in the bore even with lots of shooting, and they don't have a waxy lubricant that some companies use which picks up dirt. Seventy-eight cents per fifty-round box. How many boxes would you like?"

"We'll take a case."

"A full case is a hundred boxes. Ten ten-box cartons. Five thousand rounds for sixty-six dollars. Can you use that many right away, or do you want to start with less?"

Walter Bowman had thought that a case of .22 rimfire was 2500 cartridges, but he nodded at the salesman. "I think we'll take a full case, if that won't clean you out. Save us from having to run back here right away."

"Of course. I'll have the stockboy bring one out for you." Al Goodman rang up the sale, and Walter Bowman paid him with twenty-dollar bills and collected his change. A hundred dollars was a lot to spend on an eight-year-old, but Henry had not wanted toys that would soon be forgotten, and his birthday was so close to Christmas that in previous years his parents had only given him a cake and a few knick-knacks.

"Take you a long time to shoot all this up," the teenage stockboy said as he met them in front of the store. Walter lifted the heavy carton onto his right shoulder and took his son's hand with his left. The two of them walked towards the car, with Henry carrying his rifle in the soft cloth case in the crook of his left arm.

"I'll come back for more when it's gone," Henry replied cheerfully. The teenager, a smallbore competitor who practiced on an indoor range every day, smiled broadly. It made him feel good to see a little boy with his first rifle.

If Henry Bowman had chosen any of the other guns he had seen that afternoon on his eighth birthday, he would probably never have become aware of a quirk that was peculiar to Winchester Model 63 rifles. He definitely would not have discovered this quirk at the age of eight, when his interest in shooting was beginning to seriously accelerate, and his own preferences were crystallizing.

Henry did go home that day with the Model 63, however, and his choice would prove to have powerful repercussions that would not be ultimately felt until long after he had become an adult.

As it also turned out, it did take Henry Bowman longer than he expected to shoot up all five thousand rounds of his birthday ammunition. It was winter, and he and his parents only went to their place in the country on Saturdays.

Henry and his father would not return to Goodman's for more ammo for almost two months.

April 7, 1961

"Mr. Johnson, most law professors here at Harvard, me included, have a reputation for criticizing often and praising almost never. We do that so that students will not become complacent. Your work in my Contracts class has been uniformly excellent, and I am strongly recommending you for the Law Review.

"Although I suspect you will be successful in whatever area of the law you choose to pursue, I suggest you give serious thought to working on Wall Street. They have always needed top-flight contracts specialists, but even more so now with the Kennedy administration's apparent pro-business stance. I would not be surprised to see a substantial increase in both the required level of excellence of securities contracts lawyers, and in their compensation as well. If you are interested, I may be able to assist you in getting a summer internship at Lambert, Burns in New York. I still have a little influence there."

Raymond Johnson sat up a little straighter. Lambert, Burns was a powerhouse law firm on Wall Street, and Professor Dobbs was not known for making idle promises. "That's very generous of you, sir. I have two offers for internships right now, but neither one of them is as appealing as a summer at Lambert, Burns."

"You realize there won't be much chance to go hunting if you spend the summer in New York City." Dobbs was exhibiting a rare smile as he said this. It had become common knowledge on campus that while all of the other male students at Harvard Law School were using what little spare time they had to pursue Radcliffe undergrads, the Colorado native was apt to be out in the woods an hour west of Boston with a small game rifle.

"Upstate New York's got some decent hunting, sir. I might be able to get off some Saturday afternoon." He smiled when he said this. Both Ray and the professor knew that the pace Lambert, Burns set for its summer interns was apt to be even more rigorous than that of the Law School.

"I hope you're right. I'll make some calls and see what I can do about getting you in with them. They'd be missing a bet if they didn't make you an offer. Listen," the older man said, changing the subject, "I've got papers to grade and you've got cases to prepare. I'll call you in again when there's more to tell."

"I appreciate that, sir," Raymond said as he stood up to go. "I'm glad you think enough of my work to do this for me."

"Part of my job. Not many people know it, that's all." He turned his attention to a stack of papers on his desk.

Some days you win, as Dad always says Raymond thought as he closed the office door behind him. *Law Review. Not bad.* As he left the building he decided to go by East Bay Sports and see his friend Gene.

August 12, 1961

"Yes, sir. How can we help you today?" The proprietor smiled and faced the young man who had just entered the storefront in New York City.

Raymond Johnson looked at the man and smiled back. "Been planning to come here ever since I got to New York in the beginning of the summer, but this is the first Saturday I haven't had to work." He walked over to the older man with his hand extended, but could not resist staring around the room. "Ray Johnson," he said immediately, recognizing the man from photos he had seen. "I've wanted to see what Griffin & Howe looked like ever since I was a kid, out in Colorado."

"I hope we don't disappoint you, Mr. Johnson," the man said wryly.

"Not likely," Ray said immediately as he continued to take in the rack upon rack of beautifully finished rifles that covered the walls. He lowered his gaze to the glass case that stood waist-high in front of him. Inside it were several of the handmade steel quick-detachable scope mounts for which Griffin & Howe was internationally known. "I should warn you that I'm not in much of a position to buy one of your custom rifles right now, but it's likely I'll be moving permanently to New York in a year, and my finances are apt to improve, assuming I pass the Bar."

"Law student?"

"Start my third year in two weeks," Raymond said, nodding. "Company I'm working for says they'll probably want to hire me when I graduate, if I don't do anything stupid between now and then."

"What firm you interning with?" The question came from a man a few years older than Raymond who had been examining a rifle.

"Lambert, Burns." At this reply, the man gave a low whistle.

"Best securities firm on Wall Street. They don't hire just anybody, Jim," he said as he transferred the rifle to his left hand and extended his right in greeting. "Tony Kearns, Mr. Johnson. Anyone Lambert, Burns plans to hire who also likes fine rifles is a man I'd be proud to know."

"Well...thank you," Raymond answered, feeling a bit awkward and not knowing quite what else to say. "Are *you* a lawyer, Mr. Kearns?"

Kearns shook his head. "Please, it's Tony. No, I'm an analyst with White, Weld," he said, naming a good-sized Wall Street brokerage firm. "Risk arbitrage department. Such a huge part of the firm's business they're even thinking about hiring a second person." Kearns grinned. "When you guys draw up merger deals, I look at them after they're made public, and try to figure out which company's stock White, Weld should buy and which it should short. If any," he added as an afterthought.

"If you've been looking at merger deals, they haven't been drawn up by me, Tony. All summer I've been a research flunky, and that's all," Raymond said, wanting to change the subject. "What's that?" he asked, indicating the rifle in Tony Kearns' hands.

"Tony is one of our rather eccentric customers," the proprietor broke in, feigning a pained expression. "Despite our worldwide reputation for building graceful, perfectly-balanced rifles on Springfield, Mauser, and Model 70 actions, Tony will have none of them. He is only interested in rifles built on the big, clunky, old Enfield." He said the last word as if it were heresy to do so.

"Jim here is getting old, Ray, and he's too weak to hold up or carry a rifle unless it's a featherweight," Kearns explained with an attempt at a straight face. "His brittle old bones also can't take any more recoil than a .270 produces, which is why he'll never go hunt something that might eat him."

The man laughed. "Ray, Mr. Kearns here has taken more mental safaris to Africa than any other person on earth."

I wouldn't be too sure about that thought Raymond. "What caliber is it?" Ray asked, indicating the big rifle.

".450 Ashurst," Kearns said immediately. "Full length .375 H&H case necked up to .458 caliber and blown out straight. Holds more powder than the .458 Winchester magnum, but only if you've got an action with a long magazine. In a Model 70, a Springfield, or a Mauser, you can't seat the bullets out far enough to use all the powder capacity in the case. The receiver's too short. That's why I like Enfields. They'll handle *real* cartridges. And you'll notice that despite our host's irrational infatuation with lesser weapons, his gunsmiths manage to do quite a fine job with one of these clunky old World War One relics." He handed the younger man the rifle.

Raymond saw that quite a bit of effort had been expended to turn the military action into a worthy basis for a fine hunting rifle. The ugly 'ears' on the receiver bridge had been milled off, the dog-leg bolt handle had been replaced with a straight one, and the utilitarian trigger guard and floorplate had been replaced with a beautiful handcrafted unit milled out of a single piece of steel. All the metal parts had been carefully polished and finished in the deep rust blue for which Griffin & Howe was known. The stock was dense black walnut, with straight grain through the grip area and finely checkered in a traditional pattern. He continued to examine the rifle.

"What about a Mag Mauser, if you like big calibers?" Raymond asked.

"They make into a decent rifle, but actions alone are hard to come by. You can still buy a French Brevex, but I've always been a little leery of the frogs when it comes to steel and heat-treating methods for high-pressure cartridges. Any German Mag Mauser action you find is apt to be a complete rifle built up by one of the English makers. The Brits do damn fine work, but they aren't big on some of our magazine calibers, and their ideas of how a bolt action should be stocked differ a bit from my own. They do a beautiful stocking job on double rifles, though," he added. "But big doubles are out of my price range right now, I'm afraid.

"Anyway, I'd hate to buy a Rigby and then throw away the stock and barrel. Also, an Enfield has a true 5 degree interrupted thread for its locking lugs. A dinged case or a bit of dirt won't stop you from camming that bolt closed, which makes for peace of mind if you're in Africa. Jim's right—I've never been there, but by God I'm going to, one of these days."

"So am I. I've been dreaming about it for over ten years."

"Then you understand," Tony Kearns said immediately. "When *I* go, I'm going to be carrying a rifle like this one, built on an Enfield. One that will hold five or six rounds of something with some real steam, like a .475 Ackley or maybe even that .50 caliber John Buhmiller came up with on the .460 Weatherby case."

Ray Johnson heard this last statement from his new friend, but he was thinking about his .600 Holland double rifle, and Tony Kearns' words didn't register at the time. He would recall them twenty years later after a particularly harrowing experience, and would take them to heart.

Tony Kearns had no inkling that the words he had just spoken would one day prolong the lives of several people. Ray Johnson's would be one of them.

April 6, 1963

The Buick Riviera pulled into the driveway, and the car was unfamiliar but the driver was not. Henry Bowman had just put his clothes on after getting out of bed on the sunny Saturday morning. He ran out the back door to greet his Uncle Max.

"Picked this up half an hour ago," Max Collins said as he leaned against the gleaming blue coupe, "and thought I'd see if you wanted to go for a ride. Your mother said your dad had a teacher's meeting first thing today and couldn't be at home. Want to go get a hamburger breakfast at Steak n Shake, then go shoot your rifle some? I got a place where you might be able to try what you were talking about the other day."

Henry's grin was all the reply Max needed. "I'll go tell Mom!" Henry said as he ran back in the house to get his Winchester, shooting glasses, ear plugs, and ammo.

***

"Highway 40 used to end here at Brentwood," Max Collins said to his nephew as they sat in the parked car and chewed on their hamburgers. "They didn't extend it east until about the time you were born." Max rested the hand that held the hamburger on the bottom rim of the steering wheel. The smell of the freshly-cooked meat mingled with the Buick's new-car smell. It was a pleasant combination.

"In 'forty-eight, 'forty-nine, a kid from the West End used to hang out in this parking lot looking for races. Billy Dell. Had an Olds 88, just like your dad drove, the one with the 'Rocket V-8' engine that would run like a striped-assed ape, only Dell's was black. Used to get races lined up right here in this parking lot.

"After he and whoever he was going to race had decided what they'd run for," he said, gesturing out the side window, "they'd get on that entrance ramp there, and park for a couple of minutes, blocking it. That was the only way to get on 40, and it pissed off whoever was right behind 'em, but it made for a clear stretch of highway to race on.

"There was one cop, a highway patrolman, who made it his mission to nail Billy Dell. Waited him out one Saturday afternoon about a half-mile up the highway. That black Olds went whistling by, and the cop lit out after him, but he never could catch up. Billy was more careful after that, and he'd make a slow pass down the highway before coming back here and giving the all-clear."

"Did the policeman ever catch him?" Henry was fascinated by this story.

"No, and he did something he shouldn't have. The kid lived with his parents, down on Kingsbury near where your cousin Ruth has a house. He kept his hot rod in a locked garage whenever he wasn't driving it. Billy raced for money and he didn't want anyone doing anything to his car when he wasn't looking. He even had put a padlock on the hood. But the police know how to get into locked places without keys. One night, the state patrolman picked the lock on the garage and picked the lock on the hood."

"What did he do?"

"Well, he wanted to do something that would ruin the engine. He could have put sugar or something like that in the gas tank, but that would just gunk it up. The kid would have to take it apart and clean it, but then the engine would be back to normal. The cop didn't want that to happen.

"So what he did was, he took off the air cleaner so he could get at the carburetor. That's the thing that lets air and fuel into the engine. And he dumped a handful of hardened steel ball bearings down into the carburetor. Then he worked the throttle linkage with his hand and opened the carb, like would happen if you stepped on the gas pedal. That let the ball bearings go though the carb and into the intake manifold. You couldn't see them any more, even with the air cleaner off. Then he put the air cleaner back on, locked the hood, and locked the garage door behind him.

"The next morning, Dell got in and fired up his car, and there must have been an awful noise. Before he could shut it off the motor seized up and quit. When he disassembled the engine, all kinds of stuff was broken. Bent valves, cracked pistons, a crack in one cylinder head, and a lot of other stuff I can't remember."

"How did you find out about it, Uncle Max?"

"Hell, everybody in Missouri knew about it. Came out at the kid's trial. See, the cop couldn't resist telling one of his buddies on the patrol about what he had done. Word got out to the whole troop station. There are a few guys on the patrol--or at least there were back then--that don't much believe in giving speeding tickets at all. One of them must have thought vandalizing a citizen's car was dirty pool, because one way or 'nother, someone told Billy Dell what had happened."

"What did he do?"

"For a long time, nothing. He found out what the trooper's routine was, though. One night when the trooper was out cruising 40, the kid was on one of the bridges about ten miles west of here, waiting for him. A week before, he'd painted little white spots on the shoulder that were different distances from where he stood on the bridge, and he had practiced dropping small pebbles from the bridge when cars going at different speeds passed those marks. See, he was figuring out exactly when he'd have to drop something so that it would hit a car, not land in front of it or behind it. When he was practicing, he dropped the pebbles at the side of the road. He didn't want to ding up anyone else's car. But he paid close attention to where the car was when the pebbles hit the ground."

"What did he drop on the police car—a big rock?" Henry went to a school that pushed learning very hard, and he knew that heavy objects fell at the same rate as light ones if air resistance was not a major factor.

"No, a 200-pound oak log."

"A log?"

"Yep, and it hit the hood of the patrol car and smashed the windshield. The side pillar—this thing here," Max said, pointing to the left side of the Buick's windshield, "kept it from going all the way into the car and killing the cop. But the car went out of control and flipped. Cop broke his back and lost his right eye. He got some feeling back in his legs, but he never walked again."

"Did the man who dropped the log on him go to jail?"

"They had a big trial, and guys who try to kill cops are usually despised, but then again so are cops who break into people's homes and vandalize their property. Also, the Highway Patrol doesn't do any real police work—they mainly just give out traffic tickets. There was a surprising amount of public sympathy for the Dell kid.

"One of the local car clubs had some decals printed up of Paul Bunyan driving a souped-up Oldsmobile. Then a local cop got pissed off when he saw one on some colored kid's car, and he smashed the driver's window with his nightstick and worked the kid over, right in front of his girlfriend. Put him in the hospital. That got another big writeup in the papers.

"Eventually, the jury did send Dell off to prison at Gumbo for a few years. He's out now, but doesn't live around here. Every now and again you'll hear someone from this area say he'd like to 'pull a Paul Bunyan' or 'pull a Billy Dell'. That usually means he's

136

mad at some cop that screwed him over."

Pull a Paul Bunyan Henry thought to himself. *It's got a ring to it.*

***

"Runs pretty good, don't you think? Cuts the wind, too." The Buick's speedometer needle was hovering around a hundred ten miles an hour as they sped through St. Charles County. The 401-cubic-inch V-8 emitted a healthy roar, but there was surprisingly little wind noise. Henry Bowman had a big grin on his face as he stared out the windshield at the road.

"Had the dealer pitch the shocks that came on it and put on a set of Konis before I picked it up. Had 'em put in metallic brake shoes and make sure the alignment was dead-on, too. Watch this." Max Collins took his hands off the steering wheel and stepped hard on the brake pedal. Henry felt himself thrown forward against his seat belt as the blue coupe behaved as if the air outside had suddenly become ten times as dense. The car tracked straight on the two-lane road as it decelerated. At fifty miles an hour, Max put his hands back on the wheel and his foot back on the accelerator.

"Aren't you supposed to drive slowly when a car is brand new, to break it in?" Henry asked.

"I've never met a race mechanic that agreed with that. They've all told me that the way to scuff the rings in is to put the engine under load, like accelerating up a steep hill, and the way to seat the valves is to run it flat out. If your engine isn't all the way warmed up I think you could damage it, but I've run the bejeezus out of every car I've owned, and I never saw an American V-8 that didn't act like it was going to last forever, 'cept for maybe that blown Ford I had in '57.

"The 'drive slow for the first 500 miles' stuff is so people will get used to how their new car handles before they get too enthusiastic. Also to shake out any loose metal particles in the engine from when they put it together at the factory. Before I picked this one up, I had the mechanic put a magnetic drain plug in the oil pan, drive it twenty miles, and change the oil. He didn't find any metal on the plug, so hell, she's ready to run." He looked over at his nephew.

"We got about fifteen more miles. You want to drive the rest of the way?"

"*Yeah!*" Henry exclaimed as his Uncle Max pulled the car over to the side of the road and stopped. The man opened the driver's door and got out while the boy climbed over the console and slid into the driver's seat.

"Handle at the front right adjusts your seat back 'n' forth," Max said, pointing. "Couldn't let you do this if this car had a bench seat—I'd be squashed up under the dashboard." Henry slid his seat all the way forward and adjusted his lap belt. He stretched his arms out, looking at the dash and getting a feel for where the controls were, and adjusted the mirrors.

"Keep it under a hundred indicated," Max said in an expressionless voice.

"Can you get in trouble if we get caught?" the boy asked. Max Collins shook his head.

"Judge in this county likes to hunt pheasants, and I got him set up at Doc Wiemann's place, where we're going today." Max did not mention that he had also introduced Doc to the art school student Wiemann had been screwing twice a week. "Anything short of armed robbery, we got us a free pass."

Henry nodded as he dropped the lever into Drive, checked his left mirror, and accelerated back onto the road.

"What's the matter, you got sore feet?" Max asked pointedly as he looked at his nephew. Henry was holding the Buick at a steady sixty-two. "Get on it some, while you still got a smooth road and no traffic." Henry pressed on the accelerator, not quite enough to make the automatic transmission kick down into second gear, and the blue car smoothly sped up. At ninety, the boy eased up on the pedal enough to check the car's acceleration, but not enough to cause it to slow down. The car was holding ninety indicated, and Henry's eyes flicked constantly around the road ahead, scanning for other vehicles, objects in the road, and animals. Max smiled at the boy's technique.

"You been out flying with your dad much lately?"

"Almost every weekend," Henry replied without taking his eyes off the road.

"Never did take to being up in an airplane, the way he did." Max looked off in the distance ahead. "After this right-hand bend, there's a gravel road about a quarter-mile, up on the right. That's where we're going."

Henry eased off on the throttle without releasing it completely, and soon the car was traveling at half its former speed. He checked his mirrors and braked as the gravel road came into view, and pulled off the pavement.

"Take this 'til it dead-ends," Max instructed. "Less than a mile." The road was well-tended without ruts or potholes. Henry drove the car slowly on the loose gravel, slightly to one side so as to keep the car's undercarriage away from the high spot in the center of the road. In a few minutes the road ended at a group of white wooden buildings which appeared to serve various functions. There were three cars parked in front of one of them, and Henry pulled in and stopped next to the one on the end.

"Grab your gear and bring it in," Max said as he got out of the car and went to open the trunk. Henry retrieved his gun case and shooting gear from the floor of the back seat and got out of the car. The big engine was making soft ticking noises as it cooled in the spring breeze. The boy followed the big man into the wood frame house.

"Max!" exclaimed an older man with grey, thinning hair. He had a big smile on his face, and Henry could see that one of his teeth was missing. "Haven't seen you in a while. Come to shoot some pheasants? And who are *you*, big fella?" he asked as he peered intently at Henry. One of the older man's eyes was a milky color, and his posture showed the onset of curvature of the spine. His stained clothing was the shade of dried mud. His shirt and pants appeared to have been washed a few hundred times with very caustic soap. He looked like an aging yard man.

Henry held out his hand. "Henry Bowman, sir. My mother is Uncle Max's sister. Uncle Max brought me with him today."

"Pleased to meet you, Henry—Doc Wiemann." He gave the boy a firm handshake. "But none a that 'sir' or 'mister' shit with me. You call me 'Doc', just like ever'one else here. Your uncle bring you here today to shoot pheasants?" he asked.

Max answered for him. "Not today, Doc. I need to use your pattern board. Got a Perazzi that seems to be shooting low. Henry here hasn't used a shotgun much, but he's hell on wheels with a rifle. Brought his Winchester .22 along. Your back range free, to where he could do a little plinking?"

"Sure Max, no problem. No one's shooting skeet today, he can have that whole area all to himself."

"Okay if he uses the low house from the number seven station?"

"With a rifle?"

"You got that big hill for a backstop, if you stay on number seven."

"Hell, I'm not worried about that. How's he going to hit even one if he's not a shot-gun man?"

"Maybe he won't, but I think he'd like to try."

"Well, shit. I'll come run the thrower for him m'self. Be a sorry thing to have your nephew hit a clay bird with his rifle and me not see it." He chuckled at the thought.

"Henry, you go with Doc out to the skeet range. Doc, after I go get my things out of my locker, I'll be over behind you at the pattern board to see how much I need to bend the barrel on this thing. You need anything, kid? Glasses? Plugs?" he asked his nephew. Henry shook his head and patted the leather belt pouch he wore that contained his ammo, shooting glasses, and ear plugs. "Okay then, I'll come over and see how you two're doing when I'm all done. Shouldn't be long." The big man walked into the other room where the members' lockers were.

"This way, Henry," Doc Wiemann said with an inclination of his head. The pair walked outside and headed towards the skeet range.

Unlike the skeet and trap club in Bridgeton where Max Collins usually went to shoot clay birds, Doc Wiemann's club only had one range for skeet and trap. Few wild-fowl clubs in St. Charles County had any, but Doc Wiemann, a retired vascular surgeon, had shrewdly realized that many of the wealthy wingshooters had more money than time, and needed some quick practice to tune up their swings a bit before taking to the field. The cost of putting in two skeet houses and a trap bunker had been minuscule compared to the value of the club's land and the expense and effort required to maintain it.

"Thrower should be full," Doc opined. "I guess you've seen the way they fly. You want to stand at this station here and try to hit low house ones going away?" He was indicating the concrete pad a yard away from the opening in the righthand skeet house, where the shooter would stand with his back to the wooden structure while the clay pigeon was thrown out of the opening and flew directly away from him.

"I think I'd have the best chance here. This may not work at all. I've never tried it before. Most shotgun ranges don't have a hill to stop a rifle bullet. We were going to use a hand thrower on the riverbank, but Uncle Max was coming out here today, and said to bring my rifle." Henry reached into his pouch and took out his shatterproof shooting glasses. Doc Wiemann smiled with inward approval. He had retired from surgery when a stray pellet from a hunter in another field had blinded him in his left eye. Since that time, his own shooting glasses were perched on the bridge of his nose, just as they were now, whenever he was outdoors. Losing his left eye had cost him his practice. He could not afford to lose the right one. It was something he thought of every day.

"You hunt much with your .22, Henry?" Doc asked the young boy.

"Almost never," Henry said, shaking his head as he put his ear plugs in. "Almost all plinking, down on the river at my Mom and Dad's place. I'm pretty good on old golf balls, but since I throw them myself, they're a lot closer and slower moving than a clay pigeon will be. I've shot a few crows in the air, but they fly pretty slow." He gave the scruffy-looking man whose net worth was perhaps two million dollars an apologetic look. "This might be a waste of your time."

Doc Wiemann, who had been thinking much the same thing, quickly revised his opinion. As Henry withdrew the semiauto Winchester from the case, the man noticed that the rear sight had been relocated farther forward on the barrel, to snap shoot more quick-ly, at close-in targets. He decided this might be interesting after all. He shook his head in reply to the boy's statement.

"Henry, if it burns powder and goes bang, it's never a waste of time. You want to look at one first?" Before Henry could answer the man's question, Doc Wiemann pressed the upper right button on the heavy metal box with the black cable running out of it that he held in his hand. A whirring noise came from the wooden structure and a clay pigeon flew out of it, climbing at a shallow angle as it traveled away from them.

Henry watched its trajectory as he withdrew the magazine tube from the Winchester's buttplate and fed cartridges into the gun's loading port by feel, never taking his eyes off the target. Doc Wiemann noticed this, and his opinion of the boy's skills went up another notch. It did not occur to Doc Wiemann that this skill would one day save Henry Bowman's life.

"All set?" Doc asked. Henry stood at the ready next to the opening in the skeet house and nodded assent.

"Pull!" said the boy, as he snapped the rifle up to his shoulder and loosed a shot at the departing clay pigeon. The flight of the spinning disc continued uninterrupted, despite the crack of the rifle. Henry lowered his rifle to the ready position again. Doc Wiemann was surprised to find himself disappointed that the bird had not shattered.

"Pull!" The second clay bird followed the same path as the first, finally landing at the base of the hill which rose up at the left side of the skeet range.

"Pull!" Miss.

"Pull!" Miss.

"Pull!" Another miss. Henry lowered the rifle, withdrew the magazine tube, and dumped the cartridges into his hand. Then he opened the action and emptied the chamber. The cartridges went back into the leather pouch. He looked at the older man. "The ground's not dry, and I don't think there'd be a fire hazard. Is it okay if I use tracers? That's how I first learned on targets in the air," Henry explained.

Doc Wiemann scowled. ".22 *tracers?* Never heard of 'em."

Henry looked embarrassed. He hated trying to tell adults about things they hadn't heard of. "They're made in France. I get them from a man in New Jersey named Steen." He reached in the leather pouch, withdrew a white cardboard 50-round box, and held it out for the older man's inspection. The name **GEVELOT** was printed on it in green. "He's the only one I know who imports them. I get a lot of my shooting supplies from him. I don't think he knows I'm ten years old," Henry added as an afterthought.

Doc Wiemann took the small box in his free hand and poked it open with his thumb. The cartridges looked like ordinary .22s, except that the very tip of each bullet was painted a dull orange. "I'll be damned. How long do they burn?"

"About a hundred twenty-five yards."

"They hurt your barrel?"

"I've shot an awful lot of them, and I can't see that they've done any harm. I always clean the gun the same day when I shoot tracers, though."

"Yeah, load 'em up," the man said, handing the box back to the boy. "Let's see where you're shooting." Henry loaded the rifle with the French ammunition and stood in the ready position.

"Pull!" The rifle cracked an instant after the butt hit Henry's shoulder, and a burning red dot streaked away from him at about twelve hundred feet per second and buried itself in the hillside ninety yards away. Henry saw that his shot was high.

"'Bout eight inches over the top of it. Try another."

"Pull!" The shot was again high.

"You hold on that one the same as the one before? Both shots were high the same amount."

"Yes, I wanted to see if they'd be the same. You have to get on a lot faster than when you're just tossing golf balls in the air."

"They're coming out of the thrower at forty-five miles an hour, and you've really only got the edge to shoot at from this angle. Try putting a little daylight under the next bird. Damned if I don't think you're going to bust one in the next few shots."

"Pull!" The clay pigeon flew out of the hole to Henry's right and sailed on a leftward path away from him. The Winchester cracked and the burning dot just missed the right edge of the spinning black disc.

"Just a hair behind it. Elevation looked good."

"Pull!" As the rifle cracked, the clay bird broke into several pieces.

"*Got it!*" Doc Wiemann yelled. He was surprised to realize that he was more excited than the boy. Henry smiled.

"Pull!" This time the clay bird disintegrated in midair.

"*Perfect!* Christ, you must've nailed it dead center! I never would have thought you could smoke one like that hitting it with just one bullet. *Damn*, Henry, Max wasn't kidding when he said you were good with a rifle. Keep going."

By the time Max Collins finished his work on the pattern board and came over to see how his nephew was doing, Doc Wiemann had had to go into the skeet house and refill the thrower with clay pigeons twice. Henry had shot at a hundred twenty-four targets and had hit seventy-eight of them. He had switched back to standard ammunition after the fifty-round box of tracers was empty.

Max stood silently at the back of the range and watched as Henry hit eight birds with ten shots. As the boy pulled the magazine tube out of the Winchester's buttstock to reload the rifle, Max walked over to the two of them.

"Looks like he's getting the hang of it," Max said dryly.

"Max, if you had told me you had a ten-year-old nephew that could run over fifty percent at skeet with a *rifle,* I'd have called you a damn liar. How long you been shooting, Henry?" Doc asked the boy.

"Two and a half years."

"May I?" Doc asked, indicating the rifle.

"Sure," Henry replied, and handed the older man the gun. "Magazine's full, chamber's empty."

Doc Wiemann examined the weapon carefully. "Any idea how many rounds you've put through it?" It was obvious the rifle had seen considerable use.

"I'm on my fourteenth case of regular ammo, and just finished my fourth case of tracers. I don't know how much the first owner shot it, but it looked about the same as it does now when I got it. It's over twenty years old."

"*Ninety* thousand rounds?" Doc exclaimed, having done the multiplication. "Has anything broken on it?" The retired surgeon looked at the rifle with renewed respect.

"I've broken five or six firing pins, but that's from when the hammer falls on an empty chamber. I normally count shots and know when it's empty, but, uh, you can't do that when it's...shooting rapid fire." Henry looked uncomfortable for the first time that day. His uncle grinned at him.

"Go ahead, Henry, show Doc. He won't mind." The boy looked unconvinced. Max saw the look and went on. "He'll get a kick out of it. Show him."

Henry Bowman shrugged, took his rifle back from their host, and worked the action, chambering the first round. This time he did not hold the rifle at his waist, but instead put it up to his shoulder. He also shifted his grip slightly and deliberately inserted his trigger finger into the Winchester's trigger guard.

"Pull!" When the clay pigeon was about thirty yards away a staccato noise erupted from the rifle and the clay bird vanished in a cloud of black dust. Doc Wiemann's jaw dropped and Max Collins started laughing.

Henry opened the action to make sure the rifle was empty and gripped the rifle's takedown screw between the thumb and forefinger of his right hand. After loosening it, he pulled the buttstock off the receiver and carefully laid the barreled action in the grass. He held the buttstock and trigger mechanism up so that the older man could see it, and reached into his pouch, withdrawing a small screwdriver.

"On a Winchester 63, the sear has an egg-shaped hole in it that lets it rock back and forth, under spring tension, on this pin." He pointed with the blade of the screwdriver to the parts he had just described. "If the gun gets really dirty and that hole gets clogged up," *or if you stick a paper match in the hole and break it off* he added mentally, "the sear will stay down when you pull the trigger. That can happen on most semiauto .22s, and usually the hammer follows the bolt down on the second cartridge and the gun misfires after the first shot. That's 'cause the hammer is moving more slowly and is cushioned by the bolt, and it doesn't have enough power to set off the primer." Henry swallowed and then continued.

"On a Winchester Model 63, though, the hammer is much bigger and heavier than on other .22 autos." He pointed to the internal hammer with the screwdriver. "Even though it's slowed down, it's still got enough force to fire the next cartridge. So the gun goes full auto, like you just saw."

"But it wasn't doing it before, and your rifle doesn't look like it's all that dirty yet," Doc protested. Henry Bowman looked self-conscious, and was about to reply, but Max cut in.

"Henry figured out how to hold the gun in a certain way so that when the action cycles upon firing, the sear gets bounced out of the way of the engagement notch just from the internal harmonics of the operating mechanism."

The boy reattached the buttstock to the rifle and held the weapon with its left side facing up. "If you push your trigger finger all the way through the trigger guard so that you're pulling the trigger with the second finger joint, like this," he demonstrated, "then the tip of your trigger finger will be pressed against the left side of the receiver. That seems to transfer some of the shock of the bolt to the sear, and bounces it out of the way. At least, that's what I *think* is happening."

"Do all Model 63s do this, or just this one?" Doc asked incredulously.

"I've only tried three others, but they all did it just like mine. They don't do it as reliably if you try it left-handed," he added as an afterthought.

"Henry can dump the whole magazine onto a playing card at ten yards from the hip," Max said proudly.

"That's using a sling," Henry explained quickly. "Even a .22 on full auto will climb, because they cycle so fast. I loop a long sling over my shoulder from the barrel to the buttstock and push down on the gun with both hands before firing." He demonstrated by holding the rifle as he had described. "With a sling you can really keep them close together. With tracers, it looks like a laser beam."

"You've seen a laser?" Doc Wiemann demanded. This day was proving to be full of surprises.

"Just one in a magazine," Henry admitted sheepishly. All three laughed at that.

"It looked to me like it was getting too easy for you," Max said, changing the subject. "Let's see what you can do from the next station over." Henry moved a few yards to the left and slightly back, and stood on the concrete pad of station six. He withdrew the magazine tube and loaded the rifle with ten cartridges.

"Pull!" Henry swung on the bird and missed. "This is going to be a lot harder," he said pointedly. "I wish I had more tracers with me, but that was the last box I had left." On the eighth shot Henry connected, and a big smile crossed his face. "Okay, I think I got the lead figured out." He broke seven of the next twelve clay pigeons.

"Want to try station five?" Doc asked.

"Okay." Henry walked to the next pad over. He was in a position where the birds were flying much more from right to left than before, and were farther away from him to begin with when they emerged from the skeet house. This time it took fourteen shots before Henry connected. Out of the next forty-four birds, Henry broke seven.

"I'm out," he said finally, opening the rifle's action to make sure it was indeed empty. "I'm going to have to do a lot more practicing if I'm ever going to get any good at the middle stations." He walked over to retrieve his rifle case and slid the Winchester into it.

"Max, you bring your nephew out here any time he wants to come. I'll make sure someone runs the machine for him if I can't do it myself." The three of them started walking back to the clubhouse. "Henry, how did you get interested in shooting aerial targets with your rifle?" Doc asked the boy.

"Four years ago, Uncle Max gave me a copy of Ed McGivern's book on shooting things in the air with a revolver. As soon as I got my rifle, I started trying to hit things in the air with it. After my dad put the rear sight farther forward on the barrel, it got easier."

Doc Wiemann pulled the screen door of the clubhouse open and held it for his guests. "You do any shooting with a revolver?"

Henry shook his head. "This Winchester is the only gun I own."

"You sure as hell know how to use it. Would you like to try a revolver? I've got one I haven't shot in quite a while."

"Yes!" Henry said immediately. Then his face fell. "But I'm out of ammo."

"I may have some here. Just a minute." Doc Wiemann went into the other room. Henry and Max could hear him opening drawers. In a few moments he returned with a brown cardboard box and handed it to the boy. Henry lifted the lid and took out the blued Smith & Wesson Model 17. He pressed the cylinder latch forward and swung the cylinder out to make sure the gun was unloaded. He aimed the revolver at a spot on the top of the opposite wall, sighting along the six-inch barrel.

"I was mistaken about the ammo. Thought I had some twenty-twos here, but I don't. You take that K-22 on home and see how it shoots for you." Henry gave Doc Wiemann a worried look, but the older man shook his head. "I don't think I've put a box of shells through that thing in five years. It's just been sitting in my desk drawer. Shooting won't hurt it, and I can see you take good care of your guns. Come back with it next time and show me what you can do."

"The grips look a little big for his hands," Max Collins broke in. "I think I've got some smaller ones that fit a K-frame Smith back at my house. You want to sell that gun, Doc?"

Doc Wiemann waved the question away. "See if he likes it first. He may decide he wants a shorter barrel, or something lighter, like the Smith kitgun, built on the J-frame."

"Thanks, Doc!" Henry said earnestly as he and his uncle turned towards the door of the clubhouse.

***

"Afternoon, Mr. Gutierrez, how are you?"

Pedro Gutierrez looked startled at the question, and at being addressed in such formal manner. Pedro had never talked to a lawyer before, and now he had been hailed by Mr. Raymond Johnson, who rented an apartment in the New York building where Pedro worked as a maintenance man. Raymond Johnson was the only lawyer he had ever spoken to in his life, and he was surprised that the young man knew his name. He was about to give the standard one- or two-word reply and walk past when he saw the look of genuine goodwill on Raymond Johnson's face.

Ray smiled easily at the nervous man. Pedro reminded him of one of the ranch hands his father and uncle had employed for a few years while Ray was still in high school. A lot of the men who worked on ranches in Colorado were lean, wiry men of Spanish descent.

Raymond was about to say something else to put the man at ease when all of a sudden, the older man's face crumpled. He made a visible effort to recover, but the smile he finally put on his face was a ghastly caricature. Horrified, Raymond reached over and put his hand on the small man's shoulder. "What is it? What's wrong?"

Pedro Gutierrez, like most men, had a definite sense of pride. He had kept his troubles to himself for so long, and the young lawyer's kindness had been so unexpected, however, that words started pouring out of his mouth before he could stop them.

"It's about my daughter, Mr. Johnson," the man said. "My youngest one. She will be four years old next month. I know it is God's will, and I should be strong, but my heart is like a block of lead when I look at her."

Ray Johnson was not aware that Pedro Gutierrez *had* a daughter, let alone a sick one, but he had learned a long time before that if he let people talk at their own pace, sooner or later he would find out more than if he made the constant interjections and comments that most people uttered out of habit. Raymond said nothing, but cocked his head and raised an eyebrow to urge the man to continue.

"She is blind, Mister Johnson, blind from birth. But that is not the worst of it. When I was a young boy, I knew a blind girl in our village. A blind daughter would be a child I could show love to and help her as she grew into a woman." He gave a helpless gesture as his words trailed off. "But Rosita..." Anguish showed plainly on his face.

Raymond Johnson made an immediate decision. In later years he would wonder if his decision had been brought about by simple compassion, or by some kind of sixth sense or premonition. "What time are you done working here today, Mr. Gutierrez?"

Pedro shook his head. "Today I am off, sir. I came to pick up some things I left in my locker in the basement. Then I am going to go look for part-time work." He looked very ashamed. "We have no money for rent or food, Mister Johnson."

Raymond looked at his watch. "It's well past lunchtime and I haven't eaten. I was going around the corner to get a sandwich. Why don't you join me, and you can tell me more about it. Sometimes it can help just to talk. You'll be better able to look for more work on a full stomach." Raymond held the door for the older man, who looked startled and embarrassed, but then walked outside.

As they sat across from each other in the booth at the cafeteria, Pedro Gutierrez ate like he hadn't had a decent meal in a long time, which he hadn't. He explained to Raymond how his young daughter had been born without eyes or most of her brain. It was the first time he had talked to any caucasian about his daughter, other than the intern who had delivered her almost four years before.

"My wife Rosa, she had a very bad time when she was carrying Rosita. Not like that with any of the other three that came before. She had bad headaches, and became very dizzy. After the baby was born, Rosa did not get better. Finally, she could not work. The company she worked for, they finally had to tell her she had to go. She is still very sick, even three years later, and the doctor cannot say why. The priest says it is God's will."

It sounds like there's something seriously wrong with the mother Raymond thought. *Who do I know that might have a more accurate diagnosis than the tired intern fresh out of med school they've no doubt been using?* Ray took a bite of his sandwich and thought about what the older man had said. "Where was she working?" Raymond asked, now just making conversation while he searched his memory for a doctor that might help out the indigent family.

"Allied Chemical. She worked there for three years."

"Allied *Chemical?*" Raymond was no longer thinking of doctors. He was somewhat familiar with the firm that Pedro Gutierrez had named. The German multinational firm of Becker AG was currently negotiating to acquire Allied. Lambert, Burns, where Raymond was an associate, had hoped to get the Allied account, but had been aced out by their main competitor for the business. "What did she do there?" Raymond asked.

"At first she cleaned offices in the administration building. Then, right after we learned she was going to have another child, the company found out they were going to have to raise the wages of the cleaning staff. They decided they didn't want to have full-time employees doing cleaning work. It would be cheaper for them to hire an outside cleaning company." He stared at the lawyer. "An outside company that is not nearly so concerned as Allied Chemical about whether its workers are legally in the country." He took a deep breath and went on.

"My Rosa and many of the other cleaning women offered to work for the same wages as they had been getting, for they needed the jobs, and Allied had been a good company to work for. The company said that was illegal. It would violate the government's minimum wage law." Gutierrez gave a snort of disgust. "The government promises it is going to get higher pay for workers like Rosa, but instead it makes them lose their jobs.

"They said there were two openings for work in the plant. The personnel director said they normally didn't hire women because of the lifting involved, but one of the two jobs didn't require any strength, and he said they could take one of the cleaning women for that job. Everyone who had been on the cleaning staff more than two years put her name on a piece of paper and the plant manager drew one slip out of a hat." He knotted his hands together as he continued. "With the fourth one on the way, and Christmas coming, we couldn't afford to have her lose the job. God listened to her prayers. Rosa's name was the one that the man picked."

"How many months pregnant was she when she switched to working in the plant?"

"A little more than a month, I think."

"Did Allied Chemical know she was pregnant when they accepted her for the new job?"

"Yes," Gutierrez said, nodding. "I know they did because she told them about it and asked about maternity leave in the future, and that was when they told her the whole cleaning staff was going to be laid off."

"Mr. Gutierrez, do you think it's possible your wife was exposed to something in the chemical plant that made her sick and caused the birth defects in your daughter?" Raymond asked.

Pedro Gutierrez's eyes widened. "But she never handled any chemicals! She only did inventory work. And no one else there got sick. No, it is not possible," he said with finality.

"Did her clothes ever smell of chemicals when she came home from work?"

"Yes, always."

"Did the company issue her a respirator—a mask to filter the air she breathed when she worked in the plant?"

"She never mentioned one, no."

"Did your wife ever mention whether or not there were any other pregnant women working in the plant, or women who had been pregnant at any time when they worked there?"

"I don't think so, no."

"Mr. Gutierrez, I think it is entirely possible that the chemicals in the air your wife breathed every day at work while she was pregnant *may* be responsible for her present condition and the fact that your daughter is blind and has brain damage. If that is the case, you have an actionable claim against Allied Chemical, and it is my advice that you retain a lawyer and file a personal injury suit against the company for damages."

Pedro Gutierrez was thunderstruck. "But...the priest said it was God's will—children are born every day that have such defects."

"That may be true, but the mothers of those children don't usually get sick during pregnancy and then *stay* sick for four years after giving birth. And it doesn't matter what your priest says—it matters what a *jury* says."

"We don't have enough money to pay our electric bill right now," Pedro said with guilt in his voice. "There is no way to pay a lawyer, as you suggest."

"In personal injury cases, the lawyers typically get paid only if they win the case. If that happens, they keep one-third of the cash settlement and you get the other two-thirds." Raymond saw that this news startled his guest.

"You are right that a woman feeling dizzy and sick and a child with brain damage may not be enough to convince a jury that Allied Chemical did anything wrong. On the other hand, they might award you enough money to get long-term care for both your wife and your daughter." *And it might never even get to trial* Raymond was thinking. *Becker AG isn't apt to want to buy a company with this kind of lawsuit pending. You might get a quick settlement out-of-court.*

"Lambert, Burns does securities law—contracts between companies. I can refer you to good law firm that deals exclusively in personal injury cases."

Pedro Gutierrez was overwhelmed at the way pouring out his troubles had turned into a discussion of suing Allied Chemical for a large amount of money. In spite of this, he made a decision. "Mister Johnson, I don't want to go talk to another lawyer. I want you to be my lawyer on this thing. Will you do that?"

"Mister Gutierrez, you have to realize that what I do all day is write and review contracts between public companies that do business with each other. Furthermore, it was less than one year ago that the State of New York authorized me to practice any kind of law at all. I would be breaking my oath under the law if I were to tell you that I was the best lawyer to handle a personal injury case like yours. I am not. Since a personal injury specialist will not charge you anything up front, I can't claim to be less expensive, either.

"From what you have told me, I think you have a case against Allied Chemical for your wife's illness and your daughter's blindness and brain damage. Let me give you the name of a man to call who will do a good job for you."

"You can give it to me, but I will not call him, Mister Johnson. If you think the case is good, then you must believe you can win it. I want you to be my lawyer." He stuck out his hand for Raymond to shake in agreement.

Raymond took it, then stood up. "I have to get going. We'll talk more after I've discussed it with the partners in the firm. I can't promise you anything until I get their go-ahead."

Pedro Gutierrez nodded and smiled for the first time in weeks.

***

"I think we can do better than that," Walter Bowman said as he looked at the Smith & Wesson with the smaller grips. "Those don't feel too good, do they?"

"Not really," Henry admitted, gripping the revolver in his right hand. "They need more wood in front, like the bigger ones, but not so big on the bottom."

"I think I have an idea." Walter Bowman left his workbench and started rummaging through a box on one of the shelves in the workshop. He pulled out something wrapped in waxed paper and set it on the workbench. Then, using a small screwdriver, he removed the walnut grips from the revolver and laid the weapon on a piece of 3/8" plywood. He carefully traced the outline of the frame on the wood using a pencil, then took the pattern over to the scroll saw and cut out the shape. Walter unwrapped the waxed paper to reveal a chunk of modeling clay, which he sliced in half with his pocketknife and pressed around the wooden mockup of the revolver's frame. He trimmed the excess off the back of the dummy frame and handed the result to his son.

"Hold it like you would the real one, and work your fingers into the clay. Use your other hand if you need to. Get it to where it fits your hand exactly." Henry spent a few moments molding the clay to where it fit into his palm and fingers comfortably. He handed the wood and clay back to his father. Walter inspected it carefully. "I think I can duplicate this shape pretty closely in walnut. Do you think that would be better than either of these standard grips?"

"Much better."

"Okay then. You go up and see if your mother needs any help with dinner, and I should be able to get these roughed out before the food's ready. We ought to be able to finish them by tomorrow. I'll inlet them with the router and get them rough shaped, and I'll let you do the final handwork with the rasp and sandpaper. That sound good?" Henry beamed at his father. He loved working on projects with him.

"Can we go shoot it tomorrow?"

"I can't think of any reason why not," Walter Bowman said with a big smile.

The boy ran up the stairs to see if his mother needed anything, but his mind was not on dinner. Henry was thinking about how he intended to reread as much of the McGivern book as possible before the following morning.

***

Joe Hammond rolled over and fumbled for the telephone receiver. "Hello?" he mumbled.

"Governor's office calling. Is this Joe Hammond?"

"Yes, it is."

"Please hold."

"Joe, that you?"

"Yes, Governor, what can I do for you today?" *As if I don't already know* Hammond thought cynically.

"Joe, I won't waste words. We need your vote on House Bill 310. It's a close one, but I think that with your vote and a couple others I believe we can get, it will go through. You were in construction, and you know how important a new bridge can be to a community that's growing and finds its roads barely able to cope with increased traffic. Jackson County needs that bridge, and the state has an obligation to see that it gets built."

"I didn't realize it was that important to you, Governor." *You're goddamn right I was in construction* Hammond thought, *and I realize exactly how important it is to you, you grinning, pardon-selling mushmouth. Your wife's ne'er-do-well brother-in-law owns the land where that bridge is going to be built, and the price the state is going to pay for it will make him a rich man. By putting the bridge a hundred yards east, you could save the taxpayers almost a million dollars. And I know damn well that the firm lined up to do the concrete work is owned by your lawyer's cousin. He'll use non-union labor, which is fine, but he'll charge double what I could get the union boys to do it for, and five-to-one he goes light on the mix and pays off the engineering firm that'll be testing the casting samples.*

"I always take a strong interest in the growth of our state."

Does he think I'm an idiot, or does he realize I know the score and just expect me to play ball with him? Hammond wondered. He had not been in the legislature long enough to be able to always read all the other politicians accurately, even one as normally transparent as the Governor.

"Governor, I'm flattered you remember my construction background, but the fact is that I haven't had a chance to look into the guts of this deal and make up my mind on it."

"Joe, would it save you any time and trouble if I just told you that it was very important to me, and that I won't forget your support on this bill?"

There it is. Out in the open. No more dancing around. Hammond took a deep breath. "If you put it that way, Governor, then yes, you've got my vote."

"Thanks, Joe. I won't forget you on this one." The Governor broke the connection. *You're fucking right you won't* thought Joe Hammond as he hung up the telephone.

April 7, 1963

"Your group looks good," Walter Bowman told his son as he stared at the shirt cardboard with the black spot drawn on it. Six bullet holes were clustered in a group about an inch in diameter, three inches to the left of the spot and an inch high. "Let's adjust the rear sight. Windage first—I'm not sure what the graduations are." He took the revolver from his son and fitted the screwdriver blade into the slotted screw head on the right side of the rear sight.

"That's odd," Walter Bowman said in surprise as he turned the screw counterclockwise. The rear sight was moving to the left—the opposite direction of his intention.

"Smith & Wesson rear sights have their windage adjustments work backwards from the normal way," Henry declared. "The elevation adjustment is standard."

"So I see." *Mind like a steel trap when he reads things* Walter Bowman reflected. He twisted the adjustment screw clockwise to its original setting and watched as the rear sight moved satisfyingly to the right. Then he gave the screw another three-quarter turn. "Try it now."

His son took the gun from him and reloaded it. Then he returned to his spot on the riverbank where he sat down with his shoulders against a big rock and his knees up, and held the revolver in both hands, resting his hands on his knees. It was the position he had read was steadiest for deliberate shooting, other than resting the gun on sandbags. Henry was thirty yards from the cardboard target.

Cocking and firing the gun deliberately as before, Henry put six shots into another tight circle, about an inch left of his aiming point and still an inch high. He handed his father the revolver as they walked up to look at the target. "It needs about half again as much right windage," Walter declared, and made the adjustment with the small screwdriver. "You want the elevation changed at all?"

"No, let's leave it where it is, for now. It makes it easier to see the target if you have to hold just under it, instead of right on it, where the front sight covers half of it up." This was something he had discovered when shooting quickly with his rifle, and it was doubly true with a handgun, where the front sight was closer to the eye and obscured a larger portion of the target.

Henry took the revolver back from his father and reloaded it. Instead of sitting back down he stood and held the gun in both hands and cocked and fired it six times at the target from a slightly shorter distance than before. A two-inch group of holes appeared in the cardboard in the center of the black spot Walter had drawn with a laundry marker. "I held a little lower that time," the boy explained.

"Time to shoot something more fun." Henry walked over to a paper grocery bag they had brought along and reached into it, pulling out a 2" cube of pine. He tossed it twenty feet out into the river and brought the Smith & Wesson up into a two-hand hold, cocking the hammer as he did so. The gun cracked and the cube appeared to vanish. Henry and his father both instinctively looked up in the air, and saw the pine block spinning as it reached a height of about fifteen feet before it fell back into the water. Henry had already recocked the gun, and when the wood block bobbed back up in the water after landing, he fired again, just underneath it as before. The block repeated its flight. Henry tried to repeat his trick, but his third shot was high and nicked the top edge of the block, splintering off a chunk of pine and driving the rest of the cube briefly underwater. He looked up at his father.

"Harder to hold the sights exactly right than with the rifle." Henry could keep a floating block flying for a full magazine with his Winchester, and had taken to firing a second shot at it in the air every time it flew up, to make the trick more challenging. "This is fun." He fired the remaining three shots at the floating block double-action, sweeping the trigger through its full stroke and firing the gun without cocking the hammer first. All three shots missed the wood by a couple of inches.

It was at that instant that Henry Bowman fully realized the magnitude of Ed McGivern's accomplishments with a revolver. Decent accuracy was fairly easy for almost anyone to accomplish. Accuracy with speed was a lot harder. Henry reloaded the revolver and handed it to his father. "Hold about two inches under the front edge of the block if you want it to make it jump. Hold on the front edge if you want to try to split it in two."

Walter took the gun without comment and held it with the same technique he had seen his son use. The handmade walnut grips were a little small in his large hands, but felt comfortable nonetheless. He cocked the gun and took aim on the block. As the revolver cracked, the block vanished underwater for a brief moment, then reappeared. Walter cocked the gun again and fired a second shot with the same results.

On the third shot, he waited until the floating piece of wood rotated ninety degrees in the calm water. At the sound of the report, the block split in two and the halves floated a foot apart in the muddy water of the Mississippi River. "Hit it in the end grain to split it cleanly," the man advised his son. Both of them smiled at that. Walter Bowman fired the last three shots in the cylinder double-action, just as his son had done, and missed the fragment he was shooting at by at least six inches each time.

"I can see how you got hooked on this stuff," he told Henry. "I guess you need one of these, huh?" Henry was afraid to say anything. "I don't much believe in borrowing other people's tools, but I guess you won't hurt it any, using it for a bit." Walter Bowman realized he was talking mainly to himself. "Just the same, let's get this back to its owner pretty soon, okay?" Henry nodded. "You keep at it. I'm going to get out my camera and take some pictures."

That day on the river, Henry found he could make a 2" block jump out of the water and hit it in the air with the second shot about a third of the time. He also regularly hit a three-pound coffee can at eighty yards, which amazed Walter.

By the time they packed up and went home late that afternoon, the boy had fired 900 rounds through Doc Wiemann's revolver. Henry was hooked again.

April 8, 1963

"Arthur, may I talk to you about something?" Raymond Johnson was standing in the doorway of Arthur Lambert's office. Arthur Lambert was the senior partner of Lambert, Burns.

"Certainly, Raymond. Come in, sit down. What's on your mind?"

Raymond eased himself into one of the maroon leather chairs in front of Lambert's large mahogany desk and came to the point.

"There's a potential case that has come up, involving someone I know, and I'd like to handle it."

"A securities case? From a contact you've made?" Lambert inquired.

"No, nothing like that. Actually, I tried to refer the man to another firm, but he would have none of it. He insists that I handle the case. It's not what we normally do here, and I told him that. He doesn't want another lawyer, though. I explained to him that it would depend upon the firm's approval." He took a deep breath before going on. "I'd like to accept the case, sir, and I will make sure that it in no way interferes with my current caseload. Frankly, I don't expect it to require a lot of time."

"So what is this case, Raymond? Who's the client?"

"It's the janitor in my apartment building, Arthur. His name is Gutierrez." At the mention of the man's name, Arthur Lambert's eyes became more distant. *He's probably thinking of 'West Side Story'* Raymond thought. *George Chakiris showing off his dancing skills on the floor of a high school gymnasium, getting all the girls wet and pissing off all the clean-cut caucasian males.* He pressed on with the explanation about the daughter, and Lambert began to pay attention again after a short while.

"She has a serious health problem, and because of it he is near bankruptcy. When I learned of the circumstances, I realized that Mr. Gutierrez may have an actionable claim. I told him this, and offered to recommend a firm well-versed in personal injury cases. He insisted I take the case." Raymond broke eye contact with the senior partner.

"I don't think Mr. Gutierrez has had many breaks lately, and he reminds me of the men that Dad always hired to work at the ranch. I'd like to try to help him out. As I say, I don't think it will take much of my time. I'll keep track of my hours on it, and I can work on Sundays, since I'm not married. If there's any problem with it taking more time that I expect, I can forfeit vacation days to make it up." Arthur Lambert was startled by this last suggestion.

"We don't typically handle personal injury cases, and I don't see how this might lead in any way to further business for Lambert, Burns." Ray imagined the rest of the message, which was left unspoken. *Arthur's thinking that the last thing Lambert, Burns needs is to have one of the associates off doing pro bono work for Puerto Ricans.*

"You really think the case is a winner?" Lambert asked bluntly. Raymond shrugged.

"Any judgment at all for the plaintiff would be a huge help to the family. They're almost destitute. I seriously doubt the case will ever go to a jury. I think the defendant will make a settlement offer, and Gutierrez will take it. He regards his problems as God's will, and he's amazed at the concept that he might get any money at all."

"Lawyers need more clients like that," Arthur Lambert said with a small smile. "And the last thing I need is to have you moping around, thinking about how I said you couldn't help someone out." Fifty-nine-year-old Arthur Lambert sat back in his chair.

"When I was just out of law school, right after the Crash, any work at all had been welcome, and every case was exciting." He stared at Raymond. "Do you expect this sort of extracurricular activity to crop up often?"

Raymond could not help but smile at the question. *He wants me to get it out of my system.* "No, Arthur. I don't intend to make a habit of soliciting maintenance men for their legal business."

"Then I think we can allow you to try to help this Mr. Gutierrez with his case. Keep track of your hours, as you say, and stay on top of your regular caseload."

"Thank you, Arthur." Raymond stood to leave. "Ah...what sort of sharing arrangement do you think appropriate?"

Arthur Lambert was startled by the question. At first he thought Raymond was referring to the split with the client. "You mean with the firm?" He waved his hand in a dismissive gesture. "Just stay on top of what we're throwing at you, and keep doing the kind of work we've come to expect from you. If you manage to get your janitor any money, you're entitled to whatever share you and he agree upon." Arthur Lambert turned his attention to the papers on his desk, and Raymond left the room.

No mention had been made of the defendant in the Gutierrez case.

***

"Mr. Gutierrez, you have a lawyer." Ray Johnson said to the maintenance man. "I talked it over with the senior partner, and although this isn't the kind of case our firm handles, he's letting me run with it. We're a 'go'." Raymond handed the older man a single sheet of paper and a pen.

"This is a contract which says that you are authorizing me to file suit and negotiate on your behalf in this case. It says that I will assume all legal costs incurred in the case, and as payment for my efforts and expenses, I will receive one-third of whatever settlement is awarded, and you will receive two-thirds. It also states that you are aware that it is possible we will be unsuccessful and no settlement will be awarded at all."

"I understand." Pedro Gutierrez read the contract and put his name to it. He still found it difficult to believe that Allied Chemical might pay for any part of his family's medical problems.

"I'll need to meet with your wife and daughter, and then arrange for a medical specialist to examine them. I'll also need to talk to your wife at length about the conditions at Allied when she worked there. The sooner we can get moving on this, the better."

"We will be available whenever you need us, Mr. Johnson. When do we start? Where shall we meet you?" He was dreading having to get his wife and daughter out of their beds.

"Would it be easiest if I came to your home?"

Pedro visibly relaxed. Their apartment was tiny, but clean, and he had already acknowledged the reality that Raymond Johnson was going to have to see his daughter if he was to help her. "Yes, that would be a great help."

"How about this evening, then? After you've had your supper?"

"We will be pleased to see you whenever you arrive."

"About seven-thirty, then." They stood up and shook hands, and Raymond put the contract back in his briefcase before departing.

"Well, look who's back so soon. Don't tell me Henry's shot up that last case already? It's been, what? Two weeks?" Henry looked self-conscious.

"No, Al, it's time for another gun. A friend of Max's lent Henry a Smith & Wesson to try, and he really liked it. Did some shooting with it I wouldn't have believed if I hadn't seen it firsthand. He deserves one of his own. It's a Model 17 with a six-inch barrel."

Al Goodman looked slightly pained. He suspected that Walter Bowman was unaware of some of the facts concerning his planned purchase. With most customers, Al would not have cared, but he truly liked Walter Bowman and his son Henry.

"The Model 17 is a very fine gun. Probably the best .22 revolver made. You going to try some of that aerial stuff with it, Henry?"

"He's already hitting wood blocks in the air with the one Max's friend lent him," Walter said proudly. "Do you have one here?"

"I think we have the Model 18—that's the one with a four-inch barrel. We can order a six-inch for you, and it will be here in about a week. While you're waiting for it to arrive, you can go get your letters done."

"Letters?" Walter Bowman asked with a puzzled look on his face.

"You're not familiar with Missouri law, are you, Mr. Bowman?"

"I guess not."

"In Missouri, before you can buy a handgun, you have to get two letters of good standing on business letterhead from two 'prominent' people that you know. Then you have to take those letters to the sheriff with the make, model, and serial number of the pistol you intend to purchase. If he approves it, you come pick up your gun."

"*If* he approves it?" Walter Bowman looked at Al Goodman in disbelief. The store-owner hurried to reassure his customer.

"He'll approve your application, oh, no question, I didn't mean it that way, Mr. Bowman. No, I was just explaining what the laws were. I'm sure you know several heads of St. Louis-based companies quite well. *Of course* the police chief will approve *your* application."

"But in order to buy this revolver, I'm supposed to get two—what?—company presidents? to write letters saying they know me and that I'm a good citizen?"

"Something like that."

"What do the people who don't happen to have company presidents for personal friends do?" Walter demanded. Al Goodman, normally unflappable, licked his lips. Walter waited for an answer.

"Well, I suppose if you put that question to the sheriff, he'd say that was the whole point of the law, don't you think?" Al replied finally.

Walter Bowman was speechless. Henry saw that his father was genuinely upset, and kept quiet. "How long has this law been in effect in Missouri?" he finally said.

"I'm not sure of the answer to that one, Mr. Bowman, but it's been the law here as long as I can remember, and that goes back quite a ways. I do know that the law against carrying a pistol or revolver on you for protection has been in force here in Missouri since 1874. I only know that because there was an argument about that in here a few months ago, and a customer who's a lawyer brought in a copy of the original statute."

"It's *illegal* for an honest adult to have a gun with him for protection in Missouri?" Walter was flabbergasted. He had forgotten all about the letters of good standing required for a purchase.

"Yes, and not just a gun. Illegal to carry any defensive weapon. Also illegal to have any one of those in your car, if it's easily accessible. Has been for almost ninety years." He shook his head as if to indicate that Walter was placing far too much significance on the issue. "But no one's going to arrest you if you're carrying a gun or have one in your car, Mr. Bowman. Be realistic."

Walter Bowman looked completely disgusted, but he said nothing.

"I don't understand, Dad. What's the matter?" Henry said finally.

"Son, you remember when you asked me that time last month why there weren't any negroes at the amusement park, the Forest Park Highlands, that you went to with your friends from school?" Henry nodded.

"I didn't really answer your question at the time, but I will now." Henry's father took a deep breath. He was not enjoying this.

"You didn't see any negroes at the Forest Park Highlands because they aren't allowed in there," Walter Bowman explained. "Even though they are honest residents of this area, just like we are, they can't go to that amusement park. They would be run off if they tried to get in. The Constitution of this country says that all honest people in America have the same rights, but many places, like the Forest Park Highlands, just ignore that." No one in the room knew it at the time, but in two months the owners of the Highlands would reap the bitter results of their whites-only policy.

"Why don't the negroes just go to the police?" Henry asked immediately. Both his father and Al Goodman smiled without pleasure.

"The police are the ones keeping them out." Henry looked baffled at this answer. Walter Bowman sighed. "I hadn't expected to be teaching history on a Saturday, but this is important." He looked at Al Goodman in apology, who made a dismissive gesture. His brother Harold was in that day, and there was only one other customer at the other end of the showroom.

"You know about how there used to be slavery in part of this country—in the southern states?" Walter asked. Henry nodded assent. "Well, after the North won the Civil War, and slavery was ended, many of the people living in southern states hated the idea that former slaves could now vote and do the other things that whites could. So they passed what we now call 'Jim Crow' laws.

"These were laws which said that you had to be able to read, or pass a test, or pay a tax before you could vote. The law *looked* like it applied to everyone, but most former slaves couldn't read, and if they could, they didn't have enough money to pay the poll tax. If they had the money, then the sheriff would give them a test to pass. And they'd fail."

"What kind of test?" Henry asked.

"Shall I tell him the standard story?" Al Goodman asked Henry's father.

"Go ahead."

Al Goodman raised himself to his full five-foot, five-inch height, and began. "A colored man in Georgia went to go vote, and was told he had to go to the sheriff's office to prove that he could read," Al said in his monotone. "The sheriff handed him a newspaper and said, 'Can you tell me what that says, boy?' The sheriff was laughing because the newspaper was written in Chinese. The colored man said, 'Why yas, suh, ah kin tell you 'zactly what it says.'" Al Goodman's attempt at dialect was appalling. Walter Bowman was astonished, but he remained silent as Al delivered the final line. "'Hit says th'ain't goin' t'be no niggers votin' in Georgia this year.'"

Henry looked at his father. He was beginning to understand that no white man would have been sent to the sheriff's office in the first place, let alone handed a Chinese newspaper. Walter Bowman continued the history lesson.

"Missouri was on the dividing line between the states that wanted to have slavery and the states that didn't. There were a lot of people in Missouri that wanted the South to win the war, and who believed in slavery. That's why we still have some movie theaters and restaurants here with special sections for negroes, just like in the deep south. Where your aunt lives, up in New Hampshire, they don't have that."

"But the Civil War was a hundred years ago!" his son protested. Henry was embarrassed that he had not realized there were segregated establishments in St. Louis. He would later realize that his parents avoided them on principle.

"Time doesn't always change people's minds, Son." Walter Bowman took a deep breath. "And it isn't just about negroes. For a long time in California during the last century, there was a law that made it illegal for any Chinese person to testify against a white man. That meant that any white person could rob or kill a Chinese person, and the only way he could be arrested is if another white person complained about it."

"That was *legal?*" Henry exclaimed. Al Goodman looked startled also. He was learning some new things today as well.

"It violated our Constitution, but many states have passed laws that violate the Constitution. Even the Federal Government does it sometimes. That's why we have lawyers, like your grandfather, to defend us and get those illegal laws thrown out by the Supreme Court." Walter changed the subject back to the original purpose for their trip to Goodman's.

"What Mr. Goodman was telling us is that before I can buy this revolver for you, I have to go get two business owners to sign letters recommending me. Then I take them to the sheriff and hope he says okay. Mr. Goodman says there won't be any problem, and he's probably right, but the whole point is that the sheriff can do whatever he wants. Just like the story about voting. Henry, we still have laws written so that the police can deny negroes, or anyone else, their ability to protect themselves, and arrest them if they carry personal protection. Or arrest me, for that matter. It depends on if they like you or not."

Henry was horrified at the idea of his father being arrested. "Would they arrest Sadie?" he asked immediately. Sadie was a black woman who came in twice a week to help Henry's mother with housecleaning, and had done so before Henry was even born. Henry had always liked her. Sadie had come in two weeks earlier, badly bruised and with a cut over her eye. Two young men had knocked her down and taken her money as she was walking from the bus stop to her apartment in north St. Louis.

"I don't know, Henry. Maybe."

The boy thought of something else. "But you didn't have to get any letters with my rifle. And most rifles and shotguns are a lot more powerful than pistols." Al Goodman spoke up to address Henry's statement.

"You love to shoot for fun, Henry, but a lot of people that want to buy a pistol aren't like you, especially the women. They want a pistol to protect themselves in case someone attacks them. No one is going to carry a rifle or a shotgun around for protection. They're too big. Handguns were designed to be carried for self-defense."

Now Walter broke in. "That's why bigoted people passed the laws about voting and about guns, Henry. These bigots don't want negroes being able to protect themselves. They didn't want them voting for legislators that had their interests in mind, and they didn't want them having guns in their pockets when the lynch mob was coming." He thought a moment. "The law Al just described also gives the police an excuse to stop negroes on the street and check them for guns. Actually, it gives them the excuse to do that to anyone, but they don't do it to whites, as a rule." *Yet* Walter Bowman added silently to himself.

"Since Henry brought up the subject of long guns, I assume you know that the St. Louis police have requested that gun dealers not sell firearms of any kind to colored people," Al interjected. "And that's pretty much the standard police policy throughout the state."

"Is that the policy of this store?" Walter Bowman asked sharply. Al Goodman looked him in the eye, and when he replied, his voice carried an uncharacteristic edge to it.

"Goodman's has an ironclad rule that we have to know something about each and every customer. We turn away anyone that we do not know anything about. We turn away a lot more whites than coloreds. If your question is do we have any colored people for customers, the answer is yes. We do not have many, but we have some. It is not a policy I am particularly fond of, but it is one that my conscience can live with, and that the police accept." He paused before delivering his last statement.

"My brother and I are well aware of the horror of unchecked government, as I'm sure you can appreciate." Al waited for a response. Walter Bowman felt slightly abashed for being short with Al Goodman.

"Of course I am. Please forgive me for being rude." He decided to end the conversation on a more positive note before leaving with his son.

"Well, President Kennedy has been doing a lot of serious talking about civil rights. This time next year, maybe these kinds of unfair restrictions will all be gone."

As it turned out, Walter Bowman was half right.

"It's looking better, Pedro." Raymond Johnson had started using the more-familiar form of address with his client shortly after he had taken on the case. "We've found some documentation that Allied was aware of potential risks of chemical exposure in the plant. For several years they've had a written company policy in force limiting the number of consecutive hours employees may spend inside the plant itself. "

"My wife never mentioned that."

"She may not have known about it. Her job was such that she never was in the plant for that many hours at one time. But the fact that there was such a policy shows that Allied was well aware that prolonged exposure to chemicals was a serious health risk. It is also well-documented that Allied knew your wife was pregnant. I think we can show that common sense would dictate that pregnant women be shielded from a hostile environment to a greater extent than other employees. Which she of course was not." Pedro Gutierrez nodded, but said nothing.

"It never came up before," Raymond continued. "There weren't any women at all working in the plant before Rosa. The man they put in charge of telling the cleaning crew about the forced layoff was new. He made the decision on his own about drawing the names out of a hat for the position of inventory checker, and he didn't think about pregnant women when he did it."

"Then it is his fault, not the company's." Gutierrez had a strong sense of personal responsibility.

"He was acting on behalf of the company. If he had come over to your house and thrown chemicals in your food, he would have been acting on his own, and you would be right, Allied would not be responsible. But since it was his job to hire and fire employees in that division, it was the company's responsibility to see that he followed company policy and safeguards in the performance of his duties. They slipped up, and they are now responsible."

"How much money are you going to ask for?" It was a question Raymond had been expecting a week ago, and he was glad it had not come up until now, when he had a better feel for their chances in the case.

"Before I answer that, I want to remind you of some things I told you when we first talked about your problem. First, this is a gamble. It is possible that a jury will decide you and your wife have no claim against Allied whatsoever, and we'll all walk away with nothing.

"However, industrial accidents happen every day, and workmen's compensation generally helps with medical bills on job-related injuries. People know that. They expect it. They assume the company's insurance will cover whatever tragedy befalls a worker on the job. That never happened with you. No one connected your wife and daughter's condition with Rosa's working environment at Allied. That's good for us. It makes it look like Allied abandoned one of its loyal employees, and a pregnant one at that."

"But they thought they were helping us! The government wouldn't let them keep her at her old job for the same pay, which is what we wanted."

Raymond smiled without humor. "That doesn't matter. You can't sue the government, no matter what they do. Allied *could* have paid the new government-mandated wage to the cleaning crew. They chose instead to subcontract the work to an outside firm. That would have been fine if they had just laid your wife off with the rest of the maintenance staff." Gutierrez said nothing.

"Anyway, to get back to your question, it is almost certain that we will *not* get the amount of money that we ask for, unless we actually get in front of a jury, which is unlikely, because then we might get nothing. I intend to demand considerably more than we expect to get, and negotiate downwards from there." The lawyer took a deep breath. "I have not yet determined exactly how much Allied could be expected to pay, but I am going to file suit for at least one million dollars."

Gutierrez was speechless. *He can't even imagine such a sum of money* Ray thought.

"That's the *starting* figure. The real question is, if they come to the table with a counteroffer, and we get into negotiations to avoid a trial, what will you be willing to accept? If they lowball us, and threaten to let a jury decide if we hold out for more, what do we do? I get paid a third of the settlement, but I don't have a wife and daughter who need full-time care. Losing this case entirely will be a much greater hardship on you than it will be on me, Pedro. How low are you willing to go and not feel you were cheated or that I let you down?"

The older man stared at the lawyer and licked his lips nervously. It was obvious to Ray that Gutierrez had been hoping, these past few weeks, that a miracle would happen and he and Rosa would get enough money to help out with Rosita. The older man had been ashamed to find himself imagining that a check for ten thousand dollars would be coming in the mail. What Raymond Johnson was now telling him was entirely beyond his comprehension, and he saw how woefully unprepared he was to answer the lawyer's question.

"Mister Johnson," Pedro said finally, "if you were to call me into your apartment because the bathroom was flooded, would you tell me how to fix the pipes?"

"No, I wouldn't."

"If I worked on them all weekend and then told you that they were so badly damaged that I could not repair them, and the building owner would not pay for new plumbing, would you think I had done a bad job or believe that I did not care that you had water in your apartment?"

"No."

"I did not think so. And neither am I going to tell you how to do your job, or say that you have done it poorly if what we wish for does not come to be. Any money at all will help, but if you feel an offer is too low, then reject it. If we lose, I am in the same position, and you will have worked for nothing. You know we need any money we can get, and I know you do not want to lose the case." He felt awkward trying to express himself to the younger, more educated man. "I believe we want the same thing, and you are the one who should decide what to do."

Raymond nodded. This was the best answer he could have asked for, but also the one which thrust the most responsibility on him. *This isn't some legal opinion on a contract dispute. It's a man's wife and daughter* he thought solemnly. "That makes it clearer. Let me get back on it. I have a couple of things I want to pursue." He stood to leave.

Raymond's mind was already churning, thinking about what he should do next. He had felt ill-equipped to determine how to get a handle on the money issue, and had been reluctant to ask for help within his own firm. *They aren't getting any money out of this case, even if we manage to win* he said to himself. *I'm not about to drag one of the partners in and press him for advice.* Suddenly an idea came to him.

I wonder if Tony Kearns has ever hunted rats in a dump before Raymond thought with a smile as he walked towards the subway.

***

"Joe, I want to thank you for coming through for me on the bridge bill. I won't forget it. Let me know if there's anything I can do for you to return the favor."

"You're welcome, Governor. As a matter of fact, there is something." *Got to strike while the iron is hot* Hammond thought. *He'll forget he owes me a thing as soon as the session's over on Friday.* "I'd like you to see that a friend of mine gets a State License Bureau Office somewhere in the St. Louis area. His name is Harold Gaines." *The jerk doesn't deserve it, not by a mile, but I owe it to Linda and Harold Junior* thought Hammond. *She's stuck with the marriage for fifteen years, and she should have had a lot better. Not that you cared a lot at the time,* Joe Hammond added silently.

Joe Hammond had long suspected that Linda and Harold Gaines' eldest child, Harold Jr., was really his own. In 1948, he had admitted to the young woman he'd been involved with for two years that he did not ever intend to get married. Less than two weeks later Linda Wilson had married Harold Gaines. Harold Junior had been born eight months and ten days after the wedding. Joe Hammond had remained in contact with his old flame, but the issue of paternity had never been mentioned by either of them in fifteen years.

The Governor was startled at the suddenness of Joe Hammond's request for quid pro quo. His mind was racing to catch up. "Ah...I'm not sure a License Bureau Office will be is available in that area next session, Joe."

Hammond laughed softly. "Governor, I'm sure you'll find one available for Harold. I have just as much faith in your ability to do that as you asked me to have in your judgment about the details of the bridge they'll be building." *He probably thinks I'm an arrogant prick, but hell, I'm just playing the same ball game he is.* The Governor paused for a long moment before answering.

"Okay, Joe, I'll see what I can do. Glad to know we talk the same language, even though you just got started in the Legislature." Joe Hammond chuckled at the Governor's mild barb as he hung up the phone.

Always wise to let the other guy have the last word, as long as you get what you wanted.

May 5, 1963

"You sure this is legal, Ray?"

"I told you, it's a grey area of New York law. We aren't within city limits. It's possible we could be charged with disturbing the peace, but that's a bit unlikely. I give the guy who runs this place a fifth of scotch every month, and I think he'd stand up for me. The cops in this area know me, and join me sometimes when it's their day off. One of them even suggested I get registered as a city health official." At this last statement, Tony Kearns set down the Coleman lantern and doubled over with laughter.

"I'll never in my life say that New York cops don't have a sense of humor. *Hey,*" Tony said suddenly. "Behind that old mattress." Raymond saw the reflected red of the two small eyes and snapped the old Winchester pump .22 to his shoulder. As he squeezed the trigger, a mild crack momentarily disturbed the warm evening and was immediately followed by the sound of Raymond working the slide of the rifle, chambering another round. The rat flipped over on his back, his hind feet twitching *in extremis,* and Raymond engaged the safety and handed the rifle to his friend, taking the lantern in return.

"Nineteen," Ray said softly.

"*Damn* but you get on fast," Tony said for the third time that night.

"I keep telling you, this is perfect training for when you go to Africa. When a wounded buffalo comes at you out of the bush, you won't have time to set up for the shot."

"I'm beginning to see your point," Tony admitted as he walked over to the dead vermin and lifted the carcass by its tail, examining it. "Tell me about this ammo. Composition, you said? What the hell is that?"

"Just gallery loads, Tony," Raymond explained. "Didn't they ever have carnivals where you were a little kid?"

"Yeah, but there was a wooden wall you had to stand behind and shoot over. If you weren't tall enough, you couldn't shoot." Tony, who was a bit over six feet tall, saw his friend staring at him. "I didn't really start growing until I was fourteen, when I grew a foot in less than a year." Raymond nodded at the explanation.

"Well, if you'd ever looked close at the setup," Raymond said, returning to the previous subject, "you'd have noticed that there wasn't much of a backstop. Just a slanted piece of tin with canvas behind it. Not nearly enough to be safe with regular twenty-twos. What they use at the carnival is a special .22 Short with a bullet that's a lot lighter than normal, and made out of compressed lead dust. As soon as it hits anything at all, it disintegrates. They're quiet, no recoil, and as you can see, pure poison on rats."

Suddenly Tony swung the rifle to his shoulder and snapped off a shot. "*Got him!*" he said triumphantly. "That makes six."

"Nice shooting."

"I'm starting to get the hang of it." Tony kicked at an empty gallon paint can that lay at his feet, snapped the rifle to his shoulder, and fired at it. The can was dented by the bullet, but no hole appeared. He shook his head but made no comment. "You getting hungry? I missed dinner. If you're up for eating, I'll buy."

"Sounds good to me." Raymond took the rifle back from his friend and unloaded it as they walked to the maintenance shack. Ray loosened the takedown screw and broke the rifle down when they got there, and stowed the two sections in the short leather case he had left in the small building.

"Call a cab for you, Mr. Johnson?" said the black man who was sipping scotch from a paper cup.

"Yes, please, Robert." The man picked up the telephone, called the taxi company, and ordered a cab.

"You do all right tonight?" he asked after he hung up.

"Twenty-five," Raymond replied. Robert gave a huge grin, showing that he was missing one of his upper teeth on the right side. It made his smile even more infectious.

"They still plenty, an' there be more next time you come."

"I think you're right. Hope so. I'm not tired of it yet."

"You have a good time?" Robert asked, addressing Tony Kearns.

"I really did. Never done this before."

"Didn't know nobody who did, before Mr. Raymond here come along. He a pure terror with a rifle."

"That he is," Tony said with a grin. The three men stood in comfortable silence for a few minutes, and then they all looked out the window as the taxi pulled up.

"See you in a couple weeks, Robert," Raymond said, as he and Tony left the shack and headed for the cab.

"I'll be here," the man replied as the door banged shut behind the two men.

***

"So what's going on in your business?" Raymond asked Tony Kearns as he took a sip of his coffee.

"Only big news lately is this Becker-Allied thing." Tony Kearns took a drink of Coca Cola.

"Yeah, I heard about that. We tried to get their business, but Allied went with MacKinnon instead. Old man Lambert was one irritable senior partner when that happened, I'll tell you that."

"Interesting thing about the deal, word on the street is that there's somebody pissing in the soup. Some potential lawsuit over somebody getting injured at Allied."

"Workmen's comp?" Raymond asked.

"Hell, I don't know. That's the problem with all these rumors and 'inside dope' things. By the time you hear them, they're so watered down and rephrased, the information's worse than useless. Listen, I know you don't have any interest in the stock market, at least not yet, but let me tell you something. Everybody's always looking for a sure thing, and it ruins 'em."

"What do you mean?"

"Nobody wants to do their homework. Everybody wants to steal a copy of the answers to the test. So what happens, somebody hears something. Like, 'I know this guy who plays golf with the chief financial officer of Brunswick. He told me that the CFO said earnings this quarter were going to be almost double what they'd projected, because with these automatic pinsetters, the alleys aren't having to hire juvenile delinquents anymore, and everybody and his little brother is now going bowling.' Well, I threw in the last part, 'cause that's the kind of thinking some of these idiots are doing, but the first part, the line about the earnings, that's the kind of story that's always flying around.

"Anyway, this fellow, the one who knows the guy who plays golf with the CFO of Brunswick, he'll want to load up on Brunswick stock on margin. Margin's where the brokerage firm lends you half the money to buy the stock, so you can buy twice as much. So our hero, who has maybe four grand in savings, goes and buys eight grand worth of

Brunswick, and signs a note for four grand to White, Weld. Say the stock's at forty when he does this. He's buying 200 shares with his eight thou. If the stock goes up five points, he makes a quick thousand—five bucks times 200 shares—instead of only five hundred, which is what he's have if he didn't buy on margin and only bought a hundred shares at 40 with his four Gs.

"One big problem with this picture," Tony said as he bit into his ham and cheese sandwich. "That story from the guy who played golf with the CFO. One, it may be bull-shit. The golfer may have made it up and then told this fairy tale to our hero, for reasons of his own. Actually, that would probably be the best thing for our intrepid speculator."

"Why?"

Tony shrugged. "It would mean the stock probably wouldn't do anything, either way. Our hero would finally get sick of waiting, sell out his position about where he bought it, and all he'd lose would be the commissions and a couple months interest charges on the margin balance."

"So what would be worse?"

"It would be worse if the story was true. Say his buddy really did play golf with the CFO. What the CFO actually said might easily have been something like, 'Our earnings are going to be up a lot more than last year. Maybe almost double the year-ago numbers, if things keep going as they are.' Well, the golf buddy hears 'almost double', and that's what he focuses on, because that's the nature of people, to believe that the best possible outcome will come to pass.

"And you know damn well the golf buddy isn't the only person to whom the CFO mentioned this little tidbit. And our hero isn't the only one the golf buddy passed it on to. And in a company that size, there are doubtless some other guys in the loop who have let the cat out of the bag, too.

"So what we have *now*, is a whole bunch of people out there buying stock in Brunswick, expecting an announcement that earnings are double the year-ago same-quar-ter numbers, so then they can cash out. When our hero buys his stock, it's already three points higher than it was a month before. News comes out that Brunswick's earnings are up 40% from year-ago, which is a new record, and great news if you're head of market-ing at Brunswick. But it's terrible news if you just bought the stock at 43 and everyone who'd bid the price up to that level expected an announcement of ninety percent higher earnings, not forty. So the speculators are disappointed, and the ones who are smart enough to cut their losses sell immediately and drive the price down to 39. Our hero has an $800 paper loss, plus the commissions he's paid, plus he's paying interest on the $4300 margin balance at White, Weld.

"My absolute favorite 'hot tip' story crops up at least once a year, and if you ever start following equities, I absolutely guarantee that somebody will hit you with it, and claim it's the gospel truth." Tony Kearns washed down another bite of his sandwich with the last of his Coke and signaled the waitress for a refill.

"This is the one where some guy will tell you that he's got absolute ironclad, hun-dred-percent accurate info about a company that no one else has. The reason it's the real thing is that it came from a hundred-dollar-an-hour call girl who's been fucking the pres-ident of the company. She gives such good blow jobs, or gets the old guy hard when his wife can't, or licks his ass, or ties him up and pisses on him, or whatever, that in addition to paying her the regular rate, he's told her to put all her savings into the stock, and she'll make a bundle. Of course there's no way the guy would tell her to do that if it wasn't a sure thing, because then he'd lose his hotsy forever. So it has to be the straight goods, see?

"Now, how does the guy who's telling you this know about it, you ask? Well, he's asshole buddies with the best friend of the broad's cousin, or brother, or some such, and the guy owes him one, of course." Tony Kearns shook his head and laughed. "That one's been around so long, it's old enough to vote."

"On something like this Allied deal," Raymond asked his friend, "do you just ignore the rumor that's going around, about the workmen's comp thing?"

Tony shook his head. "I don't ignore it. There probably is something there. But since I don't know what it is, what that kind of rumor does for me, is it makes me back off and watch for a while, until more facts come out.

"I don't doubt that there's some kind of legal issue worrying the brass at Allied. The question is, is it something trivial, that will ultimately have no effect on Becker buying them? If so, since the rumor has knocked the stock down a few points, Allied would be a buy. On the other hand, if this legal thing is a deal-killer, I'd want to avoid Allied like the plague, maybe even short it. But that view's much too simplistic, as I'm sure you're aware."

"What do you mean?"

"Hell, Ray. Imagine Lambert, Burns had gotten the Allied account, and put you on it. Some guy is trying to sue their ass, and it's going to kill the sale to Becker. What would you do? You'd figure out what it was worth to Allied to buy these guys off and let the sale go through, and you'd advise the company to offer something less than that to the guy with the broken back, or whatever he's got. If the guy won't take it, Allied plays hardball and goes to court, and Becker backs off. Maybe the jury decides the asshole's faking it and throws it out. If so, then Becker's back with another offer, probably about the same, don't you think?" Raymond shrugged. He didn't want to offer anything.

"If the thing goes to court and the jury feels sorry for the guy in the wheelchair, and tells Allied to give him a bunch of money, then their insurance pays it off, and Becker's probably back with another offer, just like before. Point I'm trying to make, right now, all I've got to look at is a bunch of smoke. Who knows what kind of lawsuit it is? Even if I knew exactly, it wouldn't do me much good, because today's deal-killer can turn into tomorrow's happy compromise. Who knows what kind of back-and-forth the legal eagles are going to do, or if someone's going to pick up his ball and decide to go home? "

"So you're saying that this potential lawsuit, whatever it is, is a non-issue?"

"No, it's going to affect the deal, that's certain. I just don't intend to commit the firm's dough until if and when there's a clear way to make some money on it."

"How will you know when that happens?"

"The way I always do, which is the same way anyone who's successful in this business over the long haul does it: You spot a discrepancy between what the crowd is doing with its money, and what you understand to be the facts."

"Can you explain?"

Tony grinned. "Book you should read is *Extraordinary Popular Delusions and the Madness of Crowds*. Written over a hundred years ago by a man named Charles Mackey. I'll lend you my copy. Details all the crazy things people have done, just because everyone else was doing them. Like paying the price of a house for a single tulip bulb in Holland in the 17th century, just because it had cost half a house the week before and was apt to cost two houses within the month." Raymond didn't exactly understand what his friend was talking about, but decided silence was still the best policy for the time being.

"Crowd doesn't always lose its head, mind you," Tony said with a wolfish grin, "but it happens often enough to keep my department open and making money."

"I'm in contracts," confessed Raymond. "I have to make sure companies' legal obligations are spelled out. On a deal like this lawsuit thing you're talking about, it seems they'd need numbers guys like you fighting it out. How does the lawyer for the guy with the broken back decide what to ask for?"

Tony Kearns scowled and rubbed his chin. He loved figuring out difficult problems. "I'm not a personal injury lawyer, but you're right—guys like me always have to come up with a dollar value for the legal troubles a company has, so we can assess the appropriate impact on the stock price." He chewed his lip.

"The Krauts are very rigid, big on discipline and not very creative. 'Ve heff vays uff makink you talk' and all that. I know it sounds hokey, but that is indeed the way they run their businesses. There are a few exceptions—Volkswagen comes to mind—but Becker isn't one of them.

"First off, I'll say that Becker would definitely suspend finalizing the deal with Allied until this thing, whatever it is, is settled. They will insist Allied clean up their mess before going ahead with the deal. That will cost some money, because all the hired brains like you guys are getting paid by the hour, and the meter will be running a little longer, but I don't see that as any big deal."

"So you think Becker will just put their plans on hold, tell Allied to fix the problem, then take up where they left off?"

"That's possible, but there's still too much we don't know. For example, the Krauts aren't big on warranty claims, and shit like that. In general, they have a 'you bought it, it's your problem' attitude about that kind of thing. So, I'd say that the folks at Becker, on a personal level, won't feel much sympathy for this injured worker, even if the Allied's CEO himself shoved him into a vat of sulfuric acid and had a film crew record the incident for posterity." Raymond's spirits were sinking as he listened to his friend's words, but he kept an impassive expression on his face.

"However, these guys are buying an *American* company, and are planning to do business in America, and I have to assume that Becker has someone high up who recognizes the realities of that fact, regardless of his personal opinions."

"What do you mean?"

"Well, we don't know what this lawsuit is all about, but what if it's something that could become a P.R. nightmare? You know, something that might catch the interest and sympathy of the public? Hell, it could kill the deal permanently. The Krauts are sure to realize they've got to tread carefully, particularly in *New York*, for Christ's sake. Jesus, for all we know, twenty years ago Becker may have been a subcontractor making Zyklon-B."

"I see what you mean. If the claim was something that could be a real embarrassment if it came out, how would a lawyer put a dollar value on what Allied could afford to pay to make it go away?"

"Surely your firm has somebody who could do that."

"I'm sure we do. That's just it—I'm the new guy, and the senior partners have a game they play of asking associates to comment on cases unrelated to what they're doing. They like to see who can think on his feet about cases they aren't intimately familiar with."

"One of the senior VP's at White, Weld does that kind of shit, too."

"So you know what I'm talking about. Anyway, I'm pretty good at the game, but no one's hit me with a case involving calculating how much to try to get in a lawsuit. I got to tell you, I think I'd blank if they did."

"Well, you got to figure a lawyer's going to come out with guns blazing and demanding some outrageous figure, with punitive damages, to get their attention, right? Isn't that the way everybody does it—tell the girl you want to do her roommate at the same time, and compromise down from there?"

"I guess so, yeah."

"Anyway, I assume your question is, how does the lawyer know what to finally agree to, knowing that's as much grease as he's going to get out of that one goose. Is that it?"

"Yes. Exactly."

"Hell, for that, all he'd need would be an annual report for Allied, with a balance sheet and income statement. A sixth-grader could come up with the right figure if he had those numbers. The key for the plaintiff's lawyer would be to make Allied see that he knew exactly what their financial position was, and to give them a way to pay up that was affordable, but barely. He'd use the threat of a sympathetic jury to get them up to that level where it was still affordable, but not trivial.

"Knowledge is power in any field, yours and mine especially. If I were the hurt guy's lawyer, I'd want that company to know that I knew exactly what they could or couldn't pay, and I'd want to give them fucking nightmares about what could happen if the thing went to a jury. I'd want them to see that Becker would sooner absorb a pile of plutonium than Allied Chemical."

"You'd have been good lawyer material, Tony."

"Christ, no. Three years of law school would probably have done me in, and even if it didn't, when I got out I'd be up against all those assholes that thrive on that kind of stuff. No thanks. I like it right where I am—watching all the people do dumb things with their money, and making my moves accordingly." Tony Kearns was shaking his head, and Raymond knew he had to get him back on the numbers before Tony's mind strayed permanently to something else.

"Surely it can't be that easy to figure out what a company could absorb, just by looking at an annual report."

"Oh, you mean hidden assets, undervalued holdings, that sort of thing? Yeah, you got to do a little more research and then tweak the numbers a little to account for that stuff, but that's no big deal. Here, let me show you." Tony Kearns reached over and pulled a napkin out of the dispenser. "You got a pen?" he asked Raymond.

"Here."

"Okay, first thing, you go to the income statement and..."

Raymond Johnson, the fledgling personal injury lawyer, used every bit of concentration he had to pay attention to what his friend was saying. He was about to get a very valuable addition to his education.

May 10, 1963

"I wonder what these three heavy packages are?" said Walter Bowman in a loud voice when he opened the door to the hall closet to hang up his jacket. "They're from some place called 'Service Armament', in New Jersey," he added with a grin.

"My Mauser! Nobody told me it came today!" Henry Bowman ran from the kitchen to the front hall. He grabbed the long cardboard box, tore it open, and withdrew the well-oiled rifle, which was wrapped in newspaper. It was a WWII vintage German G33/40, the version with the short 19" barrel. Henry wiped off the excess oil with a piece of newsprint and threw the rifle up to his shoulder. The 8mm centerfire infantryman's rifle was about two pounds heavier than his Winchester .22. He operated the bolt several times without dropping the butt from his shoulder. The action was smoother than he had expected.

"Bring it on in the study and tell me about it, Henry," his father suggested. "It looks kind of like the one Dad had when I was little, that Uncle Cam gave him." Henry carried his new prize into his father's study, wiping it off further with another page of newsprint.

"It's a German Mauser, Dad. Paul Mauser designed this basic action in 1898, and it's still used all over the world. FN in Belgium still builds them for Browning. This one is a 33/40 model. The main difference between it and the Model 98 German Army rifle is that this one is even shorter and more than a pound lighter than the 98 carbine, and two pounds lighter than the standard 98 rifle. It fires the 8x57mm rifle cartridge. The bullet is a little bigger and heavier than the one our U.S. .30-06 fires, but not quite as fast. I'll get one." Henry ran out of the room. He returned and handed the loaded round of 8mm Mauser ammunition to his father.

Walter Bowman examined the cartridge. It was larger than he had expected. He had never seen any ammunition for the one his father had owned. Michael Bowman had sold the rifle, shortly after his younger brother's death, without ever having fired it.

"What about recoil?"

"I'll get used to it," Henry said. Then he added, "I bought a rubber recoil pad. I think I'll shorten the stock and put the pad on so it ends up the same length as the buttstock on my Winchester." Military rifle stocks were sized for adults and typically had steel buttplates. Many soldiers complained of the recoil of their rifles.

"Is this ammo expensive?"

"Charley has World War Two 8mm for less than three cents a round, by the case. About twice as much as rimfire."

"Does it all fire?"

"They promised it would. I bought two cases, and it looks good. Not corroded or anything."

Walter Bowman nodded. "Let me know if you need a hand in the shop on that recoil pad installation."

Henry headed for the basement stairs with his new rifle.

May 24, 1963

"Ray, you've been hinting at a claim of ten million dollars. That's ludicrous, and you know it." Ames MacKinnon III, one of the partners at MacKinnon, Reed, was speaking in a slightly patronizing tone to the younger lawyer. "Allied can't pay that kind of money! Of course they'd like to take care of your Mexican so they can get on with the sale to Becker, but you're on another planet with your dollar figure." *That's what you think, asshole* Raymond said to himself. *You think I'm a contracts man and haven't a clue as to what the company can or can't comfortably pay.*

"A jury will laugh you out of court," MacKinnon went on. "Nobody around here's ever had an award on a P.I. case anywhere near like what you're dreaming about. Pick a reasonable figure, and we'll work with you on this thing, okay? You don't want to wind up looking like a crazy man on your first real case. What do you say?"

Raymond recognized that the other lawyer was simultaneously trying to sow doubt in his mind about Raymond's abilities, point out his inexperience, trivialize his client and his claim, ridicule his lawsuit, and make Raymond revise his thinking and reduce his demands without any counteroffer from Allied. *Nervy bastard, aren't you?* Raymond thought. *I have no intention of rolling over and playing dead. You are the one who will soon be squirming.*

"Ames, I think you should sit down with Allied's CFO and come up with a serious counteroffer for me instead of dancing around with a lot of meaningless rhetoric. You're right, no one's ever paid this kind of money before, at least not around here. There's a very good reason for that. Up until now, no chemical company has ever ordered a pregnant employee to work in an environment filled with birth-defect-producing chemicals."

"There's no proof of that, and you know it. Besides, the company was going out of its way to keep her on in view of the layoffs."

"Absolute proof we don't need, Ames. You know how juries work. You need to get that CFO to sharpen up his pencil and get to work. And don't think I haven't done my homework on this one—I have. A jury is quite likely to award every nickel we're asking for, maybe even more. After all, how do you think a New York jury will vote when one of them points out in deliberation that your boys performed chemical experiments on a pregnant woman, and now is being bought by a *German* firm? Birds of a feather...? I'd hate to guess what they might ultimately decide to award."

Ames MacKinnon liked to think he was a master at maintaining an impassive expression regardless of circumstances, but Ames was unable to keep the blood from draining out of his face, which temporarily gave his skin a different hue.

"You pull anything like that, and I'll have you up on charges of jury tampering and improper conduct before you can open your mouth. You'll be parking cars for a living." Ray listened to this outburst and looked at the other lawyer with genuine bafflement.

"Ames, I'm not going to need to say word one on that subject to the jury, either before, during, or after the trial. They will see a damaged woman and child who are not white, and a bunch of caucasians who caused that damage. They will see those rich caucasians loudly protesting their innocence while at the same time cutting a big-money deal with a bunch of Germans. This is *New York City*, Ames, where you see people with numbers tattooed on their arms every day. It's the *first* thing that's going to come into the jurors' minds, even if I sleep through most of the trial. Hell, Ames, I bet it was the first thing that came into *your* mind," he said accusingly.

The color came back into Ames MacKinnon's cheeks as he flushed red. Raymond had hit it exactly, and it was what he had warned his client. The board at Allied had instructed him to get the case settled quickly for as little outlay as possible, so that the sale to Becker could proceed.

"I'll talk to my people," was his only response, and then Ames MacKinnon turned around and left.

Raymond waited until the door closed behind the departing attorney. The he started to smile. A few moments later he was laughing out loud.

***

"Dad, I can't find my set of gun screwdrivers," Henry Bowman yelled as he stepped into the kitchen after climbing the stairs from the basement. He was carrying his M98 Mauser in his left hand as he headed for the living room, looking for his father. Catherine Bowman's father, Charles Collins, had had a stroke at the age of eighty-one, and the family had stayed at the house in St. Louis, instead of moving to their place on the river for the summer.

"They aren't on your workbench, where I saw th—" He stopped abruptly when he saw the family had guests. "Sorry, I didn't know anyone—"

"That's all right, son. Your Aunt Zofia and Uncle Max just stopped by to see your grandfather, and brought Mr. Mann with them. I'm sorry, I didn't tell you I borrowed your screwdriver set to work on a chest of drawers. I needed one that fit exactly. They're up in our bedroom." Henry turned to leave the room, but his uncle stopped him.

"Let me see your Mauser, Henry. Haven't handled a 33/40 in twenty years. When did you get it?"

"Last month, Uncle Max," he said as he handed him the rifle. Max Collins opened the action, checked the chamber, and closed the bolt. He threw the gun up to his shoulder, sighted at one of the wall sconces, and squeezed the trigger. There was a loud snap as the firing pin fell.

"Who stoned the trigger? It's light and it breaks clean."

"I did, Uncle Max. I put in an overtravel screw also."

"Damn good for a military trigger," he proclaimed, and started to hand the rifle back to his nephew.

"May I see that?" Irwin Mann asked suddenly. Max Collins opened the bolt and handed Henry's rifle to his wife's brother-in-law. Irwin Mann held it in his lap and turned it in his hands at varying angles. A look of concentration came over his face as he examined the rifle. Finally he looked up at ten-year-old Henry Bowman. "This is yours?" he demanded.

"Yes."

"You have...shot it very much?" Irwin Mann's tone was intense and insistent, but not in any way unfriendly.

"About a thousand rounds in the past month," Henry explained. "Dad and I are going out shooting on the river tomorrow, and I wanted to check the guard screws first."

Irwin Mann looked at Walter Bowman. "Would you and your son mind if I were to join you tomorrow? I would very much like to see him shoot this rifle." Walter, mildly surprised at the request, looked over at his son with a questioning look. Henry gave a gesture that clearly showed it was fine with him if Mr. Mann joined them the following day.

"We usually leave about eight-thirty. Shall we pick you up at nine tomorrow?"

Walter asked.

"You are certain it is not too much trouble?"

"Don't you live a few streets over from Max? That's not even ten minutes out of our way."

"Nine o'clock will be fine, then."

Irwin Mann was not sure what he should expect from the next day's outing, but he had a strange premonition that he was going to learn something from it.

May 25, 1963

"Hello," Raymond Johnson mumbled into the phone as he rolled over in bed.

"You dog! Been trying to get you all weekend! No wonder you were so fucking interested in my analysis!" Tony Kearns was on the phone. "What I been hearing can't be right, though. Ten *million* dollars?" Tony was fishing, but Raymond remained silent. He was wide awake now. "You can't have asked for ten mil!" Raymond still said nothing. "Shit, you got big balls, you know that? Either that or you're fucking crazy."

"Listen, Tony, I wanted to be straight with you that night, but with all the laws against—"

"Hell, Raymond, I don't give a shit about that, it couldn't have done me any good anyway, but Jesus Christ, you're a contracts guy. What the hell are you doing taking on a PI case, and my God, Raymond, *ten million dollars!*" All of a sudden Tony Kearns was at a loss for words. It was an unusual experience for him. Ray was about to say something, but Tony suddenly found his voice. "You had breakfast yet? Scratch that—it doesn't matter. *I* haven't had breakfast yet, and I have *got* to hear more about this. Meet me at Bascomb's in a half hour, and you can buy this time, okay?" Raymond looked at the clock.

"Yeah, I can do that."

"Great." Tony broke the connection.

***

"Look, Tony," Raymond started to say as his friend sat down, "I really feel terrible about how I pumped you for ideas without telling you—"

"For Christ's sake will you shut up about that? If you had told me exactly what you were doing, what do you think I would have done?"

"Well, I...." Raymond's voice trailed off, and he realized he hadn't a clue.

"Exactly!" Tony said with satisfaction. "You tell me you're about to demand a huge pile of money from Allied for making the mistake of branching out into the freak-show business, what can I do with it? Nothing. Two minutes to crunch the numbers and anyone with half a brain comes to the immediate conclusion that Allied can afford one hell of a fine without breaking a sweat. All the clowns with fifty shares might dump it, but they don't have enough stock to make a dent. Did you see where Allied closed yesterday?"

"No," Raymond admitted.

"Down a quarter. A *quarter,*" Tony repeated, "and Becker's stock is unchanged. How do you make money on that?" Raymond shook his head to show he had no idea.

"That's just it—you can't. Thing I'd like to know is the same thing you would: What's going through that Allied lawyer's mind right now? He's the one I'd have to get private dope from if I wanted to profit from it. He settles out of court, sale goes through, business as usual." Tony grinned and his eyebrows went up.

"*But,* if he and Allied have a two-by-four up their ass, say 'Fuck you, let a jury decide', then Becker and their checkbook might be on the next plane back to Berlin and Allied's CEO wakes up the following morning to find his stock down ten, to thirty-eight bid, trading halted due to order imbalance."

"So you're not mad?"

"Hell, no! But listen, last night I dug into Allied's financials a little more carefully than that quick-and-dirty method I scratched out on the napkin three weeks ago, and I think their assets are more valuable than what's shown on their books. That's no real news, since Becker made the offer to buy them out, and that always requires a premium over the current stock price to do. Becker saw the hidden value as well, and if the buyout goes through, all the Allied stockholders will get paid for that value.

"Anyway, I ran some numbers a few different ways to see what kind of figure I came up with that Allied could cut a check for without losing any sleep over it, given that Becker was still going to go through with the purchase. I assume you did the same thing. What number did you come up with?"

"A little over four million."

Tony Kearns shook his head emphatically. "Don't go for less than six. I brought over some stuff for you to look at, if you're interested, that lays out my thinking on the numbers. Anyway, I assume that you're going to do a complete fuck-job on the guy from—What is it? MacKinnon?—and he probably won't be up on exactly what their financial situa–"

"It's Ames MacKinnon the third of MacKinnon, Reed," Raymond broke in, "but what do you mean you assume I'll do a 'fuck-job' on him?"

"Old man's progeny himself, eh? That's even better." Tony waved his hand in a dismissive gesture. "I just meant the lawyer stuff you guys always do with each other's minds." Raymond gave his friend a quizzical look.

"You know—he comes over to your office to discuss a potential settlement, and you've got all these blown-up pictures of the medical labs at Auschwitz lying around, and big posters showing Allied's cash flow, like you're in the middle of preparing your presentation for the trial." Tony suddenly thought of something.

"Hey, my cousin has an empty can of Zyklon-B he brought back from the war, unless he's thrown it away by now. If he's still got it, I'll get it from him. It's about the size of a quart paint can, and the label's bright orange. Have it sitting on your credenza next to a quart can of some stuff Allied makes, preferably something with an orange label. That ought to get old Ames the third's attention." Raymond was both appalled and fascinated at Tony's suggestion, and the cavalier manner in which his friend had assumed it was what Raymond had planned.

"But Tony, Allied wasn't doing medical experiments on its workers! To be accurate, there's no proof that the chemicals in the plant had anything at *all* to do with what happened to my client's wife and child." Raymond hadn't intended to make this admission, but it came out anyway. "And they're not Jews—they've been in America since they were children, and were born in Guatemala!"

Tony Kearns waved his hand again, to show that his friend was digressing onto irrelevant issues. "You can be damn sure defense counsel won't let anyone sympathetic to either ethnic group on the jury, so you're going to have a bunch of cab drivers and the like deciding your case. Guys like that would have a hard time picking a favorite between Jews and Mexicans, so the difference is immaterial. They won't like krauts, and *that's* something you can take to the bank. If you give 'em an excuse to render a decision that will make Becker put their Prussian asses on a boat and forget they ever thought about expanding into America, the jury will do it.

"Also, with all this hoo-haw going on in Washington, at least a few of 'em will want to show compassion for the downtrodden. Maybe some on the jury would prefer the downtrodden make something useful of themselves—like fertilizer—but they won't say it out loud. They may not give a damn about the bedridden lady, and what you say may be entirely true—Allied had nothing to do with it. But people don't get away with even the possibility of blinding little kids in America, not if they're about to sell out to the same guys that turned the kid in the chess club into air pollution."

"You're saying you think I should push this thing to a jury?" Raymond exclaimed, disbelieving.

"Hell, you're the lawyer, what are you asking me for? No, I assumed you wanted to get a quick settlement."

"That's right, I do."

"Well, hell, Raymond, with this Becker deal on the table, all the contracts guys are poring over the paperwork, and I got to assume there's some kind of legal clause in the agreement that says this kind of shit has to be settled before anyone signs or cuts any checks, right?"

"Yes, that's standard."

"Well, what you got here, at least from where I sit, is an absolute deal-killer of a lawsuit. MacKinnon goes back and tells the Allied brass you're going to have the jury thinking the Germans are about to set up gas chambers on Long Island, well, Christ on a crutch! The CEO's going to sprain his wrist grabbing for the pen to sign the check."

"I hope you're right."

"Thing you got to do, Ray, is make it look like you're rubbing your hands together at the very thought of a jury trial, and this needle-dick lawyer better not try to blow smoke up your ass with some chump-change settlement offer."

"And you think six million is a fair figure?"

"Maybe a little bit more. Here, let me show you what I got." Tony Kearns reached for his briefcase. "But if this all works out and you wind up with two million bucks in your pocket, I got to warn you: You're going to owe me a blow job."

***

Henry Bowman closed the trunk of the six-year-old Corvette and walked around to the passenger door to get in. "Why do you think Mr. Mann wanted to come with us today, Dad?"

Walter Bowman stabbed the gas pedal once and turned the key in the ignition. The 283 Chevy immediately burbled to life and settled down into a slightly rough idle. The valvetrain made a mild clattering noise, for the engine's camshaft acted on solid lifters, rather than the more common hydraulic ones. "I'm not sure, Henry. It's the first time I've ever heard of him showing any interest at all in shooting." Walter reflected a moment before continuing.

"He had a very rough time of it in the war. His whole family was killed, and he barely got out alive. He doesn't talk about it, although I get the impression Uncle Max has a pretty good idea about what happened to him." Walter did not need to tell his son not to ask Irwin Mann about his experiences during the war.

"I hope he has a good time with us," Henry said to his father.

***

Irwin Mann looked out his window and saw the black and silver car pull up in front of his apartment. He was not sure why, but on an impulse he went to his bookshelf and selected a volume which his put in his briefcase before going out to meet Walter and Henry Bowman.

As Irwin neared the car, he realized it had no rear seat. "Are you sure there is enough room for me?" he asked. Walter and Henry were standing by the Corvette as he came down the concrete steps.

"Catherine's going to be home all day with her father. We could have taken the station wagon, but Henry really likes this car. He rides in the middle between the two seats whenever there's another passenger. He's got his own pad to sit on. Come on—we do this all the time."

Walter took Irwin's briefcase and stowed it behind the passenger seat before ushering his son into the car. Irwin Mann slid in beside the boy, and realized that there was indeed enough room for all of them in the sports car. Walter started the engine, engaged first gear, and accelerated briskly away from the curb. The passenger side window was down, and Irwin Mann rested his right arm on the top of the door with his elbow in the breeze. He looked over at the boy sitting next to him. Henry was grinning, as was his father. Their mood was infectious.

***

"I brought some ear plugs for you, Mr. Mann," Henry said as they laid their gear down on one of the big limestone rocks on the riverbank. Irwin Mann started to wave Henry away, but the boy continued. "No, really, guns will damage your hearing if you don't wear ear protection."

"He's right," added Walter. "I didn't shoot any guns during the war, but unmuffled aircraft exhaust has taken its toll on my ears. The doctors say I've got a thirty percent loss. It won't grow back, either," he added with a rueful grin. Irwin Mann accepted the plugs Henry held out for him.

"Isn't there something they could put on the end of the gun, like a muffler on an engine, so that it would not be so...destructive on one's hearing?" Irwin asked Walter. Walter was about to say he did not know, but Henry, who was looking in the other direction and did not realize their guest was addressing his father, replied to Irwin Mann's question.

"There is, and up until the early 'thirties they were sold in gun stores and hardware stores for a few dollars. A man named Maxim invented them, and he called them 'silencers'. They didn't make the gun silent, but they took some of the blast out. They screwed on the end of the barrel, and trapped some of the burning powder gases, so the noise wouldn't be so apt to hurt your ears."

"They don't sell them any more?" Irwin asked. Henry shook his head, as he reached into his shooting bag for some ammunition for the Mauser. The 8mm cartridges were on five-round stripper clips, which slid into a groove in the top of the receiver so that the shooter could charge the magazine with five cartridges very rapidly.

"In 1934, the government made them almost completely illegal. If you want to buy one now, you have to give the government a $200 tax first. On *each* one. Almost nobody is willing to pay $200 extra just to have his gun quieter. There was a man I met out at the gun club when I was there with Uncle Max who had paid the $200 and had one on his 1911 .45 Colt automatic. He let me shoot it. The extra weight on the barrel wouldn't let the gun cycle normally, so you had to operate the slide by hand for every shot. It did make the gun a lot quieter, though. You could shoot it without plugs and it didn't hurt your ears."

"Why are they illegal?"

Henry shrugged as he dropped a handful of the five-round stripper clips into the right pocket of his shooting coat. "I don't know. Everybody says it's because silencers would make it too easy for murderers, but I never could see how that made any sense. The gun with a silencer still makes pretty much noise, just not enough to damage your hearing. Any murderer can still wrap a big piece of an old wool blanket around the gun barrel before he shoots someone with it, and that's a lot quieter than a silencer that screws on the end of the barrel—I know, I've tried it."

Irwin Mann felt the hair on the back of his neck stand up as he remembered how, twenty years before, he had shoved the barrel of the .38 revolver into the wool coat of the Lithuanian militiaman before pulling the trigger.

"Also," Henry continued, "a knife or a piece of pipe is completely silent. I never have been able to figure out why they want to have people that go out shooting make as much noise as possible and bother all their neighbors." The boy grinned. "My aunt lives up the hill from here, and I know she'd like it better if all my guns had silencers on them."

Henry retracted the bolt of his Mauser with his right hand and charged the magazine with a five-round stripper clip. He left the bolt open as he tossed the empty clip into his shooting bag and reached into the canvas sack next to it. He withdrew two scrap pieces of 2x4 pine from the sack, each about four inches long, and tossed them into the river about ten feet from shore. They floated in the water about eight feet apart.

"Got your plugs in?" he asked the two older men. Irwin Mann took the rubber plugs from his left palm and pressed them into his ears. "I've been practicing this one, Dad, but I'm still a little rough," Henry said in a loud voice so that his father could hear. He had a big grin on his face as he took his shooting glasses out of his shirt pocket and put them on. Then Henry turned toward the blocks floating in the river. He closed the bolt of the Mauser, chambering the first round, and threw the rifle up to his shoulder. He leaned forward and took aim underneath the block on the left and squeezed the trigger.

At the blast of the rifle, a geyser of water erupted and the pine block disappeared. As recoil rocked Henry to a vertical stance, he released his grip and flicked his right hand upwards, catching the round knob of the bolt handle in his palm and swiftly operating the bolt without loosening the grip of his left hand or letting the butt of the gun leave his shoulder. He slammed the bolt forward on the second cartridge as he aimed the rifle almost straight up. Walter Bowman and Irwin Mann instinctively looked up in the same direction as the gun's muzzle just in time to see the pine block forty feet in the air and almost directly overhead. The Mauser cracked again and the descending block split into two pieces, one about twice the size of the other, as Henry pulled the gun down out of recoil.

The instant Henry regained his original forward-leaning position, the gun boomed a third time and the second floating block was launched into the air. Henry repeated his rapid operation of the bolt, and when the second block was about twenty feet above their heads, Henry fired a fourth round and the wood exploded into several chunks and many splinters. The entire shooting demonstration had taken eight seconds.

Henry lowered his rifle to his waist with the muzzle pointed at the river's edge, and grinned at the two men. "Nailed that second one in the end grain, I think," he opined.

Walter Bowman, who had seen his son shoot many times before, was nonetheless very impressed. "Who needs a shotgun, right Henry?" Walter said, quoting one of his son's favorite comments. Irwin Mann was absolutely dumbfounded.

"If you shoot right under them when they're floating in the water," Henry explained, "the splash comes up more on the far side, and it throws the block back towards you, as well as up in the air. That way, if you want to shoot them in the air, you're firing almost straight up, and the bullet will land five or six hundred yards out in the water where it can't hurt anyone." The river, where they stood, was almost a mile wide, and empty fields stretched for more than that distance on the Illinois side before the first road appeared.

"How far up does the bullet go, do you know?"

"I wrote a ballistician about that." Walter Bowman lowered his camera and listened. He had not heard of this. "He said about 2400 yards for the 8x57 Mauser military round fired straight up, and that the bullet would hit the ground after about seventy seconds." Neither man made a comment, and Henry turned his attention back to his rifle.

Henry racked the Mauser's bolt a final time, ejecting the case and pushing the last round into the chamber. He did not raise the rifle to his shoulder, but continued to hold it at waist level, looking around in the water near the shore. His eyes fell on the thing they had been seeking: the larger piece of the first block, which floated fifteen feet out in the Mississippi River.

Henry made a slight adjustment to where he was aiming the rifle, which he still held at his waist, and pulled the trigger. The piece of wood vanished, and all three people instinctively jerked their faces towards the sky. The piece of pine was spinning fifty feet in the air and beginning to arc down towards the two grown men. Walter Bowman took a step to his right, reached out his arm, and caught the block in his right hand. Irwin Mann's jaw was hanging open.

"I like to shoot things from the hip, and I've always practiced that, too," Henry said with a big smile.

Henry Bowman did not know that three decades later his life would hinge on this skill.

***

After doing some longer range shooting at pieces of driftwood floating in the river and chunks of limestone two hundred yards down the riverbank, Henry handed the Mauser to Irwin Mann. "You know how to use it, don't you?" Henry asked. Irwin held the rifle and stared at it. He was remembering the efforts he and his compatriots had made long ago, trying to figure out exactly how to properly use the German weapons Irwin had captured.

"Please instruct me," Irwin said, handing the rifle back to the boy.

Henry explained how to operate the bolt and the safety before discussing how to use the sights. "You can move the rear sight for longer ranges, but that's if you have time and want to take the trouble. I usually just leave the rear sight on the lowest setting. When I want to shoot things at longer ranges, like you just saw me do, instead of lining up the sights so the top of the front one is even with the top of the rear, I hold the front sight up a little. If you hold the rifle so the front sight is about one sight-width above the rear sight, with the target sitting on top of it, you should be on at about 225 yards." Henry simulated a front and rear sight with his left forefinger held between his right fore- and middle fingers.

"Hold up more front sight if the range is longer. I can't really say exactly how much—you have to get a feel for it. Leave your left eye open, but ignore it. Focus your right eye on the front sight. Let the rear sight and the target be fuzzy, even if it seems unnatural. A front sight in sharp focus is the key to hitting what you're aiming at." Irwin was listening intently to the boy's words when Henry thought of something.

"And always use something to brace yourself on if it's available. I've been shooting from a standing position today because I'm just shooting wood blocks close up in the water, and out of the air, but if your shot has to count and the target isn't moving, always find a rest.

"Most importantly, don't guess or assume that the gun is empty, even if you just checked it. The only gun that's empty is the one that has had its barrel removed from the receiver. Every accidental shooting I've ever heard of has been with an unloaded gun." Henry felt a little awkward as he quoted his Uncle Max, but Irwin Mann's expression remained serious.

"You can use the safety if you want, but here on the river I don't load the gun until I'm ready to shoot, and then I start firing right away. If you're hunting and carrying a loaded gun around you should use the safety, but I don't think a person should rely on them. They do malfunction sometimes. Keep your finger off the trigger until you've got the gun aimed and you're ready to shoot. If you get in the habit of resting your trigger finger along the side of the trigger guard when you pick the gun up, like this," he said, demonstrating, "it will become automatic. Always point the gun in a direction so that if it goes off nothing bad will happen. If the gun fires, the bullet will be a quarter mile away in less than a second, and as my Uncle Max says, 'Oh my God, I'm so sorry' won't bring it back."

Irwin Mann nodded his understanding. Walter Bowman remained silent. "Put your plugs back in. Put these on, too," he said, handing Irwin his shooting glasses. "If a case ruptures or a primer leaks, the gas can come back in your eyes." Irwin Mann slid the glasses on his face and Henry handed him the rifle and a stripper clip. He retracted the bolt and charged the weapon as he had seen Henry do. Henry tossed a wood block out into the river.

"Hold a little under it if you want to throw it in the air." Irwin raised the gun awkwardly to his shoulder. "Lean forward a bit, and move your face a little forward. Keep your right elbow up. That's it. Make sure the butt is pulled firmly into your shoulder." Suddenly the rifle boomed and a fountain of water appeared where the block had been. Irwin looked at the water, unable to see the piece of wood. Just then there was a splash as the block landed ten feet away from where he had fired. Henry started laughing.

"You blew it thirty feet in the air, Mr. Mann. You should have been looking up. Watch the muzzle!" He yelled. Irwin had started to turn towards Henry, the rifle turning with him. Irwin Mann looked horrified and ashamed. "I'm sorry I yelled, but Dad yelled at me the first time I started to do that, and it's never happened again."

"You are quite right. It will not happen with me again, either." Irwin racked the bolt and fired at the block a second time, with similar results. He scanned the water for other floating debris and saw a log floating about fifty yards out from the bank.

"Hold right on the center of it," Henry said, when he saw Irwin's intentions. The rifle cracked and a splash appeared twenty feet on the other side of the log. "About ten inches over the top," Henry said immediately. "Squeeze the trigger slowly, so that when it breaks, it's a surprise. Forget about the bang and the thump on your shoulder. Neither one will hurt you." Irwin Mann worked the bolt and took aim again on the log. This time the splash was right in front of the log, and the bullet made it rock in the water. "You hit it, just under the waterline." Irwin Mann chambered the last round and took aim once more. As the rifle cracked, a piece of bark flew from the log. The water around the log remained calm. Irwin turned towards Henry, the muzzle of the rifle pointing towards the sky. He was smiling as he opened the bolt and ejected the fired case.

"Thank you," Irwin said with feeling as he handed Henry his rifle.

"Shoot it some more—I have lots of ammo," said Henry. "Try some longer shots.

176

Like that rock up on the bluff." He pointed at a limestone outcropping about a hundred yards away as he took the rifle from the older man and loaded the magazine. Mann took back the rifle, chambered the first round, and aimed at the outcropping, which was about eighteen inches square. "Hold right on the center of it. The rifle will hit dead-on at that range with that ammo." Irwin squeezed the trigger and as the rifle cracked, a splash of limestone fragments erupted on the bluff two feet below the outcropping. Henry remained silent as Irwin Mann racked the bolt and chambered the next round. This time his shot was high, almost the same amount. He ejected the fired case and steadied himself for a third shot.

Click.

Irwin saw the muzzle of the rifle jerk as the firing pin fell. An instantaneous wave of nausea swept over Irwin Mann and his knees sagged slightly as the metallic sound of the weapon misfiring wrenched him back to that April afternoon twenty years before. Then the moment passed and he operated the bolt. The gun was empty. He turned towards Henry with a quizzical look, still keeping the rifle pointed at the bluff.

"I only put two in it and didn't tell you. Did you see the muzzle jerk when the gun dry-fired?"

"Yes."

"You're starting to flinch—jerking the trigger because you know the recoil is coming. That's why you're missing. Hold on the rock now, with an empty gun, and squeeze the trigger." Irwin did so, and the rifle remained steady. "You would have hit it that time, I bet. Let me get you a different rifle." Henry took the Mauser from Irwin and slid it into its case. He laid it down and picked up the other rifle case that contained his Winchester .22. "I think you might like this one better," he said, withdrawing the lighter rifle and showing Irwin how to load it.

"Remember, this one's a semiauto. It's cocked, loaded, and ready to fire every time you pull the trigger. You've got ten shots before you have to reload." Irwin Mann vaguely recalled that the Lugers had operated that way, but he said nothing as he listened to the other instructions Henry was giving him.

After about twenty minutes, Irwin Mann was hitting wood blocks at fifty feet with the Winchester. He smiled at Henry and Walter as he handed the boy back his rifle. "It's time for you to get back to your own shooting. You didn't come here today to watch me."

"Hey, it's fun," Henry said, realizing something his father had known for many years: Teaching someone a skill was as satisfying as practicing it yourself.

"How far away can you hit something with a rifle?" Irwin asked.

"It mainly depends on which rifle, what kind of ammunition, and how big the target is. Many people that have never fired a gun think that if the gun is aimed in exactly the same place—clamped in a vise, say—the bullets will all hit exactly the same spot. That's not true at all. The bullets aren't all exactly the same—they vary in weight a little, and aren't perfectly round. The powder charges vary slightly, the barrel isn't absolutely uniform inside from one end to the other, and with all the parts touching the barrel, it vibrates a little differently with each shot. That Mauser we were shooting is wartime production. So is the ammo. With a perfect hold on sandbags and no wind, it will place five shots in a seven- or eight-inch circle at two hundred yards, and maybe three feet at five hundred yards. You can't do any better than that no matter how good you are, because that's as good as that gun and ammo combination can manage.

"A handmade target rifle, or one made for shooting crows at long range, using ammo you assemble yourself with bullets made to the tightest possible tolerances and powder charges individually weighed, will put five shots in an inch and a quarter at two hundred yards and maybe six inches at five hundred. Uncle Max has rifles like that, and he's let me shoot them a couple of times. I can hit a beer can with one at two hundred fifty yards or a coffee can at four hundred if I have something to steady myself on, like a log or a big rock. With my Mauser, I can hit the coffee can at a hundred, maybe a hundred fifty most shots, but that's about my limit on a target that size with a thirty-dollar war surplus rifle and three-cent ammo." He smiled at his guest. "But a heavy target rifle with a powerful scope is useless for rapid fire and moving targets. The Mauser has a smooth action, and at fifteen yards any halfway decent rifle is plenty accurate. With three-cent ammo, you can practice a lot, too."

"How much would a target rifle such as you have described cost?"

Henry scowled. "Sixty for a used Remington 722 to get the action. Another eighty or so to have it trued up perfectly by a top-flight gunsmith and barreled with a Hart stainless match barrel chambered with a match reamer. I'm saving up to have that done by a man that lives up in Baden. He's built a bunch of guns that hold world records." Henry reflected a moment.

"I don't know how much it would cost to have a target stock made. Dad and I are going to do that part ourselves. A Unertl target scope is about another ninety, but they're the best. John Unertl's dad was a sniper in World War One who killed over two hundred soldiers on the Bulgarian border. He said he'd have done a lot better with better optics. He set up a factory in New York in the 'thirties, and the scopes his son makes are better than anyone else's in the whole world," Henry said matter-of-factly.

"You two ready for lunch?" Walter Bowman asked. Henry looked at Irwin Mann, who shrugged.

"If it's okay, Dad, I'd like to shoot my K-22 some first. Fifteen minutes all right?"

"Take your time."

Henry pulled a zippered, triangular leather case from his shooting bag and opened it. Irwin Mann gave a start. "That is a—Smith & Wesson?" he asked. Henry looked surprised.

"Yes, it is. Have you used one before?"

"Only a few times, many years ago. A thirty-eight, as I recall." *And every time I fired it the muzzle was pressed firmly against the target* Irwin mentally added.

"This one's a lot smaller caliber than that—a twenty-two, like the Winchester," Henry explained. "But it's built on a .38 frame, so the gun itself is probably about the same size as the one you used." Henry swung out the cylinder, loaded the gun with ammunition he kept in the pocket of his shooting coat, and started shooting. Irwin Mann was astonished at what he saw. Henry Bowman quit talking, and for the next twenty minutes his concentration was absolute.

Henry shot with his left hand as well as his right. Using a two-hand hold, he shot at a channel-marking buoy anchored far out in the river. On all six shots, Irwin heard the dull 'thunk' as the bullets struck the steel cylinder. Irwin Mann would learn over lunch that the buoy was made out of a 55-gallon drum filled with foam, and it was almost 300 yards from shore. Henry shot wood blocks out of the water holding the revolver upside down and pulling the trigger with his little finger. He asked his father for a small metal film can about an inch in diameter with a screw-on top. Henry threw it out in the water, kicked it up in the air with the first shot and hit it in midair with the second. He hit it again as soon as it landed in the water, and then the perforated can sank.

Finally, Henry locked his elbows into his kidneys and held the revolver at waist level in a two-hand hold. He was aiming it at a medium-sized piece of driftwood about eight feet in front of him that had washed up on the shore. Suddenly a stuttering blast erupted from the revolver and fragments of the fragile wood flew into the air. Irwin thought that the noise sounded familiar, and he realized with amazement that it was the same sound made by the submachine guns the Germans had used in Warsaw.

Henry opened the cylinder and pointed the gun's muzzle at the sky. He pressed the ejector rod with his thumb, and six empties fell to his feet. "I'm down to right at one second for six shots. Ed McGivern could shoot five in four-tenths of a second, but that was with a thirty-eight. You can shoot a more powerful revolver faster than you can a .22, because pushing it down out of recoil helps you pull the trigger double-action. Sorry I wasn't explaining what I was doing, but shooting a revolver well takes a lot more concentration. Let's have lunch and then you can shoot some more."

Irwin Mann was even more quiet than usual as the three of them sat on big river rocks and ate the sandwiches Catherine Bowman had packed for them. She hadn't been certain what foods Irwin might find offensive, so she had played it safe and supplied roast beef on buns, a big Thermos of lemonade, and another of coffee.

After finishing his sandwich and lemonade, Walter got up and went over to his camera bag to retrieve his Contarex. He walked down the riverbank and started framing various shots of the river, his son, and their guest. Irwin Mann, who was now alone with his young friend, finally spoke up.

"When I was a young man, before the war started, Henry, I knew nothing at all of how to use firearms. In fact, not a single relative or person I knew had any experience at all with guns of any kind. My entire family was killed by the Nazis in that war. I could not find even a single distant cousin after it was all over. My wife's sister, your Aunt Zofia, was the only one alive, and that is because she was here in America with your Uncle Max." Henry looked at the sadness in the older man's eyes, but he said nothing.

"I was shipped off with many others to a compound in Poland. We were slowly being starved to death. Some of us fought back, finally. We captured some weapons, but none of us knew how to use them. We had to figure them out as if they were strange machines dropped from another planet. My friends were doctors, engineers, and architects, and not one of them had one-tenth of the knowledge that I have seen you demonstrate today." He kicked at a small stone near his foot.

"We fought for many days, but we were too few, too unprepared, and too unfamiliar with how to defend ourselves. I was very lucky to escape alive into a safer area, through the sewers. The others I was with were not so fortunate." He took a breath and came to a decision. "Let me show you."

Irwin Mann retrieved his briefcase and withdrew the large hardcover book from it. He opened it to a page he had marked with a scrap of paper and handed it to the boy. Henry Bowman held the book in his lap and looked down to where Irwin Mann's finger was pointing. The words were in a foreign language.

"This is the concentration camp at Treblinka in Poland. I was someplace else, but it was much the same." There was a black-and-white photo of a German soldier with a Mauser rifle slung over his shoulder, smiling at the camera. In front of him were about a dozen men, all painfully thin, dressed in clothes that were one step above rags. The soldier was dressed in a heavy wool overcoat. It was obviously very cold.

"Turn the page." Henry did so. Another photo showed a soldier holding a 9mm Luger pistol in his hand, urging another group of undernourished, miserable-looking prisoners to move onwards. Each of the captives was nude.

May 25, 1963

"Those prisoners in the concentration camp are no longer fit to work. The soldier is making them march to the edge of a big pit where they will be shot and pushed in."

"Do they know that's where they're being taken?"

"Of course. The camp prisoners, the ones who were strong enough, were forced to dig the pit themselves. Every week the ones who were not able to work as hard as the soldiers insisted were taken to the pit and executed. Those men knew exactly what was going to happen."

"This picture is a..." Henry paused, groping for the right word, "...a *reenactment* of what happened at the concentration camp. It's not a photo that was taken when this was actually happening." He was making a statement of fact.

"No!" Irwin exclaimed. "These are not actors! The arrogant Nazis were *proud* of what they were doing! They did not mind that their evil was recorded on film."

"You mean this is a photo of what you were talking about *while it was actually happening*, and a minute after this picture was snapped all these people were dead, lying at the bottom of a big mass grave, and they *knew* they were going to be killed?"

"It was a horrible, evil thing the Nazis did," Irwin said slowly.

"I know, but...that's not what I meant. These German soldiers..." Henry said, pointing at the pictures, "...none of their guns are loaded."

"*What?*" Irwin Mann was startled at how loudly he had spoken, and realized he must not have heard the boy correctly. "I'm sorry—what did you say?"

"None of the soldiers' guns are loaded, Mr. Mann. Look." Henry was pointing to the soldier with the 98 Mauser slung over his shoulder. "You can see the cocking piece at the back of the bolt. It's in the down position. That means the firing pin's down. It hasn't been cocked. No one carries a rifle with a round in the chamber and the firing pin down. Even if he did, he'd still have to operate the bolt to cock the striker before he could fire the rifle, just the same as if the chamber was empty." Henry jumped up. "Here. Let me show you."

Henry Bowman retrieved his Mauser and brought it back to where Irwin was seated. He opened the bolt and made sure the gun was empty, then closed it again. "See how the cocking piece here sticks out a half-inch?" he said, pointing. Irwin Mann nodded dumbly. "The gun is ready to shoot." He pulled the trigger and the firing pin fell with a sharp metallic sound. "Look at the picture again. The rifle's cocking piece is down, just like this one is now." Irwin Mann saw that the cocking piece on the rifle in the photograph was down, just like the one on the gun Henry Bowman held in his hands.

Henry continued, unaware of the expression on the older man's face. "And he's got his rifle slung upside down over his shoulder, and the people he's supposed to be guarding are only a few feet away. There's no way he could get that rifle unslung and rack the bolt before all those men were on top of him, if they wanted to be." He turned the page.

"And look here. This Luger the soldier's pointing at the men that are about to be executed." Henry pointed to the pistol which was in perfect profile to the camera. "Lugers have a loaded-round indicator that tells you if there's a round in the chamber. It sticks up about an eighth of an inch, and lies flat if the chamber's empty. It's not sticking up in this picture, and you said these men were going to be shot in about a minute." All of a sudden Henry thought of something.

"There must be other soldiers we can't see that are out of the picture, holding loaded guns on the men that are about to be executed, and that's why the prisoners didn't jump the guard and take his pistol."

"Maybe," Irwin said bleakly, but he knew there were no unseen soldiers backing up the guard in the photo. All of a sudden he remembered opening the captured Mauser rifle for the first time and seeing the magazine full of cartridges. *But the chamber had been empty!* he realized with a shock. *The Jews had no will to resist, and the Nazis knew it.* Irwin Mann noticed he was trembling. Henry did not notice this, for he was turning the pages, looking for other pictures.

"Look, here's a soldier with a broomhandle Mauser machine pistol in 7.63mm, with a 20-round magazine," Henry said, squinting at the photograph. "I read somewhere that that was Winston Churchill's favorite pistol," he added irrelevantly. "Must never have got his hands on an N-frame Smith & Wesson," Henry muttered under his breath. He turned his attention back to the photo. "Anyway, see how this pistol has an exposed hammer, and it's in the 'down' position? This gun doesn't have a round in the chamber either. That soldier'd have to rack the slide back and release it before he could fire the gun."

Henry moved his finger over on the photo. "And look at *this* guy. See the MP40 submachine gun he's carrying?" Irwin Mann nodded. It was the weapon that he had thought of when Henry was doing rapid fire with his revolver. "That gun fires from an open bolt. The bolt has to be held back under spring tension before you can pull the trigger and make it go off. See how the bolt handle is all the way forward? That gun's not ready to fire either. And the stock is folded. The only time you should fold the stock on a gun is when you're storing it, or packing it away someplace where space is critical, like for a parachute jump."

Henry and Irwin looked through the book for other concentration camp photos. In every picture where the soldiers' guns were plainly visible, not one weapon was ready to fire.

"Would many people notice this fact, as you have?" Irwin asked finally.

"Anyone with any knowledge of guns. My Uncle Max, for sure, and I imagine most of the people out at the rifle and pistol range. Some shotgun shooters don't know a thing about rifles and pistols, and not every shooter has read up on machine guns like I have, but yes, most shooters I know would notice that the guns weren't ready to fire."

If only we had had but one ten-year-old boy like this one twenty years ago thought Irwin Mann. *Many more of us would now be alive.*

"Henry," Irwin said finally, "I hope that you never lose interest in your shooting skills. If we had had a few less doctors and musicians in 1940, and a few more boys like you, perhaps what you see in these photos might not have been possible." Irwin Mann took a deep breath. "But Hitler and his brownshirts did not allow Jews like me to have guns."

"It's kind of the same way around here, but with Negroes," Henry replied, remembering what Al Goodman had told him.

Irwin talked to Henry a while longer, and then the two sat in contemplative silence for a few minutes. Walter Bowman was still down on the riverbank, taking pictures. He had intuited that Irwin Mann had wanted to say some things to his son.

Henry Bowman looked up at his guest, as if he had just remembered something.

"Here, show me what you can do with a revolver," the boy said, opening the cylinder of his K-22 and handing it to Irwin Mann.

***

On the drive home, Walter commented on Irwin's shooting and asked their guest if he had enjoyed himself. Irwin Mann answered mechanically, for his thoughts were on what he had seen and the things he had learned from the young boy. He felt a growing sense of shame at what he and his countrymen had allowed to happen a generation before on the other side of the globe. Finally, he wrenched himself out of this train of thought and recalled something Henry had said after lunch.

"Henry, what is an N-frame Smith & Wesson?"

"Oh, that's the biggest of the three frame sizes they make. They use special steels and heat-treat them so they're really strong for the .357 and .44 Magnum calibers. Ed McGivern shot at paper targets out in Montana with a long-barreled .357 Smith in 1937, and he proved you could hit a man-sized target at 600 yards with one, using a rest and good ammo. Uncle Max has one, and he lets me shoot it. He gave me his lead furnace, bullet molds, and loading tools, and he buys the powder, primers, and lead alloy. I load all our .357 ammo, and he lets me borrow his gun." Henry did not know it, but the boy and his uncle each viewed themselves as getting the better deal.

"Is the .357 the most accurate caliber?"

"From a rest, I can hit a coffee can at over a hundred yards every shot with a .357, but I understand the .44 magnum is even better. Big revolver bullets aren't as affected by slight imperfections as smaller ones are, and don't get deformed as much in firing. It's easier to shoot really tight groups with the .44." Henry hesitated a moment and then added, "At least, that's what all the recent testing I've read says. The .44 Magnum didn't exist in the 'thirties when Ed McGivern was doing his tests—it came out about seven years ago. Smith & Wesson doesn't make very many of them. I've only seen one in my whole life." Walter Bowman smiled at the last comment, in light of the fact that it was coming from a ten-year-old.

Irwin Mann remained silent. He was thinking of something he was going to ask Max Collins the next time he saw him.

***

"Dad, while you were taking pictures after we had lunch, Mr. Mann was telling me about what happened to him during the war." Henry and his father were down in the workshop, where Henry was cleaning his guns. Walter Bowman looked up at his son.

"Hm." Walter had never heard of Irwin Mann talking about that part of his past.

"He was telling me about how the police came and took him and his wife away, and he never saw her or any of his family again. He said that Hitler killed six million Jews like him, and would have killed all of them if the Americans hadn't fought against the Germans and beat them."

"That's probably true."

"He talked about how none of them had any way to fight back. He said first the police took away the guns that were like the ones the soldiers used, then they took away *all* their guns. He said he hoped I was always a good shot with as many kinds of guns as possible, in case the same thing ever happened here." Henry looked very upset. "Dad, I love shooting, but I don't want to kill anyone. Could something like what happened in Germany ever happen here?" he asked.

Walter Bowman, the history teacher, looked his son in the eye. *Want to take this question for me, Uncle Cam?* he said silently. Finally he answered.

"It probably won't happen here," he said, and mentally added the word *again*. "I certainly pray that it doesn't. We have a nation with the kind of freedoms that people in most other countries can only dream of. But to answer your question accurately, yes, it *could* happen here." *And it killed your uncle.*

"There are always men who want more and more power, and history has shown us that these kind of men will take all they can from the people they control. Sometimes they are finally stopped when the people fight back. Sometimes the people don't fight back, and they slowly lose their freedoms until it's too late.

"You know about the six million Jews being killed by Hitler and his police, because people talk about it. There have been many other examples of the same kind of thing, but they don't get discussed as much, for one reason or another."

"What do you mean?" Henry asked. He had stopped cleaning his 98 Mauser, and was hanging on his father's words.

"Russians, for one. Josef Stalin murdered twenty million of his own people fifteen years before World War Two, to make sure that the rest of the population would obey his will." Henry's eyes were big as he listened to what Walter said. "A few years before that, it was Armenians that were slaughtered by the Turks, in 1915. After World War II, the Chinese government murdered millions of its people, one big batch starting in the late '40s and another starting ten years later. I hear it's starting again."

Walter Bowman was unaware that over the next ten years, Mao Tse-Tung would up the ante by systematically slaughtering twenty million of his own people. This would equal Stalin's record but would be accomplished in a much shorter period of time. He also did not know of the coming genocides in other countries.

"I know you love shooting just for the pleasure it gives you. Ever since I was your age, I've been the same way about flying. I've never wanted to kill another person, and thank God I've never had to.

"But during the war, I taught hundreds of other men to fly well enough so that they could go into combat in the air, shoot down enemy fighters, and destroy targets on the ground. Those skills I learned just for the pure pleasure of it became very valuable to people's freedom, but in the course of it, a lot of people were killed.

"I really don't think you should worry about America turning into Nazi Germany, Henry," Walter Bowman said, but his face looked worried nonetheless. "At least not...not today." *Wonder what my Uncle Cameron would think if he were alive to hear me say that.* Walter licked his lips and was about to continue, but his son interrupted him.

"What's the matter, Dad?" Walter Bowman squinted, then nodded his head as he came to a decision.

"Son, I think it's time I told you about what happened to your Grandpa Mike's brother, Uncle Cameron Bowman, a little over thirty years ago, when I was a few years older than you are right now. He'd be your great-uncle, if he were still alive today.

"When he was a young man, in 1917 and 1918, he served in the Army in World War One, just like I served in the Navy in World War Two. Except when I was in the war, I stayed in this country and trained pilots on a Naval air base in Florida. Uncle Cam was in the infantry, and he got sent overseas. They sent him into combat in France, where German soldiers were shooting at him with rifles just like that one there." Henry looked at his Mauser as if it were a rattlesnake, and Walter chuckled in spite of the nature of the conversation.

"Don't look that way; he never got wounded, and he brought back some German guns for your Grandpa Mike. One of them was like that one of yours, but with a longer barrel."

"It was the standard rifle, not a carbine like mine."

"Right. Dad sold it—or gave it away, I don't know which—after Uncle Cam died. Dad said Uncle Cam always told him the Enfield was a better rifle than the Mauser."

Henry nodded.

"It is. It's stronger, and the bolt lugs are a true interrupted thread, so the Enfield will chamber dented or bent rounds when the Mauser won't."

"Then why do you have a Mauser?" Walter asked, allowing himself to get off the subject.

"Ammo's cheaper."

Walter Bowman nodded as he looked at his son, and then said something that had crossed his mind off and on for several years.

"I wish to hell Uncle Cam was still alive to see you, Henry. I've always thought you had some of his blood in you, and today reminded me of it all the more." He took a deep breath and resumed the story of his dead uncle.

"Anyway, your Great-Uncle Cam had a small farm in the western part of this state, and in 1931, he got too far into debt, and he couldn't pay back the bank that had lent him money, so he had to give them his farm instead."

"He couldn't sell the farm first, and then pay them?"

"No, lots of people had the same problem, and nobody wanted to buy his farm for as much money as he owed the bank. The bank took the farm, but they couldn't get much for it, so they lost a lot of money, too. There were other people, not just Uncle Cam, that they had lent money to who couldn't pay it back. So the bank ended up with a bunch of farms like Uncle Cam's, and when they finally sold them, the price was very low, and they lost so much money that they went out of business too. It was a bad deal for everyone.

"So your Great-Uncle Cam was broke, and he'd lost his house and property, but he had been a soldier in the war, and the government had promised that they'd give every soldier a bonus depending on how many days he'd served. In Uncle Cam's case, I think the bonus was five or six hundred dollars, which was a tremendous amount of money thirty years ago when the country was in the middle of a terrible depression and many people had no jobs.

"The problem was, the total amount the government had said they'd pay all the soldiers was over three *billion* dollars. The government had promised this money—and they *were* going to pay it, there was no doubt of that—but the agreement was that they were going to pay it in 1945, and that—"

"They were going to pay the money at the end of World War Two?" Henry broke in.

"Well, yes," Walter said, suppressing a smile, "but in 1918 no one knew then that there was going to *be* a World War Two. At that time, 1945 was just a date in the future."

"Oh. Right." Henry felt like an idiot.

"Anyway," Walter continued, "1945 was twenty-seven years after the end of the war these veterans had fought. Now it was 1931, the bonus was still fourteen years away, and fourteen more years might as well have been forever if you were someone who had lost his house and had no job.

"So in 1932, a bunch of veterans went to Washington to try to convince the government to pay them early. They jumped onto freight cars that were heading east, they packed into old trucks and marched through towns where people gave them coins so they could buy gas, and some of them even walked to Washington."

"Grandpa Mike's brother was one of them?"

"Exactly. He was one of the Bonus Marchers, or Bonus Army, as they were called then, and he got to Washington, D.C in...May, I think it was, of that year."

Walter Bowman proceeded to tell his son about all that had happened those two months in the spring and summer of 1932, when he himself had been fifteen years old. Henry listened raptly as his father described the events of that tragic period in history, and of how his father and his grandparents had read about them as the story had unfolded in newspapers and radio broadcasts across the country.

"Hoover wanted the 'Death March' to end, and he told General MacArthur to clear the Bonus Army out of the area around the Capitol. MacArthur's men did this by using tear gas, cavalry, and tanks. Then they set fire to the shacks that were there, so that the marchers wouldn't come back into the city. All that was bad enough, but it was what they did next that people remember most. There's also some argument about just who was responsible for what was about to come.

"Some people say that General MacArthur followed President Hoover's direct order, and some say he acted on his own. Hoover always took full blame for what happened that night, so it could be either." He took a deep breath.

"There's no doubt in my mind that Hoover ordered the Army to clear the veterans away from the Capitol building. But from what I've read and what I believe about the men involved, I think what MacArthur did next was exactly what the President told him *not* to do. The President took the blame, and he was *right* to take the blame, because the President is ultimately the one in charge, even if something bad happens because a General disobeys him." Walter went on.

"What happened next was, in the middle of the night, General MacArthur and Majors Patton and Eisenhower—"

"Was Major Eisenhower related to *President* Eisenhower?" Henry broke in. "I mean—was he related to the man who..." (he was about to say 'turned into') "became President Eisenhower?"

"Major Eisenhower was the man who became President Eisenhower," Walter explained, to Henry's amazement.

"So," Walter Bowman continued, "General MacArthur, and Major Patton, who would become the very famous General Patton and lead troops in World War Two, and Major Eisenhower, who would become General Eisenhower and then President Eisenhower, these three officers led the army across the river, pursuing the veterans they had driven away from the area around the Capitol building. They followed the veterans into their camp outside of the city. There were twenty thousand ex-soldiers camped there, and about six hundred wives and children were there with them."

"What did the soldiers do?" Henry asked. Walter Bowman looked his ten-year-old son in the eye.

"They fired their guns, and then they set fire to every piece of wood or cardboard there and burned the entire camp to the ground." Henry was speechless. Walter dropped his gaze and went on. "Not everyone got out alive. No one ever knew for sure how many were killed, though. Many of the veterans had separated from their families, and had nobody to ask about them."

Henry found his voice, and asked "Did your uncle die?" Walter ran his hand along the edge of the workbench and looked off towards the scroll saw in the corner of the shop before he answered.

"Not right away. Uncle Cam was burned pretty badly in the fire. He tried to make it back here to Missouri, but he had been one of the men marching near the Capitol building, and he'd gotten his wrist—or maybe it was his arm, I'm not sure which—broken by one of the horse soldiers before the Army crossed the river and burned the veterans out of their camp.

"The break was a bad one, and there was no one to tend to it, or to dress his burns properly either, and I'm not even sure it would have done any good. Burns make it easy for infection to set in, and that's what happened to my uncle. A doctor in a VA hospital in Pennsylvania amputated Uncle Cam's entire left arm, but it was too late. Dad—Grandpa Mike—took a train to Reading, and Uncle Cam held out until he got there. Dad talked to him, and then Uncle Cam died.

"Dad brought the body home and we buried him. The last time I ever saw him alive was that day in May when he hooked up with some fellows from Arizona and headed for Washington." He shook his head and forced a smile.

"That was a terrible thing, Henry, but we all knew it was a terrible thing, and the President admitted it was a terrible thing, and admitted it was his fault, and in six months, the President was voted out of office and the country had a new President," his father explained. *Who proceeded to seize even more power for the Federal Government, strip citizens of their civil rights, and do it with the peoples' own money* he added silently. Then Walter Bowman banished that course of thought from his mind and went on.

"Our Constitution and the Bill of Rights—the rules our government has to obey— were written by some very wise gentlemen who had just finished going through something very much like what Mr. Mann went through twenty years ago. Those men wrote the Constitution and the Bill of Rights to see to it that what happened to them and what happened to Mr. Mann doesn't ever happen again in this country.

"They spelled out all the things that free men have merely by being alive: the freedom to read and say what they believe, to worship in whatever way they wish, and to be free from having the police come take their property and throw them in jail without following due process of law. The men who founded our country also reminded the government, in the second article in the Bill of Rights, that free men have the right to own and carry the very same kind of weapons carried by soldiers in a modern army of the period. That put teeth in all the other promises—it guaranteed those rights by making sure all the people could fight back. That was something Mr. Mann and his family couldn't do.

"The system of government those men laid out in 1789 has worked very well for a long time—better and longer than just about any other system in any country on earth. Yes, it broke down for my uncle, and I'll never forget that.

"But what happened to my uncle wasn't the first or the last time the government ignored the rights of our citizens. You and I have talked before about how bigoted people can decide a certain group is inferior and should be treated differently, and that can be just as wrong as what the army did to my uncle. But that's finally changing. Our President has said in plain terms he intends to make discrimination illegal, and I think he means it.

"But if everything does go to hell in a handbasket here, the police start searching people's houses, seizing their property, holding citizens without bond, or trying to burn them alive—and particularly if the government starts trying to keep honest people from having guns to defend their freedoms, then Mr. Mann is dead right: the country is going to need young men with your skills to stand up to the storm troopers that want to crush them, just like it needed them almost two hundred years ago." Walter Bowman saw the worried look on his son's face, and went on.

"I think things are getting *better* in this country, Henry, not worse. By the time you're in high school, I truly believe it will be a lot different. Segregated movie theaters and restaurants, and shaking down Negroes for weapons? Those things will be just embarrassing memories that most people would like to forget." *This is turning into rather more than I had intended* he thought to himself, and decided to change the subject.

"Hey, I've been thinking about that target rig you want to have built, the one you were telling Mr. Mann about this morning. I hadn't realized how good you'd become with a rifle. You deserve good equipment, so I'll make you a deal: You save up the money for the receiver—a Remington, you said?—and I'll take care of the barrel and the scope. If you need any help making the stock, I'll pitch in there, too. Sound fair?"

"Does it ever!"

"Good. You finish cleaning your guns, then get upstairs to your bathroom and clean yourself. If we've got time before supper, I'll play a game of acey-deucey with you."

"I'll be done in a few minutes, Dad. Thanks," Henry said with a big smile as he hugged his father. Then he looked up. His face had a puzzled expression. "Dad?"

"What, Son?"

"I understand why the government didn't want to pay the money to the men in 1932, because they had to pay for so many other things that year, and they couldn't spend money if they didn't have it. But, when your Uncle Cam lost his farm, were there any people who had money? I mean, pretty much of it? People that were almost rich?"

"Oh, sure, there were still rich people in the country. But my uncle wouldn't have asked them for charity, Henry. He was a very proud man, and he felt very strongly that since the government had promised him his war bonus, it was the government that should help him when he had nothing. One of the senators tried to get the Congress to agree to pay the veterans a smaller amount of money right away instead of the full amount thirteen years later, but Congress said no."

"But the government probably didn't have that money either," Henry said. "You said even the banks were going out of business. The government didn't have even part of the three billion dollars saved up like they would in 1945—it was too early."

Walter smiled kindly at his son. "I guess my uncle still didn't want to go begging."

"No," Henry persisted, "I mean, if there were rich people around, why couldn't one of them pay your uncle some money, and then the government could give the rich man your uncle's bonus in 1945? If Uncle Cam was going to get five hundred dollars in 1945, and he needed money in 1932, why wouldn't a rich man give him...three hundred dollars, and get five hundred later? Uncle Cam would have done that instead of going to Washington and living outside for two months and having soldiers try to burn him up, wouldn't he?"

Good question Walter thought immediately. "Well...I guess there wasn't any way to transfer the bonus rights..." *That's a pretty lame answer* Walter said to himself.

"Why not? Couldn't the government give the veterans pieces of paper that said (here he lowered his voice) 'This is Mister Bowman's bo—'"

"Lieutenant."

"What?" Henry asked. His father was smiling at him.

"He was a Lieutenant in the Army, not a 'Mister'."

"Oh." He pressed on. "Couldn't they have printed up a piece of paper that said 'This is Lieutenant Bowman's bonus of five hundred dollars but we will pay it to anyone who turns in this piece of paper in 1945'? Then he could have sold it, and so could the other soldiers, and they could have had some money, and the government wouldn't have had to try to kill them to make them leave."

"That's a good question, Henry, and I don't know the answer." *Except that a free-market answer was much too sensible for the stupid cocksuckers* he added silently, then immediately felt ashamed. Walter Bowman rarely swore, even mentally. "They just didn't do it, that's all. Go on, dinner's going to be ready soon."

Walter Bowman left the shop and climbed the basement stairs to the kitchen. *Jesus! Ten years old, he's worrying about having to kill people, and I cheer him up by telling him how our government tried to burn his great-uncle alive* Walter thought. *Good thing he's too young for this mess in Southeast Asia. That's where the trouble is now, not here in the United States.*

Walter Bowman had a great knowledge of history, but he was ignorant of the existence of the obscure National Firearms Act of 1934. He also had no idea of the next piece of national legislation concerning firearms that would be written into law. It would be passed in five years, during a time of great upheaval in the country. Walter Bowman would never know of it, however. During the time of the initial discussion of the proposed legislative measure, doctors would discover that Walter Bowman had renal cancer.

By the time Lyndon Johnson signed the Gun Control Act of 1968 into law, Walter Bowman would have been dead for almost a year.

May 27, 1963

When Ames MacKinnon III walked into Raymond Johnson's office at Lambert, Burns, he did not immediately notice the items Raymond had placed strategically in various parts of the room. He was chastising himself for almost losing his last temper at their last meeting. He was determined not to let it happen again.

"Ray, good to see you. Listen, I don't have a lot of time, but I want you to know that Allied is prepared to take care of your man." Raymond noted that Pedro Gutierrez was no longer 'The Mexican'.

"They want to make sure that his daughter is set up with long-term care, and that his wife gets top-flight medical treatment. To that end, they've authorized me to make a very generous cash offer. Contingent, of course, upon the usual terms of confidentiality."

"Just how 'generous' is this cash offer?"

"Five hundred thousand dollars. I must caution you, though," Ames added quickly, "that this offer is as large as it is because Allied wants to put this unfortunate incident behind them and get on with their business. In light of that, the offer is good only until noon tomorrow."

Raymond nodded. "I can see how Allied Chemical would want to put this—as you call it— 'unfortunate incident' behind them, so that they can get on with selling their company to Becker AG." He turned and faced towards the large window that overlooked Manhattan. "Tell me, Ames, have you any idea how much each member of the board of directors is going to be putting in his checking account as a result of this Becker deal? It's all cash, remember. No stock swap."

"I don't know how many shares each board member holds, so no, I don't," he lied.

"Ellison's low man on the totem pole with a little over eighteen thousand shares. With options, Hatcher's got almost a quarter million. The others all fall between those figures. When Becker cuts their check for forty-nine dollars per share, there are going to be some very happy former directors of Allied Chemical. *If* Becker cuts the check." MacKinnon said nothing, waiting for Raymond to continue.

"Your half million dollar offer is chump change, and not only because it's tiny in relation to what's at stake here. After legal fees, my client would have less than three hundred fifty thousand dollars. At a four percent after-tax yield, that's about thirteen thousand dollars a year to provide medicine, rehabilitation, and nursing care for a blind, brain-damaged girl who had her fourth birthday last week, and a sick woman of thirty-two.

"I'm not sure that thirteen thousand dollars would cover the kind of annual costs we're talking about for 1963 alone. Mrs. Gutierrez could easily survive to see her fiftieth birthday. Given that the daughter's heart and respiratory system seem to be in good order, it is entirely possible that she could live well into the next century. In sixty years, I think a thirteen thousand dollar stipend for full-time care will look like an absolute pittance." Raymond picked up one of the two cans that were sitting on his credenza and examined it. The can he held in his hand was brand new. The one remaining on the credenza was much older, slightly dented, and its label was faded and peeling off in spots. The labels on both cans were sky blue.

"Mr. Hatcher's twelve million dollar nest egg, on the other hand, will have grown into something truly impressive, barring massive ineptitude on the part of his heirs."

"Just what are you saying?"

Raymond set the can down on top of a photo on his desk and faced the other lawyer.

"What I'm saying is that your offer is neither generous, nor fair, nor acceptable. Given what Allied Chemical knowingly did to a pregnant employee, five hundred thousand dollars is an absolute insult. Allied is obviously trying to get out of their obligation. I've been doing a little figuring, and five hundred thousand dollars is less than what the company earns in *two days*."

Suddenly the intercom crackled. "Mr. Johnson, I'm sorry, but it's a Mr. Morris from the New York Times. He's sitting here and he says he won't leave until he gets a statement on the Allied case."

Raymond pressed the button and spoke immediately. "Tell him I can see him at four o'clock. He can wait there all day if he wants, but if he wants a statement before four, tell him it's 'no comment'."

"He says that's fine, Mr. Johnson. He'll be back at four."

Ames MacKinnon III looked decidedly upset. "You can't be talking to the papers on this! We're trying to work with you! If this goes in front of a jury, you know full well you might get nothing at all." Saying the words calmed him, and MacKinnon regained his composure. It was not for long, however.

"Ames, I can do anything I want, just like you can come in here and offer my client pin money for a daughter with brain damage and no eyes. I've been doing my research, and every layer I peel off this onion makes it smell worse to me." He handed the man the quart can that sat on his desk. "Recognize that?"

MacKinnon looked at the label. He saw that he was holding a can of weed-killing powder. **HERBAMAX**, it was called. As he looked at the fine print on the label, he realized it was manufactured in Germany by Becker AG. "Becker's import for the U.S. market," he said, making a statement of fact.

Instinctively MacKinnon's eyes went to the second, older can that remained on Raymond's credenza, and he stepped over to inspect it. When he picked it up, he could tell by its weight that it was empty. The label was faded, but appeared to have once been the same shade of blue as the new can of weed killer. All printing on the old can was in German, but the layout was very similar. The part of the label where the manufacturer's name would be was torn off, but part of the address remained. It was the same town as the one printed on the new can. Up at the top was the product's name:

ZYKLON-B.

"Old can of home-market weed killer?" MacKinnon asked. Raymond reflected upon the question.

"They might have considered it that, I suppose." He handed the lawyer the photo on his desk. It was a blurred picture of a room filled with a tangle of nude bodies, hundreds of them, intertwined together in the rictus of death. "Seemed to work well enough." MacKinnon set the can down immediately and stared at Raymond. The younger man cut him off before he could speak.

"Ames, don't waste your time lecturing me about what I can or can't say in court. That's not what you should be worried about right now. I think the *Times* has got a whiff of this. They didn't get it from me, but there are some Jewish secretaries in this office. I can't think of any other particular reason for one of their reporters to try to camp out in our reception area." Raymond could see that his words had visibly shaken the other man.

"You have until four o'clock to come back with a cashier's check in the appropriate amount. If I do not have it by then, Mr. Morris gets his story, Becker gets to look for buying opportunities elsewhere, people who want to buy Allied stock get to purchase it for about twelve dollars less per share, and we get the pleasure of trying to find twelve jurors who haven't read about the U.S. company who tried to sell out to the German chemical factory that made the compound Hitler used to execute over six million people.

"If, on the other hand, I find you on the other side of that door when I open it at four o'clock, and you are holding in your hand a check for the proper amount, then my client gets to take care of his family, Mr. Morris gets to look for other stories, my firm gets to pat me on the back for a job well done, and you get the undying gratitude of the Allied board and all the other shareholders, whom you will have collectively saved over fifty million dollars in market value by averting the tragedy of having their stock return to its pre-buyout level of two months ago."

Ames MacKinnon III finally found his voice. "And what is the 'correct amount'?" He had a dismal feeling Raymond was going to laugh at him and demand ten million dollars.

"Until four o'clock, Allied gets a thirty percent discount. Seven million dollars. After four, we're back up to a full ten or let a jury decide. No counteroffers."

"I shall relay the message." MacKinnon left without another word.

Two minutes later the receptionist came in, looking very anxious. "Was I all right, Mr. Johnson? Did I buzz you at the right time, and everything?"

"You did fine, Maggie. Just fine. You can go on back to your desk."

Raymond picked up the empty can from his credenza and looked at it. Two days before it had been full of clear lacquer, sitting on the shelf of a hardware store. He stared at the faded label and recalled the odd look the printer had given him until he had explained that a stage manager cannot afford to lose his job just because some fool unwittingly throws away one of the props for the second act of the production.

Now we wait for four o'clock Raymond thought as he sat down and let his heart rate slowly return to normal.

May 28, 1963

In the sixteen hours since Ames MacKinnon III had grimly delivered the largest check he had ever held in his hand, word of the huge settlement had spread like a brush fire through the New York legal community. Raymond Johnson did his best to keep a straight face as he sat down at the conference table for the morning meeting. Every person the office had been staring at him from the moment he had come in to work that morning. Jacob Burns called the meeting to order.

"It appears that our newest associate has shown his mettle in an area heretofore untapped by this firm." He smiled broadly at the group. "Our bottom line is certainly looking better than it ever has, and for that we have Raymond to thank." Ray Johnson kept a neutral expression on his face, but inwardly his stomach was churning. He glanced around the table, and saw that everyone was smiling at him. Everyone except Arthur Lambert, who had a thoughtful expression on his face, and appeared about to speak.

"That's not quite right, Jake," Lambert said to his partner. "Lambert, Burns' bottom line looks exactly the same as it did two days ago. That was Raymond's case, not the firm's."

"What?"

"You heard me, and there'll be no argument. Raymond came to me before he took the case, to get my approval. I gave that approval, and when he asked what the sharing arrangement with the firm would be, I told him it was his case, provided he did not short us any hours. He said he would give up vacation days if necessary. Raymond kept his end of the bargain, and the firm is going to keep theirs."

"But he didn't tell you that the case was going to be worth over two million dollars to us!"

"No, and if he had, I would have laughed at him and given him the same terms. Raymond could not have known himself, at that time. I will resign as senior partner of this firm before I will renege on a verbal contract." Arthur Lambert could see that this did not please the other man, but there was no reply.

"Don't look so mad, Jake," Lambert continued with a grin. "You've still got more money than the new kid." This brought some genuine laughter from the others around the table. "Besides, aren't you always talking about how our reputation is our biggest asset?" Lambert raised his eyebrows. "Think of what it's doing for our reputation, Jake. To have a first-year associate of ours nick the company that rejected us as counsel for seven million dollars."

"The settlement was confidential—" Raymond started to say. Both senior partners fixed him with looks that told him it was the first stupid statement he had uttered in their presence. Jake Burns spoke, and a smile was starting at the corners of his mouth.

"It'll never make the papers, but you can be damn sure the real players in this town already knew the exact figure before you went to bed last night, Ray. Speaking of confidentiality, it's going to grate on you every time someone talks about the largest award that you have to keep your mouth shut. Which you're going to *have* to do. No *Guinness Book of World Records* listing for you on this one, Ray."

"I'll be sobbing all the way to the bank," he said.

"Got it all spent already, I suppose?"

Raymond laughed. "Not quite. But I do have some plans for a small part of it. I guess this is as good a time as any to bring it up—I'm going to be taking a leave of absence. There's something I've wanted to do all my life, and if I don't do it now, I'm worried that I'll never get around to it. It will require my being gone for about six weeks, and the best time for me to leave would be in about a month." He looked at Arthur Lambert. "Since you were so generous before, I'll let you set the terms. If you decide the firm should dock me a year's salary, I'll go along with your decision."

"Where on earth could you go for six weeks that would be worth a year's salary to you?" Jake Burns asked. Arthur Lambert knew the answer to the partner's question before Raymond replied. Lambert had already decided that Raymond could have his leave of absence, for six weeks or however long it turned out to be, without pay for the time he was away, but with insurance and other benefits.

Ray Johnson smiled as his eyes focused off in the distance and he imagined the butt of his .600 Holland slamming into his right shoulder.

"Africa," was all he said.

"You got that look in your eye. Tell me you're heading to Africa. If you aren't, then lie to me and say you are."

"I'm going to Kenya in about six weeks, Tony. No lie. Five week hunt."

"Hot damn! That's great news! Your bosses give you any shit, particularly since they didn't get any of the loot?" Tony Kearns asked his friend.

Raymond shook his head. "I told them it was important to me, and I'd forfeit a whole year's salary if that's what it took. They said no pay while I'm gone, but with benefits in place."

"You must live right." Tony Kearns changed the subject. "You're going to get hammered on taxes, I guess."

"That's one of the things I wanted to talk to you about before I left. I've set things up so that Allied's insurance underwriter pays both the Gutierrez family and me over a five-year period. That will reduce the chance that they'll run through the money right away, and cut my tax bill some also. Both the family and I are going to need some solid direction as to where to put the money. Your advice has been spot-on so far. What do you recommend?"

Tony Kearns took a deep breath. "First off, although it's not my specific department, I'm not ashamed to say I'm at least as good as any of the advisors you're apt to come across, and a hell of a lot better than most.

"Second, for two accounts totalling a few million bucks, White, Weld will definitely let me handle them without whining about wasting my time, if you and your clients decide you want to work with me."

"Since it's a lot of money, I was just going to put it in Treasury bills for the time being."

"In your own personal case, that's okay *if* you have a definite plan for investing the money somewhere else in the future. What is likely to happen though, is that you'll just leave the money there. T-bills are about the worst long-term investment you could make.

"For your client, that goes double. If four million bucks sits there in cash, I guarantee you it will be burning a hole in the guy's pocket, and in two years that money will be gone. I don't say that because he's a janitor, or comes from south of the border, or anything like that. This is your buddy Tony talking, the guy who spends his days watching big companies buy up littler ones.

"Whenever one of the sellers gets a big wad of cash, not stock in the new company, nine times out of ten it's gone in two years. And these are guys who built successful, thriving enterprises from scratch. If you aren't used to handling serious dough in big chunks all at once, you will lose it. And you'll lose it faster than you ever dreamed possible."

"So what do you recommend?"

"For the janitor and his family, get them set up so they get a steady and increasing stream of income for life, but the principal, or at least a big chunk of it, can't be touched. The first idea that comes to mind is a life annuity with an insurance company. For an upfront payment, an insurance company will guarantee monthly payments for life. If you die tomorrow, they win big. If you live to be 100, you come out like a hero. Either way, the customer can't do something stupid and lose all his money while he's alive. For people with health problems, the income stream is very high since payments are based on life expectancy.

"For you, you've got no dependents and are earning a bunch every year. That's a snap. Stay out of bonds or T-bills and put together a portfolio that will grow. There are equity managers who have maybe one down year out of ten, and average about double what bonds pay.

"Ray, no one ever got rich by lending his money out at four or five percent, or buying something that just holds its value. People get rich by being able to create their own wealth. You stick your money in the bank, it grows a little but you pay taxes on it, where have you gone? Nowhere. You're marching in place.

"Say you buy an apartment building or some other hard asset like a piece of real estate. Sure the rents can go up with inflation, and so can the market value, but again, you're not really getting anywhere. You get more in rent, but everything you buy costs more, too. What you'd *really* like is to somehow be able to put three, four, five times as many people in the building without having to spend any more money for land or construction, and that's not possible."

"What are you saying?"

"You, Raymond Johnson, will make more than ten times the money this year than you ever have in the past. Did you work ten times the hours? Are there ten of you now, when there was only one a few years ago? Has inflation gone up so that the things people bought in '61 now cost ten times as much? Hell, no. Your talents and abilities, and your marketing of them, have improved tenfold, that's all. You have the ability to create and increase your own wealth. That's something that no bond, or T-bill, or savings account, or apartment building, or bar of gold, or Rembrandt painting can ever do.

"Your janitor's family should invest for income because they have to. You don't. You'd still be making a decent living if you'd tried that case and lost. So don't get in the rut of putting your money in the bank and watching it grow more slowly than rising prices. Hell, keep some of it ready for safaris and stuff like that, but put the rest to work in the same way you work: creating increasing wealth without an upper limit.

"That means ownership of growing companies. Companies that are adding new products to their lines and are the dominant producers in industries that supply products to expanding markets. Companies that have patent protection on essential goods and services—drug companies come to mind—or ones that have a hammerlock on some other competitive advantage. Preferably bought at depressed prices because of temporary bad news," he added as an afterthought.

"Go on."

"Ideally, Ray, you should of course be diversified, but you should also set things up so you don't have to pay taxes on your earnings before you take 'em out and spend 'em just because your money's been growing. Assets get big a lot faster than you'd think when you let them compound without pulling money out every year for taxes.

"Also, the fact that you're getting paid in five installments is very good. It will let you invest a fixed dollar amount every quarter. That will automatically force you to buy less when the price is up, and more when the price is down. That's the way everyone operates at the department store, but for some crazy reason they abandon this winning strategy when it comes to investing their money."

"Let me get you the exact numbers, and maybe you can put together a proposal for both the Gutierrez family and for my own account."

"Sounds good to me. I may even get a chance to make a few dollars in the bargain."

"Let me call you tomorrow. Right now I've got to run an errand or two." *I've got a little surprise in store for you, Tony.*

"Will do. And let's hit the dump one more time before you ship off for Africa."

"You got it." Raymond said with a quick nod. He stood and turned to walk away.

Kearns didn't know it, but Ray Johnson was heading to a familiar address on Broadway.

***

"Morning, Ray."

"Good morning, Jim. I can't stay long, but I need a rifle."

"Well, I think you've pretty much seen what's in the rack right now except we did get a nice sporter built on a small-ring Mauser action in the other day. Let me see...here it is." The man started to walk towards the right end of the rifle rack behind the counter before Raymond stopped him.

"Sorry, I meant, I need one of your custom rifles built up. I can't stay long but I'd like to pay for it now, if you don't mind."

"Let me get the order book. If you're in a hurry, maybe you should come back later so we can go over all the specs."

"It's not for me, Jim, it's for Tony. He helped me out on a big case, and now I'm going to Africa. I want to get him a rifle built up on a Remington Enfield, whatever specifications he wants. I'd like to pay you for it now, though."

"Well, I can't quote you an exact price if we don't know what he wants done, but..." His voice trailed off as he realized that both he and Raymond could probably predict almost precisely what Tony Kearns would want in a rifle. He was impressed that Raymond wanted to do this for their friend.

"Let's see now," the older man said, pulling out a pencil and lifting his clipboard. "I suspect he'll want an elephant rifle, so that means express sights with a barrel band and no scope. Deep-belly magazine for five or six cartridges, depending on the caliber he chooses. No checkering on the bolt handle. Standard lapping of the locking lugs and smoothing the action, aftermarket trigger..."

"What about wood?" Raymond asked.

"Want to get him something nice looking, with some decent figure, but it'll have to be dense, and with straight grain through the grip to take the recoil. Most of our customers want French Walnut, but Tony's always said he liked Bastogne for the heavy-recoil stuff. Normally it's not as pretty, but I've got a stick in the back that'll knock your eyes out. Be perfect for one of the cannons you guys favor." He wrote some more on the paper.

"Point pattern on the checkering," Raymond threw in.

"I figured that," the man said as he continued to make notes. "Super Grade swivel studs, front one on a barrel band...one of our pads...probably ought to have a second recoil lug on the barrel...forend tip and grip cap out of African Blackwood...looks like about six-fifty, Ray."

"Let me write you a check, and you can tell Tony the next time he comes in. If there's any other charges, like ordering a reamer for some wildcat caliber you don't have, or one of your side mounts if he wants a plains rifle instead, go ahead with it and keep track of the extra I owe you." He pulled out his checkbook and a pen.

"What if he wants a Mag Mauser?" the proprietor asked. Raymond put down his pen and stared at him. "Right. Stupid question. Enfields..." he muttered, shaking his head.

Ray finished making out the check.

June 8, 1963

"Joe, I don't know what to say about what you've done for us. It's the first time since Harold and I have been married that I haven't been pinched paying the rent and the electric bill in the same month." It was just after 8:00 on a Sunday morning. The former lovers were sitting in the Gaines kitchen. Linda's husband had gone to Chicago for the weekend to see a Cubs game. Joe had dropped by for coffee, and the two were talking comfortably.

Twelve-year-old Richard stood on his bed and pushed the lever on the air vent to open it. He had discovered some months before that when it was open all the way, he could hear conversations held in the kitchen. It was his secret, and he took great pleasure in it, although he had never heard anything more interesting than halfhearted arguing between his parents.

"I wish it had been you, Joe," Linda said. *What're they talking about?* Richard wondered. He remained standing on the bed, where he could hear better.

Joe Hammond looked at the woman he had realized too late that he loved. Linda Wilson Gaines was thirty-eight years old, but to Joe Hammond she looked only a little different from the night he had first set eyes on her eighteen years ago. Joe, though handsome in a strong, rugged way, looked every one of his sixty-four years.

"Everyone needs a break in life, Linda. You know how many I've had. It was past time Harold had his turn." *They're talking about the license office* Richard realized immediately. *That's Dad's whole life now, just about.*

"People create their own luck, Joe." When Hammond made no response, Linda went on. "Harold isn't that sort. And he never will be. As I think you know." Joe Hammond remained silent. Richard started to feel a little ashamed. He had never heard his mother talk about his father this way.

They sat across from each other, sipping coffee and thinking their own private thoughts. *Did she leave to go to the bathroom?* Richard wondered when he heard no sounds from the vent.

"I'm worried about Richard," Linda said after a few minutes. That got her son's attention.

"How so?"

"He does poorly in school. He's no discipline problem, and the other boys like him well enough, so maybe I'm borrowing trouble. But he's....he's *slow*, Joseph. And he never stays with anything long enough to get it right or do it well." *Mom never said anything like that to me* Richard thought as his cheeks flushed pink.

"These past years have made me think hard about the future the boys will have. You always told me a person needs to plan ahead." She looked him straight in the eyes. "I don't want Richard ending up like his father." Richard wanted to close the vent and leave his room. He knew that's what he should do, and he wanted to do that, but he was rooted to the spot like a gawker at a bad car wreck.

The older man laughed unconvincingly. "I don't think a boy's character is permanently set by the time he's twelve years old," Joe Hammond lied. "Isn't your concern a little premature?" Linda Gaines shrugged, a gesture that said *No, it isn't.* "Any worries about Harold Junior?" Hammond asked, changing the subject.

"He's just the opposite, Joe. He's just like you." *That's a weird thing to say* Richard thought. "Harry has more energy and drive than he knows what to do with. He's not the one who got cheated in the gene pool." *What's a jean pool?* Richard wondered.

"I think he may even get a scholarship to Priory," Linda added, naming a local private school known for its academic excellence. *Priory!* Richard mentally yelled. *No way!* "Even if it's only a partial scholarship, I think we can afford to send him there, now that Harold has the income."

"That brings up something I wanted to talk to you about, Linda," Hammond said, glad to be on a different subject. "Those license offices may be cash cows, but they aren't permanent. Harold may have it for twenty more years, or the Governor could get beaten in the next election and his replacement could award it to someone else and Harold could be in the unemployment line overnight." *The Governor better not put Dad out of work* Richard thought immediately. *Dad needs that job.*

Linda gave him a tight smile. "I've thought a lot about that. We won't be buying a Cadillac or moving to a more expensive neighborhood. You dropped this golden goose in our laps, Joe, and I'm going to see that we keep it healthy. I've made sure the staff is competent, and I review all the paperwork myself every day. I've also seen fit to research the Governor's prospects, and assuming he isn't found in bed with a young boy, I think he may be with us for some time." *In bed with a boy? Gross!*

"Joe, don't think for one second that this license office hasn't made a tremendous improvement in our lives. I intend to see that those benefits last us for as long as we live. You have lifted a weight from my husband's shoulders, and I will never forget it." She lowered her voice and pressed on. "It's been fifteen years, Joseph, but I still want you." *What?* Richard wondered, straining to hear. *'I step on you'?*

"Not because I feel obligated," Richard's mother went on. "Because I want you in bed with me again. As often or as seldom as you like. It will be our secret." *In bed with her? Again? What is Mom talking about?* Richard screamed silently. He stood on tiptoe to try to hear more clearly.

"That would not be a good idea, Linda. But I've often th–" The rest of what he was going to say was cut off by the telephone's ring. Linda answered it, but it was a wrong number.

Hammond was very relieved at the interruption, and used it to change the subject. He looked back at Linda Gaines.

"I was just thinking, if Richard doesn't have much ability or motivation, but people like him, then it would seem he's all set for a successful career in the legislature. In a few years he'll be able to give it some serious thought," he added jokingly. His face softened as he looked at the younger woman across the table from him. "Let's stay in touch, Linda. I'd like to help you look out for Richard."

"I'd like that very much," she said in a soft voice that only he could hear.

Richard Gaines lay back down on his bed. He wasn't sure what to think about what he had just heard. *The last part sounded okay, I guess* he told himself.

July 19, 1963

On the cab ride to the airport, Ray Johnson kept having irrational fears that some-how he wouldn't make his flight. The trip was uneventful, however, and the cab driver grunted approval at the dollar tip as he handed Raymond his two rifle cases.

When Ray arrived at the check-in counter, he was sure that there would be some-thing wrong with his ticket. The young woman smiled at him, however, then handed him the claim check for his duffel bag and told him she hoped he had a pleasant vacation.

As Ray carried the two rifle cases containing his Holland, his Winchester, and ammunition for both towards the international concourse, he was sure that when he got to the gate the airplane would have been delayed and would not be there. The big white-and-red Lockheed Constellation, however, was plainly visible through the glass, sitting out on the tarmac waiting for the announcement that it was time to board.

"Hunting trip, sir?" the attendant asked, nodding towards the gun cases.

"Yes. Something I've been dreaming about for a long time."

"In England, or is Heathrow just an intermediate stop?"

"Just a quick plane-change," Raymond explained. "I'm headed for Kenya."

The attendant smiled broadly. "I'll have one of the stewardesses pre-board you, and I'll see that she stows your rifles in the first-class section where the sights won't get bumped."

"I'd appreciate that very much," Ray said sincerely. He suddenly had a flash that he had forgotten his passport, and he clutched at his shirt pocket. The document, however, was there. He saw the attendant smiling pleasantly at him.

Maybe this safari really is going to happen after all he thought to himself.

***

Henry Bowman followed his father outside into the night. He was barefoot as he stepped out onto the front porch in his pajamas, and he moved his tender feet carefully. He was not entirely awake yet. Henry followed his father's gaze and stared off into the distance. An unfamiliar hue was visible in the sky far away, giving off a dull glow and making a large section of the horizon visible even though it was the middle of the night. Walter Bowman, who often listened to the radio before going to bed, had heard the news and awakened his son.

The Forest Park Highlands was burning.

July 23, 1963

"Oh, my God." Ray Johnson's jaw dropped in awe as he reached the crest of the hill. He was looking at the first elephant outside a zoo he had ever seen in his life. The animal was immense. Thoughts of the fine impala he had dropped with a heart shot an hour earlier vanished from his mind.

Mineer, the transplanted South African, grinned at his client. The young man's ability to spot game and read sign was fully the equal of his own, and this had been a revelation for the professional hunter. Most of his clients were older, typically out of shape, and, as often as not, mediocre rifle shots. Ray Johnson had been a welcome change from that, but here he was acting like every other nimrod on his first safari at the sight of his first elephant. Mineer gave him a few moments of silent reverie before speaking.

"That one's fairly big in the body for this country," he said with a smile. "Tusks aren't much, though, as you can see. I promise we'll find you one that'll make this one look like he's still teething."

"How big *is* he?" Raymond whispered. They were downwind of the bull elephant, and with his poor eyesight he did not spot them, even though they were less than fifty yards away. Past him were two other, smaller bulls.

"About a forty-pounder, I'd say. We can do better, I promise."

"No, I mean the elephant itself," Ray corrected.

Mineer grinned. "Don't get a chance to weigh the whole bloody animal very often," the professional said drily, "so I'm a bit rusty on my estimates. Biggest one in the world was taken in Portuguese Angola in '55. It's a full mount, in your Smithsonian, by the way. That one went twelve tons, as I recall, which is about double the average for a mature male. Tusks are small in Angola, though, so they put a big set from one of our bulls in the mount. This fellow here," he said, nodding towards the beast, "he's a little bigger than normal. Say seven tons, about." Ray shook his head in wonder. He was imagining sneaking up to within fifteen yards of the huge beast and taking the tricky brain shot. An elephant's brain is about the size of a loaf of bread. It is surrounded by honeycombed bone. A head shot which misses the brain itself can enrage the animal and cause a lethal charge. Ray was mentally drawing the correct angle of penetration when his guide spoke.

"We'd best leave," Mineer said. "There's a chance he might spot us and charge. We don't want to use up one of your elephant tags on a little forty-pounder." Trophy fees for African game were payable in advance and non-refundable. Woe betide the client who shot a charging animal in self-defense without a tag for that particular species.

Ray grudgingly followed the professional hunter. Ivory weight was not what was on his mind. He was thinking that hunting North American game would never be the same for him.

***

"Here it is," Curt Behnke said to Henry and Walter as he handed the barreled action to the boy. They were in the basement of Behnke's home in the German section of St. Louis. It was the most cluttered residence Henry had ever seen, which was not surprising as there were ten children in the family. The basement shop was very cluttered, too. The gun racks and walls were covered with world record groups that Behnke had shot with rifles he had built. Some were records that had since been surpassed, and some still stood. Behnke had taped or stapled them haphazardly about his work area. He didn't much mind when one fell down or got torn. There would always be more.

Curt Behnke was a trim man of forty-seven whose hair was starting to turn grey. He moved quickly, except when he was working at his lathe or mill. Behnke was a photoengraver for the *Saint Louis Post-Dispatch* newspaper. His machinist's skills were entirely self-taught.

"Explain to me what you had done, Henry," Walter asked his son. Henry picked up a pencil and turned the custom-barreled Remington receiver over on the workbench. He pointed to where the magazine well had been.

"Single-shot 40X actions are hard to find, so Curt machined a piece of 4140 tool steel to fit here in the magazine cut. Then he had it heliarc-welded into position, with something to soak up the heat around the receiver ring so the heat-treat wouldn't change around the locking lugs."

"Why the metal block?" Walter asked. The work had been done so well that the receiver looked like it had come that way from the factory.

"It makes the action stiffer," his son answered. "Then he machined the block down so it was the same shape as the rest of the receiver, and made all the threads and everything right, instead of sloppy and crooked like they were, and reworked the trigger so it isn't real heavy and full of creep."

Behnke chuckled. "The factory doesn't do quite *that* bad a job," he explained, "but I like to true up the threads, make sure the face of the receiver is perfectly square with them, and spot-in the locking lugs on the bolt with lapping compound. Then I make sure the bolt face is square with the front of the receiver ring, and the lugs and locking area are perpendicular to the axis of the barrel. Every little bit helps when you're trying to put them all in one hole a hundred yards off."

"Tell me about the barrel," Walter asked the gunsmith.

"It's a Clyde Hart stainless blank. I've always had good results with his barrels. Much as your son shoots, I made him go with the .222 Magnum chamber instead of a Swift or a .22-250, which burn more powder. The .222 Mag will last a lot longer. In a twenty-six inch barrel, with the minimum-spec chamber I cut, he should still get thirty-six hundred feet per second with match bullets." He handed Walter a loaded round to examine. It was much smaller than the 8mm cartridges Henry shot out of his surplus Mauser. "Left the barrel eight-fifty at the muzzle," he said, speaking of the diameter in thousandths. "Never seen one left that heavy that wouldn't shoot."

Walter Bowman examined the quality of the metalwork. It was flawless. "Looks like you've got your job cut out for you making a stock that will do justice to this, Henry." Curt Behnke smiled at the compliment.

"What do we owe you for your work, Curt? I promised Henry if he saved up for the receiver and made his own stock, I'd pay for the metalwork and scope." Walter reached into his pocket and pulled out his money clip.

"Fifty-five for the blank and fifty to fit, chamber, crown, and turn it to contour. Twenty to machine the block, have it welded in, and grind it to shape. Twenty more to true up the action. Five bucks for trigger surgery. Scope blocks are free for a first-time customer. And I get fifteen for a straightline seating die made with the same reamer that cut the chamber," he added as he reached across the workbench and produced a polished loading tool with ".222 MAG." stamped on it in tiny print. "A hundred sixty-five total."

Walter Bowman counted off the bills and handed them to Curt Behnke.

"Something tells me this won't be the last time I see the two of you here."

"No, you're right. As soon as we get home, the little capitalist will probably start nagging me to find him more jobs to do to earn money."

"Drop him off here if you want, and I'll put him to work contouring barrels," Behnke said with a smile.

"Hey, I've got a *stock* to make first," Henry broke in. The two men laughed, and smiled at the boy. Henry wasn't paying attention. He was staring at the barreled action, imagining in his mind's eye how he would lay out the pattern and inlet the wood to accept the metal.

In ten days, Henry would have a complete rifle. In six more he would have developed accurate loads for it that would stay in 1/2" at 100 yards. Soon after that he would regularly be killing crows in the cornfield at ranges up to two hundred yards and occasionally farther, depending on the wind.

By the time school started, Henry would have fired over two thousand rounds through the single-shot varmint rifle. He would be very glad that he had taken Curt Behnke's advice and not specified a .22 case with more capacity, which would have shortened the barrel's accuracy life considerably.

As it turned out, Henry Bowman's .222 Magnum would not need a new barrel for almost two years.

August 18, 1963

"You ought to be working on my side of the business, my friend, as much as you understand game animals and their habits." The comment startled Raymond. It was a daydream he had found himself indulging in every day since his arrival in Kenya.

The two men were sitting by the campfire, watching one of the crew tend to an impala steak that was cooking in a plow disc that had been drafted into service as a skillet. It was the end of the sixth day of Ray's safari, and he had seen more game than he ever dreamed existed. Hundred-head herds of impala were everywhere. Zebra grazed on the plains just like the wild mustangs back in Colorado, except there were a lot more of them here. Buffalo and elephant traveled in herds also. The first time Ray had seen a herd of over a hundred elephants, he had not been able to believe his eyes.

Most enlightening to the Coloradan had been the lions. Every day he had seen a lion take down one of the thin-skinned species and start eating it while it was still alive. The big cat would gorge itself on as much of the kill as possible, then go to sleep nearby and consume the rest of it at his leisure. "They lie around like lazy kaffirs, belching and farting, for a couple weeks," Mineer had said. "Then when their fat burns off and they start to get hungry again, they go back to work." Ray had found the reality of the 'King of Beasts' somewhat different from the idealizations of his childhood.

"What does it take to become a pro?" Ray asked the white hunter. "Isn't it hard for someone not from either Africa or England to get the government's okay?"

Mineer nodded. "Most definitely, here in Kenya. Very difficult. Expensive, too," he added. His eyes crinkled in a smile. "But for an energetic young bull like yourself, there are other, more attractive opportunities that would be too much for one such as I." Mineer was forty-seven years old.

"Mozambique or Angola are where I would be looking if I were your age. The Portuguese are abysmal at managing things. A Portuguese professional hunter is—what is that word?—an *oxymoron*."

"Their governments might accept a license application from a twenty-five-year-old American?" Ray asked.

"I should think they might pay you to apply, with things as they are currently. You see, a pro in those areas is expected not only to run his hunting concession successfully, but also to provide other services to the surrounding community. To act as the local...*sheriff*, yes, that's the proper word for it." Mineer gave Ray a knowing look.

"Portuguese professional hunters are barely capable of finding their way back to base camp. You can imagine the futility of expecting them to provide any...*leadership* in the local town." He nodded his head. "Angola and Mozambique offer almost unlimited opportunity for someone such as yourself. Young man with brains and drive could make quite a bit for himself there, I should imagine." He leaned closer. "Would you like me to investigate further for you? May as well, while you're here."

"Pull up stakes and move to Africa, huh?" Ray said with a broad smile. "That's something I never thought I'd be talking about." He laughed as he imagined cabling Jacob Burns that he would not be returning. "Law office would think I'd lost my mind."

Raymond leaned back and smiled at the idea. He was unaware of the Telex which had been sent from Colorado to Nairobi two days earlier.

August 21, 1963

It was after nine o'clock in the evening when Raymond and Mineer got back to the camp in the Land-Rover. In the back was an eland which weighed close to a ton. Raymond had killed it with a single shot at about 175 yards. It was the fourteenth head of game he had taken on the safari. Both men were in excellent spirits as the headlights of their vehicle lit up the tents where the skinning crew was camped.

"*Donza, Donza, Donza!*" Mineer called out in Swahili. "Don't let it spoil!" The skinners ran to the vehicle as it rolled to a stop. As the white hunter climbed out from behind the wheel, one of the camp crew rushed up to him and handed him a folded sheet of paper.

Mineer held it so that the setting sun allowed him to read the printing, and his face clouded.

"This is for you, Ray," he said as he handed the paper to his client. "It took some time for them to find us out here. I'm sorry."

Ray Johnson took the sheet of paper and held it up where he could read it.

XMIT GJPOLDEP RCV TRADECO
15 AUGUST 1963
DELIVER MINEER SAFARIS FBO JOHNSON OF PITKIN
COUNTY COLO USA

BAD NEWS BUD AND LOUISE BOTH DEAD SINGLE CAR
ACCIDENT RED MOUNTAIN LAST NIGHT STOP CORONER
SAYS HEART ATTACK STOP FUNERAL SUNDAY AUGUST
18 STOP THIS WONT REACH YOU IN TIME SO FINISH
HUNT REPEAT FINISH HUNT STOP EXPECT YOUR CALL
FROM NYC SEPT 2 STOP WILL HANDLE THINGS HERE
STOP DONT GET EATEN STOP UNCLE CARL

Ray held the telex closer to his face and reread it three times before dropping his hand to his side. He stared out at the magnificent Kenya sunset. The news of his parents' death was a violent shock, but he was surprised at how jarring he found the reference to New York City. Ray Johnson realized right then that after he settled things in Colorado, he was going to give notice at the law firm and get with Tony Kearns about a long-term investment plan.

As soon as that was done, he was going to move to Africa.

November 22, 1963

Henry Bowman had never seen any of the teachers at Howell School cry before. Plenty of his classmates had cried over the years, especially out on the playground, but this was different. The black woman Henry recognized as working in the school's kitchen was out in the hall, sobbing openly. Henry's sixth-grade teacher was blinking back tears, and looked as if she was about to lose her composure at any moment.

"There's just been an announcement," she said solemnly. "President Kennedy has been shot. The President is dead."

There was stunned silence in the classroom for a few moments. Then the sixth graders erupted with simultaneous questions about the killing.

"Have they caught anyone?"

"Do they know who shot him?"

"How did it happen?"

"Are they sure he's dead?"

The teacher tried to smile, but the result was a total failure as she attempted to answer the students' shouted questions. Henry Bowman remained silent. His mind was not on the teacher's words, but instead was filled with a number of unrelated thoughts about the slain man. The first was of Max Collins' comments on the disastrous Bay of Pigs invasion, and his criticism of the young President for the debacle.

Henry's second thought was of some photos he had seen of Kennedy on his boat off the coast of Massachusetts, shooting the new AR-15 machine gun. The weapon had been designed by Eugene Stoner for the armaments division of Fairchild Aircraft, and was very light and easy to control. Kennedy had been grinning in the photograph, and at the time Henry had wished that he, too, could try out the new select-fire rifle that the military was talking about adopting as the standard issue weapon.

As the bell rang and the students ran out the door to recess, the boy's mind switched to another subject. Henry Bowman had substantial knowledge of firearms and was in regular contact with major importers and distributors. Because of this, his thoughts turned to Joe Kennedy, the dead President's father.

November 24, 1963

"Quick, Honey! They're about to show it again!" Catherine Bowman immediately turned the stove's heat control to a lower setting and hurried into the living room. Her husband, brother, and sister-in-law were sitting on the couch. Irwin Mann sat in an armchair to Zofia Collins' right. Henry sat on the floor in front of his father. All of them stared at the television set, transfixed.

The screen showed a crowd inside a room. The people in the scene were straining to see what was about to happen. Then a door opened and some men escorted a younger man wearing a dark sweater across the room. His right wrist was handcuffed to the left wrist of one of his captors, a fairly tall man in a light-colored suit, white shirt, dark tie, wearing a sort of dress cowboy hat. Flashbulbs popped and the noise level increased.

Suddenly a short man in a dark suit and light-colored hat with a dark hatband charged into the picture. The film footage being broadcast immediately went into frame-by-frame mode. The short man extended his right arm towards the prisoner. He was holding a revolver in his hand. In the next frame, he had fired the gun and the prisoner's mouth was open in a grimace of pain. By the next frame the young man had started to crumple to the floor. After he was on the ground, the film speed resumed to normal, and the family watched intently as the police wrestled the shooter to the floor and disarmed him. There was brief news commentary before the station cut to a commercial.

"That's the goddamnedest thing I've ever seen in my life," Max Collins said with wonder.

"According to what they've been saying on the news, he did it so that the family would be spared the ordeal of a trial." There was a hint of derision in Walter Bowman's words. Each of the adults in the group murmured comments about the killing they had just seen.

"What do *you* think, Henry?" Walter asked finally. His son's brows knitted. He was concentrating on forming his answer before he spoke.

"That revolver he shot him with. It looked like a Colt Detective Special with a hammer shroud. That's a pretty rare version. I've only seen pictures of them. Most of the hammer shroud guns you see are the Smith & Wesson Bodyguard."

"That's true," Max Collins offered. "The kid's exactly right. Installing a shroud on a Colt is no five-minute job. The factory sells you the shroud and two screws, with different thread sizes. You have to buy two drill bits and two taps to do it, and if you're not a gunsmith you'll ruin a good gun."

"What's the purpose of a hammer shroud?" Walter inquired. His son spoke up.

"It's so the gun doesn't tie up if you have to fire it when it's in your pocket. The reason some people go to the trouble of putting one on a Colt instead of a just buying a Smith with a factory-installed shroud is that the J-frame Smith only holds five rounds. The Colt carries six." Henry furrowed his brows.

"Something else I noticed, too. He was pulling the trigger with his middle finger, and laying his index finger alongside the gun. Some people use that technique when they point-shoot a revolver without using the sights." Henry shrugged. "I've tried it, and it doesn't help me any to shoot that way, but there are some people who swear by it."

"The kid's eyes are better than mine. I didn't notice that." Max Collins spoke with respect in his voice. "What he's saying is that this Ruby guy is a pro. And from the dead center shot he just made, that fits."

"Or Ruby happened to walk into a gun shop at the right time, just after the guy who had the Colt built got tired of it or needed money," Henry added quickly. "And maybe he's got a piece of wire in his index finger from some injury, like that mechanic at the gas station on Delmar, and that's why he was pulling the trigger with his middle finger." He shrugged. "After all, it doesn't take any special skills to hit someone in the chest from three feet away."

"It sure as hell looked like a pro hit to me," Max Collins said. "That 'saving the family' stuff is a bunch of crap." He changed the subject. "They still saying it was a Mauser that Oswald used to kill Kennedy? I heard that again on a news conference yesterday."

"But it was a *Carcano* they were holding up on television!" Henry exclaimed. "And the Carcano is a piece of *junk.*"

"Dallas cops said they found a Mauser, then an hour later they hold up Dago iron that isn't even safe to fire."

"What do you mean?" Walter Bowman asked his brother-in-law.

"Shoot a Carcano enough to be able to hit something with it, and it's apt to blow the firing pin back in your eye. Henry'd wear one out in an hour, if it held together. Worst rifle of the war."

"Next thing they'll be telling us is that the gun that killed the President originally came from one of his father's companies."

"Why do you say that, Henry?" his mother Catherine broke in.

"The big surplus importers, like INTERARMCO and Service Armament, that I buy from? Joe Kennedy, the President's father, owns some of them. Not those two, but he owns all or part of a couple of the other surplus-gun importing companies." The group sat in silence at the boy's statement. It was something that none of them had known. Finally, Irwin Mann spoke.

"Henry, do you have...an opinion about the assassination?" Irwin Mann was staring intently at the sixth-grader. The boy was startled by the question, but it addressed an issue that Henry had been thinking about all day.

"The way the news says it happened seems crazy to me. Someone thinking about shooting the President wouldn't use one of the worst guns ever made, unless he had no idea about what he was doing. If he knew anything at all about rifles, he'd use a target rifle, or at least a good quality surplus gun, like an Enfield or a Mauser.

"Also, anyone who had ever shot a rifle in his life would know that if you have to shoot at a moving target, it's a lot easier if the target is coming right at you or going straight away. Especially if your rifle has a cheap scope on it, like Oswald's did, and you're going to fire more than one shot in a short time. You have a real small field of view with a scope, especially those skinny ones with little lenses, and it's really hard to pick up a moving target with one in a hurry." The boy looked at his uncle for confirmation.

"The kid's right," Max Collins agreed. "According to all the pictures and drawings they've been showing about the assassination, Oswald had all the time in the world to shoot the President in the chest as the car was coming directly towards him. Kennedy was standing up and not even the windshield was in the way.

"Instead, Oswald waited until the car turned the corner and was angling away from him. And after it turned, Oswald's view was partially blocked by some trees, it looked like. Then he decided to start firing at the President with his junky, scoped Carcano." Henry nodded as his uncle went on.

"So I guess it's pretty obvious that this Oswald guy was no shooter, and didn't know that the Carcano is an unsafe junker that's really slow to operate. And we can assume he didn't know that with a cheap scope, it's even harder to pick up a target moving on a sideways angle, particularly with part of your view blocked by trees. Hell, he didn't even have the sense to take a clear shot with his target coming straight at him.

"But when this guy who obviously doesn't know anything about shooting a rifle does start firing at the President, he suddenly turns into somebody that Winchester should have put on the exhibition circuit." Max held up his hand and started ticking off his points on his fingers.

"He manages to find his moving target, fire, pull the gun out of recoil, work the bolt, find his moving target in the scope again, and repeat the process for a whole magazine. He hits Kennedy twice, once in the back and once in the head, for Christ's sake!"

"And," Henry broke in "he puts another bullet into that other guy, uh..."

"Governor Connally," Mann prompted him, still hanging on every one of Henry and Max's words.

"Yeah, Connally," Henry agreed, getting more animated, "and he does all this superb shooting in—what? five seconds?" He shook his head. "If Ad Topperwein and Herb Parsons were still alive, I don't think either one of them could do that kind of shooting with a Carcano. I know I couldn't come close."

"This nut who knows nothing about shooting but decides to kill the president anyway using the worst possible equipment and taking the worst possible shot somehow manages to do it. *Bullshit*," Max Collins spat. "No such thing as that much luck. God himself couldn't pull that one off. There had to be other shooters." Irwin Mann said nothing but nodded, fascinated by the persuasive analysis. He looked at his brother-in-law, nodding his understanding. Max added another comment.

"And now the man most likely to tell us who else was involved has conveniently been killed. He's been killed by a strip-club owner with a pro's gun using a pro's technique, who did it, we are told, out of respect for the Kennedy family," Max snorted.

"And may I also point out that this strip-club owner happens to be Jewish, and the head of the family this Jewish strip-club owner professes to respect so much is old Joe Kennedy, who never made any secret of his admiration for the Nazi regime." Max Collins laughed without humor. "Don't expect *this* deal to make sense any time soon."

"Curiouser and curiouser," Walter Bowman murmured. He was arguably the most literate person in the room.

November 24, 1963

January 10, 1964

"God *damn* it!" Harold Gaines roared at his son. "Why the hell did you have to ge—have to go cheat on a test, for Christ's sake?" the elder Gaines demanded. He had revised his question at the last moment. 'Have to get caught cheating on a test' was what he had been on the verge of asking.

"No one knew there would be a quiz the first week back from school," Richard blubbered. "It wasn't a real test or anything," he added defensively.

"All the more reason not to risk getting flunked out!" Harold replied. Richard thought it best to avoid pointing out that he was already failing the math course. "Now I'll have to go make nice with the teacher again," Harold fumed. *Dad will probably have to give him some money again because I'm so stupid* Richard thought miserably.

"Maybe you can come up with a C-minus on your next 'quiz'," Harold said in a voice that dripped with sarcasm, then turned away from his son in dismissal.

Richard Gaines hung his head and left the room. *I wish Dad would help me understand my math homework* he thought bleakly.

It did not occur to Richard Gaines that his father's academic abilities were no greater than his own.

***

"Well, good evening, birthday boy." Henry Bowman rolled his eyes as he came in the kitchen after being dropped off from sledding with some of the other boys from school. His mother Catherine knew that the phrase mildly embarrassed her son, and she laughed at his reaction. "Come get some hot chocolate. Your Uncle Max is here, and Irwin Mann is with him. They're with your father in his study, waiting for you to get back. I think they have something to show you."

Henry shrugged out of his coat, pulled his galoshes off, and put them on the porch to dry. He took the cup of cocoa from his mother and padded into his father's study in his socks. Max Collins was sipping a scotch and water, and Irwin Mann had a beer in his hand. Walter Bowman drank tea.

"Well, look who made it back! You didn't freeze your little dingus off, did you?" Max Collins was grinning his most engaging grin. Henry smiled and lowered his eyes. He knew his uncle didn't really expect an answer.

"Happy birthday, Henry," Irwin Mann said to the boy.

"Thank you."

"Henry, your uncle and Mr. Mann have some presents for you, as do I. They all go together, so we thought we'd see that you caught us all at the same time."

Max Collins held out a box that was blue-grey, about three inches thick, and roughly the size of a legal pad. "This one goes first. Was going to buy it for myself, but decided you needed it more. Let me borrow it sometime and maybe I'll decide to get one, too." Henry took the box and his eyes got big as soon as he saw the S&W logo stamped into the lid. *A Smith & Wesson presentation case.* He had heard of them, but had never seen one. He knew of only one gun that the company shipped in a presentation case, and his hands felt awkward as he lifted the lid.

His information was correct. Inside was an N-frame .44 Magnum with a 5" barrel. This was unusual. The big Smith & Wesson was catalogued with 4", 6 1/2", and 8 3/8" barrels. The gun Henry was staring at had been one of a special run of 500 made for H.

H. Harris and Co. in 1958. The metal glowed with the milk-blue finish that was characteristic of all of Smith & Wesson's best guns made while Carl Hellstrom was still in charge of operations.

Henry lifted the revolver out of the satin lining, pressed the cylinder latch forward, and swung out the cylinder. Each of the six chambers was burnished with the factory's proprietary process that allowed fired cases to drop effortlessly out of the cylinder, even when maximum-pressure loads were used. Henry closed the cylinder, cocked the weapon, and tried the trigger pull. The trigger broke without a trace of creep at what Henry judged was no more than two pounds, with a release like breaking glass. The double-action pull was smooth and positive, and Henry immediately noticed that the trigger itself was not the standard wide, grooved, target version that was best suited for slow fire, but a smooth, polished one perfect for double-action shooting.

Max Collins saw his nephew examining the non-standard piece. "Fran Longtin, in the service department in Massachusetts, set you up with that trigger when I told him the way you were apt to use the gun. Says it's their Jordan Combat Trigger, made for Bill Jordan on the Border Patrol in Texas, and anyone else that's on the company's good side."

Henry had written to Fran Longtin when the trigger stud of his uncle's .357 had broken and he had sent it back to the factory for repair. Longtin had inquired as to how many rounds had been fired through the weapon, and Henry had replied that he had shot over 20,000 rounds through the gun in the year he had used it, but had no idea how many had gone before. The service manager had apologized for the premature failure, and sent Henry a thousand fired cases along with the repaired gun as a bonus.

"This is from your old Dad," Walter Bowman said, holding out a cardboard box. Henry laid down the revolver and took the package from his father. It was heavy, and when he opened it, he saw why: Inside were a pair of eight-cavity bullet molds with handles. He did not need to read the letters stamped on the mold blocks to know that they were made by Hensley & Gibbs in Oregon. Only H&G had the skill to properly make 8-cavity gang molds.

"I was going to get you just one mold," Walter explained. "Then I wrote the folks up there, and they told me to buy a pair, made at the same time with the cavities matched to a half-thousandth, so you can fill one and let it cool while you're filling the other one. Said with practice, you could cast over 1500 bullets an hour, so you won't have to spend so much time down in the foundry." Walter used the term his wife had jokingly invented to describe the corner of the basement Henry had set up to cast bullets. "They feel a little heavy, but I guess your wrists are up to it."

"Good exercise for a revolver shooter," Henry said immediately.

"Mr. Mann has something for you also," added Walter. Irwin Mann reached behind a leather armchair and retrieved a steel 5-gallon bucket with a wire loop carrying handle. It was obviously fairly heavy. He set it down in front of Henry, who lifted the lid. It was filled to the brim with empty brass .44 magnum cartridge cases.

"Should be four thousand there," Irwin said, speaking for the first time.

"And I've got the dies, 5000 primers, and four 4-pound cans of Hercules 2400 powder coming Monday or Tuesday," Max threw in. "You can start casting this weekend, and be shooting by next Saturday."

Henry did not know what to say. He feet were still cold from sledding, but he did not notice it. His hot chocolate was forgotten. He picked up the revolver again, then looked at his father. "Can I cast some after supper, Dad?"

"I don't see why not. It's Friday. How much lead have you got left?"

"I was almost out, but Mom took me by the Goodyear place on Monday for more wheelweights. I got them all melted down, fluxed, and cast into ingots this week. I have almost 200 pounds of alloy." He was rapidly calculating how many bullets that would make. Each .44 slug was 250 grains, and there were 7000 grains to the pound. A little less than forty pounds per thousand. "That's enough for about 5000 bullets."

Max Collins laughed. "If you didn't have to wait for the molds to warm up and the lead to melt, hell, kid, you could knock those out tonight," he joked.

As it turned out, Henry turned on his three lead furnaces and started preheating the molds on a hot plate before sitting down to dinner. He got to bed a little after midnight.

When he did, he was once again out of bullet alloy.

March 12, 1964

The return address on the envelope made Henry Bowman grin. **Kane's Custom Ammo** it proclaimed. Henry had been very pleased with the first reply he had received from Allen Kane, but he had been afraid that he might not hear from the man again. In Henry's second letter he had confessed to the nationally-recognized ammunition expert that he was only eleven years old.

The envelope he held in his hand was thick and Henry tore it open. To call Allen Kane's typing mediocre was to be charitable. Henry would not discover for two years that Kane's left hand was permanently damaged, the result of a farm accident when Kane was fifteen. Henry did not care at all that the letter was littered with typos. Though his spelling and grammar were impeccable, Henry's own handwriting was far from pretty. *Kane didn't complain about the letter I sent* Henry thought. He began to read the letter which had obviously been hammered out on an aging manual typewriter.

```
Hi Henry                                        3 8 64

Eleven huh/? I got my frst 45 whn I wasd 7 but no 44mag until almost 14.
you mention Ken Bella piece in 1959 dDigest . Jim harvey is dead killd
himself but lakeville Arm s bullets still available and yes they are god
good. ProtX bore w th zincv washer ok but the JUGULAR is th one to use
for long range out of wheelgun. I was Jim' s Indiana distruibytor in
1957 and that was 8th grade HAH!
  2400 is ok in 44 but 295HP is bett4er dont care what keith syas.
Not in real cold wethr thoug h but any other time yes. Try 24 grains
with H&G 503 not with jacketed they raise pressures and will wear out
your barrel the way we shoot. Also your wallet. load 9.5 Unique and 250
keith. /Your girlfriend can shoot thiswhen you get old enough to have
one.
  Dont tell S&W but the N frames much strongr than they ever thought . I
have one with 75000 rounds all at least 3 grns over listed max. Beroke
trigger stud like you did but still shoots 6 inc h at 100 even thoug
forcing cone is ou tto the edge. Franny Loongtine wanted to replace but
I said not until the frame cracked..   Glad you got the 5" with jordan
trigger its the best for carry gun dont sellit. Get an 83/8 in for best
longrange when you get older and stronger like maybe n ext week.

  Many like the light bullets in 44 but they will wear out yr forcing
cone if you shoot a lot and wont hit hard at longrange like the heavy
ones. Most people think 300 plus yards w/a whelgun is a lie but glad to
hear you knowit just takes some practice. Was at elmers last summer a
guy called him a liar about long range work. Keith pulle$d out $500 it
looked like an d said take it count off 5oo big steps then turn around
and stand still for 6 shots. If you can walk away its yours. Guy left in
a hurry.  Keith was mad I know he wouldhave don e it.

If you want to try 5 or 6oo yds buy some 270 gra in jugulrs with jacket
vcovering lead up to shoulder no le d touching bore. they are in the
list. take off 20% all dealer prices, special discount for 5" 44 shoot-
ers who dont shave yet.. Use 22 295hp and mag primer and it should do
real well if the weathers not too cold. makes a mess out of groundhogs
too   Y es i often shoot on paper at 200 yar ds. if the load is good
and you are on sandbags then 8" with iron sightsis no big surprise. rest
the frame on the bag not the barrel or they will string vertically .
also use an old towel as blast trom bbl-cyl gap will ruin your bags. You
must have good crimp though or bullets will pull undr recoil and accura-
```

cy goes to hell even if the gun dosnt tie up. Crip in crimp groove
notover front drive band like some idiots do.

Write Star they make the best cdies and get a 7/8 bushing for your
press. Tell them you want th 2step .450"-.475" carbide sizer like mine
don't let them talk you out of it like they always try to do. Ammo may
look funny but will shoot great. Polish down your expander so it only
bells the case mouth and get a starr roll crimp die too. then you will
be all set.

Put a 5gal bucket of water by your casting setup dump the bullets out of
the mold into it. They will be harder that way and won't lead your barrel as easily. also not so many dings or dents on bullets. dings don't
matter for blasting ammo but customers complain so I shoot em myself.
Beeswax Alox mix is best lube for full power loads to avoid leqding. For
light loads anything will work ok but you dont shoot those either do you
?

Rob a bank if you have to but get yourself a star loader. 5oo roumds an
hour then you can spend more time shooting not loading. The wait on a
.44 is over a year but wel worth it so get your dad an d uncle thinking
about it now. I have used a single stage too and you need a starr.
qwrite me before you buy one and I will tell you what to tell Mock you
want when he builds it and what spare parts you will need. Also you need
to get a star sizer luber it will do a lot better job than whatever you
are using now and 3 or 4times as fast too.

If you like big guns thenyou shpld have a Solthrun like the add inside.
Shot one cople moths ag o and thyre beutigul and acurate too. Jus t an
idea
           good shooting

           Allen

Henry turned to the next page and saw that Allen had enclosed his entire price list
with a note again reminding him to deduct 20% from the printed dealer prices.

Poring over the ad for the Solothurn kept Henry occupied until his mother called
him for dinner. He knew he would probably never get one, but it was fun to dream.

The letter from Kane gave Henry something else, as well. Ever since he had walked
into his first gun store with his Uncle Max and met Al Goodman, Henry had found that
adults ignored his age and treated him as an equal when their interests involved shooting.
Al, Doc Wiemann, Irwin Mann, and now Allen Kane had proved this to him. The boy was
experiencing something that was true for all people in the gun culture regardless of age
or native language. Henry's skills and passion would one day make him a welcome guest
in the homes of people he had never met before.

In the years to come, Allen Kane would become one of his closest friends. It was
a friendship that would shape the course of Henry Bowman's life.

Henry folded the letter and put it back in his pocket. *People who take shooting skills
seriously have a natural affinity for one another* Henry thought. *It doesn't matter how old
they are.* Henry would observe this phenomenon over and over again in the coming years.

Unfortunately, the people who would become the gun culture's mortal enemies
would also be well aware of this truth.

January 10, 1967

On most school mornings, Henry Bowman was a little drowsy when he left his room to go downstairs for breakfast, and even though it was Henry's birthday, this morning was no exception. He would have tripped over the packing crate if it hadn't been quite so large. It was lying in the upstairs hall just outside his bedroom door, and for a brief instant in the dim light he thought it was a grandfather clock that was lying on its side. Then he saw the rough texture of the crate and noticed the strange markings stenciled on the side of the dark wood.

Tankbüchse S18-1000 Kal. 20mm

Suddenly Henry realized what he was looking at.

"Dad! A Solothurn! You got me a Solothurn!" Henry yelled at the top of his lungs before realizing that his father probably did not need to be told this fact. His voice was considerably deeper now than it had been a few months ago, and the sound carried throughout the house.

Walter Bowman, always an early riser, left the kitchen and climbed the stairs. He flicked on the upstairs hall light as he mounted the steps.

"Your buddy in New Jersey tried to talk me into a Lahti, because it was a little cheaper, until he found out who it was for. He said the Solothurns were going fast." Walter said this last with a wry grin. "He only had three left. Of course, he did admit that the original shipment came into the country ten years ago."

"Most people don't have a good place to shoot them, and the ammo's kind of expensive," Henry said defensively. "But I think I can get the dies and load for it."

"Well, you'll have a couple hundred cases to reload if you shoot up the two crates of ammo that're in the basement. I didn't bother to lug them up here."

"You got me *two hundred* rounds of ammo?" Henry almost shouted. That quantity of ammunition was nothing special for a .22, or even a surplus military rifle, but two hundred 20mm cannon shells was another matter. Each 20mm cartridge was the size of a large banana and weighed about a pound.

"Your favorite distributor virtually insisted on it, once he knew the gun was for you. He said you'd want 'Tracer H.E.', whatever that is." Walter looked at his watch. "I probably shouldn't have let you know about this until this afternoon. Now you won't have much concentration at school."

"Can we shoot it this weekend?"

"Only if your mother doesn't need the station wagon. I don't think we could fit this monster in the Corvette."

Henry Bowman looked longingly at the crate, realizing that there was not enough time to open it and disassemble his new prize before going to school. He grabbed the near end of it and with some effort slid the 120-pound box into his bedroom and shoved it out of the way against the wall.

Walter Bowman was exactly right. Throughout all his classes that day, Henry's mind was not on his studies. It was on the magnificent example of Swiss craftsmanship that was waiting for him back in his room.

January 14, 1967

"Mom, where's Dad?" Richard Gaines asked his mother as she handed him his orange juice. "I need to get over to Sandy's house."

"He's still asleep, and you mustn't wake him," Linda Gaines admonished her son. "He had to stay up late last night." This was almost true. Harold Gaines was, in actuality, sleeping off a major drunk.

"But Sandy and me had *plans,*" he said plaintively.

"Sandy and I," Linda corrected. "I have some errands to run today. I can take you over to your friend's house. Your father can stay in bed. He's tired."

Richard turned away. 'Tired' was his mother's way of saying 'drunk'. Richard's friend Sandy's house was not far from where Joe Hammond lived, but this fact did not cross the boy's mind.

"Let me have about fifteen minutes to fix my makeup, and I'll be ready to go."

"Aw, Mom, you don't have to put on any makeup for *that,*" Richard said, trying to be funny.

Richard's mother gave him a quick smile, then turned and walked towards the washroom.

"The hell I don't," she said in a whisper after the door was shut behind her.

***

"So, where is the intrepid field artillery off to today?" Catherine Bowman asked of her husband and son as she joined them at the breakfast table.

Her son took a breath, and immediately sang,

> *"So it's hi, hi, hee, in the field ar-till-er-ee,*
> *count off your numbers loud and strong"*

"One, two!" Walter chimed in.

> *"And where e'er you go, you will always know*
> *that the caissons go roll-ing a-long"* Henry finished.

"No singing at the table," Catherine chided good-naturedly.

"We're going to shoot the cannon Dad got me," Henry said proudly. "It's really big."

"Not as big as some of the stuff your old man got to play with when he was in the Navy," Walter said.

"What's the biggest gun you got to shoot, Dad?"

"Got to touch off some shots out of a five-inch rifle on a destroyer in '42. And I was on board the battleship Missouri when she fired all nine of her sixteen-inch rifles, later that same year. I didn't get to pull the trigger, of course, but that was just as well—the view was better from where I was watching."

"Nine sixteen-inch guns," Henry said, awed at the thought. "What did that sound like?"

"Like the absolute, no fooling, this-time-it's-for-real, honest-to-God end of the world," Walter said with a big smile. "I've never seen anything like it before or since. That whole fifty-thousand-ton ship moved sideways in the water about eight feet when those nine rifles fired."

"How accurate were they?"

"With the fire control system we had then, they could hit something the size of a small house at twenty miles, as I recall. Not bad for a gun platform sloshing around in a choppy sea."

Henry quickly did some mental arithmetic. "A forty-foot group at thirty-five thousand yards—that's almost one minute-of-angle accuracy! The best thirty-caliber thousand-yard target rifles aren't any better than that, at a fiftieth of the distance!"

"Haven't you told me that your big-caliber rifles shoot pretty well with almost any ammo, but the smallbores need careful load development to get really good accuracy?"

The boy chewed his lip. "I guess it really is easier to make a big gun shoot well, if you've got good components," Henry said finally.

"Shall we see how that rule applies to the newest addition to your arsenal?"

Henry was already out of his chair and carrying his breakfast plate over to the sink.

***

"Enough fooling around," Henry said under his breath. "It's time to touch it off." Henry Bowman took a deep breath as he lay in the grass and aimed through the telescopic sight mounted on the left side of the receiver. He started to squeeze the Solothurn's trigger with both his index and middle fingers, which was how the big gun had been designed to be fired.

The Solothurn cannon, as a piece of military ordnance designed to stop tanks, was a colossal misallocation of resources and was obsolete almost from the day it was first produced. Designed and put into production in 1938 just as tank armor was undergoing a quantum leap upwards in its ability to resist penetration, the big Swiss gun had several major things going against it.

Twenty millimeter was the upper limit for a cartridge weapon which could still be carried by two or three men and operated by one. Yet a conventional cartridge of 20mm was limited to a projectile of several ounces, and therefore had to rely on velocity and not explosive content to achieve its design goals. The high muzzle velocity, and the inherent accuracy of a close-tolerance weapon with a rifled bore, meant that the Solothurn could *hit* a tank at virtually any range where the shooter could still see the target.

When the bullet *struck* a tank, however, virtually nothing happened. The 5-ounce projectile could penetrate no more than an inch of armor plate at 500 yards, and no tank made after 1940 was so lightly protected.

In addition to being heavy, unwieldy, and ineffective on modern tank armor, the Solothurn S18-1000 had a final flaw: it was made like a 100-pound Swiss chronometer. The precise fit and finish of its tool-steel parts made it susceptible to jamming under conditions of neglect, and the man-hours and machining required to build a single example of the gun were sufficient to produce literally hundreds of cheap, lightweight, hand-carried rocket launchers capable of hitting a tank-sized object at a distance of 100 yards. The 4-pound rocket-propelled projectiles produced little recoil and carried shaped-charge warheads capable of blasting a hole through armor that was over *one foot* thick. In a modern war against WWII-era or later tanks, the Solothurn S18-1000 was an utterly useless boat anchor. For Henry Bowman, it was a dream come true.

I hope this thing doesn't blow up Henry said to himself as he prepared to fire the massive rifle. Ever since the first documented firearm had been fired in 1326, Henry's unbidden thought had been the instinctive wish of every gunner firing a large, unfamiliar weapon for the first time. When the pressure of Henry's fingers reached approximately thirty pounds, the Solothurn's sear disengaged and the firing pin slammed into the primer.

Henry Bowman had never fired a weapon that behaved anything like the way this one did. The 710-grain powder charge and the 2160-grain bullet were both about ten times as heavy as those in Henry's .375 Magnum Winchester Model 70 Max Collins had given him. As both bullet and burning powder blasted out the 52" barrel, a perforated muzzle brake which was threaded onto the end of the barrel redirected the high-velocity gases to the sides and back, reducing the 100-pound gun's recoil. The tradeoff to this recoil reduction was increased concussion felt by the person firing the weapon.

The sensation felt by the shooter, Henry would discover a few years later, could be closely duplicated by hanging a 2" diameter stick of 80% strength ditching dynamite by a thread from a tree limb, and detonating it while standing ten feet away.

Henry's first thought as the gun lifted in recoil was *how on earth could they have expected a soldier to fire this thing without any ear protection?* His second thought was to wonder how close the bullet had come to his aiming point.

As the 7 1/2-foot-long gun moved Henry a few inches back under recoil, a white streak lanced out of the muzzle and disappeared into the side of an empty 55-gallon oil drum 140 yards distant. There was a barely-visible flash, a puff of smoke, and a lot of dirt thrown into the air as the 1/3-pound bullet detonated on contact with the drum and the slug's hardened alloy core slammed into the hillside a few feet beyond.

The Solothurn's recoil prevented Henry from seeing these things as they happened, but Walter was standing directly behind his son, and saw the bullet's impact. A second later, Henry's eyes focused on the target site, and he could see he had made a center hit. The oil drum was misshapen slightly, and Henry could see that a large part of the back of it had been blasted away.

"Sights seem to be about on," Walter commented in a voice that was utterly devoid of emotion.

"This thing is *great!"* Henry exclaimed. "Dad, you've *got* to try it! Wait—let me finish out the magazine." Henry settled back down behind the optical sight, and in half a minute the ten-round magazine was empty. On the tenth shot, the magazine itself was ejected from the gun. The Swiss designers had thoughtfully included this feature for rapid reloading in the heat of battle.

Walter and Henry both looked at the distant target. It no longer resembled an oil drum. The metal was twisted and torn apart, and the hillside behind it showed the effects of the ten high-velocity explosive projectiles.

Henry was so excited he could hardly stand it. "We need some targets that are farther away," he said quickly. He scanned the area, trying to select a safe place to shoot the gun at a much longer distance, then remembered that his father hadn't yet had a chance to shoot.

"Here, let me get another magazine. "You're going to love this one, Dad," Henry assured his father. Walter obligingly stretched out behind the bipod-mounted weapon, gave a final check to make sure his ear plugs were seated properly, and prepared to try Henry's new gun.

When the magazine was empty, Walter also had a big smile on his face.

"What do you think, Dad?" his son asked.

"I think I'll tell your buddy we're going to need more ammo."

June 13, 1967

Henry Bowman did not notice the strange look in his father's eyes as they slid the hangar door open. He also did not notice that it required just a little more effort than usual to pull the big Stearman out from the T-hangar onto the taxiway. He was too focused on going flying with his father to pay attention to such little details.

Henry buckled himself in and turned around to face his father. "All set?" Walter asked his son. "Let me keep the controls for a while. I've got something I want to do that's a little unusual. Don't get too worried when you see it coming. After that, you take over and I'll take some pictures. When we get low on fuel, bring it on back and land. Oh—one more thing. I bolted the lead back in the tail in case you wanted to do a 'B-Squared' or two." The puzzled look on Henry's face that had appeared with Walter's first comment was replaced with a smile. He loved making the Stearman tumble. Walter Bowman fired up the big radial engine and prepared to taxi.

***

The recently-finished Gateway Arch loomed ahead as the Bowmans flew over St. Louis at 3000 feet. Walter had his 35mm Contarex strapped around his neck and chest with just enough slack so that he could lift the camera's viewfinder to his eye. The big Pratt & Whitney was howling along at full throttle as Walter raised the camera with his right hand and rolled the Stearman inverted with his left. He pulled back on the stick and put the biplane into a screaming inverted dive.

When the nose of the plane was aimed at the spot on the ground exactly between the legs of the stainless steel monument and the altimeter read 1200 feet, Walter aimed the camera and snapped the shutter. The plane was about seven hundred feet from the ground. The Gateway Arch was 630 feet tall. Walter was using his widest-angle lens, fastest film, and smallest lens aperture setting so as to get the greatest depth-of-field for the shot. The image centered in the Contarex's viewfinder was of the top of his instrument panel, the back of Henry's head in the front cockpit hole, and the upside-down legs of the stainless steel structure.

As soon as he felt the shutter release, Walter tensed his abdominal muscles and pushed forward on the stick with all the strength in his left arm. The Stearman flew dead center through the Gateway Arch and leveled at 200 feet above the ground, still inverted, as it passed over the bank of the Mississippi River heading towards Illinois. Halfway across the river, Walter pushed harder on the stick and raised the nose. He let go of the camera, letting it dangle on its short leash. He took the stick in his right hand and eased back on the throttle with his left.

At 2000 feet, passing over the far bank and now flying above Illinois, Walter rolled the Stearman upright and level. Only then did he feel the pain. It was like a hot poker in his right side. He closed his eyes and tried to will the agony away.

When he opened them again, his son had turned around in the front cockpit and was staring at him with a huge grin on his face. Walter lifted both his hands in the air and nodded to Henry to show that he was turning over control of the airplane.

For the next half-hour, Walter took pictures as Henry went through a number of aerobatic maneuvers. The pain in his side worsened, but Walter was too pleased with Henry's proficiency to let his discomfort spoil the pleasure he was getting. When Henry executed a perfect 'B-Squared', Walter managed to snap two frames in the middle of the tumbling maneuver before the Stearman fell into an inverted spin. Walter got off another shot before Henry reversed the controls and put the plane in a stable inverted dive before rolling it upright.

As the airport came into view in the distance and Henry cut the throttle to begin his descent into the traffic pattern, Walter Bowman did something he hadn't done for many years. He unbuckled his harness and levered himself out onto the lower wing. Henry was startled to see Walter appear at the right side of the front cockpit hole, but he leaned over to the right and angled his head, knowing his father would want to yell something in his ear.

"That was something I've always wanted to do. I think we did it fast enough that no one could have gotten proof." Henry nodded in reply. What Walter had done a half hour before had been highly illegal. "Think you can land it with me standing here on the wing?"

Henry snapped his head to the right and stared in disbelief at his father. He knew he had heard him correctly. Walter was laughing in the windblast, and motioned his son to turn his ear towards him again.

"Go ahead," Walter yelled. "Just like all the times before. You got a perfect head-wind, and I'm clipped to one of the flying wires. If it doesn't feel right, goose the throttle and make a go-round, and I'll get back in. Just remember that with the lead bolted in the tail, your CG is aft of the limit, even with me up here by you, so watch your aft stick. And don't do any inverted maneuvers on final," he joked.

All of a sudden, Henry smiled and nodded. *Mom would have a heart attack if she saw this* he thought with an inward chuckle. *If I don't crash, Dad will be fine.* He watched his airspeed and entered the downwind leg of the traffic pattern on a 45 degree angle at an altimeter reading of 1400 feet. The airport was 405 feet above sea level.

Henry scanned the pattern for other aircraft. There were none. He maintained his descent as he turned onto the downwind leg. With his father standing on the right wing, he found that he had to put in a little more left rudder to hold the Stearman in the proper attitude. Henry turned onto final 300 feet above the ground at an airspeed of 60 knots. He cut the throttle back to idle when he saw he could make the runway with no power. He was intent on the landing and did not see this father snapping pictures of him one-handed while holding onto the wing strut with the other. He also did not notice that there was no clip holding his father to any of the flying wires.

At what he judged to be about three feet over the runway, Henry increased back-pressure on the stick to halt his descent. He was jockeying with the rudder pedals to keep the nose aimed straight down the centerline of the asphalt.

The big biplane held its three-foot altitude as Henry increased backpressure on the stick. The boy was glancing every couple of seconds at the airspeed indicator, watching it wind down. As the needle swung through an indicated forty-eight knots, the stick was all the way back in Henry's lap and the Stearman settled gently onto the runway, no longer having sufficient speed to keep flying. The main gear and the tailwheel touched the asphalt at almost the same instant. With the ten-knot headwind, the Stearman was only traveling about forty miles per hour on the ground, but Henry knew that he was now at the most critical point of the landing.

With a tricycle gear airplane, which had become the most common type starting in the 'fifties, the steerable third wheel was in the nose, ahead of the airplane's center of gravity. In this inherently stable system, the plane would attempt to return to a straight path if the nose gear were turned to one side and then released.

A 'conventional' gear airplane, like the Stearman, had its third wheel in the rear, behind the center of gravity. This was better for landing on poor terrain, where two large main gear in front could endure forces that would snap off a single, more fragile nosegear. The drawback was that having the third, steerable wheel in the rear created an inherently unstable system. If a tailwheel airplane got angled more than a small amount to one side, the plane would continue swinging around so that its center of gravity ended up in front of the main landing gear.

This was called a groundloop. If it happened at any speed greater than a slow walk, the airplane would tip over and put a wingtip into the ground, causing substantial damage. Taildragger pilots had to quickly, judiciously, and continually use the rudder and brake pedals to keep the plane aimed straight until its groundspeed was down to a crawl. Henry knew if he allowed the nose to swing more than slightly out of line, he could not prevent a groundloop, for the finest pilot in the world could not repeal the laws of physics.

The problem was magnified by the tall landing gear that was installed on the custom Stearman, necessary to provide ground clearance for the oversize prop. Walter, however, had taught his son well, and as the biplane settled onto the runway, Henry held the stick all the way back to plant the tailwheel firmly on the asphalt, and he kept the nose pointed straight with quick, precise jabs on the rudder pedals.

The Stearman coasted down to walking speed, and Henry pushed gently on the right brake and turned off the runway at midfield. Only then did he glance over at his father, who was smiling broadly. Henry tapped the left brake and blipped the throttle, and the Stearman turned onto the taxiway and headed for the hangar at the rate of a man's brisk trot.

"Let's put her to bed and go get something to eat. You hungry?" Walter asked after Henry had pulled the mixture control to full lean and the engine had quit.

"Real hungry, Dad."

"Steak n Shake suit you?" he asked, naming their favorite drive-in.

"Perfect." His father jumped off the wing and walked back to the Stearman's tail to swing it around before pushing the plane back into the hangar. The pain in Walter's side had eased to a dull ache.

***

"Your maneuvers were better than ever today, Son. You really greased in that landing, too." Walter took another bite of his steakburger. His appetite wasn't what normally was.

Henry smiled at the compliment, then asked his father something that had puzzled him all morning. "Dad, when you flew through the arch, weren't you afraid of losing your license? No one else has a plane that looks like this one. What if someone reports us?"

Walter smiled, but his face was filled with sadness. "It doesn't matter, Henry. My medical is up this month, and I wouldn't pass if I tried to renew it. That was my last flight in the Stearman, Son. It's one of the reasons I wanted to go flying with you today. I needed to talk to you about it." Henry put down the french fries he had been about to put in his mouth and stared at his father.

"What do you mean you can't pass the physical? What's wrong, Dad?"

Walter took a very deep breath before answering. "I've got cancer. Renal cancer—that's when it's in your kidneys, and it's one of the really bad ones."

Henry was horrified. His father was in better shape than the parents of almost all of his classmates at school. He could not believe what he was hearing. "*Cancer...but...can't they do anything about it?*" The boy tried frantically to persuade himself that his father was going to be all right, but he knew he would not. Henry had watched his grandfather, Charles Collins, waste away to nothing from throat cancer five years before.

"They're doing it right now. That's why I'm out flying today. But I've been losing some weight, as I'm sure you can see, and the pain in my sides comes more often. It's one of those things, Henry, just like Grandpa." He smiled with genuine warmth. "I'll be around for a while—you haven't seen the last of your old Dad yet. I'm through with flying, but no aviator ever had a better send-off than the one I just had with you."

Henry stared at his lap. He had entirely lost his appetite. Walter continued matter-of-factly.

"I thought for a long time about what to do with the Stearman. I always wanted it to be yours one day, but you're only fourteen, and wouldn't be able to fly it on your own for another year-and-a-half. Also, it's got some serious expenses coming up. An airshow pilot has made me a very good offer on it. He's got a clipwing Cub with a 140 Lycoming in it, an inverted system, aileron spades, and big tires for landing almost anywhere. It's registered experimental. He's going to trade it to me, along with quite a bit of cash.

"You'll have your own acro ship you can solo on your sixteenth birthday, and the gas costs won't break you. I'm going to put the money in an account that will be yours when you turn twenty-one. Should be worth quite a bit by then." Walter didn't mention the life insurance policy, or that Henry would also start getting his Social Security. "I think that's a better plan for the long run." Henry nodded without looking up. He wasn't thinking about flying. He was imagining what his life would be like without his father.

"When did you find out, Dad?" he asked finally.

"Last week they finished up the last of their tests at Barnes. There's no doubt now. Your mother suspected ever since I first started feeling bad. She's the reason they caught it this early, and were able to give me some medicine that helps with the pain."

Henry turned to look out the window so his father wouldn't see him crying.

***

Henry Bowman was absolutely miserable as he got out of the car and went to open the garage door for his father. He watched as Walter pulled the car into its space and opened the door to get out. Henry stared at his father as he climbed out of the car. He was searching for a visible sign of Walter's affliction.

His father, however, looked the same as he always had. It was hard to believe that this strong, vital man harbored a fatal disease that was relentlessly killing him. Walter stepped over to the side of the garage where a tarpaulin hung down, covering something.

"If we can't fly together, then you and I are going to have to do more shooting."

Henry could not believe his eyes as his father pulled away the tarpaulin. There were twenty wooden crates stacked against the wall, all with German lettering stenciled on their sides. He'd have to get out his manual to decipher the words exactly, but Henry needed no dictionary to translate '20mm', and the crates themselves were familiar. Two empty ones had been sitting in a corner of the basement for more than a month.

Walter's smile broadened as he watched Henry's reaction. "There's some other calibers coming," he explained, "but I thought I'd better jump on the ammo for your Solothurn first. Your buddy made me a deal I couldn't pass up."

Henry Bowman started crying again, but this time he did not turn away.

April 5, 1968

"My dad says he's surprised it didn't happen sooner." Some of the students gathered outside the lunchroom nodded gravely at this assessment.

The Sturkes boy did not add that his father had also said '*and I hope they give the guy who did it a medal*'. John Burroughs School believed in promoting academic excellence and opening pupils' minds, but some parents differed with the institution's philosophy of racial harmony. Mr. Sturkes wasn't the only father who, in the security of his own living room, was not afraid to assert that the death of Dr. Martin Luther King, jr. was no great loss to the civilized world.

"I still can't believe somebody shot him." This was another student who, like the vast majority of his classmates at John Burroughs, came from a white, upper-class St. Louis family. Like a somewhat smaller (but nonetheless large) number of Burroughs students, if the tenth-grader had been asked twenty-four hours earlier who Dr. King *was,* he would have been unable to answer. "I'd like to kill the guy who did it," the sophomore added with great conviction.

"To spare Mrs. King from having to return to Memphis?" Henry Bowman asked, deadpan. The others looked at him oddly, but no one said anything in reply.

"Everybody at the paper's expecting real trouble," a short brown-haired girl broke in. Her father worked on the editorial page of the *St. Louis Globe-Democrat*, one of two dailies that served the metropolitan area. "Dad's afraid we'll have riots."

The girl's father was not the only person in St. Louis to hold that opinion.

***

"Jesus *Christ,* do you think you've got enough ammo?" the Mayor of Wellston asked his Chief of Police as he watched the man bring two more cans and put them on the pile. There were now over forty of the metal boxes stacked up against the air vent. It was the first time the Mayor had been on the roof of City Hall, and he marvelled at the number of cigarette butts he saw on the tarpaper. He turned his attention back to the current project.

"And do you really think this is a good idea?" The mayor was not at all sure that placing a live, tripod-mounted, heavy-barreled Browning .50 caliber belt-fed machine gun (effective range: 7300 yards) on the edge of the roof of the Wellston City Hall was the most appropriate response to local concerns about possible rioting. "We likely won't see any trouble in this area at all," he added. His tone showed more hope than conviction. Wellston was one of the poorer areas of St. Louis, and in poor neighborhoods, crime is often a major issue. Both the mayor and the police chief knew that any breakdown in security would be recognized as a perfect opportunity by potential looters.

"You're damned right we won't see any trouble," the chief said with mild indignation. His face glistened with sweat from the effort of lugging an 80-pound gun, 40-pound tripod, and several thousand rounds of linked ammunition up from the storeroom. His smile was bright. "Put ol' Ma Deuce up here where every damned one with a mind to bust windows and loot can get a good long look, with me or Jack sitting behind her. Won't be any riot here. Old Uncle drilled it into my head real well in Korea: You take care of Ma Deuce, and she'll take care of you." He looked intently at the Mayor. "You recall any riots in Wellston when they had that mess in Watts back in '65?"

The mayor shook his head. They had erected the big Browning on the roof three years earlier, during the riots in California. They had also called a meeting with local ministers and other community leaders, so that the members of their congregations could be encouraged to take similar measures to protect their homes and businesses. Delinquents in Wellston got the clear message that looting would not be tolerated, and that '*You loot, we shoot*' was official city policy. The M2 Heavy Barrel .50 BMG on the roof of City Hall had been a constant reminder of that during the Watts riots. Wellston had avoided the violence and theft that plagued other areas.

As it turned out, the strategy was once again exactly right. Would-be rioters in Wellston rapidly concluded that other neighborhoods offered more opportunity, and Wellston remained peaceful.

April 6, 1968

"Got a safari planned any time soon, Mr. Baxter?" Al Goodman asked in his nasal monotone. Most gun shop conversations across the country that day centered around the King assassination, but at Goodman's the talk, as always, revolved around fine guns and big-game hunting.

"No, got another baby on the way. Maybe in a couple of years. And when I go again, it won't be to Portuguese Angola. Those bohunks are the worst excuse for professional hunters I've ever seen in my life." The man shook his head in disgust at the memory. "They can't imagine doing any stalking on foot—they want you to do all your shooting out of the jeep. And they don't have a clue where to look for the game; I ended up being the guide most of the time."

Max Collins, who was several yards away looking at a Perazzi trap gun, listened in. He had been considering a safari himself, and the booking agent had been pushing him to sign up for three weeks in Angola. The man who was speaking was about thirty. Max had seen him in Goodman's before, and knew him vaguely. He listened as the younger man continued.

"I think Rhodesia, next time," Baxter went on. "That, or back to Kenya, but I'd like to go someplace new."

"The booking agent I've been talking to has been pushing Angola," Max said, joining the conversation.

"They always recommend whatever they've sent people on before. That's fine if they've got some basis for comparison, but a lot of these guys have never even been to Africa themselves, and push whoever'll give them the fattest percentage. I'm in insurance, so believe me, I know how that works."

"Sounds like you've got some experience there. You'd advise against Angola?"

"Don't get me wrong—there's all kinds of game in Angola right now. It's just that the Portuguese guides are atrocious, if mine was typical, and I think he was. Give you an example, the pro I had, the trigger on his rifle was screwed up, and he never had it fixed. Striker wouldn't stay cocked unless he put the safety on while he was closing the bolt. Then the gun would fire when he took the safety off."

"So he didn't back you up?"

"That was the problem—no backup would have been *fine* with me. *This* idiot used his gun the way it was."

"What do you mean? He'd...close the bolt while engaging the safety, then fire it by flicking the safety off instead of pulling the trigger?"

"Exactly." Baxter paused for effect, then added, "And he said his gun had been that way for over a year." Max shook his head in amazement. Then Baxter remembered something.

"Now, I did meet a white hunter while I was over there who was born here in the states. Don't know much else about him, only talked to him at the airport. Seemed to know his stuff, though. If you're serious about going to Angola, I think you should try to find out more about him."

"Who is he?"

"Guy from—where was it?—Colorado, I think he said. Young for a pro; about my age. His name is Raymond Johnson."

April 27, 1968

Walter Bowman was down to 105 pounds. He had survived ten months longer than the twelve weeks that the cancer specialists had privately given him to live, but it was evident that now all of his reserves had been exhausted. He had been unable to speak for several days.

Henry waved the private nurse out of the way, sat down next to the bed, and took his father's hand. He stared down at the husk of what had so recently been a very strong man. Henry looked at his father for a long time. Walter's eyes were still clear. After a time, the stricken man shook his head almost imperceptibly. Henry saw the gesture immediately. He swallowed.

"It's time, isn't it?"

Walter Bowman's head moved a fraction of an inch in a nod.

Henry nodded in reply. "Keep the front cockpit open for me, Dad. We'll go flying the next time I see you."

Henry felt his hand clasped in a powerful grip that shocked him with its intensity, and he instinctively returned it. As quickly as they had become taut, his father's muscles went slack.

Walter Bowman was dead.

June 5, 1968

"Oh, my God!" Catherine Bowman exclaimed.

"What is it, Mom?" Henry asked, racing into the family room where his mother sat in front of the television set.

"Bobby Kennedy's been shot. Just after midnight, at a reception at some hotel in California."

Her son sat down on the couch without taking his eyes off the television screen. The newsman was explaining what he had been told so far: The shooting had happened at the celebration following Kennedy's victory in the California primary for the 1968 Presidential election. A young man, apparently from a middle eastern country, had shot the senator with a pistol. The number of shots was not known. The gunman had been wrestled to the floor and disarmed. Robert Kennedy had been rushed to the hospital. His condition at the moment was not known, either.

It would later come out that pro football star Roosevelt Grier had been one of those who had thrown Sirhan B. Sirhan to the floor and ripped the gun out of his hand, and that Grier had broken the shooter's finger in the process of doing this.

People across the entire country had an eerie feeling of deja vu as they sat riveted to their television sets, watching the news. Catherine Bowman was no exception.

Henry Bowman's mother was overpowered by two very different sets of feelings. First of all, she was no fan of the Kennedy family. When she was growing up, she had watched the man who had made his fortune through stock manipulation and bootlegging liquor be appointed head of the Securities and Exchange Commission, and later Ambassador to England. She had then seen the Ambassador's admiration for the Nazi regime that had nearly killed her brother, and she had always despised the man and his obvious assumption that his sons were the rightful heirs to Washington, Jefferson, Lincoln, and the good Roosevelt.

Those feelings, however, did not change the horror Catherine Bowman felt at the thought of a woman having two of her sons slain by murderers. No one should have to experience the loss of a child, and Catherine Bowman's heart went out to Rose Kennedy for what she had endured.

Henry's mother realized with a start that she had felt exactly this way once before. More than twenty years earlier, she'd heard the news that two atomic bombs had been dropped on Japan, over 100,000 Japanese citizens had been killed, Japan had surrendered, and American servicemen including her brother Max were coming home instead of being sent to invade the Japanese mainland. Her thoughts then were the same as those she had now: *How horrible* and *Thank God.*

"It's just like his brother," she breathed in disbelief. "He's dead."

"Maybe not, Mom. We don't know how bad it is, yet," Henry said, not very convincingly.

Catherine Bowman was absolutely right in her first comment. A second Kennedy son had just been shot, allegedly by another young, disillusioned misfit with ties to a third-world country. All witnesses would state that the assailant had approached the Senator from the front, yet the three bullets had entered Kennedy's body from the rear. The number of bullet wounds inflicted upon Kennedy and five other people, combined with the number of bullet holes in the walls and ceiling of the surrounding room, was absolutely astonishing considering that the supposedly lone assassin had used one .22 caliber revolver and nothing else. Guests who told police investigators they had seen other men with guns would have their testimony ignored.

All this would be a bit much for many people to be expected to accept for the second time, and questions about both assassinations would persist for decades.

Catherine Bowman was wrong in her latter statement, however. Robert Kennedy was in fact still alive. He had been shot once in the head and twice behind the armpit with a .22 caliber revolver. Due to the low power of the .22 cartridge and the perverse fact that the human brain can often sustain damage to certain areas with minimal apparent effect, a startling number of people have survived head wounds from .22 slugs and recovered fully.

Robert Kennedy was not one of those cases, however, and he was pronounced dead that afternoon at 1:44 p.m. California time.

July 10, 1968

"Like how it runs?" Max Collins asked his nephew. He and Henry were west of Wentzville, about seventy miles out of St. Louis heading for the live pigeon shoot in Reno, Nevada. Traffic on Interstate 70 that far west of the city was almost nonexistent, and the needle on the Impala's big speedometer held steady on 105.

"It's a lot quieter than I would have thought. Not nearly as noisy as your Riviera was."

"Not working as hard. Got a lot more motor than the Buick. Ron Winterhoff said I should let him do the heads, balance the crank, open up the exhaust, and drop the nose an inch and a half. Damn if that kid didn't know exactly what he was talking about. This 427 Chevy is twice the car that Buick ever dreamed of being."

To make his point, Max pushed his right foot down until the accelerator lay against the carpet. The big V-8's exhaust note dropped half an octave, and then both it and needle on the speedometer started to climb. The pointer was closing in on the far right side of the gauge as the full-size Chevy's speed continued to increase. Max relaxed his right foot, and the noise stabilized along with the car's rate of travel. Wind noise and the sound of the engine precluded normal conversation, but the ride was remarkably vibration-free. It felt to Henry as if the car could travel all day at this rate, the Highway Patrol notwithstanding. Max held the car at this speed for almost ten minutes, during which time he and his nephew covered over twenty-two miles and passed nineteen other vehicles. Henry stretched his legs out in front of him and took a deep breath. He and his uncle were both having a very good time.

Max Collins eased off on the throttle when a cluster of five or six cars appeared in the distance. By the time he and Henry caught up to them, he had slowed the Impala so that it matched their velocity of seventy miles per hour.

"I wish the people around here would learn to stay in the right lane if they're not passing anyone. Seems like the folks in this part of Missouri have never heard of proper lane discipline." Henry waited for his uncle to start swearing under his breath at the drivers of the cars in the left lane. Max hated inept drivers. Max, however, stayed to the right and dropped back several lengths. He showed no evidence of irritation, and Henry smiled in understanding. *He's having too good a time, heading off to Reno for a big-money pigeon shoot. Even left lane bandits can't spoil his day.*

Ever since his airborne experience in the 1944 Normandy invasion, Max Collins had preferred traveling by car for any trip of less than 2000 miles. This was especially true if he himself were able to do the driving, and he was in his own car. Max Collins had great appreciation for competent, high-speed road cars that could carry him and all his gear safely, reliably, and comfortably. The ported, balanced, and lowered 1967 Impala Super Sport that he and Henry were piloting across the country was the best vehicle he had ever owned for that task.

Max Collins was not the only person in the car who was in a good mood. Fifteen-year-old Henry Bowman hadn't smiled so much since his father had been alive and healthy. Max had invited the boy to join him on the ten-day trip to Reno, and Henry had begged his mother to be allowed to go. Catherine had readily agreed. July Fourth was normally Henry's favorite holiday. Without Walter, it had been very sad for both the boy and his mother, but for Henry especially. Max's idea to invite Henry to go to Reno had been an inspired one. There was a big gun show in Reno at the same time as the highest-purse live pigeon shoot in the entire country.

Max had given Henry a Winchester Model 70 in .375 H&H Magnum two years before, and the rifle was now in a case in the Impala's trunk along with Max's pigeon guns. Goodman's had taken it in on trade from an elk hunter who thought it kicked too much, and since it had a few scratches in the buttstock, Al Goodman hadn't given much for it. Henry was delighted with the weapon, and had wasted no time ordering a thousand fired cartridge cases from the Winchester factory and variety of bullets and powders to work up loads. The big dangerous-game rifle grouped almost as well as his target rifle when using ammunition loaded with inexpensive 235-grain Speer bullets and a case full of Hodgdon's surplus 4831 powder. He'd been shooting the gun several times a week since school ended.

"Do you really think there'll be any place I can shoot a rifle at the shotgun range?" Henry asked his uncle.

"Hell, yes, kid. It's out in the middle of a goddamned *desert*—nothing but sand and cactus and maybe a few lizards crawling around. There wouldn't be any people at all in the state if the bluenoses in California had ever had sense enough to allow gambling." Max saw an opening in traffic and accelerated past the other cars, once again letting the big coupe stretch its legs.

"It's a damned shame I can't get you interested in shotguns. There's a hell of a lot more money in one major trap or pigeon shoot than in a whole year's worth of all the rifle and pistol matches put together." Henry smiled, but said nothing. *Shotguns are okay, but they're kind of boring* he thought. Max glanced over at him, almost able to read his mind. "Hell, I shouldn't say that," Max relented. "Truth is, I like rifles and pistols better myself. A damn shame you can't make any money with them, though." His face took on a look of irritation as he thought of something else.

"We'll be shooting BB guns before it's all over, if the sons-of-bitches in Washington have their way. That fucking Ay-rab. With a goddamned starter's pistol..." Max left the sentence unfinished. The weapon Sirhan had actually used was an H&R, and Max knew it, but his disgust was quite plain. The idea of an American figure and his Secret Service protectors being bested by a Middle-Eastern street punk with a weapon of only slightly better quality than the blank guns used at track meets was something Max Collins found much more offensive than the basic concept of killing a public servant.

Henry scowled at his uncle's last comments. After the King and Kennedy assassinations, which had come less than three months apart, there had been a frenzy of activity as politicians loudly proclaimed the need for new restrictions on firearm purchase and ownership. *Whatever's coming* he thought, *it's not going to be good.*

***

"I guess this one's got a vacancy," Max said unnecessarily as he pulled into the motel's parking lot. It was a little after one in the morning, local time. They were a mile off the highway, in the middle of Colorado.

"I'll get the guns out of the trunk while you're getting a room," Henry offered. His uncle handed him the keyring before easing his tall frame out of the Impala. The engine was making soft ticking noises in the cool night air as Henry went to open the trunk.

Henry Bowman had their gun cases, range kits, and both traveling bags lined up on the concrete walk by the time his uncle returned from the office, where a sleepy clerk had taken his cash and handed him the key to a double room. Max picked up three of the pieces of luggage and led the way to their accommodations.

Driving enervated Max, particularly when it was at high speeds. Now that the car was parked and a mattress beckoned, he realized how tired he was. After using the toilet and making sure his travel alarm was wound, he got out of his clothes and stretched out on the bed nearest the door. It was a little too short, but that was nothing unusual for him. He closed his eyes, knowing sleep was about to overtake him.

"Seven o'clock too early for you, kid? Shower and grab some breakfast before we get rolling again?"

Henry grinned. He had dozed off and on in the car during the last few hours of the day's drive. "It's fine with me. I'm going to go get a soda from the machine out front." He felt in his pocket for a dime as he left the room. Soda machines at gas stations and motels often had flavors that his mother refused to buy at home, and the one by the registration office did not disappoint him.

The night was quiet, and the glow of neon was the brightest light nearby. Henry looked up at the sky as he sipped from the bottle, and he realized he could see several times as many stars as he could in Missouri. This phenomenon was the converse of the one Ray Johnson had observed fourteen years before, when he had moved from Pitkin County to Boston.

As Henry Bowman stared up at the heavens that night, he had no inkling of the effect that his talent and passion would have on the lives of others. One of the people whose life would be most affected was a man who currently lived on the other side of the world, but who had grown up near the spot where a fifteen-year-old boy from Missouri was now standing, happily drinking a grape soda at 1:00 in the morning.

"Adams," the auctioneer announced. "Do I hear five hundred?" Silence. "Three hundred." Still no response. "One hundred dollars—minimum bid. Mister Adams, do you want to buy yourself for one hu–"

"One hundred!" yelled a bidder.

"Got one hundred, looking for one fifty, one *fifty*," the auctioneer declared as a hand went up. Jerry Adams eventually went for two hundred twenty-five dollars.

***

"Collins," said the announcer, when he reached the fifth name on the list. He looked up from his clipboard and recognized Max. "Do I hear five hundred?" There was a brief pause. Max was squinting, looking at the increased movement of the clouds in the sky. It looked like it might get very windy.

"Five hundred," Max said in a firm voice. "Then everybody can get on to the real shooters." He favored the group with a self-deprecating grin.

"Collins bids five hundred on himself. Any others?" As Max had suspected, there were no higher bids. If no one had agreed to meet the auctioneer's first suggestion, and the bidding had dropped, it might well have ended up higher. Max was well-known as an excellent live-bird shooter, but by his own admission he was not a full-time pro on the trap and pigeon circuit. Five hundred was a high starting bid for any amateur, and Max had gently reminded the bidders of who was coming up for auction in a few minutes.

"*Sold*," the auctioneer announced, and scribbled the number on his sheet. Henry Bowman was disappointed that no one else had wanted to bid on his uncle.

Max Collins smiled to himself.

***

"Devers!" the auctioneer almost shouted.

"Two thousand!" yelled a voice in the crowd before the auctioneer had time to suggest an opening bid.

"Three." This came from several men, speaking at once.

"Thirty-five," came another voice, and the auctioneer's eyes switched to the newest speaker.

The auctioneer was present because the Reno shoot was being run as a Calcutta. It was this fact that had drawn both the best live-bird shooters in the nation and the huge number of spectators and professional gamblers to the Nevada event.

In a Calcutta, shooters paid an entry fee, which went to the sponsors of the competition. In this case it was $100 per shooter. Before the shoot started, an auction was held, and each competitor was auctioned off to the highest bidder. If any shooter failed to fetch the $100 minimum bid, he could either drop out and get his entry fee refunded, forfeit his chance at the prize but still shoot in competition, or purchase himself for $100. No shooter ever chose the first option, and only rarely did one opt for the second. It was a matter of pride.

The revenue raised by the auction became the winning purse. The shooter who won the competition got a percentage of the purse, and whoever had purchased him at auction got the rest of it. In the Reno shoot, the split was fifteen percent to the shooter and eighty-five to the bidder who had 'bought' him. If a shooter who had bought himself happened to win, he kept all the winnings. It was rare, but it happened once in a while.

First place paid half the purse. Second took 30%, and third paid 20%. From the standpoint of prize money, fourth place was no better than dead last. For this reason, there were myriad side bets going on entirely apart from the sponsors of the shoot. Some of these bets were larger than any of the amounts the shooters were bringing at auction.

"Six thousand—do I hear six thousand for Devers?" said the auctioneer. "Fifty-five hundred once, twice, *SOLD* to Mister Burke for fifty-five hundred." Modest applause went up from the crowd. Joe Devers was the odds-on favorite to win. With the purse expected to top forty thousand dollars, Burke was looking at close to a three-to-one return if his man ended up with the high score.

Other entrants in the Reno shoot came up for bid and were duly auctioned off. Heavy bidding centered on eight shooters. There was moderate activity on about a dozen serious amateurs, who were generally thought to be about the same ability as Henry's uncle. Most of the remaining competitors were bought for a hundred to a hundred fifty dollars either by themselves, or by personal friends hoping that a miracle would happen.

"That's the last of it. We start at ten o'clock sharp, gentlemen. See you then." The meeting broke up.

July 13, 1968

July 16, 1968

"Pull!" At the command from Norm Frakes, who was the first shooter up on the third day of the shoot, the trap boy hit the button on the control in his hand and the trap just to the right of the center one snapped open. A jet of compressed air forced the disoriented bird a few yards into the air, and the pigeon immediately got its bearings and started flying with the wind. Frakes swung his Woodward-actioned Purdey to his left and fired once. His shot pattern was perfectly centered on the bird, and it crumpled in flight, dead. Its body arced through the air, rolling from the impact of the shot charge. The dead bird hit on its back in the dirt, landing less than two feet from the fence and bouncing into the wire. Murmurs went up from the crowd.

The Calcutta was a seventy-five bird event, with each participant shooting twenty-five birds each day. The first two days had been calm, and seven competitors were on the board with scores of either forty-eight or forty-nine. Max Collins, Joe Devers, and young Britt Robinson were the three leading scorers, with four others just one bird behind. Norm Frakes stood at forty-three.

"Norm's a good shot," Max whispered to his nephew, "but he takes too much time being careful. Don't be surprised if he loses six or eight birds he kills, in this wind. If that one had come out any of the traps on the left side, it would have been a lost bird." Henry nodded in understanding. He had realized this last fact the instant he had seen the dead pigeon hit the ground. As Henry considered Norman Frakes' lack of speed, a boy ran out into the ring carrying a pigeon and stowed it in the empty trap from which the first bird had been released.

Live pigeon competitions had originated in Mexico. There, human bird throwers used sleight-of-hand, feinting movements, and tremendous arm muscles to inject uncertainty into where the bird would go. In the U.S., the element of chance was provided by machines.

Norm Frakes stood at the shooter's station facing an oval-shaped dirt area which stretched from left to right in front of him. The oval was bounded by a wire fence 28 inches tall. Positioned in an arc 14 yards in front of the shooter were nine metal devices, each one about six feet from its neighbor. These were the traps, and each one of them held a pigeon. Henry thought they looked like large iron bananas. There were lead smears on some of them, and Henry wondered how often the human bird throwers down south ended up with pellet wounds.

The shooter held his shotgun aimed at the center trap, and called 'pull' when he was ready to have a bird released. When the trap operator pressed the button on his control box, the sides of one of the traps opened, releasing the bird. No one, including the operator, had any idea which one of the nine traps it would be. That was randomly determined by the electrics of the system.

As the 'iron banana' snapped open, a jet of compressed air from a fitting inside the device launched the bird out of the trap. This served two purposes: It got the bird moving much more quickly than if it were merely released, and it also disoriented the pigeon so that the bird's initial flight path was completely unpredictable. Sometimes the pigeon continued climbing, and sometimes it flew straight down to within a few feet of the ground before streaking left, right, away, or (rarely) straight at the man with the shotgun.

The shooter had to recognize which trap was releasing the pigeon, understand the bird's movement, swing on the bird, fire, kill it, and have it fall within the fenced area to have it count for score. Live pigeon shooting was the most challenging and unpredictable of all shotgun competitions, and the level of excitement was greater than Henry had ever seen before.

"Pull!"

This time the bird came out of the third trap from the left and started flying with the wind immediately. Frakes centered his shot, but it was too late. The dead bird landed a good ten feet outside the fence. The shooter swore under his breath. He and all the spectators realized this gusty weather was going to make for very difficult shooting indeed.

***

"In Mexico, like I told you," Max explained to Henry, "they don't have these nine metal traps. They've got one bird boy on a strip of concrete, kind of like a sidewalk. He can move however much he wants to, as long as he stays on the sidewalk. He'll dance around, fake throwing the bird one way and really just toss a feather out while whipping the bird in some other direction behind his back. The really good ones, they'll make some shooters a side bet that they won't score even *one* bird out of ten."

"Where does the shooter hold, before the thrower releases the bird?" Henry asked.

"Right on the thrower's head." Henry took a moment to think about that.

"Don't they ever get shot?"

"Yes, they do. Especially when you get a shooter using a release trigger, which most people use when money's involved because they're just a little bit faster. I've shot live pigeon matches down south, but I won't use a release trigger. Saw a boy get killed that way, once. He stopped on the concrete strip to grin at the shooter, a guy from Georgia who'd never used a release trigger before. The grin was part of the kid's routine to distract the guy before throwing the bird, I guess. Man relaxed his grip and took out the left half of the kid's neck. He bled out in about ten seconds."

"Did they stop the match?"

"Hell, no. Got his brother to replace him. Brother had an even better arm, in my opinion. Watching those throwers is really something, but I've never gotten used to aiming right on their heads, even using a standard trigger. I shoot a lot better when it's just those 'iron bananas' holding the birds." He smiled and wiggled his eyebrows as he used Henry's descriptive term for the pigeon traps. "I got to go get my gear, kid. I'm up pretty soon." The big man turned to walk towards the Impala, and Henry went back to watching the current shooter.

***

By the time Max's name was called, the desert wind had increased, and was gusting to thirty knots. High score so far that day was twenty-one out of a possible twenty-five, shot by Britt Robinson. The fourth- and fifth-seeded shooters were in second and third place. Joe Devers had not yet come to the line.

In an attempt to compensate for conditions, some of the shooters had taken to holding on the far left trap. With the wind blowing hard from the right, it was the left side traps that were yielding most of the missed birds. Max held on the center trap as he took a deep breath. He didn't want to alter the presentation of the birds from what he was used to, wind or no wind.

"Pull!"

The far left trap sprang open just as a powerful gust of wind blew several hats off some of the spectators. The bird's path started curving downwind even while it was still traveling upward from the compressed air. It had not even reached the apex of its launch when the bottom barrel of Max's Fabbri cracked and a cloud of feathers erupted from around the pigeon. They were carried away on the wind while the shapeless dead mass spun through the air and slammed into the base of the wire fence. *Dead bird* thought Henry, as he felt the hair on his arms stand up.

The crowd murmured its appreciation and several of the spectators who had not been paying much attention stopped what they were doing and waited to see what happened on Max's second bird. No shooter yet had gotten off a shot on the far left trap in so heavy a wind and still killed the bird inside the fence.

Max turned towards the center trap as the bird boy refilled the empty one on the end. His senses seemed even more keen than usual, and the good feeling he'd had when he stepped up to the line only intensified. He broke the gun open, ejected the spent case, switched the unfired shell from the top barrel into the lower one, and slid a new shell from his ammo pouch into the top barrel. Max raised the shotgun to his shoulder and put the front gold bead on the base of the center trap.

"Pull!"

What happened next caused a flurry of activity among the people who had been making heavy side bets as the competition continued. Max pulled the trigger the instant his brain realized that it was the middle trap that was opening. Collins' reflexes were at their absolute peak, and the center of the shot charge hit the pigeon when the bird was less than two feet off the ground. Several of the spectators thought the trap had been empty, for they had not even seen the bird.

"Jesus *Christ!*" Charlie Potts said to Ed Meers, who was standing next to him. "Did you see that?" Meers nodded without speaking.

"Shooting a standard trigger, too," another man added.

"Who is this man?" whispered a third. He was from Barcelona.

"Max Collins. Out of Missouri. Good guy, if you don't get him mad at you. See him at some of the big trapshoots, but he likes live pigeons the best. Saw him shoot in Mexico once, but he wasn't *this* fast."

"I don't believe I have ever even seen him before," said the Spaniard. "You say he likes live birds best? Why is he not shooting a release trigger? Any serious live bird shoo—"

"Pull!"

This time the pigeon came out of the trap second from the far left. Max crumpled the bird about six feet off the ground and it fell in the dirt well short of the fence.

"*Damn!* What'd this guy bring in the auction, and who's got him?"

"Bought himself for five hundred. Opening bid. No one raised it."

"Damn, that's *strong.*"

"He likes to bet, especially on himself. And the reason he doesn't use a release trigger," Charlie Potts said to the foreign visitor, "is that live birds are his favorite kind of *shotgun* shooting. He competes in rifle and pistol, too. Came in second at Wimbledon in thirty-eight or -nine." The Wimbledon Cup was the annual prone rifle match held on the thousand-yard range at Camp Perry, Ohio.

"Pull!"

The bird came out of the second trap from the far right. The pigeon was tumbling from the jet of compressed air, and when it started flying, it seemed to aim straight for the spot between Max's feet. Collins hit it with almost the entire shot column. The lead pellets arrested the bird's momentum entirely, and it fell like a stone a third of the way to the shooter.

"A rifle shooter. I never would have believed it had I not seen it myself."

"Max is hot today, all right."

Charlie's comment proved to be the understatement of the week.

***

The wind had abated slightly but was still very strong when Joe Devers stepped into position. Every shooter at the match had by now become aware of Max Collins' phenomenal score of twenty-four. It was universally accepted that Devers was the only shooter who had a chance of beating Max by going twenty-five straight without a miss.

"Pull!"

The bird was released from the trap second from the right, and Devers hit it about seven feet off the ground. As the wind carried the dead pigeon slightly towards the left side of the arena, Joe Devers centered the corpse with the shot pattern from the second barrel. It dropped directly in front of him.

"Joe's the fastest man I know on multiple shots—about as fast as Herb was with a Model 12, before he had his heart attack," Max whispered to Henry. "You should see him with a pump. I never could reliably get past four clays thrown in the air at the same time. Joe can hit five every time. He says I concentrate too much on the first shot. I need to get on to the next shot right away. That's why he's so fast on multiple targets."

Henry nodded. He knew exactly what his uncle meant. His own rifle shooting efforts faced the same dilemma. If you spent too much time getting a shot right, the next target would be on the ground before you could squeeze the trigger. If you hurried all your shots, you missed everything. The trick was to stay right on the edge of acceptable control, and gradually increase your speed.

Devers killed the next six birds well inside the fence. Though he shot each pigeon twice, only one of them had still been alive when the second shot charge hit it. Max, Henry, and the rest of the crowd watched intently as the man continued to score clean hits.

It finally happened on Devers' eleventh bird.

"Pull!"

The far left trap opened and the jet of compressed air launched the bird into the air. The pigeon was aimed upwards and started flying up and with the wind. Joe Devers swung left and shot the bird cleanly about ten feet off the ground. He pulled his Perazzi down out of recoil and fired the upper barrel. His second shot string hit the dead bird when it was four feet from the dirt. The impact gave it enough of a push that the bird landed three feet outside the fence. Reflexively, several hundred people sucked in a deep breath. They would spend the rest of the day debating whether or not the bird would have fallen inside the fence if Joe Devers hadn't fired the second shot.

"Missed bird," the official scorer called out.

"What happens if he only misses one, like you did, Uncle Max?" Henry asked in a whisper.

"Ties for high score split the first- and second-place prize money evenly, in this shoot." He looked over to where Devers was staring at the missed bird. Henry nodded. No one left on the roster could catch up, even killing 25 straight.

Henry and Max watched Joe Devers kill the next three birds well inside the fence, using a single shot on each one. Henry started to become anxious.

"Pull!"

The fifteenth bird was launched out of the extreme left trap. Just as Joe Devers swung on it, the pigeon regained its sense of orientation, pulled its wings in, and aimed its beak towards the ground to gain some momentum before starting to fly. The move caused Devers' shot string to go high. Two pellets connected with the pigeon, one in its right wing and one creasing its back. The bird, wounded but not dead, spread its wings and glided with the wind. As Joe pulled his gun out of recoil, everyone watched in fascination as the dying bird made a flared landing on the top wire of the short fence.

Henry knew exactly what was going through the shooter's mind. If Devers shot the bird where it sat, it was a virtual certainty that it would fall away from them, on the outside of the fence. The only thing to do was wait and hope that the bird, when it took flight again, came back inside the perimeter. Joe and all the spectators held their collective breath.

The pigeon was not up to flying, and it instinctively knew that the source of its troubles was upwind. It hopped off the fence wire and started walking west.

"Missed bird," the scorer called out. As noise erupted from the crowd, Joe Devers centered the wounded pigeon with the shot charge from his upper barrel.

The crowd watched with considerably less interest as Joe killed the final ten birds within the fence.

He was now fighting to hold onto second place.

**

Everywhere they walked at the range, Max drew stares and comments from the people who had heard of the money he had won in the Calcutta. Pigeon shooters clustered around Henry's uncle to congratulate him, express their admiration, and in a few cases, conceal their envy. The purse was over forty-seven thousand dollars, and Max Collins did not have to split his half of it with anyone.

"You cost Hayden here over five Gs today, Max," Denny Marks said with a laugh. The crowd had dwindled to several shooting friends of Max's, and a few others.

"Like hell he did!" Hayden Burke shot back. "When I seen how Collins here was hotter'n a monk's dream, I laid off my share of Devers for sixty cents on the dollar and put some side money on my new favorite. I got me enough scratch off'n that little wager to convince one a them girls down to the Diamond that I'm Cary Grant, out slummin'. That is, if I get me one isn't too smart." All of the men in the group laughed at Burke's joke. There might be a few cocktail waitresses in Nevada casinos who did not know who Cary Grant was, but every single one of them would recognize Hayden Burke.

"But kee-rist, son, if I had lost the five it would have been worth every bit of it watching that run Collins here had. If he'd been on 'em any sooner they'd a still been in the traps."

"You got that right," one of the men added.

"Max, would you and your nephew like to join us for dinner? Hayden, me, and a few others, we thought we'd head to Melton's about eight, eight-thirty." Doyle Patterson was speaking. He was the owner of the skeet and trap range.

"If they serve rare steaks and good bourbon, and maybe a decent hamburger for Henry here, we'd be glad to," Max answered.

"I think they can take care of both of you. And since we give them our birds, maybe Henry would like to taste one of the ones you shot. They do a good job of barbecued pigeon." Henry nodded emphatically at the suggestion. "You going in the clubhouse now, Max?" Patterson asked.

"Not just yet, Doyle. You got a free trap field up on the north side?"

"Well, sure. Nobody's shooting up there right now." He grinned at the big man. "You mean you haven't had enough excitement for one day?"

"I been having all the fun today. Henry here doesn't shoot shotguns much, but he has a Model 70 he'd like to heat up, and there's nothing but desert north of here. Think the noise will bother anyone?" Max asked. Centerfire rifles were a lot louder than shotguns.

"We shoot cannons around here, sometimes, fella."

"Grab your gear, kid." Max Collins fished his car keys out of his pants pocket and threw them to the boy. Henry rushed off to where the car was parked.

The other men in the group were trap and pigeon shooters, and had no particular interest in watching a teenage boy shoot a bolt action rifle. They were having a good time, however, and walking along with the winner of the Calcutta and reliving the excitement of the competition was a very pleasant thing for each one of them. That was the reason that when Henry and Max reached the north trap range, Hayden Burke, Doyle Patterson, and four other men were right behind them.

"What you got there, .243 Winchester?" one of the men asked when Henry pulled the rifle out of its case. Henry figured that the man's guess was because his rifle had a thick barrel. The Model 70 of the vintage Henry owned had been made in a heavy barrel version in several of the smaller calibers for varmint hunters, and Henry assumed the man had made this inference because his .375 also had a thick barrel. *He must think I shoot my groundhogs real close in* Henry thought. *Or maybe where this guy comes from, everybody puts 1 1/2 power scopes on their varmint rifles.*

In point of fact, Neal Steadman had no idea that Winchester made varmint rifles in .243, and hadn't even noticed the barrel contour on Henry's gun. He had asked Henry if his rifle was a .243 Winchester because that was the smallest caliber that came to mind. He doubted the 15-year-old was using a .270 or .30-06, although he supposed it was possible.

"No, a .375 Holland & Holland. Uncle Max has been letting me shoot it."

"*Shoot* it—hell, I *gave* it to you, kid. It's yours," Max said with a shake of his head. Henry said nothing. It made him feel awkward when people gave him valuable presents. "What load you shooting today?" Max asked.

"Two hundred thirty-five-grain Speer and a case full of 4831. Stays under two and a half inches at two hundred. Manuals say it's going about 2850." He reached into an olive-drab pouch originally designed to carry a gas mask, pulled out a cartridge, and handed it to Max for his inspection. *At least these people won't act like I'm crazy to shoot a .375 and start saying dumb things about my 'elephant gun'* he thought as he turned away and put in his earplugs. *Trap and pigeon shooters shoot more than I do. They probably all have .375s.* Henry slid his shooting glasses on and walked up towards the sixteen-yard line. He did not see the looks on the faces of the five men who stood around his uncle, staring at the cartridge Max held.

Henry carried his rifle in his right hand. Slung over his shoulder and hanging at his left side was the makeshift ammo pouch. It was divided into two partitions and held about a hundred rounds of .375 H&H Magnum ammo.

The young rifleman assumed that many of the competitors he'd seen that day had started shooting at an earlier age than he himself had. Henry was possessed of a logical, orderly mind, and he further assumed that any shooter good enough to compete in Reno's high-stakes live pigeon shoots would think it perfectly reasonable that a serious rifleman would want to sharpen his skills on moving targets.

Henry was right in his first assumption, and dead wrong on the second.

"He needs something to shoot at, Max. Want me to have one of the boys bring some cans from the clubhouse?" Doyle Patterson asked. The men watched as Henry picked up the aluminum control box that was at the end of the thick black cable and carried it with him.

"Why? You out of clays?" Max replied. Henry had walked to the sixteen-yard line. In regulation trapshooting, this was the firing position closest to the concrete bunker that housed the electric thrower. He looped the control box through the strap of his ammo pouch so that it hung below waist level on his left side. Henry transferred the rifle to his left hand and awkwardly reached into the pouch with his right. He withdrew four loaded rounds.

The Model 70 held three of the big cartridges in the magazine and a fourth one in the chamber. Henry loaded his rifle and threw it quickly to his shoulder a few times. He had mounted a Weaver K1.5 scope on his .375. Most users of the low-powered optic were shotgun shooters who attached them to their slug guns in deer season. Henry liked the wide field of view the small scope offered. He held the rifle in his right hand at waist level and touched the button on the control box with his left thumb.

The clay pigeon sailed out of the trap house. Henry looked at its trajectory without making a move to raise his gun. He wanted to see how they were flying. He had sighted his rifle in at 25 yards. That was the first point where the bullet crossed the line of sight as viewed through the scope. Past that distance, the bullet would strike higher than the point of aim, until gravity pulled it back down and the slug once again crossed the line of sight at a little over 200 yards. *I'm going to have to be awfully fast, or hold a little under them* the boy thought. *I'm 16 yards away from the bird before they even get out of the thrower.*

"The kid thinks he's going to shoot trap with an elephant rifle?" Neal Steadman said in disbelief. The entire group suddenly realized what Henry intended to do.

"Ten to one against *that* shot," Hayden Burke muttered without considering the group he was with.

"*Covered,*" Max Collins said in a loud voice as he pressed a bill into Burke's unsuspecting palm. As the others started to turn towards Max, Henry pressed the control button again and threw the rifle to his shoulder. The six men, none of whom were wearing hearing protection, snapped their heads towards the boy at the sound of the mechanical trap unleashing the clay pigeon. It flew straight away from Henry. A thunderous blast split the air and the clay bird disintegrated into black dust. As Henry rode the recoil, he racked the bolt and chambered a second round.

"*Jesus!* I never th–" Before Doyle Patterson could finish the sentence, Henry had sent a second clay sailing northwards and reduced it to fragments with another shattering blast. The men remained silent, held their fingers in their ears, and stared at Henry Bowman as he broke the next two birds as well.

As Henry was reloading his rifle, Hayden Burke suddenly remembered the bill that Max had pressed into his hand. He hadn't looked at it yet. The Texan lowered his eyes to his opened palm, and they grew wide. Grover Cleveland. Max Collins had bet a thousand dollars on his nephew.

"Didn't you always say you wouldn't give ten-to-one against the sun coming up in the morning, Hayden?" Max had a wolfish grin on his face. The others stared at the two men, wondering what would happen. Before Burke could answer, another blast made the men flinch. Reflexively, all eyes went to the trap field. Another hit.

Hayden Burke started laughing.

It took less than ten minutes for Henry to fire at forty-three clays from the sixteen yard line. Of the forty-three, Henry hit thirty-six. On the forty-fourth throw, no bird flew out of the concrete box. The trap needed to be refilled.

In the meantime, a small crowd had gathered around the men back at the twenty-five yard line. Several had come to see what was making the loud noise, and word of Burke's loss spread quickly. "While Doyle's refilling the trap, Hayden," Max Collins said pleasantly in a voice loud enough so that the men around him could all hear, "how about deciding what kind of odds you'll give me on one set of doubles." Max had no idea if Henry could hit two clay birds with a bolt action rifle, but he wasn't about to let the oil-man know it.

Burke was in a much better mood than most men would be who had just lost ten thousand dollars, in front of witnesses, right after making an impulsive decision. "You call it, this time," Burke replied. The smile was just below the surface.

"Even money, until he either hits or misses both," Max said after a moment's reflection. "One broken, it's a pass."

Burke considered this. "No bet," he said finally.

Henry walked back to the group, carrying his Winchester at the balance point with the bolt retracted. He was completely unaware of the money that had been wagered on his shooting skills.

"Henry, Hayden here wants to know if you can shoot doubles with your .375," Max said with a straight face.

"Boy, I don't know about that, Mr. Burke." *And I'm not sure I want to try it in front of two dozen nationally-ranked shooters.* "With a Garand, no problem. Even a Mauser, yeah, at least sometimes." He looked at his Model 70. "But this gun's got more recoil, and I'm afraid I'd be too slow on the second shot. Be awfully far out. Not sure where to hold on that second bird, either. I'll give it a try, though." Henry turned and walked back to the sixteen-yard line.

"I'll run the trap for you, Henry," Doyle Patterson offered when he returned from the concrete bunker that held the throwers. He had seen fit to put a pair of plugs in his ears.

"Mr. Burke wants me to try to shoot doubles," Henry explained with more than a little embarrassment. "I don't know if I'll have much luck, but..." He left the sentence unfinished.

"All set?" Patterson asked. Henry nodded.

"*Pull!*" Henry threw the gun to his shoulder and snapped off the shot when the crosshairs hit the first bird. As the rifle recoiled, Henry's left eye caught a fleeting glimpse of clay fragments in the air. He slapped his right hand up, back, forward, and down. He did not bother to grasp the bolt handle, but rather knocked it up and back with the base joint of his little finger, and then slammed it forward and shut with the hollow in the palm of his hand. The Winchester's bolt knob was round and smooth, and perfect for the rapid maneuver. Henry found the second bird in the scope and fired his second shot just as the black disc was about to hit the ground. It missed.

"Just over the top of it, and late, I think," he said, staring out at the trap field. "It took me too long to find the second one." *Maybe now that I've seen them fly, I can get on a little faster* he added silently. The boy looked out at the trap field, trying to judge how far away the second bird had been when it hit the ground. *Forty-five yards, looks like. Two and a quarter inches high.*

"Pull!"

This time Henry leaned farther into the first shot, and he worked the bolt a tiny bit faster than on his first try. As he pulled the big rifle out of recoil, he swung it slightly to the right, knowing where the second bird would be. As the riflescope's crosshairs fell through the trajectory of the clay bird, Henry pulled the trigger, hoping that his estimates of the range and the space below the bird were both right.

They were close enough. The half-ounce lead and copper projectile, which was traveling at over twice the speed of sound, caught the second bird an inch from the edge. It shattered nicely.

"Got it!" Patterson yelled. *"Damn,* but that's strong."

"Mister Patterson," Henry said quickly, "I'm not sure I could do that again if we stayed here all night. In front of the crowd we got now, can I quit on that one—quit shooting doubles, I mean?"

"Sure thing, Henry. I got an idea—something else I want you to try. Come on, walk back with me and let's see if your uncle has taken any more of old Hayden's money." Henry opened his rifle, stooped over to pick up his fired brass, and hurried to catch up with the older man. He thought nothing of Patterson's last comment.

"I may be slow, but I *do* learn," Hayden Burke said softly to Max as Henry and Doyle approached them. "Fallin' off a cliff's one thing, but I wasn't about to climb back up and jump off it afterwards."

"Max, your nephew here reminded me of something I heard years ago," the owner of the trap range said after the men in the group had exclaimed about Henry's shooting. "You ever hear the story about how when John Browning wanted the U.S. Government to adopt his BAR, he got Ad Topperwein to shoot skeet with one in front of the guys who decided what guns got bought?" Patterson had the details wrong, but the basic story was right.

"Seems I heard Topp mention something about that, once, when I was over at Olin's East Alton range in—hell, must have been the mid-'40s."

"A BAR fires from an open bolt," Henry exclaimed immediately. His mind was already working out how to compensate for the heavy bolt lurching forward before the gun actually fired.

"Think you could do it?" Doyle asked, smiling.

"I don't know," Henry said finally.

"Want to try?"

"You've got a BAR?" Henry almost yelled.

"Something even better." Doyle turned to Max. "Melton's will take us whenever we get there. You aren't starving or anything, are you?"

"We got lots of time."

"Then I'll be right back." Doyle Patterson set off for the clubhouse at a brisk walk. In the next few minutes, Max was congratulated by more shooters, and his nephew was peppered with questions about shooting clays with a high-power rifle. Henry Bowman remained unaware of his uncle's wager on his shooting.

"Here we go, Henry. Pull 'er on out of there." Doyle had returned with a gun case and a G.I. .50 caliber ammo can. He slid the zipper down on the side of the vinyl gun case and Henry withdrew the weapon. The receiver's famous silhouette was instantly obvious, but a pistol grip protruded from below, and the slender barrel had a large slotted device on the muzzle end.

"A Colt Monitor!" Henry exclaimed. The Monitor was the police version of the BAR that Colt had introduced several years after World War One had ended, in an effort to make use of a few of the countless surplus parts the factory had left over from unfinished wartime weaponry. The gun had no bipod, was several pounds lighter than the military BAR, and had a separate pistol grip for a more comfortable hold. It also had a Cutts Compensator attached to the muzzle. The Cutts reduced recoil and completely eliminated the weapon's tendency to climb under full-auto fire.

"Ever seen one before?" Doyle asked, impressed at the young man's knowledge.

"Just pictures." Henry retracted the bolt and threw the sixteen-pound automatic rifle to his shoulder. It balanced well, and wasn't as awkward as he had expected. He pulled the trigger, and the bolt slammed home. "It's definitely going to be different shooting aerial targets with this one," Henry said immediately.

Doyle opened the ammo can, revealing fifteen magazines neatly arranged on end in three rows of five. He handed one to the boy. Henry retracted the bolt again and took the proffered magazine in his free hand. He did not insert it into the weapon, for to do so would render the gun 'hot' and ready to fire full-automatic.

Henry walked back to his spot on the sixteen-yard line and slid the magazine into his right hip pocket, behind his wallet. He upended the Monitor and poked his thumbnail in the ejection port to reflect some of the fading sunlight into the barrel from the back. He looked down the muzzle to make sure there were no obstructions. The bore was clear. Henry pulled the magazine from his pocket and examined the top cartridge. The tip of the bullet was painted black, and the headstamp said LC 44. *1944 Lake City armor piercing .30-06. Probably gets it from Charley.* Henry snapped the magazine into the weapon and once again threw it to his shoulder. He drew a bead on a yellow and black fragment of broken clay bird lying on the ground thirty yards out.

When Henry squeezed the trigger, the Colt emitted two thundering blasts. *Got to get off the trigger a little faster* Henry silently admonished himself. The gun's report sounded louder than Henry's .375. This startled some of the spectators, but not the shooter. The Cutts Compensator was designed to redirect muzzle gases to reduce a gun's recoil. In so doing, the device increased the noise level for anyone behind the weapon. After the .375, the Monitor's recoil felt mild.

The first bullet struck the ground in front and slightly to the right of the clay fragment that had been Henry's aiming point. *Bolt inertia makes it hit low and a bit right when you shoot it from the shoulder this close up.* He fired a second time at the same spot to make sure, this time releasing the trigger as soon as he felt it break. Henry then slid the rear sight to the 300 yard setting and tried again. Dirt flew just to the right of the piece of compressed clay. He touched off another single round while holding on the left edge of the target. The broken target vanished in a black cloud of dust and flying dirt. He moved the rear sight up one more notch and tried again on another fragment, this time holding slightly under it and even with the left edge. The results were the same.

"Let's give it a try," Henry said over his shoulder to Doyle Patterson. "Pull!"

Henry Bowman threw the Monitor to his shoulder and loosed a round at the departing clay. It continued its journey. *Got to get my swing started sooner* Henry thought. *This thing weighs almost twice as much as my .375.* He swallowed and stood at the ready.

"*Pull!*" The gun was coming up to Henry's shoulder at the same time as the word came out of his mouth. Another miss. *Maybe I need to hold a little more left. They're fur-*

ther out than those shots I took for practice.

"*Pull!*" The bird disintegrated.

"Son of a bitch," Hayden Burke said softly but with feeling.

"Amen to tha—" Neal Steadman started to say, but his comment was drowned out by the muzzle blast of the Colt Monitor as Henry powdered another bird. When Henry called for the next bird, Doyle Patterson hit the 'doubles' button on the trap control. Henry broke both birds.

"It would appear that the kid's got his swing down," Max said dryly.

"Son of a *bitch,*" Hayden Burke repeated.

"This thing shoots great, Mister Patterson," Henry said happily. "Real smooth, once you get used to the open bolt. Okay if I keep going?"

"Have at it, Henry. You want singles or doubles?"

"Let's see, I've got...eight shots left in the mag. Count off 'one thousand one, one thousand two' and let me have eight birds spaced a second apart at my signal."

"You got it."

"Two to one he breaks at least half," Charlie Potts said to the men watching. No one took him up on his offer.

"Pull!" At Henry's call, Doyle Patterson started pressing the button at one-second intervals. The powerful machine rifle boomed out a cadence as Henry swung on each of the clays flying out of the trap. On the eighth shot, he turned the rifle on its left side and looked in the ejection port. The magazine was empty. He had broken five of the eight clays.

"I think I'm getting the hang of it," Henry said to Doyle. "Okay if I shoot it some more? I can pay you for the ammo, and I'll clean your gun. I know this wartime Lake City stuff has chlorate primers."

"Henry, you can finish out the can, if you want." There were fourteen more magazines loaded, each holding twenty cartridges.

"You don't think they're all ready to go eat?"

"Hey, all of you!" Doyle yelled. "Henry here's going to shoot some more trap with the BAR. Anyone wants to eat right away better head on over to Melton's now. We'll catch up after we're out of '06."

None of the men assembled at the trap range turned to leave.

***

Conversation at dinner revolved around the shooting that both Max and Henry had done that day.

"I cannot imagine swinging a gun of seven kilos for two hundred birds," the man next to Henry said. It was the shooter from Barcelona.

"It was getting heavy, towards the end," Henry admitted, as he took another bite of barbecued pigeon. "I was missing a lot by then." Henry's average, which was running over 80% by the third batch of twenty, had dropped to about 50% by the time he had fired ten magazines at the clays.

"Hitting a lot, too," Doyle Patterson observed. "You like that Colt Monitor, huh?" the man asked pointedly.

"I sure do." The last eighty rounds Henry had fired on full auto, from the hip, at individual clay fragments on the ground. He had hit most of them, and his hipshooting skills had further impressed the audience. "You paid the $200 NFA registration tax on it?"

Henry asked of their host.

Doyle laughed. "Hell, no. Bought that one as a deactivated gun. I keep the guts out of it when I'm not shooting it, so it's legal except when I'm out pulling the trigger. No federal boys around this area, and if any of 'em ever do show up while I'm out having fun, I'll pay the two and register the damned thing, if I have to." Doyle saw Henry's worried look and went on.

"Cops don't care, son. Hell, every cop around here has at least one machine gun in his closet, and most have a lot more than that. No one pays any attention to that crazy federal law, unless someone makes a stink about it. Then you pay the tax, if you want to keep the gun shootable." His smile turned into a frown. "This thing they got coming up now, though..." His voice trailed off. "That pig from Texas is going to fuck us good before he slinks off to his ranch."

"You got that right," Hayden Burke threw in immediately. "I'd be afraid to show my face back in Texas, was I him."

"You want that Monitor of mine, Henry?" Doyle said suddenly.

"What? No, I–"

"You ought to have it. I never shoot the damn thing, and from this evening, I'd say John Browning designed it just for you. Max, can Henry have that Monitor he was shooting tonight?"

"Sure, if you're getting rid of it. What do you want for it?"

"You said you were buying dinner, and I got a bunch of other machine guns, we'll call it even." He turned to Henry. "Just make sure you strip it when you got it in your car. Cops here in Nevada don't give a shit, but they might farther east."

"Speaking of paying for things," Hayden Burke said as he laid down his steak knife and reached into his pocket, "I'd best give you this afore I forget." He turned to Max Collins and held out a roll of bills wrapped with a rubber band.

"Give it to Henry. It's his." Burke swung his arm over towards the boy without hesitation.

Henry looked puzzled. He made no move to take the money. "What's this for?" he asked his uncle.

"Made a little wager with Hayden here on your behalf. Looks like we both made some pocket money today." Max was grinning broadly. Henry looked bewildered as he tentatively took the roll of cash.

"There's *ten thousand* dollars here!" Henry exclaimed in a shocked whisper after he had counted the ten large bills. "What did you bet on?" he demanded of his uncle. For a moment, he had forgotten about the Monitor and that there were other people at the table.

"Hayden gave me ten-to-one you couldn't hit a clay pigeon with your .375 from the sixteen-yard line, so I laid a grand on you." Max was having a good time with this.

Henry swung towards Hayden Burke. "You came to a live pigeon shoot and gave *ten to one* odds I couldn't hit *one* clay bird?" he demanded, with a look of utter disbelief on his face. Max Collins was *really* enjoying himself now.

The men around the table, who had expected Henry to be surprised that his uncle had wagered a thousand dollars on one shot, immediately saw the logic of Henry's incredulous reaction. The men erupted into laughter. For the first time since he could remember, Hayden Burke was embarrassed.

"Henry assumes everyone here could do just as well with a rifle," Max explained in between gasps for breath.

"Well, they all *could*, if they'd practice it a little," Henry said defensively. He still could scarcely believe what had happened.

"There you have it, Hayden," Max said with a look of pure delight on his face. "Anyone can do it."

"Hell, yes!" Charlie Potts threw in. "I been thinkin' 'bout gettin' rid a my engraved Browning trap gun, an' replacin' in with a *Springfield*," he said, naming the surplus World War One bolt action rifle that could be had for twenty dollars. "Rifle bullet won't glance off the clay, way some a that puny old bird shot will do."

"Me, I think I'll go with a thirty-thirty lever action," Neal Steadman added, warming to the game. "Lots lighter'n my twelve-gauge, and holds more shots, too."

"Henry here may be a strong young fella, but I'm getting on in years," Doyle Patterson said. "Sixteen-pound Monitor doesn't swing so easy, like it used to. I'm going to get an AR-15 for my wingshooting. They only weigh six and a half pounds. Glad I convinced Henry to take that old boat anchor off my hands." He turned and looked at his guests.

"Now, Gravestock, here," he said, giving a nod to a man from Wichita Falls, "he's from Texas. Down there, they got almost as much good taste as a band a drunk Mexicans. I figure Larry, now, he ought to switch from his Perazzi to a Weatherby. Since he came in fifth today, I think he needs a bigger gun. If a .375 is right for someone in high school, Larry, I think you should shoot a .460." The .460 Weatherby was the largest American-made rifle on the market.

"Yeah!" Britt Robinson said immediately. "A .460 with one a them square stocks with the slanty forend tip and all the white line spacers, and checkering that looks like a bunch a leaves and acorns. That'd be *perfect* for Gravestock. Maybe even a gold inlay on the receiver, of a one-eyed whore sittin' in a outhouse takin' a crap. Somethin' tasteful, and all." Britt was a friend and neighbor of Gravestock's. They both hated the styling of Weatherby rifles.

Soon everyone at the table was engulfed in laughter at the idea of selling their trap and pigeon shotguns and competing instead with hunting rifles and machine guns. Henry had been embarrassed at first, but the men made him feel like he was one of them.

The man from Barcelona grinned like a fool. He thought the Americans were crazy. It was one of the reasons he loved visiting the United States.

"Got anything in mind for your winnings, Henry?" Neal Steadman asked finally.

"Ten Gs ought to go a fair ways, 'less you got a girlfriend, or plan to go to the Mustang Ranch," Joe Devers offered.

"That's God's truth," said Doyle Patterson. "Just ask your Uncle Max." This comment broke up everyone at the table.

"Well," Henry said, in answer to Neal's question, "I guess I'll use some of it to buy a few more cases of ammo, and probably another Star loading tool, and some more components. I don't shoot as much as the professional trapshooters here, but it seems like I'm always just about out of ammo." His mind was on something else that he wanted, also. Something he'd wanted for nine years.

"You ought to check out the gun show tomorrow morning," Doyle broke in. "Always some good things at the Reno show, particularly for a man who likes fine rifles."

"Do you think there might be a 4-bore for sale there?" Henry asked immediately.

"Hey, that's right," Max Collins said. "You've been trying to find one of those." He shrugged. "Hey, have a look. You might run across one there."

"What's this, now?" Neal Steadman asked.

"A big English double-barreled rifle, throws about a one-inch diameter bullet,"

Henry explained. "They made them seventy or eighty years ago, and they weigh about twenty-five pounds."

"Henry's been trying to find one for sale ever since he was six years old," Max added. "We got a picture of one that a guy had in England, and that's as close as he's come."

"Christ! Doesn't the kick on those big rifles make hamburger out of your shoulder, Henry?" It was Charlie Potts speaking. "You were out there with that .375 Magnum in just a t-shirt."

"Feel his shoulder, Charlie," Max suggested. Potts reached across the table and squeezed the boy's shoulder.

"What the hell's under there?"

"It's a callus, Mr. Potts," Henry answered. "The doctor trims it when it gets too thick."

By now everyone at the table was staring at Henry Bowman. "Show Charlie your hands, Henry," Max said. Henry turned his hands palms up. The areas between thumb and forefinger of each hand had a thick callus. They were mirror images of one another. The end joint of each of Henry's index fingers were also callused.

"About a thousand rounds of .44 Magnum a week, on average," Henry explained.

"Left hand, too, I see."

"Double action from the hip only, with my left. Trying to do aimed fire with my left eye was messing up my speed shooting, so I gave that up."

"You really like those big boomers, huh?" Neal asked.

"That's nothing, Neal," Max threw out. "Henry's dad got him a damn Nazi antitank cannon for his birthday last year."

"Your father shoots too, then?" Doyle asked. Henry smiled sadly.

"Dad died of cancer at the end of April. He didn't shoot much, but he liked to watch me. What he loved best was flying. He could make an airplane do things you wouldn't believe unless you saw it. Dad said as long as he was buying avgas for himself he ought to keep me in ammo." Henry smiled again, this time with genuine happiness. "Dad gave me twenty cases of ammo for my Solothurn cannon on the last day we went flying together."

"Then you ought to go out in the desert tomorrow with the BALLS group," Doyle Patterson said. "They're having one of their shoots. In fact, if Max has other plans, I'll drive you out in the jeep. Wouldn't mind seeing their show myself."

"BALLS is having a shoot here?" Henry said excitedly. "Can I go, Uncle Max?"

"What the hell is 'BALLS'?" Max Collins demanded. He knew he was risking being set up as the 'straight man' if this was a joke.

"The 'Benevolent Artillery Loaders and Loafers Society'," Henry replied immediately. "They're mostly from California, and they shoot cannons. Not just little 20mm ones, like my Solothurn, but big ones they haul around on trailers. 'Dangerous Dave' is one of them—Dave Cumberland. I get primers for my 20mm brass from him."

"Well, sure," Max said to his nephew. "I think I might enjoy seeing some cannon shooting myself."

"Okay if I tag along too, or is this some private deal?" Neal Steadman asked their host.

"No problem."

"Then count me in too," Charlie Potts added.

"Same here."

"I'll join you as well, if I may."

"Don't leave me out of this deal, Doyle."

"Well, shoot. We'll all go, then. Two cars should do it," Patterson decided.

"We better make it three cars, in case those BALLS folks let Henry shoot their cannons," Britt Robinson said quickly.

"Why's that?"

"We need to bring plenty of clay pigeons."

Henry and Max had spent the morning at the Reno Gun Show. No one had a 4-bore for sale, but Henry found a Rigby .577 Nitro 3" double rifle with 300 rounds of Kynoch factory ammo on a dealer's table. He returned to the dealer's spot after he had seen all the tables at the show.

"May I?" Henry asked. The dealer started to say he'd rather the gun not be handled by people who just wanted to see what an elephant gun felt like, but instead he nodded his head in assent. It had been a slow day, and this kid might be the son of some high-roller just down the aisle.

Henry lifted the rifle off the table and threw it to his shoulder. He turned the rifle sideways, held it up to the light, put tension on it, and tried to see between the back of the barrels and the face of the standing breech. He lowered the big gun and examined the stock for hairline cracks in the grip area. Then he pushed the top lever to the right and opened the breech. The bores were mint. Henry closed the rifle, swung the lever on the forearm iron to the side, and removed the forearm. Then he broke the gun open again and removed the barrels. He laid the buttstock on the table and reached into his pocket, withdrawing a piece of string and a plastic-handled screwdriver.

The dealer was surprised, but said nothing. Henry hung the barrels from the string by the forend lug and held the screwdriver by the blade in his other hand. He rapped the barrels sharply with the plastic handle, and they made a deep, ringing sound. Henry was checking to see if the barrels had become unsoldered. Many people, even dealers, were not aware of the simple test. If the barrels had been less than completely joined together, there would have been only a loud clunk.

"Tight as the day Rigby finished the gun," the dealer said unnecessarily.

Henry nodded. "Got the case for it?" he asked. Max had wandered over and stood a few feet away, watching the exchange.

"No, just the gun and sixty boxes of ammo."

"How much for the lot?"

The dealer smiled. "Son, this is an expensive rifle. The only thing bigger is a .600." *In nitro calibers, you mean* Henry thought silently. "I been asking eighteen hundred, but that's because most people have something they want to trade, and I need to leave some room for maneuvering, depending on what they got. If you know of a cash buyer who'll give me fourteen, I'll give you a $20 bill for a finder's fee."

The dealer paused and reflected for a moment. "Lot of fine shotguns here this week-end. If you bring me someone who ends up trading something for it, same deal. That sound fair?" The dealer glanced at Max, smiled, and nodded to show he recognized the winner of the Calcutta. He gave Collins a look to let him know he'd be there in a moment. Max waggled his hand to show he was in no hurry.

Henry looked down the table at the rows of guns. Most of them were fine English and Belgian shotguns. "Do you have any other double rifles that aren't laid out here?"

"Got a .465 Holland back at the shop that I'm holding for a customer, but I haven't seen any cash yet. That's the only one that isn't here," he answered quickly. The dealer assumed Henry was scouting for someone who didn't want the dealers to know he was around.

Henry nodded. He reached into his pocket and pulled out his roll of cash, which was now considerably thicker since he had changed some of the large bills for hundreds, fifties, and twenties. He handed the man a thousand, three hundreds, and four twenties. "That do it? Fourteen hundred less the finder's fee?"

The dealer was startled, but he recovered quickly. He had seen stranger things than this. "Cash makes no enemies," the dealer replied as he took the money. "So let's be friends." Max Collins walked over to his nephew.

"Let me help you carry the ammo out to the car."

The dealer looked startled. "This your son, Mister Collins? I didn't know you were in the market for a double rifle."

"My sister's son, Henry Bowman," Max corrected. "And the rifle's his. He had to settle for something a little smaller than what he wanted, at least for now."

Henry handed the man a piece of paper. "Here's my name and address. I'm looking for a full-weight 4-bore, at least 22 pounds, barrels fully rifled, in good shape. Please drop me a card if you run across one." Henry had handed out several such notes that morning.

The dealer looked at the piece of paper. It had Henry's name and address printed on it, as well as a description of the rifle he wanted. "Haven't seen one of those in years, but I'll put this in my file. Here, let me help you with all this ammo," he said quickly as Henry picked up his new rifle.

Henry and the dealer were both smiling as they walked out to Max's Impala.

***

"Mr. Cumberland, you only know me through the mail. I'm Henry Bowman."

"With the Solothurn you reload for—from St. Louis—sure, great to have you out here." The slender man with slightly thinning hair shook Henry's hand.

"This is my Uncle Max, and some of his friends from the pigeon shoot. Uncle Max, this is Dangerous Dave."

"Pleased to meet you, sir," Cumberland said, extending his hand to the big man. "Your nephew apparently shoots his Solothurn as much as we do out here—he's bought quite a lot of components from us in the last year or so."

"Hey, Dave."

"Doyle! You bring these folks out here today? Great!" He swept his arm around, indicating the people and cannons assembled out in the Nevada desert. "Welcome to the irregularly held, unofficial meeting of the Benevolent Artillery Loaders and Loafers Society. BALLS, as it were. We have a wide array of historic ordnance on display for your perusal and entertainment."

He indicated a man of indeterminate age thirty yards distant tinkering with a beautifully polished brass-jacketed gun mounted on a tripod. "In this corner we have Dolf Goldsmith, our resident Maxim authority, toiling over an 1897 Argentine model he'll be warming up shortly. To his left is Ed Anthony, here from North Carolina. Ed is our visiting mortar expert, and he'll be demonstrating his skill by dropping some practice rounds into a 55-gallon drum from 200 yards away." Cumberland continued his master-of-ceremonies act for the newcomers.

"To your right is our BAR division. They'll be shooting tracers at some long range targets out a quarter-mile or so. Ditching dynamite taped onto poles stuck in the ground. Makes a satisfying boom.

"Behind that are our Hotchkiss enthusiasts. Check out the five-barrel 37mm revolving cannon when you get a chance. Made in 1895, and it's a beauty.

"All around you can see a wide array of larger ordnance, which we'll be shooting in an hour or so." He noticed that Henry had gravitated to a long, bipod-mounted weapon about the size of his Solothurn. It was a Finnish Lahti 20mm, which Henry knew fired the same cartridge as his gun. The boy bent over and was examining the scope mount on the big antitank rifle.

"Maynard Buehler prides himself on making a mount for anything the customer has. He knocked that one out for my Lahti. I've been experimenting with individually weighed bullets and segregated cases. It's a tack driver."

Henry nodded. The Lahti, while not quite as finely finished as the Solothurn, was gas-operated instead of recoil-operated, and did not have a quick-change barrel like the Swiss gun. In theory, its solid-breech design should give it an advantage in accuracy, but in issue form the Lahti was equipped with coarse metallic sights while the Solothurn had fine optics. Cumberland's scoped gun would be interesting to shoot at long range.

"Now here's the one I think you should add to your collection, Henry," Dave said, pointing to a small breechloading cannon on a wheeled mount. "Fifty millimeter Krupp Model 1902 Mountain Cannon. Disassembles in five minutes, designed to be transported on four horses or one elephant. The factory made fifty of them for Siam in that year, and I brought thirty-five of them into the U.S. in 1961. Still got a few left after seven years. Here's the round. Make the brass out of shortened 40mm Bofors cases." He handed Henry a stubby cartridge with a diameter of about two inches. It weighed about five pounds.

"Make yourselves at home, gentlemen," Cumberland suggested. "I've still got a few things to take care of before we start shooting." He excused himself and went over to one of the larger field pieces.

"This is *great*," Henry said with feeling. The men around him laughed, but they knew exactly how he felt.

Henry Bowman had not been back in St. Louis for fifteen minutes before he went to his room and started digging through the pile of back issues of gun magazines which were stacked in the corner. After several minutes of riffling through several of the periodicals, he found the ads he was looking for.

Henry Bowman stared at the various ads. He knew that any gun that was 'Dewatted' could be made serviceable very easily, just like Doyle Patterson's Monitor had been. *No use saving money* Henry decided. He got out his pen and started to check off his next purchases. There were quite a lot of them.

August 2, 1968

"What kind of sodas you got in here?" Henry Bowman asked as he climbed halfway over the back of the front seat to get at the ice chest in the rear of the 1964 Olds F-85.

"Little bit of everything. Have a look, and drag out a Coke for me," suggested David Webb without taking his eyes off the road. Henry dug a Coca-Cola and a Whistle orange soda out from under the ice. He opened two slits in the top of each with the can opener blade of the Swiss Army knife he had carried every day for the last nine years, and handed the cola to the older boy. Then he settled back down in the passenger seat and unfolded the map.

"Where should we put in?"

"South of Pershing couple miles," David suggested after a moment's thought. "Shouldn't be too many other people 'round, not this weekend at least. Most everybody'll be on the Meramec. Gasconade's not as easy to get to."

Henry turned sideways and leaned against the door, sipping his orange soda. He didn't really care where they started, or where they ended up, for that matter. He and David were going to park the car, take the 17-foot Grumman canoe off the roof, load their camping gear in it, and paddle down the Gasconade River until they either got bored, or ran out of time. They weren't apt to run out of river; it wound southwest for about 150 miles.

David Webb was eighteen, which made him nearly three years older than Henry, and had finished high school two months ago. He intended to start technical school in less than three weeks, unaware that he would be getting his draft notice two days before the first day of classes. No one in David Webb's family had ever had any education beyond that offered by rural public high schools, and David's imminent entry into Ranken Tech was regarded by his parents in the same way that the Bowman or Collins family would view a Phi Beta Kappa key.

David's father owned a welding shop in Jefferson County, where he made a decent living repairing the farm equipment that invariably broke when stressed beyond its design limits by owners bent on getting their harvesting done in the shortest possible amount of time.

Despite the age difference and their vastly different socioeconomic backgrounds, the two young men were good friends. They had met the previous summer. Henry's skill with guns impressed the older boy, as did his quick, analytical mind. Henry, who had grown up helping his father with woodworking projects, appreciated David's mechanical skills.

Unlike other people who were faced with the reality of a younger companion who was both smarter and of higher social class, David Webb harbored no hostility whatsoever towards Henry Bowman. This was because the older boy himself had a talent unusual in an eighteen-year-old and which Henry greatly admired. The country boy with the lopsided grin and the cut-rate education had thick calluses on both his hands, and they weren't there from farm labor. David Webb drove sprint cars, and he was the youngest driver in a four-state region to ever take the checkered flag while piloting one of the twitchy, violent, overpowered dirt-track machines.

Henry and David had met by chance. Walter Bowman had taken his son to one of the local races the year before, after Walter's cancer had been diagnosed. Henry had suggested they try to track down 'Anvil' Jenkins by asking around at midwestern racetracks.

The Bowmans met a few old-timers who remembered Jenkins from prewar racing days, but they never located the man himself. No one had seen him on the racing circuit after the war had ended. The Bowmans did meet David Webb, however, who was something of a racetrack curiosity at age seventeen, and the two young men had hit it off. David lived only four miles from the Collins and Bowman summer property, and the two boys often spent weekends together when David wasn't racing or putting in his hours at the welding shop.

Now the pair were headed for a three-day canoe trip in southern Missouri. Henry relaxed and sipped his soda while David piloted the Olds coupe west on Highway 100, his eyes constantly scanning the road ahead and glancing at the rearview mirror in case anyone were about to overtake them. With a canoe on the roof rack (which David and his father had welded together out of chrome-moly tubing), the young man held the car to 75 MPH. The 327 Chevrolet engine, built out of a sprint car short-block and installed using 1966 Chevelle motor mounts, loafed along at 2600 RPM.

"What we really need on this trip is a couple of girls," David said with a grin.

"They wouldn't fit in the canoe."

"If we had two canoes, it would work. A couple of sisters. Older one about seventeen or eighteen for me, and the younger one for you. One with freckles and real thick glasses, with a whole bunch of books to read, really make your heart do a back flip. Someone just your age. How old are you now, anyway, Einstein?" David demanded. "Twelve? Thirteen?"

Henry couldn't help the grin that surfaced at David's good-natured ribbing. "Yeah, and by the time we got back home, *your* girl would have the wedding invitations all printed and the baby clothes bought," he shot back. "You and she could make it a triple." Henry was alluding to the fact that each of David's two older brothers had had to get married.

"Not me, boy. Storks bring babies. I like the birds that keep babies away," David said, playing for the standard response.

"Swallows," they said simultaneously, and the two started laughing in earnest.

With the windows rolled down and his arm resting on the top of the door, Henry began to sing one of the unusual songs from his seemingly endless repertoire of obscure works. This one was to the tune of Johnny Horton's 'The Battle of New Orleans', and told the tale of boys at summer camp hoping to find girls on the other side of the lake.

"They teach you that song at that school you go to?" his friend asked facetiously when Henry had finished singing. Although Crystal City High did not have choir practice like the private school in St. Louis County that Henry attended, David Webb knew that no prep school in the nation instructed its charges in decade-old tunes recorded by the musical duo Homer & Jethro.

"Sure did. *Your* school could have a Glee Club and learn great songs too, if they could just get you and your classmates through the course where you learn to eat with knives and forks."

"Don't go making fun of the Barrows family again." Jay Barrows, who had been in the third grade when David Webb was in kindergarten, had ended up in David's graduating class. After being held back three times in grade school and junior high, he still could not quite read whole sentences.

"Why not?" Henry asked. "Is it 'Be Kind to Animals Week'?" David started laughing in spite of himself. His mixed-breed dog often exhibited more intelligence than his hapless schoolmate.

"I'd like to show you how this thing runs since Jonesey milled the heads," David said, changing the subject, "but I'm afraid the canoe'll blow off."

"Poor workmanship and shoddy welding on the homebuilt rack, I suppose."

"The rack's okay—it's the screws holding it to the roof I'm worried about, asshole."

"Ahhh, show me when we get back home—we got lots of time," Henry said expansively. David Webb nodded his agreement, took a swig of his Coke, and held the Chevy-engined Oldsmobile at an indicated seventy-five.

***

"Hey, nice job, Einstein. Last time we did this, you 'bout dropped your end. You must be getting stronger. Next thing you know, you'll be old enough to have a girlfriend."

"Just remind me to find one who spends less on makeup than I do on ammo," Henry said with an effort as he muscled the Grumman towards the water.

David set his end of the aluminum canoe down at the edge of the riverbank. "You talkin' about Mona? Yeah, I guess she did paint it on a little thick." His face brightened. "But, hey! It was a sight better-lookin' than what was underneath!" Both boys started laughing at that.

Their tent, one-burner Coleman stove, utensils, fuel, and food were wrapped in plastic and combat-packed into a single folded duffel bag, along with an empty gallon jug for flotation in case the pack went overboard. The duffel and the cooler of sodas went aft of the canoe's center thwart. The sleeping bags went behind them.

Henry wore a Smith & Wesson Model 29 with 8 3/8" barrel in an angled Bohlin crossdraw holster in front of his left hip. He lifted his G.I. .50 caliber ammo can and placed it just behind the bow seat. The steel can was half full of .44 magnum ammo Henry had loaded the week before. He had used once-fired Remington cases and 173-grain 3/4-jacketed bullets Allen Kane had made in Lakeville Arms swaging dies. A braided steel cable with a spring clip was swaged to the wire handle at one end of the can. Henry clipped it to the seat strut. The two boys threw their knee cushions in front of their respective seats, and David went back to move the Oldsmobile.

Henry watched as his friend stowed the car in a clump of trees, lifted the hood, and put the rotor from the distributor in his jeans. David locked the car and trotted back to the canoe. David's car had never been bothered before when they'd left it for a few days, but he wanted to be safe, just in case.

***

"Okay, hotshot. Think you can hit one of those?" Henry turned and saw David Webb pointing to some crows that were flying off to their right. They looked to be well over a hundred yards distant, to Henry Bowman's practiced eye. He shook his head.

"Too far. For a moving target, anyway." He laid his paddle behind him in the canoe, withdrew the long-barreled revolver from its holster, and hooked his finger under the steel headband he wore which had earplugs attached to each side. Without taking his eyes off the crows, he flexed the spring steel and guided first one plug, then the other, into his ears. He was already wearing his yellow-tinted shooting glasses. "Maybe one of 'em will land in a tree," he said, ready to take aim. He had not fired his revolver yet that day, and it was well past noon.

David and Henry drifted in the canoe, watching the blackbirds. 'As the crow flies', the euphemism for a straight path between two points on the map, is a misapplied phrase. A crow's flight is anything but straight, and Henry Bowman knew it. As he had suspected might happen, two of the birds in the group abruptly changed course. One of them flew on an angle towards them.

Henry extended his arms, and as he cocked the hammer, he drew the big revolver into the two-handed, braced position he favored for longer shots when a rest was unavailable. His right arm was straight, his left one bent at the elbow with the left shoulder forward. His left elbow was locked into his left side, and his left hand pushed firmly on the knuckles of his right. An isosceles triangle was formed from his left forearm, his torso, and his entire right arm. This technique would come to be called the 'Weaver Stance', after a shooter in the 1970's who would popularize it in competition.

"Ears, Stroker," Henry said softly. The crow was about to reach the point in its flight where it would be as close to the canoe as it was going to get. A wooded hillside loomed on the other side of the river, so Henry had a safe backstop for the shot. He was calculating his lead as his finger applied increasing pressure to the trigger. *Fifty or sixty yards out...time of flight a tenth of a second...bird's flying maybe fifteen miles per hour, call it twenty-three feet per second...lead it a little over two feet when it hits the perpendicular point...hold a couple inches low since I'm sighted in at a hundred...front sight...*

The trigger broke when the pressure exerted by Henry's right finger reached 2 1/4 pounds, and the 50-ounce blued steel revolver rose upwards sharply in recoil. As the muzzle blast echoed off the hillsides, David Webb's jaw dropped involuntarily as he watched the distant crow literally explode in flight.

"Holy shit!" he exclaimed, removing his fingers from his ears and staring at the feathers fluttering in the sky. Henry had replaced the Smith in its holster and was twisted around in the drifting canoe, a smug smile on his face. "That was a lucky shot," Webb said accusingly. Henry shrugged.

"You practice a whole lot, seems like lucky things happen pretty often. Like that last race you won," he added pointedly.

"That gun *always* do that to birds?" David asked, nodding towards where the crow had been. Henry shook his head.

"Most of the time I shoot cast bullets. You know—ones made out of melted-down tire weights and quenched in a bucket of water." Webb nodded. His friend was always scrounging wheelweights from the tire shops in Jefferson County.

"They don't deform at all, unless you hit a rock or something." He gestured out to where the feathers were drifting through the air. "That was a three-quarter-jacket 'Jugular', 173-grain hollow point designed by Jim Harvey before he shot himself. Made to blow up groundhogs at fifty yards, but Allen Kane says they seem to shoot as well at long range as the big 270-grainers. Longtin up at Smith tightened the barrel-cylinder gap down to two thousandths on this gun for me. Gives me an extra hundred or so feet per second. Gun ties up if it gets real hot, but for slow fire at long range it's great. I loaded up a thousand of the 173's with a ball powder load that's running damn near nineteen hundred feet per second, which was why that crow exploded. I got my sights dead-on at a hundred yards. Tomorrow, I want to do some 500-yard practice when we break for lunch."

"I'd like to see that."

"Great!" Henry exclaimed. "You can run across the valley and check my targets." David Webb splashed him with his canoe paddle.

***

"Ready to put in for the night?" David asked from the stern seat of the canoe.

Neither boy wore a watch, but from the fading light it was obviously close to nine o'clock.

"Suits me."

Within twenty minutes David and Henry had banked the canoe, removed their gear from it, pitched Henry's mountaineering tent, unfurled their sleeping bags, started a small campfire, and set an open can of beef stew on the Coleman camp stove. The stove was for cooking. The fire was because both boys liked campfires.

"If we had a couple of girls with us, we'd be listenin' to 'em complain about the skeeters, and we pro'ly wouldn't have the tent up or the fire built," David said, in a voice that hinted that he felt that still might be a pretty small price to pay.

"If we had a couple of girls here, you'd a pro'ly got your dick caught in your zipper, fell outa the canoe, an' drowned five hours ago," Henry suggested, unconsciously lapsing into the speech patterns of his older friend.

"I'd'a died happy," David said, laughing. He then began to describe, in animated detail, the things he would like to do with Shelly Moore, who was one of the Crystal City High School cheerleaders. Henry had heard it all before, except the part about the molasses.

"C'mon, admit it, Einstein," David said finally. "You had the choice, right now, between goin' out shooting with that big pistol of yours tomorrow, or curling up with one a them chicks in the gym class for the whole afternoon, you wouldn't study on it too damn long, now would you?"

Henry laughed and tossed a stick into the campfire. "Okay, Stroker," Henry said, using the common racer's nickname which took on an entirely different meaning under the present circumstances. "I admit it. You're right. What I'd like most of all is for us to come across some cute little blonde tomorrow, without any clothes on, who's been waiting all day for me to show up and dazzle her with my talent. *That's* what I *really* wish would happen on this trip. You satisfied?" The two boys both broke out laughing.

Henry Bowman had never been one to wish out loud for things. The last time had been when he was seven years old and had told his father he wished one of his classmates would move away. The classmate was a good friend with whom Henry had had an argument. It would not be until the next day of the canoe trip that Henry Bowman would recall what his late father had said to him at the time:

Better watch what you wish for, Son. Sometimes wishes come true.

August 3, 1968

"You ready for lunch yet?" David Webb asked as the sun neared its zenith in the sky. Henry stopped paddling and turned around.

"Not exactly," Henry said, "but this looks like maybe a good spot coming up to try out these loads at long range." He gestured off to their right. "Let's put in up there, and I'll take a walk up that valley. See if I can find a good spot up on a hill, with some rocks out four, five hundred yards." David gave a few strong J-strokes and used his paddle as a rudder to steer the canoe over towards the bank.

The older boy beached the canoe and Henry stepped out of the bow, pulling the craft up on the dirt bank of the river. David looked to make sure he wasn't about to put his foot on any glass or nails, and stepped barefoot into the shallow water.

"I keep telling you you're crazy to tramp around all the time without any shoes on," Henry said, watching his friend. He himself wore a pair of Vietnam combat boots which had a hinged piece of aluminum built into the sole. You could step on a ten-penny nail sticking straight up out of a piece of plywood without discomfort. The boots had been specifically designed to negate the effects of the 'foot-breakers' the North Vietnamese were so fond of creating: a single round of rifle ammunition sitting on the point of a nail inside a short length of bamboo, with 1/2" of the bullet exposed out the top, all firmly set into the ground in any area where American G.I.s were likely to walk. When the soldier stepped on the nose of the bullet, the primer detonated and the cartridge exploded.

A cartridge outside a rifle chamber, when ignited, acts like a big firecracker. The projectile has no more energy than a piece of gravel lying next to a Silver Salute. Henry had demonstrated this fact to a horrified David Webb on a previous trip by tossing a live round of .44 magnum ammunition into the campfire and calmly waiting for it to explode. In a VC footbreaker, the bamboo tube, though destroyed in the process, offers some containment of the explosion. This is sufficient to channel the explosive force and impart enough velocity to the bullet to break a man's foot. Word had come back to the States of what was happening, and bootmakers with government contracts had quickly responded. Henry owned several pairs, all bought through his ammunition suppliers.

"You've just got tender feet," David said in reply to his young friend's comment. Henry shrugged. David's statement was true. "How long you going to be?" he asked Henry, changing the subject.

"Depends on if I find a good spot to shoot from. Want to come along? I'll teach you to hit stuff the size of a five gallon bucket three or four hundred yards away."

"Yeah—but you go on ahead. I got to get some shoes on."

"Want me to help you stow the canoe?"

"Nah, I got that. Go on ahead and scout out a good spot. I'll catch up in a few minutes." Henry nodded. David was five inches taller, with correspondingly longer legs, and was considerably faster hiking through the woods than was Henry.

The younger boy stared up at the wooded hills, trying to decide where the best spot was apt to be. Finally he elected to break a trail in a different direction from the most inviting path. "I'm going to head up this way," he said. "Looks like a lot less traffic has been there. Better chance of no people being around if we find a good spot. I'll leave a few blazes for you, so you won't get lost." David Webb grinned his understanding as Henry turned and headed off towards one of the wooded slopes.

***

Henry had been walking for the better part of an hour, but the hill had not, as he had hoped, led to a high spot with a good view of distant rock outcroppings. So far, the terrain had been nothing but gently rolling hills, and all he had managed to discover was a small knoll that overlooked more woods. There was absolutely nowhere to do any long range shooting, at least not so far.

Henry Bowman's spirits were undampened, however. He liked walking out in the woods. He liked being on a canoe trip with David Webb. He knew by the time they stashed the canoe for the final time and walked to the nearest road to hitchhike back to get the car, he would be out of ammo, regardless of whether or not he ever found a place to shoot six hundred yards. The weather was slightly less hot and humid than usual for Missouri in August, and heat did not bother the fifteen-year-old the way it did people two or three times his age. All in all, Henry Bowman was having a very good time just as things were. He stopped and sat down on an inviting-looking log, unslung the gas-mask pouch from his shoulder, and stretched.

He looked back the way he had come. There was as yet no sign of his friend. *I must be getting a little faster* he thought with a smile. Henry had grown four inches in the past year, and now stood almost five foot seven. He reached into his ammo bag and pulled out a piece of beef jerky sealed in plastic, and a can of Seven-Up. His Swiss Army knife provided the opener for the beverage, and Henry commenced the serious business of consuming his snack.

After he had drained the last of his soda and had started occupying himself by calculating drop curves in his head, Henry decided to continue on farther. *No use making life too easy on old Stroker* he thought with a smile and stood up, donning his ammo pack as he did so. Before continuing his hike he opened his big Case knife and thoughtfully cut a large slash across the log on which he had been sitting. Then he set off again at a brisk walk.

***

Henry was several miles from the spot on the river where they had stowed the canoe, and it was looking less and less likely that he was going to find a suitable spot for long range revolver practice. Rocks and loose dirt were required at the receiving end of such shooting to allow the shooter to be able to spot his shots with the naked eye and correct his hold accordingly. So far, all Henry had seen was acres and acres of trees, with an occasional open patch of grass.

Bag it? Henry asked himself. *Hell, might as well go on a little while yet.*

Henry would later reflect on that innocuous choice, and imagine how his life might have been different if instead he had decided *Yeah, time to head back.*

***

Henry Bowman was always very conscientious about protecting his ears while shooting, which was why he heard the faint noise. He cocked his head, straining to hear. There was a faint, high-pitched keening noise, carried towards him by the same summer wind that rustled the leaves on the trees, which then drowned it out. Henry frowned, and shook his head. *Real high-pitched...scream, I think. Wounded rabbit, maybe* he added to himself, realizing that he had no idea what wounded rabbits sounded like, if indeed they made any noise at all. The young boy drew the big revolver out of the Bohlin rig and started carefully walking through the woods.

As Henry Bowman drew closer to where he believed the noise had originated, he began to make out the sound of a man's voice. He could not grasp the individual words, but the tone was that of someone giving brief orders. In another fifty yards, he could tell that there was more than one man. The keening noise continued. *Deer poachers?* he thought reflexively, then instantly rejected the idea. He didn't think wounded deer made anything like the noise he was now hearing. Henry stopped and turned back towards where he had come from, trying to hear if David Webb was approaching in the distance. Suddenly there was a bark of coarse laughter, and the keening noise intensified and became more frantic sounding. Henry didn't have a clue as to what was going on, but he was beginning to get a very bad feeling about it. He continued on slowly through the foliage.

"Fu'ther back, you two," Lowell Charles 'L.C.' Bivins commanded his brother and the one helping him, as he reached under his sagging belly to stroke himself. "Git her all the way open. Put your shoulders into it—she can't weigh much more'n half a either one a you." Trent Bivins and Gary Cort, both drained from their exertions of the previous twenty minutes, did as Trent's older brother demanded. Cammie Lynn tried to scream out in agony, but her mouth had been stuffed with a dirty shop towel and her entire head below her nose, as well as most of her neck, was bound with over a dozen wraps of black electrician's tape. Only a muffled noise escaped from her mucous-clogged nose. It sounded anything but human.

Henry Bowman stopped and turned his head, frowning. *What on earth could have made that sound?* He glanced back at his trail, then continued on towards the source of the noise.

The girl was nude, on her back on top of a fallen oak tree. Baling wire bound her wrists underneath the log and bit into the flesh above her hip bones where it had been tightened around the dead oak. A third length of wire was wrapped twice around the log and Cammie Lynn's neck, rendering her head virtually immobile. This one was looser than the other twists of wire, or else the girl would not have still been alive.

The two younger men, each holding one of the girl's ankles, had her legs bent back as far as they could. They had her feet up above her head, and had also pulled them away from each other until her ankles were almost four feet apart. Cammie Lynn, like most girls in junior high school, was very limber, but the strength of the young men and the leverage they possessed tore some of her ligaments and tendons. The baling wire around her abdomen split the skin and disappeared, leaving a bright red valley of oozing blood.

L.C. Bivins watched the wire bury itself in the girl's pale flesh and let out a short bark of laughter. He was fully erect, and now he thrust deeply into Cammie Lynn's body. He stared into the terror-filled eyes of his victim and let his pleasure build towards a climax. Then he stopped for a moment, pulled a knife out of his overalls, and resumed his efforts.

There's that laugh again Henry Bowman said to himself. *I'm getting close.* He proceeded on more cautiously towards the sound. The oak log was angled towards the direction from which Henry was approaching, with the girl's head nearest him. L.C., who stood straddling the log as he thrust in and out of the girl, directly faced the area of the woods that Henry was now carefully negotiating.

Nat Bivins was the only one of the attackers with nothing to do. He darted back and forth to either side of the victim, hopping over the log, and watching his cousins' efforts with utter fascination. Nat was the youngest of the four males. He was almost seventeen, but because of his slight build and thick glasses, looked younger. That, coupled with the fact that he had yet to pass the written portion of the Missouri driving test and thus did not have a driver's license, accounted for his older cousins' treatment of him. It was Nat who had been assigned the task of keeping track of Cammie Lynn's whereabouts so that his cousins and Gary Cort could snatch her at the proper moment.

"Remember, I get a turn," Nat whined. He had the very reasonable fear that his older cousin was going to change his mind and refuse to let him participate in the rape. It would not be the first time L.C. had excluded him from their activities.

"I ain't done yet," the oldest Bivins panted. He had let his brother and their friend take their turns at the girl first. L.C. had feigned magnanimity with this gesture, but his real motive had been twofold: First, he knew the girl would be dry, and that did not appeal to him. Secondly, he intended to kill her as he reached his climax, to heighten his own pleasure. He had no intention of letting Nat in on their fun, but Trent and Gary had certainly deserved a share.

Bivins rocked back and forth, growing continually harder. He liked the slippery feeling that the two other men had left for him, and he realized he was getting close. He held the knife up in front of his face, giving Cammie Lynn a good look at it, and taking great pleasure in the terror he saw in her eyes.

Henry Bowman finally caught a glimpse of blue denim forty yards ahead of him. He quickly moved to put a large walnut tree between himself and the strangers he knew were up ahead, and then he did something that might have surprised a casual observer: he hooked his left index finger inside the steel band and positioned the left earplug in his left ear.

L.C. Bivins slowly waved the knife in front of the girl's face as he continued to thrust in and out of her. The two other men had involuntarily relaxed their pressure on her legs. They were waiting to see what L.C. was going to do.

"Let's see if this'll make her twitch a little bit," Bivins said, and drew the entire length of the knife blade vertically across Cammie Lynn's left nipple, slicing it in half.

The girl's throat was raw, she was choking on the rag, and she was about to drown in her own mucous, but the pain of this latest act was indescribable, and she twisted with all her strength, causing the wire to bite more deeply into both her abdomen and her throat. An inhuman noise ushered from her nasal passages.

What the hell...? Henry immediately stepped slightly to the right and ducked his head to get a better look through a gap in the foliage. At first, Henry did not understand what he was seeing. There was a cluster of three men and one boy, and it appeared that the men were engaged in trying to move a fallen log, while the young boy stood with his back to Henry. Henry noticed a twelve-gauge pump gun of uncertain make lying against the end of the log. *What on earth is making that noise?* Henry wondered.

L.C. Bivins felt the beginnings of his orgasm and let out a guttural sound of satisfaction. He drew back his hand, and prepared to thrust the knife's entire 5" blade into Cammie Lynn's abdomen.

"*Wait, L.C.!*" Nat Bivins yelled as he ran around Gary Cort and grabbed his cousin's arm, wanting him to delay the damage until after he had a chance to use the girl. "I ain't had my turn yet!" Bivins dropped the knife, twisted his arm out of Nat's clumsy grasp, and backhanded his cousin on the side of head, sending the boy's glasses flying. Nat stumbled and fell to his knees behind the older man.

When Nat Bivins had run to his older cousin's side and had then been knocked away, Henry Bowman had seen exactly what was going on. He instinctively slid to the left to put more of his body behind the walnut tree, and swung his big Smith & Wesson up into the braced position, cocking it in the process. The first emotion that came into Henry Bowman's mind was gin-clear: *Kill all four of them.* Then he saw the big one shake his head as if to clear it. Reason took over once more, and Henry silently pleaded *Stop what you're doing! Go! Leave the girl! Just go!*

Henry had his front sight trained on L.C. Bivins' sternum, but his eyes darted around the area, looking for other men in addition to the four he saw. He spotted no other people, but he did see an H&R single-barrel shotgun leaning against a tree in between himself and the rapist, in addition to the twelve-gauge pump he had noticed before.

L.C. Bivins glanced with disgust at his cousin, who was feeling around on the ground, trying to find his glasses, then turned his attention back to the girl, and smiled. *Oh, shit* thought Henry. L.C. bent over, picked up the knife, and raised it in an overhand grip, as if it were an icepick.

"Freeze!" Henry Bowman yelled at the top of his lungs.

L.C. Bivins, Trent Bivins, and Gary Cort had not noticed the soft click of Henry Bowman's revolver being cocked moments before, but they would have had to been deaf not to have heard his shouted command. L.C. jerked his head up from where he was selecting the spot to sink the knife, and Trent and Gary whirled around. All three of them immediately spotted Henry.

"Get him!" the oldest Bivins commanded as he clenched his teeth and raised the knife again, preparing to drive it home. Trent and Gary were used to following L.C. Bivins' orders, and they did not elect to defy him this time. Both men ran for their guns.

Trent Bivins ran towards the sweetgum tree where he had leaned his shotgun before raping Cammie Lynn. The old Harrington & Richardson single barrel was ten feet away from him, roughly in the direction of the tree behind which Henry Bowman stood. Gary Cort took two quick steps towards the J.C. Higgins he had left lying against the log.

Henry saw L.C.'s arm muscles tense and knew the man was about to kill the girl. He relentlessly increased the pressure of his right index finger and ignored the fact that Trent Bivins was about to cross his line of fire. *Front sight* he grimly reminded himself. There was a natural tendency for shooters to focus on the target instead of the sights at the moment of letoff, especially when under pressure. L.C. Bivins was blurred slightly in Henry Bowman's vision. The 24 karat gold insert in the front sight blade which covered Bivins' heart, however, was sharp enough for Henry to see the tiny hammer marks on it, made when it had been installed by Fran Longtin in S&W's Springfield, Massachusetts service facility a year earlier.

The big revolver thundered, and the 173-grain hollow point bullet made by Allen Kane in Lakeville Arms swaging dies exited the 8 3/8" barrel at 1870 feet per second. The bullet passed less than ten inches from Trent Bivins' left ear and struck L.C. Bivins in almost the exact center of his sternum. The combined effect of the muzzle blast fifty feet in front of him and the painful crack of a supersonic projectile passing less than a foot from his ear was very disorienting to Trent Bivins, and he winced and stumbled, but kept running for his shotgun.

The effect the bullet had on Trent's cousin L.C. was more impressive.

Allen Kane had used a long hollowpoint punch in the swaging die when he had made the slugs, which made a large cavity in the nose of the bullet that extended down almost to its base. This concentrated the projectile's mass towards its outer circumference, nearer to the actual bearing surface, and was one of the reasons that the slugs had shot so accurately for the Indiana experimenter. The design had the secondary effect of destroying much of the structural integrity of the bullet.

Over the years, ammunition manufacturers would regularly use these same construction techniques in vain attempts to increase the incapacitating power of low-powered, low velocity sidearm ammunition. The results were almost always disappointing. Cartridges such as the .25 and .32 ACP usually had too little velocity to make even the most fragile bullet break up, and if the slow-moving slugs did fragment, penetration was so slight that an attacker's leather coat would sometimes stop the bullet entirely.

Frangible bullets were a different story in a high-intensity cartridge like the .44 Magnum, and in Henry's long-barreled gun with its tight cylinder gap and full-pressure handloads, doubly so. When the Lakeville Arms 173 grain 'Jugular' hollow point hit L.C. Bivins, it truly lived up to the moniker its late designer had given it. As the front half of the projectile turned itself into microscopic fragments of lead and copper, it released over one thousand two hundred foot-pounds of kinetic energy inside the chest cavity of the rapist and murderer.

Bivins' chest cavity literally exploded, and the homogenized contents of his upper torso followed the path of least resistance, just as the laws of physics dictated. In L.C.'s case, the weak point was a gash in his back made by a piece of his spine which the impact had turned into a secondary missile.

Nat Bivins, the feckless younger cousin who had been backhanded by L.C. only moments before, had just crawled to a spot directly behind L.C. when Henry fired his first shot. Nat's back was sprayed with a mixture of blood, heart tissue, and fragments of both bone and metal just before the 230-pound corpse of his late cousin landed on top of him.

In a move he had practiced some forty thousand times, Henry Bowman glanced at his second target and hauled the gun down out of recoil. While he did this, he pulled the Smith's trigger double action until the tip of his trigger finger touched the revolver's frame behind and to the left of the trigger. This was far enough to make the cylinder advance to the next chamber and lock in place, but not far enough to make the gun fire. Thirty years earlier, Ed McGivern had called this technique the 'two stage, braked trigger pull'. Twenty years in the future, shooters would call it 'trigger cocking'. As Henry finished trigger-cocking the revolver, he focused his master eye on the gold insert of the front sight.

Trent Bivins, with a searing pain in his right ear, tried to get his shotgun into action from its position leaning against the tree. At the instant the front sight of Henry's gun crossed the line of Trent's scalp, Henry Bowman gave the trigger the additional pressure needed, and his second shot hit the younger Bivins brother just to the right of the tip of his nose. The back of Trent's skull split open under the tremendous hydraulic pressure, and over one-half of his brain matter was blown out the jagged opening.

Henry Bowman did not see the effect of this shot, for he was already backpedaling and rotating his whole body—maintaining the braced position of his arms, torso, and neck—and trigger-cocking the Model 29 again as he brought it to bear on the figure of Gary Cort.

Cort had enjoyed his session with the young girl, and had been doing his best to dislocate her hip from its socket while L.C. was taking his turn. He was out of breath from these exertions, and this new development had appeared out of nowhere. Every part of Gary Cort's brain was being bombarded with stimuli, and he acted instinctively. In Cort's case, this meant grabbing the shotgun with his right hand, and sliding his right forefinger inside the trigger guard at the same time.

Sticking his finger into the trigger guard before he had complete control of the weapon was not the only bad habit Gary Cort had when it came to gun handling. He also was rather cavalier about using his gun's safety, and it was disengaged at the moment. As Cort's hand instinctively tightened around the weapon, his finger pulled the trigger, and an ounce and a quarter of number six bird shot shredded leaves ten yards above and to the right of where Henry Bowman stood.

As a flustered Gary Cort pumped the slide of his shotgun, Henry Bowman put the gold bead on Cort's center of mass and exerted a little more pressure on the trigger. He was aiming for the heart, and he got it. Cort fell as if every bone in his body had suddenly turned to liquid. He was dead before his knee struck the spot where his shotgun had been resting.

From the moment Henry had yelled until the time that Gary Cort's body collapsed in the grass was less than four seconds.

Henry Bowman saw Nat Bivins frantically trying to extricate himself from underneath his dead cousin, and he made a snap decision. He sprinted to the boy, put a knee onto his back, and shoved the muzzle of the Smith & Wesson into the base of his skull. Henry swept the area with his eyes, looking for signs of any other people, especially hostile ones. Seeing none, he clenched his teeth and looked at the girl.

He was relieved to see that she was still alive. Her eyes stared at the sky, for she was in shock. Then a strong feeling of revulsion washed through Henry when he saw what the man had done to her chest. He looked at the trembling form of Nat Bivins, saw the boy's glasses six feet away in the grass, and started to formulate a plan.

"Who were they?" Henry demanded, making sure the boy could not see him out of the corner of his eye.

"Him, that's my cousin L.C.," Nat snuffled, pointing towards the corpse a few feet away. "Did Trent 'n' Gary git away?"

"They're dead. Who's the girl?"

Nat Bivins' voice carried surprising hatred. "That's Cammie Lynn. Little bitch," he added. It was clear that he was starting to blame her for his current predicament. "Di'n't even git my turn," he muttered.

Henry inhaled slowly, thinking about this last comment, and trying to appear calm.

"Damn' ol' L.C.," Nat said with feeling. "Always keepin' me out of ever'thing, and I was th' one what got her here for 'em."

"Oh?"

"Yeah. I follered her last two, three days. Told 'em right where to git her," he said proudly. "Little bitch was going to tell on us."

"Tell on you?" At this question, Nat Bivins closed his mouth defiantly, and Henry stabbed the muzzle into his neck as a reminder.

"'Bout the business. Car parts."

"What kind of car parts?" Henry demanded.

"Any kind you need," Nat said with what might have been a touch of pride, "L.C. can git. Week, sometimes two, an' th' price ain't but half what the dealers get." He rushed on, explaining himself. "She was talkin' 'bout it to one a the people she babysits for. Little boy's big brother tole me."

A babysitter raped and murdered by some hicks running an Ozark chop shop Henry thought with disgust. *And if* she *knew what they were up to, there had to be a hundred others.*

"What was L.C. going to do with the girl after he finished with her?" Henry asked. "Leave her out here?"

Nat shook his head. "Naw, 'specially not this close to the house." Henry felt his heart lurch at this bit of news. "L.C. was going to pitch her in the hog pen, after we was through." Nat Bivins' face turned sullen again. "I was s'posed to git a turn first."

Henry felt his guts turn over, but he kept his voice level.

"How far is the house, and who's there now?" *I hope it's close by and empty.*

"Quarter mile, maybe a li'l more. No one's home right now. Aunt Char, she's gone to Cape 'til Monday. Uncle Dane, no tellin' when he'll get back." Henry didn't like the sound of this last comment, but said nothing about it.

"Where's the hog pen?"

"Oh, it's 'fore you get to the house."

"Anybody know you're here?" *With what these four had planned, I doubt it, but who knows what these cretins were thinking.* The Bivins boy shook his head.

"You going to kill me?"

"I ought to," Henry said lamely. He knew he would not. "Don't move."

Henry Bowman stood up and holstered his Smith. He fished in his pocket and pulled out the big two-bladed Case knife and opened the larger of the two blades. Without taking his eyes off the prone figure of Nat Bivins, he reached over and slid the blade of the knife in between the log and the wire which bound Cammie Lynn's abdomen to it, then dug the tip of the blade in the wood and pulled on the handle. The soft iron wire made two popping noises as the keen blade parted it. Henry dropped to his knees and carefully sliced through the wire wrapped around the girl's wrists, also. He looked at the twists binding the girl's neck to the log, then stabbed the knife into the side of the log, parting the wire as a cold chisel would.

Time to cut out he thought. *Two more things first, though.*

Henry Bowman stowed his knife, then drew his gun and held it at the ready. "Keep your face in the grass, just like you been doing," he commanded. Nat Bivins did not move.

Henry walked to where the boy's glasses had fallen, picked them up, and put them in the pocket with his knife. Then he stepped over to the crumpled corpse of L.C. Bivins, and extracted the billfold from the hip pocket of Bivins' torn, bloodstained overalls. There was a large sheaf of bills in it, and Henry removed all but $80, glanced at the driver's license, wiped off his fingerprints, and replaced the wallet in the dead man's pocket.

"Stay where you are 'til you're sure I'm gone," Henry told the boy. "Then get her some help. I'll be calling in, and if I find out she didn't make it, I'll come for you. You won't see it coming any more than you did this time. Get it?" Nat Bivins snuffled, and Henry watched the back of the boy's head as he nodded his understanding. "Don't bother looking for your glasses any more—I've got 'em." He gave a quick look around, made himself stare at Cammie Lynn's ravaged body, then jogged off into the woods.

"Came to a barbwire fence half mile back," Henry explained, throwing a thumb over his shoulder to emphasize the point. He had met up with David Webb about a mile from the site of the killings. "Got 'No Trespassing' signs all over. Thought I'd find a decent place to shoot long range here, but no soap. Let's head back, and try farther down the river."

"Suits me. You okay? You look kind of funny."

"I think I may be coming down with something—stomach flu, maybe."

"That sucks."

"That's not all. My Smith just broke the center pin inside the ejector rod," Henry lied. "And like an idiot I only brought one gun this trip."

"You can't shoot it at all?"

"Not 'til I get back to my kit and take it apart to check it out."

The two of them began hiking back towards the Gasconade. On the way, Henry had to stop and relieve his bladder. When he did, he slid Nat Bivins' glasses out of his pocket, wiped them off, and put them under a fallen tree limb lying on the ground.

***

"Can you fix it?" David asked. Henry shook his head as he stared down at the disassembled N-frame revolver.

"Not here. It's nothing serious, but I didn't bring a spare center pin. First one of those I've ever broken. Must've had bad heat-treat." *I hope I don't get hit by a bolt of lightning for that blasphemy* Henry thought. He began to reassemble the revolver.

"So what do you want to do?"

"We're on a canoe trip—let's do some real canoeing. Let's see how far we can go 'fore we get really hungry."

"Your arms are going to give out."

"Like hell they are," Henry answered with a forced grin. "Your arms may be a little stronger from jerking off all the time, but don't think you got me beat on endurance."

"Hurry your ass up, Einstein, and we'll *see* who's got the endurance."

Several times during the next three hours, Henry Bowman was close to telling his friend what had really happened. The event seemed too enormous to hold inside. Each time, however, he saw all kinds of future problems resulting, and he remembered a conversation he had overheard in Goodmans' about a front-page murder case that was baffling the police. One of the customers, a county cop, had said something to Henry's Uncle Max that Henry had never forgotten:

'If it weren't for guys ratting each other out, only busts I'd 'a made in the last ten years'd be speeding tickets, and that's the goddamn truth, Max. That stuff in the books and movies is a bunch a crap. Guy works alone and keeps his mouth shut, and doesn't do some dumb shit like cut off the dead guy's dick as a souvenir and stick it in the freezer where his girlfriend will find it and rat him out the next time she gets busted by an undercover for soliciting, hundred to one we'll never catch him. And if by some fuckin' miracle we do turn the mutt up as a suspect, and he still keeps his mouth shut, prosecution won't have enough to go to trial. And if the DA is an idiot and does take the case to a jury, and the guy still keeps his mouth shut, and doesn't try to explain where he was, and what he was doing, and all that shit, you'll never get twelve people to convict. Never.'

When the two boys banked the canoe next, David Webb was none the wiser. It was almost dark and David and Henry were both exhausted and famished. They were also thirty miles away from the site of the shooting.

After the pair returned home, Henry Bowman watched the newspapers carefully for several weeks after the incident. He found no mention of any young men being shot to death in that area of Missouri.

September 15, 1968

"Hello?"

"Yes, this is Mr. Jackson at the library calling. May I speak to Cammie Lynn, please? It's about her library card." *I feel like an idiot* Henry Bowman thought. It was his fourth call on the list of Lynns in the local directory. He had a roll of quarters in front of him at the drug store pay phone.

"Just a minute. I'll get her." Henry's heart jumped. *She's alive!* he thought. *Unless there're more than one.* He heard an adult yell for the girl and then the sound of another receiver being lifted.

"Hello?"

"Ah, yes, this is Mr. Jackson," Henry repeated, lowering his voice and feeling stupid. "At the library. Is this Cammie Lynn?" He was stalling for time, hoping the other person would hang up the other extension.

"Yes," the girl said. There was a questioning tone in her voice. She did not have a library card, and in fact did not have any idea where the nearest library was located.

"Good. The...ah, reason I'm calling is–" Henry stopped in mid-sentence when he heard the other extension click off. "I'm not from the library," Henry said quickly. "I called to see if you were all right. I met you when you were having some trouble last month." Henry heard a sharp intake of breath.

"Who are you?" the girl whispered urgently. "And why didn't you kill Nat Bivins? You let him get away," she said accusingly.

"I didn't have the stomach to murder him," Henry said with a hint of apology. "Listen, I'm not going to call again. I just wanted to make sure you...made it."

"I can't run too good yet. Have to see the doctor some more, too. But, uh, thanks for killin' the others, Mister. Dad said they needed it."

"You're welcome, Cammie," Henry replied. "I think your father was right. Good luck," he added, then hung up the phone. He felt a sense of unreality about the conversation he'd just had. His spirits, though, were much higher than they'd been just a few minutes earlier.

Henry Bowman had never been told of the concept of 'Post-Traumatic Stress Disorder.' In 1968, that theory was not popular, if indeed anyone had thought of it at all. Thus, Henry Bowman had to discover on his own what the emotional aftermath of a killing was like, without being told by any experts what to expect.

The experience with Cammie Lynn's attackers taught Henry Bowman two lessons that he would never forget. He learned that not only was it possible to kill someone and not be convicted, as the cop in the gun store had explained, but it was also possible to not ever be suspected of the killing in the first place.

The second thing Henry learned was the same truth Irwin Mann had discovered over twenty years earlier: Killing someone was not an emotionally devastating experience when the person you killed was evil.

Actually, when you got right down to it, Henry felt pretty good about the way things had worked out.

November 2, 1968

"You headed down to the foundry again?" Catherine Bowman asked as Henry excused himself from the dinner table. "You've been down there all weekend."

"Got more cutting and numbering to do, Mom," Henry said cheerfully. "This thing's going to be a one-shot deal, assuming it's not a trap."

"You sure you don't need me to sign my name to these pieces of muffler pipe you're cutting up?" Catherine Bowman joked. She found it most amusing that Henry was so adamant about how he was going to need her to become a gun dealer under these new laws that were coming.

"No, I don't think so."

"Just don't get me thrown in jail, all right?" she said with a laugh. The idea that the Federal government might arrest a middle-aged woman for agreeing to do this was, of course, utterly absurd.

"I'll try not to," Henry Bowman said, then ran down the basement stairs to his late father's workshop to wear out some more hacksaw blades.

Henry's well-focused vigor was understandable. One of the provisions of the 1968 Gun Control Act was that interstate commerce in all firearms was now going to be heavily restricted. Dealers were now going to have to be federally licensed, and would not be able to sell to purchasers under the age of eighteen for long guns and twenty-one for handguns.

In conjunction with many other restrictions soon to go into effect under the 1968 Gun Control Act, the government was promising a 30-day amnesty where National Firearms Act weapons could be registered 'live' without payment of the normal $200 tax. After the month was up, however, there would be no provision to register a weapon that was not in the system. Going one step further, non-functional weapons were soon to be registerable items under the 1968 Act. It would no longer be possible for a citizen to take the internal parts out of his Thompson to render it inoperable and expect to be left alone by the authorities.

Given that many people thought the Amnesty might be a trap, this set of circumstances posed a real dilemma to shooters like Henry Bowman who had large numbers of non-taxed NFA weapons. If the Amnesty was a trap, every gun he registered would be destroyed by the Feds. If the Amnesty was legitimate, then every gun he did *not* register would be one he wouldn't be able to take out and shoot again, for it would be contraband.

Henry was fairly sure the Amnesty was not an immediate trap, but there was another thing to consider: There were no guarantees as to what would happen in the future, and confiscation was always preceded by registration. Anyone with any knowledge of history knew this. Henry Bowman, because of the personal experiences of those in his family, was considerably better-versed than most people on what governments were capable of doing when left unchecked. That was why even if President Johnson himself had given him a document on Presidential stationery that the Amnesty Registration was on the level, Henry Bowman was not about to submit all of his machine guns and cannons for governmental approbation.

Henry Bowman had spent a lot of time thinking about what to do. Since the Amnesty involved guns owned before the passage of the 1968 Act, it did not have an age minimum, and Henry therefore did not have to involve his mother in the registration process. In the end, he had settled on a plan of action that he thought covered all the eventualities in the best possible way.

Henry had decided to register six machine guns: His .30-06 Colt Monitor, a 1918A2 BAR, a .45 caliber 1928 Thompson, a 9mm STEN, a .303 BREN, and a .30 caliber Model 1917 belt-fed Browning water cooled gun. These six machine guns were the ones he shot most, and if the Amnesty was not a trap, these were the ones he wanted to be able to use every weekend and during the summer without problems. He had a second example of five of them held in reserve in case of confiscation. Henry did not have a duplicate Monitor, but since he owned two other BAR variants which used the same magazines, he felt he was covered. He had twenty-three other machine guns of various types that he did not shoot very often, and these he was not going to register either.

In amending the National Firearms Act of 1934, the 1968 Act also reclassified military weapons with bores over a half-inch into a newly-created 'destructive device' category, which also required registration. Henry planned to register the 20mm Lahti he had recently bought, and let the Solothurn S18-1000 his father had given him remain a free-market weapon. Both guns fired the same ammo, and Henry made his choice based mainly on the fact that the Solothurn had a quick-change barrel which meant it could be broken down without tools into manageable pieces for discreet storage, while the Lahti was nine feet long and would stay that way.

What Henry had been working on the last few days involved the third area covered by the Amnesty: firearm silencers.

A $200 tax on a machine gun was very high, but a $200 tax levied on what was essentially a muffler for a lawn mower was ridiculous. Henry Bowman had only heard of one person in his life who had actually paid $200 to make his gun quieter. Virtually all registered silencers were owned by NFA dealers who paid $200 a year to deal in NFA weapons and who were thus exempted from the per-unit tariff. Henry fully intended to become an NFA dealer, but he knew he had to wait until his twenty-first birthday. He had already checked up on that.

The Amnesty was going to allow registration of silencers without having to pay the tax, during the one-month 'window'. That was why Henry was spending a great deal of time cutting and putting serial numbers on various diameters and lengths of stainless steel aircraft tubing. He had decided that fifty would probably suffice for a lifetime supply, given his high-volume shooting habits. The outer tubes were what was important. He could make the internals up later, as they were needed.

Stainless steel was a lot harder to cut than mild steel, and Henry was soon sweating again. *Christ!* Henry said to himself. *Cutting off pieces of aircraft tubing and stamping numbers on them all weekend 'cause it's the only time when you don't have to pay the Feds two hundred bucks for each one.* His hands began to sweat, so he gripped the saw more tightly to compensate. *Is this a joke or what?* Henry thought for perhaps the hundredth time as he drew the saw back and forth and watched the blade slowly make its way through the two-inch seamless tubing.

February 8, 1969

"Hey, get your own french fries!"

"Jesus, Bowman, don't have a cow. I was only taking *one.*"

"Well, take *one* from somebody else, Kerth, if you're too cheap to cough up a quarter and buy your own."

"Aw, keep your damn french fries. They're no good here, anyway." Jimmy Kerth was a notorious mooch, but it was mainly an act. He was absolutely fearless when it came to talking to girls, and because of that, his friends overlooked his minor shortcomings.

"Don't whine at me," Henry said. "I told you we should have gone to Steak n Shake, but you guys aren't happy unless the cooks salt the piss out of everything, and you get to eat off of cardboard instead of china."

"Very funny. Asshole."

"Hey, Henry!" Bill Pressler called from one of the other booths. "Come here a minute. Need your help on something." Henry Bowman shoved the last of the salty french fries into his mouth and slid off the vinyl-covered bench seat.

"What's up?"

"Sit down. Here—want some fries?"

"I'm full." *I wonder what he wants. And I wonder who this older guy with him is.*

"Dick, this is Henry Bowman, the guy I was telling you maybe could help you out."

"Dick Gaines," the older boy said, looking a little uncomfortable as he shook Henry's hand across the formica tabletop. Henry could tell Gaines was embarrassed about something. Bill Pressler took charge of the situation.

"Dick goes to school with my brother Gordon, at Hilldale." *Which means that Dick is probably a dumbshit* Henry thought to himself. "Dick's got the SAT coming up," Bill went on, "and he doesn't do so good on tests." *Now it's been confirmed* Henry said silently as he put a concerned expression on his face and nodded for his friend to continue. "I told him he ought to talk to you."

"Can you help me out?" Gaines asked, feeling embarrassed at the entire situation, and especially the fact that this new kid was younger than he. Bill says you took it a year early and aced it."

Henry shook his head. "Look, I don't think I can help on something like that, especially since it's in—what? Two weeks?"

Richard Gaines broke in quickly. "Oh, that's no problem. I can get all the stuff made up in three days—five, tops."

What on earth is he talking about? Henry wondered at this odd assertion. "Well...even if you *can,* the SAT isn't something you can really cram for. You can try to learn vocabulary for the English part, and that'll help some, but two weeks isn't much time." He took a deep breath and went on.

"The math section...well, either you can do arithmetic or you can't. I don't think I can teach you the math part in two weeks if you're really weak there. Now, what I *can* do," Henry said, warming to the subject, "is teach you to see the way the test writers *think,* which is a big part of being able to get all the way through the test before time is called." *And something that anyone with half a brain can see after reading the first two or three questions* he wanted to add. "The most important thing is—"

"No, no, you're missing the point," Bill Pressler broke in. "Dick doesn't want a tutor, that's not going to be enough, especially not now, with two weeks left, like you said."

"Then...how can I help him out?"

"Take the test for me." Henry's mouth opened as he stared at Dick Gaines. He was dumbfounded. Gaines went on quickly. "That's all you've got to do. Walk into the center, show the right ID, sit down and take the test for me. You remember what it was like—a whole bunch of kids you didn't know showing up at a place you'd never been before. A couple hours easy work, and you'll be out of there. Right?"

Henry didn't know what to say. *Getting a ringer to take the SAT for you. Jesus! Who is this guy?* he thought. *Ought to call himself 'Dickhead' Gaines.* Despite this reaction, Henry's mind instinctively went to analyzing the obstacles to pulling off such a plan.

"Well, the main problem would be the ID. When I took it last year, I wasn't sixteen yet, so I used a copy of my birth certificate. Everyone else had a driver's license, though, and I think if someone who was supposed to be seventeen or eighteen like you are tried to say he couldn't drive a car, they'd look real close at him."

"Hey, I said that's no problem. I can get a real driver's license for you, not a fake one. Your picture on it, my name, address, and birthdate." Henry thought about that for a moment.

"Yeah, sure, I go in to the license bureau, say I'm you and lost my license, they look up your address, take a new picture, and mail you off the new license. Since we're under 21, it can't be a liquor scam, and high school kids don't have any other ID anyway, so what are they going to ask for as proof—a note from your mother? Guys must pull that trick all the time for their underage brothers, sometimes even for friends, if they really trust 'em. Except I'm four inches shorter than you are, and you got blonde hair. They're sure to spot that; and even if they didn't, we still wouldn't get the thing in two weeks, not even if we went for the picture tomorrow." *Why the hell am I even talking about this stupid idea?* Henry asked himself.

Gaines was impressed at how quickly Henry had realized how to get a real driver's license issued with someone else's picture on it. "You'd be right about the clerk spotting the different description and the time it would take," he said with a broad smile, "except for one thing. My dad owns the license office. I can fill out the forms myself, stamp his signature on it, and tell 'em I need immediate turnaround. Five days, tops." Richard Gaines looked very smug.

Henry frowned. "How can your dad *own* a driver's license office?" he immediately demanded. "Those are state offices. Missouri state government owns and operates them." Henry was thinking about all the times he had gone with his father and waited while surly workers had taken their time waiting on them. The first time he had gone by himself, to license his '64 Chevy II Super Sport, the delay had been even worse.

Dick Gaines was almost laughing now, and shaking his head happily. "No, my dad owns one. The state owns the land and the building, but he owns the business. He gets the money from license fees. I can do all the paperwork for the new driver's license tonight." Henry Bowman ignored this last comment. He wanted to know more about this license office setup.

"So...if the state owns the land and the building, how does somebody get to own a driver's license office?" he asked.

"The Governor appoints him," Richard Gaines said proudly.

So that's it Henry thought. *Another damned political scam. Fits right in with our new Missouri vehicle inspection law, where you get to hang around a gas station for two hours, waiting for a gangly kid with bad skin to take your money so he can tell you that your horn, turn signals, and brakes are working.* His thoughts returned to the license office. *Wonder what the Governor got out of this asshole's dad for that little gold mine? More than a pardon?*

Most Missourians, and everyone with politicians or newsmen in their families, knew that Democratic Governors in Missouri sold pardons. Trial lawyers found this practice especially irritating when the Governor charged less than they did, as was the case currently, but there was little they could do about it.

"Yeah—my dad's good friends with the Governor," Gaines lied.

This guy talks too damn much Henry thought. He had no intention of taking the SAT for anyone, but there was no way he would ever do it for Dick Gaines.

"Look, I have to tell you, I'm not wild about this idea. There may not be much chance of getting caught, but if something happened and I did, I'd be up shit creek."

"So would I," Gaines said immediately. Henry snorted.

"Yeah, but you're fucked right now. Your grades are lousy and you're going to bomb on the one test every college uses to level out the applicants from different schools. You got to take some risk. I don't. In fact, I don't need this shit at all."

Richard Gaines was used to being talked to this way from his father, but not from someone he barely knew, and who was two years his junior. He didn't like it at all, and he wanted to get up and leave, but he was desperate.

"Look, I know that. Hey, I came to you, right? Listen, we can work something out. I'd be willing to pay you." *Oh, did you originally hope to find someone who'd do it as a favor?* Henry thought sarcastically. "But I'm not going to pay someone unless I know he's going to come through."

Trying to take control of this conversation, are we? "That's not a problem," Henry said easily. "I'm very performance-oriented. I'll guarantee you at least fifteen hundred combined score. That also means each will be over seven hundred. The math will probably be higher than the verbal." Henry's mind was working quickly to come up with terms that would be impossible for Gaines to agree to.

"F-fifteen *hundred?* Like, a—" (here he thought for a few moments) "a—a seven-fifty on *both?*" No one in Richard Gaines' high school had ever earned scores anywhere near that high.

"Yes, or seven-fifteen, seven eighty-five, or whatever. Fifteen hundred combined's the minimum. Any less, you get two hundred dollars."

"Huh?" Gaines said. Henry's last comment had made no sense to him.

"Soon as we agree to do this, I go to the bank and get a cashier's check payable to you for two hundred dollars, and put it in an envelope with your money," Henry explained. "A lawyer holds the envelope and can't release it unless we're both there. When the test scores come back, we go see him. Fifteen hundred or higher, you tell him to give it to me. If I pull say, seven-fifty, seven-thirty, then I tell him to hand it to you."

Richard Gaines was adjusting to the concept that he might *make* $200 while having 700+ scores credited to him when he realized that Henry had not yet stated his fee. "Uh, and uh, how much does my check have to be for?" he said finally.

"Two bucks a point, based on the minimum. Three grand. Have a cashier's check for it by six o'clock Monday night. If that's too much or too soon, get someone else."

"Three thousand dollars?" Richard Gaines yelled. Several tables of the people in nearby booths turned to look at him. "Are you out of your fucking *mind?*" he added in an intense whisper. When Bill Pressler had offered to introduce him to Henry Bowman, Gaines had hoped he could talk the kid into taking the test for a twenty-dollar bill.

274

"Not at all," Henry said amiably.

"Do you know what I could buy with three thousand dollars?" Gaines continued in a slightly more measured tone. *You bet I do* Henry thought immediately. *You could buy a clean clipwing Cub, stressed for aerobatics, just like mine. Or you could buy a three-year-old 427 Corvette and a Korean War Power Wagon with a ring mount. Or maybe INTERARMCO's entire inventory of 20mm Solothurn ammo.*

"Three grand's pretty cheap, considering what four years at a good college costs," Henry explained. "And I have to risk ending up where you are right now. You, on the other hand..." He finished the sentence with a shrug. "SAT makes the difference, and you know it. Otherwise you wouldn't have come looking for me." Henry saw the older boy's expression change, and realized with astonishment that Gaines was thinking about what he had said. *Jesus, he's buying this crap!* Henry thought in disbelief.

"Before 6:00 Monday," Henry said as he slid out of the booth and stood to leave. "Bill here can give you my phone number, so I can tell you where the lawyer's office is." *Since if you asked me now, I wouldn't have the faintest idea of what lawyer would want to hold an envelope for a couple of high school kids.* "Let me know, one way or the other." He walked out the door, waving goodbye to Jimmy Kerth as he went out the door.

Henry was grinning as he stepped into the parking lot. He was remembering the look on Gaines' face when he had named his fee. *Couldn't have pulled a needle out of his ass with a tractor.* Max Collins used the phrase occasionally. Henry thought it was very appropriate.

Well, after that little talk, there ought to be some good gossip around school Monday Henry told himself with a smile.

As it turned out, there wasn't. What would happen on Monday would be *much* more interesting.

February 10, 1969

"Henry, there's someone here to see you," Catherine Bowman called to her son after she had opened the front door. "Go on upstairs," she told the visitor. "His room's on the right."

Richard Gaines quickly made his way to Henry Bowman's bedroom. He found Henry sitting at a wide desk. Above it on the wall was a framed photo of a green and white biplane about a hundred feet off the ground, pointed almost straight down and obviously about to crash.

Henry had several texts open on the desk, and was bent over a piece of graph paper, making fine marks on it. He did not raise his head but held up a finger, indicating that his visitor should wait silently for a moment. Richard did not know it, but Henry was calculating extended trajectory curves for his Hart-barreled .224 Clark varmint rifle, based on the range results he had achieved the day before at one, two, and three hundred yards.

"Sorry, my head was full of numbers I didn't want to lose." He was startled to see Dick Gaines standing in the doorway. "Come on in." The older boy closed the door behind him and got to the point.

"Look, I've only got eleven hundred right now. That's all I could get in two days, but it's in cash, and I'll have the rest before you go in to take the test."

Henry shook his head. "It's almost eight-thirty," he said, nodding towards the clock on the wall. "I said by six."

"Jesus, what's *two hours?*" Richard Gaines pleaded. "Look, you don't have to do the two hundred dollar deal, okay?" he offered. "I know you'll do great. Just take the test for me, okay?"

Henry shook his head. *Have I wandered in to the Twilight Zone? I've got to come up with something that'll get rid of this moron.* He smiled sadly and said, "You don't understand. After 6:00, it was the next guy in line's turn. He's already come by with the money, so I've been hired. And no matter what kind of IDs you can come up with, there's no way I can be two people at the same time. Sorry."

Richard Gaines looked crestfallen. He nodded his head and turned to leave. Henry Bowman opened his mouth as Richard Gaines walked out the door, then shut it when he realized he had nothing more to say.

Henry didn't go back to the trajectory tables that night. Some vague beliefs he had instinctively held had just been magnified a hundredfold in his mind. It would be years before he would be able to put them into words, but they had already taken deep root.

Always deal from a position of strength. When opportunity presents itself, seize it. Take control of a situation and others will follow you, even when it is not in their best interests to do so. Political power begets corruption. But the most important lesson was the one Henry had already learned from the events of his canoe trip the previous summer: *Know when to walk away.*

June 1, 1969

"He's magnificent, but I'm afraid as soon as we stalk closer, he'll be in the woods. The wind isn't in our faces, and might change. Best to find another herd rather than waste time on this one." Raymond Johnson lowered his binoculars.

"By the time we do that, it'll be dark. I don't mind quitting for the day, but let me think about this for just a minute," Max Collins replied. His eyes scanned the area around where they stood. *Not a fucking thing I could use for a rest around here.* He looked at Raymond, and at the two trackers that were with him. *Roll up a couple shirts, still wouldn't be but three inches high, and that's not enough to keep the grip cap out of the dirt.* His eyes came to rest on a patch of ground that was very slightly higher than the surrounding area. *That might get me above the weeds.* Max Collins slid his left arm through the military sling and tightened it around his upper bicep as he knee-walked to the place he had picked out. The guide saw what he was doing and spoke up immediately.

"Ahh...Max, that's a four hundred yard shot, and I don't think—"

"Closer to four-fifty," Collins interrupted as he went from a kneeling position to one flat on his stomach. "Unless the one is normal size and all the others are stunted." Johnson opened his mouth to say something, then shut it. Max had made a perfect shot on a warthog that morning. Ray was not about to insult a client on the first day of his safari. The trackers could use some night practice anyway.

The big man stared out at the distant herd of greater kudu, looking for clues as to the speed of the wind. *Almost none, this late. Just a kiss, from the left* he decided with satisfaction. Then Collins worked himself into the same prone position he had used to place third in the Wimbledon Cup thousand-yard match in the late 'thirties. His feet were spread, and his spine, when viewed from above, made a twenty-five degree angle with the axis of the rifle barrel. Collins' elbows pressed into the dry earth, supporting his upper body, and the sling bit into his left arm as the tension on it increased.

The two trackers looked at Ray Johnson and scowled. The professional hunter did not normally let anyone take such a long shot, especially when the game was standing right next to the woods, and certainly not a half hour before dusk. Tracking a wounded animal in the dark was much harder, and their employer did not believe in letting injured game get away and take days to die. They looked at each other and resigned themselves to being up the entire night.

The grey animal with the spiral horns that faced the four men was Africa's version of a bull elk. The kudu did not come close to filling the scope's field of view at that long a distance, but Max Collins could see that he was indeed a huge example of the species. The rifleman put the crosshairs at a spot he judged to be thirty-two inches above and six inches to the left of the kudu's heart, took a deep breath, let part of it out, and began to squeeze the trigger.

The kudu took a step and started turning. It began to walk towards the woods.

Shit! Collins swore silently. *Can't shoot at moving game at this range.* He relaxed his trigger finger as he tracked the animal, willing the bull to stop for a moment. As if obeying his command, the big male kudu quit walking and sniffed the air. The kudu was now facing away at a quartering angle, and a straight line from the muzzle of Collins' Model 70 would traverse over three feet of abdominal muscle before reaching the kudu's heart or lungs.

Max Collins moved the crosshairs to a spot almost three feet over the Kudu's back, then changed his mind. *Spine's too small for this range. Too easy to miss altogether and just tear up the muscle. The kid said more than four feet. Time to see if he really knows what the fuck he's talking about.*

Max altered his aim so that the crosshairs rested on a point slightly above the kudu's back and a foot in front of the animal's right hip. It was what Elmer Keith referred to as a 'raking shot through the boiler room' and could be taken (especially on an animal as large as a greater kudu) only if the rifle and ammunition being used gave truly outstanding penetration. Typical hunting rifles firing expanding bullets normally were good for between twelve and eighteen inches of penetration on thin-skinned game.

The crosshairs were describing a regular pattern as they moved within an imaginary six-inch area containing Collins' aiming point. The rifleman got in synch with the movement, and the trigger broke just as the crosshairs passed through the spot Collins had selected. *Perfect letoff* he thought as the muzzle blast rang out across the plain.

"Miss," Ray said. The bull was just standing there.

"No, Ray. Here." Banda, the lead tracker, was staring through the binoculars, and had seen dust fly from the hide in front of the kudu's right haunch. He bent over and jabbed his index finger at the corresponding spot on his own torso to illustrate. The tracker was grinning. He knew what was coming.

The other animals in the herd began moving towards the trees when the sound of the shot reached them, but the big bull stood utterly still. Six seconds later he collapsed in a heap.

"Heart shot," Max said as he got to his feet. "Either that or he died of fright."

The guide, the client, and the two trackers started the quarter-mile walk to where the kudu lay. All four of them were smiling.

***

"So, was the first day up to expectations?" Ray and Max were relaxing by the campfire. Max was drinking scotch. The younger man preferred gin.

"Damn, but I've never seen this much game," Max said with feeling. "And I about shit when I saw that lion take down that buffalo, for Christ's sake." That morning they had seen a lion tear the throat from a cape buffalo and hang on until it bled out.

"That was unusual for me, too," Ray admitted. "Usually, they won't try it unless there are a pair that can attack at the same time. The one today must have been hungry. As I point out to everyone who comes here for the first time, nothing in Africa dies of old age." He took a sip of his drink and stared into the glowing fire. "I'm still thinking about the shot you made on that kudu. Four hundred forty steps, through the paunch and stopping just under the skin of the chest."

Max smiled. "Been practicing a little."

"I've had other clients use the .338 Winchester, but *nobody* got penetration like you did with soft points. Four and a half feet?"

"Got to give my nephew credit for that. He's become the ballistician in the family. He thought I should bring a .375 Ackley, but I wanted a factory caliber for my plains rifle, just in case my ammo got lost and I had to buy some. I was going to load up some solids for my .338 for big stuff like eland, but he talked me out of it." Max was referring to ammunition loaded with bullets that had no lead exposed and did not deform at all on impact. Such projectiles penetrated much more deeply than expanding bullets. This was necessary on large game such as the eland, which weighed over a ton. "Henry loaded the stuff I brought on this trip." Max slid a round out of his cartridge belt and handed it to Ray for his inspection.

"That's a 275-grain Speer," he explained as Ray examined the round, referring to the weight and manufacturer of the copper and lead bullet projecting from the neck of the cartridge case. "Elmer Keith's sworn by 'em for years," Max added. Keith was the 70-year-old former outfitter and firearms authority from Salmon, Idaho. Ray Johnson nodded. Keith was well-known to all serious hunters and guides. When Ray had lived in Pitkin County, he had corresponded with Keith on several occasions.

"Henry said the latest batch of 275's out of the factory would blow up. Said Speer got a bunch of complaints from deer hunters who didn't like them whistling through a mulie like shit through a goose, and they softened the core, hardened the gilding metal, and scored the inside of the jacket, if you can believe that. Henry hunted up a bunch of different lot numbers, sectioned and tested 'em all, and said this batch was good for more than four feet on game."

"Your nephew is a hunter, then?" Ray asked. Max Collins laughed at this question and took another sip of his scotch.

"Henry's dying to get over here. He shoots a .375 Ackley like a varmint rifle. Must have put five, six thousand rounds through that thing by this time. Got a Rigby .577 double he's damn good with, too. And he's been looking for a 4-bore for ten years now.

"But to answer your question, other than a few groundhogs he's potted out in the country, Henry's never been hunting. He'd rather shoot ten crows in an afternoon than sit in a tree stand all weekend and wait for a deer to walk by.

"When he promised me I'd get more than four feet penetration, I figured he'd tried the ammo out on wet newspapers or old phone books or something." Collins laughed harder at the memory.

"He was really fired up I was going to Africa, though. Turned out he—" and here Max had to get himself collected before he could continue, "—he conned some guy at the *slaughterhouse* into letting him paste a couple of their steers. Gave the guy a bottle of whisky to go on break so Henry could autopsy 'em."

"Good Lord, Max," Ray said as he laughed along with the older man, "you should have brought him along. I wish *all* my clients who'd never been hunting were like that."

"I would have, but he's still in school right now. Henry's sixteen." Max's face lit up as he remembered something else. "Henry got the whisky from my sister's liquor cabinet 'cause the store wouldn't sell him any, and had to get *me* to go buy another bottle to replace it before his mother found out."

"You did, I hope?"

"Shit, I ran out and bought him a case. Told him to work up some good cape buffalo loads for my .458."

Ray Johnson found this comment uproariously funny. Despite it being only the first day of a three-week safari, he decided that his earlier assessment of the man had been dead-on: Max Collins was the best client he had ever had in his six years working as a professional hunter.

June 12, 1969

The three big bulls were by themselves, and since the wind was blowing away from them, they were unaware that Ray, Max, and the two trackers were nearby. They were all large, but the bull in front was definitely the biggest. *45 inches at least* Raymond thought. *Seventeen, maybe eighteen hundred pounds.*

Max Collins was carrying his dangerous-game rifle, a custom .450 Ashurst built on a Czech BRNO ZKK 602 action. The BRNO action was, in Max's opinion, the best of the Magnum Mausers. Curt Behnke had fitted the barrel and milled the trigger guard and oversize magazine that held five rounds. He had also reversed the operation of the safety (no simple task) so that it functioned in the same direction, forward for 'off', as the rifles made in every country other than Czechoslovakia. Henry and Walter Bowman had made the stock to fit their big relative.

The .450 Ashurst cartridge was made from a straightened .375 H&H case. It was basically a lengthened .458 Winchester that held more powder and could therefore be loaded to more powerful levels. The chamber was cut so that lower-powered .458 factory ammo could be used in a pinch, with only a slight loss in accuracy.

"Take him," Raymond whispered. He didn't need to say which one.

Collins threw the big rifle to his cheek and squeezed the trigger as soon as the front sight settled on the cape buffalo's shoulder. The muzzle blast of the .450 Ashurst made the four men's ears ring, and the buffalo dropped as if struck by a bolt of lightning. At sixteen yards, Collins had put his shot within a quarter inch of where he was aiming, which was on the point of the animal's shoulder. The 500 grain steel-jacketed solid bullet had struck the buffalo at 2460 feet per second, concentrating over 6700 foot-pounds of energy onto an area smaller than a dime.

Henry had correctly predicted exactly what would happen if Max were to get a broadside shot at a cape buffalo. The 500 grain Winchester solid was designed to go straight and maintain its shape no matter what it struck. It shattered the buffalo's near shoulder, clipped the top of its heart, and smashed its off shoulder in a space of about three milliseconds. No four-legged creature can remain standing with both shoulders shattered, and this one was no exception.

There was another thing that Henry had predicted, but Max would not remember the boy's warning until several minutes later. A lot was going to happen before then.

Max Collins racked the bolt of the Czech Mauser without dropping the rifle's butt from his shoulder, ejected the fired case, and chambered a new round before the dust had settled around the carcass of the 1750-pound animal. Max knew that his bullet had done exactly what he had wanted, and that the buffalo he had shot was not a danger to them, but he did not lower his rifle. There were two other bulls less than fifty feet away, and cape buffalo were known to charge at almost any time.

They were especially known to charge when wounded, and that is exactly what the bull farthest from the four men did. This second bull, which weighed a mere 1630 pounds, lowered his nose and headed straight at Max Collins.

A charging cape buffalo at less than fifty feet presents a very challenging problem, particularly if the animal's head is lowered. A heart shot, where the animal will die within five or ten seconds, is not good enough. Man and lion both have all too often been killed by a dying cape buffalo in the last few seconds of its life. In order to survive a charge, the hunter must not only kill the animal, but make it collapse before it gets to him.

Shoulder and spine shots do this, but are not possible from the front.

The only shot that is certain to drop a charging buffalo instantly is one to the brain. This poses a problem in that the animal's thick horn bosses cover much of the buffalo's skull and act as a very effective form of armor against any attempted brain shots.

When the gold bead of the .450's front sight landed on the charging bull's head, Max Collins pulled the trigger and worked the bolt as the gun rose in recoil. He concentrated on his shooting and not on what might happen to him in the next few seconds.

Max's shot on the charging bull was two inches higher and an inch and a quarter left of where it should have been. It struck 1/4" above the corner of the sloping horn boss just left of center. The round nose of the Winchester bullet was deflected several degrees by the dense horn material. The bullet plowed through the horn boss on an angled path, glanced off the skull, cracking it slightly, and howled off over the Angolan countryside. In doing this, the impact of the bullet blew a baseball-sized chunk of horn material and a small amount of buffalo hide fifty feet in the air. It also made the bull considerably angrier in the process. The cape buffalo kept coming. Ray Johnson stepped to the side as he raised his .600 Nitro Holland and Holland, flicked off the safety, and prepared to try to stop the charge.

Max Collins did not notice his guide's actions. He thought of nothing except working the bolt of his rifle smoothly, putting the front sight on the center of the buffalo's skull, and squeezing the trigger. His next shot on the charging beast was an inch lower than the last one. With the chunk of horn gone, the steel-jacketed slug bored right into the brain, deflected off the inside of the skull, and traveled down the center of the animal's spinal column for a distance of almost three feet. The buffalo fell on its chest and skidded to a stop less than ten feet in front of Collins, who was racking the .450's bolt for yet another shot. The big buff was dead. It had died before its chin hit the ground, its brain destroyed and its spine cored by the steel-jacketed slug.

Max looked over at Raymond, who lowered his .600 Nitro and engaged the safety.

"Nice double, Max," Ray said with a grin.

Max nodded, but didn't say anything right away. He was feeling just a little light headed.

"Thanks for holding off," he said finally. "It felt good to drop that second one without any help." Raymond smiled. He had known that Max would want to stop the charge himself. The two men made jokes and laughed in relief after the charge, and then the guide noticed something.

"I think I see why he charged, Max. Look." Ray was indicating the side of the dead buffalo's body, and Collins had to walk several yards to his right to see what the man was pointing at.

Two feet behind the shoulder was a fingernail-sized hole with a trickle of blood running out of it. Banda, the lead tracker, stepped over to the buffalo and inserted the thin blade of a skinning knife into the hole. The knife stopped after three inches of it had disappeared.

"Your shot on the first one," Ray explained. "Broke both shoulders, exited, and went a couple inches into the bull standing behind him. Pissed him off, I'd say."

"I'll be a son of a bitch," Collins said. "My nephew told me that might happen, and I told him he was crazy."

"I've seen it before with a .378 Weatherby," Ray Johnson admitted, "but never with a .45 caliber rifle. We'll make sure your next one doesn't have anything standing around behind it."

Max Collins shook his head and laughed as he watched the trackers roll the buffalo on its side and prepare to gut it. *Damn, but it's good to be alive.*

***

The men were back in camp, eating a late dinner that the camp cook had prepared and reliving the excitement of the afternoon, when Max suddenly thought of something. He put down his fork, finished chewing, and looked at Ray Johnson.

"You know, that little bastard even told me he had a cure for it, but I didn't take him seriously."

"What's that, Max?"

"Overpenetration with solids in the .450. He loaded up some ammo for me in case I had that problem, and I thought he was kidding."

"Soft points?"

"No, we both thought those might not reach the second shoulder. Let me show you." Max Collins went to his tent and retrieved his ammo bag. He dug down in the bottom, found the ammo box he was looking for, and brought it back to the table. Ray took it from him and pulled off the lid.

Inside were twenty .450 Ashurst cartridges, but the 500 grain steel-jacketed solids had been seated backwards into the brass cases. Instead of a rounded nose, the striking end of the bullet was completely flat and full diameter.

"They're backwards!" Raymond exclaimed.

"I thought it was a joke, but he insisted I bring them with me. He said he'd found some article where John Buhmiller tried it on elephant and they killed better that way. Henry altered the feed ramp and re-throated my barrel for base-first bullets, and he says his crazy load shoots to the same point of aim at fifty yards. Said they bust up the shoulder bones on the slaughterhouse bulls better, too. "

"I have never heard of doing that, but John Buhmiller is a man I would listen to."

Buhmiller was a Montana barrelmaker who had won Montana's version of the Wimbledon cup 1000-yard match in both 1937 and 1938. He was an avid experimenter with a fondness for large calibers who had first gone to Africa when he was in his 70s. Buhmiller had taken a liking to Africa, and gone on to work game control there, shooting hundreds of head of dangerous game while in his 80s. Henry Bowman corresponded with him regularly.

Twenty years later, flat-pointed, thick-jacketed .458 projectiles would be made by Jack Carter's *Trophy Bonded Bullets* company. Trophy Bonded's 'Sledgehammer Solid' would be considered by many African hunters to be the best slug ever made for cape buffalo. In 1969, however, the only shooters loading anything like it were an old Montana barrelmaker and a 16-year-old from Missouri who liked to shoot big guns.

"I think I'll load these crazy-looking things in my .450 tomorrow, when we go out," Max said, examining one of the cartridges Henry had made for him.

"Tell me more about this nephew of yours, Max," Ray said as he motioned for one of the camp crew to refill his drink. "I have a sneaky feeling you've only given me the tip of the iceberg."

July 10, 1969

"Eight hundred, or a little bit more," Allen Kane said after turning the thumbwheel to bring the halves of the split image into alignment.

"Let's see if the sight subcontractor knew what he was doing," Henry Bowman replied with a grin.

"And the guys at Lake City Arsenal," Kane laughed as he looked up from the tripod- mounted 80 centimeter Barr & Stroud rangefinder.

Henry slid the rear sight of the 1945-era, New England Westinghouse-manufactured Browning Automatic Rifle to its 800-yard setting, checked to see that the bore was clear, made sure the wingnuts on the bipod were tight, and lay down behind the weapon. He put in his earplugs, snapped a full 20-round magazine into place, made sure the rate-of-fire selector was on 'slow', and pulled the butt tightly against his shoulder. He put the front sight on the rock outcropping jutting out from the distant mountainside and squeezed the trigger. Three blasts chugged out of the 20-pound weapon, and three red streaks curved out over the valley and disappeared into the hillside a half-mile away.

"Windage is good; you're about eight, maybe ten feet low," Kane offered, peering through the huge twenty power Japanese battleship binoculars that were also mounted on a tripod. "Shoot some more." Henry put five more bursts into the distant mountainside with very similar results.

"Tracers get lighter as they burn, probably drop more."

"Yeah, but you never know. Ball or AP might shoot somewhere else entirely."

"We'll find out after I shoot some more tracers." He adjusted his rear sight, then reached into the ammo can for another loaded magazine. He fired another burst, and the tracers bounced off the distant rock at unpredictable angles, burning out in midair as they tumbled. Henry Bowman loved tracer ammo. He fired thirteen more 20-round magazines before standing up. "Your turn," he said cheerfully as he picked up the fifteen empty magazines and stacked them neatly on end in the fifty-caliber ammo can.

"Now for the good stuff," Allen Kane announced as he lifted another .50 cal. can off the tailgate of the truck. "Blue tip."

Kane lay down behind the automatic rifle and adjusted the gun's position. He was careful not to touch the barrel, which was now at a temperature of over 700 degrees. He made sure the bolt was retracted and snapped a loaded magazine of .30-06 ammunition into the bottom of the gun's receiver.

Tracer ammunition enabled belt-fed machine gun shooters to see where their shots were going, especially at night. Standard military practice called for every fifth round in the belt to be a tracer, and the other four to be armor piercing rounds whose bullets were constructed with pointed, hardened, tungsten-alloy cores for penetrating steel armor plate. Both tracer and armor-piercing .30 caliber ammo were common on the surplus market. AP was easily recognized by the black paint on the tip of the bullet. Tracers were painted red or orange.

During the Second World War, the United States had developed a .30 caliber *incendiary* round, and had started loading it in 1943. Incendiary ammunition explodes with a flash when it hits its target, and is most useful for igniting the fuel tanks of enemy aircraft. U.S. incendiary ammo is characterized by blue paint on the tip.

Before the end of 1943, the U.S. Military had realized that since a) none of their fighter aircraft carried .30 caliber machine guns and b) the only time a .30 caliber ground gun was used in an antiaircraft capacity was by utter coincidence, there was little use for .30 caliber incendiary ammunition, and they stopped making it. Production of .50 caliber incendiary (and, to an even greater degree, silver-tipped *armor-piercing* incendiary) was summarily increased. Blue-tipped .30 caliber, however, was only found with the 43 head-stamp, and was harder to come by.

Blue tip was Henry and Allen's favorite.

Allen Kane put the rear sight back on the 800 yard setting, took aim, and squeezed off a three-round burst. A little over a second later, three bright white flashes appeared at the base of the rock outcropping. They were easily visible, even in the bright sunlight.

"Good windage. You're right at the base of the rocks. Nice, tight group, too. Looked like all three were in about five feet."

"That's the BAR for you."

Allen Kane spent the next twenty minutes putting three-shot bursts of .30-06 incendiary into the distant rocks, then picked up his Garand and took some long range shots from the standing position with the WWII semiauto.

While Allen Kane was doing this, Henry Bowman got out his 8 3/8" .44 magnum, braced himself against the rear tire of Allen's truck, and did some half-mile sixgun shooting. It took him five shots to determine the right amount of front sight to hold up to hit the Volkswagen-sized boulder a half mile away. The sun was behind them, and Henry could easily spot the puffs of rock dust that flew up when the big cast slugs hit. After getting his sight picture down pat, Henry switched to a smaller rock, one about the size of an overstuffed armchair. He found that he could hit it three to four shots out of every cylinder. *Got to ration myself* he realized, when he saw how many fired cases had piled up already. *Between us, we've only got maybe 15,000 rounds of .44s, and that has to last three weeks.* He closed the lid on the ammo can, packed his empties in a canvas bag, and stood up.

Henry stowed the ammo can and fired brass in a side compartment of the truck's camper top and went back to the giant binoculars to study the exposed rocks around him. He and Allen were on a very large section of federal land in the central part of Idaho, and the rock formations were different from those that Henry was used to seeing in Missouri. The midwest was comprised of sedimentary deposits, which were evident along the river and anywhere on any interstate where the highway cut through a hill. Idaho had many more igneous formations, and Henry realized he was unconsciously classifying the geologic structures as he saw them. Henry enjoyed figuring things out, and he was just beginning to discover that geology offered limitless opportunities in that area.

"What?" Henry asked when he realized Allen Kane had said something to him.

"I said, let's pack up and head towards the Pahsimeroi Valley, see if Elmer was pulling our leg when he told us this was the big year in the jack cycle."

"Sounds good to me." Henry began to help Allen gather up their equipment, leaving the Browning until last, to give it more time to cool. When they got in the cab of the truck and headed back down the mountain, the BAR was stowed in a felt-lined canvas drop case.

Its barrel was still too hot to touch.

July 15, 1969

"How far out do you want them?" Henry asked nervously.

"Whatever you think'd make it interesting."

Great Henry thought. *Put it all on me.* He decided to spread the targets out over various ranges. *Hundred paces ought to do it for the close ones. I can hit those, at least.* He picked up the paper sack and started walking.

Allen and Henry were thirty miles outside Salmon, Idaho. Elmer Keith was with them. When Keith had heard Allen Kane was coming to shoot jackrabbits, he had agreed to take an afternoon off from writing and do some long range shooting with the Indiana ballistician and his young friend from Missouri. Allen and Henry had picked up the seventy-year-old gun writer at his house in Salmon, and Keith had directed Allen to a suitable spot outside the small town.

Henry Bowman was nervous. Elmer Keith had been shooting revolvers for over sixty years, and he had studied and mastered many of Ed McGivern's aerial shooting feats forty years before. He was also the man who had persuaded Smith & Wesson to produce the .44 magnum, and his book *Sixguns*, written when Henry was three years old, was the definitive work on using the revolver for hunting and defense. An entire chapter of the book was devoted to shooting revolvers at ranges up to a half mile.

Henry Bowman did not want to embarrass himself in front of Elmer Keith.

In the paper sack Henry carried were two dozen 2" diameter sticks of 80% strength ditching dynamite. Allen had bought four cases of it at a truck depot in Mackey on the drive north to Salmon. They had wrapped each stick with a piece of typing paper held on with tape and then given it a quick coat of fluorescent orange paint from a spray can for better visibility. Henry was walking out across the rocks and sagebrush to put the dynamite out at various ranges for the three of them to shoot at.

When Henry had counted off seventy paces, he got nervous. *Be pretty lame if I can't hit any of them. Better stick a few close in.* He lay down three sticks several yards apart, making sure they could be seen from where Allen and Elmer were standing, and then kept walking. When Elmer Keith saw this he raised his eyebrows but said nothing.

Henry put nine sticks a hundred paces out, six at a hundred fifty, and the final six at what he judged was two hundred yards. When he got back to his two companions, the older man was smiling.

"Seventy, a hundred, one-fifty, and two hundred," Henry announced.

"Why'd you stick those first three so close in?" Kane demanded.

"So you could show us some hipshooting," Henry shot back. The old man laughed.

"Now this ought to split the real gun hands out from the ones should do their shootin' across a table," Keith said around the side of his cigar. He was obviously amused. He tipped back the large 5X beaver Stetson that had been his trademark for over forty years and looked closely at Henry. "Go on," he said, nodding.

Wonderful Henry thought. *Like we couldn't all shoot at the same time, and make it a little less embarrassing.* He slipped his earplugs in and went to the tailgate of the truck. He retrieved a .50 caliber can full of what he considered his 'match' ammo. It had been loaded using once-fired cases and bullets Henry had cast out of the alloy he had found to be most accurate in S&W revolvers. The bullet design was the Hensley & Gibbs #503, cast using the matched pair of molds his father had given him five years before, lubricated with a 50% Alox/50% beeswax mixture, and sized in straight-through Star dies. Elmer

Keith had designed the bullet in the late '20s. They shot well at all distances.

Henry Bowman put the ammo can at his feet and drew the 8 3/8" N-frame from the crossdraw holster. He had sighted that particular gun to shoot three inches high at one hundred yards. He loaded the cylinder, pulled the big sixgun into the braced, two-handed position, and cocked the hammer.

The orange targets at the 150-step range were small, but not as hard to see as Henry had feared when he had put them out there. He put the front sight on the orange speck and made sure the top of the rear blade was even with the top of the gold insert in the front ramp. Henry increased the pressure of his right index finger, and squeezed the final few ounces just as the front sight obscured the distant orange target.

The big Smith bucked in recoil. "Just over the top," Allen Kane said immediately. "I think if you'd been a couple inches lower you'd have hit it." Henry nodded and eared back the hammer for another try. This time he willed the trigger to break just before the front sight covered the orange dot in the distance.

Immediately following the blast of the magnum revolver came the distant, satisfying boom of the ditching dynamite, detonated by the impact of the 250 grain flat-nosed slug. A ten-foot cloud of dust appeared and began to settle at the spot where the charge had been. Without hesitating, Henry cocked the hammer again and loosed another round at the next charge set at the same distance. It exploded as well. Henry missed with his fourth shot, again going a bit high. He connected with his fifth, then switched to the 200-yard targets for the last round in his cylinder.

"Gonna try two hundred," he announced. He held up about a sixteenth of an inch of the front sight blade, put the target on top of it, and willed the gun to fire.

"Less than a foot right," Elmer Keith announced as Henry lowered his gun, opened the cylinder, and ejected the spent cases into his ammo pouch. "Al," Keith said, addressing the man from Indiana, "I guess young Henry here won't be calling me a liar about six-guns at long range." Kane laughed, and Henry smiled at the compliment.

"Time to see if I've still got my eyesight," Keith announced, and drew a 4" barreled Smith & Wesson from an inside-the-pants holster on his right hip. It was identical to Henry's gun except for the shorter barrel and the smaller grips, which were inlaid on each side with an eagle medallion.

Keith exploded the three remaining hundred-yard charges with four shots, missed one at 150 yards, then connected with his last round. Henry noticed that Keith fired all six rounds in about half the time that he himself had taken. *He is good* Henry thought.

"Leave me the easy ones and the impossible ones, huh?" Allen Kane said in mock indignation.

"We've got plenty of dynamite," Henry said cheerfully.

***

The three shooters had spent the rest of the afternoon shooting a variety of long range and aerial targets. Henry Bowman was especially impressed with what Allen Kane and Elmer Keith could each do with two revolvers, fired from the hip simultaneously. Keith, in turn, was surprised at Henry's skill on aerial targets, especially with the 20-pound BAR.

Henry shook the man's hand once again as they dropped him off at his house. "Thanks for taking the time to see us today, Elmer," Henry said.

Keith smiled. "You got the right idea with that .375 Ackley of yours, son," he declared as he climbed out of the truck. "No point in spending all your time practicing with a pest rifle like that 7mm Remington if you're ever going to hunt game animals." He turned and walked towards his house. Allen Kane waited until he had entered the front door, then accelerated away from the curb.

He's better than I am with a revolver Henry decided. *I need to practice more.*

"If you're looking for a department that will teach Marxism, I'd advise you to consider another school."

"Pardon me?" Henry said. He thought he had heard the man correctly, but after listening to some of the economics professors at other liberal arts schools boast of the progressive courses their departments offered, he was startled by the man's blunt declaration.

Henry Bowman was in the final stages of that ritual common to prep-school students in the summer preceding their senior year: The College Visiting Trip. In late June, Henry had removed the rear seat and control stick from his clipped-wing, 140-horsepower Cub, and bolted a cover over the hole in the floor where the stick had been. He had packed camping gear, clothes, a folding bike, his 5" Smith & Wesson, and 3000 rounds of ammunition behind the front seat, and headed east.

Henry had spent the last three weeks flying around New England, landing at local airports and bicycling to various schools. Most New England colleges had small airports nearby, and all had quoted him reasonable hangar rates if he decided to base his plane there during the school year. LaFleur airport was only four miles from Amherst College, and the people there had been very hospitable. Airport owners tended to admire aerobatic pilots, particularly ones who camped out of their airplanes.

"This department teaches Economics based on the principles of free market capitalism, and no one currently on our faculty advocates anything else."

Professor Nelson was about sixty-five, had white hair, and was slightly hard of hearing. His teeth were white and straight, and he showed a lot of them when he spoke. He was very outspoken, which Henry could see, and he had no patience for the students who attempted to 'take over' classes in the five college area of the Pioneer Valley.

This had happened often the previous year, under the guise of 'war protest'. Professor Nelson had no quarrel with those who opposed the war; he was no fan of it himself. He had noticed, however, that all protest efforts took place during daytime hours of weekdays and disappeared on weekends and vacation days. It seemed crazy to the professor that a student who was paying thousands of dollars to attend college would barricade the door to a classroom and hold the class hostage to a free-form 'rap session' about the war instead of demanding that the professor deliver every bit of his expensive expertise to the class. The only rational reason Nelson could accept was one he had overheard a demonstration leader tell another young man the previous spring: "The hell with whether you believe this shit or not—this is the best way to get good-looking rich chicks to fuck you I've ever found."

James Nelson was one of the longest-tenured professors at Amherst College, and was a nationally-recognized expert on railroad regulation. As such, he was keenly aware of the problems created when policy planners attempted to unload their own socialist agendas onto dynamic, creative people powerfully motivated by economic self-interest.

Professor Nelson smiled at Henry Bowman and added, "I tell you this now so you won't feel misled if you matriculate here a year from now. Maybe you'll want to reconsider your choice of colleges."

Henry Bowman liked this man, even though he'd only known him for twenty minutes. *He kind of reminds me of Elmer Keith* Henry thought. *That is, if Elmer Keith had lived in an eastern college town, worn a suit, and taught economics for the last forty years instead of living in Idaho, riding horses, guiding hunting parties, and shooting guns two or three hours a day.*

"On the other hand," Henry countered, "what you've said may make me want to tear up my applications to Hampshire, Antioch, and Williams, and bribe the Dean of Admissions here to make sure I get in." Nelson chuckled at this. Nobody who applied to Amherst College even considered attending any of the three schools Henry had just named.

"Thank you for taking the time to talk to me," Henry said, becoming serious again. "I've read the descriptions in the course catalog of what this department offers. There are a lot of classes I'd like to take here."

"We do a fair job," Nelson replied. Henry stood to leave.

"Can you aim me towards the Geology building?" he asked. Nelson pointed with his cane out the window.

"Corner of the quad. Two hundred yards. Make sure you go to the geology museum, too. It's the small building right next to the science center."

"Thanks. I'll do that." Henry left the man's office and found the stairwell.

Nelson smiled to himself as Henry left. He liked young people in general, and the one he had just met was no exception.

If anything, James Nelson had understated the Amherst College Econ Department's aversion to statist intervention and socialist economic policies. Eight years later, a student group devoted to campus humor and practical jokes would print up and distribute an official-looking notice of 'Recent additions to the Spring Course Catalog'. One of the entries would ostensibly be taught by the Chairman of the Economics Department, and was described thus:

Econ. 32: Constructive Alternatives to Capitalism

Professor Kohler. *Required for major.*
Room 312 Converse Hall
12:00 Noon-12:05 first Wednesday of every month.

James Nelson would find this very amusing.

***

It was the geology museum that did it Henry Bowman reflected as he stretched out on the closed-cell foam mattress, pulled his sleeping bag loosely over his legs, and reflected on what he was sure was his final choice of school.

He had entered the nondescript brick building and almost immediately been confronted with an absolutely immense mastodon skeleton that was mounted in the main room. He would come to learn that it was one of the largest in the world. After Henry had been staring at it for fifteen or twenty minutes, a geology professor with a limp had struck up a conversation with him, and had invited Henry to a screening of a film entitled *San Francisco: The City That Waits to Die*. The professor was showing it for some summer interns from the state University two miles away, and offered to let Henry join them. Henry had been fascinated by the film, and impressed that he was included with the group.

Henry checked the mosquito netting in his tent and switched off the flashlight. He was at the edge of Quabbin Reservoir, about twenty miles north of the school, where he had spent two hours shooting after dinner, until it got dark. A mile away was the Orange

Sport Parachuting Center, opened in 1959 as the first such facility in the country. Henry had taken their First Jump Course that day, at a cost of $65. It was his first airplane flight where the number of takeoffs had been greater than the number of landings.

This place is worlds better than what's in Boston Henry thought as he lay in his tent. He relived the excitement of his first parachute jump: the exhilaration of the exit, followed by the quiet, peaceful experience under the canopy. Henry knew he would make many more parachute jumps in the future.

Then he recalled the horrendous traffic that he had endured hitchhiking in Cambridge to get to what he had assumed was a tour for prospective students, only to wind up listening to a pompous nitwit explain at length about 'The Statue of the Three Lies'.

I could get to like this place Henry thought as he listened to the crickets and slowly drifted off to sleep.

October 22, 1970

"Can you hear me all right?" the voice crackled over the radio. Henry Bowman looked around at his three passengers. All were nodding their heads. He picked up the microphone and squeezed the "talk" button.

"Loud and clear, Professor Foose. This altitude suit you?" he asked the man in the six-passenger Piper a half mile ahead.

"It's good for now. It's a little bumpy this low, so if anyone starts feeling queasy, we'll have to go higher."

"Sounds good," Henry replied. "We're all ears." Henry put the microphone back in the clip on the instrument panel and leaned out the mixture on the Cessna Skyhawk until the reading on the exhaust gas temperature gauge peaked. His altimeter read 2500 feet, which was a little more than 2200 feet above the ground. He was on a southern course, flying directly over the eastern edge of the Connecticut River from Northampton, Massachusetts, to Long Island, New York.

"All right. The first thing you'll notice is what we discussed in the lecture on Thursday: the river's path is almost never straight for very long, and you can see how it has grown more and more crooked—serpentine is the official term—because of fluid dynamics." Henry dipped the right wing to give his passengers, particularly the one directly behind him, a better view of the river. "Anything which disturbs the course speeds up the water at the outside of the curve. Look at the erosion at the outside of the bend in the river about a half mile ahead, where the water is travelling fastest." Henry saw that the bank was undercut, and trees were about to topple into the river. Ann Ellis, in the front passenger seat, raised her Nikon for a photo. "Up ahead you can see a place where the river curved so much that during the next flood, the water broke over the land and made an ox-bow," Professor Foose continued on the radio.

"Can you fly down lower where I can get a better shot of the cut?" the young woman asked Henry. Ann Ellis was a Geology major in her Junior year at Smith College, taking a geo course at Amherst as part of the five-college exchange program. The hydro-dynamics class was on an aerial field trip to observe firsthand some textbook examples of maturing rivers and beachfront erosion.

Ann Ellis had been somewhat startled when she had discovered that three of the students were going to be flown by a freshman who wouldn't even be eligible to take the course for another year. She had volunteered to be one of the three when she had over-heard Henry telling Professor Foose that the visibility and photo opportunities would be much better out of the high-wing Cessna than the low-wing Piper that was being flown by a charter pilot.

"Dropping down to eight hundred for some quick photos, Chuck," Henry announced over the radio as he reduced power slightly and dropped the nose of the Skyhawk into a fast descent.

"Isn't this a little steep?" asked Mark Keller, a sophomore taking the course.

"Only if it makes you feel sick," Henry said in a voice loud enough to be heard over the increased wind noise. "We're still a good twenty knots from overspeeding the air-frame," Henry said, tapping the airspeed indicator, "and it's calm today. If I cut back on power, they'll get farther ahead of us. That Piper's already throttled back so we can keep up, and the geo department's paying by the hour. You feel funny or anything?" he asked as he glanced over his shoulder.

"No!" Keller answered, as if he had been accused of something shameful.

"Some people, it sneaks up on 'em," Henry said mildly. He levelled the plane about 500 feet off the ground and dipped the wing so Ann could get a clear shot of the under-cut riverbank.

"Perfect," she announced after she had clicked off two frames. Henry looked over his shoulder. The two men in the back seat were also taking photos. They lowered their cameras and nodded that they had both gotten their pictures. Henry added power and raised the nose slightly to return to his previous altitude.

"We're dropping down to two thousand," the other pilot announced on the radio.

"Meeting you there," Henry radioed back. He saw with satisfaction that his separation from the lead plane appeared practically unchanged.

It was an hour and a half to Long Island, and by the time the planes flew over the strip of land, Professor Foose had given the class a full narration of many of the things they had only read about before. The lead plane had alternated between two and five thousand feet four times, temporarily sacrificing optimum viewing because of upset stomachs. Henry had dutifully followed the Piper's climbs and descents, and his three passengers made cracks about what "lightweights" Foose was stuck with in the other plane. Ann Ellis, Mark Keller, and Garrett Edison were all very comfortable with Henry's flying by the time Long Island appeared. As they passed over the far tip of the island, Foose's voice came over the radio again.

"We're going to speed up and climb to five thousand on the way back, to save the geo department a little rental time."

"Okay if we take our time getting back?" Henry radioed to the other plane. "I want to make sure everyone here gets all the good pictures they want."

"Fine with me, Henry," Foose replied.

"Any requests?" Henry said, looking around at all three of his passengers. He put the 172 in a gentle turn out over the Atlantic ocean.

"Can we get down close to the beach?" Ann Ellis asked. "Closer than we were over the river when we got down low?"

"Yeah!" Garrett Edison agreed. "Uh, how low can you go? Can you get in trouble?"

"The law says minimum five hundred feet from any person or structure in sparsely populated areas, which this edge is. If I stay a little bit out from the bank, I can get as close to the water as you want. Nobody has a tape measure around here. Long as we don't make anyone think we're about to hit them, we're fine." He thought for a moment. "Seems to me you'd want a little altitude for pictures, though." The Skyhawk was a mile out over the ocean and Henry had it almost all the way turned around towards land again.

"We'd like to get pictures of the different cuts in the coastline around the jetties," Ann Ellis said quickly. "I also think it would be fun to fly close to the land."

"You got it." Henry pushed the mixture control to full rich and pulled back the power a bit. He adjusted the trim and put the plane in a 135-knot dive. "I'm not trying to scare you," he explained. "Down low, if you have an engine problem," *like it stops running* he added mentally, "you can trade airspeed for altitude and give yourself more choices of where to land. I don't ever fly low and slow unless I've got a good place to put down right in front of me." He leveled the plane at what he judged was about twenty feet off the water and fifty yards from shore.

"Man, you really see your speed down here," Mark Keller said. "How fast are we going?"

"About a hundred fifty miles per hour," Henry replied. The three passengers busied themselves taking photos as the beach raced by. As they neared the end of Long Island, Henry gave the 150-horsepower Lycoming full throttle and eased back on the yoke. Soon they had two thousand feet of altitude again.

As they made their way north over Connecticut, Ann Ellis mentioned that her family lived in a suburb of Hartford.

"Want to get an aerial photo of your house?"

"Yes!"

"Things look a lot different from the air—a whole new set of reference points. Let's figure out where the house is." They spent several minutes analyzing major roads before homing in on Ann's neighborhood. The young woman used half a roll of film shooting photos of the property. Henry grinned at how excited she became.

"Have you ever had an engine failure?" Mark Keller asked when they back on course to Northampton.

"I've never had an actual malfunction," Henry explained. "But my dad taught me to fly, and he was a big believer in emergency preparation. He'd switch the ignition off and pull the key when we were out flying, and tell me to make a real engine-out emergency landing.

"First few times he had to take it away from me and put it down himself, to show me it could always be done. He wouldn't restart the engine until we were on the ground. I got to where I was pretty good at always knowing where the wind's coming from and always noticing spots I could put down. So I must have made thirty or forty engine-out landings on bean fields and country roads. Put down on a golf course once, too."

"Isn't that illegal?" Ann Ellis asked.

"Not very," Henry said with a shrug. "We never hurt anything, and the few times anyone was around, they thought a biplane was so neat they didn't care where we'd landed."

"You learned to fly in a biplane?"

"A Stearman my dad used to teach aerobatics to Navy pilots in during World War Two."

"Do you do aerobatics?" Ann Ellis looked at the other two passengers. "Can you show us something?" Mark and Garrett were about to protest, but Henry shook his head and spoke before they could.

"Not in this aircraft—it's not approved for it. I could do a barrel roll, it wouldn't overstress anything. But an inverted maneuver's the kind of thing people can see and catch on camera, and you can lose your license. Not like flying a little too close to an empty beach shack, where no one can measure your exact distance, or putting down in a field, where you can claim you lost power.

"Flying's not like driving, where every state sets its own rules and they're all pretty reasonable. The FAA—that's the Federal Aviation Administration—they run everything, and those Federal guys can be a bunch of bastards. There's a lot more 'Federal' and 'Administration' in the Federal Aviation Administration than there is 'Aviation'. That's why there's almost no new designs coming out of the factories—too expensive to jump through all the government hoops. We're sitting in a two-year-old airplane that's no more advanced than some of the stuff you could buy in the 'thirties. That engine," he said, pointing towards the nose of the plane, "is essentially an oversized version of the 1939 predecessor to the Volkswagen. This old Lycoming is stone age compared to a Chevrolet V-8 you can buy new in the crate from GM for $700."

Henry stopped lecturing and thought for a few moments. "There is one precision maneuver I can show you that doesn't look like anything from the outside—just a climb and a dive. From inside the plane it's pretty interesting. It's how they train the astronauts." He nodded and came to a decision "Hold your camera about even with your chin," he said to Ann Ellis.

"Like this?" she asked.

"Point the lens straight forward. A little higher so Matt and Garrett can see it. Yeah, that's it. When I say 'now', let go of it, and start counting to ten in a loud voice, at about a one-second pace. Okay?" Ann Ellis looked dubious, but nodded. Her Nikon was on a wide strap around her neck. "Watch her camera, guys," Henry said to the pair in the back seat.

Henry gave the Cessna full throttle and lowered the nose until the airspeed needle was almost at the far end of the yellow arc, and scanned the air ahead and above him for any sign of traffic. He leveled the aircraft with the needle touching the end of the yellow and then pulled it up into a fairly steep climb. Ann Ellis felt her body press into the seat with three times its normal weight.

"Ready...NOW!" Henry commanded as he eased the yoke forward. Ann Ellis let go of her camera just as the pressure vanished and she felt herself levitate an inch off the seat cushion. The Nikon floated in front of her face, hovering magically in the air. She was so astonished at this spectacle that she completely forgot to count to ten.

Henry Bowman kept track of the airspeed needle with his peripheral vision as he looked at the floating camera and continued to apply precise pressure on the yoke of the aircraft while easing back on the throttle. When the needle was a half-inch from the end of the yellow arc, he yelled "Grab it!," yanked the power back to idle, and eased back on the yoke to bring the Skyhawk out of the dive.

"Man, what was *that?*" Garrett Edison yelled when the wind noise had subsided. Henry took a deep breath.

"When we were in the climb and Ann let go of her camera, from the reference point of the *ground,* the camera behaved as if it were a projectile launched at an upward angle in a vacuum. The upward angle was the angle of our climb at the instant I pushed the yoke forward, and the camera acted as if it was in a vacuum because the plane is a closed compartment, and the camera doesn't feel wind resistance any more than our faces do. With me so far?"

"Yeah..."

"The camera keeps moving forward at a constant speed relative to the ground, and that constant speed is the same as the forward component of the *plane's* speed at the instant Ann let go of the camera. Got that?"

"Y-yeah....."

"Okay, now because of *gravity,* as soon as Ann lets go of it, the camera instantly starts accelerating towards the ground, at a rate equal to that of the force of gravity— about thirty-two feet per second per second. Right?"

"Yeah, right." Edison was starting to see where this was going.

"What I just did, was fly the plane on the exact ballistic path of the camera. The trick is to arc the plane over at just the right rate so that the camera doesn't move inside the plane. Too big an arc and it would have fallen in her lap. Too tight, and the camera would have bounced off the headliner. When you make an object 'float' like that, you achieve perfect 'zero-G' conditions. For about eight seconds there, we were all absolutely weightless, as I guess you noticed."

"*No shit,*" Ann Ellis said meaningfully. Henry was momentarily embarrassed.

"That's how they train the astronauts for weightlessness," he explained. "They use a stripped Boeing 707 with padding all over the inside, and since it's a lot faster, they get a lot bigger arc. I think they can get around thirty seconds of zero-G conditions in a 707. They also do it over and over again, and the astronauts have nicknamed that particular plane 'The Vomit Comet'." He shrugged.

"It's one of the more difficult precision maneuvers, and it's not too hard on the equipment. Doesn't look like much from the ground, though." He smiled. "My dad could do that same trick while he made the plane do a barrel roll. That really looked weird. The camera—or whatever— would look like it was rotating all by itself while it floated in front of your face." He shook his head. "I'm not nearly that good."

Ann Ellis said nothing.

Obviously underwhelmed Henry thought to himself. *That's okay. She had fun when we blasted down the beach.*

In reality Ann Ellis was silent for a very different reason. The few moments of three-G pressure followed immediately by eight seconds of weightlessness had had a very interesting effect on her insides. She felt as if she were on the verge of orgasm. "Do you always have that kind of control?" she said under her breath. Henry glanced over, thinking the girl had said something. *Guess I imagined it* he decided.

Henry Bowman spent the next hour putting the plane in perfect picture-taking position over various points of geological interest. His passengers related to him some of the things Professor Foose had explained in class but not in the air.

Henry Bowman entered the traffic pattern at fifteen hundred feet over LaFleur Airport in Northampton, Massachusetts. He glanced at his gauges, pulled his mixture control to full lean, and pulled the key out of the ignition. His three passengers watched in horror as the propeller in front of them stopped spinning and came to a halt. There was still wind noise, but the geology students had grown used to the sound of the engine. To them, the airplane now seemed as quiet as death.

"I'm going to land, turn off the runway, and taxi into the spot next to that black-and-yellow clipped-wing Cub with the big tires down there," Henry announced. It was an old stunt that Duane Cole had made his trademark at the end of almost every one of his airshow routines. Henry turned on to base leg earlier than usual as he was descending faster than normal, flared cleanly, and greased the Skyhawk onto the asphalt a third of the way down the runway. As his forward momentum declined, he turned off onto the taxiway at midfield, steered over towards the tiedown spot, and braked to a halt on the centerline.

Matt and Garrett were impressed, and thanked Henry sincerely.

"Glad to do it, particularly since the department pays to rent the plane." He squinted and grinned. "And I think today has convinced me to major in geology, as well as economics."

"Best school for it," Matt asserted. Garrett concurred.

Ann Ellis had also made a decision, one that concerned Henry Bowman's plans for that evening.

It was going to make her roommate very upset, but she decided she didn't care.

***

"Hi, I'm Dick Gaines. Mind if I sit here?"

"Free country, man," one of the six students at the lunch table said.

"Great! Listen, I won't take up your time, but I'm running for class president, and

I'd like your vote," Gaines said as soon as he had put down his tray.

"President?" a young man with short black hair and acne said. "You're not even in our fraternity, are you? I know I've never seen you before."

"*Class* president, Artie. Not *frat* president," one of the others corrected as he turned towards Dick Gaines. "He got in here on an athletic scholarship," the young man explained.

"Hey, fuck you, asshole, I heard him wrong is all."

"Artie's just pissed off he didn't get laid at Stephens last week. He's been jacking off in the shower so much, every time it rains he gets a hard-on." The whole table laughed. Richard joined in nervously.

"Ah, the freshman class hasn't had much of a voice in student government, and I'd like to change that," Richard said when the laughter had died down.

"Taylor here's got a voice. Should have heard him in algebra class yesterday—'*I can answer that!*'—pro'ly the only time he's ever paid attention. Thought the teacher was goin' t' drop his chalk."

"Well, ah, I guess that must have been funny. I never could figure out algebra," Richard admitted.

"You guys ready for some hoops?" one of the boys asked.

"Sounds good," another answered, and all six of them got up to bus their trays and leave the dining room.

"Hey, remember 'Dick Gaines for class president'," Richard said to their departing backs. *Damn—I blew that one* he thought angrily. *They probably won't even bother to vote.*

Richard Gaines was only partially right. It was true that student elections were not taken very seriously, particularly at state universities in Missouri. It was also true that several people at the table would not remember his name an hour later.

In the election that would be held just before Thanksgiving break, five of the six classmates he had met that evening would indeed have other more important things to do, and would not bother to vote. The sixth would happen to be near the school post office where the balloting was being done, and would cast his vote for the one name he vaguely recognized. With about eighteen percent of the class voting, Richard's efforts at meeting every one of his classmates at the university would pay off. He would win the election with a solid four percent of his class supporting him.

His victory would not have been possible if those people had not known his name.

***

"Hey, Heinz! Remember our conversation on the Econ 11 assignment of analyzing a local business?" the tenured professor asked. The Amherst College Economics Department chairman looked up from his book at the man who had just entered the faculty lounge and called his name. "Remember you were saying all the papers on Massachusetts pizza delivery services were putting you to sleep?"

"Yes, what about it?"

"Take a look at this one."

The Chairman took the proffered paper from his associate, readjusted his glasses, and read the title page aloud.

"*The Economics of the Smith & Wesson .44 Magnum Revolver and the Pricing Strategy of its Manufacturer*". He looked over the tops of his glasses. "Another butter advocate?" he asked.

"Just read it," Nicholson said with a smile. "Take you two minutes." Department Chairman Kohler was known by his colleagues in the department for his ability to digest the printed word. He folded back the title page and scanned the paper.

"'...the only double-action revolver chambered for this cartridge'..." Kohler quoted. "Hmmm...says the Springfield plant's too small for current military demand, and all Smith & Wesson commercial guns are now backordered, but 'long before the Vietnam war was a factor, this model was hard to find and in fact has always been a rarity that commands a price in excess of retail.'" He scanned a bit further, then read "'Although the factory has always honored their listed dealer price on all guns, dealers regularly charge (and get) a substantial premium for this model, particularly in the longer barrel lengths.'" Kohler lowered the paper and laughed. "Well, that just means the CFO flunked Econ 11 and the factory is incorrectly pricing their product."

"Keep reading."

"'The factory's setting of the Model 29's price below the intersection point of the supply and demand curves would initially lead one to assume that the company's Chief Financial Officer was not doing his job'" Kohler quoted, "'...and should therefore be fired," he editorialized with a laugh, "'but there is an alternative explanation that bears consideration.' " Kohler looked up at his associate.

"I can't wait to hear this one," he said, and continued to read.

"'It is possible that the decision-makers at the firm believe that rarity adds to this model's appeal and, by extension, the desirability of the entire Smith & Wesson line.

'From my own experience, however, I believe there is an alternative explanation. The Models 29, 27, and 57 are made in a limited-production assembly facility involving large amounts of hand-fitting. These arms exhibit a quality of fit and finish even greater than that of the rest of the company's product line. By actual test, these premier models also shoot more accurately than Smith & Wesson's other offerings. I believe it is impossible to significantly increase production rates of the .44 magnum using existing production methods and facilities. Prices from the factory (currently $165.00) on this low-volume model are kept below free-market equilibrium levels likely because of fears of the substantial loss of goodwill should it be perceived by customers that Smith & Wesson has suddenly started "gouging" them.

"'Accordingly, and in light of the fact that Smith & Wesson is no longer family-owned but is a part of the South American conglomerate Bangor Punta...' Dare I detect a hint of U.S. pride here?" Kohler interjected, "'I see four possible changes in the production and pricing of this arm.'" Kohler lowered his voice and read the four suggestions.

"'One: A slight reduction in standards of overall quality. Two: Construction of new plant and facilities for increased production of all models. Three: Design changes to the weapons themselves (specifically the elimination of minor features) to lower unit production costs. Four: Substantial price increases at the factory level.' Hah! Listen to this:

"'Bangor Punta has already implemented number one, and has started on number two. I believe three will follow. The fourth change, a sudden jump in factory prices, is, in my opinion, unlikely to occur. The first three courses of action are less obvious to the public, and the present demands of war production will not last forever.'" Kohler read on silently, then looked up.

"So the sleazy South Americans have lowered the quality of recent .44 magnums, but according to your author, there are enough older guns around to satisfy the people who shoot..." and here he had to refer to the text, "'over ten thousand rounds per year, or who regularly engage targets over a hundred fifty yards away.' " He continued to scan the paper.

"Now here's some good advice for us if we decide that's what we want to do next semester. Your Mister Bowman says we should '...look for one with a serial number below S300,000.' Well, that's certainly good to know, wouldn't you say?"

"Not exactly 'local pepperoni costs have risen lately, lowering profit margins', is it?"

"Give this guy an 'A'," Kohler said as he handed back the paper.

"I already did."

***

"The first thing I have to tell you," Ann Ellis explained, "is that my...roommate is going to be upset if she finds us here together."

"Uhhh...what about the house mother?" Henry asked.

"She's kind of like the FAA," Ann replied with a laugh. "We don't want to do anything obvious that she can actually see, like running naked down the hallway. We'll keep the door locked."

"Okay," Henry said. At that moment, he didn't trust his voice with anything over two syllables.

"Seriously, if Rachel arrives, she may go a little crazy." Ann looked pointedly at her guest. Henry shrugged.

"Okay," he repeated agreeably.

"Do you understand what I'm saying?" Ann Ellis demanded. Suddenly Henry understood exactly what Ann Ellis was saying, and he started laughing.

"I'm glad to be a substitute, but I really *don't* want to get shot," he said after a moment. *Although it might be worth it* he added mentally.

Ann Ellis flushed scarlet. "Don't think of it like *that*," she said quickly. "And getting *shot?* No, no—she just throws tantrums."

"Is that why there isn't anything breakable in here?" Henry asked with a grin.

Ann Ellis was startled. She looked around the small dorm room in Northrop House and realized there wasn't anything fragile in it. "Don't miss a thing, do you?" she muttered, then turned towards Henry with a wicked smile. "Let's see if you think *this* piece of equipment's obsolete," Ann said as she moved closer to her guest.

Henry Bowman would later reflect that shooting, skiing, and flying had been the three things he had experienced in his life that had actually turned out to be much *better* than he had expected. That evening, he discovered a fourth.

March 14, 1971

"Hey, Boone! Phone's for you! Says it's the hospital!" The bartender held out the telephone receiver. A heavy, sour-looking man looked up from the pool table. He wore blue cotton twill work pants and a stained t-shirt that was stretched taut over his substantial belly. An unfiltered cigarette dangled from the corner of his mouth. He made no move towards the bar.

"Lady says your wife is in labor. Says you need to get down there."

"Tell her I'll be there in a bit. Labor always takes her a good long while." Boone Caswell gave the bartender a look that conveyed the fact that there would be no further discussion of the matter. The bartender spoke quickly into the phone, and then hung up. Caswell went back to his pool game.

***

"Congratulations, Boone. You're a father again!" The doctor smiled at the big man with an enthusiasm he did not feel. He did not like Boone Caswell. He did not know anyone in the town of Rolla, Missouri who did, for that matter. Too many people had noticed the regular appearance of bruises on Myra, Boone's timid wife. There were some which had not quite faded even when she came to the delivery room.

"Boy or girl?" the man demanded.

"You have a beautiful, healthy, seven-pound, two-ounce daughter, Boone, and Myra is doing well. Both your other daughters are in with Myra and the baby. Want to see them?" He started to usher the man into the other room, but Caswell turned on his heel.

"Maybe when they get home," he said with his back to the doctor as he headed out the door.

June 7, 1971

"Anybody here want to go on a couple of raids? Got two in the same building. Could use some extra muscle." Lou Ciamillo looked up at the man who asked the question. *Federal. Narcotics, maybe. Assholes sometimes, but hell, a raid is a raid.* He glanced around the room. *Just sitting on my ass here* he thought to himself. *Wish I had my .357, though.*

"Yeah, I'll go along. I've got my PPK with me, but that's all." The fed waved his hand in a dismissive gesture at Lou's statement.

"Don't worry about that." The federal agent stared at Ciamillo, who looked like someone you would call if you had a very heavy object that you needed lifted or moved, then nodded. "We can use you on the ram." He looked around the room. "Anyone else?" Several of the other off-duty officers hanging around the Montgomery County Police Department also volunteered to join in on the raid.

"What time we going in?" one of them asked.

"We'll be leaving in a few minutes, probably hit the first one nine-thirty or so," the fed replied. Ciamillo nodded. He was about to ask for more details about the raid when he heard another Montgomery County officer call his name.

"Hey, Lou! I been meanin to ask you about this .45 a mine. Take a look at it—I can't hit shit with it."

Ciamillo laughed. Because he liked shooting and practiced a lot, he was a good shot and very knowledgeable about handguns. Other officers often came to him with gun questions or gunsmithing problems.

"Have you considered that the problem may not be the gun, Jimmy?"

"Ah, fuck you, too. No, really, look at this. Is this too much slop in the barrel bushing, or are they all like that?" The policeman pulled the slide partway back to show Lou that the gun was empty, then let it snap forward. He demonstrated how he could wiggle the end of the barrel with the tip of his finger. Ciamillo glanced over his shoulder at the fed, who was now talking to someone else. *I doubt they need this much backup* he thought when he saw the number of officers, then mentally shrugged. *Might get in on some excitement. Sure has been a boring-ass week around here.* He turned back to the problem of the inaccurate .45.

Lou Ciamillo never did get around to asking what the raid was about.

***

The four men nearest the door could hear the sound of a television set inside the apartment. Most of the other twenty-two police agents were too far away to hear it, so Agent William Seals, who was leading the raid, made hand motions to them. He let the men know that the apartment was occupied and that they should remain silent.

"Okay, on 'three'," Seals whispered. "One...two...*three!*" Ciamillo and the other three men put all their strength behind the battering ram, and the apartment doorframe splintered and gave way. Lou Ciamillo was the second officer in the room. His adrenaline level was up, as it always was on a raid, and his senses felt unusually keen. His hand grabbed the butt of his Walther as other officers and agents poured into the room. Lou was drawing the weapon in a practiced motion when his brain registered that the only occupants of the room other than the raiding party were a young girl of ten or twelve who was sitting on a couch, and the much younger child she was holding on her lap.

The girl looked terrified, and the small child, frightened by the noise and sensing the older girl's fear, started to cry. Ciamillo kept his Walther pointed at the floor as he scanned the room. It soon became apparent that the girl, who they would later learn was ten years old, was babysitting that evening, and no one else was in the apartment.

After a quick examination to confirm that the apartment was indeed empty, the lead agent scribbled a note on a piece of paper and thrust it at the child. "Give this to your parents when they get home," he commanded. "Hope we have better luck at the next one," Seals muttered as he led his comrades out of the apartment.

The girl held the paper without looking at it and stared at the strange, disheveled men leaving through the shattered doorway. She had no idea who they were, or what they had come for.

This was understandable, as not a single one of the men who had crowded into the efficiency apartment was wearing a police uniform or had ever mentioned that he was a police officer.

Lou Ciamillo was starting to get a very bad feeling about the whole evening.

***

Twenty-seven-year-old Kenyon Ballew was taking a bath. He would have preferred a shower, as it was a chore for a grown man to wash and rinse himself in a cramped tub. The shower head still wasn't fixed, though, so a bath it was. It wasn't the difficulty Ken minded that night, however, but rather the fact that it took more time. This was relevant because as soon as Ken Ballew finished his bath, he was going to get laid. His wife Sara Louise had made that abundantly clear ten minutes earlier.

Her exact words had been 'If you aren't out of the bathtub, dried off, and in bed with me in fifteen minutes, big boy, I'm going to have to start without you. Remember the Boy Scout's motto— "Be Prepared".' Sara Louise was joking about the fact that her husband, a pressman for the *Washington Post* newspaper, was also a Scout troop leader.

Newspaper articles would later mention this fact, as a point of interest.

Ballew finished rinsing himself, flipped the tub drain to 'open', and was about to stand up when he heard muffled noises outside the apartment.

"Federal officers with a search warrant," Agent Seals announced in a normal speaking voice, making no move to knock on the door. Lou Ciamillo shot him a look, and the fed glared at the local cop as if to say, *You going to make something of it, asshole?* The man did not like being second-guessed about law enforcement procedures by a line officer in a county department.

"Ken! I think there's somebody at our door," a nude Sara Louise Ballew shouted to her husband. "And I don't have any clothes on," she added unnecessarily. She glanced at her wrist, realized her watch was lying on the dresser across the room and scowled. Neither she nor her husband were expecting anyone, and the hour was late.

"Open the door; Federal Agents," the agent leading the raid said, his voice a little louder this time.

"I'll get it," the husband shouted back to his wife. Ken Ballew thought he had heard someone say something that sounded like 'open the door', but the rest hadn't been clear. He stepped out of the tub and wrapped a towel around his waist. He intended to send whoever it was on his way post haste.

"You catch that?" one of the officers asked. The others, including Lou Ciamillo, shook their heads.

"There's two of them, I heard that much," the lead agent stated. "The second one was a man's voice. That's good enough for me." Lou Ciamillo had been about to say that if he and the agents couldn't understand what the people in the apartment were saying, it was logical to assume that the occupants had not understood the Treasury agent's command either, but Seals was already barking more orders.

"Let's bust this door open before they have a chance to get out the back or get rid of the evidence." *We got over twenty guys here* Lou thought. *Why aren't any of 'em around back already?* He shrugged inwardly. *Mine not to reason why...*Ciamillo thought as he prepared to use the ram. *Must be a narco raid.* He couldn't think of any contraband other than narcotics that could be disposed of on a moment's notice inside an apartment.

"One...two...*three!*" The battering ram crashed into the wood, but unlike the door in the previous raid, this one held. Ken Ballew had installed a door that was reinforced with steel. The doorframe cracked, but did not give way. "Again!" Agent Seals commanded.

Ken and Sara Louise, who were in separate rooms of the apartment, both heard the tremendous crash at their door and realized that they were under attack. Ken Ballew ran out of the bathroom, pulled open his desk drawer, and grabbed a percussion revolver made in 1847. Sara Louise had put on her bikini panties and was about to reach for her bra when the first impact hit the entrance to the apartment. She immediately leaped out of bed and started toward the bedroom door. Dressed or not, she was going to help her husband fight off whoever or whatever was invading their home.

Some people, particularly those with little interest in firearms, would later puzzle over the oddity that a man who felt he needed a weapon for home defense would choose a 120-year-old cap-and-ball black powder revolver for the purpose. They would correctly point out that even a 100-year-old revolver would have been a far better choice, as 1870 was the period when cartridge weapons came into common use and replaced guns that used loose powder, round balls, and percussion caps.

Ken Ballew had a loaded cap-and-ball antique instead of a 20th-century Colt or Smith & Wesson for a very simple reason: he did not at that moment own a more modern handgun. Ken Ballew, the *Washington Post* pressman and part-time Boy Scout troop leader, *did* own a modern shotgun for bird hunting. He was primarily a collector of antique arms, however, and he had a fine collection of 1840s-era cap-and-ball revolvers in addition to the one in his hand.

The Ballews lived in a middle-class, integrated apartment building. There had been a burglary or two in the area, but violent crime was not a major concern for most residents of Silver Spring, Maryland. In fact, Ken Ballew had not kept *any* loaded firearm available for protection when he had been single, for he had viewed risks from criminals as minimal. It was only under the contract of marriage that he had recognized his obligation to guarantee another person's safety.

He had thought of buying a Smith & Wesson, but monthly bills and other financial concerns had delayed that event. That was the reason that when the 27-year-old Scout leader ran naked and dripping wet towards his living room, prepared to protect his wife from whoever was breaking into their apartment, he was carrying a gun that had been made approximately fifty years before the first airplane, thirty years before the first telephone, eighteen years before the abolition of slavery, and two years before the birth of his own great-great-great-grandfather.

As soon as the door crashed open and the plainclothes raiding party poured into the Ballews' living room, Lou Ciamillo had his Walther PPK in his hand. His arms were extended and his pistol was pointed at the entrance to the narrow hallway that led to the rest of the apartment.

Ken Ballew came running down the hallway and Ciamillo put the front sight of the PPK on his head, but he held his fire until he saw that the man was armed. This was the reason that when Lou Ciamillo squeezed the trigger of his PPK, several shots had already been fired by other participants in the raid.

Ballew collapsed as shots continued to ring out in the apartment. The nude man's last act was to pull the trigger of his antique revolver, discharging the weapon at a distance of ten inches into a bookcase nearby. Then his brain function shut down and he collapsed behind a partition in the hallway.

Ciamillo watched Ballew fall behind the partition, which was made of concrete blocks. *It was a perfect letoff* he thought. *I know I hit him.* The deputy sheriff's adrenaline was pumping, but he held his fire as the federal agents continued to pour bullets at the man's body.

The painful noise of the shots was still ringing in his ears when Lou realized that some of the sound was coming from a nearly nude woman who had run to the side of her fallen husband. She was screaming, and Ciamillo started to step towards her, but a federal agent rushed past him and pulled her away from her husband's body. The agent immediately began to recite Sara Louise's rights to her, but she was hysterical and obviously did not hear or understand a word of what was said.

Ballew's wife cringed in fear, and Ciamillo suddenly realized something that troubled him greatly. *She doesn't know we're cops. Not a single one of us is in uniform.* The agent who had read Sara Louise her rights pulled handcuffs out of his pocket, then shoved the woman out the door. Ciamillo turned away and stared at the inert form on the floor. One of the feds was giving the body a casual glance as he hurried into the other room.

Lou Ciamillo took measured, even breaths. He felt his heart pounding in his chest, and willed the organ to slow down. He looked around the modest apartment, trying to take it in, as scruffy-looking federal officers and other plainclothes police agents swarmed through the small area. The feds were busy tearing the place apart, searching for evidence. Ballew's wife, wearing only panties and handcuffs, was still screaming hysterically and trying to get back in the apartment to be with the body of her husband.

"Pay dirt!" Ciamillo heard an agent yell from what he would later learn was Ken Ballew's study. "Look what we got here!" He walked proudly towards his supervisor.

The man was carrying several dummy hand grenades of the type that were sold at Army surplus and hardware stores, usually alongside the canteens, flashlights, and ammo cans. Lou knew what real grenades looked like; he and his father had set off dozens of live ones out in the country when he was a boy. He could instantly tell that these grenades were inert; they had no detonators, their bases were drilled, and it was easy to see that they were empty. One of them was glued to a piece of wood and had a numbered tag hanging from its handle. Ciamillo watched as the agent ripped the wood from the grenade and tossed it aside. He stepped over and looked at the piece that the agent had discarded.

The words **COMPLAINT DEPARTMENT—PLEASE TAKE A NUMBER** were embossed on a plaque attached to the piece of stained pine. Ciamillo smiled, then quickly sobered as he watched the federal agents racing around the place, pulling out drawers and turning things over. One was coming down the hallway carrying a side-by-side twenty gauge.

"Write this up, too," the man said, grinning and holding the eighty-dollar bird gun as if it were a million bucks worth of stolen jewels.

"I found these," another man announced. He was holding aloft a thin cardboard box about the size of a book of paper matches, yellow with blue and red printing on it. Ciamillo recognized it instantly as a box of Winchester primers for reloading shotgun shells, available for less than a dollar at any gun or hardware store.

The bad feeling Lou Ciamillo had felt earlier came back with multiplied intensity. *Who are these assholes?* Lou wondered, not for the first time that night. *Why the fuck do they care about reloading supplies and flea market junk? Who's the guy we just killed? And what did they want him for?*

Lou Ciamillo was about to find out the answers to at least some of these questions.

***

"*Tax* agents?" Lou Ciamillo demanded in an outraged whisper. The other Montgomery County police officer put his hand on his friend's arm and tried to reassure him.

"We thought you knew, Lou." Ciamillo slapped the hand away.

"Thought I *knew?* There were more than twenty of us! We killed that guy!" Ciamillo was apoplectic. "Two dozen armed men dressed like a bunch a biker trash an' carryin' a battering ram raid a guy's apartment and kill him, an' now you tryin' to tell me the feds leadin' the raid were just a bunch of pencil-pushing assholes from the ATF? Those guys are s'posed t'be checkin paperwork, for Christ's sake!" His mouth hung slack as he waited for a reply. When none came, he went on, his voice rising in the process. "What did they have on him? Huh? Tell me that— what the fuck did they have on him?"

"Ah...they did say they found a four-inch piece cut off a shotgun barrel," the policeman answered lamely.

"And I'll bet it came off that little side-by-side 20-gauge I saw one a them assholes carrying. Barrels were at least twenty inches long, looked more like twenty-two. I'd bet my badge that gun's legal." Ciamillo stabbed his finger angrily at the other officer before continuing.

"And even if the poor bastard had cut the thing down below eighteen, so what? So he's made an NFA weapon, and under the National Firearms Act of 1934, he owes the IRS two hundred bucks tax on it. You ever owe the IRS two hundred bucks, Hal?"

"Take it easy, Lou."

"*Fuck* taking it easy! You weren't one a the first guys in the door like I was, and you didn't pop a cap at that poor bastard because a them tax assholes. Answer my question—you ever owe the IRS two hundred bucks? I sure as shit have. Think maybe the tax men should bust *your* door down when you and your wife are standin around naked, and put a few slugs in you, 'cause they think maybe you owe 'em two hundred bucks?"

"Of course I've owed the IRS two hundred dollars," his friend said soothingly. "But those were ATF agents, Lou. They're a part of the IRS, but you and I both know they don't do income tax work. They're alcohol, tobacco, and *firearms.*"

"Right!" Lou exploded. "And they're a alcohol, tobacco, and firearms tax agency! They go around and make sure all the fuckin tax seals are pasted on the goddamn whiskey bottles and cigarette packs. You think it'd be fine if Agent fucking Neal rounded up some local cops to go bust in on the guy owns the Camel cigarette company? Bust his door down with a battering ram and kill him comin' outa the shower, on information from a 'reliable informant' that he had cigarettes under his bed and he owed two hundred bucks tax on 'em?"

His friend made no reply, but lowered his eyes.

"Got to be guns? Okay—how 'bout the *'reliable informant'* tells 'em Sturm, Ruger hasn't paid the government its eleven percent excise tax on a batch of .357s. Think the ATF guys should go break into Bill Ruger's house in the middle of the night? He's probably pulled a gun or two out the back door of the plant for his own use, and they'd be ones made after the Civil War. Maybe twenty-six guys wouldn't be enough. Hell, maybe they should fuck breaking down the door, an' just *burn* him out." Ciamillo shook his head in disgust, then exploded in frustration.

"Jesus! I can't believe they even let those stupid tax cocksuckers carry guns at all!" He suddenly thought of something, and his eyes narrowed.

"Who's got the warrant? I wanta see what's listed on the fuckin' search warrant!"

Lou Ciamillo was not yet aware of several things. First of all, Ciamillo did not know that the search warrant for Ballew's apartment was, for the most part, still blank. The time would be filled in as '8:31 p.m.', the last legal minute of daylight on June 7, as the blank warrant had specified that the search had to be conducted during daylight hours.

Items to be searched for would also soon be filled in, but not as 'short-barreled shotguns', for a measuring tape would reveal that the barrels on Ballew's gun were well over the 18" minimum. Instead, 'hand grenades' would be written in the proper place on the warrant, in keeping with the nature of what was seized.

Weeks later, the agency would be forced to admit that dummy grenades were not a registerable item on which tax was due. This admission would occur when a number of citizens around the country would produce proof that after passage of the 1968 Gun Control Act, they had applied to the ATF to register inert grenades identical to Ballew's, and that their applications had been returned to them rejected, with the written statement that such items were not subject to registration and taxation by the Federal Government.

Undaunted, the Alcohol, Tobacco, and Firearms division of the Internal Revenue Service would then, three weeks after the raid, retrieve the box of shotshell primers and some paper caps for a toy cap pistol from the police department storage locker. They would produce these items as evidence that Ballew intended to make *live* grenades without paying the tax on them, thus justifying their raid. The ATF agency would be forced to admit that a dummy grenade successfully jerry-rigged with a shotshell primer and some black powder would explode the instant the handle was released, not five seconds later, but the feds would insist that this minor fact was not relevant to their case in any way.

Second of all, Ciamillo did not know that Kenyon F. Ballew had not been killed in the raid. Ballew was at that moment in a coma and hooked up to life support systems at a local hospital, and would remain attached to them until his condition stabilized.

Third, Ciamillo did not know that only one of the nine bullets the raiders had fired had hit Ballew. When that single bullet had struck Ballew between the eyes, it had penetrated his brain and lodged in his cerebral cortex, instantly causing permanent paralysis and brain damage. Ballew had fallen behind the reinforced partition, and the concrete blocks had stopped the four additional shots the federal agents had fired at his unconscious body. Ken Ballew was not dead (merely paralyzed and brain damaged) after being shot between the eyes at ten feet, and this was because the one bullet that had hit him was from a .380 automatic. The .380 auto is a weak cartridge that was designed in 1908 for use in small pocket pistols for women. No police department in the entire United States issues .380 automatics as duty sidearms for its uniformed officers, but many officers carry a .380 of one make or another when off-duty because of the gun's small size.

The last thing that Lou Ciamillo did not yet know, but would eventually learn, was that of the twenty-six IRS agents and local police officers participating in the disastrous raid on Ken Ballew's apartment, only one of them had been carrying a pistol chambered for the .380 automatic cartridge. Had Ballew been shot in the brain with a more-powerful .38 or .357, he would almost certainly have been killed. Furthermore, no one would have ever been able to determine which man had fired the fatal shot, since all of the other shots fired that night had been one or the other of these two calibers.

As it was, there was only one gun from which the slug now in Ken Ballew's brain could have been fired. This fact would be learned when Ballew's condition was such that the doctors could finally extract the copper and lead projectile and give it to the police for examination.

The bullet that left the *Washington Post* pressman, Scout leader, and antique arms collector permanently paralyzed and brain damaged had been fired from a Walther PPK, and that PPK was currently resting inside the waistband of Lou Ciamillo's pants.

August 6, 1971

"Listen to this shit: 'Secretary of the Treasury John B. Connally said he had reviewed the investigative report and concluded "that the actions of the law-enforcement personnel in executing the search warrant for the Ballew apartment were legally proper under the circumstances'." Bernie Sutter put the newspaper down and snorted in derision. "The fix is in."

Henry Bowman glanced over at the man, but said nothing. Bernie was the proprietor of Sutter Sport Shop, a small, cluttered gun store in middle-class Overland, which was in North St. Louis County.

"Well, of course," said Thomas J. Fleming as he looked up from the 1887 Belgian service revolver he was examining. "Twenty-six armed men dressed in old clothes? That's the logical team to assemble when you know you're up against a shrewd adversary." He went on rapidly.

"Look—Ballew had a reinforced door, right? That's an indication he was committing crimes behind it. He sent his wife into a separate part of the house; that was probably so they could sucker the feds in a pincer maneuver. They had all their clothes off; obviously, this was to distract the officers. And the police know their own limitations—they know that their shooting skills are well below those of private citizens. They had to have twenty-six on their side, to give themselves a chance that someone would hit the man they were trying to kill. And as you can see, their strategy worked to perfection: They fired nine shots at ten feet, and just as they had hoped, one of them hit Ballew. The raid went perfectly. Not a single police agent was injured."

Thomas J. Fleming was two years out of the University of Chicago School of Law. Slender, dark-haired, clean-shaven, of medium height, and wearing glasses, Tom Fleming was the proverbial 'man who could disappear in a crowd of one'. That was true, however, only so long as Tom Fleming did not open his mouth. As soon as he started speaking, anyone listening could not avoid recognizing the tremendous store of energy the man possessed, nor were they likely to miss his biting wit. It would also be obvious that Fleming understood the Constitution better than most lawyers, and that he absolutely despised governmental infringements on his civil rights. 'There's only one real reason to become a lawyer,' he had been known to say to close friends in private. *That's so nobody can fuck with you.* He returned his attention to the 19th-century Belgian revolver.

"I wonder what the Treasury Department *would* consider 'acting improperly'? another regular, Stokely Meier, threw out.

"Using a nuke. *Maybe,*" Bernie said glumly.

Sutter Sport Shop in north county was very different from Goodmans for Guns in downtown St. Louis. Whereas the Goodman brothers' clientele tended to be well-heeled owners of finely made arms, Bernie Sutter catered to middle-class patrons who were looking for military surplus rifles or secondhand Colts and Remingtons, and who spent a large fraction of their shooting dollars on ammunition. Stokely Meier, Henry Bowman, and Max Collins were three of a small number of St. Louisans who regularly visited both stores.

Since Henry had turned sixteen 2 1/2 years before, he had become a regular visitor to the store, which was twelve miles from his house. A lot of high-volume shooters congregated there.

Tom Fleming was one of these, and he had been patronizing Sutter's since the age of eight. His father, Thomas Albert (T.A.) Fleming, had died when the boy was eleven. From then until he acquired his first car shortly before his seventeenth birthday, Tom Fleming had made the eight-mile trip to the gun shop on his bicycle. Fleming especially liked the fact that Bernie Sutter would put guns in layaway. Up until the law change in 1968, Sutter did this even for customers that weren't yet old enough to drive. He'd keep the customer's money clipped to a file card with the gun's description written on it in the store's safe until the full amount was attached. Most of Fleming's steadily-growing collection had been acquired from Bernie in this fashion.

Whereas Henry's favorite sporting arms were, in no particular order: long-range rifles, elephant guns, and .44 magnum revolvers, Fleming gravitated towards military rifles and handguns, especially the .45 Automatic Colt. Both young men liked machine guns, although unlike Henry Bowman, Tom Fleming did not own any full auto weapons on which the NFA branch of the Bureau of Alcohol, Tobacco, and Firearms had bestowed its governmental blessing.

Furthermore, Fleming owned no cannons at all; when he had been in junior high school, long before the 1968 Gun Control Act reclassified military arms over .50 caliber as 'destructive devices', Fleming had studied the ads offering Lahtis for under $100. At that time, he had never figured out how to get the 8 1/2-foot, 110-pound weapon home from the freight depot on his bicycle. By the time he got a car, college was looming, and owning a Lahti was long forgotten.

"This guy Ballew must have been doing some other stuff that isn't in the paper," threw out a local skeet shooter who bought his shotgun shells at Bernie's. "I can't believe our own government would do something like this, even by accident. Come on—twenty-six agents? They'd never put that many cops on some guy's apartment if he really was just a collector of old cap-'n'-ball guns We're not getting the whole story."

"Are you nuts?" Tom Fleming exclaimed. The Belgian revolver was forgotten as he turned to face the man. "Haven't you read *any* history, like maybe what happened in Germany in the 'thirties?" Fleming was currently involved with a woman he had first met in college. She was slender, vivacious, and possessed of a remarkable sex drive. She was Jewish, and one entire branch of her family had been executed in Buchenwald.

"This is the United States," the skeet shooter said with slight irritation.

"Which *of course* makes us immune to any violations of our civil rights," Tom Fleming immediately replied with a voice that dripped sarcasm. "Listen," he continued, his tone changing to one of exposition, "for the last hundred years, cops have known it was okay to beat on people, and sometimes kill them, as long as they only beat on and killed colored guys.

"Then, starting a few years ago, cops learned they could beat on and kill not only colored guys, but also white guys, as long as the white guys had long hair, ratty clothes, no jobs, and were out in public bitching about Vietnam.

"Now, in addition to colored guys, and white guys that have long hair, ratty clothes, and no jobs who are out protesting in public, the cops have learned it's OK to beat and kill white guys with *short* hair, *nice* clothes, and *good* jobs, *inside their own homes*, if the white guy owns guns." Fleming took a breath and raised his index finger. He realized he was lecturing again, but it was a habit he had a very hard time resisting. The others in the shop were giving him their full attention.

"'When they came for the trade unionists, I did not stand up, for I was not a trade unionist. When they came for the gypsies, I did not stand up, for I was not a gypsy. When they came for the Jews...' well, you know the rest," he said, not wanting to take up more time with the lengthy quote. "Finally, they came for the Lutheran minister, but there was no one left to stand up for him, and he ended up in a concentration camp because he didn't think his rights were in danger."

"Look, a bunch of stumblefuck cops hit the wrong apartment on a bad tip," the skeet shooter said in reply to Fleming's quote. "That's a lot different than the military carrying out the direct orders of the chief executive, which is what happened in Germany."

"Maybe so, but we've done that here in America, too."

All heads turned towards the young man who was standing by the display case holding a newspaper and a thick hardcover book. Henry Bowman met their gaze, and then the skeet shooter spoke up.

"That National Guard mess at the college was the same thing—a bunch of trigger-happy cops, not the army."

"Interesting you should say that, Sid," Tom Fleming said. "As a matter of fact, the National Guard is part of the standing army; they take their orders from the President, and they can in fact be sent into combat outside the country, which is why National Guard service qualifies as military service." Fleming smiled at Henry Bowman, but Henry shook his head.

"I didn't mean Kent State," Henry clarified. "I was talking about General Douglas MacArthur, George Patton, and Dwight Eisenhower. Patton and Eisenhower were majors at the time. MacArthur sent the tanks in to drive American war veterans out of Washington. Then he led his troops to where twenty thousand unarmed veterans were camped, and he burned them out. He set fire to their camp while they were still in it, and his soldiers shot veterans that resisted."

"The Bonus Army..." Fleming said softly. Sid the skeet shooter was looking quizzically at both Tom Fleming and the young man that had told the bizarre story about General MacArthur. Henry saw his expression and spent the next ten minutes explaining about the Bonus Marchers and what had happened to them. Everyone in the room was shocked, but not surprised.

"This Ballew thing makes me think maybe we should all listen to Mr. Forsyth here," Henry said finally. He was holding up his copy of *The Day of the Jackal*, which had recently become a national bestseller. "Been reading this the last few days, and there's a detailed description of how to procure the birth certificate of someone who died as a child, and create a new identity."

"Yeah, I heard about that," Tom Fleming said. "You're right, maybe we should all be out scouring small-town graveyards."

"Yeah." For a few moments, no one spoke.

"So how do you know so much about it?" Sid asked finally. "The Bonus Army, I mean?"

"My great-uncle was one of them. MacArthur's soldiers broke his arm, and he was badly burned in the fire. Infection set in, and a doctor at a Veterans' hospital in Pennsylvania cut off his whole arm, but it was too late, and he died a couple of days later." The skeet shooter nodded, then looked around awkwardly. No one much felt like talking any more. It was Fleming who broke the silence.

"Tom Fleming," he said, smiling and extending his hand. "I've seen you in here before, but I don't think we've met. Are you that guy Bernie's been telling me about who shoots claybirds with an elephant gun?"

"Only when I get lucky," Henry replied with an embarrassed smile.

"I got to talk to you about this," Fleming said quickly as he stepped over to the counter where Henry was standing. "I've run a bunch of training courses for cops, and I'm having real trouble getting them to hit *anything* that's moving, even if it's three feet away and the size of a refrigerator." He began to use his hands to diagram the problem. "Now, when you shoot stuff out of the air like that—say it's moving sideways, not away from you—is it better to..."

By the time their conversation ended forty minutes later, Tom Fleming and Henry Bowman were good friends. They were also the only two there that day who would remember the short discussion about new identities.

August 14, 1971

Jesus, I hate this sometimes Henry Bowman thought as his feet pounded the gravel. He had never been more than an average runner, and getting tossed off an overturning hay truck the previous summer and breaking his left leg in two places hadn't helped. *I told that moron I should drive and he should be up top* Henry thought, remembering the event. With the aid of some surgical steel, Henry's leg had healed without complications, although it still felt a little different than his right one. He had even been able to play rugby this past spring. Every time he did, though, Henry wished he had more speed. It was always frustrating to be unable to catch a rival player that had the ball.

Henry doubted that running out to the highway every night during summer break was going to make him much faster, but he hoped his endurance would increase. That would help, and not just on the rugby field. *Ought to be able to carry more ammo up the mountains out in Idaho* he told himself as the burning in his lungs increased. *Lug the Lahti around better, too.* He was approaching the turn-off that led towards a recently-constructed subdivision. Henry always took the turn and sprinted the final five hundred yards to complete his workout, then walked back home to cool down.

When Henry left the main road, the telephone pole that marked the end of his three-mile run came into view over a quarter mile off of the highway. Henry commanded his legs to pick up the pace. It was after eleven, and traffic in the area was nonexistent at that hour. Going out at night was the only way Henry could make himself run regularly during the summer months. Late as it was, the temperature was well over eighty degrees.

Henry Bowman's final effort was at a six-minute-mile pace. This was all he could muster, even knowing the end was less than a minute away. The increased wind on his face and chest felt good, but did little to actually cool him off in the August heat. *Almost there, slowpoke* he told himself as sweat filled his eyes and blurred the image of the phone pole less than a hundred yards distant. He felt a faint exhilaration in addition to his exhaustion, and was reminded of the punch line to the old joke: *It feels so good when I stop.*

Henry Bowman wiped the sweat out of his eyes and pumped his arms in the final push, commanding his legs to maintain the sprint that was threatening to make him collapse. *You fuckin' weenie* he cursed himself silently. *Half the guys on the team wouldn't even be breathing hard yet.* He pounded out the last few steps, slapped the pole, and forced himself to walk rather than flop down in the gravel. His eyes were squeezed shut and blood was pounding in his ears, and this was why Henry Bowman did not realize that he was not alone.

"Hunh..?" Henry grunted in alarm as the four men hit him almost simultaneously and drove him into the trees beside the road. For the barest instant Henry thought he was hallucinating that he was actually in a rugby game. He opened his mouth to yell, but before any sound could come out he was slammed face-first into the trunk of a maple tree. The pain was so great Henry was certain that his nose had just been broken, though in fact it had not. He collapsed facedown in the grass and twigs as one of the men drove a knee between Henry's shoulder blades, forcing air from Henry's lungs and pinning him to the earth. Henry felt that he was suffocating, and he fought off an overpowering urge to vomit. Had he known what was going to happen next, however, he would have encouraged that reflex.

Henry felt his gym shorts ripped away and all of a sudden he realized in absolute horror what was about to happen to him. An image of the ravaged young blonde-haired girl from three years before appeared, unbidden, in his mind. He flailed out with his one free arm, but the man on top of him grabbed his wrist easily and twisted his arm until an audible 'pop' signaled that he had dislocated Henry's right shoulder. The man chuckled when it happened.

Much later, Henry would decide that it was really the man's laughter that made it so awful, but at that instant, the pain was worse than anything Henry Bowman had ever felt in his life. It was several orders of magnitude greater than what he had experienced when they had slid him onto the sheet of plywood out in the alfalfa field the year before, with his leg at a funny angle and an evil-looking bulge at the side of his calf muscle.

The combination of pain, physical exhaustion, and lack of oxygen to his brain started to induce unconsciousness in Henry Bowman. *So this is what dying feels like* was Henry's last thought as a blackness began to swallow him whole.

"Fuck! I think we killed him!" came the coarse whisper as the man on Henry's back jumped off, twisted Henry's head towards him, and peered into his face. "No—still breathing," he said with relief.

"This wouldn't kill nobody," one of the others answered. "Just leave 'im a little sore." That got a laugh from all four of them. "Le's see'f we c'n wake him up." With that, the man who had made the joke produced an empty beer bottle he had brought along. He held the bottle in position with his left hand and slammed the heel of his right hand into its base.

The shock to Henry's system (coupled with the fact that his lungs had been working without restriction for fifteen or twenty seconds) brought him abruptly back to consciousness. He started to lift his head and scream involuntarily when his face was slammed into the dirt again, cutting off the sound before it could escape with any volume. The man who had been kneeling on Henry's back laid a hand gently, almost caressingly, on Henry's neck. Then he held the point of a kitchen knife at the back of Henry's jawbone, just below his right ear.

"Be still, now," the knife man whispered, softly, as if to a lover. "Keep them eyes shut tight, an' mebbe I won't hafta cut 'em."

"Don't bust the neck a that bottle off inside," one of the others advised. "That wouldn't be no fun."

"Th' ol' monster ain't *that* tough, you got that right," came the happy reply. He gave the bottle a few more whacks and then tossed it aside, noting with satisfaction that the top half of it was bloody. "Who's first?"

What seemed to Henry Bowman like an eternity was in fact well under an hour. When he realized that he was not going to lose consciousness again, Henry wished that he would die. After the first man finished and the second started in, Henry knew *that* wish was not going to come to pass, and the thought of living as a blind man filled him with a despair such as he had never imagined.

Soon after that, however, a very strange thing happened. The pain and terror and utter physical helplessness inflicted upon Henry Bowman did not diminish, but his capacity to endure those things increased a tiny bit. It increased just enough that a small part of Henry's mind was able to think of something other than how his insides and his shoulder were screaming as if they were being torn apart. He was able to think of something other than what was being done to him, and something other than how the men might well blind him when they were through.

A small part of Henry Bowman's brain was able to focus on a way to fight back and hurt at least one of these men; hurt him and maybe kill him. A spark glowed, and soon that spark ignited, like pyrite struck against steel in the presence of dry wood shavings. The small flame became a larger flame, and the larger flame turned into a roaring blaze whose heat and light did not eliminate Henry's pain, but dulled it and made it seem as if it were something that he was watching happen to someone else.

Henry Bowman realized that there was one potentially dangerous part of his body over which he still had complete control, and he intended to use it to the fullest extent possible. *One of them has to want me to suck him* Henry thought. *One of them has to.* He willed it with every shred of faith he possessed, and as he did so, Henry worked at controlling the jaw muscles that he had been spasmodically clenching in agony.

By thinking of nothing else, Henry found he could open and close his mouth at will. He found he could snap his jaw shut instantly, grind his teeth one side at a time, or slide his jaw sideways with his teeth clenched. For the next twenty-seven minutes, Henry Bowman practiced each of these exercises dozens of times. For twenty-seven minutes, Henry Bowman imagined that he was ignoring his gag reflex, as he did when the doctor stuck a dry tongue depressor down his throat every time he got strep. *Only this one won't be dry* he told himself over and over. *It'll have my blood on it. Come on, you bastards. One of you has to finish that way. It'll only take me a second to do it. I could clip six inches off an axe handle right now. Just one of you, that's all. Please. Just one.*

Henry Bowman was still praying for his chance when the high beams of a 1964 Pontiac Catalina seemed to turn night into day. Nineteen-year-old Jimmy Weir had just dropped his sixteen-year-old girlfriend Shelly off at her house in time to squeak her under the midnight curfew her father had imposed. Now he was racing back home before his own father blew a gasket. Jimmy Weir's high beams were on because he had bumped the foot switch while he and Shelly were necking. When the hour had become late and he had started the car to take her home, Jimmy Weir's mind had been filled with powerful thoughts, but none of them involved roadway etiquette.

The big Pontiac had a limited-slip differential, and when Jimmy Weir stabbed the throttle, both rear tires broke loose, slewing the tail of the car to the right. David Webb would have stayed on the throttle, given the wheel a touch of opposite lock, let the tires find traction, and powered out of the skid. David Webb, however, was not driving.

Jimmy Weir stood on the brakes.

The big V-8 stalled, and the Catalina came to rest in the center of the road, pointed about thirty degrees left of the direction it had been traveling. Its headlights illuminated an area near where the gang rape was taking place.

"Fuck! Cops!" one of the four men exclaimed, logically assuming that any car that slewed to a stop near the scene of a crime with its high beams on had to be trouble. Trees prevented a clear view of them and their actions, but the area was no longer pitch dark. All four of them ran.

Jimmy Weir was too startled to notice anything that was happening fifteen yards off the roadway. He looked frantically around the car, assuring himself that he had not damaged it in some way before turning the key, restarting the engine, and proceeding home at a much more sedate pace.

Henry Bowman tried to stand and call for help, but before he could get to his feet he heard the car drive away. He hoped that his attackers were gone for good, but he knew that there was no assurance of that. Distance was his only real ally now. *Something's wrong with my ankle* he realized. *Can't use my right arm, either.*

Using his knees and his left arm, Henry Bowman started to crawl towards home.

August 15, 1971

It took Henry Bowman almost six hours to get back to the house. He pulled himself up to the door of the wood frame building and let himself in. *Thank God Mom's out of town* he thought for perhaps the tenth time in five hours. He saw that he had dripped some blood on the wooden floor of the narrow hallway. *Got to clean that up* he told himself.

There was one downstairs bath, and it was at the end of the hall. Henry pulled himself towards it, crawled through the doorway, and turned on the bathtub taps with his left hand. For five hours he had had an overwhelming desire to wash the blood and filth from his body, and he had the irrational fear that he would never be clean again.

Henry took a steel nail file from the vanity and managed to cut off his t-shirt with his left hand. The torn gym shorts that he had tied crudely to his jockstrap came off next. Henry climbed in the tub without making any attempt to remove his shoes or socks, and let the water level slowly rise to cover his battered body. Lying in the cool water was the first thing that had felt even a little bit pleasant in what seemed like an eternity.

While he soaked, Henry focused on how the water felt and tried to ignore the fact that it was starting to exhibit a slight pink tint. He also tried not to think about his shoulder.

***

Breakfast of champions Henry Bowman thought with an inward chuckle as he noticed that the sun was starting to appear on the horizon. He was naked except for his shoes and socks, and was sitting on two towels so he wouldn't get blood on the kitchen chair.

The liquor cabinet hadn't been opened in at least a year, but Henry had found it well-stocked, mostly with unopened bottles. Henry Bowman had had ample opportunity to drink beer in college, but his first bottle had also been his last. He hated the taste. Henry had also once tried a scotch on the rocks, which was his uncle Max Collins' drink of choice. One sip of *that* had been enough to convince him that there were some personal preferences that were utterly beyond his comprehension. Looking through the dusty cabinet, he had recalled that gin and Seven-Up was a drink he had heard several people order at a party his mother had given for some of her friends. Henry liked the soft drink, and had decided the mixing it with gin was worth a try.

On the table in front of him was a quart bottle of gin that was now half full, two empty Seven-Up bottles, and a plastic bucket with a few slivers of ice floating in some very cold water.   Henry could see his reflection in the black glass of the double-stack oven across the kitchen. His dislocated shoulder was very prominent, and the bottles and ice bucket in front of him made the image surreal. *The bartender from Hell* Henry thought as he touched his glass to his lips and tipped it up.

The cold liquid coursed down his throat. *Straight from Aphrodite's breast. Tastes even better than that first one did.* He drained the glass, then poured a slug of straight gin into it and took a swallow. *Burns. Need more Seven-Up.* He looked over towards the refrigerator. His ankle felt good enough to walk on, a few yards, at least. He stood up, and dizziness swept over him. *Better do the other thing first, while I can still function* he decided.

With unsteady steps Henry made it over to the wrought iron pot rack which hung by a short length of 1/4" chain from a steel plate in the ceiling. His father had installed it in 1964, and Henry knew that the plate was held in place by two 3/8" lag bolts which went through the plaster and screwed five inches into one of the 2x10 joists that held up the second floor.

Henry smiled as he climbed on the chair. *Thanks for building a pot rack you could hook a block and tackle to and use to pull an engine swap, Dad.* He reached for the free end of the plastic-coated electrical extension cord he had earlier looped through the chain. The chair creaked under his weight of 190 pounds. *If anyone else had done it, damn thing might rip out of the ceiling and fall on my head.*

Henry tied the knot in the extension cord as best he could with his left hand. *Hope it holds.* He pulled on the cord and it bit into his skin. *Probably tear it some. No matter.* Henry made a last test to see that the cord was taut, and took a deep breath. He had thought it through for several hours now, and there just wasn't any choice. *If you got a frog to swaller, best not to look at it too long* he thought. Henry Bowman clenched his teeth and fists, and abruptly threw himself off the chair with a twisting motion.

There was a loud crack, and then blackness.

***

When Henry Bowman regained consciousness, his whole right side was screaming in protest, but it was his right hand that screamed loudest. When he opened his eyes, the room was blurred and sideways, and his stomach was doing some very unpleasant things. Henry was hanging by his right wrist, connected to the chain in the ceiling by the electrical cord. His knees were almost touching the linoleum floor. With considerable effort, Henry got his left leg under him and managed to stand up. This took all the tension taken off the cord. Henry's right wrist and shoulder still hurt, but not quite as much. He examined his right hand. It was almost the color of eggplant.

Jesus, how long was I out? Henry wondered. He rotated his shoulder, noting with satisfaction that although it hurt like hell, it seemed to work all right. Then he set to untying the extension cord from his right wrist. It took longer than he expected, for when he had tied the cord, he had had the presence of mind to wrap it tightly several times above the bone so that his makeshift technique would not dislocate his right wrist in the process of fixing his shoulder.

When he was finished unwrapping the cord, Henry was rewarded with the sensation that a thousand tiny needles were being jabbed into his swollen right hand. He flexed his fingers repeatedly, watching them closely. *Wouldn't do to lose the use of my trigger finger* he thought with a smile. It was the amusement that comes from being either exhausted or drunk, and Henry Bowman was both.

He walked unsteadily back towards his seat at the kitchen table, then remembered he needed Seven-Up to mix with his gin. He retrieved two more bottles from the refrigerator, popped the caps off on a drawer handle, and set them on the table next to the liquor. He filled his glass with ice from the freezer, and set about the serious business of finishing the rest of the alcohol.

***

The bottle was not quite empty, but Henry Bowman's bladder demanded emptying, and so he staggered to the bathroom. He leaned against the wall and began to relieve himself in the toilet. It was then that he saw the blood in his urine. *One end stops and the other starts* he thought as he squeezed his eyes shut.

Henry flushed the toilet and then lay down on the bathroom's tile floor, still naked except for shoes and socks. He curled himself into a ball, and soon his body was wracked with violent, uncontrollable sobs. *Didn't do anything!* he said to himself over and over. He was filled with an immense shame.

To be sure, Henry felt shame for the terrible thing that he had been forced to endure, but there was something else that made it much worse. It was something that Henry Bowman had been trying without success to forget ever since the moment that the car had arrived and the four men had fled.

Henry Bowman knew beyond any doubt whatsoever that the men who had attacked him would do the exact same thing again to someone else. Of this fact he was absolutely certain, just as he knew that winter would arrive in four or five months, and that it would be hot again this time next year.

Those men would do it again, and again after that, and when they did, their next victims might not be able to crawl home. Their next victims might not be left with their eyesight, Henry knew, and he had to fight to keep from vomiting.

And I didn't do anything. Didn't hurt them. Didn't mark a one of them. Didn't even keep my eyes open so I could see what they looked like.

Henry Bowman knew in his heart that he was not the final victim of the four men he had encountered that night, and he was absolutely right about that; more victims followed. There were several other things, however, that Henry did not know, at least not yet.

Henry Bowman did not know, but would eventually come to learn, that men comprised a full ten percent of all rape victims in the United States, and almost a third of the victims of gang rapes.

Henry Bowman did not know that one day he would actually consider himself lucky that what had happened to him that night had occurred in 1971 and not two decades later. By that time, the AIDS virus would guarantee that any homosexual gang rape that caused rectal bleeding was a virtual death sentence for the victim.

Last of all, Henry Bowman did not know that the reason that he had never seen his late father take a drink was not, as he had always assumed, that Walter Bowman had not liked alcoholic beverages. That was not true at all.

The reason that Walter Bowman had shunned liquor all of his life was that the people on his side of the family, particularly the men, had a genetic predisposition towards alcoholism.

November 10, 1971

"Henry, your grades have fallen off a cliff compared to what we've come to expect from you. I'm looking at a C-minus average for this semester." James Nelson knew something was wrong. Lots of students had similar grades, particularly those who spent their class hours at war protests. Few, however, had had B-plus averages the entire previous year. Henry Bowman looked at his faculty advisor. There wasn't much he wanted to say.

"I've had some...personal problems this year," Henry said quietly. *Like I have nightmares every night, I can't get it up, my girlfriend kissed me off, and I'm sick to death of classes* he added silently.

"Is it this double major you're working on?" Nelson asked. "You know, that kind of commitment...it would be much better if you eased off on one or the other, and did a real job on the one that's the most important to you."

Henry smiled sadly and shook his head. "That's not it. It's...other things. Look, I'm in a slump right now, Professor Nelson. That happens to people, doesn't it?" he asked reasonably. "It's not terminal," he added with a grin.

"I suppose you're right," James Nelson said, but he was not at all convinced.

"I'll see you on Thursday," Henry said brightly as he turned to leave the man's office. *Got to get some ice from the dining hall* he thought. *Maybe one of the guys that works there can scare up a lime for me, too. Then I'll hit a couple more cemeteries.*

December 20, 1971

Henry Bowman had never flown with a hangover before, and he didn't like it. It was the first time he could ever remember flying a plane and not enjoying himself. The fact that he had the major part of a ten-hour cross-country ahead of him did not make things any better. *Why didn't I ease off last night?* he asked himself for the fourth or fifth time since takeoff.

Winter flying was normally smooth, but there was a fair amount of turbulence in the air, and that irritated Henry also. *Since when do bumpy conditions bother an acro pilot, huh, dipshit?* He glanced at the altimeter and saw that his altitude was almost 100 above his intended level of 8500 feet, and he shook his head in disgust. *Thank God my father isn't alive to see me right now* he thought as he eased the stick forward a millimeter and put the Piper into a slight descent.

***

Feeling much better Henry thought with a smile as the city of Pittsburgh slowly disappeared behind him. He pulled the six new birth certificates out of his pocket and looked at them once more. Henry had no idea what he was going to do with the documents, but it had been an adventure getting them, along with social security numbers and other attendant proofs of legitimacy.

Henry had spent much of the last two months on his 'spy project', as he thought of it. Occasionally during that time he worried that because of what had happened to him the previous summer, he had developed an unhealthy fixation on trying to take absolute control of his future. He knew, intellectually at least, that no person could insulate himself entirely from random events.

The fact was, though, that in the fall of 1971, Henry Bowman had lost interest in almost all things in his life except drinking gin and pursuing the secret project he had undertaken. And the alternative-ID scheme was *fun*. It occupied Henry's mind and stimulated his creativity at a time when everything else seemed excruciatingly boring.

After the unexpected success of acquiring the first birth certificate, Henry had decided to get others, of slightly different ages, from other areas. The game metamorphosed into one where Henry Bowman imagined himself with a lissome female companion, and that led to getting birth certificates for three dead girls in addition to the ones of the deceased boys.

The three boys had been born in 1949, 1952, and 1956, and had all died between 1950 and 1958. Two of the three girls had been born in 1955, and died that same year. The third had died at the age of two days in 1961. The birth certificates had been sent to six different addresses in Massachusetts, Connecticut, and Virginia, which was not inconvenient for a young man who had an airplane that carried a 10-speed bike with quick-detachable hubs.

Henry glanced at his fuel gauges. *About half since the last fuel stop.* He looked over his shoulder to make sure nothing was lying in the back of the plane. Henry Bowman's classmates had been very amused by the fact that Henry had sent his clothes home ahead of him via UPS so he could fly home for Christmas break in an empty plane.

Good reason for that Henry thought as he made a few clearing turns, then lowered the nose and watched as the airspeed built to 150 miles per hour. Henry abruptly gave the engine full throttle and pulled the stick back in his lap, releasing backpressure when the plane was exactly vertical. Henry took quick glances at the horizon and the airspeed indicator while keeping the plane on the exact path with tiny movements of the stick and rudder. When his airspeed was almost zero, he gave the airplane full left rudder, executing a hammerhead turn. The clipwing Cub pivoted on the axis described by Henry's spine, and pointed straight at the ground. Henry then chopped the throttle to idle, pulled the stick back in his lap again, and gave the Cub full right rudder. This stalled the right wing, putting the plane into a vertical snap roll. After one full revolution, Henry reversed the rudder pedals and shoved the stick forward, breaking the plane out of the snap roll after 1 1/2 turns. He let the speed build for two more seconds, then pulled the stick smoothly back into his lap and pulled out of the vertical dive on his original heading.

Not bad Henry told himself with a smile. He avoided thinking about how the same maneuver would have made him feel four hours earlier.

Henry also avoided thinking about the dismal performance he had turned in on three of his final exams for the semester.

December 29, 1971

"Hello."

"Dick...that you? Joe Hammond. How are your holidays going?"

"Uh, yeah, real good, Mr. Hammond. Let me go get Mom."

"No, hold up—she's probably busy, and I've only got a minute. It's you I called to talk to."

"Oh...?" Dick Gaines said warily into the phone.

"Yeah," Hammond said expansively. He had several drinks in him. "Thought I'd see if you were interested in an internship for the first half of this coming summer. Congressman Sloan said he could use another good man the last couple of months before the end of the session, when things get kind of wild."

"Congressman Sloan in—in *Washington?*" Dick Gaines asked in amazement.

"That's the one. Actually what he needs is a couple more bodies on the payroll to help cover his tracks on the dough he's been stealing, but you don't need to know about that," Hammond added.

"YES!" Gaines exclaimed. "Yes yes yes!" Then his face fell. "I don't know if Mom and Dad will let me, though."

"I already squared it with them for you. Merry Christmas, Dick, a few days late." Dick Gaines was speechless.

"That's wonderful, Mr. Hammond," he said finally. "Thank you."

"No trouble at all. Give your mother my love. 'Bye."

"'Bye," Gaines said softly as he heard the line disconnect. *Congressman Sloan!* The thought thrilled him. Then he frowned. *Now I got to make sure I pass algebra next semester, so I don't have to take any summer school classes again.*

***

"Henry, you're an alcoholic."

"What the hell are you talking about?" The accusation had taken him entirely by surprise, and it made him very angry.

"I can smell it on you right now," Carol Weston said without backing down. "You've had a lot to drink today already, and it's barely six o'clock." Carol Weston was Henry Bowman's closest female friend from high school. They had been in dramatics class together, and Henry had thought her high school boyfriend was a jerk. Now Carol had a new college beau she had met at her school in Florida. From what she had told him about the fellow, Henry thought he sounded okay.

Henry turned sideways in the seat of his mother's Buick station wagon and took another bite out of his hamburger. He was trying to appear relaxed instead of upset. "For God's sake Carol, I didn't even drink *beer* in high school. Now I come back home from my sophomore year in college during Christmas break, there's parties just about every night, I have a few drinks like everybody else, and now, sitting here in the parking lot at Steak n Shake, you say I'm an *alcoholic?* Where the hell does *that* come from?"

"You've changed, Henry. I might not have noticed, or I might have thought it was because all of us are off in college now and we're all a little different from the way we were in high school. Except my mother became an alcoholic after Daddy left, and when I see you now, I see a difference, and it's exactly the same thing I saw with her."

"I can't believe I'm hearing this!" Henry said in amazement. "Have I been mean to you, or anyone else? Have you seen me yelling, or staggering around, or have my hands been shaking, or..." Henry tried to think of other things that alcoholics did. "...or anything like that?" he said finally.

"You were almost half an hour late to Kelly's house Monday night."

"*Late?* How can you be half an hour *late* to a *party?* That's ridiculous!"

"Henry, every party you ever went to when we were in school together, you showed up exactly at the time on the invitation. All of us girls used to laugh about it. One time I was helping with Irene Cohen's party and you showed up at her house at six minutes after seven. I told her that her clock was probably six minutes fast, and when she called time and temperature, it was."

"So since I used to show up at parties exactly on time, and now I arrive twenty minutes late, that means I'm an alcoholic." Henry was smiling, and Carol Weston wanted to join him, but she held her ground.

"When did you start drinking today?" she demanded.

"I *haven't* been drinking today," he lied. "If you smell liquor on me, it's what I had at my aunt's house last night, sweating out of me." Carol Weston nodded in acceptance.

"I'm sorry. I shouldn't have said anything. Is there any in the car right now? I could use a little something, even if you're not going to have one."

"No, I'm afraid there isn't," Henry lied again. *What made her guess I'd have a bottle under the back seat?* he wondered.

"Okay. No big deal." She picked up some more french fries and put them in her mouth. "You been flying your plane much?" she asked, changing the subject.

"Every week," he answered. *Actually more like every other week, lately.* "Flew it home," Henry added with a shrug. "That's ten hours, almost."

Carol Weston began to get an idea. "You still do those stunts?" she asked. Henry had taken Carol flying the previous summer, and had shown her a loop, a snap roll, and finally a five-turn spin. She had been both terrified and exhilarated, particularly by the last maneuver.

"Sure."

"Take me right now," she said suddenly. "Take me up in your plane and do that thing where everything whirls around and I thought I was going to die."

"It's called a 'spin'," Henry corrected. He shook his head. "Carol, it's dark out. I don't do aerobatics at night. It's not safe—you can get disoriented too easily. That's a good way to get killed."

Carol Weston snorted. "You told me when we did it that day last summer that all you had to do was push the rudder the other way and let go of everything, and the plane would start flying okay by itself. Isn't that what you said?"

"Well, yes, but..."

"Then let's go. You said you'd take me anywhere I wanted to go tonight so long as we didn't have to get dressed up. I want to go do a spin in your airplane." Henry Bowman shook his head.

"No."

"If you take me up in your airplane right now and do a spin, I'll got to bed with you," Carol said suddenly. She had not decided what she would do if he said 'yes.'

"*What?*" Henry Bowman exclaimed as he almost choked on his hamburger.

"You always had a crush on me in high school," she said quickly. "I knew it all the time, and you even admitted it to me last summer. Take me flying and then we'll go to bed together."

"Carol," Henry said, completely overwhelmed by the way the evening was going, "you've got that new guy from Rollins–Bill, isn't it?–that you're crazy about. You can't just–"

"Henry Bowman! You are the biggest liar in the whole world!" Carol Weston almost shouted. "When in your life have you *ever* cared about what some other guy felt when it came to going after a girl? Particularly a guy you've never even met!"

Henry's mouth opened but nothing came out. Carol was right, and he was dumb-struck.

"You've been drinking today, and that's why you won't take me flying now, isn't it? You can drive a car when you're about to pass out; you can go slow and maybe you'll scrape the curb but everything will be okay. I should know, Mom used to do it all the time. But if you take me flying and something goes wrong, we'll both die, and you know it."

Henry nodded. "I did drink today." Carol said nothing. "Most of the afternoon, off and on," he added. She remained silent. "I won't fly with liquor still in my system." He shook his head. "Let the nose stay down a little too long coming out of some maneuvers, you can overspeed the airframe in a hurry. Make the tail come off." He looked up at his friend and smiled. Carol saw that his eyes were wet. "I may show up late for parties now, and worry about what out-of-town boyfriends might think, but I won't fly a plane with alcohol in my bloodstream." Carol Weston took his hand and squeezed it.

"What happened to you, Henry?" she said softly.

Henry Bowman took a deep breath. He wanted to tell her, but his shame was so thick it was palpable, and he found he could not talk about the rape. He ended up giving Carol an edited version of what had happened that night in August. The attack by the four men was revised into one of terrible violence, but without the sexual component. The gang's motive was unknown, although since it was night, mistaken identity was possible.

Henry explained that he had received a severe beating, which was true enough, and that the men had run when a car had come by and shone its bright lights on them, which was true as well. Henry told Carol Weston that he had nightmares about that night, but that alcohol seemed to prevent them. This was also true. However, the last time Henry Bowman had gone to sleep completely sober had been over a month ago, so he could not honestly say that the nightmares were still returning whenever he quit drinking. He admitted this fact also.

"Have you ever gone back on your word?" Carol asked after they had talked for a while.

"No, not that I know of." *I wonder where this is heading?*

"Then I'm going to hold you to it. We're going someplace tonight where you don't have to get dressed up. I go there with Mom sometimes, and we might run into someone I'd like you to meet. He's a pilot for TWA, and he goes there a lot. They've got good cof-fee, which I know you hate, but I like it, and you can drink sodas. It's not far from here."

Guess I'd better shut up and do what she says Henry told himself. I just hope she was kidding about going to bed. I don't need another disaster tonight. "Okay. Tell me where to turn," Henry said as he twisted the key in the ignition and started the engine.

"East on Clayton Road past the movie theatre to Bellvue," she replied.

Henry Bowman was about to go to his first AA meeting.

March 10, 1972

"More dead, Ray. Near the border."

Ray Johnson looked over at his head tracker. There were three nationalist groups in Angola. The Popular Movement for the Liberation of Angola (MPLA), the Front for the Liberation of Angola (FNLA), and the Union for Total Independence of Angola (UNITA). It was this last group that was most prevalent in the local area.

Contrary to what was implied by the names of the three groups, all of them spent most of their time fighting amongst themselves despite the fact that their goals were, in theory at least, similar. More and more often, internal disagreements among the leaders and the members were turning bloody.

"How many?" Raymond asked.

"Ten, maybe twenty."

Johnson shook his head. *Damned bohunks are going to get tired of putting up with this shit one of these days. Thank God all my real funds are in Rhodesia.* He looked around at the camp he and his workers had built. *Been a good nine years. Time to get serious about moving on.*

Ray Johnson's premonition was accurate. Two years later, the Portuguese military would enact a coup and Portugal would immediately grant its Angolan colonies independence. The three nationalist groups would continue their war, with the U.S. and China supporting the FNLA, the Soviet Union and Cuba assisting the MPLA, and South Africa backing UNITA. Over a decade later, the FNLA would fade away and the other two groups would continue their fighting.

By that time, however, Ray Johnson would be long gone.

***

"Man, that was bizarre, wasn't it?"

"What do you mean?" Henry Bowman asked as they walked out the men's room and headed for the exit door. Five-hour documentaries were taxing on the bladder even when they were shown on successive nights.

"Just the whole way the French reacted. I mean, those were Nazis, for God's sake! Did you catch some of what they were saying? Unbelievable." The young man shook his head at the thought.

At Amherst, as at most colleges, films shown for specific courses were open to all students so long as seats were available. At Henry's urging, he and another geology major had just spent two nights viewing a film that one of the European History classes had screened, *The Sorrow and the Pity*. It was a Swiss documentary on occupied France during WWII.

"You have to realize, many people saw those Nazis the same way we see policemen."

"What are you talking about?"

"Well," Henry said, "cops are around, but the place isn't crawling with them, right? Here in the U.S., I mean."

"Yeah..."

"Same way in most of France, back in '42. Especially if you lived in the south part of the country. For most people, life was pretty much the same as before. You lived in the same house, went to the same grocer, same doctor, had the same job, all that. You just kept your head down." Henry thought of something.

"Look, when you glance in your rearview mirror and see a police car behind you, you wish he wasn't there, right? You don't want him around, do you? And it isn't just you. Your parents probably pay loads of taxes, and they're the same way, right?"

"Yeah, I guess so."

"But what would you or your dad do if someone riding in the back of your car said 'Oh, Christ, a goddamned cop's following us' and leaned out the window and blasted him? You'd shit, right?" Henry was becoming animated.

"And if you saw some stranger kill a cop—the same cop who just gave you a speeding ticket because he had to make his ticket quota, what would you do? Would you clap, and say 'Good riddance, asshole?' Hell, no, you'd immediately report it. You'd give a full description, and you'd read in the papers about the patrolman's fine record. You'd hear about the number of arrests he made, and how he'd been promoted to lieutenant sooner than anyone else in his class at the academy, and what a good husband and father he was, and you'd see a picture of his grieving widow and three fatherless kids, and you'd feel really sorry for them. Even though at the same time, you're trying to figure out what to do about car insurance since you got canceled.

"It was the same way with the Nazis. To most French people, the Krauts were just policemen giving out speeding tickets and roughing up long-haired war protesters, and the guys in the Resistance were kind of like the Black Panthers. Except with correct grammar and better-tasting breakfasts," he added as an afterthought.

"I can't believe *that*," the friend said. "The Nazis weren't *police!* They killed their own citizens!" Henry turned to face his friend, and shook his head.

"You don't think cops in this country thirty-five years ago helped lynch black guys? Weren't those black guys citizens here? Nazis were just police in a police state. They had wives and kids and worried about paying the mortgage and whether they'd get laid after a hard day's work at the death camp just like Deputy Billy Bob in Alabama worries about making the payment on his pickup truck while he's wiping the blood off his nigger knocker." Henry gathered his thoughts and went on.

"Look, Hitler's goal was to *rule* all of Europe, not destroy it, right? What did that mean? It meant crushing the dissenters, not killing off everyone. People like our parents? Krauts left 'em alone. Gave 'em brownie points when they ratted out the troublemakers. You're from Chicago—did your parents or any of their friends have anything to worry about during the '68 convention? No, they didn't have long hair and they weren't out holding up protest signs. I bet some of 'em were even glad to see those irritating hippies get their heads busted. Am I right?" Henry went on before his friend could answer.

"Hell, *you* know the history," Henry said, unaware that his friend did not. "After Poland in '39, Denmark and Norway rolled over for the Krauts in '40. Took a week or so. Luxembourg took a day, Holland lasted about five. Belgians held out for two weeks, then caved in. Brits sent troops to northern France to try to help the Frogs fight off the Germans. France lasted a few weeks, and the only reason it took that long instead of a day or two was that Joe Stalin kept half the German army occupied on the Russian front, losing about ten million soldiers of his own in the process.

"As soon as the Krauts drove the Brits away at Dunkirk, France rolled over and spread her legs right *now.* Germans went into Paris unopposed in June of 1940. Italy said it was neutral, but when Mussolini saw the Krauts were about to kick off their shoes and put their feet up in the Louvre, he jumped into Hitler's arms like a waterfront whore when the troop ship pulls into port.

"Churchill was determined not to cave in, but the Brits hauled ass out of Greece, and they hauled ass out of Yugoslavia. When the Brits hauled ass out of France, they managed to leave all their guns behind at Dunkirk, don't ask me why. The folks in England finally figured out they were next on Hitler's shopping list, so they hunted up all the grouse guns and hunting rifles in the country, which wasn't much against MG34 belt-feds and MP40 submachine guns. They were so desperate they even ran around to museums and got *spears,* since they didn't have anything to fight with. We shipped over boatloads of real guns, but England still would have been fucked if Germany hadn't declared war on us a few days after Pearl Harbor, which was why we went over and saved their bacon."
Henry realized he had gotten off the subject.

"Those old guys they showed in the movie? The ones who had been in the Resistance? They said right on film that the only reason they were in the Resistance at all was they were Communists, and Stalin told 'em Hitler was almost to Moscow. People in France viewed those guys as a bunch of nuts. *That* was the Resistance movement."

"How do you know so much about it?"

Henry shrugged. "Went to a good high school, my dad was a history teacher at a local college, and other relatives of mine were right in the middle of the worst of it with the Nazis. They've all told me what it was like—the way it was for them while it was happening.

"By the middle of 1941, Krauts owned all of Europe except Switzerland and England. Germany had the war won, just about.

"Switzerland, of course, would have kept its independence. Just like today, in 1941 every Swiss citizen had a machine gun and a bunch of ammo in his house. They've been practicing blowing their bridges and carrying out mountain ambushes for a couple centuries, so they were ready to slaughter the Krauts in the Alps and get back home in time for dinner. Hitler wasn't about to fuck with that country, even with Mussolini's dick.

"But Great Britain was hanging on by its fingertips, and old Joe Kennedy, our Ambassador to England, he was sending back cables to Roosevelt saying, 'Hey pal, you're backing the wrong horse in this one'." Henry shook his head.

"You don't go to sleep one night a free man and wake up the next morning to find you're a slave in your own country. It happens gradually, and when you realize it, it's too late." He looked at his friend. "You know about frogs and hot water?" The young man shook his head.

"Toss a frog in a pot of boiling water, and he'll jump out because it's boiling. That's like you looking at a picture of Jews being used for medical experiments at a concentration camp. 'AAGH! How awful!'" Henry mimicked. "But stick the frog in a pot of room temperature water, and put it on the stove, and he'll swim around happily until he's dead." Henry laughed without humor. "That's why when these people in France, and Holland, and Norway, and Luxembourg, and Denmark, and Belgium, and Yugoslavia, and Great Britain let themselves get put in a position of helplessness, they had to beg for a country which hadn't been so stupid to bail them out."

"What do you mean—those countries didn't have *guns?* I don't believe that! The Germans just had more tanks, and cannons, and bombs, and all that."

"Sure, they had guns, but almost all of them were in the military. The people didn't have jack shit. We actually air-dropped a bunch of stamped-steel, single-shot .45 pistols into occupied France to try to help them out. The damn thing didn't even have a rifled barrel—it was a smoothbore. Basically a zip gun. A real piece of junk. That was how little the French people had to protect their freedom with.

"And about the cannons and bombs—they work real well when all you've got to worry about is knocking out some fortified spots. They don't solve your problem when every single citizen of the country you're invading has a good rifle and knows how to use it.

"Hell, some Jews in the Warsaw ghetto who didn't know a thing about shooting held off the German army for over a month, and all the guns they had wouldn't fill up the trunk of that car there," Henry said, pointing to a 1969 Chevrolet Impala. "Every time German Army troops looked for 'em, a bullet would come out of a window somewhere and zap the commanding officer. Krauts finally had to burn the whole city to kill them.

"And speaking of guns and protecting yourself, I've got to get cracking. This thing I'm teaching at UMass has its first session in about twenty minutes. Catch you in geo class, rock jock." Henry Bowman started to jog towards the campus parking lot.

Henry's friend watched him go. For quite a long time he thought about the things Henry Bowman had said.

***

"Good evening. Welcome to class. I know a few of you already, but for those I haven't met, my name is Henry Bowman." He looked out at the group in front of him, and saw a few skeptical looks. "This was originally planned as a coed class, but there appears to be little or no interest among the men in the area, at least not right now.

"I suspect that at least some of you are here out of curiosity, and aren't at all sure what this course is about or if you want to take it. You can't ask anyone to advise you about it, either, because this is the first time I've taught it.

"I'm going to ask that you agree to one thing. I know that really listening carefully is extremely tiring. An hour of it, if you really do it, is exhausting. I'm going to ask that you listen to me carefully for ten minutes, with an open mind about what you hear.

"I'll warn you right now that I'm going to say some things that will almost certainly upset you, and that you will disagree with. When that happens, I want you to promise me that for the next ten minutes, you will not tune out and quit listening. I want you to promise that you will not spend all your time preoccupied with the outrageous thing I just said and miss what comes next. I want you to promise me that for ten minutes, and ten minutes only, you will pay attention to every word I say as if your life depended on it.

"After ten minutes is up, I want each of you to think about what I've said, and decide if you want to listen to anything else I have to say. If not, I won't ask for any more of your time. Does that sound fair?" There were several startled murmurs among the young women in the lecture hall. Henry saw a few tentative nods of acceptance.

"Okay. Good. Ten minutes." Henry Bowman took a deep breath and made eye contact with each of the seventeen women in front of him.

"A close relative of mine was violently gang raped. The rapists were talking about blinding her so they she could not identify them when they were interrupted by a stranger, and they ran." Henry breathed deeply and went on.

"The rape left her physically injured and emotionally devastated. The physical injuries have healed. The emotional damage will take longer. Some of you may have stories you could tell about one of your own relatives, friends, or perhaps about yourself." He nodded, deciding what would come next. "I studied everything I could about that rape and others, so that the terrible price that the victims paid would not have been for nothing. That's why I'm here talking about personal protection.

"Personal protection," Henry said in loud voice. "When you signed up for this not-for-credit course that the University agreed to offer and that I volunteered to teach, all of you had your own ideas of what personal protection meant, and those ideas were probably all different. What I think each of you shares is a realization that there are times in your life when you are not safe, and you want to do something about it. And that something, whatever it is, is important enough that you came to a not-for-credit class you know nothing about other than its title, taught by someone you'd never heard of, on the chance that it might give you something of value.

"This course is going to teach you how to avoid becoming a victim of violent crime. I am not going to tell you how to keep your dorm room from being burglarized when you are out, how to prevent the girl down the hall from stealing your checks and looting your bank account, or how to keep your jewelry from being taken while you're in the shower. Those things aren't important enough for me to bother with.

"I won't mince words here—the course I'm going to teach is how to see to it that you never ever become the victim of a violent physical attack that results in rape, crippling injury, lasting emotional damage, or death." Henry looked around and saw that he had their undivided attention.

"I am also not going to tell you how to rearrange your life so that you avoid all situations with any potential for danger. Frankly, I don't think that can be done. Even if it could, I would still not be willing to let violent predators dictate the way in which I live my life. If you're willing to stay inside a locked building and only venture out in big groups, you don't need me or anyone else to teach you how to do it.

"What I am going to teach you is how to be prepared for the sudden, unexpected, violent attack so that if it ever does come, you will instantly do the thing that has the greatest chance of stopping that attack and saving both your dignity and perhaps your life." *Still got their interest* Henry thought. *Good.* He strolled casually across the front of the lecture hall as he talked, his hands behind his back. Henry sat back against the table at the front of the room and palmed a new, white, tennis ball from his open gym bag behind him.

"I am going to help you gain skill and confidence. I am going to help you develop certain reactions until they are instinctive." Without warning, he tossed the tennis ball underhanded to a girl in the fourth row. As the ball arced towards her through the air, she looked very startled, then recovered, dropped her pen, reached out her hands, and caught the ball. Henry smiled and looked around the rest of the class.

"I'd like all of you to think about what you just saw. In less than one second, this woman did a whole list of things instinctively. She recognized that something was suddenly flying through the air at her. She identified it as a slow-moving tennis ball and therefore not a danger to her. She let go of the pen she was holding. She analyzed the trajectory of the ball, and brought her hands up to the proper position. Then, the instant the tennis ball touched her hands, she closed her fingers around it before it could bounce out. Less than one second. She wasn't born with that skill. Try what I just did with a two-year-old, and you'll be lucky if she even blinks before the ball bounces off her head." He smiled and nodded at the woman holding the ball. No one noticed that as he talked, Henry took a butter knife from his pocket concealed it in the palm of his right hand.

"The difference is that in twenty years, each of you have seen a lot of things flying through the air." He was strolling in front of the three women in the front row as he spoke. The one nearest him was a muscular, athletic-looking brunette. "You've all had enough snow balls, tennis balls, car keys, and frisbees tossed or thrown at you that you react without thinking. You duck the snowball and reach out for the car keys, even when there's no warning." As he spoke these words he stepped next to the brunette so that his hip was almost touching her shoulder and held the polished knife against the far side of her neck.

"One sound and I'll cut you bad, cunt!" Henry Bowman said in a savage whisper.

There was a collective gasp from almost the entire class. A few of the women, including the one he had addressed, froze silently in utter shock. Henry waited to a count of five, then stepped back, held up the butter knife, and ran it roughly across his hand to show how dull it was.

"None of you have had anything like that happen often enough to have developed any kind of instinctive response. Every one of you froze." Henry stepped to the table and picked up the gym bag.

"My time isn't up yet," he warned the class as a whole, then held the bag out to the woman he had just pretended to threaten. She shied away from him.

"Soap, clean towels, and fresh sweats in here. Second door on the left in the hallway. Wash your face in cold water and come back," he whispered. "Go." The girl took the bag, and Henry could see she was about to get up and run out of the room. She glared at him, then looked at her watch.

"In six minutes, when you're done," she hissed, slouching back in her seat. Henry nodded, and turned to the class.

"To cope with the situation I just demonstrated, you need three things: First, you need experience and preparation so that the unexpected does not paralyze you. You need to be ready for what I just did. You need to be just as familiar and prepared as you would be with a snowball flying at you in the middle of January.

"Second, you need to learn what to do, and then work on it, so that your instinctive reaction is the right one, and not something that will make the problem worse. Defending against violence is a lot more complicated than ducking a snowball, and because of that, it takes a lot more practice.

"The third thing you need is something that I have never seen mentioned in any discussion of personal protection and defense. It is also the one thing that is far and away the most important. For want of a better term, I call it the 'Warrior Mentality', and it's something I'm going to stress over and over in this class. If you have it, you're going to have the greatest possible likelihood of retaining not only your life and good health, but also your dignity and self-respect."

As Henry looked at the seventeen faces, he saw interest, hostility, disbelief, curiosity, puzzlement, and skepticism. He did not see boredom.

"I'm going to ask all of you to imagine something, and then I'd like one of you to volunteer to pretend you're being interviewed." He gave what he hoped was a self-effacing smile. "I won't threaten you, yell, or use bad language. I'll stand right here, I promise." Henry licked his lips and went on.

"Imagine for a moment that tonight you were the victim of a premeditated, intentional assault. It was dark. You got some bruises in the attack, and the attacker ran off. I'll let you decide the other circumstances and the specifics of the assault. The hospital people looked you over, calmed you down, and you're shaken but okay. The soreness seems to be gradually going away." He looked at each student. "Anyone willing to be interviewed?" Silence lasted a few seconds, then one young woman spoke. She was of medium height, and wore tennis shoes, cut-off shorts, and a t-shirt. Henry could see that she was lean and muscular with long, slender legs and good calves. She looked as if she spent a lot of time outside.

"Yeah. Go ahead," she told him. Henry smiled at her and nodded.

"Ma'am," Henry started, "I understand that today a man assaulted you, and you were roughed up. Can you tell me something about exactly what happened?"

"I was walking to my car. As I was getting my keys out of my purse, suddenly there was a man beside me. I don't know if he'd been following me, or what. He tried to take my purse."

"How did he do that?"

"He grabbed at it. He, uh...he just tried to rip it out of my hands. I wasn't thinking—I held on to it. It was instinctive, you know? Someone tries to pull something out of your hands, you just hold tighter." Henry saw some of the others nodding, and he did the same. He could tell the woman was getting involved with the role-play.

"So then what happened?"

"I, uh, started to scream. Before I could though, he...he hit me with his fist. He hit me in the jaw. I felt this terrible pain in my face, and...and I fell down. My wrist is sore, too."

"Did he get your purse?"

"Yes. He ran away with it."

"Anything in it he could use? Money? Credit cards?"

"Yes. Both of those."

"I see," Henry said. *Is this woman really role-playing, or did something like this actually happen to her?* he wondered. "If you don't mind my saying so, you certainly look very athletic," he said, changing the subject. "Why didn't you just run away?" The young woman actually smiled at the question.

"I was wearing heels and a long skirt at the time. I was returning from a job interview. But the man surprised me. Even if I'd had on my track shoes, I probably would have done the same thing. Holding on to the purse was, as you were talking about, instinctive."

"Any guesses why the man picked you?" Henry asked, changing the subject again.

"I was there," she said simply. "Maybe I looked preoccupied, and he saw that as an opportunity. I have no idea."

"Did you learn anything from this experience? Anything you'll do differently now when returning to your car after job interviews?"

"I'll look around more. I'll be more aware of where I am and who is nearby. I'll, uh, try to find someone to walk with me when I have to go someplace where it's dark, or where it's deserted. I don't think it would have happened if there'd been other people around. Well, maybe it still would have," she said, reconsidering, "but not as likely."

Henry nodded encouragingly. "So you've already planned a number of good steps to reduce the chance that this will happen to you again in the future."

"Yes." With his peripheral vision, Henry Bowman could see that the others in the room were nodding slightly and paying close attention.

"You're not worried about this man attacking you again?" Henry asked with concern.

"N-no. Why?" The woman was baffled now.

Henry looked incredulous. "He's got your credit cards and driver's license, so he knows where you live. He's seen your car, and he's got the keys to both it and your apartment. Knowing you'd be stranded, unable to drive your car right away, and that you'd go to a doctor, he probably went straight to your place, let himself in, and rigged a window or two so he could get in later if you changed the locks right away. But I guess you weren't thinking about your own safety. You were much too overcome with guilt." The entire lecture hall was silent.

"*What* guilt?" the young woman demanded, her eyes boring holes into his. "It wasn't my fault I got attacked."

"No, it wasn't. But you learned several things from this attack; you told us that. Well, so did the man who robbed you." Henry held up a fist and began to tick off points on his fingers.

"First of all, he learned that robbing lone women in parking lots is easy. Second, he learned that it is a viable way to get money and access to vehicles and new victims. Third, he learned that victims sometimes resist a little, so he learned to hit them to make them do what he wants. Maybe he's learned that lesson well enough that next time he'll carry a lead pipe, and hit the person first, so he doesn't have that problem." Henry pretended to have just thought of something.

"You know, I just realized, if you've got a roommate, and she was home when the attacker used your keys to let himself into your apartment, she may be dead by now. Or maybe she's just injured. If you're lucky, maybe the guy just scared the hell out of her, as he did you. If she is dead, though, then you'll have to ask the coroner to find out if she was raped first—she won't be able to tell you.

"People tend to have friends that are like them, and a woman's purse tells a lot about its owner. If your purse had an address book in it, you've given this man a bunch of names, addresses, and unlisted phone numbers of new victims to choose from.

"Maybe when the man saw how you resisted, he decided from now on to stick to older victims. Maybe he'll punch out elderly people whose bodies can't take the kind of shocks yours can. We don't know the answer to that question.

"What we *do* know," Henry said, raising his voice, "is that this man is *not* going to take your purse, go back to his apartment, and say 'Ah, my final mugging. Time to look through the want ads and find a job.' He is going to keep doing it.

"The other thing I can absolutely guarantee you is that you will not help put this man in jail now. Eyewitness testimony is the least reliable kind of evidence. If you identify a suspect in a line-up and claim that beyond doubt he's the one, you may well be helping to imprison an innocent man." Henry saw that the young woman was cowed and her eyes were filled with tears, but he pressed on.

"The time to do something is when you have the mugger right in front of you! The time to fight is when you are strong, not after you've been beaten! And the time and place to lose your dignity is in here, with me, where you'll get it back in five or ten minutes, and you won't be left lying on the ground, bruised at best and maybe permanently crippled, with guilt eating at your guts that he's going to do it again, to someone else, because you didn't stop him." Henry Bowman took a very deep breath and made eye contact with each of the pupils before him. Every one of them was waiting for his next words.

"My ten minutes are up." No one replied.

"If you elect to stay in this course, you will be forced to face more issues such as the one you're thinking about right now. You will *not* hear about rape whistles and sisterhood support groups. If you stay in this course, you will learn why the worst handgun is ten times better than the next-best choice for saving your life. You will learn how to carry one at all times when it is possible, and how to improvise other methods of defense when it is not. You will develop the will to kill a violent attacker if necessary. You will learn exactly how to do it, and you will learn when to do it." Henry looked at the woman he had just interrogated. "Are you willing to face those issues?" he asked gently.

The woman hesitated. "Yes," she said finally, with a firm nod.

"Me too," the first woman broke in. "When you stuck that knife at my throat, I wet my pants, and I wanted to rip your balls off." The other students became very animated at this revelation. "You knew it, too, didn't you?"

"That's why there's towels and sweats in the bag," Henry said with a smile. He tapped his groin area with a ballpoint pen, and there was an unexpected sound. "Also have on a plastic cup in case you did more than just think about it. Preparation is everything," he said with a smile and arched eyebrows. The class erupted, and Henry handed the woman the gym bag.

"So who's staying?" he asked the group. The response was unanimous, and Henry was startled to see expressions of raw sexual interest on several faces in the group. *Okay, fella*, Henry thought to himself as his heart rate accelerated, *don't get excited. That's the kind of thinking that's apt to screw this up big-time.*

'Bowman's Boot Camp', as it came to be known in the Pioneer Valley, was a success. In the two years before he graduated from college and left the area, Henry would teach over three hundred women and forty men. Henry would suspect, correctly, that most of the men were homosexuals who feared injury or death at the hands of 'fag-bashers'. In the period prior to Henry Bowman's graduation, several of Henry's former pupils would use what they had learned to stop violent assaults in the act and take the time to send Henry letters and newspaper clippings describing the events. Two of the letter-writers would credit Henry Bowman with saving their lives. Henry Bowman would be very proud of these letters, and would value them more than his diploma.

The sexual undercurrent that Henry Bowman noticed that first evening would be present to some degree in every class he taught, and Henry quickly came to see why so many college professors ended up having affairs with their pupils. Henry made a rule for himself that his own students were off-limits until the last of the six evening sessions was over, but *former* students were just like any other girls his own age in a college town.

Much to Henry's chagrin, he found that his female students' romantic interest in him generally disappeared after the course was over. In a few cases, though, it did not, and in the following two years, Henry ended up having three very pleasant involvements with women who had been in his personal protection class.

Each of these three women would bestow on Henry Bowman a great deal of physical pleasure. One of them, however, would do him a favor that would prove to be of more lasting value.

April 1, 1973

"Bill will never let you back on the field if he finds out," George Goveia said. "You'll have to jump at Turners Falls from now on." Henry Bowman noted with pleasure that George had not made some whiny comment about fearing for his own job at the parachuting school. It was one of the reasons that George was Henry's favorite employee at the Orange Sport Parachuting Center.

"We've *got* to do it—it's April Fool's, remember?" Henry said. "Look, we'll load up on the other side of the pumps. Bill won't see me taxi, and after that, there's no proof, right?"

"I guess you're right—no one's going to believe a chick throwing a hissy fit."

"Will the pilot go along with it?" Henry asked. George snorted.

"He'd probably pay you to do it. He's got some other flying job lined up and he's quitting in two weeks anyway."

"Then it's a go? Next jump run?"

"Yeah, but we need a fifth person. We don't want Tom. He'd probably tell Stephanie, and you know how she is. Keith might try to feel me up. Rick's not here..."

"We wouldn't want him—lightning might strike twice," Henry warned with a laugh.

"Yeah, no shit," George replied, and broke up also.

"Is Carl Beck here?"

"Haven't seen him today. Jesus, wouldn't he be perfect, though?" Carl Beck was a cadaverous, one-eyed WWII vet. He had been shot to ribbons and left for dead in the European theater, and his sewn-up eye socket, tortuous limp, ruined jaw, and wispy hair made him look like an extra in a Boris Karloff movie. Carl had done the logical thing for a man who was completely disabled: He had taken up sport parachuting. In free-fall, his disabilities vanished, and everyone on the airport liked jumping with Carl. He was a bit lackadaisical about packing his main parachute, however, and the joke at Orange was that Carl Beck was the only man around who could qualify for a Class A license (which required 25 jumps) on his *reserve* 'chute. Some years later, Carl would have his reserve 'chute fail as well, and he would land in a muddy drainage ditch at an estimated 85 miles an hour. After that, his limp became even worse, but he kept jumping.

"What about Franny, then?" Henry asked. "She's here—would she pitch a bitch?"

"Hell, no. Yeah, she'd be perfect—and Bill will believe her, if it comes to that."

"Great," Henry said. "Here, give whatsisname—the pilot—give him my helmet to wear, and make sure he knows to go rich before restart. And make damn sure that even if she freaks out, that girl doesn't pull inside the plane, okay? That would ruin your day."

"Yeah, I can take care of that. Good point. We'll stick her in the far back."

"I'll trim it up for best glide with no power before I go. And George? Since I won't be there to see it, milk it real good, okay? Act as if you're all snarled up and can't get out for a while, before letting the pilot take over, huh?"

"This is going to be a good one, Henry," George Goveia said with a big grin. Henry Bowman nodded and started walking towards the shack which served as the airport restaurant.

Like most activities that could loosely be called 'thrill sports', sport parachuting in 1973 was an activity practiced primarily by young men. College students of both sexes drove up to Orange every weekend to make the first and only parachute jump of their lives so they could say they did it. Very few women of that era, however, ever became experienced jumpers with instructor's ratings, or had jump logbooks with hundred of entries. Those that did achieve such measures of proficiency, however, were accepted as equals. 'Fast Franny' Strimenos was one of that group. Like almost all experienced jumpers, she liked a good 'gotcha', and more importantly, she felt no particular kinship to non-jumpers merely because they were of the same gender. That was important for what was about to happen.

At Orange, as at every commercial drop zone in the country, an interested party could pay the same fee that the jumpers paid for their air lift and go on an 'observation flight'. This meant that he or she got to ride in the plane with the parachutists, watch them jump out, and then land in the plane along with the pilot.

Safety regulations required that in single engine jump planes, all non-parachutists had to wear an emergency parachute in case of engine failure. Henry Bowman always thought this was a crazy rule. Jump planes stayed directly over whatever drop zone they serviced, and any pilot who had an engine failure directly over an airport and elected to abandon his aircraft did not deserve to have a pilot's license in the first place, in Henry's opinion. In spite of that, all drop zones around the country followed the rule. Pilots and observers in single-engine jump planes wore emergency parachutes.

At almost every drop zone around the country, there was an equally-important unwritten rule that the staff also followed. It took effect only when an exceptionally good-looking female signed up for an observation flight on a plane full of instructors and other experienced jumpers. The unwritten rule was that when the airplane got to jump altitude, the pilot pulled the throttle back to idle and told the observer that the engine had lost power and she was going to have to jump with the others.

This practice had been going on almost as long as there had been sport jumpers and attractive female observers. Usually the woman would turn pale, and occasionally screamed, before the pilot opened the throttle and let her in on the joke. One young lady at Orange the year before had greatly endeared herself to the instructors. When given the news, she had nodded once in acceptance and then started to climb over the right seat of the Beech 18 to get to the door at the rear of the plane. The Beech was a twin, but the instructors had put a 'chute on her anyway, and the pilot had chopped both throttles.

There were other good stories that the instructors liked to retell, but Henry's favorite was the legendary one that had occurred when the instructors had pulled the trick on a woman in a 10-person Noorduyn Norseman. The Orange facility owned three 'Norse Hogs', which were slow-flying 1940's-era military cargo aircraft, each powered by a single big radial engine. On the afternoon in question, the pilot gave the standard bad news to the observer, and then, as was custom, one of the instructors gave her the good news that it was just a joke. In this case, an instructor with the unlikely name of Rick Hustler had done the honors.

What happened next varied according to who was telling the story and how much he had had to drink. What was not disputed was that the young woman threw her arms around Rick Hustler's neck and said 'Oh, thank you, thank you', or some other equally appropriate words of gratitude. The second thing that was never disputed was that when the plane passed over the exit point, Rick Hustler elected not to jump out of the aircraft with the rest of the jumpers, and actually landed in the plane with his new admirer. What transpired between the time the jumpers exited and the time the plane landed was cause for great speculation, but there was a third undisputed fact about the incident: Within a year, Rick Hustler and the young woman were husband and wife.

Henry Bowman was about to elevate this standard drop zone prank into an art form.

He didn't know it, but in so doing, he was also going to help the pilot get what he would later say was 'the best blow job I ever had in my life.' Since Henry did not know the man well, he would be unable to assess whether this was an impressive claim or not.

Henry smiled as he bit into his hamburger. Henry thought the Orange Airport hamburgers were the best to be had in Massachusetts. When he saw through the restaurant window that the four people were standing around the Cessna 180 waiting for the pilot, Henry popped the last bite into his mouth and ran out the door.

"Sorry I'm late," Henry apologized as he slowed to a walk in front of the group.

"No problem," Franny Strimenos said immediately. "I was just telling Debbie here the most comfortable way to sit. She's never been cramped up in a plane with no seats."

"Let's get in," said the man whose name Henry had forgotten. He was wearing a single emergency 'chute. "I haven't made any jumps yet today." Henry and George bit their lips to keep from laughing.

The Cessna 180 was set up as a jump aircraft, which meant it had all its seats removed save the one for the pilot, and would now hold five people instead of four. A special jump door had been installed that hinged at the top and could be opened all the way in flight. The observer got in first and sat with her knees bunched up alongside the rear bulkhead. Fran Strimenos sat facing her, and George got in next. Then Henry climbed into the pilot's seat, and the other man sat on the floor where the passenger seat would normally have been, facing rearward.

Henry Bowman quickly ran through the preflight checklist and started the engine. He taxied the plane immediately and kept his face turned to the left. He did not want the drop zone's owner to see that the man who was flying his jump aircraft was not the person he had hired to perform that job.

The 180 was a tailwheel airplane like Henry's aerobatic Cub, and its ground handling was similar, although the pedal effort was higher. Henry taxied to the end of the runway, did his engine runup and magneto check, mumbled something unintelligible into the microphone, and pulled out onto the runway centerline. He pushed the throttle to full and held the yoke forward, keeping the plane straight with quick stabs on the rudder pedals. As the tail came up, he eased the yoke back and let the airplane fly itself off the runway. *Decent power for a spam can* he thought with a smile. Henry had a tube-and-rag pilot's disdain for all-metal airplanes.

Although modern equipment allows sport parachutists to glide to a landing virtually anywhere they choose, in 1973 many jumpers had 'chutes of limited maneuverability, and the first high-performance gliding reserve 'chutes were still six years away. Thus, jumpers always strove to exit the aircraft at the proper point upwind of their intended landing spot, so that if they ended up having to deploy a non-steerable reserve 'chute, they would still end up somewhere on the airport and not in the woods. Normally, when a jump aircraft gets to jump altitude, this is accomplished by one of the jumpers opening the door, holding his head out so he can see straight down, and giving the pilot hand corrections to put him over a spot that has been preselected based on other jump runs or a test with a crepe paper streamer. On this flight, however, Henry Bowman was going to have to guess.

It took Henry seventeen minutes of circling the airport to get to an altitude of 7500 feet above the ground. By that time, he had a good feel for the wind velocity and direction, and he turned the aircraft into the wind and flew directly over the big sand landing bowl that was in the center of the three runways.

A quarter-mile past the parachutists' intended landing point, Henry Bowman trimmed the airplane a little nose-up, pulled the mixture control to full lean, and brought the throttle back to idle position. Out of the corner of his eye he saw the jump pilot on the floor next to him draw his breath in sharply. In four seconds the engine sputtered and stopped running. Henry had just fuel-starved it. The airplane was suddenly very quiet.

"What's wrong?" Franny Strimenos yelled, her voice almost cracking. *Nice touch, Franny* Henry Bowman thought with a smile. *Perpetuate the stereotype.*

"I don't know!" Henry yelled back. "Bill warned me the jetting was off, but he said he couldn't afford to have the plane in the shop." Henry saw the pilot's face turn bright red as the man forced himself to contain his laughter. All the employees thought the airport owner was a tightwad. Henry put his right hand on the ignition key, looked at the man on the floor next to him, arched his eyebrows, and removed the key. A look of horrified comprehension came over the man's face, and he grabbed Henry's wrist. Henry slid the key back in the ignition, let go of it, and winked. *Just checking to see if you were paying attention.*

"Is the plane going to crash?" the shapely woman in the back of the plane screamed as she strained to see what was going on. Henry turned around in the pilot's seat and made sure he had solid eye contact with the girl before he spoke.

"I'm sure as shit not going to stay in it and find out," he said in a loud voice. Then he reached across the real pilot's outstretched legs, unlatched the jump door, and swung it up against the wing. Henry stared in the girl's eyes once more. "See you on the ground," he said.

Then Henry Bowman dove headfirst out of the aircraft.

Henry bent slightly forward at the waist and bent his elbows so that he would fall in a back-to-earth position. He wanted to watch the airplane to see what would happen. Since the pilot had borrowed Henry's goggles as well as his helmet, Henry squinted so that his eyes wouldn't tear. It was a full ten seconds before he saw a bright red jumpsuit appear. *There's Franny.* He glanced at the altimeter on his chest strap. 6300 feet. Henry watched the plane for another ten-count, but George didn't exit, so he flipped to a face-to-earth position, glanced at his altimeter, and got his bearings.

Four thousand-eight hundred feet. Need to get over the north edge of the farmer's field. Henry bent sideways at the waist to turn towards the field, then drew his arms in to his sides, cupped his hands forward, hunched his shoulders, and pointed his toes. He was now falling in a 'track', traveling almost one foot horizontally for every foot down. His speed through the air was over 200 miles per hour. At 3000 feet, Henry was over the proper spot, and he spread his arms and legs out wide. It felt as if he had entered a thicker layer of atmosphere as his body slowed to about 130 miles per hour. At 2400 feet, Henry pulled his ripcord and grabbed the nylon web risers that stretched out above his shoulders. He wanted to take some of the opening shock in his arms instead of entirely on the inside of his thighs.

The rectangular parachute opened abruptly with a ripping noise, and Henry was slowed to a quiet and leisurely nine-mile-an-hour descent. The 'ram-air' inflated-wing design had almost thirty miles per hour of forward speed, and Henry flew his parachute around the airport until he got within a few hundred feet of the ground. Then he aimed it upwind and stalled it out when his shoes were a few feet off the ground in the middle of the sand bowl. He ran downwind and grabbed his 'chute before the wind could catch it and drag him, then he looked up in the air.

Fran Strimenos had opened high and was flying her ram-air 'chute around the sky. George Goveia had evidently pulled at the standard altitude of 2500 feet. He was about 1500 feet above the ground, hanging upside-down in his harness. It was George's trademark; he had been a tumbler in school. George waited until he was twenty feet above the ground before flipping over and landing on his feet, then collapsed his 'chute and walked over to Henry. The two of them looked up in the sky.

"Franny did her 'terrified broad' act, and finally jumped out. I asked Dick if he wanted to jump before me. He said something about how he could see how scared the girl was, and he flew in a plane once, and he was going to try to restart the engine and see if he could land it because the observer was obviously panicked and he didn't want her to have to jump. I waited 'til he did a restart before I got out."

"So she still thinks her pilot has never landed a plane before?" Henry demanded as he stared at the descending aircraft, which was now at five hundred feet altitude on final approach. "This is really great." Then he thought of something. "Jesus, I hope she doesn't decide it's too risky and bail out about now."

"Wouldn't that be a bummer."

The pair watched as the pilot brought the 180 in for a smooth landing. When it pulled onto the taxiway, Henry stuck out his hand and grinned. "Happy April Fool's day, George."

"That it is."

May 7, 1973

"And so, Hobbes said that our lives are 'nasty, brutish, and short', and he used that as justification for the dictatorial powers of the monarch. Only by granting the State total power will we ever overcome our natural condition, which is to be perpetually at war with one another." The Political Science course the professor was teaching was listed in the course catalog with a dry-sounding title that no one remembered. Throughout the Amherst campus it was referred to as 'Right and Wrong'. Henry Bowman liked the class, mainly because the professor who taught it had a very sharp mind.

"Hobbes is just talking about our old friend, the..." and with this, the lecturer gestured with his arm to show the class he wanted someone to finish the sentence for him.

"Benevolent dictatorship," a Senior in the second row said quickly.

"Exactly, Mr. Hagner. Hobbes' *Leviathan* is just one more scholarly justification for forfeiting your rights and allowing yourself to be subjugated by the State. Learned, reasoned, articulate, and wrong. Thomas Hobbes has merely—*Mr. Bowman,*" the professor said suddenly, "you are shaking your head. That usually means you disagree with something that's been said. What is it?"

"Professor Arkes, I don't disagree with the basic principle, but it's not enough just to say, 'Totalitarian regimes are wrong, so don't let the State enslave you'. That's like saying, 'Don't get sick'. The important question is, when do you know it's going to become enslavement? When is the proper time to resist with force?"

"Please elaborate, Mr. Bowman." Henry took a deep breath.

"The end result, which we want to avoid, is the concentration camp. The gulag. The gas chamber. The Spanish Inquisition. All of those things. If you are in a death camp, no one would fault you for resisting. But when you're being herded towards the gas chamber, naked and seventy pounds below your healthy weight, it's too late. You have no chance. On the other hand, no one would support you if you started an armed rebellion because the government posts speed limits on open roads and arrests people for speeding. So when was it not too late, but also not too early?"

"Tell us, Mr. Bowman."

"Professor Arkes, I teach a Personal Protection class off-campus, where most of the students who sign up are women. I'm seeing some strong parallels here, so please indulge me in an analogy."

"Go ahead."

"A woman's confronted by a big, strong, stranger. She doesn't know what he's planning, and she's cautious. Getting away from him's not possible. They're in a room and he's standing in front of the only way out, or she's in a wheelchair—whatever. Leaving the area's not an option.

"So now he starts to do things she doesn't like. He asks her for money. She can try to talk him out of it, just like we argue for lower taxes, and maybe it will work. If it doesn't, and she gets outvoted, she'll probably choose to give it to him instead of getting into a fight to the death over ten dollars. You would probably choose to pay your taxes rather than have police arrive to throw you in jail.

"Maybe this big man demands some other things, other minor assaults on this woman's dignity. When should she claw at his eyes or shove her ballpoint pen in his throat? When he tries to force her to kiss him? Tries to force her to let him touch her? Tries to force her to have sex with him?" Henry took a deep breath and shrugged.

"Those are questions that each woman has to answer for herself. There is one situation, though, where I tell the women to fight to the death. That's when the man pulls out a pair of handcuffs and says, 'Come on, I promise I won't hurt you, this is just so you won't flail around and hurt either of us by accident. Come on, I just want to talk, get in the van and let me handcuff you to this eyebolt here, and I promise I won't touch you. I'm not asking you to put on a gag or anything, and since you can still scream for help, you know you'll be safe. Come on, I got a full bar in here, and color TV, and air conditioning, great stereo, come on, just put on the cuffs.'

"I tell women that if that ever happens, maybe the man is telling the truth, and maybe after talking to her for a while he'll let her go and she will have had a good time drinking champagne and listening to music. But if she gets in the van and puts her wrists in the handcuffs, she has just given up her future ability to fight, and now it is too late." Henry realized he had been making eye contact with all the other people in the lecture hall, just as he did when he taught a course. Now he looked directly at the professor.

"How do you spot the precise point where a society is standing at the back of the van and the State has the handcuffs out? That's the question I'd like to see addressed by one of these philosophers we've been studying, Professor."

"Mr. Bowman, that's a very good point, and I wish now that you had brought it up six weeks ago. I might have given it for the semester's final paper assignment." Most of the class laughed at this comment, and Henry smiled.

For the rest of his life, Henry Bowman would ruminate over the issue he had raised in class that day.

***

"Excellent!" Henry said as the final six bullets from the small pistol clanged satisfyingly against the circular steel plate. The metal disc was hanging fifteen feet away, suspended from a tree limb by two coat hangers.

Danielle Pelletier and Henry Bowman had been out at Quabbin Reservoir all morning. It was a gorgeous place, rocky and secluded, with no other people for over a mile. It was the first time Danielle had been out there alone, instead of with the whole class.

Danielle saw that the pistol's slide remained in the retracted position, and she looked into the loading port at the magazine to verify that the gun was indeed empty. She laid the weapon down carefully in the open hardcase next to the now-empty ammunition box. The gun's muzzle pointed downrange. Danielle stripped off her hearing protectors and shooting glasses and a big grin filled her pretty face.

"How was that? Am I getting the hang of it?" She waited for the compliment that she knew was coming.

"You don't need to ask," Henry said. "With steel plates, you can hear if you've hit the vital zone." He smiled back, but a look of concern came over his face as he started to pack up the shooting gear and put it away. He appeared to be choosing his words carefully before continuing.

"Shooting steel plates and other targets is great fun, and I have loved doing it all my life. But don't ever forget the real reason to practice. If you ever do have to use your defensive shooting skills, an awful lot of things are going to be going through your mind and body that you will never have experienced out here practicing. That's something that takes a different kind of practice, and it's why I always harp about it in the lectures." Danielle looked thoughtful.

"Mental and emotional preparation, you mean? The Warrior Mentality?"

"Exactly. And for some people, that's much harder to learn than the skills part. It's also much harder for me to teach, and I wish I knew how to improve." Henry continued to stow their gear in the back of the car. The young woman had a knowing look on her face as she looked at her companion.

"Then that explains something I was wondering about." Henry cocked his head and raised an eyebrow, waiting for her to continue. "When you didn't seem to notice that I was flirting with you, I thought maybe you were brain dead." This got a big grin out of him, and he chewed the inside of his cheek.

"You mean you didn't think I noticed you tossing your head to throw your hair back every few minutes, didn't think I realized you were standing closer to me than you needed to when I was explaining how to see if a gun is loaded, didn't think I felt you rubbing your boob against my arm when I was helping you get your grip right, didn't think I watched your nipples get hard, and didn't think I saw you clench the muscles in your ass every time you had your back to me?"

Danielle started to blush. "You realize more than I thought."

"I not only noticed, I *liked* it," he said softly. This got her attention, and she looked up into his eyes. "It's just that it would *be...wrong* if I let us get distracted from something very important that demands concentration. You said you took my course because you wanted to be able to defend yourself, and you sounded completely serious."

"I *was* serious."

"I know you were. I don't think either one of us says things we don't mean. And learning how to effectively and safely protect yourself with a deadly weapon is something that requires all of your attention." He paused and gave her a big smile. "At least while you are actually doing it. Which I notice we aren't any more."

She came over to him, put her arms around his neck, and rubbed her chest lightly against his. "So I can do this now?" Danielle asked playfully, looking up into his eyes.

"You'd better," Henry said as his hands gripped her small waist. "But first help me pack up the rest of our gear."

She opened the back of the car and looked quizzically at a large, flat metal object in the back of the vehicle, padded with black vinyl and with what appeared to be a piano hinge running its length. "What's this thing?" Danielle demanded.

"Massage table," Henry replied, sliding the gun case and range bag into the back of the vehicle. "I borrowed it from the rugby team. Have to get it back by tomorrow morning."

"Why do you have a massage table in the back of your car?" she asked accusingly.

Henry grabbed the final ammo can, put it in the back, and pulled the table out of the vehicle.

"I thought your muscles might be tired after this morning. I also thought it would be a good way to find out just what your body likes best," Henry said casually as he unfolded the padded table and set it up at the back of the car. Danielle watched as he opened the gym bag and took out a large towel which he spread on the vinyl surface.

Henry poked around in the gym bag and pulled out a large towel, a t-shirt, a can of hand cleaner, and a plastic bottle filled with what looked like shampoo. "Here," he said, holding out the large towel. "Take off your clothes and lie on your stomach," he said, indicating the table and relieved that his voice didn't crack. "Cover yourself with the towel. I'm going to go change shirts, and clean some of this powder residue off my hands." He kept his face impassive as he turned away, but his heart was pounding.

Danielle stared dumbfounded at Henry Bowman, but found herself stepping out of her shoes. Her fingers slowly unbuttoned the denim work shirt and she let it fall to the ground. She unzipped the tight, faded jeans and pushed them down her hips.

When Henry came back around the car, Danielle was standing next to the massage table. She wore matching bra and panties that were made of a fine beige material that was almost transparent. Her erect nipples were evident, as was the small brown patch of fine pubic hair five inches below her navel. She looked absolutely stunning. He stared at her, his head canted, a questioning look on his face. He started to speak, but she cut him off forcefully.

"This morning, before I got dressed in old blue jeans and a man's work shirt because we were going shooting, I planned a little surprise for you for when we came back. I put on the sexiest and most outrageously expensive set of underwear I've ever owned, and I'll be damned if I'm going to take them off, toss them in a pile, and cover myself up with a towel before you tell me how absolutely, totally hot I look in them."

She turned around to give him the rear view, and slowly, deliberately clenched the muscles in her firm ass. When she turned back to face him they were both grinning. Henry nodded his head in obvious appreciation.

"Do you want me to take them off now?" Danielle asked innocently. Henry nodded again.

Danielle unhooked her bra and stepped out of her panties. She settled comfortably onto the padded surface, stretched out on her stomach, and let her toes hang over the sides of the table.

"Start with my bottom," she instructed. Henry drew his breath in sharply. *What have you gotten yourself into here, fella?* he thought.

"This is, uh, a non-sexual massage," Henry said lamely, then immediately felt like an idiot. Danielle sighed, closed her eyes, and smiled happily.

"We'll see about that."

May 8, 1973

"So, we've talked about everything else—what's your view on the war?" Danielle Pelletier asked as she rearranged one of the pillows and propped herself up on an elbow. "You think it will end before you get drafted?" Henry Bowman stretched, put his hands behind his head, and stared at the ceiling.

"I won't get drafted, no matter how long it goes on. I tried to enlist, but they wouldn't take me. There's still a big stainless steel rod in this leg. Military won't take you with foreign metal in your body."

"*What?*"

"Yep, that's their rule, though I'm not sure why they have that policy. For some reconstructive work the steel is temporary, and they take it out after the bone's healed, but in my case they said–"

"No, no, I mean, you enlisted? You *wanted* to go? Are you out of your mind?" Danielle was sitting up now, and Henry found himself admiring her chest.

"That wasn't it," Henry said with a sigh. "Lots of things bother me about the war. Enlisting was the best way to avoid the worst part of...of the whole mess."

"What do you mean? I mean...this just blows my mind. Your whole bag, the thing you always talk about in the protection class, is that each one of us is responsible for ourselves. *Ourselves,* Henry. You always talk about personal freedom. About individual rights. About how being a policeman just entitles you to arrest people for misdemeanors." She became more animated as she spoke.

"About...about how the police are just the historians, there to write it down after it's already happened, and more interested in handing out traffic tickets than anything else. Henry, you hate it when the government says you have to go get a permit to buy a gun, or to carry it with you, and how some places they won't let you carry it for protection at all.

"Now you tell me you want to join those same people, and go over and meddle in somebody else's business in another country, when nobody has a clue as to what they're doing!" She drew away from him as she spoke.

"Everything you said is true," Henry replied, "except the part about wanting to meddle in other people's business. Let me finish," he commanded, holding up a hand.

"You are absolutely right when you say I believe that each one of us should determine our own destiny. You are also right about how our goals over there aren't particularly well-defined." He furrowed his brow, and went on.

"But the first priority is me. Volunteering to jump into a war I didn't much understand, let alone believe in, wasn't nearly as terrifying as getting drafted into that war."

"What's the difference?"

"What's the *difference?*" Henry repeated. "Jesus Christ, Danielle! Get drafted and you have no control over your future whatsoever. You can easily get thrown in with a bunch of shitbums whose only goal is to get high, and who have no reservations about lobbing a grenade into their CO's tent if they think he might give them an order to go into battle. Enlist, and you can make sure that the people you end up with are ones you can count on to back you up, not shoot you in the back." He looked into her eyes. "There's no conscripts in the Special Forces."

Danielle took a moment to think that over.

"I guess that makes sense," she said finally. "Except it still surprises me. The idea of you taking orders, I mean."

"'Girls say yes to guys who say no', you mean?" he teased as he reached between her legs.

"Stop that!" she laughed. Danielle Pelletier had participated halfheartedly in several war protests, and was well aware that most of the young men involved in them were there to get laid. Henry smiled, then became serious again.

"Sometimes taking orders, at least for a while, is your best option," he said. "But you should always keep as many options open as possible. Especially involving the government."

"Why do I have the feeling you're about to tell me something new? Something that's interesting, and maybe a little scary, like in your class?" Danielle asked.

"Woman's intuition?" Henry offered.

"I'm serious," she countered. Henry nodded.

"One of the biggest ways to keep your options open is to be able to start with a clean slate, if need be."

"Go on."

"To be able to step into another identity, and kiss off the one with the problems.."

"What, you mean like so you can get rid of a bad credit rating, or something? Skip out on the rent payment?"

"No, I mean more like not getting thrown into a concentration camp in California in 1942 because your name is Edward Anderson, with an address in Ohio, instead of Ito Hamata from Los Angeles." Henry saw her quizzical look, and went on.

"People think of fake IDs as what you use to scam people. You know, get into strip joints, get booze when you're nineteen, get a credit card and then tear up the bills, that kind of thing. You can use them for that, but then they're shot if you really get in a jam. What I'm talking about is a lot more important than ripping off some credit card company for a few extra bucks. More like ripping off the Grim Reaper for a few extra decades." He smiled at her and continued.

"Time to do something is when you can, and you got lots of time and no pressure, right? Not when the deadline's tomorrow. Krauts come knock on your door, say *'Guten tag, Frau Epstein, mach schnell to der soap factory,'* and you tell them your name's Adams, and you pull out a driver's license issued last week and a checkbook printed yesterday, and your matching luggage happens to be monogrammed with a big 'E', well, nice try.

"But if you've got a two-year-old driver's license, and a stack of paid credit card bills from the last fifteen years, and cancelled checks over the last decade, twelve year-old membership to a gym, and a copy of a birth certificate that was issued and notarized eight years ago, and all these things are in the name of Adams, well, maybe you won't end up as lather in some guy's armpit, at least not this week.

"If the krauts never come, and they probably won't, you wasted a little time over the years setting up the other 'jacket', just like the time you wasted working to pay for fire insurance all those years that your house didn't burn down."

Danielle's eyes were bright. "So what's your other identity, Henry? What name, I mean."

"I've got three."

"Three?" she squealed.

"Three males about my age, that I have birth certificates for, and driver's licenses, and credit cards, and other stuff. Each with a different address. I also have three women's birth certificates, but I couldn't very well pretend to be female and rent a post office box, apply for a driver's license, all that, so all I've got there is the three birth certificates."

"Why three women?" Danielle asked, certain she knew the answer. Henry Bowman took a deep breath and stared at the ceiling.

"Several reasons," he said. *Because I was drunk and it was fun* he answered silently. "First of all, the whole point is to plan for the unexpected in the distant future, and in twenty years I could easily be married. So I had to get several. You know, for different eye color, and like that.

"Second, even if I was single and unattached, a ready-made ID with a long history that'd stand up would be worth a fair bit of money to someone with more immediate problems, don't you think? Particularly if I could supply one that matched the person's description."

"I want to buy one of your birth certificates now," Danielle said immediately.

"Sorry, but none of the three I have lists 'world-class butt' in the official description." Henry held up his arms as Danielle started to punch him.

"Seriously," he said, after she had stopped hitting him, "I'll give you one, and help you get others if you want, if you'll help me get some of the other stuff done, like driver's licenses and P.O. boxes. It's actually kind of fun, and I've looked at the legal statutes to see how serious a crime it is. Near as I can tell, if you don't do anything with your new identity to cheat anyone, or apply for a passport, I think they'd have a tough time prosecuting you at all."

"And if they did, you'd just turn into someone else."

"Exactly."

"So when do we start?"

"How 'bout in, say, another hour?" Henry suggested, pulling back the sheet.

"Goodness! Has *that* been there all this time?" Danielle asked as she slid a pillow under her stomach and lifted her bottom slightly.

"Pretty much, yes," Henry admitted.

"Well, bring him on over here."

December 22, 1973

"This has been sitting on the mail table for two weeks," Catherine Bowman told her son as she handed him the envelope. "I was going to send it on to you but I forgot, and then it was almost your vacation." Henry looked at the flimsy paper, Rhodesian stamps and postmark, and Air Mail notices, then slit the envelope with his knife. The letter was from Raymond Johnson.

November 12

Dear Henry,

Thank you for your swift reply to my request for .458 ammunition such as your uncle used on his safari in Angola in 1969. I realized at the time that you would need to know more specifics on the gun for which it was intended, but when I wrote the letter, I had not yet secured a specific weapon.

I now have a Winchester Model 70 in this caliber. It is the old model with controlled feed, with a stock handmade out of a laminate and bedded with epoxy so it won't end up a handful of kindling. I well agree with your assessment of factory stocks in this caliber, at least concerning the first decade of production. I believe the factory has made some improvements lately, as clients have used the new model without breakage, though the extractor system leaves me cold.

Funny that you should be an Enfield man; I had a friend in New York ten years ago who felt exactly the same way. Custom gunsmithing (metalwork, at least) being relatively hard to come by on this side of the ocean, one must make do with factory offerings and modest modification.

The answer to your question about my chamber and throat is as follows: Overall length of dummy round with 500 grain Winchester bullet seated backwards (and still able to close the bolt) is 2.93 inches for my rifle. I am glad to hear that you are concerned about feeding reliability in my unmodified action and have a blunt projectile available that is not quite so square-ended as the ones Max used.

I'd prefer to keep using my .600 Holland, but I am finally out of Kynoch ammunition and there is none to be had anywhere. You could load for it I am sure but you'd need the rifle in hand to get the charge regulated properly.

You asked about Rhodesia in your letter. It is a beautiful country and I wish I had moved here earlier. The political climate would probably baffle anyone used to the U.S. system. Only South Africa recognizes the independence declared 7 years ago—the U.N. cut off Rhodesia. Because of the sanctions, Rhodesia is industrialized and self-sufficient. Not quite what the U.N. had in mind, I'd bet. Kind of like Colorado declaring independence and prospering after being cut off by the rest of the U.S., if you can imagine that. Maybe there's a lesson there.

Another novel political notion here is that you have to have a minimum quantity of assets before you can vote. One effect of this policy is that the game hasn't been slaughtered to make way for collective farming. Thank God.

Thank you once again for your help, and get over here on a trip as soon as you can. I waited until I was 25 to hunt Africa, and that was too damn long.

Let me know what I owe you on the ammo. You'll have to check out shipping on your end.

        Ray

Henry folded the letter and put it in his pocket. As Ray had pointed out, no one was loading the big English calibers any longer. Thus, the few remaining manufacturers of double rifles (mostly Germans and Austrians) were chambering their arms for available cartridges. In dangerous game calibers, this meant the .458 Winchester Magnum, which was a smaller cartridge made for bolt guns. Loads designed for use in bolt action rifles produced about 55,000 PSI of peak chamber pressure. Such pressures would overstrain the hinged action of a double rifle.

The factories soon realized that their .458 ammo was too hot for double guns, and they reduced the powder charge to bring peak pressure down to the 40,000 PSI level that double rifles could live with. Unfortunately, this also reduced the penetration of the .458 to where it was marginal on elephant and buffalo.

Ray Johnson needs some full-strength .458s loaded with flat-nosed solids Henry thought. *Three hundred ought to do him for a while.* Henry thought about whether or not he had enough components on hand to load that much .458 ammo, or if he'd have to shoot up some of his 400-grain rock-busting loads to get enough empty cases. Then he remembered two .50 caliber cans full of fired .458 brass he had put under the loading bench at the end of the summer.

No time like the present he thought as he headed for the basement stairs.

February 3, 1974

"The Regulated American Economy," James Nelson said in a loud voice. "This course is about government regulation of the free market. Much of the curriculum will focus on utility companies and other government-regulated monopolies." Nelson was an expert on industries that were most efficient when addressed by a single supplier.

"This department is known for its free-market philosophy, so it may surprise some of you to hear me advocate government-sanctioned monopolies." He saw that he had their attention, and continued.

"An existing utility company—the phone company, for example—can double its capacity and serve twice as many customers for a fraction of the cost of duplicating its entire plant and equipment. A general rule of thumb for a single entity of this type is that capacity increases as the square of the cost. This is because most of the necessary hardware is already in place." Nelson paced across the front of the room and went on.

"This fact has been known for many years, but sometimes our legislators forget it. Years ago, the local decision-makers realized Amherst was growing, and needed more water service. They passed a law decreeing that there had to be a second choice for water service in this town, and solicited sealed bids. They chose the company that offered the town the most for the privilege of competing in the water-supply business."

"They didn't dig up the streets and put in duplicate water mains!" Henry said reflexively.

"That's exactly what they did," Nelson said with a laugh. "Care to guess what happened?" No one answered. "Mister...Bowman, is it?" Henry licked his lips and took a stab at the question.

"The existing company cut their prices, maybe even to where they were losing money, and they drove the new guys out of business." Nelson smiled as he nodded in agreement.

"Then what?" the professor asked.

"Well, ah...I guess after the new company went bust, the old one was able to buy up their hardware—you know, the pipes and all—for a few cents on the dollar, and ended up in an even stronger position than before."

"Right. And on top of that," Nelson added, "the town subsidized the construction. It was a hundred years ago, and they're still paying off the debt incurred by that fiasco. Can anyone tell me what was the one smart thing the town council did in making this law?" He saw Henry grinning. "Mister Bowman, you look like you may have a suggestion."

"They were really smart to decide that there should be two water companies competing for everyone's business, and not ten."

March 20, 1974

James Nelson stared down at the term paper in his hand. He wished he'd known about it earlier. It would have made a good senior thesis, not just a mid-term paper.

The assignment had been to identify and discuss a case where government intervention had introduced a noticeable distortion into the economy. Most students chose tobacco price supports, the tax-deductible aspects of drilling for oil, or some other well-travelled area of government regulation with which James Nelson was intimately familiar and which had much in common with many other laws. Henry Bowman, by contrast, had selected a law Nelson had never heard of.

Bowman had also claimed in the very first sentence that this law forced those it affected into circumstances entirely unlike those created by any other piece of government legislation. After reading his paper twice, James Nelson believed him.

Nelson decided to do two things that were very unusual for him. The first was that he did not make a single mark on the entire paper, but instead put all of his comments on a separate sheet.

The second thing was that he gave the paper a grade of A+.

PROHIBITION'S UGLY LEGACY

Three-Tier Legal Status and
Three-Tier Pricing Caused by the
National Firearms Act Of 1934
as Amended by the Gun Control Act of 1968

by

Henry F. Bowman

Professor Nelson
Econ. 20
March 12, 1974

March 20, 1974

INTRODUCTION

A year after the 1933 repeal of Prohibition, Congress passed the National Firearms Act of 1934 and created a situation that was (and is) both unique and bizarre. The situation is unique because no other consumer good or manufactured product in the entire country is treated under the law in the same way that NFA firearms are treated. The situation is bizarre because under this law, two absolutely identical guns, consecutively produced within one minute of each other by the same manufacturer on the same assembly line, can fall into such drastically different legal categories that possession of one has the government's blessing, while possession of the other (even by the same person) merits a ten-year prison sentence. As if this were not unusual enough, a 1968 amendment to the National Firearms Act now prohibits the owner of the "bad" weapon (whichever of the two guns it may be) from placing himself in compliance with federal law.

The National Firearms Act introduced a huge distortion into the free market for all guns which fell under its scope. The result is a three-tier pricing schedule in the market for firearms regulated by this obscure section of the U.S. Code, as well as several legal questions which, to date, have not yet been resolved.

This paper addresses a distortion in the free market caused by government intervention. It is not intended to be a political science treatise. However, in order to fully understand this distortion and "how we got here", some history is in order. This is an unfamiliar area to most people, and it is quite possible that without a thorough explanation of the history behind current law, the average person would refuse to believe our present situation.

HISTORY

The issue of owning militia-type arms to protect oneself and one's freedoms was not controversial in the early days of our country's history. It was taken for granted. All citizens of this country had this basic right. Prior to 1934, there were no federal laws regulating firearms ownership[1], and prior to 1865, there were virtually no such state laws, either. All prohibitions (and attendant punishment) focused on violent criminal actions and not possession of inanimate objects.

---

1. There was a law enacted in 1920 which prohibited sending handguns through the mail except by law enforcement entities, and required that a common carrier be used instead.

Two events changed this situation on a state level: The Emancipation Proclamation, and large-scale immigration. Many lawmakers did not like the idea of foreigners and former slaves having the same rights as whites. They especially disliked the idea of these "undesirables" being able to protect themselves and control their own destinies.

Legislators didn't want blacks being able to defend their freedoms, either at the voting booth, or by having guns. Because the Second Amendment guaranteed the right to keep and bear arms, and the Fourteenth Amendment guaranteed equal protection under the law, legislative creativity was required.

Poll taxes and literacy tests solved the problem of blacks voting. Blocking Constitutionally-protected black possession of inanimate objects required a slightly different strategy. One solution to the dilemma was to require permits to possess or to carry arms[2]. These permits could then be arbitrarily denied. Another answer was for a state to enact an outright prohibition on carrying weapons for self-protection[3]. These outright prohibitions were then selectively enforced. The South Carolina legislature, perhaps pleased with the success of their poll tax, passed a law in 1875 prohibiting ownership of all firearms other than those manufactured by Colt or Winchester[4]. Since these makes were much more expensive than all others, this law was a novel way to prevent poor people of all races from having guns.

Immigrants got similar treatment. In complete defiance of the U.S. Constitution, California state law prohibited Chinese from testifying against whites in any court of law for a 20-year period in the late 1800s[5]. In New York, discussion urging the passage of the 1907 Sullivan Law made mention of how that law would make it illegal for "swarthy immigrants" to have guns[6]. Texas gun restrictions subjugated Americans

---

2.   Laws of this nature were passed in many states at one time or another. Notable exceptions were Vermont and New Hampshire.

3.   Many states, including my native Missouri, have such outright prohibitions. Such statutes rely on vague wording, such as Missouri's prohibition on carrying a weapon for protection into any "church, school, or any other assembly of persons met for any lawful purpose." (emphasis added) This last item allows police to arrest blacks and ignore whites.

4.   I have not found the actual text of this law, but there are many references to it in several publications.

5.   Stanford Lyman, <u>Chinese Americans</u> (New York: Random House, 1974) p.71

6.   This phrase became a buzzword with many politicians who wanted to expand their political power, and is found in numerous texts.

of Mexican origin[7] .

All these laws, however, were passed on a state level. It was not until 1934 that any federal law was enacted which affected firearms possession. There is some disagreement about the impetus behind this law, as will soon be discussed.

THE NATIONAL FIREARMS ACT OF 1934

The first significant federal gun law was passed in June of 1934 with minimal fanfare. It attracted little attention because it only affected a small number of arms: Full-automatic weapons (machine guns), rifles and shotguns with barrels shorter than eighteen inches (amended to sixteen inches for rifles in 1958), and rifles and shotguns with overall lengths less than twenty-six inches. These arms now fell under federal regulation. In addition, any device designed or redesigned to muffle the report of a firearm (a "silencer") also fell under the scope of the National Firearms Act[8] , despite the fact that these devices were not and are not in any way, shape, or form, "firearms".

Because of the Second Amendment, Congress realized it did not have the authority to ban these arms. Instead, the bill was slipped in as a revenue-raising measure under the Interstate Commerce Clause. Under the National Firearms Act, no person may transport, deliver, or sell in interstate commerce any firearm or silencer as described above without first having in his possession a stamp-affixed form for the firearm. The tax stamp must first be bought so that it can be affixed to the federal form when it is approved. For the form to be approved, the applicant must be fingerprinted, signed off by the local police chief, and submit to an FBI records check. The "stamp" referred to in the law costs $200. The owner of an NFA-regulated weapon must have this approved form (with the $200 stamp affixed) in his possession before the arm (or silencer) in question may be transported in interstate commerce. This $200 tax must be paid <u>each time</u> the NFA-regulated item changes ownership.

Because of the size of the tax, the frequency with which it must be

---

7.   Many people have serious misconceptions of Texas law, and think of that state as one where everyone carries guns legally. Nothing could be further from the truth. There is no provision in Texas law to carry a weapon for protection outside your home or automobile. Those who do are relying on the crony system to save them.

8.   NFA of 1934, Section 11.

paid, and the method by which it is levied, the National Firearms Act bears a strong resemblance to the Stamp Act of 1765[9] .

Being fingerprinted and forced to submit to an FBI investigation is unusual, to say the least, for a revenue-raising measure. To put this "revenue raising" tax in perspective, in 1934, $200 was more than a month's wages for a worker building Model "A"s on the Ford assembly line in Dearborn, Michigan[10] . In the '20s, silencers sold for $2 in hardware stores and Thompson submachine guns could be bought out of the Sears catalog for $125. The idea that levying a $200 tax on these manufactured goods would actually raise revenue is absurd. The demand for each of the items covered by the National Firearms Act was elastic enough that virtually no one was willing to pay the government an additional $200 for any of them. According to Treasury Department records, there was not a single tax-paid registration in 1934[11] , and there was one in 1935[12] .

Another consequence of the Act was that new development of machine guns by individual inventors stopped overnight. Given that the vast majority of full-auto weapons now in use were designed by private individuals, this is a serious issue. The U.S.'s foremost authority on machine guns, Lt. Col. George M. Chinn, has frequently described the Act a devastating blow to American security in that it has crippled all future military small arms development in this country and will continue to do so until it is repealed[13] .

After passage of the Act, there were only three classes of people who continued to buy these goods: Large companies bought the weapons for

---

9.   On March 22, 1765, Parliament levied a tax on the Colonists' newspapers and legal and commercial documents, all of which had to carry a special stamp. The Colonists formed the first intercolonial Congress which met in October of that year to declare American rights and grievances, specifically concerning the Stamp Act. Parliament rescinded the Stamp Act in March of 1766, but coupled this recission with passage of the Declaratory Act, claiming England's supremacy over America "in all cases whatsoever". The Colonists rights and their insistence on maintaining them became the basis for the American Revolution.

10. About $5 a day, according to a conversation with Arthur Wilkes, who was an assemblyline worker during that period.

11. New York Times, Dec. 25, 1934.

12. New York Times, Nov. 6, 1936.

13. Given that the most reliable U.S. designs now in use (1919A4, 1917A1, ANM2, MG52A, M2HB, BAR, M14, M1A1) were all developed by private citizens, and the guns with major flaws (M60) were designed by companies, Chinn's comment cannot be disregarded.

strike control and other labor relations purposes[14] . Police departments, the military, and special occupational taxpayers[15] continued to buy, for they were exempt from the tax. Violent criminals continued to buy these weapons outside of legal channels, just as they had obtained liquor during Prohibition.

This reality brings us to the next issue concerning this obscure federal law.

REASONS FOR THE PASSAGE OF THE NATIONAL FIREARMS ACT

In almost every published description of the National Firearms Act of 1934 is a mention of the 1929 "St. Valentine's Day Massacre"[16] , and a statement to the effect that the Act was passed because machine guns were being used with horrible results by bootleggers and other organized crime figures. There are several things wrong with this claim.

First, it is laughable to hope that people for whom murder is a standard business practice will go present themselves to the local police chief to get fingerprinted, and pay $200 for the privilege. Similarly, it is ludicrous to think that putting legal restrictions on firearms will reduce their availability to those people whose entire livelihood involves finding, buying, transporting, selling, and delivering illegal goods.

Second, the highly publicized incidents of underworld gangs machine-gunning each other over liquor shipments stopped overnight with the repeal of Prohibition, which occurred a full year before passage of the National Firearms Act.

Third, the Act also affects weapons other than machine guns; rifles and shotguns with barrels or overall lengths below a certain minimum are regulated by the NFA. It is very difficult to conceive of a reason why the owner of a shotgun with a barrel 17 1/2" long should be charged with a felony if he refuses to be fingerprinted and pay $200, when owning a shotgun with a barrel a half-inch longer is no crime at all. To compound this utter absence of logic, under the National Firearms Act a person becomes a felon if he affixes a piece of wood to the butt of his pistol

---

14. "You could not run a coal company without machine guns" is a quote widely ascribed to industrialist Richard B. Mellon. Other large companies with union problems (auto manufacturers, for example)also purchased machine guns.

15. Special Occupational Taxpayers are those who pay an annual licensing fee to actively deal in NFA-regulated items.

(doubling the weapon's physical size), for he is now in possession of a "short-barreled rifle", which is covered by the Act.

To make the final leap from the illogical to the ridiculous, the Act regulates noise mufflers, which are not firearms at all. Hollywood to the contrary, the FBI has been unable to document a _single_ case of a firearm silencer being used in a crime in the last fifty years[17] . Given that citizens fire upwards of six _billion_ rounds of ammunition per year[18] , the inclusion of silencers into the NFA is one of the greatest contributors to hearing loss in the United States and therefore must rank as one of the largest public health blunders of this century[19] .

The real reason for the passage of the National Firearms Act can be summed up in four words: Expansion of federal powers. In 1934, two major changes had recently occurred in the United States. The first was that Franklin Roosevelt had initiated an exponential increase in the size and power of the federal government. The second change was the ratification of the Twenty-first Amendment, which repealed Prohibition. Let us examine the latter incident first.

In the thirteen years that Prohibition had been in effect, there was a great proliferation of people involved in the illicit manufacture, importation, and distribution of alcohol. This in turn produced a tremendous expansion of the Treasury Department and the number of its

---

16. Al Capone, irritated at having fifteen of his men killed in three months by 'Bugs' Moran's North-Side gang, arranged a trap. On his orders, a truckload of stolen whiskey was offered to the North-Siders at an attractive price, with another truckload to follow if Moran was sat- isfied. He was, and the second truck was sent to a trucking warehouse owned by Moran. As this second delivery was being made, a car appearing to be a Chicago Police vehicle pulled up. The "officers" lined Moran's gang up against a wall, and the North-Siders assumed it was time to pay off the policemen. Instead, the men dressed as officers (but working for Capone) killed all seven of them, using two Thompson Submachine Guns. The date was February 14, 1929.

17. Pillows and blankets have been used, because they more completely eliminate the noise. Knives are also very commonly used as murder weapons.

18. Spokesmen for Olin-Mathieson and Remington-Peters state that these two companies produce over two billion rounds each for domestic consump- tion. With other companies and imports added in, the actual total is much higher.

19. Many European rifle ranges mandate the use of silencers for this reason.

agents[20] . With repeal, liquor distribution was done by legitimate businessmen, and thousands of Treasury agents were idled. Federal legislation levying $200 taxes on goods worth between $3 and $100 was guaranteed to promote non-compliance by the citizens, thereby giving former Prohibition agents something to enforce.

It is interesting to note that the original draft of the National Firearms Act included all handguns then in existence in the United States. Because of the handgun language, some of the strongest opposition to the original version of the National Firearms Act came from women, who were vulnerable to attack from stronger assailants and got the greatest benefit from being able to carry a small weapon for personal protection.

The number of pistols and revolvers in the U.S. in 1934 has been variously estimated at between thirty and one hundred million[21] . Compare this figure with perhaps one million machine guns and short-barreled long guns that fell under the Treasury's jurisdiction in the National Firearms Act's final form[22] . One can only guess at what would have happened if in 1934 the government had told every citizen to cough up $200 for each handgun he owned that he might some day want to take or ship across state lines.

The removal of handguns from the National Firearms Act may explain the odd inclusion of silencers in the legislation. In the first third of this century, silencers were commonly available in any store where firearms were sold. The term "silencer" is in fact a misnomer. It was a trade name coined by Hiram P. Maxim, an automotive engineer who applied the principles of muffler design to safety valves, compressors, blowers, and firearms[23] . A "silencer" does not make a firearm noiseless, any

---

20. The actual increase in the number of agents is unknown. The Treasury's budget for this type of work in 1932, however, was over ten times what it had been in 1918.

21. Domestic production of handguns in 1928 exceeded 5 million units. Given that firearms almost never wear out, the 100 million figure may actually be low.

22. This number takes known domestic sales and assumes that, on average, one out of every three soldiers returning from WWI brought back one machine gun. If the discussions I have had with WWI vets are typical, the 1 million figure is low.

23. Hiram Percy Maxim was the son of Hiram Stevens Maxim, who invented the first practical machine gun in 1884. No evidence has been found to indicate that the National Firearms Act was intended to single out the inventions of the Maxim family. It just ended up that way.

more than the muffler on a diesel truck exhaust conceals the fact that the truck is approaching[24] . With the 1934 Act making it a felony to transport common noise mufflers in interstate commerce without paying $200 (each!) to the government, millions of citizens were now in violation of federal law.

Although the National Firearms Act stipulated a grace period where owners could register these weapons and silencers free of charge, the Treasury reported that a grand total of 15,791 registrations occurred in this period[25] . This indicates approximately 1% compliance. The 1934 Act was thus a huge success at turning millions of citizens into criminals.

The National Firearms Act fit in perfectly with the systematic creation of government programs and deficit spending that Franklin Roosevelt immediately began to institute the instant he took office. The NFA was a model vehicle for the continued expansion of government power: It was arbitrary (i.e. the 18-inch rule); it gave the government sweeping authority over something very common; it focused on inanimate objects rather than criminal behavior; it levied draconian taxes on these objects; and most importantly, it created millions of criminals with the stroke of a pen, just as Prohibition had.

A clear example of the fact that the National Firearms Act had nothing to do with crime and everything to do with government power occurred immediately prior to its passage. Senator Hatton Sumners of Texas, the Chairman of the House Judiciary Committee, had been a virulent opponent of the proposed bill and had bottled it up because it "did violence to states' rights"[26] . On April 23, 1934, Roosevelt called Sumners into the White House for a chat. Sumners agreed to vote for passage[27] .

---

24. Noise reducers for firearms are less effective than those for engines for two reasons: first, gas pressure in a gun barrel is much higher than exhaust pressure in a tailpipe. Second, a design for a gun must include a straight, open path from the gun's muzzle to the exit end of the silencer to permit passage of the bullet. A muffler for an engine may employ all manner of reversing baffles, diffusing screens, and serpentine pathways to redirect exhaust gases that don't contain chunks of lead traveling at supersonic speeds.

25. New York Times, December 25, 1934.

26. William J. Helmer, The Gun That Made the Twenties Roar (London: MacMillan & Co., 1969) p.125

27. New York Times, April 24, 1934

ENFORCEMENT OF THE NATIONAL FIREARMS ACT PRIOR TO 1968

After the NFA was passed, sales of affected items came to an abrupt halt. Domestic firearms manufacturers stopped producing any long guns with barrels shorter than 18". They also quit making any pistols with lugs on the butt for shoulder stocks. Manufacturers of noise reducers (most notably the Maxim Silencer Co.) went out of business entirely.

After the short grace period, citizens who owned NFA-regulated items on which the tax had not been paid had several choices. The first was to pay $200 to the Treasury for each item. In 1934, no one did this. The second choice was to relinquish NFA-regulated items to the Treasury without any compensation. No one did this, either. The third option, theoretically at least, was to avoid selling or transporting anything covered under the Act outside the state. The fourth was to disassemble the machine gun, short-barreled long gun, or silencer so that it was inoperable, and keep the parts separate. In the case of short-barreled arms, the owner could also replace the barrel with one of 18" or longer, and have a legal, functional gun again without paying $200.

Short-barreled rifles and shotguns were produced in low numbers in the years prior to 1934[28] but the same could not be said for machine guns. The Colt-manufactured Thompson, BAR, and belt-fed Brownings had all been produced in large numbers and had been available on the civilian market for over a decade. Furthermore, two million American soldiers had been sent to Europe in WWI, and over half of these had served in combat units. These veterans brought home many "war trophies", as they are called, with complete legality[29]. Machine guns were a relatively new and interesting battlefield weapon in 1918[30], and captured examples were brought home by most soldiers. A conservative estimate of the full-automatic WWI weapons brought into the United States by the returning two million veterans is one million[31]. Other knowledgeable sources place the

---

28. Ithaca Gun Company produced the "Auto and Burglar" gun and Harrington & Richardson made the "Handi-gun" in modest numbers. Both are now collector's items.

29. Bringing home U.S. ordnance is technically theft of government property, but at the end of a war it is typical for a U.S. soldier to keep the weapon he carried in combat without comment from the authorities. Arms captured from the enemy have always (prior to 1968) been acceptable for U.S. soldiers to bring home.

30. WWI was the first major war fought with them.

31. Thomas J. Fleming, in a phone conversation 8/27/70

figure at over twice that[32].

The Treasury Department decreed that owners of these weapons could either register them for $200, or remove critical parts (such as the bolt) from them, which would render them inoperable. In this latter case, the gun was no longer considered a weapon subject to registration and $200 tax, but rather a "DEWAT", which was the Treasury's acronym (sort of) for Deactivated War Trophy.

When agents encountered an otherwise law-abiding citizen with a non-taxed machine gun in his possession, standard procedure was to give him the choice of paying the $200 tax and registering it "live", or removing the bolt and/or other internal parts.

As years passed, the economy improved, wages and prices went up, and the U.S. fought in two more wars. A few million more veterans returned home from WWII and Korea with a few million more war trophies. By the '50s and '60s, some citizens actually were paying $200 and getting tax stamps from the Treasury Department on weapons brought back from WWI, WWII, and Korea, and on newly-purchased machine guns from the many manufacturers around the world.

THE GUN CONTROL ACT OF 1968

In 1968, the National Firearms Act was amended by the Gun Control Act of 1968. This 1968 law enacted sweeping infringements on citizens' rights to purchase and own virtually all types of guns. In also introduced a "sporting use" test on importation of firearms and ammunition. If certain guns or ammunition were determined by the Director of the Treasury to be not suitable for "sporting use", importation of them was prohibited. The fact that the Bill of Rights concerns the preservation of freedom and not recreation is ignored in the 1968 Act. A 1939 Supreme Court decision ruling that military weapons are Constitutionally protected whereas sporting arms are not[33] was ignored also.

GCA '68 also contained language which modified the treatment under the law of NFA-regulated weapons. Since these provisions did not immediately affect nearly as many people as the rest of the new legislation, their significance was not fully understood at the time.

---

32. Lt. Colonel George M. Chinn, author of the now-declassified 2000-page work The Machine Gun for the Department of the Navy, in a phone conversation 8/30/70

33. U.S. vs. Miller, United States Supreme Court, May 15, 1939

Under the new provisions, all existing machine guns in the hands of U.S. citizens had to be registered with the NFA immediately, including DEWATS. A one-month Amnesty was instituted where the $200-per-gun NFA tax was waived. After this amnesty ended, however, registration of existing non-taxed machine guns was prohibited. Registration of machine guns manufactured in the U.S. after passage of these provisions posed serious problems for citizens and created legal questions that have not to this day been addressed.

First of all, among the millions of owners of live machine guns and DEWATS, not everyone even knew about the one-month amnesty before it was over. Second, of those who were aware of the one-month grace period, there was a tremendous fear that the entire amnesty was a trap and the guns presented for registration would be confiscated. For this reason, only a tiny fraction of machine guns and DEWATS were submitted for NFA registration during the Amnesty[34].

The 1968 amendments to the National Firearms Act and the one-time Amnesty completely ignored the fact that the Act only applies to those weapons transported in interstate commerce. The 1934 Act does not apply to a machine gun owner who never takes his gun out of state. The 1968 amendments have placed such owners in the position where they cannot now comply with the law. An owner of a machine gun on which the tax has not been paid is prohibited by the 1968 amendments from paying the tax and putting the weapon on the NFA registry. This has created a situation not duplicated anywhere else in the entire U.S. Code.

As an example of how this law introduces a severe distortion into both the economy and the lives of U.S. citizens, let us look at an example: A coal company heir owns a consecutive numbered pair of Model 1921 Thompson guns, serial numbers 1410 and 1411, which have been in his family in the same location since the mid-1920s. In 1965 (but this could be any year between 1934 and 1968), thinking he might someday want to take one of the guns outside the state, he pays $200 and registers one of them (either one) under NFA 1934. Just to be safe, he removes the bolt from the other, rendering it inoperable. Prior to GCA 1968, he was in complete compliance with the law.

Today, the taxed gun is completely transferable to other citizens, and the gun can change hands an indefinite number of times, providing

34. Many of the people I have spoken to who had a significant number (20 or more) of non-taxed NFA weapons and DEWATs decided to Amnesty-register two or three guns, hedging their bets in case of confiscation.

police and FBI checks are performed and $200 is paid to the Treasury for a tax stamp _each time_ the weapon is transferred.

Ownership of the _non_-taxed gun (the one without the bolt) is a felony[35], and there is _no_ provision in the law to allow the owner to place this weapon on the NFA registry. He can offer to pay two _million_ dollars instead of two hundred, and he will still be denied registration. Under present interpretations of the 1968 amendments, the 1921 Thompson without the bolt is contraband and it must be surrendered to BATF without any compensation. A Model 1921 Thompson is worth between $1500 and $2000 at the time of this writing if it is transferable[36].

There is another serious problem caused by the 1968 amendments to the 1934 Act. The "sporting test" section of the 1968 Act prohibits importation of non-sporting weapons and ammunition into the U.S. This includes importation of _U.S.-made_ weapons produced before 1968 but which were outside the country at the time GCA 1968 was passed. The exemption for this import ban is for military and law enforcement-related sales. Thus, a 1921 Thompson gun currently in England (there are thousands there) may only be imported into the United States by an agency of the U.S. Government, a police department, or a special occupational taxpayer who may then sell it only to one of these two types of purchasers.

THREE-TIER LEGAL STATUS AND PRICING

The example listed above makes it clear that government regulation has created three-tier status for identical manufactured goods. Machine guns made in the United States can fall into three categories: a) Fully transferable to any law-abiding resident[37] upon federal approval after FBI investigation and payment of $200 to the Treasury; b) Transferable (tax-exempt) to Special Occupational Taxpayers, police, or government agencies; and c) contraband weapons which may not be made legal.

These three different legal categories result in three different prices for otherwise identical guns. To continue the Thompson example, a transferable, mint-condition 1921 Thompson now brings approximately $1800 on the U.S. collector market[38] . An identical gun recently imported from

---

35. As the law is now being interpreted. The case mentioned before where the gun has never crossed state lines has not yet been tested in court.

36. From current price lists from six Special Occupational Taxpayers licensed to deal in these type of weapons.

37. Individual state laws may prohibit ownership.

England and sitting in a customs bonded warehouse will bring at most $150, for it can only be sold to police and government agencies, and these entities are not willing to pay much for obsolete, fifty-year-old weapons. What the third gun is worth is anyone's guess, for the only buyers for it will be those willing to risk a felony conviction[39] .

FUTURE OF THE NATIONAL FIREARMS ACT

The Gun Control Act of 1968, with its amendments to the National Firearms Act of 1934, is a recent continuation of the trend started during the Roosevelt Administration towards more government and less freedom. Recent and current Administrations show no sign of reversing this trend. When freedom is at odds with government policy, one of two things eventually happens: Either freedom is crushed, or political leaders are forced out in disgrace and replaced with guardians of individual liberty.

CONCLUSION

The National Firearms Act of 1934 is a bad law. Colonel Chinn has said on many occasions that the 1934 Act is the single most devastating piece of legislation to this nation's defense ever enacted.

From an economic viewpoint, the NFA of 1934 is a bad law because its tax is so high that it stops enterprise cold and distorts the free market. NFA 1934 is a bad law because it raises virtually no revenue at all, when a $5 tax and relaxed regulations might easily raise millions of dollars for the Treasury Department.

The 1968 amendments to the 1934 Act are bad law because these amendments actually prohibit those people who want to pay the tax on their guns from doing so. These 1968 amendments have made criminals out of people with no criminal intent, and give these citizens no option other than to surrender their property without compensation. These are the kinds of laws which led to the American Revolution. The National Firearms Act of 1934 should be repealed in its entirety.

---

38. Average of several advertised in dealer publications. Examples with a documented history (i.e. a weapon owned and used by "Pretty Boy" Floyd) command a premium.

39. Police and dealers I questioned were uneasy about estimating the "street value" of a non-taxed Thompson Submachine Gun. The only dealer who was willing to say anything at all suggested "Couple hundred bucks, tops" as an estimate.

May 28, 1974

Damn! Ray Johnson thought as the sound of his client's .375 H&H rang out and he watched a piece of hide fly off the cape buffalo's left foreleg. *How could he miss at ten yards?*

The man lowered the rifle to port arms and stared openmouthed at the 1700-pound animal he had just wounded and consequently made very, very angry. He made no effort to work the bolt and chamber another round.

"Shoot! Shoot, damn it!" Ray screamed at his client, who stood frozen, fifteen feet to the side of the professional hunter.

The buffalo instantly lowered its head, turned towards the cause of his irritation, and charged. The man then did something Ray Johnson had never seen anyone do before. Al Holbrecht turned in panic, dropped his rifle, and ran.

Ray Johnson was so stunned at his client's action that he was half a second slow getting the front sight of his .458 Model 70 on the enraged bull, even though the butt of his rifle was already on his shoulder. The buffalo was passing right-to-left in front of Raymond's muzzle. The Winchester thundered, and even as he slapped the bolt rearward, Ray knew that by the time he got off a second shot, the adrenaline-filled animal would have overtaken his panicked customer.

As Ray simultaneously hauled the rifle down out of recoil with his left hand and slammed the bolt forward with his right, he saw with amazement that the bull was down, five or six feet past where he had been when Ray pulled the trigger. He was not dead, but his hindquarters were all that would function. Both of the buffalo's shoulders were obviously shattered.

Ray put his second shot through the animal's heart and lowered his rifle. He glanced to his left, and saw that the steel company president was still running. *Hope he stops pretty soon* Raymond thought with a shake of his head. *There's a ravine in that direction, less than a mile and a half away.*

"Good shot," his lead tracker said simply as he jogged over to inspect the dead beast.

"Yeah."

It was the first time Ray Johnson had used Henry Bowman's ammo to stop a charge. It would not be the last.

***

"Richard Wescott Gaines," the valedictorian announced, and Richard stepped to the podium and took the proffered diploma. A cheer rose from a group of friends seated in folding chairs on the University lawn.

"Man, he's got it knocked," one of them said in admiration.

"What do you mean? I thought his grades sucked. Like almost flunking out."

"You didn't hear?" the first asked in surprise. "Some congressman where he lives got him a spot. His GPA doesn't matter."

"A job?"

"No. A state...not a state Senator, what's the other one? A state representative." He laughed. "Get *this:* He only has to go in four days a week from January to May, and he doesn't actually have to do anything except sit around and listen. Not even that, really. Just vote sometimes on stuff. And for five months he's getting paid more'n I'm going to get in a whole year at Monsanto."

"Shit, how do *I* get a job like that?"

"Beats me. Blow somebody, I guess." The two young men stopped discussing Richard Gaines' future when they saw that another of their friends was about to have his name called.

In point of fact, Richard Gaines did not yet actually have the state rep position his friends referred to, as the election was not until November. When that time came, however, Congressman Sloan would indeed make good on his promise, and Richard Gaines would represent a district in South St. Louis.

The rest of the young man's description of Gaines' future was reasonably accurate, although his estimate of the monetary benefits was on the low side.

***

"Well, I'm going to head back to the hotel until it's time for dinner," Catherine Bowman told her son. "Are there any of your friends that can join us, or do all of them have plans with their parents?" Henry's mother liked being able to include her son's friends when they were available.

"Marty's parents have to go do something or other that he wants to avoid like the plague. Let me find him and see if he wants to use us as an excuse to beg off on whatever they've got plotted. I think Jeff's free, too." He looked around the quadrangle at his black-robed classmates, trying to spot either or both of his friends. A number of the graduating seniors had shucked their commencement robes and were sporting purple shirts emblazoned with the slogan 'Rite is Okay', to show that they weren't ashamed for graduating without writing an honors thesis.

"Well, you go carouse with your friends for a while and then give me a call at the hotel and tell me how many, so I can phone in the reservations." Henry smiled at his mother's turn of phrase.

"If you're out, I'll leave word at the front desk," he promised.

"Oh, and I lugged this up here for you. It just came to the house, and I thought it might be important." Henry's mother opened her purse and withdrew a letter-sized envelope, and Henry smiled at the idea of her 'lugging' it up to Massachusetts for him. When he saw the return address and the absence of postage, his pulse quickened.

Department of the Treasury
Bureau of Alcohol, Tobacco and Firearms
NFA Branch
Washington, DC 20226

"My Class Three license!" he exclaimed as he tore open the envelope.

"Thought it might be important," Catherine Bowman commented, deadpan.

Henry scanned the enclosed sheet and saw that they had cashed his check and his status as a Special Occupational Taxpayer would be effective July 1, the first day of the fiscal year that had been created with the passage of the National Firearms Act in June of 1934.

"*Yessss,*" he said under his breath as he reread the document.

"First time anyone in *our* family was excited about mail from the government," his mother said drily. "See you around seven," she said as she kissed him goodbye.

Henry Bowman had just graduated with a BA in both geology and economics, and he had three firm job offers. The one he expected to accept was with an independent firm outside St. Louis that did a lot of contract work for the oil companies and whose president had complained that his geologists "still didn't understand that they've been hired to help the firm make money, not to look for fossilized Indians or some damn thing."

At that moment, however, Henry Bowman was not thinking about geology or economics. He was contemplating the fact that he had just been licensed by the feds to deal in machine guns.

December 18, 1974

Henry Bowman was not thinking about guns or shooting as he tossed the bulk rate envelopes in the trash and divided his first-class mail into 'bills' and 'everything else'. He was reviewing in his mind if there was anyone on his Christmas list he had neglected when his telephone rang.

"Hello."

"Henry! It's Ed. Glad I caught you. Have you seen the latest Shotgun News?"

Ed Barber was referring to a publication that came out twice a month. It was 96 pages of newsprint, published in Hastings, Nebraska, which was composed entirely of classified and display ads for firearms and firearms-related products.

"It's here, but I haven't looked at it yet."

"Well, you better go get it. Some guy's got a 4-bore for sale."

"What?" Henry almost screamed.

"I think he's a dealer. It's in the classified section, under 'Rifles For Sale'. I don't have my copy in front of me, but it's a Rodda. The ad said both barrels were fully rifled, and the gun weighed twenty-four pounds."

"I'll call you back," Henry said quickly and hung up the phone.

It took him four minutes to find his the most recent copy of Shotgun News, turn to the Rifles For Sale section, and locate the one-inch ad.

> R.B. RODDA 4-Bore Double Rifle. 24-pound back-action underlever hammer gun built in 1880-1882. Brown Damascus barrels, fully rifled, mint bores. Beautiful engraving (elephants, rhinos, lion), original case. Some loading tools (not original). Serious inquiries only, no collect calls. Jim, (603) 217-5543 after 6:00 P.M. EST.   1-75

Henry stared at the ad and looked at the date at the top of the page. *Damn, I hope this issue hasn't been out long.* He was kicking himself for not skimming through it as soon as it had arrived in his mailbox. The Rodda was the only 4-bore he had ever seen advertised in the *Shotgun News.*

"Hello?" the man answered on the fourth ring.

"Ah, yessir, I'm calling about the ad you ran in *Shotgun News* about a Rodda double rifle for sale? Do you still have it, or has it been sold?"

"Well, fellow said he wanted it for sure, but didn't have the money yet. Told him I'd give him 'til noon on Friday."

"I see," Henry said. *The day after tomorrow.* "What can you tell me about the gun?"

"Well, it's a full-weight four. Back-action underlever hammer gun, dual triggers of course. Twenty-four pounds empty, with twenty-four-inch barrels. Bores are mint. Extractor gun, no ejectors of course. Outside of the barrels, there's a few pits, but the gun's ninety-plus percent original finish. Action's tight—you can't pull the barrels off the face. Splinter forend, but on a four it's a pretty big splinter," the man said with a laugh. "Dark wood, nice straight grain, no figure to speak of. Got a small repair in the grip just back of the tang, but you have to look real close—it was done right, and looks as if it's been that way for a long while. Cheekpiece for a right-handed shooter. Pad's been replaced, but I don't know how long ago. Case is original, and has a bunch of real old steamship stickers on it, so the gun's been used in either Africa or India, or both. Leather straps are missing. Got one lathe-turned brass case, some fiber wads, and a bullet mold somebody made up for it a few years ago. Big 2000-grain conical job."

"What's the length of pull?"

"I'd have to measure, and it's down in the safe, but the stock hasn't been shortened or lengthened or anything, if that's what you mean."

"Have you shot it?" Henry asked.

"Not with full loads," the man admitted. "I fired a few rounds with a hundred grains of double-F. Didn't kick as bad as I thought."

No shit Henry said to himself. *The correct load's between 380 and 440 grains of powder, depending on what the gun was regulated for.* He took a breath and asked the question.

"What's the price?"

"It's the best gun I've ever owned," the man on the other end of the line said with a sigh. It was a comment that sellers used as a matter of course, but in this case Henry knew the man was speaking the truth. Henry Bowman felt that the only finer weapon in existence would have to be another 4-bore. "I wanted eight thousand five hundred for it," the seller continued. "This one fellow made me a firm offer of eight thousand, and I'm giving him until noon on Friday to get me the money. If he doesn't, and you want it for eight, it's yours."

Henry swallowed. "Okay," he said, after just a moment's hesitation. "But I have to have a one-day inspection. I don't doubt your description—it sounds as if you're very thorough. But I intend to shoot this gun, and if the stock doesn't fit me, I can't take it. I'll call you within an hour after I get the gun to tell you if I'm keeping it, and I'll pay shipping both ways if I send it back."

"Sounds fair to me. Three-day inspection's normal."

"I won't need near that long. What's your full name and mailing address, and are there any other phone numbers I should have to reach you at noon on Friday?" The man on the other end of the line gave him the information. "I'll call you at exactly noon," Henry promised, and hung up.

Now I've got to wait until Friday he thought.

December 20, 1974

"Bureau of Standards."

"Yes sir. I know you're not the bank, but I've got to set a clock to the exact time, within a second or two is good enough, and I can't get your radio signal here," Henry said into the phone. "Can you help me out?"

"What time zone?"

"Central."

"It's seventeen after ten, and about forty seconds. Hang with me, and I'll give you when it hits eighteen after."

"Thanks. I'll wait." Henry had stopped his watch with the second hand on the twelve before he made the call. Now he adjusted the minute hand to show eighteen after ten, and prepared to push in the stem to restart the timepiece.

"Riiiight—*now.*"

"Got it. Thanks a lot." Henry broke the connection.

***

"Shut that fuckin' kid up!" Boone Caswell commanded. He liked to stay in bed on Sundays after a night of heavy drinking. Boone looked at the clock beside the bed.

"Six-thirty! Christ! It's too goddamn early in the morning for this shit!" He turned over in the bed but it was no use—the crying bored into his brain, making his hangover even worse. "Myra! Can't you shut her up?"

Caswell climbed out of bed naked and marched into the living room. His four-year-old daughter Cindy sat on the couch, trembling as she cried. She wanted to tell her parents that she'd just had a terrible nightmare. When she saw she had succeeded in summoning her father, she increased the volume. To Boone Caswell, it seemed as if a hot steel needle were being thrust into his brain.

"Shut the fuck up!" he bellowed, and delivered a vicious slap across Cindy's face. The blow knocked her sideways on the couch. It was the first time Boone Caswell had ever struck his daughter, and his action had the opposite of the intended result: Cindy screamed even more loudly.

Nonetheless, Boone Caswell was smiling when he returned to his bedroom.

***

At five seconds past eleven local time Henry Bowman made the call.

"Hello."

"Good afternoon. Henry Bowman in St. Louis calling again, about the Rodda." *Please tell me it hasn't been sold.*

"Yeah...hey, I got your cashier's check this morning. Didn't know you were going to overnight it to me. Nice of you to put in an extra forty for shipping, too. Lots of folks always want the seller to pay for it."

"Did the other guy come through?" Henry asked quickly.

"Haven't heard from him." There was a pause. "Yeah, my clock says it's a couple minutes after noon."

"So it's mine?"

"'Less you change your mind when you see it."

"I mean, if this other guy shows up as soon as we hang up, and he's got eight thousand in hundred-dollar bills in his hand, it's still my gun, right?" Henry repeated. The man on the other end laughed.

"That's how I do business. I gave him 'til noon. It's past that time, his money isn't here, and yours is. You bought yourself a 4-bore double rifle, mister. Been looking for one, I take it?"

"For fifteen years," Henry said with feeling.

As it turned out, Henry Bowman had not needed to call Ft. Collins to get the exact time. The other man who had wanted the gun did not contact the owner of the big rifle to tell him he'd rounded up the money until almost 12:30, and when he did, it was over the phone and not in person. He was very upset to learn that the gun had been sold, but as a serious buyer, he played by the rules and knew that the roles could have been reversed. The seller called Henry and suggested waiting until after Christmas before dropping the package off at the UPS office.

Henry Bowman reluctantly agreed to this sensible recommendation.

December 30, 1974

Oh my God Henry thought when he lifted the lid of the 90-year-old fitted oak and leather trunk case and pushed aside the newspaper that had been used to cushion the contents. The rifle which lay inside had seen substantial use, but it had been well cared for considering it had been built for hard service. The quality of the workmanship was superb. *And the size!* Henry marveled. It was just as he remembered in the photo Al Goodman had shown him years ago. The overall length of the Rodda was no greater than his .577 Rigby, but it was much more massive.

Henry Bowman lifted the barrels out of their felt-lined compartment, swung the forend lever to the side, and removed the forend. He examined the bores. They were mint, as promised. And huge. He stuck his thumb in the muzzle of one the right barrel. It didn't even touch both sides. *They're so big I could almost...well, not quite* Henry thought.

He hung the barrels from a piece of string and rapped them with a wooden ruler. They rang like a big gong. He laid the barrels on the carpet, lifted the stocked receiver out of the case, and swung the big underlever to the side. He picked up the barrels, fitted them to the breech, and swung them shut while returning the underlever to its original position. Then he fitted the forend iron to the barrels and locked it in place with the forend lever.

He cocked the hammers and stuffed a sock in between their noses and the firing pins, then tested both triggers. They broke cleanly with no trace of creep, with a rather heavy pull, Henry was pleased to note.

Henry stood up, closed his eyes, and threw the 24-pound rifle to his shoulder with one fluid motion. When he opened his eyes, the front sight bead was resting in the V-notch of the 50-yard rear leaf. The stock would not have fit Henry any better if he had been the original owner for whom the gun was built.

He was grinning like an idiot as he carried the big rifle over to the end of the couch and picked up the telephone.

January 25, 1975

"I don't think you really need twenty-five, but I got them all done," Curt Behnke said as he let Henry Bowman in the back door of his basement workshop. "I know you're champing at the bit to go fire that monster. Matter of fact, I'd like to watch." Henry followed the gunsmith over to his cluttered workbench. Behnke reached into a box and pulled out a polished brass cartridge case, four inches long and about an inch and a quarter in diameter, which he handed to Henry.

Only a handful of makers in England had ever made 4-bore rifles, and each firm's guns used ammunition that was specific to that manufacturer. Henry had never intended to even look for the correct original ammunition for his gun. Even if it could be located, hundred-year-old ammo loaded with black powder would not likely still deliver original ballistics. If it did, it would still be too valuable to collectors to justify shooting it up.

Henry had obtained a ten-foot length of 1 3/8" round brass bar stock, and cut it in half so he could get it in Curt Behnke's basement. Behnke had used his power hacksaw and lathe to make twenty-five cases that exactly fit Henry's gun.

"Cut the primer pocket for .50 machine gun primers, like you wanted, but I think a shotgun primer'd have been plenty," Behnke opined as he went to his safe and retrieved the barrels to Henry's Rodda.

"Four hundred grains of FG black is a lot to light off," Henry replied as he dropped the oiled case into the right chamber. It fit perfectly. He extracted it and tried it in the left one with the same results.

"Near as I could tell with my inside mikes, the chambers are within a couple tenths of each other," the gunsmith said. *"When* did you say that gun was made?"

"Eighteen-eighty," Henry answered. "Little more precision work involved than on an 1873 lever action .44-40, huh?" he said with an upraised eyebrow. Behnke nodded in agreement, then moved over to his lathe.

"Here's the shell holder I made. And here's your neck sizing die, your seating punch, and your crimp die, all threaded inch-and-a-half twelve for that Hollywood press of yours. You sure it's got enough leverage?"

"It sizes my 20mm cannon brass okay," Henry pointed out.

"Oh. Right." Curt Behnke periodically seemed to forget about some of the larger guns that Henry Bowman owned and used. He himself did not own a rifle larger than .30 caliber, although that would change after his seventieth birthday, when continued exposure to Henry Bowman's enthusiasm for elephant guns would prompt Behnke to build one for himself.

Henry inspected the handmade loading tools. They were flawlessly machined. "How much do I owe you?" he asked. Behnke looked pained.

"I've got over forty hours in all this stuff. I've got to have three hundred." He did not let on, but he still thought of Henry Bowman as the ten-year-old who had first come into the basement workshop with his father in 1963.

"You take cash on Saturdays?" Henry asked as he reached into his pocket. It was an old joke.

"If that's all you got," the older man replied, deadpan.

"You busy tomorrow, Curt, or would you like to watch me break my collarbone? I'm going out to the range to see how it shoots," Henry said as he handed over the bills.

"I'll be there by eight-thirty," Behnke grinned.

January 26, 1975

"Here goes nothing," Henry Bowman said as he pulled the butt into his shoulder, tightened his grip on the forend, leaned forward, and squeezed the front trigger with his right index finger. He had placed a large, heavy wooden crate on top of the concrete shooting bench, and a cheap, loosely-rolled sleeping bag on top of the crate. The sleeping bag was in such a position that Henry could rest his left forearm on it while holding the rifle and standing straight up. It was how he shot double rifles for accuracy, for it allowed support while permitting the gun to recoil in the same way that it would when fired offhand. This was important for double rifles, for unlike single-barrel rifles, the axis of each bore on a double was to the side of the axis of recoil, not in line with it. If a double rifle were shot off sandbags, it would shoot to a different point of impact than when it was fired offhand.

The trigger broke at sixteen pounds, and the huge rifle rocked Henry's body backwards about ten degrees as a deep 'whoom' rattled the galvanized roof over the firing line. The large cloud of white smoke which had belched out of the gun's muzzle began to drift away in the wind. Henry lowered the rifle and looked at Curt Behnke.

"Not bad at all. I could shoot that load all day. Of course, it wasn't a full charge." Both men stared downrange at the fifty-yard target butt.

"No problem spotting your shots with that gun," Behnke said immediately as he hopped from one foot to the other in the cold weather. The one-inch bullet hole was very easy to see with the naked eye at the fifty-yard distance. Henry had used black spray paint, butcher paper, and a paper plate to stencil a black ring for a target. His shot was two inches outside the black at two o'clock, which put it about eight inches right of center and three inches high. He cocked the left hammer and took aim again, this time squeezing the rear trigger.

The big gun boomed again, and this shot was a mirror image of the first shot, on the left side of the target. The two holes were at the same height, spaced about fifteen inches apart.

"Hah!" Henry yelled with pleasure when he saw where his second shot had gone.

"That's good?" the benchrest gunsmith and record-holder asked dubiously. Fifteen inches apart for two shots at fifty yards was good for a bow and arrow maybe, but not any rifle Behnke would want to own.

"Elevation's identical, and the barrels are shooting apart and high with a load that's too light. That's a real good sign. The gun starts recoiling as soon as the primer goes off. With a lighter powder charge, there's more time between when the primer ignites and when the bullet leaves the muzzle. That means the right barrel should shoot right and high, and the left barrel should shoot left and high. That's the theory, at least. Remember the engineer's creed."

"When the results don't agree with the theory, believe the results and come up with a new theory," the gunsmith answered.

"Right. Let's see what results we get when we up the powder charge fifty grains." Curt Behnke winced. Bench rest shooters fired cartridges which held around twenty-five grains total. A .300 Magnum case held three times that. A cartridge where the shooter might elect to increase his powder charge by fifty grains was an assault on Behnke's sensibilities.

"What load were you shooting?" he managed to ask.

"Three hundred grains of single-eff gee. Because this gun weighs a full twenty-four pounds, I suspect it was regulated for the full sixteen dram charge. That's one ounce, or four hundred thirty-eight grains. The next pair I'll shoot is a three hundred fifty grain charge, same bullet."

"What's your bullet weight?"

"The slugs I'm shooting weigh 2140 grains out of linotype metal. Some of these old guns were regulated for a round ball cast out of pure lead, which would weigh 1750 grains. Most of them were set up for conical bullets, though, as near as I can determine. If it still shoots apart with the 440-grain charge, I'll have to shoot lighter bullets." Curt Behnke watched as Henry extracted the fired cases and replaced them with another pair. He did not ask Henry if he had brought ammunition loaded with the 440-grain charge he had mentioned. He believed he already knew the answer.

The report of the next two shots was noticeably different. It was both louder and sharper, and the older man could see that the gun recoiled with more vigor. On the second shot, he watched the target instead of the shooter, and was startled to see a large quantity of dirt and ice from the backstop thrown twenty feet in the air behind the target frame. The holes in the paper were eight inches apart, spaced equally on either side of center, and an inch high.

"Looks like your theory is holding up."

"Nice not to need a spotting scope, don't you think?"

"Recoil still okay?"

"It's definitely getting heavier. Notice the difference in the sound? Those two were supersonic."

"Eleven hundred feet per second?" Behnke said immediately. For some reason it had not occurred to him that the huge bullets could be driven that fast out of a gun which could still be fired from the shoulder.

"We're not done yet. Here comes four hundred grains." Henry pushed his earplugs in a little deeper, reloaded the Rodda, and rested his arm against the rolled sleeping bag. He made a conscious effort to grip the gun as tightly as possible. The recoil, while still manageable, was unlike that of any other weapon he had ever used, and he didn't want to drop the gun.

This time the report sounded to Henry like standing next to a tree as it was struck by lightning. A one-inch hole appeared in the paper less than two inches right of center and dead-on for elevation. Henry cocked the left hammer and took aim again. His second shot was a little higher than his first, and a little over three inches left of it.

"How high you going to go?" the older man asked.

"I loaded some at four-forty," Henry replied. I'll clean the gunk out of the barrels and give 'em a go." He swung the underlever to the side, broke the gun open, emptied it, and laid it on a blanket on the next shooting bench. Henry Bowman picked up an aluminum shotgun cleaning rod with a 12-gauge brush screwed in the end, and wrapped a large piece of rag around the bristles. He sprayed the cloth liberally with WD-40, sprayed more into the breech of the right barrel, and shoved the rod down the bore from the breech. When the wrapped brush emerged from the muzzle, it was thoroughly caked with shiny black carbon residue. Henry inspected the bore, then used a new piece of rag to repeat the process with the other barrel. "There's a lot of it, but it seems to come right out. I think the alox and beeswax bullet lube I'm using may be an improvement over what the Brits had a hundred years ago," Henry said. "Although it wouldn't surprise me if they had something just as good or better," he amended after a moment's reflection.

"Fresh target this time," Henry said as he removed two big cartridges from the bag he had labeled '440' and loaded the gun. He wiped the fog from his shooting glasses and assumed the position at the standing rest. This time he made an effort to put his feet a little farther back so that he would be leaning into the gun a little more.

The blast was tremendous, and recoil rocked Henry back until the muzzles of his rifle were pointing up at about a forty-five degree angle. Henry brought the gun down out of recoil and cocked the left hammer. He settled back into the bag and locked into position again as he switched his index finger to the rear trigger.

"It looks like you're—" The sound of the second shot cut off Curt Behnke's comment about where Henry's first shot had gone. Henry laid the gun down on the blanket, and both men squinted off into the distance. "Almost touching," the older man said with admiration in his voice.

"Let me put two more of the same load in there, see if they fall in the same group." Henry had loaded four rounds each with 400- and 440-grain charges, and eight rounds of 300- and 350- grain loadings. He replaced the fired cases with his two remaining rounds that carried the heaviest charge. Curt Behnke stepped several paces to the side, and held a camera trained on his friend. Behnke was braced against one of the roof supports, for he knew the blast would jar a freehand hold. At the shot, the gunsmith tripped the shutter, catching Henry in full recoil.

Henry Bowman recovered, cocked the left hammer, and let drive with the second barrel. He looked over at his fifty-nine-year-old companion. "Doesn't look too bad," he opined. The target showed two pairs of overlapping holes, with about an inch of space between them. Elevation was perfect.

Behnke stared at the target butt. "You going to raise the charge again?" he asked uncertainly. The barrels were obviously very close to regulating perfectly.

"I think I'll lower the bullet weight instead. Could you take an eighth of an inch off the base in the lathe without too much trouble?"

"Yeah, sure. Put 'em in the collet chuck, I could give you a half-dozen each of several different weights. You don't need a thousand, or anything like that, do you?" Both men broke into laughter at *that* idea. Henry wiped down the Rodda and laid it on the blanket.

"I think I'll give my central nervous system a rest for a while. Shall we shoot some varmint rifles? Three hundred yards, five groups averaged for record, loser buys lunch?"

"What kind of a handicap do I have to give you?" Behnke asked cautiously.

"None. I'm in too good a mood about my 4-bore." Curt Behnke just smiled.

When they were finished shooting, Curt Behnke had an average group size of 1.42". All his groups were nearly round. Henry's groups had a little over an inch of vertical dispersion, but on that gusty January day, the horizontal spread averaged almost four inches. His targets were what Curt Behnke liked to refer to as 'weather reports'.

Henry Bowman was still grinning when he picked up the check for a late lunch.

February 22, 1977

"Hey!" the man yelled out across the office, his hand covering the mouthpiece of the telephone he held. "Sloan just had a massive cerebral hemorrhage. Dead as a hammer in Washington."

His friend sat bolt upright. His mind was racing, and he was already thinking several steps ahead to the special election that would have to be held to replace the dead congressman. "Carter's only been in office a month—maybe we can make some hay on this one."

"Some other well-intentioned guy out of left field, you mean?" He began to smile. The idea was definitely appealing. "Somebody we can control?" His smile grew broader, then his brows furrowed. "Got to be someone white, though. Might backfire if we try to sneak in another Clay," he warned.

The second man nodded at this assessment. There were limits, after all. The goal was to always expand them. "Yeah," he said, nodding his head.

"What we need is somebody who can tell people what they want to hear, and doesn't have some stupid agenda that can get us into trouble."

"Shit, *that* doesn't narrow the field much."

"Yeah, but somebody young and good-looking, and who can smile without looking like Eleanor Roosevelt, so the voters will *want* to pay more taxes."

"Makes it harder..." Suddenly the two men's heads snapped towards each other.

"Dick Gaines!" they said in unison.

Missouri's next U.S. Congressman for the third district had just been chosen.

April 9, 1978

"I won't ask what was going through your mind when you signed this," the senior accountant from Ernst and Whinney said with a smile as he took the check and placed it with the other documents for delivery to the IRS.

"Please don't." Henry Bowman's face was utterly without expression, and his tone of voice told the accountant he wanted no further discussion. "You need me for anything else?"

"No, I think we're all set."

"Then I'll be going." Henry turned on his heel and left the office.

The entire way home, Henry Bowman thought about just how much he had come to despise both the socialist policies his country's government had adopted, and the people who had forced those policies on the public. *Isn't that why this nation was formed—to get away from this very thing?* he asked himself over and over.

As Henry walked into the kitchen, he hung his jacket over the back of a chair. The house still didn't feel right to him, with his mother gone. Every time he walked through a doorway he half expected to see her, especially after being away on a job for several days.

Catherine Bowman had died very suddenly of a heart attack almost a year before, while carrying a box of plants from her station wagon to the pantry off the kitchen. She was sixty-one years old. Henry had moved out of his apartment and back into the house he had grown up in, to undertake the arduous task of settling his mother's estate.

The 55% haircut appalled him. Henry Bowman had known that taxes would be bad, but losing over half of everything his parents owned was a shock. Estates of less than $175,000 were not taxed. Above that figure, taxes quickly rose to a staggering 77% on estates of over $10 million.

The law allowed nine months to come up with the money, which meant selling a lot of things. Henry had reluctantly come to the conclusion that keeping the family summer property would mean selling all the stocks and bonds, and the country place was maintenance-intensive. Without income from savings to maintain it, Henry had seen that its upkeep would bankrupt him. It was now being subdivided for development, and the entire proceeds from the sale, along with his mother's entire bond portfolio and much of the stocks, had just gone to the IRS.

And the estate tax program doesn't even break even Henry thought with disgust. He had scarcely believed it when the accountant told him, but it made sense. Very few people saved $175,000 in property and other assets. Estates of those few people who conserved and invested their assets successfully enough to rise above this level generated less taxes than the costs of administration.

The estate tax wasn't there to help pay for things the country needed, it was there to prevent Americans from passing their property and their savings on to their descendants. *Shirtsleeves to shirtsleeves in three generations. That's what Andrew Carnegie said.* Henry closed his eyes and took a deep breath. He did not like feeling angry like this. He opened the door to the basement stairs, flicked on the light switch, and descended the steps to the woodworking shop that Walter Bowman had built and that had been Henry's for the last decade.

The smell relaxed him immediately. Henry went to the partially finished gunstock that was clamped in the padded jaws of the bench vise. He ran his hand over the Bastogne walnut, taking in the wonderful scent of his favorite wood. The Enfield action, barreled in .500 Buhmiller, lay on the bench behind the stock. *This one's going to be pure poison, when I get too tired to carry my Rodda* Henry thought. Design weight for the five-shot magazine rifle was 10 1/2 pounds. It would fire a 600-grain .510" bullet at 2400 feet per second, as opposed to the .458, which threw a smaller 500-grain slug at 2250 feet per second using strong handloads. Factory .458 offerings sent the same bullet out at less than 2000 FPS.

The unfinished rifle made Henry think about his impending safari to Rhodesia, and his spirits lifted considerably. *Got to get this stock finished, if I want to practice any before I go.* His Rhodesian safari was scheduled for the entire month of September.

Henry Bowman lifted an artist's paintbrush out of a small pot of oil and lampblack, and gave the underside of the barreled receiver a thin coat of the wet mix. Then he lowered the metalwork into the stock, pressed it firmly, and lifted it out again. Henry inspected the wood closely, looking at every place that was blackened where the metal had touched it.

About 75% contact. He shook his head. *Abe & Van Horn wouldn't settle for 75%* Henry said to himself, referring to the stockmakers whose work he most admired.

He chose a round-end scraper from several dozen that were in a rack on his bench, and went to work.

***

"Have the people in this country lost their *minds?*" Congressman Gaines demanded. His aide knew better than to answer questions such as that, and remained silent. "Listen to this:

"'All across the country, a disturbing trend is taking shape. Americans are stockpiling food and rediscovering home canning in preparation for what they see as the inevitable result of runaway inflation, unchecked government spending, and the abdication of U.S. strength and respect abroad. The debate about the Panama Canal is but one of many examples of what these citizens view as a drastically weakened foreign policy, with ultimate consequences much more serious than mere loss of pride.

"'These people call themselves survivalists, and they are not wringing their hands. They are taking action. Survivalists are learning mechanical skills. They are storing massive amounts of consumables—not only food, but diesel fuel, gasoline, and goods for barter. They are planting large vegetable gardens and digging wells on their own property. Any money they have left after these large purchases of basic necessities is used to buy gold. These measures are the only protection survivalists feel they can give their families in the event that economic disaster does come to pass.'"

He put down the magazine and stared across the lunch table at his subordinate. "What kind of crap is this?" he asked rhetorically. Richard Gaines had been reading a national news magazine, quoting from one of the many current articles describing a phenomenon which was occurring all across the country. Suddenly he thought of something.

"I thought it was illegal to buy gold."

"Ah, Gerald Ford changed that when he was in office, Congressman."

"That fool," Gaines sneered.

The aide did not point out to the young congressman that gold had been the underlying asset for the world's major monetary systems for thousands of years, and it was Franklin Roosevelt, with a huge majority in both Congress and the Senate, who had unhitched the currency from its anchor and made it a federal crime for U.S. citizens to own this basic store of value. That happened in 1934, a year that saw other federal proposals with far-reaching implications for the American public become law.

"What can we do about this?" Gaines demanded. His aide opened his mouth to speak, but realized he hadn't the vaguest idea what the congressman was after. *Strengthen foreign policy? Not much the young congressman could do there. Pledge to introduce no legislation unless it repealed spending programs? It would be interesting to see how his constituents reacted to that.* The aide shrugged in reply. Richard Gaines was obviously pondering his own question.

"I could introduce a bill prohibiting ownership of more than, oh, say, a month's worth of basic necessities. Exemption for bona fide producers, of course, farmers and all that. Go through the records of all the bulk sellers, look for individual purchasers. Any excess food they've got over the one-month limit, take it and put it into a government-administered fund, to be sold at below-market rates to the people who are below the poverty line. That'd look good to the public—make these crazy end-of-the-world types give their food to people who really need it." He chewed his lip, thinking.

"Couldn't do the same thing very easily with gas or diesel, so we'd have a line in there prohibiting home storage. Make it a crime to have more than ten gallons aside from what was in your car & lawn mower. Underground tanks'd have to be filled in." Richard Gaines was pondering other elements of his bill when a large, weathered hand was laid on his shoulder.

"Son, I just finished eatin' dinner at the next table, and I couldn't he'p but hear you tellin' your friend 'bout this idea of yours for a bill." The speaker was a large man with white hair, in his seventies or early eighties. "Before you get your secretary to type it up for you, I think you might want to re-read the Constitution, 'cause right now, you got several problems that're goin' t'come up an' bite you.

"Like that plan you got to take what people's been hoarding, put it in a government fund. Going to run smack into the Fifth Amendment, I'm afraid, takin' property like that without compensation.

"Now, findin' out who to take it from, *that's* going to butt heads with the Fourth Amendment. That's the one about unreasonable search and seizure, case you forgot. Might even get some squawk on the Tenth Amendment, though that one's a little shaky.

"Anyway, thought you might want to think about those things a bit 'fore you start figurin' that since the Constitution was written a couple hundred years ago by some fellows who dressed an' talked kind of funny, it's not of much interest 'cept to college professors writin' 'bout ancient history." He chuckled as he thought of something. "Last fellow in this town who felt that way got in a whole *mess* of trouble, you may recall." The man lifted his hand from Gaines' shoulder, nodded once, and walked towards the exit.

"Who the hell was *that* old goat?" Gaines asked his aide when the older man had left the restaurant. The stranger had been exactly right in his assumption about the young congressman's view of the Constitution, and it irritated Gaines to be talked to like someone in grade school.

"Senator Sam Ervin. He eats in here sometimes. Retired four years ago after he finished up his job as Chairman of the Senate Select Committee on Presidential Campaign Activities." The aide saw Gaines' blank look, and continued. "You know—the Watergate hearings? Ended up with Nixon resigning?"

"Oh. Yeah. I thought I'd seen him somewhere before," Gaines said.

"Look," the aide said to his boss, wanting to get him back in good humor and recognizing how to do it. "What he said about the Fourth and Fifth Amendments? That's true as far as it goes. But that's only a problem when you try to do what you want head-on."

"What do you mean?"

"Well," the aide said, as he chewed a bite of steak and gestured with his fork, "when you try to pass progressive laws and do what's best for the country, a lot of times the people will resist. At least when you try to do too much too fast. You know about the Fabian Society in England?" Gaines shook his head. The aide smiled and took a deep breath. He loved political history, and didn't get to talk about it often enough. Here was a chance to look good for the boss.

"Fabian Society was a political organization founded in the 1880's in Great Britain. Their ultimate goal was to establish a socialist government in England. They knew if they came out and said that, though, their ideas would be rejected immediately by the majority of people. So they began to gradually educate the public by publishing essays that explained the benefits of socialist ideas. And they framed their ideas in terms that would appeal to the influential upper-class, because those are usually the people that can get things done.

"Anyway, because of that strategy, they were very successful. They were the major force behind the Labor Representation Committee that was founded at the turn of the century." He saw Gaines' blank look and added, "The LRC was what became England's Labour Party."

"So?" Gaines asked. He didn't see where this was going, and he was getting bored with talk about England.

"So they *got* what the Fabians had always wanted," the aide said hurriedly. "At least, a lot of it. The Labour Party won by a landslide in '45, and Prime Minister Attlee was able to finally create a welfare state in England, which was a real coup.

"Within two years they had free medical care for everyone, the government owned the Bank of England, and they'd let India, Pakistan, Ceylon, and Burma go. Within five or six years, they had nationalized a quarter of the country's industry." The aide did not mention that these policies resulted in a massive trade deficit, subsequent food rationing, and drastic devaluation of the pound sterling. It went without saying that in all socialist endeavors, certain inconveniences had to be tolerated by individuals for the greater good of the public as a whole.

The aide's eyes were bright as he stared at the Congressman. "It never could have happened all at once, and that's what I think we need to keep in mind."

"So fifty years, is that what you're telling me?" Gaines asked with irritation.

"No, no, not at all," the aide said quickly, shaking his head vigorously. "We got our welfare state over forty years ago. And what you were just talking about—you know, wanting to ban hoarding and distribute the survivalists' food to the poor? You don't have to listen to that old asshole preach about how your law would violate the Constitution. You don't even need to pass a new law at all. We've already *got* the power."

"What do you mean?" Gaines asked.

"The Emergency Powers Act. Gives the President the authority to do whatever he wants in a time of 'national emergency'. It was meant to be invoked in the event of a nuclear war, but there's nothing in it that specifies that particular circumstance. If the President wants to, he can use it. Order the Army to seize all the peoples' stockpiles of food, diesel fuel, gold, guns, whatever. Nationwide curfew, censor the press, you name it, he can do it under the Emergency Powers Act. Money, too; if the President says no taking money out of the country, even a few hundred dollars, boom—it's a crime. Freeze

378

bank accounts, seize assets, anything he wants."

"So we've got the authority already, but it takes special circumstances, huh? I guess the next step is to make the circumstances less unusual, right?" Gaines said.

"That's it," his aide replied with a grin. "The people won't give up the things they think they are entitled to if you try to take them all at once. You need to start with something that sounds so innocuous that you can ridicule anyone that opposes you. Then expand it. Do what the Fabian Society did: Treat it just as you would a salami—a slice at a time."

The congressional aide was well-versed in his political history, but he was ignorant of the National Firearms Act of 1934. If he had been familiar with this particular piece of legislation, however, he could have used it as a textbook example of the strategy he was advocating.

Do all the outfitters in Africa do this for every client that comes hunting? Henry wondered in disbelief as he stared at the preparations that had been made for his arrival. He had expected a camp similar to the ones he and Allen Kane made for themselves when they went to Idaho. What he got was something altogether different.

A 10' by 10' concrete slab had been poured, and a tent erected over it. It housed a metal-framed bed and a nightstand made of sticks lashed together. A fresh vegetable garden had been planted months before, so that fresh salads could be served with every meal. The cook tent was well-stocked, and even included a freezer that ran on propane. A fire near the cook tent was tended twenty-four hours a day, so that hot water for bathing and washing clothes was available at all times.

The water came from a two-hundred-gallon wheeled storage tank that the crew kept filled with regular trips to the river. A five-gallon can with a screw valve and shower head attached hung suspended from a tree limb near Henry's tent, and was filled with hot water whenever Henry wanted a shower. A fifty-five gallon drum of water was lashed into the crook of a tree ten feet above the ground, and was piped to a flush toilet at the back of the camp. Ray had asked Henry for his dirty clothes from the trip over, and they were washed immediately. By the end of the month, Henry would realize that he could have gone on the safari without a change of clothes, for the crew washed, dried, ironed (with an iron that was filled with hot coals), and folded his laundry for him every night.

The hunting camp that had been built for Henry Bowman was in the Charara Valley, on a million-acre tract of government land south of the Zambesi River. The land was not part of a hunting concession, and Ray Johnson had never been in the area prior to twelve weeks before, although he had been familiar with its reputation.

Most modern safaris in Africa were held on hunting concessions similar to the 200,000-acre tract Ray Johnson leased, which was two hundred miles away from where he and Henry Bowman were now standing. The professional hunter paid the government an annual fee to lease the raw land, and built his own accommodations on it. The government told him how many animals of which species could be killed in that area each year. The professional hunter then offered hunts to clients and charged them a daily rate for his services, which were all-inclusive except for trophy fees. The client paid the daily rate directly to the professional hunter. He also paid the government a nonrefundable trophy fee in advance for each animal he intended to hunt. Trophy fees varied by animal. In 1978, a warthog or baboon in Rhodesia cost $75, a male cape buffalo $500, and a trophy elephant $3000. Ray Johnson's daily rate was $400, typical for a recognized professional hunter in that area.

Countries with well-managed game departments (such as Rhodesia) would authorize the killing of only that number of animals which would ensure that the herds continued to thrive. This meant that one rhino, three or four lions, and perhaps ten elephants could be shot each year on a 200,000-acre concession. Limits for thin-skinned plains game were of course much higher. The game department typically erred on the side of caution, and every few years the numbers were temporarily raised on those species which were becoming too numerous.

The professional hunter received none of the trophy fee, and had only his daily rate to sustain his business. Because of this, and because the dangerous game was so plentiful that good specimens could be found in two or three days, professional hunters had minimum safari lengths they set for clients wishing to hunt large, dangerous game. A client could go on a six- or seven-day safari if he would be satisfied with a half-dozen head of thin-skinned plains game such as impala, duiker, oryx, and bushbuck. If he wanted to hunt elephant, buffalo, rhino, lion, or leopard, however, his professional hunter would require at least a two-week hunt. Customers wanting to hunt several of the 'big five' often signed up for safaris of a month or more.

The safari Henry Bowman was about to undertake was somewhat different than the norm, however. Each year, the Rhodesian government held auctions which were open to all professional hunters licensed in that country. The authorities would auction off the hunting rights to large tracts of government land that were *not* being leased out as hunting concessions, on a one-season basis. Again, the game department stipulated (in advance of the auction) the number and type of animals that could be killed in that area in the forthcoming season, but the auction price included all trophy fees. The successful bidder could then split up the permitted game, and hold several safaris each at an all-inclusive price.

This practice served several functions. First, elephant, buffalo, and lion populations were kept at levels which minimized the animals' consumption of the crops and residents in adjacent, populated areas.

Second, the government received additional revenues which it used for game management and anti-poaching measures, although how these funds were ultimately used was usually startling to the uninitiated.

Third, the customers ended up spending a little less money on a hunt (although the accommodations were more spartan), and the professional hunter made a little extra that season if he scheduled everything intelligently.

This was the tradeoff every professional hunter analyzed when bidding in the annual auction: Scheduling hunts in the new location required setting up a temporary hunting camp with all its attendant support crew of cooks, skinners, and laborers, and took time away from the existing hunting concession where all facilities were already set up.

Ray Johnson had made the winning bid for the Charara Valley area on the strength of a ten-minute phone conversation with Max Collins' nephew. Henry had said he was ready to go on a big hunt, and Ray had promised he'd give Henry 'a hell of a deal providing you're willing to shoot all the game on the ticket, so I don't have to run four or five safaris with four or five different clients'. Ray had also seen to it that the temporary camp provided almost as many comforts as did the permanent camp on his hunting concession, and it was this attention to detail which now amazed the young client.

"Okay, you're settled in and you know where everything is. Let's see this bloody cannon I've been hearing about." Ray Johnson, raised in Colorado and educated in Boston, had adopted some of the phraseology of his current Rhodesian peers.

"God*damn*!" he said with feeling when Henry opened the aluminum case he had had made for his 4-bore double. "Makes my .600 Holland look like a matchstick."

"Yeah, I know what you mean," Henry said with a sigh. "I used to shoot those medium bores, too, 'til I got this. That's why I left my .577 at home." Both men started laughing. "Go ahead," Henry urged with a nod.

Ray Johnson lifted the rifle and threw it to his shoulder. "Balances great," he said immediately.

"I only have twenty-five rounds for it," Henry admitted. "Is that enough?"

"Lord, I hope so. This isn't the only gun you brought, I trust?" Henry smiled and shook his head. "Look at *that!*" Ray exclaimed when he saw the ammunition. It looked like something for a turn-of-the-century field piece.

"Got a .375 Ackley Improved for the small stuff, and a .500 Buhmiller for elephant and buffalo if I get tired of lugging this boat anchor around. Speaking of which, I'd like to make sure the scope on my .375 didn't change any in transit. Where can I set up some 200-yard targets?"

Ray lifted his eyebrows. In fifteen years, Henry was only the second client he'd encountered who had wanted to check his sights before going afield. The first had been Max Collins. "Don't you want to take a nap first? Your system must be thrown off some with the time change."

"Not right now. I'm still too keyed up about being here."

"Well, let me have Kineas get some lunch together for us, and then I'll show you where you can shoot your light rifle. Fresh salad, fresh tomatoes, fresh baked bread, and roasted guinea hen all right?"

"Sounds delicious."

"Kineas can grill you a steak if you'd prefer that."

"Maybe for dinner."

"Good. I'll have one of the boys find something you can use for a target," Ray offered.

"I brought targets."

Ray Johnson raised his eyebrows. *I have a feeling this is going to be a really good hunt* he thought with a smile.

***

"You didn't bring a shotgun, did you?" Ray asked as they stopped under a tree beside the fire road fifteen miles from camp. The sun was bright and Ray recommended regular breaks to ingest fluids. They had parked the Land Rover and had been walking for about two hours. Henry had seen several zebra, which were not on his ticket, and almost a hundred impala since leaving the vehicle.

"No, I don't shoot shotguns. Why?"

"That's a pity. There's lots of good wingshooting in Africa. Especially guinea fowl, like we had for lunch," he said, nodding towards some birds in the distance. "Lot of them in this area. They're like small turkeys. Eight, ten pounds. Take a lot of killing, though. Last client I had who brought a shotgun only had skeet loads with him. They'd've been okay for doves, but guinea fowl, it just made 'em squawk and keep flying. Number eights won't do it. You need fours, at least," he said as he took a drink from his canteen.

"Wouldn't the noise spook the other game?" Henry asked as he watched the birds fly towards them. Ray laughed.

"Not plains game. There's so much of it in this area, you could detonate a bomb and you'd still find more a mile farther on."

Henry thought about that and looked at the eyepiece of the Leupold variable on his .375 Ackley Magnum. The scope was one of the new models in 1.5-5 power, with the dot reticle that Henry preferred. He noted with satisfaction that the power ring at the front of the eyepiece was set to the lowest power. Henry pulled a single earplug from the breast pocket of his khaki shirt and slipped it into his left ear.

"Hold your ears," he said softly as he held his rifle at port arms and watched the four guinea fowl fly towards the trees that he and the others stood under. The lead bird was to the left of the three that followed it. *Thirty yards, maybe less, in a second. Dead on at thirty, half-inch low at twenty.* Henry threw the Enfield-actioned .375 to his shoulder and flicked the safety forward to disengage it. He squeezed the trigger a practiced amount, then increased the pressure when the dot in the center of the crosshairs was about two inches in front of the bird's head. As the muzzle blast rolled out over the Rhodesian plains and the gun rose in recoil, Henry Bowman slapped the bolt handle up and to the rear, then shoved it forward and down as he pulled the rifle back on target. The rifle's stock obscured his face, but he was smiling.

The three other guinea fowl reacted simultaneously to the shot. Two of them broke left, but one started to turn to Henry's right, spotted the four men under the trees, and wheeled left to join the other birds. Henry swung on this one, and felt the trigger break just as the dot reticle passed through an imaginary spot four inches in front of and just slightly above the bird's beak. As the rubber recoil pad hammered his shoulder once again, Henry relaxed and watched the second corpse fall out of the sky.

"*Jesus!*" Ray Johnson exclaimed. "Banda! Grab those!" he said unnecessarily. The head tracker was already jogging out to retrieve the dead birds. "I've certainly never had a client do *that,*" Ray said to Henry, as he alternated his stares between the rifle in Henry's hands and the area out in the dry grass where the dead birds had fallen.

"A 270 Nosler at 2900 doesn't have the problem of insufficient power that skeet loads do," Henry said happily.

"Probably blew the meat all to shit," Ray said, in a tone that made it clear that he didn't care at all if each entire bird was now inedible.

"We'll see," Henry shrugged.

The tracker returned a few moments later with both guinea fowl and held them out for inspection. The professional hunter was stunned to see that the meat was not damaged at all.

Using a bolt-action rifle that most people thought of as an elephant gun, Raymond Johnson's newest client had decapitated both birds in flight with two perfect head shots.

***

"Exactly how is it you ended up a professional hunter over here, anyway?" Henry asked as they sat at the dinner table and worked on their salads. "Didn't Uncle Max tell me you were originally a lawyer, or something?"

Ray smiled. "Yeah, I had a job in New York doing securities law fifteen years ago. Lucked into an unusual personal injury case, where the defendant was a big company about to be bought out by a conglomerate. We settled out of court for a bunch of money so it wouldn't queer the sale.

"I took some of the money from my cut and went on a safari in Kenya. While I was there, I got a cable that my dad had had a heart attack while driving with my mother, and they'd both been killed in the wreck. I finished up my hunt and then went home to settle the estate. I realized that I wasn't looking forward to going back and living in New York and poring over prospectuses. Guy I'd been with in Kenya had said there were some good opportunities in Angola and Mozambique for a guy who knew a bit about game. I settled things in the States and went to Angola. That's where I met your uncle."

"Do you have any brothers or sisters?" Raymond shook his head.

"No, only other family I had was my Dad's brother, Uncle Carl. He and Dad both ran the ranch in Colorado."

"Is it still there?"

"Yeah, my uncle still runs it," Ray said, nodding his head. "I still own the half that belonged to my father. Dad had enough savings and insurance to pay the estate tax due at the time. That was in '63. I told Uncle Carl since he was going to have to hire more help, and I was fixed okay for money, he was welcome to all the profits so long as Dad's land stayed in my name. He knew I didn't have any urge to sell."

"So you've got a bunch of land in Colorado to retire to if things go to shit over here, huh?"

"That, and a mutual fund I bought with my settlement money. Dollar cost averaged over five years, and wrapped it an annuity contract so it would grow tax-deferred."

Henry nodded in understanding and sipped his lemonade. "Whoever told you to do that was smart. Feds slammed the door on that one a few years back, but guys who were in already got grandfathered."

"Tony Kearns, my broker, was really good," Ray agreed. "So, is it what you expected?" he asked, changing the subject. "Game plentiful enough?" Henry had shot a good-sized impala at a little over 200 yards, and a nice wildebeest at about half that distance, but the professional hunter was still thinking of the flying birds he had seen his client kill that morning.

"Better than I ever imagined. I can't tell you what I was expecting, exactly, but it wasn't this good, not by a jugful." He looked thoughtful for a moment, remembering how astonished he had been at regularly spotting elephant and rhino that afternoon. "How many elephants did you say there were in Africa, Ray?"

"Last estimate, about a million and a quarter. That's what astonishes every one of my clients from the United States. Apparently there's some crazy rumor over there that because of all the hunting, African elephants are nearly extinct."

"A lot of people seem to think that," Henry admitted. Raymond laughed, then turned serious.

"No one likes to say it out loud, but it comes down to the simple question of which do you like better—African elephants, or Africans?" He took a bite of his salad, and continued. "That's why every country over here has game department people on the payroll whose job it is to go kill hundreds of elephants a year—whole herds of them, babies and all. I guess a lot of the American public flunked arithmetic."

"What do you mean?"

"Well, a full-grown elephant eats about four hundred pounds of vegetation a day. That means that *per elephant*, you need between five and twenty-five square miles of free grazing area, depending on the country and how good the soil is. That's just to sustain the animals at existing levels.

"Got a little problem there, though. It's called people. They have this nasty habit of wanting to own their own property, and plant crops on it, and raise cattle, and stay alive. Those goals are not particularly compatible with having elephants and rhino and lions sharing the same real estate. You said in the summers, you grew up on a place out in the country?"

"Right."

"Cattle, chickens, pigs, corn, like that? All fenced in?"

"Yeah."

"Your mother have a vegetable garden?" Raymond asked.

"Of course."

"Any groundhogs ever get in it?" This elicited a nod. "So what'd you do?"

"Shot 'em," Henry said.

"Right. Well, imagine that instead of weighing ten pounds, those groundhogs you wanted to keep out of your fields weighed ten thousand pounds, and each one of them ate four hundred pounds of your crops every day it was alive. Imagine instead of building a fence to keep the cattle and pigs in, you had to build one that would keep lions and leopards out. And also keep them away from where your children might happen to be. Good luck," he said with feeling.

"Any place here in Africa where the people want to grow crops, all the elephant and rhino have to be exterminated first. Any place people want to have beef or dairy cattle, or raise children for that matter, all the cats have to be killed off. Every last one of 'em." He smiled sadly.

"Like if you were in Florida. Send a dozen guys off into the swamp to kill as many alligators as they can, ten years later there'll be plenty of alligators in that swamp. But drain the swamp and pour concrete for a new A&P, there'll never be another 'gator there again."

"So there's a big push to divide up the government land for the residents?" Henry asked. Ray Johnson nodded.

"With the trophy fees as high as they are, the raw land brings in enough money that the government can afford to leave huge sections of it alone. Continued profitable hunting businesses keep the land undeveloped, and that's good for photo safaris, too. The photo people don't spend any money out here, but they do a lot for the tourism in the cities. One client I had brought his girlfriend on the hunt. She wanted to know why people couldn't just take pictures of the game, and have no more hunting. I asked her if she'd be willing to pay a hundred dollars to the government for every picture she took of an impala, and three thousand for every elephant, on top of paying for her transport over here and four hundred a day for my services. She looked at me like I'd lost my fucking mind."

"The whole system usually goes to shit when they outlaw hunting. That's what we've seen in the other countries, at least. Looks like it might happen to us, with all this crap that's going on." He was referring to the civil war in Rhodesia that had been going on for several years.

"Do you think that will happen here?" Henry asked.

"Don't know. A lot of people are leaving, mostly for South Africa. What I do will depend on if the government decides to outlaw hunting and kill off the game to make way for hundred-acre farms. No read on that yet."

Henry nodded. He took a drink of water, and finished off his salad as Kineas set a thick steak down in front of him. The talk soon returned to the events of the day's hunt, and what was expected for the following morning. Political discussion was shelved for the time being, but the issues were ones Henry would ponder for the remainder of his trip.

Major changes were in store for Rhodesia. The asset-based qualification for voting would be abolished, and full independence with majority rule, along with a name-change for the country, would occur in 1980. As many had predicted, this event would immediately lead to a move towards a single-party government.

Five years after Henry's safari, Rhodesia's most productive citizens would have emigrated to South Africa. Hotels in the major cities which had averaged eighty percent occupancy throughout the course of a year would be down to fifteen percent in the tourist season. The government would levy a seventeen percent tariff on all retail sales in a fruitless effort to tax the country into prosperity.

These events would force the new leaders to recognize that hunting was one of their country's few remaining assets capable of attracting foreign dollars. Hunting concessions would still be leased to those people willing to risk a business venture in an environment largely hostile to capitalism. The handwriting was on the wall, however, and by the time the country became a one-party state in 1988, Ray Johnson would be long gone.

September 5, 1978

"Let's watch them for a bit," Henry requested.

"Sure. We'll glass them from here for a while, see if one of them's got a decent pair of teeth." Ray, Henry, the lead tracker, and two tracker-skinners were looking across a canyon at four elephants on the other hillside, about a quarter mile away. One of the bulls was pushing his head against a 12" diameter tree.

"Watch how he pushes and releases it, then pushes again, getting it rocking. He's going to get it moving farther and farther until he snaps it off at ground level." Henry watched, and just as Ray had predicted, in less than a minute the tree went all the way over, and a long cracking sound reached his ears a second later.

"Why do they do that?" Henry asked.

"No one knows. The explanation everyone uses is that the elephants do it to test their strength. They do it all the time—just look around at all the trees pushed over." Henry nodded. He was imagining a farmer trying to build something to keep elephants away from his crops. *A two-foot-thick poured concrete wall, maybe?* he thought with amusement.

"See that third one from the left? His tusks are about as big as you're going to find, at least in this area. Look like fifty, fifty-five a side from here. Want to finish that canteen, take a few pictures, and see if we can't swing around and approach them from downwind? Give your Rodda a workout?"

"Sounds good to me."

***

Ray Johnson got his client to within fifteen yards of the huge animal. He had advised Henry to avoid letting the elephant see his eyes. Henry didn't know if this was a superstition, or if his eyes really *could* give him away, like the glint off the lenses of an enemy's binoculars. He kept them shielded with his free hand. Henry had told Ray he'd take a heart shot, to see how well that would work using the huge 19th-century rifle.

Henry Bowman pulled the front trigger and held it down while drawing back the right hammer. He held the hammer to the rear as he released the trigger, then let go of the hammer spur as well. He didn't like to carry the 4-bore cocked and ready to fire, and hammer guns could be cocked in complete silence by using the method Henry had just employed. He glanced at Ray Johnson, nodded once, and threw the 25-pound rifle to his shoulder.

The animal was standing broadside to Henry, facing to the young man's right. When the front sight bead covered the proper spot on the elephant's side, Henry Bowman gripped the gun's wrist and forend with all his strength, leaned forward, and squeezed the trigger. The trackers, standing fifty yards to the rear (near some eminently climbable trees), smiled involuntarily. The huge rifle made a sound like no other whenever it went off.

Henry Bowman rocked backwards, brought the rifle down out of recoil, and thumbed back the hammer of the left barrel. He made no effort to do it silently this time. The elephant had taken two steps, stopped, and turned around so that Henry was now presented with its left side. *Did I miss the heart?* Henry wondered in amazement as he took aim again. The bull was standing still, and Henry saw a brown spot of dirt or other discoloration on the animal's skin in the proper area for another heart shot. When the front sight bead obscured it, Henry pulled the Rodda's rear trigger.

He was again rocked back under recoil, only this time Henry let go of the wrist of the stock, grabbed the knob of the underlever, and swung the lever to the side as he brought the gun down across his left knee, breaking it open. He could tell with his peripheral vision that the elephant was still standing. *I can't be flinching that badly* he thought for an instant, then closed his mind to all but the task at hand.

Without looking up, Henry plucked the two empty cases from the barrels, dropped them at his feet, and pulled a pair of cartridges out of a surgical elastic carrier he wore on his left forearm. He slid them into the chambers, swung the barrels shut, closed the underlever, cocked the right hammer, and threw the rifle to his shoulder just in time to see the bull elephant fall over on his side, dead.

Henry glanced at Raymond, who was holding his .458 in one hand at his side, grinning. He pulled the right hammer back, held back the front trigger, and let the hammer down gently. He could feel the blood pumping in his ears as he walked over and stood by the huge head of the dead creature. Henry laid his hand on the thick hide just over the eye. He felt a much stronger emotion now than he ever felt after shooting any other game animal. Ray and the men recognized this. They had seen it before. The four of them stood silently and kept a respectful distance.

"I don't know what happened," Henry said finally.

"What do you mean?"

"I must have missed with the first shot—a vital organ, I mean, not the whole elephant. He didn't go down."

"He went down faster than I've ever seen with a heart shot. They usually walk a hundred yards or so before they fall down."

"What?"

"Elephant's heart's bigger than a basketball," Ray said as he walked toward the dead bull. "Put a little pencil-sized hole in it, you'll kill the animal, but not instantly. You were talking about the Guinness book—remember that huge bull shot in Angola in '55 that's mounted in the Smithsonian?"

"Yeah...?"

"That one took three full magazines from a .416 Rigby. You don't think eleven of those shots were all in non-vital—Hey, *look!*" Raymond was pointing to the dead animal's hide. Two one-inch holes overlapped, with the right one more ragged than the left.

"My God! That's an exit wound!" Henry exclaimed, suddenly realizing that his first shot had penetrated six feet of elephant, torn through the inch-thick hide on the far side, and then sailed off over the bush. "I thought it was a spot of dirt—I used it for an aiming point!"

"With some success," the professional hunter said drily. Ray smiled to himself. Henry was staring at the hole in the hide and thinking about his 19th-century rifle's amazing penetration. Every other client he'd ever had would be examining the ivory, trying to estimate its weight.

"Damn, do you think the second shot also went through?" Henry asked, mostly to himself.

"Want to help the skinners check?" Ray asked, joking.

"Yes!"

"Better take your shoes off and roll up your pants, then."

Half an hour later, Henry Bowman was knee deep in elephant entrails. He found the elephant's heart, and saw how it was indeed larger than a basketball. The organ had sustained massive trauma from the two 4-bore slugs that had torn through its center from opposite sides. Henry tracked the path of the second bullet, poking through the vast quantity of elephant guts to determine exactly where it had gone. He found that after the slug had passed through the heart, it had clipped a rib on the off side. He pushed his finger through the jagged break in the bone, through the flesh on the side, until he found the inside of the hide. There was a hole in it, and when Henry pushed his finger through it, he touched the hard surface of rock.

"I'm all the way through to the ground," Henry announced. "Second shot went clear through, too." He stood up and began to wipe his arms and legs off with a rag that one of the skinners handed him.

"Don't you want to finish butchering him?" Raymond asked in amusement.

"No, I'm just a typical, lazy client."

Ray Johnson translated the comment into Swahili for the skinners, and they all started laughing.

September 7, 1978

Ray Johnson opened his mouth to speak, then thought better of it. *Henry can decide whether to shoot or not* he thought.

Henry Bowman had walked on ahead fifteen yards as they had climbed the hill, and was now silently cocking the right hammer of his 4-bore Rodda. Ray motioned the trackers to stay put and crouched down before moving to join his client.

On the other side of the small rise were three buffalo bulls. All were large, but the nearest one was exceptional. Ray judged it to be about 1800 pounds. It was broadside to them, at a distance of less than twenty-five yards. Henry swung the rifle to his shoulder, and the right barrel thundered. At the sound, the other two bulls ran away and to the left, up a slight incline. The buffalo Henry had shot ran with considerable effort to the right. By the time Henry had pulled the big rifle out of recoil and cocked the left hammer, the animal was forty yards away.

"I saw your shot. You went right through the lungs. You don't nee–" Ray's advice was cut off by the tremendous muzzle blast of the left barrel of Henry's rifle. *Damn, but that's a cannon* Ray thought. The buffalo did a somersault and landed on its back, dead.

"You didn't need that second shot," Raymond reproached his client. "He wouldn't have lasted a hundred yards."

"What, are you trying to lower my ammo costs on this hunt?" Henry asked. "I'm tired of shooting these game animals in the right spot with the largest rifle ever made, and then having to wait for them to get the message that they're dead. It's very unnerving."

"Where was that second shot? I couldn't tell."

"Right hip. Probably got enough penetration to get into the lungs, too."

The Rodda once again exceeded expectations. When the crew got to the big cape buffalo and examined it, they discovered that the first shot had gone in the right side, straight through the center of the lungs, and out the left side, leaving a one-inch exit hole after traversing almost four feet of flesh.

The second shot, as the bull was quartering away, had been even more impressive. It smashed the buffalo's right hip and continued forward, ripping a path through the heart and finally coming to rest under the hide in front of the bull's shoulder. The 4 1/2-ounce slug from the hundred-year-old rifle had pulverized a massive bone and then gone on through five feet of muscle. All five of the men were very impressed when they saw what the old gun had done, and they took several photos to document the event.

"Well," Henry said as he and Ray watched the trackers gut the animal in preparation for winching it onto the Land-Rover, "I hate to be a wimp, but it's been a week now, and I'm getting a little tired of lugging this boat anchor around."

"You're going to stop using the 4-bore?" Ray asked in mock horror. In truth, he had been very impressed that Henry had carried it almost all day every day, relinquishing it for his .375 only when plains game was immediately present. "Have one of the trackers carry it for you," He suggested.

"No, I like having my main gun in my hands. And I wouldn't wish a 25-pound gun on anyone who didn't get to shoot it at game." He looked down at his big rifle and grinned. "I've shot two elephant and two buffalo with it so far. That'll do for now. I'm going to start carrying my .500 Buhmiller, at least for a few days. Twelve pound gun's going to feel like a feather."

In two days, Henry was going to be glad he had made the decision to switch rifles.

"Henry!" Ray Johnson screamed. "In the truck! *NOW!"* He stepped on the starter and stabbed the throttle, revving the engine.

They had been looking for a big elephant all that morning. It was lunchtime, and very hot. The Land-Rover had no doors, windshield, or roof, and Ray Johnson had parked the open vehicle under some trees at the side of a dried-up creek bed. In the shade, he had broken out the canteens and some sandwiches for Henry and the three trackers. Banda, the lead tracker, had walked about a hundred fifty yards away on the other side of the creek bed, looking for tracks and any other sign of a good-sized elephant.

Henry, who liked the Rhodesian countryside, had walked in the same general direction as Banda had, and was about a hundred yards away from the vehicle when Ray heard the familiar sound and began yelling to his client.

Banda had heard the sound a few moments before, and he was grinning broadly. He loved showing his courage and speed in front of the other trackers.

Henry looked back quizzically at the professional hunter. Ray was standing on the seat of the Land-Rover, gesticulating wildly towards Banda, and screaming something that Henry could not understand at that distance. The other two trackers stood in the back of the open vehicle, waving their arms frantically as well.

That was when Henry Bowman heard the noise. It didn't register at first, but it grew quickly, and in a few seconds Henry realized what Ray was yelling about. He saw that Banda was standing motionless, as if rooted to his spot. About a hundred yards past the head tracker, some two hundred head of cape buffalo were coming into view around the side of a hill. They were running directly towards Banda, Henry, and the vehicle.

Henry Bowman looked over his shoulder, judging the distance to the vehicle, then brought his eyes back to the lead tracker. *Why doesn't he move? There's no trees around. He's going to get trampled in the...stampede, or whatever you call it.* Henry searched frantically for an escape route for Banda, but saw none. He realized that if he waited a few seconds more, he himself would not be able to make it back to the Land-Rover. *And Banda's another fifty yards closer to the stampeding herd. He's already fucked.* Henry Bowman made a decision.

Raymond Johnson and the two tracker-skinners stood in the idling Land-Rover and watched in abject horror as Henry Bowman unslung his .500 Buhmiller from his shoulder and began running directly towards the stampede.

Banda licked his lips and decided he had let the thundering herd get close enough. He turned on his heel and began to sprint for the truck, only to see Henry ten yards away, running straight towards him. Banda's eyes grew wide with terror. He knew the American could never outrun the herd.

Henry Bowman misinterpreted the tracker's look of fear. *About time you figured out you were going to get stomped. I thought you guys weren't supposed to choke like that* he thought as he brought himself to a halt. Henry went into the speed-shooting stance he used for rifles of heavy recoil, with almost all of his weight on his forward left foot.

"Right behind me!" he screamed to the tracker, hoping he both heard and understood. Henry flicked off the safety and swung the muzzle of the custom Enfield up and into line with the approaching herd, which was now about twenty yards away. *Fifteen feet, Uncle Max said. I hope this works* Henry thought briefly, then focused his mind on what he had to do.

Time seemed to slow down for Henry Bowman as he identified the one buffalo that was coming exactly straight at him. It was a medium-sized cow, and when it was a little less than twenty feet away, Henry squeezed the trigger. The first 600-grain Barnes solid out of the necked-up .460 Weatherby case struck within a quarter of an inch of where Henry had been aiming, instantly shutting off all the buffalo's brain function before blasting out the back of its skull and then re-entering the animal's body just in front of the base of the spine. The dead animal's head slammed into the dirt about eight feet in front of Henry Bowman and the carcass began to tumble.

As the hindquarters of the tumbling animal briefly obscured his vision, Henry worked the Enfield's bolt. A bull had been following two steps behind the buffalo cow and was now trying to jump over its dead body. Henry brought the rifle to bear on the chest of the second buffalo, slapped the trigger, and threw himself forward as the bullet tore straight through the bull's chest and shattered its spine. The buffalo died in mid-jump and collapsed on the neck of the dead cow, tearing his hide on one of the cow's horns.

Henry braced his left knee on the dead cow's back as he worked the bolt. Another bull was almost to the two dead buffalo and looked as if he might or might not break right. Henry ignored the animals that were streaming around the obstacle he had created, focused on the one headed straight at him, then slapped the trigger again. By now he was holding the rifle lightly, as he would a .22, and firing it as soon as the butt touched his shoulder. The gun hammered him with over one hundred foot-pounds of recoil, but Henry didn't feel it. His third shot hit just to the left of the bull's right eye. The bullet blew much of the bull's brain matter out of a jagged hole at the left rear of his head, just below the horn boss. Momentum carried the dead bull forward and it crashed on top of the bodies of the first two. Henry had fired all three shots in less than three seconds.

Henry stood crouched behind the three-buffalo pile with his left knee on the nearest animal and his rifle at the ready, prepared to either duck down or fire his remaining two shots. The charging animals passed on both sides of Henry and the three buffalo he had killed, like water flowing around a boulder sitting in the middle of a stream. It seemed to take a very long time, but in fact the process took less than fifteen seconds.

After the last of over two hundred animals had passed the obstruction he had created, an adrenaline-filled Henry Bowman stood up and turned around to look for the lead tracker. He half expected to see Banda's body lying trampled and lifeless five or ten yards away. Instead, he saw nothing but hoofprints in the dry dirt.

The air was filled with dust, but as it settled, Henry could still see no sign of the lean native. Henry opened the bolt of the Enfield, replenished its magazine with three cartridges from the S.D. Myers' leather carrier he wore on his belt, and engaged the safety. He stared around the immediate area, searching for the man.

He must have gotten farther than I thought Henry said to himself as he widened the scope of his visual search. There was a fourth buffalo carcass lying fifty yards away. *Looks like at least one round exited.* Later investigation would reveal that it was Henry's third shot which had struck this animal, a cow, in the lungs after exiting the skull of the second bull Henry had killed.

Henry Bowman suddenly realized his legs were quivering. He sat down on the carcass of the first buffalo he had killed, and waited for his heart rate to return to normal. That was when he heard the sound of the Land-Rover's engine approaching.

Ray Johnson could scarcely believe what he was seeing as he drove past the carcass of the dead cow. A massive jumble of dead buffalo was up ahead, and Henry Bowman was sitting on one of them, waiting to be picked up. He was actually smiling!

"Did I pick out the four biggest ones, Ray?" Henry asked with an unsuccessful attempt at a poker face when the vehicle pulled up alongside. Ray was driving, and Banda and the other two trackers were in the back.

"What the hell did you think you were doing?" his guide demanded. Henry looked sheepish.

"I guess Banda can run faster than I thought," Henry Bowman said as he stood up. He stared at the four dead buffalo, the smallest of which weighed fifteen hundred pounds, and shook his head.

"You need a bigger truck, Ray. We'll never get all four of these in the back of that thing."

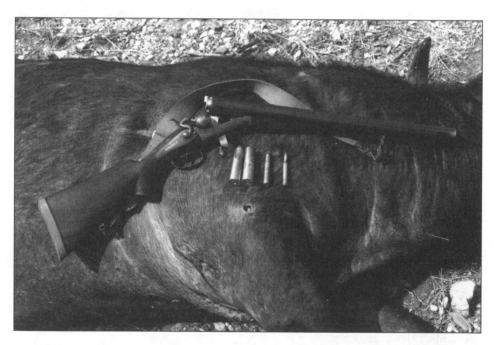

Cape Buffalo taken with shoulder shot from Henry Bowman's R.B. Rodda 4-Bore. Over entrance hole are 4-bore cartridge, fired case, and cartridges for .500 Buhmiller and .375 Ackley.

December 21, 1978

Cindy Caswell was building a snowman in the back yard. Helping her were two nine-year-old twin brothers whose father had just been transferred to nearby Ft. Leonard Wood. The boys were new to the neighborhood. Cindy always seemed to get along well with boys, especially ones that were a little older, unlike some of the other seven- and eight-year-old girls in her grade school class.

"God damn it! That goddamn kid's pissed on the couch again!" Boone Caswell yelled as he jumped up from where he'd just sat down. He ran through the kitchen and out the back door. Cindy heard him coming and cringed. *Please don't let him say anything* Cindy prayed. It was bad enough to have her father discipline her in front of her peers, without having them know exactly why he was so angry. Caswell grabbed his daughter by the arm and dragged her towards the house.

Boone Caswell's head still hurt from the previous evening's excesses, and at ten-thirty on a Friday morning, he had intended to see what was on television. There wasn't any work to be had around the holidays, at least none that Caswell was willing to do.

"Fucking brat!" he screamed as he dragged his daughter in front of the couch. "How old you going to get before you quit doing this?" He slapped Cindy hard across the face, then grabbed her by the hair and shoved her face down into the soiled cushion. "You like that smell?" he demanded. "That what you want the whole house to smell like, huh?" Caswell held his daughter's head in that position for about ten seconds. Cindy held her breath and remained motionless. She had learned from experience that whenever she resisted, the punishment increased.

Tears welled up in Cindy Caswell's eyes. *I wish he had punched me in the stomach instead of the face. Christmas is only five days away.* There were several family gatherings, and the marks would definitely show. *Mom can use some of her makeup again* she told herself. *No one will know.* But she knew that everyone would.

The two newcomers to the neighborhood could hear the man yelling inside the house. His words were muffled, but there was no mistaking his rage. They ran out of the Caswells' back yard and down the street. They had just learned what everyone in their new school would tell them as soon as the second semester started: Don't ever go over to Cindy Caswell's house. Her Dad's meaner than a snake and half crazy. That's why both her sisters live with relatives, not at home.

February 17, 1982

"The so-called leaders in the White House have an agenda that can be summed up in one sentence: Enact spending cuts to abandon the Americans who most need our help, and precipitate a world war with a massive arms buildup.

"Fellow members of Congress, this is unconscionable! We must fight to ensure that our less-fortunate citizens are not forced to starve to death because of callous disregard from some of our elected officials, under the false promise of 'tax reform'.

"We must safeguard our workers from the unfeeling devastation wreaked by the 'invisible hand' the White House so unashamedly admires.

"We must stop provoking the leaders of the Soviet Union with name-calling and blatant aggression in the form of weapons buildup! These policies can only lead to a nuclear holocaust!" Richard Gaines stopped to take a breath. His aides had advised him against the use of the word 'holocaust', but he went with it anyway.

"It is time that we accept our role as keepers of the public trust and enact legislation that meets human needs. For this reason, I am introducing House Bill number..."

Congressman Gaines went on to explain the piece of legislation he had crafted to reverse the lower-tax, free-market, strong-defense philosophy which President Reagan perpetually championed. Gaines' bill mandated additional outlays for government entitlement programs, an expanded welfare state, tariffs and other protectionist trade restrictions, and increased Federal control over the American public. Every member of Congress who heard him describe it knew that Gaines also had higher taxes in mind, although he could not put that in the bill.

Democrats held a clear majority in Congress, and most of the members of that august body would actually have liked Dick Gaines' bill to become law. The President's philosophy of self-determination held strong sway over the American public, however. Most members of Congress were loath to support a blatantly tax-and-spend measure in the current political climate. Gaines' proposal and others like it went nowhere.

The problem would be made doubly vexing to the congressman by what soon began to happen around the globe. The results of low-tax, free-market policies and a strong military were very discomfiting to Richard Gaines and those who shared his beliefs. In the ensuing six years, the United States saw its own Gross National Product rise by an amount equal to the entire economy of Germany, the wealthiest nation in Europe. It was the largest peacetime expansion in living memory. The U.S. stock market tripled in value, the U.S. dollar showed record strength, and U.S. inflation fell to a 20-year low. The Berlin Wall was torn down, the Soviet Union collapsed, and Socialist regimes in country after country toppled and were replaced by ones which embraced many of the free-market principles which America had demonstrated.

Richard Gaines and legislators with similar priorities had to wait until 1988 before they had a president to work with who was amenable to the idea of higher taxes, bigger government, and reduced individual freedom. The congressmen's jobs were secure, however. Federal regulations gave Congressional incumbents a tremendous advantage in the polls, so Richard Gaines and his friends in the House all collected substantial paychecks while they waited.

April 10, 1982

"Hey! The gang's all here. Anything interesting arrived lately in the used section, Stoke?" Henry Bowman had just walked into Kelley's Sporting Goods, seen that several of his friends were there, and hailed the store's resident gunsmith and double rifle expert. Stokely Meier had many qualities that endeared him to Henry, three of which were that he had been to Africa, liked big rifles, and was the most creative swearer Henry had ever known.

"Only little stuff—.338s and smaller. Not even a decent medium-bore in the rack. The tea-baggers that come in here tend to be a bit 'recoil sensitive', shall we say," Stokely explained with an exaggerated stiff-upper-lip British accent. A muscular man with a mustache who was standing at the end of the pistol case laughed. Rufus Ingram was one of the few Americans who had served in Britain's Special Air Service, which was considered by many to be the finest of the world's special forces units. He was standing next to Thomas J. Fleming. Henry walked over to greet his friends.

"Hey, Rufus, Tom. No Shanghai Municipal Police guns here either?" Henry asked, looking down in the pistol display case. Rufus Ingram collected handguns that had been used by the famous department, which were marked with the Shanghai crest.

"Not today. Got another safari planned anytime soon?"

"I wish. I did get a letter from the guy I hunted with, Ray Johnson, not too long ago. He's planning on moving to South Africa. As far as the economy goes, I gather that things have really gone to hell in Rhodesia. He said in his letter they have a seventeen percent national sales tax now."

"I hope he doesn't have much money there," Tom Fleming said. The new government in Zimbabwe prohibited its citizens from taking their money out of the country, which made its residents all the more eager to do so.

"No, Ray's no fool. When I paid him for my trip, I wired most of the money to an account in Luxembourg. I think he only keeps enough around to meet expenses. Probably sell off the Land-Rovers to cover the last bills right before he cuts out."

"Speaking of Rhodesia," Rufus said, "a Rhodesian friend of ours, Earl Taylor-Edgarton, is coming to town in a few weeks to help us teach a class."

"Class? What kind?" Henry asked.

"Executive protection and antiterrorist measures," Rufus explained. "I handle protection strategy, and Tom covers carry methods and legal issues. Earl's the explosives expert. It's on the weekend of the twenty-seventh. You ought to come—we'll get you a pass."

"I'm free."

"Good. I think you'll find Earl's presentation very interesting." Rufus and Tom shared a look. Henry said nothing. He knew he would find out sooner or later why they were grinning at each other.

"Earl has had some interesting experiences," Tom explained. "He was born in Rhodesia, and he was on the losing side during the recent overthrow. He's wanted in Zimbabwe for murder, violating whatever they call the neutrality act, and a few other things in conjunction with the war. He can't go back there."

"He *hates* socialist governments," Rufus added. Tom Fleming chuckled.

"Zimbabwe government still sends him his pension, though. They have to—it was part of the U.N. agreement for them to recognize the new regime." Tom Fleming looked at the book in his hand.

"And speaking of governments, have you seen a copy of this yet?" Fleming held the softbound book out for his friend.

"What is it?" Henry took the 6" x 9" booklet from the lawyer and looked at the cover.

THE RIGHT TO KEEP AND BEAR ARMS

REPORT

OF THE

SUBCOMMITTEE ON THE CONSTITUTION

OF THE

COMMITTEE ON THE JUDICIARY

UNITED STATES SENATE

NINETY-SEVENTH CONGRESS

SECOND SESSION

February 1982

Printed for the use of the Committee on the Judiciary

"The results of using the entire research facilities of the Library of Congress to determine the original basis of the Second Amendment to the Constitution," Fleming explained. "The work of some of the best Constitutional scholars in the country. The findings of the '79 and '80 Treasury hearings on ATF practices. Also some position statements from some of the national anti-human-rights organizations. For comic relief, I guess," he added.

"No, I haven't seen it. *'For sale by the Superintendent of Documents, U. S. Government Printing Office'*, huh?" Henry said as he read what was printed inside the cover of the 175-page book.

"Guess again," Tom Fleming said with a sardonic smile. "They're already out of stock and—get this—they aren't going to print any more. Think maybe someone on the Committee doesn't want the public reading the results of their research? Look at the list of Committee members on the next page."

"Boy, there are some career slime buckets here, aren't there?" Henry agreed when he saw the list of names. Then he started thumbing through the contents of the government report. He stopped abruptly on page 20, and his eyes got bigger.

"They *admit* those Treasury assholes are out of control!" Henry said in astonishment. He started reading aloud from the section on the Treasury hearings that were held two and three years earlier.

"'At these hearings evidence was received...from experts who had studied the BATF, and from officials of the Bureau itself. Based upon these hearings it is apparent that enforcement tactics made possible by current federal firearms laws are constitutionally, legally, and practically reprehensible.' Well, *that* has a nice ring to it," Henry said. He scanned more of the chapter.

"'Bureau's own figures demonstrate that percentage of arrests devoted to felons in possession and persons knowingly selling to them...down to 10 percent of their cases' Christ! I didn't know it was that low! '...BATF has primarily devoted its firearms enforcement efforts to the apprehension of individuals who lack all criminal intent and knowledge...repeatedly enticed gun collectors into making a small number of sales...then charged them with engaging in the business of dealing in guns without the required license...law permits a felony conviction where individual has no criminal knowledge or intent...numerous collectors have been ruined by a felony record...' " Henry looked up. "Which is why I've had an FFL since I can remember." He returned to the document.

"Hey, they even admit that 'Even in cases where...prosecutors failed to file criminal charges, agents of the Bureau have generally confiscated the entire collection of the potential defendant upon the ground that he intended to use it in that violation of the law.' Well, there went the Fifth Amendment," Henry added. "Jesus!" he said as he read on. "Here they document them confiscating a $7000 shotgun!"

"Probably some Pommie dick-smoker's Purdey," Stokely Meier threw out. He could not imagine anyone paying that much money for a gun with no rifling in its bore.

Henry thumbed through the section, searching for something. "I don't see anything in here about them turning Ken Ballew into a vegetable," he said. Then he had a thought. "Hey, what happened to that Maryland cop they suckered into going along? The guy that put his round right between Ballew's eyes when nine Feds missed him completely from ten feet?"

"You mean Ciamillo? Ballew's family hit him with a civil suit. Couple million bucks, I think. Feds said they'd stick up for him, but when he got to the courtroom and started looking around, he was all by his lonesome. That's one of the worst things about that department. They have just about zero loyalty downwards along the chain of command. They'll hang their guys out in the wind in a minute. And that makes for zero loyalty *up* the chain."

"I talked to Lou last year," Rufus Ingram added. "I think if you took every ATF agent and wired 'em for sound with G.I. field telephones, it'd be fine with him."

For some reason, Henry Bowman paused and thought about Tom Fleming's words for several moments, and took the time to reflect on them. *No loyalty up the chain of command, huh? Ought to be able to do something with that, someday* he decided. That thought would stick in his mind thereafter, surfacing periodically over the next decade.

Henry continued to scan the government report and soon found another item of interest.

"Says reform is needed right now, and some bill, S. 1030, will do it. Hmm...doesn't give the exact words, but looks like the gist of it is, no such thing as a non-violent gun crime."

"That bill's DOA," Tom Fleming said with a sneer.

"Yeah. Can't see that happening." Henry Bowman looked at the Table of Contents, checked a few pages, then looked again at the book's cover.

"So, our government assigned a committee to research the Second Amendment. They find out it means exactly what we've said all along. They admit their lawyers lied in the Miller case. They admit the adversarial process was absent there." He flipped some pages.

"Jesus! On page 32 they even quote the National Coalition to Ban Handguns saying that the Supreme Court has ruled that the right to keep and bear arms 'exists independently of the Second Amendment', meaning the Bill of Rights is a *reminder* to the government, not authorization." He thumbed further.

"They've got great case law in here! Here's a state decision from 1878: 'If cowardly and dishonorable men sometimes shoot unarmed men with army pistols or guns, the evil must be prevented by the penitentiary and gallows, and not by a general deprivation of constitutional privilege.' "

"The more things change, the more they stay the same," Tom Fleming commented.

"We needed *that* peckerneck on the Supreme Court in '34," Stokely Meier said.

Henry looked at his three friends. "So—they did all this research. Tom, what's going to be the upshot of it?"

"Upshot? Nothing. Absolutely nothing. It's the fox guarding the henhouse. If anyone like us reads it, it just tells us what we already know. It makes us feel good for five minutes. If Senator Arnold Katzenbaum reads it, he'll toss the whole thing in the trash after the first paragraph, and sponsor another ban." Fleming grinned as he thought of something. "I wonder if his son-in-law—the kid that has the chain of strip-mall law offices? I wonder how he did on Constitutional law in school, and what he thinks of his wife's father." Fleming shook his head and returned to the subject.

"Anyway, any reform bill that actually gets taken seriously, somebody will probably hang some horrible amendment on it, and the sponsors will agree to the 'compromise', and throw another baby out of the sleigh." Tom Fleming pointed to the government document in Henry's hand. "What they're talking about in there is just going to get worse." He shrugged. "But take it home and read it anyway. I got it for you."

Tom Fleming's prediction about a reform bill was exactly right, as the country would discover in four years. His comment about the situation getting worse also proved to be a bulls-eye.

April 24, 1982

"Sit over there. If anyone asks, you're one of the small arms instructors," Rufus told Henry. Henry took a seat about halfway back and pulled a sheet from his pocket listing the instructors' curriculum vitae and the morning's agenda.

Protection Against Terrorism

Drawing on experienced experts, the staff of DRC Services have put together lectures and field exercises to prepare governmental, military, or private security protective teams to guard their principals against kidnap or assassination. Due to the international commitments of the instructional staff, it has taken years to bring them together in the USA to offer this opportunity.

The Instructional Team

Dean Copeland has spent 15 years with the Detroit Police Department, serving as a homicide sergeant and as the weapons and tactics instructor for the Special Response Team. Dean's articles on ammunition, weapons, and tactics have made him well known as an expert on deadly encounters.

Brian Rowan is the founder of the Surrey-based DRC Services, which provides and trains bodyguards worldwide. Among Brian's assignments has been heading up protection details for the Miss World Pageant. Brian is an expert at both unarmed and armed close combat techniques.

Thomas J. Fleming served as a U.S. Army infantry officer and later as an officer commanding a CID unit. An attorney and an acknowledged expert on training military and police in close combat with firearms, Tom is the author of THE WELL-TRAINED GUNFIGHTER and DEEP COVER TERRORIST. Tom's articles have also appeared regularly in GUNS REVIEW, LAW ENFORCEMENT MONTHLY, and other respected publications.

Earl Taylor-Edgarton served in the Rhodesian Light Infantry, Rhodesian SAS, Tracker Combat Unit, and as the training officer for the Selous Scouts. Later he served as an officer in South Africa's #5 Recce Commando. A veteran of a decade of counter-terrorist warfare, Earl has now emigrated to the USA and brings much expertise on explosives, demolition, bombs, incendiaries, and close combat to this course.

Rufus Ingram was an officer with the USAF Combat Security Police and later served with the SAS on VIP protection units in Europe and the third world. He trains anti-terrorist units in this country and others. His books DEAD CLIENTS GIVE LOUSY REFERRALS and EXECUTIVES DON'T EAT AT DONUT SHOPS have become standard works on close protection and anti-terrorism.

"Humpy" Atkinson spent 26 years with 22nd SAS regiment fighting in Borneo, Aden, and was an SAS Sabre Squadron sergeant major during the Dhofar War. Later he was the senior NCO in SAS Ops Research, ran the SAS combat survival course, and ran 22nd SAS Training Wing. Humpy was on the original SAS Bodyguard Training Team and helped form the SAS anti-terrorist unit. His book SAVE YOUR BUTT NO MATTER WHAT is an outstanding text on survival anywhere in the world.

Henry Bowman turned the sheet over and saw that the morning's lecture was to be given by the fourth man on the list, Earl Taylor-Edgarton. Soon a muscular man of medium height and curly blond hair walked into the room and stepped behind the podium. In a few seconds the room was quiet, and the man smiled at the people in the class.

"G'morning," he said, in the clipped British accent of native Rhodesians. "I'm Earl Taylor-Edgarton. The last two have a hyphen between, so either call me 'Earl' or use all three, but don't dump the middle one." The audience smiled. "I've been brought on to discuss the proper use of high explosives, how to improvise when the good stuff isn't available, what to do when it is, and most importantly, the proper construction, use, and handling of detonators.

"Even if your interest lies solely in recognizing terrorist threats and not in actually blowing something up, learning how to do it yourself gives the best background for finding charges that have been set. First I'll talk about explosive types, where they are usually set, and how they are typically detonated. Then I want to take bit more time on the subject of the detonators themselves, for they are the brains, you might say, of explosive weapons." Earl Taylor-Edgarton rubbed his hands together and nodded.

"Right, then. First up on the list of products to use is what we call ANFO." Earl wrote the letters on the chalkboard and turned back to the students. "This acronym stands for ammonium nitrate-fuel oil. Anyone here who has never mixed up a bit of this and tried it out has led a very sheltered life indeed." He turned back to the board and wrote the figure 5.7% underneath the four letters.

"If you are mixing up your own batch, five point seven percent fuel oil by weight is the proper amount to give a chemically balanced mixture for best combustion, much like the fuel-air mixture on a properly tuned carburettor." Henry Bowman glanced at the other attendees and saw that they were taking detailed notes of the man's lecture. *Now comes the part about too much oil being better than too little* Henry mentally predicted. *Either that or how hardware-store fertilizer is almost as good as commercial blasting agents, but the powder companies don't want you to know that.*

"Though the five point seven figure is ideal, a bit more diesel fuel results in only a slight degradation in performance. Too little, however, reduces the force of the explosion substantially. The mixture and performance curves are provided in the handout I've given each of you." Henry saw many of the students leaf through their papers to find the chart.

"The next consideration is the source of the ammonium nitrate. The companies which manufacture the material for blasting use will give you all sorts of reasons why you must purchase their product and woe betide anyone so foolish as to expect decent results using ordinary ammonium nitrate fertilizer." He gave a wolfish grin. "While it is true that the blasting grades absorb the diesel fuel a bit more thoroughly and may be a bit more efficient, thousands upon thousands of things have been blown up quite nicely using the hardware-store product, which is much easier to get and raises no eyebrows."

All of these facts were common knowledge to Henry Bowman. He had mixed up his first batch of ANFO at age thirteen and detonated it in a hole made by a post-hole digger. Now, as a contract geologist often working for petroleum companies, blasting agents were a fact of life. Earl Taylor-Edgarton's accent got Henry thinking about British things, which instantly got him daydreaming about large British double rifles such as his 4-bore, and soon he was thinking about Colonel Fosbery's collapsing bullet. This was a 19th-century invention for large-bore rifles where a hollow slug was filled with a two-ingredient explosive mixture and solid base swaged onto it. It detonated on impact with heavy bone, or after about eighteen inches of penetration.

Henry was doodling sketches of Fosbery's collapsing bullet in his notebook when he caught a few key words that told him Earl Taylor-Edgarton was now talking about military plastic explosives. Henry started to pay more attention, for this was a subject he knew little about. He was still thinking about exploding bullets for his Rodda 4-bore, though, and was not listening as closely as he might have been, at least not at first.

"...common problem when using plastics and other high-grade agents for the first time is overestimating the amount required for the desired results. When I killed the President of Zambia, it was with a buried charge of two hundred pounds of Semtex concealed underneath the asphalt. I should say that the buried charge is one of the simplest delivery systems, and an excellent one provided that the target's route is known in advance." Earl pronounced it 'advonce'. Henry was jerked out of his daydream. *Did he just say he killed the President of Zambia?* Henry thought in astonishment.

"In this country, of course," the lecturer continued, "such a plan would be most fruitless. The President's planned route is a closely guarded secret, and the Secret Service checks every inch of it with metal detectors and other devices prior to his passage along it. However, in third-world countries, or for all U.S. officials of lesser concern than the immediate occupants of the White House, this is an excellent method of dispatch. Therefore, if you are assigned to keep some cannibal alive, you should take a leaf from the Secret Service boys' book and thoroughly examine the route prior to commencing travel. We will discuss the details of that process" (he pronounced it with a long o) "this afternoon." Earl Taylor-Edgarton looked baffled for a moment.

"Where was I, before I ran off about buried charges?" Earl Taylor-Edgarton asked himself. "Ah, yes—quantity. As I was saying, when I killed the President of Zambia, I used two hundred pounds of Semtex buried beneath the roadway. I have no excuse for what I did. I was used to using lower-grade, more universally available materials, and I did not alter my weight estimates whatsoever. The force of that explosion blew the President's car and his entourage's car over three hundred yards, which was entirely excessive and could have had tragic results. Fortunately, the flying debris did not land on any of our people.

"Two hundred pounds of Semtex was entirely too much. In contrast, I used a mere half-pound charge on the leader of the SWAPO Party. By fixing the eight-ounce block of Semtex to the gasoline tank of the Audi Fox that he was driving," (he pronounced it 'Fawkes', which Henry thought appropriate) "I accomplished the same result with far less disruption. The gasoline tank is an excellent spot for placement, and one of the first places you should look if you are assigned protective duty. Should you be working the other side, a half-pound is sufficient for a lightweight vehicle such as the Fox, but a pound should be used in the case of a full-size American auto, and perhaps two pounds for a limousine or large truck."

Henry Bowman glanced around the room and saw that everyone was rapidly taking notes. He looked at what the man in front of him had written:

Don't use too much Semtex. Gasoline tank is good spot
1/2 lb. for small cars
1 lb. for Impalas/station wagons
2 lbs. limos & trucks

Tom and Rufus weren't kidding when they said this would be an interesting seminar Henry thought. *Got to talk to this guy at lunch.*

February 28, 1985

"I don't like what I've been hearing, babe."

"I don't either, Randy. Maybe it's time you went to the courthouse and filed this, like we were talking about doing."

"Yeah. Can you watch the girls? I'll take Sammy with me."

"Of course. Can you pick up some milk when you're in town? We're about out."

"Sure," he said, kissing his wife before he left the cabin.

Randy and Vicki Weaver were in their mid-30s. They had left Iowa two years before, and moved with their three children to the mountains in Idaho. Outside Fort Dodge, Iowa, Randy had been a John Deere mechanic who supplemented the family income with an Amway distributorship. He and Vicki had been raised Baptists and went to church regularly, but they disagreed with most ministers' interpretation of scripture, and had gone from one church to another in search of a spiritual philosophy that matched their own.

Ultimately, Randy and Vicki aligned themselves with a sect known as Christian Identity, a group whose theology included the belief that European whites are God's chosen people. The Weavers, like many members of Christian Identity (and like many residents of Idaho) had no great affection for blacks, Jews, or big government. This was one of the reasons Randy and Vicki had moved to the Selkirk Mountains in the Idaho wilderness area and loved living there. Because of the remote location, Vicki Weaver homeschooled the three Weaver children.

An Aryan Nations camp was located a few miles from the Weavers' home. Randy had attended two of their meetings, and had decided that he did not want to join their group. The home schooling, the nearby white supremacy camp, and the fact that the Weavers (like almost everyone in Idaho) owned guns was a combination that elicited comment from a few of the other residents in the area. As local gossip had it, Randy was a member of Aryan Nations, owned illegal weapons, and federal agents were going to conduct an armed raid on his home. It was something that Randy Weaver wanted to avoid.

After Weaver kissed his wife goodbye, he started the drive to the Boundary County Courthouse. He was going to file an affidavit putting on record the fact that he and Vicki believed that their lives and those of their three children were in danger from what Randy termed a 'smear campaign' by some of the local residents.

The affidavit listed the residents Randy and Vicki felt were causing the problem, as well as the names of county and federal law officers that the Weavers had spoken to regarding the situation. The document also contained the sentence "I make legal and official notice that I believe I may have to defend myself and my family from a physical attack on my life."

Randy Weaver's statement exhibited great foresight.

May 12, 1985

"These niggers are really starting to irritate me. Are we all set for tomorrow morning?" the Mayor asked the Managing Director as he looked at his watch and saw that it was almost ten o'clock. "I want to get home and get to bed." Leo Brooks suppressed a wince at the black Mayor's choice of words.

"I just talked with Commissioner Sambor about an hour ago," Brooks replied. "They're ready to go in tomorrow morning, early. Between four-thirty and five."

"They have enough men and equipment on it to get it done the first time?"

"Yes, sir. The MOVE members have blocked themselves in. The police have confirmed that they've reinforced the building on Osage with railroad ties and logs. Greg's putting a demolition team in the houses on either side of them. They'll need to blast some holes in the side walls. Way the MOVE house is barricaded, that's the only shot at getting stun grenades and tear gas inside."

"They better have enough to make sure it gets done. I told Sambor I want those people *out* of there. Like yesterday."

"He knows that. He said they can blast through the side walls, and if there's any trouble getting through that way, they'll do the roof. Full load of tear gas, we should see 'em vacate pretty quick. First step's got to be explosives, though. Got to blast holes so they can get the stun grenades and tear gas in."

"Fine," Mayor Goode said to Managing Director Brooks. "I'll be asleep when they go in. Give me a call in the morning. Maybe at breakfast I can turn on the news and see them being hauled off in handcuffs." He shook his head as he turned to leave. "The last thing I need is for the neighbors to hold another goddamned news conference." Goode walked out of the room.

The situation which was so vexing to Philadelphia's mayor involved a loosely-knit group of blacks that called itself MOVE. In 1978, at another Philadelphia location, MOVE members had been involved in a confrontation with police that had resulted in the death of one officer and injuries to four policemen and four firemen. Nine MOVE members were serving time in prison for third-degree murder because of what had happened that day.

Now, seven years later, MOVE members in a house on Osage Avenue had decided to force the city of Philadelphia to negotiate the release of their jailed brethren. The group came up with a novel four-pronged strategy to achieve this goal: They reinforced their dwelling with railroad ties, tree trunks, and pieces of steel; they stopped paying their utility bills; they allowed garbage to pile up in front of their house; and they used loudspeakers to broadcast diatribes against President Reagan and Mayor Goode.

The MOVE group's plan had failed in its goal of coercing the City of Philadelphia into getting the nine men released from prison. It had, however, succeeded in irritating the other residents of the middle-class neighborhood on and around Osage Avenue.

The neighbors (who wished the radical group would live up to the name it had chosen for itself) called a news conference in late April and strongly criticized the Mayor for his failure to take action. A week later, Mayor Goode ordered Police Commissioner Greg Sambor to develop a plan to storm the MOVE house.

That plan was about to be executed.

May 13, 1985

Philadelphia Mayor W. W. Goode was not happy as he watched the live news coverage on his television set. The siege had been going on for several hours, and the MOVE members were still inside their house. He flicked off the set and headed out the door to go to his office.

***

"Brooks, I said I wanted those people *out* of there," Goode said once more into the telephone. It was perhaps his fifteenth conversation that day with Philadelphia's Managing Director, who was on the scene near the MOVE house on Osage Avenue. The MOVE group was still inside. When the police had started to break holes in the walls to set their explosives, the occupants of the house had realized they were under siege, and had fired randomly to drive off the attackers. No officers had been injured, but they were now afraid to resume their efforts in their former positions.

"Sir, you have to understand the situation here. We've had to abandon our positions on either side. They're shooting from inside, and it's too risky for–"

"You're not listening to me, Brooks," the Mayor said, cutting off his subordinate. "I've told you and I've told Sambor that all I want to know is what is *important* and *necessary.* I can see on my own goddamn television set here in the office that they're still in there. You're not telling me anything I don't already know. Sambor's supposed to drive them out, so what the hell is he sitting there jerking off for? Call me when you've got something to say," the Mayor instructed, and hung up the phone.

Leo Brooks looked at the dead receiver in his hand. He was in a position that was utterly unfamiliar to him, and he did not like it. He wished the Mayor would talk to the Police Commissioner directly instead of going through him. Brooks was tired of having the Mayor jump down his throat when the MOVE members didn't dutifully march outside to be arrested.

Brooks sighed and went to confer with the Police Commissioner once again.

***

"Sir, it's going to have to be through the roof. Sambor's got to get the tear gas in. He says that's the only way, and I believe him. The cops can't set any charges by hand— they're afraid they'll be shot at." Brooks did not point out that getting shot was one of the risks you ran when you tried to dynamite someone's house while they were inside. "He's got a bomb rigged up, and a helicop–"

"Is it going to work?" the Mayor demanded.

"Well, *he* seems to think so," Leo Brooks said. Brooks did not point out that if it did, it would be the first and only thing that had gone right that day. "He wants to make sure it's okay with you."

"I told him to get those people out of there. If that's what it takes, get him on it right now. We've been wasting too damned much time on this."

"Yes, sir." Leo Brooks hung up and went to find Greg Sambor.

***

The helicopter pilot eyed the makeshift cargo with distinct unease. In-flight fire was every pilot's worst nightmare. Having a passenger carry an obviously full five-gallon gas can as baggage was not conducive to pilot peace-of-mind, particularly when the gas can had some odd shapes taped to the side of it.

The pilot would have been even less enthused had he known more details about the package that was about to be dropped on top of the MOVE members. Attached to the gas can with duct tape was a nine-and-a-half-pound block of C-4 plastic explosive with a makeshift detonator.

Almost all of the journalists who would later write about the events of May 13th would talk about 'the bomb' that was dropped from the helicopter, but would omit or fail to mention the particular type of explosive that was used. The omission would not be by design, but rather by ignorance, for few journalists covering the story had been in active military service. Among members of the public who did have military experience or who were familiar with such matters, and who somehow learned the details of the police department's makeshift bomb, the reaction was universal: *'C-4? Jesus Christ! Where the fuck did a bunch of Philadelphia cops get ten pounds of C-4?'*

From the pilot's point of view, the delivery went well despite his earlier misgivings. The helicopter was not shot at and the pilot was able to fly the chopper well clear of the roof of the MOVE house by the time the charge was detonated.

***

"Holy *fuck!* What was that?" one of the firemen yelled. The tremendous concussion had made him lose his balance and caused windows around him to shatter. He shook his head to try to clear the ringing from his ears. Then he looked at the MOVE house, which was over 100 yards away. "Oh, *shit,*" he said as he started to run towards the truck to which he was assigned.

The entire roof of the house on Osage Avenue was on fire, and the flames were spreading to the adjacent buildings.

***

"Anyone dead in any of the other buildings?"

"No, sir, or at least, we haven't found anyone yet. We had some time to warn them, and we think we got everyone out. Of course, you never know...somebody sleeping off a drunk, that kind of thing..." He let the sentence dangle, and Leo Brooks nodded.

"Ten blocks," Leo Brooks said softly. He was thinking that if the Mayor were white, there would definitely be a race riot. A bit of gallows humor came to mind, and he smiled at the subordinate. "Right about now the neighbors are probably thinking that garbage in the lawn and incoherent broadcasts about Reagan and the Mayor weren't so bad after all." Brooks knew already that he would have to resign.

The tremendous blast had shattered everything made of wood for a considerable distance around the center of the explosion. The result had been huge quantities of tinder that the flaming gasoline vapor had soaked instantly, creating a roaring inferno that the fire department had been totally unprepared to control.

The fire had instantly spread to residences around the MOVE house. It consumed a ten-block area and destroyed sixty-one homes, leaving over two hundred fifty Philadelphia residents without any of their possessions or a place to live. Miraculously, there had been no fatalities outside of the MOVE house.

Inside the residence of the radical group, it was a different story. The crude barricades the MOVE members had constructed only served to exacerbate the deadly combination of 20th-century military explosives technology and a flammable petroleum accelerant. The reinforcements were largely made of wood, and the railroad ties were of course soaked with creosote. The MOVE house went up like a tinderbox. Only two of the members managed to escape the inferno. Seven adults and four children were burned alive inside their home on Osage Avenue.

***

The two men watched the television screen with both fascination and horror. The host, who was older than his guest by three years, kept his thoughts to himself. The sixty-eight-year-old visitor, however, found the news footage too wrenching for him to remain silent.

"It is just like Warsaw forty years ago," Irwin Mann said. "It looks exactly the same."

"They just didn't bother to build a wall around 'em first, before lighting up the torch," Max Collins replied.

The nightmares that had finally stopped disturbing Irwin Mann's sleep in the late 1950s would return that evening with a vengeance.

February 12, 1986

"Hi Mom, hi Dad," Cindy Caswell said as she walked through the back door and into the kitchen.

"Who gave you that?" Boone Caswell demanded.

"Boy at school. Valentine's Day's on Sunday," Cindy said with a big smile. *Dad is such a dweeb sometimes* she thought.

"Fella give you something, he's going to expect something back." Her father's voice had a trace of a whine in it.

"Dad, it's *just* some candy. And Kevin doesn't expect anything—if he did, I'd beat him up. I'm bigger than he is. We can eat it for dessert tonight. I think it's the kind you like, and I don't need the extra calories anyway." Cindy Caswell dropped the box of chocolates on the kitchen counter, kissed her father on the cheek, smiled at her mother, and walked to her bedroom. Her father said nothing.

In the past eighteen months, a surprising transformation had come over the Caswell family. Cindy had started going through puberty at age thirteen. As her figure had swelled and her features had become more defined, it had become obvious that she was about to turn into a truly stunning young woman.

When Cindy's breasts had started to develop and her legs had become long and shapely, Myra Caswell had been filled with dread. She had expected her husband to start in with the touching and petting that he had practiced with their two older daughters before the girls had gone to live with Myra's parents. What Myra feared most, however, had never happened.

Boone was getting older—he was almost fifty—but that wasn't the whole of it. It was Cindy. There was something about her that was much different from her sisters. Cindy Caswell had always been able to get boys to do things for her, and by age fourteen, it was obvious that she held the same kind of power over her father.

Cindy Caswell had known about her father's nighttime visits to her sisters before they had left home, and she had prepared herself for the inevitable event when he would come to her room some late night. She had planned to tell him that if he continued, it was going to be the only time it would ever happen, and that she would then be gone from the house forever. Cindy had not been sure whether her plan would actually work. She feared her father would track her down, or that she might otherwise be forced to return.

Cindy never had the chance to find out. Her father never touched her. She thought it might be because of his friends, who sometimes came over to the house. They were big, coarse men just like Boone, but when she entered the room their voices softened and their words became much less harsh. Sometimes she thought her father had somehow been shamed by the actions of these men. Sometimes she didn't know what to think. Cindy had a gift for projecting an atmosphere which surrounded her and anyone nearby. Dramatics became her strongest interest, and she shone in every school play where she had a part.

Myra Caswell, who had watched her first two daughters grow to loathe their father, gave thanks every single day that the same fate had not befallen her last child. She knew in her heart that her daughter Cindy would still be living happily in their home when she graduated from high school. She knew that Cindy would live with them until she found a decent young man to share her life with, or decided to move on for other good reasons of her own choosing.

Unfortunately, Myra Caswell was dead wrong.

March 12, 1986

The man scowled with disappointment and slight irritation as he saw the two men on the other side of the lake. Colazzo had come to the water-filled rock pit just south of the Tamiami Trail that morning to do some plinking. Soon after he arrived, the two men got in their vehicle, a white Ford pickup, and drove over to where he was standing. It was common for Florida residents in the area to target practice in the Everglades, and the man did not think anything was amiss until he saw the driver climb out and level a revolver at him. By then it was too late for him to get to his guns, and he stood there unarmed.

"Empty your pockets," the second man said. He held a Ruger Mini-14 rifle. "Slowly. We're taking your money, your guns, and your car." The unarmed man did as he was instructed, noting with dismay that the hand holding the revolver trained on him was absolutely steady. "Down by the water, spic," the driver ordered. Colazzo complied with the command, as feelings of despair washed over him.

"You a cop?" the second man demanded.

"No." Colazzo saw the first man nod, as if to himself, and realized the man was about to kill him. He had nothing to lose, so he rushed the gunman. The man with the revolver fired twice. Colazzo felt as if he had been slapped in the side, but he was charged with adrenaline and he did not go down. He grabbed for the man with the gun.

Several more shots rang out. Colazzo never knew which of the two men fired the one that hit him. The bullet struck Colazzo just to the right of his right eye, passed under the skin, and exited out the side. The blow to his skull stunned Colazzo, and he collapsed on the bank. The skin was torn open on the side of his head. Like most superficial head wounds, it bled profusely.

The two men took one look at the inert form with blood pouring out the side of its head and assumed the man was dead. They gathered up their victim's keys, money, and guns, and started walking to the two vehicles.

"What is it about spics and late 'seventies Monte Carlos?" one of the men asked the other as he got in Colazzo's black 1979 model and adjusted the seat. His friend looked blank, then grinned as he remembered. Five months before, in October, they had executed a young man in much the same fashion. His name had been Emilio Briel, and he had also been out target shooting in the area. They had killed him and stolen his car, a beige 1977 Monte Carlo. The two men had ditched the vehicle immediately after a job on January 10.

"You got me," his friend said with a laugh. He climbed into the Ford pickup, started the engine, and led the way down the dirt path out to the highway.

Colazzo was not dead and would, in fact, recover from his wounds. He would also make a complete report to the authorities about the events of that morning. The FBI would listen to his story with great interest. It would dovetail perfectly with several other pieces of information they already had about several pending cases.

Michael Platt and Edward Matix were the names of the two men who had shot Colazzo that morning and left him for dead. Some law enforcement personnel would later examine the exploits of the two criminals, as part of their police training. The FBI would go so far as to film a reenactment of what was about to come. Apart from these examples, however, it would be private citizens with a serious commitment to shooting skills who would show the most interest.

Among members of the gun culture, Platt and Matix were about to become famous.

March 29, 1986

"Hi, Stokely."

"Henry! You're just the guy I wanted to see. Everybody that comes in the store wants to know what the story is on this Volkmer-McClure bill. Adrian here was saying he's heard it's probably going to pass, but everyone tells me something different about what's in it. You've got more Federal licenses than this store—can you explain what the bill says? Volkmer's office says they're swamped." Henry Bowman walked over to the group of men standing by the used handgun display case and ran his fingers through his hair.

"Starting from the beginning, which is a habit I learned from my father who taught history, the 1968 Gun Control Act was passed in the middle of a bunch of hysteria, and was also combined with the Omnibus Crime and Safe Streets Act. Bobby Kennedy had been shot, Martin Luther King Junior had been shot, the '68 Democratic convention had resulted in a riot. All gun laws are bad, but there were some especially ludicrous ones in the '68 Act. In addition, after '68, states started passing wildly differing state laws about guns, with little or no recognition of the fact that people driving through might not be aware of them.

"The main thrust of Volkmer-McClure is to remove the most pointless aspects of GCA '68, and give people in transit a federal 'umbrella' so they don't get nailed for doing something they didn't know was illegal."

"What do you mean by that?" asked a man Henry had never seen before. "The second part, I mean."

"Well, right now you own a rifle in Missouri, and you're completely legal. Let's say you apply for and get an out-of-state moose tag to go hunt moose in the state of Maine. They're eager for you to come with your .338 Winchester. You were going to drive, but realize you'd break some state laws along the way by having your unloaded gun in the trunk of your car. So you hop on a nonstop flight to Maine with your rifle declared in checked baggage.

"A hundred fifty miles from Bangor, one engine gets low oil pressure, or is running hot, or there's something wrong at the runway, so the flight is diverted to the nearest major airport, which is Logan in Boston. TWA says they'll put you up for the night and fly you out in the morning. The plane lands in Boston.

"Under current law, the instant the wheels touch the ground you are now a felon. You are in Massachusetts with a rifle and without a firearms I.D. card, and that is a felony that carries a mandatory one-year jail sentence. It's Massachusetts law. There's no exemption just because you didn't want to be in Massachusetts.

"Volkmer-McClure says that if you are legal where you live, and legal where you're going, states in between can't arrest you in transit if your guns are cased and unloaded."

The man shook his head and laughed. "Nobody's going to arrest one of us for driving out to a hunt somewhere, with or without this new bill you're talking about."

Henry shrugged. *Dream on, Jim* he thought silently. *Stupid laws apply to everyone, even rich white people.* "Maybe not," Henry said, "but Volkmer-McClure makes it legal, so you don't have to worry. The other main provision is that all the recordkeeping requirements and interstate commerce restrictions on ammo are lifted."

"And Halle-fuckin'-lujah to that," Stokely Meier said. The Gun Control Act of 1968 had forced all stores and places of business that sold ammunition to keep detailed, permanent records of every purchase and purchaser of handgun ammunition. In eighteen years, over fifty *billion* rounds of handgun ammunition had been sold, but the record-keeping requirement had yet to account for a single criminal being brought to justice.

"There's a few other things in the bill, mostly to let old stuff get imported again, like Krags and Mausers." Henry smiled inwardly as he thought of his first centerfire, the 8mm Model 98 Mauser he had bought when he was ten years old. He still put a few hundred rounds through it each year.

"Anything bad in it?" one of the men asked.

"Not that I know of. I think I would have heard if there was. It's just straight repeal of some bad stuff."

Henry Bowman was right. The Firearms Owner's Protection Act, which was the official title of the Volkmer-McClure bill, contained no new infringements. That would hold true right up until thirty seconds before the bill was passed by the United States Congress.

"Okay, let me recap what we know and how we're going to proceed," Special Agent Gordon McNeill said as he stared at the thirteen FBI agents under his supervision. "These two men have hit five banks or armored cars that we know of in a six-month period. In two of those five instances, they shot guards without provocation. One of them they shot three times in the back. They also shot two citizens execution-style down in the Everglades to get their cars." He looked at each of his men. "These guys like to kill people," he added meaningfully.

"On October sixteenth, two men in ski masks hit a Wells Fargo armored car parked in front of a Winn-Dixie on Dixie Highway. They had a shotgun and a .45, yelled 'Freeze!', then shot the driver in the leg and ran off without getting any money.

"November eighth, two men in ski masks grabbed two employees at the drive-in of the Florida National Bank on Dixie Highway. They never got in the bank because the teller fumbled with his keys, but they got away with ten thousand dollars that was being brought from the bank to the drive-in window.

"An hour and a half later on the same day, two men in ski masks hit the Professional Savings Bank on Dixie Highway, eighteen blocks away from Florida National. They did a little better at this one—forty-one thousand dollars." One of the other agents whistled at the dollar amount. "Right. Witnesses said the men were armed with a large-frame revolver and an AR-15, and escaped in a 1977 Monte Carlo." McNeill stopped to clear his throat.

"January tenth of this year, two men, again in dark clothing and again wearing ski masks, held up the Brink's armored car in front of the Barnett Bank on Dixie highway. One of them shot the guard in the back. When the guard collapsed, the other shot him twice more in the back with an AR-15 and took his gun. This time they got $54,000 in cash." This figure drew even more murmurs of appreciation. "Witnesses saw the men escape in a beige Monte Carlo with a light-colored vinyl top. One of them followed the car, and–"

"*What?*" one of the agents exclaimed.

"Yes. One of the witnesses followed the two men and saw them abandon the Monte Carlo and continue their flight in a white or beige 3/4-ton pickup truck. He thinks it was a Ford."

"What, he didn't follow that one, too? And tell us where they went? Or better yet, arrest 'em while he was at it?" Gordon McNeill said nothing. In a few moments he had their attention again.

"The abandoned Monte Carlo was recovered. It was registered to a Mr. Aureliano Briel. Mr. Briel's son, Emelio Briel, was reported missing in October. Emilio Briel was last seen on October fourth, when he took the Monte Carlo and told his father he was going target shooting with a .22 rifle in the Everglades. On March first, skeletal remains of a decomposed body were found seven-tenths of a mile south of the Tamiami Trail. Analysis confirmed that it was the body of Emilio Briel, who had been killed by a large-caliber handgun wound to the head.

"On March twelfth, we got a break. Mr. Jose Colazzo was out target shooting on a small lake south of the Tamiami Trail, in the same general area that Briel's body had been found. Colazzo was accosted by two men driving a white Ford pickup who held him at gunpoint, took his money, guns, and keys, and shot him several times. They left him for dead and took his car. Colazzo survived. He has given us a description of the two men, and you have the artist's sketches in front of you. Colazzo's car is a black 1979 Chevrolet Monte Carlo, license plate NTJ 891."

"These scrotes got a thing about Monte Carlos or what?" one of the agents joked. Supervisory Agent McNeill ignored him.

"Seven days after the attempted murder of Jose Colazzo," McNeill went on, "on March nineteenth, two men wearing ski masks and dark clothing robbed the Barnett Bank on Dixie Highway."

"Same bank as before?" one of the agents asked.

"Right. They got away with $8,000 this time, and their getaway car was a black two-door Chevrolet Monte Carlo." Gordon McNeill looked at the thirteen agents in front of him. "All five of these bank and armored car robberies were committed in a small area along Dixie Highway, by two heavily armed men in ski masks. The FBI is certain that the same two men committed all five robberies, and were also responsible for the murder of Briel and the attempted murder of Jose Colazzo. Accordingly, the fourteen of us are going to set up a ten-car rolling stakeout along Dixie Highway with the goal of spotting and apprehending these two assholes. We've got two good vehicle descriptions and one license plate number, and we'll be in constant radio contact with each other. We've got a good chance of finding these scumbags."

"You really think they'll be in the same car, and not have ditched it, or changed the plates?" asked one of the agents. "After this much time, I mean?"

"Good chance of it. Briel's beige Monte Carlo was abandoned January 10. That was more than three months after Briel was killed and the car stolen from him, and it still had the original plates on it. They ditched that car only after shooting the guard. On the bank job three weeks ago, no one was shot. These guys may still be driving that car around. They think Colazzo's dead, remember." McNeill flipped to a map and went on to the next phase of his briefing.

"Here's how we're going to work it. Tomorrow morning, we're going to spread the ten cars out along a five-mile stretch of Dixie Highway, and..."

The briefing session continued for another half hour.

"Attention all units, we are behind a black vehicle, two-door, Florida license NTJ 891, we're headed south on South Dixie...North on South Dixie," he corrected, *"it's a black Monte Carlo, two males in it, NTJ 891."* Ben Grogan had spotted Colazzo's stolen car and was directly behind it. The FBI had lucked into the two bank robbers in the first half-hour of the first day of the surveillance. Grogan was calling all the other cars on the rolling stakeout.

"Oooh, that's it, lift up a little...yeah, right there," the FBI agent told the waitress, then resumed his thrusting. She was lying on her back on the table in the closed-off back room of the restaurant on Dixie Highway. "You like starting the day off this way, honey?" he asked teasingly.

"She can't talk with her mouth full," laughed his partner on the other side of the table. "But I'd say she's enjoying it."

"Mmm-hmm," the girl mumbled in agreement.

"Watch those teeth, now, darlin'," the second man said as he pushed down her bra and squeezed the woman's full breasts.

After a few minutes, the first agent raised his hand up for a 'high five'. The second agent saw this and mirrored his partner's move. "Readyyyy—*shift!*" the first man yelled as he slapped his partner's hand. The two agents simultaneously disengaged themselves from the woman's vagina and mouth, and rapidly exchanged positions.

Cop groupies are great the first man thought with a grin. *And it's good to be able to share it with your partner.* He briefly thought of the Heckler & Koch MP5 submachine guns, and a look of concern passed over his face. The two weapons were lying underneath two sets of body armor on the back seat of the unmarked sedan out in the parking lot. *Hell, nobody's going to steal them in broad daylight. Not in the next hour or two, at least* he decided, and returned his concentration to the situation at hand. Much later, after the two agents had finished their exertions, had a few cups of coffee with their friend, and returned to the parking lot, the first man would discover that he had been right. No one had given the parked sedan or its contents a second look.

"They're making a right turn on 117th...right on 117th," Jerry Dove, Grogan's partner continued over the radio. "We're burned. They're onto us. They know we're cops. Moving around, lots of activity in the front seat."

Special Agent Richard Manauzzi had been close by, and in less than a minute he had maneuvered his vehicle in behind Grogan and Dove's car. Within moments, agents John Hanlon and Edmundo Mireles, in their unmarked sedan, had joined the other two FBI cars following the black Monte Carlo.

"Keep on 'em," Agent McNeill, the supervisor, said on the radio to the other cars when he heard the exchange. "I'm heading north on Dixie. I'll turn east on 120th and parallel you." The Monte Carlo, however, had made one right turn and was about to make another.

"We're turning west on 120th Street," Dove, in the lead FBI car, announced. Platt and Matix in the Monte Carlo, followed by three FBI cars, were about to pass Supervisor McNeill, who was headed in the opposite direction on 120th Street.

"Hey, we're right behind you," John Hanlon, driving the third FBI car called. "If

414

you want to do it, let's do it."

The FBI supervisor saw the four cars headed towards him. Agent McNeill looked at the driver of the black Monte Carlo and saw what he would later describe as 'the face of a man on a mission.' He also saw that the man in the passenger seat was putting a magazine into what McNeill recognized was a Ruger Mini-14 rifle.

"Guy in the passenger seat has a long gun he's loading, looks like a Mini-14," McNeill called over the radio as he passed the Monte Carlo and the three FBI cars. McNeill braked his sedan to make a U-turn and join the other three federal vehicles as the Monte Carlo turned left and began to head south on 82nd Avenue. "Let's do it," McNeill ordered over the radio. "Felony car stop. Let's do it."

John Hanlon, behind the wheel of the second FBI car, drew his Smith & Wesson .357 magnum and put it on the seat beside him. Then he stomped on the throttle and pulled around Ben Grogan and Jerry Dove's vehicle until he and his partner, Ed Mireles, were parallel to the black Monte Carlo. Hanlon rammed the Monte Carlo, trying to force it off the right side of the road. Jerry Dove, in turn, pulled around both John Hanlon's sedan and the black Monte Carlo, and pulled directly in front of the two felons, to keep them from outrunning the car that was trying to force them off the road. Richard Manauzzi, in the third FBI vehicle, was now immediately behind the black Chevrolet. Michael Platt and Edward Matix were boxed in.

Those two have a clear shot at blasting all four agents Manauzzi thought grimly as he drew his revolver and put it on his lap. *Got to distract them.* He floored the accelerator and rammed Platt and Matix's black Monte Carlo from behind.

When Agent Manauzzi slammed his sedan into the back of the Monte Carlo, he caused several things to happen. The first was that as per Newton's Law, Manauzzi's revolver flew off his lap and the driver's door flew open. Manauzzi was carrying no back-up gun, and a feeling of horror suffused him as he visualized his only weapon lying yards behind him, out in the street.

The force of the impact also disengaged the Monte Carlo from Hanlon's vehicle, shoving it forward. Matix, the Monte Carlo's driver, had cranked his wheels to the left to counteract Hanlon's attempt to push him off the road. Thus, when Manauzzi's car bunted the Chevy on ahead, the black two-door immediately spun out counterclockwise. Matix rode the slide back onto the pavement and punched the throttle when the car was facing in the opposite direction. Platt and Matix were now heading back north on 82nd Avenue.

Hanlon and Mireles' car, on the other hand, had had its wheels cranked right, to force the black car off the road. When the Monte Carlo was knocked clear, Hanlon's sedan spun to the right in the gravel at the side of the road, and slammed head-on into a concrete wall. Newton's Law was still in effect. As with Manauzzi's gun, Agent Hanlon's revolver flew off the front seat and out of reach in the impact.

Agent Richard Manauzzi saw the black Monte Carlo headed towards him. The two men were about to escape, and he was now unarmed. He knew Grogan and Dove were up ahead of him, and they still had to get turned around. *Not this time, pal* he thought as he spun his wheel hard left and rammed into the driver's side of the approaching Monte Carlo, forcing it into a tree on the side of the road. His own car slewed to a stop parallel to the black two-door, in a position similar to two cars side-by-side in a parking lot.

Agent Manauzzi was hyperventilating as he looked over at the Monte Carlo. The driver's window of the black car was rolled down. One man was bringing a 12-gauge shotgun to bear on him and the other was raising a rifle. It was then that the full weight of realization hit FBI Agent Manauzzi: *I am in deep shit.* He flung open the door of his sedan and ducked his head as he bailed out of the car. The shotgun boomed and the muzzle blast of the .223 rifle rang in his ears as the two men fired at him from six feet away. The shots had to come through the glass on the passenger side of Agent Manauzzi's sedan, however. The high-velocity rifle bullets fragmented, and the shotgun pellets were slowed. Manauzzi was taking his first step when he felt lead fragments dig into his shoulder and torso. He gritted his teeth and kept running for the other side of the street, where he hoped to find his lost revolver.

Supervisory Agent Gordon NcNeill, who had passed the others in the opposite direction less than a minute before, had gotten his car turned around and was almost to the bank robbers' vehicle when he saw Manauzzi force the Monte Carlo into the tree. He swung his car in at an angle to Manauzzi's sedan. A few seconds before, McNeill had managed to throw his vest on over his head, but had not been able to secure it with the velcro straps to his torso. Like all of the agents, he had been carrying body armor. Also like all of the agents but one, he had not been wearing it, but had left it lying on the seat of his car.

McNeill knew that the two men were already shooting at him, for he could hear the bullets striking his car even before he came to a stop. He wanted the shotgun that was lying on the floor of the back seat, but when shots through his windshield sprayed him with glass fragments, Gordon McNeill changed his mind. He couldn't afford to expose himself by retrieving the more effective weapon, so he drew his 2 1/2" Smith & Wesson .357 magnum and ran for cover. His unsecured bullet-resistant vest flapped around him as McNeill took a position behind the engine block of Manauzzi's wrecked car. That put Supervisory Agent Gordon McNeill about eight feet from Platt and Matix, directly facing the deafening muzzle blasts coming from their guns.

As McNeill exited his car and ran for cover, more agents joined in the fray. Ben Grogan, who had gotten his car turned around and had resumed pursuit, slammed on the brakes and brought his white Buick to a screeching halt behind the black Monte Carlo. Newton's Law reasserted itself once more. Under the car's abrupt deceleration, Grogan's eyeglasses flew off his face and lodged under the sedan's brake pedal. Grogan and Dove both jumped out of the car and started firing at the men in the black Monte Carlo, although Grogan was essentially blind. Neither Grogan nor Dove, however, had lost their weapons. Each man was carrying a Smith & Wesson model 459 semiauto that held fifteen rounds of 9mm ammo.

Platt and Matix could not open either door of their stolen vehicle to escape. The right one was caved in and jammed shut from the crash, and the left was blocked by Manauzzi's FBI car. As McNeill, Grogan, and Dove began firing at the two men trapped in the front seat of the Monte Carlo, Hanlon and Mireles jumped out of their car, the one that had spun and crashed into the concrete wall.

Mireles was carrying a Remington 870 shotgun as he ran over to join Gordon McNeill. Hanlon, who had lost his main gun in the crash, drew his 5-shot Chief's Special backup gun from his ankle holster and ran to join Ben Grogan, who was firing blindly from the left rear of his Buick.

As Mireles ran towards McNeill, he realized his shotgun was pointing straight at his fellow agent, and he instinctively took his finger out of the trigger guard and raised the muzzle towards the sky just as Platt fired his Ruger .223 at the center of Mireles' unprotected chest. The move saved Mireles' life. Raising the shotgun put Mireles' left arm directly in front of his heart. The high-velocity bullet struck Mireles' upraised forearm, shattering both bones and turning the flesh almost inside out. The 280-lb. agent fell to the ground and looked at his ruined left arm. White bones were sticking out for a distance of over three inches. *Puta! It's turned inside out. Have to be amputated* he thought, then turned his mind to matters he could control. *Funny how it doesn't hurt* Mireles realized distractedly.

As Mireles hit the asphalt, Platt continued to fire his .223. One of his next few shots hit Gordon McNeill's gun hand, throwing the agent's right arm to a vertical position. *Oh, Jesus!* McNeill thought as he looked at the horrendous ruin of his right hand. *Well, it doesn't hurt, and I didn't let go of my gun.* He brought the gun back down and kept firing at Platt and Matix. The FBI agent watched Matix jerk when one of the Winchester Silvertips out of his .357 magnum hit him. Then the agent's gun snapped on a fired case. Gordon McNeill felt utterly deflated. *I'm empty, and they're both still firing.* He forced himself to run to his own car to reload. His mind was fully occupied, and he did not notice Ed Mireles heave himself to his feet and follow him, carrying the shotgun and cradling his ruined left arm.

"Where is everybody?" Ben Grogan screamed from the left side of his white Buick, behind the black Monte Carlo. He was firing his Model 459 in the direction of Platt and Matix, but he could not see without his glasses. His partner, Jerry Dove, crouched behind the right side of their car and continued to fire 9mm bullets out of his own 15-shot Model 459. So far he had not hit either of the two men in the black Monte Carlo.

This is a fucking nightmare thought Agent Ron Risner. He and his partner Gil Arrantia had stopped their car across the street and slightly north, to block an escape. Risner, who had been riding in the passenger seat, was now crouched behind the right front fender of the car and firing his 15-shot 459 over the hood at the two men in the Chevrolet. Risner was the only agent who had been wearing his vest when the two FBI vehicles had rammed the black Monte Carlo.

Gil Arrantia had remained in the driver's seat of the car, and was firing his .38 revolver over the windowsill. The two agents were a little over twenty yards away from Platt and Matix. This was much farther away from the two bank robbers than any of the other agents in the shootout.

Matix realized he was in a two-door coffin with a vinyl top. He slammed his shoulder into the driver's door of the Monte Carlo and got it open enough to squeeze out.

"Get out the window—I'll try to cover you," Matix said to his friend, then slid out of the car and sent a load of buckshot at Grogan and Dove's car to pin them down. Michael Platt began to climb out the Monte Carlo's passenger-side window with his Mini-14 and several spare magazines.

Perfect thought agents Risner and Dove from two very different locations as they saw the man climbing out the car window. Both fired their S&W 459 semiautos at Platt's center of mass. Platt felt Risner's Silvertip plow into his chest muscle, and he let out a grunt at the force of the impact. *Fucker* Platt thought, just as the second Winchester Silvertip, this one from Jerry Dove's gun, hit him in the arm and tore through the brachial artery leading to his heart. Michael Platt, his arm wound pumping blood like a small hose, rolled across the hood of a Cutlass sedan parked next to the Monte Carlo and landed on his feet. He was still holding his rifle and his loaded magazines as he crouched behind the vehicle.

As Matix exited the driver's side of the Monte Carlo while firing his shotgun, Gil Arrantia across the street realized his own gun was dry, and he flattened himself on the seat to reload his revolver from a belt pouch.

Gordon McNeill was lying on the ground by his car. *Got to keep from being hit* McNeill thought as he saw bullets kicking up dust around him. He began rolling back and forth on the ground between his own car and Manauzzi's vehicle, trying to reload his revolver with his ruined right hand as he did so. Blood and bone fragments were getting into the rear of the cylinder, and McNeill realized in dismay that his gun might not close. *Got to get the shotgun* he told himself. *Can't take the time to get all six in this cylinder.* The agent stopped after he had put two rounds in the gun. *That'll do 'til I get the 870* he thought and began to close the revolver. *Which way does it turn?* he asked himself, then snapped it shut so that the two cartridges were to the right of the firing position when viewed from the rear. He pushed himself to his feet to get to the shotgun lying in the back seat of his car.

When McNeill had been lying on the ground, his vehicle had concealed him from Michael Platt. Now he was exposed. McNeill realized in horror that the man was aiming his Ruger Mini-14 straight in his face from fifteen feet away, and was actually *grinning* at him.

Michael Platt, with two Winchester Silvertips in his chest and his heart pumping blood relentlessly out of his body, smiled at Gordon McNeill. Platt squeezed the trigger of his rifle three times in rapid succession. McNeill felt the air from one .223 bullet passing, and a flick to his ear from the second, before the third slug struck him in the side of the neck. The bullet ricocheted off his spinal column and lodged in his chest cavity. McNeill dropped as if he had been pole-axed.

Gordon McNeill lay on the asphalt, completely conscious but unable to move anything below his neck. *I'm paralyzed* the supervisor thought. *I'm paralyzed from the neck down and these two are going to kill my men and get away.* For the first time in the twenty-one years since he had joined the FBI, Gordon McNeill felt utterly and completely helpless.

Michael Platt thought he had just killed the agent. He took a few steps back, unaware that he was bleeding to death. The FBI would later claim that the wound from Dove's bullet would not have been survivable even if Platt had surrendered immediately and been air-lifted to a hospital. This was not strictly correct. If Michael Platt had pinched off the wound (and somehow managed to avoid further bullets while retreating to safety) he could have survived.

As it was, Michael Platt stood under some trees, out of sight of the agents who were pinned down by the shotgun fire from his partner Matix. *Time to smoke the rest of these pricks* he thought as he reloaded his Mini-14 with a fresh magazine and started walking towards where Grogan, Dove, and Hanlon were crouched behind Grogan's Buick.

Jerry Dove ejected the empty magazine from his S&W 459 and inserted a full 14-round replacement. He stayed crouched behind the Buick and resumed firing.

"Where is everybody?" Ben Grogan shouted again. His voice was full of sorrow and frustration. He was standing at the left rear of the white Buick, firing his 15-shot S&W Model 459 towards the sound of Matix's shotgun. Ben Grogan was utterly blind without his glasses.

Agent Hanlon, seven feet to Grogan's right and crouched behind the right taillight of the white Buick, saw Michael Platt emerge from behind cover and come towards the three agents who were firing at him and his partner. Hanlon emptied his five-shot Chief's Special revolver at Platt. He cursed himself once more for losing his main weapon when he ran his car into the concrete wall. Hanlon dropped into a crouch and started to reload his gun when a slug from Platt's rifle just missed his arm. He felt it pass, and moved to the left. Platt's next shot shattered Hanlon's right hand, tore through his forearm, and lodged in his bicep.

"Aagh!" Hanlon screamed in agony as he rolled over onto his back. "I'm hit!"

Ron Risner, across the street, had emptied his 15-shot Model 459 at Michael Platt. His partner, Gil Arrantia, had emptied his revolver twice, and had been wounded, though not critically. Risner drew his 2" barreled backup .38 as Arrantia frantically threw open the glove compartment, looking for the spare 50-round box of ammunition kept in every FBI vehicle.

Risner fired one shot from his 2" Model 60, and realized he could not shoot the short weapon accurately at that distance. He put a fresh 14-round magazine in his 459 and extended the weapon in front of him just as Hanlon went down.

Oh, fuck Risner thought as his stomach turned over. Michael Platt had left his position behind the parked car and was headed for the white Buick that Ben Grogan and Jerry Dove were hiding behind. He was firing his Mini-14 as he approached. Ron Risner could not shoot because from Risner's vantage point across the street, Grogan and Dove were both between him and Michael Platt, directly in Risner's line of fire.

Hanlon was lying on his back at the rear of the Buick, clutching his arm. He turned his head so he could see underneath the car. He saw Platt's feet, wearing Nike running shoes, walking towards him. Hanlon dug his heels into the asphalt and began to slide himself towards Jerry Dove and away from the approaching Platt.

"He's coming behind you! He's coming behind you!" Risner screamed from across the street. Grogan and Dove had all their attention focused elsewhere, and they did not hear him.

Platt swung his rifle on Ben Grogan. "Oh, my God," Grogan screamed, and then fell dead. Platt had put three slugs into his torso from seven feet away.

"See how your wife likes this," Michael Platt said as he leaned over the fender of the Buick. Platt fired his Mini-14 once into Hanlon's groin from a distance of about five feet. The .223 bullet missed Hanlon's penis, but struck the joint of his pelvic bone, sending a hail of bone fragments into his guts. Platt then turned his attention to Jerry Dove.

"Your turn, sonny," Michael Platt added as he shifted his aim and squeezed the trigger twice more. The bullets caught the young agent as he was trying to turn towards his attacker. Dove dropped his Model 459—through which he had just fired 29 rounds—and fell face-first on the asphalt. Agent Dove pushed against the ground, trying to get up. Michael Platt leaned over the trunk of the Buick, covering it with the blood pumping out of his upper arm, and fired two quick rounds into Dove's brain. Dove's head made a thudding noise as it hit the pavement a few inches from John Hanlon's ear.

That's the worst sound I've ever heard John Hanlon thought before he lapsed into unconsciousness.

"Nice of you guys to leave your car here for me," Michael Platt mumbled giddily as he stepped over the corpses of Grogan and Dove towards the open driver's door of the white Buick. He had suffered a tremendous amount of blood loss, and it was starting to make him light-headed.

Ed Mireles, lying behind McNeill's car with his ruined left arm, watched as Michael Platt prepared to get in the two dead agents' vehicle. Mireles had not yet used the 12-gauge 870 because Grogan and Dove had been in his line of fire. Now they lay dead. Mireles pointed the shotgun in Platt's general direction with his right hand and pulled the trigger, firing his first shot of the firefight. The gun was hard to hold well one-handed, and the shot string was low. It skipped off the asphalt and put four .33 caliber 00 buckshot pellets into Michael Platt's left foot. Mireles pulled himself to a sitting position. He was still well-concealed behind McNeill's cruiser.

Platt thought dreamily about how it felt good to sit down as he slid behind the wheel and closed the door. His foot was throbbing from the buckshot wounds.

Ed Mireles watched as Platt prepared to drive off in Ben Grogan's car. He put the butt of the 870 on the asphalt, gritted his teeth, held the receiver between his knees, and worked the action with his one good hand. Then he steadied the shotgun on McNeill's rear bumper and pulled the trigger. Instantly he saw the holes made by the nine 00 pellets appear in the sheetmetal in front of the Buick's left door.

That's not going to do it Mireles thought as he turned away, put the butt on the ground again, and pumped the action. As the wounded agent with the ruined left arm was cycling the weapon, Matix ran to the passenger door of the white Buick and joined Michael Platt in the front seat.

So the other one's still alive, too Mireles thought as he rested the Remington's forend on the corner of the bumper and took careful aim down the barrel. He lined up the front sight bead with where he thought Platt's left nipple should be, and then squeezed the trigger. *That's more like it* Mireles thought as he saw Platt thrown back in the seat from the impact of the buckshot striking him in the face. *Now to get the other one.*

"Shit, where is that fucker?" Michael Platt asked his partner as he spit a tooth and one of the buckshot pellets out of his mouth. Mireles had ideal cover behind McNeill's vehicle. Platt tried to turn the key in the ignition, but his right arm and hand would not work properly. One of Risner's 9mm Silvertips had gone clear through his right forearm. Platt reached over and tried to turn the key with his left hand. Matix was trying to help him when Mireles' next load of buckshot blasted through the windshield. Platt and Matix both were sprayed with buckshot and broken glass.

Mireles methodically pumped the shotgun's action again, chambering the final 12-gauge shell, and took aim as he had before. *One more through the windshield* he decided. *Get the guy in the passenger seat.* Another nine-pellet load of 00 buckshot roared out of the Remington and blasted through the Buick's windshield, spraying Matix in the face. Mireles saw the man thrown backwards. Then the big agent dropped the empty shotgun and slumped to the side.

Michael Platt looked at Matix's ruined face. "Guy's dead meat," he mumbled to his friend, and threw open the door.

Agent Grogan and Agent Dove did not see what happened next, for they were both dead, each shot four times by Michael Platt with his Ruger Mini-14.

Agent Hanlon did not see what happened next, for he was lying unconscious with his pelvis destroyed and his right arm shattered by two shots out of Michael Platt's rifle.

Agent McNeill did not see what happened next, for he was lying on his back behind his own vehicle, paralyzed from the neck down and with his right hand a shattered mess from being shot twice by Michael Platt with his .223.

Agent Mireles did not see what happened next, for he was slumped facing away from the white Buick, with his left forearm destroyed by a bullet out of Michael Platt's rifle.

Agent Manauzzi did not see what happened next, for he was still looking for his lost revolver while forcing himself to ignore the glass and bullet fragments that had burrowed into his flesh when Michael Platt had fired his rifle through the window at him.

Agent Arrantia did not see what happened next, for he was hunkered down in the front seat of his car across the street, trying to get more cartridges out of the box in the glove compartment to reload his revolver, and gritting his teeth against the pain of a wound inflicted by Edward Matix's shotgun.

Agent Risner did not see what happened next, for he was across the street, running behind his and Arrantia's car and trying to find a spot where he could shoot at Platt and Matix without hitting Agent Mireles in the process.

A private citizen, watching from his apartment window, saw what happened next.

Michael Platt twisted a six-inch S&W .357 magnum out of his shoulder holster with his left hand. Michael Platt, who had two 9mm slugs in his chest, one 9mm slug through his right arm, several 9mm and .38 grazes, four .33 caliber lead buckshot in his left foot and six more in his face, got out of the white Buick that had been issued to the late agents Grogan and Dove and started walking towards Ed Mireles.

The private citizen would use the word 'stealthily' to describe the manner in which Michael Platt walked towards Ed Mireles. Intellectually, the citizen knew that Platt's gait was a result of his wounds, but he would never shake the image of Platt sneaking up on the unsuspecting agent.

Michael Platt stopped two paces from where Mireles was slumped. Platt felt his vision clouding as he stared at the big man's broad back. He held the L-frame Smith & Wesson awkwardly out in front of him with his left hand and pulled the trigger three times. Then Platt turned and limped back to the Buick.

All three shots missed.

Ed Mireles did not hear the three shots fired five feet from him, or feel the concussion of the muzzle blasts. He was in a private world of planning and determination. When Ed Mireles got to his feet and drew his revolver, he had no idea that Platt had gotten out of the car, walked over to him, fired three shots, and returned to the driver's seat. He only knew that Platt and Matix were still alive.

Mireles drew his .357 revolver, which he had not yet fired, and held it out in front of him as he walked towards the driver's door of the white Buick. His vision was getting black around the edges, and Mireles knew that 'tunnel vision' was a sure sign that loss of consciousness was imminent.

Front sight Mireles thought as he focused on the front blade, put it over the center of Platt's face, and squeezed the trigger. *Pinwheel* he thought as he saw Platt's head jerk. *One more.* Mireles repeated the process a second time as he continued to walk towards the car.

When he was close enough to the car to see Matix with his ruined face in the passenger seat, Mireles switched targets and fired three more times, hitting Matix in the head with each 158-grain lead hollowpoint. *Last one's for you* Mireles thought as he stopped a few inches from the door of the Buick and fired his sixth round into Platt's face at a distance of one foot.

The first round out of Mireles' revolver had killed Michael Platt; the other three had been superfluous. Platt had seen the big man coming towards him with the gun extended, but he had been momentarily stunned at the sight, for he had been sure he had just killed him moments before.

Michael Platt had fired a fair amount of ammo in his lifetime, but there was one shooting exercise he had never once practiced: He had never done any point shooting with his weak hand.

"So what does this Hughes amendment you're talking about mean, exactly?" Stokely Meier asked when he saw Henry Bowman and his uncle Max Collins enter the store. Henry Bowman sighed.

"No one's really sure. Word I get is that it was added in the last thirty seconds of discussion by a voice vote, and there's strong evidence that parliamentary rules weren't followed, so some people think maybe it'll be overturned. I think whatever it is, it won't be tossed out. It involves people who own machine guns, and we're an embarrassment to both sides." He closed his eyes for a moment before continuing.

"The wording—if the version I heard was accurate—is redundant. It doesn't make anything illegal that isn't already."

"So what's the problem?"

"The problem is, we know what Hughes wanted, even if he wasn't smart enough or know enough about guns and gun laws to have it written out properly before jumping up and down and waving his hands in the last minute of discussion.

"What the amendment says is that after the effective date there shall be no machine gun transfers quote 'except under the authority of an agency of the United States Government' unquote. Well, *every* machine gun transfer is *already* done on a federal form signed and approved by the Director of the Treasury, and has been ever since June of 1934."

"So what's the problem?"

"The problem is, we know that what Hughes meant is no transfers of guns made after the effective date except to an agency of the U.S. Government. He wanted to freeze the supply. BATF is going to start rejecting all transfer forms for machine guns made after the effective date, except to police and government agencies. And there's nothing we can do about it."

"Is freezing the supply really so bad?" asked a man Henry did not know. "I mean— aren't there enough machine guns in the system for you to get what you want?" Tom Fleming expelled his breath in a loud bark of derision at the man's comment, then quoted Winston Churchill.

"Those who appease a tiger do so in the hope that the tiger will eat them last." Henry Bowman nodded, then decided to answer the man's question.

"The politicians have just accomplished something they have never been able to do before. They have taken a whole class of small arms and made it so that no newly manufactured ones can be owned by private citizens ever again. Hughes or anyone else can now easily claim there are more than enough shotguns and rifles around to justify the same kind of law on them. Remington has produced about three million 870 shotguns alone. That's *thirty times* as many of just one model of shotgun as *all* the machine guns put together. Are you starting to realize that maybe the things *you* like are at risk, too, and not just mine?" The man looked embarrassed, but said nothing.

"There have been approximately one hundred thousand Class Three firearms placed on the civilian registry since June of 1934. In that fifty-year time period, not a single machine gun transferred on a federal form has ever been used by its owner in a crime of violence. Not one. But that record wasn't good enough for William Hughes. Paying two hundred dollars to the Treasury each time they change hands wasn't good enough for William Hughes. Making the applicants get fingerprinted, photographed, and investigated by the FBI wasn't good enough for William Hughes. Having no machine guns at all in the hands of honest residents of Hughes' home state, because New Jersey has a state prohibition on them, wasn't good enough for William Hughes." Henry stared at the man who had asked him the question.

"No government agency ever invented a decent machine gun. Every truly outstanding small arms design I know of was the work of an individual gun designer, usually working without a nickel of government money until *after* they bought his design, except maybe in combloc countries. John Browning in his workshop in Utah gave us the 1895 Colt, the 1917 watercooled, the BAR, the 1919A4, the AN-M2, the watercooled .50, the M2 heavy-barreled .50, and the 37mm automatic cannon. That was just one guy. Throw in all of Hiram Maxim's guns next. Then the Vickers, the Thompson, the Kalashnikov—Russians would've been screwed without him—all Gene Stoner's guns like the AR-10 and AR-15, Degtyarev's designs, Vaclav Halek's ZB 26 and the BREN copy of it, Hugo Schmeisser's guns and all the copies of them, the STEN, the Patchett, Uziel Gal's 9mm UZI and .308 Galil, the Steyr AUG—hell, every one of them." Henry shook his head in frustration.

"The United States cancelled most of its future full-auto small arms development in 1934 with the National Firearms Act, by making inventors pay $200 a year. And it was development that our country was getting for free. When $200 finally got to where it wasn't that big a deal, some of that development picked up again, like Gene Stoner in the '50s. Now this Hughes guy has cancelled it altogether. He ought to be charged with treason." Henry was livid. "Barring that," Henry Bowman said softly, "I'd like to handcuff him to one of the steel I-beam supports in my basement, and wire him for sound."

Stokely Meier's head jerked up and he stared, wide-eyed. He had never before seen his friend become truly angry at anyone. He was seeing it now, and he well understood it.

"One of these days," Pete Malloy said, "this is really going to blow up in their faces." Pete was a retired cop that hung around the gun store on Saturdays.

"And speaking of *that*," Tom Fleming said, "I got a bunch of dope from my buddy Evan last night about the FBI shootout in Miami."

Everyone in the shop turned to look at the lawyer. Tom Fleming currently ran police firearms training courses with Rufus Ingram and gave lectures on legal aspects to police departments. He had also headed a military police agency in Illinois when he was in the army. On matters involving police procedures and police weapons training, Tom and Rufus were the two most knowledgeable people Henry knew. Rufus was ex-SAS.

"What's the story?" Henry asked.

"FBI got clobbered, is the short version," Fleming said. "And they're scrambling like hell to keep from looking like bumbling idiots.

"First of all, they set up this ten-car surveillance looking for two bank robbers that they *know* always carry at least one AR-15 and several handguns, and who they know have already killed several people. Fourteen FBI agents get in ten air-conditioned cars to go cruising around looking for well-armed, known killers, and not one of them has a rifle-rated vest. Not one. They all have pistol-rated vests, but get this, only one guy bothers to put his on. The rest have 'em lying on the seats.

"One of the Fibbies spots the bad guys fifteen minutes after they start looking for them, and what does he do? Tailgates them in the middle of a residential area, and then calls in a bunch of the other cars. Then two of the cars ram the suspect car."

"*What?*" Henry said.

"That's just what I said—What? That's exactly what Evan said. He works in Detroit, and they stop eight or ten cars a night. Cruiser wouldn't last a whole day using those tactics. Anyway, three FBI cars ram these guys off the road. But before they do, two of the agents thoughtfully take their guns out of their holsters and put them on the car seats. So the guns fly off the seats and get lost as soon as the agents start the ram-a-thon. One of those two isn't even carrying a backup gun, so he's running around the whole time looking for his revolver while bullets are whizzing through the air."

"Couple of agents got killed, I heard on the news, along with the bank robbers. Also, didn't they fire some crazy number of shots?" Stokely asked.

"Over a hundred forty," Tom Fleming replied. "One of the guys who got killed had a 459 Smith and fired it dry twice. Only got one hit that they know of, out of twenty-nine shots, and died with the slide locked back."

"Jesus, how far away was everybody? A hundred yards?" Henry asked. Most semi-auto handguns weren't good for better than 18" groups at that distance under ideal conditions. Henry was visualizing the FBI agents pitted at long distance against someone with a rifle.

"Six of the eight agents, including both of the ones that were killed, were between six and twenty feet from the two suspects. The other two Fibbies were about twenty-five yards away, shooting from across the street."

"One hit out of twenty-nine from less than twenty feet?" Henry shook his head. "Sounds like spray and pray, big-time," he said finally. "What kind of guns were the feds using?"

"Three 459s. Three .357 Smiths. Two .38 Smith Model 10s. Two Chief's Specials as backup guns. One 870 Remington."

"Out of eight agents, seven of them don't wear body armor and six of them only had one handgun?" Henry asked. "Going after known killers who had centerfire rifles?" He was incredulous. "Why only one shotgun? Why no rifles or subguns?"

"Funny you should ask that. There was a second shotgun there. The supervisor had it. It was in the back of his car, where he couldn't get to it without exposing himself to being shot. When he tried to, one of the bad guys put a .223 round in his neck that bounced off his spine and left him paralyzed for a few hours." Tom Fleming laughed at what he was about to say next.

"Subguns, you asked? As a matter of fact, the FBI did have two H&K MP5s in one of the cars. Problem was, the two agents that had them were busy double-teaming some broad at the restaurant where she worked. They didn't get their pants up in time to get to the gunfight."

Henry was incredulous. "Wait a minute," he demanded. "I thought you said the feds found the suspects fifteen minutes after they started their surveillance!" Henry's uncle spoke up.

"I guess those two agents got started early on breakfast." At seventy-three, Max Collins was still powerfully built and in excellent shape, but his sex drive had declined as he had aged. It had gotten to where every other day was plenty.

Fleming saw Henry Bowman's expression. "I keep telling you, Henry. It's the biggest problem Rufus and I have doing our training courses. Cops get used to people doing whatever they tell them to. They get used to routine. That's why they are absolutely undone when they come up against someone that doesn't do what they're supposed to."

"He's right, Henry," Pete Malloy said. "And I was a cop for twenty-seven years. Lot of faith in the badge, and all the back-up. Every cop has to cool down drunk assholes that want to take a swing at him. That's what the mail-order pacifier's for. Very few coppers ever come across some hard-on that's ready to kill him even if he dies in the process. I know I never did. Every cop I ever knew came across someone like that is dead now."

Malloy thought a moment. "You had better gunfight training on that trip to Rhodesia than any police officer in this country." Before Henry could answer, Tom Fleming spoke again.

"Pete, you hear about those two Secret Service agents on the stakeout in, uh, San Diego, I think it was?"

"The ones staking out the place where some counterfeiters were printing up food stamps? Everybody knows that story."

"That the one where they were screwing and got mugged?" Stokely asked.

"What are you talking about?" Henry demanded.

"Couple a Secret Service agents, man and a woman, got assigned to watch this place where some guys were holed up," Pete Malloy explained. "Guys were suspected of printing up food stamp coupons, startin' their own welfare program. Next day, the two agents don't call in. Secret Service can't find 'em. Meanwhile, local coppers have come on a car with two dead bodies in it, mugging victims. No I.D. on the bodies, so they get hauled off to the morgue, an' the car gets towed away. VIN number says the car's registered to the government. Coroner's report comes in, couple was fucking in the car, some dirtbag killed 'em, took their money an' wallets. Meanwhile, Secret Service is still tryin' to find their two stakeout agents. Then word finally filters back to the Secret Service that one a their cars is in the impound lot, an' they finally find the missing stakeout team down at the morgue with toe tags."

"They were screwing in the car and the counterfeiters snuck up on them and killed them?" Henry asked.

"Hell, no!" Pete roared. "Service tried six ways to Sunday to pin it on the food stamp guys, but they didn't have anything to do with it. They'd never been involved in a violent crime in their lives, just printin' paper. No, the two agents were screwin' in their car, an' just like the report said, some stranger walked along, iced 'em for what they had in their wallets, then took their I.D. an' all the guns in the car. Feds were lots more upset 'bout losin' two sets a creds than they were about losin' two agents. The Service never did find out who did it. Coulda been anyone."

Henry was still thinking hard about the ex-cop's last two statements when Max returned to the subject of the Miami incident.

"On this Florida thing, it's a fucking miracle no one around got hit by a stray bullet. A hundred forty rounds fired in less than five minutes in the middle of a residential area in Miami and no one around gets hit. That's an act of God."

"And speaking of that," Pete Malloy asked, "Tom, can you imagine what the FBI would have said if it had been the local Miami coppers that had gone after known, heavily armed killers, and left their vests and shotguns in the back seats of their cars, then rammed the suspects' vehicle to precipitate a hundred-forty-round gun battle in the middle of a residential neighborhood?" Fleming considered the concept, then tucked his chin into his chest and lowered his voice when he replied.

"A spokesman for the FBI said, 'These actions show that local municipal police departments do not have the knowledge, training, or expertise to handle highly motivated, heavily armed career criminals with a history of deadly violence. That is why the apprehension of such dangerous men should always be left to the trained professionals of the FBI whenever possible.'"

Fleming switched back to his normal voice and added, "You could actually argue that the FBI guys got off easy. The suspect who did almost all the damage used a Ruger Mini-14. He killed the two cops, bounced a round off the supervisor's spine and paralyzed him for a few hours, wounded one agent with fragments when he shot him through his car window, hit two guys in their gun hands, and smashed one fed's left arm when he had it in front of his heart. Guy hit in the arm was the one who ended up finally killing both of the suspects. Worked his shotgun one-handed and wounded them, then finished them off with .357s to the brain from a few feet away when they were in an FBI car trying to escape."

Henry saw his friend's point immediately.

"So if the suspect had been shooting a *real* gun..." Henry said, thinking out loud.

"Like a Garand," Max broke in.

"Yeah, like a Garand, he would have shot right through that fed's arm and into his heart. And the fed wouldn't have been alive to kill him."

"Right."

"And if he'd been shooting a Garand, he would have killed the guy he hit in the neck, too, instead of just putting him on the sidelines for a few hours."

"Right."

"And if he'd been shooting a Garand, he would have also killed the guy he shot through the window glass instead of just peppering him with fragments, because a .30 caliber ball round wouldn't have come apart."

"Right."

"So now we've got five dead agents instead of two. And one of the remaining three is still running around looking for his gun, so he's no threat. And I take it the suspects were not wearing body armor, and if they had been, they would have sustained far fewer wounds?"

"Right again on all counts."

"Shit," Max Collins said. "When Frank Hamer killed Bonnie and Clyde in the 'thirties, they found all kinds of stuff in the Model A. Couple BARs, bunch of pistols, and a shitload of ammunition. Couple thousand rounds, as I recall."

"You're kidding," Pete Malloy said.

"No, I'm sure of it."

"You know," Stokely Meier added, "we got a book here on Frank Hamer I was reading the other day." He grinned, walked over to the bookshelf, and opened a volume. It took him a few seconds to find the spot he was looking for.

"Over a dozen guns and over five thousand rounds of ammo. Three BARs with a hundred loaded magazines, which shows a certain sense of style for a couple of inbred Okies. Also seven .45 autos with a bunch of loaded mags." He looked up at the group. "I guess bank robbers in the 'thirties were a little more hard-core than they are today." Henry and Tom looked at each other. Henry thought that John Browning's BAR was the finest small arms development in history. Tom Fleming felt the same way about the Browning-designed .45 Automatic.

"The feds lucked out that only two of them are dead," Max declared.

"You could say that," Tom Fleming admitted.

"They lucked out one other way, too," Pete Malloy added. The group turned to look at the retired cop. "The feds went after a couple of bank robbers. Bank robbers are pretty uncommon, and nobody I know has any sympathy for 'em."

Everyone in the shop knew what Pete was getting at. It was an issue that was being discussed that afternoon in gun stores all around the country:

If this is what happens when the feds go after a couple of bank robbers who know they're in the wrong, what's going to happen to the feds when they go after a couple million trained, motivated, heavily armed citizens who haven't done anything worse than exercise their Constitutional rights?

May 19, 1986

"This bill will remove bad laws that were passed during a period of hysteria," announced President Reagan as he signed the Firearms Owners Protection Act of 1986. He made no mention of the Hughes Amendment. This was not surprising, for he was not aware of this last-minute addition to the bill. Virtually the only people in the country who were aware of the ramifications of the measure were those people licensed by the government to deal in or manufacture Title II (National Firearms Act) weapons.

Henry Bowman had been exactly right about how the feds would interpret the new provision: BATF had stated flatly that they would not approve any transfers of weapons made after the cutoff date. The result of this was that before the supply of machine guns was frozen, it was first doubled. Licensed manufacturers had a one-month time period where they knew the cutoff was imminent, and they worked 24-hour shifts manufacturing machine gun receivers and remanufacturing semi-auto guns to select-fire status. Temporary services charged (and got) triple overtime for their stenographers to work round-the-clock typing up Form 1s, the federal form that manufacturers of Title II weapons must submit in duplicate for each machine gun made. It had taken fifty years to get 90,000 NFA weapons on the civilian registry. It took another month for that number to grow to just under 200,000.

Doubling the number of machine guns on the NFA registry would not be the only unintended consequence of the Hughes Amendment. Since 1934, a slow trickle of gun inventors had paid the high annual fee and done machine gun development work. It was nothing like what had gone on before the 1934 Act, but a few men, such as the M16's designer Gene Stoner, had produced decent designs. As Henry Bowman had accurately predicted, almost all of the spiritual successors to John Browning doing machine gun development work were put out of business overnight, just as they had been 52 years before. Colonel Chinn, the U.S. Armed Forces' foremost expert on machine guns, was livid, and in private he accused Rep. Hughes of treason.

Hollywood was also affected. The movie industry was the largest non-military consumer of machine guns in the U.S., and the Hughes Amendment made it impossible for the gun rental companies to get new military designs or replace worn-out guns for action films and documentaries.

Prices of existing guns were driven up, and this caused the unintended consequence of government corruption. One ATF examiner in the Washington NFA office became well-known for falsifying documents after the May 19 cutoff, using his access to official approval and date stamps to line his own pockets.

The biggest unintended consequence of 'Black Monday', as the NFA dealers called it, was something else, however. May 19, 1986 was an alarm. Though the alarm did not ring as loudly or as rapidly as that famous one of four-and-a-half decades before, it did its job.

The May 19, 1986 alarm, just like the one on December 7, 1941, awakened a sleeping giant to a terrible resolve.

June 20, 1986

Wind's almost gone Henry Bowman thought as scanned the vast prairie. *Let's try to end on one that's a real challenge.* He twisted the power ring of the Leupold scope up to its highest setting. The optic had originally been a 6.5-20 power variable. It now magnified the target between 14.5 and 35 times, depending on what the shooter wanted.

As Henry rotated the ring, the dots and crosshairs increased in size along with the image of the distant prairie dog. The reticle was in the first focal plane of the variable-power optic, so the relationship of dot size to target remained constant regardless of the power setting. This was not the way the scopes worked when they came from the factory, but it was the way they operated after Dick Thomas in West Virginia performed his magic on them. Thomas also boosted the power with an additional lens, and installed the fine multiple-dot crosshairs with whatever dot size and spacing that the customer requested. The center dot on Henry's scope was 1/2 minute-of-angle in diameter; it covered 1/2" of the target at 100 yards, 1" at 200 yards, 1 1/2" at 300, and so on.

Damn, that's a long ways Henry thought when he saw that the top dot was wider than the prairie dog he was looking at. The body of an adult prairie dog in the standing position was about 2 inches wide. *More than 400 yards.* He moved the rifle so that the next dot, which was 1/3 minute in diameter, was centered on the squirrel-like creature. A tiny bit of hair showed on either side of the black dot. Henry switched back to the half-minute dot, and extrapolated. *Closer to 600 yards than 400. Call it 560 yards* he finally decided.

Five hundred sixty yards would be out of range for someone shooting a factory varmint rifle at a full-sized Idaho rockchuck. On a Wyoming prairie dog, it was a tremendous distance to expect to connect on the first shot, even for a varmint hunter shooting the finest handmade rifle. The vital area of a prairie dog was about the size of a playing card. With any kind of crosswind, it would have been ludicrous to hope to make a first-round kill. A five-mile-an-hour breeze would move the bullet Henry was shooting a full eight inches at that range. It was close to dusk, however, and the wind was nonexistent.

The gun Henry Bowman was shooting was, for legal purposes, the same one that Henry, his father, and Curt Behnke had built in 1963. The rifle had undergone several changes in the ensuing twenty-three years, however. First of all, it was on its fifth Hart barrel. Second, the barrel was larger in diameter and fluted, which made it stiffer without making it heavier. Third, the caliber was no longer .222 Remington Magnum. The modified Remington action was now fitted with a barrel chambered for the .244 Ackley Improved cartridge, and employed a 1-in-9" twist, instead of the 1-in-12" or 1-in-13" pitches favored by top bench rest competitors shooting bullets of 6mm diameter. The fast twist (theoretically) reduced accuracy a tiny bit, but it stabilized long, streamlined bullets that would tumble if fired out of a 1-in-12" barrel. These slender, boat-tailed, 103-grain VLD projectiles (for Very Low Drag) drifted much less in the wind and shot more accurately at extreme distances than the lighter slugs that bench rest shooters used in 100 and 200 yard matches.

Third, although the rifle still wore its original walnut stock that Henry and his father had made when Henry was ten years old, there was now no wood touching the steel of the barreled action. This was because the action was supported on two solid blocks of aluminum that Curt Behnke had fitted into the wood at each end of the receiver and anchored in place with epoxy. It was a technique known as 'pillar bedding', and it resulted in a stock that was just as stable as one made entirely of fiberglass, though about a pound heavier. Everyone used fiberglass stocks in competition classes where there was a weight limit, but prairie dog hunters had no such constraints, and Henry liked the look and feel of the stock he and Walter had made years ago.

Last of all, the Lyman Super Targetspot scope had been replaced with what was now the state-of-the-art in long-range varmint glass, the Dick Thomas-modified Leupold target variable.

Henry Bowman had fired this rifle for group at a measured 600 yards, and had achieved a number of five-shot groups under 3" in diameter in no-wind conditions.

Henry consulted the trajectory chart he had taped to the side of the stock. His chart told him that he would have to hold 29" high at 560 yards to strike his target. Henry settled in behind the rifle and adjusted it on the sawdust-filled 'sandbags' he carried in the field. The dots Thomas had installed in the reticle had a three-minute-of-angle spacing. At 560 yards, that meant the dots were 16.8" apart. Henry moved the rifle on the bags so that the second dot down from the horizontal crosshair was at the base of the animal, then gently touched the trigger. The sear broke with less than two ounces of pressure, and the rifle cracked.

The report was short and flat-sounding, for there was nothing within ten miles to reflect the sound. Two seconds after the gun fired came the unmistakable *whock* that told Henry he had connected. When one of the thin-jacketed hollowpoints struck a prairie dog, it made a noise unlike when the bullet hit dirt. It sounded like a paper bag bursting.

Henry repositioned the rifle and peered through the scope. Next to the dirt mound lay two halves of a dead prairie dog, spaced about two feet apart. Henry Bowman opened the bolt, picked the fired case out of the action, and put it in the right compartment of his three-section ammo bag. From the time he had first spotted the distant rodent to the moment he dropped the fired case into his pouch was about twenty seconds.

A good one to end the day on Henry thought. He heaved himself to his feet, picked up his rifle, slung the ammo pouch over his shoulder, and hung the two sawdust-filled leather bags around his neck by the leather cord that connected them. Then he started to walk back to his truck.

***

"So how'd you do?" Curt Behnke asked when Henry walked in the door of the main house. "Tommy was afraid you'd decided to stay out there all night." Tommy was Curt Behnke's eleven-year-old grandson. It was his first trip hunting prairie dogs.

"Let's find out," Henry said, dropping the ammo pouch on the table. He scooped out the fired cases in the left-hand pocket and dumped them on the table in front of the boy. "Count the misses for me, and I'll add up the hits." Tommy started counting the empties in the pile in front of him while Henry reached into the righthand pocket of the bag.

"Man, you did a lot of shooting," the rancher said when he saw the pile of brass. He leased the twenty-eight thousand acres of Wyoming grazing land that Curt, Henry, and Tommy had been hunting on all day. Prairie dogs lived in colonies. Left unchecked, the animals multiplied and would strip grazing land of edible grass, drastically reducing the number of cattle a rancher could raise. Most ranchers resorted to poison. Some, like the host, encouraged serious long-range shooters to come try to make a dent in the dog population. Curt Behnke had a permanent invitation to shoot prairie dogs on the property, and could bring whomever he wanted.

"A hundred forty-seven," the boy said finally.

"A hundred eighty-eight kills," Henry replied when he finished counting his pile. The rancher shook his head and grinned. Prairie dogs did not come out of their holes when someone was within a hundred yards of them, and a prairie dog was harder to hit than a beer can. The rancher had often shot at prairie dogs with his lever-action carbine, but he had never hit one. He had watched Curt Behnke (who was now seventy years old) shoot one entire afternoon five years before, and he had never gotten over watching the man connect at what the cattle rancher thought were absurd distances.

"Dinner will be ready in about ten minutes," the host announced. He turned to Curt Behnke. "Looks like your friend's almost as good a shot as you, Curt."

"Not really à fair comparison," the older man said, shaking his head. "His eyes are better than mine ever were, even when I was twenty years old, and the cartridge he shoots has a lot less wind drift than the Improved .223 case I've been using. On the other hand," Behnke said with a smile, "Henry won't take any shots on prairie dogs closer than three hundred yards." The rancher laughed at this and returned to the kitchen.

He thought that Curt Behnke was joking.

September 27, 1986

"I can't believe the way all the cops are going nuts about this guy," Stokely Meier said, shaking his head. "They've got such an almighty hard-on right now, you'd think the entire prison population of the three-state area was on the loose, raping and pillaging."

"Papers are telling everyone to stay inside, bolt their doors, say a few 'Hail Marys', and God knows what else," another man added.

"They even called up Ed's department," Tom Fleming said. "See if any of the coppers there wanted to get in on the action."

"Ed *Seyffert?* From *Troy?*" Stokely demanded. "Haven't they already got enough guys running around in the woods?" Fleming shrugged.

"They asked anyway. Ed was smart and said no thanks."

It was a typical Saturday afternoon at the gun store, and much of the usual crowd was present, including Henry Bowman. The subject of greatest interest that day was Michael Wayne Jackson. He was wanted in Indiana for a double homicide and had escaped to Missouri. Five days previously, Jackson had killed a local resident. He was still at large.

Jackson had last been seen near Wright City, Missouri, a town in Warren County about forty miles from St. Louis. A massive manhunt was underway to locate and apprehend Jackson, and front-page newspaper articles covered the situation daily.

"What's the big fear, anyway?" Henry asked. "Jackson's still running around in the woods, right? They've checked all the houses, and didn't find anybody dead or tied up. He's no wilderness survival expert. Hell, the guy's probably so hungry right now he's been trying to eat his shoe leather. And he's no danger at all if you're more than a hundred yards away from him."

"What do you mean?" Stokely asked.

"Well, he's on foot, and they know what kind of gun he's got. It's a sixteen gauge side-by-side. How much ammo can he have? He can't have more than a handful of shells aside from the two in the gun. I'd bet even money he doesn't have *any* spares." Henry paused, then went on.

"And remember, it's a sixteen gauge. Nobody carries slug or buckshot loads in sixteen. So the biggest shot size he could have is twos, and that's real unlikely. You got any sixteen gauge twos here in the store, Stoke?" Stokely Meier shook his head.

"So fours or sixes at most, and probably seven-and-a-halfs." Henry laughed. "We got one starving guy running around in the woods with two shells in his gun, and neither one will break the skin at a hundred yards. Hell, guy with a good arm can throw a baseball a lot farther than 7 1/2s will draw blood." Henry snorted. "Way I see it, this Michael Wayne Jackson is practically unarmed."

"Shit, maybe *that's* what they ought to do," Stokely said with a huge grin. "Send the outfielders and the pitchers from the friggin' Country Day varsity baseball team out to Warren County on the weekend. Make sure they got shooting glasses, so their eyes don't get hurt, and a couple bushel baskets full of old baseballs. Have 'em throw at this peckerwood 'til he wastes his ammo and has to surrender 'fore they charge in and all start throwing at his head."

"The school would probably charge the parents for extra coaching hours," Adrian Baker added drily. This idea made Stokely Meier double up with laughter. He and Adrian were alumni of the local high school, and were forever receiving letters from the institution asking for money.

"That many cops running around, it'll be a miracle if none of them get shot," Tom Fleming threw in. "You get a few hundred cops all looking for one guy, two things happen: One, chances of any particular cop running across the guy are really small, so they all just go through the motions. Two, the chances of *somebody* running across him are very high. Mr. Jackson is in what the army refers to as a 'target-rich environment' right now."

"Good thing for the cops the guy isn't a prairie dog hunter with a decent varmint rifle, Henry Bowman commented. The other men were silent for a moment.

"Man, isn't *that* the truth," Stokely breathed. "Coroners wouldn't get any sleep at all."

"The police are also fortunate that the fugitive Mr. Jackson is a murderer wanted for double homicide," Tom Fleming said, "and not someone with whose plight folks like us might empathize."

"You mean, like if Jackson was just some guy who didn't fill out a stupid yellow form, or maybe a Monsanto executive with an M3 that he brought back from Korea stashed in his closet?" Henry asked.

"Right."

"Holy pecker," Stokely said with feeling. "He'd have a couple thousand folks running interference for him then."

Everyone in the shop was silent as they pondered these last few comments.

"So you're really going to vote for him? Guy that teaches his kids at home 'stead of sending 'em to school?"

"Yeah, I am. Don't see that the teachers we got 'round here are so all-fired great a fella couldn't do as well himself. Maybe even better." The man smiled. "Also says he'll only enforce the laws people want him to enforce. That sounds pretty good to me."

"You mean, no speeding tickets, rolling stops, stuff like that?"

"Right."

"I could go for that," the second man agreed.

"Here's what he's been handing out," the first man said as he reached in his pocket and withdrew a credit-card sized piece of white pasteboard.

The second man looked at it.

> **Vote *Weaver***
> for
> **Sheriff**

He turned the card over and looked at the other side.

> **Get Out of Jail—**
>
> **Free**

"Least he's got a sense of humor," the man said with a laugh. "We could use that again."

"You got that right."

Randy Weaver had a definite following among the local residents in his race for sheriff of Boundary County, but not a big enough one to win the election.

May 18, 1989

"These deadly assault rifles are the weapons of choice for drug dealers and street gangs. The President has shown great courage in standing up to the gun lobby. He has taken an important first step to get these terrible weapons off the streets. Our children are being slaughtered and—"

"Lying scum," Henry Bowman said as he hit the 'OFF' button on his remote. He looked over at his friend who he had invited for dinner. "Irwin, I think we just watched Mr. Bush lose five or six million votes in the 1992 election."

Irwin Mann looked startled. "You believe so?" he asked.

"I may be all wrong, but yes, I think that's what just happened. Americans expect to be lied to about taxes, and how they'll have better jobs, and things like that. All politicians do that. But Americans don't like being told their rights are being rescinded, and they absolutely despise politicians who promise to protect their rights and then sell them out. I don't know who the Democrats are going to run in three years, but whoever they trundle out just got a huge boost today."

"The President has..." Irwin Mann made sure he had the correct metaphor, then smiled and said, "shot himself in the foot, you might say?" Henry Bowman laughed in spite of himself.

"More like the liver."

May 19, 1989

"All right, we've got almost a half hour before our bus gets here. If you want to walk around in the immediate area, that's fine, but don't go far. You need to be back right here at noon sharp. Everyone clear on that?" The students from the Rolla high school all nodded or spoke their assent.

Like most of her classmates from Rolla, Missouri, Cindy Caswell had never been far from home. She had been south to a few of the lakes just across the Arkansas border, and her family went to St. Louis two or three times a year, but Chicago was a new and fascinating city. Its size and energy dwarfed anything else she had experienced.

The honors students taking the senior-year elective drama history had been offered the chance to go on a three-day field trip to Chicago for the price of plane fare and lodging. TWA had a $64 round-trip shuttle, and the school had arranged low-cost rooms at one of the hungrier hotels. To Cindy's amazement, her parents had agreed without an argument to let her go on the trip. They had not even suggested that she pay for all or part of the trip, which she had been fully prepared to do. Getting their blessing for the trip had been one of the happiest moments of her life.

Cindy Caswell walked slowly down the sidewalk, staring into the sky at the tops of the impossibly tall buildings that lined the street. She had no inkling that her life was about to change forever.

***

"Let's get this done," Eddie Viglisi said to the driver.

"Seen nothin' but skanks so far," the man behind the wheel pointed out. The white van was windowless behind the front doors, and was lettered with the logo of a nonexistent painting contractor. "Sal likes 'em young an' fresh, not these wore-out street kids landed at the bus station a month, two months ago. The AIDS thing has got him all goosy."

"Head up towards the West Side. Around Carson's."

"Bunch a housewives out shoppin' 'round there. Mall would be better." The driver thought a moment. "But yeah, you're right. We could go there after. Carson's is on the way." He made a left at the next light. The two other men in the back of the van remained silent.

***

"There! That one. She's *perfect*," Eddie exclaimed. The two men in the back sat up and looked out the front window so they could identify their target. "Look for parents, or a boyfriend, or something," he instructed.

The van circled the block to check for local patrol cars. There were none, and when the driver returned to the original block, he stopped and let the two men out of the back of the van. They were about fifty yards north of Cindy Caswell. The girl was walking slowly southbound along the sidewalk. She was taking in the grandeur of the city itself, thinking of the play they were going to see that night, and ignoring her immediate surroundings. She did not see the two men or the van with the side doors open until it was much too late.

***

"Almost didn't need the junk," Eddie Viglisi commented as he glanced at the doped-up teenage girl sprawled in the back of the van. Cindy Caswell had been so surprised she had scarcely resisted, and then the synthetic heroin had hit her system like a freight train.

The two men who had pulled her into the van looked on Cindy with undisguised anticipation. Sal Marino would be done with her soon enough, and then it would be their job to kill her and dispose of the body.

What they did before she died was their own business.

***

When the mild dose of heroin worked its way out of her system and Cindy Caswell regained her ability to think and reason, she found that she was handcuffed by the right wrist to a metal bed. She was in a small room with no windows and a single ceiling light, which was switched on. She had no idea what time of day it was. Her head felt woozy and her stomach was heaving. It took all of ten seconds for her to come to the conclusion that immediate escape was pointless to even consider. The bed was sturdy and made of steel pipe. The handcuffs were equally strong, and obviously designed to hold much more dangerous people than drugged, eighteen-year-old high school girls.

Cindy knew instinctively that she was in more danger than she had ever been in her life. Her parents had no money to speak of, so the kidnapping had not been for ransom. Even if it had been, and the men had grabbed her by mistake (very unlikely), they would probably kill her when they discovered their error.

Cindy knew that the reason she had been grabbed off the street would almost certainly involve forced sex, or worse. Cindy did what she had done for much of her life and closed her mind to any eventualities over which she could have no possible control. *Focus* she told herself. *I've got to make them want to keep me alive and healthy. That's something I can control. Maybe.*

Although Cindy Caswell had more than a little experience defusing the ardor of predatory men, she suspected, correctly, that the man or men she would soon have to handle would be several orders of magnitude past anything she had experienced in Rolla, Missouri.

Looking nice and showing what those books say is 'inner strength' isn't going to be good enough she said to herself. Then she realized that was the only thing she really knew, so that was where she started.

The room had no mirror anywhere, but Cindy found that she could see her reflection in a convex section of the large glass stone of the ring on her free hand. She began to use the fake stone as a mirror. *Well, that's a start.*

Cindy looked at her image, used her hand to straighten her hair and wipe her eyes and nose with the sheets, checked the results, and repeated the process until she was satisfied. Then she set about straightening her blouse and smoothing her skirt. Finally, she pulled her underwear down, spat repeatedly onto the first three fingers of her left hand, and transferred as much of her own saliva as possible to the inside of her vagina.

By the time Eddie Viglisi came to fetch the captive for his boss, what he found was a very composed, calm-looking young woman of striking beauty with what actually looked like the hint of a smile on her face.

If they want someone who's terrified and screams all the time, that won't be hard to switch to Cindy thought. *If they think it's really a big adventure for me, maybe I'll stay alive for a while.*

"C'mon, Princess. Your dream date's waiting for you," Viglisi said as he took out the ring with the handcuff key on it and released the metal restraint. Cindy nodded once in acceptance. She stood waiting beside the bed for Viglisi to show the way.

May 20, 1989

"I never did a thing," Boone Caswell whispered sullenly. "No reason for her to run off. No reason," he repeated, wanting it made clear that this was not his fault. Myra's eyes were an angry red from continued sobbing. The sheriff hung up the phone and walked over to where they were sitting. His face was red and he looked uncharacteristically ill at ease. He took a deep breath and let part of it out before speaking.

"The, ah...Chicago police. They're not willing to say any crime has been committed—least not yet," he added hastily. "Cindy's eighteen, and she's legally an adult. They got no, uh, evidence that anything bad's happened to her. Only that she's not where *you'd* like her to be."

What the Chicago desk sergeant had actually said was *'Look, ace, if we tried to track down everyone who ever got a wild hair an' said adios to the hick town they grew up in, well, shit—we couldn't do it if we had twice the men an' didn't do nothin' else. And if the kid's eighteen, forget it. That's the kind of shit can get our asses slapped with a lawsuit right now. She may turn up of her own accord. I got the description an' your number. I'll check the Jane Does in the morgue every day or two for a couple weeks. That's the best I can do.'*

"She didn't run away from home," Boone Caswell said with a conviction he did not feel. He was actually more concerned with taking the blame for his daughter's departure than he was with the fact of her disappearance. Myra Caswell continued to cry.

***

Much to the disappointment of his two hardboys, Sal Marino had not yet grown tired of Cindy Caswell. If anything, he was more interested in her than when Eddie had brought her to his room in the penthouse the previous afternoon.

She had been a virgin, which had surprised the mob boss. She had also been genuinely wet, and had exhibited a sort of shy enthusiasm, which had been a real shock. That was something he had occasionally gotten from the very best whores, but never from one of the young 'throwaways' he sent Tony out for when he was feeling especially tense.

Sal Marino was not feeling tense now. He sat on the couch with a champagne bottle in his right hand and his left hand between Cindy's legs. She was rhythmically squeezing the man's middle finger, using the Kegel technique.

Cindy did not know that was its proper name. She had read about in one of the skin magazines she had found that her father kept hidden in his closet. 'Hong Kong Fuck Muscles' was what the article had called them. *Good thing I practiced those exercises,* Cindy thought as she watched the mob bosses' erection start to grow. She took the champagne bottle from him, pulled back his robe, and poured a few ounces on his exposed groin. Then she set the bottle aside and bent over, taking him in her mouth.

"I'm going to have to keep you around for a while," Marino said as he closed his eyes. "Get you some decent clothes, take you back to Vegas with me, show you off."

A wave of relief passed over Cindy Caswell, but she did not allow it to spoil her concentration.

"You really expect anyone to buy this boat anchor?" Henry Bowman grunted as he helped Allen Kane lift the 12.7mm Russian DSHK heavy machine Gun onto its armored mount. "At—what? Twelve thousand dollars?" Allen Kane shrugged.

"Never can tell. There's only seven of them, I think, on the registry, and this one's never been cut. But even if I knew no one would be interested, I'd bring it anyway," Allen said as the gun slipped into position. "Big display'll draw guys who've only got a couple Gs to spend."

"I guess you got a point," Henry admitted. Allen Kane, with seventeen eight-foot tables, was the largest exhibitor at the Indianapolis Gun Show. Kane's usual assistant had been unavailable, and Henry had driven to the show early to help his friend set up before the show opened, and help field questions from the thousands of showgoers. Allen had almost a hundred machine guns and other NFA weapons on display, including about two dozen belt-fed weapons. Henry's eye fell on a 20mm Solothurn S18-1000, and he thought of the one Walter had given him for his fourteenth birthday. *Mine's in even better condition* he thought proudly as he noticed the minor blue wear on the sharp edges of Allen's gun.

"Is that why you brought the Gatling?" Henry was nodding toward a beautiful full-size replica of an 1873 Gatling Gun on the correct oak field carriage. The entire assembly weighed about 500 pounds.

"Well, partly," Allen said, "but this is a big show, and there's a good chance that someone will take that home with him, since there's no Form 4 involved." Henry nodded. A crank-operated Gatling did not fall under the machine gun classification, as it did not 'fire multiple shots with a single function of a trigger', which was the definition of full-auto fire.

"I usually sell one at about every other big show. I sell at least one at every big California show," Allen added. "Sometimes Mike can't build them fast enough for me." The Gatling guns were made by Thunder Valley Ordnance, a shop whose sole owner and master machinist was a muscular perfectionist named Mike Suchka, who had a penchant for 18-hour work days.

"You set up in *California?*" Henry asked, surprised. Although California state law had a provision for private ownership of machine guns, the state blanketly rejected all applications. Only Stembridge Gun Rentals, which served the Hollywood movie industry, and a handful of importers and police distributors like Armex International, met with state approval.

"I don't normally set up at gun shows in non-machine-gun states, but California's an exception."

"What, you do business with Stembridge?"

"Yeah, usually a little bit, but that's pretty trivial. I do a fair amount of night vision gear, rangefinders, and stuff like that, but the crazy thing is the quantity of parts I sell to individuals."

"What?" Henry asked as he put down the night vision scope he had been examining and turned to face his friend.

"I know it sounds nuts, but those people out there will buy shit that won't move anywhere else in the country. It's the damnedest thing I've ever seen. Last batch of parts I got from Charley, his guys threw on a bunch of torch-cut .50 barrels by accident. Didn't charge me for them, but the damn things added a few hundred pounds to the weight. I called him up to bitch about having to pay the freight on a bunch of scrap I didn't want, he said throw 'em away and he'd knock a hundred bucks off my next order."

"Charley's like that," Henry said with a laugh. "I bought my first centerfire from him, a 98 Mauser when I was ten years old."

"You and about a million other kids in the early 'sixties," Allen said with a smile. "Anyway, I still had the barrels in the truck when I hit the L.A. show, so I threw 'em on my table and stuck a price of twenty bucks each on 'em. They all moved the first day."

"That's crazy. Torch-cut barrels? They're useless."

"That's what I said. But it happens every show out there. They'll buy anything—wooden buttstocks for machine guns where every known example has been destroyed, magazines for Swiss subguns where no known example exists in this country, you name it." Allen Kane shook his head.

"Way I had it explained, California's got so many people in it, a lot of them were there before '68, and remember the way it used to be. Back when you could buy anything you wanted, take it out in the desert and shoot it, and nobody cared. Now they get hit with a new state ban on something every few months or so, and they'll buy anything.

"Also, with the new people, a lot of them have lots of money, and figure they'll get a state permit somehow, 'cause they think rich people can always figure out ways around the rules."

"On gun stuff, it's the other way around," Henry broke in. "In Missouri, black guy in an old Fairlane gets stopped and the cops find an old piece-of-shit .22 auto with the sear ground down so it'll run the clip out, they take the gun and tell him to get lost. Same thing happens to a millionaire in the high-rent district, it'll cost him fifty, sixty thousand bucks and maybe he'll avoid a felony conviction, maybe not. Happened to a Ralston Purina heir last year. Damn near lost everything he had over an original Maxim silencer his old man had bought for three bucks back in the 'twenties."

"Yeah, well, it takes rich people a while to learn that cop courtesy goes out the window on gun stuff. When they do, and if they live in California, they get another place in Nevada, buy and keep their squirt guns there, or maybe they sit tight and hope the laws will all get repealed, ha ha. Point is, I sell a lot of parts and stuff in California that are of no earthly use to anyone, but the folks out there buy 'em 'cause they still can." Allen Kane shook his head, marvelling at the concept of people eager to buy machine gun barrels that had been demilled with a cutting torch.

"Speaking of getting nailed," Allen said, "you guys in Missouri having trouble with feds at gun shows?" Henry scowled.

"Yeah, some that I hear about, but I haven't set up at a show for a couple years now. I sell subguns to police departments now and then, but it's so hard getting Form 4s signed in my area, it's not worth it for me to pay for the table space. What's been going on around here? Standard scam about dealing without a license? Conspiracy bullshit?"

"Those, yeah, but they got another one now. Remember how ATF ruled you couldn't have spare suppressor parts, like wipes, even if you had a suppressor registered to you, unless you were a manufacturer?"

"I heard about that, but I thought someone made it up, it sounded so crazy," Henry answered. A suppressor 'wipe' is a rubber disc with a hole in it slightly smaller than the bullet diameter, installed just under the front end cap of a suppressor. The rubber stretches as the bullet passes through, then snaps back, trapping the sound a little more effectively than a metal baffle. Wipes have to be replaced often as the rubber quickly wears out, and accuracy is much worse than with baffle-only designs, because the bullet hits the rubber before leaving the suppressor. All of Henry's suppressors were wipeless designs, and even so, he still wore out baffles periodically with high-volume shooting.

"Believe it, it's true. A few guys in Indiana and Ohio didn't take the feds seriously. Thought that having spare rubber washers for their registered suppressor would be okay, 'cause they wear out so fast."

"Oh, shit," Henry said. He could see what was coming.

"Oh shit is right. First guy got sentenced to three years in prison, and the others became ATF informants like right now. Dealer at the Columbus show last month caught one of these assholes trying to slip an auto-sear and some suppressor wipes into his parts box to set him up. That's why I started keeping everything besides the guns in these cases." Allen gestured to the large, flat, plexiglas-topped, compartmented cases that covered three of his tables. They were filled with bolts, springs, extractors, magazines, and other gun parts. The cases were hinged at the spectator side and latched at the side towards the exhibitor. The goods were clearly visible to the show patrons, but only someone standing behind the table could get at them.

"I'll watch out for that kind of crap," Henry promised. He looked at his watch. "Should open in about fifteen minutes. You want a Coke before the crowd hits?"

"Breakfast of Champions," Kane said. Henry headed for the concession stand.

***

"Mister Blair, I gotta say, I'm kind of nervous about this," the ATF agent said with an apologetic look. "Hey," he added, noticing that the senior man was parking in a loading zone. "Should we be parking here?"

"What, you think I'm going to have to pay a parking ticket?" Blair laughed. *This kid really is new* he thought. "You don't want to have to walk to hell-and-gone, do you?" He gestured to the myriad pedestrians that were all headed towards the Indianapolis Convention Center. Many carried cased long guns, and one man had a shotgun under his arm without any case at all.

"I've told you before," Wilson Blair went on, speaking to his protege's fears, "you can't screw up gun show duty. It's not possible. And you'll actually be better at this than some of the guys who've been doing it for a while, 'cause there's no way anyone could recognize you on your first day undercover. Right?" The young man nodded. "You'll be fine," Blair told him. "Trust me." Wilson Blair shut off the ignition, then turned to the young agent. "You want me to run through everything again, before we go in?"

"Yes, please. That would help me a lot."

"Okay. Blending in's a snap. When we get in the door, immediately go to one corner of the hall and start there. Just walk down the aisle, looking at everything on all the tables. Ignore all the non-gun stuff, just like a gun nut would do. When you get to the end, go to the next row and walk down it in the opposite direction, and so on. That way you'll make a path that goes by every table, just like the customers do."

"I know that part, but what about what I'm supposed to *do?* Should I concentrate on the people who're set up, or the ones walking the aisles, or–"

"I'm getting to that," Blair said with a smile. "Bear with me."

"Sorry."

"Don't worry about it." *This kid acts scared to death* Blair thought with amazement. "Like I've told you before, there's no risk here. None of these people are going to do anything to you if they find out who you are. You're not DEA, for Christ's sake. These people don't think they're doing anything wrong. Remember what I told you?"

"Yeah," the young man said sheepishly. "Like writing parking tickets, only a lot more fun."

"Right. Okay, priorities," Blair said. "There's all kinds of things we can nail guys for, but it'll be easiest for you if you divide it in your mind into two categories: Number One, dealing firearms without a federal license, and Number Two, conspiracy to violate federal firearms laws." He saw the younger man nodding, and had an idea. "Why don't you tell me about how to catch someone for dealing without a license?" The younger man licked his lips.

"Uh, okay. As I walk through the aisles, I watch for anyone buying a gun from someone at a table. I pay attention to what it is and how much he pays for it, and I listen in to make sure he's not a dealer. If it's something that costs less than $400, I trail him from a distance until he's well away from the man he bought it from. Then I come up to him, say 'That's a nice...whatever, I'll give you...blank for it', and quote a figure $200 higher than what he paid."

"Right. Then what?"

"Then, if he says no, I offer to go a little higher. If I make the deal, I pay him, then ask to see his license. If he doesn't have one, I arrest him, and call you over." The agent looked worried.

"What's the matter?" Blair asked.

"Well, suppose it turns out he is a dealer, and never mentioned it when he bought the gun? Then I've wasted a bunch of ATF's money."

"Five, six hundred bucks? Don't worry about it. One solid bust will make up for fifty that turn out to be dealers." *Has this kid forgotten everything?* Blair wondered when he saw the young agent's quizzical look.

"You're forgetting that when you arrest the guy, you seize all his cash, which with some of these gun nuts is a bundle. Then you seize whatever guns he has. Then we go out to the parking lot and seize his vehicle. You might pick up thirty, forty grand on one bust."

"Won't the case get thrown out? You know, entrapment?"

"Who cares? Only way that'll happen is if the guy hires some serious legal muscle and spends fifty or sixty thousand bucks. And frankly, no one with any sense takes a chance in court on gun stuff. Everything's a felony, and the public's sick of these gun guys. A judge or a jury might slap him with ten years as soon as turn him loose. You watch—nail some guy good today and see if he doesn't agree to hand over his cash, guns, and car in return for us not pressing charges." Wilson Blair smiled and went on. "Now tell me about how you get someone for conspiracy."

"Well, uh, that's mainly finding someone that's talking about how you can, you know, do something that isn't legal to do."

"Such as?" Blair prompted.

"Uh, like taking the thumbhole sporter stock off one of the recently-imported semi-autos, and putting an old pre-ban style buttstock on instead."

"Hey," Wilson Blair said, impressed, "you even *sound* like one of these gun nuts." The young agent blushed.

"I've, uh, been reading up," he explained.

"That was a good example you gave," Blair told him. "What are some other felonies these people might conspire to do?"

"Well, talking about how to sneak in one of the guns they don't allow you to import any more, uh...talking about, you know, uh, how to put a bayonet on one of the military rifles that came in after the Bush ban, uh, talking about how to make brass bullets for handgun ammo, uh..." The agent finally shrugged to indicate he had run out of ideas.

"You're forgetting the best one of all," Blair told him. *Actually the second-best* Blair thought, *but we won't get into the suppressor-parts tactic until you're farther along.* "That's conspiring to convert Title 1 firearms into machine guns."

"Right!" the young man said immediately. "I blanked on that one."

"That's the big kahuna," Blair said. "You'll see several Class 3 dealers set up at this show, and the smallest one will have fifty thousand bucks worth of guns on his table. You get one of those jerks explaining to someone how to convert a gun to full auto, we can put him out of business for keeps." Blair stared at the younger agent. "You ready?"

"Yessir," the young man said as he zipped up his blue nylon windbreaker. Blair nodded and opened the car door.

"Then let's go do some good."

***

"Man, you got a beautiful set-up here. I've never seen a machine gun display before."

"Thanks," Henry said, "but I'm just helping out at these tables. My friend's off looking around the show. But I'm a Class 3 dealer too, and I know most of these guns pretty well, so I can probably answer any questions you have. Other than swap offers, and stuff like that," he added. The man Henry was talking to had greying hair and looked to be about fifty. He was very well dressed. *That platinum Rolex probably set him back as much as a new Corvette* Henry thought absentmindedly.

"I don't mean to be rude, but some of these guns seem ridiculously expensive. Like that STEN gun there for a thousand dollars—didn't those cost about six dollars to make during World War II?"

"They actually cost less than that," Henry agreed, nodding. "And you're not being rude at all. The problem is that the supply is fixed. And small," he added. Henry noticed that a few other people had gathered around, listening to what he said to the man. "If you'd like, I'll explain."

"I'd like to know, even if he doesn't," one of the others said.

"Okay," Henry said, swallowing. "The STEN gun was a military weapon made in a foreign country. The Gun Control Act of 1968 banned importation of all foreign-made machine guns. Some STENs, like that one, had already been brought in before that. In duffel bags of GIs returning home in '45, mostly. However, there was a two hundred dollar tax on machine guns, and no one paid that kind of money back then just to have a piece of paper for a junky old STEN gun.

"Then, in '68, our government gave anyone with non-taxed machine guns a one-month grace period where they could register them for free. A few people heard about this amnesty before it was over and actually did that. The problem was, anyone who didn't register his guns was out of luck forever; After '68, you couldn't do it even if you were willing to pay the two hundred. And remember, additional imports were banned. So the only *original* STEN guns you can buy—like this one—are ones that were brought back by GIs and amnesty-registered. There are probably less than a thousand of them on the registry, and there can't be any more, even though the guns are available overseas for a nickel a pound." He held the weapon out for the man to examine.

"Now, after 1968, existing machine guns could not be registered or imported, but domestic manufacturers, here in the U.S., were still allowed to make and register weapons. A STEN gun receiver is a rather simple thing to make, so you will see many STENs like this one," Henry explained, as he lifted a second example off the table, "and they sell for about half of an what an original goes for. The receiver is recent U.S. manufacture, the rest of the parts are military surplus." Henry handed the man the second STEN so he could compare the two.

"The next thing you'll probably tell me is that five hundred is still awfully steep for the new-receiver gun, and that it couldn't cost more than fifty bucks to make. The reason it's five hundred is that on May 19, 1986, all U.S. manufacture of machine guns for non-government use was banned. So the supply of *non*-original STENs on the market is now fixed as well. As an Economics major would say, this is a textbook example of the government introducing a huge distortion into the free market."

"Does this new-receiver gun function as well as the original?" the man asked Henry. "I can't tell them apart."

"There's no difference," Henry agreed. "So now you're thinking that no one's apt to find this piece of iron 'collectible', and five hundred versus a thousand dollars seems like an awfully big price difference, right?"

"Well, yes, actually."

"The reason for that is yet another government-mandated distortion in the system, this time on the demand side. World War II and earlier weapons, if they use the original receiver, are considered 'Curios and Relics' by the U.S. Treasury Department, which regulates these things. Guns that are still standard issue like the M2 .50 don't qualify, but everything obsolete, yes. Curios and Relics may be sold directly interstate between holders of Curios and Relics licenses without going through a dealer. That in itself is no big deal, but some states have laws that say the only machine guns that private citizens may own are the ones on the Curio list. I forget how many states there are like that, five or six maybe, but Michigan is one that I know of for sure."

"So if I lived in Michigan, I could buy this one," the man said, holding up the first STEN, "but not this one?" he asked as he raised the other.

"Right. So the demand for Curios is much higher in those states, ergo the high price." Several of the people listening snorted at this, but the wealthy man's expression did not change. *Guy's got a lot of self-control* Henry thought.

"If you are interested in a shooter, and I mean any shooter, not just a STEN, I recommend the less expensive gun. With an AK47, for example, you can pay five thousand for an Amnesty-registered pre-1968 Vietnam bringback like this one here," he said, pointing, "or half that much for a semiauto that was remanufactured to full auto and registered prior to May 19, 1986 by a licensed NFA weapons manufacturer, like this one. If by some miracle they reverse that manufacturing ban, the price will go back down to $150 for the machine work and registration on your semiauto, done by a licensed machine gun manufacturer, but right now, with a fixed supply, the price is way up there." Henry turned his hands palms up in supplication.

"Fact of the matter is, dealers like me have a hard time finding decent guns to sell with the laws as they are, and if you can find someone with an original STEN or AK, and all the federal documentation intact, I'll pay 80% of the price shown here, less the $200 tax, of course, regardless of condition. That's how hard they are to find."

"What $200 tax?" the man asked.

"Feds get that every time a machine gun changes hands, other than dealer-to-dealer, inheritance by lawful heir, or sale to or from a police department." Henry watched as eyebrows went up with this last bit of information.

"With the laws you've described, how do you guys stay in business?" the man demanded. Henry laughed.

"Good question. There are a few people who manage to make a full-time living out of it, like my friend Allen. This is his display, not mine," Henry said for the benefit of the newcomers who were listening to the discussion.

"Remember that all these guns were twenty or thirty dollars each back in the 'sixties, and a lot of guys who've owned them since then are now retirement age. Major player like Allen will buy hundred-piece machine gun collections from guys who've owned them for thirty or forty years, with a cost basis of next to nothing, when the guys want to cash out and spend the money in retirement. He'll pay up front, maybe seventy percent of retail, and then sell off the guns over the next six, eight months.

"Won't that game dry up?" the man asked, mixing his metaphors.

"Yeah, eventually." Henry took a breath and went on. "The other thing dealers like Allen do is travel overseas, looking for the correct accessories that the serious collectors demand. You can still import rare tripods, and stuff like that. This gun here," Henry said, laying his hand on a tripod-mounted German MG34, "is worth $3500. The tripod it's sitting on, which is a rare Alpine version, sells for about $4000 'cause the Krauts only made a handful, and I bet you can't find another one for that price.

"Allen's the best man I know at finding indirect-fire sights, wheeled mounts, and all those other things they made in limited quantities for these guns before the wartime factories had to revise their production priorities."

"So serious collectors buy these guns, just like pre-war Purdey shotguns and English double rifles?"

"Sure," Henry said. *I bet he's got more doubles than I do* he thought with a small smile, remembering the four double rifles in his gun safe. "Thompsons can be worth over ten grand, and I know more than one person with a million-dollar machine gun collection. For people like that, I recommend only buying all original guns, like the first STEN I showed you, not guns with new-manufacture receivers. However," Henry went on, stressing the word heavily, "I strongly recommend that you do not buy any machine gun with the expectation that it will increase in value over time, like you might with other guns."

"Why not?"

"One law change, and your whole collection could be worthless. Personally, I think confiscation is unlikely. It would outrage too many influential people. But proposals have already been made to ban all further transfers. You'd keep what you had 'til you died, basically, then the government would seize the guns from your estate and cut them up."

"No one would stand for that!" another man in the group exclaimed. Henry shrugged.

"Lots of people already have, on a local level. In several cities they've already banned certain rifles based on appearance, not function, and there haven't been any riots. In 1986 the feds banned further manufacture of an entire category of gun. That's pretty drastic, but you don't see anyone doing much except whining."

"You're the most straightforward dealer I've met," the wealthy man said abruptly. "And it sounds as if you know your machine guns. Which ones do you like best?"

"Well, I'm a dealer, and I own or have owned over fifty different types of squirt guns," Henry explained, lapsing into Class 3 dealer jargon. "If you're asking which half dozen or so I'd sell last, you need to understand that I shoot a lot, so I like guns that are very controllable on full auto, last forever, and use inexpensive magazines. On any gun I really like, I plan on spending between fifty and one hundred percent of the gun's cost on magazines. It's nice when that means getting a few hundred magazines, instead of only a couple dozen. I pay kids to load them for me, and I always have at least ten thousand rounds in magazines, ready to shoot." *That got their attention* Henry thought as he saw eyebrows go up. The man with the Rolex listened attentively without any reaction to what Henry had said.

"I also prefer rifle-caliber machine guns. With those...personal preferences in mind, last gun I'd get rid of is the Belgian FN Model D. It's the final refinement of John Browning's BAR, with a self-cleaning gas regulator, quick-change barrel, and a clock-type rate reducer. My shooter is a police-only demonstrator with over a hundred thousand rounds through it. I've worn out four barrels and broken a dozen firing pins, and that's it. There are less than ten on the civilian registry that can be sold to private individuals, like this one here," Henry said, touching a gun to his left. "Allen's got $7000 on this one, and he'll get it. That's with five hundred magazines, by the way. If that's too much dough, I'd get the U.S. BAR, which are much more common, for about half the cost.

"Gun number two would be a 1917A1 watercooled Browning, like this one. They run like clockwork, don't burn the barrels out, and shoot much more accurately than the aircooled version because the barrel's supported at the muzzle. Five thousand on the correct mount with a hundred belts, two spare barrels, spare bolt, and a belt loader.

"After that, I'd have to have an original Colt Thompson and a hundred mags, which would be about five grand for a 1921 model in decent shape, like this one here. Then a British BREN gun, that's this one over on this table, which would be six Gs or so after I got done buying a few spare barrels and a hundred magazines. BREN gun is the British version of the Czech ZB26, that this one over here, and both these guns'll go a half million rounds without breaking ten dollars worth of parts. That's not counting wearing out barrels," Henry added quickly.

"Next I'd have to have a .50, and I like watercooled guns, so I'd get the original Colt MG52A, over there, instead of the aircooled heavy barrel gun most people choose, down here on the end. That M2 mount is the wrong one, but no one's seen an MG52 tripod in this country for thirty, forty years." Henry remembered something and went on. "Allen got the documentation on that old Colt, and it originally went to a coal company, back in 'thirty-one. "

"A *coal* company?" one of the people standing there said. "What for?"

"Labor relations," the man with the platinum Rolex answered, before Henry could say anything. "That's how it was done back then."

"Exactly," Henry added. "They didn't spell it out in their annual report, though." He went back to answering the man's original question.

"For a 9mm, I'd want one that used cheap STEN mags, so I'd get a Lanchester, like this one here, which would be about $1500. The gun's heavy and the bolt doesn't bottom against the back of the receiver, so the gun's real controllable. I like the Lanchester—and the STEN, for that matter—a lot better than the UZI. STEN magazines are two bucks each, five hundred at a whack.

"If I wanted a .223-caliber gun, the M16 is the way to go. Parts are everywhere, you can swap uppers to change barrels in five seconds, and used mags are three dollars each in quantity." Henry pointed at a half-dozen M16s on the table behind him. "I'd rather shoot a BAR, but '16s are good for girlfriends to shoot. Two grand for a nice original Colt, fifteen hundred for a remanufactured semiauto.

"Last of all, and this may sound weird, I'd want a rimfire machine gun. Guy in Arkansas named Norrell designed a beautiful conversion of the Ruger 10/22, and made a bunch before the '86 ban. Works like a champ, fires from a closed bolt, and uses the 50-round aftermarket magazines. Barely any recoil at all—it just vibrates. Those full-auto trigger groups go for about a thousand, and can be installed in any 10/22 with no receiver modification. The trigger group is the registered machine gun; your gun is unaltered." The man with the Rolex nodded.

"Those are the guns I'd keep for shooting," Henry said. "There's others I'd want just because they're pretty, like this 1897 Argentine Maxim with the brass jacket, but I'd get the blasters nailed down before I concentrated on the museum pieces."

"Your advice sounds well-reasoned," he said to Henry as he lifted an aluminum attache case onto the table in front of him. "And I think I'll follow it. I believe I brought that much cash with me today. Do you or your friend here have one of those .22 triggers you were talking about? All the other suggestions you made look like they're available."

"I've got one back in Missouri I can transfer to you," Henry answered, then licked his lips. "I don't mean to sound like a bait-and-switch sleazeball, but the prices I threw out at you, which are taped on all the guns here, do not include the $200-per-gun federal transfer tax." The man waved his hand in dismissal.

"I'd never expect your posted prices—or anyone else's, for that matter—to include tax. I assume you—or your friend—will handle all the paperwork?" he asked as he opened the case to reveal stacks of hundred-dollar bills. "What kind of identification do you want? Driver's license?"

"The procedure's more involved than that," Henry said evenly. "If you were hoping to take any of these home with you, I'm afraid that's against the law."

"Five-day waiting period, huh?" the man said. "Asinine law, but I can live with it. How much of a deposit do you want, then?"

"Ah, mister..."

"Recht. Sam Recht," the man said, sticking out his hand for Henry to shake. "It's Doctor Recht, actually, but I'd just as soon you call me Sam."

"Henry Bowman, Dr. Recht," Henry said as he shook the man's hand. "Lot of successful doctors I've met like guns. What I mean to say," Henry explained, "is the procedure is a lot more involved when you buy these things, and it won't be any five days, either. We've got to submit the forms in duplicate, with a passport-size photo of you on each form, so that's fourteen photos for the seven guns. Then you'll have to go to your local police station and get fourteen copies of your fingerprints taken—we'll give you the fingerprint cards you need to use. Then you–"

"*Finger*prints? And *fourteen* sets of them?" Recht exclaimed. "That's absurd!"

"It's federal law, Doctor," Henry said gently. "After you get your prints done," he continued, "you have to get your local police chief to sign all fourteen of the forms, saying that he has no knowledge of you intending to use the guns for criminal purposes. That's where the trouble–"

"Wait a minute wait a minute," Dr. Recht broke in. "I have to get *permission* from a guy who didn't even finish high school?" he asked, shaking his head. "I'm a *neuro*surgeon. I cut on people's *brains,* for God's sake, and I can check out any drugs I want from the lab. The police chief in my town has a tenth-grade education, and last year his wife came into the ER with a subdural hematoma. Said she fell down the stairs, but since they live in a trailer, I'd say he slugged her."

"Regardless of whether or not he's a wife-beater," Henry said, "you have to get all the forms signed, and that's where people run into trouble. Some chiefs refuse to sign any forms for anyone. Chief in Olivette, Missouri, near where I live, refused to sign for one of his own officers. Fortunately, there are other people who can sign that the feds will accept, like the sheriff where you live or the local Prosecuting Attorney. But it sounds as if you might have a little leverage over your chief, what with having worked on his wife, and knowing her condition. If everybody you go to still says no, I suggest you talk to the people who manage the DA or the sheriff's reelection campaigns, and make a five hundred dollar contribution. That'll often get you your forms signed. But if you're thinking of buying more guns later, I recommend you have the guy sign a bunch of extras, or you'll end up coughing up another five hundred on the next go-round." Sam Recht stared at Henry.

"Is that it?" Recht demanded. "Or do you have some other little surprise for me, such as only being allowed to buy one gun a year?"

"No, you can buy all the guns you want, as long as you go through all that crap for each one, and you already know about the $200 tax per gun the feds get. But there is one other thing you won't like, that I started to mention before: The wait."

"How long?"

"There's no set time period. The forms, fingerprint cards, and money get sent off to the feds, and they send the prints to the FBI, who does a background check. That's why the cards have to be perfect—any smudges or incomplete impressions, they'll kick 'em back, demand new sets, and that delays the process.

"Assuming the prints are okay, and assuming the FBI doesn't turn up any skeletons in your closet, ATF will keep one copy, and send the other one back to the seller with the $200 tax-paid stamp stuck to it usually within five months, though sometimes it takes close to a year."

"Five months to a year?" Dr. Recht almost yelled.

"That's what it takes for a first-time buyer. On subsequent transfers I always enclose a copy of a prior approved Form 4, and then it usually takes six to eight weeks. But not always," Henry added. "Dealer-to-dealer transfers also use duplicate submissions, without the police signature, prints, or photos. I've had some of those take six months, although six weeks is probably more normal." Henry looked at the flabbergasted doctor.

"I know it's surprising, first time you hear about it, and if you want to blow off the whole idea, you'll have a lot of company."

"I'll have to think about it," Dr. Recht said slowly. He still looked stunned by the whole conversation.

"Where do you live?" Henry asked. "When Allen gets back, I'll see if he's done any transfers in your area. Maybe one of the people the feds will accept to sign your forms is someone he's used before, and you won't have any trouble."

"I doubt it," Dr. Recht told him. "I live in a small town near Urbana." *Oh, fuck* Henry thought.

"Urbana, Illinois?" he asked. Recht caught his worried look.

"Yes. Why?"

"You're screwed," Henry said simply. "Illinois state law bans private ownership of full autos with the singular exception of police officers. Sorry."

"I see," Dr. Recht said. His expression was hard to read. Then he leaned over so that his words would not be heard by anyone else standing nearby. "Tell me, Mr. Bowman," he said softly, "do you ever wish you could watch the people in our government be boiled in oil?"

"Not more than four or five times a day," Henry answered. He was not smiling when he said the words.

"Excuse me, sir," a boy who looked to be about eighteen said, and Henry pulled away from Dr. Recht.

"Yes, how can I help you?"

"Can I look inside this AK, see how it's different from mine?" *Here we go* Henry thought to himself. *Kids always want to see how machine guns work, just like I did more than twenty years ago.*

"No."

"No?" the young man asked, startled. Henry shook his head.

"Remachining semiautos to select-fire is a felony. Discussing how to do it can be interpreted by a court as conspiring to violate the law."

"But–"

"I suspect," Henry said loudly, cutting the young man off, "that you are genuinely interested is seeing how a machine gun functions. I should know, because I was the exact same way when I was fifteen. Problem is, we can both get in big-time trouble, because when it comes to guns, the Constitution is out the window, including the First Amendment. So I don't discuss differences between semi- and full-auto guns with anyone except federally licensed machine gun manufacturers. Ever. Period. I'm sorry."

"But just looking at–"

"I'd listen to this man if I were you, son," Dr. Recht broke in. "I think he knows what he's talking about." The young man turned and walked away. The crowd that had been watching the exchange lost interest and moved on.

"Thanks for backing me up," Henry told the doctor. "I hate to be a jerk, but talking about conversions is a real bad habit. That's one of the easiest ways to spot an ATF informant. They get nailed for doing something careless like making replacement suppressor baffles," he explained, "and all of a sudden they're looking at never owning another gun, or being able to go shooting, or anything. So the feds dangle this deal, agree to let the guy walk if he helps them land some bigger fish, and big Class 3 dealers are the biggest fish of all. Allen tells me he's seen several people who used to set up at shows now walking around machine gun dealers' tables, asking leading questions and moving like a tape recorder was glued to the small of their backs."

"You think that kid was an informant?" the doctor asked, startled.

"Not a chance. That was a kid who wanted to know about machine guns. There'll be twenty people who'll ask me or Allen that same question before the day's over. I don't care who they are, I'm not going to give anyone eavesdropping even the slightest idea that I'm helping someone learn how to break the law." Henry shook his head. "I'm sorry about the damn state ban, Sam, but that cesspool called Chicago sets the rules for the rest of the state. If you get some property in any of the forty machine gun states, give Allen a call.

"Even where it's legal, some people find the ridiculous transfer process so offensive, they won't have anything to do with machine guns, and I can't blame them. I decided it was worth it a long time ago, but as I said, I really like to shoot."

"In Illinois, I could own this stuff myself if I was a cop?"

"Yeah. Crazy, isn't it? There's probably not a bent neurosurgeon in the whole state, but you could throw a rock in Chicago and hit a crooked cop. Friend of mine ran a department near there, and he had to quit. Said it was the most depressing job he'd ever had.

"I know it probably sticks in your craw, but talk to the sheriff about having him make you a deputy. Even if you decide not to buy any machine guns, it'll help you out.

Illinois is like Missouri in that it's a felony to carry a gun for protection as a private citizen. A lot of people who wear Rolexes and carry fifty thousand bucks in briefcases think that only applies to black guys," Henry said, glancing down in the vicinity of Doctor Recht's waist. "I'll tell you, in this political climate, a revolver in your pocket can cost someone like that everything he owns."

"That what you do? Carry a deputy badge?" Sam Recht asked, reflexively putting his hand over the bulge made by the .38 Chief's Special in his right pocket. Henry shook his head.

"I've gone a step further than that. I'm on the force at three small departments in rural Missouri as the weapons instructor and armorer. Got on the first one when I was eighteen, after I got mugged."

"I'm learning more than I expected to at this gun show," Dr. Recht said. "Do you have a card?" Henry handed him one. "A geologist?" Recht said, surprised.

"Like we were talking about before, damn few people in this country can make a living just by selling guns. And I'm not one of them," Henry added with a laugh. "Here, take one of Allen's cards, too. He'll do a good job for you if you get police creds and decide you want to buy some Class 3 stuff."

"I've enjoyed talking to you, Henry," the doctor said, and continued resumed walking down the aisle towards the tables he hadn't seen yet.

***

"See anything you couldn't live without?" Allen Kane asked as Henry returned from wandering around the show. It was early afternoon.

"Saw a nice custom .460 on a Remington 30-S action, but the guy wanted about double what the thing was worth. Did you see the dealer that had the ZB37 barrels for sale?"

"No...barrels for a ZB? Which caliber, and how much does he want for them?"

"They're 8mm, they look new, and he has 'Make Offer' on the tag. My guess is either he wants some crazy high price and he's ashamed to show everybody, or he doesn't know what the things are, and hasn't a clue what to ask for them. I didn't talk to him 'cause I knew you'd have a better feel for what to pay. Go on, I'll stay here. They're at a table about two rows past that big Glock banner over there," Henry said, pointing to a spot halfway across the exhibition hall, "and a little bit to the right. Next to a table where a guy has about a hundred wooden rubber band guns for sale that he's letting people shoot at tin cans on strings in front of an old bedsheet."

"Want me to grab you a Coke on my way back?"

"Yeah. Maybe see if Andy needs one, too," Henry suggested, nodding toward the man set up next to them who was selling nothing but parts. "He's been here a while with no break." Allen stepped from behind an early Colt Maxim gun and headed off in the direction Henry had indicated. Henry stepped behind Allen's row of tables and looked around for anyone who might want a question answered.

"Excuse me, do you sell AK parts?" Henry turned around. The man who had spoken to him was in his late twenties, slender and clean-shaven, wearing a blue nylon windbreaker.

"Some. Got mags, spare barrels, op rods and springs if you shot your gun with corrosive ammo and didn't clean it. I think Allen's got an RPK rate reducer here somewhere, cut down the cyclic about 200 RPM–"

"Is that a full auto part?" the young man broke in.

"Yeah. No use on a semi. We don't sell semis, as a matter of fact," Henry explained. "Only full autos and other high-dollar rare stuff, like that Gatling replica over there."

"That thing you mentioned is a full auto part?"

"It's only used on the full auto," Henry said, mentally adding *you half-wit.* "It's from the heavy RPK version of the AK. They use the same receiver. It slows down the cyclic rate on full auto. It obviously wouldn't do you any good on a semi. You could install it, and it would then increase the time it took for your bolt to cycle from seven-hundredths of a second to nine hundredths, but so what. You'd still have to pull the trigger again. Understand? What kind of AK do you have?" he asked, changing the subject. "Is something on it broken?" *Or more likely did you take it apart and lose something after you couldn't figure out how to put it back together?* Henry had had almost a whole day of politely answering questions from people for whom the four-dollar admission charge was a stretch.

"Uh, it's a regular AK. A semi. So, uh, you sell full auto parts, huh?" the young man said quickly.

Alarm bells went off in Henry's mind. *Goddamned informant, trying to set me up* he thought. Henry took a deep breath and spoke calmly and deliberately. "We don't have any parts here that can be used to alter a semiauto and make it fire full automatic. The government has decreed that as of May 19, 1986, such conversions are illegal for anyone except government agencies."

"It's real easy, though, isn't it?"

"I wouldn't know. I'm not a gun designer."

"Some of your guns are converted from semiautos, aren't they?"

"I only know what the transfer form from ATF says on it: 'Machine Gun'," Henry replied levelly. "It says machine gun, then that's what it is."

"But lots of people sell the parts to convert, don't they?"

"I've never seen any for sale, and wouldn't know what they looked like if I did." He stared at the young man. "Haven't even seen any shoelaces, super glue, or paper clips for sale here."

Got him Henry thought as he watched the young man's expression. In a recent case where ATF had charged a man with selling 'illegal conversion parts', an expert witness for the defense had used his shoelace to make a 40-year-old military rifle fire full auto. Then he had taken super glue and a paper clip and done the same thing with several .22 pistols and rifles. ATF had tried to suppress the videotape of these feats, but it had ended up in wide distribution. Henry Bowman made as if to scratch a spot over his right kidney, and started to pull out his shirttail so that he could reach the itch.

"Uh, well, uh, who here do you know that has some AK stuff of any kind for sale. Like, uh, another dealer like y–"

"Not one more word," Henry commanded as he brought the 5"-barreled Smith & Wesson .44 to bear on the young man's chest. "Put your hands on top of your head and nod if you can see the white things inside the cylinder." The man obeyed. "Good. Those bullets are turned out of nylon bar stock. They make a huge wound cavity at this range but they won't exit. No one behind you is in any danger at all." Henry saw in his peripheral vision that other show patrons were backing away, pointing at the spectacle in front of them. He also saw that the crotch of the young man's pants was soaked. His bladder had let go.

"Jesus, Henry, what'd this guy do?" Allen Kane said as he ran up to where his friend stood. Allen had spotted Henry holding the man at gunpoint from two rows away.

"He's soliciting to violate federal firearms laws," Henry told Allen without taking his eyes off the man. "Go over to Andy's table, get me a Garand clip with no ammo in it."

"You got it," Allen said without asking questions.

"Turn around slowly, then put your palms together with your arms stretched out behind your back," Henry commanded his captive as he climbed over the table, trying not to step on guns as he did so. He held the man's wrists with his left hand and holstered the big revolver. "Hands together like you were praying. That's it." He took the Garand clip Allen held out for him and slid it over the tips of the four middle fingers of the young man's hands. Then he balled his fist and drove the sheetmetal holder down to the base of the man's fingers. The young man grunted in pain as the steel scraped off a fair amount of skin.

"Field handcuffs," Henry said to Allen. "I haven't searched him yet. Take any guns or knives he's got on him, then grab your camera and get a few pictures of this asshole. I'm going to get on the PA and see if any feds are here." Henry left at a brisk walk while Allen patted the man down, using a STEN mag on the urine-soaked areas.

"Your attention please," Henry's voice boomed out over the Convention Center's loudspeakers, *"Would any agent of the Bureau of Alcohol, Tobacco, and Firearms present in the hall please go to Table G-nineteen, repeat, G-nineteen. We have a criminal in custody who has been caught attempting to violate the National Firearms Act. Any ATF agents in the hall please go to table G-nineteen. Thank you."*

"Special Agent Wilson Blair," the ATF man said as he stepped in front of Allen Kane and flashed his credentials. "I'll take over here," he added as his eyes bored into those of the prisoner. A crowd of perhaps forty people was gathered around the three men. "I'll take whatever weapons you took off him also." A crowd was standing around, snickering.

"Didn't find anything," Allen Kane said, deadpan. "No ID, even, and none of these people here have ever seen this man before. I guess he's just another scumbag criminal, trying to make machine guns without paying the tax." His brows knitted together.

"I didn't search too carefully down at that wet spot," he admitted, "so you better check there." The crowd erupted into laughter. Blair gave Allen Kane a look of pure hatred, then turned it towards the dozens of faces which surrounded him. No one made a move to say anything. Blair stood there for a few moments, his jaw muscles working.

"Better watch where his hands are bleeding, too, when you take that clip off him," Allen said helpfully. "He might have AIDS." The crowd laughed even louder at this comment.

"Give me his gun and his creds right now, you son of a bitch," the ATF supervisor said in a whisper of barely-controlled fury. Allen Kane stared at him for a moment, then pulled the Model 19 Smith and Wesson from his pocket, opened the cylinder, dumped the six rounds into his left hand, and handed Blair the empty gun. He pulled the agent's badge and wallet from his other pocket and relinquished them, also.

"Happy now?" Kane asked, amid jeers from the crowd.

"You just fucked with the wrong guy, asshole," Blair told him under his breath, then turned and ushered the younger agent away. Tears ran down the young man's cheeks as he shuffled off ahead of his supervisor, his hands still secured together behind his back by the Garand clip. Catcalls followed the two men as they headed toward the exit.

"I can't fucking believe you let those sons-of-bitches take your gun and your badge!" Blair yelled as they walked along the concrete ramp outside the convention hall. Administrators in Federal agencies viewed relinquishing a badge as the greatest sin an agent could commit. J. Edgar Hoover had once tried to have two slain FBI agents ejected from the Bureau posthumously because their credentials had been taken. Such action would have cancelled all death benefits for the two surviving families, and Hoover had reluctantly been forced to officially assume that the badges were taken after the agents had been killed, and not before.

"I...I couldn't do anything about it," the young man cried as he turned his head and wiped mucous on his shoulder. "Everyone there saw him take my gun and my badge, and no one said a thing." His tears were ones of shame, but the physical pain from where Wilson Blair had tried to take the Garand clip off his fingers didn't help. His screams had convinced the older man to wait until they could use a hacksaw.

"Right," Blair said tightly. "I'm sure you did every fucking thing you could." He turned his head right and left as they reached the loading area. "Where did I park that goddamn car?"

"You fellas have that white Chevy four-door?" a grizzled black man in a maintenance uniform asked. He was staring, obviously not knowing quite what to make of their appearance. "This here's the loading dock, for folks who has tables inside. Manager checked his list, saw you wasn't no exhibitor, called a tow truck. Here," he said, proffering a business card. "That's where you can get your car back. Forty dollars. No checks."

Blair snatched the card and shoved the other agent towards the concrete steps without a word.

***

"So no official reprimand in his file. That's very kind of you, sir," Wilson Blair said. "I know he'll be grateful."

"He's new to that detail," Dwight Greenwell told his subordinate over the phone. Greenwell was the Deputy Director of the ATF in Washington. "Can't throw him to the wolves when he's just starting out. I'll flag all of Kane's transfers, see if we turn up anything irregular. Was he the only one involved?"

"No, sir, it was another dealer who pulled the gun on him, although he had left by the time I got there and I did not ever see him. Name of Bowman, sir."

"Bowman. Got it. We'll flag his transfers, too, and you keep a file on both of them on your end." There was a pause before Greenwell spoke again. "We'll get them," he assured Blair. "No one embarrasses us and gets away with it."

"Yessir," Blair said. The smile in his voice was evident a thousand miles away in Washington. "And once again, I'm sorry to have bothered you at home, sir," he repeated. "But I wanted to know what to do."

"You did the right thing," the Deputy Director assured him. "Goodnight."

"Goodnight, sir," Blair said, and hung up.

***

"Good evening, Mister D'Onofrio," Cindy said with a dazzling smile as she extended her hand. "I'm Cynthia."

"Hey, what's with this 'mister' stuff, huh, doll? It's 'Marty,' okay?" He smiled but did not get up.

"Marty it is." Cindy Caswell turned the wattage up a notch on her smile as she slid in next to the man, but made no move to rub up against him or put her hand on his thigh the way most of the girls would have.

"Jimmy, bring us a bottle of Dom. And another when we get low, all right?"

"Right away, Mister Marino," the waiter said and hurried to the back of the restaurant.

Sal Marino had not grown tired of Cindy Caswell, at least, not in the way he had expected to. The newness and novelty had diminished of course, but that had happened more slowly with her than it had with any of the others before or since. Rather, Sal Marino had become aware that it was much easier to negotiate with his associates and competitors when Cindy was part of the process. They expected a girl as part of the deal; that was a given, especially in Vegas. With Cindy, though, their minds weren't always so focused on the agreement's bottom line. As a result, Cindy Caswell had taken on a new role in Sal Marino's organization. She was still Marino's slave, to be sure, but it beat the alternative, which was to star in one of the organization's snuff films. *At least it has so far* Cindy thought grimly as she beamed at her boyfriend for the evening.

Sal Marino saw that Marty D'Onofrio was paying a lot of attention to his new friend, and he smiled expansively. Cindy noticed Sal's expression as he casually fingered the redhead he had brought along for dinner.

No mystery what Sal's thinking right now she thought humorlessly. *Pussy's pussy, but an extra point-and-a-half is something you can put in the bank.*

June 12, 1990

"Randy Weaver?" called the man in the U.S. Forest Service truck.

"You're talking to him." The two men in the federal vehicle looked at one another, then got out of the truck and walked to the house.

"You weren't home," the man who had been driving said. Weaver shrugged at the accusation. He had driven over to a friend's house not far from his own cabin in the Idaho wilderness. He hadn't been expecting anyone, least of all Forest Service employees, to come calling.

"We're with the Bureau of Alcohol, Tobacco, and Firearms," the second man volunteered. Weaver's eyes narrowed at this bit of information.

"Yeah?"

"Last summer, you sold a shotgun that was under the minimum length. The man you sold it to was one of ours. We have it on tape." Weaver said nothing. He had indeed sold a shotgun the year before, a Harrington and Richardson single-barrel. Randy Weaver knew that the barrel had been over the 18" federal minimum, but that didn't mean anything. The buyer could have easily cut the barrel off a little more after Randy left.

The two federal agents looked at each other nervously. Finally one of them spoke.

"Look, you're in serious trouble, mister. Ten years in prison and a ten thousand dollar fine. How's your family going to like that?" Weaver still said nothing.

"We've come here to offer you a deal," the other man said. Weaver stared at him. "We want you to work for us. Get in the Aryan Nations camp—we know you've been there—and tell us what they got, what their layout's like. We'll give you all the stuff you'll need, and tell you where to put it. Do that for us, and we mi–"

"Forget it."

"Listen, Weaver, you can't act li–"

"I said forget it."

"You're the one who's forgetting something, tough guy," the other agent broke in. "You're forgetting who we are and what we can do. You had that shotgun in your house before you sold it, and we'll just say that's where you cut it down. Then you transported it in your truck to sell it. Under the seizure guidelines, both your house and your vehicle were used to facilitate the commission of a felony. That means they're ours, whether we prove you sold our man that gun or not. What you got to say to *that,* tough guy? *Well?"*

"Fuck off and die," Weaver said, then walked past the agents, climbed into his truck, and drove away.

***

"I'm going to write them a letter," Vicki Weaver told her husband. "Tell them to watch out for anyone new." Randy Weaver shook his head in disgust.

"I thought we headed off this kind of crap in '85," he said angrily. He turned and walked into the other room.

Randy Weaver was not now and had never been a member of Aryan Nations. He had made that fact clear in his sworn affidavit five years before. That did not mean, however, that Randy was ready to become a spy for the BATF and plant contraband to help the feds facilitate a raid. Vicki agreed, and she insisted on warning the white supremacy group of the attempt to coerce her husband into infiltrating their organization.

The lever that the feds were vainly attempting to use on Randy Weaver to make him do their bidding was the National Firearms Act of 1934. The BATF claimed that Weaver had sold their informant a shotgun upon which Weaver had failed to pay a $5 tax to the Treasury, as per the 1934 Act. The shotgun, a Harrington & Richardson single-barrel worth about $50, had a barrel eighteen and one-half inches long, which was eminently legal. However, the overall length of the weapon in question was twenty-five and five-eighths inches, due to the fact that the buttstock had been shortened. This was 3/8" below the federally approved 26" minimum overall length for Title I firearms, making it a Title II 'Any Other Weapon' and subject to NFA regulation.

It would never be officially determined just who was responsible for shortening the piece of wood this final three-eighths of an inch. Some would claim that Randy Weaver, like most proficient shooters, had been well aware of the 18" barrel rule but was ignorant of the 26" overall length regulation, which was much less well-known, even among the most ardent of shooting enthusiasts. Others (including Randy himself) would maintain that the gun was legal when Weaver sold it to the BATF informant, and that either the informant or someone else in the agency had whittled the wood down the final 3/8" after the gun was no longer in Weaver's possession.

There were several things that were *not* in dispute, however; things that virtually everyone on both sides of the issue agreed with.

Everyone agreed that belonging to a religious sect which believed its members were God's chosen people was not a crime. Everyone also agreed that moving to a sparsely populated rural area whose few inhabitants were of the same racial and ethnic background was not a crime. Not one person had ever accused Randy Weaver of assault, robbery, theft, verbal abuse, littering, or any crime which harmed any other person physically, monetarily, or emotionally.

Every person involved with the case agreed that at most, Randy Weaver had committed one crime, and one crime only.

All subsequent actions of federal agents involving Randy Weaver and his family were based on the presumption that Weaver was guilty of failing to pay the Treasury a $5 tax on a $50 shotgun, and that tax was due the government because a piece of wood was 3/8" too short.

January 17, 1991

"That's a hell of a place to break down," Vicki Weaver said when she saw the truck stalled in the middle of the bridge, blocking both lanes. She and Randy were heading into Naples, Idaho, five miles from their home. The stalled truck's hood was open, and a man and a woman were peering into the engine compartment.

"Let's go give them a hand. If I can't get it running, four of us ought to be able to push it over into one lane, at least," Randy said as he slowed his vehicle and pulled over to the side of the road. He and Vicki got out and walked up to the other motorists.

"What's the problem?" Randy asked as he walked up to the stalled vehicle. "Can we give you a ha–"

"Federal Agents! You're under arrest!" the man yelled, cutting Weaver off in mid-sentence as he whirled around and held a gun to Randy's head. The woman, on cue, grabbed Vicki Weaver at the same time. "You have the right to remain silent. Anything you say can and will..." The agent droned on reciting the Weavers' Miranda rights as he and the woman agent handcuffed Randy and Vicki's wrists behind their backs.

Randy and his wife were herded into the back of the camper by the woman as the male agent lowered the hood and got in the driver's seat of the truck. Randy Weaver smiled grimly at his wife and settled in for the drive to the federal magistrate in Coeur d'Alene.

Because neither he nor Vicki had criminal records, Vicki would be released immediately and Randy would spend one night in jail. The judge allowed Randy to go home after signing a $10,000 property bond.

Throughout the proceeding, Randy Weaver silently vowed that the feds would never fool him again.

February 19, 1991

"Looks like Weaver's not going to show up, your honor." The federal judge slammed his gavel on the bench in reply.

"Issue a warrant for his arrest. Order the federal marshals to bring him in. Next case." Neither of the men realized that the date on the summons they had sent Randy Weaver had been the wrong one.

The stakes had just been raised for the entire Weaver family.

December 16, 1991

John Lawmaster wondered what his wife was up to as he hung up the telephone. He shook his head as he reached into his pocket for his car keys and headed for the garage. In the tradition of divorced men everywhere, he reminded himself that he was lucky not to have a real crazy psycho hate relationship with his ex. That was something to be grateful for. Lawmaster got in his car and pulled out of the garage.

Ted Royster smiled as he watched John Lawmaster drive away. Lawmaster's ex-wife had done her job perfectly. He picked up the microphone to his mobile radio.

"Okay, we're all set," he announced. "Lets do it."

Royster was the head of the regional office of the Bureau of Alcohol, Tobacco, and Firearms, located in Dallas. The Dallas office controlled all ATF operations in Texas, New Mexico, and Oklahoma. Royster liked to participate in ATF's high-profile raids, and that was why he was now sitting in his government car with blacked-out windows on a Tulsa street, waiting for his agents and the news crew to arrive.

It did not take long. In a few minutes a several large vans with their sirens screaming pulled up in front of John Lawmaster's house. Thirty black-clothed agents carrying machine guns, cutting tools, and a battering ram emerged from the vehicles. Patrons of the Sonic fast-food restaurant across the street stared as eighteen of the men prepared to smash the front door while the rest ran around to the back of the house.

"On three," Agent Ward commanded. "One, two, three!" The dry wood of the front door made a sound like several small-caliber gunshots as it splintered under the onslaught of the 300-pound ram. Neighbors watched in horrified fascination as John Lawmaster's front door was torn off its hinges and the black-clad invaders streamed into the empty house.

The ATF agents pulled out or tore open every drawer, shelf, and cabinet in every room in the house, and dumped the contents in the center of the floor. They broke through walls looking for potential hiding spots. They tore tiles out of the ceiling. Finally, they cut the locks off Lawmaster's gun safes and threw every firearm in the safes out on the floor.

One of the guns was a Colt AR-15, a lightweight rifle Eugene Stoner had designed for the ArmaLite division of Fairchild Aircraft 35 years earlier, now made by Colt Industries in Hartford, Connecticut. Supervisory Agent Ward picked up the rifle, opened it, and inspected the mechanism carefully. *Shit, no M16 parts* he said to himself, and tossed the weapon back on the floor.

"Check the shed out back, and then that motor home," Ward commanded, in spite of the fact that neither was listed on the search warrant. Two agents, one with a pair of bolt cutters, ran out the door. They were met by a Channel 7 news crew that had arrived on the scene. The cameraman got some quick footage of the destruction inside the house before he filmed the agents breaking into John Lawmaster's tool shed and throwing the man's tools and fishing equipment out in the yard.

"Nothing here," the first agent said. Undeterred, he examined the lock on the motor home. "Bring that sledge over," he asked of his companion.

"Hang on, that's mine," Lawmaster's neighbor said quickly. He had been watching the proceedings with undisguised astonishment. "I got the key right here," he added helpfully. He did not mention that he was also the owner of the house, and that Lawmaster was renting it from him.

"You his neighbor?" the agent demanded.

"Yeah, my name's–"

"Has Lawmaster got an AR-15?" the agent interrupted.

"Uh, yeah," the neighbor answered, momentarily taken aback by the unexpected question. "Unless he sold it."

The agent grinned. He knew John Lawmaster owned an AR-15, for he had seen Ward inspect it.

"And he has an auto sear and M16 parts for it, doesn't he?" the agent demanded.

An auto sear was a machined piece of steel about the size of two sugar cubes. When combined with five M16-specific Colt parts, an auto sear enabled an AR-15 to fire full auto. ATF had banned the manufacture of unregistered auto sears in 1981 by ruling that any of these half-ounce chunks of steel made after that date would by themselves be classified as machine guns. ATF had banned the manufacture of registered ones five years later, except of course for government agencies.

ATF had further ruled that if one of these six pieces of steel (i.e. a loose M16 trigger) were possessed by a person who also owned an AR-15, it was a felony, regardless of whether the part was installed in the gun and despite the fact that all six items had to be present to make the gun function.

"I don't know," his neighbor shot back as he glared at the fed. The agent stared at the cap the man wore, which was imprinted with the logo of a local pistol range.

"Lapse of memory, huh?" He nodded at the cap. "You're one of them, and you don't know what an auto sear is?"

"I know exactly what an auto sear is," the man said irritably. "I don't know if John Lawmaster owns one or not." The agent turned on his heel and joined the other ATF men.

The thirty agents systematically destroyed almost everything inside John Lawmaster's home. They searched in vain for any NFA-regulated article on which Lawmaster owed but had not paid the $200 NFA-mandated tax. Royster, Ward, and the other ATF agents did not find one single such weapon, because John Lawmaster did not own any NFA-regulated weapons, taxed or otherwise.

"Sorry there was no story," Ward said to the film crew. His voice carried more than a trace of irritation. He had promised the news people that his men would find 'illegal guns' in the home of the federally-licensed Tulsa dealer, but he had let the media people down.

The ATF men who had devastated the inside of John Lawmaster's house had carried machine guns as they conducted their raid. Not one agent or any of his superiors had paid any taxes on any of these NFA-regulated weapons.

Not one agent had been made to undergo an exhaustive FBI records check and get a local police chief to sign a transfer form.

Not one of the agents or any of his superiors had paid the $500 special (occupational) tax that people such as Henry Bowman were forced to pay annually in order to buy or sell NFA weapons without paying the $200-per-weapon fee.

Not one of the agents or his superiors kept a bound book listing the seller, the seller's license number, and the date of acquisition of the machine guns they carried, as someone such as Henry Bowman had to do.

Not one of the agents or his superiors would ever be charged with the crime of failing to maintain such a bound book, as someone such as Henry Bowman would have been.

The agents did not have to worry about any of these failings. They didn't have to. They worked for the government.

The ATF operations commander scribbled the words 'Nothing Taken - ATF' on a piece of paper, dropped it on the floor, and called his men to gather up their things and return to headquarters. He and the other ATF agents left Lawmaster's house with the front door broken off its hinges, his safes cut open, and all his guns lying in piles in the middle of the devastated residence.

John Lawmaster was never charged with any crime.

January 6, 1992

"I don't get it with the broad, Sal. Why give him a piece first? What's the point?"

"Mikey-Mike's going to do this one, become a made man. I know the kid's got big balls, but Fat Tony Farratto ain't exactly some runner with sticky fingers like mosta the guys learn on. Up to me I'd bring in a mechanic and who cares about payin' the extra twenty gees. But Carmine says his son Mikey-Mike has to do it. So okay, I understand, it's a pride thing, I respect that. But this is my territory. Fat Tony never minded gettin' wet, an' I know he ain't forgot how. Mikey-Mike gets iced here, I look bad. Don't matter Carmine said it was the kid's play, don't matter I said let us handle it and Carmine said no. I still look bad. So I soften Fat Tony up a little, first. Let him have Cindy, get him relaxed, keep his mind on pussy and not on the fact I still got a lot goin' on with Carmine."

"Sal, Fat Tony like to hurt broads when he fucks' em."

"Shit, Nine-ball, who doesn't? Slam it in hard when they ain't quite ready? You 'n' me both done that lots a times."

"Sal, Fat Tony likes to hurt broads when he fucks 'em like by cuttin' em. He licks their blood for Christ's sake! Sometimes he burns 'em with cigarettes while he's doin' it. Bit halfway through some whore's lip in Atlantic City." Sal Marino looked pained.

"Sick fuckin' bastard. There's no knife on him—he was clean for the meet." Rules of etiquette dictated no weapons of any kind were allowed during territorial negotiations. The same rules prohibited killing a rival while he was a guest in your home. That meant that Fat Tony Farratto was safe as long as he was inside the building. This was why he had two hardmen waiting for him outside the front door.

"Shoulda given him someone else, Sal."

"We got a doc full-time, for Christ's sake, just two floors down. Any burns or bruises, he'll take care of her. Anyway, it'll be the last time Fat Tony ever pulls that kind a shit."

***

Cindy Caswell saw it coming long in advance, and she tried to defuse it. Fat Tony Farratto was not the first man she'd encountered in the last three years who had not been able to enjoy himself unless he was hurting her. Others had slapped her, bit her, jerked her hair, and in one case, punched her in the stomach hard enough to make her vomit blood.

Cindy had learned to move with the slaps. She had learned to endure the bites until the pain was severe, then deliver an ear-splitting shriek to stop the man from continuing. She had learned that if she moved her head so that when her hair was jerked it was pulled to the rear, it almost didn't hurt at all. She had learned to do all these things while at the same time coaxing more arousal out of whomever she had been commanded to pleasure.

Cindy Caswell realized in the first thirty seconds with the man now in front of her that she was in serious danger, but all of her experience was proving useless. Most men stroked themselves or reached for her when she came to them. The first thing Fat Tony had done after she had undressed entirely was to lick his lips. That was not unusual.

The second thing he had done was to take her left nipple in a firm grip between the thumb and forefinger of his right hand. That was not unusual either.

The third thing he had done was to try to tear it off. Cindy had remained silent, but her eyes watered furiously. She realized now that the only reason Farrotto had not succeeded was that she always rubbed her skin with almond oil before she presented herself to a new master. In spite of the oil, she felt that the man had almost drawn blood. She knew that at the very minimum, Anthony Joseph Farratto was going to leave her with permanent scars.

"Oh, *my*," Cindy said in a husky voice as her eyes watered and she frantically tried to think her way through this crisis. "You're a man that wants a girl to remember him."

"You will," Fat Tony assured her.

When she heard those two words, Cindy Caswell made a decision. She knew she was probably writing her own death warrant. Had it been three years earlier, or two years earlier, or perhaps even only *one* year earlier, she might have decided otherwise. She might have elected to alternately beg and scream, and endure whatever outrages the syndicate man inflicted upon her flesh while hoping that someone would come stop him before he killed her. She might have chosen acquiescence then, but now she did not.

Cindy Caswell had been the personal sex slave of Salvatore Xavier Marino for three and a half years. For all but the first few months of that time period, she had been a 'perk' for whomever the mid-level Mafioso wanted to keep happy. Her services were required twice a week on average. Sal had made it clear that so long as she performed this duty adequately, she would continue to have her own suite in the hotel, room service meals, cable television, and elegant clothes to wear when they went out. As soon as her performance was not up to expectations, Sal had explained, the organization would have no more use for her. There were hints that if age eventually diminished her appeal, she would be given a job in a casino, with a bank account as a retirement bonus. Cindy did not for one second believe this would ever happen.

Sal himself liked variety, so after the first two months he rarely had sex with Cindy Caswell. One thing Sal Marino never grew tired of, however, was watching two women in bed together. On many evenings when she was not otherwise occupied, he would call Cindy in to his bedroom to introduce her to whatever young woman was there with him. Women were safe, Cindy quickly learned, and sometimes she was almost able to forget that Sal Marino was even there.

For the first year, Cindy had concentrated on staying alive. In the second year, she had looked for every possible avenue of escape, and concluded that there were none. She could not possibly get out of Vegas before the word was put out and she was spotted. Cindy was forced to admit that she probably couldn't even get out of the hotel.

In the third year, Cindy Caswell had decided that she would endure her servitude for as long as possible, but when it became intolerable, she was going to die with her own self-respect intact. She was not going to die alone.

Cindy Caswell was not permitted to have anything in her room which could effectively be used as a weapon. When room service delivered meals, a single knife was included, and it was always removed with the dishes. Every time she went out with Sal or one of his guests, she was expertly frisked after dinner by one of his soldiers. After years without ever finding anything, she thought Sal would abandon the practice, but he had not.

Five months before, Cindy Caswell had taken to wearing her hair up in a chignon. She pinned her thick brown tresses in place with two tapered wooden dowels that looked like chopsticks, only a bit shorter. The first day she had come out of the salon with the new coiffure, two two-inch sections of wood were plainly visible angling out of the knot at the back of her head. No one had thought anything of it.

Over a one-month period, Cindy Caswell had used several paper emery boards altering the taper of the two dowels and making their tips much sharper. The change was gradual, so no one had noticed that, either.

Cindy's hair was held up with the two tapered hardwood dowels as she stood naked in front of Fat Tony Farratto. She turned her body slightly to the left, presenting him with her right breast.

"Please don't ignore this one," she breathed. Fat Tony obliged her by savagely twisting her right nipple as he had her left. "Ohhhh...." she exclaimed, trying to make her cry of pain sound like one of sexual release. She saw that the man was now fully erect inside his slacks. *I'm only going to get one shot at this* she told herself. *Better do it right now, while he's just been aroused.* "Bed," she sighed. "Let's get in bed."

Cindy Caswell led Anthony Farratto to the king-size bed. He allowed her to push him onto his back, remove his shoes, and unzip his trousers. Cindy climbed astride the obese Mafioso, saying, "I want you to watch how wet I get when you spank my bottom." She moved her body up his so that she was kneeling with her thighs on either side of the fat man's neck. Her vagina was two inches from the tip of his nose. "I shaved it for you, so you could watch."

Fat Tony swung his right arm and slammed the palm of his hand into the girl's bottom, but he had no leverage at that angle, and the impact had little force. Cindy moved slightly with the blow and let her pelvic area cover more of the man's face.

"Harder!" she demanded, arching her back, tightening the muscles in her thighs, and throwing her hips forward. Fat Tony's eyes were now covered by Cindy Caswell's crotch. When she looked down, she could see only the top of the man's forehead and his oily black hair. *Only got a couple of seconds she thought.* "Slap my ass!" she said, breathing hard. Anthony Farratto was not going to try to slap Cindy's bottom. He had something else in mind.

Cindy Caswell pulled one of the tapered maple dowels from the coil of hair at the back of her head, seated the dowel's flat end into the palm of her right hand, and made a fist. The sharpened end stuck out five inches between the knuckles of Cindy's second and third fingers. She felt Fat Tony's hands reach up and grab her hipbones. *One shot, girl* Cindy said to herself. *Got to lift yourself straight off the bed.* She gripped the back of her right hand in the palm of her left, then pulled her hands in until her thumbs touched her abdominal muscles, with the tapered wooden spike pointing straight down. She knew instinctively that the man was about to pull her down onto his mouth so that he could bite off her labia.

Fat Tony pulled his lips back to expose his teeth, dropped his jaw, and used all of his considerable might to pull the girl towards his waiting mouth. Cindy sat back slightly, and as soon as she saw the man's eyebrows come into view below the swell of her pubic mound, she drove the wooden shaft straight down with all of the strength in both her arms.

Anthony Farratto had just started to close his jaws on Cindy Caswell's vaginal lips when the point of the sharpened maple spike entered the top of his left eye socket. With one hundred thirteen pounds of force behind it, the small wooden lance passed between the bone and the top of the eyeball, pushed the optic nerve aside, and drove straight through the man's brain. In less than three hundredths of a second, the sharpened wooden tip bottomed on the inside back of Anthony Farratto's skull and blunted itself as it slammed into the bone.

Cindy Caswell, her system charged with adrenaline, locked her elbows, flexed her shoulders forward, put every ounce of her weight on her palms, and did indeed manage to momentarily lift her knees off the bed.

Most of Fat Tony's right side went numb, and some of his voluntary motor functions on that side were shut down as if a huge switch had been thrown. His left eyeball was rotated upwards, but the vision in his right eye was still good. When Cindy Caswell got off his chest, he thought he could see something sticking out of his head just left of his nose. His left eye hurt, but other than that, there was little pain. He was trying to figure out what was going on, and why the girl was smiling at him.

Cindy Caswell reached for the protruding end of the wood spike. She saw with satisfaction that Fat Tony's good eye followed the movement of her hand. Cindy gripped the end of the round maple spike and pulled. The tapered dowel started to come free, and she stopped after she had withdrawn it about an inch. With her left hand, she grabbed the man's still-rigid penis, threw her leg over his hips, and sank onto his erection. An unintelligible sound came from Fat Tony Farratto.

"You like that, huh?" she said with a smile as she rocked back and forth on him. To Fat Tony, her voice sounded as if she were in a big steel drum, but he heard what she said. She picked up the pace and realized with surprise that she was close to a climax. "Don't look so surprised, Mister Farratto," Cindy chided as she reached once more for the protruding end of the wooden dowel. "Sal *told* you I was going to fuck your brains out."

As she felt the first wave of her orgasm start to course through her body, Cindy Caswell grabbed the end of the dowel, closed her eyes, and stirred vigorously.

***

"Hey! Tony! You still in there?" Sal Marino looked at his companion, then swore under his breath. "They been in there for hours. You hear water runnin', Nine-ball, or is that my ears?"

"No, it's water. Probably takin' a shower, wash the blood off," he said darkly.

"*Christ!* Don't say that!" Sal blurted out. The other man shrugged. Sal Marino shook his head and came to a decision. "Give me the passkey." Marino took the key, used it to open the door, and peered inside. He closed it softly and turned to his companion. There was a smile on his face. "Fat Tony's in the bed, under the covers. Must be sleepin'. So that's Cindy in the shower. I guess she worked her charm on him, huh?"

"I guess so, Sal. What do we do now?"

"Hell, let's hit the tables. He'll probably want to go for seconds when he wakes up. Let him have some fun. It's got to last him a long time."

The other man laughed at that, and followed Marino to the elevator.

"You three know where you're going?" Deputy Marshal Arthur T. Roderick, Jr. asked the members of the other three-man team. "The north peak?"

"Yeah, no problem."

"Looks like it's going to be a hot one. You guys going to wear body armor along with all that camo gear?" one of the group asked.

"Screw that. It's a big enough pain in the ass we got to lug around all this other shit every day, 'specially in the heat."

"That's the truth."

The six deputy marshals all decided to forego body armor that day.

What was going on that morning was nothing new. Federal marshals from the U. S. Marshal's Service had been spying on the Weaver house for eighteen months, ever since Weaver had failed to show up for his court date in February of 1991. For the first year, the Weaver 'mission' had been run by the northern Idaho office of the U.S. Marshal's Service.

In March of 1992, however, control of the federal operation was handed over to the Marshal's Service headquarters in Arlington, Virginia, two thousand miles away. In that month, Deputy Marshal Arthur T. Roderick, Jr., a member of the Marshal's Service's Special Operations Group, was sent from Arlington headquarters to Idaho to take command of the Weaver operation.

Roderick was heading a six-man unit. He had split the group into two three-man teams. One team's job was to watch the Weaver cabin from the distant vantage point of a mountain peak. The other team, which included Roderick, planned to penetrate the dense woods immediately below Randy Weaver's house.

The other two members of Roderick's team were William Degan and Larry Cooper. Although Roderick himself had made over two dozen clandestine trips to the area around Randy Weaver's cabin in the past six months, Degan and Cooper were new to this part of the operation. Roderick's plan was to move an undercover agent onto the land adjacent to Weaver's, and, over the next few months, have him gain Randy Weaver's confidence. Degan and/or Cooper were potential choices for this role, and Roderick intended to familiarize them both with Weaver's property and the land around it.

"All set?" Arthur Roderick asked.

"Yeah, I guess."

"Hope it doesn't get too hot, with all this gear."

The three men on the penetration team wore camouflage over their entire bodies. On their heads were night vision goggles. In their packs they carried still cameras, movie cameras, and electronics gear for surveillance. Clipped to their harnesses were secure-voice radios. Roderick, Degan, and Cooper each carried both a pistol and a machine gun. Roderick and Degan had Colt M16s, while Cooper's machine gun was a 9mm with a sound suppressor. Between the three of them, the marshals were carrying four NFA weapons—three machine guns and a silencer. None of the three men had filled out any registration forms or paid any taxes on any of the four NFA weapons they carried, nor were any of the agents special (occupational) taxpayers.

Randy Weaver had been under constant federal surveillance for eighteen months. The cost of this operation would exceed what the government would spend on intelligence gathering before the invasion of Haiti.

Federal agents carrying machine guns and over $50,000 worth of surveillance gear (but no search or arrest warrants) were once again about to invade Weaver's property. All this was due to the feds' claim that a piece of wood had been 3/8" too short, and Weaver had not paid a $5 tax on it.

The appalling irony of this situation was lost on Deputy Marshals Roderick, Degan, and Cooper.

***

"Oh, shit," Larry Cooper said. The three of them were in the woods below the Weaver family's cabin. It was a little before 11:00 in the morning, and a dog had just started barking.

"Must've caught our scent," William Degan said.

"Let's get out of here," Arthur Roderick suggested. "Your machine gun has a silencer," he said to Cooper. "You shoot the dog." The three heavily armed deputy marshals began to run down the hill.

"Sounds like Striker's found a deer," Kevin Harris said to Sammy Weaver. Harris was a twenty-five-year-old logger, a family friend who spent much of his time at the Weaver cabin. Sammy and Kevin grabbed their rifles from the wall rack and ran out the door towards the sound of Sammy's yellow Labrador retriever.

As the dog approached, the three feds crouched down in the heavy brush and remained still. They were all but invisible, for they wore not only camouflage clothing from head to toe, but also camo face paint. The three men watched as the dog approached.

The yellow lab was much more of a pet than a guard dog. Striker had been around people all his life, and because of the constant federal surveillance, the land around the Weaver cabin had been loaded with traces of human scent for over a year. The dog had a good nose for birds and animals, but human scent did not set him off. Striker had started barking not because he had smelled the deputy marshals, but because he had heard them moving through the brush below the house. Now they were silent.

Roderick, Degan, and Cooper watched as the dog approached where they were hiding. Sammy Weaver and Kevin Harris followed about sixty yards behind the yellow Lab.

No point in shooting now Cooper thought as the dog walked past the hiding place and continued down the mountain. The Lab was no threat, and the 9mm machine gun Cooper carried, even with its sound suppressor, would easily be heard by the two approaching young men. *Best to wait here until they all go away* Cooper told himself as he watched the dog walk away from him and his two companions. Larry Cooper was completely unprepared for what happened next.

Why doesn't he kill it? Deputy Marshal Arthur Roderick thought as the Labrador passed by their hiding place. Sammy Weaver and Kevin Harris were almost to the three agents when Roderick stood up, flipped the selector lever of his M16 to 'semi', shouldered the rifle, and shot Weaver's dog in the rear. The animal yelped once loudly enough to be heard over the rifle's tremendous muzzle blast, then died. Its spine had been shattered by the high velocity rifle bullet.

"Sammy! Kevin! What's going on?" Randy Weaver shouted from above when he heard the shot.

Sammy Weaver and Kevin Harris were taken utterly by surprise as the sound of the .223 blasted in their ears. The Weaver boy had been watching Striker, and when he saw his dog killed, he whirled towards the source of the shot and instinctively fired two quick rounds from his rifle in that general direction, then ran towards the cabin. Neither shot hit anything other than brush.

"I'm coming, Dad!" the boy yelled. He had taken three steps before two rifle bullets slammed into him. The first struck him in the upper arm, very nearly severing the limb from his body. The second hit him in the back. Sammy Weaver's legs carried him two more steps before he fell on his face, dead. He had just recently turned fourteen.

Randy Weaver, up on an adjacent logging road, was carrying a shotgun when he heard the shots ring out. A shotgun was useless at that distance, so he started firing the weapon in the air as he ran towards the cabin. He hoped to distract the feds from Sammy and Kevin and allow the two boys to escape. Randy Weaver did not realize that his son was already dead.

Kevin Harris watched in horror as the boy he had known for nine years died before his eyes. Instinctively, with his rifle held at waist level, Harris fired from the hip at the man who had killed Sammy, then turned and ran. Kevin Harris proved to be more proficient at point shooting than his young friend had been. The bullet hit Degan in the rib cage, smashing several ribs and exiting behind his armpit. The bullet caused massive trauma and hemmorhage into Degan's lung, killing the man. Kevin Harris made it back to the cabin safely.

As a terrified Roderick and Cooper stayed hidden in the bushes, the weather turned colder and it started to rain. The two deputy marshals huddled by the body of their dead companion, shivering in the cold rain as they waited for someone to come save them. Finally, after nightfall, an Idaho State Police SWAT team rescued the two men and recovered the dead marshal's corpse.

When sworn testimony was taken, Roderick and Cooper would repeat their initial statements that they had made to the FBI. The two men said that Harris had fired the first shot, hitting Degan in the chest, and only after Harris had killed their fellow marshal did the two feds return fire.

There would be several problems with this claim: The first was that both 14-year-old Sammy Weaver and his yellow Labrador had been shot from behind. The second was that if Harris *had* fired the first shot of the firefight, killing Degan, it was certainly an odd response for Roderick to shoot the dog and let the young man who had just killed his partner get away.

The final and most troubling fact that did not square with the marshals' claim was that seven pieces of .223 brass would be found next to where Degan's corpse had fallen. These fired cases had come from Degan's M16 which, according to Deputy Marshal Cooper's sworn testimony, had been set on 'semi-automatic' when Cooper later picked it up. William Degan had fired seven shots before he died. Many would claim that Degan could only have fired these rounds before Kevin Harris fired the single shot that tore through Degan's chest and killed the marshal. Others quickly countered that Degan had held his fire, then pulled the trigger of his weapon seven times as fast as he could before falling down dead.

Another deputy marshal, a man named Jack Cluff, would do his part to exonerate Marshals Roderick and Cooper by giving the *Salt Lake Tribune* yet another version of what had happened on that morning. In an article that the Utah newspaper published two weeks later, Cluff explained that after Degan had been shot, Roderick and Cooper '...dove into a natural depression in the ground...held their guns overhead and cranked off rounds blindly in front of them. Presumably, Samuel Weaver was killed in the exchange.'

Though Cluff would fail to mention it, presumably the dog was also killed in this panicked spray-and-pray maneuver. Cluff would also fail to mention how he came by this proprietary knowledge about the incident, given that he was not present when the shooting occurred.

***

Midnight was approaching as Randy Weaver and Kevin Harris went back down the mountainside to retrieve the body of Randy's 14-year-old son. Randy wrapped the body in a sheet and the two men carried it up the hill then laid it out in a shed near the cabin. As Randy looked at the mud- and blood-stained corpse, he thought his heart would break.

Randy Weaver did not realize that things were about to get a lot worse.

August 22, 1992

This is not good at all FBI Agent Alex Neumann thought to himself as he surveyed the mountainous terrain around him. Neumann was a member of the FBI's Hostage Rescue Team, or HRT, pronounced 'hurt'. He had been with the Bureau for eighteen years, and he had never seen anything like what was happening now. More than three hundred law enforcement officers from both federal and state agencies had swarmed into the area since Marshal Degan had been killed the previous morning. These agents that surrounded the Weaver residence wore camouflage clothing and face paint, and were armed with machine guns and sniper rifles.

Along with the hundreds of armed police agents was an impressive array of vehicles and other equipment. There was a huge command post set up on a neighbor's property, complete with satellite links, communications trailers, motor homes, and wall tents. There were fourteen Humvees, two armored personnel carriers, three 2 1/2-ton cargo trucks, two medevac helicopters, one Hughes surveillance helicopter, two army field kitchens, six water trailers and four field generators. The aerial photos that the agents were using had been taken by an Air Force F-4 Phantom pilot.

I don't want to be a part of this Neumann told himself for perhaps the tenth time. *No way they're going to get out alive now. All-wood cabin up on the hill...sun ought to be out before long...everything'll be dry in a few days...this many agents...* The man felt an overwhelming sense of dread about what was to come. *I don't want to be here when they burn this guy and his family alive.*

The HRT man was thinking of the 1974 raid in California, when he had only been with the Bureau for three months. There, the Bureau's final assault on the so-called Symbionese Liberation Army had resulted in the fiery deaths of five people. He was also thinking of 1983, when tax protester Gordon Wahl of the *Posse Comitatus* had been burned to death by the Bureau. Neumann was remembering the courses the FBI gave its agents on the use of fire to burn out adversaries.

Maybe I can get a lateral transfer to Cheyenne, Wyoming. Take a few cuts in benefits if I have to. I'm getting too old to watch this kind of shit any more.

As it turned out, although Alex Neumann was right in his prediction of disaster for the family on the hill, his fears of fire that morning were premature. Randy, Vicki, their three daughters, and Kevin Harris were indeed surrounded by hundreds of agents. Up on the mountain they had some freedom of movement, however, and were not completely trapped in the cabin. The FBI did not elect to burn them out.

Alex Neumann would have to wait another six months before the Bureau would once again demonstrate its expertise with incendiaries.

***

Special Agent Lon Horiuchi of the FBI's Hostage Rescue Team in Quantico, Virginia, was settled in behind the scope of his bolt action, .308 caliber police sniper rifle. The gun rested on sandbags and was aimed at Randy Weaver's cabin, about 200 yards away. It was close to six o'clock in the evening. Horiuchi and the other FBI snipers had been watching the Weaver cabin for several hours, waiting for a target to present itself. He had already been given clearance to shoot.

Randy Weaver sat at the kitchen table. He was thinking of his son, whose body lay in a shed outside. He heard one of his two remaining dogs barking, and instinctively thought of Striker, Sammy's yellow Lab who was also dead.

"Sounds like he's behind one of the sheds," Kevin Harris said to his friend.

"Probably smells Sammy," Randy Weaver said forlornly. He stood up and took a deep breath. "I'm going to go check. To make sure Sammy...make sure Sammy's body's okay."

"I'll go with you," Harris said.

"Me too, Dad," Sara Weaver insisted. "I want to see Sammy one more time." Randy Weaver started to protest, but Vicki, who was nursing their youngest daughter, ten-month-old Elisheba, cut him off.

"Let her go, Randy."

Her husband nodded. Sara Weaver, who at sixteen was Randy and Vicki's eldest child, followed her father and Kevin Harris out the cabin door.

"Cleared to fire," came the FBI order when Randy, Kevin, and Sara came out of the cabin and started hurrying towards the shed. One FBI sniper waited until Randy stopped at the door to the shed, then the federal man pulled the trigger. Randy Weaver was reaching up to unlatch the shed door when the sniper's bullet creased his right armpit and slammed into the shed. Randy's other hand flew to the site of the wound as the muzzle blast rang out over the mountainside.

"*Daddy!* Get back in the house!" screamed Sara Weaver as she grabbed her father and began pushing him back towards the cabin. Kevin Harris followed quickly after his two friends.

Vicki Weaver, still nursing the ten-month-old she cradled in one arm, held the kitchen door open for Randy, Sara, and Kevin.

"You bastards!" Vicki screamed as the last of the three, Kevin Harris, ran past her into the kitchen. It was then that Agent Horiuchi of the Hostage Rescue Team pulled the trigger and fired the shot that would make him famous.

The bullet struck Vicki Weaver squarely in the temple. Brain matter and large skull fragments were blasted out the opposite side of her head as the heavy .30 caliber slug exited her skull and continued on, tearing through Kevin Harris' left arm and smashing two of his ribs before finally lodging in his chest. Vicki Weaver's corpse collapsed on the floor, clutching the baby in a rictus of death.

Sara Weaver turned at the sound of the impact and took in the grisly scene. Her mother was obviously dead—part of her head was gone. Kevin Harris' arm was torn open and he had a bad-looking chest wound. He was doubled over, trying to get his breath, for his lung was collapsing. Her father, Sara believed, was seriously wounded from Horiuchi's first shot. Sara Weaver looked for the baby, and realized Elisheba was under her mother's lifeless body, still clutched in the dead woman's arms. Sara grabbed her mother's corpse by the shoulder and pulled it over enough so that the baby would not be smothered, and then rushed to her wounded father.

In a space of thirty-six hours, federal agents had killed Randy Weaver's wife and also his son. The FBI would claim that Horiuchi had been authorized to shoot because when Randy, Sara, and Kevin had come out of the cabin, they were about to open fire on a surveillance helicopter hovering overhead. One problem with this claim was that several government witnesses testified that when Horiuchi fired the shot that creased Weaver's armpit, Randy Weaver was reaching to unlatch the shed door. He was not and could not have been shooting at a helicopter.

The killing of Vicki Weaver was much harder to justify. The two men and the girl had been running into the relative safety of the cabin, and they had already gotten inside when Horiuchi fired his fatal second shot. No one could claim that the three were doing anything aggressive—they were simply running for their lives.

Furthermore, Randy Weaver had been the first one in the door. No one could make a credible claim that the hostage rescue specialist had been shooting at him. The official report would be that Horiuchi had been trying to shoot Kevin Harris in the back as he ran into the kitchen, but had been late with the shot and then jerked the trigger. That was why the agent had shot the nursing mother in the head: purely by accident. It was also pure luck that Kevin Harris had been seriously wounded in the process.

***

"What do you suppose they're doing up there?" one of the agents asked as he looked up the hill at the cabin. "Why don't they come out? The mother's dead. You'd think they'd give up."

"I'm getting tired of standing here in this rain," his friend said. "Let's see if we can get a rise out of anyone up there." The agent cupped his hands to make a megaphone for his voice.

"Vick-eee, oh, Vick-eee! What are you going to cook us for breakfast tomorrow, Vicky? Your husband loves it when you cook for him, doesn't he? Have you got enough for everybody? Vick-eee..." The agent shook his head and chuckled. "Guess it's not going to work."

"Try again later," his friend suggested.

***

I hate this job Alex Neumann thought as he stood in the cold night rain and watched the scene in front of him. He was standing by the barricaded Ruby Creek bridge, four miles below the Weaver cabin, where dozens of state and federal officers faced an angry mob of area residents and friends of the Weavers. Included in the group were Kevin Harris' parents.

The situation was more volatile than anything that Neumann had experienced in eighteen years with the FBI. The feds had set up the barricade that morning to deny access to the Weaver property, and had evicted over thirty nearby residents from their homes, some of them at gunpoint. The people absolutely hated the massive federal invasion. They were demanding answers, and they weren't getting any. *Thank God they don't know about the dead boy* Neumann thought. *Yet.*

The veteran FBI man stood up straight in the cold rain and kept his face from showing any of what he felt inside.

He had not yet heard about what had happened to Vicki Weaver five hours earlier.

September 19, 1992

"Good afternoon, my name's Henry Bowman, and I'm an alcoholic."

"Hi, Henry!" a chorus of people replied simultaneously. *I swear that's the most moronic part of this whole organization* Henry thought with an inward smile. *But I guess I'd miss it if they didn't do it. Maybe.* He cleared his throat and went on. There were about twenty people seated in front of him in the church rectory.

"It's been a while since I came to a meeting. A couple things have happened lately that made me realize it would be a good idea to find one and go. One of them was that I'm the sponsor for this young guy who just got out of a chemical dependency program at one of the hospitals, and he wanted to talk to me about something they'd gone over in class. One of the counselors was talking about secrets—secrets about things in our past we're ashamed of. He was saying to the class that these things have a lot of power over us mainly because they're *secret,* not because of what they *are.*

"Anyway, this kid told me that some of the people in his class had volunteered to tell some secrets about themselves, and after they did, they seemed to feel a lot better for having done it. Only he couldn't bring himself to, in front of all of those people. So he asked me could he tell me his secret, which would be easier for him than 'fessing up in front of a whole bunch of people, some of them women. I guess I was kind of a practice run." Most of the people in the room laughed at that comment.

"I said 'sure', and was hoping it would be something interesting, because it had been a slow day, but he ended up telling me about how he'd stolen something worth about ten dollars from someone a long time ago and he was really ashamed because the person was his best friend. We talked about it some, and he seemed to feel a lot better, and if I was disappointed because his secret was really boring, I tried not to let on." A few more people chuckled at that.

"After I hung up, I got to thinking about the whole 'secrets' thing, and did I still have any. Came to realize there was one. I'd never thought of it in the way this kid had, because it wasn't something I'd done to somebody while I was drinking. It was something that happened to me twenty-one years ago, when I was cold sober and my drinking consisted of maybe a glass of champagne at Christmas."

Henry Bowman went on to tell the group about the summer night in 1971 that he had been gang-raped while out running. He told the story quickly and without embellishment. He was surprised at how easy it was. *Maybe the counselor at that program is on to something* Henry thought. When he finished the story, several people were looking at the floor. There was one woman, however, who could not take her eyes off Henry.

"That was twenty-one years ago. It was the real start of my drinking, and I was just lucky that someone took me to an AA meeting before I got into some disaster that couldn't be reversed.

"After I got sober, I started teaching personal self-defense classes, using what I had learned. I told all of my students about what happened. Only thing is, I lied. I told them it was a severe beating, which it definitely was, but I left the sex part out of it. The classes were a success, and I have received letters over the years from former students saying that what they learned from me kept them alive and unhurt when they were attacked.

"Thing is, why did I lie? It wasn't because I'd done anything wrong. I hadn't committed a crime. You could argue that it wasn't my duty to air dirty linen in public, except I didn't tell *anybody* what really happened, not for over twenty years. Not until right now.

"I haven't had a drink for seventeen years. Some things are happening right now that make me feel powerless—very much like the way I felt that night in 1971—and I really wanted a drink last night." Henry paused and shook his head.

"I take that back. I didn't want *one* drink last night, I wanted a full bottle of gin, and about a quart of fresh tonic water, and a whole lime to slice up, and a place to drink it with no phone and no television. But I knew if I did *that*, I'd have the same set of problems today, along with a great big new one: losing twenty years of sobriety. So I ate an ice cream cone instead, and came here tonight."

One by one, many of the people in the group thanked Henry for what he had said, and related something they had gotten out of hearing it. Several told secrets about themselves. Henry thought they were all pretty mundane, except for one member's confession that after he had been fired from his job for drinking, he'd had a printer run off some labels for a wear-reducing engine additive, slapped one on a can of lapping compound, and sent it off with a "here's your free sample" letter on dummied-up Valvoline letterhead to his ex-boss. The man's Mercedes had gone almost a whole week before the entire engine was ruined.

"You sure your boss didn't keep a bottle of gin in his desk?" Henry asked when he heard this story. "I wouldn't dump some strange crap in my engine if the letter that came with it was from God Himself."

***

"I'd like to speak with you for a few minutes," the young woman said to Henry. "I haven't had dinner yet, and the coffee shop down the street has good milk shakes, if you like ice cream." Henry smiled.

"Sure, I could go for that. I'm sorry, if you said your name before, I didn't catch it."

"No, it's only my fourth or fifth meeting here. We've never met, and I didn't say anything tonight. My name's Cindy. Cindy Caswell." The two shook hands and Cindy led the way out the door.

***

"There's a secret *I* have that I wasn't quite ready to tell the whole group," Cindy said after they had been seated and had ordered their food. "I think you might understand, so I'd like to talk to you about it." Henry nodded his head and Cindy Caswell told him about her abduction and subsequent three-year ordeal in Las Vegas.

When she got to the part about Fat Tony Farratto, she told Henry that her last 'assignment' had been an overweight man who'd had a heart attack during sex. She said she'd taken the considerable sum of money he'd had in his pocket (which was true) and managed to get out of town before anyone knew he was dead. Cindy Caswell was not about to confess to murder, not to someone from an AA meeting, or to anyone else. She did, however, mention the date of the event, and Henry Bowman made a mental note of it.

"So, you went through all that for three years straight in Las Vegas, but didn't start drinking until you got back here?" Henry asked after the waitress brought his milkshake and Cindy's hamburger. He was reserving judgment on the story the girl had just told him. Alcoholics tended to lie when it suited their purposes, just like the rest of the population.

"There, I didn't have a choice. I might as well have been kept in a cage. When I got back here, well..." she let the sentence hang.

"So why AA?" he asked critically as he sipped his milkshake. "You don't look too bad off to me. And it certainly didn't seem you were all too keen to be at the meeting tonight."

"Judge's orders. I wrecked a car when I was drunk. Just an old junker—ran it off the road into the woods, no one hurt—but I totaled it, and when the police came and I was babbling, they did a test and I came up more than double the limit. It was AA or women's detention."

"And sometimes it seems to you that all this 'higher power' stuff is a bunch of Jehovah's Witnesses crap, right? 'Let go and let God', serenity prayers, and all that?"

"Exactly."

"Well," Henry said as he took a deep breath, "I got news for you. It is."

"What?" she exclaimed, putting down her hamburger.

"It is a bunch of crap, if you look at it that way. Simplistic phrases repeated endlessly by people who probably got shorted in the genetic lottery to begin with? Not apt to engender confidence in the program, if that's what you're focusing on. But there are a lot of good people in AA that just about anyone would look up to. Go talk to *them*. Find out what *they* get out of the program. Don't ask the sappy-sounding moron that says he's got his recovery all figured out, when he's only been sober three weeks. And if you think you aren't an alcoholic, well, driving off into a tree doesn't strike me as normal behavior. You've got enough problems, like getting snatched off the street, without making more trouble for yourself." Cindy nodded.

"So what works for you?" she asked.

"Law of physics. That's *my* higher power. Energy equals one-half mass times velocity squared. Immutable. Constant. Stand in the way of a freight train, you get clobbered. All the good intentions, or will power, or careful planning won't change the train's effect on your body. Same thing with alcohol. My body has a biochemical addiction to a drug. Period. If I have one drink, I want another. I want another one a lot more than I wanted the first one. All the good intentions and careful planning can't change that. Other people may not have that biochemical addiction, but I do. Just like my cousin is allergic to penicillin—one injection and his heart stops beating. Mine chugs along with no problem.

"I can't change those things. Going to AA reminds me of that. Keeps me from thinking maybe that freight train won't hurt me, if I'm real careful. It's also a chance for me to see just how good life is when you stay sober. Those people in there tonight? Lot of them had one foot in the grave and the other on a banana peel, when they first came in." Henry chuckled. "People been sober a month can't wait to tell everybody all the terrible things they did when they were drunk. People been sober a long time like to talk about all the great things that've happened since they stopped wandering around in a gin fog."

"I'd like you to be my sponsor," Cindy Caswell said suddenly.

"No," Henry Bowman said immediately, shaking his head. "Bad idea. Opposite-sex sponsors are strongly discouraged, and with good reason. Sexual tension is real bad news tossed on top of recovery. More than a few of the young babes new to AA get 'thirteenth-stepped' by guys in the group. Some guys even go to AA meetings for that reason. They don't put that in the literature," Henry added. "And being a girl's sponsor makes it that much easier. So no." As he was saying this, Cindy Caswell was shaking her head vigorously in disagreement.

"After those three years in Las Vegas, I don't have *any* desire for men. I much prefer women, so *that* wouldn't be a problem, if you were my sponsor."

"Hell, that doesn't matter!" Henry exclaimed. "We're not talking about your sex drive. Jesus, it wasn't your urges that caused you three years of grief." He gave a short laugh. "A few months after my little incident in Jefferson County, *my* interest in the female gender came back with a goddamn vengeance, and it's been that way ever since." Cindy Caswell laughed heartily when she heard this.

"That's good," she said with a smile.

"Yeah, no shit."

"Look, I, uh, don't really know anyone around here," Cindy said, changing her tack. "And things are kind of...up in the air for me right now. Can I still call you to talk about stuff? Like we did tonight? Call you on the phone?"

"Yeah, sure. That's okay." Henry pulled a business card out of his pocket listing the consulting firm where he worked, and wrote his home number on the back. "Don't worry about the time. I live alone and I keep weird hours."

"I've got a roommate, but so do I."

"What about your family in Rolla?" Henry asked suddenly. "Have you seen them?" Cindy Caswell looked distinctly uncomfortable at the question.

"I called there from a pay phone, but the number had been disconnected. I guess they're gone."

"Why don't you just run down there? It's only a couple hours from here. You'd be sure to find *someone* you know—it's only been four years, right?"

"I don't want to be...seen. Sal knew I was from there. I'm not sure they're still alive now. He may have had them killed. You know—because I ran away."

That doesn't make any sense Henry thought immediately. *Go two thousand miles to track down and kill the family of one of their captive whores 'cause she took off after three years? Whole story's probably made up. White-trash parents threw her out, or something.* Henry nodded as if agreeing with her.

"This Sal guy..." Henry said, as if trying to remember, "...he wasn't the one who died, was he?" Henry was hoping some more names would shake loose.

"No, that was Fat Tony. Sal Marino was the guy who told me who I had to screw." *Fat Tony and Sal Marino* Henry thought. *Sounds like a high school production of Guys And Dolls.* Henry nodded, and then changed the subject back to the AA meeting.

He kept the two names filed in his memory.

September 21, 1992

"Okay, I got some dope on those two you asked about Friday," Dean Copeland said over the long-distance phone line. "I don't suppose you're going to tell me what this is about?"

"Sure I am," Henry replied easily. "Probably not today, but before too long, yes."

"Well, it looks like ancient history, anyway. The 'Fat Tony' you referred to would be one Anthony Farratto, of Atlantic City. Former up-and-comer in the organization with a nasty habit of disfiguring and crippling prostitutes. He was killed January seventh of this year in Las Vegas." *January sixth* Henry thought. *That's the date she told me he had a heart attack.*

"Mister Farratto was shot four times with a nine millimeter, three times in the chest and once in the left eye. Winchester 115-grain full metal jacket, if it matters. His action in New Jersey was taken over by a Mister Carmine Mangini, also of the Atlantic City area. The killing was done while Anthony Farratto was in the back seat of his car. Killed along with him were two of his torpedoes, one of them in the driver's seat. All three of the men were bound hand and foot. Want the names of the other two?"

"No, that's okay," Henry said. "Uh, you find anything out about that Sal Marino?"

"Yeah. He's in Vegas, mid-level type. Lives in a hotel, the, uh...." Henry heard papers rustling as Dean Copeland went through his notes. "The Vegas Moon," he said when he found it. *That's the name she told me* Henry thought.

"Marino's still around, but he's getting pressure from some of the mutts in California and right now it looks like he's trying to keep his powder dry." Henry digested that and then asked another question of the Detroit detective.

"What's Marino's connection to the dead guy, Farratto?"

"Funny you should ask. Farratto came to Vegas to talk business with Marino. Michael Mangini, known as 'Mikey-Mike', and son of Carmine Mangini, was working as a kind of apprentice to Marino. A training program, you might say. With the intention of returning to Atlantic City after a period of time, to work for his dad. Which is exactly what he did as soon as the three guys turned up dead, and conventional wisdom has it that Mikey-Mike made his bones on the hit."

"So the son shoots Farratto and his two soldiers, and Dad takes over Farratto's business. Sal Marino still friends with Mangini? Was he in on it, you think?"

"Yes, he still does a lot of business with Mangini, and it'd be a miracle if he wasn't involved in the killing."

"I see," Henry said, not understanding where Cindy Caswell fit into all this. "Ah, Dean, was there anything...*strange* about the whole thing—the killing, who did it, anything like that? Anything that didn't look like a typical internal power grab?"

"You tell me, Henry." There was a long pause, and then Henry Bowman sighed into the phone.

"Dean, the story I heard, told to me by someone who is afraid she's going to be hunted down and killed because of what she might have seen, is that this Farratto guy did *not* die from being shot four times while tied up in the back of a limo."

"Bingo. I talked to the medical examiner, guy named Wong. No accent, probably fifth generation American. Anyway, I called him 'cause I thought I might get some useful dope on the wound ballistics for my database." Dean Copeland had gathered more empirical data than any other person in the country on real-world performance of handgun ammunition in gunfights. His findings were being used more and more by serious individuals to dictate what loads they carried in their self-defense weapons.

"What he told me was very interesting. According to him, your Mister Farratto died quite some time before the other two men. It was also his best estimate that whatever killed Mister Farratto, it was not any of the four 9mm Winchesters."

"Oh?" Henry said, now even more interested.

"That's right. The wounds are consistent with the results we get when we fire into cadavers. The most interesting thing was the head wound. Wong autopsied Farratto's brain. Said the path of the bullet was obvious, and that there was substantial trauma to the brain that absolutely could not have been caused by that one full-jacketed bullet. He said he found minute wood particles—sawdust, you might say—in the damaged part of the brain that was away from the path of the bullet. Ran them through a mass spectrometer, and came up with rock maple as the material."

"Why did this Farratto's death merit such a big-time investigation?" Henry asked. Dean Copeland laughed.

"I asked the same question. The short answer is it didn't. Far as the cops are concerned, Farratto died same time as the other two, of multiple gunshot wounds. Mikey-Mike did it, even though he has a hundred witnesses saying he was somewhere else at the time. Case closed.

"No, this pathologist apparently takes great pride in doing as thorough a job as possible, even when nobody asks him to. He told me his lab partner in tenth grade chemistry class needled him once about making up the results to some experiment, and he's never forgotten it.

"There's one more thing he told me. Seems Farratto was fortunate enough to get laid shortly before he died, although not fortunate enough to get off."

"The pathologist told you that?" Henry demanded in amazement.

"Said any second-year med student could have called that one."

"Then I'm glad I went into geology." Henry thought a moment. "The pathologist give you his opinion on what really happened, if the guy didn't die from gunshots?"

"Yes. He said that in his best judgment, Anthony Farratto, either during or immediately after sexual intercourse, died while lying on his back from the effects of having a long wooden object—a long maple object, to be exact—thrust into his eye socket and wiggled around enthusiastically. Eight to twelve hours later, his corpse was placed in the car and four shots were fired into it."

"You got a theory why they'd do it that way?" Henry asked.

"Only one. The wiseguys don't kill their competition in their own house. It's bad form. Also, they usually leave the soldiers alone, when there's going to be a new boss."

"So why do it inside the hotel in the first place? Why not wait?"

"That's the one that no one can answer right now." Henry was silent for a few moments before speaking.

"I may be able to give you an a possible explanation before too long, if it means anything to you."

"Only academically, but yeah, I'd like to hear it." Copeland laughed. "What other Detroit cop do you know that could get you the inside poop on a Vegas syndicate hit?"

"You the man, Dean. You the man."

Henry Bowman thought about the conversation for some time after Copeland broke the connection.

September 23, 1992

"I don't think Sal Marino is looking for you."

"What?"

"I talked to a homicide cop I know with some good contacts in Las Vegas. Fat Tony Farratto's body was found January seventh in the back of his car, shot once in the eye and three times in the chest. The bodies of both his guards were in the car with him. One of Sal Marino's buddies has taken over Farratto's action in Atlantic City." Henry paused, and then went on.

"Medical examiner said he'd been dead when the bullets were fired. My cop friend seems to think that Marino had already planned to have him killed. Then, when he died in the saddle, Marino set up the dummy murder scene. Did you order me a chocolate malt?"

"Yes. Uh...why?" Cindy Caswell asked. "I mean, why fake a shooting?"

"Because having Farratto expire in the hotel while he was Marino's guest is against the Mafia rules of etiquette, apparently." Cindy Caswell thought for a while about that, then nodded her head in acceptance.

"Henry," she said, "there's something I didn't te–"

"You know about Joe Columbo's attempted murder?" Henry broke in.

"What? No. Who's that?"

"One of the most instructive events in American history. A lawyer friend of mine thinks it should be taught in grade school. Ah...here we go," Henry said as his malt was delivered. "Damn, these are good," he said, savoring the first few sips. "Where was I? Oh yes—Joe Columbo and the guy that tried to kill him.

"Joe Columbo was a big wheel in the organization in New York City in the early '60s. Some other big wheel or wheels decided to take over Joe's part of the business. He or they hired a contract killer—some black guy—to shoot Joe in the middle of a New York City parade. I don't know what they paid the guy, promised him, or threatened him with, but he did it. Shot Joe Columbo in the middle of the parade, just like he was supposed to. Didn't kill him, but left him paralyzed and confined to a wheelchair. A few thousand witnesses were there to see it, and a couple or three television cameras filmed it as well." Henry took another sip of his malt and smiled. "What happened next is the interesting part.

"As soon as the black guy shoots and paralyzes Columbo, five big Sicilian gentlemen jump on top of him. The black guy is buried underneath them. Don't forget—cameras are filming all this. Okay, so there's this big dogpile of six people, and all of a sudden, *Whump! Whump!* Two muffled shots. The five guys stand up, and there's one dead black guy lying on the ground with two .38 slugs in him, and a .38 revolver lying on the ground next to him. Smith & Wesson, I think it was.

"Anyway, the serial numbers on the gun have been destroyed with a punch, and every place on the gun that the shooter would have touched is wrapped with friction tape, including the trigger.

"Cops haul in the five big Sicilians, find out all of 'em test positive on the nitrate test. Also find out none of 'em have Social Security numbers. Guess which one they decided to charge with the murder of the black guy?"

"Uh...I have no idea," Cindy said.

"Neither did the cops. So they let them all go."

"What?"

"They let them all go. Had to. Not one of the Sicilians said anything. Not one single word. Soon as one of them claimed something—anything—the cops could go to work on that one thing, find out if it was true or not, get the guy on the stand, nail him for perjury if nothing else, whatever. Take hold of the one loose thread and unravel the whole cloth. But there was no loose thread."

"What about that test?"

"It tests for nitrates, which are found in both gunpowder and fertilizer. Cops knew if they looked hard enough, they'd find someone who'd seen all five of the men carrying bags of fertilizer that day. Even without the fertilizer, proving all five of them shot a gun since their last bath doesn't make them guilty of murder. State had no case. They had to let all five of them go." Henry stared at Cindy Caswell.

"You understand the significance of this event?" he asked pointedly.

"I think so."

"How did Fat Tony Farratto die?" Henry demanded.

"He had a heart a—"

"Wrong!" Henry cut in. "How did Fat Tony Farratto die?"

"I don't know a Fa—"

"Wrong!" Henry said again. "How did Fat Tony Farratto die?" There was utter silence. "How did Fat Tony Farratto die?" he repeated. Still silence. "Were you forced to have sex with Fat Tony Farratto?"

"I hear the meat loaf here is good also," Cindy said pleasantly.

"Was Fat Tony Farratto a sick bastard who liked to maim and torture the women he had sex with?"

"I can't decide if I should have dessert or not tonight."

"Were you relieved when he had his heart attack? Were you glad he was no longer able to bother you?"

"I was..." She started to say something, then changed her mind. "...going to have dessert, but I think I'll pass tonight." Henry smiled.

"Good idea. I think I'll order something else, though." He opened the menu. "Oh, and one more thing. The medical examiner said that one of the reasons Farratto's heart may have stopped beating was that after he had sex, but before he had a climax, someone shoved a piece of wood—maple, to be exact—into his left eye and scrambled his brains." Henry watched as Cindy Caswell's eyes widened and her skin went slightly pale. "You know anything about that?"

"I..." She started to speak once again, then caught herself. "...think you should try their french fries. They're really good here."

"French fries it is," Henry said, and signaled for the waitress.

October 10, 1992

As his GMC sport-utility silently rocketed up the interstate's entrance ramp, Henry Bowman thought once again about how his old friend David Webb would have loved the boxy hot rod. It was exactly the kind of vehicle Henry had always felt the auto manufacturers should make for the kind of wealthy people who lived in St. Louis county. *Stroker would be out racing people for money every time it rained* he thought with a smile. Henry pulled onto Interstate 64 East and kept his speed at sixty-five or a hair over.

The back of Henry Bowman's GMC Typhoon was riding only slightly lower than usual under the load Henry had placed in the back. He had only 4,000 rounds of ammunition in the vehicle, along with all five of the machine guns he was taking. The other 12,000 rounds, all in belts, was being hauled by Steve Brush, another St. Louis shooting enthusiast. Steve had never fired a full-automatic, and he had jumped at the chance when Henry had suggested he go to the big Kentucky machine gun shoot. Steve had left St. Louis in his 1-ton pickup a half-hour before Henry. Steve had detailed directions to the range, but Henry expected to catch him on the highway before he hit the Kentucky border. *With a full tank and an empty bladder,* Henry thought, *I ought to be there in three hours.*

Henry glanced in his rearview mirror and saw a bright yellow car approaching at about a thirty-mile-per-hour speed advantage. *Looks like a slope-nose Porsche* Henry thought as he watched the car move over into the left lane in anticipation of passing Henry's slower vehicle.

Under normal circumstances, Henry Bowman would have ignored the other car. At the moment, though, Henry was heading for a big national shoot where he would get to see a lot of friends from around the country, and he had been thinking about David Webb only a few moments before. Henry Bowman was in an exceptionally good mood. *If Stroker were here he'd insist on making that guy hate life* Henry thought with a smile as he reached down under the driver's seat and turned a lever-operated valve on the floor. As the yellow sports car swept past him, Henry pushed the GMC's throttle to the floor.

The four-speed automatic dropped down two gears as the turbo rapidly spooled up. The tach jumped to a bit over 5000 RPM and the needle on the boost gauge moved into positive territory as Henry felt himself pressed back in the leather seat. At 6300 RPM the transmission shifted into third and the boost needle blipped up another 3 PSI as the turbine wheel suddenly found itself pressurizing a slower-turning engine. At 115 MPH the Typhoon shifted into high gear and the boost needle held steady at 8 PSI. Henry saw that he was steadily gaining on the yellow German car.

The cheap stuff ought to be burnt out of the lines by now Henry thought as he reached down to turn a knob unobtrusively located at the bottom of the dashboard. When Henry had flipped the lever on the floor, he had switched to his auxiliary fuel tank. Aftermarket tanks were designed for people who wanted to extend their range of their trucks and sport-utility vehicles, but Henry had installed his for a different purpose: The twelve-gallon bladder was always kept topped off with 108-octane race gas that Henry bought in 55-gallon drums from a local Unocal distributor.

The knob on the dash controlled an adjustable wastegate. It was part of the GMC's new, larger exhaust system that had been installed at the same time that Henry had had the Typhoon's heads ported, the block decked and O-ringed, the crank balanced, the turbo scroll housing reworked, the pistons and rods replaced, a bigger intercooler and radiator installed, and the electronics reprogrammed for a different fuel curve.

As Henry twisted the knob clockwise, the boost needle started climbing and the GMC reacted as if a giant had poked the rear bumper with his finger. When Henry saw 20 PSI on the gauge, he let go of the knob and put his right hand back on the steering wheel.

Mike Garland was listening to the Porsche's compact disk player, and like all people who are exempt from speed limits, he almost never used his rearview mirror. One hundred was a comfortable speed for long-distance cruising, and his only thoughts about driving concerned the sparse traffic that lay ahead of him. Out of long habit, he stayed in the right lane when possible and only switched to the left when overtaking a slower vehicle. Like fast drivers everywhere, he hated left lane bandits that clogged the interstates, but the fact was that Mike Garland had never been passed when traveling in the ninety-plus range where the Porsche seemed happiest. He was totally unprepared for the black GMC wearing truck plates that blew by him with a solid 40 MPH edge. He stared at his own speedometer, then watched in amazement as the rapidly disappearing truck signaled with its right blinker and returned to the right lane.

Henry Bowman focused his eyes far ahead of him on the highway and was relieved to see that the nearest vehicle was well over a mile away. He did not like to pass people at wildly extralegal speeds unless those people were also flagrantly disregarding the posted limit. A lot of people on the roads were fundamentally envious and resentful of high-speed travelers, and the proliferation of cellular phones had given these drivers the ability to act on their frustrations. *Got at least another minute* Henry decided. *More than enough time.*

Mike Garland downshifted and gave the German sports car full throttle as the GMC became a shrinking spot in the distance. The European-spec 3.3 liter engine was capable of pushing the sleek vehicle to a top speed 20 MPH higher than that of the hot-rodded GMC, but Garland faced three huge obstacles to catching up with the vanishing truck: First, it would take time to accelerate up to a speed greater than the truck's, and until the Porsche got there, the GMC would relentlessly increase the already substantial gap. Second, the Porsche had not had a good front end alignment since it left Germany, and although the toe-in was not off enough to notice at normal highway speeds, by 130 the car became disturbingly twitchy. Last of all, although Mike Garland had spent a lot of time driving at speeds over 100 MPH, he had virtually no experience in the 140-and-up range. At about 145, discretion became the better part of valor and he backed off.

Mike Garland held the yellow car at an indicated 110, and watched in amazement as the distant GMC continued to grow smaller and then vanished from his sight entirely. He reached out and tapped the speedometer, then immediately felt foolish for doing so.

Henry Bowman kept an eye on the water temperature gauge and noted with satisfaction that it did not rise above 180 degrees, despite the lengthy full-throttle blast. The GMC was reassuringly stable at two and a half times the speed limit and the exhaust note was not excessive, but the wind noise was something else. *Back to the real world* Henry thought as a clump of cars came into view and rapidly grew larger as he closed on them at an 80 MPH speed differential. Henry Bowman slowly eased off the throttle and the boxy vehicle slowed down instantly under the tremendous aerodynamic drag. *Would've helped if the guys in styling had rounded the corners a little on the S-10 before the GM skunk works dreamed this thing up* Henry thought. Then he reminded himself that the GM's project planners' hair would have stood on end if they had been told what the boys at Kenne-Bell were going to do with their creation. Henry slid in behind a flatbed truck traveling about 60 MPH in the right lane. The left lane was filled with four cars traveling the same speed. They were closely trailing a brown Lincoln whose driver was oblivious to the line of cars behind him.

Henry was looking for a decent station on the GMC's radio when he heard a horn sound and looked to his left. It was the man in the yellow slope-nose 911. He was waving and motioning to Henry with eating-and-drinking gestures. It appeared that the man wanted him to pull off at the next exit where they could grab some hamburgers and talk about cars. Henry nodded agreement and held up two fingers, to indicate the second exit coming up. He had never seen a slope-nose 911 up close.

***

"What on earth's *in* that thing?" Mike Garland asked as he climbed out of his car. The two men were in the parking lot of a Hardee's restaurant just off the interstate.

"This is the Typhoon," Henry explained. "Engine and trans out of a Grand National, hooked up to full-time four-wheel-drive." Garland stared at the vehicle, and Henry went on, speaking with the courtesy that comes naturally to a victor.

"It's the most sensible car I've ever seen. Lot of guys I know with cars like yours also have rural property, with a half-mile of rutted, rocky, dirt road leading from the state-maintained pavement. So they buy a Wagoneer, Blazer, or Bronco, and they end up driving the 'beater' on two-hour interstate trips because the last half mile would rip the undercarriage out of their good car. I always thought the solution would be if BMW would put an on-board air compressor and air shocks on their high-speed sedans. Let the driver raise the ride height four or five inches for negotiating farm roads. Might cost $300, and it would be easy to incorporate an electronic governor so that the car couldn't be driven over 35 MPH when it was jacked up." Henry laughed.

"No one in marketing at any of the car companies ever approved *that* idea, but GM came up with an even better solution. Took their S-10, and put in full-time four-wheel-drive, independent front suspension, lowered ride height, wide wheels with Z-rated tires, and that intercooled turbo V-6 out of the Grand National. Hit a hundred in thirteen seconds in the rain, by my watch, with no wheelspin."

Henry grinned and laughed when he saw the man shaking his head. "I surprised you," he assured him. "You'd've caught me easily with a little more room. This thing's a barn door compared to your 911." Like any good street racer, Henry wasn't about to let on about what had been done to his engine. "Henry Bowman," he said as he stuck out his hand.

"Mike Garland." Henry eyed the license plate affixed to the rear of the German car. "You work for the government?"

"Yeah—U.S. Customs. Confiscated vehicle—guy was trying to smuggle drugs in it."

"Mmm-hmm," Henry nodded. *This would be a good guy to know for ironing out problems with ammo import deals* he thought. A recent import shipment of Yugoslavian surplus ammunition had been held up for three months because the declaration form had not listed the importation of 'Yugoslavian straw' in addition to the ammunition. The shippers had used straw as packing between a few of the crates, and the storage fees had tripled amount the ammunition had ultimately cost Henry.

"Can I see the engine compartment? Not that I'd know anything about one of these," Henry added.

"Sure," Garland replied, and lifted the rear deck lid.

Guy would have to be brain damaged to use a car like this as a smuggling vehicle Henry thought to himself when he saw the mechanicals. *Customs would be all over it anyway. It's not even federalized.* "How much dope did he have in it, and how much time did he get?" Henry asked.

"Uh, there was a lot less coke than we expected, and, uh, he had a sharp lawyer and we couldn't prove he had put the stuff in there himself."

Henry nodded. *So what really happened is some schlepp tried to bring in a Porsche that didn't pass your rules about air pumps and crash standards, and you snowflaked him so you could steal his car and keep it for yourself without actually bringing charges.*

"You ready to go eat?" Garland asked.

"Yeah, just let me get my road atlas." Henry opened the back of the GMC and then swore. "Damn, it's buried under these crates. Hang on just a second." Mike Garland looked on in astonishment as Henry hoisted three obviously heavy wooden crates out of the back and poked around in the vehicle before emerging with a battered Atlas. Then Henry lifted the crates back into his truck and locked the back.

"How much weight you got in there?" the Customs agent demanded.

"Oh, hell, not all that much," Henry said with a shake of his head. "Maybe twelve, thirteen hundred pounds. Going to a big military weapons shoot and demonstration in Kentucky, and I got to have plenty of ammo for all the demos they've got me signed up for." He turned towards the restaurant. "Let's make sure we sit somewhere with a view of the cars," Henry added over his shoulder. He knew Mike Garland was still slack-jawed over the GMC's weight penalty that he had just discovered.

The pair had a pleasant lunch together, and ended up exchanging business cards. Garland had promised that if he was given advance warning, Henry would not have any more problems like he'd had with the Yugoslavian shipment. Henry told him to give him a call when Customs wanted a live-fire demonstration of the latest full-auto weaponry.

***

Henry Bowman pulled off Route 31 and passed a liquor store painted bright pink. Steve Brush was parked in the store's lot, and started his engine when he saw his friend. In about a half-mile they came to the big, familiar sign at the entrance to the range that the range crew always erected for the shoot. Henry took the turnoff and was dutifully followed by his friend in the pickup truck.

The Knob Creek Range was about 40 miles south of Louisville, on property which adjoined Fort Knox. Decades earlier, it had been an artillery testing range, before it had outlived its usefulness to the military and the government had sold the property. The old steel tracks leading up to the firing line offered mute reminder that railway cars had been required to bring in the big guns and pallets of ammunition for testing. The hillside four hundred yards away had an awful lot of metal buried in its face.

Twice a year, in April and October, the owners of Knob Creek put on a machine gun shoot. Spectator admission was a few dollars, and spots on the firing line were eighty dollars for the entire weekend. There was a ten-year waiting list for the latter, and most shooters ended up paying a reduced fee to get on the line as a 'helper'.

What the annual EAA fly-in at Oshkosh, Wisconsin, was to people who loved to fly, or the Cologne Show in Germany was to people who liked exotic cars, the Knob Creek event was to people who loved to shoot. Two million rounds went downrange in a three-day period. The organizers put out stacks of old tires, stripped cars, and junk appliances to shoot at. What made it more interesting was the bundles of ditching dynamite the explosives crew thoughtfully taped to the front of many of the targets. It was like a giant fireworks display, but with active involvement.

Soon the two Missourians passed some big, open fields filled with parked cars, and a man in an orange hunting vest and orange cap stopped them. Henry already had his window down.

"Got a bunch of guns and over fifteen thousand rounds of ammo to unload up at the firing line," he said, jerking his thumb towards Steve to show the man that the two vehicles were together. "We know the drill." The range worker smiled and waved them through. He liked people who brought large quantities of ammunition to send downrange. They were what made the shoot so successful.

Henry and Steve slowly threaded their vehicles through the maze of cars, vans, pickups, motor homes, deuce-and-a-halfs, half-tracks, armored cars, and tanks. Thousands of people were milling around, many with small children on their shoulders. It reminded Steve Brush of the big riverfront fair in St. Louis on the July 4th weekend, except that he had never in his life seen such an array of ordnance as was packed together along the 350-foot firing line.

Henry stopped a short distance down the line and got out of his vehicle.

"We'll just be a minute unloading—then we'll be out of here," he said to a range officer who looked like he was about to tell Henry he couldn't park there. "Unload the buckets right here, Steve. This is where we're going to shoot." The belted ammunition Henry had loaded for his water-cooled Browning was stored in 5-gallon plastic buckets. Each bucket held four coiled 250-round belts. It had taken Henry fifteen hours to belt up twelve thousand rounds of .30-06 and 8mm ammunition that Steve Brush was now unloading from the back of his truck. Henry had filled the forty-eight cloth belts using a John Browning-designed hand-cranked belt filling machine that had been made in 1918. Some people brought their ammo loose to the shoot, and loaded it into magazines and belts during the many cease-fires during the day. Henry preferred to load everything in advance, and have free time to talk to friends and see who had what for sale.

"Is this your spot?" Steve Brush asked, still a bit overwhelmed by the entire spectacle.

"No, I'm still on the waiting list, after six years. This spot belongs to John Parker, but we're going to shoot on it. He's from St. Louis, so you may have seen him around. Although he dresses like a bum when he's here."

"What's he do?"

"Senior partner in a brokerage firm. Parker, Gates, & Company. He's pretty well-connected. Knows all the bigshots in St. Louis, particularly the ones in finance and investments. I've sold him a bunch of machine guns. Like that water-cooled Browning there."

Sitting to the left of the chalk line that designated the right boundary of Parker's six-foot spot was a 1917A1 Browning on an A1 tripod with custom, double-length legs. There was a pile of fired brass under it that Henry estimated numbered about six thousand. *Looks like he's shooting mid-'50s Egyptian 8mm Mauser ammo* Henry thought as he looked at the shape and color of the fired cases under the gun. 8mm Egyptian was corrosive, and could be had for about ten cents a round, if you bought in half-million round lots. This was less than half the cost of surplus .30-06 ammo. Henry looked at the feed tray of Parker's gun. The homemade spacer there confirmed his suspicions.

"Hey, Henry!" a voice called in greeting. "You bring your Colt Monitor this trip?

Shoot Landies' parachute flares out of the sky and piss him off again?"

"Of course. What would Knob Creek be if we couldn't irritate Bob?"

"How 'bout your Minimi?"

"Yep. Got one of Reed's fancy suppressors on it. Supposed to outlast an M16. I'm going to see how it holds up on a real gun." The man grinned at this reply and moved on.

"Who was that?" Steve Brush asked.

"Some guy that's here every time. Half the people that say 'hi' to me, they've never told me their names." He looked at the crowd. "We better get the rest of the stuff unloaded and get the vehicles moved. The parking gestapo here have no sense of humor." Henry opened the back of his vehicle and started unloading the five guns he had brought with him.

"Follow me," Henry said when he was done. "I'll show you where we can park that's not to hell-and-gone from here."

"Is it okay to leave your guns right there on the ground?" Steve Brush asked with a worried look.

"Do you think anyone's going to steal guns in the middle of this bunch?" Henry asked, waving his hand at the hundreds of people milling around the firing line, over half of whom were carrying loaded handguns on their persons.

"You got a point. Okay, lead on."

"Hey, Henry Bowman!" another voice called. "You gonna turn your FN-D red tonight, like you did last year?"

"Probably," Henry said with a smile as he looked up at the man. The man turned to his companion.

"This guy Bowman here, he likes BARs. Shoots shit out of the air with 'em. Put his Belgian one on a tripod last fall and ran—what? Twenty magazines?—through the damn thing fast as he could. Turned as red as your electric stove and never missed a beat."

"BARs are like that," Henry said cheerfully as he got into his vehicle.

***

"Can you believe they're not even going to charge that FBI asshole?" one of the men said in disgust.

A lengthy cease-fire was in effect while targets were set up, and the men and women at the range were, as always, talking about what guns people had brought to shoot, who had the best bargains on ammo, and which statist politicians needed to be thrown out of office in the upcoming Congressional elections. In addition to these standard topics, talk that day at Knob Creek Range often turned to the disastrous FBI raid in Idaho that had ended seven weeks earlier.

Randy Weaver, his friend Kevin Harris, and Weaver's three daughters, aged ten months to sixteen years, had remained in his cabin for nine days after the FBI sniper had killed Vicki. During the standoff, and at the urging of neighbors, thousands of citizens had converged on the area to keep an eye on what the feds did and to implore Weaver and Harris to surrender so that they and the girls would not also be killed by the federal agents. Messages to Weaver had been smuggled in to the cabin by friends and sympathizers, and after considering that his friend Kevin Harris was seriously wounded, Weaver had come out peacefully on August 31.

The entire Weaver incident, starting with the wood buttstock that was 3/8" too short, had disgusted everyone at the Kentucky shooting range. Ever since the Ken Ballew raid, however, serious shooters had come to expect disaster when the ATF claimed a paperwork or tax violation had been committed. Weaver and Lawmaster were only the most recent examples in a long list of this kind of storm-trooper behavior.

Up until the Weaver incident, however, citizens had always understood that even if the tax agents destroyed a man's house or smashed his door in and shot him in the head without a proper warrant, the gunowner's family was off-limits. Federal marshals killing fourteen-year-old Sammy Weaver by shooting him in the back and an FBI sniper blowing Vicki Weaver's brains out as she nursed her baby were a new development. The people at Knob Creek, and at ranges, gun shops, and sporting goods stores across the nation, found this escalation of federal force extraordinarily repellent.

"Ought to at least slap that FBI bastard with a manslaughter rap," the man continued. "Hell, in *Time* magazine, feds claimed their HRT guys could put a bullet within a quarter inch of where they wanted at two hundred yards."

"Maybe that was a misprint," one of the other men suggested derisively. "Maybe what the feds said was two yards." He thought a moment, then added, "Or maybe that guy did put his bullet exactly where he wanted."

"Yeah, killing a man's wife while she's nursing their baby daughter is a damned effective negotiating tactic. I can't believe that Yamaguchi fucker, or whatever his name is, gets to just walk away without so much as a ten-dollar fine."

"Joe, you're not thinking straight," Henry Bowman said to the man. "The FBI has huge public support. Hoover started a massive PR campaign sixty years ago, and it's continued ever since. Jimmy Stewart movies, Efrem Zimbalist, Jr. in his TV show—the public and the press love the feds."

"I don't."

"Maybe not, but everybody else does. Most of the adults in this country can tell you exactly where the FBI shot John Dillinger."

"In front of the Biograph theater."

"Right. But how many people know that the FBI also managed to shoot two bystanders in the process? Go to your library and see how much ink that got in '34." Henry shook his head and continued.

"Six years ago, was there one word of official criticism or apology for the way they handled the Miami shootout? FBI's official conclusion was that their guns weren't powerful enough. Did you see one newspaper article about how two of their stakeout agents were too busy banging some waitress to help their buddies who were getting blasted? Did you see Time magazine saying something like this?" Henry lowered his voice in a parody of a news anchorman.

"'The FBI has a thorough training program for handling vehicles they suspect contain heavily armed, known killers. Their state-of-the-art tactics include sex breaks to relieve tension, leaving their body armor and shotguns on the floor of their back seats, taking their pistols out of their holsters and putting them on the front seats so they can fly off and get lost, tailgating the suspects to let them know they have been spotted, and ramming the suspects' vehicle off the road in densely populated residential areas to precipitate a gunfight.'"

Humorless laughter followed Henry Bowman's mock news segment. Though none of the facts he had mentioned had been highly publicized, they were common knowledge among people seriously involved in the shooting sports. Serious shooters invariably had a number of contacts inside law enforcement agencies.

"Way I see it," one of the other men in the group said, "it's a goddamn miracle

Weaver and his daughters are still alive. I'd've expected them all to come off that mountain in body bags, instead of just the mother and the boy."

"Feds must be getting slow," another man in the group offered.

In six months, the FBI would be back up to speed.

***

"I see your watercooled's working okay," Henry said to John Parker as he sipped from a paper cup full of soda. Parker was sitting on the seat he had made which fit on the extended rear leg of the 1917A1's tripod. Parker's girlfriend Karen Hill, a paralegal who was with him for the weekend, sat on one of Henry's ammo buckets. Henry and Steve were leaning against one of the concrete benches. They were waiting while the dynamite crew went downrange to make sure there were no unexploded charges left from the three o'clock shoot.

"Yeah, I'm glad you talked me into buying a '17 instead of an A4. You were right— with the muzzle supported in the front bearing of the water jacket, it's a lot more accurate at long range than the aircooled guns. As I think I demonstrated," Parker said with a grin. Using the click adjustments of the 1917A1 tripod, John Parker had managed to hit two of the fifteen dynamite charges the crew had set out downrange. That was exceptional, considering that there were over fifty belt-fed machine guns on the line, and they had all begun firing continuously as soon as the range officer had given the command.

"Haven't seen a single Bush bumper sticker," Henry Bowman said calmly as he took another drink of his soda. John Parker nodded.

"No shit. I think he's going to lose."

"Lose, hell," Henry said. "He's already thrown the election." Parker raised an eyebrow in a questioning gesture. Henry continued. "We'd've been much better off with Michael Dukakis, from a civil rights standpoint, at least."

"What do you mean?" This came from a slender man in a khaki shirt who had overheard the conversation.

"Bush banned semiauto imports by executive order in '89. Got his 'Drug Czar' buddy to say it was a wonderful idea. Could Dukakis have gotten away with that? Hell, no. He wouldn't have dared try it, because the Republicans in the House and Senate wouldn't have played ball. They'd have screamed bloody murder. Bush got away with it, though, 'cause he's a Republican, and now it's going to cost him the election."

"Come on, Henry," Parker said, forcefully but without rancor. "Bush has all kinds of problems. The economy is lousy, and people haven't forgiven him for breaking his 'no new taxes' promise."

"And let's face it," Karen Hill added, "a lot of voters, particularly women, don't like his anti-abortion stance. Those are the things that're going to end up costing him the Presidency." Henry Bowman was shaking his head. A crowd was starting to gather, but no one interrupted.

"I'll give you the taxes thing, but that's still only a small factor, and I'll prove it to you in a second. Your other issues are curtain dressing. Economy? The economy was terrible in 1982, and the public didn't turn against Ronald Reagan. Reagan was also at least as much against abortion as Bush, and more women voted for him than Carter in '80 or Mondale in '84. The reason George Bush will lose in three weeks is because he sold us out on gun rights." Henry Bowman and John Parker both saw a number of the people around them nodding in agreement. John Parker began to protest.

"That may be a part of it, but–"

"No 'buts', John. I'll prove it to you. Look around. How many guys do you see here right now who you know saw active duty and are proud of it? I don't mean everybody wearing camo—anyone can buy that at K-Mart. I mean guys wearing boonie hats and dog tags with their division numbers on 'em, or guys in Gulf War uniforms, or old guys with tattoos and shrapnel wounds and arms missing. How many do you see around here right now? A lot, right?

"George Bush is a genuine war hero from the Second World War, right? And last year he got a half million men over to Iraq, ran Hussein out of Kuwait, and only lost— what? Eighty soldiers? That's less than I would expect would get killed in a half-million-man training exercise with no enemy." The people gathered around were nodding in agreement.

"So?" John Parker said.

"So Bush is a war hero—I really mean that—and look who he's running against. Should be no contest among vets proud of their military service, right?" Henry grinned wickedly at John Parker. "Just go around and ask some of these vets here if they're going to vote for the President in three weeks. Take your own poll."

"I'm not!" shouted a veteran of Korea who had been listening to Henry's argument. "Your friend's dead right."

"Me neither," spat another. "He sold us out." A half-dozen other veterans grunted in agreement. No one contradicted what Henry Bowman had said.

"Is anyone here—not just veterans, but anyone—planning to vote for Bush?" Henry asked in a loud voice. No one volunteered with an affirmative answer. John Parker's mouth opened in amazement.

"Too many Republicans have this crazy idea that since their party usually isn't quite as much in favor of throwing away the linchpin of the Bill of Rights, they can take our votes for granted," Henry said to what was now a crowd of forty or fifty people. "In a few weeks, they're going to find out that taking us for granted was the biggest mistake they ever made in their lives. Except that the news will undoubtedly focus on the abortion issue, or the bad economy, or how Bush didn't seem compassionate, or some other horse-shit, and miss the real story."

"You really think we're the ones going to cost him the election?" a man in his fifties asked. "Not sayin' I disagree with you, but...everyone always acts like all the other issues are the real important ones. You know—the ones that get elections won or lost."

"Let me ask everyone here a question, then," Henry said. It was obvious he believed in what he was about to say.

"Pretend I'm George Bush, and it's Monday, the day after tomorrow. The first debate—which is tomorrow night—is over. I didn't say anything at all about the gun issue in the debate. It's now Monday, okay? Since I'm still the President, I tell the networks I'm going to give a State of the Union address, or a press conference, or whatever you call it on short notice. I'm going to give it that night, since the second debate isn't for a couple of days. I get up in front of the cameras, and here's the speech that goes out over every network Monday night." Henry looked over at John Parker. "Cut me some slack if I get some details wrong; I'm winging it here, okay?" He cleared his throat.

"My fellow Americans, I would like to address a serious issue which faces our country today: the gradual erosion of the individual rights of our honest citizens. Our government, including my administration, must shoulder much of the blame for this problem. It is time for me to acknowledge and repair the damage that has been done."

Henry paused for a moment to collect his thoughts before continuing.

"The Soviet Union has collapsed. People around the world are throwing off their yokes of oppression and tasting freedom for the first time. It is an embarrassing fact, however, that our government has forgotten about individual rights here at home. It is time to acknowledge and correct the infringements we have inflicted upon our citizens in the name of 'crime control'.

"Decent, honest Americans are being victimized by a tiny fraction of the population, and it is our government's fault. It is our fault because we politicians have continually passed laws that stripped the law-abiding of their rights. As a result we have made the crime problem much worse.

"Our great economic power comes from the fact that Americans determine their own economic destiny. It is time we let Americans once again determine their own physical destiny." Henry Bowman saw the audience hanging on his words. He took a breath and went on.

"In 1989 I prohibited importation of firearms mechanically and functionally identical to weapons made before the Wright Brothers' invention of the airplane in 1903. I hoped that banning these guns would reduce crime. It hasn't. The only people denied the weapons that I banned are those citizens in our country who obey our laws. These are not the people our government should punish, and I now see what a terrible decision that was.

"Some politicians are now calling for a national 5-day waiting period to purchase a handgun. The riots last spring showed us the tragedy of that kind of policy. One congressman has even introduced a bill to repeal the Second Amendment to our Constitution. The Bill of Rights *enumerates* human rights, it does not *grant* them. That is something that we in government have forgotten. Repealing the Second Amendment would not legitimize our actions any more than repealing the Fifth Amendment would authorize us to kill whoever we wanted."

Henry noticed several people smile at the notion of George Bush acknowledging his responsibility for government intrusions in a State of the Union address.

"All dictatorships restrict or prohibit the honest citizen's access to modern small arms. Anywhere this right is not restricted, you will find a free country.

"There is a name for a society where only the police have guns. It is called a police state. The Second Amendment in the Bill of Rights is not about duck hunting, any more than the First Amendment is about playing Scrabble. The entire Bill of Rights is about individual freedom.

"In my recent trip to St. Louis, Missouri, I found that violent criminals have a government guarantee that honest people are unarmed if they're away from their homes or businesses. It's a felony for a citizen to carry a gun for protection. Giving evil, violent people who ignore our laws a government guarantee that decent people are completely helpless is terrible public policy. It is dangerous public policy. Our Federal and State governments have betrayed the honest citizens of this country by focusing on inanimate objects instead of violent criminal behavior, and I am ashamed to have been a party to it. It is time to correct that betrayal.

"Accordingly, I am lifting the import ban on weapons with a military appearance, effective immediately. I am abandoning any and all proposals to ban honest citizens from owning guns or magazines that hold more than a certain number of cartridges. I will veto any bill that contains any provision which would make it illegal, more difficult, or more expensive for any honest citizen to obtain any firearm or firearm accessory that it is now lawful for him to own. I will also encourage the removal of laws currently in effect which punish honest adults for mere ownership or possession of weapons or for paperwork errors involving weapons. I will work to effect repeal of the Gun Control Act of 1968 and the National Firearms Act of 1934 in their entirety.

"Tomorrow I will appoint a task force to investigate abusive practices of the Bureau of Alcohol, Tobacco, and Firearms. I will ask for recommendations as to how that department can be made to shift its focus from technical and paperwork errors to violent criminal activity. I will demand the resignations of all agents and supervisors who have participated in any entrapment schemes or planting of evidence.

"Our government has betrayed its citizens and tomorrow morning I intend to start correcting that. Good night."

Screams of "Yeah!," "Damn right!," and "That's it!" came amidst tremendous applause from the several dozen people who had been standing around listening.

"Okay, that's the speech," Henry said in his normal voice after the applause had died down. He did not notice the look on John Parker's face. "Then, the next morning on the news, you see that Bush has indeed rescinded the import ban, he's named the people on the Task Force, and he's fired Bill Bennett. A couple of senators have offered to draft legislation repealing the National Firearms Act and GCA '68, and you hear Bush say on camera that he's all for it, and you hear him encourage other legislators to support this much-needed reform.

"Question number one: What are all of you going to do now?"

"Do everything we can to get George Bush re-elected!" one man yelled immediately. He was joined by a dozen similar responses. Henry Bowman laughed.

"Not bad. And we haven't even asked question number two, and it's the real clincher: If George Bush gave the speech I just gave and did the things I just described, how many people who were already going to vote for him do you think would change their minds? How many people do you think would say 'Boy, I was going to vote for Bush, but now I'm not going to'?"

"Nobody," John Parker said under his breath. "Anyone who didn't like your speech would already be against the President." John Parker was thinking frantically.

"Exactly. So he picks up four or five million votes, and loses none."

"A damn geologist who likes to shoot has just laid out how Bush can pull it off," John Parker said. "I wonder if it's too late." He looked over at Karen Hill.

"You bring your laptop?" Parker asked his companion. "Is it in the car?" She nodded, and a smile came over her face.

"John Parker, are you thinking what I think you're thinking?" the young woman asked her friend. "Bucky?"

"You got it. Any objections to taking dictation?"

"Hell, I'll sit on Henry's lap and undo a couple buttons on my blouse if that's what it takes." Parker laughed, and then explained what he planned to do.

"Worth a try," Henry answered. Others in the group readily agreed.

In the midst of the large crowd of shooters, all of whom had been listening intently, no one paid any attention to the man who left the group abruptly and began walking towards the parking area.

***

"Hello?" the Deputy Director of the ATF answered as he picked up the private line in his office in Washington. *Working on Saturday's unheard of in this building* Dwight

Greenwell thought. *But I like having the entire place to myself.*

"It's Rivera, sir. In Kentucky. Something's come up here I think you should know about."

"What is it?"

"Man from St. Louis at the shoot here knows the President's brother. Guy's name is John Parker. Some dealer—I don't know his name, but like all these guys here he shoots machine guns—this dealer was shooting his mouth off like they always do. He was going on in front of a big group about how he wished the President would change his mind on the gun thing. This John Parker was listening, and he gets the idea to get hold of the brother." The agent explained about the rough content of the speech Henry had made, and John Parker's plan to contact the President's brother in time to save the election.

"Shit, that'd be just what we need," Greenwell said after he had listened to his undercover agent describe what the two men had in mind. George Bush had given ATF a huge boost with his Executive Order banning imports of military lookalikes. His expected successor promised to be even more receptive to expanded ATF power. *The President do an about-face and urge repeal of not only the import ban, but all the other laws we enforce, then win reelection?* Greenwell thought. The prospect was not a pleasant one, especially in view of the current internal problems that plagued the agency, and the imminent threat of budget cuts. He sat contemplating all this when his thoughts were interrupted.

"Do we, uh, have anyone that could...intercept the FAX?" the agent in Kentucky asked after the silence became too much for him..

Goddamned fool Greenwell thought immediately. Breaking into the office of the brother of the President struck the Deputy Director as a good way to get his agency disbanded and himself a visit to a federal prison. Talking about it on the telephone was equally stupid.

"Everyone said you had a good sense of humor," the fed assured his undercover man, for the benefit of anyone who might be recording the call. "I doubt the President is going to reverse his position on the strength of some stranger's advice, particularly a gun nut, even if it does get brought to him by his brother." *At least I hope he won't* he added mentally. "If he is, there's nothing we can do about it anyway. Get back there and keep your ears open, though. This is exactly the kind of intelligence we need, to know what we're up against."

"Yessir," the man said, and folded up his cellular phone.

Dwight Greenwell sat back in his chair, thinking. Wiretapping and electronic eavesdropping, when it involved high-up politicos, was a very risky proposition. The hoped-for benefits almost never outweighed the potential for disaster. *John Parker* he thought, as he called up a screen on his computer. *Haven't heard that name before.* He tapped the name in on the keyboard and waited for his computer to find the file. *No wonder. He's not a dealer.* John Parker had a number of machine guns, but he had bought all of them as a private individual with a $200 tax stamp on each transfer.

What is it about these damned gun nuts? he asked himself. It was a question he contemplated daily, and it baffled him no less now than it had when he had first taken the job. He sat in his chair, thinking about what the undercover agent in Kentucky had told him, and decided to do nothing. *A sitting President's businessman brother is one sleeping dog I'm going to let lie.* His mind returned to the specter of budget cuts, and Greenwell smiled. A plan was well underway at ATF to solve that little problem.

Six months from now, he thought happily, *we'll get anything we ask for.*

***

The night shoot was as spectacular as usual. The crew set out drums full of used printer's solvent with explosive charges in front. Railroad flares burned nearby.

At the 'Commence firing' command, thousands of tracers laced out into the night. Dynamite charges exploded and vaporized the liquid in the drums. The flares ignited it, and huge fireballs erupted one after another. The heat from the fiery explosions warmed the faces of the spectators two hundred yards away. The fires died out as the solvent was consumed, only to be followed by more explosions as other shots found their marks at the bases of the remaining drums.

"Just like a James Bond movie, huh?" Henry yelled happily. He was shooting belts of straight tracer in his 1917A1. The precise support of the muzzle end of the barrel and the constant stream of tracers made the watercooled Browning shoot like a laser. Henry hit four charges, causing an equal number of explosions.

Despite the magnificent display, John Parker was only half paying attention. He was thinking about the FAX he was going to send as soon as he got to his motel room.

October 12, 1992

The President's brother stared at the FAX he had taken from his machine. The time-stamp showed it was sent after midnight Saturday night, when the office was deserted, and had come from the 503 area code. Bush checked and saw that 503 was Kentucky.

Parker, Gates & Co.

7700 Maryland Avenue
St. Louis, MO 63105
(314) 728-9000 FAX (314) 728-9013

October 10, 1992

Mr. William H.T. Bush
120 S. Central Ave.
Clayton, MO 63105

Dear Bucky,

It's worse than anyone ever thought. Today I was in Ft. Knox, Kentucky, attending a military show, shooting competition, and historic weapons demonstration that is held there semiannually. News crews and reporters from England, Belgium, Japan, and other countries were interviewing people. There were over 2,000 active participants in the shooting activities, and over 10,000 spectators.

Every person I talked to felt absolute betrayal on the part of the President regarding their individual rights. There wasn't one Bush/Quayle bumper sticker, campaign button, or T-shirt anywhere. Several Gulf War and Vietnam vets were looking at a restored White armored car when the election came up. One said, "I'd rather cut my throat than vote for Bush. No one stabs me in the back and keeps my vote, the son-of-a-bitch." These were Desert Storm vets!

I asked people what it would take to get them to vote to re-elect. The answers were remarkably uniform and amazingly simple. The President can still get another four or five million votes with the right program. I can lay it out for him to see in fifteen minutes, and it won't cost a nickel to implement.

Bucky, we need to see your brother or James Baker soon. I know the first debate is tomorrow night. He may say something that will lose these people forever, and won't be able to retract it. He can get the votes back, but he needs to see how. Call me 24 hours a day here, at home 747-2164, or my car 701-7332.

John

Bucky Bush read the FAX over several times. It sounded like an idle fantasy. "Never known John Parker to blow smoke, though," he said under his breath. "Be a miracle if even I can get through right now. He picked up the phone and began to dial.

Bucky Bush's fears proved accurate. The White House was in a frenzy, and the President did not return his sibling's call. The brothers did not get together, even on the phone, until after the election.

By then the issue was academic.

February 28, 1993

"It's show time," ATF agent Steve Willis said to the driver sitting to his left as the truck pulled up in front of the door to the large complex. Willis was riding in the passenger seat of one of two longbed pickup trucks, each of which was towing a gooseneck cattle trailer. He flipped the selector lever on his suppressed Heckler & Koch MP5SD submachine gun from the semiauto position to full automatic.

The German H&K 9mm SD was one of the best submachine guns in existence. The integral suppressor added weight to the weapon and eliminated the gun's muzzle blast. Both the additional weight and the blast suppression reduced the subgun's recoil and made it one of the easiest-to-shoot full-auto weapons in the world.

Henry Bowman, like most serious NFA weapons dealers, owned several 9mm H&K submachine guns. He used these as 'demonstrators' for police departments, many of whom elected to order additional examples after they had seen how well the guns performed. Henry referred to his suppressed H&K as his 'girlfriend gun', because his girlfriends had always been able to roll cans with it or put an entire 30-round magazine on a man target after only a few minutes of instruction and practice. The German-made weapon was very popular with law enforcement on both federal and state levels, and was a much better choice for officers with low gun skills than larger machine guns such as the Colt M16.

Above the four-structure compound, three Texas Army National Guard helicopters circled. One of them, the command chopper, held Ted Royster, the head of the regional ATF office and the man who had overseen the Lawmaster raid. Royster smiled as he saw that the news crews were in position. He noted with satisfaction that the cattle trailers blocked the news cameras' view of the front door. He did not want what was about to happen next to be recorded on film. *This'll make up for that fiasco in Tulsa* he thought happily.

Up on the second floor of the building, Jaydean Wendel was taking a nap. She had just finished nursing her 11-month-old baby. The baby was now in its crib, and Wendel had dozed off in an overstuffed armchair. Nursing always made her sleepy.

As the two trucks with cattle trailers attached pulled to a stop in front of the main building, David Koresh opened the front door. He held his two-year-old daughter in one arm as he opened the door with the other. Koresh was a slender, bespectacled man, cleanshaven and with a full head of curly hair which reached almost to his shoulders. Koresh was thirty-two years old, which made him the same age as ATF agent Willis. Unlike Willis, Koresh carried no weapons. He glanced up in the sky at the circling helicopters, looked over at the two huge trailers attached to the pickup trucks, and grinned.

"Think you fellows brought enough pe–"

Koresh's comment was cut short as Willis poked the 1 5/8" diameter muzzle of the suppressed machine gun out the passenger side window of the pickup truck and squeezed the trigger.

Like virtually all members of tax collection departments, and the vast majority of law enforcement personnel (other than the FBI and Secret Service), Willis had minimal skill and experience with firearms. He was further hampered by the somewhat awkward left-to-right shooting position inside the cab of the pickup truck. Finally, Willis made the mistake common to people whose real-life experience with machine guns was largely limited to movies and comic books: he assumed that since he had a gun that fired twelve bullets per second, he could not fail to miss a man's chest at a distance of ten feet.

ATF agent Willis was excited. He hurried the shot, and he did not push against the weapon as he fired to counteract the muzzle's slight tendency to rise and move away from the shooter's body as the gun chattered away on full-automatic.

The first shot of Willis' eight-round full-auto burst hit David Koresh in the left side near his waist, also clipping his wrist. The second slug was twenty inches left of the first and a foot higher. It hit David Koresh's two-year-old daughter in the center of her chest, killing her instantly before exiting out her back and slamming into the far wall inside the building. The third bullet smashed through the doorframe just to the right of Koresh, splintering it. Shots four through eight stitched a rising, angled pattern of holes into the outside wall of the building.

The H&K's suppressor effectively eliminated the muzzle blast of the pistol-caliber weapon, and the cab enclosure of the truck shielded the distant news crews from the lesser sounds of high-pressure gas coming out the gun's ejection port. The half-dozen bullets slamming into the building at seven hundred miles per hour made a sizable racket, but the position of the cattle trailers blocked much of this noise from the newspeople who were about 300 yards away.

The residents inside the building, however, were only a few yards away, and they knew exactly what was happening. David Koresh, bleeding from his arm and still holding his dead daughter, jumped back inside the building and slammed the door.

"He shot us," Koresh gasped. "She's dead." Two of the other residents of the large building were standing near the windows, and had seen Willis fire the burst at David and his daughter. When they saw that the girl was obviously dead, they shouldered their rifles and fired at Steve Willis as he was getting out of the cab of the pickup. The two men from the Mt. Carmel religious group took the trouble to aim their weapons, and they killed the ATF agent instantly.

When David Koresh had been retreating back into the building after being shot, the livestock trailers had opened, discharging their cargo. One hundred armed tax agents from the Bureau of Alcohol, Tobacco, and Firearms had poured out onto the ground. They were wearing dark jumpsuits and tactical gear, and screaming at the tops of their lungs. They were not shouting words, but rather emitting the attack noises they had learned in the simulated assaults they had practiced during the previous weeks.

Most of the screaming agents began hurling concussion grenades at the windows of the compound. Before the attack, there had been brief discussion of issuing everyone on the raid fragmentation grenades, but that idea had been abandoned in favor of restricting their use to the specialized 'entry teams' assigned to penetrate the building and kill anyone resisting. It was fortunate for the ATF men and women that the decision had gone that way; about a third of the grenades the tax men were throwing were going wide of the windows, bouncing back off the building, and landing on the ground directly in front of the federal agents.

At the same time as the grenades were exploding on the first floor and the ground outside, men in the helicopters began firing down into the roof of the building. Jaydean Wendel was abruptly awakened by all the noise. Like all mothers with infants, she immediately thought of her baby.

"Huh? Wha...? Sweetheart, are you all ri–" The woman's half-awake thoughts were cut short by a 7.62 slug that tore through the ceiling and struck her in the top of the head. The bullet shattered her skull, penetrated her brain, and lodged against her jawbone, killing her instantly. Jaydean Wendel was the third person killed in the first thirty seconds

496

of the assault.

The ATF agents from the first livestock trailer concentrated on the west wall of the building where the two trucks were parked. They threw grenades, took cover behind cars in the dirt parking area, and fired their pistols and submachine guns at the windows of the Mt. Carmel compound. One of the agents, Dan Curtis, who owned one of the pickup trucks that had pulled the trailers into position, was taking aim with his 15-shot 9mm pistol when he saw Koresh briefly through one of the first-floor windows. Curtis altered his aim and squeezed the trigger. He smiled as he saw Koresh spin and fall under the impact of the 9mm slug piercing his abdomen.

While the load of tax agents from the first trailer concentrated on the main entrance, some of those from the second trailer ran around the southwest corner of the building and threw ladders up to the second floor. An entry team commanded by Agent Bill Buford of the Little Rock, Arkansas ATF office was trying to get to the section of the building where they thought Koresh had his bedroom and a weapons locker. There was a shallowly-sloping roofed area over part of the first floor, and the ATF men threw two ladders up to it. Once they were standing on it, the second-floor windows would be at waist level.

"McKeehan!" Buford commanded, "You and those four ladder up to that window! Rest of you follow me." What happened next was captured by the news cameras of KWTX-TV and shown on news broadcasts hundreds of times around the nation in the following days.

Agent Conway LeBleu drew his gun from his belt holster when he was halfway up the aluminum extension ladder. His finger was inside the trigger guard when his foot slipped on a rung of the ladder. For a horrible instant he realized that he had come very close to shooting himself in the thigh. After hesitating a moment, the shaken agent continued his climb and made his way onto the roof. The agents massed on the projecting rooftop while one of them smashed the window, threw the curtain aside, and looked in to make sure it was clear.

"Shit, I hope those guys in the choppers watch where they're shooting!" one of the agents yelled. A man in one of the Army helicopters was now hosing down the roof of the compound with long bursts from an M60 belt-fed machine gun.

"Keep your head down! Guys in front are goin' nuts, too!"

"Okay, all clear! Let's move in!" Robb Williams, Todd McKeehan, and Conway LeBleu climbed through the window into what they had been told was David Koresh's bedroom. Their information was out of date. Koresh had moved to a different section of the compound some time before. Bill Buford led the other group through a different window into an adjacent section of the building.

Williams, McKeehan, and LeBleu moved cautiously through the darkened room. Their nerves were strung tight as they listened to the helicopter rake the roof with full-auto fire and heard the bullets ripping through the ceiling several rooms away. *I wish that guy would stay up by the northwest corner instead of shooting so close to here* Todd McKeehan thought as he waited for his eyes to adjust to the darkness. Muffled sounds of gunfire from the agents in front of the building continued unabated. As he visually identified his two companions in the dim light, McKeehan subconsciously contemplated the body armor and ballistic helmet he was wearing. *They're heavy enough, but will they stop rifle bullets coming through the ceiling? Maybe, if the wood and plaster is thick enough to really slow them down. Jesus, if it isn't, and if that guy up there in the chopper isn't care—*

No one ever knew why the agent outside on the roof decided to throw the stun grenade into the room. Some who later saw the film footage would claim he must have thought the men inside had moved into other parts of the building and were no longer in the bedroom. Others would say that he knew the agents were wearing ballistic helmets, which would protect their ears from the concussion. Neither argument explained the logic of throwing a bomb into a room that was either empty, or occupied by your own men.

Three of the members of the religious group had just finished checking on the children's dormitory. They left the two dozen children huddled underneath their beds and were running towards the stairwell at the southeast corner of the complex when the grenade went off in Koresh's former bedroom.

When the grenade exploded, the tax agents inside the empty bedroom reacted instinctively. They all began firing their submachine guns blindly, spraying the dark room in all directions with 9mm bullets. Seven rounds came through the wall near the man who had thrown in the grenade, and viewers across the country saw him cringe as the holes appeared in the outside wall just a few feet from where he sat.

The aramid fiber ballistic armor that the agents inside the bedroom were wearing was designed to stop standard lead-core, copper-jacketed pistol ammunition. Like most body armor, it offered little or no protection against rifle bullets. It was rated to stop most 9mm handgun ammunition, and the H&K MP5SD submachine guns that the agents were firing at each other were chambered for this round. However, there was one problem: the tax agents were not shooting standard 9mm ammunition.

Fifteen years before, in an effort to develop a more effective 20mm projectile for air-to-air combat, an engineer at the Army's Edgewood Arsenal had come up with the idea of a bullet made of a hardened steel tube with the leading edge sharpened to a circular razor edge. During testing, this projectile bit into metal aircraft surfaces at angles where other rounds glanced off.

An offshoot of this development was that the concept was scaled down to handgun ammunition. The result was a 9mm bullet which acted like a tiny, spinning, razor-sharp cookie cutter which went through soft body armor, as one government engineer put it, 'like shit through a goose'. The feds were very excited about this finding, and commissioned a subcontractor to produce the specialized ammunition in limited numbers. The round was nicknamed the 'Cyclone' by federal agents that used it.

It was these Cyclone rounds that the tax agents inside David Koresh's bedroom were now firing at each other, and their MP5 submachine guns were each spewing them out at a rate of twelve per second.

Bill Buford and the other men heard the chattering of the suppressed submachine guns in the other room, and saw bullets come through the wall in front of them. The subguns sounded like several electric typewriters.

"They've found 'em!" Buford yelled as he took cover behind an oak chest and looked for something to shoot at.

The three members of the religious camp knew that none of the residents were in that corner of the building. That meant that all the gunfire was coming from the raiders, and that there were a lot of them. The three men crept up the stairwell, dropped to their knees, and began firing their AR-15s upwards through the ceiling and wall towards the attackers. The sound in the enclosed space was ear-splitting, but the three men gritted their teeth and ignored it.

The defenders were shooting inexpensive Chinese NORINCO .223 ammunition in their AR-15s. This ammunition was uniform, reliable, and functioned well, but it did not have a steel core like the current military issue loading. Michael Platt had fired the same

498

ammunition seven years before in his Ruger Mini-14 during the Miami shootout with the FBI. There, the slugs had been stopped or destroyed on impact with a man's arm, and also on auto glass. At least two FBI men were still alive because of this lack of penetration.

At the Texas religious complex, penetration of the NORINCO round was even less than it had been in Miami. The barrels of the AR-15s that the three men were firing had 1-in-7" rifling twists designed to stabilize military steel-core ammo. This twist spun the bullets almost twice as fast as the 1-in-12" pitch of the Mini-14. The bullets exited the muzzle spinning at over 300,000 RPM, and the tremendous rotational force caused most of the slugs to break apart when they hit the wood-and-plaster wall. One fragment hit Bill Buford, and he grimaced.

With bullets now coming through two of the walls instead of just one, the men in ATF agent Buford's group started firing in all directions. One shot hit a defender in the thigh. He fell against the wall near the top of the stairwell, still clutching his AR-15. Then he pulled back as his two companions continued shooting.

Agent Buford ignored the burning pain of his wound and peered through a doorway, where he saw Robb Williams huddled behind an old safe. *He's been hit* Buford thought. *More than once.* Buford watched as Williams collapsed on the floor. Williams was dead, as were Conway LeBleu and Todd McKeehan.

"Pull back!" Buford screamed as a feeling of dread swept over him.

The raid was not going the way he had planned.

***

In six separate living rooms many miles apart, Henry Bowman, Irwin Mann, Thomas J. Fleming, Rufus Ingram, Curt Behnke, and Earl Taylor-Edgarton watched in utter horror at the spectacle on their television screens. All of them were appalled and sickened at the federal invasion of the Branch Davidian compound, which was the term the newscasters were using for the Mt. Carmel camp located outside Waco, Texas.

What on earth have the people in there done? all six of the men wondered.

It's just like the attack on us in '44 Irwin Mann thought as his stomach turned over. Tears came to his eyes as he watched the black-clad agents with their German machine guns and their coal-scuttle helmets attack the compound, and Irwin Mann was filled with a silent rage.

Why the hell are tax agents carrying submachine guns and grenades? Tom Fleming silently demanded as he clenched his teeth. *What possible tax violation deserves sending in a hundred armed feds with guns blazing?*

Henry Bowman, Curt Behnke, and Rufus Ingram were staring at the scene of ATF agents crouched behind cars parked in the dirt driveway in front of the Branch Davidian compound. Most of the feds were firing their weapons as fast as they could pull the triggers.

Why are these idiots panicked? Henry Bowman wondered. *The people in the building aren't even shooting back. There's not a single puff of dust anywhere on the ground around them, and it's a dirt driveway!* Henry Bowman had rolled plenty of cans in his parents' dirt pasture. Even a .22 Short threw up a noticeable spout of dust when it hit the ground. Centerfire rifle and pistol rounds would throw lots of dirt in the air. In the area around the wildly-firing feds, there was not a single bit of evidence to indicate the Branch Davidians were returning fire.

"Who taught these morons how to shoot?" Rufus asked the woman who lived with him and sometimes helped with his training courses. Several agents were blindly firing their pistols in the general direction of the building. "If any of them were in my combat handgunning class, I'd flunk them out and recommend they be removed from the force. And where's the return fire?" Rufus demanded, pointing at the screen. None of the vehicles the feds were crouched behind exhibited a single bullet hole in either the sheetmetal or the glass.

Earl Taylor-Edgarton watched the footage of the raid, then listened to ATF's regional head, Ted Royster, explain why the raid had been such a disaster.

"They were tipped off," Royster said emphatically. "They were tipped off beforehand, and they had us outgunned," Royster said into the newsman's microphone.

"Those bloody imbeciles," Earl Taylor-Edgarton said to his wife. "They don't know how lucky they are."

"No one's shooting back at them," the woman agreed.

"If they'd had me to deal with instead of a bunch of silly Jesus-freaks, they'd find out about 'outgunned'. A little buried surprise would have been waiting for those cattle trailers." He snorted. "That cannibal would have a hundred more grieving widows to explain himself to before he climbed back up on his dung-heap." He reached for the phone to call one of his contacts in Texas.

Seventy-seven-year-old Curt Behnke was also watching the scene of the agents firing at the building, which ran and re-ran on several television stations.

"Why are they shooting, Grandpa?" his youngest grandson Nathan asked. "What are they shooting at?"

"I'm not sure," Behnke answered slowly, without taking his eyes off the screen. He was counting the number of ATF men hiding behind the parked vehicles. *Eleven* he decided. *Probably a lot more around, but the news camera only shows this one area.* Each of the tax agents had at least half his head exposed to the compound, and most of them were exposing a lot more of their bodies than that. Behnke thought of the rack of single-shot target rifles in the basement next to his lathe. He thought of the thousands of one-hole groups he had fired in his lifetime, and of the countless prairie dogs he had killed. Any one of his match rifles would be far better than necessary for shooting at distances of less than a hundred yards. *Take me about thirty seconds to fire eleven aimed shots* the retired photoengraver with fourteen grandchildren decided.

"I don't really know what's going on, Nathan," Behnke said to the six-year-old sitting next to him on the couch. "About all I can tell you is those men behind the cars are very lucky."

March 5, 1993

"Cindy, would you come in the office, please?" Cindy Caswell put down the rate card and worksheet she was analyzing and got up from her desk. She walked across the sales area to her boss' private office and took a seat inside after closing the door.

Rebecca Williams was a striking-looking woman in her early forties. She had a mane of red hair and a spectacular figure, and her clothes were selected to accentuate these assets. She was the owner of the Williams Agency, a St. Louis County firm that designed and sold promotional materials, ad specialties, and incentive awards for local businesses. The shelves in the crowded office were filled with thick catalogs from suppliers that wholesaled imprinted pens, embossed clocks, silkscreened T-shirts, electronic equipment, baking tins, tool kits, and thousands of other things that companies could sell or give away with the goal of increasing their own business.

Rebecca Williams was an ex-model. As owner of the agency, she believed strongly in one overriding business principle on which she had built a successful company: Good-looking women were the salespeople most likely to make male decision-makers want to do business with her firm. This was especially true in marginal cases where the product the men were buying only had a slight chance of improving their firm's sales. In keeping with this philosophy, all of the Williams Agency's salespeople, like Cindy Caswell, were young, attractive women, and they were paid on a straight commission basis.

Rebecca had taken a chance on Cindy Caswell the year before. Despite her complete lack of sales experience, the young girl had exuded an unquestionable appeal. Men gravitated towards Cindy, and much more importantly, wanted to do things that would please her. There was a constant erotic undercurrent between Cindy Caswell and the people she dealt with. It was more subtle and yet much more powerful than the normal sexual tension found whenever men were in the proximity of sharply-dressed young women with good figures. Rebecca Williams herself had felt the physical attraction Cindy's presence created; for reasons of common sense she had done nothing about it. Cindy Caswell was, after all, second in the office in production.

"Cindy, I have some bad news," the owner said from behind her desk as the girl looked at her brightly. "You know about the tug-of-war I've been having with the IRS." Cindy nodded.

Rebecca Williams treated all of the salespeople as independent contractors. They were free to take days off, make sales calls from their homes, and work on weekends, for they received no salary, hourly rate, or 'draw'. They were paid only on the sales they made.

The IRS had recently taken the position that these facts were not sufficient to prove independent contractor status, and that the Williams Agency was going to have to institute withholding, Social Security, and other federal mandates to stay in business. Rebecca Williams had been fighting bitterly with the Service on this issue for several months.

"We've come to an agreement," Rebecca told Cindy. "All prior years are okay. Up through now, they'll let things stand. But from now on, they say I have to play their game." Rebecca Williams smiled at Cindy, but the look on her face was wistful. Cindy Caswell had a feeling that the other shoe was about to drop.

"This is a small office," Rebecca continued. "I suppose I could hire someone to do all the new paperwork, and we could switch over to the way the IRS wants things to be. But now there's all this talk about making business owners pay for health care. I don't want to go to the expense and effort of setting up a whole new system, just to have all my salespeople leave."

"What do you mean?" Cindy asked. She couldn't see where this was going, but it didn't sound good.

"Right now, the company takes in the money from the customer, and writes you a check for your commission. You handle your own tax preparation and buy your own health insurance, right?" Cindy nodded. *Actually, H&R Block does my income tax return for me* she thought silently.

"If the company has to start doing those things, I'm not going to be able to pay you and the others as much, because buying health insurance for everyone and putting an accounting firm permanently on-line will cost the firm a lot of money." Cindy nodded again. She still did not see why this would be a problem.

"When that happens, you and the others are going to quit and go work elsewhere. Maybe not immediately, but soon."

"Why, Rebecca?" Cindy asked immediately.

"Because salespeople, like everyone else, go where they are paid the most for their work. There are only eight people in this office, but the Williams Agency pays the same licensing fees as a company with a hundred workers, so it hurts us a lot more. When we have to start doing all the things the government says we now have to do, it will cost us almost the same dollars in additional overhead as a firm ten times our size. I won't be able to afford the payouts that the bigger firms will be able to offer. In six months, I won't have anyone working here. So I've decided to close the office."

"Rebecca, I'm happy to do my own taxes and pay my own insurance," Cindy said quickly. "Out of what I earn here, that's been easy."

"I believe you. But even if you never left, I wouldn't be able to keep all the others. And with just a couple of salespeople, the overhead here would eat us alive." She shook her head. "No, the new rules mean that there will be two kinds of businesses: Big companies with hundreds of employees, and sole proprietorships where people work out of their living rooms and don't hire anyone. The IRS will let me keep the doors open until the end of the month. April first, the Williams Agency will be no more." Cindy looked down at her feet. She knew she could get another job, and she had some money saved up, but she liked Rebecca and she liked working for her.

"It's no consolation to you, but there's one person who's going to be happy about this," Rebecca said with a grin.

"Who?"

"Roger. Tonight we're going to Baker's for dinner, and I'm going to tell him I'll marry him." Roger was a local real estate developer that had been trying to persuade Rebecca to accept his marriage proposal for almost two years. Cindy Caswell smiled.

"Babies?" Cindy asked.

"My God, I'm forty-three years old!" Rebecca laughed. "Can you imagine what that would do to this body?" Cindy shrugged. "But since you asked, yes."

"Yes?" Cindy asked, raising her eyebrows in delight.

"Yes. Absolutely. Hugh Hefner, Jack Nicholson, and Warren Beatty? They had the easy part, becoming middle-aged parents. This old broad is going to show them women can do it too."

Cindy Caswell gave her boss a huge hug. She knew she'd find another job.

Rebecca felt a warm glow in her pelvic area. "If I had ten more like you, Cindy, I might be willing to play by those stupid new federal rules."

April 9, 1993

"The situation in Waco, Texas remains unchanged. The FBI controls the situation, and as you can see, behind where I am standing, army tanks have been moved into position a half mile from the compound. The Branch Davidians, however, have not agreed to any of the terms offered. Just this afternoon, FBI spokesman–"

The sound and picture of the news broadcast were abruptly cut off as Henry Bowman hit the button on his remote. "You didn't need to hear any more of that, did you?" he asked his friend.

"Not until something changes," Tom Fleming replied.

"The way to resolve this thing would be for the feds to admit they really screwed up, and just leave," Henry said.

"They'll never do that. ATF started demonizing those people in that building five minutes after the news showed everyone what kind of thugs our federal agents really are. Now they've got too much time and money invested. Those people inside are very close to all being dead, in my opinion." Fleming thought a moment, then brightened.

"You know, the way you could get those people out of there would be to have ten thousand civilians walk up to the compound, let the Branch Davidians mingle in with them, and walk out."

"Think the group could get by the police line?"

"If we had the numbers, yeah, I think so." Henry Bowman considered the idea, then changed the subject.

"Is the ATF still saying there's a crank lab in there, along with Jesus and his multiple teenage wives?" Henry asked.

"I don't know. Couple weeks ago I saw a press conference where they were still saying that. Some guy claiming to be an ATF intelligence officer, if you can believe the gall of that title," Fleming snorted. "You ask me, these guys have incompetent legal counsel. I'd be disbarred if my clients stood up on television and said some shit like that." Henry nodded at Tom's assessment.

Tom Fleming and Henry Bowman were discussing the issue that had been on the minds of people in the gun culture all across the country. The Waco attack and subsequent standoff had captivated everyone in America who had to deal with the ATF on a regular basis. For this reason, it was even more compelling than the Miami shootout in 1986.

The February 28 ATF assault on the Branch Davidians had been broadcast live on the television news, and viewers had been appalled at what they had seen. At the time of the initial raid, the public had not been told what crimes the residents of the religious camp had committed.

The ATF had realized how it would sound if they admitted that they had sent three helicopter gunships and 100 agents armed with grenades and machine guns to attack 85 men, women, and children over a $200 tax matter. A different 'spin' was needed, and fast.

The federal agency had immediately started explaining that their raid would have gone off 'perfectly' if the Branch Davidians had not been forewarned. The ATF then justified their actions by telling the public that David Koresh thought he was Jesus, had multiple wives, and was having sex with most of the women in the camp, especially underage ones. They also said other child abuse was suspected, and implied that it was this concern which had required such urgent and violent action.

The ATF did not explain why a federal tax agency was involved in these areas in the first place, let alone with explosives and machine guns. The ATF also failed to elucidate how their concerns for the safety of two dozen children within a wooden building squared with firing over seven thousand rounds of ammunition, much of it armor piercing, into that same structure.

In the disastrous initial raid, the ATF had suffered twenty casualties, and the Branch Davidians even more. All Davidian casualties and two-thirds of ATF's were caused by ATF bullets. These numbers were not precisely known at the time of the raid, but there were so many witnesses, it was obvious that 'friendly fire' had accounted for the lion's share of dead and wounded feds.

Compounding this monumental embarrassment were several other revelations. The first was that the search warrant authorizing the raid did not show probable cause. It listed non-NFA firearms and parts that were legal to own with no special registration or federal taxes. These included dummy grenades which the Davidians had been known to mount on plaques and sell at flea markets, inviting immediate comparison with the Ken Ballew case over twenty years earlier.

The second revelation was that the ATF had lied to Texas officials in order to borrow three Texas National Guard helicopter gunships in the raid. Texas law prohibited lending state-controlled aircraft to federal agencies except in drug cases. In order to get approval, the ATF had told state officials that the Branch Davidians were operating a methamphetamine lab within the compound. When copies of the search warrants were made public, there was no mention of drugs, and the lie was obvious.

It had been apparent from the outset that regardless of jurisdiction or the validity of the search warrants, the Bureau of Alcohol, Tobacco, and Firearms was in well over its collective head in the Waco debacle. Within 48 hours of the February 28 disaster, the FBI was called in.

Rightly or wrongly, the public as a whole viewed the FBI as an elite organization that was especially competent at negotiation during critical situations. The FBI had promised America almost daily that a peaceful end to the standoff was imminent. Now, more than a month after the initial attack, many observers were coming to the viewpoint Tom and Henry had held for five weeks: *Be a goddamn miracle if the feds let any of those people out of there alive.*

***

"Buy you a hamburger and a chocolate milkshake?" Cindy Caswell asked Henry Bowman as they walked out of the AA meeting. "I'd like a chance to pick your brains about something."

"Best offer I've had in ages," Henry replied. "Food tastes better when it's free. You buy, I'll drive." Henry led the way to his GMC and unlocked the door for the young woman.

"You've been going to more meetings lately," Cindy commented. "Seems I've seen you several times in the last month."

"This mess down in Texas has really got me down," Henry said as he started the vehicle and pulled out of the parking lot. "Everybody seems horrified, but I'd bet anything I own that when it's all over, the only changes will be that a few officials resign or are put on a leave of absence, probably with full pay."

"You been tempted to get drunk?"

"Actually, no, not really. That's not the reason I've been going to meetings so often.

It's more for...inspiration, I guess you'd call it." Henry cut the wheel and stabbed the throttle. The GMC silently shot around a Buick that was crawling along in the right lane, its driver searching for an address.

"AA has been a great success for over half a century. The worst thing I've ever heard anyone say about it is they don't like the religious undertones. No one has ever claimed that the program has made somebody's chemical dependency worse. And the one thing the program has never, ever done is blame the distilleries or liquor stores. AA never tries to get the grocery stores to stop selling vodka or the ballpark to stop selling beer. That's not the problem. The problem lies with the alcoholic and his alcoholism, and that's where the solution is, too, not with the liquor manufacturer, the grocery store, or the drinker who is not an alcoholic.

"Now, I know that the line is to turn it over to God, put your faith in Him, and all that. But ultimately, it's still the individual alcoholic who elects to do that, not the distiller, the store, or the other people in the community."

"And...?" Cindy asked.

"And that's a source of strength for me. Seeing a group of people who take personal responsibility for their problems, and who don't try to fix the blame on others? That's a very positive thing for me. It's a good antidote for constant exposure to the socialist slime that want the government to tax me and then use my money to take away more of my freedoms in the pursuit of some nebulous 'greater good'." Henry took a deep breath as he pulled into the lot of the coffee shop. "More specifically, it's a much-needed break from the news reports of the federal storm troopers in Texas."

"I've been reading the papers about that. It sounds awful, and it doesn't look like they're about to agree to anything," Cindy said as she got out of the car.

"What's to agree on?" Henry Bowman snorted. "The religious group wanted to be left alone, and thinks it had every right to shoot people who were attacking their home with grenades and machine guns. The feds think everyone inside should have submitted to the attack, and since they didn't, they should all be charged with murder."

"Koresh does sound kind of weird," Cindy threw out.

"Several dozen friends, relatives, and business acquaintances of mine practice symbolized cannibalism once a week as part of their religion. To be blunt, I find that practice a lot more bizarre than some guy wanting to set up a community where the women take turns going to bed with him." Henry chuckled as he held the door to the restaurant, and added "Hell, if the feds made that a hanging offense, most of the guys I went to college with would be on death row."

"I see your point."

"So what's up with you?" Henry asked as they took a booth.

"I lost my job. The office shut down last week." Cindy Caswell went on to explain about the IRS' argument over independent contractor status, and Rebecca Williams' decision to close the agency.

"What are you going to do now? I assume one of the other companies in the same business would give you a job. Successful salespeople willing to work on straight commission can always get work."

"Yes, I've already found two places that will let me start work immediately. That's not what I wanted to talk to you about." Cindy stopped talking as the waitress arrived and took their order.

"I've had enough time in the business to see that there's going to be a limit on what I can earn selling promotional materials. I'm saving money every month, but not as much as I'm going to need for the catering business I want to start. I've had another offer, from one of my customers, for part-time work. I wanted to talk to you about it." Cindy Caswell looked as if she was getting up her courage to tell him something. Henry thought he knew what it was.

"The president of Caldo Electric wants me to be his mistress." There was a slightly defiant tone to her voice. Henry nodded and casually took a pen from his shirt pocket.

"Has he said what kind of arrangement he has in mind?"

"No, Ted...only talked in general terms. It was more than hinting, though. He was clear about what he wanted. Sex, not a new wife."

"But it did involve a...salary, you might say?"

"A check every month."

"No figure mentioned?"

"He kind of let me know that if I was interested, we could talk about it."

Henry Bowman was a geologist, not a lawyer or a private investigator, but he had a habit that would have stood him in very good stead in either of those other two professions: Whenever people told him something startling, and particularly when they wanted an opinion, Henry was absolutely disinterested. His manner implied that the issue in question was commonplace. It was this reaction, or lack of it, that Cindy Caswell received after explaining what her client had suggested.

"Did you want me to have him checked out?" Henry asked. "See if he's beat up any women and had it hushed up, get a look at his history, find out if he might try to use you as a perk for his best customers, things like that?" The request startled Cindy Caswell, for she had not expected it. Now that it came, she saw the logic behind it.

"Ah...I don't think that's a problem." She grinned suddenly. "You recall I've got some experience in spotting that kind of thing."

"So...what can I do about this for you?"

"Just give me your opinion." Henry rubbed his chin with the end of his pen before answering.

"No good way to evaluate an offer that hasn't been made yet. You thought about how much money you're looking to get, and what you're willing to give up?" Cindy considered this question.

"I don't know what he has in mind, but if I can't make an extra ten thousand in a year, I'm not interested."

"That'd be once a week, mutually convenient time, your place for a couple of hours?"

"I guess. You think it's a terrible idea?"

"I don't really have an opinion right now. Need more information for that. Let me make a few guesses, and you tell me how I'm doing."

"Okay." The food arrived and Henry put ketchup and pepper on his hamburger and fries before continuing. He took a bite from the sandwich and sat back in the booth.

"Our executive is forty-five or fifty, married, with kids. People like him, and think he's a good guy. That includes his family, and also includes you, or you wouldn't even be considering his offer."

"Dead-on so far," Cindy told him. Henry nodded and went on.

"Okay, since I got the age right, he would have been in his twenties during the 1970s. That was after it became okay to have a bunch of sex partners, but before the newspapers started telling everyone that a blow job might turn into a death sentence. So I see three possible situations. Number one, your boyfriend got married young, maybe because

506

he had to, missed out on swinging bachelorhood, and now he wants to make up for it before he's too old to get it up any more. I don't see that one as likely. Guys like that are usually scared to death around young women.

"Number two, he had a swinging bachelorhood, fell in love with a woman who he married, but he likes variety, and wants someone new. Also not too likely, because then he wouldn't be talking about a mistress, he'd be trying to talk you into one weekend with him at the lake.

"The other guess, which is the one I'd put my money on, is that he likes his marriage and monogamy suits him okay, but his wife's sex drive has shot craps. I'll bet that having good sex with a friendly, good-looking woman is one of his all-time favorite things. He always knew he'd have to give that up eventually, but he was thinking maybe age seventy or so, not forty-five."

"I think you've hit it exactly right," Cindy Caswell said with a voice that showed she was impressed. "From what I know of him, I don't think he wants to divorce his wife. I think he loves her. Likes her, too," she added.

"It fits with wanting to pay you. I take it this guy is decent-looking?"

"Yes."

"So if he wanted to, he could fish for somebody who'd be impressed by him, and drop not-so-subtle hints to her that his marriage was on the rocks and if she stuck around, she'd be the one who didn't have to worry about car payments and the phone being turned off and all that, right? But if he did that, the girl might get impatient and call his wife, or bitch at him all the time, and more problems is not what he's looking for.

"So instead, he looks at you. You're successful, sharp, understand business, and have a firm grasp of the concept of 'added value'. And he makes you an offer that he hopes will benefit you both."

"So you think it's an okay idea?"

"Maybe. Question is, though, what are you going to have to give up, hm?" Henry sat back and sipped his malt. "That's always the issue that the girl doesn't think about until it's too late." He remembered something and nodded.

"Friend of mine's sister, girl named Holly, she went to the Muny Opera with her girlfriend when she was eighteen, summer before her freshman year of college. Had a seat in about the fifth row. Intermission, guy comes up to them, says the star would like to see them backstage afterwards, gives them both passes. It's only Holly he's interested in, you understand, but he invites them both because he knows that's the way to start. I forget the guy's name, black song-and-dance man about forty-five, fifty. I'm sure the guy's in Vegas all the time—I just can't remember his name." Henry scowled, then waved his hand in dismissal.

"Anyway, Holly goes backstage, and the guy turns on the charm, wants to take her and her girlfriend out to some clubs in his limo."

"I think I see where this is going."

"Right. The girls are both virgins, but they love the attention, and they know he's not going to rape them both in a limo or a club, so they go. He takes 'em dancing, orders 'em champagne, the whole bit, and all the while people are recognizing him and wanting his autograph. The girls have a great time, and when they go home, that's all they can talk about for days.

"So then this guy calls my friend's sister every day from New York, wants her to come visit. Of course she says no, the guy's black, married, and has four kids older than she is. But this guy's no beginner, so he keeps up the charm, calls her every day, sends her plane tickets, all that.

"In a few weeks, she goes off to college. She had some scholarship money, and student loans lined up, and a part-time campus job like a lot of college kids. For most eighteen-year-olds, that's a big adventure, but Holly decides it sucks compared to running around with a star. So one weekend, she goes to New York."

"Let me guess," Cindy said. "She becomes his mistress."

"Right. And then college gets really boring, and her grades go to hell, so she drops out before the end of the first semester. And then three years later, guess what?"

"The star finds another eighteen-year-old."

"Exactly. And he's been supporting Holly, but it was all apartment rent, and car lease payments, and clothes. She has zero assets to show for those three years, no degree, no ability to get scholarship dough, or student loans, or an on-campus job, nothing. She's just a high school graduate that's three years older with no money and even less ambition.

"Now, I've got no moral objection to an eighteen-year-old being some black entertainer's mistress. Point is, though, my friend's sister gave up some things that she'll never get back. So if she'd asked me what to do before moving to be near Mr. Soft Shoe, I would have told her to insist upon a fixed monthly contribution to a good mutual fund. Thousand a month, she'd have fifty Gs as a nest egg right now, and she'd have choices. She could take charge of her life instead of being stuck in what I'm afraid is likely to become a cycle of poverty." Henry ate the last of his french fries and continued.

"Your case is a lot different. You aren't in awe of this guy at Caldo Electric, and don't have the hots for him. In fact, for sex, you'd rather be with another girl, right?" Henry continued without waiting for an answer. "So you've got different issues involved, but they still involve what you have to give up. Is this guy going to demand you be on call, where you can't make plans for yourself? Can you have another lover, male or female, or will that piss him off? Get that stuff nailed down and set your price accordingly."

Cindy Caswell stared at her plate. "I don't know what he has in mind exactly. "I'll have to talk to him." She looked up at Henry. "You don't seem surprised at the whole idea." Henry shook his head.

"What you're talking about's not terribly unusual. Several stewardesses have told me about identical setups they've got. Stew on a standard route will get together with a guy in another city two, three times a month for an extra thousand. She knows and likes him, so it's good for both of them." Henry laughed. "I'm the one that suggested the monthly mutual fund contribution, instead of just cash, to make sure the girls were really building for the future. That made sense to all the parties involved." Henry turned serious again.

"There's one thing you should always keep in mind: You're talking about an enterprise that rewards youth, not experience. You will not be able to earn what you can make now in ten, even five years. Your present financial compensation should reflect that fact." Henry switched to a different area of the subject. "What are your long-term goals here?"

"I want to be economically self-sufficient. Period. On top of that, like I told you before, I want to open a catering business. There are a lot of businesses doing a bad job at catering. I think I can do better."

"So you're looking to raise a bunch of money in a hurry, get a stake to work with?"

"Yes, but I don't want partners," she insisted. Henry started laughing. "What's so funny?"

"I think I've got a lot better idea for you than skimming an extra thousand a month from some frustrated executive, Cindy." He looked at his watch. "You got an extra couple hours to kill?"

"I'm a woman of leisure, at the moment." Henry handed her the check and then stood up.

"I'll get the tip," he said, reaching for his wallet. "You know those stupid government rules that encouraged your boss to close up shop?" Henry asked. "I think the same kind of regulations may offer a big opportunity for a motivated young woman like you. Any time they slam the door in one place, some other area jumps in to take up the slack. Come on."

* * *

"We're going to a strip joint?" Cindy Caswell demanded when Henry Bowman pulled into the parking lot on the Illinois side of the Mississippi River. "That's not my idea of a step up."

"Ever been here?" Henry asked.

"No, but I know what—"

"Ever heard about this place—specifically, I mean?" he interrupted.

"Not exactly."

"Then don't pass judgment yet. I think you're going to be very interested at what you see here tonight. Come on." Henry opened the door and stepped out of the GMC. He waited until Cindy got out also, then punched the power lock and closed the door behind him.

Henry paid the man at the front desk a four dollar cover charge for himself and he and Cindy walked inside. Women got in free. The inside of PT's Show Club was dark, but there was enough light to see that the place was clean. There were four raised, hexagonal 'stages' on the lower level, and two more on the smaller area up three steps at the north end of the room. Fifteen or twenty chairs were around each stage, and small tables with upholstered armchairs around them filled up the rest of the large room. A deejay in a booth at the east side of the room was announcing the next number as Henry led Cindy to one of the tables near the steps leading to the raised section at the north end.

"All right, now we're going to switch things around just a little bit, bring up four more stages of lovely Dreamgirl entertainment. How many guys out there want to see more naked ladies, let me hear a big 'Hell, yeah!'"

"Hell, yeah!" a number of men in the crowd yelled obligingly.

"PT's in Sauget: You know you're there when you can taste the air. Naked ladies, cold beer, and complimentary matches—it just doesn't get any better than this. Don't be shy, gentlemen, move on up to those stages, and be sure to ask your favorite Dreamgirl about one of those private, private table dances up in the Love Zone. Don't forget, too, we've got party shots here at PT's, just ask your waitress for a PT's party shot, my favorite is tequila—no salt, no lime, chase it with a cigarette, it'll do you just fine. Now it's time to switch things around a little bit. On Stage Two, Thunder's private playground over by the bar, Stage Two, we've got T.J., lovely T.J. on Stage Two; on Stage Three there's Nikki, long and lean and sometimes mean Nikki on Stage Three over in the pinball corner; coming up next on Stage Four, clap your hands for Tiffany, Tiffany on Stage Four; and our feature for the next three numbers up on the mainstage, her first time up tonight, let's hear a nice round of applause for Destiny, Destiny on Stage One."

As each girl's name was called, the dancer already on stage took the new girl's hand

and welcomed her up onto the stage before stepping down. The girls getting onto the stages were clothed, one in a cocktail dress, one in a nurse's uniform, and two in Vegas-type costumes. The girls getting off the stages were naked except for G-strings and high heels, and carried their outer clothing. The music started, and Cindy saw that three of the four departing dancers had each taken a man from her stage by the hand. All three pairs passed by them and walked up the steps to the empty, elevated area at the north end of the large room. The fourth dancer who had just finished her set went back to the dressing room.

Cindy looked around the darkened club. Some of the dancers not on stage were sitting on men's laps, talking to them, while others were walking around the room, asking questions of men at the tables. Sometimes the man would stand up, pick up his drink, and the woman would lead him by the hand to the north section of the room. Other times, the woman would rub up against the man for a few moments, and the customer would then slip a bill under the elastic of her G-string.

"Okay, what's going on here," Henry explained, "is that the girls pay the management for the rental of the stages, and—"

"What?" Cindy exclaimed, interrupting him.

"It's not very much," Henry added quickly. "About twenty-five dollars for an eight-hour shift. Then, the girls go onstage for three-song sets. Depending on how crowded it is, they'll be down to G-strings by the second or the third song. Anyone sitting at the stage is expected to slip at least a dollar in the girl's G-string when she dances in front of him. Friday and Saturday at midnight, that might mean forty, fifty bucks in tips for three songs. Monday afternoon, it might be less than ten. But the real dough comes in when it's not your turn on stage." Henry gestured to the girls walking around the room.

"What they're doing is dollar dances. The girl wiggles around on the guy's lap and rubs her boobs in his face for a few seconds, and he puts a dollar in her G-string. Maybe then she goes on to the next guy. But what she's really trying to set up, same as when she's onstage, is a 'private', over there in the back," Henry explained, nodding his head towards the elevated section to their right. "That's where she sits on his lap and climbs all over him for a whole song, maybe more if he's a good customer or she likes him because he's friendly and not a jerk."

"How much is that?"

"Twenty minimum. Most girls charge twenty-five. A couple girls charge more, which pisses off some of the other dancers who assume they're letting the guys feel them up or squeeze their tits, or do something else that's not allowed."

"Are they?" Cindy asked, amazed at the dollars involved.

"Absolutely not. Owners can get in all kinds of trouble if the customers do anything more daring than rub the girls' backs, so the managers watch real carefully, and they got a couple hidden cameras in the walls and ceiling with monitors in the office. They'll toss the guy out and tell the girl she can't work here any more if they see anything illegal. And what dancer's going to let a guy do something that could get her in trouble? Way it's set up, the girls break no laws, have a safe place to work, have no risk of getting hurt or catching anything other than a cold, and make a pile of money. Watch."

The song ended, and Cindy watched as one of the girls in the 'private' area walked back past the two of them, grabbed another customer, and took him back up to the 'Love Zone'.

"She obviously had more than one 'private' lined up, and she's taking them in turn. The other two girls that're still up there? Obviously the guys they're with were willing to

510

spring for more than one."

"Twenty-five dollars again?" Cindy demanded. Henry shrugged.

"Maybe. Maybe forty-five for two, or sixty for three. Up to the girl, but six songs for a hundred is about as cheap as they'll go." Suddenly he looked to their left. "Hey, Kitty! Come here!" Henry called to a tall blonde girl he recognized. She was nude except for a G-string and heels, and had a deep tan with no tan lines. "A woman that was in one of my self-defense classes," Henry explained to his companion.

"Henry Bowman! I haven't seen you in months! Who's this?"

"Kitty, this is my friend Cindy Caswell. You and she have a lot in common," he added with a grin.

"Well, now," Kitty said as she pulled a chair up facing Cindy, sat in it, and ran her hand between Cindy's thighs.

"The rules are different with women customers," Henry said with a laugh.

"I don't have a dollar," Cindy said as she blushed crimson.

"This one's for free," Kitty said as she leaned over, kissed Cindy on the mouth, then gently bit Cindy's nipple through her shirt. Henry noticed that quite a few of the patrons were surreptitiously staring at what was going on between the two women. All of them were smiling.

"The dancers who are friendly make more money," Henry explained as he signaled the waitress for two Cokes, "and the dancers who are friendly and bisexual make the most money of all. If you were up on stage with her right now, you'd each make over fifty for a set."

"We'd do a lot better than that, Henry," Kitty corrected, then added, "I've got three privates that're waiting for me, so I can only stay for a few minutes."

"Lord, shouldn't you be taking care of them?" Cindy asked, trying to keep her composure as the woman stroked her crotch. The dancer laughed.

"They're all watching right now, and I guarantee they're more turned on than they were two minutes ago. Probably get an extra twenty from at least one of them. Maybe all three." She reached over and gave Henry's crotch a quick squeeze. "Come find me later, and I'll give both of you a special." The dancer stood up, went over to her eager-looking customer, and led him away.

Cindy Caswell looked around the club, focusing on the dancers that were onstage. "Some of these girls have no rhythm," she said immediately.

"Look at their faces," Henry instructed.

"The one there looks like she's into it. Those other two look bored to tears."

"Think you could do better?"

"In my sleep."

"Check out the girls doing private dances." Cindy Caswell stood up and looked over the brass railing at the girls in the north end of the room.

"Your friend Kitty is laughing and climbing all over her guy. The other girl looks like a robot."

"And she's still getting at least twenty dollars for four minutes work," Henry said with raised eyebrows. "Kitty, on the other hand—she probably won't be free until after her next dance set, in maybe an hour."

"Lord, how much does she make in a night?"

"Busy weekend night like it is now? Thousand bucks. More if some guy wants to play big shot. Maybe five hundred on a Monday or Tuesday." Cindy Caswell's jaw dropped, and Henry grinned. "Pissed-off-looking girl like the other one up there? Half that much."

"But...that's crazy!"

"It's what I wanted to show you. Missouri legislature bans it on our side of the river, it throws a big distortion into the market, and the few places that don't ban it have a license to print money. Like cigarette advertising. They ban it on television, and it all goes to billboards. Drives the price way up. Same deal here. Couple of the girls, like Kitty, they've got their heads together, invest a big chunk of the money they make. After she went through the self-defense class, I told her to talk to the investment guy I use. She says her portfolio's worth about two hundred Gs now. Lot of the other girls, they blow every nickel they make. Some of 'em support shitbum boyfriends, some of 'em have a couple kids, some get into coke, and get fired. Ones that really look at it like a business, and they're in the minority, they make out like bandits." Something caught Henry's eye, and he started laughing.

"That girl over there?" he said, nodding at a slender, well-tanned blonde that was sitting on an older customer's lap. "She was in a class I helped teach. Different one, though. She works here once a week, or did when I met her. Care to guess what she does the rest of the week?"

"Dental technician. Nursing student. Housewife," Cindy guessed. "Advertising specialties sales," she added with a laugh. "No? Then I have no idea."

"Springfield police officer," Henry announced.

"No."

"Ask her. Only keep it quiet—the department doesn't know." He watched his friend as she stared at the moonlighting policewoman straddling the man in the business suit. "Getting some ideas for how to finance your catering business?"

"Damn right," Cindy said with feeling.

April 19, 1993

"The tanks are defensive only," Bob Ricks' image on the television screen asserted. He was answering a reporter's question about the armored vehicles being used to smash the walls of the 50-year-old wood-frame building that housed the Mount Carmel religious group.

Bullshit Alex Neumann though as he tipped up his beer bottle and took a long swallow. *You've smashed a fifth of their building into kindling. Defensive, my ass.*

The newsmen clustered at the 10:30 press conference started talking all at once, but the FBI spokesman motioned for them to be silent. "We're not negotiating. We're saying 'come out'."

They got no food, no water, and no power Neumann thought, shaking his head. *You want 'em to come out, Bob, send everybody home 'cept one guy with a folding chair, some suntan lotion, a good book, and a cellular phone. Smashed-up wood-frame building pumped full of CS doesn't say 'come out', Bob. It says 'you're dead.'* Neumann finished the beer and set the bottle on the floor. *Thank God I'm a thousand miles away for this one.*

Bob Ricks wanted to step down from the podium amid myriad shouts and questions from the television reporters. Then he decided to make sure his point was understood. He leaned over and brought the microphone close to his mouth. "We're telling them that this matter is over."

"Yeah, no shit," Agent Alex Neumann said aloud to no one in particular.

* * *

"'Bout fuckin' time," the FBI man muttered when he saw some smoke appear from one of the second-floor windows of main building in the Branch Davidian compound. The tanks had been smashing first-floor walls for over an hour. The gym roof had collapsed a half hour earlier after tanks had knocked out most of the load-bearing wall in the gym area at the back of the building. During the time since the collapse of the roof, the feds had been firing pyrotechnic tear gas canisters through the sheetrock interior walls of the building. This had driven most of the adults and all of the children inside the building up to the second floor. Then stairwells had been destroyed by the battering ram, and the wood-frame structure was just now beginning to catch fire.

"I guess we better call the fire department," the agent next to him commented, but made no move to carry out the suggestion.

"Give it a few minutes," his superior said as he looked at his watch. The time was 12:01. "When you do, route the call through the sheriff's department. And make sure they know they got to go through the checkpoints."

"Yeah. Got it." While he was waiting, the agent remembered something he had wanted to ask his boss. "Think anyone will ask why we didn't already have fire crews standing by, along with all the armored vehicles, and waited so long to get them out here?"

"Fuck 'em. Let 'em wonder," his superior replied. "And don't forget, we got a tame ATF agent, friend of that first guy killed, Willis, all lined up to be the independent fire investigator. Besides, who's going to challenge us on procedures?"

"Good point."

The news guys might also figure out that we sent the fire-suppression helicopters home the supervisor thought with a smile. *And waited for the windiest day in six weeks to shoot pyrotechnics into an old wood-frame building. After we filled that building full of stuff that produces mustard gas when it burns.* His smile grew a little wider. *Fuck 'em on that, too.*

***

"Jim, the stairwell's gone! We can't get out!" the woman screamed at her husband as she clutched her daughter. She was choking and nearly blinded from the tear gas.

"I'll jump down," he gasped. "Find something to...prop up...climb down on...catch you if I have to." His lungs felt as if they were on fire as he swung his legs out over the hole in the floor and dropped down. An exposed lag bolt from the broken stairwell raked his side, making a ragged gash up his ribcage. The man cried out in pain just as his right foot wedged itself in the shattered lumber on the floor and his ankle snapped with an audible *crack.*

Nausea and searing pain washed over the man as he collapsed, but he forced himself to his feet, determined to get his wife and daughter to safety. He inhaled deeply, and it was then that his lungs filled with hydrogen cyanide. The man's face turned a shade of blue, and he fell to the floor, dead.

"Jim! Jim!" his wife screamed, gasping for breath. She could not see her husband through the smoke, and he did not answer her. It did not matter. The Branch Davidians were all getting their final chemistry lesson, and it was going to kill every one of them in the building.

The CS tear gas which permeated the building was not itself classified as flammable. Nor was the solvent used to carry it. However, when the solvent evaporated, the remaining CS material was suspended in the air. As any high school chemistry student can attest, virtually any fine material will burn when it is uniformly suspended in air because of the tremendous amount of surface area exposed. A pinch of powdered aluminum tossed in a fireplace will prove this. A handful of cornstarch sprayed from a squeeze bottle will do so even more spectacularly. Grain dust explosions in grain silos and sawdust explosions in sawmills are more serious examples of this phenomenon.

The pyrotechnic devices fired into the old wood-frame structure had started several fires, which were spreading rapidly. When the fire hit the fine CS material suspended in the air inside the building, the CS burned, releasing deadly hydrogen cyanide gas. In less than a minute, the woman and her daughter were dead, as were others trapped in that section of the second floor.

***

"Sheriff's office."

"Yeah. FBI calling. Ah...listen, you'd better call the fire station and have 'em send some trucks to the checkpoints. It's a pretty good fire. The entire compound is going up right now."

"You got it."

The time was 12:16.

***

"Sheriff's office dispatch here," announced the man from the McLennan County Sheriff's Department.

"Yes?" said the fireman on the other end of the line. He had been wondering when the call was going to come.

"This Hawthorne?"

"Yeah, it is," the fireman replied.

"They've got a fire at the compound."

"Tell me about it!" the fireman said immediately. *No shit, Sherlock* was what had been going through his mind. He could see the flames from where he was standing.

"Are y'all en route?" the dispatcher asked.

"No, we're looking at it. Just waitin' for you to call."

"Okay...take off, then." The dispatcher at the sheriff's office broke the connection.

In six minutes, two pumper trucks pulled up to the FBI checkpoint, but the feds ordered the fire trucks to stay put. It would be 12:40 before they were allowed anywhere near the burning building.

The FBI's delaying tactics worked perfectly. By the time the trucks arrived, the hellish inferno and the deadly hydrogen cyanide had done their job. Pathologists who later examined the charred corpses would find hydrogen cyanide in the burned bodies. Since hydrogen cyanide cannot be absorbed into a person's body after death, the pathologists would correctly conclude that many of the people trapped in the building, both children and adults, were already dying from inhaling poison gas by the time the flames finally consumed them.

The firemen, standing at a distance, felt the blast of heat on their faces and stared helplessly at the monstrous blaze. One of them summed up the situation with a single sentence:

"Even God Himself couldn't put that bitch out."

Part Three

HARVEST

"Jesus, what happened to you?" Cindy Caswell said as her roommate came into the apartment, sobbing almost hysterically. One of the buttons on the girl's tuxedo shirt was torn off.

"It...it was *awful,*" she got out, then burst into renewed spasms as she fell into her lover's arms. "Th-three of them. They...they tried..."

"Hey, now," Cindy said gently, instinctively using a phrase her mother had used to comfort her when she was little. "Hey..." She rubbed April's back and held her as sobs wracked the girl's body.

Fucking St. Patrick's Day Cindy thought disgustedly. *Green beer and stupid music, and every drunken Irish asshole thinks the rules don't apply today.*

"Let me get a shower going, and we'll get you all clean and fresh and wrapped in a warm blanket. Then you can tell me about it, if you want." April Lassiter nodded as Cindy led her towards the bathroom.

Hope Henry's home Cindy found herself thinking. *We may want to talk to him.*

***

"Can't do it," Henry Bowman said for the third or fourth time. "It's a felony. If you were a juvenile, I'd say go for it, but you're not. A felony conviction will fuck up your whole life, and that's no exaggeration."

"So would- "

"I know what you're going to say," Henry interrupted, "and I agree with you. But carrying a gun or a knife or a sap for protection is like wearing a seatbelt: you have to do it every single day. If you do it every single day where it's illegal, you are going to get caught, period. Then, if you're lucky, the cop who arrested you will let you off if you blow him and his partner. How does that sound? Not much better than three drunks slowed down by fifty bucks worth of green beer, does it?" April closed her eyes and shuddered.

"Look," Henry said, "I'm not trying to be a jerk. I'm trying to make you see the whole picture. Bar parking lots are dangerous places. Particularly the ones in so-called 'nice' neighborhoods.

"Place like Cindy works, behind a chemical plant and under so many high-voltage lines it hurts to touch your car when the ground's wet? Where the girls have to pretend every shitbum that walks in gives her a wide-on? Management knows there's a risk there. That's why there's a guy weighs two-eighty with a bunch of scar tissue on his knuckles standing in the parking lot, another one at the door, and a cop who's screwing one of the dancers cruising by in a squad car every five minutes. Place is probably the safest bar in a three-state area.

"But where you work, with the cappuccino machine and the forty different kinds of beer and all the college kids in the shirts and pants that look sloppy but cost a hundred bucks each, that's a different story. Guy could punch out every waitress in the place, take all his clothes off, jump up on the bar, and smoke a cigar with his butt, nobody would do a thing. Ninety-pound busboy would stand there with his mouth open, black dishwasher with the do-rag would be saying 'be cool, bro', and the owner would be staring at the cash register to make sure the bartender with the coke habit wasn't dipping into the till. And that's inside the building. You expect security in the parking lot? Maybe after we pay off the national debt, but not before." April was seething.

"So you're saying just lie back and enjoy it?"

"Not at all," Henry said gently. "I can set you up with a couple things that the cops can't nail you for. Pepper spray, stuff like that. Nothing like a decent gun, but better than nothing." The girl nodded.

"When the hell is this stupid state going to change the law?" April asked.

"I don't know. Third time's the charm."

"The way those bastards in the Capitol treat us, it makes me want to sandpaper a few more maple dowels," Cindy said softly. Henry's heart lurched in his chest, and April gave her lover a questioning look.

"Vampires," Cindy explained to the younger girl. "You know—blood suckers? Wooden stake through the heart?"

"Oh sure," the younger girl said, now understanding. Henry Bowman stood up.

"I have to get going. I'll get back with Cindy as soon as I can, probably by tomorrow afternoon. Then we can talk some more, okay?"

"Yeah, that would be great. And I really want to thank you for coming over right away."

"I'll see you out," Cindy offered, and walked with Henry to the door. At the doorway she turned to face him. "'Smoke a cigar with his butt'?" she said in a low voice. Her whole face threatened to break into a smile.

"Hey, it just popped into my head," Henry said defensively.

"Thanks for coming over," she said as she squeezed his arm. "I owe you one." Henry nodded and turned toward the stairs.

He was still thinking about politicians and wooden dowels. Vampires did not figure in these thoughts.

May 12, 1994

"We're not going to make it, folks," the State Rep's aide said. "Flanagan's running out the clock." Cindy Caswell winced when she heard the words, but she knew they were true. She glanced at her wristwatch. It was 4:15.

"That bastard," Cindy said in disgust, and others in the group nodded agreement. They were gathered outside the door to the Senate chamber. *God but I hate it here* she thought. It was the seventeenth full day Cindy had spent in the State Capitol building, and she had grown to loathe the place.

"Too late to get a law, but not too late to get a vote," one of the others in the group said. He looked up at the Rep's assistant. "We've got to have a Senate vote, people. Win, lose, or draw, these spineless bastards have got to be forced to go on record, one side or the other."

"We'll have that, no question," the aide assured him. "Some of these senators are afraid they're going to be boiled in oil by their constituents if they don't prove they're in favor of the rights of the citizen."

"Too bad fear is the only thing that seems to work on these jerks," Cindy said.

"Fear may be the only thing that bothers these guys, but when they feel it, it works great. We do have these guys scared. Flanagan's so terrified of this thing landing on his desk that he's called in every chit he has out to get it voted down in the Senate. Senators are more scared of the voters than they are of him, though. What does that tell you, huh?" Cindy smiled a little, and the aide, seeing the change, pressed on. "Come on, let's go put the fear of God into a couple more of them before they let out for the year."

Cindy Caswell and seven others followed the aide down the hall of the Capitol building in Jefferson City, Missouri. They were in the Capitol on the last day of the 1994 legislative session because of a bill known as the Missouri Public Safety Law. Under existing Missouri law, it was a felony for a citizen to carry any sort of concealable weapon for protection, either on his person or readily available in a vehicle. The only exemptions were for police officers, judges, and officials authorized to execute process.

This law had been passed in 1874 during Reconstruction, and had obviously been designed to keep former slaves from being able to protect themselves. Prior to 1967, no white person had ever been arrested for violating this Missouri law. Al Goodman had explained this to Walter Bowman when Walter and his son Henry had come into Goodman's For Guns in May of 1963.

In the three most recent decades, however, all the other Jim Crow laws in Missouri had been stricken from the law books, and blacks had been elected and appointed to many positions of power in the state. Gradually, the prohibition on self-protection outside the home was applied to all Missouri residents, not just minorities. By 1992, Missouri led the nation in arresting people for carrying weapons for protection.

Just before the start of the 1992 session, two well-to-do citizens (who carried police credentials and were therefore exempt from the prohibition) had decided that they'd had enough of waiting for the NRA to do something about the problem. They had hired a lobbyist to help get this last bit of Jim Crow legislation off the Missouri books.

A number of grassroots human and civil rights organizations had immediately thrown their entire weight behind the effort. *Missouri Citizens for Civil Liberties,* the *Second Amendment Coalition of Missouri,* and the *Western Missouri Shooters Alliance* all went into high gear to get the Missouri prohibition on self-defense repealed.

The next groups to throw in their support were business organizations. Under existing law, criminals had a government guarantee that merchants heading to the bank with the day's receipts had nothing except their fists with which to deter robbers. Every Missouri storeowner whose customers paid cash wanted that deplorable state of affairs changed immediately.

Not surprisingly, many women's groups followed suit. These groups had learned that men who commit rape upon strangers were statistically very likely to have spent time in prison and for that reason were likely to carry the AIDS virus. Missouri women knew that following the standard advice to 'give the attacker whatever he wants so he won't hurt you' could easily turn into a death sentence when rape was involved. Suddenly, thousands of women realized what Henry Bowman had told John Parker at Knob Creek: Giving violent criminals a government guarantee that potential victims are defenseless was very bad public policy. Parker had become involved in the issue and had spent much of his own money even though he, too, carried police credentials. Since he still had to work for a living, Parker could not be there for the last day of the session.

Because of the overwhelming support from these varied groups, the Missouri reform proposal had been constantly in the news in the Spring of 1992.

The lobbyist had been utterly baffled at the idea of wealthy citizens spending tens of thousands of dollars out of their own pockets to change a law from which they had already secured exemption. Despite this, he had initially done a decent job of developing strategy and guiding the bill through Missouri's House of Representatives, where it passed by a monumental 3-to-1 margin.

At that point, however, the lobbyist had been overwhelmed by the magnitude of the issue and the depth of police officials' animosity towards the effort. The lobbyist had other clients with strong ties to the police chiefs, and he had resigned near the end of the session.

Missouri law enforcement officials were unanimous in their opposition to the proposed Public Safety Law for three very embarrassing reasons: The first was that no police chief wanted to advocate any anti-crime measure if it undermined his ability to get a bigger budget and/or more authority. The second was that the monopoly on non-uniformed security jobs that off-duty police officers had under the existing law would disappear if the bill was passed. The final reason was that police chiefs in Missouri had spent long years creating the myth that the police controlled the citizenry, rather than the reverse. The last thing police chiefs in Missouri wanted was to have citizens realize that the main difference between private citizens and police officers was that police officers were authorized to arrest people for traffic violations and other misdemeanors, while private citizens could only make arrests for felonies.

The police officials could not make these reasons public, and instead embarked on a campaign of hysteria, claiming that every minor argument was likely to result in a homicide if the law was passed. The chiefs insisted that although doctors, nurses, pharmacists, brake mechanics, bus drivers, cooks, and the like were already entrusted with serious public safety and health responsibilities, these same people would suddenly become seething cauldrons of homicidal rage if allowed to defend themselves outside their homes. The civil rights groups countered that this had not occurred in the thirty-four states which issued permits to their citizens, nor had it happened in Vermont, where no permit for defending oneself was required at all. The chiefs stonewalled.

Many Missourians were offended by the notion that they were not as trustworthy as the residents of other states, but the fix was in. When the bill went to the Senate, the senators claimed they'd have to see the results in other states before they'd consider the proposal, and the Citizens' Self-Defense Act of 1992 never got out of committee.

In 1993, the civil rights groups were without a lobbyist, and through ignorance and other missteps, allowed their bill to get delayed by the senator who claimed to be championing their cause. Once again, the session ended before the Missouri Senate was forced to vote on the proposal. It was in that legislative session that Cindy Caswell first became involved in the issue.

In 1994, things heated up. One of the groups published some of their research entitled *Self-Defense Laws and Violent Crime Rates in the United States*. The document cross-referenced the FBI Uniform Crime Report with the concealed-weapons laws of every state in the union. It also showed the population densities and ethnic composition of each state, and compared the crime rates of states that were similar to each other in all ways except their self-defense laws.

The report came to an inescapable conclusion: States with non-discriminatory laws allowing citizens to carry concealed weapons for self-defense were much safer than those where the citizens were, by law, defenseless when outside their homes.

The Missouri civil rights group also took the trouble to contact the Attorney General in each of the 34 states which issued licenses. The organization asked for documentation as to how many concealed-weapon licensees had been convicted of a violent gun crime after being issued their license. No state AG had been able to provide a single example, and the civil rights group tactfully pointed out to the media that this record was far better than that of any major Missouri law enforcement body.

For Missourians, there were two especially eye-opening things in the report. The first was that the safest state in the union, Vermont, allowed *every* U.S. citizen (not just Vermont residents) to carry a handgun or other self-defense weapon for protection. The fact that Vermont shared a long border with the state of New York made Vermont's low crime level even more interesting.

The second thing that startled Missourians who read the report was the comparison of their state with Indiana. An unspoken assumption among many residents and legislators was that states with high densities of blacks and/or Hispanics could not risk letting their citizens carry guns, especially not without lengthy training requirements and convoluted licensing procedures. The Indiana data blew this theory away.

With the same proportion of blacks and Hispanics as Missouri but double the population density (and therefore double the blacks and Hispanics per square mile), Indiana had only two-thirds the homicides and assaults, and less than half the robberies of the Show-Me state. Furthermore, Indianapolis, Fort Wayne, and Terre Haute did not have the gang problems of St. Louis and Kansas City.

The only significant difference that anyone could find to account for this disparity in crime rates was that Indiana had enacted a non-discriminatory Public Safety Law in 1973. Indiana's concealed-carry license cost only $25 for four years and required no special training. Just as with the right to vote, the Indiana authorities were required by law to issue the license to any applicant who satisfied the objective criteria. Arbitrary discrimination by the issuing body was illegal.

With these facts in hand, the pro-rights groups went back to their senators. In 1992 and 1993, the reformers had been new to the game, and had allowed all sorts of discriminatory elements into the bill in the mistaken belief that it would win support from their enemies.

In 1994, they were a lot wiser, and knew they could win even if every police chief in the state opposed them. The reformers refused to consider $500 fees, police chief discretion, or any other discriminatory measures that the chiefs wanted included in the bill. Their initial proposal, which had strong support, was to adopt Vermont's law: no license at all. Eventually (and reluctantly), they agreed to offer a bill similar to Indiana's law, for there were still pockets of strong racism in the state, and some legislators could not stomach the notion of letting black citizens defend themselves without some form of government regulation.

The theme of the 1994 Public Safety Law was 'I Trust You', and it was very successful. Missouri police chiefs and anti-self-defense politicians were forced to admit that no, they did not trust the people they served.

In the middle of this controversy was a growing awareness among Missourians of the corruption within their law enforcement community. In 1992, the Highway Patrol was found to have set up illegal wiretaps. This revelation utterly baffled most residents of the state, who saw no possible reason how wiretapping related to radar traps. In 1993, the St. Louis prosecuting attorney, who had spent most of his tenure fanatically prosecuting video stores that rented X-rated tapes, was arrested paying a prostitute in a motel room near the airport. He stayed in office for several months after the arrest, refusing to resign even after it was learned that he had paid for many such liaisons with public money and maintained a private phone line in his city office that he answered with an alias to schedule paid sex appointments.

In 1994, the dam broke. The newspapers documented that city cops were systematically extorting money from motorists. The public learned that juvenile history was ignored in the police officer application process, and that many police officers in St. Louis and Kansas City had extensive juvenile rap sheets, including gang affiliations and murder charges. All efforts to force the departments to open the juvenile records of their officers failed, but the public got the message.

Then word got around that one of the officials close to the St. Louis police chief was expunging *adult* criminal records from the system for applicants to the force. The message to the public was clear: Some city cops were still gang members, and the police chief is trying to avoid being indicted.

With the police chiefs utterly devoid of credibility, the only remaining stronghold of resistance to the Public Safety Law within the Missouri legislature was the Governor himself.

Ken Flanagan had been one of several weak Democratic candidates in the 1992 election who had suddenly found himself in the Governor's mansion through sheer Providence. There had been two very strong Republican candidates for the office, and one of them, the state's Attorney General, had outspent his opponent and won the primary. After the primary but before the election, revelations of insurance fraud had been published in the newspapers, and the Attorney General had been indicted. It cost him the election.

Flanagan, as Governor, had backed many socialist proposals that the public rejected, and he was determined not to suffer the additional embarrassment of vetoing the Public Safety Law and then having his veto overridden by the legislature. Flanagan had called in every favor possible to get the senators to vote against the bill, but those in favor were still in the majority.

The Governor's final tactic had been to get an unrelated section of the Senate bill changed slightly from the House version (which had once again passed overwhelmingly), so that when the bill was approved by the Senate it would have to go to conference committee. Then he had convinced the main sponsor of the bill, Senator Gene Brenner, to delay a vote on the bill until the last possible moment. The carrot Flanagan used on Brenner was a quarter-million dollars of money the Governor controlled, which he promised to direct to Brenner's upcoming fall campaign for State Auditor.

It was now 4:30 on the last day of the 1994 Missouri legislative session. Cindy Caswell and other supporters of the bill were calling senators out into the hallway for some last-minute checks on how they intended to vote.

***

"All discussion has been considered on Senate Bill 592," the Speaker of the Missouri Senate announced. "Senator Adams...?"

"Aye."

"Senator Arnold...?"

"Aye."

The Speaker continued down the list as Cindy Caswell and the others sat in the gallery and watched.

"Where are Jackson, Leland, and Wuertz?" Cindy whispered. "They're 'yes' votes."

"In the men's room. They're hiding out. They won't come out 'til the vote's over. That was their promise to the Governor." *Spineless scum* Cindy thought as she shook her head in disgust. The Senate restrooms had several loudspeakers in them wired directly to the Senate chamber. The absent senators knew exactly what they were doing. "Don't worry," the aide whispered. "We've still got the votes without them. These guys are all up for re-election in six months. They'll be history then." The man stopped talking and concentrated on the count. "That's it," he whispered. "It passed."

Cindy Caswell looked at her wristwatch. 5:43. The session ended at 6:00 p.m.

"Seventeen minutes left," she sighed. "Not enough time for the bill to go to conference committee. Looks like the Governor won." One of the others in the group looked at her. He was a big man, with a beard. His name was Arthur Bedderson.

"I don't know about that," Bedderson said slowly. "I think Flanagan may have signed his own death warrant on this one."

Cindy Caswell had no idea exactly how prescient this final comment would prove to be.

June 25, 1994

"In preparation for our landing in New York, please make sure your tray tables are stowed and locked and your seat backs are returned to their full upright position. To speed your clearance through U.S. Customs, please have your customs declaration cards ready to present to the Customs agent, and follow the signs to the proper aisle."

Ray Johnson looked around the airplane as the stewardess repeated the message in German, French, Spanish, and Japanese. He absentmindedly wondered how long it would take three hundred passengers to clear customs. Ray had not been to the United States for many years, and then he had travelled with only a carry-on. He glanced at his declaration card to make sure he'd filled out each portion, then tucked it back in his shirt pocket.

***

"That real?" the Customs agent asked with a scowl as he tilted his head toward Raymond. *Why does he think I might be wearing a toupee?* Ray thought, mystified by the man's question. "Let me see it." The Customs agent waited, and Ray belatedly realized the man was talking about the hat Ray was wearing. The battered bush hat had kept the sun out of his eyes for almost twenty years.

Ray handed the hat to the man, and the agent inspected the worn, dirty, leopardskin band at the base of the crown. "Can't let you in with this," he said with a note of finality. He set the hat on a table behind him.

"Wait a minute!" Ray exclaimed. "What's the problem?"

"Leopards are protected, sir," the agent said with forced politeness. "Whoever sold you this obviously didn't tell you that you can't bring it into the United States."

"No one sold it to me," Ray said immediately, letting his irritation show. "I shot that leopard fifteen years ago. Leopard are not prohibited from being hunted." *There're so damn many of them in some areas, they've cut the trophy fees to encourage people to shoot them* he thought but did not say.

"I am a professional...hunting guide," Ray explained reasonably, in terms he hoped the man would understand. "Surely you've had leopard hides come through Customs before?" The agent nodded.

"Got your paperwork on it?" the Customs man asked in a bored tone.

"For a fifteen-year-old hatband?" Ray asked in exasperation. It was the wrong reaction, and Ray immediately realized his error, but the words were already out of his mouth.

"I'm sorry, sir," the agent said in a tone that made it clear that sorrow was the one emotion he did not feel. "You can talk to my supervisor, but I can tell you right now what his answer will be. U.S. Customs cannot allow this in the country without the proper documentation." Ray took a deep breath, but before he could apologize, the agent added, "Let's take a look at the rest of your luggage." He motioned to the gun cases and the large duffel.

Ray Johnson unzipped his duffel bag and the agent began inspecting his clothes. While the man was doing this, Ray selected a key on his keyring and unlocked the padlocks on his three welded aluminum gun cases. The cases had been made on an Indian reservation in Montana. Henry Bowman had had a set of them sent over after Ray had admired the ones Henry had brought with him on safari in 1978. They bore the luggage tags of several African airlines and all showed evidence of much use. Ray opened the first one, which contained his Holland & Holland .600 Nitro double rifle. The agent was feeling around the foam that lined the case as Ray opened the other two rectangular aluminum boxes.

Finding nothing else in the case, the Customs man lifted the big English rifle out of the foam padding and began to examine it carefully. He paused in his inspection when his gaze fell on the muzzle end. A small smile crossed his lips and he laid the gun down on a table behind him, next to Ray's hat.

"What else we got here?" he said as he moved to the other two cases.

"Winchester Model 70 .458 and another one in .338," Ray said as he opened the first case. The pair of 35-year-old rifles lay facing in opposite directions. The .338 was scoped with an out-of-production three-power Leupold, while the .458 wore only open sights. Both guns were well cared-for but showed the long-term effects of constant use. Again the agent felt around in the foam. After finding nothing, he gave the rifles a brief inspection, left them where they were, and moved on to the third and final aluminum hardcase.

"Semiauto FAL and two Smith & Wessons," Ray announced as he opened the metal container. The inspector stared at the guns.

"Did you buy these guns overseas?" he asked. Ray shook his head.

"No, I've had them since I left the United States in '63."

"Got your registration papers on them?" the man asked. Ray looked blank.

"Registration...?"

"If they were already imported into the U.S. when you left in 1963, I can let them back in, but you have to show proof that they were already in this country." The agent picked up the FAL and the .38 Smith & Wesson and laid them next to the .600 double rifle and the hat on the table behind him.

"You mean you want me to pay import duty on my own guns?" Ray asked. He was starting to get irritated again. The agent smiled humorlessly.

"No, sir. These three guns," he said, indicating the .600 Nitro Holland, the FAL, and the S&W .38 Chiefs Special, "they're prohibited from importation. They're contraband. I can't let them in the country at all, unless you can prove you already had them here in the United States before you left."

Ray Johnson was dumbstruck.

"Contraband? Prohibited from importation?" he said when he finally found his voice. "How is that possible?"

"The Gun Control Act of 1968 prohibits importation of handguns that do not meet certain size criteria. This .38 Smith & Wesson cannot be imported unless it has a three inch barrel on it."

"But it obviously was made in the United States...in Springfield, Massachusetts, to be exact," Ray pointed out.

"That may be, but it is in your luggage and you are getting off a flight from a foreign country. I have to assume that this was a gun that Smith & Wesson sold for export, and you are now trying to import it in violation of the Gun Control Act of 1968." The agent switched his attention to the Belgian rifle on the table.

"This assault rifle has been prohibited from importation since 1989," the Customs agent said with a note of satisfaction.

"No, it isn't," Ray said immediately. "It's not a machine gun—it's the civilian version. It fires semiauto only, just like a kid's twenty-two. I can demonstrate," he added, starting to walk around the table. The Customs agent held up his hand and stopped him.

"President Bush signed an executive order in 1989 banning all imports of rifles that look like military machine guns. We get a lot of people trying to sneak them in in their luggage," he added.

"I'm not trying to sneak anything in!" Ray exploded. "I bought that gun in late 1962, and the serial number will prove that FN made it over thirty years ago!"

"If you can prove you had the gun here in the United States prior to 1989, I'll be glad to release this weapon. Otherwise..." he let the sentence drop unfinished. Ray took several deep breaths, and forced himself to remain calm before speaking.

"And my Holland & Holland double rifle?" he asked finally. "Did the President ban that, as well?"

"There is a ban on the importation of elephant ivory, sir. And I see that the gun has an ivory front sight."

"So you want to take the front sight off my eighty-year-old English gun because the bead is a piece of ivory half the size of a grain of rice?" Ray asked incredulously. One of Ray's last hunting clients, a jeweler from Milwaukee, had offered Ray forty thousand dollars for the rifle when he had seen it. The idea of knocking the front sight off the beautiful Holland and Holland rifle offended Ray greatly. Again the Customs agent shook his head.

"U.S. Customs has a policy of zero tolerance. That front sight is an integral part of the rifle. The whole gun is contraband." Ray saw that the hint of a smile was starting to appear on the agent's face. Suddenly a memory from thirty-five years ago came flooding back. Gene Corson at East Bay Sports in Boston had issued him a warning on the day he had decided to spend his college graduation money on the big rifle, and Ray now recalled his words with almost perfect clarity:

"You got to realize, Ray, a lot of people operate on envy. Guy like that jerk would never spend the money to buy a rifle like this, let alone the cost of a safari, no matter how much he had in the bank. Even if someone gave it all to him, he wouldn't have the nerve to go, which is also why he'll never have any real money in the first place. He works for some steady wage, and always will. Guy like that gets very uncomfortable at the notion of someone who makes things happen for himself. Suddenly he feels like his own life is pretty shabby. Problem is, people like him, they get half a chance, they'll do their level best to screw it up for anyone else. You got to watch out for them all the time. Envy and resentment are terrible things."

Ray Johnson had not practiced law for over thirty years, but his legal instincts finally took over. His face was impassive, and he chose his words carefully before he spoke.

"I see that there are several things that need to be resolved here. As I say, I have been out of the country for some time and was not aware of the current procedures involved with clearing Customs. Will you please put my things aside for a moment and handle some of these other travelers while I use a phone? I think I will be able to produce the kind of documentation or authorization you're looking for."

"All right, sir," the Customs agent said with forced civility. "You can use one of the phones behind you." Ray nodded as the agent shoved his bags to the side and turned on his heel to find the bank of pay phones. There was one person he knew in the United States that he thought might be able to help him.

Ray glanced at the clock on the wall as he stepped up to a vacant phone. *Almost midnight. That's eleven o'clock in Missouri. I hope he's home and not over at some girl's house.* Raymond poked through his wallet and found the slip of paper he was looking for, then dialed the operator and told her he wanted to make a collect call. He heard Henry Bowman pick up the phone on the second ring. He sounded wide awake.

"I have a collect call for anyone from a Mister Raymond Johnson. Will you pay for the call?" the operator asked.

"Yes, I will," Henry said immediately.

"Go ahead," the operator instructed.

"Ray!" Henry exclaimed, sounding not at all sleepy. "Where are you? Here in the States?" Henry knew that Ray was moving back to America, but he had not known exactly when.

"Yeah, I'm at LaGuardia in New York, and I've got a problem. Did I wake you up?"

"No, not at all. Spent all evening doing some geo shock-wave chart analysis, and now I'm down in the shop resizing some bullets before I go to bed. What's the trouble and how can I help?"

"I'm at Customs, and they won't let my guns through."

"Shit," Henry said immediately, but his voice showed no surprise. "You don't have any papers showing you left the U.S. with them thirty years ago, so they're trying to stick you with the duty on them, right?"

"Worse than that. My Holland has an ivory front sight, which the agent says makes the whole rifle contraband—"

"Jesus!" Henry almost shouted. He knew that the .600 Nitro was currently worth more than a new Corvette, and rising in value by the month.

"—And he says they have to confiscate it. Then there's some kind of ban on my FN, so I can't bring that one in either. My Chiefs Special is too small, or something like that, so they have to take it, too. And they're taking my hat," he added.

"That beat-up old thing you always wore?" Henry asked.

"Yeah. That's how this whole mess got started. The man told me he was taking my hat because of the leopardskin band on it, and things went downhill from there." While Ray had been talking, Henry had been scribbling on a pad of paper.

"Okay. Let me get this straight. They're trying to steal your Holland, your FAL, your Smith & Wesson, and your hat. Anything else? Particularly guns?"

"No. The only other guns I've got are two old Model 70s."

"And they didn't say you had to pay duty on them? Claim they were Winchester exports you were bringing back in, or some shit like that?"

"Not yet."

"How many guys did you piss off?"

"Excuse me?"

"Is there a whole division of Customs agents standing over your stuff, rubbing their hands together and telling you you're about to spend the rest of your life in Leavenworth, or have you got one semi-literate GS-three with a high school equivalency degree telling you 'no' because that's his answer to everything?"

Ray Johnson chuckled despite the situation. In the middle of the night, in response to a completely unexpected phone call, his geologist friend was sounding like a lawyer. It was a good sign.

"Ah, closer to the latter, I should think," Ray answered. "I was only dealing with one fellow. He may have gone to get his boss when I went to make this call, but I think he was busy processing some of the other passengers on my flight."

"Good. Okay—first things first," Henry said, thinking rapidly. "Let's look at each thing individually and see what we can do about it. Your Holland is worth forty to fifty Gs, so it's priority number one. Holland and Holland keeps records of all the guns they've ever made, but unless the original buyer was an American, which is possible but not terribly likely, that won't do you any good with the feds here. Didn't you tell me you found that rifle in a Boston gunshop back in the late '50s?"

"Yes. Gene Corson's East Bay Sports."

"I can find out if they're still around, and I can probably locate Gene Corson if he's still alive, and I bet he'd remember that gun even if he doesn't have any records left, so he could sign a statement." Henry took a deep breath and continued. "But that's our fall-back plan, which I'll elaborate on in a minute.

"Number two, your FAL is a Belgian G Model you bought in—what? Sixty-three? Sixty-four?"

"Sixty-two. Before I left the United States."

"Okay. That's one of the early ones that Browning brought in and sold for about a hundred fifty, hundred sixty bucks, right?"

"Exactly."

"Those bring three to five thousand now, depending on whether they're mint or have been beat to shit. I know a guy at Browning, so there's a chance that I can get you the import recor–"

"It's worth *how* much?" Ray demanded in astonishment. Henry laughed.

"Browning brought in a few FALs guns with semiauto parts in them, and had a bitch of a time selling them. Hundred sixty bucks was a lot of dough in '63. That would buy you a Model 70 Match rifle, which was a lot more accurate. If semiautos were your thing, you could have four or five Garands for the same dough, and '06 ammo was more pow-erful and lots cheaper. If full autos turned you on, you could pick up six or eight good ones from Fenwick's or Interarmco for a hundred and a half total, and all of them shot cheap surplus ammo, remember?

"Anyway, that first batch of FALs came in, and it took a long time to sell 'em all. Then, years later, when Browning decided to try to sell a few more, our old friends at the ATF decided the guns were too easy to switch back into machineguns. So FN redesigned the receiver so it wouldn't take the full auto parts without major surgery.

"The guns out of that original batch are legal semiautos with full auto receivers, with Browning's import markings. They get military collectors all excited. They're more valuable than the registered full auto FALs that are in the country.

"The reason Customs won't let you bring it in is because five years ago, King George decreed there would be no more imports of guns that looked like military rifles, even though they couldn't fire full auto. All imports were stopped overnight, and only those factories that were willing to put stupid-looking thumbhole stocks on their guns so they wouldn't look like military issue could resume shipping. Krauts and the Chinese went along with that nonsense, other countries decided the U.S. civilian market wasn't worth the trouble, and said screw it.

"So, they're going to confiscate your G-model, or at the very minimum make you stick on a stupid-looking stock so that it won't look like an FAL any more, unless we can show that it was here prior to '89." Henry sensed that Raymond was about to protest the senselessness of this policy, and quickly went on.

"Don't ask me to justify this crazy shit—I'm just telling you the score, okay?"

"Right," Ray said, and clamped his mouth shut. *He's a hell of a lot more on top of this than I am* Ray told himself.

"Now, your Chiefs Special is on the Customs shit list because of the Gun Control Act of 1968. That law followed in the tradition of the National Firearms Act of 1934 by using physical dimensions as determining criteria for legality."

"What do you mean?"

"The '68 Act decreed that any handguns whose aggregate sum of certain specific dimensions fell below a certain total could not be imported. I forget what the minimum total has to be, but a Chiefs Special with a two inch barrel falls just below it. The same gun with a three inch barrel is okay.

"So what that means is that foreign companies can only import Chiefs Special copies if the barrels are three inches or longer. So what they do is bring in three-inch guns, ship in a bunch of two-inch barrels, switch them in this country, and re-export the three-inch barrels so they can do the whole thing over again."

"That's the most ridiculous thing I've ever heard."

Henry chuckled without humor. "Then you haven't read many of our country's present gun laws. Anyway," he said, returning to the primary subject, "I'm telling you this so you'll understand how you can get that Smith back in the country if all else fails, by swapping barrels. It shouldn't come to that, because Smith might have records showing that gun was not exported." Henry took a breath.

"But personally, I'd let the Customs guy steal it if it would get him off my back about the other stuff. Chiefs are decent guns, but they're less than three hundred bucks, and the quality difference between early-sixties J-frames like yours and present day ones isn't enough to worry about like it is on N-frames. I can have one or a hundred in your dealer's hands in Aspen long before your five-day waiting period is up–"

"What five-day waiting period?"

"That's another story I won't get into right now. Anyway, what I was saying was, unless your .38 was a gift from Grace Kelly in appreciation for letting her blow you, I'd kiss it goodbye without a second thought." Ray Johnson found himself grinning in spite of the situation.

"Which brings me to the most important point concerning your problem. I'm going to make a phone call to a guy I know, a Customs official used to be here in Missouri and now works out of New York, see if he can make all this go away. But I think I can tell you right now what he's going to say, and I'll tell you right now that I agree with it: These government guys have to get something, or they look like idiots, and they hate looking like idiots more than anything in the world." Henry went on before his friend could reply.

"IRS audits you and throws out ten Gs in legitimate deductions, doesn't matter you can document each one five ways, doesn't matter you got twenty thousand more you forgot about and could use to prove they owe you money. Forget it. They will spend half a million bucks, if that's what it takes, to get you to agree to throw out a few lunches and write 'em a check for fifty bucks in taxes and a hundred in penalties. When they challenge you, you have to concede something. It's not their money, but it is their pride. So don't stand on principle over a hat and a .38 Special, okay? Let's get your Holland and your FAL and your Winchesters cleared and let's get you on your way and out of there. You got one guy right now that's about to make your life a nightmare. Let's make it stay at one, and fix the problem before we have to deal with the whole fucking Customs Bureau.

"Let the guy steal the hat and the Smith, if that's what it takes to wave you through. The hat he can turn over to his boss. They'll stick it in a glass case with the banjos made out of turtle shells and the fake Rolexes from Bangkok and show everyone what a great job they're doing, and the agent will get a pat on the back. The .38 Smith he can stick in his pocket, sell on 42nd street for tax-free cash. His boss is happy, he's happy, and you're happy 'cause you get to get out of that shithole and back to Colorado with your good stuff. Everybody wins. Are you with me on this, Ray?"

"Yes, but..." His voice trailed off, not knowing what to say.

"You thought things only worked like this in third-world countries, not America?" Henry asked with a laugh, accurately reading his friend's thoughts.

"Exactly."

"Things have changed a lot since you lived here. Lot more stuff is illegal, which means there's a lot more money to be made if you're the one who enforces the law." There was a pause in the conversation before Raymond spoke.

"Do you really think it'll work?" he asked, getting back to the most pressing issue.

"I have to make a call. Maybe more than one."

"At this hour?"

"Ah, Mike keeps weird hours, same as me. He's probably busy with some girls who want to earn Green Cards. Give me your phone number there, but don't hang out by the pay phone. Go back to your stuff, and don't let it out of your sight. You don't want anything else suddenly appearing in your bags or stuffed down the bore of your rifle, okay?"

"Got it." Ray read the number off the telephone and thanked Henry for helping him.

"I'll get on this, and if I can't get hold of Mike, I'll work on some other angles, okay?"

"Okay. And thanks again, Henry."

"Don't thank me 'til you're out of there with your stuff," Henry said as he hung up the phone.

***

"Hello?" the voice said sleepily.

"Mike, Henry Bowman in Missouri. You awake yet, or you want me to wait while you get your head together?"

"Mm, Bowman, geologist from Missouri who's a gun expert and likes fast trucks. I'm awake, what's the story?"

"Got a pencil? Here's my phone number," Henry said, reciting it. "Call me back on your cellular."

"What do you mea–"

"Come on, Mike, I know the drill. You think I'm a moron?" Henry repeated the number and hung up. In less than a minute the phone rang.

"Okay, what's the deal?" Mike Garland asked after Henry answered the phone.

"I won't waste your time. Good friend of mine's at LaGuardia, returning to the United States after thirty years in Africa as a professional hunting guide. He's a U.S. citizen. Name's Ray Johnson. One of your guys at Customs won't let three of his guns back in the country because he didn't fill out any registration forms in 1963.

"Number one is an elephant gun, made in England seventy years ago that Ray bought in a Boston sporting goods store in 1959. Customs guy's not asking for duty, he's trying to steal the whole gun because of the front sight. It's a piece of elephant ivory about the size of half a grain of rice. Holland and Holland made the rifle that way and they have good records, so we can prove that one's already been imported, we just can't do it instantaneously since they're in London." Henry was bluffing. If the original purchaser had not been an American, it would be very difficult to prove that the rifle had already been in the country, as thirty-year-old sales records did not exist.

"Number two's a Belgian Browning FAL he bought in New York in 1962, now subject to the Bush 1989 ban. Browning only brought in a handful of that model thirty years ago, and Fabrique Nationale's records are impeccable, so we can prove that one, too, but again, not this very second since FN's in Belgium." This claim was slightly more accurate than the previous one.

"Number three is a .38 Smith & Wesson Chiefs Special. Gun has a two inch barrel, which is in conflict with the import section of the Gun Control Act of 1968. Serial number will prove that it was made before 1968, and Smith & Wesson records will show that it was not part of any export shipment. Take me a few days to get my contacts at the factory in Massachusetts to copy the documentation." Proof on the S&W would be easiest of the three to obtain.

"Last item is the hat my buddy's worn for–"

"His hat?" Garland broke in.

"Right. Ray's a professional hunter, and it's got a leopardskin hatband. The man's guided maybe two hundred leopard hunts in the last thirty years, and he cut a piece of hide off one of his clients' skins, a torn-up section by the exit wound. Been on his hat ten years or so, but he doesn't have any papers, of course.

"So here's the deal: I know the way this works, which is why I had you call me back on a cellular, in case the internal affairs guys had your place wired. I'd like you to call the airport, talk to the agent that's holding my buddy up. Tell your guy he can confiscate the hat, and the .38 revolver, if he'll let Ray through with his other guns. Otherwise, we'll get documentation on all the guns, make your agent go through a bunch of busy work, and leave him with just the hat. Okay?"

"Wait a minute, Henry," Garland said over the mobile phone, "if he can show that all his guns have already been in the United States, then there's no reason he can't get all of them through Cus–"

"Mike," Henry interrupted, speaking slowly, "I know the way this works. I'm trying to save everyone some time here. My friend Ray Johnson is a lawyer. He hasn't practiced in thirty years, but he's still licensed in New York and he still has friends at the silk stocking firm where he used to work. Just think of the .38 as an out-of-court settlement. Or a gesture of goodwill, just like my suggestion about the phone.

"If the guy at the airport wants to be a prick and make Ray miss his plane and have to get a hotel, fine, but he'll eventually get all his guns back. If you tell him to let him go now, your guy can keep Ray's .38 as consideration for expediting his clearance, okay?

"But Mike? As we speak, Ray is watching his guns. There is *no way* that any drugs are going to miraculously appear inside any of them, as can happen sometimes with vehicles. Particularly expensive, fast, German vehicles. Okay?" There was a long pause, but Henry remained silent.

"I'll see what I can do," Garland finally said. Then he hung up.

***

"Jesus Christ, what did you do?" Ray demanded over the phone. "The guy at Customs waved me through with everything."

"Some days you win," Henry replied. "What are you going to do now?"

"I left my ticket open, since I wasn't sure how long it would take to get through everything. Got to go find a flight to Denver now, but I wanted to call you back, first."

"Go to the TWA desk and see what they've got for St. Louis—that's their hub. Stay here at my place for a day or two before you head for Colorado," Henry offered.

"You sure that's all right?"

"I live alone, and by the time your plane arrives, I'll have this stuff all done for the driller. Find the next flight, and before it leaves, call here and leave me the flight number. Doesn't matter what time it gets in, just grab the next one out. If I'm sleeping, the recorder will be on and you can leave a message, but I'll be there to pick you up. I'll call the airline to make sure when you're getting in, then meet you at the airport."

"Well...okay. I'd like that."

"See you tomorrow, then," Henry said, and broke the connection.

June 26, 1994

"Better put your seatbelt on, Ray," Henry said as he pulled out of the airport parking lot. "Cops'll write us up if they don't see your shoulder belt across your chest. Which reminds me—how much cash you got on you?" Henry Bowman's serious tone was much different from the delighted welcome he had given his friend when he met him at the baggage claim.

"About eight thousand," Ray replied with a baffled look as he fastened his shoulder belt. "Why do you ask, and what do you mean the cops will 'write us up'?"

"Lot of states, including this one, it's a crime to drive or ride in a car without wearing a seatbelt." Henry pressed several buttons on a welded steel box bolted to the floor of the GMC and lifted its lid. "Give me your dough so I can put it in here. If we get stopped, they'll have to get a search warrant to cut this open."

"You're welcome to put this in your box," Ray said as he held out the roll of bills, "but why is it necessary?" Henry did not answer the question, but instead glanced at the face of one of the bills and pulled onto the entrance ramp to the highway.

"I hope you don't have a lot more like these. These are the old ones—the ones the banks are destroying. Don't deposit many of these, or they'll write you up, and God knows who'll be at your door next."

"What are you talking about?" Ray asked, utterly confused.

"Turn on the overhead," Henry said as he put down Ray's money, reached into his right pocket, and pulled out his own money clip. With one hand he slipped the clip off the folded cash and selected a bill that felt nearly new. He glanced at it, and saw that it was a twenty. "Find one of the freshest-looking bills in your roll," Henry told his friend. "Hold it up next to this twenty, about five inches from your nose."

"Yeah...?"

"All right, the light isn't the greatest, but do you see a thin line around the outside of the oval around the portrait of Jackson? It's on my bill, but not yours." As Ray examined the bills, Henry took the remainder of Ray's large roll of cash, dropped it into the metal box, and closed the lid. The box locked automatically.

"Yeah, I see the line you mean."

"Okay, my eyes are better than normal, and most people need magnification to see it, but that line is actually the words 'THE UNITED STATES OF AMERICA' repeating over and over."

"I can't make that out with this weak dome light."

"That's okay. You can see it later. That's the first change. Hold the two bills up to the light and you'll see the second change. Look at a spot about an inch from the left-hand side of each one."

"There's a strip running through yours, about a tenth of an inch wide," Ray said immediately. "Looks like it's actually inside the paper. It says, 'USA TWENTY', both normally and inverted mirror image."

"Right. The official explanation for those changes is that they make the bills much more difficult to counterfeit. And that's absolutely true. It would be a cast-iron bitch to duplicate those changes exactly. Those two changes have received minor mention in the press. Everyone hates counterfeits, and the money doesn't look any different, so nobody cares. It's no more of a change than switching to the current Secretary of the Treasury's signature, like they do with every new series."

"But...?"

"But there's a third change. The supermarkets in Johannesburg have those scanners that read the funny black lines on packaged products, don't they? The ones where the checker just drags the box of laundry soap over a glass plate, or points a plastic gun at it, and the description and price pops up on a screen?"

"Yes, we've had those for several years."

"Those machines mostly work on optical bar code recognition, but it's all the same kind of technology. That strip you found in my twenty is magnetic, and it has a magnetic code embedded in it. That's fact, not rumor," Henry said forcefully.

"If you run a magnetic code reader over any bill, five dollars or larger, Series 1990 or later, you will get a unique reading. If you run the magnetic reading over another bill of the same denomination, you will get another unique reading.

"In 1985, if you wrote a $5000 check for cash, you'd get four or five different series, and generally one or two bills from the 1930s. Do that today, and I guarantee you there won't be a single bill older than 1990 in the pile except ones and twos. Take fifty crisp pre-1990 bills in for deposit, and have a friend behind you in the same line hand the same teller a check for cash in exactly the same amount as the money you just deposited. Your buddy won't get a single one of your bills back. The banks have orders to turn in all pre-1990 bills regardless of condition."

"So the United States government is now able to track the actual flow of cash..." Ray thought aloud.

"Not only that, but I told you that was a magnetic strip, right? Guess what happens if you have a bunch of bills together."

"They set off magnetometers at airports!" Ray exclaimed.

"Bingo."

"But what does that have to do with storing my money in your lockbox inside your car?"

"Nothing at all. I did that because of the seizure laws," Henry explained as he exited the highway onto a four-lane state road. "Cops are seizing property without bringing charges, and their favorite property to seize is cash. Way it works, cops stop a car—or for that matter, a guy walking on the street. They confiscate his wad, say 'Prove you got this legally if you want it back', and let him go with no arrest."

"That's absurd!" Ray exclaimed, thinking immediately about the $50,000 worth of rifles in the back of the vehicle. "Where's due process? Where's their probable cause?"

"If they see a bulge in a guy's pocket, that's their probable cause for a search. People who pay for things with cash—like us—are now assumed to be criminals. And the car stop doesn't have to be for a seatbelt. All the cops have to do is say the vehicle fit a 'profile', and that was why they pulled it over. This car? Hell, the latest ghetto craze is small trucks and four-wheel-drives with alloy wheels and low-profile tires. That's enough to stop this thing and search it, especially at four in the morning.

"And since the person isn't charged with anything, just the property, the prosecution doesn't have to prove shit. The owner has to prove he didn't get the money or the car by illegal activity. Cops are seizing cars all the time now. They see one they like, they'll pull it over, 'find' a little something in it, and seize the vehicle. Tell you you're lucky they aren't charging you with something serious. Then, if you ever manage to get your car back, you'll discover it's junk because they've used it to haul stuff, left it outside with the windows open, never changed the oil, et cetera."

"You can't be serious! Who would stand for that?"

"Everyone. This isn't some secret I'm telling you about. There was a front-page article a while back in *USA Today*, which is our national newspaper sold on every street-corner in the country. Big write-up on all the abuses. Gave a bunch of examples. All white guys, by the way.

"My favorite was a man with a wood-splitting and equipment business who likes to fish. He carries cash when he goes on fishing trips in case he finds any deals on used equipment along the way. Cops stopped him in his pickup for five over, saw the bulge in his pocket, found eight Gs, so they searched his whole truck. Wasn't so much as an over-due library book, but they kept the cash, and he still doesn't have it back." Henry laughed humorlessly. "So they do this big article, but they might as well have been reporting the weather. Nothing changed."

Ray Johnson said nothing. What his friend was telling him seemed difficult to believe. Ray looked at Henry and saw him smile humorlessly and nod towards the front of the car.

"And speak of the Devil..." Henry said with a sardonic chuckle. Up ahead on the right shoulder of the highway were seven police cars, all with their lights flashing. A uniformed officer was waving a flashlight, motioning the car ahead of them to pull over. Henry slid in behind the Oldsmobile and braked to a stop.

"What the hell's this all about?" Raymond asked.

"'Safety Check' is what they call it," Henry replied. "They stop everyone, see if they're wearing seatbelts, look for open liquor bottles, sniff the driver's breath, check out the inside of the car, all that. Just keep your hands in plain sight and act like nothing's going on," Henry advised as he pressed the button to lower the driver's side window, then put both his hands back on top of the steering wheel.

"Good morning, gentlemen," the Missouri Highway Patrolman said with an air of superiority as he swept the beam of his flashlight around the inside of Henry's GMC.

"'Morning, officer," Henry said, breathing heavily in the man's direction so that he could immediately know that Henry had not been drinking.

"Been to the airport, I see," the man said.

"Cheapest fares are at the worst hours," Henry said with a smile. The officer nodded.

"Drive safely," the patrolman commanded, and waved his flashlight to send Henry and Raymond on their way. Henry checked his mirror, cut the wheel, and accelerated back onto the highway.

"I don't believe what just happened," Ray said after Henry had rolled up the window. "I can't believe anyone here stands for it. They sure as hell wouldn't in South Africa."

"The hook they use is drunk drivers," Henry explained. "There's all sorts of people keep harping on drunk driving and demanding all sorts of shit: lower blood-alcohol level limits for drivers, mandatory jail time for convicted DWI offenders, legal liability for bar owners, legal liability for distilleries, you name it.

"The interesting thing about it is that the death rate from DWI cases is lower than it's ever been. It's been declining every year for several decades. I don't know the exact figures, but when you left the country, back in the early 'sixties, the rate was three or four times what it is today. Does that make sense? You have a condition that you seem to accept, then after three-fourths of the problem goes away by itself, then you declare a crisis, and toss out the Constitution?" Henry shook his head, as if to clear it.

"Now, I'm an alcoholic who hasn't had a drink for more than twenty years, but twenty years ago, I drove drunk, and I remember what it was like. I don't mean to sound like an advocate for drunk driving, but I don't think drunk drivers as a group have worse vision, reflexes, and motor skills than eighty-year-old sober drivers. Fair number of fatal accidents are caused by old people having strokes and heart attacks behind the wheel." Henry heard Ray draw his breath in sharply at this comment.

"No, I didn't forget about your parents. I'm sorry if I was tactless, but my point is that I expect to have to watch out for that kind of thing. I don't want to live where jack-booted lackeys stop cars with white-haired drivers and make them get out and demonstrate their reflexes, and if they're slow or clumsy, arrest them."

"Is that why everyone drives so slowly?" Raymond asked.

"What do you mean?"

"Well, it's four in the morning, there's only a few cars around, we're on a four-lane highway, and I don't see anyone going over about fifty. Are they all worried about these random stops?"

Henry laughed. "They're driving fifty-five, Ray, because that's the national speed limit."

"Fifty-five miles an hour on a road like this?" Ray Johnson almost yelled.

"That's right, Mister Van Winkle, sir. Thirty years ago, seventy-five was fine in a solid-axle car with drum brakes, a single master cylinder, lousy steering, no seat belts, and tires with a little more grip than the ones on a shopping cart.

"Today, most cars have rack-and-pinion steering, four wheel discs with anti-lock, and will stop from eighty in the rain quicker than a '58 Mercury would in the dry. The tires have gotten so good that this truck will go through a slalom course faster than a big-block Corvette could in the '70s. We've got dual air bags, more impact protection, and car phones to call in accidents and other road hazards so we don't need nearly so many highway patrol cars driving around. So the fifty-five makes perfect sense."

"But...why?" Ray asked in utter bewilderment.

"The law was passed in '73, supposedly to save gas during the 'energy crisis'. Any state refusing to comply didn't get any federal highway funds, which nobody bothered to realize was our own money the feds were so graciously returning to us.

"So they all shut up and spread their legs, 'cept one or two states that got creative. I'd've liked to've seen Missouri say 'fuck off' and raise the limit to eighty, but our legislature loves federal power even more than most state governments do. Montana, which had no daytime open-road speed limits at all went along with the law, then said that under a hundred, you were guilty of 'wasting a natural resource', but not a moving violation, and the fine was five bucks. Gave the cops a stack of postpaid envelopes so the driver could just stick a five in it and be on their way. Nevada had no open-road limits day or night prior to the fifty-five, and I hear cops there pretty much ignore speeders. I haven't been there since '68.

"Anyway, the country endured this nonsense for about ten years or so, and a giant new consumer electronics industry was built around ever more effective radar detectors. Made Mike Valentine a multimillionaire, and he deserved every penny.

"Then, after a lot of pressure, the feds decreed that sixty-five was okay, but only on interstates and even then only on sections way the hell outside of cities. Never mind that the whole point of the interstate system was uniform, limited-access roads to allow safe, fast travel everywhere, and the roads were all engineered for a safe seventy-five in cars built in the late '50s." Henry quit talking for a few moments, then made a final comment on the subject. Raymond thought he sounded almost apologetic.

538

"Normally, I'd drive a little faster than I am right now, 'cause I carry police creds that'll usually get me some professional courtesy. But the guns you got in the back would bring twice what this GMC is worth, and you've already had them almost stolen once today. I don't think we should tempt the cops any more than we have to. They're greedy enough as it is."

Ray Johnson nodded.

***

"Let's leave your bags in the car until I show you your room," Henry said, sniffing. "I think Allen's cooking something." He ushered his friend into the back door of the house. Ray brought his carry-on bag with him as they stepped into Henry's kitchen.

"Hope you guys want breakfast," Allen Kane said. "I made enough for about five people."

"I hadn't expected you up this early," Henry replied. "Yeah, it smells great. Ray, this is my friend Allen Kane from Indiana. He's on his way to a gun show in Reno, and stopped here yesterday so we could shoot a little. Allen, Ray Johnson."

"Pleased to meet you," Kane said as he put down the spatula and shook Raymond's hand. "I've seen Henry's pictures and video footage from Rhodesia. You gave him the best hunt I've ever heard of." Ray smiled at the compliment as he reached into his bag and pulled out his shaving kit. "I wanted to get going early, so I thought I'd get breakfast done before you two got back from the airport. Grab a plate."

"Need to take one of these asthma pills first," Ray said as he unzipped the battered leather kit.

"You've got asthma?" Henry said, glancing over from the counter where he was pouring himself a glass of juice.

"Real mild case, acts up once in a while, mainly when I change climates."

"I guess we are all getting older, come to thi—Holy *Shit!*" Henry almost shouted. "You went through Customs with *those?*" His eyes were wide. "And had them in the car with us?" he added unnecessarily.

"What?" Raymond asked, as his eyes went back and forth between Henry and the flat cardboard box in his hand. "These? They're just over-the-counter antihistamines, made by an international drug company. Just like aspirin."

Henry shook his head. "Not here they're not. That's Clenbuterol, and it's a controlled substance in this country. Might as well be cocaine. If the customs guy had noticed it, you'd be in a cell right now. If that Highway Patrol guy that stopped us had found it, my car and all your guns would be gone forever. They would have been used in the transportation of a controlled substance, and taken under the seizure laws." Henry took the package from his friend's hand, pulled the plastic heat-sealed packet from inside it, and handed the pills back. Then he began to methodically tear the pasteboard box into tiny pieces and drop them into the garbage disposal. "Grab a plate and I'll tell you about it while we eat." He picked up his glass of juice and went on.

"Whole story: A few years ago, this guy named Bill Phillips, out in Colorado, had a newsletter he put out for athletes. He gave them straight, unbiased information on nutrition, natural supplements, and drugs, as they related to strength training, using empirical evidence instead of opinion. Had a lot of info on various anabolics.

"Then the DEA reclassified anabolic steroids, and put them in same category as cocaine, LSD, hashish, and all that. All of a sudden, to get anabolics, instead of having your doctor or vet write a scrip for you and going to a drugstore and buying something made by a drug company like Merck or CIBA-Geigy, you had to deal with the same people that smuggle crack. And you were probably getting God-knows-what, brewed up in a filthy garage in Mexico and stuck in a used bottle with a counterfeit label. Anabolics are much harder to make than amphetamines, so 99% of the stuff coming in had no steroids in it at all, just bathtub speed, which is a hell of a lot harder on your system.

"The only guys getting the real stuff made by real drug companies were the people that had enough dough to be wired in to the feds, like pro football players, pro wrestlers, and pro bodybuilders. So this newsletter writer began to dig into obscure medical papers, trying to find any info on over-the-counter stuff like caffeine, or aspirin, or whatever, that documented side effects that would be of interest to athletes.

"And guess what? He found this clinical test on a European over-the-counter asthmatic called Clenbuterol. Clembumar, in South America. The report noted that patients who took the drug, in addition to having their bronchial passages dilated, also experienced increased fat loss and a slight gain in lean muscle mass. Not much of a gain, but a detectable one. Athletes started to use the stuff, since it was made by a real drug company and it didn't screw up your system like caffeine or other stimulants. So DEA reclassified it. Now it'll get you sent to prison in this country."

"Unbelievable."

"Was probably a good thing you had that hat on, to take the Customs guy's attention away from your shaving kit." Henry turned to Allen Kane. "Ray had a little run-in with Customs over his leopardskin hatband, then they tried to steal his Holland, his G-model FAL, and his two-inch Chiefs Special 'cause he didn't have proof he'd bought them here before he left the States. Had to call in a favor with a supervisor I know in New York. Told him to let the agent keep the hat and the .38, but Mike yanked his chain, I guess, and Ray got through with everything." Allen Kane nodded, then scowled.

"What was wrong with the Chief? Oh, that's right—short barrels can't be imported after '68, 'less you bring 'em in with long barrels and swap the parts after they're here. Let me take a look at that G-model after we're done eating," Allen said to the new guest. "See if you got a real early one."

As the three men devoured the biscuits, Canadian bacon, fresh cantaloupe, scrambled eggs, and orange juice, Allen Kane asked Ray about hunting in Africa. From Kane's questions and comments, it became apparent to Ray Johnson that although Allen Kane had never hunted big game, he was even more expert than Henry Bowman on firearms design. Like Henry, he lived on a property where he could shoot whenever he wanted to, and he fired large quantities of ammunition almost daily.

"As you know, Ray, I'm licensed to deal in machine guns," Henry explained to the professional hunter. "Allen here has a license above that. He's a destructive device manufacturer and DD ammo manufacturer. I do a decent business selling squirt guns to police departments and rich collectors, but it's still only part-time. Allen really does it as a business, and he knows more than anybody in the country about making machine guns and cannons work right. He reworks stuff for the Secret Service, does swaps with the Enfield Pattern Room in England, you name it. Last year he did a big demo where he showed one of the SEAL teams how a bunch of foreign belt-feds worked, ones they hadn't been able to get to fire more than two shots straight. They thought it was a miracle." Kane laughed and shook his head.

"Fat lot of good it's done me. I can't even get this goddamned Israeli .308 ammo cleared. I wish someone on the SEAL team could call Imports branch and tell them we're all on the same side. Maybe hurry them up a little. It's been six months, for Christ's sake."

"What's the problem?" Ray asked.

"It's AP," Kane said, in a tone that showed he thought his two-word answer was sufficient explanation.

"And...?" Ray said, raising his eyebrows.

"Allen," Henry broke in, "Ray's been out of the country for thirty years. There've been a lot of changes since '63 that don't make sense to him."

"Thirty *years?* Shit, you must think you're on a different planet!" Kane exclaimed. "Okay, AP ammo—better give you the whole story." Allen Kane took a final bite of biscuit, wiped his mouth, and leaned back in his chair.

"Ever since '34, and especially since a little after you left, there's been a push to ban guns, put more restrictions on them, all that crap, on a federal level. Lot of shit has gone through, but of course not as much as the Big Government folks wanted.

"Then, back in the early 'eighties, a couple of politicians who'd had some of their proposals shot down decided to take a different tack and focus instead on the ammunition. But they needed a hook. Like 'Saturday Night Specials' in the 1970s and 'Assault Rifles' in the late 1980s, the fuckers knew they needed some evil-sounding term to describe a type of inanimate object that would fail their straw-man test of 'sporting purpose'. The phrase these jerks settled on was 'Cop-Killer Bullets'. Once they got that label into common use, they were home free. Who could oppose a ban on bullets that were specifically designed to kill police officers? Only dangerous lunatics, right?" Kane leaned back and took a drink of his Coke.

"Once they had set the terms," Henry broke in, "the prohibitionists then set about to define which bullets were 'cop-killers', and which were not. The beauty of this strategy was that once the legislation was passed—and it was—the definition of the types of bullets that were banned could be broadened by BATF decree, bypassing the annoying legislative process. It was like putting atheists in charge of deciding which religions are acceptable to practice."

"Of course," Kane threw out, "the way the news played it up, everyone who watched television got the idea that criminals were regularly killing vest-wearing cops by shooting them with exotic ammunition specifically designed to shoot through police body armor." Kane laughed. "Fact was, at the time the stupid 'cop-killer bullet' ban was passed, there had never been one documented case of a police officer wearing body armor being shot through his vest, let alone killed." Henry nodded vigorously in agreement, then broke in again.

"Any thirteen-year-old in science class could tell you that basic physics made the entire argument ludicrous for two reasons. First, and as you well know," Henry said, looking at Ray, "in a given caliber at a given velocity, you can trade expansion for penetration, but you can't increase both. Say for example a standard .44 Magnum round will cut maybe twelve layers of Kevlar. It depends on the particular weave, but say it'll go through twelve, and fifteen layers will stop it. An enthusiastic twelve-year-old with an icepick can zip right through thirty layers of the same material, no sweat." Henry raised his eyebrows and continued.

"So now you, Mister Exotic Ammunition Manufacturer, decide you're going to load some armor piercing .44 mag ammo. What do you do? You give the .44 bullet more penetration by making it more like the icepick: sharp and pointed instead of blunt, and made of a hard, non-deforming material like steel, titanium, or tungsten, instead of soft and malleable copper and lead. You decide to go whole hog and make centerless-ground, sharpened tungsten bullets, then coat them with Teflon so they won't ruin the barrel. Using your $5-a-round superduper ammo, the .44 will penetrate a 15-layer vest but not an 18-layer one. Big change, right, and on top of the huge cost, your new, pointy, non-deforming bullet is much less deadly when it hits flesh, because it causes much less trauma than a bullet that's either blunt, or designed to expand on impact."

"And the second reality," Allen Kane broke in, "is that any bullet, regardless of its construction, will go through all known soft body armor if it's going fast enough. Henry's got some .38 Special ammo he loaded with plastic bullets and a bunch of Winchester 230. They're so light, they won't even go the length of a football field, fired like this," Kane said, demonstrating by pointing his right index finger at a forty-degree angle.

"Yeah, and at five feet, fired out of your little two-inch-barreled Chiefs Special," Henry broke in, "they'll chop a dime-sized hole in a vest rated to stop a .44 Magnum. Velocity's the key. Doesn't matter what you make the bullet out of."

"Which is why every modern rifle round will shoot through both sides of a typical vest, regardless of what the bullet's made of. Hell, the .243, .270, 7mm Magnum, .338, .375, and .458 loaded with goddamned softpoints will cut half-inch steel plate, for Christ's sake. Half-inch steel's a lot more bullet-resistant than any soft body armor I ever saw."

"So...what are 'cop-killer bullets'?" Ray asked. "For legal purposes, I mean."

"Legislators decided that for legal purposes, AP ammo would be defined as any handgun ammunition loaded with bullets that were primarily composed of any metal harder than lead or copper," Henry answered. "Sale of this ammo was then restricted to law enforcement entities, like the ATF agents who shot each other down in Waco, Texas. They were using MP5s loaded with some steel 'Cyclone' rounds made up for a government contract."

"Which they shot each other with while diligently trying to execute ninety members of a religious group," Kane threw in.

"Over a suspected $200 tax liability," Henry added.

"I read about that," Ray said, nodding.

"Wait 'til you see the footage the news crews shot before the feds made 'em move back a mile," Henry said meaningfully. "Anyway, back to the AP bullet thing. Way the law's written, federally-licensed dealers, even those like me who are authorized to deal in machine guns, are looking at a $250,000 fine and ten years in prison if we sell one round of pistol ammo loaded with a steel bullet."

"That's ridiculous."

"Yeah, but it gets worse," Allen Kane said. "One by-product of the whole mess was the news people gave a postgraduate education to all the violent criminals in this country. Most of them didn't know so many cops wore vests, 'cause most of the vests out there are made by New Lease up in Michigan, and they make the most comfortable vests, that don't show when you wear 'em under your clothes."

"Yeah, that's Dave Richards' company. He's always told everybody, 'If they see the armor, they shoot for the head.'"

"Which is exactly what all the bad guys started doing," Allen Kane interjected. "Press told 'em all the cops were wearing vests, which was actually a crock, since lots of cops leave 'em in the trunk even if they've got 'em, but the bad guys believed it, and started shooting 'em in the head."

"What does this have to do with your .308 ammo?" Ray asked immediately.

"This is where it goes from stupid to insane," Henry said, "and lots of people, me

542

included, think this was the main plan all along. ATF started adding rifle ammunition to the ban list. Every time the ATF discovered a single example of a handgun made to fire a rifle caliber, all steel-cored ammunition in that caliber became *verboten*. Some guy built a single shot handgun on an XP-100 action for long range shooting in .308 Winchester, and when the ATF found this out in 1983, all importation of steel-cored military .308 ammo was halted, and selling a single round of it suddenly became a felony."

"Same thing happened to 7.62 x 39 rifle ammo ten years later," Allen Kane added. "In 1993, despite everybody begging them to scrap the idea, the dumb cocksuckers at Olympic Arms in Washington State built several prototypes of a five-pound repeating 'handgun' based on one of their AR-15 type receivers. So ATF immediately put that caliber on the ban list, for any ammo that had steel cores. Which was ninety percent of the stuff coming in the country."

"And the only reason the steel-cored ammunition was made that way was because steel's cheaper than brass or lead," Henry explained. "Which was why the stuff was loaded in steel cases, too."

"There's some lead-core stuff out there," Kane went on, "and it's much deadlier. Goes through vests like cardboard, just like any high-velocity rifle round, and fragments inside the wearer. ATF didn't give a fuck about that. They were the experts. They said one pistol made it a pistol caliber, so it was banned."

"The only exemption to the 'cop-killer bullet' ban, like the immunity from most laws, is for government and law enforcement transactions," Henry Bowman explained to Ray, who was still looking baffled. "And this exemption applies, in some circumstances, to situations where the ammunition is not actually sold to the government or law enforcement agency. And that's where Allen's deal comes in. He's got this deal going that came about because of design work he's been doing on the U.S. M60 machine gun."

"Bottom line," the Indiana man said, "the M60 sucks. It's the worst machine gun ever adopted in the last fifty years by a major army. United States Army adopted it in 1960 to replace the recoil-operated .30-06 Browning 1917 and 1919 models, and whoever signed off on that decision ought to have his balls cut off and fed to him."

"What's wrong with it?" Raymond asked. Allen Kane took a deep breath.

"It's as if someone looked at ten early-design machine guns, and incorporated all the worst features into a new design.

"They took the unsupported bolt and piston post design from a Lewis gun, only instead of using good quality heat-treated steel like on a Lewis, they made it out of soft, shlocky shit that falls apart right away.

"They claim the M60 is based on the German MG42, but what they really mean is it's made out of stampings. That's fine, but the designers left out the MG42's sear trip. Instead of making it so the bolt slaps the sear trip when you release the trigger, and slams the sear into the 'engaged' position, the sear on the '60 is connected directly to the trigger. As you let go of the trigger, the sear tries to gradually engage. The bolt is flying back and forth all the while, hammering the engagement edge. So the sear gets worn immediately, and pretty soon the gun starts running away on you.

"To close the top cover, the bolt has to be cocked. If you try to close it when the bolt isn't, you bend stuff.

"The front sight's fixed and the rear sight's adjustable, which is the exact opposite of what you want on a gun with a quick-change barrel. Put on a new barrel, and your gun no longer shoots where it used to. By the same token, they put the bipod on the barrel instead of the receiver, so you have to carry a spare bipod with every spare barrel, which is stupid.

"There's not enough locking lug area on an M60, so after fifty rounds the gun has ten thousandths excess headspace, which makes it batter itself harder as it fires and causes frequent case-head separations that tie up the gun.

"To compound that problem, the chamber's cut so that the case head protrudes 150 thousandths, instead of the more common 125 thousandths of other NATO caliber machine guns. That means you have to shoot ammo with extra-thick case heads. If you shoot stuff designed for the normal NATO chamber, like all the U.S. ammo loaded for the GE Minigun, the case head blows right in front of the web. That blows the extractor into the barrel extension, and you need a workbench, a vise, and a power grinder just to get the gun apart and the broken pieces out of it.

"If the gun has the right ammo and does keep shooting, then the gas regulator will vibrate off. That's why the factory tells you to safety-wire the regulator, but that means you have to cut the safety wire off every time you want to clean the gun.

"The regulator itself is what they call 'self-adjusting', which really means it does not adjust at all. If it works okay when the gun's dirty, then it flows too much gas when it's clean and the gun beats itself to death. If it flows the right amount when the gun's clean, then there's not enough gas volume when the gun gets dirty, so it quits firing.

"The extractor and ejector springs are weak, so cases drop into the receiver instead of being kicked out. The receiver's tiny, with a side ejection port, so you can't get your fingers in to clear it. John Browning's belt-feds all have big receivers, and they eject out the bottom, so gravity keeps 'em clean.

"On other belt-feds, the cartridge is brought halfway into position in the feed block when the bolt goes back and extracts the round from the belt, and the cartridge is moved the rest of the way as the bolt goes forward to chamber it. On the M60, though, the entire positioning is done on the rearward bolt stroke, and the belt remains stationary as the bolt goes forward. That's why the M60 belt jerks so much as it goes through the gun, unlike other guns that spread out the movement.

"I always point out that a good indication of the quality of any weapons design is the number of different countries that have made it their standard issue weapon. Practically the only countries other than the United States that ever adopted the M60 were ones like Vietnam and the Philippines, where we gave the goddamned things to them. The Australians bought some without us breathing down their necks, probably when they were drunk, but now they've wised up and the '60s are history.

"On the other hand, about thirty countries have outfitted their soldiers with Belgian MAG-58 machine guns and paid for the weapons with their own money. The MAG-58 is basically the receiver of the 1918 BAR turned upside-down and adapted to use linked belts instead of detachable box magazines. Henry likes BARs," Kane added.

"And Allen likes MAGs," Henry threw in.

"Damn right. Field trials showed that the MAG would outlast the M60 by a factor of about forty to one, and about four years ago, the United States Marine Corps said fuck the M60s and replaced 'em with MAG-58s." He paused and drank some orange juice.

"Anyway," Kane continued, "SACO Defense is one of the primary contractors now supplying the Army's M60s, and they want to keep the business. They also want their guns to function better and last longer before breaking. One of the executives at SACO was at Knob Creek in '93. That's a big machine gun shoot in Kentucky. He was at the shoot in 1993, and he saw all the junk M60s that guys had pieced together and registered before the 1986 ban." Kane stopped and looked at Henry. "Does Ray know about how they fucked us in '86?"

"No, but I'll tell him later. Go ahead."

"Okay. Anyway, all of these guns had been functioning even more unreliably than factory-produced M60s, except the two I was shooting. So this guy comes up to me, and he starts asking me how I got them to working so well and I told him tha–"

"Nononononono," Henry broke in immediately. "That's not how it happened." He turned to Ray and grinned broadly. "What really happened was, there's a cease-fire so they can go put out more junk to shoot at, and this guy comes over to where we're shooting, and he says something to Allen like, 'These other people with their rewelded M60 are having all kinds of jams. Your guns must be original', or something like that.

"So then Allen here, being such a diplomatic devil, what does he do? He immediately says, 'Shit, no, mine's not original! The originals are even worse than those other rewelds you see on the line. The design itself is bad enough, but the dumb bastards who built the thing didn't even bother to machine the parts right. I played with the cam angles and changed the timing; mine'll go two, three times as long as a factory-new one before it breaks. If I could try a little different heat-treat on a couple parts, I think I could double that again. It's still junk next to a MAG, but the dumb bootlips at SACO Defense can't even put the sears in right-side-up.'"

Kane was laughing at Henry's imitation of him. "That's right, I did say that to him didn't I?" he admitted. "Well, hell, I didn't know who he was," Allen Kane added defensively.

"And that's when the guy tells Allen that he works at SACO, and he's in charge of quality control, or some damn thing, and would Allen fly up there and show them what to do," Henry added.

"So I go up there," Kane explained, "and I look around, and I tell 'em I need a million rounds of ammo and ten of their guns, and I'll figure out how they can make them better, given the constraints of their tooling. They just about shit when I told them that much ammo for ten guns, and I'm thinking 'Jesus, don't you guys shoot any of this stuff before you ship it out and expect some kid to bet his life on it?' That's when they tell me that all ammunition at SACO Defense is technically the property of the U.S. Government, and can't be released to a private citizen."

"Keep in mind that Allen is offering to do this work for free," Henry threw out, "and at the same time, the government is burning billion-round stockpiles of .308 ammo to destroy it."

"Yeah, and I even offered to return all the fired brass to prove that I hadn't taken the ammo and sold it. They still said no."

"So what did you do?" Ray asked. He found the entire conversation appalling.

"That brings us to the current situation. SACO finally agreed to pay for the test ammo out of company research funds, but I had to get it cheap. So I found some out-of-date Israeli .308 AP for a nickel, delivered. It would go for more than that in this country, except they won't approve it for importation 'cause it's a so-called armor-piercing pistol round, as we were explaining. I've applied for an import permit based on the fact that it will be used for government testing, but it hasn't been approved yet. And I'm not holding my breath."

Ray's eyes narrowed in fury at the whole bizarre situation. *I don't know what the hell I was expecting to come home to* he thought angrily. *But it sure as shit wasn't this.*

***

"I like your friend Allen," Ray told Henry after Kane had left. The two men were sitting in Henry Bowman's study. Ray Johnson looked around the room. Floor-to-ceiling shelves of books lined two walls. On a long table in the corner sat an extensive computer setup, complete with two printers, a flatbed scanner, and an office-quality copy machine. A drafting table stood in the corner.

"I wish he lived closer. We try to get together to shoot every couple months. And there's Knob Creek twice a year, but that's become a zoo, with all the interest in historic weaponry that's sprung up in the last decade or so."

"You work out of your house?" Ray asked, nodding towards the electronic equipment.

"Yeah. All these articles in magazines were saying how everybody was going to start working at home, but I think it's a bunch of crap. If I had a family there'd be no way it could work. As it is, I can turn off the phone and it's just like being in an office.

"But what you see here is typical for lots of people, just for personal use. Take out the extra printer and the drafting table, and swap the copier for something smaller, and you're looking at a setup millions of people use for non-business stuff."

"Are you on this new thing, the...the Internet?" Ray asked, remembering the name he'd heard. Henry chuckled.

"Yeah, but I hardly use it. All this stuff about the 'Information Superhighway' is a bunch of hype. 'Information Cow Path' would be much more accurate. Anybody can send anything anywhere, which is good, but it results in three problems:

"First, unlike making a thousand identical phone calls or addressing and sending a thousand identical letters, you can send a message, long as you want, to a thousand addresses with just a few keystrokes. There's mountains of junk to wade through, and the temptation is to blow it all off.

"Second, assholes take particular advantage of the increased ability to send messages. Sending someone a hostile message is now called 'flaming' him. There's been more and more of that, too.

"Last of all, and partially because of what I just mentioned but mainly because it's in their nature, our old friends the feds are real keen to get into the act. The government has actually proposed that a device called a 'Clipper Chip'—and I don't know where that term comes from or why they call it that—be installed in every privately-owned computer in the U.S. It would have an encryption code in it. To prevent theft, or some damn thing, that's the supposed selling point.

"The thing is, the government would have all the master encryption codes. This electronic gizmo would give the feds access to all information stored in every privately-owned computer in the country."

"*What?*"

"That's right. Sort of like–"

"But that's an absolute violation of the Fifth Amendment!" Ray broke in. "The Fourth and First, too."

"No, it isn't, Ray," Henry said patiently, with a sickeningly sweet smile on his face. "This is for everyone's own good, don't you see? You'll still be able to write things down with pen and paper. You'll still be able to get together and talk about things in private. For now, at least," he added with an evil grin.

"But back when the Founding Fathers wrote the Constitution, they could not possibly have foreseen the advent of computers. They never would have imagined a time when just anyone could express his views to a huge audience, just like they never would have imagined guns that fire more than one shot without reloading. If they had, they never would have written the Bill of Rights so broadly. This 'Clipper Chip' is for our own good, don't you see?

"And besides, now we have the Drug War. The Founding Fathers never imagined huge illegal businesses using computers to hide their money. Why, they never even thought anyone would want to hide their money in the first place—they wrote that old Constitution over a hundred years before we realized we had to have a federal income tax.

"The President himself said last month that we have too much freedom in this country, and we need to look more towards the greater good for our society as a whole." Henry smiled without humor as he watched Ray shake his head in wonder and disgust. "I keep forgetting that you've been gone for thirty years, and this is like stepping out of a time machine for you." He leaned back in his chair. "Nineteen sixty-three," Henry mused as he looked at the ceiling.

"In 1963, I was ten years old. I'd had my first gun, a Winchester semiauto my dad gave me, for two years by then. In the Spring of 1963, Dad bought me my first revolver, a K22 Smith. About the same time, I bought my first centerfire, a 98 Mauser I got from Charley Steen, with money I'd saved up helping Dad with photography work.

"Six months later, my dad, my uncle, and an old friend of our family all got together and gave me the best birthday present I've ever received in my life. Uncle Max gave me this original 5" .44 made on that special run for H.H. Harris in Chicago," Henry said, patting his hip. "Dad gave me a matched pair of Hensley & Gibbs 8-cavity number 503 molds, and Irwin Mann gave me five thousand cases to load. I've still got a few hundred of them, and I guess I've loaded and shot about quarter million .44s since then. No, that's only eight thousand a year, so it would be more than that. Half million, maybe." He took a deep breath, and reflected some more.

"In 1963 and 1964 I was shooting about every other weekend during the school year, and at least every other day during the summer. I don't think anyone else in the sixth grade was shooting as much as I was, but I'd say about half the boys had their own .22 rifles, and at least two of them had handguns. Ted Swenson had a nickeled Smith & Wesson Kitgun and Beau Hadley had a Government Model his dad gave him with a .22 conversion kit in it. He couldn't hit moving targets very well, but that gun was as accurate as any .22 conversion I've seen, and Beau could put the whole magazine on a five gallon bucket at a hundred yards.

"When you left this country, Ray, every time a bunch of gun guys got together in somebody's study like we're doing now, or more likely in somebody's basement, or in a gun shop, they only did one thing: they talked about guns, or reloading info, or going shooting. At least, that's the way it was here."

"Yeah. Same way in Colorado, and Massachusetts, and New York City. I used to hang out at Griffin & Howe, and that's all anyone ever did there."

"That's not what happens now," Henry said simply. "Now they all talk about how to fight the constant onslaught of legislation." He pointed to his computer and printers. "My high-tech electronic stuff over there? In actual fact, I use my word processor, FAX, and modem twice as much to fight for my civil rights as I do for anything that earns any money."

"Really? How so?" Ray asked. Henry shrugged before answering.

"Grassroots civil rights groups have popped up all over the country. Lot of them have computer bulletin boards, and if you've got a FAX line on your computer, you can log in and see what the latest outrage is that your state or national legislators are trying to sneak by. Here in Missouri, we get ten or fifteen bills a year trying to make just about anything involving guns illegal. Every year we see bills that would make it a crime to have a cased, unloaded gun locked in the trunk of your car within a thousand feet of school property. Last year, some kid in St. Louis County got a map and drew a line 1000 feet outside every school boundary. You should have seen what it looked like. Every time you drove somewhere to go shooting, you'd be breaking the law. Legislators didn't give a shit. Same bill comes up every year.

"There's bills that would prohibit owning more than five hundred rounds of ammo. Bills that would make you pay a thousand dollars a year if you own more than ten guns, and make it flatly illegal to have that many if you live in a community of more than 250,000 people. Proposals for ten thousand percent taxes on handgun ammo. Bans on clip-fed semiautos with threaded muzzles, bayonet lugs, or pistol grips, not just imports but domestic guns, too. Bans on the magazines themselves.

"A perennial favorite here in Missouri is a bill that would make it a crime if you ever had a gun somewhere where a minor could gain access to it." He snorted. "So much for teaching gun safety and proficiency to anyone under eighteen." Ray Johnson sat there with his mouth open. What his friend was describing was almost impossible to believe. Henry wasn't looking at him, and didn't notice.

"If you're really gung-ho, like more and more groups are becoming, you get some legislators that understand the issue, and you introduce reform legislation. Take the offensive, instead of always fighting defense. That's what the guys around here have been doing. I give 'em ten thousand or so a year, but that's just a drop in the bucket against all the free ink the press gives our enemies," Henry added sadly. He looked out the window and breathed deeply.

"You know, my grandfather grew up in a farming family at the end of the last century. His family never got a nickel from the government, which I know was exactly as he thought it should be. He worked his way through college and law school, and he saved much of his earnings from his law work. Patent law was his field.

"In the 'twenties, a man came to him who had designed a better plow disc. He was looking for backers. Grandpa knew something about plowing, so he watched the man demonstrate his design, and helped him get the financing. Some of the money came from Grandpa's savings—enough to where he owned about a seventh of this start-up business.

"The company did well. The crash came in '29, but they were still in the black, they had no debt, and since they were a private firm, no one had bought stock on ten percent margin and gotten caught in a short squeeze.

"The big ag products companies were all being hit by the raft of farm foreclosures, and they took notice of this private company that was still enjoying decent sales and making money with a good product that had patent protection. One of them made a buyout offer. This was in 'thirty-two.

"The big company was strapped for cash like everyone else, and its stock price was in the basement. Knowing that, and also knowing that getting the rights to produce the new disc could put the big guys back in the black, Grandpa talked his board into demanding an all-stock deal. That appealed to the buyers, except with the market value depressed, they had to give up more of their company than they really wanted to, but they did it. Grandpa ended up with a little less than one percent of the company."

"What company was it?" Ray asked. "Are they still around?" Henry smiled.

"Yeah, as a matter of fact, they are. Had a name change not too many years ago. Deere & Company. John Deere, to you." He became serious again.

"Point of all this is, whenever the little company made a profit, which was every year except the first one, they paid taxes to the government. When John Deere made a profit, it gave a big part of them to the government, too. Right now their corporate tax rate is about forty percent.

"Now, John Deere, after they pay all that corporate tax, they almost always declare a chunk of what's left as dividends. Guess what? The money gets taxed again. In the '60s and '70s, the rate was seventy percent, both for my grandfather, and then my mother, after Grandpa died. Reagan managed to twist Congress' arm and get the personal rates down to twenty-eight percent, but with the corporate rates thrown in, the feds still got about half our share of the company's profits by the time all the subtracting was done." He stared at Ray Johnson.

"Then Bush caved in and kicked rates back up in '90, and in '92, this new slime bucket succeeds in getting Congress to raise the rates retroactively to before he took office, and–"

"What?" Ray interrupted. "Retroactively? What are you talking about? That's unconstitutional!"

"Tell that to the President," Henry said with a grimace. "You're the goddamn lawyer. I'm just a geologist, so what the hell do I know?" He laughed humorlessly. "Did you just think your ranch had had an especially good year and your deductions were down when you got your last tax bill from your accountant?"

"Actually, that's exactly what I thought," Ray admitted.

"Yeah, well the retroactive section probably cost you an extra few thousand, over and above the time after he took office. Anyway, point I'm trying to make, the feds have taken over half of my family's share of the profits down through the years. But that's just the tip of the iceberg." Henry began to tick off his points using his fingers.

"Taxes on John Deere's profits had already been levied twice each year, once on the corporate earnings and then on the dividends paid out of the after-tax net. Then Grandpa's earnings as a lawyer were taxed every year. Grandpa was pretty frugal, and out of what was left, he bought four residences and several cars over a forty-year period. Then he had to cough up real estate taxes and personal property taxes on those things every single year. Then, every time he sold one house at a higher price than he'd paid because of inflation, he paid taxes on the so-called profit, even though the new house he was buying was even more expensive.

"We haven't even gotten to the big one yet. When Grandpa died, there was estate tax due, and the bill came to forty-seven percent of everything he owned. My parents had to sell off half of everything he had just to cut a check to the feds. The house, all the cash, all the bonds, all the stocks other than Deere, and a bunch of the Deere stock vanished overnight.

"My father died five years later, my mother, ten years after that. In '78, at age twenty-five, I had to go through the same process to settle her estate, only in my case I had to cut a check for fifty-three percent of the value of everything my family owned. Mom had two houses that I sold, but there wasn't much left besides the Deere stock, so almost half of that got liquidated."

"That must have been right around the time you came on safari with me," Ray said after doing some figuring.

"I settled up with the feds just before I went," Henry agreed. "So by now," Henry went on, "the government has taken over half the earnings of the company my grandfather helped build. They've also taken about two-thirds of the value of the company itself.

"On top of that, they take close to forty percent of everything I earn as a geologist and forty percent of all the profits from any successful venture cap deals I finance. On the Deere stock I have left, they take forty percent of Deere's earnings, and forty percent again on the cash dividends I get, which are paid out of what's left. If I want to diversify my investments, or raise capital to finance a start-up business, I better get the money somewhere else. If I sell Deere stock, the feds take about a third of the proceeds right away, since I've held the stock for so long and its value is a lot higher than my cost basis.

"The thing to remember is that during all of these years that we've paid all these taxes to the government, not a single member of my family has received one nickel in subsidies of any sort. We have not gotten a penny from Medicare or Medicaid. We have not burdened the public school system with even one student. My grandfather and father paid in to Social Security for a total of fifty years without drawing a single check. After Dad died, I got his Social Security for seven years, but an average of ninety bucks a month that ended when I got out of college was nowhere near as much as he'd paid in, let alone expecting any interest or growth.

"I figured it up a year or so ago. Totaled up the taxes I've paid to date on earned income alone. Didn't count taxes on dividends or interest or gains or estate tax on inheritance, just earned income. The total was six times the taxes on all sources of income paid by the President of this country and his wife added together. And I'm five years younger than either of them!" he added emphatically.

"I have never lied about my income, or knowingly wronged any person in any way. And you know something, Ray?" Henry said, looking at his friend. "I've paid every one of those taxes without complaint, even when the President announced that people like me weren't paying our fair share of the nation's bills.

"I've been a damn good sport about it, and you'd think the government would leave me alone to make money so they could continue to take half. But instead, they pick the one thing I really like to do, something that's a fundamental right supposedly secured by the Constitution, and they do everything they can to take that away from me." Henry shook his head, and Ray suspected that his friend was not quite finished.

"I've never said this out loud, but you know all those hours I've spent developing my shooting skills? All the money I've spent on ammunition, and club memberships, and on my private range here, and all the time I've spent training other people to protect themselves, including lots of women and police departments, always for free? I think the government should say, 'Hey, Henry Bowman, good job! We want people to be skilled and safe with guns. We want them to be able to protect themselves from harm. We want everyone to be self-reliant. We wish we had more people like you, with good gun skills and a lifetime of experience to pass along to others. Keep up the good work!'

"Instead, they have treated me and others like me with utter contempt. They have confiscated our property and put people like me in maximum-security prisons over ownership of fender washers, claiming they were unassembled silencer parts. Over pieces of muffler tubing. They have shot a man's wife in the head because his gun's buttstock was too short. They beat another man's pregnant wife until she miscarried, over a gun collection on which the guy had done all the stupid paperwork things the ATF wanted, but the feds temporarily lost the records. They burned ninety people alive over a disputed two hundred dollar tax.

"If you believe you have the right to buy, own and shoot small arms in a safe man-

550   *June 26, 1994*

ner, as much and as often as you want, and you exercise that right regularly, our government has branded you as the enemy. They will pursue you more relentlessly and attack you more severely than they do the people who pick up teenage runaways in the bus station and torture them to death on camera for black-market 'snuff' films.

"These statist thugs are zeroing in on the most important thing in my life. Being able to exercise my right to buy guns and shoot them is more valuable to me than all the millions of dollars of mine they've taken. The federal and state governments are doing everything in their power to take away my most important right, and they are doing this every single day." Henry Bowman closed his eyes and shook his head. Ray Johnson scarcely knew what to say.

"What you are describing is much worse than anything I ever saw in South Africa," Ray said levelly. "I have not practiced law here for thirty years. But from a legal standpoint, I would think these things you tell me about would be utterly impossible in this country."

"They aren't," Henry replied. The anger had seeped out of him, and he was left with a pervasive sadness that lay in his body like a deep bruise. "I have never wished ill of anyone," Henry said softly, "but by God I hate these bastards. And there's not a damn thing I can do about it."

Ray Johnson stared at his friend, and his mind went back to 1978. *Sixteen years ago,* he thought to himself, *I watched this man face down a stampede of buffalo with a bolt action rifle because he thought the herd was going to trample one of my trackers, and he did it with a smile. Now he feels beaten by his own government.* Ray opened his mouth, and the words came out without conscious thought.

"When you get to where you start shooting them, give me a call." *Jesus, where did that come from?* Ray thought in astonishment.

"I'm sorry, Ray," Henry said after a few moments, not looking at his friend. "I just unloaded about twenty-six years of anger on you, right there." He smiled and pinched the bridge of his nose. He laughed softly. "I'm not going to do anything like shoot anyone. And if I did, I'd hire a trial lawyer, not a contracts or personal-injury guy who's spent the last thirty years in African hunting camps. No offense."

"I didn't mean I'd represent you," Ray explained slowly. "I was talking about helping pull the trigger." Henry looked at his friend for a long time before speaking, and he chose his next words with care.

"Don't say things like that out loud. Ever. Everyone that's been charged by the feds with some stupid gun-law violation has been slapped with a conspiracy charge on top of it, and that's the one they usually make stick. It's a hundred times worse than the airports—jokes really will get you sent to prison." He looked at his guest for a few seconds, then jumped to his feet.

"Screw it," Henry said suddenly. "I'm being a lousy host. Let's pretend it's 1963 again. I'll show you my shop, then we'll go to my quarry. I've got a gun you'll get a kick out of shooting. Come on." Henry got up and ushered Raymond towards the basement steps, his voice once again full of pleasure and enthusiasm.

"You're going to like my shop," he said happily. "It's one of the best I've ever seen, if I do say so myself."

"What you got going here?" Ray asked as they stood by the smaller of Henry's two metal lathes, a 10" Hardinge. Gripped in the machine's collet chuck was what appeared to be a steel cylinder about 3/4" in diameter with a copper ridge encircling it near the exposed end. In a cardboard box on top of the machine were several more of the cylinders. They were pointed on the other end, and Ray realized they were large bullets.

"Guy at the scrap yard called me when he got in a big pile of fired brass from some military installation. Wanted me to see if there were any I could use before he sent it to the smelter.

"Along with all the fired .50s and Vulcan brass were a couple dozen unfired rounds of U.S. 20mm he told me to take. I've never had a U.S. twenty, but if you pull the bullets and turn the drive bands nine thousandths in a lathe, you can load the U.S. projectiles in the bigger 20 x 138mm case and shoot them in Finnish Lahti or a Swiss Solothurn.

"I wasn't up on what the tip colors meant, especially the newest stuff. I thought these might be depleted uranium, but they're not dense enough for that. They're definitely not ball ammo—there's too many paint bands on the nose. I've been told that some of the newest rounds are spin-armed, and I heard that some of the new explosive rounds automatically detonate in the air after a certain number of revolutions, so our pilots in dogfights don't send stray explosive rounds into our ground troops by accident.

"That would seem to be a fairly complicated mechanism to put in a little 20mm slug, but I don't doubt it's possible. So I spun 'em real slow, like fifty RPM, when I cut the drive bands down."

"Prudent of you," Ray said drily. "So what do you think these bullets do when they hit?" Henry removed the projectile from the Hardinge's chuck, put it in the box with the others, and handed the box to Ray.

"I thought we'd go find out. Take these over by the big loading press on the far end of the loading bench. Solothurn dies are in the rack bolted to the shelf. I'll go dig up some Solothurn brass and the right powder."

"Got it."

The two men began to assemble the ammunition for the old Swiss weapon.

***

"Got your ears on?"

"Have at it."

"Watch the middle of the big limestone boulder. Would look better at night, but let's see if we can spot anything in daylight." Henry Bowman wriggled on his stomach and fitted his right eye to the rubber eyepiece of the big gun's scope and aimed at his target three hundred forty yards distant. He squeezed the big trigger with the first two fingers of his right hand, and the fifty-five-year-old gun thundered.

"Cool," Ray said with feeling. "You got a whole bunch of little flickering things that showered the whole rock. Looked like a bunch of little fireflies. Made a big shower about the size of a one-car garage."

"I caught a little bit of it out of my left eye," Henry said as he turned towards his friend. "I think these must be the 'firestarter' rounds I heard about, from some guys in Desert Storm. They've got thermite particles in them, and burn real hot. Let me pop another one, then let you shoot a couple. After that, I'd kind of like to save the rest for the night shoot at Knob Creek. I bet they look great in the dark."

"You got a great set-up here, with this old quarry."

"Yeah, it's safe to shoot anything. Rock face on the far side catches any slugs that skip off the surface. That's what made me buy the place. Every serious shooter should have his own rock quarry."

"Get any swimmers, or is it all fenced and posted?"

"No swimmers, and yes, it's posted, but that's not what keeps them out. Lawyers warned me about having an attractive nuisance, but it's a funny thing: nobody wants to trespass where there's machine gun fire." Ray and Henry both started laughing.

"Hey, I brought plenty of ball 20mm we can shoot up. Vulcan practice bullets with the drive bands turned down. That stuff's really fun to shoot into the water. We'll go throw some small logs in, see how far you can pitch 'em in the air."

"Sounds like a deal."

***

"Did you actually handload all of these?" Ray asked as he helped Henry collect all the banana-sized fired cases that lay strewn around on the ground.

"Had to. Original surplus twenty mil is almost all gone. Goes for twenty, thirty bucks a round now. I found a huge pile of it in Europe, like five hundred tons, practically for free. Nothing modern shoots it. Only guys can use it are the collectors like us that happen to have one of the few hundred old Lahtis and Solothurns brought in over thirty years ago. Could've bought it for a quarter a round, but Imports Branch turned down the application. Not 'sporting' ammo, that stupid clause they threw in in '68. So I use U.S. practice projectiles that end up on the scrap market after the government demils the ammo, and swage the drive bands down in a die I made. I didn't use the die on the ones today 'cause I wasn't too keen on putting an incendiary bullet under pressure.

"I also have to anneal the necks on the brass, 'cause it's fifty-five years old, and swage the primer pockets in a hydraulic press so I can use .50 primers."

"You load and shoot it a hell of a lot more than I ever did," Ray said, "but did you ever stop to think about how much time and money people like us spend, scrounging components and reworking brass and machining new parts and shit like that, just so we can make the best possible ammo for every different kind of gun we happen to come across, just to blow it out the barrel?"

"Only three or four times a day," Henry said with a grin.

***

"It's *cultural*. That's what I keep telling Henry," Thomas J. Fleming explained as he cut into his steak.

"What do you mean?" Ray thought he knew what Fleming was talking about, but he wanted to hear the man's rationale for what he said. The three men were eating dinner at a private club where Henry was a member. The mounted head of one of the buffalo he had shot sixteen years before hung on the wall over the fireplace.

"People who don't shoot guns have this image of a fat guy in overalls with a sixth-grade education, drinking a six-pack of beer in the front seat of his pickup while driving back from a wedding where two of his cousins married each other. That's what some people think of when they hear 'gun nut', or 'NRA'. Or alternatively, they envision some moron with a shaved head, wearing camo, distributing Klan literature and bragging about how he's going to shoot any colored guy he sees with a white girl. To many people, those two stereotypes represent the gun culture." He took a drink of iced tea and went on.

"Now there are a few of those stereotypes around, but they're just a handful compared to the rest of us. The real members of the gun culture are the kind of people that are sitting at this table." Fleming paused a moment to let that sink in, and then went on.

"You might think Henry here is an extreme example, but you'd be wrong. There are a lot of guys like him. You know what IPSC shooting is, don't you? They hold the world championships in South Africa."

"Sure," Ray answered easily. "Before that, they were in Rhodesia." Fleming and Johnson were referring to the International Practical Shooting Conference. It was an established series of handgun matches where competitors ran through a course and encountered both 'hostile' and 'friendly' targets, designed to simulate real-world situations.

"Right," Fleming said, raising a finger. "Well, there are over fifty thousand registered IPSC competitors in this country. Typical serious competitor shoots between forty and a hundred thousand rounds a year practicing, and his competition gun costs two thousand minimum. You shoot IPSC, Henry?"

"No."

"Me neither. So Henry and I aren't part of that fifty thousand." Fleming raised a second finger. "Handgun silhouette, there's between thirty and forty thousand competitors. They shoot almost as much in practice as IPSC guys. You shoot silhouette, Henry?"

"Entered a couple matches a few years ago, but there's no range around here."

"No to that one too, then. Me, I've never tried it." He raised a third finger. "PPC, Practical Pistol Competition. At least as many competitors as IPSC, at least as much practice, guns are cheaper. You shoot PPC, Henry?"

"Never tried it."

"Nor I. Next we got bowling pin," he said as he raised a fourth finger, "which I know Henry's done, and those guys practice all the time. Then there's bullseye competition, rimfire silhouette, cowboy shoots for black powder guns, and a bunch of other stuff different organizations have dreamed up.

"Mind you now, that's just organized competition involving centerfire handguns. Now we move to rifles," he said as he folded up his fingers and started over. "We got twenty or thirty thousand bench rest shooters shooting dime-sized groups at two hundred yards. We got almost that many in rifle silhouette. We got high power shooters and DCM shooters lying on their stomachs shooting prone. We got a ton of smallbore shooters using rimfires, and we got more rimfire shooters in the GM Sportsman's Truck Challenge. Then there's the centerfire action matches for the semiauto guys, just like IPSC."

"I won one of those with a bolt action last year," Henry said with a smile.

"Show-off. We've also got a bunch of long range black powder shooters like in the Coors Schuetzenfest, plus frontier competitions, and even black powder benchrest.

"Finally, with shotguns, the numbers really go nuts. Skeet, trap, and sporting clays, well over two billion rounds fired last year. There's also crazy quail, plus bowling pin and other combat matches held with shotguns. How many rounds of shotgun ammo did you fire last year, Henry?"

"None."

"How much hunting?"

"None."

"So what we've got to look at now," Tom Fleming went on, "is the biggest part of all: the people like me or like Henry who shoot just to keep their skills up. People shooting just because they like it, without any particular interest in competition." Fleming took a breath, then saw that Henry was about to take over.

"Tom's exactly right," Henry jumped in. "Last year the ammo manufacturers sold over three billion rounds of rimfire ammo. Centerfire rifle and pistol was about two billion. Imports another billion.

"Then there's reloads. I don't have the figures from component companies, but I can make a fair guess. Almost nobody buys U.S. commercial centerfire ammo several cases at a time, but everybody buys primers a few thousand at a whack. I bet there's three or four rounds of reloads shot, minimum, for every factory metallic centerfire round fired downrange. And I haven't even considered shotshells in that estimate.

"So that's—What? Fifteen billion rounds of ammunition fired every year?" Henry asked.

"Sounds right," Tom Fleming agreed. "And this lisping moron in the U. S. Senate wants to put a ten thousand percent tax on it." He shook his head.

"It isn't out-of-work high school dropouts firing all that ammo. It isn't guys with maxed-out credit cards who drink beer and watch sports all the time. It's educated, serious guys just like you, and Henry, and me. We've all got high incomes, or we wouldn't be able to afford to shoot all that ammo. None of us are on the dole. A few gun guys drink, but I don't know a single one that goes to football games or even watches sports on television. Do you, Henry?"

"Nobody I know."

"And if you think back to when you were a kid, I bet almost all your best memories are of when you were out shooting, or talking about it when you were done."

"You're dead-on on that one," Ray admitted.

"Boy, that's the truth," Henry broke in. "I went out to Reno with my uncle when I was in high school. Best time I ever had. Those live pigeon shooters all watched me shoot trap with my .375, and then went with us out in the desert to a cannon shoot. Had a hell of a time. They never shot anything but shotguns up until that day, and I bet a bunch of them now shoot big rifles.

"See what I mean?" Fleming said. "We're all the same. And the kicker is, every single one of us believes that as honest adult citizens, we have the absolute right to own any and all small arms and shoot them just as often as we want. We have a specific culture. Guns and shooting are very important to us, just like living as nomads and hunting buffalo was important to the Indians. We are willing to work hard and have the government confiscate half our money and use it for things we never get any benefit out of, if only we can continue to buy our guns and our ammo and our components, and shoot a lot.

"Our culture is important, and we're willing to pay for it. We have above-average educations, above-average incomes, and almost nonexistent criminal involvement. We pay far more in taxes and receive virtually no subsidy payments. You'd think Washington would be happy, but instead they are doing everything they can to destroy our culture.

"In the '20s, soldiers sat on their bunks in the cold at Camp Perry, cleaning the handmade .22 target rifles they would compete with the next day. When the President proudly announces that today, seventy years later, he is ordering these same guns thrown into a blast furnace, we in the gun culture feel powerful emotions. They are the same emotions a Native American would feel if the President proudly ordered the destruction of war clubs and other sacred tribal artifacts. They are the same emotions that Jews felt watching newsreel footage of Nazi *Sturmtroopen* gleefully burning intricate copies of the Torah.

We offer to buy the government's surplus guns, and instead they pay to have them cut up. We offer to buy their surplus military ammo, shoot it, sell the brass to a smelter, and give the government the proceeds, and instead they pay to have it burned.

"These government slugs ban our guns and they ban our magazines and they ban our ammo. They ban suppressors that make our guns quieter and then they ban our outdoor shooting ranges because our guns are too loud. They ban steel-core ammunition because it's 'armor piercing', then they close down our indoor ranges where people shoot lead-core bullets because they say we might get lead poisoning.

"The people in the gun culture have a better safety record than any police department in the nation, but in several states actually prohibit us from using guns for self-protection, and in all the other states except one they make us buy a license. They tax us so we can have more cops, and when crime still goes up, they tax us more and ban more of our guns.

"People in the gun culture endure waiting periods that no other group would stand for. We undergo background checks that no legislator, judge, doctor, or police officer has to tolerate, and we submit to it not once, or once a year, but over and over again. Then, after we yield to this outrage, they smile and forbid us from buying more than one gun in a 30-day period.

"If we sell one gun we own that's gone up in value, they can charge us with dealing in firearms without a federal dealer's license, which is a felony. If we get a dealer's license, they say we are not really in business, and report us to our local authorities for violating zoning ordinances by running a commercial venture out of a residence.

"If the steel or the wood on our guns is too long or too short, they make us pay $200 taxes and get fingerprinted and photographed. They make us get a law enforcement certification from the local police chief. If he refuses to sign we have no recourse. If he takes the forms in the next room and brings them back out, signed, he can later claim the signature is not his, and the feds will charge us with the felony.

"We in the gun culture have played all their stupid games on NFA weapons for over half a century, without a single violent crime being committed by any person in the system. So when a bill comes up to keep travelers with guns locked in the trunk of their cars out of jail, what happens? A scumbucket from New Jersey, where NFA weapons are illegal already, puts an amendment on it that closes down the whole NFA process.

"Then, if they even suspect we've ignored the $200 tax process altogether, on the guns where the wood and steel is too long or too short, they'll spend over a million dollars watching us for months, then they'll shoot our wives and children or burn us all alive. When the public gets outraged by these actions, the government issues letters of reprimand and sends the guys who did the killing on paid leave. In the decades that the feds have been raiding and killing people in the gun culture over suspected non-payment of $200 taxes, not one federal agent has been fined a single dollar or spent even one night in jail." Fleming stopped for a moment and took another drink of tea.

"And you know something else that's never happened, Ray? To this day, not a single person in the gun culture has ever dropped the hammer on one of these feds. Not once.

"Then, after these statist bastards have done all these things, they grin and tell us how they like to hunt ducks, and how the only laws they want to pass are 'reasonable' ones." Henry and Ray both looked at their friend. Neither had anything to add at that moment. It was Ray Johnson who finally spoke.

"I now know everything you say is true," he said. "I still can't quite believe it." He was quiet again, then asked a question. "What do you think is going to happen?"

"One of two things," Fleming said with a sigh. "One of the political parties is going to have to wake up, smell the coffee, and start restoring and reaffirming all the articles in the Bill of Rights—the Second, Fourth, Fifth, and Tenth Amendments."

"And if that doesn't happen?" Ray asked gently. Fleming took several moments before he spoke, though it was obvious he knew exactly what he was going to say.

"Then we're going to have a civil war."

July 31, 1994

"Uh, hello? This on?" The paunchy, balding, middle-aged man asked nervously. It was obvious that the huge crowd could hear him perfectly. "Testing, testing..." David R. Hinson said, trying to delay the inevitable. A few calls came from the crowd, telling him that the sound system was working fine and to go ahead. The Administrator of the United States Federal Aviation Administration glanced at his staff standing slightly behind him, licked his lips nervously, and took a breath.

"Let me right at the outset...ah...get to the Bob Hoover issue, because I know–"

The rest of his sentence was drowned out by thunderous applause from the audience. When the outburst died down, Hinson continued.

"...that's on your mind, because I know you're not going to like what I have to say, but, I've got to say it. I've known Bob Hoover for many, many years. Because it's in the United States Court of Appeals and because it's in litigation, I am precluded from commenting." For a moment there was stunned silence from the crowd as the audience waited for Hinson to say more. When he did not, murmurs rippled through the audience.

"That is fairly standard to protect, ah, his interests," Hinson said finally, "and I will follow that time-held rule. And I simply cannot comment about Mr. Hoover. Subsequent to this issue being resolved, in any forum that's appropriate, certainly next year, I'd be more than pleased to engage in dialogue about this issue. I hope you will understand," the administrator said, hesitating and choosing his words, "it is not because I have faint heart or I will duck the issue...uh, I hope you will respect and understand that." The undercurrent of noise from the crowd increased with this bit of doublespeak. Hinson quickly began to introduce his staff, then started in on another unnecessary sound check.

The old man at the side of the crowd narrowed his eyes, turned his head, and spat a thick wad of phlegm onto the floor.

"Dickless cocksucker," he said in a voice that carried well. His eyes never left the man on the stage.

In any other part of the Experimental Aircraft Association's massive annual fly-in and airshow in Oshkosh, Wisconsin, the old man's conduct would have been cause for instant reproach. With over one million attendees during a nine-day period, it was impossible to find even one speck of litter at Wittman Field, let alone rude or uncouth behavior.

The old man's actions would have been disdained anywhere else at the huge facility. On the flight line, at the builders' workshops, or at any of the other EAA-sponsored forums, he would have instantly become a pariah, and others would have turned their heads in disgust at the vile nonagenarian.

This was not the flight line, however. It was the annual "Meet the Boss" forum, co-sponsored the EAA and the FAA, and this year EAA members had come for one reason only. They had come to hear the head of the FAA explain why the Federal Aviation Administration had grounded Bob Hoover. The old man's coarse words had accurately mirrored the thoughts of the majority of the people in the audience.

No point in hanging around for the rest of this dog-and-pony show the old man thought to himself, and turned to leave. He saw that all but a handful of the people in the room were staying, obviously hoping that somehow their sheer numbers would cause the FAA to relent. *That ain't the way it works with these pricks* the man thought as he turned towards the exit. *Somebody ought to kill the two punks started this fuckin' crap. Ought to gut 'em, and peel the hide off 'em, and tan it into parchment, and use it to write a nice clear letter to the U.S. Governm-*

The old man stopped dead in his tracks, and his jaw dropped. He was staring at a man wearing khaki pants and shirt who had been standing at the back of the room, and who was now making his way along the back wall, heading for the exit.

It's Blackout! he thought in utter disbelief. He blinked twice, but the image did not change. The same man was still there, and he was almost to the doorway. *It can't be!* the old man told himself. *He looks exactly the same as the last time I saw him fifty years ago!* The old man opened his mouth to yell, but no sound came out. He stood there transfixed, and in a few seconds the one who had so profoundly influenced his life was out the doorway and gone.

The old man sagged against the wall. His eyes were unfocused and his breathing was shallow. Then a moment of pure clarity infused his entire body, and the resulting surge of adrenaline made him feel less than half of his ninety-three years.

Haven't seen the inside of a church since I left home in '15, and after eighty years of whiskey, and cigarettes, and beer for breakfast, God sends me a sign. He raised his eyes to the ceiling, and his backbone straightened perceptibly. *I heard you, Lord. Loud and clear. No 'somebody ought to' about it. Those two government bastards railroaded Bob Hoover are dead men.*

As he walked out of the EAA forum room, Buell 'Anvil' Jenkins realized that he hadn't felt as good in close to fifty years.

August 1, 1994

"God *damn*," Jenkins said under his breath when he saw who was peering into the rear cockpit hole of the airplane. "I *did* see him." The old man began walking as fast as he could toward the biplane that had drawn him like a magnet every day of the airshow.

"Shit and God *damn*." His steps quickened as he made his way towards the ghost from his past.

"You kept the brass plaque in it!" Henry almost yelled.

Terry Mace turned around. He was about to tell the guy to get off the lower wing of his airplane when something about the stranger's expression made him change his mind. The man was climbing down anyway.

"The one on the instrument panel?" Mace asked. "Was there when I bought it. Why, you ever heard of the guy? Man I bought it from couldn't tell me anything about the plane or the original builder. He bought it out of some airshow pilot's estate, then groundlooped it first thing and busted a wingtip when it tipped over. Stuck it in storage. Didn't have any logs when I got it." Mace noticed that the fellow he was addressing looked as if he were about to cry.

"Uh...have you seen this plane before?" the show pilot asked uncertainly. "I'm trying to find out more about it."

"Walter Bowman—that's the name on the plaque—he was my dad." Henry blinked and shook his head to clear it. "I used to fly this plane when I was a kid. Dad sold it in 'sixty-seven, when he found out he had cancer. I was fourteen. He swapped it for a clip-wing Cub and cash, for my schooling. I've still got the Cub." Henry swallowed. "Every time I've come to Oshkosh, I always hoped I'd find it." He ran his hand along the fuselage. The Stearman was now painted solid white, finished in flawless Imron polyurethane. Henry turned to the owner. "I'm Henry Bowman."

"Terry Mace," the pilot said, shaking his hand.

"So," Henry said with a grin, his composure regained, "How do you like the power?"

"Oh, man!" Mace said with feeling, "Got the motor back together 'bout six months ago, and I damn near put the left wingtip in the asphalt the first takeoff I made.

"Listen, what can you tell me about the engine? The pitch on the prop is awful flat, and some guy painted a new redline on the tach, which is crazy. On top of that, compression was too high to do more than idle on the best avgas around. Pulled the heads off and found they'd been shaved and ported like a Reno Unlimited, but none of the builders I talked to had any idea who'd done the work. Not many guys around doing full-house jobs on Wasps, and we found all kinds of parts we'd never seen before when we pulled it down. Got a decent set of stock heads on it now.

"Crazy thing is, my wife said some old goat came around when I was over at the pilot's meeting, said he built the motor when he was in the Navy in World War II. She said he–"

"Anvil Jenkins is still *alive?*" Henry broke in. "And he's *here?*"

"Goddamn right I am," Jenkins said. The pair turned to look at the man who was standing behind them. "Thought I was seein' a ghost when you was there on the wing, mister," he said with a smile. "You look just like your dad did, last time I saw him."

"Well, this is something," Henry said as he shook Jenkins' hand. "When I was a little kid, Dad talked about you all the time. We went around to some of the dirttrack teams and tried to find out where you were. Found one guy who'd seen you in the late 'thirties, but that was it."

"You and your old man shoulda looked where he saw me last," Jenkins told him. "I stayed in. Those big motors kinda grew on me. Navy finally cashiered me in 'sixty-nine, as a Master Chief.

"Liked the kind a work your dad done on this plane here, so I went into the FAA. Got my Inspector's ticket. Did sign-offs on homebuilts 'til 'eighty-three. Been comin' up here for twenty-five years. Always thought I might see the Lieutenant and this old girl one more time." He stared at the airplane, then turned toward Terry Mace.

"You put a set of stock heads on that engine, you're down a good two hundred horsepower. Can't unmill 'em, I know, so I'd try to swap 'em out to Zeuschel, trade him even for a good porting job on the stockers. Tell him you want as much flow as on the good heads, but a combustion chamber volume 25% bigger to knock the compression down for the junk gas they got now.

"Tach's not wrong—she'll live forever that high up, unless somebody screwed around with the reciprocating weights. That's why the prop's so flat—we built her to climb."

Terry Mace nodded. He had not expected the original engine builder to walk up to his plane and tell him all about it, and this was a real bonus. The three men talked for a while about the plane's history. Jenkins related the stories about Walter as a flight instructor. He told of the time he had offered to help the lieutenant try to pull the wings off of one of their trainers, and of Walter's unorthodox instruction techniques.

"Since your dad owned the airplane," Mace said to Henry, "and Mr. Jenkins, you built the engine, maybe you two can tell me why when I came to own this monster, there was a metal bulkhead in the tail section, and a block of lead machined to size, with mounting holes that matched it. New engine's heavier than the original Continental, but when we recalculated the weight and balance with that lead block installed, it was way past the aft limit. That come after your dad sold it?"

"No," Henry said, "it was there for a reason. Needed to get the weight back that far if you wanted to do a lomcevak."

"What?"

"Didn't call 'em that back then," Jenkins broke in. "I told the lieutenant if he was going to fuck around with the CG, try it on one a the trainers first, out over the palmetto grass, case he had to get out. Worked out okay, 'cept he had to stay up high, 'cause that old Continental didn't have enough guts to get out of its own way, forget pullin' out of one a those tumbles without losing a bunch of altitude."

Terry Mace was about to protest, but Henry Bowman was pulling a small photo folder from his flight bag. He showed the pictures to Jenkins first.

"I'll be damned. That's that arch thing you got in Missouri." Jenkins was looking at the photo Walter had taken as he had aimed the Stearman in an inverted dive between the monument's legs. The old man looked at the rest of the photos carefully until he came to one where the airplane was pointed straight at the ground with what he judged was less than a thousand feet of altitude. The image of the ground was smeared sideways, but the instrument panel was in sharp focus. A piece of yarn on top of the windscreen was flowing sideways also.

"Here you go," he said to Mace, handing the photo to the younger man. "Look at the airspeed indicator."

"Reads zero."

"Plane's tumbling."

"I'll be damned," Mace said, echoing Jenkins' earlier comment.

"Shit, look at this!" Jenkins exclaimed, staring at another photo. "This you, Henry? Your dad did this all the time with cadets. Son of a bitch, here you are landing the damn thing." Anvil Jenkins was looking at the pictures Walter had taken of Henry flying the Stearman while Walter stood on the wing. "Were you flying when he took that other one, doing the lomcevak?"

"Yeah," Henry smiled sadly. "Last day we ever flew together, right before they yanked his medical. He took it through the arch, then he turned it over to me and concentrated on pictures." The three men were silent for a few moments, then Terry Mace spoke.

"Can you make me copies of these pictures?" he asked, holding out two prints that showed the Stearman in profile sitting on the ramp.

"Sure. Why?" Henry asked.

"I put the white on as a base coat, and was trying to decide what trim color I wanted." He nodded firmly. "This settles it. I'm going to paint it just like it was."

***

"I'm going to kill all three of the sorry little pricks," Anvil Jenkins said softly with a small smile. He had been smiling ever since mid-morning, when he had found Henry by the custom Stearman.

"What?" Henry looked around the outdoor cafeteria to see if anyone was eavesdropping, then stared at the man across the table form him. "Who are you talking about?"

"You know who I mean. I saw you at the FAA meeting yesterday." Henry cocked his head in silent query, and Jenkins went on.

"Clint Boehler and Jim Kelln, they're the ones got together and wrote those fuckin' 'independent' evaluations of Bob Hoover. Then that Glen Nelson, he made up a bullshit story about one a Hoover's airshow routines he didn't even see, an' told that fairy tale to the Airman Medical branch." Jenkins turned and spat on the ground.

"Nelson, he's Accident Prevention Program Manager for the FAA. S'posed to maintain proficiency, and stay current in the operation of FAA and rental aircraft. Shit. That sorry bastard hasn't been current since I got laid.

"Jealous little snots. And the feds bought into it, even though every one of 'em knows it's bullshit. Afraid the whole FAA will look bad if they throw 'em out. Cocksuckers. Ashamed I ever had anything to do with 'em. Guy in the service pull that kind of shit, try to get a man dishonored, brass would feed him to the sharks. Fuckin' feds." His smile was gone.

"I've always thought it was crazy having to have a medical in the first place," Henry told the old man. "Skies are empty compared to the streets."

"Hoover's got a Australian license now," Jenkins went on, not hearing what Henry had said. "Flies some shows with 'nother exhibition pilot in the left seat, but it ain't the same." Jenkins shook his head.

"I seen him do that thing you always did, Lieutenant. With the glass of water on the panel. Like to see the two of you fly together. Yes I would." Jenkins eyes were focused on infinity. "Been a while since I done anything that made a difference." He tried to take a sip from his glass, but it was empty.

"Boehler, Kelln, and Nelson, they ain't the whole of it, not by a long shot. But they'll do." He laughed for the first time in months. "What're the feds going to do to me, Blackout? Hm? Give me a life sentence?" He laughed again, then he leaned forward and his eyes bored into Henry's. He grabbed the younger man's arm, and Henry was startled at Anvil Jenkins' surprising strength.

"You going to try to stop me, Lieutenant?" Jenkins challenged. "Talk me out of it?"

"No, I'm not."

Anvil Jenkins let go of Henry's forearm and sat back in the molded plastic chair.

"That's good," the old man said softly. He had a distant look in his eyes.

"Let me get you another iced tea, Anvil," Henry said, and stood up.

Henry Bowman heard the shouts when he was waiting at the cash register. He left his tray and ran to where Jenkins was sitting.

Anvil Jenkins lay slumped to the side in the molded chair. His eyes were open but lifeless.

"Does anyone here know CPR?" a man shouted.

"I do!" came a quick reply. "Get him down on the ground!"

Be a sin to let him check out at a damn fast food tent Henry Bowman thought. He stepped over to the second man, put a firm hand on his bicep, and squeezed hard.

"Let him be."

"But–"

"He does this sometimes. Just a little too much walking, that's all. C'mon, Anvil," Henry said as he scooped Jenkins' corpse into his arms. "Let's find us a golf cart, get you back to the car." Henry carried the body out of the tent and away from the crowd. A couple of the people stared, but in a few moments they interested themselves in other things.

The Navy's Blue Angels tent. That's less than a half mile he said to himself. As he walked toward the distant shelter, Henry Bowman considered the plans Anvil Jenkins had been making when his heart gave out.

"You were lucky, Master Chief Jenkins," Henry said quietly to the corpse in his arms. "Not everybody dies happy."

August 14, 1994

"Not a bad turnout," the man said as he looked from the Lincoln Memorial out over the reflecting pool towards the Washington Monument. "Looks like eight, maybe ten thousand people."

"More than that," the photographer for the *New York Times* said. "Close to fifteen. Paper won't run an article on it, though. Not unless there's a riot or something." His companion nodded. A national rally in support of restoring gun rights to the citizenry did not fit in with the editorial policy of the nation's largest newspaper. "The people I've talked to here don't seem as excited about the crime bill going down as I would have thought," the photographer said, changing the subject. His companion shook his head.

"It's just been delayed, and they all know it. President'll loot the Treasury if he has to, to buy the votes he needs to get it passed." The man shook his head ruefully.

"You know, I grew up with a fellow who wasn't ashamed of his racism. Lot of people are like that, but Jerry was one of my best friends. He had a favorite joke you've probably heard: 'How do you keep five niggers from raping a white girl? Throw them a basketball.' Wherever he is, Jerry's probably laughing his ass off right now, since our Administration has seen fit to adopt that strategy as a major part of its anti-crime policy."

The man was referring to one of the many controversial provisions in the proposed 'crime bill' which the House had three days earlier voted not to consider and which would, if passed, cost the taxpayers over thirty billion dollars. Among other things, it called for taxpayers' money to be spent to fund midnight basketball in the inner cities in the hope that this would reduce crime.

The provision that was of most immediate interest to the fifteen thousand people massed at the Lincoln Memorial that day was the proposed bill would ban the manufacture of over 200 types of firearms and several thousand types of magazines.

"Yeah, well let's just hope the people who voted this down show some spine and don't cave in on this one," the photographer said. "I've heard more than one person say that if this 'crime bill' passes we'll be a lot closer to a civil war." He looked at the podium and said suddenly. "Hey, I hear this guy is really good."

The two men turned to look at the next speaker, who was being introduced by the Master of Ceremonies. The speaker was a man of medium height with short dark hair, who wore a navy blue suit and a light-colored yarmulke. His name was Jay Simkin, and he was a Holocaust scholar speaking for the civil rights organization *Jews for the Preservation of Firearms Ownership*.

"There have been many genocides in the last century," Simkin said. "The Holocaust was not the largest. There have been at least two other genocides, one of them much more recent, which have been even larger. The Holocaust has received much more coverage and discussion than any other genocide, for two reasons. It is the only genocide that has been carefully researched and documented, and it is the only genocide where the ones responsible have been brought to public trial for their crimes."

The two men listened, along with the rest of the crowd, as Simkin discussed the Holocaust and all the other genocides of the twentieth century. The *Times* reporter was familiar with much of the speech, for he had read Simkin's first book *Gateway to Tyranny*, which included the entire text of the Nazi gun law of 1938, printed next to the U.S. law passed thirty years later. The domestic legislation appeared to have been copied verbatim from the German.

The other, less-familiar genocides were covered in Simkin's second work, *Lethal Laws*, which had just been published. In each case, the mass killings had been preceded by gun bans, and Simkin's book documented this. The two men watched as he held aloft a copy of the book and began talking about a current genocide in the central African country of Rwanda.

"I hold in my hand at this moment as I speak the authentic text of Rwanda's gun control law passed 21 November 1964 as published by the Rwanda government. This document is the key to the murder of over 250,000 people in the last several months. During all the tremendous news coverage of the slaughter in Rwanda," Simkin thundered, "there is one simple question that no journalist from any national publication has addressed. It is a question that goes to the heart of every genocide that has ever occurred. That question is this: How is it physically possible that so many people could be murdered in a so short a time by a mere handful of oppressors? The answer is gun control.

"There is a downside to gun control, and it is not, I repeat *not*, inconvenience to hunters, and it is not inconvenience to people who want to buy a gun for the purpose of target shooting. The downside to gun control is *genocide*. *Mountains* of corpses. In each of the seven major genocides in this century in which over 56 million people were murdered, including millions of children, there was, on the books, prior to the onset of the genocide, at least one and in most cases several gun control laws. You cannot have a genocide without having gun control." The applause the audience gave Simkin was overwhelming.

"Wouldn't Carl Schaumberg have apoplexy if he heard this guy talk?" commented the photographer. He was referring to the U.S. Congressman who chaired the crime committee and who was the principal architect of many of the recent proposals to prevent U.S. voters from owning guns.

"I always look at it the other way. What do Holocaust survivors make of Jews like Schaumberg? Misguided? Well-intentioned? Courageous? What?"

The news photographer shrugged in reply and shook his head. He had no idea how to respond to his companion's question.

Though few would realize it when they saw it printed, the correct answer to the man's inquiry would eventually be found on the front page of the same newspaper that had sent the photographer to the Lincoln Memorial rally.

August 20, 1994

"Hello."

"Henry—Tom Fleming. Go turn on C-SPAN. Stick a tape in your recorder if you've got one handy. It's on right now."

"I'll call you back." Henry Bowman hung up and went to his study, where he grabbed a blank tape from the stack on the shelf. He slipped it into his VCR, turned the recorder and the television set on, punched in the channel for C-SPAN on the VCR's tuner, and pressed the RECORD button. He set his television set to 'Video', then sat back to watch.

There was a podium and a large crowd around it. Henry recognized the Lincoln Memorial in the background, and realized that he was looking at footage of the Gun Rights Rally that had been held in the nation's capital the previous Sunday. A bearded man in a grey suit was delivering an address to more than 10,000 people that were gathered around the reflecting pool. He was squinting in the bright sunlight, but his voice carried great conviction.

"...heard a lot of good history today, and I'm not going to repeat it. What I'm going to do is tell you some things you haven't heard. Some of them are shameful things, but you must face them. After that, I'm going to tell you what you can do instead of just coming here and feeling good. First though, I'd like to add to what other speakers have said about freedom. The Second Amendment is about freedom, and the people fighting for it—you people—are on the cutting edge of the human rights issue.

"In some countries, the people have not yet wrested control of their destiny from tyrants, and America has become the adopted home of many of the world's oppressed people. That's why the Founders wrote the first ten articles of our Bill of Rights to remind the government of the freedoms that all people have merely by drawing breath. They knew firsthand what can happen when the government, its standing army, and the police have too much power. They wrote the Bill of Rights as a reminder to the government of where it had no authority. Nine of those ten articles were promises to the people. The other one was the Second Amendment, and it wasn't a promise. It was the guarantee that backed up all the promises.

"The guarantee was and is very simple. Every citizen over sixteen is a member of the militia, and the founders wanted every one of us to have the same basic weapon as a soldier in a modern military. In 1775, that basic weapon was a flintlock musket. In 1925, it was a bolt action rifle and a BAR. In 1945, it was a BAR and a semiautomatic Garand, and in 1995 it will be an M16A2 and an M249 Squad Automatic. The army may have cannons, mortars, and explosive shells, but if every citizen has the basic infantryman's rifle, no army, foreign or domestic, can ever prevail. That was true in the eighteenth century when the cannons fired round balls and the bombs were filled with black powder, and it's true in the twentieth century when the cannons shoot twenty miles and the bombs carry nuclear warheads. In Switzerland, every household with a male over eighteen has at least one machine gun, identical to those used by the military. Anyplace on earth where the citizens have the same small arms as the soldiers to defend their freedoms, you will find a free nation. Anywhere there is tyranny you will find that the people were first disarmed.

"America has served as a beacon for oppressed people all over the world. We have led by example, and we have watched our example of individual freedom be embraced by others who cherish liberty. It is a bitter irony that today, as we watch the Soviet Union disintegrate and we watch people all over the planet throw off their yokes of oppression, we ourselves stand meekly by while our own government slowly strips us of our final guarantee of freedom.

"What can you do about this? Several things. One: Always remember that freedom isn't free, and freedom is much too precious to expect someone else to secure for us. The NRA was founded 120 years ago to promote safety, proficiency, and competition. Those are good things, but they're still recreation. Even today, the NRA spends only a fraction of its budget on civil rights. Don't expect anyone else, particularly not a group whose primary focus is recreation, to safeguard your freedom.

"Two: Don't ever think it can't happen here. It *has* happened here. We have a shameful history—don't ever forget it. In 1932, twenty thousand World War One veterans peacefully assembled here in Washington to urge Congress to give them their war bonus early. The military drove them out at gunpoint. General Douglas MacArthur had full armament, including foot soldiers with rifles and bayonets, cavalry with pistols and sabers, and tanks. MacArthur led his troops into a place where twenty thousand unarmed American war veterans were camped, and he burned them out. The soldiers shot and bayonetted some of the veterans, their wives, and children. Babies died from tear gas inhalation. The result of this horror was that Hoover was defeated and Franklin Roosevelt was able to seize power and drastically expand the government's reach into your lives. Part of that meant passing the unconstitutional National Firearms Act of 1934, which was the beginning of the terrible situation we now face. What happened at Waco and the disaster we face now is nothing new. It started sixty years ago with Franklin Roosevelt, it's gotten worse ever since, and we let it happen!

"Another shameful thing involves those of you who have always thought of yourself as supportive of law enforcement. You must realize that when the police are ordered to violate your rights, they are not your friends. That brings us to number three: Do not hope police officers will resign instead of carrying out orders they dislike. They will not. The State Police did not resign thirty years ago. Instead, they used tear gas, billy clubs, and German Shepherds on civil rights marchers. Federal Police in Waco, Texas last year did not resign. Instead, they used machine guns and tanks on a group of people they suspected had not paid a $200 tax, and then burned all eighty-six of them alive. In Los Angeles, St.Louis, and Chicago, the police are not resigning. Instead, they are conducting warrantless searches in public housing projects. They are seizing guns that have not been stolen, and they are seizing them from people who do not have criminal records. Federal forms for applicants to the Special Forces contain the question 'Would you seize weapons from U.S. citizens if ordered to do so?' I guarantee the answer they're looking for is 'Yes', not 'No'. The so-called crime bill contains a measure to hire thousands of Hong Kong police. Why? Because these officers are already highly trained in confiscating arms from Chinese, and won't resign when ordered to confiscate them from us.

"Number four: Guns are our ultimate guarantee of freedom, but to take back these rights we need to band together with the millions of people in our country who don't think about how important their gun rights are, but who despise other government intrusions into their lives.

"Millions of people don't want government lawyers telling them what doctor they have to use. Millions of people don't want the police seizing their property without even charging them with a crime. Millions of landowners think they should be able to build a tool shed on their property without risking the government jailing them for destroying wetlands. Millions of business owners don't think Congress should dictate what they should charge for their services, what they should pay for raw materials, what products they should sell, or how much they should pay their employees. Millions of residents of blighted areas in this country think the government should let them work for low wages instead of promoting factories in Mexico. Millions of drivers don't think it's any of Congress' business where their state sets its speed limits or what motorcyclists should wear on their heads. Millions of people think they are the ones, not government, who should decide whether or not to have plastic surgery.

"We must continue to forge alliances with these people. The things these people want may not be of particular interest to us, but we all share a common bond: None of us want our lives controlled by faceless, uniformed, jackbooted bureaucrats.

"Fifth, stop fighting a defensive battle. Get informed, and then get pro-civil-rights people elected and pro-human-rights laws passed in your state. It's working. In the last two years, more states have repealed the Jim Crow laws that were designed to disarm blacks and that now give violent criminals a government guarantee that citizens are defenseless. Thirty-seven states now allow at least some of their citizens to protect themselves outside their homes. For over 200 years in Vermont, not just Vermont residents, but every U.S. citizen has had the right to carry a gun for self-protection without asking the government for permission, just as our Founders promised. Vermont, which shares a long border with New York, is the safest state in the union in which to live. *Self-Defense Laws and Violent Crime Rates in the United States* documents how armed citizens, not police, reduce crime and engender freedom. Get copies of this and force your legislators to read it. We must make every state return to Vermont's law. We must elect representatives which support human rights and who will repeal the 1934 National Firearms Act and the 1968 Gun Control Act. We must continue to identify the statist slime in our local, state, and national legislatures and throw them from office!

"Sixth, take advantage of the great improvements in technology that are now available to all of us. If you're not on a network now, get on one immediately! When you hear of a politician introducing a bill that restricts your freedoms, spread the word, mobilize, and fight! When a legislator introduces a bill to restore your rights, mobilize and help.

"ATF now has Bradley Fighting Vehicles, and the FBI has just bought over two thousand silenced sniper rifles. They decided after Waco and Ruby Ridge that they need more firepower. If you don't want more Wacos, and you don't want your neighbors to be the next Weaver family, it's up to you to keep it from happening. Internal security at ATF is dismal. When you hear of an impending raid near you, and I guarantee some of you will, get the word out to every person you know in the area. Be there with video cameras to record everything. A photographic record of their actions is the last thing these storm troopers want. Statist thugs view video cameras the way vampires view crosses and sunlight.

"Last of all, I know that every one of you here has felt discouraged at each new government attempt to take away your freedom. I know you have felt helpless when you hear that the people responsible for burning eighty citizens alive over a $200 tax dispute go unpunished.

"Whenever you feel this way, I want you to take heart. I want you to remember that these policies of tyranny have ultimately failed everywhere they have been forced on the people. Josef Stalin was willing to murder twenty million of his own people trying to make socialism stick, and he still failed. People will always move towards freedom. Even farmers in Albania know that, so don't you forget it.

"The recent policies of raising your taxes, banning your guns, seizing your property, and chilling your freedoms are the last gasp of an evil monster. That evil monster is socialism, and it is dying. I want to see every one of you at the funeral. Thank you."

The applause was thunderous, and as the man stepped down, the moderator began to announce another speaker. As Henry watched, his phone rang again. It was Tom Fleming.

"What did you think? That guy wasn't even the best one. I saw someone else who was even better. Apparently the whole rally was filled with speakers like that. The speakers had their history down cold. You'll see more on C-SPAN."

"Why hasn't there been any other coverage on local or national news? Jesus, it looked like there were ten or fifteen thousand people there when they panned the crowd. Haven't seen word one in any newspaper."

"Does that really surprise you?" Tom Fleming asked. "Hey, like the guy said, cheer up. Socialism's dying all around the globe. Washington just wants to give it one more try."

"They better hope it doesn't kill 'em first," Henry said before hanging up the phone.

May 12, 1995

"What are all these Highway Patrol guys doing here in the Capitol?" Cindy Caswell asked. "Are they all here to lobby against our bill?" Cindy had just arrived in the cafeteria of the State Capitol building in Jefferson City. It was the last day of the 1995 Missouri legislative session, and once again a final vote on the concealed carry measure was imminent.

"Hi, Cindy," one of the group said in greeting. "You didn't hear? Senate Majority Leader claims his life was threatened. Highway Patrol's here to protect him. The legislators are all in a dither." Everyone there knew the Senate Majority Leader was adamantly opposed to anyone other than the police and himself carrying guns for protection. He owned a security firm in the ghetto, and a concealed carry law would be bad for his business.

"Why does everybody look so bummed out?" Cindy asked. "Don't we still have the votes?"

"Yeah, but it may not come up now. The Senator is claiming the death threat came from his biggest fundraiser, about concealed carry."

"*What?*"

"Word is the Governor promised him the moon to do it."

"Yeah," another person interjected. "Everyone knows his district's just a breeding ground for the prison system, and that's the way he wants it to stay. His business employs all those cops that get suspended from the St. Louis Police Department for shaking down motorists."

"We're trying to figure out what our next move here is," a big man with a full beard explained. His name was Arthur Bedderson, and he was the owner of a medical instruments manufacturing company located in St. Louis. Bedderson's nickname was 'B.I.', a moniker he had acquired in college, and which stood for 'Bad Influence'. Those who had met him in the mid-1980s had thought that it was a takeoff on 'Bad Attitude' Baracas, the character on the television program *The A-Team*, but Bedderson's sobriquet actually predated the show by almost a decade.

"So what are we going to do?" Cindy asked.

"Damned if I know."

The concealed carry bill in the 1995 session had originated in the Senate, where it had passed overwhelmingly. In the year since the 1994 vote when the Governor's stalling tactics had prevented the measure from becoming law, four more states had passed concealed-carry legislation, bringing the total to 41. The mood of the country was strongly in favor of individual rights, and former Texas Governor Ann Richards' November 1994 defeat was widely attributed to the fact that she had vetoed concealed carry in Texas the year before. Her challenger, former President George Bush's son, had successfully campaigned with the pledge that as soon as a concealed carry bill hit his desk, he would sign it. Missouri remained one of only nine states which absolutely prohibited honest adults from protecting themselves outside their homes, and this state of affairs was due to the singular efforts of Governor Ken Flanagan.

After passing in the Senate, the 1995 Missouri bill had gone to the House, where it had been amended and then passed by a three-to-one margin, just as it had in the three previous years. Now the bill was back in the Senate for a final vote. The death threat claim had been a surprise for everyone. The leaders of the various grassroots organizations were gathered around a large table in the Capitol cafeteria, trying to determine their next move.

"The Governor will do anything in his power to keep our bill from hitting his desk," said the president of the Kansas City Cab Driver's Union. "He knows if he vetoes it, he's out, just like in Texas."

"Somebody's pointed that out to him?"

"Only about ten of his big-money supporters," Arthur 'B.I.' Bedderson answered. "He's trying to get a deal cut where the conference committee will stick a public referendum on it, and send it to a statewide vote. That way it bypasses his desk."

"I thought we had the votes to override a veto," Cindy said.

"We do. That's why Flanagan's pissing blood," explained the president of the St. Louis County Realtors Association. "He promised Todd Barnes and Donny Rivetts the same prison if they voted to send the bill to referendum, and then we stripped that measure off in the house."

"Man, I'd hate to fight the smear campaign they'd fund with public money on a referendum deal," another man said. He was referring to the letter the Missouri Police Chiefs Association had sent out the week before. The MPCA letter claimed the supporters of the concealed carry bill in Missouri were in league with the people who had blown up the Federal building in Oklahoma City.

"Civil rights are not subject to a majority vote," Thomas J. Fleming pointed out. "I think someone should explain that to the Governor."

"Yeah," Arthur Bedderson said. "If the Civil Rights Act had been put to a vote here in Missouri in 1964, our current Senate Majority Leader wouldn't be allowed to eat in this cafeteria." Then he thought of something.

"Did you say the Governor promised the same prison to two different legislators, and they both sold us out?" Bedderson asked.

"Yeah. Rivetts is the biggest whore in the Senate. His district's down near the Arkansas border, where a lot of the family trees are straight lines. Barnes is a freshman from just outside St. Louis who hasn't figured out how the game is played. He's the one who'll get fucked."

"Anything we can do to Rivetts?" Bedderson asked.

"Not politically. No one runs against him. Last election he got 80% of the vote."

"There's got to be something," Bedderson wondered aloud.

***

"Okay," the young man said to the assembled group. He was the aide to the Democratic senator who had sponsored Missouri's concealed carry bill. "Here's the deal. The Majority Leader is going to fuck us. He's going to cry about this made-up death threat and filibuster until the clock runs out. Only way to avoid that is to turn the bill over to the House members, who have promised the Governor to put the referendum on it. If we do that, though, Harold loses control of the bill entirely."

"You mean it isn't his any more? He can't withdraw it?" Cindy Caswell asked.

"That's right. He wants to know what you people want him to do."

"Kill it."

"Kill it."

"Damn right. Kill it."

"Have him tell Flanagan we'll be back next year. The referendum is going to be on his Governorship, not our bill," Tom Fleming said. "Civil rights issues don't go away."

"Anybody disagree?" the aide asked. No one did. "I'll tell him," the young man said. Then he smiled. "The Governor is going to be pissed."

***

"Can you believe the long faces of our opponents?" the president of the Retailers Association asked. "You'd think they'd be happier. The bill's dead."

"Yeah, but only temporarily," a man named Greg pointed out. "It'll be back next session, which is during an election year, and these guys were all counting on being able to duck it permanently with that referendum scheme. I think the Governor just lost the next election."

"I don't know if that'll be much consolation to Linda Kravis," Arthur Bedderson said. He was referring to one of his employees who had been beaten and raped by a gang while she was leaving the St. Louis Union Station shopping mall. She had lost the vision in one eye during the assault.

The others nodded. Kravis' story was familiar to everyone in the group. Also well-known was Bedderson's wish to open a second plant in North St. Louis, which was a blighted, high-crime section of the city which the businessman felt was ripe for economic development. Arthur Bedderson refused to go ahead with his plans until he could be assured that all of his workers could legally protect themselves while traveling to and from their place of employment.

"B.I., you've just pointed out the thing that's always bothered me the most about this whole 'throw-the-bums-out' process," Thomas J. Fleming said.

"How so?"

"I mean, let's face it. We send Ken Flanagan packing next year, and what happens? He gets to keep all the campaign funds he's got left over from his failed re-election effort. Put that together with what he's been able to pile up selling pardons and doling out State contracts and other favors, and he's a rich man. Rich for rural Missouri, at least," he amended.

"Self-protection isn't just some political difference, subject to majority vote, like a bond issue or a speed limit," Fleming went on. "It's a fundamental right. Flanagan swore an oath when he took office to defend our fundamental rights, and he's violated that oath. Flanagan can retire and live damned well, while Linda Kravis and a hundred other decent citizens are maimed or dead because of him.

"My wife's Jewish," Tom Fleming reminded Bedderson, "and I look at this situation just like when I read they'd finally located Klaus Barbie. A lot of folks said, 'Hey, the guy's eighty years old, he's not bothering anyone, let him be.' My reaction was, we should have executed him fifty years ago. This bastard's had fifty years of good living while the people he's murdered have been six feet under. If he draws breath one more day it's one day too many."

"You got a point," Bedderson agreed, "but I think we'll have to settle for returning Flanagan to the private sector."

"I guess so."

June 15, 1995

"So what's this thing we're going to, again?" the girl in the back asked. "The leasing company, or something?" *Theresa, do you have to be such an airhead?* Cindy Caswell thought. In the front seat, Henry and Cindy looked at each other.

"You know, it's great to have a girl around who'll do whatever you want, no questions asked. 'Want to go with me?' 'Sure.' 'Need to know where we're going, what we're going to do, where we're going to stay, what kind of clothes to bring?' 'Naah.' I tell you, Cindy, Theresa's the ideal companion."

"Well, I figure we'll...have a good time," the young woman said with a laugh. "And clothes? You said we wouldn't be going anyplace dressy. My thong, couple T-bars, cut-offs, and a few tops—in this weather, what else am I going to use?"

"What else indeed," Henry agreed. "But to answer your question, we are going to the annual New Lease Body Armor Shoot. It is run by a good friend of mine, David Richards. David makes what most people call 'bulletproof vests', and every year he has a big-*Goddamit*, Theresa, don't *do* that," Henry yelled, glancing at the girl in the rearview mirror. Cindy Caswell turned around in her seat and looked at their companion. *Every boy's fantasy...*she thought.

"Babe, the back's all full of guns and the last thing we need is to have some radar cop pull us over for contributing to the delinquency of a minor," Cindy said gently. "Those people might have a car phone," she added, as Henry accelerated away from the station wagon in the next lane. Inside the other car, a wide-eyed junior high-schooler was getting yelled at by his mother.

"Sorry," Theresa said as she once again faced the front of the vehicle and put her halter top back on.

"What I was saying was, every year David has a week-long competition up near the factory. Bowling pin shooting, where the shooters see how fast they can shoot five bowling pins off a table with a pistol at twenty-five feet. It's three feet to the back of the table, and so your gun has to have enough power to throw the pin that far. The timer doesn't stop until the last pin hits the ground. The more effective your gun is at clearing the pins off the table, the harder it is to shoot fast, because of recoil. Just like real life."

"I've been practicing at Henry's place for the 9mm event," Cindy said. "That's a newer class where they put up nine pins instead of five, but only a foot from the back of the table, because the guns hold more cartridges, but they aren't as powerful as a .357, .44, or .45."

"She's pretty good," Henry admitted to Theresa. "David has a bunch of other competitions to enter. Two-person teams, a shotgun event, and the Book Depository shoot."

"What the hell is that?"

"David set up a mock-up of the Texas School Book Depository window up on a hill, with a couple old convertibles, some department-store mannequins, and an armored tractor with a long cable to pull the vehicle at the right speed through a clearing. You have to use a 6.5 Carcano with a four-power Tasco scope from 1962. The idea is to see if anyone can duplicate what Oswald is alleged to have done, because a lot of people have said it's impossible."

"This Richards guy sounds like a piece of work," Theresa said with a laugh. "So what did you two invite me along for, kinky sex after all the shooting's done for the day?"

"Basically, yeah," Cindy Caswell admitted.

"I could go for that," Theresa said agreeably.

June 16, 1995

"Shooters ready...guns on the rail...timers ready..." David Richards shouted from the announcer's stand. Then he fired a blank pistol in the air. At the sound of the shot, the three timers pressed the buttons on their electronic stopwatches. Henry Bowman had been holding his 5"-barreled .44 Magnum Smith & Wesson with its muzzle touching the waist-level barrel rest in front of him. When he heard Richards' muzzle blast, he swung his gun up into firing position, locked into the Weaver stance, and began to shoot pins off the table twenty-five feet away. The bowling pins flew eight feet off the back of the table before landing on the ground. Big splinters blew out the backs of the pins as they flew through the air. The fifth pin split in two as it bounced in the dirt.

He's slowed down a tiny bit Cindy Caswell thought as Henry removed the five empties and the single loaded round from his revolver.

"Four point one."

"Four point two."

"Four point one."

"Four point one it is," David Richards announced for the official scorer, throwing out the odd time of the three. There were seven separate ranges set up with tables of pins to shoot. Five of the tables had a single worker with a stopwatch at each. One table used two timers. David Richards stood on a platform that overlooked the table reserved for the fastest guns. The better the shooter, the more timers Richards put on him. A couple of the fastest shooters would have five watches on them by the final round.

"That's a four point oh average for the string," the scorer called out.

"Nice shooting, Henry," Richards said as Henry Bowman stepped off the line. "Maybe I'll develop a Magnum event." Then Richards went to check the schedule.

This is really fun here Cindy Caswell thought as she looked around at all the shooters. A number of the competitors were women, and that had surprised her.

"Congratulations," Theresa said as Henry walked up to where she and Cindy were standing. "That's the fastest I've seen." *Yesterday she couldn't have cared less about what was going on during the daytime* Cindy thought with a smile.

"The really good shooters aren't up yet. Jerry Miculek shoots in the high twos."

"Is he a cop?" Theresa asked. Henry and Cindy both started laughing.

"No," Henry said, after he had calmed down. "Very few cops shoot enough to get any good. Almost none of them show up here—it's too embarrassing."

"How come your gun blows the pins so far off the table, and splits them apart sometimes?" Theresa asked.

"I don't load down for this event. I shoot the full-power load in the .44, which is more than you need to take the pins off the table. When I tried loading down, it was screwing up my timing, because I've been shooting this one load since I was a kid. I could practice a bunch with mid-range ammo, but I'd still never get as fast as the top guys. How'd you do?" Henry asked, turning to Cindy.

"Twelve point three."

"That's pretty fast for nine pins and no more practice than you've had with that Glock. How'd my loads work for you?"

"Great. No rollers." Cindy was referring to loads with low momentum knocking the pins over but not off the table.

"What was the fastest you saw anyone shoot in the nine class?"

"High eights. Mr. Richards said I was best time so far in the 9mm Novice Division."

"Good deal. Although he may be trying to make time with you. He's getting a divorce, and I think it's been a while for him."

"Hmm," Theresa said, "maybe we should invite him over. What's he look like?"

"You haven't met him? He was just here. He's that guy over there in the gym shorts and shower flip-flops."

"Oh, he's adorable!" Theresa said. "Like a teddy bear." Henry laughed, and then thought of something.

"You two want to get his heart rate up a little? I got an idea." He told them what he had in mind.

"I've got a better one," Cindy said when she heard it. Henry agreed with her assessment.

**

"We clear?" David Richards asked over the PA system. He looked out over the seven ranges. "Range four? Yes? Good. Okay, people, we're going to take a one-hour break, give the timers a rest and give the pin sorters a chance to cull out the bad ones. Got plenty of barbecue, plenty of soda, we'll hit it again at two o'clock. All ranges are now closed." Richards put down the microphone, switched off the amplifier, and used his cap to fan himself. The midday sun was warm for Michigan, and he had been going nonstop for almost four hours.

David Richards climbed down from the platform and headed towards the large storage building where the used bowling pins were kept. He wanted to see how the supply was holding out, and if he needed to have more brought up from the other facility.

"Here he comes," whispered Theresa as she and Cindy peered outside through the space between the door and the frame. The two women quickly stripped off their shorts, underwear, and T-shirts and threw them under the table in the corner eight feet to the right of the doorway. Cindy jumped up on the table and lay back with her legs spread. Theresa climbed on top of her, facing in the opposite direction, and started giggling.

"Shh!" Cindy hissed. "We don't want him to notice us right away." Theresa bit her lip and fell silent.

David Richards opened the door to the storage building. As he walked into the structure, instinct made him reach for the light switch until his brain registered that he had left the fluorescents on. The boxes of used pins were on pallet racks against the far wall, and so he headed straight towards them without looking to either side. David Richards was just about to pull down one of the boxes when he heard a sharp intake of breath behind him, to his right, and so he turned around.

"Oh!" said Theresa, rising up to a kneeling position and bringing her hand up to her mouth in a gesture of surprise. "Oh, I'm...oh, this is so...listen, I know we shouldn't be in here, but...we weren't going to steal anything, I promise." *Like he could possibly think that's what we were doing* Cindy thought as she fought to keep from being convulsed with laughter.

"Well, uh..." David Richards stammered, "I–".

"Please, don't get us in trouble, we'll get out of here right away. Listen, I am really sorry, I hope you won't say anything about this to the manager, because–"

"I'm the manager," Richards said in his best 'Here's-some-candy-little-girl' voice. "And who might you be?"

"I'm Theresa, and this is my friend Cindy," the girl said as she hopped off the table. "Cin, we better get dressed." She bent over to look for their clothes, giving David Richards a rear view where he could confirm her lack of tan lines.

"I hope we haven't embarrassed you, Mr. Richards," Cindy said as she sat up. "We meant no harm. We were just...in the mood."

"Oh...sure," Richards said to her, trying to sound as if this sort of thing happened regularly between rounds at the New Lease shoots. "That's fine. I'm glad the building was unlocked, ha ha. No harm done whatso–" He stopped in mid-sentence as he recognized Cindy's face. "You're... Henry Bowman's girlfriend."

"Well, yeah," Theresa said, "but Cindy knew him first, so..." She shrugged as she left the sentence unfinished. *Now we've got him completely confused* Cindy Caswell thought with a smile.

"Look, I've got to, uh, get back outside," David Richards said as he backed towards the exit, "so...uh...put something to block the door, and you can...uh...whatever..." He closed the door behind him as he left. The two women hurried to the door after he had closed it and waited for half a minute. Then they peeked through the crack.

"Henry's walking up to him!" Cindy said merrily. "He's asking him about us." Cindy and Theresa watched as Henry Bowman hailed the nervous-looking David Richards.

"Hey, David! Have you seen my girlfriend Theresa? She and Cindy were supposed to meet me back near the ranges, and I can't find either one of them." Henry gave the other man a conspiratorial look. "I think Theresa's up for something other than shooting tonight."

"No, no, I've just been rounding some gear up from storage. Can't help you, got to run," he said quickly, and hurried off. Henry made a show of looking around until David Richards was out of sight. Then he opened the door to the shed.

"Did it work?"

"I think your friend David Richards may be in love, Henry," Cindy Caswell said. Cindy's judgment about people had always been excellent, and this time did not prove to be an exception.

***

"Shooters ready...guns on the rail...timers ready..."

When Richards fired his blank pistol, the two men with Remington 1100 shotguns raised the muzzles of their weapons and began shooting at the ten bowling pins standing on the long table twenty-five feet away. They worked from opposite ends, which was the way they had practiced for the Unlimited Two-Man event. Both men shot well under pressure and did not rush themselves, and neither missed any targets. The shooter on the left was faster than the one on the right, and so both men's shot strings hit the sixth pin from the left at virtually the same time with their last shots. This bowling pin was driven violently off the table and came to rest some twenty feet back, in the grass.

"Three point eight."

"Three point eight."

"Three point seven."

"Three point eight."

"Okay, good job, timers, score is three point eight, scorer," David Richards called out as the pinsetters hurried to put up ten more targets. "Looks like right now, that's the time to beat. Next shooter," he called out. Then David Richards started laughing when he saw Henry Bowman step up to the line.

"Well, it looks like either we're going to need five watches on this one, or just a sundial. Where's your partner, Henry?"

"Cindy, come on up." Henry turned to his rotund friend on the announcer's platform. "Rules don't say both shooters have to have guns. Got your ears and glasses on?" he asked the young woman. "This brake throws a lot of shit out the sides." Cindy Caswell nodded and moved over to the side, then took a step back. "Perfect," Henry told her.

The gun Henry Bowman carried was an FN Model D, the final refinement of John Browning's BAR and Henry Bowman's all-time favorite machine gun. The particular one in his hands was the last variant made before the full-auto-only Model D had been completely superseded by lighter, less-expensive machine rifles. It had been made in the 1950s for Israel, and unlike earlier versions, it was barreled in 7.62 NATO caliber and used FAL magazines.

Henry Bowman had removed the weapon's bipod, and in its place on the front of the gas tube had attached a sling swivel originally designed for a shotgun. He had also installed a sling swivel on top of the buttstock just in front of the steel buttplate. Attached to the two sling swivels was a long, padded M60 sling made of black nylon. The sling went around Henry's shoulder and neck, and put the gun at waist level. Screwed onto the weapon's muzzle was a stainless steel muzzle brake designed by Henry's friend Bruce McArthur who was also friends with David Richards.

Henry snapped a loaded magazine in place, gripped the gun for firing from the hip, and pushed with his arms to put tension on the sling. He was settling in with the weapon, making his concentration absolute.

"Point shooting, huh?" Richards asked. "You might do it. Six watches to the timing stand," he yelled. David Richards had grown up point-shooting an M-1 carbine from the hip, and he was very good at it. He knew that with the FN-D on its slow rate of 350 rounds per minute, it was easy to tap off single shots by releasing the trigger, shooting the gun like a semiauto.

"Shooter ready...gun on the rail...timers ready..." Richards called as Henry pressed the Belgian BAR down and forward, putting tension on the sling looped over his shoulder and down his back. Then David Richards fired his blank gun.

At the sound, Henry Bowman raised the muzzle while keeping tension on the sling. He squeezed the trigger and held it down as he swung the Model D in a smooth arc. The 18-pound gun chugged away with almost no recoil and ten bowling pins were swept away one after another, as if a giant invisible hand had brushed them off the table.

"Jesus!" one of the spectators yelled.

"Damn," echoed another.

"One point eight," cried out the six timers almost in unison. Henry removed the half-full magazine, which rendered the open-bolt gun safe.

"Set 'em up again," Henry Bowman yelled cheerfully as he put the magazine away and pulled a fresh one out of his BAR belt. "I've got the range."

The next two sets yielded identical results. The rules called for shooting four tables of pins and discarding the worst time, but Henry declined to shoot his final table.

"No point. Only way to shoot a different time is to miss one. Time's set by the cyclic rate."

"You going to let his time stand?" one of the other competitors in the Two-Man Unlimited class asked. "With a machine gun?" David Richards gave out guns for prizes to most of the top finishers in the various classes, which in part accounted for the heated competition.

"The official judge will take it under advisement," Richards announced imperiously. Henry laughed. He didn't care about prizes and he knew his friend would dream up some way of needling him at the awards ceremony.

"Hey, Henry. How'd you manage that, anyway?" Richards asked.

"I saw Steve McCreary do it with his Thompson in the subgun class a few years ago, and so I practiced a little at my range at home with my Belgian jackhammer here," he said, patting the FN-D. What Henry Bowman did not mention was that it had taken him thirteen thousand rounds of concentrated practice to time the first shot and match his swing to the pin spacing and the gun's cyclic rate.

"Bloody amazing," said a man with curly blond hair and a broad smile. The speaker was standing behind David Richards, and Henry Bowman did not notice him. If he had, he would have stopped to talk.

"So, shall we go find our girlfriend?" Cindy asked.

"That's a plan," Henry said easily. David Richards watched them walk away, not listening to what one of his timers was asking him.

***

"You should have seen his face when he saw us, Henry," Theresa said as she stepped naked out of the motel bathroom, toweling her hair.

"It was a really good 'gotcha'," Cindy agreed, smiling at Henry and stretching out on her side of the king-size bed. She, too, was naked.

"Do you think we went too far?" Theresa asked as she slid in bed between her two lovers. "I mean, was it rude? He's our host, after all."

"I don't think he minded too much, babe," Henry told Theresa as he molded his body alongside hers and began to massage her bottom.

"No, I think Henry's right," Cindy agreed as she also pressed against the young woman, nuzzling her throat. "Gun people are all pretty easygoing."

June 20, 1995

"Anybody do it yet?" Henry asked as he and Cindy approached the mock-up of the 'sniper's nest' of the Texas School Book Depository. It was the last day of the New Lease shoot, and the awards banquet was that evening.

"Nope," one of the competitors answered. "Got three guys out of over a hundred entrants who've made the three hits, but they're all at least a second-and-a-half too slow. Couple of 'em said they'd have a better chance with open sights." The man was referring to the fact that the scope made it very difficult to get back on target quickly after the gun fired and the shooter worked the bolt. "Go on and get in line if you want to give it a try. Take one of those Carcanos and do some dry-fire practice while you wait."

Henry took the man's suggestion. When his turn came up, he was able to score the three hits on the mannequins in the moving convertible in six seconds flat.

"Damn," one of the spectators breathed. "With a borrowed junker."

"I seen that guy shoot before," another said. "He can beat yourn with hisn, and hisn with yourn."

"Looks like you're the second-fastest so far," the scorekeeper told Henry when he finished. "Only one point four too slow. You win a bottle of Coke. That's David's prize for anyone that scores all three hits." Cindy looked puzzled, and Henry explained the joke.

"Two minutes after the shooting, Oswald was seen calmly drinking a Coke five floors down from where they found the rifle. And the rifle was at the opposite corner of the sixth floor from where it was supposedly fired."

"Yeah," another man broke in, "David was going to make the shooters run over, dump the rifle, run down some steps, and put money in a vending machine, but he was afraid someone would have a heart attack and sue him."

"Was it what you expected?" Cindy asked, referring to the results Henry had achieved.

"Pretty much. I mainly just wanted to see if my assessment when I was eleven years old was accurate."

"Which was?"

"If Oswald did what the Warren Commission said he did, he was the best man with a bolt action in the whole country. And it's really hard to feature that the fastest bolt man in the entire United States would have a brain tumor."

"You mean because that's the only possible explanation for why he would try to assassinate the President?"

"No, I mean because that's the only possible explanation for why he would try to do it with a Carcano."

***

"In the 9mm Novice class, our top shooter is Cindy Caswell," David Richards announced in his rapid-fire speech pattern. Cindy stood up and went to claim her plaque as the others in the dining room applauded.

"Thank you, David," she said, shaking Richards' hand.

"Here, take a number," the host said, holding out a top hat. Cindy reached in and drew out a slip of paper with a number on it. The winners of all the classes drew numbers, which determined the order in which they would choose their prizes from the awards table. There were a number of guns in the $500-$700 range to choose from, many more which were less valuable than that, lots of body armor, and enough shooting accessories for almost everyone who had entered.

"Good job," Henry said when she sat back down at the table. David Richards was announcing the next winner.

"What number did you get?" Theresa asked.

"Eleven."

"Have you looked over the stuff?"

"Yeah. He's got all kinds of good things. I'd like one of the .40-caliber Glocks, if they aren't all taken. Or a Seecamp."

"The Seecamps will go quick, I bet," Henry told her. "There's a long wait from the factory."

"Yeah."

"Well, worst case," Henry said with a laugh, "you can get one of his new light-weight women's vests. Use it for one of your outfits on stage, with a cop shirt and hat."

"Oh, the person who should do *that* is Theresa! Do you think he could fit her?" Cindy asked, looking at their friend.

"David can fit anybody. And he'd probably pay to fit Theresa." The young dancer laughed. She had a twenty-two inch waist and a chest of which she and her surgeon were both very proud.

"If the guns I want are taken, that's what I'll do," Cindy decided.

"And finally, the Two-Man Unlimited class," David Richards announced. "As Supreme Administrator-For-Life, I declare Guy Arnold and Tom Battle the winners in this category, with a time of three point nine seconds. Congratulations, gentlemen," he said as the two men walked up and shook his hand.

"What about you, Henry?" Theresa whispered. She looked around and saw that others in the room were talking amongst themselves, asking the same question.

"Don't worry about me," Henry told her.

"Thanks, great shoot, David," Guy Arnold said.

"Yeah, thanks," his partner agreed. The two men both drew numbers from the top hat.

"And now I would like to make a special announcement," David Richards said quickly. "In the Unlimited event, I am starting a new 'Outlaw' class, like the 'Run-what-you-brung' class in drag racing. Some of our competitors live in non-machine-gun states, and are restricted to using inferior shotguns when they practice before coming up here for the big shoot. So I'm putting machine guns in the Outlaw class. I've called it the Outlaw class because you have to shoot so much ammo practicing, it puts you in violation of all these crazy 'arsenal' laws they're talking about." Catcalls came from the audience at this comment.

"We're all in the outlaw class, David!" shouted one man.

"That's the truth," the host agreed. "And the winner of the first annual New Lease Outlaw competition is Henry Bowman. For this one, Henry doesn't draw a number, he gets his own special prize. Come on up here, Henry." The crowd cheered as Henry walked up and accepted the long cardboard box.

"Open it!" someone yelled. Henry did, and held up a break-open, single-barrel shotgun with rifle sights. It was worth about ninety dollars. The crowd howled.

"Concurrent with the new outlaw event," Richards announced, "I am creating the Shootaholic Rehab class, where you will be required to use a weapon like the one Henry Bowman has just won. You'll notice that this H&R shotgun is fully rifled, so you have to use slugs. The Rehab class is for guys who are trying to quit. It is a three-pin event. You will be allowed only three rounds of ammo, and you'll have to use slugs, because the rifling will give you donut-shaped shot patterns with a hole about four feet in diameter at twenty-five feet. Oh, one other thing: you start with an empty gun." Gales of laughter came from the crowd as they imagined competing with a single shot weapon under those rules. Henry Bowman laughed along with them, and started to return to his seat.

"Wait a minute, Henry, you haven't claimed the rest of your prize," Richards said. "Boys!" he shouted.

From the other end of the dining hall, pinsetters and other shoot workers began filing into the room, one after the other. Each carried an identical cardboard box about the size of an airline carry-on bag. Each box was obviously heavy. As soon as each worker set his box down by the podium, he went out to get another. Soon there were three stacks of boxes, each as tall as a man.

"This event is going to require plenty of practice," Richards announced, "so along with the gun, I'm including twenty-five cases of twelve-gauge slugs. I hope you brought a trailer." The crowd went wild, cheering and stamping their feet as Henry shook David Richards' hand once more and went back to sit with the two women. Everyone there knew Richards had spent over two thousand dollars on Henry Bowman's prize. It was the kind of thing David Richards liked to do at his shoot.

"That's it for the awards," Richards announced. "Dessert should be out shortly. Have at it," he instructed, and went off to find a seat at one of the tables.

"Earl!" Henry said when he saw that his chair next to Theresa had been taken by a lean, muscular man in his fifties with short, curly blond hair. "I didn't know you were here. Lord, I haven't seen you in ages!" Earl Taylor-Edgarton stood up and clasped his old friend's arm.

"Didn't want to interrupt while you were enjoying the company of these two charming ladies, but when you went up to the front, I judged it was every man for himself."

"Cindy, Theresa, this is Earl Taylor-Edgarton, formerly of Rhodesia, and a man who I haven't seen in years."

"Are you the man who teaches those classes about guarding against terrorism and assassination attempts?" Cindy asked.

"Yes, that's how Henry and I met, actually, years ago. It's slacked off a bit in the last few years," he admitted, pronouncing it 'lost'. "Though business has picked up again of late," he added with a meaningful look.

"Will you excuse me for a moment?" Theresa asked. "Mr. Richards is waving at me and I think he wants something."

"Certainly," Henry said. He and Earl rose as the young woman got up and left the table.

"I think David is keen on your friend," Earl said to Henry and Cindy. Both of them started laughing when they heard this. Then Henry turned serious.

"Earl, before we get talking about other stuff, what's your read on this Oklahoma City thing? I've used more explosives than most people, and there's a lot of things that don't look right to me, but I'm no authority on blowing up urban targets with improvised charges. Everybody's been talking about it ever since it happened, but I haven't heard an opinion from a real expert. What do you think?"

"It's interesting you should be skeptical, Henry," Earl Taylor-Edgarton said. "There are a number of things which don't sit right in my mind, as well. I can say this with authority: if Mr. McVeigh did in Europe what he is alleged to have done here, he would be hailed by every newspaper and magazine on the Continent as an absolute 'Master Bomber'."

"Why?" Cindy asked.

"For one, because of his faultless construction of an improvised shaped charge on such a grand scale. The blast in Oklahoma City was a directional one. A car bomb sitting in an open area normally radiates its force equally all 'round. However, in Oklahoma, the devastation directed towards the Federal building far exceeded the damage on the other side of the bomb. I saw a quick mention of the theory that the bomber used sandbags inside the vehicle to direct the blast, but I'll tell you straight, there's quite a bit more to it than that." Henry and Cindy both nodded in understanding.

"The next troubling bit," Earl went on, "is the fertilizer issue. As you well know, ANFO is a low-grade explosive. It's good for shoving big heaps of earth aside when you put it in a series of holes in the ground, but to set it out in the open and expect it to shatter a structure meters and meters away with nothing but air between? No," he said simply. "Those vertical steel supports were sheared off by a high-level explosion, like Semtex."

"That's why the news reports kept upping the amount of fertilizer that was in the van," Henry said immediately. "It started out as a one-thousand-pound bomb. Then fifteen hundred, then twenty-five. I think they've levelled off at five thousand pounds now."

"And that provokes another major issue. The five thousand pounds had to be in a number of smaller containers. It wasn't two and a half tons poured into the van like so much oatmeal. Say our master bomber built compartments holding five hundred pounds each, which would be a feat in itself. It's not that bloody easy to get ten large quantities of fertilizer to detonate simultaneously. Last month I read a theory that the ANFO was in a hundred forty 5-gallon buckets. No. It's virtually impossible to get good simultaneous detonation on a hundred charges, without top-quality commercial detcord or other high-level detonators that are harder to get than high-level explosives themselves."

"Could you...improvise a bomb that would shear off the steel girders?" Cindy asked.

"Perhaps. And again, this is where it would indicate that a 'master bomber' had engineered this explosion. There are ingredients which can be added to the basic ANFO mixture to increase its shock, but I don't know if I could create such a result as we saw in Oklahoma. Not with ANFO as the base. If Mr. McVeigh accomplished such a feat, he is a genius with explosives."

"It's just like what Henry was saying today at the Oswald shoot," Cindy Caswell said. Earl Taylor-Edgarton nodded in agreement, and a reflective look came over his face.

"You know, in 1969, I believe it was, a group of eight young people blew up the U.S. Army mathematics laboratory at the University of Wisconsin. In that case as well, the explosives used were considerably more sophisticated than you'd expect to see a bunch of disenchanted students produce. The authorities caught seven of the group, and as you'd expect, they were all near the bottom of the food chain. The seven all agreed that the technical work had been done by the one other member, who no one seemed to know much about. The FBI found a false birth certificate, as I recall, and other identification that led nowhere. What's so funny?" Earl asked.

"You reminded me of something, that's all," Henry said, thinking about the stack of alternate ID, addresses, and credit cards he'd acquired in his college days by scouring cemeteries. "It's nothing. Go on."

"They never did find him," the Rhodesian continued, "but now it's assumed he was an *agent provocateur.* Your government did those kinds of things back in those days. I'd forgotten all about that math lab until just now."

"That's not the only historic precedent, Henry said. "Hitler's men burned the *Reichstag* to make it look like they had more opposition and justify violent retaliation. That worked like a charm. And at Amherst College, a few years after I graduated, someone burned a cross in front of the black fraternity when the campus Afro-Am organization was about to get its student funding reduced. Guess who finally confessed after his girlfriend ratted him out?"

"The President of the Afro-Am organization?" Cindy guessed.

"I must've told you the story before."

"Did they lynch the bugger?"

"No, but it did put a strain on race relations at the school for a while, from what I hear. Anyway, I think it does look a little suspicious that our master bomber picks a federal building with a day-care center in it, and that the ATF people were all conveniently out of the building when the bomb blew up."

"What?" Cindy asked. "I hadn't heard that."

"Yeah. They were all off at a conference somewhere out of town. Office was empty. Then, of course, there's this master bomber's so-called flight from the scene. He drives away, speeding, in a car with no license plate. He's wearing a shoulder holster with a Glock in it on top of a T-shirt, which is another big red flag. And when a cop stops him, after he's just killed a hundred people, does he blast him and leave? No. He lets the cop arrest him. Not for the gun; he had a carry permit for that. For a pocketknife. That was the concealed-weapon charge."

"You can't be serious," Earl Taylor-Edgarton said, astonished.

"Yep. So they got in a dig at the few states that are still trying to get carry laws, too. 'Oh, my God! The Oklahoma Bomber was carrying a gun, and it was legal! How awful!' Governor Flanagan in Missouri was rubbing his hands together."

"You think it was the ATF that did it, Henry?" Cindy asked.

"I don't have a clue. But it seems hard to feature a lot of those guys being in on it. Someone would rat out the rest of the group. I confess that my first reaction, when I heard what had happened and that ATF was out of the building, was that it was an accident."

"*An accident?*" Earl and Cindy both asked, not understanding.

"Not an accident that a bomb went off, an accident that any people were killed. That's why I wanted to ask you about the explosives end of it, Earl. I mean, I wouldn't think a bomb out in a parking lot would make a big building collapse, would you? I'd think you'd need to get the truck inside, like in a basement parking garage.

"See, my first thought was that maybe a couple of individual agents were scared of losing their jobs what with the upcoming hearings on ATF, Waco, and Ruby Ridge. So they go stick a bomb in a van out in the middle of the parking lot on the Waco anniversary, figuring they'll break a bunch of windows, scare the shit out of everybody, and shift attention towards the militias and the gun guys, and away from ninja-suited tax agents with machine guns.

"Except that it's a government building in a Democratic state, and when it was built, the contractor gave the Governor a big kickback, then left out a bunch of rebar and went real light on the mix. And instead of just having a bunch of windows break, the whole building fell down. Hell, in Chicago, back when I was nineteen or twenty, a whole highway collapsed for that reason. Had one-fourth as many reinforcements in it as the prints said it had. As I said, I didn't have any expertise on the explosive end of things, so maybe

582

that accident theory won't work. But I'm a big believer in history repeating itself."

"I've not seen your theory advanced in the press," Earl Taylor-Edgarton said with a smile. "Perhaps you should suggest it to the FBI."

"There's an idea," Henry said.

"This McVeigh person is keeping his mouth shut, from all the reports I've read. Smartest thing he could do," Earl Taylor-Edgarton declared. Henry shot Cindy a look, and she smiled almost imperceptibly, remembering.

"I wonder how he spends his time in prison," Cindy said. Suddenly, the Rhodesian grinned.

"If our friend Henry here is right," Earl said to her, "and history repeats itself, Mr. McVeigh has plenty to do."

"Why do you say that?"

"Well, this McVeigh fellow is said to have been angry with a government he felt was oppressing him, so he allegedly set a bomb at a nerve center for government activities, and blew it up, killed dozens of government employees, women, and children.

"After World War Two, Menachem Begin led the Irgun Zvai Leumi guerrilla movement against the British government because the Brits were occupying Palestine. In 1947, Begin blew up the King David Hotel in Jerusalem, which was a center for British government operations. He, too, killed many dozens of people—army officers, wives, children, and hotel workers."

"So?" Cindy asked. Henry smiled tightly because he saw where Earl was heading.

"So if history is our guide," Earl Taylor-Edgarton said with raised eyebrows, "then Mr. McVeigh is undoubtedly working on his acceptance speech for the Nobel Peace Prize."

June 21, 1995

"Look, I'm, uh...really embarrassed," Cindy Caswell said as she reclined her seatback another few degrees. "I didn't see this coming." Henry started laughing, took his hand off the steering wheel, and squeezed his friend's leg.

"You know, kiddo, it reminds me of the old joke about the guy whose wife dies, and he's just crying his eyes out at the funeral. His friend tells him to get a grip, and the guy says, 'No one to hold close, and kiss, and cuddle, and make passionate love to, and, oh, God, I can't stand it!' And the friend says, 'Look Harry, you're only thirty-five, you're in great shape, and people really like you. I'm sure that some time in the future you'll find another woman and you'll have all those things again. Buck up, man.' And the guy looks at his friend and says, 'Sure, but what am I going to do *tonight?*'"

"I still can't believe she's moving in with him without even going back home first," Cindy said. "It's my fault. I never should have suggested that stupid joke."

"Hey, David looked happier this morning than I've ever seen him. Right now, he's probably got on his English horseman's outfit, is swatting Theresa's butt with his riding crop, and trying to figure out how to work the scene into the next New Lease Body Armor instructional video. So chill out—you'll pick up another player for us, right?" he asked, looking over at Cindy. She turned her head, and then Cindy and Henry spoke in unison:

"Sure, but what are we going to do *tonight?*"

"Hey, been a while since you were in town," Stokely Meier said as Henry Bowman came through the door of the gun shop. "Anything new going on?"

"Just looking at rocks for people, when I'm working."

"And turning them into powder with your 4-bore when you're not?" Stokely said, laughing.

"Something like that. I got a 2-bore, as a matter of fact."

"No."

"Yes. A single-barrel Farquharson a guy in Vermont made up. Shot it a bunch last week, with a 3145-grain turned brass bullet at a little over twelve hundred. You'll love it."

"Well, bring it on in next time, damn it. Hey—you see today's headlines?" Stokely asked as he tossed that morning's *St. Louis Post-Dispatch* onto the glass-topped pistol case next to the cash register. Henry Bowman looked down at the newspaper.

FBI Targets Four More In Weaver Case

Freeh's Ex-Deputy Included; Criminal Inquiry Launched

"I heard about that on CNN last night, Stoke. They're throwing a few more babies out of the lifeboat, hoping to keep the sharks occupied until they can get to land."

"Four more paid vacations for those peckernecks." Stokely was referring to the last sentence of the lengthy article, which admitted that the four agents were receiving full pay for the duration of their suspensions.

"They admit to destroying evidence," Henry said as he scanned the news piece. "That's always good for public opinion. And I see Potts is *mucho* pissed about being demoted from Deputy Director," he commented, referring to the supervisor in charge of the Weaver fiasco.

"You should've heard what some of the guys who come in here were saying when they read Potts got the same letter of censure for Ruby Ridge as he did for losing a cellular phone."

"I can imagine. And if I were Lon Horiuchi," Henry said, referring to the FBI sniper who had shot Vicki Weaver in the head, "I would hire myself the best damn criminal defense lawyer in the country. I'd move to a state like New York or New Jersey, and I'd blow the Governor so that he wouldn't let me be extradited to Idaho. If that boy doesn't watch it, he's going to find himself facing a prison sentence."

"No shit. Hey, if you really want to get sick, read this." He handed Henry a copy of the latest *Gun Week*, a national weekly newspaper focusing on firearms-related issues.

BATF Gets Its Own 22-Plane Air Force

Here's news that may make some people sleep a little less soundly at night: the Bureau of Alcohol, Tobacco, and Firearms (BATF) is getting its own air force.

The Washington Times, quoting confirmation by BATF spokesperson Susan McCarron, reported on July 18 that BATF has obtained 22 counterinsurgency, heavy-weapons-capable military aircraft.

However, the confirmation to The Times seems to have come only after unofficial sources had reported on the transfer of planes to BATF, and only after *Soldier of Fortune* magazine had gone to press with their September 1995 issue in which reporter James Pate disclosed that the aircraft deal had been consummated under rather murky circumstances. (The September issue of Soldier of Fortune hit the newsstand circulation system just prior to the publication of The Times report on July 18.)

What The Times did not disclose and what SOF did report was that the aircraft deal began in a somewhat covert manner last September, almost a year earlier. That's when the Federal Aviation Administration (FAA) recorded conveyance of title to at least two of the OV-10D Broncos from the General Services Administration to Mid-Air Salvage Inc., of Franklin Park, NJ, and on the same day from Mid-Air Salvage to America Warbirds Inc. of Gaithersburg, MD. The FAA documents obtained by Soldier of Fortune relate directly to two specific aircraft serial numbers.

The 300-mph OV-10D planes—one of several designations used by the Marine Corps during the Vietnam War for gunfire

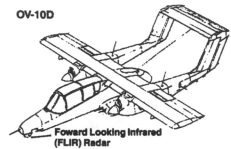

OV-10D

Foward Looking Infrared (FLIR) Radar

and missile support of ground troops, and by the Air Force during Operation Desert Storm for night observation—have been transferred from the Defense Department to BATF.

The turboprop aircraft, which will be used for day and night surveillance support, were designed to locate people on the ground through their body heat. When used by military services, the planes were equipped with infrared tracking systems, ground-mapping radar, laser range-finders, gun sights, and 20mm cannons.

BATF spokeswoman Susan McCarron confirmed that the agency had obtained the aircraft but noted that they had been stripped of their armament. She told The Times that nine of the OV-10Ds were operational and that the remaining 13 were being used for spare parts.

'No Weapons'

"We have nine OV-10Ds that are unarmed; they have no weapons on them," Ms. McCarron said. "They are being used for surveillance and photography purposes. The remainder are being used for spare parts."

Ms. McCarron said the aircraft were obtained from the Defense Department "when DOD was getting rid of them," and that other agencies had also received some of the airplanes. However, there had been no confirmation that the planes acquired by other agencies are exactly the same models. The BATF has confirmed that they type of aircraft they have acquired features a longer, pointed nose which houses the Forward-Looking Infra-Red (FLIR) system used to detect heat emitted by people and heat-producing objects.

The Times pointed out that "The transfer of the aircraft to ATF comes at a time of heightened public skepticism and congressional scrutiny of the agency's ability to enforce the law without trampling on the rights of citizens."

The Times noted BATF's image suffered greatly in the aftermath of its 1993 raid and subsequent shootout at the Branch Davidian compound in Waco, TX, during which four agents and six Davidians were killed. It sustained another public-relations blow after it was revealed that BATF agents helped organize a whites-only "Good Ol' Boys Roundup" in the Tennessee hills. (See Gun Week, Aug 4, 1995)

One Senate staffer said there was "some real interest" in BATF's acquisition of the aircraft and that questions "probably will be asked very soon of the agency" about the specifics of their use and the locations where they have been assigned.

Michael Pruitt, foreman at Business Jet Designs of Shawnee, OK, confirmed that two of the BATF aircraft had been painted at his facility and that at least one more of the OV-10Ds "was on the way." Pruitt said the aircraft were painted dark blue with red and white trim. The sources said the paint jobs cost about $20,000 each.

The firm's owners, Johnny Patterson, told associates in June that he expects to be painting at least 12 of the BATF aircraft but was unsure whether he could move all of them fast enough through his shop.

Infrared System

According to The Times' sources, the BATF's OV-10Ds recently were overhauled and were equipped with a state-of-the-art forward-looking infrared system that allows the pilot to locate and identify targets at night—similar to the tracking system on the Apache advanced attack helicopter.

Designed by Rockwell International, the OV-10D originally was outfitted with two 7.62mm machine guns. It also was modified to carry one Sidewinder missile under each wing, bombs, fire bombs, rocket packages, and cluster bombs.

The OV-10D can carry a 20mm gun with 1500 rounds of ammunition.

During the Vietnam War, the OV-10Ds flew over 200 combat missions in which they were credited with killing 300 enemy troops.

As Soldier of Fortune pointed out, the BATF's Bronco squadron is troubling for two main reasons:

First, the Bureau apparently was trying to hide ownership of the OV-10Ds by transferring title through one phony company to another. A check of the two company names showed that the address given for Mid-Air Salvage was a town house with no apparent commercial activity; American Warbirds' address belongs to an electronics and radio office for BATF's special operations division.

Second, an air of suspicion surrounds the financial transactions and the secretive allocation of government funds.

These are questions which Congress may want to address during appropriations hearings. If BATF has a legitimate use for such aircraft, why the furtiveness of the acquisition?

"Boy, now doesn't this give you a warm, fuzzy feeling about the future, hm?" Henry asked when he had finished the piece.

"It's worse than when ATF busted into that Maryland gun show promoter's house and the woman agent stomped his cats to death earlier this year," Stokely agreed, referring to a recent outrage that had made some of the papers.

"Warplanes for a bunch of stumblefuck tax agents? What's it going to take for these guys to get the picture, Stoke?"

"Damned if I know, Henry. Damned if I know."

"What the hell is that?" Thomas J. Fleming's brother-in-law demanded, pointing his finger at a prominent billboard ahead of them on the right. Fleming had just picked up his wife's sibling at the airport, and they were sitting in rush-hour traffic on the inner belt headed south. There was a worker on a scaffolding on the left side of the large sign.

FLANAGAN DEATH CLOCK

117 honest adults *Murdered* because

The Governor Doesn't Trust YOU!

Paid for by the family of the late Elicia T. Boulton

"You haven't heard about that?" Fleming asked as he turned up the car's air conditioner. "Not surprising, I guess, since you don't live here. For that matter, it's been getting almost no local press, either. The papers and news editors hate it, but they can't disagree with the facts, so they ignore it. It's been paid for by the family of a murdered carjacking victim. Some woman with the bad judgment to buy a Jeep Cherokee instead of some other sport utility that African-American gang members find less desirable."

"What's the deal?"

"The woman was unarmed, and after the murder one of the gun groups unearthed a letter the victim had written the Governor six weeks before. Told Flanagan to change his position on the concealed-carry issue and support a licensing system for honest adults. Sent along a bunch of documentation that licensees caused no problems in any of the 41 states where permits are available. Said the legislature trusted her at the hospital with other people's lives, but not out in the parking lot with her own."

"She was a doctor?"

"Nurse anaesthetist. That was a big enough embarrassment to the Governor, but then the hospital supervisor told the papers that she had also taken several days of unpaid leave to travel to Jefferson City. Woman went to see her legislators about the issue, and tried to get into the Governor's office, but had no luck there. All this got a lot of press after the murder, and then the dead woman's family ponied up for the billboard. That '117' figure is the murders since Flanagan took office in '92."

"I thought there were about two hundred killings a year."

"They only count unarmed victims over twenty-one that have no criminal record, and only when the victim is killed outside his or her home. The felon-on-felon killings and victims under 21 are excluded, 'cause neither group would be eligible for a carry license. At home you can protect yourself, and if you don't, it's your decision, not the government's."

"That kind of information on victims is readily available?"

"The newspapers don't print it, if that's what you mean. But there's hundreds of thousands of hard-core supporters in this state, some of them cops with access to crime databases. Every time someone hears of a killing, it gets checked out immediately.

Researched and documented, whether the papers picked it up or not. Lot of editors have egg on their faces because of it."

"Are they about to take it down?" the guest asked, pointing at the worker on the scaffolding.

"No, the family's promised to keep paying for the space until the law gets changed or the Governor gets thrown out. That guy's just going up there to change the number."

"Think it'll make any difference in the election?"

"Maybe make Flanagan's defeat humiliating instead of merely embarrassing. Guy's pulled a George Bush and cut his own throat, politically. With or without the 'Death Clock'."

Present Day

"I think this may be what we're looking for," the technician said to his superior. "There's a bunch of crap about ammo first that you can ignore, then it gets interesting. Listen." He punched the 'play' button on the tape recorder.

"So, did you get your taxes done on time?" came the voice from the machine.

"That's Kane talking to Henry Bowman in Missouri," the technician said quickly.

"Yeah. Last thing I want to do is file an extension and have it hanging over me for another five months, or whatever it is," Henry Bowman answered. "Besides, that's why God invented accountants—so they can deal with it and all I have to do is write the check. We got any ammo coming from anywhere?" he asked, changing the subject. "Last I heard, a shipment of West German .308 was about to come in, and Dale was supposed to get a bunch of it."

"Yeah, but it was fifteen cents, and turned out that a lot of it had been stored underwater. Got a whole bunch of head seps and now Dale's trying to blow it out for components at a dime."

"Shit, that's twenty-five grand a container down the toilet, and he still has to hump it around to get rid of it. How many containers did he get stuck with?"

"Don't ask," Kane replied. "Anyway, feds aren't approving many Form Sixes right now. China's still out, but I'm working on some 7.62 x 54R from Russia."

"How much?"

"A nickel, in Goryunov belts."

"Man, that'd be the nuts. I've got a couple of top covers for my 17A1s, and I've still got that pair of Chinese Maxims. But can we get it in that way?" Bowman asked suddenly. He was referring to the magazine ban in the so-called 'Crime Bill' which Congress had passed in September of 1994. The fact that the ammunition was loaded in metal belts would likely cause Imports Branch to refuse the application.

"We'll have to see. I'm not paying for it until it lands on my doorstep."

"If it's good stuff, I'll take a container at any price under six cents," Henry said. "That's what—twenty thousand dollars?"

"Something like that. Belts and cans add to the weight." A standard container load was twenty tons, which was deliverable in one semi-trailer. "It's kind of a weird deal," Kane went on. "The stuff's in Israel, and I–"

"What the hell were the Israelis doing with a bunch of 7.62 Russian?" Henry broke in.

"Beats me. They've got a zillion rounds of it, though. I came across it 'cause I'm still trying to get that Israeli .308 AP on an exemption certificate for that deal with SACO Defense."

"You mean you don't have that .308 yet?" Henry demanded in disbelief. "From 1994?"

"No, this is some more, 'cause they still got problems. Probably have to wait forever again on this batch, too, though."

The federal agents listening to the tape did not grasp what Allen Kane and Henry Bowman were talking about, beyond the fact that they were having trouble getting ammunition approved for import, nor did they care. Imports was not their department.

"Anyway," Kane went on, "reason I called, I talked to Phil, and this summer is the peak of a cycle and supposed to be the best one for jacks in more than twenty years. Don't know it'll be *that* good, but you want to go back to the Pahsimeroi, like we did in '69?"

"When you going?"

"Probably leave here early June. Going to take my deuce-and-a-half. Want to come?"

"How long you going to be out there?"

"A month, maybe, if my ammo holds out that long." There was a long pause before Henry replied.

"I doubt I can stay more than two or three weeks. Okay if I fly back a little early?"

"Yeah, sure."

"Then I'm in, partner."

"Great."

"Just keep me posted if your timetable changes, 'cause I'm going to have to juggle some things to take off for that long."

"No problem. Hey—dumb question, but did you ever transfer me those A4s? I got three guys screaming at me, and I can't even give them serial numbers, and–" Kane's voice was cut off as the agent snapped off the tape recording.

"The rest is just gun talk," the agent explained.

"When did this conversation take place?" the supervisor asked.

"Last night. We'll be continuing to monitor Kane and Bowman to make sure they don't change their plans. But based on what we've observed and past history, Allen Kane sticks to schedules he has made, and he is not apt to let anything interrupt his western trip."

"Keep the tap on Kane's line, and get one put on Bowman's. We still got Millet wired?"

"Yes sir."

"Good. Keep monitoring him, too." The supervisor smiled. "Get a proposal drawn up and submit it for my approval," he instructed. "I want it by Tuesday."

"I'll get right on it."

April 20

"Okay, fittings are all tight—start pumping," the man from Wingfoot Dry Cleaning Supply in Kansas City said as he stood up and prepared to put the orange-and-white sawhorse in front of the driveway. It was 5:58 a.m. and Ace Cleaners would open in two minutes. Before the man could block the entrance to the Ace Cleaners lot, the first customer of the day pulled in. The driver of the late-model Cadillac cut the wheel sharply just as the car's left front tire rolled over the high-pressure hose at the junction of hose and brass fitting. The combination of the weight of the car, twisting motion of the tire, and rough asphalt was enough to tear the high-pressure line. Dry cleaning fluid began to pour out of the torn hose, forming a puddle underneath the car. The man did not notice this immediately. He had already gone inside the office with his paperwork.

"Excuse me, Ma'am," the Wingfoot employee said as he walked back out of the building. "Would you mind pulling your car up about another ten feet? We've got to get at the—*Oh, Christ!*" the man yelled when he saw the pool of fluid. "Ronnie! Shut 'er off, *now!* We got a busted line!" The man at the truck did as he was told.

"What's the problem?" said a short, balding man named Billings as he stepped out of the building and squinted in the bright sunlight. Billings was Ace Cleaners' owner. "Ahh, hell," he said, shaking his head when he saw the eight-foot diameter pool of fluid soaking into the hot asphalt. He was imagining the horrendous amount of paperwork he was going to have to do.

"There goes my morning."

April 21

"Dig up the entire parking lot?" the owner of Ace Cleaners yelled into the phone. "For five gallons of fluid? You've got to be kidding!" Billings listened with mounting dread as the government employee explained the new EPA regulations. The entire Ace Cleaners parking lot had to be removed and the contaminated asphalt processed to remove all traces of the spilled fluid. "But we're in an industrial area—it's all paved over and there isn't a tree for blocks. Do your people think it's going to get in the water table? Our parking lot has had cars drip oil on it for forty years, and even if they didn't, there's petroleum in the goddamn asphalt itself, for Christ's sake." Billings held his tongue as the man on the other end began telling him to call Wingfoot, the cleaning supplies company, and get them to contact their insurance carrier.

The dry cleaning shop's owner would soon learn that Wingfoot's rates had long ago become unaffordable, and the company was 'going naked'. Ace and Wingfoot were now jointly and severally liable for cleaning up the toxic spill. The initial estimate for this procedure would be over a half million dollars.

April 27

"You're kidding."

"Dead serious, Alex. Everyone has to go through it. New department policy."

"Sexual Harassment Awareness Training. SHAT, huh? Sounds a lot more like 'shit' to me, sir." Alex Neumann put his hand over the receiver, laughed, and made a face at the other FBI agent in the Cheyenne office, Trey Mullins.

"That's not the kind of attitude the Bureau likes to see its men display, Agent Neumann," the voice on the other end of the phone said sternly. Neumann stopped laughing and took his hand away quickly.

"I understand, sir," Alex Neumann said, "but there aren't any women FBI agents here. None. And it's not like I'm some twenty-year-old kid. Hell, sir, I'm not all that far away from early retirement." Trey Mullins began doing an old-man-with-a-cane pantomime.

"No exceptions, Alex." The man in Washington chuckled. "And age has nothing to do with it. Who knows? You might be the Bureau's Lyndon Johnson."

Agent Neumann made one final plea. "Look, does it matter that here in Cheyenne, there are practically no women to harass period, let alone women FBI agents?"

"Not at all, Alex. It's just like any other training the FBI requires. You may not think you'll need it, but the Bureau's not about to take that chance. You could get transferred again. Think of it as an insurance policy for us."

"So when do I have to take this SHAT class?"

"It's a ten-day course at Quantico that's being–"

"Ten days?" Alex Neumann almost yelled into the phone. "What the hell are they going to talk about to a bunch of old guys for ten days? Best pickup lines to use with the forensic staff?" The voice on the other end of the phone turned icy.

"The course is ten days long. It will be given at the Quantico facility starting at 8:00 a.m. sharp on June 9. Our travel office will mail you an airplane ticket for a June 8 departure. Agent Mullins can take care of the office while you're away. Don't miss your flight." FBI Agent and HRT member Alex Neumann started to apologize, but realized he was holding a dead receiver.

"Did you have to go through this crap?" he asked his friend, Harker Edward Mullins III, whom everyone called 'Trey'. Mullins shrugged.

"Yeah, they had some stupid course I had to take a while back. Wasn't ten days long, but it seemed like it. Guess they've changed things some. Cover Your Ass is the name of the game, pal."

"Waste of time."

"Yeah, well, it's not like we're overwhelmed with work. Even by myself, I won't have much to do around here."

"I'm going to be bored to tears in D.C. You know that, don't you?" Trey Mullins shrugged in reply.

Both men's predictions would prove to be dead wrong.

***

"Hello?"

"Curt! Orville Crocker up in Wyoming. I'm not interrupting your dinner, am I?"

"No, we eat about 6:00 around here," Curt Behnke said with a smile. "And I was going to call you in the next day or so. I've finished that piece for your cannon."

"You're kidding—it's been less than a week."

"Well, since I retired, there's more time for gun work. And I still had my sketches from the one I made for Henry Bowman. The second one always goes a lot faster."

Orville Crocker was a Class 3 dealer in Laramie, Wyoming. He owned a Finnish Lahti gas-operated 20mm antitank cannon like the one Henry Bowman had bought from Potomac Arms in 1968. The obsolete Lahti/Solothurn ammo could be had in Europe for 50 cents a round, but the 1968 import ban on non-sporting cartridges had dried up the U.S. supply, and the domestic price was now over $30 a shot. Reloading the brass with resized U.S. Vulcan projectiles was the only option for serious 20mm shooters such as Henry Bowman and Orville Crocker.

The problem with the Lahti was that unlike the Solothurn, the gun ejected spent rounds straight down when it fired, and the case mouths got torn up when they hit the ground. This ruined them for reloading. Henry's solution was to have Curt Behnke make a new gas regulator for the gun, with no holes in it. The tolerances were such that Henry had elected to have Behnke do the work, rather than machine one himself.

The undrilled regulator deactivated the Lahti's gas operating system, leaving the fired case in the chamber. This turned the semiautomatic gun into a manually-operated repeater, where the shooter had to retract the 11-pound bolt manually every shot by cranking the charging handle several revolutions. It was not nearly as convenient as aiming and pulling the trigger, but it saved the brass. Crocker had seen Henry's setup at the Knob Creek shoot, wheedled Behnke's name out of Henry, and convinced the St. Louis gunsmith to repeat his efforts.

"Well, that's a nice surprise," Crocker said into the phone. "I'm not used to getting gun work finished ahead of schedule. But that's not why I called. Henry said you're a prairie dog hunter. Good friend of mine has a ranch about fifty miles from here, leases something like ten thousand acres to graze cattle. He's been after me to come hunt prairie dogs up at his place, but all I've got to shoot are pistols and NFA stuff—you know, machine guns and cannons. I've wanted to get a good varmint rifle built, and Henry says you're the best.

"How'd you like to come up here for a few days, we'll drive out to his place in my truck, and you can show me how it's done. I've got good binoculars and a tripod, and I'll spot for you. You can drive here if you want, but what I thought you might rather do is ship your guns and ammo up ahead by UPS, and fly into Cheyenne. Save you a lot of boring hours on the road."

"Well," Behnke said, thinking about the offer, "I don't have a hunt planned yet this summer..." Henry Bowman had told Curt Behnke his summer schedule looked pretty full, and Behnke's son that liked to shoot was unable to get a week off of work at that time of year. The gunsmith could tolerate a 1600-mile highway trip, but like most people he preferred to have someone along to share the driving and provide company. Orville Crocker's offer sounded good.

"Are you sure your friend wouldn't mind?" Crocker laughed at the question.

"He'll complain there aren't more of us. What time of summer you want to come up? Mid-, late June?"

"Sure, that would work. I'll have to call the airlines and see what flights they've got."

"While you're doing that, make up a list of stuff you want me to have when you get here. You know, sandbags, screwdriver sets, things like that. I already have most of that stuff around here, and anything I have to buy I probably ought to own anyway. That way you won't have to ship anything except guns and ammo."

"We'll mostly shoot off folding bipods, but that's a good point. If you're serious, you ought to order a portable shooting bench from Armor Metal Products. I'll send you their ad with your gas regulator. And I can ship up a couple extra rifles and match ammo I've loaded for them. If you like the way either of them works for you, I'll make you a good price on it. Cost a third of what it would take to build one up new. It's got so in my old age I've ended up with more match rifles than I know what to do with."

"Sounds great. Let's plan on sometime around the end of June, and I'll be talking to you about the details between now and then."

"I'll send that part for your big gun out tomorrow. Then I guess I'd better get to my loading bench," he joked.

"I'm looking forward to meeting you, Curt."

"Same here. 'Bye, now," he said, and hung up the phone.

May 2

"Taylor Lowell?" the man in the suit asked.

"That's me," Lowell answered as he straightened up from inspecting the left brake rotor on his 1994 Pitts S2-B. "Actually, Taylor Lowell is my dad. I'm Taylor Lowell, Junior." He wiped his right hand on a shop towel and extended it towards the stranger, who ignored the gesture.

"Mendez, FAA," the man said, unfolding his credentials. "Here for a ramp check. Is this plane registered either Experimental or Exhibition?" he asked abruptly.

"No, it's straight factory," Lowell said, taken aback. He had purchased the immaculate 260-horsepower aerobatic biplane seven months earlier for $104,500, with less than 300 hours total time on its Hobbs meter. The seller had ferried it from his airport in Houston to Lowell's local strip outside Phoenix. Since that time, Lowell had put 110 hours on the craft. Flying, particularly aerobatic flying, was the US West executive's one indulgence.

The FAA inspector stepped up onto the lower wing and peered into the cockpit. "What's this?" he asked, pointing at the seat.

"That's a trickle charger I've got hooked to the battery. To keep the Gel Cell at full charge, if I miss a couple weekends."

"Got an STC for it?" the FAA man demanded, referring to the Supplemental Type Certificate that the FAA required before any modifications to a factory airplane could be legally performed.

"No, I take it out before I go flying. I've got it hooked up for right now, 'cause I haven't been up in two weeks." Then, because he was eager to go flying and the FAA man's ramp check was cutting into his air time, Taylor Lowell made a huge mistake. "I mean, Jesus, it's just a little trickle charger." His tone of voice implied tolerant amusement.

"You have the unit bolted to the battery terminals, which—"

"That's so it can't spark, like spring clips can do," Lowell broke in quickly.

"It also makes it a permanent installation," Mendez said smoothly.

"Christ, I'm not going to go flying with it still hooked up. Jesus, talk about the Princess and the Pea," Lowell said with a laugh as he imagined having to fly his airplane while sitting on a metal box the size of half a loaf of bread.

"It's still a permanent installation," Mendez said with a smile as he reached into the cockpit and withdrew the small piece of FAA cardboard from its clear plastic pouch. "I'm afraid I'm going to have to revoke your airworthiness certificate. For now," he added as he stepped off the wing.

"What?"

"We'll need some time to check for other airworthiness violations, and more people. We'll need to go over this aircraft carefully, Mr. Lowell." The Pitts pilot's jaw dropped, and his face turned bright red.

"You can't ground my—"

"And I'm going to recommend that you be given an up-to-date medical evaluation. Your appearance indicates that your blood pressure may be over FAA limits. I also want to see the results of a neurological exam. I'll tell the tower your pilot status is no longer current." With that, Inspector Mendez turned on his heel and walked away.

Taylor Lowell, Junior, had over two thousand flight hours in a dozen different types of private aircraft. He had inherited his passion from his father, who had first taken him flying shortly after the boy had learned to walk. Taylor Lowell, Senior, was an ex-Navy pilot who had had to quit flying in his late sixties when his eyesight began to go. He had never forgotten the instructor who had first instilled in him the combination of respect, awe, and delight for what an airplane could be made to do.

The old man always smiled when he talked about his flight school days in 1944. His son's favorite stories were the ones his father told about the instructor who liked to climb out on the lower wing of the open-cockpit trainers, where he could talk right in the student's ear and use his one free hand to punctuate his lessons.

As Taylor Lowell, Junior, stood on the flight line, hyperventilating and willing his heart rate to subside, he cursed himself for speaking his mind to a government agent who held such power over his future. "I'm a goddamned fool," he said under his breath. Then he thought of what his father's reaction would be, and he closed his eyes. "Dad doesn't need to know."

May 21

Irwin Mann sipped his coffee and turned to the obituary section of the *St. Louis Post-Dispatch* before looking at the rest of the paper. It was a practice he'd observed for many years. Face death and accept it, then move on. Mann scanned the listings, but saw no one's name he recognized. Satisfied, he closed the paper and started in on the front page. A news item near the bottom caught his eye.

Sol Schenker, Govt. Holocaust Historian and Advisor, Dies

President Lauds 'Unyielding Commitment', Seeks Successor

Compiled From News Services

WASHINGTON, D.C. - Sol Schenker, whose calm but relentless dedication to recording the facts of the Holocaust, died Sunday. He was 92.

Mr. Schenker, who underwent cancer surgery in 1993, died at Cedars Sinai Hospital, his grandson Alvin Rosenfeld said. He said Mr. Schenker had had a stroke on Thursday. When doctors could detect no remaining brain function, family members requested that Schenker be removed from life-support systems, Rosenfeld said.

At the time of his death, Schenker was the spokesman for the Washington-based Center for Holocaust Studies, and served as the primary link between the Center and the White House. "It will be very difficult to replace Sol Schenker," the President said in a news conference last night. "He filled a vital role. We will need the same serious, unyielding commitment to history

See SCHENKER, Page 3

Irwin Mann folded the page back and finished the article. The President said he needed someone to fill the void left by Schenker's death. For a brief moment, Mann wished that he could apply for the position. Then he laughed at himself.

"Old man, they want a scholar to make the people remember the tragedy," he said aloud. "Not an old fighter to shame them with talk of what might have been."

Irwin Mann went on to the other articles in the newspaper, but his mind would not focus on them.

June 2

"We just picked this up this morning, sir. It looks like everything's on schedule," the ATF agent said as he hit the PLAY button on the tape recorder.

"Hello."

"You got all your ammo loaded?" came the voice that all the men in the room knew was Allen Kane's.

"As a matter of fact, I do. I actually got done a little ahead of schedule. You still coming by on the fifth to pick me up?" Henry Bowman asked.

"Yeah. Probably blow out of here about five in the morning, should wheel into your place about noon. Then we'll load up all your shit and hit the road. That still okay?"

"Yeah. Perfect."

"Good. Hey, I wish you were here right now—I just got the breech ring for my 105. Damn thing took nine months to clear. They're a bitch for one guy to put together."

"Hell, just hook the 105 to the back of the deuce-and-a-half, throw the breech ring in the back, we'll put it together here at my place, and we can take it with us. Shoot it out over Mormon Gulch." There was a long pause, as Henry Bowman realized his friend was actually considering the idea.

"Allen, I was just kidding! Jesus, it's eighteen hundred miles each way! We lunch a bearing in that thing and we're fucked big-time."

"Yeah, I know..." his friend said wistfully. It was obvious from his tone of voice that he wanted to reassemble and test the howitzer as soon as possible.

"Look," Henry said, I'll make you a deal. Since you're coming here to pick up me and all my stuff on the way out, and probably dropping it off by yourself on the way back, here's what I'll do: Soon as you get back to your place next month, I'll whip on over for a couple days and we'll get that thing up and running. Take it out to the reservoir, or the old strip mines, and give it a workout. That way you won't be tempted to try putting it together tonight, drop it on your foot, and ruin the trip for both of us. And it'll give you something to look forward to when you're driving back by yourself. That fair?"

"Yeah—that's a deal."

"Okay. I'll look for you in three days, then, around lunchtime."

"Make sure you got plenty of ammo for your wheelguns. Phil says the jacks are so thick there's a dead one every ten feet on all the roads around Mackey."

"Well, for the .44s, I've got twelve thousand Hemsted hollowpoints, hundred-sixty-five grain with the cavity that goes almost to the base. Goes 1850 out of my Smiths and stays in three inches at 100. New Winchester brass with the old fast lot of H110."

"You still got some of that?"

"Bought sixteen hundred pounds of it from Jurras when he went bust in '73. Got two kegs left."

"Wish we could still get powder at a buck a pound."

"That's the truth. Hey, I got to run. Anything else?"

"Nah, just making sure you were all set."

"Yeah, I'm in good shape. See you in a few days."

"Bye." There was the sound of two receivers being hung up, and the agent hit the STOP button on the tape player. He looked up and grinned at his supervisor.

"When Mister Kane gets home," he said with a laugh, "he's going to have quite a little surprise waiting for him, isn't he, sir?" The senior man shook his head in reply.

"He'll be national news long before he gets back to Indiana."

***

Henry Bowman set the alarm to his house and walked out to the detached six-car garage. He carried a nylon bag in his left hand and a thin plastic case in his right. The bag contained some papers, his shaving kit, a pair of running shoes, clean socks and underwear, and his cellular phone and battery charger. The plastic case housed his laptop computer, portable printer, and other related accessories.

Henry put down his computer case, unbolted the walk-in door to the garage with his key, reached in, and pressed the leftmost of the three buttons that operated the overhead doors. He closed and bolted the walk-in door and walked to the far end of the garage, where he kept his motorcycles.

The BMW was the least powerful of the six bikes Henry owned, but it was the only one he had that was truly an all-purpose machine. While the other five were made purely for on-pavement use, the 1989 GS1000 was designed from the start to be a competent mount on asphalt, dirt, gravel, sand, and (in a pinch), snow. It had over eight inches of suspension travel on each end, knobby tires, and was lighter than any other 1000cc machine available from a factory. It also had a seven-gallon tank that gave it an over-300-mile range, integrated bags and luggage rack, and a complete set of maintenance tools. It was one of the few factory-built motorcycles designed to carry a rider and a quantity of gear comfortably over substantial distances, regardless of whether the route was pavement, unimproved terrain, or both. Several similar bikes, in modified form, had competed successfully in the Paris-Dakar rally over the years.

Henry had acquired the BMW in a trade for a 1921 Thompson with mismatched serial numbers three weeks before, and he had put less than 100 miles on it. The bike's former owner would not receive federal approval to take possession of his gun for three to twelve months, depending on the whim of the feds, but he had done business with Henry Bowman before, and he knew that Henry wanted the BMW for his Idaho trip. He had agreed to let Henry take immediate possession, and Henry had thrown in a spare 50-round drum and five 30-round stick mags for good measure.

Be good to put some miles on this thing and shake it out a little before I rely on it as an emergency vehicle Henry thought as he slid his laptop case into the BMW's right hand luggage bag. The computer took up about half the volume of the compartment, so Henry also threw in six nylon tie-down straps for securing the bike in Allen Kane's 2 1/2-ton truck. The nylon bag with his other things in it fit easily into the left side compartment. A folded rainsuit was already stored under a cargo net on the bike's luggage rack.

Henry Bowman put on his jacket, helmet, and gloves, wheeled the bike out of the garage, set the garage alarm, and pushed the button which lowered the overhead door. He threw his right leg over the tall saddle, flicked up the sidestand, turned on the fuel, set the choke, turned the key in the ignition, pulled in the clutch lever, and hit the starter button with his right thumb. The one-liter opposed twin caught on the second revolution and settled into a fast idle. Henry fumbled his sunglasses out of his shirt pocket with gloved fingers and slid them onto his face, then lowered the visor. He snicked the shift lever into First, opened the throttle, and eased the clutch out until it caught.

As Henry rode towards the gate at the end of his property, he glanced at his fuel gauge and remembered that he had topped off the tank the last time he had ridden the GS. *Wonder if I can make it all the way without a fuel stop* Henry said to himself as he eased the choke off, opened the throttle, then tested the brakes. *Be dark by the time I get there. I hope Allen hasn't given himself a hernia already.*

***

"What have you got for me, Ben?"

"We've received something I thought you should know about, Mr. President. A letter from a man in Missouri who is interested in filling Sol's position at the Center."

"What are his qualifications?"

"He says up front that he has no teaching experience and done no research in the last twenty years."

"Death camp survivor?"

"Actually, no. Although from what he was able to learn after the war, it would appear that his entire family died at Treblinka and Auschwitz." The Assistant Director of the Center for Holocaust Studies gave a small smile before dropping the other shoe.

"What I thought you might find interesting, sir, is that Mr. Irwin Mann, if he is to be believed, is a survivor not of the death camps, but of the Warsaw ghetto uprising."

"The Warsaw Uprising? I thought there were no survivors." The Assistant Director shook his head.

"That's a common misconception, Mr. President. Almost everyone died when the Nazis burned the ghetto to the ground, but there were a few who managed to escape through the sewers. Most who tried it died from suffocation or drowning—the storm troopers put poison smoke candles in the sewers, and in some cases pumped them full of water also. But a few made it. That has been well-documented.

"What makes Mr. Mann so interesting, assuming his story is true, is that he was part of the uprising itself, not merely a resident of the ghetto at the time of the uprising. All known survivors of the ghetto—or I should say, all known survivors who are still alive today—were living in the ghetto but did not take an active role in the insurrection itself." The Assistant Director's eyes were alive.

"Can you check on the...authenticity of his claims?"

"We are doing that right now. From the names he gave us of the participants in his group and their occupations before the war, our researchers should be able to tell very shortly whether or not Mr. Mann is what he claims to be. From what they have found so far, it looks like Irwin Mann is the genuine article."

"How do the others at the Center feel about him for the position?"

"Mr. President, I would be less than honest if I told you all of them were as enthusiastic as I. There are some who would prefer a Holocaust scholar over any candidate who is not a full-time historian."

"But this Mr. Mann would be your first choice, Ben, provided his bona fides check out?"

"Yes, sir."

"Even if the alternative was to offer you the spot?" The Assistant Director was startled by the question, but he answered quickly.

"Yes, Mr. President. No question. Some day I hope to be Director of the Center, I'll admit that. But for the Presidential liaison, the Center needs someone who can...inspire those not normally interested in our cause. America likes heroes. They're a big help with funding, if nothing else." He paused, then added what he suspected the President was already thinking. "And to be blunt, sir, I myself would prefer a position that would endure through a number of administrations."

"Good point," the President admitted. "His health okay?"

"He says it is, and he certainly doesn't have arthritis. His letter was hammered out on a manual typewriter as neatly as a government secretary from fifty years ago would have done it."

"You'll check him out for skeletons in his closet?" the Chief Executive asked. The Assistant Director smiled faintly.

"Yes, sir. We're fairly good at that."

***

"Hey, Eugene. Hey, fella," Henry Bowman said as he petted Allen Kane's dog, which was wagging his entire hindquarters along with his tail. Eugene was a mixed-breed that was half Australian Shepherd, and the animal was using every ounce of his self-control not to jump on his friend from Missouri.

"What the hell are you doing here?" Allen Kane yelled with a grin when Henry had removed his helmet and Kane saw who had ridden into his yard. Kane was in jeans and a sleeveless T-shirt, and was very greasy. He had been working on his howitzer, which was in between the old barn and the house, using the halogen floodlights mounted on the barn to illuminate the entire yard. "Afraid I'd forget to pick you up?" Henry squinted at his friend, who was only a silhouette. The brilliant lights made everything throw long shadows across the yard.

"The thought crossed my mind. No, after I hung up, I figured you'd be unable to resist working on your 105, so I came to help. I wanted to put some miles on this bike anyway, see if there were any bugs in it. I thought we'd take it with us; if we have any vehicle trouble out there, it'll sure beat hiking out for parts or help. I've still got some paperwork to do before we go, but I brought it with me. And I can help you load up."

"You just wanted an excuse to ride your 'sickle somewhere," Allen Kane laughed.

"That was part of it."

"Well, I'm glad you showed up. I got in a couple new night vision scopes that're supposed to be the nuts. SEAL Team Six wants a second opinion before they buy a bunch of 'em. I wanted to take at least one of them with us, but they've got to have them both back right away, so I'm shipping them out before we leave. I was using one of them last night, and the clarity was something else. I'll get cleaned up, and we'll see what you think." Henry nodded in reply, but he was staring at the howitzer sitting in the yard.

"Tell me about this thing."

"Oh, man, you're going to love it," Allen Kane said enthusiastically as he turned toward the surplus field piece. "Fires a thirty-seven pound bullet at fourteen hundred feet per second. Bore's mint. Got a little machining to do to fit the breech ring, but with the two of us, I think we can have it up and running tomorrow. Hey, quit standing around— I thought you said you came here to help." Henry smiled and walked over to his friend.

"Okay, Boss. Show me what to do."

June 4

"What are you doing with golf balls?" Henry asked his friend when he noticed the box of Titleists on the workshop shelf. Allen Kane laughed.

"Guy I know told me they were just a little bigger than 40mm. I'm going to try to make a steel case that holds a .32 blank, or something like that, and see if I can shoot them out of an M79. Should be a fun practice round, if it works."

"Hey, that sounds like something I'd think of," Henry said with a laugh. "Tell me if it works."

"Got anything for me today?" they heard the UPS driver yell. Allen Kane got up from his chair inside the old barn which now housed his shop and went to the door.

"Yeah," he called back. "Just a second." He came back to where Henry was sitting. "That stuff of yours ready to go?"

"No, I've got a couple more hours of work yet. I'll stick it in an overnight envelope tomorrow, on our way out."

"Okay." Kane went to his shipping bench, where he picked up two long boxes, a square box, and his UPS shipping record book. He carried these out to the waiting truck and returned in less than a minute.

"UPS come here every day?" Henry asked. Allen Kane's house in southern Indiana was about forty miles from the Kentucky border, and was situated amid lots of farmland.

"Mm-hmm."

"They charge any extra?"

"No, standard weekly rate, just like for an office building in Indianapolis."

"Yeah, same with me, but I'm not quite this far out in the sticks. Always surprises me all these overnight guys can give people like us the same service and still make money. What'd you just ship out?" Henry asked, changing the subject.

"The night vision stuff, of course. Shame it won't take it on a real gun," Kane observed. Allen and Henry had mounted one of the two prototype units on a single shot .50 caliber rifle the previous evening, and the image intensifier had broken after a hundred sixty rounds.

"Also a new-in-the-box M16 I nicked a guy thirty-five hundred for. Guy went nuts when he found out I had one hadn't been touched since '83. And a BAR that I re-watted for Stembridge."

Henry nodded. Stembridge Gun Rentals in Hollywood was the largest and oldest supplier of correct period weapons to filmmakers, and they relied heavily on Allen Kane and his unparalleled ability to restore old, incomplete machine guns and make them function better than they did when they were new.

The BAR had been a registered DEWAT with the chamber plugged and welded and the bolt welded open. Allen Kane had applied to re-activate the gun, then machined out the welds, replaced the bolt and barrel, fitted the correct bipod and flash hider for the period that the weapon had been manufactured, reparkerized the metal and refinished the wood. It was one of his least-involved restoration jobs.

"You doing any cheap DSHKs for them to rent to Stallone?" Henry asked with a grin.

"Fuck you," Allen replied good-naturedly. Henry had repeated a standing joke among NFA weapons dealers and manufacturers, and it was one that he himself had created.

The makers of modern action/war movies prided themselves on their attention to detail regarding the weapons used in their films. NFA weapons experts such as Henry and Allen could forgive artistic license, as when one of the characters in *Predator* fired long bursts from the hip out of a hand-carried GE Minigun fed from a backpack. They also understood that allowances had to be made if a movie included scenes involving weaponry of which no single remaining example existed. They drew the line, however, when big-budget films with well-known stars showed weaponry that was absolutely wrong for the scene.

The example that had made NFA dealers howl was *Rambo III,* a 1987 movie set in Afghanistan. The Russian heavy machine gun which the Soviets were using against the Mujahadeen was, of course, the 12.7mm DSHK, which had been put into service in the USSR in 1938. The gun had been revised slightly in 1946, and though the guns were rare in the U.S., several good examples were present at every Knob Creek shoot. Henry and Allen each owned both a 1938 and a 1946 model. The guns weighed well over 100 pounds without the mount, and fired a cartridge similar to but slightly larger than the U.S. .50 Browning.

The moviemakers, however, had not used DSHKs in the film. Instead, *Rambo III* had depicted Russian soldiers firing .30 caliber U.S. M60 machine guns (weight: 25 pounds) fitted with dummy barrel shrouds crudely fashioned to resemble the silhouette of the 12.7mm DSHK. Henry Bowman had immediately spread the rumor (utterly false) that it was Allen Kane who had effected the makeover and convinced the producers that no one would know the difference. Henry was amazed at the number of otherwise intelligent people who still believed this story, and Allen Kane still got razzed about it.

"You still doing a lot of business with Stembridge?" Henry asked.

"More than ever," Kane said immediately. "They really got fucked in '86." The 1986 ban had made it impossible for the studios or their designees to legally manufacture full auto weaponry from scratch or from semiauto variants, as the Hollywood entities were not government or police agencies.

"Some of the studios are just ignoring the law entirely now," Kane went on. "Tim says they're hiring machinists to set up on-site, and manufacture machine guns for the duration of filming, then cut 'em up after all the gun scenes are done."

"Damn! Aren't they worried some fed will want to make a name for himself?"

"You'd think so, but they got so much money, they can probably buy off anyone. Anyway, it's not everyone doing it that way. Stembridge has been calling me all the time for stuff lately." Allen looked over at Henry. "You 'bout ready for lunch? I was going to go in the house and throw something together."

"Yeah, let me work on this a little longer. Twenty, thirty minutes, say?"

"You got it." Kane left the shop and walked towards the house.

Henry Bowman sat up in the straight-backed wooden chair and turned his attention back to the papers and yellow legal pad. He had been using one of Allen Kane's loading benches as a desk ever since he had arrived. So far, Henry had spent more time with a pen than with the keyboard of his computer. He was almost done with his assessment of a 3-D geologic imaging process that his stockbroker had asked him to evaluate.

The process was one patented by a small company, Petromag, whose stock was followed by only a handful of analysts. Henry's broker, who was always looking for companies that would grow faster than the economy as a whole, had picked up on it. Petromag's proprietary technique involved spatial analysis of belowground sound waves to determine the location of oil deposits. The company hired out its technicians to drilling companies for an up-front fee and a percentage of the future revenues of any wells that were drilled based on data generated by Petromag.

The company also had a small oil company which was a wholly owned subsidiary. This oil company had drilled seventeen exploratory wells in the past two years. Only three of them had been dry holes.

Henry's broker had explained that such results could still be due to luck, and wanted an impartial opinion as to whether the new process might possibly be as superior as the company claimed. The discovery that the broker had made was that the firm maintained a "library" of all the geologic data they had analyzed using their 3-D imaging process, but for accounting purposes, they were assigning a five-year life to each set of data.

Unless the maps were no good whatsoever, they would be valuable for an indefinite period of time, for the oil was not going anywhere. Thus, if the process worked at all, the current price of the stock did not reflect the true value of the company's 3-D map library.

Henry reached over to the battery charger sitting at the back of the bench and retrieved the cellular phone he had brought from Missouri. Allen Kane didn't like to be interrupted while he was working on guns, and he did not have a phone in his workshop. If he had, Henry would probably still have used his own cellular unit, as he did not generally use other people's things when his own were available. He folded out the mouthpiece, hit the POWER button, and tapped in the number.

"Bartram, Meeks."

"Yeah, Tina, this is Henry Bowman. Is Mitt there?"

"Just a moment."

"Hey, Henry. Where are you? I've been trying to get hold of you for two days now."

"I'm over at a friend's house right now. I've been studying the dope you sent me on Petromag–"

"Yeah, that's what I've been trying to call you about. They–"

"Look, bottom line," Henry broke in, "I think the guys at Petromag are on to something. It may not be as vastly superior to previous technology as they claim, but it does look like an improvement over prior art.

"Put it this way: In Organic Chemistry final exams, college professors write down the beginning compounds and ending compounds, and ask you to write down all the intervening chemical reactions. When you don't know the answer and make something up that you think sounds plausible, they like to take a big red marker and write 'Magic!' in big letters on that part of your exam book.

"From what I can see, if these guys submitted the explanations you got for me to the appropriate professor, I don't think he'd get out his red pen. Nothing in the technical description is of the lead-into-gold type of science. That's the best I can do with what you sent, okay?"

"Well that's good news, but you're not finished. Petromag just announced a new addition to their process that they says gets rid of some of the false positives they were getting. Talked to their chief engineer yesterday, and he sent me a bunch more scans I want you to look at."

"Hell, Mitt, I'm about to go on vacation," Henry said plaintively. Even as he uttered the words, Henry Bowman knew he would find some way to do what his broker wanted. Stewart Mittendorfer was very thorough in performing his own analysis, and he used any experts he could to get at the truth. His recommendations had tripled the value of Henry Bowman's portfolio over the last eight years. He was particularly good at judging when it was time to get out of a stock.

Mitt did not answer, and Henry knew that he could hold the phone for ten minutes and the broker would not speak until Henry broke the silence.

"Okay, I admit it," Henry said, "you got me really interested. How soon do I have to look at this new stuff? Yesterday?"

"Pretty much. This thing might pop any day now. Nobody follows this company right now, but..." he left the rest of the sentence unfinished.

"Let me call you back in an hour or so," Henry sighed. "I need to get my other messages first."

"Your recorder wasn't turned on the last few times I tried to reach you," the broker said. "And you didn't have your cellular on, either. That's why I was going nuts."

Damn Henry thought. *I did forget to turn on the recorder before I left.* He began to mentally review who he needed to talk to before rendering himself incommunicado for two to three weeks.

"You going to be in the office for the next hour or two?" Henry asked.

"All day."

"Let me call you back." Henry thought a moment, then reconsidered. "Nah, screw that. How many pages is this stuff?"

"Uh, six, I think, is what I've got right now. There's more coming, but it won't get here 'til tomorrow. Some time before 10:30."

"Okay, anything oversize, stick on your copier and reduce it to letter size. Then FAX everything you've got so far to my cellular number. I'll hook it into my laptop as soon as I hang up here. If any seismic charts or stuff like that are too hard to read, I can have you send me the originals overnight mail if I have to. If your FAX doesn't go through right away, keep sending. I'll be using the phone while you're using your copier, and you may finish before I do."

"Good deal," the broker said with obvious relief in his voice. Henry disconnected and began to dial his home number, to confirm that he really had failed to turn on his phone recorder, before making his other calls.

"Change of plans, Allen," Henry said with a very embarrassed look on his face as he came in for lunch. "And I feel like a real dick-brain."

"Well, that's understandable," Kane replied with a smile. Allen motioned to Henry to help himself to one of the thick hamburgers Allen had cooked. "What's the problem?"

"Two things have come up," Henry said as he filled a glass with water from the tap and ignored the dig. "I've been doing analysis on a seismic process being used by an oil services company, and I just found out that I need to do some more. I could blow it off, but I've already done most of the work, and I think I'm going to end up buying a big chunk of stock for myself. So I want to finish up. Probably take me another day."

"I can wait an extra day," Allen said immediately. "Hey, you like spicy food—put a little slice of one of these on that," Kane said as he handed Henry a red pepper about the size of a .458 bullet. "But just a little bitty slice. I mean like half the size of a grain of rice. That's a Habanero. Friend of mine has a garden where he grows nothing but peppers. He says that's the hottest one in the world." Henry gave his friend a dubious look, pulled his knife from his pocket, and flicked open the double-edged blade with one hand.

"An Applegate?" Allen Kane asked, eyeing the metal's satin finish and the two names laser-engraved on it.

"Right. Leave it to Colonel Rex to design a pocket knife that'll get you arrested in forty-three states," he joked. Henry was referring to the fact that the knife he was holding was designed to be opened with one hand, and its blade was double-edged--a feature almost unheard-of in a folder. On the market since 1996, Henry's knife was the last blade designed by Col. Rex Applegate, the fullback-sized ex-OSS officer who had been assigned to train Americans in close quarter battle in WWII. Applegate had taken his wartime job to heart, and had seen no reason to slack off on his efforts merely because the Second World War ended. Applegate continued to train people until his death in August of 1998. Colonel Rex had been one of Henry and Allen's favorite people.

"Last time I saw him was in early '98, about six months before he died. He was signing a copy of *Kill or Get Killed* for a friend of mine. Had some big gold coin on a choker, looked like it weighed a couple ounces."

"You know why he wore that, don't you?" Henry asked as he sliced a small piece off the pepper and put it on the edge of his hamburger. "It was to bait the street punks into trying to mug him, to keep in practice. Some moron outside the SHOT show back in '96 thought a guy in his eighties with a bad limp would be easy pickings," Henry continued as he prepared to bite into his sandwich. "He ended up on the ground, screaming like a woman, with the sorest set of—*Jesus Christ!*" Henry exclaimed around a mouthful of food.

"Don't say I didn't warn you," Allen Kane said, and then became utterly overcome with laughter at Henry's facial expressions. "Too hot for you?" he finally asked.

"No," Henry said, swallowing, "but you weren't kidding about how much to use. I guess that's why you never see these things in the supermarket—not too much profit margin when one of them is enough for a thousand people." Henry judiciously sliced four even tinier pieces off the Habanero and arranged them on the rest of his hamburger. He took a long drink of water and eyed his sandwich cautiously before taking another, smaller bite.

"What I was saying earlier," he continued, getting back to his change of plans, "remember I was telling you about that refueling company I capitalized?"

"Wasn't that the deal where your fuel trucks would go fill up semis at night that were operated by union drivers, and charge the company double for the fuel? Something about when it was after hours and the union's depot was closed, the unions wouldn't let their drivers fill their own trucks at a self-service?"

"Yeah, that's the one, except the drivers weren't completely prohibited from self-service, but it was such a horrendous extra charge that our setup was cheaper. Anyway, we locked one truck line into a five-year contract less than three years ago, and now the drivers' union has gotten hungry and changed their policy, and the truck line wants out of their contract with my guy. They just read the fine print on the contract, and went ballistic. Hack Carter—that's the president of the refueling company—just had his tires slashed and started getting death threats."

"Jesus! That's just what you need."

"Oh, it's not quite that bad," Henry said as he gingerly took another bite from his hamburger. "I don't have any active role in managing the company, and I think I can handle it with a phone call to a fellow I know, if I can ever get through to him. He seems to be away from his office, too." Henry then drained his water glass and went to the sink to refill it.

"So you telling me you're out for Idaho?"

"Hell, no, not that. What it looks like, though, is that this crap might take more than a day or two. I wasn't planning to go for a full month anyway. What say we flip it around—I'll come out ten days late, instead of leaving ten days early."

"What about your guns? And how are you going to get from a major airport to wherever I happen to be ten days from now?"

"I thought about that. Since you're bringing the belt-feds and the 20mm, all I've got is a half-dozen wheelguns, three bolt action rifles, and a BAR. They'll fit in my Cub, no problem. I'll check my charts, but there's apt to be a local airport or a duster strip within ten miles of anywhere you're likely to be camped." Henry paused, and he could see Allen was considering the idea.

"Would you be able to do your stuff from here for a few days before going back to Missouri?" Allen asked.

"I guess I could," Henry said with a puzzled expression. "Why?"

"While you were out in the shop working, Dale Price called. You've met him—he's the hog farmer lives about five miles west of here, likes big-caliber single shots."

"The guy with the .577 built on a Fix action, wanted to see my 4-bore?"

"Yeah, that's the guy. Anyway, he was supposed to come by tonight and pick up Eugene, take care of him 'til I got back," Kane said, scratching the dog behind his ears. "He just called from Pennsylvania, said could I leave him tied up with plenty of food or water and he'd be by in a couple days. No way I'm going to do that, but I don't have anyone else I can leave him with."

"I'll stay here a couple days, work on the Petromag stuff, and when I have to go, if Dale hasn't shown up yet, I'll take Eugene back to Missouri with me." Allen Kane laughed.

"On a motorcycle?"

"Of course. I'll bolt a wooden box with the top open to the luggage rack. He'll love it."

"You know, this may actually work out okay," Allen said, thinking. "What about your ammo? Where is it?"

"All my ammo is inside the door to the garage, ready to throw on your truck, if you still don't mind stopping by the house and picking it up. I can give you my alarm codes."

"Sure. No problem."

"Then let's plan on meeting in Mackey ten days from today," Henry suggested. "That's where Lindbergh Truck Lines is, remember? Where we used to buy our dynamite? Ten days should be plenty of time for me to clear up this newest headache. Let's just plan on meeting at Lindbergh's June fourteenth, ten days from today. When you're near a phone a day or two before, give them a call. If some disaster hits and I can't make it, I'll phone them and leave a message. Give them a call on the twelfth. If I haven't called in to cancel, I'll be there. That sound good?"

"Yeah...that'll work," Allen replied. "And after lunch, you can help me load the deuce-and-a-half."

"Somehow I had a feeling you were going to get around to that."

June 7

"Gentlemen," the supervisor said. "Ladies," he added, nodding to acknowledge the two women agents present in the briefing room, "I can't stress strongly enough the importance of the mission you are about to carry out. A successful, three-pronged raid will break the back of the largest obstacle to our authority and ability to do our jobs: independent Class Three manufacturers." Wilson Blair wasn't telling his people anything he hadn't said before, but he was a strong believer in the benefits of a final pep talk before an important raid.

"Between them, Grant Millet and Allen Kane account for almost one-third of the annual dealer-to-dealer transfers of NFA weapons in this country. Nailing both these guys at the same time will be the death knell for all the people in this country who think that just because they get a bunch of federal licenses and pay a bunch of taxes, they have the right to manufacture and own guns that should properly be restricted to the government.

"Together, Kane and Millet have over two thousand machine guns and destructive devices registered to them. I guarantee that the haul you take from those two places is going to be plastered on the front pages of every newspaper in this country," he said. *And this time, there'll be no goddamn disasters like we got back in '93* he added silently.

.   "Henry Bowman is not a manufacturer like Kane and Millet, and compared to those two, his Class Three business is tiny. He is nonetheless the third-largest NFA weapons dealer in Missouri, and you'll still get a great photo opportunity with what you'll find at his place. According to the current NFA registry, Bowman has over one hundred Title Two weapons registered to him.

"Henry Bowman's great importance to this raid is that he is a lifelong friend of Allen Kane's, and is also close to Grant Millet. As such, we can safely assume that he knows as much or more about Kane and Millet than anyone else in the country. He is also a wealthy man who has considerable assets other than his firearms inventory.

"Kane and Millet have only their guns to lose," Blair said airily. He was ignoring any concepts of personal freedom or dignity, but none of the agents in the room noticed. "Because of that," he went on, "we have less to trade with the two of them.

"Bowman, however, has several million dollars in securities and real estate in addition to his guns. Further, he has never held a manufacturer's license. He has a lot smaller stake in the gun end of things and a lot more to lose overall than his two friends. It is Bowman that we believe we can get to roll over and hand us Kane and Millet. And hitting all three of them at the same time is the way to do it."

"Bowman is currently en route spending three weeks in the Idaho Rockies with Kane. Our surveillance has confirmed that Kane's 2 1/2-ton military truck left Indiana two days ago, and was seen in Wyoming this morning. Their destination is somewhere in the Pahsimeroi Valley in central Idaho. They should soon be there, if they are not already. That is some eighteen hundred miles away from Kane's house, and fifteen hundred miles from Bowman's.

"They are camping out of their vehicle, and their exact location is unknown, not only to us but to anyone. That gives us a great advantage, for it means that no message can reach them for a minimum of several days and perhaps as long as several weeks.

"Similarly, Millet is currently in Ecuador. He is halfway through a three-week trip to Central and South America, where he is looking for surplus tripods, optics, and gun parts for future importation. As with Bowman and Kane, Millet's exact schedule is unknown to anyone, and the fact that he on a different continent makes it a certainty that by the time he learns of our actions, we will have an airtight case against him.

"Bowman is single, and at the moment he lives alone. Kane has been separated from his wife for almost a year; she lives with another man in Indianapolis, and their two children are grown and live out of state. Millet's wife and their three children are at the present time in Orlando, Florida, and will soon be visiting Disney World, where Millet will meet them on his way home to Ohio." The supervisor smiled broadly.

"None of the three targets' houses are occupied at this time. We have an opportunity here, people," the supervisor said emphatically, "like we have never had before." *This one's going to finally make up for all the screw-ups that have gone before* he added to himself.

"We are going to nail these three bastards, and we are going to have them up on a list of charges three feet long before they even know they've been raided."

***

Henry Bowman was sitting in an old armchair next to the loading bench. He had turned out the lights and was sitting in the dark thinking about the most recent FAX concerning Petromag when his cellular phone rang. He looked at his watch. *11:17 p.m. I hope it's Sam.* Sam Ashton was a private investigator and skip tracer who brought back bail jumpers for bail bondsmen. With the possible exception of Earl Taylor-Edgarton, Sam was the first person Henry would choose to have on his side in a fight where he was greatly outnumbered.

"Hello."

"Yeah, man, what do you need?"

"Sam!" Henry exclaimed. "Thanks for calling me back. Listen, I'm out of town, and I've got a problem. St. Louis company I've got some money in, named On-Site Refueling, out near the airport, off of Dunn Road. They've got a long-standing contract with a truck line and now the union drivers are pissed and want On-Site to tear it up. On-Site's president's name is Hack Carter, and he's had his tires slashed and some death threats on the phone. That was when I talked to him a couple days ago—maybe more shit's happened by now. Here's his home number," Henry continued, and recited an exchange in Bridgeton.

As he finished repeating the number, Henry heard Eugene barking loudly outside. *Hope that's Dale Price* he thought.

"Sam, there's someone just pulled up, so I'll have to call you back. But can you talk to Hack for me and maybe help him out? He's been going kind of nuts." Sam Ashton laughed in reply.

"The way you sounded on the recorder, I thought this was going to be something difficult. I've got to leave town in two days, but those union bosses are all so dirty, first-time investigator could fill up a legal pad by then. Give me a day, and your guy won't have any more trouble. Probably won't run you over five hundred."

Eugene was barking more frantically now, and Henry heard what sounded like several voices at the far edge of the yard.

"Sounds great. I'm sure Hack'll jump at that deal." *What the hell's going on out there?* Henry wondered as he stood up. "Sam, let me call you back. Somebody just drove up, and I've got to see who it is."

"Don't bother—I won't be here. I got all the info I need. This time tomorrow, the problem will be solved. Bye." Sam Ashton hung up.

Henry Bowman pushed the END button on his cellular phone and reached out in the darkness for the doorway to Allen Kane's lead casting room. His hand found the edge of the door frame and he slid his fingers along the loading workshop wall to where he knew the light switch lay. Henry's fingertips had just touched the switch plate when he heard a most distinctive noise, and Eugene suddenly fell silent.

Henry Bowman felt the hair on his back stand on end, and his hand instinctively went to the 5" N-frame in the sharkskin Ken Null holster at his right kidney. *There's only two things I know of that make that sound* he thought to himself as he pulled his hand away from the light switch. *And one of them requires a constant source of compressed air. Somehow I doubt that whoever's out there just happens to have an air tank and a pneumatic nail gun. And I don't think Eugene just happened to get tired of barking.* Henry knew that Kane's pet was almost certainly dead. He forced his mind to focus on preserving his own life instead of mourning the dog.

Need to be able to see first Henry said to himself, thinking of the two latest-design night scopes that Allen had shipped back three days earlier. *Goggles'd be best.* He walked silently in the darkness towards the other end of the room. There was enough moonlight coming in through the curtains for Henry to see the larger things in the crowded shop, but he shuffled his feet and extended his arms to avoid crashing into anything smaller and causing a racket.

The eight night vision devices that Allen and Henry had used as a comparison with the ones sent by the SEAL team were on the shelf next to a boxed set of collets for Allen's milling machine. Henry felt around until his hands recognized the familiar shape of the AN-TVS-5 dual-tube night vision goggles, then he lifted them off the shelf and slipped them on his head. The newer-generation TVS-7 single-tube version was newer and supposedly better, but Henry wanted the -5 for two reasons: First, Henry owned a pair of TVS-5s, and so was familiar with the layout of their controls. Second, Allen had been the last one to use the -7 in their comparison, while Henry had been the last person to wear the -5. Henry knew the dual-tube unit was already adjusted for his head and eyes.

Henry Bowman pulled off the lens caps and switched on the power. He was rewarded with a blurred green video image of Allen Kane's shop. *Focus is set at infinity* he realized with satisfaction. *Now for some ears.* He took one of the amplified headsets off a hook on the wall, put them on his head over the NV goggle harness, switched them on, and turned up the gain. Only then did Henry draw his .44 Smith and make his way to the large sliding doors that separated him from Allen Kane's yard.

"Should one or two of us go check the storage buildings?" Ralph Compton asked as he nudged the carcass of Allen Kane's dog with the toe of his boot. He was mentally congratulating himself on the chest shot he had made from ten feet. The 147-grain 9mm slug from Compton's suppressed H&K MP5 had killed the dog instantly.

"No, won't take us but a minute to get in here. After we've had a look around the main house, then we can all spread out and check the rest of the property."

Allen Kane's two-acre plot contained his house, the barn he had turned into a shop, two sheds he used for storing tripods and heavy mounts, an old blacksmith's shop where he kept his lead ingots and .50 caliber 'burnouts', and two modern-era steel buildings; one where he stored all his belts and magazines, and the other full of smokeless powder for reloading. His guns were kept in safes inside an underground vault, accessible only from the house.

Henry Bowman stood a few feet back from the gap between the sliding doors and looked out into the night towards the house. What he saw filled him with dismay. A white van was parked on the gravel to the side of Kane's house. *And shit! There's...six of them!* he said to himself, after counting heads. *At least six* he corrected when he realized there could be more men out of sight. *No night vision gear, and they drove right up by the back door of the house. They know where the guns are and they think the place is deserted.* Henry saw Eugene lying dead by the back porch, and saw the unmistakable shape of a suppressed MP5. *Six guys with MP5s* he thought in utter horror. Suddenly the Smith & Wesson in his right hand felt about as potent as a muzzle loader.

Got to find something better Henry thought frantically as he looked around the shop. The green image was blurred at the close distance, and Henry reached up and focused the image tubes for an eight-foot distance and turned on the tiny IR bulb which lit up the video screen like a floodlight.

Allen Kane kept almost all of his guns in his vault, except when he was working on them or shooting them. There were usually one or two lying around the shop, but Allen had left for Idaho, and the only gun Henry could remember being out was a .22 pistol Henry had been shooting the day before. It was a Hi-Standard Olympic in .22 Short, loaded with CB caps. CB caps were .22s loaded with a light 29-grain bullet and a tiny amount of powder. Their velocity was well under the speed of sound, and close up, they would penetrate only about 3/4" into a pine two-by-four. They also made very little noise. Allen kept the gun and the pipsqueak loads around to shoot mice.

Better than nothing Henry thought as he hurried to the cleaning table where he had left the Hi-Standard. The bolt was locked back on an empty magazine, but there were four loaded ones next to it that Henry had not yet gotten around to shooting. He swapped the empty magazine in the gun for a full one, put the remaining three loaded magazines in his left pocket, and continued to look around the shop. *Didn't Allen have a Garand up here?* he thought, before remembering his friend had taken it with him in the truck. Then Henry spotted the one other gun in the room, a rifle standing in the corner behind the drill press. *Mag's missing* Henry observed, and almost left it where it was. Then he realized it would be foolish to do so. *At least I've got ammo for it* he thought sardonically as he grabbed the rifle and returned to his vantage point by the sliding door. The electronics in his muffs magnified the sounds of his footsteps and made him wince.

"Door looks pretty solid, sir," Peter Hagedorn said, shining his flashlight around its perimeter.

"G.G., grab the shotgun out of the van," Wilson Blair commanded, and one of the agents immediately hurried towards the white Ford.

G.G. Jackson was one of many women employed by agencies of the federal government. She had been born in Chicago's South Side in 1963. Her mother, Shavonna Jackson, had been fifteen at the time. Like many 15-year-old single mothers, Shavonna Jackson had not thought much about the realities of motherhood, including the immediate problem of what to name her offspring.

Concurrently, overworked interns on rotation in ghetto hospitals did what they could to entertain themselves amid 20-hour days in depressing surroundings. In 1963, as in all other years, one of the standard gambits among interns assigned to inner-city delivery rooms was to see who could cause the most outrageous name to be printed on the birth certificate of children born to ghetto teenagers.

The second week of February, 1963 saw some serious competition among interns in south Chicago. In a five-day period, there were Chicago-area births registered for Madison Avenue Washington, Epluribus Wilson, Nosmo King (inspired by a waiting room sign), Simian Cook, and Anus Brown. The award that week, however, went to a young doctor from Grosse Pointe, Michigan, who hated working in the Chicago facility. He had suggested to Miss Jackson that she give her infant daughter a distinctive, happy-sounding name, and offered one he thought appropriate. He pronounced the first name with the accent on the second syllable, and Shavonna thought it sounded nice. Like 'Gloria', only fancier. People who read the name would pronounce it differently, but Shavonna could not read, so the impact of the intern's joke was not felt for some time.

When Shavonna learned the truth two years later, she started addressing her daughter by her first and middle initials, and the Jackson girl grew up pretending she was named for a pretty lady in a movie. To this day, G.G. Jackson was unaware of what was actually typed on her birth certificate.

Henry Bowman had been making his way to the sliding barn doors and had not heard Wilson Blair call Agent Jackson by her first name. *That pudgy black guy runs like a girl* Henry thought as he watched the intruder jog back to the van. The reflection of the flashlight on the back door of Allen Kane's house made it look like green daylight in Henry's night vision goggles. Although the goggles offered no magnification, Henry could make out a number of details at the 60-yard distance. He reached in his left pocket, withdrew one of the 10-shot magazines for the Hi-Standard .22 pistol, and began to unload it so that he would have ammo for the rifle. Henry analyzed the weapons he faced as he put the ten cartridges in his mouth.

White guy with the MP5. Tall black guy with an AR-15 or M16. Probably a -16, if they've got a suppressed H&K. White guy with an attache case, not wearing a hat like the others, seems to be giving the orders, probably has a pistol under his coat. White guy with a flashlight and a pistol in a belt holster, small guy—girl, maybe?—standing off to the left, also with a belt holster, fat black guy coming back from the van with a thin padded case, not wide enough to hold a scoped rifle, no holster visible on this side, maybe he's a lefty.

A multi-gender and multi-racial assault force armed with automatic weapons and invading Allen Kane's home in the middle of the night meant only one thing to Henry Bowman. *Some kind of terrorist organization looking to outfit their troops* Henry decided as he stared at the six intruders. *Possibly a drug ring. Outlaw motorcycle gang?* he thought briefly. *No, not with two black guys. And the hair's too short. What's that guy got in the briefcase? Burglary tools?*

Henry thought a moment about the timing of the assault. *Probably found out at a gun show when Allen'd be gone. Likely from out of state. Probably California.* Allen Kane set up at gun shows from California to Florida to advertise his business. California state law prohibited private ownership of machine guns, and banned the sale of most semiautos, but Kane did a large business with the movie studios and the rental companies that served them.

Henry scanned the area to the sides as far as his vantage point would permit, but saw no other people. *Allen's storage vault is better than the local bank's, but you can get into anything if you have enough time. Van's probably full of equipment. They've got all the time in the world, and they'll kill me if I try to make a run for it.* He considered using his cellular to call the local sheriff. *Out here in the middle of a bunch of farmland, probably only have one cruiser to send, with a couple deputies they'll have to roust out of bed.*

God knows how long that would take, and then these guys would cut them to ribbons before they got out of the car.

Henry came to a decision. *It's time to take the advice you've been giving people for over twenty years, fella. Strike back when you're strong, and still have your wits about you, and the enemy isn't expecting it. Give them your teeth, not your belly.* Henry's mind went into overdrive, trying to determine how to mount an effective defense against the six invaders. A plan was beginning to take shape, and Henry Bowman was completely focused on how to stop all six terrorists and stay alive in the process.

One of the white men was removing a gun from the case that the other had brought from the van, and Henry saw it was a long-barreled Remington 870 12-gauge. *Doorbuster!* Henry thought. He immediately knew what was going to happen next, and he had an idea of how to make it work for him.

Henry Bowman stripped the amplified earmuffs and the night vision goggles off his head, laid the goggles on top of a turret lathe to his left, and replaced the muffs. The Hi-Standard was tucked in his pants with the bolt still back. Henry ignored it and picked up the rifle he had brought from the far end of the shop. It was a Remington Model 37 .22, a boy's target rifle made in 1946. The magazine was missing, and to load the rifle Henry had to angle it downwards, take a cartridge out of his mouth, and manually insert the round into the breech without letting it fall into the magazine cutout. He took a step backwards, leaned against the turret lathe to make his position even more steady, and raised the .22 rifle to check his sight picture. The flashlight beam on the back door put all six of the intruders in stark silhouette.

"Prop the screen door open with something," agent Peter Hagedorn said as he looked at the main door to Kane's house. "You don't want to be standing there holding it." Agent Elena Martinez spotted a 5-gallon bucket in the yard and went to get it. As she did, Hagedorn examined the edge of the door carefully to determine exactly where he was going to shoot.

Henry Bowman lowered the rifle and took a step back. He put his finger in his mouth and rearranged three of the .22 rounds so they poked out between his lips, rims facing out. As he raised the gun, five of the six intruders backed up several steps away from the door. All but the white man with the 870 and the black man holding the M16 put their fingers in their ears. The man with the suppressed H&K submachine gun let the weapon dangle on its sling as he held his ears. One of the others held the flashlight trained on the left side of the door with one hand and covered one ear with the other.

From three feet inside the barn, Henry Bowman took careful aim at the man holding the M16 and placed the white bead of the front sight on the base of the man's skull. He squeezed the trigger with about a pound of pressure, which was as hard as he dared, and waited.

Peter Hagedorn raised the 870 to his shoulder. From a distance of about four feet, he took aim at the spot on the door that concealed the lower hinge, and pulled the trigger. As flame leaped out of the shotgun barrel and the slug slammed into the lower left edge of the hardwood door, Henry's finger tightened involuntarily on the Model 37's trigger, and the gun fired.

Twenty-two CB caps, such as the ones Henry had removed from the Hi-Standard's magazine and put in his mouth, are loaded to a velocity of about 800 feet per second. This is less than the speed of sound. Any bullet traveling below the speed of sound makes no sonic 'crack' as it passes through the air. The only real noise is the muzzle blast, which is why subsonic ammunition is preferred for suppressed weapons. A .22 CB cap, however, only uses about one one-thousandth of an ounce of propellant, which is completely consumed in the first 10" of barrel. When fired in a bolt action rifle with a barrel 24" long, a .22 CB cap round makes a trivial amount of noise compared to a 12 gauge shotgun. The report of Henry's single shot .22, fired from inside the barn, was inaudible. It was completely drowned out by the muzzle blast of the 870, the echoes of that muzzle blast bouncing off the barn, and the sound of the one-ounce slug tearing through the wood door and impacting the steel hinge on the other side.

Henry Bowman had already flicked the bolt open and ejected the fired case by the time the echoes of the larger gun had died out. He plucked a second round out from between his lips, bent forward sharply at the waist, and pushed the cartridge into the chamber without dropping the butt from his shoulder. As he prepared for his second shot, Henry's vision registered that his first target was down and that the shotgun man was taking aim again. He put the front sight on a spot behind the ear of the man with the MP5, tightened his trigger finger, and held his breath.

The five spectators had been watching the illuminated spot on the door, and Elena Martinez was the only one of the five who noticed Agent Levar Williams fall down. She logically assumed he had been struck with a slug fragment.

"Hey, I think Levar got–" she started to say, but Agent Hagedorn was concentrating on his aim, and his ears were ringing. The second blast of his shotgun cut off the rest of what Martinez was trying to tell them. This time, Agent Compton collapsed.

"Hagedorn!" Agent Martinez screamed. "Stop shooting! Williams and Compton are hurt! I think your slugs are ricocheting! They may be hurt bad!" This time the man heard her, and he lowered his shotgun and started to turn towards the other agents. Agent G.G. Jackson was shining the light on the corpse of Levar Williams, and Elena Martinez was still screaming about ricochets when Henry Bowman's third shot hit Peter Hagedorn a half-inch to the left of the bridge of his nose.

The human mind can only process a finite amount of information in a given amount of time. When the brain is expecting to receive one set of inputs and gets something entirely different, the process takes several times longer. Supervisory Agent Blair and Agent Jackson had been watching their companion fire a shotgun at the door of a house whose owner was known to be almost two thousand miles away. They had been fully expecting to see the door sag on its remaining hinge.

Instead, Blair and Jackson found themselves staring at two bodies on the ground, and listening (with ringing ears from two shotgun blasts) to Agent Martinez screaming about ricochets. When their minds had grasped the fact that two of their men were hurt, their brains were overwhelmed with the new data, and the common phenomena of auditory exclusion under stress occurred. Neither Wilson Blair, G.G. Jackson, nor the nearly hysterical Elena Martinez had been able to hear the first two soft sounds from the direction of the barn. With Martinez's increasing volume, the jarring sight of the two men on the ground, and the onset of auditory exclusion, they did not notice the third.

As Agents Blair, Jackson, and Martinez stared openmouthed, Agent Hagedorn dropped the Remington 870 pumpgun on the concrete pad just outside the back door to the house and collapsed on top of it. The three agents who were still on their feet looked around wildly, but it was dark, and their night vision was nonexistent from staring at a white door illuminated by a flashlight.

"Weapons out!" Blair finally yelled as he dropped his briefcase and drew his 9mm Beretta. He was about to give the command to run for the cover of the vehicle when night turned into day. Henry Bowman had switched on all four of the halogen spotlights mounted on the roof of the barn. The three ATF agents that were still functioning stood frozen in the blinding light.

"Drop your weapons!" Henry Bowman yelled as he drew his 5" .44 Magnum and cocked it as he brought it to bear on the center figure. His voice was loud enough that it activated the circuitry in his hearing protectors, shutting off the amplifier. Henry's words sounded muffled to him, then the electronics cut back in and the night sounds were once again amplified.

The three intruders squinted in the bright light, and Henry saw that the pudgy black one was female. She was the only one of the three who obeyed Henry's command. The other two still gripped their 9mm Berettas. The man was holding his hand out in front of his face as if to shield his eyes from the light. With his amplified earmuffs, Henry heard the man whisper to the two women.

"On my signal, we break for cover," Wilson Blair instructed softly. "Martinez, you go for the van, Jackson, you get around the side of the house." Henry Bowman heard the command in his amplified earmuffs, saw the two women turn their heads reflexively towards their superior, and made a quick decision. *It's still three to one. They split up, they can get me in a whipsaw. The leader's the one I want to talk to.* He took aim on the woman nearest the van, put the front sight of his N-frame on the hinge of her jaw, and squeezed the trigger.

G.G. Jackson watched in horror as Elena Martinez's head seemed to burst, and the black woman's bladder let go involuntarily.

Wilson Blair, who had been steeling himself to give the command to run, flinched at the sound of the high-powered revolver discharging sixty yards away. He heard the sickening *thwock* of the bullet striking home, and at the edge of his vision he saw Martinez's body collapse in the grass. Blair let go of his Beretta as if it were radioactive. It fell next to his briefcase.

"Much better," Henry Bowman yelled. "Now, both of you—hands on top of your heads. Good. Now turn around and face the house." Blair and Jackson obeyed. Against the floodlit back wall of Allen Kane's house the two agents saw the shadow of one man approaching with a pistol in his left hand and a bag of some sort in his right. Wilson Blair found his voice.

"We are agents of the United States Government," he said, his words wavering at first, then beginning to gain strength.

Yeah, right Henry thought when he heard the man's claim. *And I'm Santa Claus.* He looked at the body nearest him. The black man's eye was open and a trickle of blood ran from the base of his skull where Henry's first round had struck its mark.

"The Treasury Department, Bureau of Alcohol, Tobacco, and Firearms," Blair continued. *What a moron* Henry thought immediately. *If you're going to pretend to be a cop, pretend to be a real one.*

Henry had left his amplified hearing protectors in the shop. He held his 5" Smith in his left hand as he stood twenty feet from the two invaders. The barrel of the Hi-Standard .22 was in the right pocket of his blue jeans with the gun's action and grip protruding. The pistol had a round in the chamber and the safety was on.

"Keep your hands on top of your heads, and turn around slowly." The white man and the black woman did as they were instructed. Henry Bowman was a dark silhouette standing between them and the bright lights.

Henry glanced at the four bodies on the ground. The man with the M16 was a clean kill, and the woman he had head-shot with his .44 was obviously dead also. *But I can't see any blood on the shotgun guy, and he and the MP5 guy are both lying on top of their weapons.* He considered the two sprawled forms that might still be alive. *Shotgun's the biggest threat* Henry decided. *Then the MP5.* He saw that the man who was staring down the muzzle of his Smith was licking his lips, getting up the nerve to speak.

"I am Supervisory Agent Wilson Blair of the Bureau of Alcohol, Tobacco, and Firearms," Blair said as Henry dropped the canvas bag and drew the Hi-Standard. "And I demand that you–"

Blair stopped in mid-sentence as Henry Bowman pulled the trigger on the .22 and sent a bullet into the center of the crown of Peter Hagedorn's facedown corpse. The gun spat like a loud air rifle. Before it registered on Blair what had happened, Henry had swung the muzzle onto his second target.

The inert form of Ralph Compton was no longer inert. When Henry had shot him earlier, Compton had been moving slightly and the 29-grain bullet from the old .22 target rifle had hit the back of his head at a shallow angle. It had glanced off his skull, chipping the bone slightly and tearing a gash in the skin without doing any real damage. Compton had initially been stunned by the blow to the back of his head, and had ended up lying chest-down, with his face turned away from the man who had stopped their raid. Compton had heard every word his enemy had said, and now correctly estimated that he was about ten feet away. The agent tried to roll over and bring his weapon to bear on the man who had shot him.

At ten feet, Henry Bowman didn't need to use sights. In nine-tenths of a second he put three rounds into a three-inch circle immediately in front of Ralph Compton's right ear.

"I'm afraid I outrank you, Mister Blair," Henry continued in a conversational tone as he put the Hi-Standard's safety back on and slid the barrel of the weapon back in his pocket. "And I have to say, I don't hold much respect for you guys in F Troop. None of us do." He saw that the black woman had closed her eyes and was clenching her teeth.

"Who sent you? What are you doing here?" Wilson Blair was starting to become hysterical, and he hated it when other feds referred to ATF as 'F Troop'. "We had this all set up!" he yelled, then managed to calm himself.

"You don't know what you've meddled in," he went on. "We're going to get Kane, Millet, and Bowman all at the same time, and now you people are mixing in." *Bowman!* Henry thought. He felt as if he had been hit with an electric prod at the mention of his own name, but he remained silent.

"Call out the rest of your squad, and let's get our stories straight about what happened here," Blair said beseechingly. "And, uh, what agency sent you?" he added as he lowered his hands.

"Put your hands back on top of your head," Henry Bowman instructed as his mind furiously tried to accept the implications of what the man was saying. *What the hell is going on here?* Henry asked himself. The great relief he had felt at still being alive, healthy, and in control had been replaced by a feeling of dread. *What's this guy talking about? He really does believe I'm a fed. But he's not afraid I'll arrest him—he wants us to get our stories straight, for Christ's sake. And that can only mean...* Henry looked over at the black woman.

"What's your name?" he demanded.

"Special Agent G.G. Jackson," the woman snuffled.

Oh, fuck thought Henry Bowman, and then he remembered the old saying common to both resistance fighters and criminals: *The first one's expensive, but after that, they're all free.* He sighed inaudibly. *I guess I'll figure out what I'm going to do while she's taping him up.*

Suddenly, Henry remembered something from many summers ago, before he was old enough to drive. *What was that kid's name, that I let go? Nat, that was it.* The barest beginnings of a plan were starting to form in his mind. *Maybe I can use what he and his cousin were fixing to do, before I came along and broke up their party. Got a lot of stuff to get done before I start in on that, though* he told himself. Then he smiled.

"Well, Special Agent G.G. Jackson," Henry Bowman said brightly as he reached into the canvas bag and pulled out a roll of duct tape. "You've just received a temporary interagency lateral transfer."

Part Four

WAR

That he which hath no stomach to this fight,
Let him depart. His passport shall be made
And crowns for convoy put into his purse.
We would not die in that man's company
That fears his fellowship to die with us.
This day is called the feast of Crispian.
He that outlives this day and comes safe home
Will stand a-tiptoe when this day is named
And rouse him at the name of Crispian,
He that shall live this day and see old age
Will yearly on the vigil feast his neighbors
And say, "Tomorrow is Saint Crispian."
Then will he strip his sleeve and show his scars,
And say "These wounds I had on Crispin's Day."
Old men forget, yet all shall be forgot,
But he'll remember with advantages
What feats he did that day. Then shall our names,
Familiar in his mouth as household words,
Harry the King, Bedford and Exeter,
Warwick and Talbot, Salisbury and Gloucester,
Be in their flowing cups freshly remembered.
This story shall the good man teach his son,
And Crispin Crispian shall ne'er go by,
From this day to the ending of the world,
But we in it shall be remembered—
We few, we happy few, we band of brothers.
For he today that sheds his blood with me
Shall be my brother. Be he ne'er so vile,
This day shall gentle his condition.
And gentlemen in England now abed
Shall think themselves accursed they were not here,
And hold their manhoods cheap whiles any speaks
That fought with us upon Saint Crispin's Day.

W. Shakespeare, *Henry V*

Every normal man must be tempted, at times,
to spit on his hands, hoist the black flag, and
begin slitting throats.

—H.L. Mencken

June 7, continued

"Here's the way it works," Henry Bowman said to his prisoner as he rolled the foam earplugs between his fingers, compressing them. "I've got a few things to do. I'm going to let you sit here and think about what you're going to say to me when I get back. Jackson's taped up, same as you, on the other side of the barn. I'm going to ask her a bunch of questions, and I'm going to ask you the same questions. I already know the answers to most of them, but you won't know which ones. When you lie or hold out, it's going to get a lot worse." Henry slipped the plugs, one at a time, into Blair's ears. They started to expand slowly.

Wilson Blair could not see his captor, nor in fact had he ever gotten a look at his face. Blair was sitting on the ground with his spine against the six-inch diameter trunk of a silver maple. His arms were behind him, taped together from the wrists to the elbows. He had zero leverage, and it hurt. Duct tape also encircled his forehead and neck, binding his head to the tree and rendering it almost immobile. The roll was still attached to the last wrap around the trunk.

"Open up," Henry commanded from Blair's back as he reached around the tree trunk and showed the man a golf ball in one hand and the wicked looking Applegate knife in the other. Blair grudgingly opened his mouth, only half noticing that the golf ball seemed to be dripping with moisture.

Henry popped the golf ball past Blair's teeth and shoved the point of the knife firmly against the flesh behind the man's chin to force his mouth closed. He held the knife there as he grabbed the roll of duct tape with his free hand and wrapped four layers around Blair's mouth, neck, and the tree trunk, then covered the man's eyes with the last turn.

"I'll be back in fifteen minutes," Henry Bowman said in a loud voice so that Blair could hear him through the earplugs. "Remember, it can get a lot worse." As Henry walked over to the side of the barn where G.G. Jackson was similarly restrained, he heard Blair making tortured, guttural noises through his nose. Wilson Blair was now acutely aware that the liquid coating on the golf ball in his mouth was not water.

Henry had taped Jackson to a wheeled platform truck that Allen Kane used to move ammo crates. He pulled another pair of foam earplugs from his pocket, and spent the next two minutes administering the same treatment to the woman agent.

"I'll be back in fifteen minutes," Henry lied again as he wrapped the duct tape around Jackson's head. Before he covered the woman's eyes, Henry saw them bulging and beginning to water, and her nostrils flaring. After wrapping the tape over her eyes, Henry checked once more that all her bonds were secure and there was no way she could escape, and walked quietly back to where Wilson Blair sat against the tree.

Blair's upper body was heaving, and the cords in his neck stood out as he tried to move his immobilized head. His jaw was working, trying to move the golf ball around to a different spot in his mouth, in the vain hope that such action would lessen his agony. At the angle his arms were held, Blair had no leverage, and the many wraps of tape were not about to fail.

Henry smiled and walked back around the house. *I don't think you can die from Habanero juice in your mouth* he thought to himself. *But I guess we'll find out.* He looked at his watch as he trotted back to the barn. *Almost midnight. Good thing I never needed all that much sleep* he told himself. What Henry Bowman had to do next was going to take a lot longer than fifteen minutes.

June 8

It took more effort than Henry ever would have imagined to get the jacket and shirt off the black corpse, but when he finally accomplished this and tried them on, they were a decent fit. Levar Williams had stood a good four inches taller than Henry, and Bowman knew that the black agent's pants would be much too long. The ones worn by the white man who had the MP5 looked to be a little big in the waist, but about the right length. It turned out that they were, and after he cinched the belt tight, Henry decided they would pass muster. Henry took off the jacket and shirt, and put the collar of the shirt in a basin of cold water to soak out the bloodstains. Then he used his double-edged folding knife to cut the rest of the clothes off the four dead ATF agents.

Now for the bad part Henry said to himself as he stripped to his underwear in the back corner of the shop, put his shoes back on, and reached up to the section of pegboard where Allen Kane hung his various types of hand saws. His eyes then fell on a kukri, the curved weapon used by the Ghurkas in Nepal, that lay on Kane's workbench. Henry had once used a kukri to cut a yellow pine two-by-four in half with three strokes. *Might as well try them all* he thought, as he took two saws from the pegboard, and grabbed the heavy blade with his other hand.

***

By the time Henry had finished his grisly chore, he was covered with blood. He washed himself off with the garden hose before loading the cargo in the back of the van. Then he washed up again, returned to the shop, and started to go through the personal effects of the six government agents.

In addition to their badges and federal ID, each of them had the usual assortment of family photos and personal items. Seeing those things made Henry feel worse about what he had done. He put them aside and popped the latches on the briefcase Wilson Blair had been carrying.

What he found inside made him forget all about family snapshots, and he put his head in his hands. *What am I going to do now?* he asked himself. Then he remembered something that he seen when he was twenty years old.

For a period of about two decades, the men of the Amherst College Glee Club had gone on goodwill concert tours every other summer, singing in a number of foreign countries. Henry Bowman had gone to Europe one summer with the Glee Club, and during the time the group was in France, Henry and a friend had rented a car on one of their few free days. They had visited the museums and beaches at Normandy, where Henry's Uncle Max had landed in a glider on June 6, 1944.

There had been restored gliders, period photos, descriptions of the planning of the invasion, and many other impressive exhibits at the various museums, along with the terribly moving sight of the vast expanse of perfectly aligned crosses in the cemetery. The thing that Henry Bowman remembered most vividly, however, was a small exhibit of memorabilia from past D-Day anniversaries that one of the museums had assembled.

One of the items was a June 6 clipping from an American newspaper printed many years after the war. It showed a paunchy man wearing glasses and sitting in an overstuffed armchair in his living room, drinking a beer. The story focused on the human-interest angle, describing how, in May of 1944, the man's family had been sent a telegram saying that he had been killed in action. Several months later, the family had learned that their son was still alive. The reason for the error was that the young G.I. had been captured by the Germans in France, but had later managed to kill one of his captors, change clothes and I.D. with him, and bluff his way to safety in a German uniform. In the meantime, the Nazis had found a corpse dressed in U.S. fatigues with U.S. dogtags around its neck, and had dutifully notified the proper authorities.

The author of the newspaper item had focused on the family's joy those long years ago at learning their son was alive and well, and on what the man had done with his life since. Henry Bowman, however, had found something much more amazing in the yellowed article. In telling his story to the reporter, the man had used barely a whole sentence mentioning what he had been doing in France several weeks before the Normandy invasion, before detailing his capture and escape. He had parachuted, alone, into occupied France in mid-April. His assignment had been to destroy and disrupt German communications in any way he could, while avoiding detection or capture.

"I can't believe this!" Henry Bowman had said to his friend. There was a smaller photo of the man that the paper had printed, taken at the time he had enlisted. He looked like he worked in a gas station. Henry had stabbed his finger at the small picture in the framed clipping.

"Here's some nineteen-year-old kid from Moosefuck, Georgia. You know he doesn't speak a word of any foreign language, and probably hasn't ever been a hundred miles outside where he was born, before he joined the army.

"Now they slap a 'chute on him, hand him a pair of wire cutters and a couple tins of beef jerky, and say 'Good luck, Duane. Go knock out all the radio transmitters you can, and cut a few phone lines while you're at it, but for Christ's sake don't get caught. Food? Shelter? Krauts everywhere? Everybody speaking languages you don't understand? Hell, boy, you'll figure something out. Reinforcements? Well, son, that's top secret, and fact is, it's still in the planning stage. Let's just say you shouldn't count on any backup for, oh, a couple months, okay? See you later,' and they boot his ass out the door of a Gooney Bird at ten thousand feet in the middle of the night over enemy territory. Jesus!"

"Looks like he did okay," his friend had said.

"No shit," Henry had replied. Henry Bowman had never forgotten the enormity of what that young man had been expected to do, and had done willingly.

Well, Duane Henry said to himself as he looked at the contents of the open briefcase, *you got lots more'n a set a wire cutters, plenty to eat, and there ain't but two enemies in this territory, and they's tied up. Whatcha bitchin' for, boy?*

***

"Okay, it's time to talk," Henry said to G.G. Jackson after he had used one of the keys on his keyring to snag the foam earplugs and pull them out of her ears. He flicked open the blade of his knife and carefully sliced through the layers of tape covering her mouth.

An hour and a half of extreme discomfort coupled with sight and sound deprivation had taken its toll. G.G. Jackson had barely enough strength to weakly spit out the golf ball. She made a series of horrendous hacking noises as she fought for breath through the layers of mucous that had been draining down her throat. Henry held a dipper of water to her lips, then followed it with a piece of bread.

"Long as I keep getting answers, you can keep getting more. If you stop, well, I've got another golf ball here."

"No!" she gasped. "No, I'll tell you. 'S nothin' to me. 'Spect you know most of it a'ready," she panted. Then she began to talk.

In less than ten minutes, G.G. Jackson was repeating herself. It seemed obvious to Henry that she was a foot soldier, and had not been a part of the strategy session where the raid had initially been planned.

"Which agents were on the other raid teams?" Henry asked suddenly. Jackson replied immediately.

"Don't know none of 'em. Blair, he picked 'em all. Talked 'bout how good this was going to look, how we was all going to get on the news, like it would mean a big promotion. Was another team in Ohio for Millet's place, an' one in Missouri for that other fella. You want names, get him to turn on that computer of his he so proud of. It pro'ly tell you name, address, an' what they eat f'breakfast. It's under the front seat of the van."

Computer? I missed the laptop when I loaded up the van Henry though, reprimanding himself silently. *I'll give it a once-over while he stews a little longer.*

"What about the funny money?" Henry demanded, suddenly changing the subject to keep the woman off-balance. Jackson looked blank, then shook her head.

"Wasn't no money," she said as she spat and swallowed. "Wasn't gettin' paid no extry. Blair promised us two more days off, full pay, for workin' at night. Just bust in an' drag out all the guns. Take lots of pictures."

Henry nodded. He had found enough camera gear in the van to outfit a mobile news crew. He decided not to mention the pictures he had found to Agent Jackson. He was virtually certain that she knew nothing about them.

"I think it's time I had a talk with your boss," Henry said, and began walking towards the house. It would only take a minute to find the computer and see if any of the files on it were encrypted before interrogating the ATF supervisor.

***

Wilson Blair had had an even stronger reaction to the hot pepper juice and had been in even worse shape than G.G. Jackson. It took almost fifteen minutes before he was able to communicate intelligibly. That was more than enough time for Henry to position the small tape recorder behind him in the grass. The battery-operated unit was one that Allen Kane, like most firearms dealers, used whenever he talked to ATF agents on the telephone. When Blair did start talking, he began spilling his guts.

Henry had suspected that Blair would know a lot more about the raid than the young black woman. He had not counted on the fact that Wilson Blair was the one who had conceived and designed the entire operation. Over the next half hour, he told Henry about the entire three-part raid, starting with the phone taps. Henry's guts turned over when he realized that it was only because he had used his cellular instead of Allen's phone that he'd been able to surprise the six-agent raiding party.

Henry Bowman knew that his life was now irreversibly altered, and that this would be the case regardless of where he had been that evening—at home in Missouri, with Allen Kane in the mountains in Idaho, or sitting in Kane's Indiana shop. Henry cursed his luck, then flashed back to what he had told Danielle Pelletier more that two decades before when she'd found out he'd tried to enlist in Vietnam: *When you get the opportunity to control more of your own future, grab it with both hands.* He nodded to himself. *At least this way,* Henry thought as he stared at the back of Wilson Blair's head, *I've got some say in what happens next.*

At about one-thirty in the morning, Wilson Blair finally decided that maybe this man was not going to kill him as he had the four others, and the ATF supervisor risked asking a few questions of his own.

"What is your name, and what agency do you work for?" Blair finally demanded. "Why have your people interfered with our operation? And why won't you let me see your face?"

Jesus! Henry thought. *This guy still thinks I'm a fed!* He considered this for a few moments, trying to figure out how to make it pay off for him. The beginnings of a plan were starting to take shape in his mind. *Take some brass* Henry thought, then smiled sardonically to himself. *Brass, hell. After the first one, the rest are free. Right, Duane?*

"I suspect you know the reason I have not told you or Miss Jackson my name, nor let either of you see my face," Henry said evenly. "And you should take great comfort in it. When we are done here, I am authorized to arrange for your safe pick-up, and entry into the Witness Protection Program if, and I stress the word, if I determine such action does not pose an unacceptable security risk.

"Frankly, Mister Blair, I dislike unnecessary loose ends, and I would just as soon dispose of your corpse at the same time as the others." *There's the stick* Henry thought with a grim smile. *Now for the carrot.*

"Our Commander-In-Chief, however, feels that those who help him resolve a difficult problem should be protected, even when those people are themselves the original cause of that problem. That is why, on my orders, you will be given a new identity and a new job in a new location."

"What about my family?" Blair asked reflexively.

"They would go with you, if that is what you want. Some of the entrants into the program are not particularly attached to their families, and prefer to start fresh." *Let him think about that for a while* Henry thought.

"You must realize," Bowman went on, "that I have less than glowing admiration for the Witness Protection Program. It is run by sloppy amateurs who understandably don't care much about the future of Mob accountants and other typical...participants. They shoot their mouths off with alarming regularity, which is one of the reasons why the program's record of protecting people from truly motivated enemies approaches a 100% failure rate.

"In your case, however, the only person who would want to find you and kill you is me, and I will already have your new name, Social Security number, address, and other particulars. That is why I suggest you not do anything now that might piss me off later. Like giving me wrong info," Henry added pointedly.

"As to why I interrupted your little raid-in-progress, I suspect you know the answer to that question also, but I'll spell it out for you.

"For many years now, you fools have been using blank search warrants, planting evidence, and perjuring yourselves in court. You've reinterpreted your own rulings and used entrapment to put people in prison over paperwork disputes. You've killed citizens over suspected non-payment of $200 taxes, and burned their children alive. You've tried to frame a man and threatened him with prison because a piece of wood was a half-inch too short, and when he wouldn't roll over for you, your buddies at the FBI shot his son in the back and blew his wife's head off while she was nursing their ten-month old daughter. You illegally invaded the house of a man who pays more taxes in a year than the President and his wife have in their whole lives. Then you jacked that man's pregnant wife up against her living room wall and made her miscarry, and you did it because your own people fucked up the Washington records of his machine gun collection." Henry took a breath and squatted a foot or so behind where Wilson Blair sat with his arms taped around the tree.

"It has finally dawned on certain people inside the Beltway that your band of inept storm troopers are responsible for the ultimate atrocity: You have been costing them votes. The President wants this problem solved in a way that won't embarrass him, so he had a little chat with my supervisor. That's why I'm here."

"You're alone?" Blair demanded in astonishment. Henry Bowman smiled as he remembered the old story about the Texas Ranger. *There's only one riot, ain't there?*

"Have to be, for a job like this," Henry answered aloud. "Bunch of others around, word would eventually get out as to what really happened, and that would embarrass the President. And, there'd be no way to let you live. Too many who'd know about you and what you did." He stood up.

"Time for me to go get Miss Jackson. Got some things I need to say to both of you." Wilson Blair had many things he wanted answered as he listened to his captor's receding footsteps, but he held his tongue.

***

"He didn't kill you, neither," G.G. Jackson said flatly. She was duct-taped to a platform truck which Henry had wheeled to a spot a few feet to the side of the ATF supervisor. Wilson Blair did not reply.

"Okay, folks, here's the deal," Henry Bowman said briskly after he had checked to see that both his captives were securely bound. "Both of you have been a great help to me. Miss Jackson, you knew much more about this operation than I had been told you would. I had thought that only your supervisor knew about the materials that he planned to plant in the house. And volunteering the info about the other agents in the system, and where Blair left his computer—that was good, too, although I had already found the laptop and copied all the files." Blair jerked at the words he was hearing.

"You told–" he started to say, then stopped when he felt the muzzle of the Hi-Standard .22 behind his right ear.

"And Agent Blair," Henry went on, acting as if nothing had happened. "You spelled out exactly what you intended to do, and what the other raid teams' instructions were." He paced back and forth behind his two captives, letting the tension increase.

"Point is," Henry said reasonably, "I can only take one of you in the Witness protection program. Those are my orders. So the question is, which one of you is it going to be? Hmn? Which one of you is going to be willing to help me out the most? Which one of you really wants to stay alive?"

"You the big man, struttin' 'round with the gun," G.G. Jackson said.

Obviously a short memory Henry Bowman said to himself, but remained silent and let the woman continue.

"You makin' all the rules. You decide. Ain't gon' be makin' me start cryin' 'bout how much I want to live."

"Sir," Wilson Blair said suddenly. "I can and will tell you much more than she did, or ever could. There are all sorts of things that aren't in my computer, that I can tell you about. You didn't ask me about my computer," he said desperately. "I forgot. I would have told you—and there's probably nothing on it that you don't already have anyway. Roster of the other agents, other raids that are scheduled, you already have that, I know, but I can tell you much more—anything! Anything you want to know about any agent, any mission, I know or I can find out. She doesn't know anything—for God's sake, take *me!*"

"I guess that settles it, then," Henry said softly. *It's obvious who here has the spine.* He grabbed the grip of the Hi-Standard, released the safety as the barrel cleared the top of his jeans pocket, and pulled the trigger twice. The double-tap put both 29-grain slugs within a half-inch of each other, just behind and below the left ear.

Gonorrhea Gaily Jackson, originally from Chicago's south side, was dead.

***

"Okay, Blair," Henry Bowman said from behind the floodlight. "I got lots of video-tape, and I got lots of time. We're going to do this until you get it right. I know you're a good bullshitter, so if at any time this starts sounding like you don't mean it, I'm going to stop, rewind, and we'll start all over from the beginning. When you see the red light above the lens, that means I'm recording. Get ready."

Wilson Blair sat in a folding metal chair in Allen Kane's living room. In front of him was a 3' by 6' table with folding legs. It had come from Kane's basement, next to the dryer, and was covered with a white sheet. On it sat Blair's briefcase, and a glass of ice water. The wood-paneled wall behind Blair was also covered with a white bedsheet that Henry Bowman had nailed to the paneling near the ceiling.

The image through the viewfinder of the tripod-mounted video camera showed Blair sitting behind one side of the covered tabletop, with a white background behind. The camera's position cropped off the left half of the table and all of the wall that was more than a foot above Blair's head. There would be no way that someone viewing the tape would be able to tell anything about the room, how long the table was, what kind of legs it had, or if indeed it was a table at all, or just a packing crate turned on its side.

"Three seconds, then go," Henry Bowman instructed. Blair saw the red light appear, and licked his lips.

"My name is Wilson Blair," he said in a clear tenor. "I am a regional director for the Bureau of Alcohol, Tobacco, and Firearms. The government of this country, through the efforts of my agency, has been engaged in a systematic program of lies, coercion, and evidence planting, with the ultimate goal of disarming the citizenry. Our actions have chilled the freedoms of this country's strongest defenders of individual rights." He paused to take a sip of water, then went on.

"In April of this year," Blair said, "I initiated what was to be a three-part raid on the homes of three U.S. citizens who had never in their lives committed any crime more serious than traffic violations. In order to plan this raid, I employed a number of illegal wire-taps, and I was prepared to use three blank search warrants which had been signed in advance by a federal judge who has signed many blank warrants for us in the past."

Wilson Blair laid the briefcase flat on the table and opened it. He withdrew three pieces of paper, held them up, then put them away.

"I scheduled the three raids so that they would take place when the...subjects of these raids were thousands of miles away. I wanted to see that these three people would be jailed without bond. To make sure that would happen, I obtained several things that I planned to plant in the three houses at the time of the raids, which would then be found by other agents during the ensuing searches." Blair scowled, remembering that his captor had spelled out exactly how he had to explain this section clearly, and took a deep breath.

"I have planted evidence after the fact on many prior occasions," he said quickly, "but these were always firearms-related objects: an auto-sear, a barrel we had cut off to a length below the legal minimum, a bunch of muffler tubing and fender washers that we could say were illegal silencer parts, dummy grenades that a paid informant could testify were being illegally reactivated, or metal dies and stamps that we could claim a citizen had been using to re-number firearms.

"These tactics always resulted in indictments, but in each case the accused was free to hire lawyers and gather evidence of our wrongdoing. Almost invariably the citizen would eventually plead to a charge of conspiracy after having spent a few hundred thousand dollars in court costs and legal fees, and be sentenced to a few years in prison.

"This, however, was expensive for the government, and in the raids I was planning, I wanted all three of the suspects to be jailed without bond. That was going to require much more serious charges, and therefore much more serious evidence." Blair saw his captor's arm come up from behind the floodlight with the muzzle of the Smith & Wesson pointed at Blair's face. He quickly amended his last sentence.

"Much more serious *planted* evidence," the ATF man said meaningfully as he reached once more into the briefcase. "The first item," he explained, "was not gun-related at all. Instead..."

Henry Bowman watched from behind the spotlight as Blair proceeded with his presentation. *His delivery is smoother than I expected* Henry thought with a small smile. Although Blair was hardly in a position where he could launch an effective attack, Bowman held the 5" N-frame at waist level, trained in the general direction of the ATF man's nose.

***

"I have quit my position at the BATF, I no longer work for the Federal Government, and I cannot be contacted," Blair said as he concluded his presentation. "I may, however, transmit additional messages. They will not include my image, for my appearance will change drastically immediately after this recording is made." He swallowed. "Future communications will, however, contain information that only I and a few other people could know." Blair sat motionless in the chair, and Henry Bowman switched off the video camera. Wilson Blair breathed with relief when the red light blinked out.

"Don't move, Mister Blair," Henry instructed as he tossed a dishtowel to the man. "Mop off your face, then throw the towel on the floor. We're going to do it again, this time with a few changes." Bowman popped the tape out of the camera and inserted a new one.

"We'll have to rehearse a little more, but basically you're going to change the tone of what you're saying. It's not a personal confession this time. Now you're a man who's been given direct orders from his superior. Only you've become disgusted with yourself for letting it go this far. You're not going to wait until your own Nuremberg trial and then claim you were 'just following orders'. You're going to come clean. You're going to name names, and then you're going to give a little pep talk to the American public." Henry Bowman explained in detail what it was he expected Blair to say.

Wilson Blair was horrified. "I can't say *that!*" he protested.

"Sure you can," Henry said easily. "You've been making up worse bullshit all your life. And it's not like it's actually going to get used," Henry lied. "I just need my own insurance policy, if you get what I mean."

Wilson Blair didn't, but he wasn't going to argue about it. He was almost home free.

"Excellent!" Henry Bowman said as he switched off the camera for the final time. "Stand up, turn around, keep your hands behind your back where I can see them, and walk slowly towards the back door. We're going out to the van, and get you on your way to your new identity."

As Wilson Blair followed the instructions, Henry transferred the revolver to his left hand. With his right, he reached over to the back of the couch where he had laid the hammer he'd used to nail up the backdrop. He picked it up and adjusted his grip on the leather handle. The tool was an Estwing, like the one Walter had given him when he was a toddler, but several ounces heavier. Allen Kane, like Henry and Henry's late father before him, liked good tools.

"You must tell me what agency you work for, that planned all this," Wilson Blair said with what he hoped was a smile in his voice. He was emotionally and physically exhausted.

"You haven't heard of us," Henry answered from behind him as they stepped out into the night air. Then, because he, too, was tired, Henry Bowman thought of an utterly frivolous lie, and he allowed himself the one bit of whimsy. *Guy probably doesn't read the same authors I do* Henry told himself.

"We answer to the President," Henry said, "though I've got a lot more respect for my immediate superior. The few people who know about us call us the Wrecking Crew."

Henry swung the sixteen-ounce Estwing in a smooth arc, giving his wrist the practiced snap at the end of the swing that his father Walter had taught him decades before. The polished face of the hammer struck ATF agent Wilson Blair dead center on the occipital protrusion at the back of his head, and he collapsed as if pole-axed.

Did I kill the fool? Henry wondered as he bent down to feel for a pulse at the man's neck. Henry suddenly had an image of his fifth-grade class, where he had learned to find a pulse both on himself and on others. *I guess my expensive education has some practical uses after all* he thought as he felt the faint throb through the man's skin. For an instant, Henry longed to be sitting in Allen Kane's 2 1/2-ton army truck, driving on mining roads in Idaho, miles away from his current predicament. Then he abandoned that indulgence and went back to his current tasks.

Henry Bowman backed the white Ford van up to the house and opened the dual back doors. With considerable effort he got Wilson Blair in and on top of the plastic garbage bags he had loaded in the van earlier. The man weighed no more than Henry, but by the time he was lying in the back of the van, Henry was breathing hard. *Now I know why they call it 'dead weight'* he thought distractedly. The corpse of the young woman agent out by the side of the building proved less difficult to handle.

Henry walked back to the workshop. When he returned, he was carrying a plastic 5-gallon bucket, which he tossed in the back of the vehicle on top of the hand saws and the kukri knife. *Gloves* Henry remembered, and went back in the workshop for them.

Henry Bowman returned to Allen Kane's house, where he retrieved some clothes and also towels from the washroom. He put the clothes next to him on the passenger seat as he climbed into the cab of the van. Then he released the parking brake, dropped the idling vehicle into DRIVE, and drove out of the yard.

***

"Little midnight snack, guys," Henry said softly to the snuffling animals as he climbed out of the van. "Have it ready for you in a few minutes." He had changed into the pants and shirt he had taken from the house; his own clothes lay on the van's passenger seat. *If you got a frog to swallow...* Henry told himself for the fourth or fifth time as he pushed his thumb against the checkered stud on the blade of his Applegate folder. The two-edged blade swung open and locked into place, and Henry went to work. In less than ten minutes, G.G. Jackson's corpse was nude, and a pile of shredded clothing and duct tape sat under the back end of the van. Wilson Blair lay nude and unconscious in the back of the van with his head hanging over the back edge of the rear bumper.

Henry Bowman put his gloves back on, placed the bucket he had taken from the workshop directly under Wilson Blair's head, then found the man's pulse in the side of his neck. He looked at his Applegate fighting knife, on which he had always maintained a near-razor edge. It was a habit he had learned long ago from his Uncle Max.

Your turn's come up, ace. Wish the Colonel was here to see this Henry thought irrelevantly. *He'd probably show me how to do it more efficiently, not break so much of a sweat.* With a decisive movement of the hand that held the sharp blade, Henry Bowman opened up a large incision in Wilson Blair's carotid artery, then quickly adjusted the position of the bucket so as to catch the blood which pumped relentlessly out of the wound in the man's neck.

It took over ten minutes for Wilson Blair's heart to stop beating. By that time, there was over a gallon of fresh blood in the bucket. Bowman stowed the folding knife, picked up the big, curved instrument from Nepal, and relieved the fresh corpse of its head, hands, and feet. Blair had been larger than four of the other five, but by this time, Henry had had enough practice to have his technique down. He had learned back at Kane's house that the Ghurka kukri was far more efficient than a hacksaw for some of what was required, although it was slightly messier.

How I Spent My Summer Vacation he found himself thinking. *If I get tired of geology and start-up companies I can always find work at the slaughterhouse.* It took less than three minutes to remove all of the identifying attributes from the man's body and pack them in a plastic trash bag.

"You didn't really think I was going to let you back in the gene pool, did you?" Henry found himself saying out loud to the disembodied head as he pushed it into the sack. *Jesus!* he thought as he clamped his mouth shut. *I'm losing my mind—talking to a dead man's head!* He squeezed his eyes shut and shook his head violently. *Come on, guy* he said to himself. *Lots more work to do here.* Then he started in on the corpse of G.G. Jackson.

Henry Bowman was literally drenched with sweat and blood when he stopped to take a break. A pang of intense hunger swept over him, followed immediately by a wave of nausea at the idea of eating under the circumstances. He closed his eyes and waited for the feeling to pass. Henry was suddenly reminded of something a rugby teammate from college had told him during a game when Henry was doubled over, exhausted, and the play was halfway down the field: *'You're wiped out and you need rest. You can't run to where the play is. That's okay. You don't have to. Walk towards the ball—you'll get there, and you'll get your rest on the way. But if you just stand here, you'll never get back in the play.'*

Henry smiled at the thought, opened his eyes, and let the smile vanish. *You were right, Randy. You got to keep moving, even if it's real slow.* He grabbed the biggest section of what was left of Wilson Blair under the arms and with an effort dragged it out of the van and let it fall in the dirt. Henry glanced involuntarily around him, then turned towards Blair's body. Suddenly, Henry bent over and grabbed the dead man's penis and scrotum with a gloved left hand. With a strong sweep of his right arm he cut off the shriveled member and tossed it backhand into the hog pen. Henry watched as it flipped over in the moonlight, revolving around its center of gravity before falling with a faint slap into the dirt of the pen. The nearest hog snuffled once and immediately began devouring the unexpected delicacy.

Fuck it Henry thought. *Six of 'em shouldn't take as long as one cape buffalo. They knew what they were doing, and they died quick. Not like the kids in Mt. Carmel.*

When he thought about it that way, gutting out and quartering the bodies of six headless, handless, and feetless ATF agents and feeding them to Dale Price's hogs didn't seem so bad.

***

Dawn was threatening to break by the time Henry Bowman had cleaned up again, stripped the two machine guns to bare receivers, rearranged Allen Kane's living room, and stowed the dead agents' weapons and other useful effects in the BMW's saddlebags. He looked at the back door, with its lower hinge blasted away. *Drive partway to Ohio, and sack out in the van?* he wondered. *The hell with it* he decided. *I'm about to pass out on my feet.* He drove the van behind one of the outbuildings, threw a tarp over it, and returned to Allen Kane's bedroom for a nap.

As Henry set the alarm and laid the set of ATF garb and credentials on the floor beside the bed, he thought of one more thing. He retrieved the battery-powered tape recorder from the living room, rewound it for a few seconds, and listened until the end. Then he switched it to Record, and repeated the words. He rewound it, hit PLAY again, and listened to the two versions of Wilson Blair. *A little higher, but less nasal* Henry thought. He rewound the tape back to the start of his impression, recorded another attempt, and listened again. *Better,* he decided. *I'll practice some more in a few hours* he promised himself, and fell back onto the bed.

In thirty seconds he was snoring softly.

***

"Coffee, sir?" the stewardess asked. Alex Neumann opened his eyes and looked up.

"Oh. Ah, no thank you," he said with a faint headshake. The FBI man went back to the calculations he'd been doing in his head.

Roundtrip airfare, even if they got it dirt cheap, got to be a few hundred. Ten nights lodging, another few hundred. Food, maybe a hundred. Transport, fifty bucks, maybe. He chewed his lip. *What does a Sexual Harassment Awareness Training instructor make, I wonder? Couple thousand? Call it two hundred for my share. Twelve hundred so far. Other staff, maybe? Use of the facilities?* He closed his eyes again. *Probably add up to more than two thousand by the time it's all over. That's more than a semester of college cost me.* Neumann sighed. *That's not even counting the fact that they're still paying my salary. And I won't be doing jack shit for the Bureau for the next two weeks.*

FBI Agent Alex Neumann was wrong about the total per-agent cost of the special course he was about to attend. His estimate was much too low. He was also wrong in thinking that for the next two weeks, the Bureau was going to do nothing but waste his time.

***

"I'm sorry," the middle-aged man said to the eight employees standing before him. There were tears in his eyes.

"Mr. Billings, if I lose this job, I could lose my house."

"I know Jackie," he said softly. "But there isn't any job any more. Ace Cleaners is bankrupt. I don't own this place any more—the bankruptcy trustee holds the title."

"What are they going to do with it?" another woman asked. Billings licked his lips.

"I don't know. Probably level the place."

"Isn't it those other people's fault, over at Wingfoot?" another asked. Billings sighed.

"It's both of ours. We had the fluid. If we hadn't, they wouldn't have been here. And this has put them into bankruptcy, too." There were reluctant nods of understanding.

Billings looked around at the faces of the people who had worked for him, some for over twenty years. It was the saddest moment of his life.

***

It was almost 10:00 a.m. by the time Henry Bowman pulled out of Allen Kane's driveway and headed east. He was wearing the dark blue clothing from two of the slain agents, and was carrying Wilson Blair's credentials in his right hip pocket. On his head he wore a dark pair of sunglasses, and one of the ATF agents' navy blue billed caps. He was convinced that no one seeing him through the dusty windshield would be able to later give any description more detailed than "clean-shaven white man, somewhere between thirty and sixty-five."

Henry had spent ten minutes in Kane's shop loading eighteen very low-velocity rounds for his .44. He had also scrounged every one of Allen Kane's jerrycans that he could find, and filled them from Kane's storage tank. An extra forty gallons of fuel gave him a few more options, if things did not go well.

On the way to Columbus, Ohio, Henry Bowman used the portable tape deck and practiced mimicking Wilson Blair, even after he felt he had the man's speech pattern down cold. *Extra practice never hurt* Henry told himself, then smiled. *Hey, hotshot, it's why you're still alive.*

***

"Hello?" said the accented voice.

"Cruz, it's Blair," Henry Bowman said into the mouthpiece of the pay phone, then held his breath.

"Hey, how'd it go at Kane's?" the man asked immediately.

"Perfect," Henry answered, determined to keep his sentences short. "But there's a possible problem at Millet's house. Millet may have set a trap."

"What?"

"Yeah. I'm sending a specialist—guy used to work bomb squad—to go in first. He's on his way to pick you up and go over everything. Name's Eric Cutter. He's on his way right now, driving a white van. Where are the others?"

"J.P.'s here with me. Heywood and Mary are over at Heywood's place, I think."

"Good. I'll have Cutter pick them up, too. There's a lot you'll have to go over, from what we found at Kane's, and it tightens our schedule, so don't make Cutter sit out by the curb." He paused, then gave his parting comment. "We're a third of the way there, Cruz.

Let's nail these bastards."

Henry Bowman used his index finger to disconnect the call, dropped more coins in the slot, and dialed the second number. A black man answered on the second ring.

"Heywood? Wilson Blair. Listen carefully," Henry Bowman said, and then went through the same presentation as he had with Lorenzo Cruz.

When he was finished, and after he had heard Heywood Downing hang up, Henry took a heavy pair of pliers from his pocket and clipped the metal cable holding the receiver to the pay phone. Heywood Downing's phone would be out of service until someone pressed down the lever on the pay phone's receiver. Then Henry closed his eyes and sagged against the aluminum shield surrounding the public phone.

Now for the really tricky part he thought.

***

"You must be Cutter," the tall man with the pockmarked face said as he opened the passenger door of the van, reached over the stack of Halliburton aluminum hardcases, and extended his right hand. "J.P. Stewart. And this is Lorenzo Cruz," he said, indicating an hispanic man of medium height standing behind him.

"Eric Cutter," Henry said in his own voice, shaking Stewart's hand. "Sorry about all this gear, but Blair said get cracking, and I just threw it in the front."

"No problem. We'll just hop in the back." Stewart slid the side door open and the two men climbed into the van's middle seat.

"You'll have to help him with the door," Henry said helpfully to the tall man who had entered first. "Push on the top edge while Mr. Cruz slams it shut hard, or it won't close all the way."

"Goddamn Fords," Stewart muttered as he leaned across the bench seat and began to push on the top of the door. He did not notice the slight movement in the driver's seat. Lorenzo Cruz grabbed the door handle, gave it a mighty heave, and the sliding door swooped rapidly along its track.

As the door slammed shut, Henry Bowman shot Jedediah P. Stewart in the back of the head. Stewart's corpse folded across Lorenzo Cruz's knees, then became wedged against the front seat.

"Hey–" Cruz started to say, but his words were cut off as Henry put two 29-grain bullets into his left eye socket. Cruz died with his mouth open, still sitting upright in the seat.

Thank God this van doesn't have any windows back of the front doors Henry Bowman thought as he laid the Hi-Standard on the passenger seat, dropped the lever into DRIVE, and pulled away from the curb. Then he switched his 5" Smith & Wesson from his left hand to his right, and slid it into the inside-the-pants holster on his right hip.

Four grains of Bullseye still would have made a hell of a mess. Glad I didn't have to use it Henry thought as he gave silent thanks that the .22 functioned reliably with CB caps.

In over three decades of shooting, Henry Bowman had still never gotten to where he was willing to trust his life to any semiautomatic handgun designed by someone other than John Browning.

***

Hope my luck keeps holding Henry said to himself as he pulled onto the street where Heywood Downing's apartment was located. It was in a more densely populated part of the city than Cruz's house, and cars lined the curb in front of the two-story walk-up. He honked the horn after bringing the van to a stop. Several black faces on front stoops stared in his direction. *That's it, guys* he thought. *Burn this into your memory for when they come to your door with questions in a week or so.*

After a little over a minute's wait, a black couple in dark blue uniforms came out of the front door.

"You Cutter?" the man said.

"Yeah. Blair's got a problem. We got to go pick up the other two and meet him before tonight. Hop in."

"We need anything?" Heywood Downing asked.

"Nah, you'll have time to come back here. Blair needs to see everybody right now, 'cause he's got to be somewhere else in an hour, or something like that." The black couple nodded in understanding as they climbed into the van. Wilson Blair liked to play the role of workaholic supervisor.

"What's that smell?" Mary Bright asked, sniffing the air as the van accelerated down the city street.

"Lysol and cedar shavings, " Henry answered. "Blair's kid puked in here, or at least that's what he told me. For all I know, he did it himself," Henry added with an undertone of irritation. "I'm just the goddamn clean-up crew." Downing and Bright looked at each other knowingly. Wilson Blair was not one of their favorite people.

"So where do you come in on this deal?" Downing asked.

"The Indiana team found something at the house. A letter, or something like that. Blair's afraid this guy—Millet?—he's afraid Millet may have rigged his house before leaving the country. And that's my specialty: Bomb disposal and disarming boobytraps."

"Man, ain't there an easier way to make a living?"

"You sound like my ex-wife," Henry said, laughing. "She's afraid I'll let my insurance lapse, and then get sloppy."

"See why I say we should just live together, baby?" Downing teased. Mary Bright glared at him. Henry laughed at the comment, and scanned the area ahead. The next intersection was a four-way stop with a boarded-up gas station on one corner and a burned-out brick building on the other. The only person visible within a hundred yards was a kid on a bicycle, pedaling across the intersection with his back to the van. Henry checked his mirrors and saw no car behind him.

"Say, is my briefcase back there?" Henry asked as he braked for the stop sign and twisted around to face the two agents. "Under your seat, or on the seat behind you maybe? It's not up here." Heywood Downing turned around to look over the back of his seat, and Mary Bright bent over to look underneath where she was sitting.

"There's nothing under here," Bright finished saying just as Henry Bowman shot her lover in the back of the head with the .22. As Heywood Downing fell sideways across the bench seat, Henry triggered two quick shots into the crown of the woman's head, and sent his fourth round into Downing's ear canal. Henry engaged the safety on the Hi-Standard and put the gun under his leg. Then he reholstered his Smith & Wesson, and accelerated away from the stop sign.

The four-person raid team Wilson Blair had handpicked to break into Grant Millet's house no longer existed.

***

"Listen carefully and don't talk," Henry Bowman said into the mouthpiece of the pay phone, speaking softly and using his Wilson Blair voice. "Grant Millet's in South America and the ATF has a raid scheduled for his place sometime in the next ten days. They've got a pile of stuff they're going to plant, and it's enough so that he'll be held without bond. Might be as early as tonight. Got it?"

"Jesus! Tonight? Who is thi–"

"Shut up. I could lose my job for this, or worse. Do what you want with this info," Henry said, and broke the connection.

Henry Bowman knew exactly what Keith Werner, another NFA dealer in Ohio, would do with the information. It was what Second Amendment advocates around the country had been doing on a regular basis since the Waco disaster, whenever word leaked out of an impending raid.

Keith Werner, Henry knew, was at that very moment on the phone, organizing a round-the-clock watch of Millet's house. The watch would be manned by between ten and twenty local Federal Firearms License holders and other gun enthusiasts, all armed with video cameras.

How did that guy put it? Henry thought with a smile. *ATF agents treat video cameras like vampires do crosses and sunlight. Yeah, that's what he said.* He laughed, dumped a bunch of quarters into the phone, and became serious again. This call was going to be a lot more critical.

"ATF, Brown speaking."

"Wilson Blair. Let me talk to Hernandez."

"Hang on." Henry waited for a few moments before the other man came on the line.

"Hernandez here. What's going on?"

"I'm in Ohio. Kane's went like clockwork, but what we found there changes a few things. Schedule's been changed on the Millet raid, and I may not be able to get back with you until you see me. Are the choppers all set for tomorrow?"

"Yeah, and they even got the gun mounts installed. We're all ready to rock and roll." For a moment Henry Bowman was speechless. *Gun mounts?* he thought, then realized the man was probably waiting for a verbal pat on the back.

"Good job." Henry Bowman was thinking frantically, trying to cope with this new development. "What time you going in?" he asked, stalling for time to come up with a plan.

"We're still on for 2:00, if you can still be at the airport by then. We can push it back 'til later in the afternoon, if the team there is running behind."

"That's what I called about. I won't be able to meet you at the airport, and two o'clock's a little early. Like I said, we found some stuff here that'll make our case even stronger—broaden the scope quite a bit. I'm meeting some guys from Washington tonight that I'll be bringing with me."

"What's going on?" Hernandez asked.

"I'll tell you about it in person." *Nothing like tossing in a little dose of paranoia* Henry thought. "Got your aerials of Bowman's place handy? If not, go get 'em."

"Here in front of me."

"Okay. The old quarry pit on the northeast corner of his property—See it?"

"I got it."

"There's a clearing on the west side of it. It's big enough for the choppers to land, but there's no houses around, and I can get to it without being noticed. Pick me up there at 4:00 sharp. You won't see me 'til you land. I need to brief you on some changes, so get everybody on the ground as fast as you can—no screwing around. Clear?"

"Yes, sir." Henry heard the hesitation in the man's voice, and knew it was time to give a little more.

"And make sure you're all carrying max fuel and lots of ammo. Our three-part raid just turned into a four-part raid."

"Yes, sir!" Hernandez replied enthusiastically. "Four o'clock at the clearing by the lake. All choppers on the ground, with full fuel and loaded for bear."

"See you then," Henry Bowman promised, and broke the connection.

***

It was a little after 7:00 p.m. when Henry Bowman made it back to Dale Price's property in southern Indiana. Henry noted with relief that Dale's truck was not visible, and he immediately drove over to the large hog pens and got out of the van. He looked over every inch of the inside of the pen, but could not see anything resembling a bone fragment.

Damn he thought. *Those things really do eat every last piece. Guess I'll risk it with the hands and feet. Not the heads, though.* The hogs snuffled and looked at him.

"Hang tight, girls," Henry said out loud. "I'll have four more for you after it gets dark." He turned and walked back to the van.

***

After going over everything several more times in his mind, and convincing himself that he had not forgotten anything, Henry Bowman pushed his BMW up the 2 x 12 and into the now-spacious rear section of the van. He used the tie-downs he had brought from Missouri to secure the bike. Then he picked up the pieces of the van's seats, which he had unbolted earlier and then cut apart with Allen Kane's disc grinder, and wedged them between the BMW and the sides of the van.

The full jerrycans came next, followed by the plastic bag containing Eugene, the dead dog, and then the covered plastic bucket. Last of all, Henry loaded the two large cardboard boxes that were heavily wrapped with duct tape. He felt his gorge rise as he put the two heavy packages into the vehicle, and he slammed the back doors quickly. *Not now, you idiot* he said to himself. *That part's over. For now, at least* he amended.

***

When he neared Indianapolis, Henry Bowman started looking for an all-night supermarket in a busy section of the city. It did not take long to find one, and he pulled the van around back, next to the dumpsters where the store disposed of its rotten produce. He was ready with a story about how his dog had gotten loose and been run over in the street, and his wife was hysterical and wouldn't get in the van until he'd gotten rid of the body.

No one came around the back of the building, however, as Henry heaved the boxes into the half-full dumpster. He popped the lid on the bucket of rotten foodstuffs, poured the foul contents over the two packages, and threw the bucket in also. Then he lifted Eugene's corpse from where it lay on top of the gas cans and dropped it on top of the pile of garbage.

Ten minutes later, Henry Bowman was several miles away from the supermarket. It was almost 11:00 p.m., and he had a good four hours of traveling ahead of him. Four hours to think about what he had accomplished, and what he still had to do. *Two more things to do right now* he reminded himself, and pulled into the parking lot of a Walgreens drug and convenience store. His first stop was the pay phone.

There was no answer at the first number, but a sleepy voice picked up the phone when Henry made his second call. Bowman gave the man on the other end the same warning he had passed along in Ohio, only this time it was Allen Kane's house that was due to be raided in the next few days.

The response was almost identical, and Henry Bowman smiled as he hung up the phone. *Just what the doctor ordered* he thought with satisfaction. *A dozen camera-toting friends of Allen's, camping out on his property, hoping to catch crooked feds red-handed. And tramping around, destroying any tire tracks, bloodstains in the grass, or other evidence I might have missed.* He pulled the door open and went into the store.

"Can I help you?" the cashier asked as he came in. It was a slow night.

"Pack of cigarette lighter flints," Henry answered. "And where are your padlocks, and things like that?"

"Aisle six, far end on the left."

"Thanks." Henry followed the woman's directions, and thought of a few other things that would come in handy.

***

Henry Bowman stuck to state roads instead of taking the interstate. He knew that the patchwork of local agencies would have poorer radio communications amongst each other than the Highway Patrol which cruised I-70. The cars and trucks which used secondary roads hopped on and off more often than those cruising at a legal 65 miles per hour on the interstates. People coming back from a tavern or taking a girlfriend home had more on their minds than long distance travelers. It was easier to be invisible among the former group.

Well, Duane Henry said to himself as he flicked on his high beams, *you've come this far with your wire cutters and your tin of beef jerky. Don't back down now.*

June 9

East St. Louis, Illinois, took its name from the Missouri city which stood just across the Mississippi river, but any similarity between the two ended there. The Illinois town was an utterly blighted ghetto of tarpaper slums and broken glass, interspersed with liquor stores and barbecue shacks.

It was a community which had achieved brief national fame in the mid-1980s when news services picked up the story of a resident who had found, in her grandfather's effects, a $200 bond issued by the city around the time of the Civil War. The terms of the note were that it was to accrue at 10% per year, compounded annually, until redemption. The City of East St. Louis had not yet paid the bondholder, and quick calculation indicated that the amount due was over one hundred fifty million dollars.

The town's mayor at that time was flamboyant, controversial, and corrupt, given to putting personal bodyguards on the city payroll and waving at police cars while driving his Jaguar coupe past them at 100 MPH. He had made the story even better. He had been widely quoted as saying 'City of East St. Louis pay this woman a hundred fifty million dollars interest? Shit, we ain't even got the two hundred bucks!'

It was on a rubble-strewn lot at the end of one of the gloomy streets in this area that Henry parked the BATF agents' van. He wiped the vehicle of fingerprints, left the passenger-side window down, and rolled the BMW down the 2 x 12 onto the asphalt. He started the motorcycle, and after it had warmed up and was idling with the choke off, he went back to the van, opened all of the jerrycans, and tipped all but one of them on their sides. The remaining can he used to soak the upholstery of the vehicle, including the cut-up sections of the back seats. Then he closed the back doors, put on his helmet, and rode to the far corner of the lot. Trees and overgrowth concealed him from every direction except the quadrant facing the vehicle.

Henry lowered the side stand, retrieved the Hi-Standard .22 from the right saddle-bag, and extracted three .22 rounds from his shirt pocket. *One ought to do it, unless I miss and hit the seat or something* he thought as he examined the noses of the .22 slugs. There was enough moonlight for Henry to see that the flints were still in place. He poked one of the homemade rounds into the pistol's chamber and dropped the bolt.

It was a trick Henry had discovered when he was eleven years old, and Walter had been mightily impressed. A cigarette lighter flint, bought in 5-packs at the grocery store and inserted into the nose of a .22 hollowpoint, made a surprisingly large flash when fired against rock or steel. In 1964, Henry had written the Ronson company, asking for a price quote on ten thousand of the tiny, red, cylindrical flints, packed loose instead of in those irritating yellow plastic holders. The Ronson company had not been interested in selling them that way, or in bypassing its normal distributors. When Henry had bought these at the Walgreens in Indianapolis, he saw that they still came packed five to a yellow plastic card.

The van was about eighty yards distant. Henry used a two-handed hold, took aim at the top of the opening of the van's passenger-side window, and squeezed the trigger. The .22 slug passed through the open window and slammed into the steel reinforcing pillar behind the driver's door, converting the tiny flint into a geyser of white-hot sparks. The gasoline vapor filling the van ignited instantly with a solid *whump!* that blew out the windshield and driver's side window and bulged the sheetmetal sides of the vehicle's body. Then the van began to burn in earnest.

Henry stowed the Hi-Standard in the saddlebag, hopped on the bike, and rode away from the blazing vehicle.

In addition to the ATF van, small fires burned on several vacant lots, tended by residents of varying ages. There were a surprising number of people, both young and old, still up at three o'clock in the morning in East St. Louis. They paid no attention to one more burning stolen car in their neighborhood or to the lone rider piloting his motorcycle towards the bridge which spanned the Mississippi River.

***

The biggest dilemma Henry had been wrestling with all the way from Indiana was where to park the motorcycle so that it wasn't too far away from the airport, and yet wouldn't be noticed by anyone. *If I screw up this part* he thought, *I'm fucked.*

Decker Field was a private airport south of the city of St. Louis which catered to private pilots, particularly those interested in sport flying. There were several homebuilts based on the field, and five or six aerobatic aircraft, including a Stearman. Henry Bowman flew in there fairly frequently, and he and his black-and-yellow clipwing Cub were well-known to the regulars at Decker.

At any small airport with lots of private planes, there are always some planes whose owners don't have much time to fly, and quite often, these planes are for sale. The situation at Decker Field was no exception. Henry knew of at least two and possibly three Cessna 172 Skyhawks on the airport that were for sale. He wanted one with an autopilot. Given that, he wanted the most neglected-looking one there.

Henry rode his BMW down the taxiway with its lights off and pulled in almost at the far end of the flight line. He parked the bike, took a small Mag-Lite from his saddlebag, and shone it in the plexiglas side window of a blue-and-white 1973 model that had a 'For Sale' sign taped in the window. *No autopilot. And the outside's cleaner than I'd like.* He jogged thirty yards to another 172 and repeated his once-over. *Autopilot. Kind of dirty.* He shone his light on the brake rotors, and saw they were rusty. *Hasn't been flown in quite a while. Battery might be dead.* He ran down the rows of planes and found three more Skyhawks, but one had a custom paint job, and the other two Henry recognized as planes that were flown regularly. One of the two was on a leaseback arrangement with the airport owner. He jogged back to the second plane he had looked at.

It's down to this one Henry Bowman decided as he grabbed a wingtip and pulled it up and down. It felt heavy, and there was a slight sloshing sound. *Almost full* Henry thought with a smile. He looked around the deserted airport on the off-chance that someone else was on the field, and might be able to see him. Henry had a story ready about checking out the 172 for an out-of town friend that was in the market for one. The fact that it was four in the morning was somewhat unusual, but everybody knew acro pilots were different, and nobody would suspect Henry Bowman or any other tube-and-rag acro pilot of trying to steal a tri-gear 'spam can'. Any interruption would nonetheless destroy his plan, however, and Henry stayed in shadow as he worked on the door lock.

Light airplanes in general and older ones in particular are ridiculously easy to get into and start without the key. Private aircraft are of necessity lightly constructed, and theft has never been a big problem since there are relatively few pilots, and almost all airplanes have to be based at airports. Theft-for-export is a risk, and the drug business has forced some owners of transport aircraft to take stronger measures, but low-powered, four-place planes based in the midwest are generally ignored by professional criminals.

Henry Bowman had a pocketful of small keys he had either scrounged from Allen Kane's shop or bought at the Walgreens several hours before. It took him less than a minute to discover that a Craftsman toolbox key would open the door of the 1973 Skyhawk, and less than two more minutes to jump the ignition and learn that the battery was in fact sufficiently charged to turn the engine over. Once he was convinced the airplane would fly, he transferred the contents of his saddlebags to the back seat of the plane, and rode the BMW off the airport to the adjacent industrial park. He parked it behind the end building in the row of offices nearest the runway, and began the 15-minute jog back to the plane.

***

The 150 horsepower Lycoming caught on the third revolution when Henry Bowman pressed the starter button. He fed the mixture control to full rich, leaned it out slightly, released the brakes, and began a fast taxi. Henry pressed the right rudder pedal to the floor and pulled onto the south runway, cycling the yoke to make sure the controls were free. *Steers like a goddamn car* he thought distractedly. Henry was used to planes that could turn around in their own length on the ground.

Henry dispensed with a mag check and gave the engine full throttle as he kept it centered on the runway. At 70 MPH the airplane lifted off the ground. He checked his oil pressure and fuel, fiddled with the mixture for best power, and turned onto a compass heading that would take him straight to his house.

***

After dark, things look much different from the air than they do in the daytime, but Henry Bowman had spent enough time flying in and out of his place at night that he had no trouble finding it or setting up for a landing in the somewhat unfamiliar craft. The Cessna, with flaps extended, had a steeper approach angle than his flapless, clipped-wing Cub, but that was to be expected.

Dad would have been proud of that one he thought as his mains kissed the grass strip at less than 60 MPH.

Henry looked at his watch as he got out of the Skyhawk and saw that it was quarter to five. He pushed the airplane into his spare hangar, closed the door, and trotted up the hill to his garage. After deactivating the alarm, Henry pulled the door closed, flipped on the fluorescents, and began searching his tool shelf.

"Bingo," he said aloud when he spotted his electric die grinder. He pushed a 1979 Kawasaki Z-1 out into the middle of the floor, plugged his grinder into a retractable-reel extension cord that also housed a trouble light, packed several semi-clean shop towels between the bike's frame and fuel tank, and began to relieve the motorcycle of the serial numbers on its frame and engine.

That done, Henry inflated the bike's tires using shop air, checked the tank to see that he had fuel, set the choke, flipped on the petcock, turned the key in the ignition, and pressed the starter button. Nothing happened. *Dead. Well, I guess that would have been too much to expect, wouldn't it?* he thought to himself, and popped the seat so that he could attach his booster to the Kawasaki's battery. With the airbox open, he sprayed a three-second shot of ether starting fluid into the carb throats before hooking up the cables, turning the dial to **200 AMP CRANKING ASSIST**, switching the booster on, and pressing the starter button.

The 1000cc motor caught after a few seconds of high-speed cranking, and settled into a fast, ragged idle. *Sounds like the pilot jet's gummed up on at least one carb* he thought. *No matter.* Henry disconnected the cables, shut the seat, turned the lights in the garage off, and hit the button that opened the east overhead door. *Shit, no plates* he realized. The Z-1 was a spare that he had never licensed. It took another minute to take the plates off his 1452cc GSXR with the 210-horsepower Gatlin motor and affix them to the back of the slower bike. By the time he put his helmet on and pushed the Z-1 outside, the motorcycle was warmed up, but still threatened to die when the choke was switched off. Henry closed the garage door, climbed on the old Kaw, and headed back to the airport to retrieve his BMW.

***

It was just after 7:00 a.m. when Henry Bowman wheeled the yellow-and-black BMW in front of his garage with his GSXR's plates in his jacket pocket. It felt like he had been up forever. *Stay with it, hoss* he told himself. *About two more hours worth of prep, then you can sack out for a good three, maybe four hours.*

The first order of business was to strap the three aluminum cases onto the BMW. The second was to outfit the Skyhawk for long-range travel.

Like Randy said Henry reminded himself, *just keep putting one foot in front of the other.*

***

It was a few minutes past 4:00 p.m. when he finally heard the helicopters coming. The wind was blowing gently towards him, and it carried the sound well. *Two choppers,* he judged from the pitch of the engines, *possibly three.* Henry realized that his first emotion upon hearing the sound of rotor blades approaching was not one of anxiety, or even sadness, but rather an overwhelming sense of relief. The waiting was over.

His next thought concerned the relatives of the men that were about to die. The surviving spouses and children would never comprehend that their loved ones were dead because a little man in an out-of-control federal agency had wanted to be a hero. *Actually,* Henry thought, *Blair was just the last straw. It started when the government got just a little too heavy-handed in June of '68.*

That isn't right, either he reflected. *It started a long time before King and Kennedy got killed. The death sentence for the men in the helicopters was handed down a lot earlier. In June of 1934.*

Henry settled in behind the big Solothurn and checked his field of view through the optical sight. The example of Swiss craftsmanship had been manufactured in 1939. That irony was not lost on Henry Bowman. 1939 was the year the Supreme Court had ruled on the Miller case, after the defense had declined to show up.

Supreme Court's been ducking that issue ever since Henry thought as he strained to hear a change in the approaching noise. *Well, guys, the tide has turned. It's time you thugs had a little history lesson. I don't suppose you're familiar with what happened in the Warsaw ghetto in 1943.* A small smile appeared on his lips, as Henry remembered something. *It's just like the story Uncle Max told me when I was a kid. About Billy Dell, pulling a Paul Bunyan.*

Henry Bowman's right hand tightened around the walnut grip of the Solothurn S18-1000. He twisted his head methodically and arched his back as he lay there on his stomach, working the stiffness from his body. He had lain prone for over an hour with his face pressed against a pair of binoculars, and he needed to be loose for what he was going to have to do.

The helicopters appeared over a ridge that Bowman had previously determined was a little more than two miles distant. They were following a heading that would take them to the spot that he had selected, next to the old water-filled quarry where he did most of his shooting. Henry steadied the binoculars by resting his right wrist on the top of the Solothurn's receiver, and cranked the zoom control from ten power all the way up to twenty. The binoculars amplified the heat waves in the air that are invisible to the naked eye, and called 'mirage' by competition shooters who use high magnification optical sights.

The boiling, shimmering image in the glasses gave a surrealistic appearance to the approaching choppers, but Henry could make them out well enough. *Three of them. Bell turbine model, Jet Ranger or its descendant. A door gunner with a belt-fed machine gun poking out of the right side of each one. Possibly the Belgian MAG-58, but more likely M60s,* he thought with derision.

They should have brought armored Apaches carrying napalm, he thought. *Or nukes.* A grin split his face.

Oh, those poor bastards.

"I'll put down on the east corner, near the water," the pilot of the lead helicopter announced over the radio. "Two, you take the south edge, Three, you land in the north-west corner." The other two pilots acknowledged as all three rotorcraft throttled back and began their descents.

Calron Jones, crouched behind the M60 in the third helicopter, had been feeling uneasy ever since boarding the aircraft. It was his first time flying in anything other than a commercial jet airliner, and the wind blast and the open door did nothing to relieve his anxiety. He nervously flicked the safety off of the belt-fed gun, without consciously realizing he had done so. His right hand gripped the weapon's black pistol grip more tightly as the turbine helicopter descended.

Jaime Hernandez, in the lead aircraft, visually scanned the ground below for signs of Wilson Blair. He saw nothing but wooded rolling hills, and the open grassy area next to the water-filled quarry pit. The gravel road leading from the state highway to Henry Bowman's house was over a half-mile away from the clearing, straight line. Hernandez scowled, trying to figure out how Wilson Blair could have come to this remote location. Walking was the only way, as far as he could see.

Just like ducks flaring out to land in the decoys Henry thought as he watched through the optical sight of the 20mm. The three choppers were in a stairstep descent, aiming for the clearing west of the limestone pit. Henry Bowman tightened his right index and middle fingers around the Solothurn's two-finger trigger, and waited.

The hilltop on which Henry Bowman lay was, by actual measurement with a laser rangefinder, four hundred twenty-three yards from the center of the clearing by the pit. The 20mm was sighted in at 300 yards, and would place all its shots in an area the size of a large dinner plate at that range. At 425 yards, the slugs would hit about 15" lower than they would at the 300 yard distance for which the gun was zeroed. At 600 yards, they would be 45" below point of aim.

Henry centered the most distant helicopter in the scope. It was about 300 feet off the ground, flying straight at him, and was perhaps 650 yards away. He switched his aiming point to the swash plate on top of the chopper's whirling mainshaft, and tracked the aircraft's gradual descent.

Send helicopter gunships to my house, will you? Suck up to your buddies in DEA and Secret Service so you can snowflake my friends? Not today, guys Henry said silently as he began to squeeze the trigger. *It's hammer time.*

The big gun lifted about an inch off the ground as it thundered, and pushed Henry back half a foot. The quarter-pound thermite-filled incendiary slug took less than a second to traverse the one-third mile distance. It was traveling at twice the speed of sound when it struck the thin aluminum skin below the helicopter's plexiglas windshield, and detonated on the back side of the instrument panel just in front and to the left of the pilot.

The fifteen thousand foot-pounds of kinetic energy the projectile already possessed due to its forward motion was greatly amplified by the small explosive charge inside it. The explosion vaporized the left side of the pilot's torso just above the hip, ruptured six of the eight eardrums on board the aircraft, and blew out all the windows on the left side as thousands of tiny, white-hot thermite particles were propelled at supersonic velocity throughout the chopper.

The pilot's body shielded Calron Jones from much of the shrapnel, but the force of the blast blew the gunner out the open doorway even as his hand clamped onto the M60's pistol grip and his index finger reflexively grabbed the trigger. The M60 was bolted into a 360 degree swivel mount, and for a brief moment, Jones was outside the helicopter, hanging onto the M60 and spraying the inside of the aircraft with 147-grain armor-piercing .308 projectiles traveling at 2600 feet per second. In less than two seconds, the centripetal acceleration from the spinning, out-of-control chopper exceeded the strength of Jones' grip, and he was flung away from the doomed craft.

The M60, like most M60s that were not brand new, had a worn sear. It was worn enough that the gun did not stop firing even though no finger remained on the trigger. The continued stream of .308 slugs tore additional holes in the helicopter's fuel tanks, and suddenly the aircraft became one huge fireball. The M60 kept chattering away, finally running out of ammo seconds before the flaming mass of steel and aluminum slammed into the trees at over 200 MPH.

"What the fuck?" the pilot of the second helicopter said as he heard the noise behind him and swung his aircraft around to see what was the problem. His jaw dropped in horror and disbelief as he watched the flaming wreck fall out of the sky.

"They're on fire!" he screamed into the microphone as he gave his engine full throttle and increased the pitch on the collective to stop his descent. "Davis is on fire and he's–"

The pilot's transmission was cut off as Henry's second shot penetrated the left side of the #2 aircraft and detonated on the engine's turbine scroll housing. The turbine wheel was spinning at tremendous speed, and when its structural integrity was destroyed, it disintegrated like an overrevved flywheel. The resulting shrapnel tore through the helicopter, killing one passenger instantly and wounding the others. The chopper fell two hundred feet and tore through the top of a 60-foot oak tree. Then it caught on fire.

The lead helicopter had been about fifty feet off the ground when the pilot of the second aircraft had broadcast that the third was on fire. When the transmission had been cut off in mid-sentence, the pilot of the lead chopper had swung ninety degrees to the left to see what was going on. Both the National Guard pilot and ATF Agent Jaime Hernandez saw the explosion in the woods to their left, and the other fire burning several hundred yards behind it. "Get us out of here!" Agent Hernandez screamed at the pilot. The door gunner dove onto the floor, and the fourth man curled into a ball next to him.

The chopper pilot was good, but he was up against the laws of physics. He'd had almost zero forward motion because he had been setting up for the landing. Now he needed as much horizontal speed as possible, and he did the only logical thing, just as Henry had anticipated. The pilot flattened the pitch of his rotor blades, gave his engine full throttle, and dove for the edge of the quarry pit, trading what little altitude he had for horizontal speed.

In the two hours he had lain on the hill, Henry Bowman had calculated leads and holdovers for various target speeds and ranges. One of the scenarios he had considered was a hovering helicopter over the landing site suddenly trying to get away as quickly as possible. Henry had reasoned that in such a situation, the aircraft would not be able to accelerate to more than sixty miles per hour before he got off a shot. Sixty miles per hour was eighty-eight feet per second. This dictated a forty-foot lead at 425 yards if the helicopter was flying straight across his line of fire, and less if the aircraft was angling towards him or away. In the angled case, the holdover would change slightly, but not enough to matter.

The pilot had the chopper's nose angled down and was aiming for the spot at the far end of the water-filled pit, where there were no trees. That heading put him on a left-to-right path that was not quite at right angles to Henry's position. Henry Bowman got the fleeing chopper in his sights, maintained a lead that was a little less than one helicopter-length in front of the aircraft's nose, and squeezed the Solothurn's trigger for the third time.

He had been hoping to hit the helicopter's engine bay, but Henry Bowman had picked up the target more quickly than his earlier calculations had assumed, and the chopper was only accelerating through 40 MPH when the S18-1000 fired. The bullet went well forward of the engine bay, hit the plexiglas side window, and detonated as it was entering Jaime Hernandez's shoulder.

The explosion killed Hernandez and the pilot instantly. The rotor tips touched the surface of the water, shearing off both blades and sending the helicopter cartwheeling across the surface, its engine screaming. The door gunner broke his neck when his head slammed into the pilot's seat upon impact, but the fourth passenger was still alive, paralyzed with a broken back, when the aircraft began sinking towards the bottom of the limestone pit one hundred twenty-eight feet below the surface.

The trapped ATF agent tried to use his arms to extricate himself, but the impact had knocked the wind out of him, and he was disoriented in the sinking tangle of metal. Unwittingly, he used his last bit of strength to pull himself farther inside the helicopter, away from the opening in the fuselage where the gun was mounted. The wreck continued to sink towards the bottom.

By the time the doomed man could hold his breath no longer and began inhaling water, Henry Bowman had picked up his three fired cases, started his BMW, and broken his Solothurn down into its three main components. Ten minutes after that, the BMW was in the locked garage, the Solothurn was stowed behind him with the rest of his gear, and Henry was easing back on the yoke of the stolen Skyhawk, lifting it off the grass runway.

Henry had the radio set to the UNICOM frequency, 118.3, that was used by pilots in uncontrolled airspace. He keyed the mike, put a North Carolina twang in his voice, and spoke excitedly.

"*Mayday! Mayday!* Midair and they're in the woods, burning! Two west of the river, going to investigate." He released the TRANSMIT button and listened. Sure enough, chatter overlapped on the channel. Other pilots tuned to the frequency had caught snatches of the hurried transmission and started talking, asking for more info.

By the time the local police and fire departments had responded to the reports of what was variously reported as a forest fire, a gas explosion, and a plane crash, Henry Bowman was twenty miles west, climbing through an altitude of six thousand feet.

***

Henry leveled the Skyhawk at 10,500 feet, which complied with the FAA-approved even-thousand-plus-500 feet guideline for westbound flights. He fiddled with the throttle setting and mixture control until he had the engine at 2000 RPM and what he judged was 40% power, then looked at his portable GPS receiver.

GPS stood for Global Positioning System, which had come into widespread use around 1990. It referred to a series of orbiting satellites that were used for navigation. The Garmin 95XL GPS receiver was about the size of one of the larger personal cassette decks worn by joggers. Henry had bought it in late 1994 for less than $1000. When he had switched it on before taking off, it had taken about thirty seconds to receive signals from the three nearest satellites. It had used the data to triangulate, and then had displayed his exact position on the liquid crystal screen. The GPS receiver was accurate to within about thirty feet.

Now that Henry was in the air and moving, the GPS receiver's internal computer continually sampled data from the satellites and calculated his true heading as well as his groundspeed, and displayed both on the 2" screen. The groundspeed function was especially useful, for winds aloft could cause huge differences between a pilot's true airspeed and the progress he was actually making across the countryside.

The receiver Henry held in his hand had the coordinates of all U.S. airports loaded into memory, as well as information about each one, and also had a map function. The map mode displayed all airports within a user-specified radius from the airplane's position. Perhaps most importantly for in-flight emergencies, the GPS receiver had a 'nearest airport' function, which listed the five closest airports at any given instant, the distance to each one, and the heading to take to get there. The user could specify a minimum runway length for the function, so that the receiver would not list airports with 2000' runways for a pilot flying a corporate jet.

Looking at the GPS screen, Henry compared the figures he saw there with those on his instrument panel. *Getting a little push to the north* he thought when he saw that his compass heading was twelve degrees less than what the GPS receiver showed as his true course. *Eighty-two knots. That's not bad, for burning a little over four gallons per hour. Ought to be there before they get their reconnaissance planes off the ground.*

Henry Bowman had taken the plane up high where the air was thin and set up an extremely low power setting to minimize fuel burn and maximize miles per gallon, willingly sacrificing cross-country speed. He had a long way to go, and he did not want to land a stolen airplane at an airport unless he absolutely had to.

Satisfied that he was on a course that would take him over no Terminal Control Areas, Henry reset the autopilot and took his feet off the rudder pedals and his hands off the yoke. In ten minutes, his heading was unchanged, as was his altitude. Satisfied, he pulled a U-shaped piece of foam from under his seat, fitted it around his neck, and switched his sunglasses for a pair that had duct tape over the lenses.

Henry Bowman then did something that few lone pilots have ever done intentionally while flying an airplane: he fell asleep.

***

"Damned lucky they got the fire stopped before half the county was turned to charcoal. Those volunteer guys ought to get medals for what they did," Sheriff Krause announced.

"They'd probably prefer beer," the deputy answered. Then he motioned the sheriff over. "Take a look at this, Skip." The Jefferson County Sheriff turned and walked towards the wreckage of the helicopter.

"What you got, Dee?" the big man asked.

"This make any sense to you?" the younger man said, pointing at a spot inside the twisted hulk of the helicopter. The coroner's office had already removed the charred bodies of the three men that had been inside. The shattered carcass of Calron Jones lay undiscovered in the woods almost a quarter mile away.

"Bullet holes," Krause said immediately. "Thirty caliber, looks like to me," he added, moving to look at the outside of the aircraft, where the shots had exited. "Lots of 'em, and close together, too."

"And they're all on the inside, going out," the younger man pointed out. "No entrance holes on the outside skin anywhere."

"Mmm-hmm," he said, poking through the ashes on the floor of the helicopter. He came up with a symmetrically bent piece of charcoal grey metal. "M60 link," he announced. "Sift through these ashes, we'll find more, I bet. Brass, too. Other chopper's got a mag box fulla cook-offs. This one's empty."

He bent to inspect the gun, which was still locked into the pintle mount. The plastic forearm guard and buttstock had melted in the fire. The sheriff peered inside the bore from the muzzle end. "Purt' near plated with copper," he stated, then swiveled the gun in its mount and nodded his head.

"What you thinking, Sheriff?"

"I think the damn thing ran away on 'em."

"You think maybe this chopper shot itself down? From the inside? What about the other one?" Up until that moment, the discovery of the two crashed helicopters in the middle of a forest fire had spelled *Midair Collision* to the men who arrived on the scene.

"I don't know," he said slowly. "And even more than why they crashed, I'd sure like to know what two helicopters with M60 door guns and a bunch a armed guys in 'em were doing over Henry Bowman's place while he's on vacation." He squinted and looked around the burned area. "Yes, I surely would like to know that."

No one knew about the third helicopter, which was lying at the bottom of the flooded quarry pit.

June 10

It was past midnight, Missouri time, when Henry Bowman finally awoke from his slumber. *Damn* he thought when he looked at his watch. *Almost eight hours. Just like a transatlantic commercial flight. Guess I really did set a course that didn't hit any TCAs or MOAs* he told himself. The alarm on the GPS which sounded when getting too close to restricted airspace had remained silent the entire time.

A quick glance at his compass, altimeter, and gauges confirmed that the autopilot had kept him on the proper heading and at the same altitude, and nothing was amiss with the engine. The fuel level showed less than 1/4 of the original 40 gallons remaining. *About 4.2 gallons per hour. Right on spec* he thought with a smile.

Having ascertained that he was on-course and that everything was running smoothly, the well-rested pilot fumbled for an empty half-gallon orange juice jug and set about attending to the next most pressing matter on his agenda: his bladder.

Much better Henry thought as he screwed the lid on the plastic jug and carefully zipped up his trousers. *Now let's see where the hell I am.* He addressed the Nearest Airport function on the GPS receiver and found that the closest field was almost 40 miles away. *Bridgeport, Nebraska. Well, that's no surprise* Henry said to himself, though he was nonetheless relieved to learn that he really was still on course. He hit up the airport identifier for Arco, Idaho and pressed the GO TO key. The screen informed him that it was 517 nautical miles to that airport, and he needed to change his heading by nine degrees farther to the north.

After making the slight heading correction, Henry turned on the Skyhawk's faint cockpit light. *Now for the tedious part* he said to himself as he reached down on the floor beside him where the passenger seat had once been and selected the materials he would need for the next phase of his plan.

Henry Bowman had chosen a Cessna 172 Skyhawk as the plane in which to make his escape for several reasons, all of which were important ones. The first was that the Skyhawk was the most common private plane in the world. On top of that, the factory had never been much on changing the paint schemes. White with blue trim or white with red trim covered 90% of the 172s in the country, whether the plane had been made in 1959 or twenty-five years later.

The second reason Henry had chosen the 172 was that it was known for its reliability, stable and forgiving flight characteristics, and load-carrying ability. Four normal-sized adult passengers and their luggage was the standard payload in a 172. Pilots with cavalier attitudes toward such matters regularly overloaded their Skyhawks or flew them with the CG past the aft limit, and usually got away with it.

Third, later-production 172s had 150-horsepower Lycoming engines just like the one that had been retrofitted to Henry's Cub when the wings spars were cut. Henry knew exactly what that motor's fuel consumption was at all power settings, including those that were lower than the lowest ones listed in the operator's manual.

Last of all, the Cessna 172, like Henry's Cub, was a high-wing aircraft. The fuel in the wings did not need a fuel pump, but used gravity to get to the engine. Furthermore, there was a crossover fuel line above the windshield which joined the two tanks, just like in Henry's Cub. In the Skyhawk, the line was covered by plastic interior trim, but that had taken less than a minute to remove when Henry had prepped the plane back in Missouri.

After he had exposed the crossover line, Henry had spliced in a tee fitting and connected a hose and hand pump to it. The tee fitting had come off his GSXR Suzuki. The hand pump was the one he normally used to pump Union 76 high-octane race gas for his Typhoon and motorcycles out of the 55-gallon drums it came in. Now he was going to use it to refill the main tanks from inside the aircraft.

After draining his GMC, his Kaiser 715 one-and-a-quarter ton, all his motorcycles, and the partially-full drum of race gas, and then topping off the 172 on the ground, Henry had been left with fifty-three gallons of gasoline. That was what he was now carrying inside the cabin of the 172. There were four plastic 5-gallon jerrycans in the back of the plane, as well as a round 6-gallon unit marked 'Race Gas Only', one 2 1/2-gallon metal gas can, nine round metal screw-top containers that 24 hours earlier had each held eight pounds of pistol powder, seven one-gallon milk jugs, four half-gallon orange juice jugs, and a 1952 Moet et Chandon Jereboam that Walter had given Henry (empty) for his fifth birthday because the boy had liked bottles.

The fuel containers, along with his Solothurn and other important gear, were where the rear seat had been. Henry had unbolted the rear and passenger seats, cut them up with a reciprocating saw, and packed them into the luggage area at the back of the plane at the same time he had made the fuel line modifications.

Henry reached back, grabbed one of the 5-gallon plastic jerrycans, and slid it up next to him. He unscrewed the lid and poked the loose end of the hose into the mouth of the can. The other end of the hose was attached to the suction side of the hand pump. Henry unsnapped the Vise-Grip pliers he had clamped onto the spliced-in line, and began to operate the pump. *I think this thing's only rated for twenty or twenty-five gallons an hour* Henry silently reminded himself. Then he laughed.

"Hell," he said out loud, "it's not like I've got a lot of better things to do."

***

"Three National Guard helicopters left St. Louis a little after three o'clock yesterday," Sheriff Krause announced after he had hung up the phone. "They were on loan to the Treasury Department," he added, "as part of some quote 'comprehensive, multi-part mission' unquote. The mission coordinator of this comprehensive, multi-part mission, according to the guy I just talked to, is a fellow named Wilson Blair, who is based in Ohio."

"Ohio?" one of the deputies said immediately.

"What do the guys in the third 'copter say they were doing here?" another man asked.

"That's what they'd like to know," Krause answered, ignoring the first deputy. "You see, the third helicopter has not yet come home." He looked at his watch. "And since it's been a good sixteen hours since he took off, it seems safe to assume that by now he's put down somewhere. And the feds do wish he'd call," Krause added in a high-pitched girl's voice. The other men in the room laughed heartily. Like most local law enforcement men, they had no great love for federal police usurping their authority.

"What's this Blair guy say about all this?" one of the other men asked.

"He is 'currently occupied elsewhere', according to the pencil-pusher I talked to," Krause answered. "Sounds to me like they can't find him, either."

"So what do we do?" asked one of the deputies.

Krause shrugged. "Tate checked Henry's property. Everything looked okay, didn't it, Spud?"

"Gate was locked, like I expected, so I hopped the fence and walked in. House looked okay—no windows busted or doors jimmied. Same with the garage. Pried the hangar door out a little, shined my flashlight in, and his plane was still there, didn't look like nobody had bothered it. When's he due back, Skip?"

"He told me end of June," the Sheriff answered.

"So what do we do?"

"Hell," Krause said in a tone that showed he didn't know what to make of all this, "looks to me like Henry's okay, and his property's okay, except for some trees. Let the feds hash it out."

***

"Pass your quizzes up to the front of the room," the SHAT instructor told the class of FBI agents. "I'll grade them over the lunch hour. Let's break for lunch, and when we come back, we'll do a role-play involving some of the material you read for today. See you in an hour."

Oh goody Alex Neumann thought as he heaved himself out of the classroom chair. *Just like fucking grammar school.* He looked around at the middle-aged men who were also standing up to stretch their legs. *There's one other guy here younger than I am. Wonder what the role-play's going to be this time. Probably have to put on a dress and take turns playing grab-ass.* Neumann smiled involuntarily at the mental image. Then he laughed out loud, and several of the other agents turned to stare at him. *Probably think I'm cracking up. Hell, maybe I am.* He was out in the hall when he felt a hand on his arm.

"Agent...Neumann, is it? Angela Riggs." Neumann turned to face a tall, brown-haired woman of about thirty-five with a slender figure and an engaging smile. *Great eyes* he thought. Her suit was tailored to fit, and although Neumann focused on the woman's face, the second thought that came into Alex Neumann's head was that Agent Riggs had a nice-looking chest.

"Alex," he said, shaking her hand. "Pleased to meet you."

"Would you like to join me for lunch, Alex?"

"Think the teacher might give us any demerits? Two agents having lunch together?"

"I'm not an FBI agent. I'm a psychologist. I've been asked to audit this class because they're thinking of having me teach it."

"And you picked me to have lunch with because of my obvious disgust for the whole process."

"Actually, I picked you to have lunch with because you were the only man in the room within twenty years of my own age who wasn't wearing a wedding band. And you have a flat stomach." Alex Neumann laughed, and he had a third thought: *I like this woman.*

"So let's go eat."

***

The 172 was showing a little over three hours fuel remaining at 65% power. Henry did not want to use a power setting much lower than that with mountains around. Henry Bowman had found Borah Peak, the tallest in Idaho, and had been flying a zigzag search pattern over the Pahsimeroi Valley which lay below it. He'd been at it for a little over an hour when he spotted the 2 1/2-ton Army truck.

Flew right over it the first time he thought with a grin. *I should have figured Allen would try to find some shade.* He brought the Skyhawk down to about 500 feet and made three passes, but saw no sign of his friend. *Probably hiked off somewhere* he decided. *Well, with three hours fuel, I can afford to look around some more, now that I've found his camp.* Henry Bowman gave the airplane full throttle and climbed another two thousand feet.

While he was out over the open valley he uncapped a felt-tip pen and wrote a message on one of the plastic orange juice jugs to which he had earlier tied one of his T-shirts. It was a shirt that Allen Kane had given him at Knob Creek a few years before. The black fabric had a yellow silkscreened logo on it which said

DON'T TELL MY MOTHER
I'M AN NFA DEALER—
SHE STILL THINKS I OWN
A CHAIN OF WHOREHOUSES

That way he won't think I'm some fed from the Bureau of Land Management, going to nail him for salting a lead mine Henry thought with a smile as he began a back-and-forth search of the lower levels of Borah Peak, which rose up from where Kane had made camp.

He had just finished making a one-eighty at the far edge of the area where he thought his friend might be when red streaks in the distance caught his eye. Henry Bowman grinned.

Nothing like a magazine full of tracers to announce your position he thought as he guided the plane towards the source of the pyrotechnics. Just then, another, much longer burst of red dots arced out down the valley and peppered a dark spot on a distant rock face. This time Henry Bowman laughed out loud. *He's got a belt-fed. Allen Kane carried a belt-fed gun up the mountain so he could shoot tracers out over the valley.*

Henry eased back on the throttle and lowered the nose to maintain airspeed. *Let's not slam into the mountain* he admonished himself. *That would be most embarrassing.* He flew parallel to the slope of the hill with the mountain on his right, and when he passed over Allen Kane, he banked to the left and waggled his wings several times. As he headed out over the valley, Henry stayed in a very gentle turn to the left. He wanted to make a big circle and come by the same way he had before, now that he had his friend's attention. Flying near mountains was nothing to take lightly, especially in a non-aerobatic aircraft. Air currents were unpredictable, and he was going to be flying low and slow, close to the hillside when he dropped the plastic jug.

Allen Kane watched the aircraft fly directly over him and turn left, over the valley. "Stupid buttfucker ought to mind his own business when a guy's shooting tracers," he said out loud. Kane figured the pilot was using the radio to report him when he saw the plane waggle its wings and come around for another pass.

By the time the aircraft had circled around and was about to fly over Allen Kane again, it was considerably lower and its engine made a lot less noise. Just before it passed over him, Kane saw something appear below the white-and-blue aircraft and fall towards the ground as the plane accelerated away. The way it fell through the air, it was obvious the object did not weigh very much, and Allen saw it land behind some rocks on a talus slope about a hundred yards in front of him. He realized it was probably some kind of message as he started walking over to where the thing had fallen. Henry Bowman was the first person he thought of, but it didn't make sense that his friend would be this early, and flying a strange airplane.

Allen Kane found the plastic jug in the rocks, and when he saw the t-shirt tied to it, he knew who was flying the aircraft. He looked at the message written on the plastic, and his brows knitted together. **FIND ME IN THE VALLEY** it said simply. Underneath those words were the letters **RFN**, printed much larger than the message itself.

Allen Kane did not know anyone with the initials R.F.N. He did, however know another meaning for those three letters, an abbreviation that he and Henry Bowman used occasionally.

It stood for Right Fucking Now.

***

Henry Bowman was stretched out in the grass, lying under the shade of the Cessna's right wing when Allen Kane drove his deuce-and-a-half up to where the plane was parked, a mile down the valley from where Kane had made his camp. Henry got up and brushed himself off as Kane climbed down out of the big military vehicle.

"You're here early," Kane said with a big grin. "With new wings." The grin faded when he saw the look on his friend's face.

"I got problems, Allen. Serious ones. Some people are dead. You want to risk being charged with harboring a fugitive?" Henry said without preamble. "If not, I'll fly out of here right now."

"Was it anybody I liked?" Allen Kane asked with a skeptical expression on his face. Henry smiled involuntarily.

"No, I don't think so."

"Then spell it out, dipshit."

"Before I do, is there anyone you talked to on your phone before you left, that you told I had planned to drive out with you, but couldn't?" Allen thought for a moment, then shook his head.

"I turned the recorder on a day or two before you changed your plans. Wanted to pack up without a bunch of guys bothering me. Only calls I made out were a couple to guys that were transferring guns to me. Nobody that knows you."

"Well, was there anyone you talked to, about that? Guy at a gas station near your place? Someone near my house when you picked up my ammo, or at Lindbergh's in Mackey when you were buying dynamite, or anything like that?" Kane considered the question.

"No, I don't think so. Haven't been to Lindbergh's yet. Talked to a guy in a cafe in Arco who asked about my truck, and told him I was out here to shoot some jacks. Said 'I', not 'we', and didn't mention you or anyone else, and I guess he figured I was out here alone, but that doesn't mean anything. You could just have easily been back at camp, or across the street getting a haircut, or whatever, and I just didn't mention it."

"What about when you went to my house?"

"Didn't see anybody. Unlocked your gate, drove in, got your ammo out of the garage, locked up, locked the gate on the way out, drove here." Henry nodded in understanding, then smiled and licked his lips.

"And if anybody did see you, it was our plan to go by my house and pick up my stuff anyway. If they saw just you in the truck and not me, I could have been asleep in the back, or picking something up off the floor—"

"Or giving me a blow job," Allen suggested agreeably. Henry shook his head and took a deep breath.

"Right. Anyhow, if that's the case, then you are the only living person who knows that I stayed at your house instead of riding with you when you left Indiana driving this truck. You are the only living person who knows I was not riding with you the entire way across the country, and you are the only living person who knows that I have not been out here in Idaho with you the last seventy-two hours. And I would like to keep it that way," he added.

"Okay," Allen said. "I understand. Now *what happened?*"

Henry told him.

Kane listened without comment, although his eyebrows went up and his nostrils flared several times. When Henry had finished, Allen Kane was silent for a moment, then he asked one question.

"How'd they decide to hit us right then?"

"I forgot to mention—all three of our phone lines have been tapped for more than six months now."

"Six *months?* All of us? Christ!"

"Yeah. This Blair guy had a hard-on for everybody with an SOT number, but especially us, 'cause of that thing at the Columbus show back in '90," Henry added with disgust. "Anyway, the reason they didn't know I was still there was 'cause I was out in your shop most of the time, and every time I called somebody, I used my cellular."

Allen nodded. "And now there's nothing left. After you shot them, you butchered all six feds and fed them to Dale Price's hogs."

"Ten, actually," Henry admitted. "There were six at your place. I killed four more in Columbus."

"Right. Ten ATF agents, butchered and fed to Dale's hogs."

"All except the heads. The heads I wrapped up with duct tape and newspaper, and put in boxes, and taped the boxes up real well. Then I threw them in a dumpster behind a supermarket in Indianapolis and dumped some rotten food on top." He shook his head, remembering something he'd left out.

"Before I wrapped the heads up, I knocked the teeth out with the back side of a hatchet, and drove the van over them a couple times. I don't think they could be IDed, even if they ever got found, which seems unlikely anyway. " Henry shrugged. "I mean, the way I tried to set it up, everyone thinks these guys have split." He paused, then went on. "Oh, and I checked the hog pen a while after I put in the first six. Didn't see any bones left." His stomach turned over at the memory.

"I really think from the feds' viewpoint, those ten have just vanished," Henry repeated. "And with the tape Blair made, and the other stuff I plan to do, they'll be trying to figure out where they ran off to, not where the bodies went." Henry chewed his lip.

"I'm more worried about what they'll make of the three crashed helicopters at my place, and if anyone saw me take off right after they crashed. But hell," he said, shrugging, "what have they got? A 172 taking off, or more likely, just flying in the area. Could have been anyone. Especially someone coming down for a look-see, after that Mayday." Kane nodded, then thought for a while.

"What're we going to do with this?" he asked, pointing to the plane. "Cut it up and throw it in a ravine?" Henry shook his head.

"ATF's got those damn OV-10s, with the trick radar for spotting people on the ground. They're going to come looking for us, Allen, to make sure we're here. They could be on their way now, and I don't want them spotting this 172 from the air.

656

"We'll drive the truck into town, fill up the gas cans, come back and fuel up the plane. I'll take off, set it on autopilot heading west, and bail out. Brought my 'chutes with me. Thing should be about three hundred miles over the Pacific when it runs out of fuel. I better hustle up and do it now," Henry explained, "because they might come looking for us any minute." Allen Kane smiled when he heard the plan.

"I like it," he said after a few moments. "It vanishes forever, and you've been here all this time, with me. Only we don't need to drive back to Mackey to get fuel. I've got fifty gallons with me, if that's enough."

"Lord, that's twice as much as I need," Henry said. "But I thought this was diesel?"

"That was the other one," Kane explained. "This one's gasoline."

"Then let's get cracking. I'll tell you more about what I've got planned while we're getting my stuff out of the plane. Then we'll gas it up, and while I'm in the air, you can watch the tapes I made, see what you think about my plan." Henry stopped for a moment and looked at his friend.

"You realize what you're getting into, don't you, Allen?"

"Yeah," Kane replied. "And it's about fucking time."

***

It took Henry Bowman about half an hour to get to altitude, circle around from the east, and set up the airplane for straight and level flight at 2100 RPM. He was sitting at an angle in the single remaining front seat, for the dual rig on his back was a good 7" thick.

The 172 had been 'sanitized' so that any plane flying nearby could tell next to nothing about it. Henry had spray-painted the 172's side windows gloss black from the inside after he and Allen had unloaded everything of value from the plane, and the entire interior smelled like enamel. *Be just perfect to pass out from paint fumes* Henry said to himself. The N-numbers on the tail were painted over as well. All interior surfaces had been wiped clean of prints, and Henry was flying with gloves on. These precautions were just in case the Skyhawk somehow crashed before reaching the ocean. Allen had asked about the Emergency Locator Transmitter, designed to activate on high-G impacts, but Henry had explained that he'd removed the ELT's batteries before leaving Missouri.

Henry engaged the autopilot, let go of everything, and made sure that the airplane stayed on course. Satisfied that the electronics were functioning as designed, Henry looked at the instruments one final time and grabbed the door handle. *Now for the hard part* he told himself.

Skydiving schools that use Cessnas for jump planes invariably replace the factory door with a 'jump door' which is hinged at the top, and can be easily opened in flight. Henry had jumped out of a 172 with a standard door once before, when a friend had flown him over a college football game in a rental plane, and he had jumped in at halftime. On that jump, however, the pilot had chopped the throttle, crossed the controls, and slipped the plane to the right to reduce the windblast. Henry had none of those luxuries this time.

No screwing around. One good shove he told himself as he turned the handle and got his fingers between the door's trailing edge and the fuselage, then crouched on the floor next to the pilot's seat

Now! he said silently as he pushed off the pilot's seat with both feet, slammed his left shoulder into the door, and protected the handle of the pilot 'chute on his belly band with his left arm.

Henry got most of his torso out past the edge of the door as the 100-MPH wind tried to clamp him between the door and the fuselage. He sank down a few inches lower and gave a second violent thrust with his legs, while pushing against door and fuselage with his shoulders and upper arms.

Don't rack your balls on the main gear Henry thought as his body exited the doorway on a 45 degree angle to the rear of the Skyhawk. His left thigh slammed painfully into the plane's right wheel pant, and then he was tumbling free.

Henry Bowman bent at the waist and relaxed his arms, and immediately started falling in a back-to-earth position. For a five-count he watched the Cessna proceed across the sky. Then he pulled in his left arm, flipped over, and went into the arch-and-spread position. He saw that he was west of Allen's van, so he pulled his arms into his sides and hunched his shoulders to put his body in a 'track' towards the spot where he wanted to open.

Allen Kane had intended to try to observe Henry's exit and opening, but he had started watching the Wilson Blair videotapes on the 9" DC-powered TV/VCR Henry had brought. The portable color unit was running on batteries since Allen's truck had a military-standard 24-volt system, and now the Indiana firearms expert was utterly engrossed. He was almost through the second, more explosive tape Henry had made of Wilson Blair.

"This stuff is pure plutonium," Allen whispered to himself as he watched the screen. Then he heard the unmistakable sound of a parachute opening. It sounded like one second of violently fluttering nylon ending in a loud *whop!* Kane hit the STOP button on the player and watched for the ninety seconds it took his friend to fly his gliding 'chute around the center of the valley and make a stand-up landing fifty feet away from the truck.

Henry gathered up the parachute and walked over to where Allen stood at the back of the truck. He was favoring his left leg slightly from where he had slammed his thigh exiting the plane. There was a big smile on the younger man's face.

"I see it opened," Allen said drily.

"Of course," Henry replied happily. "I packed it."

"I watched your tapes," Allen said, changing the subject. "Almost through the second one. Good diversion."

"Did my best on short notice."

"You know, Bowman," Allen Kane said with a smile, "when you first flew in here and told me what had happened, all I could think of was you spending the rest of your life in prison. But after seeing this," he said, indicating the portable television, "I think you got a real shot at dodging this thing altogether, and showing the whole country what those sons-of-bitches have been up to. I think this tape here might make a real difference." He sucked at his teeth.

"And they won't have a clue who did it," Henry added.

"Right. Your scheme seems to've worked okay so far," Allen continued. "So I don't guess you were jerking off the whole time it took to fly up here. You got some plan, I suppose? Of what we should do now?" Henry's spirits rose at Allen Kane's choice of pronouns.

"First I got to repack this 'chute, so we can bury it, and the Solothurn, too," Henry said. "Then, when we get to town, I want to call Ray Johnson in Colorado."

"The guy moved back from Africa I met at your house that time?"

"Right. I think the time has come to get some legal counsel on this. As backup, if nothing else. Then, I think, we'll let ourselves get found by the feds."

"Sounds like a plan."

"No, I haven't heard from Blair!" the man in Chicago almost shouted.

Dwight Greenwell, seven hundred miles east, gritted his teeth as he listened to his Regional Director give him the bad news. *Don't you realize that raising your voice to the boss is not the way to get ahead in government?* he thought acidly. His Washington office was becoming more and more cramped, and Greenwell could feel his blood pressure hitting new levels.

"I'm sorry, sir," the man on the other end of the phone continued, as if reading Greenwell's mind. "It's just that we don't have much of anything on this end. Initial reports out of Missouri have been saying the crash out by Bowman's place was a midair collision, but we still don't have any word on where the third chopper went, and the Guard is screaming bloody murder. On top of that, one of the local guys in the sheriff's department noticed that one of the two wrecked choppers on the scene was all shot up with machine gun fire from the inside."

"What?" Greenwell sat bolt upright in his chair.

"We're still trying to put that part together, sir, but apparently the door gun malfunctioned and spun on its mount. It sprayed the inside of the helicopter, causing it to go out of control and hit the other one."

"And the third pilot decided to take a vacation in Mexico," Dwight Greenwell said with obvious disgust.

"Apparently Blair had an elaborate plan, which included raids in Ohio, Indiana, and Missouri, all in a space of three days," the man in Chicago replied, ignored his superior's sarcasm. "I've spoken with people in the Columbus and Indianapolis offices, and Blair had a total of ten agents, counting himself, slated to raid the homes of a Mr. Grant Millet, and a Mr. Allen Kane. Millet's place is in Columbus, and Kane's in out in the country in southern Indiana. Both of these men are licensed Class Two Manufacturers, and carry DD licenses as well." He took a breath and went on.

"Kane is presently in Idaho with Bowman. Millet is in South America. The raids were scheduled for the seventh and eighth, but apparently never happened. "Uh...it appears that word of the raids leaked out to friends of both these men. There are between ten and twenty people with cameras camped out at both locations."

"*Sonofawhore!*" Greenwell spat. "I despise it when those yellow, chickenshit bastards do that!" He calmed down and asked another question. "Is that why the raids weren't carried out? Because the element of surprise was lost?"

"We don't know, sir."

"Well, what do the agents on the raid teams say?" Greenwell sometimes felt he was a kindergarten teacher.

"None of them can be located, sir," the man in Chicago answered miserably. "We know, or we strongly believe, that Blair contacted at least two members of the Ohio raid team on the day that the raid was supposed to take place. We do not know what was said, but no one we've talked to heard any mention of the raid being cancelled. Shortly thereafter, however, the four agents vanished.

"We have one report," the Regional Director went on, "of two of the Ohio agents, Heywood Downing and Mary Bright, getting into a white van that matches the description of the one Wilson Blair was driving out two days before. The driver was a white male, wearing dark clothing and sunglasses. Witness doesn't think he had a beard or mustache. We assume it's Blair."

"Well, where do you assume he is now? And where do you assume the agents from Indiana are?" Greenwell demanded.

"I have no idea," the subordinate answered truthfully.

"Find all three of them," Greenwell said suddenly.

"Three...?" The man did not realize what his boss meant.

"Millet, Kane, and that other one," the director explained, as if to an idiot child. "Make damn sure they really are in South America and Montana, or wherever. Get those OV-10s up in the air and find the two that are in this country. Find those two men, debrief them, and get back to me."

"Yes, sir," the agent said, then realized he was speaking into a dead line.

Dwight Greenwell sat in his office pondering the situation. *Didn't want to say it out loud,* he thought, *but I'll bet Blair took a nice, fat bribe from those two men. If I were asked how to get a raid cancelled and have the agents all go on a long vacation, that's what I'd recommend. A large application of money.*

June 11

"Well, look who finally showed up," Allen Kane said with a smile as he squinted towards the sky. A dark blue twin-engine turboprop airplane was circling the valley. As it got closer to them, Henry could see the plane had red and white trim. "Think you could hit it?" he asked.

"With the Solothurn? Yeah, if he kept circling, and if I had one of those wheeled mounts like you got in Indiana. Never get enough elevation with the little bipod. Have to wait 'til he got a lot closer, but it looks like he's heading this way. I'd stick one right in his windscreen."

The conversation Allen and Henry were having was purely theoretical. Henry's free-market 20mm cannon was at the moment broken down, wiped clean, wrapped in hydrosorbent paper, packed in airtight plastic bags, and buried in the National Forest, with the location logged and encrypted inside his GPS receiver. Henry knew he might never be able to return to get the big gun his father had given him in 1967, but he believed in thinking positively.

"He's checking out the truck."

"Yeah."

"What now?" Allen asked, after the plane had finally left the area.

"Let's shoot for a while, but then I think we should head into town. I hate making life easier for these assholes, but wouldn't you rather they found us in public, instead of out here with no witnesses around?"

"Good point," Allen agreed.

June 12

"Some folks been asking around about you two," the man behind the counter in the service station said as Allen and Henry came in to pay for their fuel. "I didn't tell 'em nothing, but they been asking all over. Tax men, I think they was. Not from around here."

"Tax guys?" Henry replied. "What would they want us for out here?" Allen Kane looked equally puzzled.

"Don't know. Seems like they was more interested in knowing if you two was really out here and had anyone seen you. Didn't act like they had to get holt of you right away. You fellas in trouble?" the man asked dubiously. "None a my business if y'are." Henry and Allen both shook their heads.

"I'd like to know what they want," Kane said evenly. "If you see them again, tell them we're heading back to the Pahsimeroi, then up towards Blue Dome." He handed the man a hundred-dollar bill, collected his change, and followed Henry back to the vehicle.

"Let's hit a few more places, get something to eat, maybe," Henry suggested in the cab of the truck. "Give them a chance to find us before we head out." The man at the filling station was the third person that morning to tell Allen and Henry about the federal agents. People in Idaho had no great love for government men, and that had been true even before Randy Weaver's wife and son had been murdered.

"Sounds like a plan," Kane said as he started the engine.

***

"Are you Allen Kane and Henry Bowman?" Allen and Henry looked at each other, then at the two men in suits standing at their table in the cafe.

"Yes we are," Kane said. "What's the trouble?"

"We're with the Treasury Department," one of the men said as he produced some credentials.

"You're ATF out of Boise," Henry said as he read the printing on the identification. "If somebody's reported machine-gun fire, we're both Special Occupational Taxpayers, and we've got copies of the registration papers for all the machine guns we brought with us." As Henry said the words, Allen Kane reached into his battered leather valise. Henry Bowman noted with interest that the two agents paid no attention to the action. Allen extracted a sheaf of ATF Form 3s and laid them on the table. The two feds ignored the documents.

"Could, uh, could we see some identification?" the second of the two ATF agents asked uncertainly.

"What's this about?" Henry said as he slowly reached for his wallet. "We've got all our papers. Idaho doesn't have any law against firing full auto on state land. We haven't shot anything except a bunch of jacks, and those were with revolvers, but it wouldn't matter what we'd used. You federal guys wouldn't drive all the way to Salmon from Boise to look into a possible game violation or a noise complaint anyway. What's the story?"

The agent took Henry's driver's license, looked at it, did the same with Kane's, and handed both to his partner. His expression was one of disappointment. "It's them," he said to the second man, shaking his head.

"What?" Allen asked again, more forcefully this time. "What are you here for? What's the charge?"

"We don't know the details," the second agent admitted. "We were told to find you, if you were up here. Director seemed to act like you wouldn't be." He furrowed his brow which went against the training he had been given to remain impassive.

"Three days ago, two government helicopters crashed on your property," he explained, nodding to Henry. "Everyone on board was killed."

"I don't understand," Henry said to the man. "What happened? And why did they send you to come find me? That's not the Treasury Department's jo- Did they crash on my *house?*" he demanded, as if suddenly realizing the implications of what the men were saying.

"We don't know," the agent said truthfully. "We were sent to find you, since the men were from our department," he added lamely. Both agents had already learned from a dozen local sources that the big army truck had driven into the area two days before the time of the helicopter crash, and that the men in it were on vacation to shoot jackrabbits.

"Well, I'd like to find out!" Henry announced as he quickly slid out of the booth and walked briskly to the pay phone near the cashier's station.

"When did you two get to this area?" the second agent asked Allen Kane.

"Last week," Kane said. "Wednesday, I guess it was, we went through Arco, in the late afternoon," he added, confirming what the feds had already found out from several sources. "Made camp that night in the Pahsimeroi." Kane looked the two men in the eyes.

"What's going on here, guys?" the Indiana weapons expert asked reasonably. "Why send you two all the way from Boise? Has Henry's place been burned to the ground? Are you here to find out what guns he brought so you can tell your records guys in Washington which serial numbers to keep in your system, and which to report as destroyed?"

The agents were startled by this question, and it showed in their faces. They had not bothered to think how their presence might be interpreted by the two men.

"We were told to find you," one of the agents said diffidently.

"Mister Kane," the other agent said in a more friendly tone, "the fact is that we don't know much more than you do about this deal. Like we said, we're out of Boise. We get a call to hotfoot it over here and make sure you two are all right." The man smiled. "And I'm glad to see that you are."

"So who said we were in Mackey? Or anywhere else in this state, for that matter?" Kane demanded. "Both of us are single, and I didn't give my ex any idea where I'd be— how'd you know where to look?" Both agents' faces instantly became blank.

"We got our orders from Washington," the first one said finally. His tone implied that he expected Kane to be impressed by that bit of news.

"So now you're all done?" Kane asked. "You call up your boss on the east coast and say 'Yep, they're there, all right' and hang up the phone? *What* is going on?" Kane repeated. The two agents were starting to plead ignorance again when Henry walked up

"Talked to Skip Krause," Henry said to his friend as he slid back into the booth. "He's the sheriff where I live. Feds aren't talking much, but they told him more than they told these guys. ATF borrowed three National Guard helicopters with pilots. Two of 'em crashed in the woods on my property. They don't know where the third one is. He hasn't called in and they have no idea where he flew off to." The two agents looked at each other. This was indeed more than they had been told. "He hasn't crashed, though," Henry went on. "There was no ELT signal like there was from the other two." The Emergency Locator Transmitter on the third aircraft had indeed been activated on impact. However, ELTs did not work underwater.

"Sheriff Krause says that ATF doesn't want to talk about what they were doing there, but that it was some special project they were working on." Henry paused a moment, and his eyes narrowed. Kane thought he saw just the hint of a smile threatening to form, but it vanished. Then Henry dropped the bomb.

"The interesting part is that Krause says, according to the FAA, it looks like the ATF guys shot themselves down."

"What?" Allen and one of the two agents said almost simultaneously.

"All three choppers had door gunners and M60s on swivel mounts. The two that crashed were blackened wrecks, but one had a ton of bullet holes in it, going from the inside out."

"What are you talking about?" the first agent demanded.

"One chopper was almost cut in half from .30-cal fire that came from the inside. First they figured it was a midair, and that's what set the gun off and spun it around. Made sense, 'cause the gun was an M60, and those things run away all the time. But the FAA inspector told the sheriff that since the two wrecks were far apart and each helicopter's rotor blades were still attached to the mainshaft, it wasn't a midair.

"And on the one with the inside-out bullet holes, they only found three bodies at the crash site, and all the helos took off with four men in each. Deputies finally found the door gunner's body a quarter mile away in the woods. Sheriff said it looked like he climbed out on the skid and hosed down the others inside, then bailed out."

"That's ridiculous," the second agent said indignantly. Allen Kane shook his head.

"No it isn't," the Indianan said. "In fact, it makes a lot of sense. Henry, what did the guy say about the second helicopter—did it have a bunch of holes in it from the outside?"

"He didn't mention anything about that, either way. Just said that they were both burned-out wrecks."

"What I bet happened," Kane went on, "guy probably fired his first burst at the other chopper and shot it down. Then he jumped out on the skid and hosed the rest of the belt into his own helicopter, and dove out before all the fuel caught fire." The two agents looked mightily offended at this, and began to protest.

"That's absurd! You don't know anyth–"

"Makes sense, Allen," Henry went on, cutting off and ignoring the two feds who had now lost control of the discussion. "It fits with what's happened before. Out in California that time."

"Right!" Kane said. "That ATF guy in Los Angeles." One of the agents at the table spoke up.

"What are you talk–"

"Best indicator of future behavior is past behavior," Henry Bowman said, once again acting as if the two government men were not there. The other agent put his hand on his partner's arm.

"I'll explain later," the first agent said to the second fed.

"Oh, you new to the department?" Henry asked as he widened his eyes and looked at the ATF man. "Happened a while back out in Southern California. An ATF guy in one of the local offices shot his partner in the head and then killed himself. Word the office tried to put out was it was an accident. When no one bought that line of crap, they came up with the claim that the guy was despondent 'cause he hadn't gotten laid. A single guy in Southern California," Henry added, and he and Allen both broke out laughing. "It's no wonder the other chopper pilot booked out of there and hasn't been heard from since. He probably wasn't ready to die for the glory of F Troop." Henry abruptly became serious and stared at the senior agent from Boise.

"I notice that in all this time you haven't bothered to tell me what three armed helicopters loaded with ATF agents were doing over my property in the first place." There was a long pause before the agent spoke.

"We're not at liberty to say."

Henry and Allen exchanged a look. They both knew that there was no way the two feds from the local field office would be told anything about a raid over a thousand miles away. What they were now hearing was blatant posturing and nothing more.

"You want to pack up and head back?" Allen Kane asked his friend. Henry shook his head.

"I still got plenty to shoot, and the jacks are unbelievable. Sheriff said he'd check my property every few days, shoot anyone that tried to loot the place. Let's stay 'til we run out of ammo. Maybe check out what's over in Montana."

"You got anything more you want to ask us?" Kane asked the two feds. "If not, we're leaving. It's past the time we'd planned to head out." He and Henry both stood up. Kane picked up the check. The older fed opened his mouth, then closed it again. He had been about to tell Henry and Allen not to go anywhere they couldn't be reached, but had realized he had no authority to make such a demand. The fed hadn't liked the way the conversation had gone, but there was nothing to do except report back to Washington. He and his partner turned without speaking and left the cafe.

"Them two fellas from the ATF give you boys any trouble?" the woman behind the cash register asked. Henry grinned as he handed her a twenty. The woman was only a few years older than he was, and at least five years younger than Allen Kane. She had dirty-blond hair, and a little smile that told the two men that no matter how many unwanted come-ons she might receive every day, she still enjoyed male attention.

"No more than you'd expect," Allen told her. "They been bothering you?"

"Can't say that. They just been hangin' around, askin' about you two, and makin' everyone edgy. People 'round here, they don't think much of that bunch. After what happened to the Weaver family, and all."

"I hear you."

"Two of their helicopters crashed on my property back in Missouri," Henry explained. "They wanted to tell me about it."

"Well, hallelujah to that." Henry and Allen turned to see a weathered-looking man in faded blue jeans and a battered Stetson rising from a nearby table. "Didn't mean to listen in, but them two have been asking around about you for a couple days now, and I recognized the name. You're Allen Kane, aren't you? I been reading your stuff for over twenty years now." He held out his hand, and Kane shook it.

"Folks thought Elmer Keith was a liar, about shooting pistols at real long range, but you were telling everybody the same thing. I bought me a Super Blackhawk .44 back in 'seventy-one, tried it for myself. Saw you guys was telling the truth. Then this metal silhouette game come along, and the ones was calling you a liar seemed to shut up right quick. It's an honor to meet you, Mister Kane. You say some of them ATF men crashed their helicopters on your property?" he asked, looking at Henry.

"That's what they said. I called the sheriff a few minutes ago. Both the choppers had M60 machine guns mounted in them. One of the wrecks was full of bullet holes going from the inside out, and they found the body of the guy who had been the door gunner a quarter mile away in the woods. He said it looked like the door gunner shot the other chopper down, swiveled the gun around and dumped the rest of the belt into his own aircraft, then bailed out. They're looking into his history right now, from what the sheriff tells me," Henry said, making an educated guess. "See was he on drugs, or what." Henry turned to his friend.

"I got to make some more calls. Allen, sit down with this man and tell him about the hundred- and two hundred-yard groups you been getting with that new nose design." Henry turned towards the pay phone.

"They say why them two helicopters with door gunners was coming to your place?" the stranger asked. Henry stopped and turned back towards him, shrugging.

"Those two guys wouldn't say, but I got a lot of guns, and I guess that's reason enough."

"They find out what stuff it was that guy was on," the man said, "maybe we could put it in the water, up in Washington."

***

"Goddamn it, I said I wanted a complete blackout on this fucking mess!" ATF Director Dwight Greenwell screamed at his staff as he slammed down the phone.

"That's the fourth call I've gotten in the last half hour from a newspaper, and they're all asking about Calron Jones and what made him shoot down his own helicopter. 'Did he have a drug problem? Is this related to the murder-suicide in Los Angeles a few years ago?' Jesus!

"Then they want to know what the two choppers were doing there, and of course they want copies of the search warrant. And on top of that, they all seem to know about the third one, that's gone missing."

"How do they know about that?" one of the staffers asked.

"Hell, anyone could have talked about it. But this last guy wanted to know if *Blair* was on it. Said an agent gave him that tip. Where the fuck is the loyalty in this agency?" He shook his head and looked around at the others in the office.

"I want you people to get on the phones to every one of our field offices. Find Blair. Call every goddamn airport where a National Guard helicopter might refuel. That sonofabitch is going to have some answers for me." He looked each of his subordinates in the eye.

"I don't need to tell you that none of you is to say word one to the press about any of this." Greenwell's staff was not about to disobey this last order, but the damage had been done. Nine well-placed phone calls from a cafe in Idaho had started a line of inquiry that was not going to go away.

***

"You had a ZX-11, and it got *stolen?*" the young man asked Henry as the two men stood looking at the 1981 Kawasaki which Henry had spent twenty minutes going over. The ZX-11 was the fastest motorcycle Kawasaki had ever made. It had been tested by several magazines at over 170 MPH in utterly stock condition.

"Right outside my motel room in Idaho Falls. Had my gear in the room with me, but the bike's gone for good, I'm afraid. Had a padlock on the brake rotor, so I guess it got lifted into a pickup. Best road bike I ever had," Henry said wistfully. He shrugged. "Got to finish my trip, and the insurance won't pay off for a couple months, at the least."

"That sucks."

"Yeah." Henry stared at the thirtyish man whose classified ad he had spotted in the local paper. "Look. You're asking absolute top dollar for a bike this old. But you've always garaged it, the oil's clean, the electrics all work, the engine sounds good, the tires aren't bald, and Z-1's don't break. I know—I had one before I got my 'eleven. I got to buy something soon, 'cause I got to be moving, and I'm over a barrel. You got saddlebags on it, and that helps, too.

"I'll pay your price, in cash, but you got to do one thing for me."

"What's that?" the seller asked.

"I can't be riding all the way back to Pennsylvania with no plates. And I'd rather not trust that long a trip to one of those pieces of paper that says 'License Applied For'. Insurance is no problem—I'm insured on anything. But riding with no plate is asking for trouble. Call your agent and cancel your coverage right now if you want, but leave the plate on. The bike'll still be in your name until I get home and mail the title off to the DMV anyway."

The young man thought a moment and then nodded. "Yeah, okay," he said, smiling. "That sounds fair." Henry pulled out his money clip and began peeling off hundreds.

∗∗∗

It was almost 10:00 p.m. when Henry Bowman pulled in to the long-term parking lot at the Salt Lake City airport. Henry lifted the Kawasaki onto its center stand and bent over to check the oil level through the sight glass. *Doesn't look like it used any.* He smiled. *Motorcycles are the perfect way to travel anonymously* Henry told himself. *Pick one with no trick paint and wear a full-face helmet, and you'll never get a positive ID on the bike or the rider.* He pocketed the key, unstowed his bags, and began the long walk to the United Express ticket counter.

June 13

"You made it a little earlier than I thought," Ray Johnson said into the phone. He did not use any names. "But that's good. I can pick you up in about twenty minutes. Ah..." Ray hesitated, about to say more, then decided against it. *I got a funny feeling about this* he thought silently, remembering the time when the roles had been reversed and he had been the one calling from an airport. "...I'll see you then," he finished, knowing the questions he had could wait until he and Henry were face-to-face in private.

***

"So what's going on?" *He looks a little tired, but otherwise in good shape* Ray decided. Henry smiled.

"Are you still a lawyer, Ray?" he asked as he turned in the passenger seat of Ray's pickup so that he could face his friend. "You still belong to the New York Bar?"

"I told you that on the phone. It was only twenty bucks a year to stay a member while I was in Africa. I figured that was a screaming bargain compared to taking it all over again if I ended up wanting to practice law when I got back to the United States. You want to tell me why that's important?"

"I want to retain you." He reached in his shirt pocket and withdrew a thin sheaf of bills. "Here. That's a thousand dollars." Ray waved the money away.

"Lawyer can be on retainer without actually getting any cash up front. He just has to be convinced the client's good for it." He yawned quickly, then closed his mouth. "Okay, I'm working for you, now. Anything you say is protected by the attorney-client privilege. What's the scoop? You in trouble?" At this question, Henry Bowman started laughing and Ray felt the hair on his back stand up. He turned to look at his younger friend.

"Watch where you're going, Ray," Henry said gently. "Be embarrassing to drive into the Roaring Fork River sober and in broad daylight. To answer your question, to the best of my knowledge, no, I am not in trouble. Not yet, at least. But that could change any time."

"This sounds like it might be interesting," Ray said as he pulled off the road onto the gravel shoulder. "And maybe I'd better concentrate." *How to start?* he wondered as he turned to face his friend. "Ah, what do you...anticipate that you might be charged with?" Ray asked. "Lawyers need to know what the charges are and what evidence the prosecution has. They don't need to have the client confess his guilt or innocence." *Although I never met one yet that didn't want to know, whether he needed to or not* he added mentally.

"You remember my friend Allen Kane?" Henry asked.

"Sure. Guy from Indiana. Met him at your place that time."

"Right. ATF tapped his phone this past spring. They have recordings of us planning a trip out to Idaho to shoot jackrabbits. Here's what ATF knows and/or suspects." Henry took a deep breath and started in, speaking with the minimal inflection of a newscaster.

"On the morning of June fifth, Allen Kane was seen leaving his house in southern Indiana in his Army deuce-and-a-half. That afternoon he was seen driving onto Henry Bowman's property in Missouri.

"On June seventh, six ATF agents including Regional Director Wilson Blair left Indianapolis to execute a search warrant on Allen Kane's property. None of the six agents or the white van they were in has been seen since. However, Wilson Blair is believed to have contacted one or more agents in the Columbus, Ohio ATF office the following day. Four agents from that office, who were under Blair's supervision and planning to execute a second raid on an NFA dealer in Columbus on June eighth, have gone missing as well.

"Two, and possibly all four of the missing agents in the second group were last seen in Columbus, getting into a white van similar to the one Blair and the other five agents from Indianapolis were last seen driving. Witnesses said the driver was a white man whose physical appearance and manner of dress is consistent with Wilson Blair's. The raid, which was to be made on the home of an NFA dealer who is currently in South America, was supposed to be a secret. However, a number of NFA and Title 1 dealers were camped out at the site of the raid the day after it was to have taken place, and they had apparently been there for over 24 hours. It is clear that they were 'tipped off'.

"The following morning, June ninth, Blair or someone claiming to be him phoned the ATF office in Missouri to talk to an agent who was going on a third raid with him, this one scheduled for that afternoon. The raid was on Henry Bowman's property in Missouri, and because of the terrain, the agents had arranged to be transported there in three National Guard helicopters borrowed for the occasion.

"Two of the helicopters crashed in the woods on Bowman's property before reaching his house. The third is missing. Examination of the wrecks revealed that one helicopter was riddled with machine-gun fire which came from inside the aircraft. The body of the door gunner was found a quarter mile away in the woods. One theory gaining merit is that the door gunner shot down the other helicopter, swung the gun around and shot up his own aircraft, then either committed suicide by jumping out the door, or was blown out of it when leaking fuel in the plummeting craft ignited. No one has as yet come up with a satisfactory explanation for the third helicopter and the men in it, all of which remain missing.

"Upon learning of the crashes and hearing the FAA's preliminary evaluation of the evidence at the crash sites, the ATF Director in D.C. called the ATF regional office in Boise. He gave instructions to the agents there to look for Kane and Bowman in Idaho. The Director wanted to determine if the two men were indeed in that state.

"The agents were finally able to locate Kane and Bowman eating breakfast in a cafe in Salmon, Idaho on June twelfth. In the two days prior to that encounter, however, the ATF agents had spoken with numerous people in several towns who had seen the big green army truck and had talked to the two men who had come to Idaho to shoot running jackrabbits with revolvers.

"Several people interviewed place both Kane and Bowman in a remote section of the Pahsimeroi Valley on June tenth. One of these witnesses was a cattle rancher living at the base of Borah Peak, who recalls the two men stopping at his cabin on their way out of the valley that day. He accurately described Kane's injured left hand and the flecks of brown in Bowman's right eye. He said Kane drank coffee with him while Bowman played with his dogs, a pair of Australian Shepherds.

"Grant Millet, the owner of the property in Columbus, Ohio, which was scheduled to be raided on June eighth, was located in South America, where he had been for more than two weeks. Thus, none of the three NFA dealers scheduled to be raided appear to have been actively involved in the disappearance of the ten agents in Indiana and Ohio, or the deaths or disappearances of the twelve agents and Guardsmen in Missouri.

"At the present time, efforts are being focused on investigating other NFA dealers known to or friends of Kane, Bowman, or Millet. No promising leads have been discovered as yet." Ray waited for Henry to go on, then realized his friend had finished. *He's trying for a poker face, but I can see something in his eyes* Ray thought.

"Do you...expect to be charged with a crime?" Ray asked finally. Henry shrugged.

"I didn't expect to have three Guard choppers with door gunners attack my place, but it looks like it happened." *Yeah, no shit* Ray thought.

"I get the distinct impression you know more about what happened than anyone in the ATF. Or the FAA, for that matter." *He's thinking how to answer that one. Or whether to say anything at all.* Ray waited him out. *What have you gotten yourself into, Henry Bowman?* Ray wondered. The dangerous game hunter had not felt so much alive since before his return to the states.

"Let's just say," Henry said deliberately, "that none of the events which I have just described baffle me." When he heard those words, Ray Johnson felt something click inside.

"I'm in."

"What?"

"I'm in. Whatever part you had in what you just told me about, you're not finished. You're planning something on top of it, aren't you?" *I got him there* Ray thought when he saw Henry's reaction.

"I want to be part of it," Ray said baldly. "As an accomplice, not legal counsel." He turned the key in the ignition and restarted the car. *Damn, I feel twenty years younger* Ray thought happily.

"Uh, Ray, I don't think—"

"Hey, wait 'til we get to the house," Ray said, cutting Henry off in mid-sentence as he pulled back out onto the road.

***

"We're done dancing around," Ray said as he put down his coffee and leaned forward in his chair. "There were twenty-two feds you mentioned when we were in the car driving up here. Twelve dead and ten missing. I assume you killed some of them?"

"Not some," Henry explained, shaking his head. "All twenty-two."

"Damn," Ray said, "This is worse than when you got caught in that buffalo stampede."

***

Ray sat silently, thinking about everything Henry had told him, and about the videotape he had seen. *Feds'll be looking for men that don't exist* he thought. *Even if they find the chopper in the quarry, it doesn't change anything. Same theory would still fit perfectly. And if they analyze the wrecks and find traces of thermite, like Henry's afraid they'll do, so what? That just makes their whole mission even more bizarre. He's home free.* Ray squinted his eyes shut and rubbed his temples. *But he's got that whole list, and all that other data from Blair's files...* Ray opened his eyes and stared at his friend as he delivered his assessment.

"It's good, but it's not good enough," he said finally.

"I can't think of any more safeguards or cut-outs," Henry said, shrugging helplessly. "Either it'll work, or it won't. I can't go back and redo any of the things I set up, so no use playing coulda-shoulda-woulda. I'm sure Allen won't let me down on the alibi end of things."

"That's not what I meant," Ray corrected. "Your plan's a winner, far as it goes," he said, nodding. "You've eliminated the evidence and made it look like you were out in Idaho when it happened. You got the ringleader on tape, admitting that ATF was going to plant stuff and lie so they could arrest the three of you, and he stopped it. That call to action you have him giving was a damn stroke of genius. You're dead right that a few copies of that tape in the right places will drive the whole department batshit and throw them off any theory that it might've been you that killed those guys in the helicopters. You're basically home free," the older man said. "But it doesn't go far enough. It doesn't solve the problem."

"Doesn't solve the problem? Not just staying out of prison, but not being arrested in the first place—what do you call that?" Henry said immediately. *He doesn't see it* Ray thought. *At least not yet. I wonder if he'll think I've lost my mind.*

"It doesn't solve the problem of the ATF, and all these other government assholes. There'll be an investigation, and then it will go back to the same thing. That's the first thing I thought of when you told me what happened." Ray sat back in his chair and stared out the big window that overlooked Aspen Mountain.

"Henry, when I left your house back in '94, I didn't quite believe all the things you and your friend Allen had told me. I didn't think you were making anything up, but I figured there was more to the story than you knew. So when I got back here, I took some of my own money and I made my own inquiries. And I found out things were a lot worse. I found out that what you told me was just the tip of the iceberg.

"There were a lot of things I learned that bothered me, but the one that really did it was what I found out in early '95. The papers then were full of articles about how the FBI was being investigated for shooting Randy Weaver's son in the back, and blowing his wife's brains out while she was holding the baby she was nursing. I got transcripts of everything, and as you said, it was all stonewall and whitewash, and 'our brave agents acted heroically under tremendous adversity'. That didn't really surprise me, although I admit I had expected better.

"The last straw was what I discovered next. At the same time they were saying Horiuchi maybe shouldn't have murdered Vicki Weaver, and they would keep much closer control on their 'rules of engagement', the FBI had just ordered almost two thousand suppressed .308 sniper rifles with night vision scopes.

"Henry," Ray said, leaning forward as he spoke, "We get that kind of information out, along with that tape you made of Wilson Blair, we can stop these bastards. Put them all on the run, in fear for their lives, and–"

"Those rifles," Henry broke in, "were they made by Brown Precision, with AWC suppressors and STANO image tubes?" Ray's eyes grew wide. *How did he know?*

"Y-yes," he said, caught off guard. "How...?"

"Everyone knew. Hell, those three companies were months behind in the last half of '94 and the first half of '95. None of us with NFA licenses could get anything out of them for a long time. Was like trying to get semiauto pistols out of Smith & Wesson at the end of the Vietnam war."

"Yeah, well, I called those places, because I wanted to find out why the FBI thought it needed two thousand suppressed, night-capable sniper rifles. You know what one of them said?"

"Let me guess—when you talked to the guys at AWC and STANO, they either said it was confidential, or gave you a bunch of crap about the FBI meeting the terrorist threat, and used those morons who bombed the World Trade Center as an example. They got the order long before the Oklahoma City bombing, or they'd've used that one as an excuse, too.

"If you talked to anyone at Brown Precision, they probably half-joked that it was so the FBI could kill civilian members of the gun culture, like me or Allen, with less risk of dying in the process. And they probably sounded half apologetic that they were doing business with the goddamned feds in the first place, 'cause Chet Brown is an old-time prairie dog hunter and bench rest shooter, but the company needed the business and they figured it wouldn't hurt to get on the government's good side."

Ray Johnson's mouth hung open. "How did you know?" he asked, dumbfounded. Henry shrugged.

"Common knowledge. While you were doing research, did you check out the Bill Fleming case, happened about the same time? Machine gun manufacturer in Oklahoma, no relation to my friend Tom the lawyer. Bill used to do business with a bunch of police departments, developed a bunch of HK variations the factory had said were impossible, like an MP5 in .45 auto, and ended up going to prison?"

"Yes," Ray said with great animation. "That was another one I was going to tell you I found out about. He got three years in prison for a $1200 tax dispute—$200 taxes on six guns. I looked into it, and he was exempt from the tax because the transaction was with a police department. Henry, when people find out what our government's doing, they–"

"Everybody knew that," Henry cut in. "Did you find out the real reason Bill's in prison?"

"What do you mean?"

"Bill acted as an expert witness a few years earlier, in a case the ATF was trying to make against some guy, involving suppressors. He made the jury see the feds didn't have a case. If that was all, he might've been okay, but Bill rubbed their noses in it, made 'em look like idiots in court. They never forgave him for that. He knew he'd fucked up, and for a while, his ads had a picture of him and his family dressed up like feds on a raid, ready to break in the back door of some cheap tract house. They were all holding machine guns, with Bill toting a G.E. Minigun, which everyone thought was hilarious. He was trying to suck up to the feds, but it was too late and they got him.

"Jerry Drasen, over in Illinois, feds bought an AR-15 barrel from him. Not a gun, just the barrel. Was one of those short military ones, and Jerry had a long flash hider on the muzzle, welded in place to make sure the length was over 16". Feds put the thing in a vise, stuck a pipe wrench on the flash hider to try to bust it off. It turned in the jaws, so they threw the barrel on a milling machine, milled a couple flats on it to keep it from turning, went back to the vise with their four-foot Stillson, and snapped the welds. Hit Jerry with a couple hundred counts of selling short-barreled rifles, 'cause that's how many barrels he had in stock, then threw on a couple hundred more counts of conspiracy to violate federal tax laws, 'cause that's what the NFA is officially—a tax measure."

"I thought you said it was just as barrel, and there was no gun with it."

"There wasn't, but Jerry did have AR-15s for sale, so that was good enough. After spending half a million bucks fighting it, he finally pled to a few of the counts, and they let him off with a hundred-thousand-dollar fine. Since he's a felon, he can never own or sell guns again. Only reason he got off that easy is that while all this was going on, he got in a car accident when a tire came through his windshield. It almost killed him, and he's disabled now with brain damage.

"How 'bout Aron Lippman?" Henry asked. "You check on him? Jewish guy in his late fifties, NFA dealer who sold guns to police departments and made self-defense videos. Goes to Florida with his girlfriend, and when he gets back to Pennsylvania he finds this guy who was working for him has sold a bunch of his inventory and made off with the money. Aron has him arrested, and to save his ass the guy tells the cops he'll cut a deal with the feds. Says Aron's making suppressors and machine guns without a Class 2 manufacturer's license, and shows them a bunch of steel tubing lying around the shop and a junky old semiauto M-11 MAC that he says is now full auto. Feds seize the tubing and the MAC, and every other gun in his inventory, hit him with eighty-seven counts of illegal manufacture, and conspiracy to violate federal firearms laws, or tax laws, I forget which. Prosecutor saw it was a bullshit case and kicked it, but the feds kept all Aron's guns, which were worth about sixty grand. The dumb bastard sued to get them back, so the feds had to give it all they had to keep from looking like idiots."

"And...?"

"Guilty on eighty-seven counts. He's in the federal slam right now." Henry cocked his head to one side. "Dave Green, at Springfield Armory, and Jack Birge, over in Ohio—you know about that one?"

"No," Ray said, his anger mounting. Henry scowled.

"There was another guy in there, too, I forget his name 'cause I never met him. Anyway, all three of 'em were NFA dealers like me. Dave was supposed to transfer twenty M60 machine guns to one of the others, I think it was the third guy, but Dave's secretary gets the message wrong and fills out the forms transferring them to Jack Birge instead. Dave realizes the error when the transfers come back approved and he sees the wrong name on them. So he calls Jack, explains the fuckup, and Jack says he'll transfer them to the third guy, where they should have gone in the first place. Jack grabs a stack of transfer forms, fill 'em out, signs 'em, and sends 'em off to Washington. Dave calls the third guy, explains his mistake, tells him the delay will only be a few weeks, and he'll ship the twenty guns as soon as Jack gets the papers back approved. Guy says that's fine. Papers clear in three weeks, Jack mails them to the guy, and then Dave ships the guy his guns."

"So what's the problem?"

"Problem is the feds found out, from somebody who heard about it and ratted out those three to save his own butt."

"Ratted them out for what?" Ray demanded. "What was the crime?"

"Jack Birge was hit with twenty counts of filling out transfer forms to transfer NFA weapons which were not in his possession. All three men were charged with twenty counts of conspiring to violate federal firearms laws, since they discussed the screwup on the phone. In point of fact, I don't think any one of them thought Dave should ship nine hundred pounds of stuff worth forty thousand dollars to the wrong guy, so that he could then ship it to the right one. Anyway, all three of them spent a pile of money, saw they were fucked, and pleaded to a few counts with six-figure fines. None of 'em have licenses any more.

"You could talk for weeks without running out of examples. Guy named Lamplugh in Pennsylvania, he was a guy organized gun shows. Fifteen feds broke into his house, tore the shit out of the place, and left. On the way out, walking across the yard, a lady fed stomped the wife's kitten to death in front of her and other witnesses."

"Stomped her *cat* to death?" Ray almost shouted.

"Yeah. Laughed at her while she did it, and told Lamplugh and his wife to count themselves lucky.

"Louie Katona, you find out about him? He had a machine gun collection, taxes all paid, the whole deal. Police chief who signed his paperwork got in a jam about child molestation, so he hands 'em Louie. Says he never signed any of the forms—his secretary did it for him, so they're not legit. Feds bust into Katona's house, jack his pregnant wife up against the wall, and she miscarries. He eventually got his guns back, but it cost him a hundred thousand or so, in addition to the miscarriage.

"There are literally thousands more cases—I'm just giving you the ones I knew personally." Henry quit talking, and Ray stared at him. *Looks like he's about to cry* Ray thought in surprise. He kept his peace and waited for his friend to speak.

"Worst one of all, at least in my opinion," Henry said finally, "was Chris Lee. Chris was an NFA dealer and manufacturer lived up north of Allen in Indiana. Never saw a gun he couldn't fix. Got swamped during all the cease-fires at Knob Creek, 'cause he'd work on everybody's stuff for free. Just for the challenge, I guess," Henry added as an afterthought.

"One year at Knob, this big fat guy from Michigan sees Chris on the firing line and says 'Hey Chris, where can I find Dan Hunter? I need to talk to him.' Chris says 'At the other end of the line,' or whatever, and the fat guy goes off and finds Hunter.

"Turns out what the fat guy wants to talk to Hunter about is getting some 'paper' for guns he's got. That means registration paperwork that somebody typed up and got approved before May 19, 1986, when the feds slammed the door because of that stupid New Jersey cocksucker Hughes. We're talking about paperwork that was typed up and approved, without there ever having been a gun to go with it. Paperwork that manufacturers planned to use after the cutoff, so they could do some business while they looked for other employment, since the law change abolished their livelihood.

"Now Dan Hunter was a fucking squirrel, and he always seemed to have a virtually limitless supply of pre-May 19th approved paper. I guess those two things together should have been a tip-off, but back then the guys he was selling it to weren't thinking along those lines.

"So the fat guy buys the paper for some gun or other that he's built up, and Dan Hunter rats him out. Dan Hunter rats him out 'cause ratting guys out is what Dan Hunter does for a living. You see, Dan Hunter is the highest-paid informant in the history of the whole fucking ATF, and that is why Dan Hunter always has a supply of Pre-May 19th paper—the feds make it up for him whenever he wants, with all the proper date stamps and official signatures on it.

"The fat guy from Michigan shits when the feds come down on him, and he starts blubbering that he'll rat anyone out that they want if they'll pleasepleaseplease give him immunity. Who do they want? Chris Lee.

"Now most people might not think that Chris Lee had committed a crime, but most people don't work for the ATF. Chris Lee was charged with our old friend conspiracy, the all-purpose charge. You see, he told the fat guy at Knob Creek where to find Dan Hunter when the fat guy asked him."

"But that wouldn–" Ray broke in, but Henry cut him off.

"Don't argue with me Ray, I said the same thing until I got a copy of the indictment. I read it." *He's furious* Ray thought as he watched Henry get himself back under control. Ray's own outrage was continuing to mount.

"So they break into his place with a dozen agents, one guy shoves his gun in Chris's mouth, and they cut open his safes and take maybe $200,000 worth of guns. They go to one prosecutor after another, and none of them would touch it, but finally they get some cunt from Detroit who thinks that no one but the cops should have guns, and she says okay.

"What everybody hoped would happen, Chris included, was that the feds would offer to let him plead to an infraction and pay a big fine, like a quarter million dollars or so. No soap. The feds were bound and determined to get at least one felony count. You see, Chris Lee is the most serious shooting enthusiast on the entire planet, bar none, and everyone, feds included, knows it. He makes you, me, Allen, and Tom put together look like we're bored with shooting. He fires upwards of half a million rounds a year. And there is no way Chris Lee will ever rat out or set up another gun guy, and everyone knows that, too. So it is a matter of pride for the feds to make it so that Chris Lee can never own or shoot another gun in his life.

"Chris hires Bob Sanders, the former head of the Chicago ATF office. Sanders quit ATF in 1982 when he got proof his agents were planting evidence and committing perjury against guys like us, and his bosses in Washington told him to shut up about it. He quit and went into private practice doing nothing but defending gun guys on this kind of stuff. Chris also hires Jim Jefferies, former prosecutor who nailed Agnew in the '70s. And Chris hires Stephen Halbrook, the country's top legal scholar on the Second Amendment.

"These three guys are the best there is, and they are not cheap, especially for a guy who tries to make his living selling something the government banned the manufacture of in 1986. The feds hit back by getting indictments in several other districts so he has to fight those too. They hit him with an IRS audit the next day. They drag their feet on his transfers. His lawyers file suit for harassment, get documentation of a bunch of illegal actions by all the agents involved, show that the warrant's a joke, and get a court order stating that any agent discussing the case is committing a felony as he is divulging confidential tax information.

"Then Waco happens, and the public is outraged, and we start thinking Chris's case will get dismissed. Nope. Feds have unlimited money, and they're going to bankrupt him and make him plead to a felony." Henry sat back in his chair. His eyes were focused far off in the distance.

"Is that what happened?" Ray asked finally.

"I don't know," Henry answered, without shifting his gaze. "I'm ashamed to say that. Last I heard, it was still getting delayed, with the feds hoping he'd go bust before they had to go to trial, 'cause they were afraid they'd lose. But that was a while ago.

"See, in '95, I found out that there were over three thousand people in federal prison for gun paperwork violations, and I figured that sooner or later, I would be next. I quit going to Knob Creek, and I quit going to gun shows, and I quit selling guns, and I damn near quit buying them, too. Other than the people in Missouri, I lost contact with every gun guy I used to see except Allen Kane. Mainly, I would just shoot on my own place. Figured the feds would leave me alone, that way." Henry drew a deep breath.

"It's the only thing I've ever done in my life for which I am truly ashamed." He laughed mirthlessly. "And you can see how well that plan worked."

"That's just what I've been wanting to tell you," Ray said, finally seeing an outlet for the intense feelings that had been building up within him. "The time for passive resistance and legal redress is past, and the time to take up arms has come. We can't let these feds keep getting away with this kind of outrage. With what you've done and that tape you made, we can reverse this. If you're willing to continue the fight, I'll sign on with you. If you fade into the background now, it'll just keep happening."

"Two of us take on one whole branch of the government?" Henry said with a soft chuckle. "That's just a little too lopsided for me, Ray. I'm not that eager to die."

"I'm not talking about just the two of us, Henry. There are at least five or six million serious Bill of Rights advocates in this country who understand the importance of the Second Amendment. There are at most—what?—ten or twelve thousand people in the government trying to dismantle the Bill of Rights. That's a 500-to-1 advantage. And you, one person, have managed to kill twenty-two of those enemies. There'll be no contest."

"I got thrown into that," Henry said quickly. "I had to do something. No one else is in that position." *He doesn't see* it Ray thought. *I'll try a different tack.*

"We're at a crossroads here, Henry. And we've got history to guide us, to tell us which road to take. Think of how the last fifty years would have been different if the Jews in Germany had chosen the other road. There were German Jews who fought in France in World War One, and you know some of them brought home guns. Twenty years later, when the SS guys came for them, they had a choice, and the choice they made was to roll over and get ready to die.

"What would have happened if after *Kristallnacht*, they had swept up their broken glass, dragged out their twenty-year-old war souvenirs, and said 'Okay, those guys didn't wear masks. We know exactly who they were. They're dead meat', and blasted the storm troopers the next time they saw them alone? What if every time there was a raid, a couple of those fresh-faced blond twenty-year-olds got carried off to the morgue, and the others got marked for later execution?"

"I can't argue with you there; I've said the same thing many times."

"Right. And what about the Ku Klux Klan here in America? They had serious power for sixty or seventy years. What if every time five or six guys in white sheets came to toss a firebomb in a black church, or burn a cross on a guy's lawn, somebody with a ten-dollar .22 shot one of them in the leg to keep him from running away? And then held a straight razor against his balls and asked the man nicely for the names and addresses of his friends? And then popped each one of them in the back over the next few weeks, while they were on their way to church, or the drug store? Klan wouldn't have lasted seventy minutes, let alone seventy years.

"Look, I know that with the Jews, there's been a hundred or so generations of knuckling under. And Jews have always succeeded mentally, not physically. Say Sandy Koufax and Mark Spitz, and you've about exhausted the list of the world's Jewish athletes. Blacks had a history of subservience too, Jim Crow laws in many places kept them from having guns, and where it was legal, they didn't have any money to buy anything but junk single-shots.

"But shit, Henry, the people at the crossroads now don't have any of those problems!" Ray looked at his friend, who had obviously been thinking about what he had been saying.

"I've said many of the same things, to various other people, over the last twenty or thirty years," Henry admitted.

"So you agree that this problem is not going to go away, and it is only going to get worse until it turns into a real shooting war?" Ray asked.

"I think that's already been proven. But how are you proposing we make this 'call to arms', Ray? Organizing against the government, we'd get nailed in a New York second. Someone will always sell you out to save his own ass."

"We don't organize. Who were you organized with in the last week? Nobody. You can't get sold out if no one knows what you're doing. We use the Internet, and electronic bulletin boards. We get the message out, about who the targets are, and how easy it is to kill them and get away with it when working alone.

"We don't have to get much participation, Henry. Hell, take that figure of five million I used before, which I think may be low. If only one out of every five thousand thinks it's a good plan, and pops one fed, don't you think a thousand dead ATF agents would get these guys to revise their priorities?"

"Let's see if I've got your plan straight, here. You want to log onto the Internet, or a bunch of bulletin boards, or both. Anonymously, of course. Then you want to issue an 'Immediate Release' to all ATF and government offices." Henry thought a moment, then went on.

"It'll say something like, 'ATF, you've had your fun and up 'til now your only risk has been a letter in your file or a few days of paid suspension. That's over. Thousands of decent American citizens are in prison or dead because they didn't fill out a line on one of your stupid forms, or a piece of wood or metal was longer or shorter than you said it should be, or some other stupid thing. No more. The party's over.'" Henry thought a moment. "Won't do much good to kill the janitors in the federal buildings, so let's put a limit on our ultimatum, say, GS-7." He went back to his announcer's voice.

"'From now on, any ATF employee with a Government Service classification of GS-7 or higher is a party to the treason the ATF has committed and is now subject to execution, as are all ATF informants. No exceptions.

"'Second, any judge who upholds any gun law shall also be guilty of treason and subject to execution. No exceptions. From now on, guns will be treated the same as books.

"'Third, since elected officials and law enforcement entities have a duty to defend the Constitution, any elected official or police agent who supports or enforces any measure, past or present, which violates the Second Amendment shall be subject to execution. Private citizens may freely advocate any policies or ideas that they want, as per the First Amendment.'" *Not bad, actually* Ray thought, but Henry was talking again.

"Then I suppose you'd want to post a list on the Internet of all the ATF agents and their home addresses. Informants too, and maybe throw in the national politicians who've voted for antigun bills, so the people wouldn't have to track down all that info themselves. And then a few tips about tactics, and acting alone, and not talking to anyone, and how you should refuse to make any statements at all to cops. That about what you had in mind?" Henry asked his friend.

"Oh, I almost forgot—I guess you'd want to give all these thugs an alternative to being executed, so you'd throw in a graceful way out, like 'Public notice in the *Wall Street Journal* classifieds of resignation from government service or from law enforcement duties shall secure absolution from past crimes. Any return to government service shall reinstate the death sentence'.

"Would that do it, Ray?" Henry asked with raised eyebrows and a faint smile. "Shall we let them keep their pensions?"

"You don't think that plan would work?" Ray asked. His face was entirely devoid of expression. Henry's face became equally serious, and Ray watched him inhale deeply before answering.

"No, I don't think it would work. Let's leave out the fact that no System Operator in his right mind would run that kind of message on his bulletin board because he'd be soliciting murder. Assuming you could get your message out exactly the way you wanted it, your revolt would still never happen, and here's why:

"You might get a few guys from the fringes of society. A fellow like Randy Weaver might go for your idea. You might get a Tim McVeigh or two. And out-of-work guys who spend all their time talking about forming militias might buy in, but they'd blab about anything they were even thinking of doing, and they'd get caught before they accomplished a thing.

"For your plan to really work, you need intelligent, thoughtful, motivated people to embrace it. You need leaders, not losers." Henry took a breath and shook his head slowly, thinking.

"That's not going to happen for two reasons. First, you are asking people to do the hardest thing in the world, and that's to be completely alone with no support. You're asking people to go into enemy territory alone, like a guy parachuting into France before the Normandy invasion.

"Except your soldier won't have anyone on his side who knows what he's up to and who might be able to help him. Your soldier can't look forward to getting out of enemy territory when his mission is accomplished. Your soldier can't talk to his buddies about how scared he was and how glad he is to be safe. Your soldier has no commanding officer. Your soldier is winging it.

"I can't think of a single person I know who'd sign on to that deal on the basis of an anonymous message over the Internet." *I guess he's right* Ray thought, and a feeling of helpless rage came over him.

"There's another problem," Henry said, "and it's even more serious than the first one. You are expecting your volunteers to go out and kill people who are just like them. You aren't saying, 'See that guy over there, by the barbed wire? The one wearing a strange uniform, talking in a language you don't understand, and laughing while his German Shepherd tears the baby out of that naked woman's belly? Go blast him.'

"That would be easy. That would be like sitting in your living room in Bozeman, Montana, seeing some Italian U.N. troops in blue berets smash in the door across the street. Take about three seconds to decide what to do there: Boom! Bunch of dead Italians. Ninety-four Crime Bill, where the President had that provision in it to hire a bunch of Hong Kong Municipal Police 'cause they'd be good at seizing guns, I had to laugh. Talk about hazardous duty, Christ! You send a bunch of Chinese police to go seize guns from folks in Kentucky, undertakers'll be working three shifts.

"But what *you're* telling people, Ray, is 'See that guy over there, waiting for the bank's loan officer 'cause his wife want to remodel the bathroom? The one wearing the suit a little more wrinkled than yours? The guy who just dropped his kids off at Little League and then ate lunch with his wife at Shoney's? Yeah, that's the one. He's an ATF field agent. Last week he inspected the inventory of a local gun store. Found a single-shot .22 with a 16 1/2" barrel. Looked at it close, saw it was a smoothbore, made for .22 shot loads, so he called his supervisor. Sixteen inches is the limit for rifles, but under 18" for smoothbores without the $200 registration is illegal possession of a sawed-off shotgun. Store owner and his employees are now in jail, trying to raise a $250,000 bond, charged with violating the National Firearms Act, conspiracy to violate federal firearms laws, and violating RICO. The entire contents of the store as well as the building itself have been seized under the new forfeiture laws. The agent's about to go to the bank's parking garage now. Pop him in the back of the head with a .22 when he fiddles with his car keys, then walk away.'

"Ray, no one is going to do that. History proves it. You are not going to get intelligent, thoughtful, level-headed leaders to declare violent war on people that live in their neighborhood and whose kids go to their kids' school. It's hard enough for most people to fight complete strangers when they invade their country. Frogs wouldn't do it in '42. Italians, Yugoslavians, Greeks, same deal. Hell, even the Czechs, back in the '30s, they didn't do anything, and the Czechs had some of the best guns in the world, built at the ZB factory there.

"The *Reichsprotektor* of Czechoslovakia rode around in an open car with only a driver for security, and all the driver had was a P38 in a flap holster. Finally, after a few years of occupation, a handful of guys decided to pop Heydrich, and they blew up his car. Blasted pieces of horsehide from the seats into him, and he eventually died from blood poisoning, 'cause they didn't have any penicillin. But guess what? Heydrich was a hero, and got a hero's funeral and a huge monument on his grave. Kraut's'd won the war, he'd be in the history books as a hero today."

"I'll grant you your points," Ray said. "Let me get us a couple more sodas 'fore we talk ourselves hoarse." He left for a few minutes and returned with two cans and a brown paper bag. Ray handed Henry his Coke and sat back down.

"My idea wouldn't work the way you described it, you're right about that. I'll also admit that it is much harder to initiate a war when your enemies look and talk just like you do. But you're forgetting one thing.

"This isn't Germany or France or Czechoslovakia. It's America. Americans are people who don't want government running their lives. That's why we're here. The Colonists fought the finest army in the world for that reason. Immigrants came here and made this their home because of that philosophy.

"You're right that I wouldn't sign up after reading an anonymous call to arms. But I would sign up when I saw with my own two eyes that it was time. And I see that right now, with what happened to you. You got the names, addresses, and a lot more, and I've got the resources. I want to fight these bastards, Henry. Don't you?"

"Ray," Henry said, as he watched his friend fiddle with the paper sack, "I came here because I wanted your help, ideas mostly, on making sure I stayed out of prison. The fact is, I'd like to keep blasting these guys, and I haven't completely made up my mind to quit just yet. Not when the first twenty-two went so well," he added.

"But you're in a lot different position," Henry went on. "I got thrown into this, and I can't turn back the clock. I don't think you should voluntarily jump into something that can get you put away for life." Henry Bowman shifted his position in the overstuffed armchair.

"I'm not up on my Aspen land values, but my guess is your net worth is fifteen or twenty million bucks."

"No, you're not up to date," Ray said, "and that money from my settlement that I put in a mutual fund wrapped in an annuity? Over a hundred million now."

"You're kidding."

"No, that's just fourteen percent a year, which piles up when you defer the taxes instead of having to lose principal every year."

"Well, that's my point. No matter what our government does, I can't see them nationalizing all your real estate. And your fund is still worth sixty million after the feds take forty percent. Guy in your situation can insulate himself from Washington." Henry cocked an eyebrow as he continued. "Might burn up most of your money by the time you die, but that's a damn sight better than having the feds confiscate it all under RICO and send you off to prison to have your asshole stretched by a bunch of lifers with AIDS."

"I know that, Henry. I also know that in the eighteenth century, the principals in the American Revolution didn't have AFDC, and Social Security, and unemployment, and

Welfare to fall back on. If they lost their house and their land and their livelihood, they had nothing. The taxes the Colonists paid in America were lower than the ones the Brits paid in England, but that didn't cut any ice. The Colonists said 'enough'. And when the time came to shoot those guys that looked the same and talked the same as they did, they shot them.

"What I want to do is modest compared to what the Founders did. Every one of the men who signed the Declaration of Independence knew he might be signing his own death warrant. And many of them were captured, tortured, and killed. I'm not as brave as they were. But I will put my money where my mouth is. One of those brave men was a landowner who makes me look like a bit player. He owned more land than anyone else in the entire state of Virginia, and his property extended all the way to Ohio. I'm sure he could have cut a deal and kept all or most of what he had by siding with the King, but he didn't.

"George Washington could have relaxed on his estate, screwing his wife when she was in the mood and his slave girls when she wasn't, but instead he chose to risk death by starvation and exposure in the winter, and fever in the summer, fighting in the woods alongside a bunch of his field hands. If you'd gone to law school, you might have learned that," Ray said with a grin.

"In Africa, I kept having to move from one country to another because the governments always ended up stealing the wealth their most productive residents created. I move back here, where that kind of shit doesn't happen, and as soon as I get to the airport I discover that while I was gone the federal government of the United States started modeling itself after Germany's brownshirts in the 'thirties." He held out the paper bag. "So I'm in, pal."

"What's that?" Henry made no move to take the sack.

"Went to one of my safes while I getting our sodas. This is a piece of our war chest."

"I appreciate it, but I've got about forty Gs with me."

"Then an extra quarter million ought to help out quite a bit," Ray said with a smile as he threw the bag in his friend's lap.

"Jesus," Henry said as he peered inside. He looked up at his friend. "You are serious."

"That's what I been telling you." *I got his wheels turning now* Ray said to himself. "Your estimate of the land value here was short by about half, and I sold off a chunk of it last year and banked it offshore. Money's not a problem. You're the idea man—you still think it's impossible?"

"Whoooo..." Henry said, exhaling. "This is a whole new ball game. Can't do it without getting a bunch of people to take the plunge, but..."

"But what?"

"But they don't have to be the first," Henry said slowly, then nodded his head. Ray remained silent and waited for him to explain what he meant.

"The kind of intelligent leaders we need are often motivated by two emotions, opposite sides of the same coin. You just showed that."

"Which two are those?"

"Inspiration's the big one. You think about what the Founders went through, when they could have taken the easy way out, it makes you want to be a better person. The other motivator is shame. Shame at how little you've done, always letting someone else carry the water. We tap in to those two sentiments, we might not need to ask for any help or give too many instructions. The people just might do all those things I said would be too hard for them. They won't do them based on just a verbal or written plea for action, but they just might be inspired by seeing someone else first."

"The two of us?" Ray asked. Henry shook his head.

"Need more than just us. You and I can kick it off, but we'll need one other person. Shouldn't have to get more than that, if you're serious about the bankroll." Henry stared into the distance, his eyes unfocused.

"Any ideas?"

"I think he's already joined up."

***

"I wasn't counting on the use of a jet," Henry said as they broke through 20,000 feet. "When did you get this thing?"

"Last year. An old guy like me can't get laid in Aspen unless he has at least one private jet. Bought the little Citation since it only needs one pilot."

"You normally go places on the spur of the moment like this? Pilot won't think anything of it?" Henry said softly in his friend's ear. Ray shook his head.

"Bill's an ex-drug pilot. Crashed in the Everglades and it cured him of his thirst for adventure, shall we say. Now he sells home furnishings in the off season, and flies for me when I want to go somewhere. He doesn't mind sitting around in motels or at the airport when we're on the ground. It gives him a chance to work on his proposal for a TV series."

"You're kidding."

"No, one of his friends in town hit it big that way, and Bill's convinced he can do better."

"Hm. Maybe he can."

"Right. Anyway, to answer your original question, Bill thinks I'm going to look at some potential sites for strip shopping centers, on a swap deal. You're along as a second set of eyes. I told him I've got friends in all three cities, and I could stay an hour or a couple days in each place, depending on how things go. He's used to that." Ray saw his friend scowl faintly. "What's the matter?"

"I better pay attention to the approach speeds and bone up on the manual for this thing," Henry said. "It probably won't be a problem this trip, but unless your boy Bill ignores all forms of news media, he'll figure it out before too long. Either that," Henry said with a big grin, "or he'll start to think one of us is awfully bad luck." He saw Ray's look.

"What, you think I'd crunch it?" Henry asked in mock indignation. "Come on—fortune favors the bold." He stood, stooping in the low cabin, and moved up to the righthand pilot's seat.

God, I hope so Ray Johnson thought as he stared at his friend's back.

***

Rush hour had not yet started when they arrived at the Tulsa airport. A quick look in the Yellow Pages gave Henry the name of a serious computer-supply store, and it took the cab driver less than fifteen minutes to get there. He left the meter running. A half hour after that, Ray and Henry were sitting at a table in a Denny's restaurant. Ray was drinking an iced tea while Henry attached the newly-acquired device to his laptop computer.

"What's that for?" Ray asked. He was looking at a small piece of equipment whose label said it was a Konnex Coupler.

"You mean what do normal people who aren't planning to start a war use them for?" Henry laughed. "They're big with anyone who takes his laptop out of the country and has to access a computer back home. Most places don't use modular jacks like we do here. Some guys will actually bring their tools and add a modular jack to their hotel system, but that can get you in trouble in a place like Mexico. Next thing you know, you're coughing up *mucho mordida* to the local *federales*.

"This widget takes the old-tech approach, sends the signal through the handset microphone. Much slower, but it works. It's like what insurance agents had in the early '80s. They'd carry this heavy thing into the customer's house. About the size of a suitcase, and it incorporated a typewriter keyboard and a printer. They'd jam his phone receiver into it, dial the number of the home office, and type in the stuff like age and gender and smoking status and how much face amount. Then the computer in the home office would figure the proposal and tell the printer what to print, all through the handset. Nobody uses them any more in this country—you get much faster and cleaner transmissions wiring in direct through the jacks."

"Then why are you using one?"

"Because they'll let you hook your laptop up to a pay phone."

"Oh. Right." Ray was silent for almost a minute before he spoke again.

"I remember you once said there was a lot of garbage to wade through on the Internet. Is that still true?"

"Yes, but less so. This'll get some people's attention, and they'll talk it up. Plus, I got eight bulletin boards and Internet sites I'm going to call up next with the exact same message."

"How about if they trace it back?"

"I've got a free trial with a fictitious name and address. In two weeks, they'll cut me off unless I come up with some money and subscribe, but by then, we'll have another way in. Be back after a while." He finished what he was entering on the laptop's keyboard, then stood up and carried his equipment towards the public phone by the men's room.

Henry hooked the coupler to the pay phone's receiver, deposited five dollars worth of quarters, entered a ten-digit number on the phone's touchpad, and waited. After a few moments, he resumed entering keystrokes on the small computer. He stared at the screen and smiled.

That's got it Henry said to himself after about two minutes. *Now for the bulletin boards.* In the ensuing twenty minutes, Henry Bowman logged on to eight electronic bulletin board services and uploaded the exact same material.

"All done?" Ray asked.

"For right now. Let's eat, and then I'm going call each of the system operators on the telephone, tell them to check their boards."

***

"Holy shit," the young man in the Houston apartment said under his breath as he stared at his computer screen. "This can't be for real." The Sysop of the Texas Freedom Fighters Bulletin Board did not normally talk to himself, but these were not normal circumstances. He was almost through the message when his telephone rang.

"TFF," he said automatically.

"You the Sysop?"

"Y-yes." Henry laughed at the man's involuntary stutter.

"You sound nervous. I take it you've checked your 'in' file?"

"In front of me right now. Who are you? Is this on the level?"

"I'm ex-ATF, and yes, it is. You're one of eight Sysops I've flashed this to. I'll be using the 'net also, until Washington closes it down. Then it'll be just you guys. You want in on this deal? If not, say the word, delete what I sent you, and you'll never hear from me again. No B.S. here—it's apt to get hot."

"Yes. I want in," the young man said after a moment's hesitation. The temptation was irresistible.

"Okay then, listen up. First, you'll get floppies in the mail duplicating every upload I make. That's so you can verify they're really from me. Second, any calls I make to you from now on will be with a voice synthesizer, one of the cheap ones that came with the first multimedia kits. Third, the word I want you to use to tell me the feds are actively trying to get you to help trap me is *understaffed*. As in, I say, 'Any trouble with feds on your end?' and you say, 'No, I think they're way too understaffed to bother with a BBS operator.' And only use it if they're trying to make you do something. I know they'll be trying traces. Clear on that?"

"Yes. Understaffed."

"Last point. I'll call this number once more, sometime tomorrow. Between now and then, find a pay phone you can get to easily, and record the number. Make sure it's a fair distance from your house or business. That's 'cause the feds typically tap all the pay phones within two or three blocks of someone's house when they really want him. I'll contact you there from that point on. I'll flash you on the system with a message that contains the word 'turnaround', one word, not two, and a date and time. 'Turnaround' lets you know it's me. Ignore the rest of the message, other than the date and time. That clear?"

"Got it. Uh, one question: You really expect them to close down the 'net?"

"Wouldn't surprise me. Keep watching the papers."

"Okay."

"Things get too hot, you use that word. Remember it?"

"'Understaffed'."

"And my message code?"

"'Turnaround'. One word."

"That's it. Keep your powder dry." Henry broke the connection and began to dial the number of another Sysop, this one in Michigan.

The Houston man slowly hung up the phone. He had some skydiving experience, and he now felt like he had just gone into free-fall and was still accelerating, waiting to reach equilibrium. He stood up, planning to go look for pay phones, then sat back down.

"Let's read this over one more time," he said aloud as he turned his attention back to the monitor's screen.

```
                    STOP WHINING, AMERICANS
                  by Wilson Blair, ex-ATF agent

Up until last week, I worked for the government. I was a bureaucrat. I
handled producer-tax paperwork involving tobacco companies. It wasn't an
exciting job, but it wasn't a bad one either.

Not too long ago, I was transferred out of the Tobacco division and into
Firearms. I was told that many Americans didn't like the ATF agents in
the Firearms Division. I assumed it was because individuals always com-
```

plain about paying taxes, while corporations know that complaining does-n't do any good. I soon learned that paying taxes had nothing to do with why the public didn't like us.

As an agent in the Firearms Division, I was ordered to entrap private citizens at gun shows by offering them inflated prices for guns they had just bought, and then arrest them for dealing without a license.

I was told to pose as a neophyte, ask about the mechanical differences between semiautos and machine guns, and then arrest the person who talked to me and charge him with "conspiring to violate federal firearms laws."

I was given a machine gun, and told to intimidate family members when a man's house was being raided with a blank warrant.

In April, I helped monitor illegal wiretaps on the phones of three deal-ers in three midwestern states. The taps told us that all three dealers would be out of town in mid-June. I was ordered to plant evidence which would result in the three dealers being held without bail.

This was the last straw, for me and for most of the others involved in two of the three raids. I and other agents stopped these two raids from ever happening.

The third raid involved helicopters armed with belt-fed machine guns. Only one of the agents on that raid was bothered by what he had been ordered to do, but he was not a man to sit back and do nothing. This man, who was also new to the Firearms Division, saw only one way to stop the assault on an American citizen's home. When he told me what he was going to do, I knew it was suicide and begged him to reconsider. He did what he thought was right. He used his machine gun on the other heli-copters before they reached the house, then turned the gun on the inside of his own aircraft, shooting it down also. He knowingly gave his life for what he believed in: Freedom.

I think of this young man who gave his life to defend your freedom. Then I think of the successful, well-off, gun-owning citizens like yourselves who have criticized the ATF for so long, and I am disgusted.

QUIT WHINING, people! You have bleated like a bunch of sheep for decades now. "Our guns are our guarantee of freedom," you cry, but you'd never know that from your actions. You outnumber your oppressors 500 to 1, yet you continue to let them vote away your freedoms and march you off to prison. You meekly submit time after time, letting people with GED cer-tificates consign you to the penitentiary because a piece of wood was too short or too long, because a bullet was made of brass and not lead, because you owned steel tubing or rubber washers, or because a barrel had threads on it.

You have complained about ATF agents for long enough. Stop it if you are unwilling to be part of the solution. One agent has already given his life for your freedom. There are several others who intend to stay alive as they undertake the obligation you have shunned. Don't dishonor these men and women with your petulant whimpering.

The following list of current Firearms Division agents and ATF infor-mants will be of interest to anyone who wants to keep track.

The Houston Sysop scanned the remaining pages in the transmission. Quick calculation showed there were over six hundred names and addresses of ATF agents. He was startled at the number of informants listed.

The young man was not aware of the fact that the names of six agents from Indiana and four from Ohio were absent from the list.

***

"Hello?"

"Agent Shawn Montoya, please."

"You got him."

"This is Getz, from the Chicago office. I catch you at a bad time? With your family?"

"Here alone watching the tube, having a beer. What can I do for you?" *Bingo* Henry Bowman thought. *And on the first call, too.*

"Got a situation involves one of your local informants and something we've been working on back in our area. Boss is pissed and he wants it face-to-face, which is why I'm down here now. Shouldn't take long—can you spare a few minutes, let me show you what we got?"

"Sure, uh...you want to meet somewhere, or what?" Henry smiled. It was exactly the question he wanted.

"Since you're off the clock and I'm still on Chicago's dime, why don't I come by your place, get this stuff out of the way. Then you pick a spot where we can get a decent dinner and a few drinks, and we'll let my office pick up the tab."

"Sounds good to me. You got my address, know how to get here?"

"Let's make sure what they gave me isn't five years out of date," Henry said, then recited the address that had been on Wilson Blair's portable computer, followed by the directions he had written for himself gleaned from a Tulsa street map.

"That's it," Montoya said pleasantly.

"Good deal. Should see you in ten or fifteen minutes, if I don't get lost." *I could imitate that voice in my sleep* Henry thought with a grin as he broke the connection.

***

"This makes my place look like a rathole," Henry said with feeling as he stared around the middle-class apartment. *Looks like he's about twenty-five* Henry said to himself, then grinned broadly as he stared at the younger man's left hand. "You've obviously never been married," Henry said as he slipped his third finger through the loop of the leather sap he carried in his hip pocket. Montoya laughed.

"Gringa girls from the University think Shawn *muy exotico*," he said with an exaggerated Speedy Gonzales accent, then switched back to his normal voice. "Can I get you something to drink?"

"Whatever you're having." Montoya turned towards the kitchen as Henry pulled the lead-filled weapon from his pocket. In a fluid motion very similar to throwing a baseball, Henry Bowman snapped his wrist as he brought the sap down on the back of Montoya's head. The ATF agent fell like a marionette whose strings had been cut. Henry slipped the sap back in his pocket and bent over to inspect his work.

In the movies, this guy would wake up with a headache Henry thought with a sardonic smile. He well knew that any impact to the head forceful enough to knock a person unconscious was, by definition, almost strong enough to kill him. Henry had put every bit of his substantial upper-body strength into the blow he had delivered. He slid the dead man's wallet, keys, and credentials out of his pockets, then pulled a pair of thin cotton socks out of his own jacket and slipped them on his hands.

It took less than three minutes for Henry to dump out every drawer in the place, empty the closet, throw every chair cushion on the floor, and leave the refrigerator/freezer open and unplugged. Then he reached for the telephone. *Time for an appearance from Rich Little* Henry thought as he dialed a number from his notebook.

On the third call, he found another Chicago ATF agent who was home alone that evening.

***

"Damn, that was fast," Ray said as Henry slid into the passenger seat of the rented Buick. "Nice hat." Henry had on one of Montoya's hats he'd found in the man's closet. The brim was pulled down and it obscured much of his face,

"Make a right out of the lot, then go straight 'til you hit Madison. Should be ten or twelve blocks." Ray nodded and slowly pulled out of the supermarket parking lot.

***

Perfect Henry thought as the door opened to let him in. The man before him was in his fifties and was the fattest person Henry had seen in more than a month. He was holding a thick sandwich in his left hand. His jaws moved methodically.

"You must be Getz," the man said around his food, then swallowed and smiled. Henry was starting to unfold his wallet to display Wilson Blair's badge, but the obese agent waved his hand. "Pancho Villa explained everything, said you were on your way. C'mon in." He motioned Henry into the apartment.

"Hope this isn't inconvenient for you," Henry said with what he hoped was the right blend of apology and disinterest. "I won't take long, and then you can get back to your family." Getz waved a hand.

"Sharon won't be back from bingo for a couple hours, kids're grown and moved out. Have a seat while I go to the kitchen," he said as he turned around. "You want a beer?" he asked over his shoulder. "I got Stag, and I think a Schae–"

The rest of the man's sentence was cut off as Henry Bowman wrapped his arms around the obese agent's body and clamped his fists into the man's chest. The electronic stun gun in Henry's right hand sent 90,000 volts into the ATF man's central nervous system. The agent collapsed in a 440-pound heap with Henry on top of him.

Lucky he didn't break my damn arm Henry thought as he let go of the stun gun and extricated his right arm from beneath the agent's bulk. The man's head was turned to the side. His jaw was working but no sound came out. Bits of chewed sandwich fell from his mouth onto the carpet.

Henry reached into his own inside jacket pocket and grabbed the wooden handle of the icepick. He had used a section of plugged rubber fuel line to cover the steel shaft, and this sheath stayed inside his pocket as he withdrew the tool from his coat. Before the agent could see what was happening, Henry slid the icepick straight into the man's ear and smacked the butt of the wooden handle with the heel of his hand. The metal ferrule clamped around the base of the tapered 6" shaft bottomed inside the agent's ear.

A look of surprise came over the man's face, and he made a hissing noise in the back of his throat. Henry smacked the side of the icepick's handle several times with his fist, pounding in a different direction with each blow. A stench suddenly filled the air. The man was dead. The smell was much worse than when Agent Montoya had died. *Like that's a big surprise* Henry thought grimly as he withdrew the icepick.

No blood he noticed with detachment. The steel shaft was wet with clear cerebrospinal fluid. Henry slid the icepick back into the rubber tube in his jacket and reached into his pants for a piece of cellophane. He unwrapped the plastic and exposed the lump of 50/50 Alox/beeswax cast bullet lube, which he then smeared into the dead man's ear canal. Henry was careful not to let his fingers touch the brown, waxy material, lest he leave prints. He twisted the corpse's head enough to perform the same procedure in the opposite orifice, then put the remainder of the bullet lube back in his pocket.

Henry sat up straight and surveyed his work. *Analysis'll show that stuff's not a product of the human body, but I doubt the coroner will bother* Henry thought. *Looks like any other fat guy with ear wax whose heart let go.* He considered for a moment whether multiple deaths would arouse suspicion, then mentally shrugged. *Pretty soon they'll know they're all executions. Still best to keep the methods different.*

Henry climbed off the huge mass and walked to the door to the apartment. He cracked it open, using the tail of his sport coat to prevent his skin from touching the doorknob. No one was in the hallway. Henry let himself out, made sure the door locked behind him, and walked out to the street.

Twenty-four he said to himself with grim satisfaction. *And the day is far from over.*

***

"Who can we get?" FBI Director Roland Lemp asked. "President wants a meeting in two hours and I damn well intend to have a good field agent along to take the heat. Got to be somebody has some experience on this gun stuff, but nobody that was part of that Waco disaster." Lemp sucked his teeth. "We have anybody around here with experience on that Idaho thing in '92? Anybody besides the sniper, I mean?"

"I doubt it, sir. I'll check the agent transfer records, but I don't think any of the local agents we've got here now were stationed in Idaho then. They did pull some men from other areas, but from around here? I don't think so. Wait a minute. That sex harassment course they're running this week at Quantico—there's agents from all over. Might find an experienced man in there, someone who was on the Ruby Ridge detail. Want me to check it out?"

"Yeah, and if there are any, check their files and get back to me before you call down there. I'd rather go it alone than find out too late I'm carrying extra baggage. If we find someone who reads clean, let's get him out of whatever class he's in and get him up here."

"Yessir."

June 16

"Mr. President? You said to wake you if there were any more...messages from this Wilson Blair."

"Exactly right. Has there been another?" he asked softly through the gap in the bedroom door. He did not want to wake his wife.

"This was distributed over the Internet some time in the last few hours." The Secret Service agent handed the Chief Executive the sheet of paper.

"Thanks, Ron," The President said. "Tell them I'll be there in twenty minutes." The agent nodded once and left.

The President began to read the message. The Secret Service agent had treated it like a privileged communique, but in fact it was already in tens of thousands of households across the nation. The President grimaced as his tired eyes finally focused on the paper. He was still not used to the concept of instantaneous national distribution of information by any person with access to a personal computer and a phone line.

```
                    Post-Op Briefing
                         by
                    Wilson Blair

To those of you who took my last message to heart, a quick critique:
Good jobs in Houston, Little Rock, and Pittsburgh. Keep at it and
they'll eventually get the message. I've heard rumors that some of them
want immunity, and we're working on how to deal with that issue.

Some of you other guys obviously want to be famous more than you want to
be successful. A standard velocity .22 on the way to work in the morning
is smart. An icepick in a movie theater is smart. An AK in an office at
the Federal Building is stupid. If you need a complete instruction set,
you shouldn't be tackling this kind of project. On a more upbeat note, I
hear noises that some of you want to cast the net wider. Sounds good to
me, just use sensible tactics.

END
```

"Immunity?" the President asked himself aloud. He folded the sheet of paper and closed the door softly so as not to wake his wife. She was still not used to emergencies cropping up at odd hours of the night. He wondered what the Internet author was talking about as he went back into his bedroom to shower and get dressed.

He knew it was going to be a very long day.

***

"Any problems?" Henry asked as Allen Kane slid into the booth across from him. He spoke softly without moving his lips very much.

"Just been shooting up your ammo," Kane said with a smile.

"Won't bitch at you for that. This time," he added with a raised eyebrow.

"How 'bout you—things go okay?" Allen Kane sounded concerned.

"Yeah. Better than I expected, actually." Henry took a deep drink of water. "Old Z-1 ran like a clock both ways." Mention of the motorcycle made him remember something. "You get a two-by-twelve to use for a ramp, and some tie-downs?"

"They're in the truck." Allen looked at his friend closely. He felt a sense of energy in Henry that was stronger than usual. "You seem more keyed-up than before." Henry nodded.

"Ray had some things to say that made me, ah...revise my immediate plans. I'll tell you about it later, see what you think."

"You want to head home today? Take turns and drive straight through? We could make it to your place by late tomorrow night—the truck's all loaded." Henry looked at the clock on the wall and considered the suggestion.

"Yeah," he said, his mind made up. "Let's do that. I'll meet you out of town, we'll roll the bike in the back where no one can see us do it. First, though, I want to eat. Lost my appetite the last couple of days, but it's come back with a vengeance. Does this place have steaks for breakfast?"

"We can find out," Allen answered as he picked up a menu.

***

"Charlie, I don't know any more about this than I did when you called half an hour ago, and I–"

"Sir?" the subordinate interrupted.

"Hold on a second," Dwight Greenwell said into the phone, then covered the mouthpiece as he looked up at the agent standing in his office doorway. "What?"

"Sir, they've found another one."

"Where?" he demanded. Greenwell's flared nostrils showed his rage, but the ATF Director did his best to hold it in check. He was too professional to shoot the messenger.

"Outside Pittsburgh, sir. An Agent Karbo. They foun–"

"*Pitts*burgh!" Greenwell almost yelled. He composed himself, took his hand off the phone's mouthpiece, and spoke into the instrument. "Charlie, I'll have to call you back." The Director hung up the phone and glared at the agent. "Talk."

"Police in Pennsylvania got a call there was a wrecked car upside down in a ravine. When they got to it, there was no sign of a driver. Wrecker was winching it up the hill, the trunk popped open, and Agent Karbo's body fell out. Hands were bound behind him with a coat hanger, and he'd been shot once with a .22 behind the ear. Cops checked the vehicle's VIN number, it was Karbo's agency car."

"I don't suppose the forensic guys got anything," Greenwell said, rubbing the bridge of his nose. The agent shook his head.

"No, sir. Not with all the people tramping around, and the car was wiped clean. Police even checked for prints on the inside of the trunk, but..." he shrugged, indicating there had been nothing to find.

"*Sir,*" Greenwell's secretary's voice crackled over the intercom. *"The President's on Line Four."*

"Got some newspapers," Henry said as he climbed into the elevated cab of the 2 1/2-ton army truck.

"I'll trade you," Allen said as he reached for the *USA Today* and handed Henry a hamburger. "Have they got that idiot Michael Gartner in there again, bleating for the repeal of the Second Amendment?" He looked at the paper's headline.

ATF Death Toll Continues To Rise
Suspect In Tibbs Killing Released

"Looks like they caught some guy and let him go," Allen said. "Says here, 'A man detained in Tuesday's killing of Ronald Tibbs has been released from custody and is no longer a suspect...'" Kane read aloud. "Says this guy got pulled over for speeding, cop noticed a 'strong gasoline smell', found a pressurized weed sprayer full of unleaded in the back of his car. Hmmm... 'Also in the suspect's vehicle was piece of notebook paper with the names and home addresses of four local ATF agents handwritten in blue ink.' I wonder why blue is significant," he added.

"Means the guy doesn't have a printer for his computer," Henry said. "Why did he put gasoline in a weed sprayer?"

"Let's see. 'Bomb and arson specialists say Tillotson intended to use the weed sprayer as a homemade flamethrower. "He had it all planned out," one officer said, who asked that his name not be relea-'"

"A homemade *flame*thrower!" Henry broke in. "Even Ragnar Benson wouldn't try *that!* Where's this guy from, Arkansas?" Allen Kane looked up.

"You already read the story," he said accusingly, then turned his attention back to the article.

"'Agent Tibbs' name, address, and unlisted telephone number were written on the paper found in Tillotson's vehicle, along with those of three other agents. A large "X" was drawn through Tibbs' name, and authorities initially considered Tillotson a prime suspect in the June 15 murder. At the time of the slaying, however, Tillotson was attending a wedding seventy miles away in Hagenport. "It was just a coincidence" the arresting officer said. Tillotson was fined $250 for unsafe storage of a flammable substance and released.'"

"So somebody beat him to it?" Henry asked.

"Looks that way. Says here 'Related Editorial, 18A'." Allen Kane turned the paper over and folded out the back page.

Today's Debate:
Terror On The Information Highway
Should Internet Access Be Restricted?

"Now they're talking about closing off the Internet," Kane said.

"That ought to make the public feel all warm and fuzzy about the government," Henry told him. "Where does USA Today stand on the issue?"

"'Our View: Don't Violate the First Amendment'."

"Guess that one hits a little too close to home," Henry said with a chuckle. He finished the rest of his hamburger and picked up the *New York Times*. Allen craned his neck to read the headline.

President To Appoint Task Force
Vows 'Justice Will Prevail' on ATF Killings

"The President playing CYA?" Allen asked, using the initials for Cover Your Ass.

"Looks that way. I'll read this in a minute," Henry said, handing the section to Allen. "I want to see what a good newspaper has to say about the ATF's current problems." He picked up the *Wall Street Journal* and turned to the editorial page.

Who is Wilson Blair?
Coworkers Silent About Electronic Message

"This is more like it," Henry said as he scanned the piece. Then his brows knitted together and a look came over his face that Allen could not interpret.

"What's it say?"

"For once, ATF has clammed up tighter than a bull's ass in fly time," Henry said, using one of Max Collins' similies. "Not one person in the whole agency is willing to say one word, on or off the record, about your old friend Wilson Blair. Director must have come down on them like a ton of bricks. This article is nothing but questions raised by the guys who write the editorial page." Henry chewed his lip. "I think ATF is scared."

"There's a news flash."

"No, I mean, I figured they'd say Blair couldn't possibly have written that Internet piece. Instead, they refuse to comment. That makes it look to all the world like he really did do it and it's a huge embarrassment to them."

"You going to release that tape?"

"Not yet." Henry closed his eyes, thinking. "Maybe the *Journal* could find the space to run a guest editorial."

"From that recent convert to civil rights issues, Wilson Blair?"

"None other." Henry took some french fries and nodded at his friend. "They probably won't run it, but hey, you never know. Damn, but I'm hungry," he said, finishing off the fries.

"Want me to get another round? I'm not full, either."

"That's not a bad idea. Let me have the *Times,* there." Allen Kane handed the heavy paper to his friend.

"*Jesus!*" Henry yelled when he saw the headline to an article at the bottom of the front page. "Look at this!"

Warsaw Ghetto Vet To Fill Post At Holocaust Center

Irwin Mann To Be Presidential Liaison

UPI

WASHINGTON, D.C. - Irwin Mann, one of the few survivors of the Warsaw ghetto resistance of April 1943, has been made spokesman for the Center for Holocaust Studies in Washington. He replaces Sol Schenker, who died in April of this year.

Mann, who has lived in Missouri since the late 1950s, was actively involved in the armed rebellion against the Nazis that resulted in the Warsaw ghetto being burned to the ground. Mann and a few others escaped through the sewers. Over 60,000 perished in the blaze.

The appointment has drawn criticism from some officials at the Center. "I myself would have expected an historian," said Michael Stix, a researcher at the Center. "And understand that Mr. Mann's actions, are, in part, what

See MANN, Page 5

"What is it? You know him?"

"That's my friend. Known him since I was a little kid. He and my uncle married sisters from Poland, back in the 'thirties." Henry read the article quickly.

"I can't believe it," Henry said as he finished the piece. "What's the next presidential appointment? Charlie Askins heading the Department of Immigration?" At this, Allen Kane broke out laughing and began to choke on his food.

"So what's the deal?" Kane said after he had recovered. "What's the story on this Mann guy that you're sort of related to?"

"Haven't I told you about Irwin?" Henry asked. "Nazis sent his wife off to be killed and tossed him into the Warsaw ghetto. When Irwin figured out that everyone in the ghetto was gradually getting sent off to the death camps, he joined up with a few others that wanted to fight back. Had about a dozen guys in his group, with a handful of guns they'd scrounged. Irwin killed a bunch of Krauts one at a time with a revolver, and got their group some more ordnance. There were a few groups like his—Mordecai Anielewicz was the overall leader. They held off the whole German army for a couple weeks with about one-tenth of what we got in the back of this truck. Irwin managed to get out through the sewers when the fires got close, but the others died. Krauts burned the whole Warsaw ghetto to the ground."

"Boy, doesn't that sound familiar."

"Yeah."

***

"What do you think about this guy on the computer network?" the man in the wheelchair asked. It was a question that was being posed around the country wherever people gathered, and the crowded Kansas City VFW hall was no exception. Billings sat at the end of the bar, sipping his beer silently. He was the only Korean War vet in the room, and was not a gregarious man in any case, but he liked the company of other ex-servicemen.

"Some kid, fooling around on his toy," one of the others answered.

"Homer thinks anything with more electronics in it than a Jeep alternator is some crackpot invention we don't need," a Vietnam radioman said with a laugh.

"Yeah, well, we did okay without all that fancy stuff George Bush had in Iraq."

"I wish we'd had some of those 'smart bombs' in '44."

"Amen to that." Others in the room put in their own comments.

"But what about this government fella sending computer messages?" the man in the wheelchair repeated. "What do you men think?"

"I got no quarrel with what he's saying."

"Me neither. My grandson came back from Iraq with a bunch of Ay-rab hardware, had to give it all up. Feds said he was lucky they wasn't goin' to put him in prison. Couple of men in suits never spent a day in the service."

"Far as I'm concerned, he should add a bunch a other federal agencies to his list." The owner of the now-defunct Ace Cleaners froze when he heard the words, the mouth of the beer bottle barely touching his lips. Billings sat the bottle down on the bar and turned his head towards the speaker.

"My son's 'bout to lose his farm," the man continued, "because he graded an acre and a half, and the government's sayin' he destroyed wetlands, or some such nonsense. Snotty little shit with a fifty-dollar haircut come out to his place with some kind a legal papers. If I had any sand, I'd poke the muzzle of my Garand in that bastard's ear, pull the trigger, an' say 'Fuck the lot of you, cancer'll get me 'fore you put me in front of a jury'."

"They'd go after your estate. Your kids wouldn't get a dime."

"Yeah, well maybe that's part a the reason I got a yella streak runnin' up my back," the man said with a look of disgust. Billings took a sip of his beer and watched silently as the others reacted to what had been said.

"What do you mean, Skeets?" one of the oldest men there said suddenly, "Federal government's paying most of the medical bills for the people in this place. You included."

"I'd pay my own bills with a smile if the bastards would leave me and my family alone." There were grunts of agreement around the room. Billings took a long pull from his beer and set the bottle down on the bar. A faint smile was on his face. For the first time since he had learned he would lose his dry cleaning business, his life had purpose.

June 19

"The President and the First Lady will be here in a few minutes," the Chief of Staff announced. "Please make yourselves comfortable." He turned around and left the room.

Roland Lemp gave Alex Neumann a look. The Director of the Federal Bureau of Investigation had not expected the President's wife to be present at the meeting for which they had been summoned. Both FBI men stood as if at attention.

George Cowan, the Director of the CIA, remained impassive. Cowan, a spare man in his late fifties with thinning brown hair, wore his trademark grey suit. Cowan's clothing always fit as if the man had recently lost fifteen pounds. He stood relaxed, with his hands in his pockets. He seemed personally untroubled by the current situation, and this was indeed the case. George Cowan had no intention of laying even one finger on the tar baby that currently faced the President.

Richard Gaines, the Democratic Congressman from Missouri, continued to stare around the room. It was only the second time he had been in the White House, and he had an uneasy feeling that he didn't belong there. The Secret Service agents that had looked at him when he had come in the room had made him especially nervous.

Lawrence Mills, the hawk-faced Secretary of the Treasury, stared at ATF Director Dwight Greenwell. Greenwell forced himself to hold the man's gaze yet remain impassive. He imagined that Mills held him responsible for the current situation. That assumption was fairly accurate.

Harrison Potter, the retired Chief Justice of the Supreme Court, smiled at Helen Schule, who was the only woman in the room. Potter, a widower, was an exceedingly handsome man who looked much younger than his seventy-nine years. His navy chalk-stripe suit was the most expensive garment in the room. Potter had a full head of white hair and strong features that sagged almost imperceptibly to one side. The Chief Justice had suffered a mild stroke the previous year. The doctors had correctly told him he was likely to enjoy a complete recovery. Only some muscle control had been affected and not Potter's substantial mental ability, but he had retired immediately from the Court. For Harrison Potter, it had been a perfect exit.

Helen Schule returned the smile. She was a freshman Congresswoman from Vermont, a Republican, and she was not at all certain why the President had summoned her to the White House. She had met the man only once, and that had been for all of ten seconds. Helen saw that the look in the Chief Justice's eyes seemed to acknowledge her puzzlement, and her smile involuntarily grew broader.

Carl Schaumberg, the long-standing Democratic Congressman from New York who was on the House Committee for Criminal Justice, leaned against the wall and smiled also. The effect, however, was not nearly so pleasant as with Helen Schule or Harrison Potter. Schoolmates when Schaumberg was a child had tagged him with the nickname 'lizard face', and as he had aged his visage had grown only more reptilian in appearance. He was the only person in the room who had specifically asked to be included on the task force.

Andrew Ward, the Republican Congressman from Indiana, and Jonathan Bane, his Democratic counterpart from Ohio, stood off to the side. Neither had any close ties to the President, but each man understood why he had been asked to participate.

The eleven people in the room quickly stood to attention as the President and his wife walked through the door. The First Couple were followed at a discreet distance by two Secret Service agents. Harrison Potter bowed slightly towards the First Lady. The President's slim, dark-haired wife gave him a warm smile in return. Like most people who met Potter in person, she could not help but like the man. Then she stepped to one side and faced her husband along with the rest of the group.

"Thank you," the President said without preamble, as his eyes scanned the twelve faces before him. "Thank all of you for dropping everything and coming here to help me tackle this problem." The way he said the words made each person feel that he or she really had made a conscious choice to join the Presidential task force, instead of merely jumping at the President's signal.

"I can only stay here a few minutes, as I have a press conference to go to. I expect you to plan on spending some serious time with me here tomorrow morning, however. I want everyone to be up to speed by then, and I want your thoughts well-organized." The people in the group nodded. They all knew the President's insistence on being given concise briefings.

"I think everyone here knows everyone else, but just in case any of you do not, I'll make quick introductions. All of you have met the First Lady, of course," he said with a smile. The Chief Executive then gave each person's name and position, pausing slightly each time to let the words sink in to anyone who might not have already known them.

"We have a serious problem on our hands, ladies and gentlemen. Twelve federal agents from the Bureau of Alcohol, Tobacco, and Firearms and one Missouri National Guard helicopter pilot are missing," he said, glancing down at the piece of paper he was holding, "along with the helicopter itself. Twenty-six ATF agents and two National Guard helicopter pilots are dead, and–" the President stopped when he noticed Roland Lemp's face twitch.

"What is it, Roland? Did I get something wrong?" the President asked. Roland Lemp was startled at the question, but he recovered quickly.

"I'm sorry, Mr. President," Lemp said, cursing himself silently for having let his face show any emotion, "but we just got word less than an hour ago. Two more ATF agents were murdered in Nebraska this morning. A suspect is in custody."

"Twenty-eight ATF agents, then," the President corrected himself. "Furthermore, someone claiming to be one of the missing agents has distributed inflammatory material via the electronic media, with the implication that he is at least in part responsible. Those are the known facts, and if I have left anything else out you can tell me about it later." He took the time to look each person in the room in the eye.

"Presidents have always been quick to appoint committees, as my predecessors often demonstrated. If ever there was a time when a Presidential Task Force was called for, though, it is now. Furthermore, there is a very good reason why I asked each one of you to be a part of it.

"I don't need to explain why I've called in the directors of the FBI, CIA, and ATF. Director Lemp asked that Agent Neumann be placed on this committee. Alex is a member of the FBI's Hostage Rescue Team and has field experience with terrorist situations. Since the FBI will be doing most of the actual investigating and is the primary federal law enforcement agency in this country, I readily agreed. I suspect that both men will still be overworked.

"Similarly, I asked Lawrence here to be a part of this team since the ATF is a part of Treasury, and it is his men who are being killed." Secretary of the Treasury Lawrence Mills nodded curtly. His face was respectful, but he would have preferred the President to have used the word 'murdered' instead of 'killed'.

"Harrison Potter, as retired Chief Justice of the Supreme Court, is going to keep me advised on the legal aspects of this situation. Several of you are lawyers, but Harry has a background in constitutional law no one here can match." The others looked at the white-haired man. Everyone knew the President trusted Potter's judgment, and listened to him more than he did anyone else in the room, with the possible exception of the First Lady.

"This committee also needs bipartisan support from elected representatives who have more contact with the public than do I or any of the Agency directors. Carl Schaumberg has served in Congress for many years, and has extensive experience on the house crime Committee." Schaumberg smiled at the recognition.

"Jon Bane, Andy Ward, and Dick Gaines," he said, nodding at the three men in turn, "I asked each of you to be here because the agents who initially turned up dead or missing all vanished from or died in Ohio, Indiana, and Missouri. I may need to be in even closer contact with the people in those states than I do with the rest of the nation. I hope the three of you can help me out." His eyes fell on the Republican Congresswoman from Vermont. It was obvious she was waiting to hear what he was going to say about her.

"Helen, there will be those in the media who say that you are on this task force because you are a woman." Helen Schule smiled. That thought had crossed her mind, along with the fact that three of the other four congressmen were Democrats, and another Republican was needed for balance on the committee. She also thought that being a freshman legislator might count in her favor here.

"They may say that," the President continued, "but the real reason you are on this committee is that Chief Justice Potter told me you should be on it, and I have learned to listen to Harry when he tells me I should do something." The President did not elaborate any further on the matter.

"One final thing: I encourage all of you to draw on any resources you can, but it is ultimately your assessments that I want to hear. Don't quote me any outside experts unless you're willing to defend what they say." He turned to the two FBI men.

"Roland, Alex, please bring the rest of the group up to date on what you have learned so far." His eyes scanned the eleven faces. "I'll see all of you tomorrow morning," he said in parting, and then the President and his wife left the room.

***

"I don't understand why you're having a dinner party for that...for the former Governor," Arthur 'B.I.' Bedderson amended.

"If you're going to talk that way about him, I'll take back my offer to put you on the guest list," his mother said with a smile. "He doesn't talk that way about you."

"Not to you, he doesn't," the big man shot back with a laugh. "We don't know what he says about me to *his* mother. Probably calls her up every day to tell her I cost him the election." The elderly woman laughed out loud at the image of Ken Flanagan dialing up his mother to whine about her son.

"To answer your question, I am having this dinner because I had promised that I would. If I had known at the time how the Governor treated you and your people, I might not have agreed to it. But I did, and I'm not about to go back on my word."

"Like he did, you mean." Lois Bedderson frowned at her son's comment. She had been outraged when Flanagan had appointed the legal counsel from one of the casino companies to head Missouri's Gaming Commission. It had made her consider, for a brief instant, that her son might be right about the man. But Lois Bedderson had been a

Democrat for over sixty years, and so she had championed Flanagan while wishing he had character.

"You just don't like him because he's a Democrat," she came back, but her retort lacked conviction.

"That's not the reason, and you know it, Mom. I'd back Harold in a heartbeat," he said, referring to the Democratic Missouri Senator who had championed concealed-carry legislation in 1995 and kept his promise to his supporters. "I don't like Flanagan because he's a *statist* Democrat," the man corrected. "And for the same reason, I don't like that jerk Jerry Abel because he's a statist Republican."

"Well, Abel *is* a jerk," she agreed, embracing common ground. Her son displayed both strong support for and virulent opposition to candidates in both parties, depending on how he squared their actions with the Bill of Rights. Lois Bedderson found this absence of allegiance to one party very unnerving.

"Hey," the big man said as his gave his mother a hug, "I won't do anything to embarrass you at your dinner. I'm always friendly to all these guys in the legislature. When they find out you got more juice than they thought, lot of times they change their tune. It's a lot easier for them if you haven't burned any bridges." His mother nodded in understanding.

"Flanagan's Chief of Staff told me how polite and decent you and your friends were up in the Capitol." She smiled sadly. "He even went so far as to tell me the Governor said he wished he'd been willing to talk to you. I think he regrets shutting you out."

"Of course he regrets it," Bedderson laughed. "It cost him the election."

***

"Hm, gh, wh...what?" Cindy Caswell mumbled as she came fully awake. It was the sound of a shot that had brought her out of her light sleep, but she did not know that. Then, a few moments later, she heard the distant sound of a large vehicle on the gravel road that went from the edge of Henry Bowman's property to his house. *Seats aren't too bad for this* she thought as she opened the door of her dark red Toyota, stepped out, and stretched. *Damn. Why didn't I remember he wouldn't be alone?* Henry Bowman was in the passenger seat of the approaching army truck. A man she had never seen before was driving.

Allen Kane killed the engine and the two men opened their respective doors and climbed down out of the tall vehicle.

"You just get here?" Henry asked. "We've just come straight-through from Idaho. Cindy, this is Allen Kane from Indiana. Allen, this is my friend Cindy Caswell."

"I wish I had a welcoming committee like this at *my* house," Allen said with a laugh. Cindy smiled.

"Pleased to meet you," she said as she held out her hand. Allen shook it before he realized that his own hands were far from clean. Cindy did not notice. "I've been checking on your place every night before I go in to work. I read about all that stuff in the papers, and I thought you could use an extra set of eyes here until you got back."

"Krause was supposed to be taking care of that. Speaking of which—how'd you get in? They had a new lock on the gate, which I just shot off to get through." Cindy smiled and held up a key.

"I talked the Sheriff out of a copy. He believed me when I told him we were friends. UPS dropped off a package for you. It's in my trunk."

"Grab it, and let me open up the house and get the alarm turned off, and you can sit in there if you want while Allen and I unload my stuff. Then I'm going to take a long-overdue shower and put on some fresh clothes, and after that I'm going to throw some steaks on the grill. Allen and I haven't had much to eat today."

"Show me where they are and I'll take care of that while you unload and clean up." Henry gave her a look. *Just because I overcooked them once* Cindy thought as her face flushed.

"That's okay, Cindy."

"Henry Bowman, I am perfectly capable of cooking steaks for you and your friend without ruining them," she said irritably. "Just because I don't often eat meat myself, and one time I let the hamburgers stay on a little too long is no reason to assume I can't be trusted at a barbecue grill. I watch your house for you, and the first thing you do when you get back is act like I'm an idiot."

"Tell Cindy how you like your steaks cooked, Allen," Henry said. "'Well done' would be a good answer," he added in a stage whisper. The three all started laughing.

***

"Henry, have you been reading the papers?" Cindy asked as she flipped the steaks over on Henry's aluminum thawing plate. The sound of Allen Kane's shower running came faintly through the open door. "Do you know what's been going on while you've been away?" *You'd have to have been on an island not to have heard about it* she thought. Henry sat at his kitchen table and sipped at his orange juice.

"Something about ATF agents shooting themselves down over my woods, and some others gone missing, and now one of the missing agents is sending out messages on the Internet about how ATF is corrupt and out of control, and he's going to do something about it. Some guy named Blair. It's in all the papers, and Krause filled me in on what happened here."

"Not 'going' to do something about it, Henry," she said as she sat down across from him. "He's been *doing* it. Killed something like eight or ten ATF agents in a few days, and published the whole list of all the other ones in the country on the Internet. Some people have apparently been jumping in to help." *Damn I wish he was alone* Cindy thought again.

"Didn't they catch a couple of those guys? That's what I heard somebody say."

"Two of the copycats. And they were stupid." *Might as well spell it out* Cindy thought when she saw Henry staring at her. "Look," she said, glancing in the direction of the guest room where the water was still running, "I wanted to talk to you for a while in private, but it looks like I'll have to give you the short version while your friend's still in the shower. I think this Wilson Blair guy is on to something, but he's focused on the wrong people. He's concentrating on ATF agents 'cause he was one, but they're not the real problem. The ones who really ought to squirm are those reptiles up in the Capitol building."

"I assume you're talking about getting screwed over in Jefferson City year after year on the concealed-carry bill."

"That's exactly what I'm talking about." *At least he hasn't yet told me I'm nuts* she thought.

"Why are you telling me this? Isn't that how the other guys got caught—running their mouths? If you want to go pop Governor Flanagan, you should just go do it and keep your mouth shut. Nobody knows, nobody can rat you out. Keep your mouth shut and you'll never spend the night in jail. Goes double if you're a woman."

"I know that," Cindy said. "But I don't think you'd sell me out, and...I need your help. Not help doing the actual killing," she said quickly, "but...advice beforehand. So I don't do anything stupid." *God, didn't that sound moronic* she said to herself.

"You mean anything stupid apart from plotting murder in the first place, I assume," Henry said mildly. "You're forgetting that helping plan a murder makes me equally guilty, and now I'm the one who has to worry the rest of my life that you'll get your tit in a wringer about something else and serve me up to the cops to get out of it. Headlines would read, ' Machine gun dealer forces stripper to do his killing'. Forget it, Cindy." *He still hasn't said he's against the principle* Cindy thought. *Time to go for broke.*

"You have a guarantee that that won't happen," she said softly. "When I met you at AA and told you about what happened to me in Vegas, I didn't give you the whole story. I think you suspected that, and I think you did your own checking and found out most of the truth. That was when you told me about the killing of Joe Columbo's would-be murderer, and of the benefits of keeping one's mouth shut."

"I remember that."

"Well, just in case you didn't find out exactly what happened, I'll tell you. While Tony Farratto was lying in bed and I was sitting on his face, I took out one of the hardwood spikes I was using to hold my hair up and I drove it straight down his eye socket and into his brain, where I stirred it around until I was sure he was dead. Then I turned on the shower, got dressed, and left town. I know from you that Sal Marino took his body somewhere and set it up to look like Tony was shot to death, and then took over Tony's business. Sal isn't looking for me and wouldn't care if somebody told him where I was.

"But Tony Farrotto still has living relatives, and I think you could easily get word to them about what really happened, and I think they would know who to ask the right questions of to see if the story was true. And I think that after that happened, I would have a more unpleasant death than I can possibly imagine, and there would be nothing I could do about it." Henry nodded, but remained silent for a long while.

"What you did then was survival. That's a lot different from killing a man because of how he voted on something." Cindy Caswell shook her head.

"Not on those kind of votes. Wheelchair ramps, or warning labels on cigarettes, sure." *Got to make him see this* she thought. *Don't want Henry to think I'm this psycho killer bitch from hell. Then again, maybe I am, now.* Cindy took a deep breath.

"I was snatched off a street in Chicago when I was eighteen years old. At that time I didn't realize that no one besides me had any compelling interest in stopping something like that from happening. So for the next two and a half years, I was passed around like a plate of cookies to a bunch of men who order people beaten or killed as easily as you or I would order a pizza. These men were free to do anything they wanted to me. Which they did. Slapping was pretty common, and a few liked to use lit cigarettes. Any one of them could have killed me for pleasure, and my owner—that's what he was—would have acted the same as if his best friend had spilled grape juice on his carpet.

"I manage to get out of that living nightmare with most of my sanity, and all I really want to do is keep the same thing from happening again. But the wise men in our state government say 'Guns are for the police, honey, they're the professionals. Maybe you and that girl you live with should stay inside at night'." She stared Henry in the eye, and at that moment the sound of running water stopped. Allen had just finished his shower.

"I'll sleep like a baby afterwards," Cindy told him, "but I need you to tell me what to do." *Say yes, damn it.*

"What makes you think I'd have a better plan than you would?" he asked. Cindy rolled her eyes.

"Henry, you know about that stuff. You just do. You also have a very...orderly mind. What? What's so funny?" she demanded as Henry broke out laughing.

"Thank you. I think," he added. "One question," he said, after he had regained his composure. "Will you do whatever I say?" Cindy thought about that for a moment. *It's what I've been begging him for, isn't it?*

"Yes," she said finally.

"Then I want you to sit down with Allen after he gets dressed, and I want you to tell him exactly what happened to you in Las Vegas and I want you to tell him what you want me to help you do. And while the steaks are cooking, you're going to watch a video-tape I made that I think you'll find very interesting. Then over dinner, we're going to talk about some things."

"But I don't wan–" Cindy stopped in mid-sentence. "I know what I said, but..." *Why bring this other guy into it?* she thought, but left the fear unspoken.

"The other thing is," Henry said gently, "the Missouri legislators are going to have to wait. There's bigger fish to fry in Washington." *Washington!* Cindy thought. *If Henry wants to go after the feds, he and his friend must have been thinking about this too.* She nodded once.

"I'll go tell Allen." She stood up and walked into the living room.

***

"I still can't believe it," Cindy Caswell said as she finished the last of her salad. "And the third helicopter isn't off missing somewhere, it's at the bottom of the quarry out there? Jesus!" Henry pushed his chair back from the table and drained the last of his ice-water.

"The question now is, do you really want to hook up with Allen and me on this deal? If you pull some solo number on your own and keep your mouth shut, you'll never get caught. The two of us, on the other hand, are going to be setting off a whole raft of alarm bells, and right now the feds are standing around at a bunch of murder scenes where I've already been." Henry scratched his jaw as he stared at the floor, then looked up.

"For all we know, the President will invoke the Emergency Powers Act and make everyone in the country give the feds a hair sample for DNA matching. I was pretty careful, and looked real close, but I might well have left a hair or two at one of those places. And that's just one possibility. There are probably another hundred I haven't thought of." Cindy nodded as she considered that.

"Won't they be stretched pretty thin?"

"That's the plan," Allen Kane broke in, "but Henry's right. These guys have an ungodly amount of manpower. Everything else just got put on next-to-zero priority. Counterfeit team, organized crime case squad, auto theft crew, all those feds have been yanked off what they're doing and put on the Who's Whacking ATF Guys detail."

"I'm in, fellas. I found out in Vegas that I was one of Sal's throwaways, and it was just a goddamned miracle that he decided to keep me around instead of leaving me in an alley with a bullet in the back of my head. Ever since I learned that, it's seemed like what-ever time I've got left is a bonus. I'm going to take the advice I saw on a license plate, once: Live Free Or Die."

"New Hampshire," Allen said. "Used to be, at least."

"That may sound good," Henry said quietly, "but you're going to feel a whole lot different in your guts when the time comes—a whole lot different than you do right now. This isn't an Outfit wiseguy who's about to torture you in the middle of a rape. This is premeditated murder of people with families, and lovers, and kids in nursery school, and worries about the future, just like us. And on top of that, these are people who champion the democratic process. You are going to be killing a man because he voted the wrong way."

"No," Cindy said without hesitation, "I am going to be killing a man because he voted away something that was not his to vote on in the first place. The people making the laws think that anything is okay if they can get 51% of the legislators or the people to go along with it. One hundred per cent of the people making the rules in the Vegas outfit thought it was just fine for me to be locked in a room and taken out when it suited them. I've had enough of that."

"Sounds good in theory," Henry agreed. "However, if you told *People* magazine the story of your Las Vegas ordeal and what you did about it, you'd be hailed as the country's bravest woman. When we get found out—and let's not mince words, we probably will— we are going to have well over one hundred million American citizens believe we are the most evil people this country has ever seen."

"There'll be a few who think differently."

"I think she's with the program," Allen said. Henry smiled in spite of himself.

"In that case," he asked, "How do you feel about having sex with some of these guys? It'll make it a lot easier."

"No problem," Cindy said immediately. She turned to Allen. "I enjoy sex with women. With men, there's no pleasure for me, but it's no worse than, say, shoveling snow off the sidewalk."

"Wish my ex-wife had liked it that much," Allen said dryly. *I like this guy* Cindy thought as she burst out laughing. Allen and Henry joined in. Breaking the tension felt good to all three of them.

"What do you have in mind?" she finally asked Henry.

"Got a few ideas. Can you take time off on short notice without raising any eyebrows?"

"No problem. I haven't had a vacation in almost a year. That's almost unheard of among the girls at the club. I'll tell Troy tonight."

"How about we shove off tomorrow, then? Allen and I can work out the details tonight while you're at work. When do you have to be at the club?"

"Eleven-thirty. I've been working midnight-to-close lately."

"Four hours," Henry said, looking at the clock on the wall and chewing on his lip.

"What're you thinking?"

"Want to do a little tune-up run before you go in to work, get your adrenaline going?" Henry asked.

"Such as?"

"U.S. Congressman Jerry Abel, guy who the gun groups around here got elected a while back. Soon as he got in office, he went and voted for that stupid magazine ban in '94 and the bill to throw out the Fourth Amendment in '95."

"The dorky-looking lawyer? Lives west of St. Louis?"

"That's the one. His wife's a lawyer, too, and I don't think he'd still be married to her if he wasn't afraid it would hurt his career. Jerry likes to drink, and I'm pretty sure I know where. Think you could pick him up, get him to take you somewhere for a quickie in his car?"

"Worth a try. I've got a bunch of different outfits for the club in my bag. What kind of girl would be most apt to get his motor running, do you think?"

"Rhonda's a frump that looks like she'd rather suck a hundred lemons than one cock, so almost anything should work. I would say that athletic, cheerful, and straight-forward about liking sex ought to do the trick on Mr. Abel. And on 98% of the rest of the men in this country, for that matter."

"Say a young girl in a thin cotton dress, impressed with his important position and who finds boys her own age childish? Something like that?"

"You clearly don't need my advice."

"Anything I can do to help on this?" Allen Kane asked.

"Yeah—help Cindy practice. Go sit on the couch, like it was a car seat. You're going to be the esteemed Congressman. I forget what he drives, but it's something big and American. Cindy, you're going to get him to move away from the steering wheel and into the passenger seat so you can get astride him. Allen, when she's on top of you, have her practice finding the 'V' under your ribcage in a hurry. Heart's the way to do it, I think," Henry said as he went into the kitchen.

"What're you going to be doing?" Cindy asked.

"Putting one of my halfway-decent kitchen knives on a coarse grinder. Turn it into something that a crackhead whore from East St. Louis might carry, with friction tape on the handle. Best place to leave a murder victim is in an area with a lousy forensics depart-ment, preferably in such a condition that it looks like he brought his troubles on himself."

"I told you you had an orderly mind," Cindy said. She turned to Allen Kane, who was sitting on the couch and looking nervous. "Don't look that way. We'll practice with-out the knife." *Men are so predictable* she thought cheerfully.

"That's not what's worrying me."

"Oh, *that*," Cindy said with a smile. "Don't worry. I'm a professional." She settled onto Allen Kane's lap. "Well," she said, laughing. "Let's hope the Congressman has the same reaction."

***

"Third time is indeed the charm," Henry said as he looked over Allen's shoulder and through the window of the crowded West County restaurant. The bar was four-sided, with two women in open-necked tuxedo shirts standing in the center serving drinks. "He's about five feet from the corner on the far side. Wire-rimmed glasses, blue suit, white shirt, red tie, talking to the bald Jewish guy."

"Got him," Cindy said. *Skinnier than I expected* was her first impression.

"Call me when they leave," Henry said to Allen, then turned and headed back out into the parking lot as his friends walked towards the bar's entrance.

Allen went in first and immediately walked to the men's room. Cindy waited a few moments, then opened the door and headed for the bar. Jerry Abel's eyes slid reflexively across her, as they did with every new entrant to the room. *Smile, and look him in the eyes, but hold it just a beat longer than normal.* She found a stool at the bar with a half-finished drink and a few bills in front of it, and asked for a seltzer with lime.

Jerry Abel's eyes fell on Cindy Caswell repeatedly over the next twenty minutes. Each time, she held his gaze, but then glanced nervously towards the area where bar patrons sat at small tables. *That ought to about do it* she thought as she patted her mouth with her napkin and slid off the stool.

"Excuse me," Cindy said as she squeezed past the Congressman on her way to the women's room.

"They're probably violating the fire code with this size crowd," Abel said with a big smile. "May I b–" He stopped what he had been about to say in mid-sentence as he felt the young woman press a folded business card into his hand. His fingers closed involuntarily around it as she brushed past him with a nod.

Congressman Abel took a sip of his scotch, looked absentmindedly around at some of the other bar patrons, and then unfolded the card under the bar rail and read it. *My ex-husband's best friend is sitting at a table over to your left, so I'd rather not stay here. If you'd like to go somewhere else, bring your car to the southwest corner of the lot.* Congressman Abel turned the business card over and read the name and company printed on it.

"Check, please," Abel said to the bartender. He paid his tab, left a generous tip, glanced in the direction of the rest rooms, and headed for the exit.

***

"I'm glad you wanted to leave," Cindy said as she slid into the front seat of the Lincoln and extended her right hand in greeting. "Christine Weld," she added, using the name of the woman realtor whose card Henry had found in his desk drawer.

"Pleased to meet you. Jerry Abel."

"I hope you're not too surprised. I know you're married—I mean, I can see you're wearing a wedding ring. But I was staring at you, and..." She let the sentence hang, then looked down in her lap. "I just wanted to go in for a quick drink, talk about something besides real estate, but my ex-husband..." She shivered. "He's got a restraining order, but I don't trust him to obey it. He likes to spy on me, and one black eye and one broken eardrum was plenty. Thanks for meeting me out here," Cindy said again with a warm smile.

"I'm co-sponsoring a federal anti-stalking law," Abel said. "Your case is just one more example of why we really need it."

"Do you think you'll have the votes to pass it?" Cindy answered. *Like making one more thing against federal law will do anything about the problem* she thought. *Idiot.*

"I'm almost sure of it. There are a lot of women in your situation, and it's time we did something for them," Abel said. Cindy smiled. *He's happy that the adoring girl recognizes his position in the legislature.*

"I'm always worried about it, particularly when I'm out showing empty houses to men I've never met before."

"Then you're the perfect example of why we need the new law."

"Thank you." *For nothing* she added mentally. *You didn't do a damn thing to help us get a concealed carry law here. Asshole.*

"Where shall we go, Christine?"

"You decide," Cindy answered as she laid her hand on the Congressman's thigh.

***

"God, I can't believe how long you can last," Cindy said as she rode Jerry Abel's erection and pinched his nipples. "And it's been such a long time for me." Before he could reply, Cindy covered his mouth with hers and resumed probing with her tongue. She ran her fingers through the hair on his chest and pushed his unbuttoned dress shirt farther apart. "I want you to come in my mouth," she said suddenly as she uncoupled herself from the Congressman and slid to her knees on the passenger-side floorboard. Abel made a noise in the back of his throat.

Cindy Caswell quickly peeled off the condom she had put on Jerry Abel ten minutes earlier, and threw it on the floor. Holding him with her left thumb and forefinger, she took his entire length in her mouth with one smooth motion as she reached into her purse with her free hand. Cindy had no difficulty finding what she wanted; there were only two items in the handbag.

"I want to try something," she said a few moments later when she took a break from her efforts. The object she had in her hand looked like a miniature bicycle clip for securing a cyclist's trouser cuffs. It was a circle of spring steel with a slight gap where the ends were bent in tiny reverse curves. *I wonder what other things Henry keeps in the drawer on his nightstand* Cindy thought as she pulled the ends apart with her fingers and slid the metal loop over Abel's erection. The spring steel was under tension and it firmly encircled the base of his shaft. "This will keep you hard even afterwards." *Like for the rest of your life.*

"Lean back and close your eyes," Cindy commanded as she smudged the fingerprint she had left on the metal. "I'm going to see if I can do this with no hands." *As if that takes any particular skill* she added mentally. She glanced up to make sure that the Congressman was complying with her instructions, then her lips once again traveled down the length of his penis, this time until they touched cool metal. Cindy's heart was beating faster as she slid her right hand into her purse for the second time. Her fingers closed around the handle of Henry's reground kitchen knife. *Feels almost sticky. Tacky, that's the word* Cindy thought as she felt the cloth friction tape wrapped around the wood. Cindy increased both the movement of her head and the suction she was applying. Soon it was obvious that Jerry Abel was on the brink of orgasm.

"Hold it..." Cindy urged him. Abel clamped his teeth and eyes shut in a grimace, trying to delay the climax that was about to burst from his loins. As the Congressman threw his head back and tried to halt the impending release, Cindy Caswell held the six-inch blade so that the flat side was up. Without hesitating, she jammed the knife into the soft spot just below Jerry Abel's sternum. When the steel was all the way in, Cindy yanked the handle sideways, to Abel's right. Congressman Abel opened his eyes and his jaw dropped as the cutting edge neatly bisected his heart.

Cindy pressed against the dashboard, wanting to stay away from any torrent of gore that was going to gush out of the corpse. With the heart cut in half, though, Abel's circulatory system was shut down, and gravity alone had a much milder effect. A small trickle of blood slowly oozed from around the blade and ran down the late Congressman's chest and into his lap. *Just like Henry said it would, if I wrecked the heart straight off* she thought. Cindy reached over to her left and pulled the passenger-side door handle. Then she rose up off the floor and got her legs out onto the pavement. *Whatever you do, don't vomit inside the car. That's what Henry said, too* she reminded herself. *Funny, I don't feel queasy at all.* Cindy slid the rest of the way out of the car, reached back in and retrieved her purse, then closed the door behind her without letting it latch. When she turned around, she saw Henry and Allen walking towards her across the near-empty parking lot.

"Nice job," Henry said with a nod as he looked at the corpse. "Where's the rubber?"

"Oh. Uh, on the floor somewhere."

Henry knelt down beside the open door and began rummaging.

"It's, uh, over on the driver's–" She stopped in mid-sentence when she realized that Henry was going through the dead man's pockets. It was easy, as Abel's suit pants were already off and wadded into a ball on the floor.

"Here," Henry said, holding his hand out behind him without turning around. In it was the business card Cindy had used to pick up the Congressman in the bar. Next, Henry handed Allen the dead man's billfold, money clip, and address book, and Allen put them in his own jacket pocket. Then Allen stepped back as Henry dropped the condom onto the pavement. Allen wiped the door handle with the corner of a terrycloth towel, then handed the towel to Henry. He quickly ran it over the door panel, lock, and handle before pushing the door closed.

"You touch anything else?" he asked as he walked around to the driver's side and opened the door.

"I don't think so. No."

"Probably won't need this at all," Henry said as he rolled up the towel and wedged it between the driver's seat cushion and the body. It was to prevent any blood from seeping over onto where Henry was going to sit. He looked carefully at the corpse, realizing something.

"You didn't let him come."

"No. I did it right before." Henry thought about that for a moment.

"I like that even better," he said. "Okay. Follow me, and if a cop gets behind us, one of you do something mildly illegal like driving twenty over. Probably be better if it was Cindy, since she's in her own car." Henry reached in through the driver's door and pushed Congressman Abel's corpse so it fell over on its side across the passenger seat, then checked to be sure the towel made an effective barrier. "We get across the river, Cindy, you peel off and head up north to the sex-shop strip. Then we'll meet you at the Denny's south of the club. You know where it is." He turned to Allen. "Don't lose me, okay?"

"I'll try not to." Henry nodded at this, then slid in behind the steering wheel of the late Congressman's Lincoln and started the engine.

***

"I got everything we needed," Cindy said as she sat down in the booth next to Allen. "I think I made the cashier's day."

"The rest of the clientele in there all a bunch of shitbums?"

"A lot of guys in business suits, as a matter of fact. Couple women, too. You know— hair in curlers, too much makeup, hoping for a miracle."

"Like we all need," Allen broke in.

"So no trouble finding one open this late?" Henry asked.

"Jesus, Henry, where have you been? They're *all* open this late—this is when they do their best business. People in Brooklyn, Illinois, would all be on welfare and the city would be broke if it weren't for the titty bars, massage parlors, and sex-toy shops."

"Sorry. I wasn't thinking." Henry tipped up his glass and finished his orange juice. "Is the next part going to be a problem?" he asked.

"If management finds out, I'll get fired, but I don't guess that's what you meant."

"No," Henry said with a small smile.

"I'll be fine. I have a few 'regulars' who I think would do anything I asked them to. For a couple of free private dances..." She laughed as she left the sentence unfinished. "The problem will be what they expect the next time I see them." Cindy looked over at

Allen. "You know, this idea sounded crazy at first, but now it makes perfect sense. I never would have thought of it, though."

"Most people's minds don't work like his."

"Sometimes I feel lucky it works at all," Henry said good-naturedly. "How about the time off part? If that's a problem, I can do this alone."

"No, they'll give me a few weeks off on short notice. I've been the most reliable one there for a long time now. Some of the girls are no-shows every few days."

"Just like anything. Treat it like a real business and you end up with real money." He turned to Allen. "Cindy now has a stock portfolio worth over four hundred thousand dollars." Allen Kane's eyes grew wide.

"A dollar at a time," Cindy Caswell said with a smile.

"I guess I'll stop wondering if you feel exploited," Kane said. "How do you avoid the government giving you a hard time?"

"I buy money orders at Seven-Eleven, and deposit them in a variable annuity. No reporting requirements and no taxes until I take the money out. Henry found that deal for me," she added.

"Interesting," Kane said, clearly impressed. "And that reminds me," he said as he reached into his pocket. "Here." He slid Congressman Abel's money clip off a sheaf of bills and handed her the money. "You earned it." Cindy looked at Henry, who nodded.

"Allen's right. This is going to go a lot better with you than if we were winging it, as you demonstrated an hour ago. And whatever's there," he said, nodding at the bills in Cindy's hand, "is going to look like peanuts when the feds start offering rewards."

"How high do you think they'll go?" Allen Kane asked with a smile. Henry considered the question for a while before answering.

"Not high enough."

***

"Would you like a private, David?" Cindy asked as she sat on the man's lap and ran her index finger down his chest.

"Of course, Dusty."

"Then I've got a surprise for you. Three for the price of one. I want to make you come tonight." The customer's eyes got wide. Cindy smiled as she felt him start to grow hard underneath her thigh. "Here," she said, gently slipping a condom packet into his hand underneath the table. "Go in the men's room, take your underwear off, and put this on so you don't stain your suit." She grinned wickedly. "I'm really horny tonight," she added, and stood up to let the excited insurance agent out of his chair.

***

"Ohhh...you know what I'm going to do after we've both come?" Cindy whispered as she rocked rhythmically astride her customer, grinding her G-string against his crotch. *He's getting ready* she thought as the third song started. David had his teeth clenched and his eyes shut. "I'm going to wait for you by the men's room so you can give me the rubber. Then I'm going to take it in the dressing room and rub your come all over my chest. Oh, God, I can't wait to do that." *That did it* Cindy thought as she felt his erection pulsate.

"I'm coming," she moaned, and flexed her vaginal muscles several times. *Just in case he's really paying attention* she thought with a smile.

June 20

"Shit," the patrolman said, drawing out the word until it was several syllables long. "Look at this." He used his flashlight to lift up the door handle and open the Lincoln's door. "Looks fresh."

"Damn right," the second man agreed. "Never saw no dead man still had a hard dick." The first cop started laughing.

"White boy, look like he got all the money in the world, want to come over here to East St. Louis, get him some twenty-dollar strange stuff. Crazy damn world."

"You got that right. I'll go call it in. Then we go look for Lawanda, and maybe Sharlene. See what they know."

The two East St. Louis policemen would start laughing even harder when the registration on the vehicle came back over the radio. Neither, however, would be particularly surprised.

***

"Five of them?" Henry asked incredulously as Cindy handed him the condoms, each one knotted about halfway down.

"Best night I've had in months. None of them would let me leave with just the twenty-five. One guy gave me two hundred. I made twelve hundred dollars tonight, after tipping all the bartenders and staff. What's the plan?" she asked as she watched Henry pack the condoms in an ice-filled vacuum bottle.

"Allen's off getting two airline tickets," Henry said, tamping more ice into the glass-lined container and screwing on the lid. "Commuter flights are about fifty bucks, so they don't bat an eye when you pay cash. You and I are going to Chicago. Once we get there, I'll book us to D.C."

"Sounds like a winner."

"I guess I better check this through, with the other goodies," he said, holding up the bottle.

"Oh, I don't know, Henry. They probably get people carrying things like this on board all the time, don't you think?"

***

"You're up early."

"Hard to lose a thirty-year habit," Billings cheerfully told his wife. "And I got a few errands to run. You need me to pick up anything on my way home?"

"Some paper towels, and we're almost out of soda."

"Okay." He kissed his wife and was out the door. The errand he planned was one that he had attempted before, but there had always been a snag somewhere. Billings didn't mind. With the dry cleaning business gone, he had lots of time, and he was a patient man.

At the end of the block, Billings came to a complete stop before proceeding through the intersection. He was driving a six-year-old Chevrolet four-door sedan. There were two large cardboard boxes full of old newspapers sitting beside him on the front seat. A steel tube spanned the width of the car above the rear-seat windows, and on it hung three suits and a dozen shirts that blocked the view out the back. These accessories would serve an important function when he was ready.

For now, Billings concentrated solely on reconnaissance.

***

"Returning the twenty-fourth?" the American Airlines ticket agent asked.

"That's the plan," Henry answered as he handed her the credit card, "but we may end up staying longer. Will there be any problem exchanging the tickets for a later return date?"

"No. Since you're paying the full fare, there aren't any restrictions." She looked at the name on the credit card before handing it back. "Vous etes francais, Monsieur Kreyder?"

"Seulement technicalement," Henry said, inventing some pidgin French before switching back to English. "I was born there, but my family left France for good when I was less than a year old, and I haven't been back since. Where am I headed?"

"After you take your tickets and bags over to the other counter, you'll be going to Gate 57 on the 'B' Concourse," the agent said with a smile. "You have a little over half an hour. Enjoy your trip," she added, almost as an afterthought. The way she said it implied she could not fathom why anyone would want to travel to the nation's capital, but wished the best for anyone who actually did.

"Thank you," Henry said as he palmed the tickets. "I will." He slipped one of the tickets to Cindy as he passed by her on the way to the check-in counter.

"Any luggage to check through?" the agent asked. Cindy Caswell gave her a grin as she slid the single bag through the opening in the counter. It was of popular manufacture and had once been advertised in a TV spot that had featured a gorilla. The identifying tag attached to the handle was a cardboard one provided by Trans World Airlines, folded over for security. Inside, it listed a fictitious Chicago address.

"Have you ever met a woman, other than a stewardess, who could travel with just a carry-on?" *Particularly when she wants to travel with a bunch of bondage equipment, butt plugs, and a quarter-pound of cocaine* she added silently.

"I have to ask," the woman said, laughing as she hooked the routing tape around the handle. "It's my job."

Two queues to Cindy's right, Henry Bowman was checking an identical suitcase with another airline employee. His bag was packed with nondescript clothing, a small shaving kit, and some reading material. Nothing inside it gave any clue as to its owner or origin. The TWA tag on the handle listed the owner as Didier Kreyder, whose address was a post office box in the Boston area. In about five hours, the tag would be gone and the suitcase would be placed in the Unclaimed Baggage office at Dulles airport, where it would remain.

The real Didier Kreyder had died of influenza in 1955 at the age of five months, and was buried in a cemetery outside Paris. His birth certificate was one of four Henry had acquired while on a European concert tour with the Amherst College Glee Club in the summer of 1973.

***

Billings followed the other car until it pulled into the lot of the tall office building. The route was the same as it had been the day before. This time out, Billings had spotted another likely site for what he had planned.

He smiled as he cut the wheel and drove away from the parking lot.

"This is going to take some time," The President said as he unbuttoned his collar. "You men might want to loosen your ties. The air conditioning in here is a little weak." Some of the people in the room shifted slightly in their chairs, but the men's hands all stayed in their laps or on the notes they held. No one there was about to look less than his best in front of the President of the United States. "Talk to me," the President said as he scanned the faces before him. Dwight Greenwell cleared his throat. The task force had decided the previous afternoon that Greenwell should speak first. What he had to say was important background for what was to follow.

"Mr. President, I knew Wilson Blair for sixteen years," the ATF Director began. The President raised an eyebrow at Greenwell's choice of tense for the verb he had used, but said nothing. Greenwell took a deep breath and rushed on.

"There is no possibility that the man I knew could have been responsible for the message that was sent out over the Internet. Blair would have had a list of agents at ATF, however. That leads me to the inescapable conclusion that Wilson Blair is dead, and whoever killed him stole the list and distributed it." Greenwell saw that the President expected him to explain.

"Wilson Blair did not, as the message claimed, work for years and years in the tobacco section of ATF and suddenly get transferred to firearms. Lower-level agents at ATF are trained in all three sections from the moment they are hired and rotate departments every few months. Supervisory agents such as Blair almost always remain in one section. Wilson Blair had been a supervisory agent in the firearms division since 1987, and he had worked in the firearms division for quite some time before that."

"I see."

"Wilson Blair was also one of ATF's most dedicated men. I checked his record, and his agents have been responsible for over eight hundred arrests for federal firearms law violations. The conviction rate on those arrests is 99.7%, which is the third-highest at ATF." Helen Schule turned her head at this number, not certain she had heard correctly.

"I'm sorry, but—a ninety-nine point seven percent conviction rate?" she broke in. "And that's *third* highest at ATF?"

"That's correct, ma'am. Wilson Blair was a professional, and some gun nut killed him for it. It could have been any one of them. The bombing in Oklahoma in the Spring of 1995 showed us that." The two men from the FBI nodded at this comment. The Chief Executive remained impassive.

"Mr. President, anyone who saw that Internet message knows it was a transparent attempt to incite people to attack ATF agents. The gun nuts in this country stick together, and that is one of the things that makes this situation so dangerous." He licked his lips nervously.

"So far, we have refused to issue any official comment on the Internet message, and that has been a public relations nightmare for us. With your permission, sir, we would like to issue a press release that the Internet message was not authored by Wilson Blair or any other member of ATF, and also counter the outright slander of the ATF that the message conveys." Greenwell was trying to sound as mild as possible, but half the people in the room knew that the President's 'No Comment' order had made the ATF Director furious.

"I know it's been tough for you, Dwight," the President agreed, without speaking to his request. "What about the claims of entrapment, and the part about three raids using illegal wiretaps, blank warrants, and planting evidence?"

"Complete lies. The paranoid gun nuts in this country have been saying that about us for decades."

"I'm not sure I understand—were there actually three raids scheduled or was that made up as well?"

"No, no sir, I'm sorry," Greenwell said hurriedly. "There *were* three raids planned, but they didn't happen. Well, the third one did, but..." His voice trailed off as he realized he had nothing to say about the disaster involving the helicopters.

"So who were these three men Blair's team planned to raid?"

"Three machine gun dealers, Mr. President," Greenwell said confidently, feeling himself on firmer ground now. "Three of the largest in the country, as a matter of fact."

"And who had these men been selling machine guns to—terrorists? Drug gangs? Organized crime syndicates?"

"Uh, no, Mr. President. Not to my specific knowledge, although that is certainly possible," he added quickly. "Wilson Blair was in charge of the investigation, and I'm still looking into the particulars of it."

"You don't know what the raids were for?" The Chief Executive asked. "What kind of business were these men engaged in, Dwight?"

"Mr. President, our regional supervisory agents have the authority to initiate and conduct investigations and raids without my micromanaging them. If Wilson Blair were alive and in his office instead of having vanished into thin air, I would have the answers to all your questions. As it is, we're still looking." Harrison Potter chose that moment to clear his throat, and the President glanced at him.

"Yes, Harry?"

"Mr. President, I know nothing of the raids in question, but after our meeting yesterday, I paid a visit to NFA Branch over at 5100 Pennsylvania, and made a few other inquiries. Being retired, I'm always looking for something to do," he said with a smile. Potter's face became serious. "I, too was interested in who these three men were selling machine guns to."

"Go on, Harry."

"The three men Director Greenwell is describing are licensed by the Treasury Department to deal in weapons regulated by the National Firearms Act of 1934," the retired Chief Justice explained. Potter referred to a small, leather-bound notebook in his hand before continuing. His notes in it were written in fountain pen ink.

"It seems almost all of Grant Millet's customers are other Treasury-licensed dealers around the country, and a few police departments also. Millet apparently has a talent for finding rare military accessories in foreign countries, and the majority of his business is actually in obsolete gun parts for collectors and museums."

"So Millet is an importer of machine guns as well as a dealer in them."

"That's correct, Mr. President," Dwight Greenwell broke in.

"Actually, it's not," Potter said mildly. "Since 1968, it has been illegal to import any machine gun receiver except for government or law enforcement use. Millet is a...Class 2 manufacturer," Potter said, referring to his notes for the correct term, "and he was manufacturing receivers in Ohio, importing other parts, and assembling and selling guns to other dealers.

"However, on...May 19, 1986," Potter went on, once again referring to his notebook, "manufacture of machine guns in this country became illegal, again with the exception of arms made for sale to government entities. Millet has manufactured or imported a few of these firearms since 1986, but all were for police departments. Most of his business is now importing spare parts. He has some weapons for sale to other dealers, but no good way to replenish that inventory once it is gone." Harrison Potter turned several pages over until he found the notes he wanted.

"Allen Kane, according to the kind people at ATF who researched this for me, has sold more machine guns to police departments in this country than any other single licensee in the United States save the Colt factory. I also learned from them that Kane does a lot of business with...Stembridge Gun Rentals in Hollywood," he said, checking the spelling of the name. "This is a firm which supplies the movie industry with props for films.

"I then called California to speak with this company. The gentleman I spoke to said that Mr. Kane has regularly acquired historic machine guns for Stembridge that the company had been previously unable to locate, let alone purchase. The man at Stembridge also had high praise for Mr. Kane's mechanical and restoration abilities. He said every machine gun he had bought from Kane worked flawlessly, even turn-of-the century pieces.

"Apparently, then, in addition to police sales, Kane makes much of his living buying large machine gun collections from private individuals and dealers who are leaving the business, and then selling these weapons one at a time. He also holds a manufacturer's license, although since the 1986 prohibition his activity in that area has been next to nothing.

"Which brings us to Mr. Bowman," the retired Chief Justice said as he flipped to another page. "Henry Bowman is licensed to deal in machine guns, but unlike Kane and Millet, he does not hold a manufacturer's license. Selling guns is also not a significant source of income for him. Bowman's selling activity has been minimal in the last few years. He did sell...twenty-seven machine guns to a police department in Missouri last year," Potter added as he peered at his notebook, "but he makes only a handful of sales to other dealers a year, and sales to private collectors are even less than that.

"Bowman's current inventory is seventy-three machine guns, with little duplication as to make and model. According to a man in your Firearms Technology department," Potter said as he looked at Dwight Greenwell, "many of Bowman's guns are ones of which only a handful of examples exist on the civilian registry. Many of these he acquired from Allen Kane, and some from Grant Millet, according to NFA records."

"We know that all three men are good friends," Greenwell broke in.

"Typical gun nuts," Carl Schaumberg muttered under his breath. Only Helen Schule heard him.

"So he's a collector, and when he sells any machine guns, it's to a police department," the President summarized. "Thanks, Harry," he said with a smile, then turned to the ATF Director. "Dwight, I'm still waiting to hear what these men were being raided for."

"Mr. President, the only people who can give you the exact answer to that question are at this moment either dead or missing. I hope to learn the answer to your question in the near future. However, I can tell you right now why other machine gun dealers and manufacturers with exactly the same credentials have been arrested by our agents and are now spending time in prison."

"Please do."

"What I suspect Wilson Blair may have uncovered," Greenwell went on rapidly, "is evidence to indicate that Millet, Kane, and Bowman were conspiring to violate federal firearms laws. Chief Justice Potter just explained that it is illegal for any citizen to own a machine gun manufactured after May 19, 1986. Manufacturers—and here I mean individuals with manufacturer's licenses, Mr. President, not companies like Colt—often conspire to falsify records. They'll make a gun and claim it was made before the cut-off. Then they sell it at a big profit."

"Why don't they just sell it to a police department and be legal?"

"Well, then it wouldn't be worth as much. Machine guns that are transferable to individuals are worth a lot more, because the, uh, supply is fixed."

"Then how can these manufacturers make more and register them? I thought you said the cut-off was in May of 1986?"

"It was sir, but, uh, some manufacturers registered a bunch of guns on paper before President Reagan signed the bill, but after it had been passed by the legislature. These were guns that they hadn't actually made yet. Again, I'm talking about manufacturers like Kane and Millet, not Colt."

"You're saying that before the law took effect, these small manufacturers typed up registration forms to create a paper inventory to work on in anticipation of us putting them out of business?"

"Exactly, Mr. President." The Commander-In-Chief scowled and nodded to himself.

"And all this registration of then-nonexistent guns happened prior to May 19, 1986?"

"Correct. We call them 'paper receivers', sir," he added helpfully.

"I had been led to believe," the President said slowly, "that ATF performed regular compliance checks on federally licensed dealers. I was also told that in the case of the small number of machine gun dealers and manufacturers in this country, those compliance checks included a complete check of the licensee's entire registered inventory."

"Are you telling me, Dwight, that there are licenseholders in your system that you think have stacks of these 'paper receivers' on their desks, but that your agents have not even checked their inventory since before 1986? And that instead of scheduling the manufacturer's long-overdue inventory assessment, your agents plan a raid? Is that what you are saying?"

"Uh, no, Mr. President, I'm sorry, I didn't explain everything, uh, we don't...we don't think there are very many paper receivers left around, not at all. But, uh, the manufacturers will still falsify their records, and, uh..." Greenwell saw the look on the President's face and quickly blurted out, "I can explain it better with an example, sir."

"All right."

"Okay. A manufacturer like Kane will have a machine gun in his inventory. And it'll be some gun that's worth maybe a thousand, fifteen hundred dollars. He'll get hold of another machine gun out of some veteran's attic, or maybe one somebody smuggled into the country sometime, that would be worth a lot more than the gun he's got except that this second gun is not registered so the manufacturer can't sell it."

"Why doesn't the manufacturer register it and then sell it?" the President asked.

"That's illegal."

"It's illegal for a machine gun manufacturer to register a gun made before 1986?"

"It's illegal for anyone, except government agencies. And not just since 1986. That was part of the Gun Control Act of 1968," Greenwell explained.

"Go on."

"So the manufacturer or dealer will stamp the serial number of the first gun on the second one, and then cut the first gun in half and throw it away. Now he's got something worth maybe ten, fifteen thousand dollars to sell."

"Isn't that an IRS matter?" the President asked. "Not reporting the additional income on the sale?"

"That's not the crime, sir. It doesn't matter if the manufacturer or dealer declares every nickel of profit. Putting a new serial number on a gun and claiming this new gun is the one described on the registration form is a felony."

"Since the registration form describes the gun, isn't it obvious that the gun is not the right one?"

"Well, yes, but some guns are the same length and caliber, and have the same model number, like 'Mark II'."

"So the manufacturer or dealer finds a gun someone brought back from the War, and it just happens to be a very rare type that would be worth ten or twenty thousand dollars, except the owner is prohibited from registering it. This gun also just happens to loosely fit the description of a registered weapon the dealer just happens to already own. So the dealer transfers the serial number, destroys the less-valuable gun, and sells the more-valuable one to a collector, declaring the income from the sale and paying the tax on it. Is that what Millet, Kane, and Bowman were suspected of doing?" the President asked pointedly. Dwight Greenwell shrugged with a helpless expression.

"It's possible, Mr. President, but as I say, I don't know what charges he was bringing against the three men. The warrant disappeared with him and his men."

"One last question then, Dwight, before I move on. I understand that all three men were out of town at the time their homes were raided, and that your people knew this. Is it standard practice for ATF to execute warrants on charges such as you have described when the premises in question are known to be unoccupied? Isn't the purpose of an arrest warrant to make an arrest?"

"That's up to the supervisor in charge, sir," Greenwell said. The President nodded once, coming to a decision, and spoke quickly.

"We'll maintain the 'No Comment' reply to questions about Blair, at least for now." He turned to the Director of the CIA. "George?"

"There is no indication that any of this originated outside the United States," George Cowan said. Everyone in the room knew the CIA's charter prohibited domestic operations. "God knows we learned our lesson with Oklahoma City on that score. I think we can learn a lot from what's gone on overseas, however, so I've called Hap Edwards in to help with this. Hap was the head of the CIA Center for Counter-Terrorism up until last year, and he's coming in with one of his top guys from northern Ireland to talk about tactics."

"Very good," the President said with a nod. He switched his attention to the FBI Director. "Roland, tell me what your people have on the Internet messages and on the killings themselves." Lemp, already sitting ramrod-straight, spoke without notes and in a voice devoid of inflection.

"The first message was distributed on the Internet over land lines which originated at a pay phone in the Tulsa area. The caller used a fictitious name and a temporary, free-trial-period ID number to enter the system. In addition to the Internet, Blair also sent the same message to eight electronic bulletin boards popular with the shooting community." Dwight Greenwell glared at the FBI Director's use of Wilson Blair's name. Greenwell knew the FBI viewed ATF as incompetent. Roland Lemp paid no attention to him, and continued.

"This is significant because it shows us that Blair fully expects us to shut down the Internet. The system operator of one of the bulletin boards told us that he was contacted on the phone at about the same time as Blair's electronic message arrived. The caller told the man he was ATF, and that the bulletin board was backup for when the Internet was closed. That tells us he's going to be sending more messages. We assume the caller contacted the other seven system operators as well, but they are refusing to answer our questions. We have telephone traps on all the incoming lines at all eight bulletin board sites, and are investigating every incoming transmission." Roland Lemp did not say what a Herculean task that was.

"Concerning the killings, of which there were two more yesterday afternoon, three suspects have been taken into custody so far, and of these, one has been released. None of the three have any ties to each other. Neither do they have any conceivable connection to the Internet messages, other than having read them. The suspect who was released had been apprehended with a list of local ATF agents in his possession, the top name crossed off. The agent in question had been killed the day before, but–"

"I know what I read in the newspapers, Roland," the President interrupted. "Tell me what isn't there."

"What isn't there, sir," Lemp said smoothly, "is that the killings can be loosely divided into two categories: Amateurish efforts, sometimes centered around ATF offices in federal buildings and almost always involving shootings; and professional-quality executions in which the killers have employed a variety of techniques, almost all of them silent and untraceable.

"Some of these murders almost exactly coincided with the transmission of the first Internet message. This is strong evidence that these killings were the work of those who were responsible for that message, the 'core group' as we have been calling it. We also believe this core group is responsible for the disappearance or deaths of the agents in Ohio, Indiana, and Missouri. The group may include Blair and possibly some other missing agents. We are still looking for evidence to support or refute this theory.

"We believe that any of the missing agents not in the core group are now dead. The first Internet message listed the names and addresses of all current ATF agents but did not include the twelve missing ones or the six killed in the helicopter crashes. The names of the agents in the helicopters were published in the media, but the missing ones from Ohio and Indiana were not." The President nodded. He saw the logic of the FBI's conclusion.

"You said some of the so-called 'professional executions' appeared to be the work of this core group. Not all of them? What of the others?"

"Two of the pro-quality killings have occurred too far away from each other in too short a time period to be the work of one group, unless that group is larger than our current best estimates suggest. We believe some of these deaths to be the work of ex-military and/or police, who got the message and acted independently. At the moment, eyewitness testimony is sketchy and varied. Forensic evidence is nonexistent." A thick silence hung over the room as the members of the task force contemplated the enormity of veterans and policemen taking up arms against agents of the United States government.

"Who are these people?" the President said softly.

"I'm going to let Alex take over on that one, sir," The FBI Director answered. Agent Neumann took his cue.

"Mr. President, the first Internet message contained inside information, specifically the agent list. It is therefore certainly possible that the core group includes one or more of the missing agents, including Wilson Blair. On the other hand, the message is also an obvious propaganda attempt to garner support for killing ATF agents. We have thoroughly examined the past history of Calron Jones, the door gunner who supposedly died shooting down the two helicopters. There is absolutely nothing we have found that points to such an action."

"So what brought those choppers down?"

"Jones' own helicopter was riddled with .30 caliber bullet holes and a few slugs were recovered from the wreckage of that aircraft. His machine gun was empty, and the barrel was severely eroded. This is consistent with the theory that the gun fired an entire belt of ammo nonstop, swiveling on the mount and shooting up the helicopter. Examination of the second wreck, though, indicates that Jones did not fire at the other helicopter. Some kind of explosion occurred. Our forensic experts are still doing tests, "

"What explains this machine-gun fire?"

"The weapon in the helicopter was a model that is known to 'run away', as it is called. To continue firing after the trigger is released. We believe Jones was blown out of the aircraft in the explosion. Either he jerked the trigger first, or the blast jarred the mechanism into firing."

"So what kind of people are we up against, Alex?" the President asked. "One of these militia groups?" Alex Neumann shook his head and swallowed.

"No, Mr. President, it's not the militias. The FBI has undercover agents in every militia organization in the United States. That's been the case since well before the building in Oklahoma blew up in '95. If there were even a hint of something like this, we would have heard about it long before it ever happened. Nothing," he said emphatically.

"Since the attacks on ATF agents started one week ago today, our undercover people have overheard several militia members talking about working down the agent list. We have put surveillance on each of these men, and so far we've been wasting our time. At this time I would say that the most logical use of our database of militia members would be to eliminate potential suspects from pointless scrutiny."

"Yes, Dick, what is it?" the President asked, seeing the Congressman's agitation. Richard Gaines looked very uncomfortable.

"I didn't mean to interrupt, Mr. President, but I thought these militias were almost certainly behind what's been happening. And now Mr. Neumann is telling us they're not a factor at all? And the FBI was inside them even before the Oklahoma bombing? How can that be?"

"I'd like to hear the FBI explain that myself," Carl Schaumberg echoed. "These gun-crazy militia lunatics are the greatest danger this country has ever seen."

"Wasn't that the whole reason we expanded the FBI's authority?" asked Andrew Ward, the Congressman from Indiana.

"Alex?" the President prompted. Neumann glanced at Director Lemp, who nodded. The President, seeing the FBI man's reluctance, added, "Go ahead. Nothing said here will leave this room." Neumann shrugged and cleared his throat.

"It's no big secret. You can find what I'm about to say in any number of sources. Just not the newspapers or *Time* and *Newsweek*, is all." He looked around the room at each of the task force members in turn.

"The militias are almost entirely comprised of men who want to play soldier, feel good about it, and stop at 4:30 so they can go grab a few beers. They put on camo and do calisthenics and 'drill' out in the woods, but you will go a long time before you find a militia member who has served in the infantry." Neumann let that sink in for a few seconds.

"The next time we have a flood, hurricane, or other natural disaster, I would not be surprised to see militia groups in the affected area muster their troops to give aid,"

Neumann admitted. "Aside from things like that, however, these men have no more effect on serious matters than the kids who put on goggles and play with paintball guns."

"But they're all gun nuts!" Carl Schaumberg exclaimed. "Worse than street criminals. They're banding together to shoot people like us in twisted defense of their beloved Second Amendment." Neumann shook his head.

"The majority of them are shooting enthusiasts, yes," the FBI man said evenly. "And it's true that they are mostly one-issue voters on the subject of gun rights. It's also true that they have a great distrust of the federal government. It's even true that some of them talk about armed rebellion. But that's all it is—talk. Tim McVeigh went to one militia meeting in Michigan, one, and as soon as he talked about 'striking back', the members threw him out. After the Oklahoma City bombing in 1995, every militia group publicly disavowed the bombers, just as you're seeing them distance themselves from the people responsible for these current killings. I am absolutely convinced that the militias are not involved."

"Aren't the militias full of white supremacists like Randy Weaver? Isn't he their poster boy, along with the Waco cult?" Neumann winced at Jonathan Bane's mention of Weaver and Waco. He was mightily ashamed of the FBI's conduct during both events.

"Militias that are racist in nature do not exist," Alex Neumann said flatly. "There are a few 'Aryan Nations'-type groups around, but their focus is on white supremacy. Making race-mixing illegal, things like that.

"The militias, as Congressman Schaumberg pointed out, are largely comprised of people who think that gun laws should be abolished. Walk into any gun store in any state in the union, buy any gun you want with no wait and no paperwork. That's the last thing white supremacists want black people to be able to do." He stared at the Congressman. "I should also point out, though it gives me no pleasure to do so, that Mr. Weaver was not a white supremacist, but a white separatist. God knows I have very little respect for the man, but to give him his due, he didn't want to live around black people, so he moved someplace where there weren't any. If that's a crime, an awful lot of rich people should be in jail. Including some of those in this room," he added.

"Let's get back on track here," the President said firmly. "Alex, you're saying the militias are a nonstarter on this thing, and you don't want to waste any manpower on them. Roland, is that your opinion as well?"

"Agent Neumann and I differ on this issue," Director Lemp said as he furrowed his brow. "Although we cannot rule out his viewpoint. I thought from the very outset that a militia group might have been responsible, and that we should use that as a focus point for our investigation. That, in fact, is exactly what we have done. And I must admit that thus far it has led us nowhere. So I think we should all listen to what Alex has to say. His theory may well prove to be the correct one."

"Mr. President," Neumann jumped in, emboldened by his superior's vote of confidence, "Militias are open to anyone. Our agents walk up to their recruiting tables at gun shows and sign on, and the person there smiles and welcomes them. Some of our agents have even admitted working for the FBI. Not one has been asked to leave. These people talk openly about what they believe in. Any plans for violence, we would learn about long before anything was carried out." He took a deep breath and went on.

"Any organization that intends to successfully conduct illegal activities on an ongoing basis must have a method of ensuring both the loyalty and the silence of its members. The more heinous the crimes, the more drastic these internal measures must be."

"You're referring to the Mafia?" the President asked.

"The organized crime families are an example of what I am talking about, but much of what they do is, in fact, socially acceptable to most of the population. Bookmaking, vending machines, and the like don't raise many eyebrows. Even drugs. The violence committed by drug distributors is almost entirely confined to competitors and informants. Also, the Mafia and the drug cartels are themselves very large and control a huge amount of money. That in itself commands obedience and makes it possible to monetarily encourage law enforcement to look the other way and get the courts to render appropriate verdicts." The President looked closely at the FBI man. He had not expected him to so readily admit that the police and judges were regularly bought off.

"A much more drastic system of internal security is necessary in a small group with limited resources which intends to carry out activities guaranteed to elicit a massive police response. An organization that's done what we've seen this last week would have to have some very severe safeguards in place to prevent infiltration."

"Can you give us an example, Alex?" the President asked.

"The most hardcore of the various outlaw motorcycle gangs around the country are the first groups that come to mind."

"The Hell's Angels?" Dick Gaines asked. Alex Neumann shook his head.

"The Angels' initiation generally involves wearing clothing that the existing members have urinated and defecated upon, which the initiate may not remove for a period of weeks. Some chapters add other forms of discomfort, and most gangs' initiation procedures are along these lines. Others use sexual pain and humiliation—being whipped on the genitals with belts, or performing oral sex on a woman with venereal disease. One gang requires recruits to have both passive and active anal sex with a Great Dane, in front of the assembled membership.

"While humiliating, these acts are endurable, and the FBI has undercover agents in all of the organizations that have similar initiation requirements. There are a few gangs, however, which we have been unable to penetrate. To join them, you must commit a murder in front of witnesses." The task force was silent as they considered what Neumann had said.

"These outlaw motorcycle gangs aren't suspects in this case," the FBI man assured the group. "My point is that whatever group is behind this has a system of internal discipline that is better than anything we have ever seen before. It has been one entire week since the Internet message went out, two entire weeks since twelve ATF agents and a government helicopter vanished into thin air, and we have no hard evidence whatsoever. We'll get a break in this case—we always do—but we're probably going to have to create it, not stumble across it."

"How?" the President asked.

"Money," Neumann said immediately. "Lots of it."

"Something like the two million dollar reward they offered on the Oklahoma City bombing in '95?" the President asked.

"I think it's going to take a lot more than that," Neumann came back. "We're up against something we haven't seen before, sir. These people are good. They don't talk about what they've done, and they don't leave tracks. If anyone not involved had any knowledge and was going to tip us off, he would have done it by now. Mr. President, the reward's going to have to be enough to break loose one of the principals, and nothing they've done so far indicates they're motivated by money. A hundred million might cause one of them to revise his thinking."

At the mention of the dollar figure there was a collective intake of breath, and every head in the room save one swiveled to face the FBI agent. Harrison Potter, the retired Chief Justice, was watching the President.

"Roland, do you agree with this recommendation?"

"Mr. President...the FBI does not support the concept of making terrorists into centimillionaires. However, Alex's arguments have a logic to them that cannot be ignored. I think we should be prepared for the eventuality of having to offer such a sum, if other measures prove ineffective. I would recommend against it at this time. If other avenues which we are currently pursuing prove successful, it may not need to be made at all."

"Are you of the opinion that a hundred-million-dollar offer should be made immediately?" the President asked of the younger FBI man.

"Yes, sir. The murders are an outrage, so we lose no face by being visibly and seriously outraged over them. We will almost certainly catch the men eventually without the reward. But the reward will speed things up, and that means saving lives. Also, if we wait until other methods fail, then we look terrible. That's a PR nightmare.

"Remember when O.J. Simpson's ex-wife and that waiter were killed? O.J. was stoic at the funeral, and didn't seem too outraged that someone had sliced up the mother of his children. Does he offer a reward for finding the killer? No, not until it's obvious that he's the only suspect, and he's botched his getaway wearing the fake beard and carrying a bunch of cash. That reward offer made him look terrible." He shook his head. "Mr. President, I think we should offer a hundred million right now, not after we've exhausted everything else." Neumann glanced around the room, then returned his gaze to the President.

"You make some good points," the President conceded. "Has there been any progress on the investigation? Any leads at all?"

"It is true that we have no hard evidence as to who is responsible. However, the things that these people have done, and just as importantly the things they have *not* done, are giving us some very definite direction to our search. I'll have a full report for you at our next meeting, Mr. President."

"Very good. George, when is your man coming in?" the President asked the CIA Director.

"Hap and Nigel should arrive tomorrow morning, sir."

"Tomorrow at 2:00 too soon for you to have that report ready?" the President asked Alex Neumann.

"Not at all, Mr. President."

"Does that time suit ev–" The President stopped in mid-sentence as a Secret Service agent opened the door and walked over to him.

"You said you were to be notified immediately, sir," the agent said. "This hit the Internet less than two minutes ago." He handed the President a thin stack of laser-printer output. "There are fifteen copies, sir, in case you need them for the whole group."

"Thanks, Bill." The Secret Service man nodded, then brought his head closer and said something that the others could not hear. The President's eyes widened slightly, but he gave no other visible reaction. The man then turned on his heel and left the room.

"It appears you were right, Roland," the President said as he read the words in front of him. Then he handed the pages to the FBI Director. "Give everyone a copy."

The Lessons of the Joe Columbo Shooting
by Wilson Blair

Joe Columbo was a well-guarded organized crime boss who operated in New York in the '60s and '70s. In 1972, a mob rival paid someone to murder Columbo during a New York parade. Knowing that the man might be caught and reveal who had hired him, the employer took additional precautions to silence the killer.

As planned, the hired assassin rushed Columbo during the parade and shot the mob boss. Columbo did not die, but was permanently paralyzed and soon lost control of his crime syndicate.

When the gunman tried to make his escape, however, five large Sicilian gentlemen tackled him and covered him with their bodies. When the five men stood up, the man who had shot Columbo lay dead with two bullet holes in him. A revolver wrapped in friction tape lay on his body. The entire incident was captured on film by several television cameras.

The five Sicilian gentlemen refused to talk to the police. So thorough was their refusal that the police were not sure whether the men spoke English, or any other language, for that matter. Attempted interrogations in various dialects were all fruitless.

All five men tested positive for nitrates on both hands. None of the five, as near as could be determined, had a Social Security number. All five were released by the police after being held for less than 20 hours. None of the five were charged with any crime.

Some people might ask why a charge of conspiracy was not brought. The fact was that since no one said one word to the police, there was no starting point from which to build a case. The five men could have been tackling the assassin to disarm him, and the trigger of his gun got squeezed twice in the struggle. Without testimony, the prosecution could not prove anything, and the DA knew this. The five men walked away.

The lessons of the Columbo shooting are clear and uncomplicated:

1. Eyewitness testimony is the least reliable in court, even when the actions are filmed. There can always be multiple explanations for what someone saw.
2. Forensic evidence is much harder to refute, but it can be completely neutralized with a little foresight.
3. You pick the time and place for action if you want to succeed--don't let someone else dictate the terms.
4. Never talk to the police. Ever. About anything. You will only give them rope to make a noose for you. This is just as important to remember when you are completely innocent. Open your mouth and a case may get built on some fragment of your testimony, and you will take the fall for someone who was smart enough to keep his mouth shut.

Keep these lessons firmly in mind. They will serve you well in all circumstances, including the times when you've done nothing.

Lastly, I have learned that some of my former colleagues want immunity from the current program. That's easy—resign, and announce the fact in the Wall Street Journal classified section under "Jobs Wanted."

END

"God bless the Information Superhighway," the President said with a grimace. He looked very tired as he put down the sheet of paper. "I am informed that this Internet transmission originated in Lincoln, Nebraska. Roland, I'd like you and Alex to get on this. Maybe you can have something for us by tomorrow. I understand you're bringing in your expert with a psychological profile of the terrorists?"

"Yes, sir."

"George, your people all set for tomorrow?"

"Yes, Mr. President."

"Dwight, what about you?"

"I have two people giving testimony. Uh, Mr. President?"

"Yes, Dwight?"

"Uh...do you think maybe by tomorrow we'll be able to announce that whoever's doing this is not anyone in the Treasury Department? Morale at ATF is at an all-time low."

"We'll see," the President said noncommittally. "Looks like tomorrow's going to be 'Outside Expert's Day'. Anything else before we break?"

"Mr. President?"

"What is it, Helen?"

"Would it make sense for us to put an ad in the *Journal?* To ask Wilson Blair—or whoever he is—what he wants?"

"He wants to kill ATF agents!" Carl Schaumberg interrupted. "That's what he's been encouraging people to do, and now he's telling them how to get away with it," Schaumberg said, shaking the photocopy in his hand. The Congresswoman from Vermont looked back and forth between the New York Congressman and the Chief Executive.

"Congressman Schaumberg, Mr. President—if all this man wanted was to kill people, why does he now distribute *this* announcement?"

"What are you saying, Helen?"

"I'm saying that his first message seemed to me to be both a veiled threat and a call to action. His second one was a pat on the back to the people that listened to him and some advice on the...tactics his followers should use, but there was also that sentence about 'immunity'.

"Now we get a third message, and it's mostly this Columbo story—more advice on how not to get caught. But here at the end," she said, pointing, "is this instruction to put an ad in the *Wall Street Journal.* What's that for?"

"You mean you don't know?" Harrison Potter asked. All heads turned toward the retired Chief Justice. "I thought it was obvious."

"Tell us, Harry," the President said.

"This man who calls himself Wilson Blair doesn't want ATF agents to all die. He just wants them to go away."

***

"'Evening, Ray. Been a while. Gin?"

"Just a draft beer, Peter, and some huevos rancheros." Ray Johnson casually looked around the Woody Creek Tavern. It had been almost a month since he'd dropped in. "Been in Boulder the last few days. Anything new going on?" he asked.

"Other than the dead narcs?" Peter asked, setting the beer glass on the bar in front of his customer. Ray's eyebrows knitted in query. *Dead narcs?* he thought. *Around here?*

"You mean you haven't heard about that?" the barman asked in surprise. "Three of 'em," he explained. "Gutted like deer and dumped in the woods. Guy on his mountain bike found 'em last night."

"Where?"

"Up near North Starwood."

"North *Starwood?*" Ray asked in disbelief. "What about the guard?" Starwood was the private drive on the shoulder of Red Mountain eight miles northwest of the town of Aspen. John Denver had a house there, and the constant flow of drifters in the '70s who had dropped in to meet him had prompted the singer to erect and staff a guardhouse at the drive's only entrance. Starwood's other, less-famous residents had welcomed this addition and were more than happy to assist in the expense of a 24-hour gatekeeper to keep out unwanted visitors.

"Guard says he doesn't know a thing. Logs show the only people he let in were ones lived there. Word is the three narcs were tortured to death."

"Who'd they piss off?" Ray asked as he lifted the bottle to his lips. The bartender shrugged.

"You know those transformers you see on utility poles?"

"Yeah?"

"You weren't here then, but back in '79 or '80, I think it was, it came out that one of those transformers was a dummy. Inside it was a surveillance camera. Feds had put it up so they could watch this guy's house in Missouri Heights, and they'd been watching it for something like six months. Guy found out when his neighbors were flipping around on their satellite dish, and one of the channels was this guy's house. They called him, he came over to look at the screen, and they figured out where the camera had to be. Pissed off a lot of people."

"Yeah, I can imagine."

"Right. Well, word is, it's been a long time, and the feds thought they'd do it again. Only on a larger scale. Ten or twelve of them, this time."

"Damn."

"Damn is right. Feds'll nail some guy at Denver International every now and then with a hundred kilos in a steamer trunk, but they've pretty much left everyone around here alone. Aspen cops won't cooperate with them—you know that. Guy with ten, twenty million dollars comes here and buys a place to live, he assumes he's buying a little privacy, least around his own house. Then this comes along."

"But, three feds *tortured* to death? Who around here could've done it?" The bartender shook his head in reply as he picked up another glass to polish.

"A week ago, I'd've said nobody. Today? Shit. Could be any one of a couple dozen people. I tell you, Ray, this thing with the ATF guys has got a bunch of people thinking. Lot of folks around here just want to be left alone, but they always jumped to attention with 'Yes, sir' and 'Yes, ma'am' when the feds came in. Not now." The bartender smiled. "I guess you don't know about Hunter," he said, referring to the Woody Creek Tavern's most famous regular patron.

"No, what?"

"Started a pool on how many dead feds there'd be by August first. Hundred dollars a guess, enter as many times as you want before the cutoff on July fourth. Winner takes the whole pot, earliest guess wins if there's a tie. I keep the money in the safe. Pot's over twelve thousand as of this morning. He's–"

"*Twelve thousand dollars?*" Ray interrupted.

"Yeah. Hunter won't tell me what his own guess is, but he did say it was three figures. He said it wouldn't be just ATF agents. Looks like he was right. You want in?"

"I'll pass." The bartender shrugged.

"Oh, and one other thing. There's a rumor going around, and a lot of people think it's crazy, but I don't. What some folks are saying is that on this surveillance deal, the feds weren't looking to make a coke bust."

"What, then?"

"Steroids." The bartender saw Ray's look, and continued. "Think about it, Ray. It makes sense. A bunch of those action-film muscleboys have been coming out here for a while now. And the studio heads've been buying up acreage like bandits. Hell, you know that, some of it was yours."

"And...?"

"And steroids are just as illegal as coke now, so they get imported from South America, too. Only the labs making the stuff are legit pharmaceutical companies like Searle and Upjohn and Parke-Davis, not a bunch of beaners in a dirty warehouse." *Henry was right* Ray thought in astonishment as the bartender continued.

"The studios have a huge investment in their stars. You think they're going to let some squirrels from the DEA throw a few hundred million bucks of their money out the window just 'cause a couple of their box-office studs are on the juice?"

"You sound rather knowledgeable about this, Peter," Ray said with a smile.

"Hell, it's no big secret. Half the guys in the Aspen Club have been on the juice at one time or another. Probably more than that, crazy as this town is about strong bodies. The girls, too." He smiled conspiratorially. "You trying to tell me you've never come across an Aspen chick with a clit like the end of your little finger? Ah-ha! Gotcha!" he said in triumph when he saw the look on Ray's face.

"So you think it was the head of a Hollywood studio who tortured federal agents to death and dumped their bodies up by Starwood?" Ray Johnson asked, deadpan.

"I think it could've been anybody. I know that nobody I've talked to thinks it's particularly terrible, and that if it keeps the feds away from here from now on, they're all for it. Even the local cops don't want any part of this mess. And the folks the feds have questioned? You'd think they all of a sudden turned into those stupid street mimes you see at the music festival." The bartender looked down at the hundred-dollar bill Ray had placed on the bar.

"You want your check? Your huevos aren't out yet—you got to go?"

"No, I'm in no hurry," Ray said, pushing the bill towards the man. "I just thought I'd take a chance in Hunter's pool."

***

"Mr. Neumann, I think we've found something."

"What is it?"

"That one in Philadelphia—the ATF agent who got burned up in his car. Remember how you said you thought somebody bumped him off the road, then went in on foot and lit his gas tank?"

"Yeah...?"

"We may have found the bump vehicle." The FBI agent picked up a legal pad and consulted the notes he had just taken so as not to forget anything. "Mid-1970's Chevy Suburban. Big mother. Philly cops ticketed it next to a mall parking lot for no plates, then saw the keys were in it. Went to check the VIN, and the tag had been removed. Front corner was bashed in some, and it looked recent. That set off some alarm bells with one of the officers that had seen your FAX."

"Glad to see somebody in local law enforcement pays attention to us. Call 'em up and tell them to hold that vehicle for us."

"I already did, but there's more. When they went to check the serial number on the frame, it was gone, too. Not ground off, like they usually do. If it had been, the cops could acid-etch the steel and bring the number back up. This guy had used a hammer and punch and stippled the whole area to displace the metal."

"Cute."

"So next they look for the number on the engine block, and one of the gearheads on the force tells them it doesn't have the original motor in it."

"The guy put in a new motor?"

"No, it had been in there a while, but it was a rebuilt job." He consulted his notes. "They said the big boat had a hundred forty on the clock."

"How about on the body, or anywhere else—any numbers there?"

"They didn't do that back then. The build tag on the rearend's gone, and the keys are hardware-store dupes, so there's no code there, either. That's why the cops aren't sure what year the thing is. Oh, something else: The guy checks the oil, and it's damn near new. Said it had to've been changed a couple hundred miles ago, at most. And all four tires were new. The car guy said they were really good ones. Lots better than he'd put on an old cancered-out Suburban. They checked for prints, but the whole thing had been wiped clean, they think with gasoline." The agent looked at his boss. "What do you think?"

"I think we may have gotten a break. Get our Philadelphia office on it. Find out who locally sells those kind of tires. Check the big chains first. Try to find the guy who waited on him. Maybe he can give us a description. Get hold of copies of the want ads from the last three weeks. See can they find who sold it. It'll probably be a private seller, not a dealer." Neumann thought a moment.

"Get hold of the locals in all the other cities where ATF agents have been killed. See if they've come up with any other sterile vehicles that've been abandoned."

"I'll get on it."

"Good job," Neumann said, and was about to say more when another man came up to him.

"Sir, we've run up against a wall on what blew up the helicopters."

"What's the problem, Joe?" Neumann asked.

"Choppers have been cut up. Hauled off and dismantled for scrap."

"You're kidding. Who gave *that* order?"

"Don't know, sir. Somebody pretty high up, I'd guess."

Greenwell Alex Neumann thought in disgust. *He could get it done.* The FBI agent considered this newest bit of information. *Did ATF agents take out the choppers? It's a crazy theory, but even if it's true, would Dwight Greenwell have known about it?* Neumann asked himself. *No way. He would have stopped it* Neumann decided. *Greenwell's just as clueless as the rest of us. He had the wrecks destroyed to save face. Just in case.*

"...matched with one of the readings we got from–"

"What was that, Joe? Sorry, my mind was elsewhere."

"I was saying that I ran the results from the mass spectrometer against all known U.S. and foreign explosives and explosive ordnance for which we've got prints. I got one match that's dead-on, sir."

"What is it?"

"It's the compound inside a particular 20mm incendiary projectile used by the Air Force. Loaded for the multibarrel cannon mounted on some of their fighters, for air-to-air combat. The 20mm Vulcan. M246 is the military designation of that projectile."

"How big is the gun that fires it?"

"I can't give you an exact answer, since I've only seen pictures. But I'd say it's about eight feet long, and weighs three hundred pounds or so. Maybe more."

"Could one have been put on that third helicopter—the one that's missing?"

"That's out of my department, sir, but the Vulcan has an awful lot of recoil. I don't think so."

"How about the back of a pickup truck?"

"Maybe..." the agent said dubiously. "But how would you aim it? And according to the guys I talked to, the Vulcan runs at sixty or seventy rounds a second, which is the only way to hit a flying target. Sounds like the Devil's own impact wrench when it fires, and no one in the area that day heard anything like that. Also slows those big jets down twenty miles an hour. Probably rock on the springs of any civilian vehicle it was mounted on, if it didn't flip it over."

"Just thinking out loud, Joe. So now we're looking at a bomb made out of disassembled 20mm slugs?"

"Maybe," the agent said, not satisfied with that idea, either. "I sure as hell wouldn't want to cut one apart, just to get a third of an ounce of something anyone with half a brain could mix up himself."

"Hm." *These guys got a lot more than half a brain* Alex Neumann thought. "Wish we still had those wrecks to look at."

June 21

"Feeling the slings and arrows of outrageous misfortune today, Mr. President?" Harrison Potter asked as his old friend stepped into his office and sat down. The President had come to discuss task force issues with Potter before the meeting. His two Secret Service men remained outside the door.

"Only a few little ones, Harry," he said with a smile, which abruptly vanished as he thought of something. "Not like that poor woman in Missouri." Potter nodded in agreement.

"The headlines and the articles this morning were actually restrained, I thought. They could have been a lot worse." The President cocked a skeptical eyebrow.

"You wouldn't say that if you were the one who'd just had to offer condolences to the widow." He shook his head. "As if it really matters how the papers handle it when your husband's body gets found in the ghetto with a knife in the chest, wearing a cock ring and not much else."

"What?"

"It's a piece of metal or plastic that's made to—"

"I know what one is, sir," Potter interrupted with feigned irritation. "I didn't know the late Congressman had been...using one."

"Oh. Well, he was."

"Is that common knowledge?"

"Somehow I have the feeling it will be before the day's out," he sighed. "Harry, why is it that so many politicians are...?"

"Willing to engage in self-destructive behavior?" Potter suggested.

"Thank you, Harry. That's much better. 'Pussy hounds with no more brains than a load of gravel' was what I had been about to say. No matter," he said with a wave of his hand. "Rhetorical question. I guess my main surprise is not that it happened, but that it wasn't someone else. The Senator from Massachusetts, for example."

"Mr. President, I believe that gentleman prefers, as they say, the higher-priced spread."

***

"Good afternoon, everyone. I'm running a little late, so let's get started. Roland, you want to go first?"

"Yes, Mr. President," he said, walking over to the door and opening it to whisper to the Secret Service agent standing on the other side. *Here comes Sigmund Freud* Neumann thought. The agent ushered in a balding, bespectacled man who looked exactly like the way most of the people in the room expected a psychiatrist to look.

"This is Dr. Morris Berkowitz. He has been of great help to the Bureau, developing psychological profiles of criminals being sought by the FBI," Lemp said. Dr. Berkowitz nodded at the group and sat down at the front table, behind an aluminum pitcher and a full glass of icewater. He referred to some handwritten notes before speaking. Like most people speaking before the President of the United States, he wasted no time.

"For purposes of psychological evaluation, psychiatrists prefer spontaneous spoken testimony. At the moment, we have none from this person claiming to be Wilson Blair. We have only three written communications. Written words, especially those prepared on a computer before being delivered electronically, are subject to unrestricted revision and editing before they are sent. However, this in itself can be of benefit. What a person chooses to say after having a long time to think about it can tell us a lot.

"First of all, the three Internet messages were not written by Wilson Blair. Director Lemp has provided me with videotape footage of Blair speaking, as well as reports and other communications he has written. The Internet messages were not sent by the same man."

"You're sure of that?"

"Positive. Aside from substantial differences in style and construction, nothing in Blair's past indicates dissatisfaction or disillusionment with government service. The Internet messages are undoubtably the work of someone who has his own reasons for claiming to be Blair. He may believe, and with justification, that his words carry more weight if the public hears them come from a high-level government official. More importantly, however, the man who wrote these words is thumbing his nose at the federal government. He is taunting us, putting his own words in the mouths of our people." Berkowitz took a sip of water.

Here it comes Neumann thought. *I wish Angela were here. I bet she'd have a better handle on it than this guy.* Alex Neumann had spent quite a bit of time with the psychologist he met at the Quantico class on sexual harassment awareness training. He had taken Angela Riggs to dinner on three occasions in the last week, but was finding it harder to see her with the increasing demands of this new assignment.

"I can go into detail and explanation if you want," Berkowitz continued, "but my opinion is that the person who wrote these Internet messages is intelligent, well-educated, and thinks of himself as much smarter, more clever, and generally better than the people he normally deals with. He looks down on those with less education, and he likes to show how witty he is. In his first message, he sneered at government employees with GED degrees.

"In his last message, he used the phrase 'Sicilian gentlemen' to describe Mafia thugs. He also offers this 'suggestion' that ATF agents resign publicly by placing an ad in the newspaper. This is a smug person who likely has no close friends. His familiarity with computers is consistent with this. Ultimately, this man wants to be caught. He wants to be caught so that the whole country can see the clever individual who made the giant federal government look foolish." During this testimony, Neumann suddenly realized that the President was looking at him. *Shit. Hope I wasn't rolling my eyes.*

"Roland, do you concur with this assessment?"

"Mr. President, we really need more to go on, but yes, I do. And Dr. Berkowitz's psychological profiles have been dead-on in the three most recent terrorist-bombing cases the Bureau has solved."

"Any other comments, Doctor?"

"No, Mr. President. Not until we get more communications to evaluate."

"Thank you for your time." A Secret Service agent escorted Berkowitz out the door.

"Alex, you look unconvinced."

"Mr. President, I have great respect for Dr. Berkowitz's judgment. But this case is different. This is not some malcontent computer nerd sending letter-bombs to people he imagines have wronged him or his world. Forget for the moment all the agents who have been killed. Mr. President, a dozen people are *gone*. Disappeared without a trace. A National Guard helicopter has vanished into thin air, and we don't have a clue as to what happened. Dr. Berkowitz's psychological profile not only fails to explain these things, it doesn't even fit in with them."

"You have an evaluation from a psychiatrist which differs from the one we just heard?"

"I'm in the middle of getting one, sir," Neumann explained, stretching the truth. "I've gathered what we have and will be presenting it for evaluation later today."

"Do that. Anything else?"

"Yes, sir. On the helicopter crashes, it was on-board explosions, not gunfire, that brought both aircraft down. Forensics ran some of the material from both crash sites through a mass spectrometer. They found residue of burned thermite particles, and trace evidence of a high-velocity detonating compound used in explosive military ordnance. We now believe there was a bomb on each of the two helicopters, perhaps detonated by a transmitter on the third." Neumann frowned. "Usually in cases involving small bombs, Mr. President, we can tell quite a bit about the precise construction of the bomb by the forensic evidence remaining at the scene.

"In this case, however, we did not know that we were looking for a bomb until the spectrometer results came in, which was last night, so now we'll have to guess as to the type of detonators or the casing used. Other aspects remain puzzling as well. The combination of the two materials is a very odd choice for a homemade explosive. Inconceivable for an amateur and very unlikely even for a person with extensive military experience. Still possible, however. Our best current guess, given that we can't see the wrecks themselves, is that one bomb was placed under the instrument panel of the first helicopter and wired in to the electrical system. The other one was positioned somewhere on the engine of the second aircraft. That turbine wheel came apart like a king-sized hand grenade."

"Why can't you examine the wreckage?" the President demanded. Dwight Greenwell cleared his throat.

"I'll answer that, Mr. President. The FBI's forensic staff informed me that they had all the necessary samples and photos from both wrecks, and the manufacturer of the engines wanted assurance that their product was not at fault. They were concerned, I believe, about their next military contract. I had the engines removed and turned over to the manufacturer. The remainder of the wreckage was disposed of."

"I see," the President said, his eyes narrowing as he opened his mouth to say more. *Now he's going to nail him* Alex Neumann thought, but instead the Chief Executive just nodded.

"Keep your men working on it, Alex," he instructed. "George?" the President said, turning to George Cowan. The Director of the CIA straightened slightly before speaking.

"Mr. President, members of the Task Force, I've asked Hap Edwards to brief the group today." Cowan opened the door and in walked a lean, dark-haired man in his fifties. He wore a navy blue suit, and his face was all but devoid of expression. Following him into the room was a much larger man some ten years younger, tall and muscular with sandy-blond hair and a look of mild amusement on his weathered face.

"I think most of you know him already, and for any of you who don't, Hap is the retired director of the CIA's Center for Counter-Terrorism." *The 'Hit Squad'* Neumann thought. *Wonder how many people this guy's killed.*

"Mr. President," Edwards began, "I realize that I am here solely in an advisory capacity, and in addition to that I am retired from all duties at the CIA. Despite those facts, I would like to state at the outset that as the CIA is prohibited from engaging in domestic operations, I feel that my presence here, along with the presence of any other current or past employees of the Agency, is inappropriate and uncalled for. Domestic crimes are the province of the FBI, and I see that you have the Bureau's top man here already. In light of those facts, Mr. President, I request that I be dismissed from this forum."

"Relax, Mr. Edwards," the President said with a smile. "I'm not going to violate the CIA's charter or ask you to compromise national security." The smile vanished and he became utterly serious. "This administration is a little different from the one you remember." Edwards gave a quick look that took in the four Congressmen and the ATF Director. The President saw it, as he was intended to.

"None of these people are going to talk to the press about what you say in here, Hap. And if they did, what of it? Do you really think it would make things worse?" the President asked with arched eyebrows.

"I would still like to reiterate my position that my presence here is inappropriate. Certain elected officials have in the past soundly criticized the CIA for becoming involved in events of this type. And some of those criticisms have cost CIA agents their lives and careers." *Might you be referring to the Church Commission, Mr. Edwards?* Neumann thought as Edwards' eyes bored in to each of the four Congressmen and Dwight Greenwell in turn.

"But you want to know what I think," Edwards continued, nodding as if to himself. "And you want advice on what to do. With me today is Major Nigel Hume-Douglas," he said, indicating the tall, muscular man to his right. At this, the second man smiled at the rest of the group. "Major Hume-Douglas is with Britain's Special Air Service. He has been on active duty in Northern Ireland for the past nine years. His experience at combatting domestic terrorism exceeds that of any man I know or know of. We have discussed the current situation at length, and I agree completely with the Major's assessment of where we stand and what we will be able to do about it. Nigel, tell these people about the IRA in Northern Ireland."

"Not much to tell, I shouldn't imagine, that these folks don't already know." He looked at the President. "The IRA gets much of its funding from citizens of this country. Your predecessor, sir, invited Gerry Adams to come here and be his guest. In March of 1995, I believe it was. For St. Patrick's Day."

"Tell them about the way the IRA operates, Nigel," Edwards prompted.

"Quite a bit like these chaps you're now facing," the SAS man said. "Those in active service kill British soldiers at every possible opportunity. As, of course, we do them," he added with a tight smile.

"Excuse me?" Helen Schule said.

"Not much secret about it," Hume-Douglas said to the Vermont Congresswoman. "Different rules of engagement for us than you folks have over here in the States."

"The SAS has none of our restrictions on wiretapping, opening mail, and other forms of surveillance, Congresswoman Schule," Hap Edwards explained.

"Normal procedure for us is to identify an active IRA member through those methods, or a word from an informant. Then we follow him, if possible, to see who he'll be chatting up. Get more of them identified, you see. Then we snatch him. For interrogation, of course," Nigel Hume-Douglas explained. "We try to get as much as possible out of the fellow before he dies." Several of the task force members appeared visibly disturbed by this revelation. *He got their attention there* Neumann thought.

"British Army officers identify and murder IRA members?" Jon Bane of Ohio asked. "Is that what you are telling us?"

"Just so."

"Are you saying you believe we should adopt those tactics in this country?"

"Mr. Edwards and I were having just such a discussion last night," the SAS officer said easily. He glanced at the President, then continued. "There are several bits about the IRA you must remember before you start thinking of these American chaps in the same way." He looked around at his audience. Many were scowling. The President's face was blank. The white-haired man in the Savile Row suit showed a glimmer of a smile.

"Right, then. The IRA are Marxists," Hume-Douglas said in a strong baritone. "They want Ireland to be ruled by their own Socialist government at a time when Socialist governments are collapsing of their own weight all around the world.

"Next up, the IRA are operating on a small island, where our people control all normal means of exit and entrance. A small island about the size of your Arkansas," he added helpfully, using the example Hap Edwards had suggested earlier in private. "You can see how that makes things a bit easier on us." Harrison Potter was smiling openly now, a lopsided grin that was full of delight.

"The IRA also has to go elsewhere to do most of its training. Shooting practice, to you folks," he added. "They go to Libya for that, which must be a bit of a nuisance, come to it."

"Why is that necessary?" the President asked.

"Guns must be kept at shooting clubs," the Major explained with a trace of surprise. "Almost no one may have them at home. Anyone we suspect might have any connection at all to the IRA is prohibited from belonging to such a club, so practicing is a bit dicey. Ammunition's forbidden as well, so it's a bit scarcer now and not to be wasted except on important things like assassinations. Most of the kneecappings we've seen in the last few years have been done with those cordless power drills you Yanks are so keen on. Come to it, the Black and Decker seems to be more of a deterrent on informants than the Walther. We've had the Devil's own time recruiting squealers since the drills got popular." Alex Neumann noticed that Dick Gaines looked like he was going to be sick.

"Tell them how many active IRA members there are, Nigel," Hap Edwards prompted.

"Most recent estimates put the number at a bit under two hundred."

"Thousand?" Dick Gaines broke in.

"Two hundred," Hume-Douglas repeated. "Not two thousand," he added, not realizing what the Congressman had been asking. "And those two hundred Marxists on that little Arkansas-sized island have held the British milit'ry at bay for close on to a century, now. I expect when I go to my grave I'll still be fighting the buggers. Begging your pardon, ma'am," he said to Helen Schule.

"Are you saying we have the beginnings of our own IRA-type terrorist organization forming here in the United States?" Congressman Bane asked.

"Not in the slightest. The IRA are Marxists," he repeated, stressing the word. "Not much enthusiasm for unilateral government control over here, now is there?" he said with a chuckle. "Look what happened to that last fellow." The SAS Major turned to the President.

"Do I have it right—these chaps who've been such a nuisance here have made no demands? Mr. Edwards tells me that the only thing they seem to want is for your gun police to leave them alone."

"We've had no direct communication with them, as yet," the President said slowly. *Nice answer* Neumann thought. *And I see old Dwight Greenwell doesn't much care for the Brit's characterization of ATF.*

"Because if all these chaps want is to be left alone in a free market," the Englishman went on, "I should think they'd get quite a bit more public support in this country than our band of Marxist socialists do at home. Gun clubs for folks who like to shoot rifles and pistols—you have them everywhere over here. Just one of them might easily muster more men than the entire Irish Republican Army."

"Last rifle and pistol club I belonged to had a membership of twelve hundred," Hap Edwards agreed. "Many others are bigger."

"Right, then. And come to the skill level, I should expect the clumsiest of the entire lot to stand head and shoulders above what we face in Ireland. Saw your Mr. Richards in the other room, chap who puts on that New Lease Body Armor bowling pin shoot each summer in Michigan. Went there m'self in '93, had my eyes opened a bit, I did. You Yanks know how to shoot, I'll say that straight out. Saw many a man I'd trust in the killing house with the PM. Women, too," he amended. "And not a copper or milit'ry man in the bunch, to my eye."

The 'killing house' to which Hume-Douglas was referring was the building where SAS men ran hostage-rescue drills. The drills were very realistic, with live ammunition in the soldiers' submachine guns and live humans for the hostages. During at least one drill a year, the 'don't-shoot' targets were the actual Prime Minister and members of the Royal Family.

"Mr. Richards...?" the President asked, cocking his head slightly. He did not know any such man.

"David Richards is here at my request, Mr. President," Dwight Greenwell said. "He's the owner of New Lease Body Armor, and he has a lot of contacts in the gun culture. He's in the other room, in case we need him."

"I see." The President turned back to Major Hume-Douglas. "Let me summarize: Ireland is an island two percent of the size of the United States. Residents there have to store their weapons at government-sanctioned gun clubs. Anyone with a relative even suspected of belonging to the IRA cannot own a gun, cannot belong to such a club, and must go outside the country if he wants to shoot at paper targets. The Special Air Service has quite a bit more...latitude in dealing with terrorists than we have here, and the SAS is one of the finest fighting units in the world. It is fully the equal of our own Special Forces. And for decades, the SAS has been held at bay by a group of Marxist-Socialists similar in number to the spectators at an average American Little League baseball game. Is that about right?"

"Spot on," the SAS Major said without a trace of embarrassment.

"So you have no advice on how we should deal with this...situation."

"None at all, sir."

"Mr. Edwards, have you anything to add to what the Major has said?"

"No, sir. I completely concur with his evaluation." *Jesus, he's grinning!* Alex Neumann thought as Nigel Hume-Douglas began to smile.

"Something to add, Major?" the President asked.

"Just thinking what you people must be wishing. That our chaps hadn't made such a hash of it at Concord Green, don't you know."

"You might want to keep that thought to yourself," the President said drily. "Although I suspect Congressman Schaumberg might agree with you." He took a deep breath. "Major Hume-Douglas, thank you for your time," the President said in dismissal. "Mr. Edwards, I'd like you to stay for the rest of the meeting." He gave a nod to the Secret Service agent stationed by the door, who quickly ushered the SAS man out of the room. *Now what?* Alex Neumann wondered just as the President's gaze fell on him full force.

"Alex, has there been evidence of coordination or cross-linkage with the killings we've seen here? Not the ones done by the core group, but the others?"

"No, Mr. President. None that we have been able to detect. They've all been individual acts, prompted, we believe, by the messages from the man claiming to be Blair."

"So if we can find the man sending these messages, and the people in his group, we should be able to stop all of the killings?" *How to answer that one?* Alex wondered.

"Ah, that is possible, Mr. President. But I would say that our window of opportunity will not remain open indefinitely. The longer any subversive movement progresses, the less important its originator becomes to the survival of the movement as a whole." The President nodded.

"Have you a plan for narrowing the list of suspects from the entire U.S. Census to a more manageable group?"

"We have, sir, and we have begun to implement it."

"Tell the task force about this plan, please."

"Mr. President, do you want the entire methodology, or just the final number on the list?"

"Let's have the whole thought process. That's why we're here—to share our insights. Perhaps Mr. Edwards will even offer some of his own." *The President didn't think much of that last bit of Cover Your Ass* Alex Neumann thought. *Wonder if he'll like my testimony any better.*

"There are certain assumptions we can make about our primary target," Neumann began, "but if we make too many of them, we run the risk of excluding the very man we want to catch. We should only use the more stringent criteria to prioritize suspects in our investigation, not exclude them.

"The first and most logical filter is current and former members of the National Rifle Association. That organization is the largest group of individual gun advocates in the country. It would be hard to imagine our core group being comprised entirely of people who have never belonged to the NRA."

"How many people are we talking about here?"

"Four and a half million." *That got their attention* Neumann thought grimly, and hurried to continue. "That includes women shooters, junior members, octogenarians, and others we can logically eliminate from our pool. If we narrow our focus to men between the ages of twenty-five and sixty, the number shrinks to less than three million. Priority should be given to life members, and especially life members who have resigned their membership."

"Like George Bush?" Jon Bane of Ohio said sarcastically. *I should have expected that* Neumann thought with irritation.

"There are two reasons life members resign from the NRA," Neumann explained. "One is that they are offended at NRA's printed attacks on ATF and FBI, and think that NRA should spend all of its money, instead of just most of it, on hunting and target shooting. There are a handful of former members who fall into that category, and former President Bush, who publicly resigned in May of 1995, is one of them.

"However, the vast majority of life members who have quit the NRA in disgust have done so for the opposite reason—because they felt the NRA was spending *too much* money on target shooting and not devoting enough of its efforts on so-called gun rights."

"What are you talking about?" Dwight Greenwell broke in. "This is the organization that ran ads in *USA Today* calling us 'jackbooted government thugs'. Your agency as well as mine."

"And now you expect them to hand the FBI their membership list?" Congressman

Ward of Indiana interrupted.

"We'll get it," Neumann snapped. *I hope* he added silently. Then he turned to the ATF Director. "That's a more recent phenomenon, excoriating a federal agency in full-page ads. Those ads were supposedly the reason George Bush resigned in '95. But we need to remember that Bush had only joined the NRA in 1988, I think it was. He needed them to win the '88 election, because some of the NRA people had long memories. Remember the bumper stickers? 'Defend Firearms--Defeat Dukakis', blue and red."

"What do you mean, 'long memories'?" Ward asked.

"Bush was anti-gun before most of us were old enough to vote," Neumann explained. "Before many of us were born, for that matter. He was about the only legislator in Texas that was in favor of the Gun Control Act of 1968, aside from Johnson. So in 1988 he sent in five hundred dollars and became a life member, then as soon as he got in office in 1989 he issued the semiauto import ban by presidential edict. Almost immediately, a large contingent of NRA members petitioned their Board to revoke Bush's life membership and refund his money, because of the ban. That's the point I'm trying to make. Prior to 1995, NRA had seen thousands of members resign because the organization was focused on recreation rather than so-called civil rights. That 'jackbooted thugs' campaign was the most successful recruiting effort in their history." Neumann scowled.

"But we can't concentrate just on former members. Most of the hard-core advocates were and are life members, and only a handful of those actually wrote in to resign. Most of the dissatisfied life members quit sending in additional contributions, but did nothing to terminate their affiliation.

"To the group of 25-to-60 year old male NRA members, past and present, we need to add the membership rosters of the smaller national organizations which focus solely on gun rights and spend no funds at all on recreational issues. The membership overlap between these groups and the NRA is large. However, we are finding that at the bottom end of our age cut-off, there are some strong supporters of these groups who have never had any NRA affiliation at all."

"To what groups are you referring, Alex?"

"There are several, Mr. President. *The Gun Owners of America* has around a quarter million members. The *Second Amendment Foundation*, and the *Citizens' Committee for the Right to Keep and Bear Arms* are somewhat smaller, but have a substantial membership. Probably the most aggressive of the national groups is *Jews for the Preservation of Firearms Ownership*, which--"

"*Jews* for the preservation of firearms ownership?" Jon Bane broke in, reflexively glancing at Carl Schaumberg, who was seething. "Is that a joke?" The others in the group were giving him reproving looks, but he did not catch them. Neumann shook his head.

"For its size, it's probably the most effective pro-gun organization in the country. They've put up billboards of Adolf Hitler saluting, with the caption 'All Those in Favor of Gun Control Raise Your Right Hand'. They also published the 1938 Nazi laws, in both German and English, side-by-side with the Gun Control Act of 1968. The wording is virtually identical, and they claim Dodd copied the Nazi code."

"I heard about that, but I thought it was NRA propaganda."

"That's been a major complaint among all the smaller groups. Their independent efforts are often assumed to be the work of the NRA." Neumann turned back to the President. "JPFO is based in Milwaukee. Their Executive Director is a man named Aaron Zelman. A Washington news reporter asked him on-camera why almost all Jewish legislators favored more gun control laws. Zelman said many Jews had a quote 'gas-chamber mentality' unquote. The station didn't air that segment, but I have a copy of the raw footage." The President was momentarily speechless, but when he saw that Carl Schaumberg was about to break in, he recovered quickly.

"Let's get back to your list of suspects, Alex. Adding these other groups in, it's up around three million?"

"A bit over that. Now we begin to pare it down using other considerations." He held up a finger. "First, education. Every expert we've consulted agrees this guy is well-educated. College graduate almost a certainty. Even though NRA members have above-average levels of education, restricting ourselves to graduates of four-year colleges cuts us down to about a million and a quarter suspects." He held up a second finger.

"Next we have to factor in income. Our boy is computer-literate, and knows his way around the system. We also believe that on at least one occasion, and perhaps several, he or his group has bought a used car for cash, put fresh tires on it, and abandoned it after using it in a killing. That's not something factory workers are apt to be able to do with what they carry in their pockets. Again, NRA members have higher-than-average incomes, but if we use a cut-off of $50,000 a year adjusted gross, it should bring us down to around a half-million suspects. On top of that–"

"Excuse me," Harrison Potter broke in, "but is the FBI planning to access the income tax records of a million U.S. citizens for the purpose of fishing for a killer?" *I was hoping to avoid that issue* Neumann thought.

"We were going to discuss that with the President."

"Invoke the War Powers Act?" Potter asked. "I see."

"From that half-million," Neumann continued, "there are several other filters we can use. One that we are considering is holders of Federal Firearms licenses. Of the 300,000 licensees in the country, perhaps half of them would fit the other qualifications I've laid out. However, there are serious people in the gun culture who do not hold dealer's licenses, so making dealership status a requirement may backfire on us." Neumann took a drink from the glass in front of him.

"The most aggressive screening, Mr. President, would be to restrict our search, at least initially, to people who have at one time or another been licensed by the federal government to own or deal in NFA weapons. People like Kane, Millet, and Bowman. That would cut our sample down to less than thirty thousand people. NFA weapons dealers and collectors have borne the heaviest brunt of the federal antigun laws in the past decades. Most of the dealers were put out of business in '86. A lot of the ones remaining got stuck with huge losses when ATF reclassified their 7.62x39 ammo as armor-piercing and told them they had to eat it. And every one of them risks a prison sentence if he leaves a date out or makes a clerical error on one of his federal forms. These are the people with the most to be angry about."

"Thirty thousand," the President said slowly. "What about when you use the income test? How many does that reduce it to?"

"It hardly changes it at all, sir. NFA weapons are very expensive. Median income of NFA weapons collectors and dealers is a little over two hundred thousand dollars a year." There was a sharp intake of breath among the people in the room.

"That's more than I make," said the President. *No one's laughing* Neumann thought. The task force members sat in stunned silence until Andy Ward of Indiana spoke up.

"If I'd known that, I'd've campaigned a little differently," he said with a grin. The rest of the group laughed nervously, then the President regained control of the discussion.

"So what we have here is a situation where there are thirty thousand suspects. Every one of these suspects legally owns at least one machine gun, and perhaps several. Each of the thirty thousand almost certainly owns a number of other weapons as well. These thirty thousand will be well-educated men that are especially adept at coping with government regulations. And every one of them will have lots of money, and therefore substantial influence and excellent representation. How many FBI agents are there, Alex? Five, six thousand?"

"That's about right."

"So now every FBI agent in the United States has to investigate five well-armed, wealthy, influential citizens who hate gun laws and who view the agent as a jackbooted government thug. Is that what's going to happen?"

"It's our job, Mr. President," Neumann said.

"So it is." Just then, the Secretary of the Treasury cleared his throat. Lawrence Mills had been silent during all of the meeting.

"Mr. President, whoever is doing this seems to have substantial skills that I, for, one, associate with military or police training. I didn't hear Mr. Neumann say anything about narrowing his list to people with military or law enforcement experience."

"Alex?"

"Mr. President, you should know that Director Lemp shares Secretary Mills' opinion." He took a deep breath. "It is my fear, however, that if we use military or police experience as a screen, we may miss our man. Many if not most of the people in this country who have exceptional shooting and other combat skills have never been in the armed forces or worked in a police department. Major Hume-Douglas was talking about it earlier—the top competitors in the various combat shooting matches held throughout the country are always private citizens. If David Richards is coming in to speak, ask him for his opinion. Police tactics and procedures are also widely known and understood by gun enthusiasts. Articles in gun magazine discuss them on a regular basis."

"Roland?"

"What Alex says may be true. However, I think those on the list who are veterans or have police experience should be given priority."

"I agree with that," Alex Neumann said. *Time to play it safe* he thought.

"Dwight, I guess you might as well call in this Mr. Richards."

"Yes, sir," Greenwell said as he got out of his chair. "Uh, Mr. President, he's not sympathetic to our agency, or the government in general. And he's very vocal on that subject. Richards hates the government's involvement in the body armor industry. He claims in his sales literature that government standards on body armor have gotten policemen killed. I don't believe that will affect his testimony on the terrorist killings, but I thought I should warn you." The President frowned, but made no comment.

"The main reason I've brought Richards in," Greenwell explained, "is that he is a serious shooter and has many friends in the gun culture. As a matter of fact, he personally knows Kane, Millet, and Bowman, the three NFA dealers Wilson Blair was investigating when all this started." The President nodded as Greenwell walked towards the door and ushered in his expert witness.

David Richards was a cherubic-looking man with thinning sandy hair. He wore a blue suit that had obviously been expertly tailored to fit his barrel-shaped body. His smooth skin made him look younger than his fifty-two years. Alex Neumann found himself thinking of a vaudeville entertainer dressed up to get married and now, standing at the altar, wondering if it was really a good idea after all.

"Mr. President, this is David Richards, the president of the New Lease Body Armor

Company. Have a seat, Mr. Richards," Greenwell added, nodding towards the chair Dr. Berkowitz had occupied.

"Mr. Richards, Director Greenwell asked you here because he felt your knowledge might help the task force with this terrible situation we're facing. However, before we get into that, I understand that you have some grievances about government standards involving your business. I've been told that your sales literature contains serious allegations against the government. Is that true?"

"You mean, how the NIJ standard kills cops? Sure, I explain that to everyone, but they still keep doing it." Richards' speech pattern was a stacatto burst of words that ended as abruptly as it had started.

"Would you mind explaining it to me?" The President spoke more slowly than usual, unconsciously trying to set an example for the man in front of him. "NIJ stands for...?"

"National Institute of Justice," Richards rattled off instantly. "Mr. President, anybody can design a vest that will stop a bullet. Take the cartridge you want to defend against, and keep making your vest thicker until the bullet doesn't go through any more. Not real complicated, right? Anybody can do it. Hard part's making a vest that a guy would be willing to wear all the time, that doesn't feel like a sandwich board. That's what we do, make comfortable vests, right? Make them in whatever level the customer wants. Guy wants a T-shirt that'll stop .32s and .380s, fine. Guy wants something to stop armor piercing .357s, with a ceramic insert over the heart that'll defeat AP rifle rounds, no problem. We say one of our vests will stop such-and-such, that means I'll put it on and let someone shoot me with that cartridge. Not like I'm going to lie about what our vests will stop, right? Not like I'm going to close up shop and leave town when the first guy actually gets shot wearing one of my vests. We've been in business over twenty years and have over a thousand 'saves' so far—more than all the other manufacturers put together. That doesn't count the two hundred times I've been shot demonstrating my vests. Last time was day before yesterday," he threw in as an afterthought.

"So maybe I know a few things about designing a comfortable vest and proving that it works. I mean, I'm not hypnotizing these people." Richards laughed at his own joke, shifting his eyes up and to the side to imply he was now considering the concept.

"Anyway, in 1980, NIJ decides to set 'standards' for body armor, to certify vests. They decide blunt trauma's important, but they don't have a clue as to how much blunt trauma is too much, and they don't have any way to simulate human flesh. So the day before the standards get written, their head guy decides to use his kid's modeling clay— Roma Plastilina # 1—as the official standard. Why? 'Cause it's oil-based and convenient to use and he found some in his kid's room. Nobody ever said it acts like human tissue, but he's got some of it, so that's what they use for the simulation.

"So they pound this Roma Plastilina into a block, cover it with the only vest they happen to have lying around—they don't even say in their documentation who made the thing—and shoot it ten times with a .38. Then they measure the 'Backface Deformation Signature' in the clay. 'Backface Deformation Signature' is the government-funded word for 'dent'. They measure this dent in a bunch of different directions and add up the dimensions, and that's the NIJ blunt trauma standard. Any vest that makes a bigger dent in the Roma Plastilina fails the test with that caliber. Never mind that no cop in history has ever been shot ten times in the same spot. Never mind that no cop in history has been permanently injured from blunt trauma after his vest stopped a pistol bullet. NIJ makes the rules. No arguing.

"But NIJ wasn't done yet. They decided the vest had to pass their test when it was soaking wet, and that standard's killed even more people."

"These government standards may irritate you as a manufacturer, Mr. Richards, but I fail to see how they are 'killing people', as you claim." The President was clearly not favorably impressed with the man's complaining. David Richards was undeterred.

"You got different levels of protection, okay, based on what each vest will stop. NIJ-tested vest that'll stop high-velocity .44 Magnum fired out of a rifle gets their Level IIIA rating. I'll sell you a comfortable vest you could wear all day that'll stop .44 Mag out of a rifle, and I'll put it on and let you shoot me before you buy it. Except it won't even pass NIJ's Level 2 test, because the 'backface deformation signature' in kid's modeling clay will be too big. The vest will be too flexible, even when it's dry. Wet? Forget it. Every synthetic fiber known to man bends a lot more when it's completely drenched.

"Never mind you're going to wear a shirt and jacket over it, and if it's raining out you probably got sense enough to put on a raincoat, too. Never mind you're willing to get bruised instead of killed. NIJ says to get that Level 3A rating, the vest has to pass its test after you've jumped into a swimming pool. So the manufacturer—that's me—has three choices. One: Make the vest with three times as much material, which means you'll never buy it 'cause it's a lot more expensive, and even if you did you'd never wear it 'cause it'd be a boat anchor. Two: Cover it with waterproof material and stitch it everywhere so the layers are locked together. That's what my competitors do, and it makes the vest feel like a board. You can't wear it for five minutes without the edges rubbing your skin raw. Three: Sell the vest with no rating, and explain to you the facts of life in my ads and literature. Problem with that is that almost every department now requires an NIJ rating to cover its butt on liability. So they buy someone else's vest that's so uncomfortable the cop throws it in the trunk." He jerked a thumb at Roland Lemp.

"Ask him. Miami, 1986. A dozen FBI agents on special detail go out looking for two bank robbers that've killed some people. Five FBI cars—eight agents—find the killers twenty minutes later. Only one of the eight feds has his vest on, and guess what? It turned out the robbers could shoot. Two agents dead, five wounded. Vests were so stiff, only one guy was willing to wear his for twenty minutes in an air-conditioned car." Richards nodded at Roland Lemp. Lemp looked decidedly uncomfortable.

"We do have a vest that passes NIJ's stupid water test, most days at least, called our Tyrant model. Like the name? I thought of it myself. It's pretty comfortable, but expensive 'cause of what we have to pay for the Gore-Tex outside fabric. Lot of departments won't pay the price, so they buy our competitors' stuff that ends up in the trunk of the squad car. We got over a thousand saves, more than the rest of the whole industry, almost all with non-rated vests—a tiny fraction of the market. Why? People wear our vests, and they work." His face lit up as he thought of something.

"You wear a vest once in a while, and I know it's not one of mine. You like the way it feels? Or does it rub a hole in your skin after an hour and a half? See, I knew it," Richards said with a grin when he saw the President's expression. "Here, feel this one." David Richards stood up and began to remove his suit jacket and tie.

"Mr. Richards–" Roland Lemp began in protest.

"Hey, it's okay, I got a T-shirt on under it," Richards assured him as he undid the last button on his dress shirt and shrugged out of it. Then he pulled the satin-like nylon carrier over his head and walked up to where the President sat, pulling his undershirt down to cover his ample midsection as he did so.

"Here," he said, proffering the garment. "This is the 'Deep Cover' model. Stops .44

Magnum. Feel it—you don't have to put it on," he assured the Chief Executive. "No rating at all, but I'll put it back on and let one of your FBI guys shoot me with a three-round burst out of his 10mm MP5 submachine gun from a foot away."

"I don't think–"

"You know how bad NIJ is?" Richards interrupted as he remembered something. "Head trauma surgeon for the entire armed forces, Martin Fackler, got interested in body armor and requested NIJ's testing protocol. They wouldn't give it to him. Had to get it under the Freedom of Information Act. When he did, he immediately said the kid's clay test was a joke. But that wasn't all. Fackler ran the numbers and found that back in '80, when they added up the different dimensions on their backface deformation signature, NIJ even did their addition wrong!"

"Mr. Richards," the President said, handing back the body armor, "I was unaware of the controversy surrounding government standards in your industry. Perhaps we can go into this another time, when we can give this issue the attention it merits. Director Greenwell asked you to speak before us today, I am told, because he hoped you could help us with the threat ATF is now facing."

"You want vests?" Richards asked, incredulous. "For all the ATF agents? The guy told me you wanted to talk about–" He stopped abruptly. "Oh. Yes, of course. Got sidetracked with the stuff about NIJ standards. Wishful thinking." His brow furrowed. "It's only been, what? A week and a half? FBI already go through all of the suspects? Jesus, I didn't know they had that much manpower." Now it was the President's turn to appear puzzled. Dwight Greenwell looked miserable.

"Mr. President, Mr. Richards made an offhand suggestion last week that I of course did not take literally. I knew that the FBI would have its own criteria for finding–"

"Didn't take it literally?" Richards said in surprise. "Did you think I was kidding? And the FBI has its own criteria—you mean they have some better group of suspects to choose from? What have you people been doing here all this time?"

"Mr. President," Greenwell went on quickly, "Mr. Richards thinks that the most likely group of suspects would be the friends and relatives of people ATF has charged with firearms violations."

"Not 'charged with firearms violations'," Richards said, vigorously shaking his head. "I said 'killed or put in prison'. Those're the first people I'd look at. You stick some 25-year-old kid in the slam 'cause he put a folding stock on his SKS, and now he gets to be Darnell's wife every night, you think his dad's going to go, 'Oh, I'm glad he's learning about another culture', and send his new son-in-law a nice card?" He laughed. "You want to find this guy, check out the friends and relatives of the people ATF has shot or burned to death. Then go check out the friends and relatives of the ones they've put in federal prison because some piece of wood or steel on their gun violated ATF's rule-of-the-day.

"Guy watches his best friend go to prison on some conspiracy charge based on fender washers or bayonet lugs he had in his workshop, charges made by some government jerk who wants to pump up his arrest record, you don't think he's a likely candidate for what's going on now?"

"That's the purp–"

"What do you think people in this country are?" Richards asked, interrupting the President with another question before the man could answer the previous one. "I got a dog, loves everyone, never heard her growl once. Kids on the block love to play with her. I stop feeding her, let her run with some other dogs no one feeds, throw rocks at 'em when they come around to be petted, what happens? I end up with something acts more like a wolverine than a puppy the neighborhood kids like to play with.

"Why're people any different? Wartime, feds grab a kid just out of high school, issue him a rifle and tell him to kill another kid just out of high school 'cause the other kid's got on a different-shaped helmet. He does it 'cause fighting is what you do when you have to, and the feds've made him believe in the cause. We got thousands of war vets did just that when they were eighteen, and nobody thinks twice about it.

"Now, instead of an eighteen-year-old, you got a guy maybe thirty, forty, fifty years old. He sees his friends get their lives ruined by some trigger-happy government jerks who get promoted instead of fired when they screw up. Does it amaze you that this grown man might actually on his own decide this was something worth risking his life for?" Once again, Richards rushed on without waiting for an answer.

"Some Army choppers with door guns crashed on Henry Bowman's property two weeks ago. This Blair guy writing stuff on the Internet says Henry was being raided, along with two other dealers. Greenwell here says the other two were Grant Millet and Allen Kane. Is that true?"

"Yes, it is."

"Well, I know all three of those men, and between them, they got maybe a hundred friends who'd be mad as hell ATF was attacking them with helicopter gunships. I also know that at least two of those three men each paid more in federal income tax last year than you did, Mr. President. Why were Bowman, Kane, and Millet being raided? Hm?" he demanded, his words pelting the President rapid-fire like hail on a metal roof. "Aside from the fact that Bowman likes to drive over a hundred on the interstates, I've never known any of them to break one single law. What the hell'd they do, anyway?" There was a long pause, and the President finally decided to tell Richards the truth.

"We don't know, Mr. Richards. Wilson Blair was the supervisory agent in charge, and he and the agents who have vanished were the only ones who knew the particulars of the raids. We believe Blair may be dead, and whoever is sending the messages is someone else. But we don't know that for a fact." He smiled sadly. "To be blunt, Mr. Richards, we were hoping you could help us figure out who that person is."

"Mr. President," David Richards said slowly, which surprised everyone in the room, "has the FBI even *started* looking at relatives and associates of guys ATF has put in federal prison?"

"Roland?" the President asked. The FBI Director frowned.

"Not specifically. No."

"Dwight, how many people are there who fit Mr. Richards' description?"

"I don't have that information with me, but I can have it for you shortly. I'm sure it's a manageable num–"

"It's over sixty-two hundred people now," David Richards broke in, "that're in prison on technical violations. And he knows it. The crime is almost always 'conspiracy to violate federal firearms laws'. Bunch of guys I've done business with are in lockup right now for selling fifty bucks worth of SKS ammo. That stuff ATF declared was AP pistol ammo. Day before, you could buy it in any hardware store. Day after, dealer gets a felony count for each *round* he sells. At ten cents a round, that was five hundred counts of conspiracy, which comes out to about ten life sentences. One of the five guys turned rat for ATF, so he got off, but the others wouldn't, and they're doing ten-to-fifteen, which their lawyer said was a good deal." Richards eyes narrowed, and he was no longer the pleasant cherub talking about bureaucrats with their modeling clay.

"Guys one step away from welfare get ignored. Director Greenwell here and his band of merry men are trying to put every serious dealer out of business, starting with the NFA manufacturers. Forget about the failed raids on Kane, Millet, and Bowman for a second. Let's talk about ATF's 'successes'. Bill Fleming, Fred Vollmer, Jerry Drasen, Chris Lee, Dave Green, Jack Birge, Aron Lippman—every one of those men is a friend of mine. Every one of them was doing a few million dollars a year business, a lot of it to police departments. And the ATF gun thugs spent more than that trying to railroad them into prison for the rest of their lives. Not for shooting anybody, not for selling guns to felons, and not for lying about how much money they made. The hundreds of counts of 'conspiracy' were for steel washers, or pieces of wood, or forms ATF said weren't filled out right. Some of those cases are still open—Greenwell knows they're losers, but he's still spending money, trying to bankrupt these guys 'cause he found out they won't roll over like most of the fucking snitches he's got." Richards smiled without pleasure.

"You don't hear him contradicting me, do you, Mr. President?" he said as he nodded toward Dwight Greenwell. "That's because he knows as soon as you check it out, you'll find everything I've just said is true. You want to catch these guys? You tell Mr. Lemp there to get started on a list of all the acquaintances of the people I just named. The guys who're whacking ATF agents are smart, motivated, and they got money, so tell Mr. Lemp not to bother with anyone that doesn't have a few hundred thousand bucks in the bank, minimum. My name'll be on the list, 'cause I fit the profile. The guys you're looking for are people just like me." Richards stood up and put his suit jacket over his arm.

"Mr. Greenwell called me in so that I could give you my opinion. Well, here it is. ATF screwed the pooch. What's happening now is long overdue, and I'm not a bit sorry it's started. My advice? Try to make contact with these people and negotiate with them. You might find their demands very reasonable. I know mine would be." He walked to the exit and had his hand on the doorknob when he turned for a final comment.

"Keep the vest. Whoever's killing ATF agents doesn't want to kill you, Mr. President, but you might need it on an overseas visit, or something."

"Why do you say these people are not a threat to the Oval Office?"

"Because if they were, you'd already be dead."

***

"Give me somewhere to start from," Alex Neumann said. "I just don't buy what that guy Berkowitz was saying."

"From what you've told me, I don't either," Angela Riggs agreed. "Not the part about the egotism and thumbing his nose at the government." Riggs was wearing faded jeans and a yellow T-shirt, and sitting barefoot and cross-legged on the floor of her apartment. A glass-topped coffee table separated her from Alex Neumann. On the table were a half-dozen open cartons of Chinese food.

"So what's going on?"

"Well, first of all," she said, digging into the spiced pork with her chopsticks, "I think you are looking at the work of one man. The planning and strategy, I mean. Not the execution."

"So to speak."

"What? Oh. Right. Unfortunate word choice." She chewed and then continued, gesturing with the chopsticks. "I mean, everything I've seen and everything you've told me points to a coherent overall plan. A plan with defined goals, and an overall strategy specifically designed to achieve those goals. That indicates a single leader with vision. Fair statement?"

"Yes."

"Okay then. A coherent plan with defined goals and a strategy to achieve them is not the mark of a crazy person. This is not some guy who thinks he's Jesus or gets told what to do by his dog. He may be egotistical, but so was Patton. We may be able to exploit that, but we may not. So let's concentrate on this guy's goals. What are they? Most important ones first."

"Make the ATF go away," Neumann said hesitantly, remembering Harrison Potter's comment. "Well, let me rephrase that. If ATF were disbanded and their duties turned over to us, or back to the IRS, that wouldn't change anything. This guy's goal is to make the government get out of the gun-regulation business."

"Is it bigger than that? The allusions in his Internet messages to killing other federal agents? Is this man's ultimate goal to overthrow the government?"

"I don't think so," Neumann said, scowling. "I think that's mainly to pull others into it, and give us more to do."

"So you'll be so busy putting out fires, you won't be able to concentrate your assets on finding him and arresting him?"

"Right," Neumann said around a mouthful of rice.

"Alex, does that sound to you like someone who, deep down, wants to get caught?" Neumann quit chewing.

"No," he said quickly, remembering his 20th-century history. "It sounds like a leader in the middle of a war with a stronger enemy, calling on others with parallel interests to join in. America was fighting both the fanatical Japs in the Pacific and the German military machine in Europe. So we linked arms with Josef Stalin and let the Soviets lose twenty million soldiers keeping Germany's finest busy on the Russian Front. That spread Hitler too thin, and he couldn't hold France."

"And the more people he pulls in, the more likely he'll accomplish what he wants and the less likely it is that you'll figure out who he is." Neumann nodded as he considered this, then thought of something else that had been bothering him.

"What if there's another agenda, besides changing federal gun policy? Something bigger."

"Such as?" Riggs asked.

"I don't know. It's just that the facts of the case don't add up. Not yet, at least. Raids are planned, but they don't happen, and the agents that are supposed to be on them disappear. Okay, possible explanation: Someone in the government has a change of heart, or undergoes a conversion like Saul on the road to Damascus. He sabotages the raids, kills the others involved, and gets on the Internet with a call to arms. Two problems: One, there isn't an ATF agent alive who would want to do that. Two, there isn't an ATF agent alive who could pull it off if his life depended on it.

"Second explanation: Somebody running a hardcore gun rights group gets wind of the raids, and makes a preemptive strike, and then goes on-line. I could almost buy that, except for what happened in Missouri. How'd they blow up those two choppers in the air? So let's say we find an answer to that—what about the one that's missing? Any way you slice it, somebody in that helicopter had to be in on it. Otherwise, we'd have another wreck, or the men on it would have called in. What we got is straight out of the Twilight Zone."

"Is it?" Angela Riggs asked. "I mean, a jet, yes. You need an airport. But a helicopter, those men could have landed it anywhere. It's probably sitting in the woods somewhere, where they had a four-wheel-drive stashed."

"Right, but who was in on the plan? We've checked out all three ATF agents that were on that chopper. Might as well have been the Three Stooges. That leaves a National Guard pilot. Now he's in on this conspiracy, too? Doesn't add up."

"A stowaway?" she offered. "Holding a gun to the pilot's head? I know it's weak, but..."

"But we don't have anything better," Neumann agreed. "That's what makes me think this is something bigger. I can't help but believe that we've got hold of the tail of the elephant, Angela."

"What do you think the rest of it looks like?"

"I haven't the slightest goddamn idea."

***

"Aaron Siteman? You mean Congressman Aaron Siteman? From New Jersey? Oh, this is so exciting!" Cindy said, clapping her hands like a little girl.

"Hey, it's not that big a deal, Ellen," the young man said, preening. *He wants me to think it is a very big deal* Cindy thought.

"But this is so amazing. I've been here three days, and I get to meet you. It's amazing."

"Where are you from?" the Congressman asked as he sipped his vodka.

"California. And I've gotten so I just can't stand it there."

"Really?" Siteman asked. He had never been west of Pennsylvania.

"Oh, yeah. It's terrible. In San Francisco, I mean, all the guys are gay. And then I was in Marina Del Rey, and I'm like, give me a break. You know, all the surfer types, where you just want to yell, 'Hey, get a life!'" Cindy arched her back slightly and tossed her hair. "It's just gotten so plastic there, you know?" *That's it, check them out* she thought when she saw where Siteman's eyes were aimed.

"I've heard that," he said agreeably.

"My God, I still can't believe I'm meeting you." She lowered her voice and moved her head close to his. "Aren't you afraid, going out like this alone?"

"What do you mean?" Siteman asked, puzzled, as he glanced around the crowded bar.

"I mean, you don't have a bodyguard. Everybody important in California has bodyguards. I mean, there was this one guy that wanted to go out with me, and I'm like, no way. He had these two big guys hanging around him all the time, and I'm like, yeah, right. Your carpet cleaning business makes you just sooooo cool. No way I wanted to hang around with him and his two muscleheads."

"Well, I–"

"Teddy Kennedy has bodyguards," she said suddenly. "I've seen them. They carry UZIs and everything." She flashed him her most dazzling smile and moved in closer so she could whisper. "Can I be your bodyguard? For tonight?"

Aaron Siteman started laughing at his amazingly good fortune, and he put his arm around the young woman's waist.

"You can guard it all you want."

***

"Mmmm...you're a good kisser," Cindy Caswell said when he finally broke for air. They were outside the third Georgetown drinking establishment they had visited that evening. "Do you have a place we can go?"

"Well, I, uh–"

"That's all right," Cindy breathed softly. "My hotel's not too far, but I don't want to embarrass you, if there's anyone there that might see you, you know?" *Probably wishes the whole House could see him right now* she thought to herself.

"No, no, I don't think that would be a problem. Your hotel would be great."

"Mmmm...let's walk for a little while first," she whispered as she rubbed her breasts against his chest. "I like walking with you."

***

"God, I feel such an infinity with you," Cindy said, using the most inane-sounding line she could think of on short notice. She pulled Aaron Siteman away from the light of a streetlamp and into the shadows of an oak tree. "Ohhh, kiss me some more," she demanded, and arched her back as her mouth found his. The Congressman pulled her to him with his right arm and with his free hand began squeezing her firm breasts.

Cindy Caswell opened her left eye and looked over Congressman Siteman's shoulder. A figure in a dark business suit was walking silently towards them on crepe-soled shoes. She scanned the area behind and to the sides of the approaching form, searching for any other people. There were none. She pointed her right thumb up in the air behind the Congressman's back as she broke the kiss and moved her mouth up next to the man's right ear.

"Oh, that feels so good," she said, knowing her whispers would cover any sound Henry might make as he crossed the last few yards to where they stood. "Oh, I love it when you rub me like that, don't stop, that feels wonderful, a little harder, I like it firm, you've got such strong hands, oh, that's so good when you do it like that, God, I think I might even come this way, oh, I can't believe what you're doing, don't stop, just like that, oh, that's just r–"

Cindy Caswell kept her passionate monologue going right up until the last instant, when the polished face of the sixteen-ounce Estwing framing hammer shattered the back of Aaron Siteman's skull. She tensed her leg muscles as the Congressman collapsed against her, so that he would not drag her to the ground.

"Go," Henry said softly, and Cindy Caswell turned and walked away. Henry stayed another seven seconds, which was more than enough time to beat the Congressman to death with the tape-wrapped hammer. As he strolled off in the direction opposite of where Cindy had gone, he dropped the tool onto the rear-seat floor of a rusted out Fiat whose window was rolled down.

A block later, Henry started whistling.

"How the hell did they run this without our knowing it?" Roland Lemp demanded, waving the newspaper. "And what's this crap about how it came from Blair or someone close to him?"

"The cover letter had Blair's fingerprints on it. In ink, so you couldn't miss them," Alex Neumann explained. *Now he's going to ask how the Journal staff could verify whose they were without calling the Bureau* Neumann thought.

"Then how the hell did the editorial staff at a goddamn newspaper check them, without us knowing what they were up to?"

"We're still looking into that, sir."

"This makes us look like fools, Alex."

"Sir, I don't think it does. We have never said anything for publication about this subject. The only things we've put in print are generic comments about the investigation. It's Dwight Greenwell who's apt to be pissing blood, sir." The FBI Director listened to this comment, then smiled in spite of himself.

"I can't say I feel particularly sorry for him."

***

"Your breakfast, sir, and the four newspapers you wanted."

"Well, thank you. It's a pleasure to stay in a place with such excellent room service," Henry said with a faint French accent. "Here," he said, slipping the waiter a twenty.

"Thank you, Mr. Kreyder. Just ask for me if you need anything. My name's Jimmy."

"I'll do that," he agreed as the young man closed the door behind him.

"You are such a ham," Cindy Caswell said as she walked out of the bathroom. She wore a man's white terrycloth bathrobe, belted at the waist. "What did you order for me?"

"Little bit of everything. Fruit, melon, pancakes, toast, eggs, bacon, hash browns, juice, coffee." Henry held the chair for Cindy as she sat down at one end of the wheeled cart, then he picked up the stack of newspapers to scan the headlines. *USA Today* sat on top of the pile. Henry stared at the headline.

$50M REWARD FOR TERRORIST LEADER

"Looks like they're trying to get our attention," Henry said.

"Fifty million?"

"Yeah. They're a little vague on the terms, though," he added after scanning the article. "Like what exactly has to happen for someone to get it." He read further. "It also doesn't say if it would be considered taxable income or not." He tossed Cindy the paper and looked at the *New York Times* and the *Washington Post*.

"Hm. Here we go." At the bottom of the page of the second newspaper was a short article.

SITEMAN SLAIN IN GEORGETOWN
MOTIVE UNKNOWN IN CONGRESSMAN'S DEATH

"Nothing here," he said after he had skimmed the article. "That they're printing, at least."

"Is that good?"

"Who knows?"

"Henry?" Cindy said slowly.

"What?"

"Does it...ah...is it a turn-on for you?"

"Last night?" he asked, startled by the question but not enough to get careless and talk about murder while sitting in a hotel room. "No." *But I think I know what you're talking about* he thought to himself. "Why?"

"Just wondering. I didn't think it was for you, or anything. I didn't mean that. It's just that, well...that first time, in Las Vegas, it was..."

"It was different. The whole thing."

"Yes. You're right. It was." Cindy looked off at a point in space a few feet in front of the opposite wall, then shook her head and turned to look at her friend. "The President got anything to say about this reward business?" Cindy asked.

"Not much. Mostly talk about the task force meetings."

"Be nice if we could know what's going on in them."

"I got an idea about how to do that," Henry said as he picked up the *Wall Street Journal* and glanced at the front page. Then he turned to the editorials inside the back of the paper's first section.

"By God, they printed it," he said in a voice that held a tinge of disbelief. "And they didn't tell anyone they were going to." Cindy cocked an eyebrow. "Take a look," he said, and handed her the paper.

Free-Market Terrorists?

By Wilson M. Blair

This piece arrived at WSJ offices shortly before the ATF press conference yesterday. We believe it came either from Wilson Blair or from someone who was at one time in close contact with him. The Journal does not normally provide a forum for those who commit violent crimes. In this case, we have made an exception.

Since I first condemned ATF and explained my intentions, media comment has taken three forms: 1) Outrage that any American might use systematic murder to effect a paradigm shift; 2) Horror that some American citizens do not share this outrage, and 3) Speculation as to whether ATF Agent Wilson Blair is really the one leading the charge.

Conspicuously absent is a rational discussion of the philosophy behind the killings or the fundamental beliefs of the killers. The 'terrorists' are invariably assumed to be either white supremacists, paranoids who believe in massive

Like it or not, millions of intelligent, rational Americans think guns are exactly the same as books.

government conspiracies, or weird loners who would trade their lives for the elusive fifteen minutes of fame.

The unspoken and unchallenged assumption is that anyone who kills employees of the U.S. Government is at best an irrational, paranoid, right-wing fanatic and at worst certifiably insane. The idea that the killers might be logical people acting in a reasoned manner is too horrible for guardians of the status quo to contemplate. Unfortunately, dismissing a growing movement as irrational and ignoring the basis for its existence will not make it go away. Like it or not, our leaders are going to have to examine the reasons behind our actions.

There are a lot of promises in the Constitution, but only one thing guarantees these promises: The Second Amendment. A large number of people in America believe that honest adults have a fundamental right, which they possess by merely drawing breath, to buy, sell, borrow, own, transport, carry, lend, or give away whatever small arms they want without any restrictions whatsoever. It does not matter to them how long the buttstock is, whether there are threads on the barrel, how many shots the gun holds, or what date the gun was made.

To these people, murder, robbery, and assault are made no more or less despicable by dint of the instrument used. A knife-wielding murderer should receive no less punishment nor less speedy trial than one who uses a gun.

These people believe government has no more authority to restrict their gun rights than it has the right to ban the sale of automated printing presses. For years, these people have grudgingly submitted to ever more ludicrous measures, and then been vilified as fanatics any time they tried to say "enough!" Most importantly, when these people disobey these laws they so detest, they do not believe they are doing anything wrong.

The printing press parallel is not made idly; If you want to really understand these people, imagine your reaction if the government enacted the same laws on books as it has on guns.

What if the government required every book to have a serial number? What if it were a felony for any person to sell a book at a profit without a federal license? What if anyone (except government agents) who bought a book from a federally-licensed book dealer had to fill out a federal form listing his name, address, and the book's serial number, then wait five days before taking possession? What if anyone (except government agents) who wanted a book under a certain size had to pay a $200 federal tax, get fingerprinted and photographed, and wait months for government approval, and the penalty for noncompliance was 10 years and $10,000? What if it were a felony for anyone (except government agents) to buy or sell books whose

pages were made out of anything other than a specific type of paper? What if some states made it a felony (except for government agents) to buy more than one book a month, and banned outright (except to government agents) books with more than a certain number of pages? What if it was a common occurrence for government agents to destroy someone's house, seize all his property, and imprison him for suspected violations of these book laws? What if government agents planted banned books in people's homes and shot the citizens or burned them alive?

You may think this comparison is crazy, and that is your privilege. Like it or not, however, millions of intelligent, rational people think guns are exactly the same as books.

Any gun? you ask. What about an atomic bomb? Should the people have those? The

---

[ATF] has made millions of citizens realize that they have nothing left to lose.

Federalist Papers discussed this very issue. Freedom will always be assured if the people have the same basic arms as are issued to a soldier in a modern military. In 1789, that was muskets but not field pieces. Two centuries later, it's M16s, not nukes. Prior to June of 1934, the federal government understood this.

Who are these people that hold such radical beliefs? Not white supremacists. State antigun laws took root in the Jim Crow era after the Civil War. White supremacists want to strengthen their hold over hated minorities, not diminish it.

Nor are these people conspiracy theorists. They don't think the world is run by the Trilateral Commission—they know it is all but impossible to get a half-dozen

egotists to agree on anything, let alone keep their mouths shut about it. They know there was no huge conspiracy when General Douglas MacArthur burned indigent WWI vets out of their D.C. camp in 1932. No secret 'master plan' when U.S. government doctors conducted radiation experiments on unwitting citizens in the 1940's, and gave poor blacks with syphillis a placebo so that they could be the 'control' group in a VD experiment. No complex plot when the Philadelphia mayor dropped a bomb on some irritating residents and burned ten square blocks of his city to the ground in 1985. No overarching scheme when federal agents killed an Idaho man's wife and son (over the length of a shotgun buttstock) in 1992, or burned eighty citizens alive over a $200 tax in 1993.

These events were all simply powerful government officials exercising that power the way they wanted to. The people who view guns like you view books understand this. They understand Lord Acton's simple, fundamental truth: Power corrupts, and absolute power corrupts absolutely. Those in power will always try to maintain and increase that power, and try to crush anyone who challenges it.

The Constitution may enumerate the areas where the government has no authority to pass laws, but many legislators think a 51% majority vote negates any basic human right. Americans want to live in a free society. ATF jails them, seizes their property, and even kills them over things that do not merit even a one dollar fine. We have made millions of reasonable citizens realize they have nothing left to lose.

Final point: Some will continue to claim that Wilson Blair, former ATF Supervisor, would never say these things, and that this author is really someone else. Rather than debate the issue, ask yourselves this: *Does it matter?*

"Think it'll help?" she asked after reading the piece.

"Can't hurt," Henry said as he pulled up a chair and dug into the food on the cart.

"So what's our schedule?"

"Do some reconnaissance around town today, get set up for our next...engagement. Catch a five o'clock flight to Denver and then Aspen. Check in with Ray, find out if he's heard from Allen. Tomorrow I'll see if I can fly that jet of his."

"Busy day."

"No rest for the wicked."

***

"Congressman, it's some reporter from the *Washington Times*. I tried to get rid of him, but he says he needs your approval to run a story. Something about SAT scores...? You want me to hang up on him?"

"Nonono, I'll take it. Let me, ah, go in my office, where it's quieter. What line is he on?"

"Two."

"Okay. Thanks." Richard Gaines went into his private office and closed the door. "Hello?" he said into the phone.

"Congressman Gaines?"

"Speaking."

"Yeah, Jim Howard at the *Times*," Henry said, making up a name and saying it in a rush so Gaines wouldn't catch it. "I got a very interesting phone call from a man named William Pressler in Missouri not too long ago. He says he knows you, or used to, at least. He's got an interesting story about why your SAT scores were so high. Says you would-n't have gone to Washington University otherwise. Would you care to comment?" There was a long silence. *That's it* Henry said to himself. *Get that old mind working. I'll wait you out. First one to talk is the loser, and I intend to win this one, Congressman.*

"I don't think you have much of a story. Not after all this time, certainly." Henry heard Gaines swallow and inhale.

"I think you're wrong, Congressman. The public loves to hear about it when you folks pay your babysitters in cash, and this is a lot more interesting than that, don't you think?"

"Ted Kennedy was thrown out of Harvard for paying someone to take his test for him, and that didn't hurt his political career." There was a whine in Gaines' voice, and Henry smiled. *Wouldn't that make a great quote* he thought. *Wishful thinking if ever I heard it.*

"As to some unproven allegation about something that supposedly happened back in the 'sixties..." Congressman Gaines left the sentence unfinished, but laughed nervous-ly.

"Congressman, I'd say you were right if your last name was Kennedy. But it isn't. Unless you got a few million stashed away I don't know about, this thing could be very bad for you." *There's the stick.* "Thing is," Henry went on, "I agree with you. Who cares if you bought your SATs? Not like there's a minimum score you have to have before you can be a Congressman. But I need a story. That's my job." *Now the carrot.* "So help me out here. Tell me what's going on with the task force."

"Those meetings are private. With the President."

"Of course. But all the agencies are in on it, and some of those guys are already talking, like they always do. Give me something, and I'll go to them for verification."

"You won't mention my name?"

"Never. Won't even say it's from one of the people on the task force. I'll make like it came from inside ATF or FBI, wherever. We always protect our sources." There was another long pause where Henry held his tongue.

"Okay," Gaines said finally. "There's not much to report. Everybody says Blair is dead, and it's some terrorist group that's doing the killing and pretending to be him. The suspect list sounds huge, like a couple hundred thousand people. They're going after some special kind of dealer or something first, which gets it down to thirty or forty thousand."

"What kind of dealer?"

"NSA, I think they said. Not just dealers but something about dealers and people with NSA licenses. They said there were over 30,000 of them. Oh, and the FBI found a car in Philadelphia they think was used in one of the killings, with all the serial numbers ground off."

"Do they have anyone in custody?"

"No, it was a dead end. But they're looking for more abandoned cars. Then the CIA had some British guy in, talking about the IRA. You might could get hold of him and talk to him. Nigel something. Had two last names. Laughed at us and said since his soldiers can't stop the IRA, there wasn't anything we could do about these people here. He was a real jerk. ATF brought in some guy from Michigan who makes bulletproof vests." *David Richards?* Henry thought. *Bet he gave them an earful.*

"He complained a lot about the rules his company has to follow. Oh, and he told the FBI to go check out the friends and relatives of the people ATF had killed or put in prison. He said they were the most likely suspects. Talked about how he had a bunch of friends in prison, which kind of surprised me, that he'd say that in front of the President."

"Congressman, one of the things I'm trying to get a handle on is the human angle, and you just touched on that. What's the dynamic inside this task force? Can you tell how the people in it feel about each other?"

"Well, I don't think the President likes Dwight Greenwell. He hasn't seemed too impressed with anything Greenwell has said. He seems okay with the FBI guys. The younger one, Neumann, has been doing a lot of the talking and it looks like the President is listening. Schaumberg talks a lot sometimes, and I don't think the President likes him much, either. It's Harrison Potter, the old Chief Justice, that the President seems to respect the most. The rest of us don't speak much. Nobody likes Schaumberg," he added after a moment. *No shit* Henry thought.

"What's Potter's role been, so far?"

"It's kind of weird. He doesn't say much, but when he does, it usually makes someone nervous. Not the President, though. And he seems to be smiling sometimes when no one else is." There was a pause, and Henry decided Gaines was thinking. "He did talk a lot in the first meeting, about the gun laws and ATF procedures. He'd gone over to their office and asked a lot of questions. I don't think Greenwell liked that at all."

"You're saying some things I've heard from several of my other sources, Congressman," Henry lied. "Let me ask you something. What's the problem with Greenwell? Why don't people like him?"

"I think maybe some of the people blame Dwight Greenwell for what has been happening. Like it's partly his fault. I think maybe even the President has that feeling. A little bit, at least." *Just wait* Henry thought with a smile. *It gets better.*

"Congressman, I think I've got a much better story to write than that other one. Let me see what I can get from inside the various agencies, and talk to my editor. He may not want to blame Greenwell in print, but you've given me several angles to work. There are also some other reporters covering this, but none of them knows about the SAT stuff, so you can hang up on them. In fact, I'd prefer it."

"Okay."

"Good deal. And you can call me Bud. My friends do."

"But that...other story is dead?" Gaines asked quickly, before the other man could hang up.

"Dead as Jerry Abel," Henry said immediately, and broke the connection.

June 23

At the end of the block, Billings used his outside mirrors and saw that no one was around. He pulled the Chevrolet over to the curb, and stopped. The two cardboard boxes full of old newspapers were still on the front seat, and the rack of suits and shirts still obscured the rear window.

Billings reached down, picked up the leather sandbag off the floor in front of him, and set it atop one of the boxes. Then he leaned over the driver's seat and retrieved the rifle he had stowed on the floor in the back the night before. It was a Marlin lever action in .45-70 caliber, a rifle many Missouri deer hunters favored. An old cotton dress shirt was wrapped around the buttstock and secured with tape. Another covered the entire barrel. The back half of the action, including the hammer, was exposed. Billings laid the wrapped-up weapon on top of the sandbag with its buttstock touching his chest and its muzzle pointed towards the right window. Then he dropped the car back into Drive, checked his left mirror, and pulled back out into the street.

At a few minutes before 7:00 CST, as Billings had learned to expect, the Cadillac appeared up ahead on the right, coming down the cross street. The Regional Director of the Environmental Protection Agency was a man of routines, and that fact made a simple task even easier. The Cadillac slowed for the 4-way stop and made a right turn onto the street where Billings was parked. Billings took his foot off the brake and drove up to the empty intersection where he made a complete stop. Then he accelerated to a point where he was about seventy-five yards behind the other man's car and maintained that distance as he followed the other vehicle through the suburban neighborhood.

The driver of the Cadillac stayed in the center lane heading west and braked on the gentle downgrade as the electric signal changed from yellow to red. Billings pressed the control for the Chevrolet's passenger window and lowered it all the way as he steered his vehicle into the left-turn lane and came to a stop beside the other car. He was familiar with all the lights in this area, and knew that at this one, left-turning traffic got a green arrow for about fifteen seconds while the straight-ahead signal remained red. Billings glanced over at the Cadillac to make sure of who was driving. Then he turned his attention to his own driver's side mirror, willing that no cars pull up behind them as they waited out the red light.

Billings adjusted the position of the rifle on the sandbag and disengaged the Marlin's safety. That done, he split his attention between his outside mirrors and the cross-traffic signal to his left.

When the light for the cross traffic turned yellow, Billings took a deep breath and swiveled his head to the right. He held the grip area of the Marlin's buttstock in his left hand, tilted his head so that his eye was directly above the barrel, and squeezed the trigger.

The 405-grain flatpoint traveled three feet in 1/400 of a second and deformed slightly as it chopped a jagged hole in the safety glass of the Cadillac's driver's-side window. It then struck the EPA Director just above his left ear with a remaining velocity of a little over nine hundred feet per second.

The blast inside the enclosed space was deafening, and Billings winced as his eardrums suffered the expected momentary agony. He saw the starred hole in the other car's left front window, within an inch of the spot he had intended, and the spray of blood on the passenger side of the Cadillac's interior. Then the other car began to roll out into the deserted intersection as the corpse's foot slipped off the brake pedal and the body slumped across the front seat.

The retired dry cleaner glanced once more at his mirrors, looked each way for anyone running a red light, then waited the final two seconds for the arrow. When it turned green, Billings cut his wheel left and accelerated at a normal rate. The other car was all the way across the intersection, gradually picking up speed on the gentle slope as it slowly drifted over into the empty oncoming-traffic lanes.

Two hundred seventeen yards past the signal, the EPA Director's Cadillac was traveling thirty-eight miles per hour when it slammed into the left front corner of a GEO sedan parked at the curb. The smaller car's right-side wheels caught on the curb and the GEO overturned before both vehicles came to rest on the sidewalk, locked in a twisted metallic embrace.

It would be twenty-one minutes before the police arrived. They would scratch their heads at the two deployed airbags and the dead driver with massive head injuries lying across the floor. Then they would discover that the crash was not what had killed the man in the Cadillac.

***

"You're sure about this?"

"Getting nervous, Ray?" Henry Bowman asked as he cycled the Citation's controls and continued working his way through the lengthy pre-takeoff checklist. "Want to get out, and I'll take Cindy to breakfast in Denver, meet you back here in a few hours?"

"Okay, I'll shut up."

"Good," he said, then keyed the mike. "Sardy Tower, Citation two-niner Alpha Whiskey ready for takeoff, destination Denver International, I have Tango."

"Citation two-niner Alpha Whiskey, cleared for takeoff runway two-eight, eastern departure approved."

"Two-niner Alpha Whiskey," Henry acknowledged, then stowed the mike and gently advanced the throttles of the idling engines. He gave the aircraft hard right rudder, and the big jet turned as it rolled onto the runway. As the nose swung onto the centerline, Henry fed in left rudder and gave the Pratt & Whitney turbojets full throttle. The white business jet was several thousand pounds under gross weight, and it rapidly gathered speed as it rocketed down the asphalt. The nose lifted, and a few seconds later the mains broke free of the ground. Henry checked his compressor RPM, exhaust gas temperature, and airspeed, then retracted the gear and adjusted the trim.

"All we need's a stewardess," Henry said happily as he banked the jet to put it on an easterly heading. He had to shout to be heard over the noise of 5900 pounds of thrust. "Looks like we got about a fifty-knot tailwind. Should make Denver in less than twenty minutes if they're not stacked up in the pattern."

Ray Johnson relaxed a little.

June 24

"Thank you for making time to see me, Mr. President."

"Quite all right, Alex."

"Sir, that article in the paper is really hurting us. We're up to forty-seven dead, and it's not just ATF any more. A Regional Director of the Environmental Protection Agency was murdered in Phoenix yesterday, and an EPA field agent was killed this morning in California. A message on one of the bulletin boards now says all EPA agents carrying guns will be shot on sight. But the–"

"What are you talking about, Alex? EPA agents don't carry guns." *Oh, Christ* Neumann thought. *Now I get to explain this mess, too.*

"Yes, they do, Mr. President. At least, they're authorized to carry guns. Just like employees of most federal agencies."

"What? Which federal agencies? FBI and DEA, you mean."

"Not just them, sir. The State Department, Department of Labor, Department of Agriculture, Department of En–"

"*Agriculture?*" the President shouted. "What do *they* need to carry guns for? What are you talking about, Agent Neumann?"

"Ah, I assumed you knew, Mr. President. It's common knowledge, at least among those who are involved in this, ah, gun issue. The gun magazines are constantly running editorials complaining about it. Would you like me to get you a list of the agencies?"

"Immediately."

"Yes, sir." *Come on, Alex* the FBI agent told himself. *Keep cool here.* "Ah, sir, the problem is getting worse with ATF as well. Three ATF agents killed and one wounded in the last twenty-four hours. One of the three had announced his resignation the day before. It's in today's *Wall Street Journal*. The *Journal* informs me that there have been nine more resignations phoned in to their classified ad department since this time yesterday."

"Tell me about the suspects you have," the President demanded. *From bad to worse* Neumann thought as he delivered more bad news. The FBI had few leads, and the suspects and possible witnesses absolutely refused to speak. Then Neumann made his pitch.

"Mr. President, I know this is not a hostage situation in the strict sense of the word. But I think it's time to treat it like one."

"Negotiate?"

"Yes, sir. I think you should contact the man that's behind all this, and find out what he wants. Apparently it isn't money. Maybe if you talked to him before...before things go any farther..."

"And how shall we contact this man? A full-page ad in the *Wall Street Journal?*"

"Sir, I'm not sure how to do that. I mean, without setting off a PR nightmare."

"Agent Neumann, the public is going to turn more against these terrorists, not more in favor of them. And if the FBI would just–" The President stopped himself in mid-sentence and took a deep breath.

"I didn't mean that. I'm proud of the job you and your men have been doing. And this negotiation idea is a fair suggestion. Maybe if we put our heads together we can think of some way to contact these people without the media eating us for breakfast. Are you willing to work with me on this?" the President asked.

"I'd be honored, Mr. President."

As it turned out, the two men's efforts proved to be unnecessary.

June 25

"This thing really handles great, Ray," Henry yelled over his shoulder. "I'm glad you got it. Is Bill pissed?"

"Haven't seen him for a while. He was living down valley with some aerobics instructor, but I think she got tired of him running up her charge cards. I don't know where he is now." Ray stepped up between the two pilot's seats. "How you doing up here?" he asked Cindy.

"He's letting me fly it," she answered. "Is that okay?"

"Sure," Ray said, his heart rate and blood pressure climbing slightly with this bit of new information. *Hard to believe this girl is such a skilled assassin* he thought for perhaps the tenth time. Like most men, he was quite taken with Cindy Caswell.

"I bet girls love this plane. You ever get laid while you were in it?" she asked with a grin.

"I'm too old for that," Ray said with a laugh. *Not.*

"Don't believe it, Cindy. His pilot told me they have to put it in the shop at Sardy twice a year just to get all the come stains out of the carpet."

"Henry is an incurable optimist, Miss Caswell."

"Listen, I know a couple girls at the club, Kimmy and Olivia? You get them in here, you'll need new carpeting. Bring this to St. Louis, and I'll set it up, when this is all over."

"Yeah, when it's over. Sounds good." *When it's over* he thought. *That might be a while, Cindy.*

"Stop getting Ray horny and pull your power back for a descent. We're coming up on Washington."

***

"Come in, Mr. President," Harrison Potter said as he opened his office door. The Chief Executive looked exhausted, which was very unusual. Potter scowled quickly as the President headed for a leather armchair. He followed a few steps behind the President and sat down on a couch across from the younger man.

"I damn near bit off Alex Neumann's head yesterday," the President said without preamble, "and all the man was doing was telling me the latest facts. I ought to be ashamed of myself." The President sighed. "Harry, do you know the story about President Truman, when that music critic wrote the bad review about his daughter's singing, and Truman blasted him in print?"

"Of course, sir."

"You know the facts behind it?"

"Tell me," Potter answered. He knew what the President was going to say, but also realized the President needed to say it out loud.

"Harry Truman's Press Secretary was a boyhood friend that Truman had always respected, man named Charles Ross. Whenever something really made Truman mad and offended him personally, he'd dictate a letter. Charles Ross, I'm told, never made any attempt to reason with the President, to talk him out of doing something that was beneath him. He'd take down verbatim whatever the President said, and have the letter typed up without changing one word. Except he never handed it back to the President for his signature until twenty-four hours later. And the President always tore it up.

"Charles Ross never took a vacation while Truman was in office, and he probably didn't think Truman would fire him without warning, so he never told anyone about the procedure he used when the President got hot under the collar about something personal."

"And then Charles Ross had a massive heart attack and died while Harry Truman was still in office," Potter said.

"Right. And the new man didn't know the drill, and when that music critic said Margaret sang like a mockingbird in heat, the new Press Secretary had Truman sign the angry letter on the spot, and he sent it off in the morning mail. You know the story."

"I like hearing it again."

"I don't have a daughter, and if I did, I don't think I'd feel compelled to defend her in print against music critics. But I sure as hell think every President should have a Charlie Ross to talk to. And in my case, you're it." The retired Chief Justice nodded in acceptance and gave the President his asymmetric smile.

"Harry, this Wilson Blair mess has made everyone absolutely crazy. I just had a meeting with Alex Neumann. Seven ATF agents murdered in the last twenty-four hours. That makes fifty-two total, not counting the thirteen that are missing, with another dozen or so wounded. That also doesn't include family members that in some cases have been executed at the same time. On top of that, two EPA officials have been murdered, one outside Kansas City, and–"

"What?" Potter interrupted, which was something he did very rarely.

"The EPA's Regional Director was shot in the head on his way to work two days ago. It probably didn't make the papers here, what with all the others. Out in California, an EPA field agent was shot in the back this morning as he got out of his car. In his own driveway, Harry. Neumann says it's two different killers. There are no specific suspects; I have been told that the FBI is looking at small business owners who have had large fines levied on them by the Agency, things like that. The list of people with possible grudges in the Kansas and Missouri area is apparently quite large—several hundred names. In California it's ten times that many. Privately, Alex Neumann doesn't expect an arrest on either murder any time soon. At about the time of the second shooting, a message appeared on the computer network that all EPA agents that carry guns were now fair game."

"How many is *that*, Mr. President?" Potter asked. "What EPA agents carry guns?"

"Funny you should say that, Harry. I asked the same question. You were in the hospital for a while a few years back, so you may be forgiven your ignorance, but I don't have an excuse.

"For several years now, Mr. Neumann informs me, employees of the EPA have been armed while on duty, and with full government sanction. And they are not alone. Neumann sent me a copy of an FAA memorandum to its Aviation Security Divisions. Those are the folks that operate the metal detectors in the airports. Would you be interested to know which federal employees these Security Divisions are supposed to wave through without checking?"

"Yes, I would." This was news to the retired Chief Justice.

"Let's see here," the President said, pulling a folded sheet of copy paper from the pocket of his suit coat. "In addition to the FBI, Secret Service, and DEA, which you probably already knew about, employees of the Environmental Protection Agency are now authorized to carry guns. As are employees of the Departments of Agriculture, Education, Immigration, Labor, Energy, and Commerce. To that, add the Bureau of Land Management, the FAA, the Department of Health and Human Services, Department of Housing and Urban Development, and the State Department. And, of course, the IRS," the President added. "People from those agencies may be armed anywhere in the country.

Including, as I said, while they are traveling on commercial airlines. Surprised?"

"'Horrified' would be more accurate."

"My thoughts exactly. I was made aware of this startling fact less than an hour ago. Apparently it has been common knowledge among members of the gun culture since the late 1980's." He shook his head in disbelief. "I won't say this to anyone else, but it's no wonder these people are so angry." He scowled.

"Where was I? Oh yes, dead federal employees, and how their numbers increase daily. Concurrent with the murders, over a hundred ATF agents have resigned. About half of them in the last seventy-two hours." The President smiled without pleasure. "Of course we haven't yet exhausted the supply of applicants to replace them, but that pool is shrinking also.

"On the other side of the ledger, Treasury agents did kill a man yesterday in Minneapolis who walked into the local ATF office and started spraying bullets. There were a similar case in another city this past week. Atlanta, I think."

"I read about those."

"Right. That took care of the murderers of four agents. For all the rest of the killings I just mentioned, we have a total of fourteen suspects in custody . Two of them know each other, and those are the only two that are talking. They are apparently responsible for killing an agent in Florida. Alex Neumann tells me that if the other twelve suspects in other killings continue to keep their mouths shut, at least ten of them will be released within the week." The President paused to let his words sink in.

"Harry, part of me wants to invoke martial law and send the Marines in to shoot anyone even suspected of killing federal employees." He smiled sadly. "But that feeling usually lasts about five seconds." The President took a deep breath, and Harrison Potter knew what his old friend was going through.

"Alex Neumann wants to try to get Blair, or whoever he is, to contact me. No plan that suits me, yet. A full page ad on the back of the *Wall Street Journal* might work, but would kill me in the polls, I'm afraid." The President shook his head. "I'd prefer to give the FBI a little more time, see if they can find him first."

"Sounds reasonable."

"What the hell am I going to do here?" the President asked rhetorically. Potter inferred that his friend was not through thinking out loud, so he held his tongue. "My predecessors would probably have called for more federal authority. Burn the midnight oil and draft another sweeping 'anti-terrorism' bill, all dressed up like a Thanksgiving turkey."

"You don't want to do that?"

"Sometimes, as I said, I want to do a lot more than that. And then I'm ashamed of myself. So no—I don't want to see more legislation. But there's another reason, the one I'll have to use on the people in Congress who don't have any of those moral reservations." The President stared at Potter, and the older man realized he was expected to answer.

"Laws like that don't work."

"Exactly. You know, Harry, I never would have thought when I took this office that I'd have to become a virtual expert on terrorist groups."

"But you have," Potter said with a smile as he glanced involuntarily at the engraved plaque on his office wall. It said **Those Who Refuse to Remember History Are Destined to Repeat It.**

"I have," the President agreed, "and I have learned things I had no idea were true. I won't confess my ignorance in public, but no sense keeping it from you. When that Brit told us there were only two hundred active IRA members in all of Ireland, it was all I could do to keep my jaw from hitting the floor."

"The others were less adept at concealing their own astonishment, Mr. President."

"Yes, well, I called Major Hume-Douglas in for a little private chat later in the day, and got an even bigger earful. Then I tapped some researchers from three different universities, and got them to bring me up to speed on the philosophies and practices of terrorist groups around the world. The Red Brigades and the Baader-Meinhof in particular, in Italy and Germany. Do you realize that both those organizations do things to force the government to be more authoritarian? That that's one of their goals?" Potter nodded.

"Common strategy. Make the government crack down on more people, and you'll get more converts to your cause, or so goes the theory. Doesn't work too well when the revolutionaries are viewed as a handful of crackpot kids, whining about how big industry controls the government. Socialist youths in Italy haven't proven to be any more effective at turning the public against the government than American college kids here in the late 'sixties, bombing ROTC buildings.

"And as for Germany..." Potter gave a shrug, and laughed softly. "Using that strategy on the Teutonic mentality strikes me about like plotting to throw Br'er Rabbit in the briar patch."

"The Germans' supposed natural affinity for authority?" the President asked with a cocked eyebrow. It was the same theory the University researchers had offered. Potter nodded gently.

"Laugh if you want to, Mr. President, but some people actually like rigid organization and being told what to do. Remember back in '86, when Kurt Waldheim was elected President of Austria, and some U.S. journalist found out he'd been in the SS during the war? The big hue and cry was all in this country, not Austria. I half-expected to see a full-page ad in *USA Today* from the Austrian Chamber of Commerce saying 'Hey, Americans, get it through your thick heads: WE DON'T CARE!'" The President smiled ruefully at this and shook his head.

"I'm in a bind, Harry."

"I know that, sir," the older man said, becoming completely serious once more.

"Congress is pressuring me to declare martial law." Potter looked at the President sharply when he heard this. "My feelings exactly," the President said when he saw Potter's reaction. "Several other presidents have been accused of suspending the Constitution. I don't want to be the one who makes it official."

"Don't blame you." The former Chief Justice closed his eyes. "You know, I've always felt the American president who faced the single most difficult challenge as leader of this country was Abraham Lincoln. And your current problem, while similar in many ways, does not yet compare to the one that confronted him."

"Go on," the President said, resisting the urge to comment on the modifier Potter had used for the word 'compare'.

"The Civil War might have been averted if Lincoln had realized two fundamental facts. First, the South had a different culture from the North, and placed a high value on preventing that culture from being destroyed by federal edict and government troops. Second, slavery as an institution was already being pulled into a deep grave by its own economic weight. All it needed was a little free-market push, and it would have been dead and buried."

"Explain that, Harry." The older man took a deep breath.

"A slave was a huge capital investment. In 1850, an eighteen-year-old buck would bring upwards of a thousand dollars at auction. On top of that, the owner had to keep him fed, clothed, sheltered, and relatively healthy. That wasn't free. He also had to keep him working and prevent him from running away, which meant hiring an overseer. And then, the slave had an incentive to do just enough work to avoid a beating. So slave labor was not very cost-effective, and became less and less so the more rigorous the work. The railroads showed that."

"Enlighten me."

"Immigrant labor built the railroads, not slaves. Slaves were too valuable to risk. Railroad companies worked their men 'til they dropped at twenty-five cents a day. Man lost an eye from flying metal chips, or a foot from a dropped rail, that was his problem. Drag him off the line and call in another. Company wasn't out a nickel, let alone a thousand dollars."

"I hadn't realized that."

"Sure. Lots of workers died building the railroads. The old saying was that the railroad lines had 'an Irishman under every tie.' Out in California, it was Chinese." Potter shook his head. "Owning a machine made sense. Owning a human who could get sick, die, run away, or choose to work as slowly as possible didn't make any economic sense at all. Which was why only a tiny fraction of southerners still owned slaves as of 1860. The issue was ultimately a cultural one, and it was central to the whole secession movement. Southerners who would never have been able to afford even one slave didn't want the government telling them how they had to live. Lincoln could have easily solved the problem in the marketplace, but he chose the battlefield."

"How so?"

"By having the government buy all existing slaves from their owners. The number of slaves was finite; slave importation had ended a half-century earlier in 1809, as proscribed in the Constitution." Potter laughed mirthlessly as he thought of something.

"Now, that in itself is an amazing thing, when you think about it. The men who ran slave ships didn't get a nickel of government money, yet they agreed that in twenty years they would go out of business entirely. Forget forcing companies out of business—can you imagine the reaction today if you just proposed a bill that would abolish government subsidies completely in twenty years and force all industries to cope with a free market?" Potter shook his head, as if to clear it of the heretical thought.

"Anyway, with slave importation in 1860 having been dead for over half a century, the only new supply was slave women giving birth. Buy all slaves their freedom, and the slavery issue vanishes without a shot being fired. Not to mention avoiding that pesky issue of seizing property without compensation."

"Would've been expensive."

"Dirt cheap compared to fighting a war," Harrison Potter said as he leaned back in his chair. "Not to mention the huge cost in lives. This mess we've got now is also a cultural issue. A month ago, I hadn't realized how true that was. Whoever wrote that piece in the *Journal* hit it right on the head—these people don't think they're doing anything wrong, and we've taught them they have nothing left to lose."

"And unlike slavery, the government can't take the moral high ground on this one," the President said quietly. He looked around Potter's extensive library. "Do you have a book on Lincoln you could recommend?" he asked his friend. "Right now I could use some inspiration."

June 26

"You shouldn't even be talking about this, Ray."

"We have to, Henry. Ultimately, negotiation is going to happen. We might as well open up the discussions now." *He's more upset than I've ever seen him* Ray thought. *Much worse than when I insisted on getting involved with this.*

"No."

"But we can't go on indefinitely like this without letting them see that there's a way out for everyone."

"If you go in the White House to talk to the President about what we've been doing, you will never come out alive. And you will die the worst death you can possibly imagine. I am absolutely certain of that."

"That won't happen." *It can't. Not in this country* he added silently.

"Why? Because this is America?" Henry said sarcastically, as if reading his friend's thoughts. "That's *exactly* what will happen. What would you do, Ray, if you were in their place?" he asked. "Hm? Your people are being killed every day and you don't have shit. Fifty million dollar reward gets ignored. Every day it's getting worse. Your agents are resigning and your apparent leadership ability is going straight into the toilet. Your approval ratings are in the basement, and suddenly a guy appears on your doorstep saying he represents Blair and company. You going to make nice? Shit, no. You'd call in old Hap Edwards with his bolt cutters and tell him to find out whatever he could, don't worry about the blood."

"Henry, I—"

"Ray. Listen to me. I am not making this up. I know Hap Edwards. Not personally, but gun people have lots of connections in law enforcement, including FBI and CIA. There's always a few shooters in those groups, even if they're not as good as the serious guys. You remember Tom Fleming, my friend you met in St. Louis, the lawyer who helps run the training courses with those other guys?"

"Yeah...?"

"Tom knows Hap, and he told me a story about Hap Edwards from a few years back. While you were over in Africa during the Reagan Administration, there was some reporter from New York who was making a nuisance of himself. Hap Edwards was carrying State Department creds, 'cause that was his standard cover, even though anyone that knew anything knew Hap was head of the CIA hit squad. So some administrative aide of Reagan's was whining about this reporter, and he says to Hap, 'I want you to take care of this guy for us. This is embarrassing the President', or words to that effect. Hap says okay, and the guy leaves. So five minutes later, the aide is walking down the hall, Hap's office door is open, and the aide smells this funny smell that you and I would instantly recognize as Hoppe's # 9 coming from the open door. He walks in to investigate, and there's Hap, cleaning the baffles on his suppressed Ruger .22 pistol. The aide says, 'What are you doing?', and Hap says, 'You told me to take care of this asshole reporter, right?', and the aide about has a stroke right there." Henry laughed.

"If Hap had been in the habit of cleaning his gun after every job instead of right before, or if he hadn't left his door open that day, that reporter would have been dead as a hammer inside of twenty-four hours. Hap Edwards travels all around the world for that very purpose. Torturing people for information and then killing them is what he does, Ray. Hell, look who he brought in to testify on his behalf at the last task force meeting—

Nigel Hume-Douglas. That guy was wiring IRA guys' nuts to field generators when I was in diapers."

"Henry, you yourself would agree that the President of the United States is not likely to order the torture of a citizen worth two hundred million dollars."

"That's an interesting point. Suppose somebody planted an atomic bomb in New York City, and Ross Perot showed up out of the blue at the White House, saying he was representing the terrorists. You don't think they would wire him for sound, and after they got what they wanted announce he'd had an unexpected heart attack, DOA at Walter Reed? You think that's absolutely impossible? Maybe you're right. But Ross Perot is very well known, and he has a family that would use his money to fight what had happened to him. You don't have a family, and no one has any close ties to you. You wind up dead, Ray, and some distant relatives are going to be ecstatic. You go into the White House, and the first thing Hap would do is take off five of your fingers with a set of bolt cutters. Then he'd ask what you had to say. You'd be dead meat, with me and Cindy and Allen about two days behind you. Forget it."

"What if I insist on a different spot?"

"Then they'll know who you are, and snatch you later. Same deal."

He's right Ray thought grudgingly. *But there still has to be a way.* Then he thought of something, and asked Henry a question.

"How about if we used a cut-out?"

"Have to be someone who won't rat you out, and that Hap and his men won't torture. I doubt such a person exists."

"What about Harrison Potter?" There was a long pause before Henry answered.

"Can't call him and set up a meeting. Word might get back to the President, or Neumann, or Hap Edwards, and they'd follow him and snatch you."

"What, then?" Ray asked. Henry thought for a few moments.

"You'll have to run into him, and get his attention. A chance meeting, but that you orchestrated. At a gas station, or a drug store, something like that. Five minutes to give him the pitch and get his phone number, then you're out of there, and you never meet with him again. Phones only from then on. I got a way to beat those. You'll want to change your appearance some, glasses, wear a Hawaiian shirt, that kind of thing. Best if no one else is around, 'cause if there are other witnesses, like in a restaurant, the FBI will interview everybody and get a better composite than just Potter's recollection." Henry looked at his friend. "You up for tailing him for a day or two?"

"It's not even 8:30 yet," Ray said, looking at his watch. "So we got a whole day ahead of us. Let's get cracking."

***

"Judge Potter?" Ray asked. It was late afternoon and Harrison Potter was looking at the new arrivals in the biographies section of the Barnes & Noble book store.

"Sir?"

"My name is Jones. I'm a lawyer representing some people in a rather delicate matter. It concerns what the task force has been working on. My clients do not wish to end up on the wrong side of Mr. Edwards' field generator or Major Hume-Douglas' cordless drill. Neither, I confess, do I." Harrison Potter did not surprise easily, but he was surprised now.

"Your client wants to provide information so that he may claim the reward."

"Turn back and face towards the book shelves, please. Thank you, sir," Ray whispered politely. "No, to answer your question. The fact that the President offered such a sum convinced us that the White House is now willing to negotiate. But we don't want money." Ray gave Potter a quick rundown on his own history, changing several details and being vague about others.

"I understand your reluctance to explain how you and Wilson Blair got together," Potter said as he pretended to look at the titles, "or exactly how many people you represent. Since you say you've spent most of the last thirty years living outside of the United States, they were logical questions, but I won't bring them up again. But surely your involvement in this matter is founded on something about which you can tell me."

"It is, Judge Potter," Ray agreed. "You're familiar with the efforts of the Fabian Society more than a century ago in England?" The old man was startled by the question, but he latched onto it quickly.

"Yes. They wanted to establish a Socialist government in Great Britain. The group the Fabians founded became the Labour Party, and the rest, as they say, is history."

"Their tactic was to promote incremental change," Ray said. "Like boiling the frog. It worked very well."

"And when you came back to America a few years ago, after being gone for thirty years," Potter said with a nod, "you were the frog that got thrown in all at once."

"Exactly." Without mentioning Henry or the Customs incident in New York, Ray described how he had learned about the new currency, regulations on cash, warrantless searches, and seizing property without an arrest or conviction. Then he talked about the tremendous number of people in federal prison for technical violations of the ever-expanding federal antigun laws. Potter nodded again, then frowned.

"And what you're negotiating for your client or clients is not the reward money?"

"Have you ever studied the Miller case, Judge Potter?" Ray asked. "From 1939?"

"I know of the ruling. I have not researched the case itself."

"It was one of the things I did before agreeing to this job. When the Western District threw out the case and the Government appealed to the Supreme Court, Miller was long gone and neither he nor his lawyer showed up. No one was there from Miller's side, Judge Potter. Nobody filed a brief on his behalf. And with no one to call them on it, the government's people lied, Judge Potter. Has that ever happened before, do you suppose?" he said before plunging on.

"They lied and said a gun like Miller's wasn't a type used by any militia. The Court said, 'Okay, since we haven't been shown any evidence that it could have a militia application, it's okay to restrict it under the 1934 Act,' and let the original conviction stand. So the ruling says that militia-type weapons should not be restricted, but the government ignores that and passes more antigun laws, ultimately in 1986 banning one class of militia weapons entirely.

"Remember that the 1934 National Firarms Act was allowed to pass in the first place only as a revenue-raising measure. And the Supreme Court has ruled that for a tax statute to be constitutional, its prime consideration has to be raising revenue, not regulation or prohibition."

"Drexall Furniture..." Potter said softly, remembering the landmark Supreme Court case.

"Right. Punitive tax rates cannot be used for the primary purpose of enacting regulatory policy. But with the NFA we have a $200 tax on a twenty-dollar STEN gun. A $200 tax on a ten-dollar auto-sear. A $200 tax on a two-dollar piece of wood. And a $200 tax on a one-dollar soda bottle adaptor. No decent person dares fight it in court, because you have to risk spending life in prison if you lose. Then the 1986 ban comes in, and we get more case law. Three different judges rule that since the government refuses to administer the paperwork and collect the tax on post-May 19, 1986 machine guns, the whole NFA is null and void. Government ignores that ruling, too.

"Then the Supreme Court hands us the Lopez case. Suddenly, the feds can't claim everything on earth falls under interstate commerce. And finally, we get Bownds, where the Court ruled the law was now irrelevant to a man who made his own STEN guns and kept them in one state.

"So now the feds are put in a box, and the only way out is to say 'Yeah, okay, all this stuff really is unconstitutional, sorry about everything, we'll go home now.' Only they don't. Instead, they ignore the rulings. They pass more bans and they issue their tax agents more surveillance aircraft and more machine guns. The tax agents put on more ninja suits and black ski masks, and trash more people's houses and slam more pregnant wives up against the wall and stomp more cats to death and plant more evidence and throw more people in prison.

"And finally, Judge Potter, one of those tax agents says 'enough'. The government has refused to clean up its own mess, so he takes the only option left and issues a simple ultimatum: Shape up or die. And horror of horrors, it's working. It's drawing all kinds of decent people in. That should come as no surprise--if you'll check your history, you'll see that the same thing happened on a smaller scale in 1946. The Battle of Athens, Tennessee." Before Potter could say anything, Ray changed the subject.

"To get back to your original question, sir, no one I represent wants to sell out a friend to collect thirty pieces of silver. No matter how much those pieces weigh."

"What *do* you want?"

"A solution to both sides' problems. The government wants their people to stop dying prematurely. We want our people to stop being sent to prison, shot, or burned alive over $200 taxes on pieces of wood and steel. I don't see why we can't come to an agreement that satisfies both parties."

"It will be a tough sell, I'm afraid," Potter sighed.

"Well, of course it will be a tough sell, Judge Potter," Ray whispered to the man's back, a little more loudly than he had intended. "If it wasn't, my clients and I wouldn't need you."

With that, the old man burst out laughing, and Ray Johnson looked around to see if anyone was paying attention to them. No one was.

"I worry that I may have put your own life in jeopardy by telling you as much as I have."

"From what source?"

"The White House, Judge. Do you think I'm crazy for saying it?"

"No...not necessarily. Though I really can't imagine *that* happening."

"I understand, but I think it's possible. So do my clients. That's why this is the only time you'll be seeing me. From now on, I'll call you. I assume you have a cellular phone?"

"Yes. Let me give you the number." After he had done so, Judge Potter turned his head slightly. "I assume Jones is not your real name." Ray shrugged, but said nothing. "Well then," the Judge said, "perhaps you'd better tell me what kind of terms you have in mind on this 'negotiated peace'."

After Ray had finished explaining his position and the two men had talked further,

Ray pulled a manila envelope from his coat pocket and dumped the contents on the floor.

"You'll find some corroboration there," he told Potter. As the Judge bent down to pick up the wallet and badge case, Ray Johnson turned on his heel and left the store. By the time he was three blocks away, the glasses and Hawaiian shirt were in two different trash cans, and Ray's heart rate was slowly returning to normal.

***

"Mr. President, Jones is in an unusual situation. He represents, and I believe that is indeed the proper term, more than one person. No one that he represents has been arrested or indicted, and he intends to keep it that way. Divulging their names or identities can in no way benefit any of them, and he did not tell me who they were."

"Surely he doesn't represent all of the people who are behind what's been happening," Edgar Loverin said. Loverin was White House Counsel. "His clients could be looking at, shall we say...modest sentences in return for information that would help us wrap this up. Perhaps even complete immunity, in some cases." He paused and smiled. "And of course there's the matter of the reward." Potter nodded and shifted his gaze to the President.

"I'm glad Mr. Loverin brought that up early on," Potter said easily. "I said the same thing, and I believe I can quote Jones' response exactly, or close to it: 'No one that I represent has any interest in helping the federal government arrest and convict any private citizen. I did not contact you to represent an informant in the exchange of information for payment of a reward. Each side wants something, Judge Potter, and each side has something to offer, but money is not on our list. Neither is betrayal'. Those were his words." The President looked thoughtful and scratched his chin.

"What, then, is he proposing?"

"He believes that the interests of both sides are...compatible, Mr. President. The government finds the killings unacceptable and wants them to end. Jones' clients truly believe that the federal government has enacted legislation in areas over which it has no authority. They believe Government agents who enforce these measures share equally in the blame. The Nuremberg defense doesn't cut any ice."

"Go on."

"Jones' clients take no pleasure in killing, but neither do they find it repellent. And they have a saying—a philosophy, if you will: 'After the first one, the rest are free'." The President frowned as he considered that.

"Jones also points out that the killings are working, Mr. President, and on two fronts: First, they discourage evil behavior. Every day, more agents resign and more legislators get religion about the Second Amendment. Second, he believes the killings remind the public that the behavior really *is* evil. Every time a specific agent or politician is executed, it shows the public that rights violations have serious consequences, not just a two-week paid leave and a letter in the agent's file. That is why, he feels, support for what is happening has been growing exponentially. If you want to stop the killings, you, Mr. President, will have to bring about the same or better results through other means. Jones doubts you would be willing to do that. He thinks it virtually impossible you would be willing to publicly tell the American people that certain laws and government policies are fundamentally evil, before demanding that they be reversed."

"In what areas? Give me an example."

"With the exception of the FBI, Secret Service, Coast Guard, Marshal's Service, and possibly DEA, Jones says all government agents should be prohibited from carrying weapons while on duty. According to him, tax agents who carry machine guns and wear ninja outfits, body armor and ski masks are the textbook definition of 'jackbooted thugs'. They are evil." The President did not reply for several long moments.

"I might be able to work something like that," he said finally. "What else?"

"Several things," Potter said, and listed them. It took a few minutes. The President's eyes narrowed as the retired Chief Justice enumerated Jones' demands.

"That's preposterous!" Edgar Loverin blurted out when Judge Potter had finished. "I'm sorry, Mr. President," the White House Counsel added quickly, obviously abashed by his instinctive response.

"That's all right, Ed," the President said evenly. He turned to Potter. "I'm afraid what he asks is out of the question. A pardon for his clients is within the realm of possibility, but it could only occur if Blair calls for an immediate cease-fire while these negotiations continue. I think that's the only way we can proceed in good faith." Potter scowled and looked at his notes for the first time.

"Mr. President, Jones says that we, the government, have unlimited money, unlimited manpower, unlimited access to the media, and unlimited authority to make whatever rules we want. His clients have none of those things. The only way they can even the odds is to attract more supporters. Which, he points out, is happening daily. A cease-fire would be counterproductive to their interests."

"Then I'd say we were at an impasse with these people, Harry. We'll have to wait until you can talk to this man Jones some more. When's your next meeting?"

"I don't believe there will be one. I can only wait for him to call me."

"Then we'll have to wait for them to come down on their demands, Harry. We'll let the FBI work the case some more."

"Jones told me he suspected as much," Judge Potter said as he reached into his suit coat. "My instructions were to give you this envelope, Mr. President. I do not know what is in it, except to say that I have been promised it will not explode." He held out the thin white rectangle, which the President took reluctantly.

"Jones says he will have a short message for you tomorrow morning. I don't know if I will be the one delivering it, or what." The President nodded. Then he pressed a button, and a Secret Service agent stuck his head in the door.

"Get Alex Neumann for me." When the FBI man came in, the President told him about the envelope and handed it to him. Neumann was careful to touch only the edges as he looked at it. Then he held it up to the light.

"Just one piece of paper, with a number on it. I'll have the techs check this out, but don't hold your breath. The number is 324452651, for what that's worth. We'll see if we can make anything of it, sir."

"Very good," the President said. He had the unpleasant feeling that this first contact with the terrorists had accomplished absolutely nothing.

***

"Potter was a little nervous when he first sat down, Mr. Edwards," one of the two technicians said as he reran the videotapes of the meeting with the President and Edgar Loverin. "Got a jump in his heart rate early on. That's par—reaction to the opening round, especially when it's the President of the United States. The VSA started to settle down a few words later." The technician was referring to the Voice Stress Analyzer that detected changes in frequency and pitch in a person's speech.

"No iffy spots?" Edwards asked.

"No, sir. By the time he was talking about Jones' demands, his stress level was next to nothing."

"You're positive?" Hap Edwards asked. The technician shrugged.

"If I'm wrong, Mr. Edwards, then we ought to throw this hundred thousand dollars worth of electronic equipment in the trash and hire a gypsy with a crystal ball." The technician looked ashamed. "I'm really sorry, sir, I shouldn't have run my mouth, but what I meant was—"

"Don't worry about it," the retired CIA man said brusquely. "I got what I need."

***

"The ID all checks out, Mr. President. Bunch of prints on the credit cards and other things inside the wallet, some Blair's, some unknown. Probably store clerks, things like that. Judge Potter's are on the outside."

"Can you tell us anything else, Alex?" Neumann glanced at CIA Director George Cowan, Hap Edwards, then back to the President.

"Only things that didn't happen, sir. Wilson Blair didn't get drowned somewhere with his clothes on, or get his wallet soaked in his own blood. His wallet didn't spend any time exposed to unusual environmental conditions, like a PCP lab, or a coke-processing plant. And there's nothing we can use as a lead inside the badge case or the wallet. No scraps of paper with phone numbers on them, receipts, or anything like that."

"Mr. President," George Cowan said, "our only link to the terrorists is Potter. Can't you persuade the Judge to tell us what he knows of this Jones character?"

"As part of his role in these negotiations, Judge Potter promised to keep any personal information about Jones confidential. Frankly, I don't think Jones told him anything of use."

"He told him *something,* Mr. President," Cowan said immediately. "And he knows what he looks like. If we knew what was in Potter's head, we could find this guy and squeeze him. We'd have the names of the people who are behind this."

"Harry gave his word. He's not going to go back on it."

"I could find out what he knows, Mr. President," Hap Edwards said without a trace of inflection. The President's jaw dropped and his head snapped around to face the former head of the CIA's Center For Counter-Terrorism.

"Are you implying that I should authorize the torture of a retired Chief Justice of the Supreme Court?" Hap Edwards stared at the President without saying a word. The President squinted and a horrible parody of a smile appeared on his face. "Aren't you afraid his heart would give out, Mr. Edwards?" he said in the most caustic tone he could muster.

"I'd keep it going long enough," Edwards said softly.

"You're excused from these proceedings, Mr. Edwards. Get out of this room." Hap Edwards shrugged, and then he left without another word.

June 27

"Hap Edwards offered to torture you to get information on this Jones person, Harry," the President said without preamble. "It was the most offensive thing I have encountered since I took office. And the most surprising. I think Hap Edwards is a certifiable psychopa—Harry!" he said suddenly. "Why on earth are you smiling?" The President was horrified.

"*You* may have been surprised, Mr. President, but at least one person will not be, when I tell him. That was exactly what our Mr. Jones told me I could expect, when he asked if I was sure I wanted to be the liaison on these negotiations. I, too, thought the possibility ludicrous." Potter's face took on an expression that was hard to read.

"You know, Mr. President, for nine years, during the entire American Revolution, Benjamin Franklin lived in Paris. Think about that for a moment. The British never kidnapped him and tortured him to see what he knew. I mentioned this to Mr. Jones, after he said he would contact me only by phone from now on, to protect his safety. He laughed. He laughed and he reminded me that Franklin had a penchant for pleasures of the flesh.

"You know what Jones said then? 'Judge, today Hap Edwards would have Ben Franklin in a honey trap before his bags were unpacked. If that didn't work, Hap would hook him up to a field generator and give him a new education on electricity, beyond what he learned with his kite and his brass key.'" The Judge's face turned utterly serious.

"These...terrorists," Potter said, his voice indicating he was not entirely comfortable with the word, "often seem to know more about our people than we do, Mr. President. I find that more and more disturbing."

"As do I."

"Jones also told me this wasn't about guns, it was about everything. I thought he meant the dead EPA director, but he mentioned our current seizure laws and told me to research an incident he called the 'Battle of Athens', in 1946 in Tennessee."

"I've never heard of it."

"Neither had I, but our Library of Congress has. There's a book, now out of print, that tells all about it."

"Tell me," the President said.

"McMinn County, in Tennessee, between Knoxville and Chattanooga. In the late 1930s and up through the Second World War, the local government got more and more corrupt. The Sheriff's Department was financed by fines. Speeding, public drunkenness, that sort of thing. I guess I don't need to tell you what an incentive that was for false arrest."

"Our expanding seizure laws?"

"It's a good parallel," Potter agreed. "At any rate, both parties were fixing local elections and stuffing ballot boxes, but this was during the Roosevelt Administration, so the Democrats were better at it than the Republicans. The sheriff from '36 to '42 was a man named Cantrell. He became a state senator in '42, saw he couldn't win again in '46, so he decided to run against the incumbent sheriff, a man named Mansfield, I believe it was. Elections were held in the town of Athens.

"Only problem was that there were now three thousand ex-GIs in Athens, back from the war. A quarter of the registered voters. They'd had recent experience with dictators, and they held both Mansfield and Cantrell responsible for the police policy of false arrests, beatings while in custody, bribe-taking, and vote fraud. They ran an all-GI, non-partisan ticket for the local political offices, and they promised a fair election with no vote fraud." Potter drew a breath and collected his thoughts.

"On election day, the sitting sheriff deputized two hundred of his cronies, issued them guns, and told them to help him out. They wouldn't let the blacks vote, and they shot one black man who wouldn't back down. They held guns on the ex-GIs who insisted on observing the count, and took the ballot boxes into the jail. Wouldn't let anyone watch. They shot people who came near the building."

"Oh, shit."

"Exactly. The GIs weren't having any of that. They got guns from the Guard armory and pinned down the deputies inside the jail. Finally dynamited the jail's porch, and the deputies panicked and surrendered. Gave up the ballots, which were then counted in front of everyone, and Mansfield and Cantrell were both defeated. The police who fled the town were replaced, and the newly elected officials accepted a pay limit."

"Where was the Governor when all this was going on?"

"He mobilized the State Guard, but a lot of those men were ex-service. He held off on sending them to Athens. The Guardsmen might have agreed with what the GIs were doing and joined them."

"Jones knew about this obscure bit of history..." The President said. "Might he have come from the area?" Potter shook his head.

"It's not obscure any more. Just about everyone in the gun culture knows all about it. Jay Simkin, a researcher for *Jews for the Preservation of Firearms Ownership*--that Milwaukee group Alex Neumann mentioned the other day? Simkin dug up the history and did a detailed piece in JPFO's newspaper in January of 1995. Spelled out exactly what happened."

"Our old friends," the President sighed. "Do they really have that big a circulation?" Potter shrugged.

"Big enough, and getting bigger every day. They sell reprints, and apparently you see them everywhere that gun people gather. Along with the reprint comes a list of questions that police and other public servants have to answer under the Privacy Act of 1974. Recommended for when the police ask for citizens' help." The President closed his eyes but said nothing.

"Oh, and then later that year, Simkin did a shorter piece on the 'Battle of Athens' for *Soldier of Fortune,* which has a lot of readers. Then a two page treatment on it ran in the October 1995 issue of *Guns and Ammo* magazine. They're part of the Petersen Group and they have a huge circulation." Potter watched as the President rubbed his temples. There were a few moments of complete silence, and then Potter took a deep breath.

"They'll be listening for notice of your agreement tomorrow, on the radio, Mr. President. Are you sure you want to turn them down?" It was the closest that Harrison Potter had ever come to verbally questioning the President's judgment.

"I can't accede to what they're demanding, Harry," the President said. "I just can't. We'll have to wait for Jones to call you, and carry on from there."

Harrison Potter thought of the conversation he'd had with the President only two days before, about how the issues involved had gone beyond ones based on the Second Amendment. Potter feared that very soon it was not going to matter what demands the President agreed to; it would be too late.

The old man also knew, however, that he had already pushed as hard as he dared. Further suggestions would have to wait for another time.

June 28

Sitting in the hotel room with the radio on, Cindy Caswell looked again at her watch. It was time. She listened to the radio for another twenty minutes, but the innocuous news message she had been told might be broadcast at ten minutes past the hour never came on. Cindy switched the radio off and left the room. Fifteen minutes later she was at a pay phone three blocks away, punching a number in Ohio onto the keypad. She fed a fistful of quarters into the instrument and waited.

"Hello?" came Allen Kane's voice after the third ring.

"They didn't go for it. You're on."

"Got it," Allen said, and broke the connection.

***

Arnold Katzenbaum, the retired U.S. Senator from Ohio, had reached the age where just getting around was an effort, but he still took a short walk every night. He reached the corner of the block and had just turned around to head back to his house when a shiny late-model Ford Crown Victoria pulled up across from him on the other side of the street.

"Sir, I'm lost," the driver said in a voice that indicated some kind of childhood speech impediment, not quite overcome. He was dressed in a business suit and held a map in front of him. Katzenbaum saw the frustrated look on the man's face. The retired Senator glanced both ways, then stepped out into the street and walked over to the driver's window.

"Can you show me where I am?" the man asked, turning the map towards the window but holding it inside the car so they could both see it. Katzenbaum peered at the map. He barely had to lean over, for he had severe curvature of the spine.

"Let's see," he said, reaching his right arm through the window to touch the paper with a gnarled finger. "Right here is, uh–"

Katzenbaum's words turned into a grunt of pain as the driver grabbed the Senator's wrist and pinned it to the inside of the door panel. Allen Kane took his foot off the brake and pushed the accelerator down about halfway. The sedan accelerated almost noiselessly down the suburban street. The speedometer was passing through 45 MPH when Allen heard something pop inside the old man's shoulder as his frail body flopped helplessly against the side of the car.

Allen made a slight steering correction with his right hand, and let go of Katzenbaum's wrist with his left just as the speedometer touched 60 MPH. He had been prepared to smash the man in the face with his left elbow, but that had not been necessary. Under the best of conditions Arnold Katzenbaum would not have been able to hold on to the speeding car for very long, and with a dislocated shoulder, it was hopeless. Katzenbaum tumbled eighty-seven feet before his body came to rest in the gutter. When it did, his limbs, head, and spine were all at odd angles.

Allen Kane let off the accelerator, checked his rearview mirror, and continued on his way at a more sedate 30 MPH.

***

The National Guard helicopter lay silently on the limestone floor of Henry Bowman's quarry pit. The pit had never been stocked, so no fish lived there, and there were no underwater currents to move the wreckage. After two weeks, however, the bodies of the four men trapped in the twisted hulk had begun to decompose. The methane gas made the corpses buoyant, enough so that the wreckage began to tilt slightly from where it had settled, until the opening in the fuselage faced up towards the surface. One of the bodies was not belted or wedged in place. It was the ATF agent who had broken his back and drowned while trying to get out of the sinking helicopter. His corpse floated out the opening and slowly rose to the surface, where the bloated skin glistened ripely in the moonlight.

"Hello?"

"Judge Potter? This is Jones. I have a message for the President. I don't know what it means, but my clients seem to believe he will be able to make some sense of it. Have you a pen?"

"Go ahead, Mr. Jones."

"The message is, 'Step one: Reverse the order. Step two: Add three to each of the first four digits. Step three: Add one to each of the last five digits.' That's the instructions, then there's three words: 'Just like Nuremberg.' And that's all."

"As in the war crimes trial?"

"Exactly." Ray listened as Judge Potter repeated the instructions back to him. "That's it," Ray said. "Plan on hearing from me again in about three weeks." Ray broke the connection.

***

"It's Arnold Katzenbaum's Social Security number, Mr. President," Alex Neumann said grimly.

"The retired Senator from Ohio?" Both the President and Alex Neumann were well aware that Senator Katzenbaum had pushed for every antigun bill that had ever been mentioned in the Senate.

"That's right, sir. He was pronounced dead at 12:31 this morning, Central time." The President closed his eyes and rubbed his temples.

"How was he killed?" he asked.

"We're not sure. His body was found three blocks from his house, in the middle of the street. Emergency room techs all say he looked like one of the real bad one-vehicle motorcycle accidents they get every once in a while. Both arms and legs broken, neck broken, severe road rash, and a whole bunch of internal injuries, any one of which by itself would have killed him. They said part of his spine was actually sticking out through the skin on his back." Neumann paused. *Got to stay professional here* he thought.

"The theory, at least for now, is that he was thrown out of the back of a pickup truck. Guys on the scene said it looked like he tumbled close to a hundred feet. They say the truck must have been going close to 70 MPH."

"Was he alive when it happened?"

"Yes, sir. They tell me there's no doubt about that. The other bad news is on the phone call. Our equipment traced it instantly, but it originated at a bulk wholesaler in New York."

"Explain that." *He's going to love this one* Neumann thought.

"A company buys phone time in bulk. They resell it in blocks with different access codes for each block. The end user calls the company's 800 number, punches in this access code, then the number he wants to reach. The call is actually made by the equipment at the bulk wholesaler's facility. The person placing the call could be five states away, at a pay phone."

"Can't you get the name of the customer who has that access code from the company?" the President asked in a voice that showed his irritation.

"That's just it sir, we can't. The company couldn't give them to us if they wanted to—they don't have them. You see, what they do, they print up a paper card with a twelve-digit access code on it, and seal it in an opaque wrapper like a candy bar. The wrapper lists how much air time the card inside is good for. Twenty-five minutes is common, and that would retail for fifty dollars. The company wholesales bunches of these wrapped cards to retail chains, just like boxes of candy bars, at half that. Guy walks in off the street, at a drugstore or a QuikTrip, he buys phone privacy for two dollars a minute. After he's used his access code for twenty-five minutes, or whatever the card was good for, his call gets terminated by the company's computer. The company never uses that access code again. Using twelve digits, they could print a billion cards without using the same access code."

"There's that big a market for long distance service at two dollars a minute?" the President asked. Neumann shrugged.

"Yeah, for people who don't like to have their calls traced. I'd pay a lot more than that to keep Hap Edwards away from my door, sir." Neumann immediately regretted making the comment, but the President did not give any appearance of having heard it.

"I'm beginning to wish I hadn't cut the reward to half of what you recommended, Alex."

"I'm not sure that's the problem, Mr. President," Neumann said uncertainly. *If they won't take fifty million* Neumann was thinking, *they probably aren't human.*

***

"Arnold Katzenbaum was killed last night," the President announced to the assembled members of the task force, "in a most horrible manner. And this event bears directly on the job we are doing here." He went on to explain the details of what had happened, without mentioning Harrison Potter's meeting with the so-called Mr. Jones, or the coded number that showed the murder had been carefully planned.

"I bring this up now because the FBI has strong evidence to indicate that this killing was premeditated, and done personally by the core group of terrorists who have been fomenting this...rebellion."

"I knew Arnold Katzenbaum," Ohio Congressman Bane said. "What evidence does the FBI have?"

"That's confidential, Jon," the President answered. "But I think that we must face up to the fact that all legislators, both active and retired, are now at risk. Especially those who have supported stricter gun control measures," he added.

"You're leaving something out, Mr. President," Carl Schaumberg almost shouted. "Two legislators have now been killed. Aaron Siteman was beaten to death in Georgetown, barely a week ago. These people are not just killing legislators, they are killing Jews!"

"Ah, Congressman Schaumberg," Dick Gaines broke in, "there was actually another murder a few days before Siteman's. Congressman Jerry Abel, from my state. He was a gentile, I think. And a Republican."

"That was a cheap sex thing," Schaumberg said in dismissal, "and everyone knew he was drunk all the time." Then he turned back to the Chief Executive. "Mr. President, this is the beginning of another Holocaust!"

"Carl, let's you and I have a talk after the meeting. I see your point, and I have an idea of what to do until we get a better handle on this." He turned to the rest of the group. "We have some things to go over here, people, and I'd like to get through them."

The task force meeting lasted less than half an hour. Every person there left with the vague feeling that it had been a waste of time.

***

"Congressman, it's Bud again, at the *Times*. How are you today?"

"I'm okay."

"Listen, my editor didn't think we should kick Dwight Greenwell too much while he was down, so he killed the piece I did for him."

"Look, I told you everything I knew, it's not my fault he didn't like your–"

"No, no, that's all right, Congressman." *Don't get your bowels in an uproar, dickhead* Henry thought. "I'm not about to run that other thing. I just thought I'd see if anything new happened with the task force."

"Oh. Well, nothing really went on today, except about Senator Katzenbaum. The President warned us that other legislators might be at risk, and then Carl Schaumberg went ballistic and said it was another Holocaust."

"A Holocaust? He used that word?" Henry asked, as a smile formed on his face.

"Yeah. Because of Congressman Siteman getting killed a week or so ago. I reminded him that Congressman Jerry Abel from Missouri got murdered, too, but he didn't seem to think that counted."

"What happened then?"

"Nothing. Oh, at the end of the meeting, I heard the President talking with Schaumberg. He was trying to talk him into taking some time off for a couple of weeks."

"Congressman Schaumberg? Taking time off?"

"Yeah."

"Hm. You know, that makes me wonder about something, Congressman Gaines," Henry said thoughtfully. *Let's see if I can orchestrate this*. "Has the President suggested bringing on someone to address this issue? Someone from the Holocaust Center, for example?"

"No, not that I remember."

"Really. That surprises me." Then Henry made a few comments and asked several more questions. Dick Gaines talked a little longer, then the two men ended their conversation.

When Henry Bowman hung up the pay phone, he was smiling.

July 4

The dog was gun-shy, and for an animal with that condition in rural Missouri, the first week of July was a terrible time of the year. Independence Day itself was the worst. Firecrackers and bottle rockets popped incessantly. There seemed to be no escaping the distant explosions which made the mixed-breed named Betsy so miserable.

When the two oldest boys in the family started lighting firecrackers out in the field behind the house, Betsy shot out from under the porch and ran. She ran northwest, which put the house between her and the two boys, then angled through the woods when she heard noises off to her right a half mile away. Ten minutes later, she was more than two miles from home, and the sounds were almost inaudible.

The dog continued trotting west, and barely slowed when she came to the barbed-wire fence with the NO TRESPASSING signs every hundred feet. Betsy slipped between the second and third strands without touching a single sharp point, and kept going on the unfamiliar terrain.. She was not lost, for her homing instinct was excellent, but she was on a section of land where she had never strayed before, for obvious reasons.

After several more minutes, Betsy was thirsty from her run. She stopped, raising her muzzle in the air to sniff. She smelled water, and something else. The water smelled good, but the something else smelled absolutely wonderful.

Betsy took off towards the smell at a fast trot.

***

"Dad, Betsy's got something dead again."

"Well, you go take it away from her and put it out in the burn barrel. If she's rolled on it and she stinks, take her over by the welding shed and wash her off. Take the nozzle off the hose, so it doesn't spray her, and be careful when you wash around her eyes. Then you come in and get a bath. Your mama's going to have dinner ready soon."

"Okay," the boy said, and ran off. In a few moments he returned to the window and again spoke through the screen. *"Dad,"* he said, "Would you do it? It really stinks bad."

"Okay, Mr. Sensitive Nose," he said, laughing. "Probably another groundhog she killed a few days ago. They'll get ripe in a hurry in this heat. You go get cleaned up for dinner."

"Thanks."

The man could smell the stench when he stepped into the kitchen. There, on the other side of the screen door at the base of the back steps, was Betsy. She was panting and wagging her tail happily, waiting to be praised for the treasure she had deposited on the doorstep for her master. It was torn and rotten, and missing a section. To the Vietnam combat veteran, however, it was also unmistakable.

Betsy had brought home a human hand.

The man grabbed a piece of newspaper off the kitchen table and wrapped it around the decaying flesh. He thought for a moment about the disassembled select-fire ChiCom AK47 that was in his footlocker in the shop, brought back from Southeast Asia in his duffel bag in 1970. Inviting the police and maybe the feds over to the house would serve no good purpose, and might get him in a world of trouble.

He threw the hand in the trash can, put some other things on top of it, and tied the trash bag shut with several wraps of duct tape. Then he dragged his two trash cans out to the end of the drive.

Because of the holiday, pick-up would be the following morning.

"That was barbaric. An appalling thing you people did."

"It wasn't my doing, Judge Potter, but that's of no consequence," Ray Johnson said over the phone. "I confess I wasn't sorry when I found out," he admitted. "But name-calling isn't going to get either side what they want. Has the President thought about my clients' offer?"

"Yes, and he thinks he was perhaps too quick to decide last time. He also wishes that you would have called sooner. Things have gone on too long with no dialogue between us." *The President's starting to sweat already* Ray realized. *Henry was right about making them wait.*

"The move is his, Judge Potter. What we want is the same thing we wanted three weeks ago, back when a lot of dead federal agents were still alive. No money, just action. Action and reform. What do you think he will say?"

"There are a number of areas on your list of demands where you and he can reach complete agreement. Let me get my notes." Ray heard the sound of papers shuffling. "Here we are. The President has already drawn up the new policy guidelines for federal agencies concerning the carrying of weapons while on duty. Would you like to hear the language?"

"Not right now, Judge Potter. What else?"

"On the issue of federal inmates currently serving time for firearms law violations, he is prepared to set up a judicial review committee whose sole function will be to assess each case and determine if the early release of the convicted prisoner would pose a risk to the community. The committee would have the power to expunge the criminal record, in some cases."

"I see. And ATF?"

"They would be under tighter supervision. A review of their practices will be held in open committee hearings. New appointees would be put in key positions, such as Director, and also the head of Imports branch. Your designees," Potter added.

"Judge, that's unacceptable," Ray said quickly, "and although I only met you once, I suspect you're a little embarrassed at having to deliver the news. What the President is offering is a syphilitic whore conducting business as usual, with a little extra lipstick and eyeliner to pass inspection in bad light." *That got Potter's attention* Ray thought to himself as he heard the intake of breath. "You have our list, you are losing this war, and what you offer to do is trivial. A joke. Some sham hearings and vague promises of 'reform' that will never occur." Ray heard Potter sigh.

"Mr. Jones, I don't think that you understand the way things have to be done in the legislature."

"Judge Potter, I understand exactly the way things are done. Deals are cut, and compromises are made, and everybody shakes hands when they come to a final agreement. And then if things don't work out and they have to change the agreement, then the standard line is, 'Oh, we made the best decision based on the information available at the time.'

"And that all works fine if you're negotiating a new lease on an office building, or an end to a baseball strike, or who's going to get the contract to build the new interstate highway overpass, or how to divvy up some tax money.

"But it doesn't work at all when the issue is fundamental rights, Judge. The Branch

Davidians were burned alive, and when hearings finally happened two years later, the government says 'Koresh was having sex with children, and ATF made the best decisions possible given the information available at the time.' No one said, 'Tax agents should not use machine guns and grenades to attack citizens for any reason. That is morally wrong.'

"A law that puts men in prison because a piece of wood is too short isn't 'the best decision given the information at the time.' It is morally wrong, and always has been. The federal government has painted itself into a corner on this issue, Judge, and you know it. In order to fix the problem, the President needs to shout something that no one in Washington is willing to even whisper. He needs to say to the public, 'What we have been doing is morally wrong.'

"That's what the problem is, isn't it, Judge?" Ray asked. "Robbery is robbery, assault is assault, and murder is murder, but for decades, Washington has done its best to turn our most valuable, productive, honest citizens into felons."

"Those are the issues we need to be discussing, Mr. Jones. That's why these talks are so important." *Sounds like a line they told him to say* Ray thought. *His heart wasn't in that one.*

"There's not much to discuss, Judge. The people I represent would much rather risk being caught or killed by the FBI than accept what the President just offered. Why? Because they will accept no less than freedom, and what he has suggested is a nicer-looking set of shackles."

"Mr. Jones, I really think we should discuss this further."

"We will. Three weeks from today. August eleventh. That should give the President time to think about what I've said. In the meantime, my clients will be listening to the radio for the President's answer. If the President isn't going to insert the fluff news piece we talked about before, at 12:10 tomorrow, then you need to give him this exact message. I assume this call is being recorded?"

"That's not my area of expertise."

"Well, in case the FBI's equipment is malfunctioning, please write down the message I've been asked to convey: 'Both ends? What a player!' Is that clear?

"Both ends question mark, what a player exclamation point."

"Right," Ray Johnson said. "I'll call again on the eleventh." Ray was about to hang up, then stopped to add one more thought.

"A lot can happen in three weeks, Judge."

***

"You need me to bring anything for your party for the ex-Governor?" Arthur 'B.I.' Bedderson asked his mother as he prepared to leave. "Folding chairs? More tonic? A bail bondsman for his kid? Give me some notice, it's coming up in two weeks."

"Now you hush," Lois Bedderson scolded. "I threatened to rescind your invitation, and I can still make good on that. Bail bondsman..." She shook her head and fought back the smile that threatened to form. "I've got plenty of everything. Just make sure your beard's trimmed and you wear a suit that's been recently pressed."

"Yes, Mom," he said, and gave his mother a hug before departing. "I'll talk to you tomorrow."

***

"Come in, come in," Congressman Schaumberg said pleasantly as he opened the door to his apartment. "I must say, you people are prompt. I just got back in town not twenty minutes ago. Are you on the tactical squad also?" he asked the woman. Schaumberg spent longer eyeing her than he did her male companion.

"Yes, sir." The two agents on bodyguard duty glanced at each other and smiled faintly. It was obvious to them that Congressman Schaumberg liked the idea of two full-time protectors.

"Congressman," the man said softly, glancing around as he and the woman put away their ATF credentials, "Director Greenwell doesn't want to take any chances. Particularly someone who gets around as much as you do and who lives in a place this size."

"*This* building?" Schaumberg said, pleased that his concerns were being given such serious attention and that the agent was impressed with where he lived. "I don't think so. This place is quiet as a tomb," he said, laughing as he ushered the pair inside his apartment. "That's the main reason I live here," he added as he closed the door. The man and the woman shared a look.

"The first thing you need to do is show us the complete layout here, Congressman," Cindy Caswell said, nodding her head in the direction of the short hallway.

"Follow me," Schaumberg said, and turned his back on Henry Bowman.

"You get a lot of your hot tips from fruits, Brad?" the policeman asked with a chuckle as the five of them climbed the stairs. "You their favorite reporter?" The man from the *New York Post* ignored the question and asked one of his own.

"You got a phobia about elevators or something, Jack? Afraid the cable's going to snap?"

"Hey, we're not rich like all the New York swells you write about. No high-dollar health clubs with a Stairmaster room on our expense accounts. Besides, cops learn fast that the scrotes think it's fun to chop the power and leave you stuck."

"It's this floor here," the superintendent said, breathing hard. "Down the hall on the right." Brad motioned the press photographer to go ahead of him, right after the two police officers and the building super. He could already detect the faint odor, which became stronger as they made their way toward the apartment. He was in no great hurry to see what he felt fairly sure was waiting for them.

"Okay, now don't touch anything," the second cop said to the photographer as he wrinkled his nose.

"Yeah," the first cop agreed. "And as soon as you get your pictures, get the hell out of here. I'm going to have enough explaining to do to the Captain as it is. Unless your 'hot tip' turns out to be a waste of time." The reporter laughed.

"Come on, Jack. You'll think of a good story to tell him. I didn't drive all the way here with one of our photographers just to enjoy the beauty of this city."

"There we go, gentlemen," the super said as he pulled out his key and pushed the door open. "All yours." The smell of death hit all five men at the same time. The D.C. police officers led the way in, followed by the two men from the *New York Post*.

"Looks like he had a party, and somebody cleaned up real quick," the second police-man said as he scanned the living room with a practiced eye.

"Bingo," the *Post* photographer said from the bedroom doorway. "Looks like your tip was good, Brad." The policemen shouldered him aside, and then all five men stared at the tableau in front of them.

The king-size bed, which took up a good part of the bedroom, looked like a cyclone had hit it. The covers were bunched at the footboard, and the bottom sheet was pulled away from one corner, exposing the mattress pad. Various leather restraints lay on the floor, and a ball gag poked out from under the tangled bedspread.

Congressman Schaumberg's body lay facedown across the stained sheet. The corpse was nude. A framed photo of Schaumberg with the former President lay a few inches from his face. Traces of white powder dusted the glass, and a single-edged razor blade lay in the corner of the frame. White powder was also visible at the edges of Schaumberg's nostrils. A pound can of Crisco stood on the nightstand, next to a white candle that was burned down to a two-inch stub.

"DNA boys will love this one," the first policeman said. He spotted something on the bed. "Looks like the Congressman had himself some decent cuffs." He was referring to the pair of stainless steel Smith & Wesson handcuffs which lay next to Schaumberg's left knee. The *Post* photographer was busy snapping pictures of the body from various angles. "Don't touch anything," the policeman admonished him once more.

"You think I'm out of my goddamned mind?" the man shot back. "I'll use up a whole bar of soap when I get out of here. You couldn't pay me enough to work the forensic team on this case," he said as he reloaded the film back with deft fingers. He was nodding to a molded latex object about fifteen inches long which lay in between Schaumberg's feet. It was a replica of a child's forearm, with the hand clenched into a fist. The sex toy glistened with what all five men fervently wished was just vegetable shortening.

"I haven't seen that trick before," the second cop said. "With the candle, I mean." Hardened wax lay in the cleft in Schaumberg's buttocks.

"Stay on the force and it won't be the last time." He shook his head. "Poppers 'n' coke. Hell on the old heart," he said reflectively as he used the clip on the cap of his pen to scrape up a tiny amount of the white powder from the glass. He touched the clip with the tip of his tongue. "Damn. I doubt the Mayor gets stuff this good," he said as his eyes grew wide. "You better go call this in. Brad, your guy got his pictures? Two of you better shove off now."

"Thanks, Jack. You're a good guy to work with."

"Right. Just don't tell that to the Captain."

"Looks like your buddy decided to make a splash on his way out," the FBI Chief-of-Station said to Alex Neumann as the visiting agent walked towards him. "*The New York Post* is showing its typical restrained sensitivity." He handed Alex Neumann a FAX copy of the paper's front page that had been sent down from New York. It was a little after 7:00 a.m. Eastern time, and hard copies would not be available in D.C. for several more hours. Neumann stared at the reduced-size image. The headline was still huge.

WHAT A WAY TO GO!

SCHAUMBERG DIES IN GAY SEX-AND-DRUG ORGY

"He was no buddy of mine," Neumann muttered unnecessarily as he scanned the article. "Hmmm... 'An autopsy confirmed that shortly prior to his death by a cocaine overdose, the late Congressman had had sexual relations several times.' How do they know that? His balls were empty, or something?"

"You haven't heard? Semen samples from multiple partners in both his stomach and rectum."

"*What* did you say?" Neumann asked softly. He felt his blood turn to ice as he remembered the cryptic wording Jones had given to Judge Potter. *Both ends? What a player!*

"Yeah. One of the other dick-smokers that was there when it happened called it in. To a reporter, not the cops."

"A reporter?" Neumann demanded.

"Am I not talking loud enough? You sound like a parrot. Yeah, a reporter. Guy rings up some fella at the *Post,* who comes down and tells some District cop he knows, on the condition the *Post* guy and his photographer can tag along when they open up his apartment."

"Locals here consider that it might be premeditated murder?" Neumann asked.

"No sign of forced entry, so the cops presume he knew whoever it was, and Schaumberg was coked to the gills. You figure the Congressman might have had a few people over for a little suck-and-fuck party, but his blowjob technique was so bad they forced enough coke up his nose to kill him?"

"Well, what I–"

"Or maybe it was somebody planning to whack him all along, some guy runs a company that's getting fucked over by the government. Say a boat company that's going out of business 'cause of that new higher luxury tax Schaumberg's been yelling for. 'Stead of sticking a knife in him on the street, the Chairman and the rest of the Board of Directors go up to the Congressman's digs, fuck him and make him blow them before they OD him on coke. So's it won't look like murder. That your idea, hotshot?" Neumann said nothing. *This jerk's still mad the Director tagged me to be on the Presidential Task Force instead of him* he thought with the part of his brain that wasn't focused on the murder. As if reading his mind, the Chief-of-Station spoke again.

"Hey, that was shitty of me, Alex. Fact of the matter is, locals don't know what to make of it. Nobody saw anyone unusual go in or out of the building. Whoever was with him cleaned the place up pretty good before they left, which isn't too surprising. I did hear they had enough residue lying around to do a good work-up on the coke, though. Good stuff, apparently. 'Better than the Mayor gets' was how D.C. forensics put it. And it won't be the first time one of our esteemed elected officials has stepped on his dick. Had one last month, as a matter of fact, 'cept Congressman Abel liked ghetto hookers, and he liked to pitch instead of catch." Neumann nodded. *So Abel's death may be part of this, too.*

"If bad things come in threes, I wonder who's the next Congressman we'll find dead with his pecker hanging out," Neumann said.

"We'll see."

"Yeah." *Might as well get used to it* the FBI man told himself. *Things can't get that much worse.*

Alex Neumann was wrong.

***

"Good to see you again," the President said, shaking hands. "Thank you for coming on such short notice. I hope it was not a burden for you."

"As one grows old, new tasks become the food of life. Old people with nothing to do wither and die, Mr. President. I am sure you have seen it." He smiled. "I intend to live to be one hundred."

"If I'm still around then, Mr. Mann, I hope you will invite me to the celebration. Please, have a seat." Irwin Mann sat down in a straight-backed chair and waited for the Chief Executive to tell him why he had been summoned.

"As I'm sure you are aware, Mr. Mann, Jewish legislators make up a very small fraction of our legislative body in Washington. One night last month, Congressman Aaron Siteman of New Jersey was beaten to death on a street in Georgetown. There are no suspects in the case, and the motive is unknown. However, in light of the current national situation, it is entirely possible that he was killed because of his voting record on gun legislation."

"He favored more restrictions?"

"Yes. We have checked his record back to the time when he was first elected a State Representative in New Jersey. The only piece of gun control legislation he had ever voted against was eight years ago, when he opposed a measure to institute an instant-check system on gun purchases."

"I see."

"Then, one week later, Arnold Katzenbaum, the retired U.S. Senator from Ohio, was murdered outside his home. Thrown out of a vehicle traveling at high speed. We know for a fact that this killing was related to his record of supporting gun legislation.

"Immediately after Katzenbaum's murder, Congressman Schaumberg very vocally stated that we were facing a Holocaust, that someone or some group was systematically killing off Jewish federal legislators. I insisted he leave Washington for three weeks, to take himself out of the danger zone, and to give the FBI time to solve the murders. I did not, however, follow another suggestion another congressman on the task force made, and solicit your input. And I should have." The President looked pained, but continued.

"Congressman Schaumberg returned to Washington four days ago. Yesterday, his body was found in his apartment. I assume you have seen the newspapers?"

"Yes, I have."

"A month ago, the White House was given a message that made no sense at the time. Now it is obvious that it was a reference to the Congressman's death. We now know beyond doubt that Carl Schaumberg was murdered by the same people who killed Arnold Katzenbaum. Mr. Mann, I want you on the task force."

"Mr. President, I don't know what help I can be to you. And I do not hold the same strong political views as the men who were killed."

"Mr. Mann, that doesn't matter. I'm not supposed to say things like that, but you're too old and I'm too tired for me to use a bunch of Washington doublespeak on you. It's something that would be obvious to anyone who's been around the Capitol for any length of time, so I'll say it straight out: I need to cover my ass.

"I don't expect you or anyone else besides Alex Neumann and his men to solve these killings, that's an FBI matter. But it would be political suicide to announce that there's not a damn thing we can do about these killings of Jewish legislators, beyond what the FBI is already doing. However, if I announce that in response to these horrible murders I have asked the Presidential liaison to the Center for Holocaust Studies to join the task force, then I look all right." The President smiled.

"This cynical decision is made much easier by the fact that I admire you, Mr. Mann, and I actually think it is possible you will offer some insight that all the others have missed." Irwin Mann sat a tiny bit straighter in his chair.

"I would be proud to accept your offer, Mr. President. I promise I will do everything I can to help this country."

July 26

"Now that you have all had a chance to introduce yourselves to Mr. Mann," the President said, "let's get down to business." He scanned the faces of the people on the task force. "Alex, you were talking to me yesterday, and I recall you said that your people do not believe the person behind this is really Wilson Blair. Is that right?"

"That's correct, Mr. President. Too many things have happened which would be virtually impossible for Blair to have arranged."

"Is there anyone at the FBI who disagrees with that assessment?"

"Not to my knowledge, sir."

"Is there any person or any agency represented here who has reason to believe that Wilson Blair is actually the one leading these terrorist attacks?" The President scanned the room, but saw nothing but shaking heads. "All right, then. Dwight, your agency may issue that statement you've been asking for." *Best news that guy's had all month* Neumann thought.

"Thank you, Mr. President," Greenwell said with feeling. "I would like to call a press conference tomorrow, if I may."

"That will be fine. Now," he said, addressing the rest of the group, "let's review the latest bad news." The President glanced at his notes and started the meeting in earnest.

July 28

"Put your bathrobe on. You're about to give me an erection."

"So why are you complaining?" Cindy asked as she sipped the orange juice that Room Service had delivered.

"Bad things have been happening to guys who get erections around you." Cindy began to choke as she unsuccessfully tried to stop laughing.

"It's...it's...not really funny," she gasped, "but...I can't help it. I'm...punchy, I guess." She regained her composure, then stared out the large window that surveyed downtown Atlanta. Finally she looked Henry straight in the eyes. "I'm really horny, too."

"You mentioned that once before, about a week ago, and I pretended not to hear you. I changed the subject. I'm sorry, that was a stupid thing for me to do." He lowered his eyes, slightly abashed. "It's a life affirmation. It happens when you see people die." Henry chewed his toast thoughtfully as he remembered something.

"Back when I was in school in the 'seventies, and parachuting a lot, one weekend I was at the drop zone up in Orange, Massachusetts. Late April, I think it was. It was a beautiful Saturday, sunny and about seventy-five degrees, and there were tons of people there. Must've been a couple hundred. One of the guys had planned a big clambake, and had maybe fifty pounds of clams he'd bought, and they'd been cooking all day. Everybody was invited.

"Well, about three o'clock, one of the instructors, a little Italian guy, he puts out a load of students on static line, and after they're all open okay, he jumps out last. His main 'chute streamers, 'cause he had just bought it and wasn't up on how to pack it right. You're supposed to release your main when something's wrong, and go back into freefall. He didn't. His reserve 'chute had been packed by a licensed rigger, but this instructor had second-guessed the manufacturer and jury-rigged the reserve container with a 'last hope rope', which he had hand sewn to the flap. Supposedly, this was the thing you pulled if your reserve didn't come out. And last of all, the kid had tied the last hope rope to his reserve ripcord, so it would get pulled automatically when he pulled the reserve.

"You can probably guess where this is leading. The reserve release handle snagged a line as the 'chute was coming out, which would have been no problem, except the last hope rope was tied to it, and so it held the whole mess right on top of his pack instead of letting it fly up in the air and open. If all that sounds confusing and unlikely, I agree with you, but it's what the FAA report that came out a couple months later said had happened.

"Anyway, this guy hit the ground at maybe 80 MPH and bounced about four feet in the air, and I know that's true because I saw it. Bill got to him first, in about thirty seconds, after almost running over a couple people with his station wagon, but the kid was obviously dead. So the ambulance came, and Bill got on the loudspeaker and announced there had been a fatality, which everyone already knew, and he closed the airport for the rest of the day. A bunch of the women and a couple of the men there were crying, and no one really knew what to do."

"And all those clams were cooking."

"Yep, all those clams were cooking, and maybe a couple people blew it off and went home, but not very many. The clambake went on as scheduled, and there were a whole lot of people there. And a fair amount of liquor was consumed, but I don't think it was much more than it would have been if nobody had died.

"The weird thing was that people couldn't keep their hands off each other.

Everybody was necking, and feeling each other up, and going off with someone they'd just met. George Goveia would usually end up with someone when he went to a party, but that night he had three different girls. And I'm sure it's true, 'cause it was the three women that told me about it, not George. He always kept his mouth shut, which was one reason he got laid a lot.

"Anyway, Cindy, the point is I think it's some kind of instinctive thing, left over from when there was always the possibility of the race dying off. You're not kinky," Henry assured her. "Well, not that way, at least," he amended.

"That's good to know, because since the two yesterday, sex is all I can think of."

"Then let's go find a titty bar somewhere. That's the breeding ground for foxy bisexuals."

"Oh, so you have the same condition?"

"I didn't say that," Henry told her, trying to keep a straight face. "But I'd feel terrible if I let you out of my sight, and something happened to you." Then he grinned.

"We'll see how it goes," Cindy said as she, too, tried to hide her smile. "What's in the newspapers?"

"Here's *USA Today*," Henry said, tossing it to her and turning serious.

BLAIR DEAD, SAYS GREENWELL
ATF Chief Says Missing Agent "One of Our Finest", Calls for Public Support to Fight Domestic Terrorism

"So the feds finally decided Wilson Blair isn't the person behind the killings," Cindy said as she read the article. "Dwight Greenwell held a press conference yesterday. I told you we should have turned on the news. We missed it."

"Yeah, but Allen didn't."

"You think he got the tape to CNN?"

"I know he did. I talked to him while you were asleep," Henry said. "From a pay phone down the street. Some real fireworks ought to start tomorrow."

"You sure they'll air it?"

"You don't think a tape of a missing agent that the feds all claim is dead is newsworthy?"

"Well, of course, but what he says is so..."

"Trust me, they'll play it. They know if they don't, one of the other networks will," Henry assured her as he scanned the newspaper article. "Hey, here's a great quote: 'Wilson Blair exemplified the very best of dedicated government service. These terrorists will be found, arrested, and tried. The public is behind us 200%, but right now we need even more.'" Henry snorted. "What Greenwell really needs is a remedial math course." Henry set the paper aside and looked at the *New York Times*.

ATF Press Conference
Director Lauds Supervisor, Agency

"Damn!" Henry exclaimed as he scanned the article. "This is unbelievable."

"What?"

"They don't mention that Blair is dead until halfway down the column, and then it's as a quote only." He looked up at Cindy. "I think the goddamn *New York Times* is hedging its bets." He put the paper down, picked up the *Washington Post,* took note of the headline, and scanned the article below it.

ATF Director Speaks
Federal Agency Still Under Fire

"More of the same," he said as he tossed the paper aside and reached for his orange juice. "Tomorrow should be interesting."

July 29

"Agent Neumann, I think you'd better come look at this," the man said in a loud voice. Alex stepped into the D.C. agent's office and stared at the television, which was tuned to the Cable News Network. Most people in the CIA or State Department had CNN permanently on in their offices, but the practice was not nearly so widespread in the FBI building.

"They claim they got some exclusive footage of Blair coming up," the agent explained. "This is from yesterday." Neumann stepped over to the corner of the man's desk. The man he had been talking with followed, and another agent joined them as well. The four FBI men stared at the screen, which showed a clip from Dwight Greenwell's press conference.

"...encourage the FBI in its efforts to find the persons responsible for Agent Blair's fate and see that these evil terrorists are brought to justice." The camera cut back to the news anchor.

"That was yesterday," the announcer said. "Today, CNN obtained exclusive footage of Agent Wilson Blair, who has been missing since June 7. Blair makes some shocking allegations both about Director Greenwell, who you just saw praising him, and the entire Bureau of Alcohol, Tobacco, and Firearms." The image of the anchorman was replaced by that of a man sitting behind a desk or table covered with a white sheet, with a similar piece of fabric covering the wall or partition behind him.

"That's our boy," one of the agents said.

"What do you think the ransom will be, couple hundred bucks?" another joked.

"My name is Wilson Blair," the man onscreen said in a clear if reedy voice, and the agents became quiet. "I am a regional supervisor for the Bureau of Alcohol, Tobacco, and Firearms. The government of this country has been engaged in a systematic program of lies, evidence planting, and coercion. My agency has been at the forefront of this deception. Our actions have chilled the freedoms of this country's strongest defenders of individual rights."

"Somebody's got a gun on him," Neumann said as the man on the screen stopped to take a sip of water.

"I'd bet money on it," another answered.

"In April of this year," Blair went on, "Dwight Greenwell, the Director of the Bureau of Alcohol, Tobacco, and Firearms, spoke with me at length. He explained the difficulties ATF was having trying to enforce more and more gun laws. He also told me that many legislators and former legislators who had voted for these laws were blaming their losses, or their declines in the polls, on ATF's bad image as a bunch of inept bunglers.

"Director Greenwell reminded me that the most vocal of ATF's critics were people licensed under the National Firearms Act of 1934. This was not news. For many years, and particularly since 1986, ATF has targeted NFA manufacturers and dealers, but many of our raids and legal battles have not gone well. Director Greenwell said we had to put every independent NFA manufacturer and dealer out of business if we were ever to accomplish anything. He said that our previous efforts had not gone nearly far enough. Then he explained that the first step we had to take was to select several well-to-do, successful, high-volume independent dealers and manufacturers, and crush them. He intended to see to it that these men and women would be prohibited from ever owning another firearm for the rest of their lives. The rest would then follow.

"Acting on Director Greenwell's specific orders, my office began planning a three-part raid on the homes of three U.S. citizens. These three men hold federal licenses to deal in and manufacture firearms, issued by the Secretary of the Treasury pursuant to the National Firearms Act of 1934, as amended by the Gun Control Act of 1968. They have never in their lives committed any crime more serious than traffic violations.

"In order to plan this raid, my office employed a number of illegal wiretaps, and I had three blank search warrants signed in advance by a federal judge, Ellett Stevens, who has signed many blank warrants for us in the past." Blair pulled three pieces of paper from his jacket and held them up in front of his chest. The camera zoomed in on the documents.

"Jesus," Neumann breathed.

"Blank warrants, all right," one of the agents in the room said. "You can even read the signature." The camera panned out, and Blair resumed speaking.

"ATF scheduled the three raids so that they would take place when the dealers were thousands of miles away. And we intended to plant evidence in all three houses, to be 'found' by our agents during the searches."

"Put-up job, no question," one of the agents commented.

"ATF has planted evidence on prior occasions, but it was always firearms-related. An auto-sear, a barrel we had cut off to a length below the legal minimum, muffler tubing and fender washers we could say were illegal silencer parts, dummy grenades a paid informant could testify were being illegally reactivated, or metal dies and stamps we could claim a citizen had been using to re-number firearms." The man on the screen paused again to take a drink of water.

"He's got a script," one of the men in the room said quickly. "Those warrants are no big deal. Everybody knows that shit goes on. Nobody'll believe the stuff about Greenwell." *He's trying to convince himself* Neumann thought as he glanced at the other man. *This does not look good.*

"We always get our indictments," Blair said as he put down the water glass, "but in too many cases, the accused dealers hire top lawyers and private detectives to get proof of what we've done. We bankrupt them eventually, and after they've gone through all their assets paying legal fees, they plead to charges of conspiracy and go to prison.

"This, however, takes time and uses up government resources. The men we were going after have a total net worth of over ten million dollars, and we fully expected them to use it all to prove their innocence. Dwight Greenwell said that because of this, all three of the men had to be jailed without bond. That would make it much harder and more expensive for the three men to work with their lawyers. Jailing the men without bond was going to require very serious charges, and therefore some very serious planted evidence. That was no problem after Director Greenwell obtained the cooperation of the DEA and Secret Service."

"Now what?" one of the FBI men asked as he watched the man on the television screen pop the latches on the briefcase. "He looks a little nervous," another answered as Blair lifted out several stacks of bills and two brick-shaped blocks of white powder wrapped in white plastic. Alex Neumann clenched his teeth as his guts turned over. *By this time tomorrow, a hundred million Americans will have seen this tape* he thought grimly.

"DEA provided six pounds of pharmaceutical-grade cocaine," Blair said, lifting up the two bricks. "Of course, there's no way to prove on film that this isn't powdered chalk. The authorities can check out my story if they want to, though. This coke came from a raid last February in Titusville, Florida, where the principals escaped before they could be captured. DEA Agent Herbert Salvest was in charge of the property seized that day. Salvest claimed he destroyed the cocaine, but in reality sold most of it back to the original owners, and kept the rest for future use. He used the proceeds to buy a house on Halifax Avenue in Fort Lauderdale titled in the name of the Paris Corporation. Agent Salvest is the sole shareholder of that company. Paris is the middle name of his current primary mistress, Jennifer Fannon, who also lives in that city." Blair laid the two bundles down on the sheet-covered table and reached once again into the briefcase.

"These stacks of counterfeit hundred-dollar bills came from Agent Kenneth Lenstrom of the Secret Service. Agent Lenstrom was in charge of the detail which arrested a counterfeiter in Los Angeles in December of last year. I have forgotten the man's name, but that should be easy to check. Lenstrom said the counterfeiter made some crack to the newspapers that since the government wanted to increase the money supply, he thought he'd help." The FBI agents watched the screen raptly as Blair broke a stack of bills and selected several from it.

"Unlike the coke, I can easily show this stuff is counterfeit." He gripped the short stack between his thumbs and forefingers and held it taut with the bottom edges of the bills against the white cloth of the table. The camera zoomed in until a blurred image of the front bill more than filled the entire screen. Then the focus adjusted and the image became sharply defined.

"Notice the serial number," Blair's voice continued. "H10273160A. Every single one of these hundreds has this number." The hands slid the first bill off the stack and laid it aside, paused, and did the same with the next bill. The process went on until all the bills were discarded. Each one clearly had the same serial number. "This next stack is all H33724233A." He demonstrated once more. "Director Greenwell instructed us to make sure the bills were found in stacks of like serial numbers to strengthen our claim that the men could not have received them from a bank." The voice on the television cleared its throat.

"Notice also the series, 1993. Look closely at the border around the image of Franklin, however, and you will see there is no third line surrounding it, which, under magnification, would show the words 'The United States of America' over and over. Check the bills in your pocket—the third line is present on all currency series 1990 and later, five dollars and larger. Also present on 1990 and later bills over $5 is a vertical magnetic strip inside the paper for tracking the movement of currency. This coded vertical strip is an inch from the left side. Shine a light through the bill and you will see it." Alex Neumann and his companions watched in fascination as the bill on the screen moved and went out of focus, then became sharp again. Now the left half of it was being held taut against the illuminated face of a powerful flashlight. No strip was visible. "Here's what it should look like," the voice said. "This is a bill out of my pocket." The hundred was replaced by a ten, and everyone in the room saw the thin vertical stripe in the paper. Then the camera panned back out.

"In addition to the drugs and counterfeit money, I have here news clippings of an upcoming speaking engagement planned by the former Attorney General, and photographs of several federal buildings in three states. The photos have strategic areas circled in ink." Blair held up the photos and clippings for the viewers.

"This planted evidence was designed to paint the picture of licensed dealers and manufacturers heading a terrorist organization funded by drugs and counterfeiting. This would get all federal law enforcement agencies involved, cause the suspects to be held without bail, and encourage the public to support greater government authority, particularly for ATF.

"I was the 'cut-out' for this operation. Dwight Greenwell will claim I and my people were acting alone. If that were true, why would I now confess? A guilty conscience?

"This is a warning to the American public. The problem is not that a bad man occupies a position of authority in a government agency. The evil is much greater, for it has become institutionalized. On October 18, 1995, the former head of the NFA Branch lectured at an ATF training seminar. He admitted ATF's own registration records are grossly inaccurate. Then he told the agents that in any trial, they were to perjure themselves and always testify under oath that the registry was 100% error-free. This lecture was videotaped and a former federal prosecutor obtained a transcript under the Freedom of Information Act. These transcripts are now in wide circulation among NFA dealers.

"Parts of our government now operate without regard to the rights of citizens, and this philosophy of unlimited authority is taken for granted by everyone involved. Federal agents have put citizens in prison, gassed them, shot them to death, and burned them alive over tax issues involving trivial amounts of money. Not one government employee has spent one night in jail or paid one dollar in fines. Instead, they are given paid leave, get promoted, and garner even more authority to do as they please.

"Worst of all is that the men and women who commit these atrocities are not acting out of deep moral purpose. It is only a job to them, a paycheck, a way to make the next VISA payment. That makes these people even more despicable, but it also makes the strategy for stopping them very simple." All four FBI agents stared at the screen, waiting for Wilson Blair to say the words they knew were coming.

"Kill them," he said simply. "Individually, without risk to anyone else. Take it from someone who knows—government employees have a strong instinct for self-preservation. Kill fifty or a hundred of them around the country, and many more will resign and look for less hazardous work. But kill them one at a time, when others are not around. The blood of innocents helps the wrong side.

"One at a time," he repeated. "Pick your spot, use a piece of pipe, walk away, and keep your mouth shut. It's ridiculously easy when the Constitution is on your side and you outnumber the enemy over five thousand to one. Good luck." Blair smiled, and was then suddenly replaced by the Cable News anchorman.

"CNN obtained that footage from an anonymous source this morning. Director Greenwell was unavailable for comment. We'll have more as the story unfolds, but at the moment it appears that Agent Wilson Blair may indeed be alive and well at this time.

"In Los Angeles today, city administrators met once again to discuss–" The image vanished and the screen went black as Alex Neumann reached over and punched the button on front of the set.

"How'd you like to be in Greenwell's shoes about now?" one of the men asked. "Or that Secret Service, or DEA guy, hmm?"

"Guys are fucked."

"Yeah, but we'll probably have to run the investigation on them." The others grunted. They hated having to go after their own.

Alex Neumann was not listening. His mind was elsewhere. *This time tomorrow, every person in the country will have seen that clip. Several times* he mentally amended. *Blair didn't mention FBI* he reminded himself. *Thank God.* The Bureau was very proud that its agents had never stooped to planting evidence on those they investigated. *Like that's a real reason for us to hold our heads high after what we did in Idaho and Texas* he reminded himself grimly.

***

The doorbell chimed just as Orville Crocker finished setting out the last of his pistols. He had spent the whole morning moving his inventory from the vault and arranging his paperwork so that the annual inspection would go as quickly as possible. He had to leave for the Cheyenne airport that afternoon to pick up Curt Behnke, who was flying in from St. Louis. Crocker had not turned on a television set or radio since the previous day. He knew absolutely nothing of the Wilson Blair tape.

"Good morning," the ATF compliance inspector said as Crocker opened his front door. "Vonetta Ecks, Bureau of Alcohol, Tobacco, and Firearms," she continued, extending her right arm. A look of slight surprise and disgust briefly flashed on Orville Crocker's face as he shook the young woman's hand. His reaction was due to the zircon-studded, two-inch synthetic nails the woman wore on all ten of her fingertips. Vonetta Ecks misinterpreted the fleeting expression, and her attitude towards Crocker changed abruptly. He did not realize this.

"Orville Crocker. Come on in," he said. "I've got everything laid out. Would you like some coffee?"

"No, thank you."

"Everything's in here," he said, ushering her into his dining room. The large table was covered with a white sheet, and twenty-seven submachine guns were laid out on top. Eleven of them were Thompsons, mostly 1921 models. Near the end, next to a Swedish Suomi, was a Mauser 712 select-fire machine pistol. It looked out of place among the shoulder-fired weapons. Two card tables were set up a few feet away where thirty-nine handguns were neatly laid out, and a pair of rimfire rifles lay across one of the chairs. The 20mm Lahti sat on the floor against the far wall. Crocker picked up his bound book which documented all the acquisitions and dispositions of firearms since his Federal Firearms License had first been issued eleven years before.

"You've got twenty-three NFA weapons, according to our records," Ecks said briskly. Her back was turned and she did not notice Crocker's reaction. "Let's start with them. Is this your book?"

"Uh, yeah, but I've got more machine guns than that." He looked at the table and began rapidly counting in his head. "Thirty," he said after a few seconds, "Not twenty-three. And the 20mm Lahti makes thirty-one, but it's not in my bound book, since I had to buy that on a Form 4." Crocker paid $500 per year for Class 3 status, but that did not entitle him to buy Destructive Devices on a tax-exempt basis. He had purchased the Lahti as a private individual with fingerprint cards, photographs, police signature, a five-month wait, and a $200 tax stamp.

Vonetta Ecks scowled. "You have the transfer forms for all of them?" she asked.

"Right here," Crocker said, holding out a sheaf of papers. The woman took them and began cross-checking the serial numbers with her own list. After a minute or so she began making corrections to the sheet she had received from Washington. It was obvious that Crocker's records were correct, for in each case he had both the gun in his physical possession as well as the individual transfer form bearing ATF's date stamp and a hand-stamp of Dwight Greenwell's signature.

"Damn computer," she muttered quietly.

The discrepancy between the two sets of records was not, strictly speaking, computer-related. Turnover at NFA in Washington was high, and disgruntled soon-to-be ex-employees often deleted, altered, or "lost" machine gun registration records. In other businesses this would be a colossal nuisance. With NFA weapons,the problem was much more serious.

The law dictated that an NFA weapon be registered once and maintain that registration forever. At the same time, the law prohibited registration of existing unregistered guns. Taken together, these two constraints reversed the doctrine of "innocent until proven guilty." When a machine gun dealer or collector possessed a gun that ATF did not show in its records, it was up to the individual to prove prior registration. If he, like ATF, had misplaced his paperwork, ATF would confiscate the weapon and have it destroyed. If the individual was lucky, that was all that would happen. In many cases, however, ATF would bring charges and the person would go to prison. There were many people in the gun culture serving time because they had learned this lesson too late. Orville Crocker was acutely aware of the rules of the game, and kept all his paperwork in a locked safe.

Crocker saw that the compliance inspector was going to be a while, and he was about to go out to the kitchen when the telephone rang. He reached over and picked up the receiver.

"Hello? Hey, Doug." Crocker smiled when he heard his friend's question. "Funny you should ask, I'm right in the middle of my ATF compliance inspection. No, that's okay, they just need to check my records and make sure all the paperwork's right. Theirs, mostly," Crocker added with another laugh. Vonetta Ecks glared at his back. "Should be up at your place tomorrow."

There was a lengthy pause while Crocker listened, and Vonetta Ecks noticed the lone pistol sitting on the table of machine guns. She picked it up and held it at chest level to look at the German markings on the top of the gun. Like almost all ATF inspectors, Ecks had absolutely no experience with firearms other than writing down their serial numbers. It did not cross her mind that she should keep her finger off the trigger, point the muzzle in a safe direction, and check the action to see if the gun was loaded. She was not part of the gun culture.

Crocker listened to the man on the other end of the line, then snorted with amusement. "Doug, I promise I won't machine-gun any of your cattle. I haven't yet, have I?" he asked with a grin. "And I don't think I'll need to go in your house, but I'll put the key back if I do." He listened some more. "Good deal. Okay. Bye." He hung up the phone and started to turn around.

"If you need license copies for the dealers that–*JESUS!*" Crocker yelled in horror when he saw the machine pistol that was pointed straight at his heart. Then reflex took over. He lunged forward, swung his right arm in an arc from right to left, slapping away the weapon. At the same time, he grabbed the barrel and violently twisted the gun away from his body in one instinctive motion. The move bent the compliance inspector's hand backwards, and she released the Mauser. Her index finger on the trigger was also bent back, and the gun would have fired into the wall if it had been cocked and loaded. As the machine pistol's trigger guard slid off the tip of Ecks' index finger, the only thing left blocking the gun was the two-inch artificial fingernail. The synthetic nail was epoxied to Vonetta Ecks' natural growth, and both the plastic and the epoxy were stronger and more durable than Mother Nature's best effort.

Vonetta Ecks screamed as part of her real nail was torn to the quick in the fraction of a second before the gun was ripped free. Orville Crocker went down on one knee clutching the Mauser 712 as momentum carried him off-balance.

"*Ofay mothafucka!*" Ecks bellowed.

"Look, goddammit," he said, breathing hard and with a violently elevated heart rate, "you were—"

"You mothafuckin white devil!" Ecks screamed in a dialect entirely unlike the one she had used at the front door. Tears filled her eyes and she was literally shaking with pain and rage. Then her face changed with a sudden internal recognition, and something that might have been a smile flashed briefly across her face. "See what happens now," she said triumphantly. Vonetta Ecks grabbed her briefcase and rushed out of the house without another word.

***

"You believe CNN showed that tape?" Stokely Meier asked of no one in particular.

"That Blair guy, you think he's really the one behind all this?" one of the men in the St. Louis gun shop asked.

"Doesn't really matter, does it?" asked another.

"Guess not."

"Liked to piss myself, when that peckerneck started pulling stuff out of his briefcase. Cocaine, counterfeit hundreds, newspaper clippings—shit, he had everything there but a map of Dealey friggin' Plaza."

"Feds left one thing out." The others in the gun shop turned to look at Thomas J. Fleming, who was examining a 1937 National Match Government Model. They did not notice the large bearded man standing two aisles away behind a rack of graphite fly rods. "When I saw that tape of Blair and his briefcase full of goodies," Fleming said, "next thing I expected him to say was that they'd gotten the Postmaster General to hand over some child pornography the Post Office had confiscated." Arthur Bedderson, standing by the fly rods, cocked his head to listen to the lawyer.

"Feds seize kiddie porn all the time," Fleming explained. He shrugged. "Maybe the ATF Director didn't think of it." The others grunted agreement. Bedderson smiled tightly and turned away. He had just had an idea.

"We'll see some serious resignations now," one of the men suggested. "You get the *Wall Street Journal* here in the store, Stoke? I wonder what their advance time is for classifieds?"

"There's one in the back," he answered. "Lead time's only a day or two, I think, but maybe they got a special deal for feds. Got a couple more in yesterday's paper, but my favorite was today."

"What was that? I must've missed it." Everyone had been watching the 'Jobs Wanted' section, following the dozens of resignations and early retirements.

"Some ATF guy's wife," Stokely answered.

"What?"

"Yeah. Took out an ad to say she'd filed for divorce and moved out of the house. Thought everyone should know. I guess she was afraid Blair and company might decide to include her, like the Colombians do in the drug wars."

"That's not what she was worried about," Tom Fleming said immediately. "More likely she was afraid her husband would pop her, and try to make it look like the ATF execution squad did it. That's what she wanted to head off. His alibi." Two of the men present laughed uproariously at Fleming's comment.

"You got problems at home, Tom?" one of them said after he had calmed down a bit.

"Not at all. Used to do a lot of divorces, though." The men laughed some more.

None of them paid any attention as Arthur 'B.I.' Bedderson slipped out of the store and walked around the corner. At the end of the next block was both a camera store and a newsstand with a large adult section.

***

"Sir, you said to bring to your attention anything irregular concerning NFA dealers and manufacturers."

"What is it?" Dwight Greenwell snapped.

"One of our people says she was assaulted during a compliance check this morning. Out in Laramie, Wyoming. Apparently it happened when she discovered a discrepancy in the dealer's records. She thinks he may be, uh, connected to...what's been going on," the man said finally. He was uncomfortable mentioning anything related to the day's newscasts. Greenwell closed his eyes.

"This shit is going to stop right goddamn now," he said in what was almost a whisper. "Is the woman all right?"

"Yes, sir. I believe so."

"Thank God for that. How many tactical people can we put on the ground?"

"Two, from the Cheyenne area. We can get more if we bring them up from Denver."

"Do it. Every man we can muster. It's time to turn this thing around." Greenwell looked up as he thought of something. "Cheyenne's where Alex Neumann came from. Call the FBI office out there and have them give us some backup. Get back with me if they give you any shit."

"Yessir."

***

"You can still fly an ultralight, sweetheart," Jenny Lowell said with a sad smile when she heard the news. "I checked, and they've got some now that are aerobatic." From another person, the comment might have brought a sarcastic response, but Taylor Lowell hugged his wife and kissed the top of her head. She knew exactly how miserable he was.

"Maybe it'll come to that," he said. His most recent attempt to get his pilot's license reinstated had failed, just like the others.

Jenny Lowell's suggestion was now the one remaining way that Taylor Lowell could stay in the air. Single-seat aircraft weighing less than 254 pounds with level-flight top speeds of less than 60 miles per hour could be legally flown without a pilot's license. These $15,000-$20,000 powered hang gliders were the refuge of those who did not have the money to buy a 'real' airplane, did not want to submit to ever-increasing stacks of equipment regulations, or who, like Taylor Lowell, had been grounded by the FAA despite every attempt to remain in compliance.

"Would you like me to fix you a drink?"

"Thanks, babe," he said as he patted his wife's bottom. "Just a Coke. I think I'll go veg out in front of the tube for a bit." He picked up the newspaper from the kitchen counter and walked into the living room.

The projection television was already on and tuned to CNN. The Blair tape was running again, and the newsman then gave an update about reactions from around the country. Outrage at the government was high on the list. Lowell sat in his armchair and scanned the paper's headlines. The lead story in the *Kansas City Star* was on the killings, but not the Blair tape. That story had broken too late for that day's deadline. Lowell listened to the news report as he skimmed the Star article.

The paper mentioned how closed-mouthed the government was being about leads in the case. The author had thrown in a few quotes about the evil nature of the killers, and Taylor Lowell thought these comments sounded tired and obligatory. In light of the Blair tape on CNN, they were almost embarrassing. The last part of the article addressed the rumors surrounding the recent violent deaths of two Congressmen. Each of the dead legislators had a record of vigorously advocating gun bans.

"They don't have shit," Lowell said under his breath, then smiled, stood up quickly, and headed for the back of the house.

"Where are you going?" his wife asked as he entered the kitchen. "Here's your Coke."

"Thanks," he said, gulping it. "I'm heading over to the library. Just remembered some things I want to look up." He grinned and thought of something else that would divert further questions. "And I want to run by the newsstand, get one of those ultralight magazines. Moping won't put me back in the air, and I might as well find out about those aerobatic jobs you mentioned, right?" He kissed his wife and headed for the door before she could respond.

Jenny Lowell's spirits lifted as she watched her husband depart. It was the first time she had seen him looking happy since his Pitts had been grounded and his airman's medical certificate revoked.

The drive to the library took less than ten minutes, and Taylor Lowell found what he was looking for sooner than he had expected. Several aviation magazines had discussed the four most recent bills which had expanded the FAA's power, and listed how every U.S. Congressman and Senator had voted on each of them. One of the U.S. legislators from the Phoenix area, Congressman Heebner, had supported all four.

The pilot was about to leave when he thought of something else. It took a little longer than it should have because Taylor Lowell was not initially sure how to find what he was looking for. In about twenty minutes, however, Taylor Lowell learned that Congressman Heebner had also supported a number of proposed federal bans on guns and ammunition, and had vocally opposed the state-level concealed-carry legislation which had recently passed in Arizona.

When Taylor Lowell discovered this, his initial reaction was to marvel at his good fortune. He did not own a gun and had no interest in shooting sports, but Taylor Lowell did not want the police department's list of suspects to be entirely composed of private pilots. Then, on impulse, the aviator cross-checked the list of legislators who favored more restrictions on pilots with the list of those who had voted to further restrict gunowners. The tallies were very close to identical.

***

"Hey, little boo," Arthur Bedderson said as his two-year-old daughter pushed open the door to his study. He turned away from the computer keyboard and pushed his chair back from the desk.

"Daddeee," the little girl said happily, reaching out her arms towards her father's beard as he bent over to pick her up. "Whatchoo doin, Daddy?"

"Playing political spin doctor, little thrasher," he answered.

"Doc-tor?" she asked.

"That's right," he said, as he clicked the mouse button and saved his work that was on the screen. "Want to see the new camera your old man just got?" Bedderson said as she let go of his whiskers. He unfolded the ten-year-old Polaroid single lens reflex he had bought for $90 and held it backwards at arm's length. "Watch this—big flashy thing, boo," he said, making a face. Bedderson pressed the button with his thumb and the electronic strobe discharged. Then the camera whirred and ejected the print. "Wait a minute, and you'll see it," he told the little girl. She stared for a few seconds at the shiny surface of the undeveloped photo.

"Oy?" the girl said quizzically.

"Unh huh," Bedderson answered agreeably. "Now let's do one of you. Squint your eyes shut tight," he told her, demonstrating. The little girl giggled happily and imitated her father. The big man snapped another photo and laid the print on the table next to the first.

"Daddy," she giggled. Then the image of her father in the first photo started to appear, and the little girl opened her mouth in wonder. "More, Daddy," she said insistently, pointing at the camera.

"You want more? Take more pictures?" Bedderson asked.

"Yes!"

"Okay, we'll take some more," 'B.I.' Bedderson assured his daughter, who was making faces for the camera. She was used to having people take pictures of her, but instant results were something new. Soon Bedderson had used up all of the ten-shot film pack, and he replaced it with a new one as his daughter Rachel looked back and forth in fascination at the images laid out on the coffee table.

"Uh-oh," Bedderson said in mock horror. "Do I smell a poopy diaper?" He scooped her up in his arms. *"You are my poopy diaper, poopy diaper baby of mine, diaper baby, ooooh, diaper baby,"* he sang, doing an excellent imitation of a song on a children's tape Rachel liked.

"More, Daddy," she said insistently.

"More?" he asked. "Does the little babe want more pictures? Okay, but first we have to change your little diaper and give you a little bath to get you all clean before bedtime. Let's go get your bath started, little stinkbottom," he said, carrying the giggling little girl upside down towards the changing table in the other room. He folded up the instant camera and carried it in his free hand.

After disposing of the soiled diaper and bathing Rachel, Arthur Bedderson wrapped her up in a fluffy towel and carried her to the bedroom. The little girl threw the towel aside and turned around in a sort of pirouette.

"An X-rated session, huh?" Bedderson commented as he unfolded the camera and prepared to shoot some more pictures. "We'd better stick to family-oriented shots. I don't think they'd believe it with a two-year-old. Maybe if you were ten."

"Pic-ture," she said happily when she saw her father holding the camera.

"Okay, little smiler," Bedderson said, moving in close and framing his daughter's face in the viewfinder. The autofocus SLR camera bounced an infrared beam off Rachel's face and the lens adjusted to the fourteen-inch distance. Bedderson snapped off two pictures and set them at the foot of the bed. "That's all for now," he announced. "Got to save the rest of the film." He handed the photos to his daughter. "Take these into the kitchen and put them on the breakfast table where Mama will see them when she gets home tomorrow. Then I'm going to put you in bed." Rachel grabbed the prints and ran off naked towards the other end of the house. When she came back, Bedderson took her upstairs, put a diaper on her, then returned to his study. This time he locked the door before sitting down at the computer.

After a few marginally satisfactory attempts, 'B.I.' Bedderson hit on a combination of settings on his photo-morphing program that gave him startlingly good results. A CD-ROM of public-domain clipart had given him a number of photos of girls between the ages of eight and ten. Copies of the magazines *Shaved Clean, Barely Legal, Asian Sluts,* and *Anal Bike*r had provided images of small-bodied, flat-chested, nude women without pubic hair. The pictures in the last magazine showed women being penetrated by male subjects. The morphing program combined these into pictures of nude ten-year-olds. Bedderson's color inkjet printer using purpose-made paper turned out photo-quality prints of the computer-generated composite images.

"Now for the final test," Bedderson said as he laid the first print out on his desk, held the Polaroid over it, and pressed the red button. The results were what Bedderson had expected. The focal plane of the Polaroid was ten inches from the print. This distance was proportionally different, compared to the size of the subject, than the camera-to-subject distance that had existed when the magazine photos had been taken. Since the print was laid flat, the focal distance to the center of the print was considerably shorter than it was to the sides of the image. The Polaroid photo looked just like what it was: A picture of a picture.

"Not done yet," Bedderson muttered to himself. Like most serious shooters and ballisticians, he had a facility with math, numbers, and objects in three-dimensional space. What he knew he needed to do was digitally alter his final computer-generated image so that each pixel would appear to be the same distance from a point that was exactly over the center of the image. That dimension had to be the same as the distance from the center of the print to the Polaroid's film plane.

After two hours and fifty minutes of manipulating the program inputs, he had what he needed. The color printer ejected a picture that appeared slightly concave. When Bedderson laid it on his desk and copied it with the Polaroid, the proper geometry of the image was restored. Arthur Bedderson studied the final result, then took another instant photo, this time intentionally moving the camera slightly after the autofocus mechanism had done its job. This made the picture very slightly out-of-focus, and rendered the image even more realistic. The final result was better than Arthur Bedderson had dared expect.

"Better living through technology," he whispered as he applied the same digital distortion to the other morphed images and sent them to the color printer. In another ten minutes, Arthur 'B.I.' Bedderson had a short stack of Polaroid photos of nude ten-year-olds in blatantly sexual poses.

'Bad Influence' Bedderson was not normally bothered by unpleasant tasks or distasteful photographs, but the last computer-generated image made his skin crawl. He had used a photo of a tiny young woman on her back with her feet held up around her head, being anally penetrated by a large, hairy, well-endowed man whose face was not visible. The young woman in the magazine had had a look of sexual ecstasy on her face. Bedderson had digitally grafted on a new head from a clipart shot of a child crying because she had dropped her ice cream cone. What had been tears of frustrated disappointment became, in the new setting, a look of abject terror and excruciating pain. The final Polaroid result was even more horrifying.

Arthur Bedderson picked up that photo and two others by their edges, and slipped them into an envelope. The other photos and all the prints he wrapped in newspapers, carried over to the fireplace, and burned. The envelope with the three Polaroid photos went into his gun safe.

Bedderson encrypted all internal data from his morphing program, including all the intermediate steps he had used, before saving it to his computer's hard disk. Then he went to bed, but sleep was a long time coming.

***

Back at home from the library, the first thing Taylor Lowell did was sit down at his computer and log onto a web site. After a few false starts, he found some discussion about the mysterious Wilson Blair and his advice to those who were unwilling to endure more government in their lives. The next time Lowell looked at a clock, it was 2:07 a.m.

After he got in bed, it took Taylor Lowell over an hour to fall asleep. That was not unusual, for in recent weeks he had been consumed with anxiety. Tonight, however, his insomnia was caused by a mind thoroughly occupied with planning an important task.

"Dwight, I've got to handle this now. I've got a press conference this afternoon."

"Mr. President, Wilson Blair was not acting of his own free will."

"Maybe not when he made that tape, but the drugs and the counterfeit money are a real problem for this administration, even ignoring the blank warrants. And Blair said you arranged for it all."

"Mr. President, I had no knowledge whatsoever that Wilson Blair was manufacturing evidence."

"Kenneth Lenstrom, formerly of the Secret Service, and Herbert Salvest, who used to be at DEA, tell a different story. But that's not the issue. You are responsible for the actions of your men, Dwight."

"Mr. President, I–"

"I expect your resignation on my desk by tomorrow at noon. Dwight, please don't make me publicly fire you."

***

"Need a hand?"

"That's okay. It isn't as heavy as the Unrestricted guns I used to shoot in competition." Curt Behnke carefully laid the 28-pound rifle on the sandbags and prepared to push a dry patch through the bore from the breech end. It was still fairly early in the morning, and there was not even a hint of wind in the air. At the Missouri gunsmith's suggestion, the two men had started out at first light to make the most of their first day of prairie dog shooting. With the Wyoming man helping, Behnke had just finished making sure that all four of his light rifles were properly zeroed at 250 yards.

Curt Behnke stowed his cleaning rod, removed the rod guide from the receiver, sat down on the stool, and squinted at the target frame he had set up in the distance. It was 500 meters away, according to the rangefinder. *Five hundred forty-seven yards* he thought. *That ought to be far enough to get an idea of whether I've been wasting my time.*

"Tell me about what you've got there," Orville Crocker asked the old man.

"Long range gun I built up," he said, opening one of two hinged plastic boxes next to the gun. Inside were thirty-seven fired cases unlike any others on the planet, made for a rifle that was one-of-a-kind. "Six millimeter on a .348 case. Probably burn out the barrel in a few hundred rounds, but right now I got a load stays under an inch at three hundred yards, which is all the longer my range is in Missouri, and it's the flattest shooting rifle I've ever built." He took out a screwdriver and made sure the scope mounts were tight.

"A couple of these crazy guys in *Precision Shooting* magazine wanted to shoot Idaho rockchucks out at a half-mile and beyond. They talked the custom bulletmakers into ordering special dies and extra-long jackets to make real long varmint bullets," he explained. "Hundred grains and up in .243" diameter, with boattails and long, fifteen-caliber ogives, instead of a normal eight-caliber radius. Don't lose velocity as quickly or drift as much in the wind. Now they're making low-drags in .22, .25, 7mm, .30, and .338 calibers, but the 6mm has the most choices.

"Hitting out at those crazy ranges, you got to have an accurate rangefinder. Estimates won't work. If you misguess the range by twenty percent on a shot at two hundred yards, you'll be off by an inch and a half. Misguess the range by twenty percent on an eight hundred-yard shot and your bullet will miss by four or five feet. So you also need a scope with exact click adjustments of known value. It gets to be a miniature version of what artillerymen do," Behnke said with a smile. "Most folks shooting 6mm low-drags use the .284 case, to get enough velocity with heavy bullets. I thought I'd see what something even bigger would do." He handed Crocker a fired case from his box.

The shiny brass had started life as an unfired .348 Winchester case. The .348 was a cartridge for which only one factory rifle had ever been chambered: the Model 71 Winchester lever action, introduced in 1937 and discontinued in 1956. Browning had made a limited run of reproduction Model 71s in 1992 for fanciers of the obsolete weapon.

Behnke had selected the .348 case as the basis for the long range cartridge he had designed because it was the 'fattest' commercial cartridge case made by a domestic manufacturer. This meant that for a given powder capacity, any cartridge based on the .348 case would be shorter than one made using another parent case. Match shooters had shown through constant experimentation that short, fat cases created more uniform combustion than long, skinny ones. The .348 was also of 'rimmed' design, which made for a strong case head and had allowed Behnke to sort the brass by rim thickness.

Two months earlier, Behnke had fitted an old 6mm barrel to a match action and chambered it with his special 6mm-.348 reamer. Then he had measured a thousand factory Winchester .348 cases and obtained a little over three hundred with exactly the same rim thickness. He had necked these down using a die he had made, seated a primer in each, put in a small charge of fast-burning pistol powder, filled the rest of the case with Cream-of-Wheat, and fired each case with the gun's muzzle pointed towards the sky. The result was several hundred formed brass in this special caliber.

Using a wall-thickness checker he had made, Curt Behnke had found a hundred forty-seven cases whose wall thickness at the case body varied less than .001". He had then put each of these cases on a mandrel in his lathe and turned their necks so that the wall thickness of each case neck was exactly .014", then trimmed each case so that the overall length of each one was exactly 2.080". Behnke had deprimed all 147 cases, cleaned them with carbon tetrachloride, and drilled the flash holes to the same size. Finally, he had weighed each of the finished cases. Thirty-seven had weighed exactly the same, and these had been set aside. Fifty-eight were within two-tenths of a grain, and this was close enough to use for load development. The rest had gone in the trash.

Behnke had removed the barrel he'd used to form the cases, and chambered and fitted a Hart match blank to the Hall 'Express' single shot match action. Then he had removed the barrel and sent it to a firm in Illinois called 300 Below, which specialized in cryogenic tempering of metal parts. This company had slowly brought the barrel to negative 318 degrees Fahrenheit, held it there for eleven hours, and then slowly brought it back up to ambient temperature. The procedure removed all internal stresses from the steel, and also made the material more wear-resistant. Behnke had read of the process in *Precision Shooting,* and tried it himself, sending the company one of his best-shooting barrels, and a mediocre one. Both were markedly more accurate after cryogenic tempering. When Behnke saw the improvement, he made sure that every rifle he built from then on got a cryogenically treated barrel.

The gunsmith had then epoxied the Hall action into a heavy Lee Six fiberglass stock with a 4" wide forend, screwed the barrel back in, fitted a scope rail to the receiver, mounted a scope, and begun working up loads for the rifle. He had used a laborious technique that called for thorough cleaning after each round fired to 'break in' the bore. Curt

Behnke was now about to demonstrate the results of all this work.

"What's your load?" Crocker asked as Behnke sat down at the bench.

"Case full of some slow-burning surplus ball powder Henry got for me, and a 115-grain Berger bullet. Velocity's over 3700, which is marginal for the strength of these thin match jackets. I molycoated the bullets, which seems to make them shoot a little flatter at long range, but I mainly did it to cut down on fouling and make the bore last longer. I molycoat all my match bullets now."

"I wondered why they were that dull grey color."

"That's NECO's lab-grade moly. Tumble them in steel shot with just a pinch of the stuff to coat the bullets. Then some lab-grade carnauba wax, with more shot in another tumbler, to keep it from rubbing off on your fingers. They're really slick now, boy." Crocker smiled as he watched Curt Behnke unscrew the steel scope caps, pull the Unertl target scope to the rear to make sure it was seated, and settle in behind the rifle. Behnke plucked a cartridge from his second box, slid it into the loading port, and closed the bolt.

"When the barrel was brand new and the rifling at the throat was dead sharp, sometimes the bullets would come apart in the air about fifty, a hundred yards out. The moly seems to help. Still does it once in a while, especially when it gets hot." The gunsmith was referring to how the bullet's thin copper jacket, stressed from being engraved by the rifling, would sometimes rupture under the rotational force of being spun at 350,000 RPM as it left the muzzle. When it did, the bullet would leave a blue-grey trail of vaporized lead as it disintegrated in mid-flight.

Behnke touched the trigger as he stared over the top of the rifle without looking through the scope. The gun thundered and slid back three inches on the sandbags. "The fouling shot held together," he said with a nod. "Now for the group." He opened the bolt, extracted the fired case, and put it back in the box with the other second-quality brass. Then he selected five rounds from his box of thirty-seven and laid them carefully on the folded towel next to the butt of the rifle.

In the no-wind conditions, Curt Behnke fired carefully and let the barrel cool between shots with the bolt open. His aiming point was a five-inch black dot on a three-foot-square piece of butcher paper tacked to the folding target frame over a quarter mile distant.

"Too far to spot my shots from here," Behnke said, standing up. "We'll have to drive down."

"How 'bout I take the truck and one of the walkie-talkies, tell you where you're hitting. Then I'll move over to the side a bit and you can adjust your sights while I spot for you."

"Okay."

Orville Crocker closed the tailgate and the camper's rear window, climbed into his GMC, and drove off across the prairie. Two minutes later he was staring at the butcher paper from ten feet away, and he could not believe his eyes. Three of the five shots were almost touching. The other two enlarged the group so that it was just a little too big to be covered by a quarter. Crocker hit the Transmit button on the portable radio.

"Ah, it looks like an inch, maybe an inch and an eighth," he said in wonder.

"Where is it?" Curt Behnke came back.

"Oh—uh, right. You're about, uh, nine inches low and three inches right. I'll move over to the side." Crocker put the truck in Reverse and backed ten yards away. A minute passed, and then there was a loud *crack* that startled the Wyoming native, and a quarter-inch hole appeared a half-inch from the center of the black spot. A moment later the rolling boom of the muzzle blast echoed in cab of the truck. In half a minute, a second bullet cut the target, almost touching the first. Thirty seconds after that, there was a third distant boom, but no supersonic crack and no hole in the paper.

"That one make it to the target?" Behnke asked on the radio.

"No."

"Okay, give me a minute, and I'll try one more." Crocker waited, and was rewarded with a crack-boom.

"How do those three look?"

"Dead center, it looks like from here. Want me to go check?"

"Yeah. I've got the bolt out. Go ahead." Crocker dropped his truck in Drive and pulled up to the target frame.

"Your group's about a half-inch high. Windage is perfect. Three shots in well under an inch. Looks like about three-quarters. Want to shoot some more?"

"No, we'll save the barrel for prairie dogs."

"Okay, I'll pack up the target." Crocker lowered the walkie-talkie and stood staring at the two unbelievable groups for a long moment. Then he began carefully pulling down the butcher paper and disassembling the target frame.

***

"Hildebrandt, ATF," the black-clad man said, extending his right hand. "Local office. Kellogg here is my partner. Ruiz and Figueroa," he added, cocking his head towards the two men slightly behind him. "They've just come up from Denver."

"Trey Mullins," the FBI agent answered. He had hesitated just a fraction before taking the ATF man's hand, and was staring at what the ATF agents were wearing. All four men wore black "ninja" outfits, black combat boots, black body armor, and carried black machine guns. On their heads were knit black ski masks, pulled up and worn like caps for the moment. Mullins was thinking about how hot the four men were likely to be before too long.

"You've confirmed that Crocker is out shooting on the Pertzborn property?" Hildebrandt asked. "We've checked his house, and no one's home." Trey Mullins forced his face to remain expressionless as he developed a mental image of that little scene.

"Talked to some folks who saw his truck headed that way," Mullins lied. "I phoned Pertzborn's house, but there's no answer," he added, which was the truth. "Whether Crocker's still up there now..." He shrugged and let his voice trail off.

Trey Mullins had never liked the idea of being involved in any ATF action. After CNN's bombshell video footage of the day before, the four ATF men were about as welcome in his office as a wheelbarrow full of plutonium. The notion of an armed, unannounced raid on a man who was an alderman in his community struck Trey Mullins as very bad public relations. To execute this raid while the man was out on someone's ranch plinking with his Thompsons looked to Mullins like a good way to initiate another Ruby Ridge disaster. He had spoken with his friend Alex Neumann on the phone, and although Alex had sympathized with his old partner, he'd explained that there had to be cooperation between the agencies. Neumann had told him to provide backup only, and that is exactly what Trey Mullins intended to do.

"We'll find him," the ATF leader said confidently. "You going like that? On a deployment?" Trey Mullins looked down at the cotton work shirt, blue jeans, and cowboy boots he was wearing. He shrugged.

"I'll have on my windbreaker. I'm just going to stand in the background, remember? This is your boys' show." Agent Hildebrandt gave a look of mild disapproval, but said nothing. "Let me go sign out a rifle," Mullins said, "and we'll get going." The FBI man walked into the other room and unlocked the gun rack. He lifted out the Brown Precision bolt action rifle, which was the most accurate weapon in the Cheyenne office. The rifle had a Remington 700 action, Douglas barrel, and fiberglass stock. An AWC suppressor was screwed onto the threaded muzzle. The rifle had originally come with a night vision scope, which Neumann and Mullins had immediately replaced with a more conventional Leupold variable optic. Once in a while they used the NV scope by itself for midnight observation, but neither man had ever envisioned an occasion where they'd want to shoot someone from a long distance in secret after dark.

The sound suppressor was another matter. The moment Mullins fired the .308 and discovered that it had the report of a little .22 rimfire, he'd fallen in love with the glass-stocked rifle. Agent Mullins had grown up in western ranching country, and subscribed to the rancher's "Three S" creed regarding wolves: Shoot 'em, Shovel 'em, and Shut up. The noise-suppressed rifle was tailor-made for wolf control. Any wolf that got within two hundred yards was as good as dead if Trey Mullins had the suppressed .308 handy. Agent Mullins was well-liked by the ranchers he knew.

The AWC suppressor which made this possible was about the size of two frozen-juice cans, and made the gun a foot longer and much less convenient to transport and carry. However, the one time Trey Mullins had taken it off, he discovered that the rifle's point of impact changed radically. The gun was equally accurate; shooting off his coat thrown over the hood of the car, Mullins had still put his three shots in 1 1/4" at 100 yards. The group, however, was almost a foot above and to the right of where he had expected to see it. When he'd screwed the suppressor back on, point of impact returned to the point of aim. From that moment on, the suppressor had remained attached.

Hildebrandt's look of disapproval at Mullins' casual civilian garb changed to one of pleasure when he saw the suppressed sniper rifle the agent carried under his arm. Trey Mullins picked up his blue nylon FBI windbreaker, adjusted his cowboy hat, and opened the door leading out of the office.

"Let's go."

***

"Man, this little seventeen is great!" Orville Crocker said happily as he walked up to the vehicle. He had just connected with yet another prairie dog at over 300 yards. "Maybe I ought to have you build me one of these." The day before, Crocker would have considered a fifth of a mile an absurd range at which to expect to hit a prairie dog with any rifle, let alone one that weighed only nine pounds. He was still amazed that it could be done with a gun whose recoil was so slight that the shooter could watch the bullet strike through the scope. The rifle he was shooting was chambered for the wildcat .17 Mach IV, a case made by reforming .221 Fireball pistol brass to the smaller neck size and sharper shoulder. Most of the .17s Curt Behnke had built had been chambered for this custom cartridge. The .17 Remington was the only factory round which fired .172" bullets, and while it had slightly higher velocity than smaller-cased .17s, Behnke had never achieved the stellar accuracy with the bigger case that he had with the Mach IV.

"It took me a long time before I was willing to believe a .17 could keep up with a good .22 centerfire varmint rifle. Twenty years ago, nobody made a decent .17 barrel, and there weren't any match-grade bullets because no one made match jackets. Now Ed Shilen and Ken Johnson make .17 barrels just as good as their .22s, and Walt Berger talked J4 into doing a big run of match jackets."

"Are the benchrest shooters using .17s now?" Crocker asked.

"No, those guys take the barrel off and throw it away if the gun won't stay under two-tenths, and the little .17s won't quite average that, no matter how careful you are." Behnke was referring to the center-to-center group size, in fractions of an inch, for five shots at a hundred yards. "But three-tenths is plenty good for prairie dogs." He squinted in the bright sun. "If you really want me to build you one like that one you're shooting, I can rebarrel the .223 you were using this morning. Only drawback is you won't be able to buy match bullets at your local gun shop, like you can with a .22 centerfire. And you'll need to make your own cases, but I can get my grandson to form as many as you want while I'm fitting up the barrel."

"Let's keep that .223 I shot earlier the way it is, and build up a second gun," Crocker said as he chambered another round. "Like you said before, the .223 is the most sensible caliber. And I mean, if you lived out here, would you want to own just one prairie dog rifle?"

Hooked after half a day the old gunsmith thought as he answered with a laugh. *A man after my own heart.* "Better watch it. Next thing you know, there'll be a dozen of them in your gun cabinet. You ready to take a break?"

"Sounds good. It's about time to clean the rifles, anyway."

Guess I already got him trained about cleaning, too Curt Behnke thought. He had impressed upon Orville Crocker the necessity of keeping a match rifle's bore free of copper fouling. Some prairie dog shooters would let a gun go fifty and even a hundred rounds before scrubbing the bore, but Behnke's long years of match competition had made cleaning a religion. It was what made the difference between hits and near misses out at four hundred yards.

"Let me handle the cleaning chores. You can stop me if I do anything wrong."

"All right. And while you're doing that, I'll prep some cases for the big gun. You can take some more crazy long shots off the bench this afternoon. Maybe we can find another good long range spot after lunch."

"Can't wait," Crocker said. He had made one kill at over five hundred yards that morning, and was still marvelling at the event.

Curt Behnke smiled as he stood by the tailgate and opened the bottom drawer of the machinist's chest he used for a shooting kit. He took out his loading tools and began reassembling thirty-seven more rounds of ammo for the 6mm-.348.

***

"I've never been on this part," Orville Crocker said as he and Curt Behnke approached the foot-deep stream in Crocker's truck. "Want to go farther?"

"Sure. We can always come back."

"Right." Crocker put the truck in low gear and took his foot off the gas, letting the engine do the braking as the truck's front wheels dropped down into the stream. The thick steel rear bumper scraped loudly on the rocky ground as the rear wheels followed.

"Sharper drop-off than it looked," Behnke said in surprise as they bumped across fifteen feet of stream bed and climbed up the opposite side.

"Think it messed up your sight settings?" Crocker asked, worried.

"No, no, not in foam hardcases. I was just thinking of your bumper."

"That's what it's for," Crocker said as he accelerated down the track worn in the prairie over the years by other vehicles before him. A long, rolling hill topped with a rock outcropping rose up in the distance. It was over a mile away. The path through the sagebrush aimed straight for the hill, then veered left around it at the base. "Shall we go up there, see if we can get any good long-range shots down the other side of that hill?"

"That's a good idea. It's easier to use the rangefinder on any kind of downward angle than it is on the flat. Prairie dogs don't stick up much." *Got to see if maybe Henry will sell me that Russian gadget* Behnke thought. *Best piece of equipment a long-range shooter could ask for, next to his rifle.*

"Good point." Orville Crocker drove on, then brought the truck to a stop where the path bent left around the hill. He cut the wheels right, put his truck in low gear, and engaged the shift lever for the transfer case. Then he eased out the clutch without touching the accelerator. The GMC 3/4-ton began to idle up the gentle slope.

"I always take it easy out in the middle of nowhere," he explained. "Lot of guys would race up here in two-wheel-drive. You spin a wheel, and one of these rocks can cut your tire right to the cord. Not so easy when it's dry, like now, but it can happen 'fore you know it, especially right after a rain." Curt Behnke nodded. Minutes went by as the truck slowly made its way up the hill. When they got to the rock outcropping, Orville Crocker drove around and parked on the far side of it, with the nose of the truck aimed west, in the direction away from where they had come.

"Now let's see what we've got in the cooler," the younger man said as he opened the back of the truck. "Ham and cheese on rye sound good? And what do you want to wash it down with, Coke or iced tea?"

"I'll take a Coke," Curt Behnke said absentmindedly. He was using the 7x26 binoculars to check the area below them for dog towns. "Looks like we got some real barrel stretchers west of us. Six hundred yards to the nearest one, looks like." He chuckled. "Watch that rangefinder make a liar out of me."

"I'll set up the portable bench," Crocker offered. It worried him when the old man started doing any kind of heavy lifting, even though Curt Behnke didn't seem to show any strain.

***

"They're over on the other side of this creek."

"How deep is it?"

"Less than a foot, I'd say."

"Want me to get out and check?"

"Nah, I can see from here," Hildebrandt said quickly as he took his foot off the brake. Trey Mullins opened his mouth to suggest that they all get out of the van to lighten the vehicle, but it was too late. The undercarriage scraped noisily as the front wheels dropped into the creek bed. The driver reflexively took his foot off the accelerator, and the van slowed to a crawl just as the dragging stopped and the rear wheels neared the edge of the short drop-off. Before Agent Hildebrandt had the presence of mind to speed up, the back of the van dropped eight inches and there was a loud, jarring *clunk* as the van's rear bumper landed on the rocky creekbank. The driver stepped on the gas pedal, but the engine just revved freely. Both rear wheels were spinning in the water.

"Shit."

"You'd better get out and push," the driver said. "Four of you should be able to get this thing unstuck." Trey Mullins and three ATF agents clambered out of the van and got behind it up on the rocky bank of the creek. Try as they did, the van wouldn't budge.

"Let's find something to put under the wheels," Hildebrandt said as he got out of the van. The men searched the area, but there was nothing suitable to plug the seven-inch gap between the tires and the slippery bottom of the creek bed. The largest loose stones were fist-sized at best.

"Got a pry bar in there?" Mullins asked in a voice that showed he did not hold much hope for an affirmative answer. The lead agent shook his head. Guns were the only tools the ATF agents had brought. "We'll have to go find Crocker on foot, then. Use his truck to pull us out."

"What if he doesn't have a chain in his truck?" Agent Ruiz asked.

"Then we'll drive and get one," Mullins said with just a hint of exasperation in his voice.

"Let's try piling up those smaller rocks, first," one of the others suggested. "Before we have to go off on a long hike." The agents set about gathering up the stones and trying to wedge them *en masse* under the tires.

"Get behind and push, when I give it the gas," Hildebrandt said as he climbed back into the cab. Sweat was beginning to soak his body armor and black clothing. There was a very slight wind blowing to the west, but it helped only a little. "Get ready," he said as he started the van's engine and dropped the lever into Drive. "Okay...now!" The driver took his foot off the brake and pressed down on the accelerator. A bubbling whine cut through the air as the left tire spun on the wet stones and the pile collapsed. The wheel spun impotently as the right remained stationary.

"I think you broke an axle," ATF Agent Kellogg said. Trey Mullins rolled his eyes. "The van's just got an open differential," he corrected. "No limited-slip."

"Whatever, it's not going to work," Hildebrandt said. "Let's get going. Hoods down, men. We're deploying."

Curt Behnke paused with his sandwich held halfway to his mouth. "You hear that?" he asked.

"Sounded like a car winding out. Or something," Crocker said with a scowl as he turned his head. Both men walked to the side of the rock outcropping and looked out over the path from which they had come.

"Van's stuck in the creek, looks like," Curt Behnke said as he reached for the little seven-power binoculars he wore around his neck. He lifted them to his eyes and adjusted the focus. "Hm."

"What is it?"

"Take a look," Behnke answered, pulling the carry strap over his head and handing the binoculars to the younger man. He was frowning. "See what you think. That's over a mile off. I'll get the big set." The old gunsmith walked back around the rock outcropping towards where Crocker's truck was parked.

Crocker steadied himself against one side of the gap in the rocks and turned the focus wheel with his finger. "Oh, Christ," he breathed softly. What he saw looked for all the world like four men dressed in black with black hoods over their heads, carrying short weapons of some sort. They were followed by a fifth man in a dark jacket and cowboy hat holding a gun that was longer than the others. Reflexively, Crocker stepped back and to his left, concealing himself behind the upthrust rock.

"Let's try these," Curt Behnke said as he set the camera tripod down. Attached to the top of it were a large pair of observation binoculars weighing twelve pounds. They had 100mm objective lenses, and were fitted with 45 degree eyepieces for more convenient use while on a mount. Behnke loosened the tripod's head and adjusted the position of the big twenty-power glasses until he had the five men in his field of view. There was almost no mirage present, for it was the middle of the afternoon, and the hottest part of the day was past. Through the binoculars, the hooded men looked like they were about 130 yards away. The gunsmith's eyes narrowed as he stared at the five of them walking along the path worn in the prairie. *Black hoods and machine guns* he thought. After what was not quite a minute but seemed much longer, Curt Behnke looked up from the twin eyepieces.

"Take a look. You'd be better at identifying the guns they're carrying than I am." He stepped back to let Orville Crocker have his position behind the big glasses.

"Suppressed Heckler & Koch MP5s," Crocker said softly after a few seconds. "The four in black are ATF, I'd bet anything on it. The fifth man has a scoped bolt action with a suppressor screwed on the muzzle. I don't know who he is. Local, maybe." Crocker gave a long sigh. "It's me they're after."

"The fifth man is FBI," Behnke corrected. "I saw him turn around and his jacket has 'FBI' in big white letters across the back." He closed his eyes and spoke very carefully. "Why are they coming after you, Orville?" *Now he's going to tell me he's one of the fellows who's been doing all this killing.*

"I had my annual compliance check yesterday, right before you got here. I didn't want to talk about it, so I didn't say anything to you." He rubbed the bridge of his nose, where his shooting glasses sat.

"The field agent they sent out was this black woman who I don't think had ever touched a gun before. I wasn't thinking about that at the time, though. Anyway, she picked up a Mauser 712 Schnellfeuer and pointed it at me. Not on purpose," Crocker said quickly. "She was probably just looking at it, but I haven't had a gun pointed at me since Vietnam, her finger was in the trigger guard, and I just went ballistic." *Oh Lord* Curt Behnke thought. *So you drew your gun and shot her.*

"I slapped the barrel to the side and twisted the gun out of her hand," Crocker continued, nervously glancing past the edge of the rocks at the approaching men. "She had these real long glued-on fingernails, like a lot of black women wear. You know—the kind with the little fake diamonds stuck to them? Anyway, her finger was on the trigger, like I said, and when I twisted the gun out of her hand, it tore that big long nail off. She screamed bloody murder and called me a few things you don't hear on television, even if you got cable. Maybe I said something—I don't remember. She got this kind of crazy look on her face, and said 'I'll fix you' or something like that, and stormed out.

"I guess I should have called the Cheyenne ATF office and told them what happened, but..." He looked at the ground. "Probably would have made things worse." Crocker licked his lips. "We better pack up and drive down to where they are." He started to step towards the truck, but Curt Behnke put his hand on the younger man's arm, stopping him.

"Is what you told me really all that happened?" Behnke asked. Orville Crocker considered the question.

"I guess it's possible I broke her finger, but I don't think I did. I've broken a few fingers in the last thirty years—couple of them mine and one on someone else. You usually hear it let go. I'm pretty sure it was just her nail torn partway off. But that can hurt like a bastard, too."

Assassination team. I can't believe I'm seeing it Behnke thought in amazement. *Time was, I'd've called a man crazy if he came up with a notion like that* the old gunsmith said to himself. *Not now.* Curt Behnke was remembering the news footage he'd seen from Waco, and the description of what had happened at Ruby Ridge. He was also thinking of two helicopter gunships on his friend Henry Bowman's property.

"Those men are coming here to kill us," Behnke said slowly. "I might not say that," he continued, "if there were only two of them, or even three, and they weren't wearing those hoods, and they didn't all have silencers on their guns. But what else would four men be doing with silenced submachine guns and their faces covered?"

"I don't know."

"That fifth man is there for backup," Behnke found himself saying. "I'm sure of it." The gunsmith squinted. "The thing that doesn't make any sense is why anyone carrying a pistol-caliber weapon would be crazy enough to climb up a hill out on the wide-open prairie after a couple of fellows with varmint rifles. There's absolutely nothing for any of them to hide behind." Orville Crocker's jaw dropped suddenly.

"They don't know we've got varmint rifles," he said immediately. "In fact, they don't know that you're here at all. They think I'm alone."

"How can that be?"

"ATF knows the guns I've got from checking my records every year. They're all handguns and submachine guns. All pistol-caliber stuff, except my Lahti. The only rifles I've got are a couple of twenty-twos." He glanced past the rocks. The five men were still a long ways off.

"But you're out here shooting prairie dogs."

"Nobody knows that. This is my first time. But I *have* been out here at Doug's place several times before, shooting machine guns. Thompsons, mostly. They're my favorite, and he likes 'em, too. Folks in the area know that." He looked down at his feet. "I can't tell you how sorry I am I got you into this. Why don't I just show myself, and wave my undershirt, or something?" Behnke considered the suggestion. *Nowhere to hide* he thought. *They need his truck, to pull their van out.*

"They're all on foot," the gunsmith agreed. "I guess I could take your truck and go for help. But with no witnesses there'd be no reason they couldn't shoot you and say you attacked them." He paused, considering. "We could both pack up now, and drive away..." His voice trailed off. *Run away from this two-bit assassination team?* Behnke found himself thinking.

"But I'm not going to do that," he finished. "Help me bring the shooting bench and my gear over around on this side," he said briskly. "Then you can get in your truck and drive out of here if you want." Orville Crocker saw the look on the old man's face and shook his head.

"I think I'll stick around."

"Then grab that old army blanket from the truck," Behnke told his friend. "Gun needs a fouling shot," he said in reply to Crocker's puzzled look.

The two men wrapped the blanket around the front half of the barrel and folded it over. Behnke put on his earmuffs, lifted the heavy rifle off the sandbags, carried it to the cab of the vehicle, and climbed in. With the butt sticking out the passenger window and the wrapped muzzle over the middle of the front seat, Behnke chambered a round, closed the bolt, and pulled the trigger. There was a muffled *whump* and a snowstorm of wool scraps flew inside the cab and out the driver's window where the gun had been pointed.

Behnke climbed out of the truck and returned to the shooting bench.

FBI Agent Trey Mullins cocked his head. He thought he had heard something. A shot, perhaps. If so, it was a long ways off. Miles, maybe. He looked to where the others were, more than fifty yards ahead of him. None of the ATF agents appeared to have noticed any sound. Then he saw the head man stop and turn around.

"You coming with us?" the ATF leader yelled, pulling down the opening in his hood to better expose his mouth. Agent Mullins was standing at the spot where the tire tracks of Orville Crocker's truck left the dusty path. The four ATF agents had begun to head up the gentle slope, following the apparent course of the vehicle.

"I'm going to hang back here, I think," Mullins called. "In case he comes driving around the side of that hill before one of you can cut him off."

"Good idea," the ATF man yelled with a nod, then told his three companions to spread out on their long uphill march. The grade was very gentle, but all four men were already sweating heavily in their black ninja suits, ski masks, and body armor.

"Looks like that last guy is staying put. About where we turned off."

"He's the only one that really bothers me," Behnke answered, chewing his lip. "Hand me the rangefinder." Crocker uncased the binocular-shaped instrument and handed it to his friend. The device was a Russian copy of a British unit made for artillery battalions. A few had come into the country after the collapse of the Soviet Union, and Henry Bowman had snapped this one up in 1994. It employed a capacitor, a rechargeable battery, and a high-powered infrared laser. Behnke switched it on, pulled the cap off the front lens, and adjusted the power setting to its lowest level. The unit had a maximum range of 25,000 meters, or about sixteen miles.

Behnke rested his elbows on the shooting bench and looked through the eyepieces. The right side held the optics and imposed a reticle, which could be illuminated for night use, on the magnified target. The left side contained the LED electronics, and was black at the moment. The gunsmith centered the reticle on the tiny figure in the distance and pressed one of two buttons on the top right side of the rangefinder with his right index finger. He held it down until a small green light appeared, seen by his left eye. Then he released the button.

Pressing the button had sent current to the capacitor, and the green indicator had told Behnke when it was fully charged. Releasing the button discharged the capacitor, sending a two-million-watt laser pulse of infrared light towards the target. The pulse lasted about seven nanoseconds, and the laser spread very slightly with distance. IR-sensitive electronics in the front of the unit caught the reflected scatter from the first object the laser beam contacted. An internal quartz clock had started running at thirty million cycles per second when the laser fired, and shut off when the reflection returned. The rangefinder performed the necessary math in less than a millisecond, and red LED numbers appeared in the left eyepiece of the unit. *Damn* Behnke thought as he looked at the digits. They told him the FBI sniper was 1065 meters away. He repeated the process twice and was rewarded with a reading of 1070 and then another of 1065. Five meters was the smallest increment the rangefinder could display.

"Eleven hundred seventy-five yards," he said, doing the math in his head. "Never tried a shot that far away." He bit his lip. "Target's bigger than a prairie dog, though."

"Here's the computer," Crocker said as he unfolded the laptop and put it on the shooting bench. It, too, was on loan from Henry Bowman.

Many men in their eighties had an aversion to joining the computer age, at least on a personal level. Curt Behnke, the self-taught machinist, was inherently comfortable with numbers, however, and embraced any technology that increased the precision of his work. Both his lathe and mill now had electronic spars mounted on them with digital readouts for all axes. Behnke had immediately seen the virtues of a trajectory program that would calculate exterior ballistics based on the exact set of prevailing conditions. After using the laptop computer in the field for several hours the day before, he had vowed that as soon as he returned to St. Louis, he would outfit himself with just such a setup.

After the computer booted itself up, Behnke called up the ballistics program which had been written by a ballistician named Pejsa and began entering data. Because the program did its calculations based on the range in yards, Behnke did the conversion from meters in his head from the Russian rangefinder's figures. He had an exact ballistic coefficient for the 115-grain Berger bullet he was using. A month earlier he had fired the rifle over two different chronographs set exactly three hundred yards apart, and had determined exact velocities at both ranges. From these figures, and with known temperature, pressure, and humidity values, another Pejsa computer program had derived the projectile's precise drag coefficient.

"Need the barometer," Behnke said to Crocker. His friend retrieved it from the truck and gave him the current reading. "Same as yesterday," the gunsmith said as he typed in the number. "Don't have a humidity gauge, but it's dry. I'll call it ten percent." He rechecked all the figures he had entered, used the rangefinder once more to be sure the FBI sniper had not moved, and hit RETURN on the keyboard.

"Thirteen and three-quarters minutes more elevation from my five-hundred-meter zero," he announced. "Bullet will drift about six inches for every one mile per hour of crosswind." Behnke pulled a calculator from his shirt pocket and typed in some numbers. The Unertl target scope used external click-type micrometer adjustments, and the shift in impact depended on the spacing between the front and rear mounts. When Curt Behnke had machined the mounting rail, he had tried to get a spacing that would yield .200" of adjustment with each click of the windage and elevation knobs. Range testing on a grid after the rifle was completed revealed that the actual value was .194" per click.

"Seventy-one clicks elevation," he declared, and carefully began to turn the knob counterclockwise. "Make sure those binoculars are lined up exactly over the barrel," the gunsmith told Orville Crocker as he settled in behind the rifle. "Just like yesterday."

"Hang on, I'm not set up exactly right," Crocker said quickly.

"Take your time, I'm not going to shoot just yet," Behnke amended. "Not 'til those four are a little closer. In case they decide to all run in different directions."

"Oh. Right. Okay, I'm all set." Crocker had positioned the tripod as Behnke had told him, and aligned it so that the FBI agent was slightly below the center of the big observation binoculars' field-of-view.

"You asked me yesterday why I use an old two-inch Unertl on this gun, instead of a more modern scope with internal adjustments."

"Yeah, and I can see your point now—about how you need more elevation adjustment for real long shots."

"It just occurred to me, do you know the story behind the Unertl Optical Company? It's...appropriate, you might say."

"I don't," Crocker answered, glancing nervously through the binoculars.

"John Unertl was in World War One. He was a German sniper stationed on the Bulgarian border. He didn't think much of the rifle scopes that had been available then, even the best German ones. Said he would have done a lot better shooting with better optics. When he came to the United States, he decided to fix that. Unertl Optical always made every single part of each one of their scopes. Lenses were still ground in this country, in Pennsylvania, when the factory closed in '91 or '92. Everyone else's come from Germany or Japan. If you don't mind the three-pound weight, Unertls are still the best." His eyes narrowed. "When John Unertl applied for U.S. citizenship, back in the early '30s I think it was, one of the standard questions was 'Have you killed anyone?'"

"Did he say 'no'?" Crocker asked.

"He wrote on the papers, 'Two hundred forty-seven Bulgarians'. They let him in." Orville Crocker nodded, but said nothing.

Curt Behnke picked up the rangefinder and used it on the most distant ATF agent. *They're spread out more now* he noted. *585 meters. Back down sixty-eight clicks.* "Use plugs and earmuffs both," he told the other man. "Don't want you flinching at the muzzle blast. You're going to have to call my first shot right on the money. I'm figuring the crosswind component at three miles per hour average over the distance. That's eighteen inches, and the three miles per hour is a guess. Be pure luck if I connect on the first round at this range."

"Shooting for center of mass?"

"No," the gunsmith said as he slid a round into the action. "Don't know what he's got on under that jacket, and I've heard Henry talk about some kind of ceramic stuff that will stop .308 AP rounds at ten feet." Behnke paused. "I'm going to try to put it on the bridge of his nose."

"All set."

Curt Behnke adjusted the position of the big rifle on the sandbags with gentle nudges until the dot in the center of the Unertl's reticle was two headwidths to the right of the FBI man's nose. Behnke touched his finger to the trigger and began exerting slight but ever-increasing pressure. Orville Crocker gritted his teeth and willed himself to ignore the coming concussion.

Trey Mullins jumped reflexively and almost dropped his rifle. *"What the...?"* he said to no one in particular as he shook his head. It was as if someone had fired a cap pistol an inch from his right ear. He twisted his neck and had the irrational thought that a vertebra had popped when his subconscious registered the faint *boom* that was rolling across the prairie.

"Just a little left—like less than three inches from his ear," Orville Crocker said excitedly. "Saw it all the way in. Perfect elevation." His voice was quivering. Curt Behnke had already opened the bolt and plucked out the fired case; the match action had no ejector. He slid another round in the loading port, closed the bolt, pulled the scope back to its original position, slid the gun forward on the sandbags until the stock touched the forend stop, and once again began making minute adjustments to the rifle's position.

"Watch close," Behnke said in a normal tone of voice. It did not occur to him that Crocker, with two sets of hearing protection, might not hear him. *Little more wind than I figured* he thought as he adjusted his hold one head-width farther to the right and once again began exerting slight but relentless pressure on the two-ounce trigger.

FBI Agent Mullins' first instinct, after he realized that it was a high-velocity rifle bullet which had passed by his ear, was to look for the ATF agents a third of a mile in front of him. Three were immediately visible, then he saw the fourth off to the left. It was hard to tell, staring into the sun the way he was, but it looked like they were all facing the rock outcropping far in the distance.

Agent Mullins second instinct was to throw himself flat on the ground, but that was overridden by the instantaneous realization that there was absolutely no cover. Mullins had no idea where the shot could have possibly come from, but that did not matter. Presenting himself as a stationary target was a sure way to get killed, and the FBI man knew it. Mullins' leg muscles started to contract, and he was just about to push off into a sprint when Curt Behnke's second shot found its mark, 1172.34 yards from where it had originated.

"*My God...*" Orville Crocker breathed.

"Where was it?" Curt Behnke demanded as he pulled the scope back and repositioned the rifle. He had already reloaded.

"You got him. He's dead." Crocker continued to stare through the big binoculars at the inert form crumpled on the prairie two-thirds of a mile away. He did not pay attention to Curt Behnke, who was twisting the Unertl's elevation knob clockwise at a rate barely slow enough to counts the clicks.

For the rest of his life, Orville Crocker would remember what he had seen through the big twenty-power glasses. The sun had been at his back and he had been positioned in the exact plane of the bullet's flight path as it traveled away from him. Under those conditions, and with top-quality optics, it was often possible for a spotter to 'see' the bullet as it headed for the target. What the spotter was actually observing was a moving tube of compressed air as it was formed around the high-speed projectile, like a tiny heat wave arching out into the distance. Twenty-power magnification compressed the entire viewing distance twentyfold, revealing a visual effect that was invisible to the naked eye. Trained spotters with their scopes directly behind shooters at 1000-yard matches were usually able to 'call' each shot within three or four inches of its point of impact, even though the holes in the target were much too small to discern at that distance. These spotters sometimes referred to the phenomena as 'laser beams', or 'contrails.'

Orville Crocker had never heard these terms, but he saw the streaks firsthand. Crocker had watched Curt Behnke's first shot from the 6mm-.348 rise up near the top of his field-of-view, then drop back down into the center. It passed by the FBI agent's ear at the end of its descending arc and disappeared into a clump of sagebrush in line with his collarbone. The time-of-flight was one and four-tenths seconds.

With the magnification making it appear that the FBI man was only 58 yards away, Crocker had seen the agent's reaction to that near miss. Surprise, indecision, fear, and resolve had appeared and metamorphosed on the FBI agent's face as the second contrail had streaked towards him, ending on his upper lip. Trey Mullins' head had exploded in a fan-shaped geyser of red mist larger in diameter than a man was tall.

"Get with me, now," Behnke said, removing the rear sandbag and replacing it with his left fist. "Far man, over on the left."

"Right," Orville Crocker answered, wrenched back to the reality that there were still four men out there who were planning his death. "Got him," he said when he had the ninja-suited agent in his field of vision.

That's it, talk to your buddies Curt Behnke thought as he watched Agent Hildebrandt bring his radio up to his mouth and speak into it. The 36-power Unertl target scope made the man appear fifty feet away. At the actual distance of 633 yards, and with plugs in his ears, the gunsmith would not have heard any of the words even if Hildebrandt had been yelling. *Guy doesn't know his backup's dead* Behnke thought, making the inference from gestures and body language. The black-clad agent had not turned around to look behind him. *Wind should only push the bullet a quarter as far at this range.* Behnke moved his left fist under the rifle's butt until the dot reticle was on the right edge of the man's head. The black-clad agent was raising his left hand towards the top of his ski mask as Curt Behnke touched his finger to the trigger.

"He's shooting up in those rocks," Hildebrandt said into the radio. He was midway between Behnke and the dead FBI man. For that reason, the sound of the bullet's impact had reached his ears at about the same time as the much louder muzzle blast, so he did not hear the bullet strike. "Still too far to see anything. Spread out and we'll surround him. I'm going around this way to the north. Move in closer, but make sure you maintain a safe distance. Call me when you get him spotted. Out."

Agent Hildebrandt slid the radio back in the black nylon pouch and brought his hand up to shield his eyes as he faced directly into the late afternoon sun. Hildebrandt squinted, and thought he saw something at the very edge of one of the large rocks more than a third of a mile in the distance. Reflexively, he opened his mouth to say so, even though there was no one nearby.

The thin-jacketed 115-grain Berger match bullet at 600 yards was still traveling at a higher velocity than a .30-06 at the muzzle. It struck Agent Hildebrandt's left front tooth. Still spinning at over 250,000 RPM, its copper-alloy jacket ruptured in less than a microsecond. The lead core disintegrated like an overrevved flywheel and dumped over two thousand foot-pounds of energy inside Agent Hildebrandt's head.

"Center hit," Orville Crocker said clearly as the distant *thwock* confirmed his assessment. "Next target." The image the had just watched through the binoculars had not been nearly so unnerving as the one he had seen fifteen seconds before. It had taken barely a half-second for this bullet to reach its mark, and when it had, the elasticity of the agent's black ski mask had reduced the spray of brain matter considerably. Braced for a replay, Crocker found himself unmoved by the second killing.

"Get on the computer, hit the letter 'R' key on the keyboard," Behnke demanded as he reloaded the rifle, pulled the Unertl scope back into position, and picked up the laser rangefinder. *Hope he doesn't choke.*

"Now what?"

"Hit the RETURN key until it asks for the sight-in range. Then enter six hundred thirty." As he talked, Curt Behnke aimed the Russian device at the most distant of the three remaining figures.

"Done."

"Where's the bullet at...five hundred twenty-eight yards?" he asked, after mentally adding ten percent to the figure in meters displayed in the left eyepiece. *Should be around a foot, or less.*

"You're eight inches high at 550, eleven-and-a-half at 500. Split the difference, and it's..."

"Nine and three-quarters," Behnke answered. "Get back on the binoculars," he instructed as he settled in behind his rifle. "Now, if he'll just stay still..."

Agent Ruiz had been steadily trudging up the gentle grade. The slope was very slight, but Ruiz was a lifelong smoker whose idea of cutting back was setting a two-pack-a-day limit. He was breathing hard and drenched with sweat. His level 2A body armor, which would stop 9mm and .45 pistol bullets, was rubbing his skin raw just in front of his armpits. His whole head itched from the black wool-and-nylon ski mask.

When he had heard the third distant report, Ruiz stopped in his tracks and stared at the rocks over a quarter mile away. As he caught his breath, he turned his head over to the right. He was looking for the team leader from the Cheyenne office who had summoned him up from Denver, but there was no sign of him.

Ruiz squinted, trying to see where the terrain could vary enough to obstruct a six-foot human. It appeared nearly flat until much farther away than the spot he had last seen Agent Hildebrandt. He looked at the other two men a hundred yards ahead. They were both fully visible from the knees up. One of them began waving his arms and shouting, and Ruiz realized he should turn on his radio. He looked down at the radio pouch on his belt, and the 115-grain 6mm boattail slammed into his forehead over his left eye at almost three thousand feet per second.

"He's got a rifle!" Agent Kellogg screamed when he saw Agent Ruiz's body slam into the dirt. "Run!" Agent Figueroa hesitated, for he saw no place where a man could have positioned himself to be shooting at them. The nearest cover was over a quarter mile away. "Run, damn it!" Kellogg shouted, waving his left arm. "I'll pin him down!"

Figueroa turned and ran. Kellogg flipped the selector lever to full auto, raised the H&K to his shoulder, and pointed it at the rocks.

"You got him, but the other two saw it," Orville Crocker reported.

"Mm-hmm," Behnke agreed as he removed the fired case, chambered a new round, and returned the Unertl to its proper position. "What're they doing?" he asked. Orville Crocker adjusted the position of the big glasses. With their minimal eye relief and 20X magnification, their field-of-view at the 400 yard range where the near man stood with his suppressed H&K was almost a hundred feet wide. Crocker was able to see both men at the same time.

"Looks like the near guy's yelling to the one behind him. The far guy is to his left a bit, now he's starting to run. Now the closer guy's got his gun pointed towards us. With not near enough elevation," he added. It still unnerved Orville Crocker to see the magnified image of the ninja-suited agent pointing a submachine gun at him.

The big Unertl target scope mounted on Behnke's 6mm-.348 was 36 power, and like all riflescopes, it had a lot more eye relief than a pair of binoculars. Its field of view was only about twelve feet at 400 yards, and it took practice to locate targets quickly. Curt Behnke had half a century of experience picking up crows, groundhogs, rockchucks, and prairie dogs in scopes with narrow fields of view. It took him about three seconds to spot Agent Kellogg, who had a submachine gun pointed towards him, and another two seconds to shift the butt of the rifle slightly and pick up the awkwardly running form of Agent Figueroa.

The man was angling slightly to the right from where Behnke sat, and the gunsmith knew he was going to have to lead his prey in order to hit him. By the time he made his shot, the range would be a little longer than the last shot but not as far as the 630 yards for which the gun was now zeroed. *Flight time about a half second he thought.* Behnke put the dot on the man's left side as he mentally counted *'one thousand one'*. As he finished the word *'one'*, there was almost two torso-widths of space between the dot and the left edge of the agent's black suit.

Time to see how bulletproof those vests really are Behnke thought as he put the dot half a bodywidth to the right of the agent. He maintained that distance on the running target with a tiny movement of his left hand under the rifle's butt, and brought his right index finger to bear on the two-ounce trigger.

The sear on the 6mm-.348 broke just as Agent Kellogg squeezed off a nine-round burst from his MP5. The muzzle blast of the long range rifle masked the muffled clattering noise of the submachine gun, but through the binoculars, Orville Crocker saw the H&K vibrate in the agent's hands.

"Bullet blew up!" Crocker yelled as he saw the grey-blue smoke streak lance out halfway to the running man and then disappear. The view through the binoculars got hazy as dust was thrown up by the 9mm bullets landing some 300 yards in front of their position.

"Next one won't," Curt Behnke predicted as he removed the fired case and reloaded the gun without moving from his position behind the scope. "And that other guy should be holding a hundred feet over our heads if he expects to do any good."

Kellogg turned and saw that Figueroa was still running. The ninja-suited agent aimed his submachine gun at the top of the distant rocks and held the trigger down until the bolt slammed closed on an empty chamber. Then he saw the dust from his spray of shots and realized he was still several hundred yards away from where Crocker had to be. He crouched down, ejected the empty magazine, and glanced over his shoulder to check on the other agent. Figueroa was still pumping hard, almost two hundred yards farther down the gentle hill. Then a loud crack split the air, and the running figure slammed forward onto his face as if struck between the shoulder blades by an invisible sledgehammer. A half-second later the distant boom rolled out over the prairie, and Agent Kellogg simultaneously emptied his bladder and threw himself facedown in the dirt.

"Nice shot," Orville Crocker said softly. Curt Behnke, wearing earplugs, did not catch it, but he had heard the sound of the bullet hitting. "The other one's thrown himself flat," Crocker said in a louder voice.

"He'll keep. Got to see if this last one's dead, or just knocked down," Behnke said as he made minute adjustments to the rifle's butt while peering through the scope. He found the man crumpled in a heap with his head against some sagebrush. Figueroa's spine was destroyed, for the pistol-rated body armor was no match for the high velocity target bullet. Neither man could tell this, however, for blood did not show up on the black cloth that covered the ATF agent's whole body.

"I don't know if he's dead," Crocker said judiciously as he looked through the binoculars, "but I thi–" He flinched as the concussion from the big 6mm cut him off. The black-hooded head moved an inch against the sagebrush. It was now slightly different in shape. Two seconds after the gun's report came a sound like a paper bag bursting.

"He's dead now," Behnke said as he extracted the fired case and laid it next to the other six on the benchtop. "What's the last fellow doing? Can you tell?"

"Just lying there, looks like."

"Is he using his radio?"

"Hard to see. I don't think so."

"Let's see if I can pick him up in the scope." Behnke began adjusting the position of the rifle on the sandbags. "There he is," the gunsmith said as he stared through the powerful optic. Behnke could not be certain because of the black ski mask, but he thought the man was crying. He chambered another round, checked to be sure the scope was all the way to the rear in its mounts, and made minute final corrections to the rifle's position. Suddenly he stood up and started to tug Orville Crocker by the arm, but the younger man was already moving. He had seen the same thing through the binoculars.

"No use tempting fate."

"My thoughts exactly," Behnke answered as they stepped completely behind one of the large rocks. The two men listened for the distant sound of the suppressed submachine gun, but both were wearing ear protection, and it was inaudible. Crocker stripped off his muffs and pulled the plug out of his left ear. He could hear the faint clatter of the action and the sound of slugs landing in the dust somewhere between them and the ATF agent. The noise stopped, and ten seconds later, there was another thirty-round burst. This time, a few of the bullet strikes were closer.

"Man's a fool to leave his gun on full auto," Crocker said. "He's probably never shot it at long range."

"I doubt he's ever fired it at all," Behnke said with a shake of his head.

"You may be right." The two men looked up as they heard the sound of several slugs traveling through the air far above their heads.

"Now he's got it aimed like a howitzer. You count how many magazine pouches he had?"

"No."

"Neither did I. Enough of this nonsense." Curt Behnke sat back down at the portable shooting bench and put his cheek against the stock. "Ears," he commanded, and Orville Crocker slipped his muffs back on. The 6mm-.348 thundered for the last time. Curt Behnke pushed the gun back in position and checked the results through the rifle's scope. Satisfied, he stood up, removed the bolt, and began to lay out his cleaning equipment. The old gunsmith had just eliminated the entire Cheyenne, Wyoming ATF office, half the Denver ATF office, and half the Cheyenne FBI office.

"What now?" Orville Crocker asked. Curt Behnke had been thinking about that question before it had been voiced.

"Why don't you pack up your truck, while I clean the rifle. Then let's go down and drag that van loose. I'll drive it back and leave it in town somewhere—supermarket or shopping mall parking lot. Or maybe I'll drive it partway back home. Dump it in another city, take a bus the rest of the way."

"Have to check all the bodies, find the keys," Crocker pointed out. Curt Behnke gave him a look.

"I brought my tools," the gunsmith said pointedly.

"Oh. But, uh, shouldn't we go pick up their guns?" Behnke shook his head immediately.

"Bunch of stamped steel things shooting a little 9mm pistol round? What do we want them for? The most worn-out target rifle I own is better than all of them together. And that way, we won't leave any tracks near the bodies. Why, you want 'em?"

"No, I agree with you. Be better not to leave any more evidence than we already have. And nothing they've got is as good as a Thompson, and I don't need to take the risk anyway. Can you use that bolt action the one guy had?"

"I could, but like you say, why bother?" Crocker nodded, then licked his lips.

"Ah, Curt, how do you think we should, uh, handle this now?"

"I'll box up my guns, ship 'em back at one of those mail service places. You got those out here?"

"Yeah, a bunch of them."

"That's what I'll do, then. You keep your mouth shut, no one can prove you had anything to do with this," he said, waving his hand in the general direction of the five dead men.

"Tire tracks..." Crocker thought aloud, "but that doesn't prove anything," he said, answering his own question. "And I've got a set of mud-and-snows mounted up I use in the winter. I could throw them on," he suggested.

"If you do that, make damned sure you get rid of the others where they can never be traced back to you. That's the kind of thing could hang you."

"Maybe I'll just leave 'em," Orville Crocker said. "But what about when they find out you came to visit?"

"*I'm* not going to tell anyone. If you don't mention it, how're they going to find out? They won't even know what they're looking for." He continued to scrub down the bore of the long range varmint rifle. "And if they do get lucky, what're they going to do with some old retired guy in his eighties?"

"There's that." Crocker agreed. Then he frowned. "What about the bodies?"

"Leave 'em for the coyotes."

"You really like those?" the man asked as he eased up his stride. He was breathing deeply as he jogged. "I see a lot of folks using them." Taylor Lowell nodded to the runner who had come up from behind. He'd been asked before about the red, D-shaped hand weights he used when he ran.

"Yeah. They give me an upper-body workout, so I get equally tired all over, instead of just my legs. And when my knees start hurting, I can just walk and still keep my heart rate jacked up. Your joints ever complain?"

"You kidding?" the man snorted. "Almost all the time."

"Try a set of these, and just walk while pumping your arms hard. Only start light on the weight. Five pounds is the most I ever use running, and two pounds will wear you out if your arms aren't used to it. But any weight at all will definitely slow you down, so you'd best run alone or with somebody a lot slower."

"What, different weights screw on those handles?"

"Yeah. Ones I got here are three pounds a hand." The other jogger looked at Taylor Lowell's upper body. It was much more muscular than his own.

"You lift weights, too?"

"No, just this."

"I think you may be on to something," the man said with a smile. "You have to order those special?"

"No, you can get them all over."

"Thanks," the man said, nodding, and resumed his quicker pace.

***

"What's the story on that guy out in Wyoming that ATF was going after?" Alex Neumann asked.

"They haven't checked in."

"Jesus, it's been, what? Three days? Call our office, see what Trey Mullins has to say."

"We can't reach him, either."

"Well, where are they?"

"We don't know, sir."

"Where's their vehicle?"

"It's missing, too."

"Is there anything we *do* know?" he asked. *Jesus, is this another Wilson Blair?* Neumann wondered.

"Yes sir, we know that Orville Crocker is at home in Laramie, because he is answering his phone, and the local sheriff confirms that Crocker is indeed on the premises. We've asked the sheriff to question him, and all he'll say is that Vonetta Ecks of the ATF pointed a gun at him and he took it away from her. He refuses to speak on any other subject. Uh, we really need some more of our own men on the scene, sir. The local sheriff is helping us as little as he possibly can without risking an obstruction charge."

"So what else is new. Locals have never liked feds, and after that CNN piece, we might as well all have AIDS." He thought a moment, chewing his lip. "I'll have some men sent up from the Denver office and have them contact us directly the minute they have anything." The younger agent nodded and left.

Christ Neumann said to himself. *You'd think I might be due for a break by now.*

"Hey, Boss?" a new voice said. Alex Neumann looked up at the agent who had appeared in the doorway .

"What now, Jud?"

"They're getting grim. San Antonio, Texas. Somebody set fire to an ATF agent's house at 2:00 this morning. Obvious arson job. Accelerants all over the front of the house, especially the front door. When the firemen got there, they find the whole family in their pajamas, in the back yard. The agent, his wife, and three kids. All dead. Each one shot at least three times, and all of them once behind the right ear."

"A finisher."

"Right. All the slugs were twenty-twos, but forensics says they came from two different guns. Both bolt actions, from the looks of the fired cases. One's a Marlin, they have that special kind of rifling with lots of little grooves. The other's a Winchester, looks like."

"Which narrows it down to maybe ten million guns."

"Yeah." The agent looked away from Alex for an instant, then turned back to face him. "Guys from the San Antone office questioned four sets of neighbors."

"And?"

"And nobody knows nothin' about nothin'. One old guy with a walker came to the door, told the San Antonio SAC he wasn't about to talk to him, and to get a warrant if he wanted to come inside. The wife's behind the old guy, and she's sitting in a wheelchair, so the SAC asks *her* for a statement. Did she hear anything, see anything out the window? She says, 'You want a statement? Okay, Mister FBI man. People who play with fire sometimes get burned.' Then she laughs and shuts the door in his face." The agent took a deep breath. "Sir, cooperation was low before that tape got aired, but now it's nonexistent."

"I know, Jud. And thanks for the update. I know it's hard, especially for the guys in the field. But make sure you get all the reports to me as soon as you can, no matter how bad they are. And let me know if they get any breaks on this last one."

"Yessir." The man nodded and left Neumann's office.

I've got to talk to the President again Alex Neumann thought as he stood up from his desk.

August 3

"Sir! They've found the missing chopper!" Alex Neumann jumped out of his chair when the other agent came into his office and blurted out the news.

"Where is it? Any sign of the men that were in it?"

"All dead, sir. Found it a couple of hours ago. A diver verified the bodies were all there. And you're not going to believe where it was—Bowman's property in Missouri."

"*What?*"

"At the bottom of the old quarry that's at the northeast corner of his land. Been there all along, apparently. Must've crashed at the same time as the other two."

"Son of a bitch. Why didn't we spot it from the air?"

"Water's pretty deep, sir. Over a hundred feet. One of the bodies floated up and drifted over to the bank. Must've been there a while. Up on the bank, I mean. Scavengers had picked it clean, down to the bones. Skeleton with a flak jacket on it."

"Who found it?"

"One of the local deputies. He was checking on the property while Bowman's off on some geology dig, and decided to go over to the old quarry pit while he was there, and shoot his M16."

"Call the St. Louis office, and the National Guard in that area. We got jurisdiction and authority, and by God I'm going to use it. I want our people there when that thing gets dredged up. I want it done today, I want every piece of it tagged and put on a cargo plane, and I want it here in our lab by midnight tonight. The same goes for the corpses. Have our best bomb people and our best forensic pathologists ready and waiting to go to work the second everything gets here. You have my authority to do whatever it takes to see that that gets done. And make damn sure none of it gets lost or thrown away this time."

"Yes, sir."

"We been due for a break," Neumann said with real enthusiasm. It was the first time he had smiled for many days. "We got ourselves another chopper to work with. Let's see what Forensics can do with one that didn't burn up."

***

Taylor Lowell increased his pace when he saw the familiar figure ahead of him in the distance on the jogging path. He glanced around without breaking stride to confirm that no one else was around. On this, his sixth attempt, Lowell had timed it almost perfectly, and there were no other runners in sight. With a little more speed Taylor Lowell would catch up to the man just as the path entered the grove of trees. The air was dry, but the heat that morning in Phoenix was as hot as it had been all month, and the runner up ahead was not in the same physical condition as the USWest executive with the revoked pilot's medical certificate. Taylor Lowell continued to close the gap.

Congressman Heebner was breathing hard and plugging along at a ten-minute-mile pace when the path bent left and into the welcome shade. He wiped sweat from his brow and stopped squinting quite so hard as the morning sun was intermittently blocked by the trees. The soft *thup-thup-thup* of another runner approaching joined the early-morning sounds of insects and distant automobiles. Without breaking stride or turning his head to look, Congressman Heebner automatically moved to the right side of the path to give the faster runner plenty of room to pass.

Taylor Lowell flicked his head left and right, looking over his shoulders for final confirmation that no one else was anywhere around. Then he increased his pace and adjusted his stride slightly so that it would be his left foot that would be leading at the moment he shot past Congressman Heebner. As Lowell closed to within a few yards of the slower jogger, he lengthened the swing of his arms so that they extended their full length, each moving in concert with the opposite leg.

The sole of Taylor Lowell's right shoe landed three feet behind the jogging Congressman as the five-pound handweight in Lowell's right hand reached its full rear-ward extension. On his next stride, Lowell brought his right hand up and forward, describing an ellipse in the air with the same motion that a person uses to pound his fist on a table. At almost exactly the same instant that Taylor Lowell's left foot slapped against the pavement to the side and just ahead of Heebner, the five-pound weight slammed into the back of the Congressman's skull with the sound of forceful impact. Congressman Heebner skidded on his face as Taylor Lowell blew past him.

Taylor Lowell continued on for several more strides and then looked back. Heebner was crumpled on the ground. The executive and former pilot put an expression of concern on his face and trotted back to the fallen man. He squatted on the asphalt and rolled the Congressman over on his back. He knew that the man might still be alive, although he suspected the legislator had a fractured skull. Lowell looked around in a pantomime of frantic anxiety, preparing to shout for help and ready to volunteer to run for a doctor if anyone was nearby. When he was sure there was still no one approaching, Lowell dropped the act.

With an economy of motion that belied the power of the blow, Taylor Lowell swung the handweight once more, crushing Heebner's larynx. Then he stood up and resumed his seven-minute pace, enjoying a 'runner's high' as he contemplated the FAA supervisor who was next on his list.

August 4

"Right in here," the aide said, and ushered Alex Neumann in through the doorway. Neumann spoke before he got a good look at the President's face.

"Mr. President, I'm glad you called me in. We're running 'round the clock, and–"

"Slow down, Alex. I called you, remember?"

"I'm sorry, Mr. President." *Shit! Stupid idiot!* Neumann thought. "Of course you did. What can I do for you?"

"I asked you to keep me up to speed on any new assaults on our people, outside of ATF," the President said. "Alex, you let me down. I just got blindsided at my press conference. Did you see it?"

"No, sir," Neumann said miserably.

"I got blindsided, Alex, on national television, by a reporter who asked me what the White House response was to the fact that the killings had spread to the FAA, what we were going to do about 'Hoover's Revenge', and whether the White House approved of the current FAA medical standards. The goddamned *FAA,* for Christ's sake!" he exploded. Openmouthed, Neumann shook his head in bewilderment.

"I'm sorry, I...I don't know anything about that," the FBI man said finally, then stared at the floor. The President closed his eyes, most of his rage obviously spent.

"Alex, things have gone crazy in the five days since CNN ran that damn footage of Blair," he said slowly. "It's spreading way beyond ATF now. Congressman Heebner's killing yesterday was apparently not because of his voting record on gun laws." Neumann looked up quickly.

"That's right. An FAA official was shot to death this morning, also in the Phoenix area. Two hours ago someone posted an anonymous message on the Internet, calling for the assassination of other FAA officials and legislators who have given the FAA more power. Legislators like Congressman Heebner," he added pointedly.

"The Internet message referred to this...engagement, as 'Hoover's Revenge'. When I first heard that, I thought it referred to J. Edgar Hoover."

"No?"

"No," the President said, shaking his head. "Bob Hoover, not J. Edgar. Some air show pilot that was a World War II hero. Back in '93, someone in the FAA used an 'emergency procedure' to revoke his medical certificate so he couldn't fly any more, and apparently every private pilot in the country thinks we railroaded him. I just had a talk with an FAA lawyer and looked at the evidence Hoover's people have. It looks like they have the proof that FAA fabricated all of it, with an FAA Inspector's sworn testimony, and the government's strategy has been to bankrupt them. I'm beginning to think the Director is another Dwight Greenwell."

"Mr. President, do you want me to put an FBI team on this? It won't take me long to get up to speed, sir. On these medical standards, or whatever they are."

"I can brief you right now, Alex," the President said with a sigh. "Apparently, pilots have to meet medical minimums to keep their licenses. I hadn't realized it, but that includes everyone, not just commercial pilots. The FAA has set blood pressure limits, and things like that, and a lot of people flying these little two- and four-place planes for pleasure have lost their licenses. That's our pool of suspects, and it's a big list."

"You lose your right to fly your little plane around an empty sky over open ground because your blood pressure's elevated, but you can go drive your Cadillac in the business district at lunch hour?" Alex Neumann asked, startled at the news. "How low does it have to be?"

"Lower than mine is right now. I talked to a lawyer for a pilots' rights group, and that was exactly his point." The President rubbed his temples. *It would give me a headache, too* Neumann thought.

"Alex, this is a parallel situation to the gun issue, and it's just starting to accelerate. I do *not* want another Wilson Blair preaching rebellion, but that's exactly what we're about to get. God knows how many other groups are going to spring out of the woodwork. No one's targeted anyone at the IRS yet, but they're getting very nervous." Neumann nodded. *Guys at the Bureau have all been predicting the same thing.*

"Judge Potter is expecting the next call from this Jones bastard on the eleventh. I'm going to be there when he takes it." The President flared his nostrils, breathing in and coming to a decision.

"Alex, since CNN showed that tape, another seventy-plus agents have been killed and over a thousand have resigned. I don't know what the total deaths are now in all branches and on a state level, but with legislators added in it's well over two hundred. This thing is on the verge of turning into a real civil war, and I am not going to let that happen. You and Judge Potter are the only ones who know this, but I am going to come to some kind of agreement with Jones on the eleventh. He is not going to put me off for another three weeks. The eleventh is one week from today. I should have agreed to what he wanted a month ago, but that was then and this is now. The one thing that would strengthen my position is if we had Jones' client in our hands before I have that final meeting."

"Mr. President, Forensics is poring over the wrecked helicopter they pulled out of the quarry pit, and I'm going to get something out of those people today. But you know I can't promise an arrest by the eleventh. It's been—"

"I know it's been a long time, but we're down to the wire here. You have my authorization to do whatever it takes. Am I being too vague?"

"No, sir. Ah, there's been some talk about...encouraging Judge Potter to tell more about this Mr. Jones..."

"And that's what it will stay, Alex. Talk."

"Yes, sir."

"We'll have at least one more meeting of the whole group. I believe it's scheduled for the eighth."

"Ah, Mr. President?"

"Yes?"

"Forensics should be done long before then, and I will have already given you their findings. If they turn up anything major, do you want me to give a full report in the meeting, or should we keep it private? Sometimes I'm concerned about leaks."

"Everyone in the group realizes the gravity of what we're facing, Alex. That negotiation session with Jones is in a week, and after that, everything is apt to be out in the open for all the historians anyway. At this point, I'm inclined to have everyone in the group know what we're working on. Better that than risk being accused later on of holding Star Chamber proceedings in secret. You get a specific lead on one or a few suspects, keep it confidential. Otherwise, let's be aboveboard."

"Yes, Mr. President. And I can't tell you just how ashamed I am I let you down on that FAA killing."

"That's all right, Alex. Pitchers throw no-hitters once in a while, but nobody bats a thousand."

820

"Uh, sir? Agent Neumann?"

"What is it? We got a read on what brought down the chopper?" Alex Neumann asked quickly.

"Uh, no, sir," the agent in the doorway said, looking uncomfortable. "They're still picking it apart, but no firm conclusions yet. Maybe in a few more hours. Uh, that wasn't what I came to tell you. They found the four ATF agents assigned to pick up that guy Crocker out in Wyoming," the agent said. Alex Neumann saw the man's expression and prepared himself for the worst.

"And my partner, Trey Mullins?"

"Yes, sir. They found him, too. They're all dead."

The words hit Alex Neumann like a hammer blow straight to his chest. He had told himself that his friend Trey was probably dead, but the news about the third helicopter had driven the Wyoming case from his mind. Now, in the midst of the anticipation that the third aircraft might yield some solid clues, came the blunt realization that his worst fears were true.

"How?" Neumann managed to say.

"Shot," the younger man replied. "Beyond that, they don't know yet." There was a long pause before Alex Neumann finally spoke.

"Have them call here or FAX me a report as soon as they have anything."

"Yes, sir." The agent turned on his heel and left the office. Alex Neumann sat and stared vacantly at the FAXes and reports strewn across his desk. He suddenly became acutely aware of how detached he had been from the entire investigation. Alex had shed no tears for the dead ATF agents. He had seen Dwight Greenwell as a sterling example of a small-minded man in a position of power, and had viewed the whole mess as a challenging puzzle.

With the killing of his friend and partner Trey Mullins, Neumann's mindset changed dramatically. At another time and under different circumstances, he might have focused his anger on the root cause of the problem. As it was, with his position on the task force, the President's one-week deadline, and the growing and understandable us-versus-them attitude of federal agents, Alex Neumann's response was emotional and predictable: *I'm going to get the people that are behind this.*

Perhaps it was due to his police instincts, or maybe it was because the one piece of good news had come just the day before word of Trey Mullins' death. In any event, Alex Neumann was convinced that the solution to the mystery would be found in the submerged helicopter.

"This is one for the books, Alex," the leader of the forensic team said. "You're damn lucky the chopper crashed in the water. If it had hit the ground and burned like the other two, we'd never have figured it out."

"What can you tell me, Smitty?"

"The helicopter broke up when it slammed into the water at maybe a hundred miles an hour or so. Virtually all of the damage to the aircraft was from this impact. The man in the right seat, however, was killed by an explosion. ATF Agent Jaime Hernandez was literally blown in half at the chest level."

"A bomb? Where was it?"

"You might call it a bomb," he said with a humorless smile. "The pathologists told me that when it went off, it was inside his body."

"*What?*"

"The National Guard pilot was killed at the same time, by the same explosion. That helicopter was shot down by a single explosive round from a U.S. 20mm cannon. The projectile came through the right side of the helicopter and blew up as it was entering Agent Hernandez, somewhere in the vicinity of his shoulder. His body contained most of the blast, but those antiaircraft slugs are much too heavy to be stopped by one human. We found this lodged against the bone in the Guard pilot's left shoulder." He handed Neumann a short steel cylinder about 3/4" in diameter and less than a half-inch long, with a groove running around it. One end was jagged and melted-looking.

"That's the base of the bullet. It carried through and killed the pilot. Here's what it looked like before it hit." The forensic pathologist handed Neumann an unfired projectile. It was not quite three inches long, .80 caliber, with a conical aluminum nose cap which contained the detonator. The body was painted yellow for an inch in front of the copper drive band, with the lot number and the designation M246 printed at the bottom of the yellow segment. In front of the yellow section was a 1/4" brown stripe, and the remaining 3/16" behind the nose fuze was painted red-orange.

"Thermite firestarter," the man went on, "that's what the military guys call it. Mass spectrometer test of the residue we got out of the corpse confirms it. Same stuff they found from the other two wrecks. Here's the loaded round." He handed Neumann a 20mm Vulcan cartridge.

"Any doubt?"

"None."

"How many of these rounds hit the helicopter?" Neumann asked.

"That's the only one, to the best of my knowledge. I only examined the cockpit area and the corpses myself, but I asked that same question, and the other boys went over every inch of every part they recovered, which was maybe 98% of the aircraft. No evidence of any other round impacting the helicopter. A one-shot kill."

"Thanks for the quick work-up, Smitty," Neumann said distractedly. "Okay if I keep these?" He held up the unfired projectile, the loaded round, and the jagged base fragment.

"You got more juice than the Director on this one, Alex. A guy in Ordnance scrounged up the new bullet and the whole cartridge for me, so they're no big deal. But that other one killed four people. Do me a favor and sign it out, so it's not my ass if you lose it."

***

"I need to know what guns could fire this cartridge," Alex Neumann said as he held out the Vulcan round. "Anything that's ever been made, and the smaller and more portable, the better. Experimental stuff, foreign prototypes, whatever. We're looking for something that could be carried and quickly aimed by one man. And I need to know yesterday."

"Yessir."

"And when you find that out," Neumann continued, "see if any have been reported stolen from government depots."

"I'll get right on it," the ordnance man said, turning the Vulcan cartridge over in his hand to examine it as he spoke.

He had no way of knowing that Alex Neumann had asked him to solve the wrong problem.

***

"Here's a FAX for you, sir. It's marked 'Urgent'." Alex Neumann took the papers and saw it was the preliminary report on the deaths of Agent Mullins and the four ATF men. *Focus here, guy* he thought. *You can get back to the mystery 20mm later. Work the problem in front of you.* He stared at the drawing of the scene where the bodies had been found, and began to silently scan the sterile-sounding words. His brows knitted together in an expression of perplexity.

All head shots, with one of the ATF agents from Denver also shot in the back. Neumann stared at the diagram and blinked when he saw the distances that were marked. *Five dead men spread out over an area half a mile wide, and only one of them fired his weapon.* Neumann read further, and the report became even more bizarre. He picked up his phone and dialed the number of what up until recently had been his office.

"Cheyenne FBI, Masters speaking," came the voice on the other end.

"Masters, this is Alex Neumann in Washington. I've got your FAX in front of me."

"Yes, sir."

"It says here Agent Kellogg fired 173 rounds out of his H&K, and died with seven rounds left in his gun. According to the position of the body and the fired brass, you're saying he was shooting almost due west, and the only cover in that direction was some rocks four hundred yards away. And Trey was eight hundred yards behind him."

"That's basically correct, sir. That bunch of rocks was the only substantial cover for well over a mile in any direction. It is possible that two or more shooters were spread out and all wearing camouflage amidst the sagebrush. They remained motionless, and were undetected by Mullins and the four ATF agents until it was too late. If that is not what happened, then that bunch of rocks was the only place the shooters could have been."

"That puts the closest agent a quarter mile away and Trey almost three times that far. How the hell is that possible? Were they killed somewhere else and dumped out on the prairie?"

"Forensics says no. Lots of blood soaked into the ground by every corpse. The coyotes had picked the bodies over pretty bad before we got to 'em, but forensics says there weren't any tire tracks or anything leading up to or away from them. Course, it's been a few days, and what with the wind..." Neumann could almost hear the man shrug over the phone.

"They were all killed where they stood, is the way we're reading it. There's a couple things not in that preliminary report, sir. We did find some tire tracks behind the rocks, and a bunch of footprints. Whoever made them mussed them up, or maybe it was the wind, but it looks like at least two people were up there, probably more."

"They leave anything behind? Gum wrappers, beer cans?"

"Found one used cleaning patch, and that's it. It's been sent off for analysis. Other than that, zip. Oh, another thing. The guy who was shot twice? The bullet that hit him in the back is the one that killed him. Forensics says the one in the head came second, while he was lying on the ground. They think he was shot in the back while he was running away from the rocks. Second shot, in the head, was to make sure."

"But that's..." Neumann paused to consult the diagram of the crime scene. "...Six hundred yards!"

"Tell me about it."

"Agent...Kellogg," Neumann said, again consulting the FAX, "was the only one who fired his gun, and he fired it quite a bit. Does anyone there have an explanation for that?" There was a long pause, and then Masters cleared his throat.

"Ah...sir, we've got a dozen theories and not much else. A local cop thinks Mullins was killed first. His theory is that the shooters planned to kill all five agents, and the text-book way to do that is to shoot them in order, farthest one first."

"If that's the plan, wouldn't you wait a little longer? The closest one was still over four hundred yards away."

"His guess is that Agent Mullins wasn't advancing along with the ATF agents. He was staying in one spot. The agents all knew that the shooters were up in the rocks, and ATF went after them, but Mullins hung back, at what he thought was a safe distance."

"That's quite likely. I told him personally that he was there to provide backup only."

"Well, that jibes with the way he was dressed—jeans, cowboy boots, cowboy hat and a windbreaker. No body armor. He was also carrying a silenced .308 sniper rifle. Chamber was empty.

"Anyway, the way this cop thinks it might have played out is that one or more of these guys maybe has his rifle sighted in at five hundred yards, so they wait 'til the four are right around that range. Then one of the others shoots Mullins and gets lucky. The ATF guys hear the shot, but they don't turn around to look at their backup because they think he's way out of range. Then the fellows up in the rocks open up on the four ATF agents. They kill Hildebrandt and Ruiz, Figueroa starts to run, and Kellogg starts shooting back. Figueroa gets hit in the back, Kellogg takes it in the head, then they give Figueroa a finisher." Masters took a breath.

"Before you say anything, sir, I know it's full of holes. I checked some ballistic tables, and a .30 caliber sniper rifle like the one Mullins had, even if it was dead on the money at 500 yards, you'd still be a foot and a half high at 400 and three feet low at 600. Twelve hundred yards? No one makes a table that goes out that far, but it wouldn't surprise me you were fifty or a hundred feet low at that range. But with this deal, every one of the five dead men was head-shot like the gun was sighted in just for him. Haven't even mentioned wind drift." Masters paused, then went on.

"Five shooters, each one just happens to have his gun sighted in at exactly the range of one of the agents? We actually had someone suggest that as a theory."

"How many shooters do you think there were?" Neumann asked.

"Had to be more than one, to have three agents killed before the other two knew what was happening. Two or three is the consensus here. More than that runs into big logistics problems."

"Was Crocker one of them?"

"Don't see how he could have been. He's not saying a word, but I think that's just on principle. We got a warrant and went through every inch of his property. He's got a couple dozen machine guns and a cannon, but not a single scoped centerfire rifle to his name. Now, I know that doesn't mean shit, in and of itself, but the folks we've questioned have all talked him up as a machine gun shooter. All of a sudden he's a world-class thousand-yard rifleman? Hard to feature. Tires on his truck are far from new, and they don't match the tracks we found out on the prairie. ATF thought he was out there, and he may have been out on the prairie shooting machine guns at some point, but sir, those five men weren't killed with Thompsons."

"What about the bullets? You must have recovered some."

"Fragments. Got vaporized lead and little bitty flecks of jacket material, like you'd expect with high velocity varmint rounds."

"So who did kill those men?"

"Only theory anyone's come up with is that the ATF agents heard shooting up in the rocks, thought it was Crocker, and closed in. Instead of Crocker, it was some men who were out shooting prairie dogs with their varmint rifles."

"Prairie dog hunters."

"Yes, sir. They saw four guys coming towards them in black suits and hoods, carrying machine guns, and they panicked."

Panic's not the word I'd use Neumann thought, but he made no comment. "What about the agents' vehicle?" he asked, changing the subject.

"Vanished. Keys were in Agent Hildebrandt's pocket, though. Maybe it was a spare set."

"One more mystery." Alex Neumann sighed. "Masters, I want the bullet fragments from the dead agents segregated and sent up here overnight for analysis. Then I want your men to go back and scour that area for fired brass and any other evidence. Widen your search past where the men were shot. If the shooters were prairie dog hunters, they may have been shooting in other spots and been less careful. Get back to me as soon as you have anything."

"Yes, sir."

I have my own theory Alex Neumann thought as he hung up the phone. *We're not going to win this one.*

August 6

"This party is like being in the losing team's locker room after the Super Bowl," Arthur 'B.I.' Bedderson whispered to his mother. "We're the only ones smiling."

"Hush," she said, biting her lip to keep her composure. "They'll hear you." The elderly woman often disagreed with her son's libertarian political views but he could always make her laugh.

"They'll probably loosen up after they knock back some more of the free booze," Bedderson offered.

"Ken Flanagan told me he had a nice talk with you," his mother said. Bedderson shrugged.

"No percentage in me being mean-spirited. And in any event, I only talk politics to the opposition when I'm in the Capitol. Certainly not at my mother's dinner party."

"I think he's still bitter about losing. And especially that 'Flanagan Death Clock' billboard."

"I was neutral on that one. You shouldn't let sensationalism overwhelm reason, even when they say the same thing." His mother nodded. It was one point on which they agreed. "As to the election," Bedderson went on, "you'd think some of these guys would figure out that ultimately, people always move towards freedom."

"You planning to point that out to them, are you?" She asked. Bedderson laughed.

"As I said before, no discussion of politics here. At least not from my lips," he amended. "Shall I go over and strike up a conversation with Mrs. Kinser? I could tell her how much I admire Billie Jean King," he suggested innocently. Representative Kinser and his wife were both at the party for the ex-governor, amid rumors that she was leaving him for another woman.

"You're terrible," Bedderson's mother said, turning her head so no one could see her smile. "I should have insisted you stay home."

"I think I'll get a drink and go mingle." Bedderson headed for the bar and ordered a tonic water with lime. He wasn't about to put any chemicals into his system until well afterwards.

***

"Have you been upstairs?" Bedderson asked. "Mom keeps her parties on the first floor, but I know she'd want you to see the rest of the house."

"No, I haven't," the ex-Governor said.

"I'll give you a quick tour. Oh, wait—I told Mom I'd check on something in the kitchen." He smiled suddenly. "Won't take a minute. Go on up the front stairs and I'll meet you in the upstairs hall." He nodded towards the far end of the seventy-foot marble hallway, past the door to the living room where most of the guests were gathered. "Mom's got some artwork up there she's very proud of." Before the older man could answer, Bedderson had turned on his heel and headed towards the kitchen. Ken Flanagan hesitated a moment, then began walking towards the marble stairs.

"Beautiful," Flanagan said as he looked at one of the sculptures in the upstairs hallway. "Not just this sculpture, but the whole house." In both architectural design and interior furnishings, the quality of Lois Bedderson's home far eclipsed the Governor's mansion in Jefferson City that Ken Flanagan had inhabited for one term.

Flanagan was from a town in rural Missouri where it was unusual to find two graduates of a state university in the same family. He was still not entirely at ease with some-one whose parents, grandparents, and great-grandparents had all received degrees from Ivy League institutions. This was particularly true when Flanagan was on the other man's turf, and even more so given that Bedderson was three inches taller and outweighed the ex-Governor by almost a hundred pounds.

"Built in 1912," Bedderson said of the house, nodding to acknowledge Flanagan's compliment. "Just before the creation of the Federal Reserve."

"Did you grow up here?"

"Yes, my parents bought it before I was born. When Dad died a few years ago, I thought Mom would move someplace smaller, but she likes being able to hold parties. Like this one."

"She's very kind." Bedderson smiled at the compliment, then shrugged.

"As I say, Mom likes putting the house to good use." Flanagan nodded. There was a long silence, and Ken Flanagan began to look more and more uncomfortable.

"Ah, listen," he said finally, "I, uh, don't have a problem with...you carrying a gun," the ex-Governor finished quickly. "If you had come to me originally, I'm sure I could have accommodated you." Bedderson gave the older man a puzzled look.

"I could have given you a special dispensation," Flanagan continued. "Several of my aides have them."

"Oh, that's not the problem, sir," Bedderson answered with a dismissive wave of his fingers when he understood what Flanagan was talking about. "I carry police creds. Have for more than fifteen years." Now it was the ex-Governor's turn to look baffled.

"I'm on the force of three different departments," the younger man explained. "Give them weapons instruction a couple times a year, that kind of thing."

"Then why...?"

"Why spend twenty thousand dollars out of my own pocket pushing for a carry law? Because my having police creds doesn't do any good for the people who work for me at the plant. It doesn't help my wife when she's away from me, like tonight. It doesn't help the two women that clean this house for my mother, who both live in fourth-floor walk-ups in north St. Louis. And it won't help my daughter when she grows up. I wanted a law for them." Flanagan looked dumbfounded for an instant, then quickly recovered.

"I understand what you're saying, but having people carry guns is not the answer. It's what I've always believed, and I'm not going to change my mind."

"Well, that's something we can agree on completely," B.I. Bedderson said with a genuine smile as he scratched his beard. "A person should always stick with what he truly believes in, and fight for what he thinks is right. And I also think that's enough political talk for me for a social occasion." Bedderson took a deep breath as he looked around the upstairs hallway. "The people downstairs are probably waiting for you, and—oh, hell."

"What's the matter?" Flanagan asked immediately.

"The back of your suit jacket. There's something smeared on it. No, don't take it off here, let's go in the bathroom. There's some soap and towels in there, and I'll bet we can find some spot remover if we need it. Josephine always kept some in every bathroom when I lived here. It's probably just something from one of the food trays. This way," he urged, indicating the third of four doors evenly spaced along the seventy-foot wall.

"This used to be my room, years ago," Bedderson said as they walked by the four-poster bed. "Now it's a guest room. Over here," he said, pointing the older man towards a door in the far corner.

The bathroom was one of two on the front side of the second floor. The big stone house had been designed with four large bedrooms comprising the entire south face of the second story. Each bedroom door locked from the inside with a deadbolt. The two east and two west bedrooms were connected by a shared bathroom between each pair. To facilitate privacy in a bathroom with two doors opening into two different bedrooms, both doors were fitted with dual, opposite-side deadbolt locks. Thus, a person using the bathroom could prevent entry from either or both bedrooms, and someone in either bedroom could secure himself from someone inadvertently entering from the bathroom.

As he ushered Flanagan into the large tiled room, Bedderson glanced at the handle for the deadbolt on the opposite door. It was where he had set it, in the locked position. He also noted that the shades and drapes on the window were drawn shut, as was normal.

"Here, let me take that," he offered as he closed the door and simultaneously shot the bolt. The century-old mechanism was a precision one, and like all the locks in the house, it was well-lubricated with the synthetic gun oil Break-Free CLP. The sound of the bolt was completely masked by the noise of the latch snapping into the recess, just as it had been on Bedderson's numerous practice runs.

Flanagan shrugged out of his grey suit jacket and let the younger man behind him slip it off his arms. Before the ex-Governor could turn around, Arthur 'B.I.' Bedderson clamped his arms around the older man in a powerful bear hug and lifted him a few inches off the floor.

Ken Flanagan opened his mouth, but before he could cry out, his central nervous system was hit with a 120,000-volt blast from the stun gun Bedderson had jammed against his throat. Flanagan lost voluntary control of every major muscle group in his body, and would have collapsed on the tile but for the fact that Bedderson was holding him aloft.

Flanagan's mouth was open and quivering as Arthur Bedderson eased him onto the floor by the toilet. As a precaution, Bedderson twisted the ex-Governor's left wrist in such a way that attempted escape would cause bones to break. Then he laid the stun gun down on the tile. As he knelt by the incapacitated man, Bedderson unbuttoned the left cuff, pushed up the sleeve, then reached into his own jacket pocket for a nylon pouch closed with Velcro. With a move he had practiced dozens of times in the last week, Bedderson opened the pouch one-handed, grabbed the hypodermic inside, shook the pouch away, then exposed the needle by holding the plastic cover in his teeth and unscrewing the syringe. Bedderson slipped the needle into the proper spot on Flanagan's left arm and depressed the plunger until it bottomed.

"See how that feels," he said softly to his captive. "I hear it's great while it lasts." Ken Flanagan's eyes opened wide, and for an instant a beatific expression appeared on his face. "One thousand one, one thousand two..." Bedderson counted under his breath as he let go of the syringe and relaxed pressure on Flanagan's wrist. When he got to 'nine', the ex-Governor closed his eyes. A few seconds later, the man stopped breathing. Bedderson let go, but continued to watch as he opened the medicine cabinet. He removed a zippered vinyl case, being careful to touch only the corners as he did so. The case had previously contained a set of computer tools. Now it was set up as an addict's 'works'. Bedderson forced the dying man's hands around the vinyl, smudged the prints, and left the open case on the floor.

Then Bedderson withdrew the envelope with the three Polaroid photos from his right inside jacket pocket and shook them out onto Flanagan's open palm. Bedderson pressed the slack fingers onto the glossy emulsion several times, smudging some of the prints and making the photos well-handled. He used the empty envelope to scoop up the pictures, and slid them into Flanagan's trouser pocket. By this time, ex-Governor Ken Flanagan's heart had stopped beating. Bedderson wiped the syringe that was still in the corpse's arm, then repeated the process of putting Flanagan's fingerprints on the plastic tabs and his thumbprint on the plunger. He did the same with the protective cap that had been on the syringe.

"We've all got to fight for what we believe in, Ken," Bedderson whispered as he stood up and stretched. "Now all the dead victims can rest in peace," he added, thinking of Tom Fleming's comment about Klaus Barbie. He glanced around to see if he had forgotten anything, then unlocked the far door and stepped into the end bedroom. The room was dark, but Bedderson knew its layout. He made his way to the only other door, which led to the hallway, unlocked the deadbolt, and cracked the door. No one was in the upstairs hall.

Bedderson closed the bedroom door behind him and walked quickly to the back hallway. He was in what had been the servants' wing when the house had been built in 1912. He softly descended the back stairs, walked through the back hallway, and into the kitchen area. A half-dozen men and women were busy with food preparation.

"Arthur! I didn't know you were here tonight."

"Hi, Harold," Bedderson said cheerfully to the man who had been catering Lois Bedderson's dinner parties since her son was in diapers. "Running out of anything?"

"Not yet," he answered, laughing at the old joke. "Get you a drink?"

"Psychic as always. Just Seven-Up for now."

"Coming up." Harold went into the pantry where the bar was set up and came back shortly with a double rocks glass made of Baccarat crystal.

"Thank you, sir," Bedderson said as Harold handed him the glass. He snared a couple of the hors d'oeuvres from one of the silver trays, then went back out to mingle.

***

"Where's the Governor?" Lois Bedderson asked.

"Probably having dinner in the Governor's mansion."

"Smarty. You know who I meant."

"Probably in the bathroom," her son suggested.

"I haven't seen him for quite a while. His wife's looking for him."

"Maybe he went outside to smoke a cigarette, or something."

"He can do that in here—I don't have any rule against it."

"Sometimes people go outside anyway. Hey, it was just an idea. I don't even know if he smokes or not." Bedderson furrowed his brow. "Want me to go check outside?"

"Would you?"

"Be glad to," he answered, and got up from his chair. Lois Bedderson glanced around the room, then started talking to one of the other women at her table.

"No luck," Arthur Bedderson said when he returned.

"I'll ask around."

"Don't do that yet," her son said quickly. "Have you noticed anyone else missing?" he asked under his breath. "A woman, most likely, although it doesn't have to be."

"What do you mean?" his mother asked, her eyebrows going up as she caught the implication.

"Got a better explanation? I'll go get one of his former aides and we'll hit the gu rooms quietly."

"What can I do?"

"Keep his wife occupied," he instructed. Lois Bedderson nodded and stood up from the table as her son walked away in search of Flanagan's entourage.

Arthur Bedderson spotted a slender man with slicked-back hair and grabbed him by the elbow. "Is Flanagan off humping someone?" he asked abruptly. "His wife's looking for him."

"Uh, no, of course not...well, I mean–"

"Look, I've got my mother keeping her busy, but if he's got his dick out somewhere, I suggest we find him before she does. He's not outside and he's not anywhere here on the first floor."

"Right," the man agreed, recovering quickly. "Ah...," he added, not sure what to say.

"What do you want to hit first, basement or second floor? Basement's all storage space. Upstairs is all bedrooms."

"Upstairs."

"Okay," Arthur Bedderson said, and led the way towards the marble stairway. The aide paused at the landing and surveyed the guests in the hallway below him, hoping Flanagan would somehow come into view. Then he continued up to the second floor.

"Check those four rooms at the front. Doors should all be unlocked. I'll hit the back of the house and the old servant's wing." Bedderson hurried off down the hallway. The aide stepped over to the first door and rapped on it gently with his knuckles.

"Uh, Ken?" he whispered. "Ken?" he repeated, a little louder this time. When there was no answer, he turned the knob and opened the door an inch. Lois Bedderson's bedroom was empty. The man closed the door and went on to the next one on his right, where he repeated the procedure. This room was dark. "Ken?" he said once more. When there was no answer, he felt around until he found a light switch and discovered the room was lined floor-to-ceiling with bookshelves. It was obviously the family library. The man saw a door in the far left corner, so he walked to it and slowly turned the knob. It was Lois Bedderson's bathroom, and was twice the size of the one the aide used at his own home. The man closed the door and went back out to the hall.

Flanagan's aide stood in the corner of Arthur Bedderson's old room, trying the knob to the bathroom. "Ken? Ken, you in there? It's Mark. *Ken?*" he repeated, more loudly this time. The aide turned to face Arthur Bedderson, who had just walked into the room.

"No sign of him in the back wing," Bedderson announced.

"The knob turns, but this door won't open."

"Bolted from the inside. Someone forgot to unlock it when they were done and left by the other door. We'll have to go around." The two men walked back out into the hallway, knocked on the door, then entered the bedroom at the west end of the house. Bedderson flicked on the light switch. The aide walked over to the bathroom door and knocked.

"Ken? You in there?" He turned the knob and opened the door.

"*Ohmygod!*" he almost screamed, and stepped back.

"What is it?" Bedderson said quickly, rushing to the doorway. "Shit! He's not a pussy hound, he's a fucking junkie!" Arthur Bedderson bent over the corpse and felt for a pulse at both the wrist and throat. "And he's dead as a hammer."

"But...he can't be...I mean, he's not...he doesn't...I've known Ken Flanagan for–"

"You think that's an insulin syringe there, sticking out of his arm?"

"Oh God...are you sure he's...?"

"Dead? Christ, take a look. You want to practice your mouth-to-mouth, see if maybe

Schaumberg murder buried Neumann thought. *Got to head this guy off.*

"The real chicken-dinner winner is this Schaumberg thing," Alex Neumann went on. "OD'ed on coke, and just happens to have the semen from three or four different guys inside him when he checks out. At both ends, no less." Remembering the note from Ray Johnson, Neumann realized the smile on his face felt like it was molded in plastic.

"So you think that one's a legitimate OD?"

"What else could it be?" Neumann asked.

"I'd have a lot easier time believing the way it was laid out if it weren't for the way the body got found. Come on, Alex—after the fags clean the place up, one of them calls a reporter at the *New York Post?* When was the last time someone did that to report an accidental sex-and-drug death?"

"Well, I–"

"Maximum negative press," the older agent interrupted. "That's what our boy's been hitting us with. It's just like that Wilson Blair tape. Was it released when the Internet stuff first hit? No. Why not? Because if it was done after Greenwell publicly said Blair was dead and told everyone the Internet author was someone else, then Greenwell is an utter liar and what little credibility ATF might have left goes straight out the window.

"Then, take a look at those other two. Jerry Abel gets murdered with his pants off in an Illinois ghetto, and an ex-Governor OD's on heroin with kiddie porn in his pocket. Come on, Alex. If you and Mick here held a contest to see who could make up the set of circumstances most likely to discredit a dead politician, do either of you guys think you could do better than what we're looking at?"

"Got me there."

"Yeah."

"And this guy understands the beauty of laying out a simple story for the media," the agent added. "The papers and networks run with it, and the public buys it instantly. Schaumberg a gay cokehead? That's just Barney Frank and Marion Barry rolled into one. Jerry Abel likes cheap black whores? So did that Brit actor a while back, and he had Estee Lauder's top babe back at home waiting for him with her legs spread. You say Ken Flanagan's a heroin junkie with short eyes? Boy, that's really over the top. Wish he'd gone a little lighter on his last fix, maybe we could've seen him on the Tonight Show."

"So you want me to go public with this murder theory?" Neumann asked, challenging the older man.

"That's just it, Alex. We can't. The way it's laid out now is too believable, and we'll look like idiots. Remember Vince Foster? Look at that case. You had a guy who knew things that could cripple the Administration, and he's about to get subpoenaed on them. His own *notes* said 'This is a fucking Pandora's box', or something like that, when the investigators were trying to get his records. He's got a hundred times more power and prestige than he did back in jerkwater Arkansas, but he's so upset about how mean people are in Washington he decides to commit suicide. As chance would have it, he elects to kill himself in a place he's never gone to before in his life. This tiny area just happens to be under the jurisdiction of the Washington department least capable of investigating a suspicious death. It just happens that he's managed to walk to the spot in this park where he killed himself without getting any dirt on the soles of his shoes."

"It just happens there are carpet fibers all over his suit," the young agent named Mick broke in. "Maybe he rolled around on a floor somewhere before hopping in his ca to go kill himself in the park."

"Right," Butch agreed. "It just happens there's no blood on the scene but his cor has less than half the normal amount of blood in it. Knowing that he was going to die, I guess Foster did the charitable thing and donated six pints of blood before killing himself. And he must've had superhuman motivation to get to that park to kill himself, 'cause every doctor I've asked says no one could remain conscious with so little blood in his system.

"He just happens to use an old piece-of-junk revolver no one has ever seen before. There's no way he could have bought it legally in D.C., so this high-powered lawyer must have brought the piece of junk all the way from Little Rock, and kept it a secret."

"Maybe it had sentimental value."

"It just happens that there's no bullet ever recovered, and the guy is found with his arm stretched out by his waist with the gun laying on his open palm."

"Which would make it the first suicide on record where *that* happened," Mick said.

"And finally, the instant he's dead, the people who had the most to lose if he talked go clean out his office and destroy all his records before we can seal the place. Only they leave this torn-up note that says, 'I did this all by myself, nobody else did anything bad, ever, they're all innocent of everything, I didn't have anything on them, I'm just depressed.'" The man took a breath.

"I've never seen a suicide case with as many red flags on it as Foster's," said the agent named Butch. "But anyone who even hinted there should be an investigation was called a right-wing lunatic with a personal vendetta against that administration. If we jump around yelling 'murder', we look like the same old bunch of government sleazeballs trying to whitewash the truth and make the feds look better."

"I guess we'll keep the murder theory in the same box as UFO sightings," Neumann said, secretly relieved. He shook his head in frustration. "Two things are becoming more and more clear."

"What's that?"

"Number one, the guy we're up against is goddamn good. And two, things keep happening in Missouri."

***

"Sir, this is Special Agent Alex Neumann of the Federal Bureau of Investigation in Washington, D.C. We're in the middle of a very important murder investigation, and we believe you may be able to help us. Normally we contact people in person, but I wanted to give you a preliminary call before one of our agents came by from the Little Rock office. Could I please speak to whoever is in charge of your company?"

"This about them ATF agents killed out in Wyoming?" the man asked.

"Well, ah–"

"Heard it was somebody using the long six millimeter J-fours. I guess you folks want to find out who made the bullets. Boss says he'll be glad to turn over our customer list for the sixes we make, soon as we see a warrant." *Shit!* Neumann thought. He wasn't at all sure he could get one based on the evidence he currently had.

"You know, we been talking 'bout that bit of shooting," the man continued, "and some of the boys think maybe the VHA ought to come up with a new patch."

"I don't follow you." Alex Neumann did not yet know that the Varmint Hunters Association issued a cloth shoulder patch to members who provided documented proof that they had, in front of witnesses, killed a rockchuck at a measured distance in excess of 1000 yards.

"No matter," the man said with a chuckle. "Mr...Neumann, was it? If it'll help you out, I will tell you who our biggest customer is for our Very Low Drag sixes. They buy a ton of 'em. You got a pen?"

Alex Neumann felt his bowels loosen as the man read off the name and address.

***

"Agent Neumann is here, Mr. President."

"Send him in." The President remained seated as Alex Neumann entered the room.

"Good afternoon, Mr. President." The Chief Executive nodded curtly.

"Alex, what's the story on the evidence from the Wyoming killings? My meeting's in three days. Do you have anything I can use as a lever over Jones?" *He sounds like he's pleading* Neumann thought. *Not too surprising, with between five and ten feds getting killed every day, if you add in all the branches besides ATF.*

Word of the 'Laramie Massacre', as it had come to be known, had spread throughout the country. It was the largest known single killing of federal agents in a gun battle, and it had attracted more comment among serious shooters than even the Miami shootout of 1986. The President had been hoping that with evidence from the site, the FBI would be able to get a lead on where to find at least one of Mr. Jones' clients. Alex Neumann was about to deliver some very bad news.

"Mr. President, the agents scoured the entire area, every foot within a half mile from where the men were killed. They found forty-seven fired cartridge cases. Three were from a .45 automatic, which is a handgun caliber, Winchester-Western factory loads, all fired from the same gun. Two were .30-30 Winchester brass, which is a relatively short-range round normally fired out of lever-action rifles, also factory ammunition fired from the same gun. Ten were twenty-two rimfire cases, made by CCI, also from one gun. Six were .22-250 Remington, which is a very high velocity varmint cartridge, usually chambered in heavy-barreled bolt action rifles capable of hitting prairie dogs at ranges of up to three hundred yards. The six shells were from Remington factory ammunition fired from two different guns, four from one and two from the other." *He doesn't need all this detail* Neumann thought, *but I can't just hit him with the bottom line.*

"The remaining twenty-six cases were U.S. Government 5.56mm, the M16 round. In sporting arms, this same cartridge is called the .223 Remington, and is very popular as a varmint cartridge, although its velocity and range is less than the .22-250. Prairie dog shooters who fire a lot of rounds like the cartridge because surplus brass for reloading is cheap, and the smaller powder charge does not wear out barrels as quickly as the larger and more powerful varmint cartridges.

"The 5.56mm brass we found was all the same headstamp, from the Lake City Arsenal, made in 1972. Each of the twenty-six cases had the crimp removed from the primer pocket, and the spent primer was not a military item but a commercial primer made by the Federal Cartridge Company. In addition, the case necks had been trimmed, which is also standard reloading practice. All cases were within .001" of the same length.

"All twenty-six cases exhibited signs of having been fired and reloaded many times; our resident authority on interior ballistics says at least ten reloadings and perhaps as many as fifty. All were fired, the final time at least, in the same gun. All cases exhibited thinning of the interior case wall in front of the case head, which will ultimately result in the case breaking in half and leaving the front section in the gun." Neumann licked his lips. He saw that the President was looking impatient.

"The logical conclusion is that these cases were fired by a serious prairie dog hunter, and intentionally discarded as they were near the end of their useful life. We were able to lift partial prints from many of these cases, as well as the others. None of them match any of Orville Crocker's fingerprints. Or Wilson Blair's, or any of the other ATF agents missing since June."

"Your conclusion, Alex?"

"These cases we found had nothing to do with the killings. They had been lying out there long before our men were killed. It appeared that the .223 brass had been fired the most recently, but it still was slightly tarnished, and we can assume a serious prairie dog shooter would have pristine ammunition to fire. Our metals expert thinks those cases have been out there at least a month. The killers took their brass with them, sir." Alex Neumann hurried on before the President could comment.

"Our next analysis was of the bullet fragments recovered from the bodies of the dead agents. No bullets were even partially intact; all had disintegrated. This is typical of thin-jacketed varmint bullets fired at high velocity. We–"

"I thought the men were shot at extreme ranges," the President interrupted. "Wouldn't that mean the bullets were traveling much more slowly than at the muzzle, and would remain intact?" *Guy's been doing his homework* Neumann thought.

"Yes, sir, that's partially correct. And the answer surprised me. A projectile fired from a rifle loses its forward velocity much more rapidly than its rotational velocity. A bullet fired straight up will hit the ground base-first, still spinning. Long-range cartridges require rifling twists which impart higher rates of spin than short-range cartridges, so the effect is even more pronounced. The only thing holding the soft lead core together at these high spin rates is the thin copper-alloy jacket. When the jacket ruptures on impact, the lead flies apart. It doesn't matter that the bullet is only going half as fast as it was at the muzzle; it's still spinning at over two hundred thousand RPM." Neumann took a breath.

"And that brings us to the caliber itself. From a base fragment of one of the bullet jackets we recovered, the projectile appears to be a boattail design in .243" diameter, or 6mm. The size and shape of the boattail base is different from any 6mm bullet produced by a major factory such as Winchester, Remington, Sierra, Hornady, or Nosler. Also, from the fragments recovered, we know that the bullets were heavier than one hundred grains. We cannot get an exact weight because scavengers had...eaten some of the flesh at each wound site, but the bullet weight was definitely more than one hundred grains. This is heavier than any factory-loaded boattail design."

"So all five men were shot with custom-made bullets?"

"Yes, sir. And using neutron activation analysis, which gives the precise composition of the metal itself, we have determined that all six of the bullets were made using jackets manufactured by the J4 corporation in California. J4 jackets are acknowledged as the most uniform in the industry, and are used almost exclusively by all of the top custom bulletmakers who produce match-grade bullets. One of our people at Quantico shoots competitively, and has a good relationship with the company. With his help, we isolated the lot number. The jackets were manufactured some time during a three-month period in late 1993."

"Excellent, Alex," the President said, pleased. "That narrows it down quite a bit, I would think."

"Yes, sir. However, part of the company's reputation for uniformity comes from the ·ct that it alloys very large batches of material. The lot we are looking at is a run of ·roximately nine million jackets." Neumann saw the President's reaction, and hurried to continue. "That's for all calibers," the FBI agent amended quickly. "Less than one million were .243" jackets in the length suitable for making bullets of over one hundred grains in weight. Almost all those were sold to four custom bulletmakers: Berger Bullets, Hammett's, Jef Fowler, and Jimmy Knox."

"So you got their list of customers?" Neumann looked pained at the President's question.

"We tried to do that, sir, but after our research with the J4 company, the word was out."

"What do you mean? These people wouldn't help?"

"No, sir. Their basic response was 'You want out customer records? Get a warrant.' ATF is not admired by any segment of the shooting fraternity." Neumann did not relate to the President the specifics of the conversations he'd had with the various custom bulletmakers.

"We also contacted the top manufacturers of match-grade 6mm barrel blanks that offer twist rates fast enough to stabilize the long boattail bullets: Hart, Shilen, Lilja, K&P, Wiseman, Obermeyer, and McMillan. Three of the seven makers sell barrels to the government, and we got the list of gunsmiths who have bought barrels of this type in the last two years. The other four said 'get a warrant'.

"We are lucky that the weapon used was such a specialized piece, Mr. President, but there are still major problems with this type of investigation. First, even with complete cooperation, we would only be able to trace the million 6mm match bullets from the manufacturer to the first purchaser. In some cases this is an individual, but in many instances it is a target shooting club or gun store that serves such a club."

"And the trail vanishes there?"

"Pretty much. Looking for the end users of the match barrels might have a better chance of success, but again, the custom rifle in question could easily have changed hands several times since the gunsmith first built it. And even if we could be sure that it hadn't, we're still stuck. There is no way to prove a given rifle was the murder weapon."

"Your ballistic tests can't determine that?"

"No, sir. I'm afraid television has misled everyone. On low-velocity handgun bullets, the rifling marks are distinguishing characteristics, but they are not fingerprints. Fingerprints have a pattern; the striations on a fired bullet are random. And running a stainless steel brush down the bore of a pistol will result in a new set of random striations on the next bullet fired. Visual analysis is really only useful to eliminate handguns as suspected murder weapons. A recovered bullet with six rifling marks on it could not have been fired from a Smith & Wesson revolver, for example, because barrels on those guns have five lands and grooves."

"I see."

"The higher the velocity, the more the bullet is deformed, and the less useful this sort of comparison becomes. When you are dealing with high-velocity target and varmint rifles, it's pointless. Those bullets literally vaporize when they hit. With the occasional exception of the base of the jacket, you are unlikely to find a single fragment larger than the head of a pin.

"We can continue to try to trace the match barrels, but unless someone feels guilty and confesses, I don't hold out much hope." Neumann paused, letting the President digest what he had said. *Time to drop the bomb* he thought.

"And there's one other thing, Mr. President."

"Go on."

"Through more...anonymous methods, we have discovered the major purchaser of both 6mm low-drag match bullets and 6mm fast-twist match-grade barrel blanks. It's the U.S. Marksmanship Unit at Quantico. The Secret Service trains with them. We cannot dismiss the possibility that the killer or killers might be members of that group. And that puts us in a difficult position for further investigation." The words hung in the air, like the smell of a person who needs a bath but whose friends are unwilling to tell him. Finally the President spoke.

"I need some time alone, Alex. You've done an excellent job."

As Neumann turned to leave, the President lowered his head and began to rub his temples. Ever since news of the Laramie Massacre had reached the White House, the President had been thinking about the personal implications of the existence of expert riflemen capable of hitting a human target two-thirds of a mile away.

Neumann's report had just amplified that concern exponentially.

August 8

"And so, after much discussion, I believe that White House may soon be able to negotiate some sort of truce with the instigators of this current anti-government rebellion. That information is not to leave this room, but within several days, I should be talking with a person who represents...our main opponents." Most of the task force sat there, stunned by the news. It was Helen Schule from Vermont who first found her voice.

"Mr. President, is it really Wilson Blair who has been behind all this?"

"I can't say anything further on that, Helen. And since we have not negotiated an agreement as yet, the FBI is still working three shifts to track down the principals. Alex, why don't you tell us where you are on that?"

"Right, Mr. President. After recovering the third helicopter from the bottom of the flooded quarry in Missouri," he said, addressing the group, "our forensic team has determined what brought the three aircraft down." *That got their attention* Alex Neumann thought as he surveyed the looks on the faces of the assembled members. "They were shot down by explosive U.S. 20mm antiaircraft rounds. One shot for each helicopter, as nearly as we can determine."

"The Vulcan?" Congressman Andy Ward of Indiana asked. He knew a little bit about military ordnance. "That's a multibarrel Gatling-type weapon. Would have shredded those helicopters." *Shit!* thought Neumann. *I didn't expect this.*

"Ah, that's correct, Congressman, as far as it goes," the FBI man said smoothly. "There are several other guns which fire the same round, however. The T160 revolver cannon is a single-barrel weapon with a revolving, multi-chambered cylinder that uses the same cartridge, and there are others.

"Five of these automatic 20mm cannons are known to be in civilian hands, three of which are at a movie rental concern in North Hollywood. All five guns have been accounted for during the time period that the helicopters were shot down. We have inquired about any such weapons being reported stolen or missing from government arsenals, and have found no leads there, either. However, reporting such thefts is problematic. There could easily be a hundred such guns missing.

"In addition, Congressman Ward is exactly right. The Vulcan is a multibarrel weapon that fires sixty-five to a hundred rounds a second. The single-barrel T160 made by Oldsmobile is slower, but it still delivers about fifteen rounds per second. Other designs which fire this round have cyclic rates between these two extremes. This fact is incompatible with the helicopters being struck by only a single round apiece. In addition, the noise generated by these automatic machine cannons is impossible to overlook. No one anywhere near the area recalls hearing anything that could have been a burst from one of these guns. All our reports are of a few single explosions, and the belt of .30-caliber ammunition fired by Calron Jones in the third helicopter. Nothing else. Initially, the single explosions were assumed to be the sound of the helicopters crashing. Now we believe that they were single 20mm rounds being fired.

"At this point, we are exploring the possibility that one of these type weapons was rigged to fire single shots. Mounted on a helicopter, it could have been used to down the three unsuspecting National Guard aircraft.

"On the massacre in Wyoming, we have a number of leads, but nothing solid to report at this moment." Neumann was about to continue when he saw Irwin Mann begin to rise from his chair.

"Excuse me, please," Mann said softly as he stood up and left the room. From the expression on his face and the way he carried himself, it was obvious he was headed towards the men's room. *Getting old must be a bitch* Alex Neumann thought before resuming his briefing.

Neumann had finished talking about the Laramie Massacre and was going over the slight progress being made in other killings when Irwin Mann returned. Out of respect, Neumann stopped talking and waited until the elderly man had reclaimed his chair. As he sat down, Irwin Mann spoke.

"Agent Neumann, I know little of such matters, but many years ago, I saw a young boy with a rifle shoot targets thrown in the air. While I was out of the room just now, I remembered watching this feat." *I do some of my best thinking on the toilet, too* Neumann concurred silently.

"Would it be possible that the weapon used to shoot the helicopters was something much less complicated than one of these automatic aircraft cannon you describe? A simple gun made to fire only one round of this same ammunition? If so, perhaps it could have been used by someone on the ground, and not in another helicopter."

"Yeah," Jonathan Bane of Ohio said suddenly. "Agent Neumann, didn't you tell us in one of your early reports that Wilson Blair was supposed to meet the three helicopters there on the ground? Maybe he was waiting for them while they tried to land, and shot them then. Or someone who was with him did," Bane amended.

"Why would someone go to the trouble of building a single shot 20mm?" Congressman Ward of Indiana asked. "If the guy was a good shot, and on the ground, a normal rifle would be more accurate and easier to use than a 20mm. That thing would kick him to death."

"I know little of guns," Irwin Mann said quickly. "I do not even know if constructing such a single-shot weapon would be feasible."

"Congressman Ward," Jon Bane said condescendingly, "a regular rifle would be worthless against a helicopter."

"Are you *kidding?*" Ward almost yelled. "Have you ever been in one? Pilot's got to control a helicopter every second, or it'll crash. Unless you're talking about armored choppers like the Apache, you can bring most helicopters down with a .22 if you can hit the pilot anywhere. Don't have to kill him, or even hurt him very bad. That's why we hated being in helicopters in 'Nam. I should know, I was in one that was shot down by a fifteen-year-old girl with an old Russian bolt action. Bullet came through the windshield and clipped the tip of the pilot's left index finger off. We were flying at about thirty feet, between the dikes, and she was on a rope bridge. Bullet clipped his fingertip, he lost control for a few seconds, and we went in. If we'd been a little higher I'd be dead now.

"Shooting choppers down is *easy.* Those guys who pulled off that bit of business in Wyoming? With a couple boxes of ammo and a good elk rifle, they could knock down every Guard helicopter you threw at 'em." Ward stopped talking, and the other members of the task force sat awkwardly in the ensuing silence.

"We'll find out about the gun," Neumann said, breaking the tension.

Irwin Mann looked pale and weak. The others in the room took no notice of this, for the Presidential liaison to the Holocaust Center was an old man. There was nothing wrong with Irwin Mann's health, however. His illness was emotional. Irwin Mann had given his word, and kept it, but he was now very afraid that he had just done a terrible thing.

August 9

"You want to keep doing this, Fred?" Alex Neumann asked. He and another agent had checked with all licensed Destructive Device manufacturers in the country, but none had ever made a weapon like the one Irwin Mann had suggested. Now they were working through the list of custom gunsmiths published in the *Gun Digest,* looking for someone who could make an extra-large single shot rifle. After being stonewalled by the 6mm bullet- and barrelmakers, Neumann had decided to take a different approach with this part of the investigation.

"Yeah, I can pull it off," the other agent said. "I think the trick is to admit your eccentricities. Then you don't sound like you're an idiot."

"Okay, well, go for it." The FBI agent named Fred picked up the phone and made sure the microphone pickup was attached and the tape recorder was running. Alex Neumann put the earplug in his ear and nodded that he was ready.

The two FBI men had had no luck with any of the gunsmiths they had called so far, but the last shop they'd tried had suggested a man in Vermont, so the two men skipped ahead to that name. Neumann watched as the agent punched in the number.

"Bischoff here," answered the man on the other end.

"Ah, yes, sir, my name is Evans," the agent said, "and a fellow up in Alaska said I should call you. I forget his name, but I met him at a gun show, and he told me you make big single shots."

"Probably Kirby you talked to. He's been thinking about having me make up a .600 for him, to go with his double. That what you interested in, or is a .600 too small?" The two agents looked at each other. *This sounds promising* Neumann thought.

"Ah, well, actually, I wanted to talk to you about making something even larger. I was—"

"I'm two years behind on my 4-bores," the gunsmith interrupted, "but that's not as bad as that guy in Colorado. He even makes 2-bores, but I hear he quit that. Don't blame him. I don't want to make any more of those damn things, either. But then again, I said that after the first one," he added. *What the hell is he talking about?* Neumann wondered. He made a rolling gesture with his forearm, imploring the younger man to keep the gunsmith talking about the subject.

"Ah, what size is that, exactly?"

"The 4-bores, we use a barrel with a groove diameter of exactly one inch. Now, on the 2-bores, you got a hell of a time getting barrel blanks. That one goes 1.325" on the groove diameter."

"What I was, uh, thinking about, was could you make a rifle for the U.S. Air Force 20mm round?"

"You know, I wouldn't've believed it twenty years ago, but in the last few years I must've had three or four people ask me about that."

"Really?" Fred prompted. *Pay dirt!* Neumann thought.

"Yeah, I think it's because of all these folks with .50 caliber shoulder rifles. Some fellas, now they want to try a twenty. But there's three problems. First, the 20mm is a military cartridge over a half inch diameter. So what you're building is what them idiots up in Washington call a 'destructive device', and that means you got to go get fingerprinted and get your picture took and whatnot, and you got to pay a $200 tax.

"Now, maybe that don't bother you, 'cause you're the buyer and it's going to be expensive anyway, but if I build one and sell it, I got to have a license to make destructive devices, and that costs $3000. And I got to deal with them sons a bitches from the machine gun part of ATF, sniffing around here and all, and I won't have that at my shop. I don't care if you pay for the license and I'm not out a nickel, I won't do it. I've played all their stupid games and filled out paperwork for .22 ammo for twenty years and paid all the damn excise taxes and made folks wait for five days when they got a trunkful of pistols already, and now on my last renewal they made me give them my fingerprints and a floor plan of where my safes were. By God I hope every damned one of them bastards gets killed, and it looks like we're a good ways there. But that's off the subject of the twenty you want built, isn't it?"

"You said there were three problems."

"Right. The second problem is all those U.S. cases are electric primed, except the earliest ones, so you got the nuisance of taking the ammo apart and bushing the case for a .50 Browning primer, or building an electric ignition system, and I don't have a clue how to do that, although it probably wouldn't be too hard.

"Anyway, on your 20mm, the thing that shoots the whole deal in the head, even if you could talk me into getting a license to build it, is the recoil. That shell throws a 2000-something grain bullet out at about 2600 feet per second. That's the same bullet weight as the 4-bore, but at twice the velocity. The 4-bore's low pressure. Not too many folks want to shoot a 4-bore, and I only know of two men in the whole country that've fired a 2-bore. The third 2-bore rifle I built just hangs on the wall. One of the two men is the guy did my load development on both the four and the two, and so when that last fella called me about building a 20mm, I called up John and asked him what the gun would have to weigh before he'd be willing to shoot it. He done some figuring, and said with a real good muzzle brake on it, it ought to kick like the full-load 4-bore if it weighed 75 pounds.

"Now, a few fellas can handle a 25-pound rifle with heavy recoil, maybe 30 pounds even, but I don't think there's a man on the planet could shoot a 75-pound gun offhand and hold onto it when it belted him with two hundred foot-pounds of free recoil. So now what you're talking about is some hundred-pound rifle you'd shoot off a rest, and your best bet there would be a big bolt action. I don't build bolt guns; no challenge in it and they aren't as pretty as a Farquharson. That last guy called me about a twenty mil, he might've gone ahead and had a bolt action built. I don't know. Seems I heard someone talk about wanting to build up a big rifle for that 14.5mm Russian round. Now there would be a caliber maybe you could shoot from the shoulder, I don't know, but at least it uses percussion primers. Still would be a destructive device, though; it's military and a .60 caliber if I recall. That what you're looking for, a big monster bolt action to shoot off sandbags, blow up rocks at a thousand yards?"

"Uh, yeah, that's about it, something new to fool with," the agent said quickly. "Could you tell me who this man was, the one you think might've had the 20mm bolt action built? I'd like to talk to him about it, see how it worked out."

"He was out of Pennsylvania, I remember that. Murdoch, I think, was his last name. Can't give you any more than that."

"Do you have any idea who might have built the rifle? Maybe I could call him."

"Don't have a clue. It'd have to be someone who had paid that crazy $3000 tax, and I don't know anyone who'd be willing to do that. Those ATF bastards might come kick your door in and stomp your cats to death."

"Or burn you alive, right?" the agent said with a forced chuckle, trying to keep the man talking.

"Yeah, if they brought the FBI into it, that might happen," the gunsmith answered. The two agents jumped when they heard that. "But give Nelson a try, too. Out in Colorado," the gunsmith went on. "He's worth a call."

"Listen," the FBI man said quickly, "you've been very good to talk to me about this, and–"

"Oh, hell, no problem. Didn't help you out much. But if you're really serious, I got one last idea."

"What's that?"

"Build the dang thing yourself. Get you one of these Asian mill-drills for about fifteen hundred, new, and a decent used lathe for thirty-five hundred, four thousand. Be only five parts you'd have to make. Couple hours a night, you'd have your action in two, three months. Damn sight sooner than any gunsmith you'll find to build it, especially me. You'll still have to get all those stupid forms and pay the $200, but you got to do that anyway. Wouldn't have to pay the $3000 'less you built one to sell."

"Ah, I'll think about that."

"Okay. Well, good talking to you—I got to get back to the shop. Good luck." The man in Vermont hung up.

"Let's keep going on the list," Alex Neumann said with an enthusiasm he did not feel.

"Maybe the shooter built it at home, like he said."

"I don't even want to think about that."

August 10

"What the hell is *this?*" Alex Neumann demanded as he stood, openmouthed, by one of the desks. "Where's the guy that sits here?"

The day before, ATF had given Neumann and his assistant the list of all the licensed destructive device manufacturers in the country. After eliminating General Electric and other similar government contractors, there were only a handful of small independents. One of them from Texas had indeed made several bolt action single shot rifles for the 14.5mm Russian round, but neither he nor anyone else had made a single shot 20mm.

Now, on the morning before the mysterious Mr. Jones was due to contact the President, Alex Neumann was standing by one of the desks in the Washington office. Next to a picture cube holding photos of some agent's wife and children sat a fired 20mm projectile. It was the same shape as the M246 'firestarter' Smitty at the FBI forensic lab had given Neumann, including the aluminum nose cap. The projectile body, however, was not painted. Instead, it was bare steel that was covered with a patina of rust. The copper drive band just above the base of the bullet was engraved with rifling marks, but otherwise, the bullet looked like it had never been fired. It certainly showed no evidence of having struck anything.

"That's Polvecki's desk, sir. Shall I go find him?" another agent asked.

"Yes. Immediately." The agent hurried off, and in a few moments he returned with a very worried-looking man.

"Where did you get this?" Alex Neumann demanded, holding up the rusty 20mm projectile.

"One of the crew that came from the helicopter crash site gave it to me, sir. I think he got it from one of the divers."

"Get hold of your friend, and right now. I want to talk to that diver immediately. Get me as soon as you have him on the line. I'll be over with Smitty." *I hope I'm not clutching at straws here* Alex Neumann thought as he hurried off to deliver the projectile to the forensic people.

***

"Ah, sir, I think I know the one you're talking about, but I picked up a whole bunch of different bullets off the bottom of that pit. Just for souvenirs. I mean, they were all over, just lying there on the limestone floor. They weren't part of the helicopter crash, or anything. Somebody's been shooting into the water in that quarry pit for a hell of a long time, sir."

"Were there others like the one you gave Agent Polvecki?"

"I really don't know, sir. I was concentrating on finding helicopter parts, and I just scooped up a few bullets off the bottom and put them in my pocket while I was looking for pieces. I didn't see any harm in it."

"No, you did fine. It's just that this bullet you picked up may have some bearing on the case, we're not sure. I want you to take a team back there immediately, and this time I want your search to be specifically for bullets at the bottom of the pit. You're probably right about people plinking there, so don't waste your time on anything that looks like it came out of a normal pistol or rifle; I want only big stuff. Don't just confine your search to where the helicopter was found. Look all over. Then get everything you got up to Lambert Field in St. Louis and to an air cargo company with next-flight-out capability.

Don't spend all night picking up bullets. Give it an hour or two with a big team, so you get a lot done, then ship up what you've got. We have a deadline."

"Yessir," the man said, and Alex Neumann broke the connection.

"We may have more samples in another eight or ten hours, Smitty," Neumann said to the forensics specialist. The tall, balding technician tossed the bullet a few inches in the air and caught it.

"It's a Vulcan projectile all right," he said, scowling, "but it's a practice round, not H.E. or incendiary, like the ones that shot down the helicopters. This thing would just make a hole when it hit." He thought a moment and revised his statement. "I take that back. If it hit steel, or rock, you'd probably get a mild pyrotechnic effect, from the aluminum nose cap vaporizing into aluminum oxide under the impact. That's what the ordnance experts tell me, at least. But this one obviously didn't hit anything other than water. One other thing—this wasn't fired out of a Vulcan or a revolver cannon."

"What?"

"It came out of something else. Rifling marks aren't the same width as either of those two guns. Those guns have a gain twist. Whatever shot this had conventional rifling. Diameter of the drive band's not the same, either, but that might be just manufacturing tolerances. We really need more than one bullet to look at."

"I'm hoping that in about ten hours, you'll have others."

August 11

"Ah, sir, we're starting to sort the bullets that just came in from Missouri, but, there's an awful lot of them. Maybe you better come look." Alex Neumann closed his eyes and gripped the receiver more tightly.

"Did those goddamn divers pick up a bunch of rifle and pistol bullets?" Neumann demanded. "I told them nothing that would have come out of a pistol or hunting rifle."

"No, that's not the problem, sir," the man on the other end assured him. "Looks like it's almost all .50 caliber and up."

"Well, set aside all the .50s. We're interested in the bigger stuff. How many bullets did they ship us, anyway?"

"We got no idea of the count, sir," the agent told him truthfully. "But the weight's more than four tons."

***

"That might be him," the President said quickly when he heard Harrison Potter's cellular phone ring. Potter nodded and pressed a button on the instrument.

"Hello?" Potter listened, then nodded to the Chief Executive. "Ah, Mr. Jones, I think it's time you talked directly to the President. I'm giving the phone to him."

"So I finally get to talk to you, Mr. Jones," the President said. Neumann nodded, letting the President know their devices were tracking the call.

"I hope you understand my caution," Ray told him.

"I now wish I had...considered your points more carefully," the President confessed. Both men knew that the lawyer's negotiating position was stronger than ever. The government was in a virtual state of siege. Every time anyone opened the newspapers or turned on the news, another federal agent or antigun politician had been shot in the back while on his way to work, had his house firebombed, or been knifed to death on vacation.

"Before we work out the details, Mr. President," Ray Johnson said, "There is now an additional demand that is absolutely non-negotiable. My clients were pleased at the public reaction to Senator Katzenbaum's death. Apparently, many people in this country felt that he should have been tried for treason years ago. There is another person now in the private sector who must face similar judgment, with your unofficial sanction."

"I cannot use the office of the Presidency to carry out contract murder," the President said levelly. Ray Johnson gave a short bark of laughter.

"You do it all the time. You just don't want to do it to one of your own. And anyway, your people won't have to do a thing, just look the other way and not interfere, then let the verdict of suicide stand without picking at the details too closely. The White House has some experience in that area," he added.

"I won't allow the assassination of a former President of the United States," the President said firmly, mainly for the benefit of the recording devices.

This time Ray's reaction was genuine laughter. *I can tell he's considering it* Ray thought with amusement. "You won't have to do that," Ray assured the Chief Executive. "He has it bad enough, with what he's got to live with, and all. My clients will settle for smaller fish." Then he told the President what he wanted.

"I see. Well." He chewed his lip. "That shouldn't be a problem," he said finally. "And the Secret Service isn't involved in...in that instance."

"I know," Ray said. "Now that that's out of the way, let's get back to where we were

August 12

"Alex, we've figured out your mystery weapon," the forensic man said with a hint of triumph in his tired voice. It was 3:50 a.m., and he and his crew had been up for thirty-three hours. "Come here." He led Neumann to a table where there were several stereo microscopes. Another man stood nearby.

"This bullet," he said, handing Alex Neumann one of the projectiles recovered from Henry Bowman's quarry, "was made in 1939." Neumann scowled as he examined the solid steel projectile with the radius ogive that came to a sharp point.

"I don't understand."

"Tell him, George," the forensic chief instructed.

"That's out of a German 20x138B Armor Piercing round used during WWII," the ordnance tech explained. "Here's the loaded cartridge," he added, handing Neumann a complete round of ammunition. The 20x138B was substantially longer than the U.S. 20mm Vulcan shell he was used to looking at. "Several guns used it," the ordnance man continued, "probably the best-known was the FLAK 30, which was a full-auto antiaircraft cannon that was towed behind vehicles. That wasn't what fired this one, though.

"In addition to the Germans, the Finns also made weapons that fired this cartridge. There were other 20mm rounds in use during the late '30s, but the 20x138 had the largest capacity and the most power. A little more than our own current Vulcan round," he added.

"There were two man-portable weapons which fired this cartridge," the ordnance tech explained. "Two that I know of," he amended. "The first was the German Solothurn S18-1000, which was made in Switzerland because of the restrictions on Germany laid out in the Treaty of Versailles. It's a ten-shot semiautomatic rifle weighing about a hundred ten pounds, fired off either a bipod or a wheeled mount. The second gun is a Finnish Lahti Model 39, which is similar in size to the Solothurn, also a semiauto, and fires off of either a bipod or short skis.

"The barrels of the Solothurn and the Lahti have slightly different interior dimensions than our current weapons which fire the Vulcan round. The groove diameter is about eight thousandths smaller than the Vulcan, although the bore diameter is almost identical. The Lahti and Solothurn use conventional rifling, not gain twist, like more modern 20mms used around the world.

"These bullets," he said, pointing to two small piles of 1939 German projectiles to the right of his microscope, "came from Lahtis and Solothurns. The bullets in the left pile were fired out of Lahtis. The bullets in the right pile were shot out of Solothurns."

"How many different guns?"

"Who knows? Could be one of each, could be fifty. Both weapons are very high quality with almost no dimensional differences between examples. Throw in the fact that the bores wear as you shoot the guns more, one gun could give you a bunch of different samples over time. Plus the barrel could have been replaced. You know all that."

"Yeah. Sorry. I guess I was starting to believe TV for a minute." The technician laughed at Neumann's comment and walked over to a table with two much larger piles of projectiles on it.

"Now we get to the interesting part. These bullets here are U.S. practice rounds. They don't blow up, or anything, but they were made for the Vulcan. However, all of them were also fired out of Lahti and Solothurn barrels, just like the German rounds." He handed one to Alex Neumann. It was like the one he had found on Agent Polvecki's desk.

"Somebody chucked it up in a lathe and cut the copper drive band down eight thousandths, then loaded it in a 20x138 case."

"Could you do that with High Explosive or Incendiary bullets from the Vulcan?"

"Absolutely. I'd want to be damned careful with the spin-armed ones in a lathe, though."

"Why would someone go to all that trouble with the solid steel practice bullets?" Neumann asked, staring at the huge pile of fired projectiles.

"So he could shoot his guns. Original ammo from WWII is almost nonexistent, but our government sells brand-new Vulcan practice bullets for scrap. It's obvious that somebody likes to shoot," he said, waving his arm at the 400 pounds of bullets on the table.

"These aren't all the bullets that were down there, either," the head of Forensics interjected. "Not by a long shot. Divers only covered part of the quarry pit."

"You've done a hell of a job," Neumann said, obviously impressed. "Can you tell me more about these Lahti and Solothurn guns?" he asked the ordnance man.

"Sure. A bunch of them came into the States in the '50s and '60s, and got sold mail-order. The Lahtis were a hundred bucks, if I remember correctly. You had to register them with the IRS in '68, with a tax stamp, 'cause they got reclassified. Sixty-eight was a few years before ATF took over that stuff. Only a few people did, of course. Registered them, I mean."

"How is it you know so much about these two guns?" Neumann asked curiously. The ordnance man smiled.

"Had a Lahti when I was in high school. We had it in the rec room in our basement, on the skis. My little brother and sister would use it as a teeter-totter. Dad took the barrel off it when he saw that law was coming."

"Did you ever shoot it?"

"Oh yeah. I shot up all the ammo that came with it, and then Dad got one more crate, but it was pretty expensive. Seventy cents a round, I think it was. A lot of money back in '67."

"Could you have hit a flying helicopter with it?"

"You mean like one of the traffic copters flying around over the city? That'd be a real trick. Main problem would be elevating the gun enough. On the bipod or skis, you can only shoot five or ten degrees off of level."

"What about if the helicopter was setting up to land?"

"Then you could do it. Although you'd be better off with a good hunting rifle, I think. The Lahti was pretty accurate, but not like a good scoped bolt action; a 250-grain Silvertip out of a .338 Winchester would be how I'd take down a chopper. And the sights on the Lahti were pretty crude, as I remember. You could fix that, though. Dad was talking about mounting a scope on ours, but then that law came along."

"If you had to guess which weapon a man would use to shoot a helicopter out of the air at long range, which would it be, the Lahti or the Solothurn?" The ordnance tech looked pensive.

"The Solothurn has an integral optic sight—a scope—and that would be a great help, but like I said, you could put a scope on the Lahti, no problem. Anyone who shoots a Lahti this much," he said, indicating the piles of converted bullets, "would probably want a scope. The Solothurn is recoil-operated and the barrel slides back, whereas the Lahti is gas-operated and the barrel's fixed. The Lahti should be more accurate, but the reports I've heard, the Solothurn was pretty good, too.

"It could be either one," the ordnance man said finally, "unless the shooter had to get out of there in a hurry and didn't want to leave his gun. Then it would be the Solothurn, no question."

"Why's that?"

"The Solothurn has a quick-change barrel. You can take it off and break the gun down into two fifty-pound, four-foot-long pieces in fifteen seconds. The Lahti is an eight-foot-long, hundred-pound boat anchor."

"I guess I'll head over to the ATF office and see if I can check their registrations of Lahtis and Solothurns."

"Ah, sir? Are you sure you want to do that?" the ordnance man asked.

"What do you mean?"

"Well, ah...NFA records are tax records, sir. NFA isn't supposed to release them to other departments for non-tax reasons. Like if you just call up the IRS and want to know how much money a guy made last year 'cause you think it might help your investigation out—they won't do it. That's a felony. A woman prosecutor up in Detroit is in all kinds of trouble for just that reason, blabbing about a gun dealer's NFA records.

"But on top of that, sir, what would be the point? Hundreds of those guns came in the country, but only a few people papered them in '68. If you find a guy with a gun, maybe you can nail him if it's not papered, but why go to NFA now? To see if the guy who owns the quarry has a 20mm cannon? That seems pretty obvious, doesn't it?" he said, nodding towards the piles of projectiles. "To find out which gun he owns, and match a bullet to it? Like I said before, we can't do that, even if you had an intact slug from one of the choppers, which you don't."

"I see your point," Alex said softly. "Thank you for your work. You've done quite a job."

"No problem," the ordnance man said cheerfully. "Hey, and when you catch this guy, ask him why he didn't use a .338 or a .375 instead of a big clumsy 20mm. That'd be something to know."

***

"I'm not supposed to do this," the sleepy NFA branch Senior Examiner said as she unlocked the door and let Alex Neumann into the office on 650 Massachusetts Avenue. She had never been there at 7:00 a.m. before. "What you're about to learn didn't come from me."

"I keep my promises," Neumann said irritably as he watched her turn on her computer. *I'm only doing this so the President can't ask me why I neglected to* he reminded himself. A moment later the video screen lit up.

"Henry Bowman, Rural Route One, that the one you want?" the examiner said as the information scrolled across the monitor. "Whooo-eee, he's got a lot of stuff."

"We're looking for a Solothurn S18-1000."

"Got a serial number?"

"No."

"Then it'll take a little longer. You know if he's had this gun for a while?"

"Yes, I think so," Neumann said, thinking of the pile of bullets and how long it would take to shoot them all.

"Then I'll put the guns in the order they were registered," she said, tapping more keys. "Well. Got some Amnesty stuff." Five entries listed 1968 as the year that the NFA weapons had been registered to Henry Bowman.

"No Lahti, either," Neumann said after he had scanned the list. He and the examiner spent twenty minutes looking through each one of Henry Bowman's registrations, but there was no 20mm destructive device of any type listed. Henry had in fact registered his Lahti during the 1968 Amnesty, but ATF had inadvertently lost the record of this twelve years later, along with his Amnesty-registered Thompson. Henry's copy of each registration was currently sitting in one of his safes.

"It's not there," Alex Neumann said finally.

"Ah, sir," the woman said, "you got to realize that from 1934 up through about 1981, all this stuff was on one Rolodex, not a computer. Lot of these records been lost over the last fifty, sixty years. Our best guess is maybe a third of them are gone. This man could easily have the guns you're looking for. It's just not in our records."

"Well then, how would you know?"

"If there was ever a problem, he'd just show us his papers, and we'd put the gun into the computer."

"What if he's lost his papers, too?"

"It's not up to me what they do, then."

"Wouldn't the gun have shown up during a compliance inspection sometime since '68, and have been put on the computer system?"

"No, because if it was an amnesty registration, it wouldn't be part of his dealer inventory. It would be registered to him personally, like these others, on a Form 4."

"So he might have one, but you have no way of knowing, because the records might have been lost out of the Rolodex twenty years ago."

"Or somebody we let go deleted or changed a bunch of stuff in the computer. We get that all the time, when we got to fire someone." *Jesus* Neumann said to himself. *And I thought the Bureau was bad sometimes.*

"Thank you very much. You've been most helpful."

***

"With luck, it should all be over tonight," the President said gravely as he finished describing what he had planned for the State of the Union address that evening. The members of the task force sat silently, considering the implications of what the President had told them. Congressman Jon Bane of Ohio was the first to speak.

"Maybe Blair or whoever it is will stick to their end of the bargain and call off the dogs, but this thing is beyond that, now. I mean, it's not just guns anymore. EPA officials and people who work for the FAA are being killed, too, all across the country. And the legislators who supported them," he added forcefully. It was obvious that it was this last fact which Bane found by far the most disturbing.

"I talked to him about that, Jon. Mr. Jones said that while he had no direct control over the people involved in those killings, he believed that they would stop, along with the others, because of the terms I agreed to. I think he's right."

"Why wouldn't they just start up again?" Bane demanded. The President looked pained, and Harrison Potter chose to step in and answer the question.

"Congressman Bane, implicit in Mr. Jones' prediction was the assumption that the legislators in question use the recent events as a productive learning experience." Bane stared at the retired Chief Justice, then closed his mouth and sat back in his chair.

"The families of the murdered agents will want your head, Mr. President," Secretary of the Treasury Mills said softly. "Especially the ones where a suspect's in custody."

"I know that, Lawrence. It goes with the territory."

"Mr. President–"

"Alex," the President said, cutting off the FBI agent, "I've told you that the agreement has already been made, and I am not going to renege on it under any circumstances."

"I understand that, Mr. President, but isn't it true that it does not take effect until you address the country at nine o'clock tonight? That means Jones' clients are still going to be killing our people for thirteen more hours. If that's the case, sir, I don't want to be pulled off this detail until nine o'clock."

"But when nine o'clock comes, Alex, your efforts will have been pointless, regardless of what you accomplish."

"We don't know that for sure, Mr. President, but there is something we do know: Henry Bowman shot down those three helicopters that crashed on his property. He killed twelve of our men. Bowman did that, Mr. President. Not Wilson Blair, not Calron Jones, and not some phantom. Henry Bowman. ATF found him up in Idaho soon after the choppers went down and said he couldn't have been involved. I checked the logs, Mr. President, and the earliest that a reliable witness can place him in the mountains in Idaho is one full day after the three helicopters crashed. The bottom line is he had time to do it and get up there right after. When we have more time, we'll find out how.

"Bowman may have the 20mm cannon that did it, and we have every reason to believe he's been practicing with that gun since before 1968. Our divers recovered over a thousand 20mm projectiles from the bottom of his rock quarry, and there were a lot more they didn't bring back. I talked to Ken Hackathorn this morning, and he has seen Henry Bowman shoot military parachute flares out of the sky with his BAR at a shoot in Kentucky. Helicopters would have been easy for this man. Other people may have had motive, but no one but Bowman also had the means, the ability, and the opportunity.

"Will he keep his mouth shut and refuse to talk until it's too late for us? Maybe, but maybe not. Maybe he's dying to confess, Mr. President, but we'll never know unless I get a chance to pull him in. Give me until 9:00 to do that, sir."

"'Dying to confess', Agent Neumann?" the President asked pointedly. "Were you planning on taking Hap Edwards with you?"

"N-No," Neumann said, surprised by the question.

"Good. Don't," the President told him. "So how do you propose to find him?" the Chief executive asked, switching gears.

"Half an hour ago he was answering his phone at his home in southern Missouri. If I get on one of our jets, I could be on his doorstep in four hours, tops. That would give me nine hours before your speech, Mr. President. A person can accomplish a lot in nine hours," he added, unwittingly mimicking what Ray Johnson had said to Harrison Potter. Before the President could reply, Irwin Mann spoke up.

"Mr. President, we do not know the extent to which these people may have...infiltrated parts of the government. Word may get out that Agent Neumann is taking an FBI aircraft to Missouri, even with strict internal measures. In Warsaw, it was a problem we...confronted constantly, Mr. President, and I think Agent Neumann faces it now."

"Alex?" the President asked.

"I doubt we have that problem," Neumann said quickly. "But it is possible. Mr. Mann, what alternative do you suggest? Commercial airlines?" he asked sarcastically.

"Not at all. If I may make a phone call, it is possible that the Holocaust Center's aircraft is available. It flies just as swiftly as the commercial airliners, but can land at the airport closest to where Agent Neumann wishes to go, instead of in St. Louis. If it is not currently away from the city, I might be able to arrange for it to be ready by the time Agent Neumann got to the airport."

"I'm not sure that would be appropriate use of the Center's jet, Mr. Mann."

"But it would, Mr. President," Irwin Mann said with an enthusiasm he did not feel. "Else why was I asked to be on this council? To date I have been of no help at all, but now there is something I can do. Agent Neumann is not some fat Chief of Staff who wishes to go to a stamp collecting auction; he is searching for the person who may be indirectly responsible for the deaths of three Jewish legislators. In any event, none of that will be known. The purpose of the trip will be to take me to Missouri, which is my home. If you are still worried about the appearance of...impropriety, put your mind at ease. No government monies are involved. The airplane is privately owned, and its use has been donated. The Center has many friends, as you know."

"Well...all right."

"I must check. Please excuse me." Irwin Mann rose from his chair and left the room. As he walked out the door, he had the powerful urge to go sit in the men's room for five minutes and return with the report that the airplane was out of the area and unavailable. Irwin had grave misgivings about taking Alex Neumann directly to Henry Bowman, particularly now that he knew the content of the President's upcoming speech. Irwin Mann had made a promise, however, and so he went to place his telephone call.

The President stared into Alex Neumann's eyes. Each man knew the other had a singular agenda. The President's priorities included the health of the nation as a whole, but also his own political future. For Neumann, other more personal issues had come to carry the greatest weight. From his days at Ruby Ridge to the current investigation, Alex Neumann had seen firsthand the governmental outrages which had fueled the movement he had been so powerless to stop.

When Trey Mullins had been killed, however, Neumann's empathy for those who had reached their emotional limit had mutated into something less stable and much more dangerous. His professionalism had kept this force in check, but now it threatened to explode. The President recognized this, and wanted to prevent it, but the Chief Executive's main concern was to make sure he was nowhere around when it happened.

"The airplane will be ready before we get to the airport," Irwin Mann announced as he reentered the meeting room. "I have business in Missouri myself, which I will attend to after Agent Neumann's needs have been addressed." Irwin Mann and Alex Neumann both looked at the President for confirmation.

"If the Center has no objections, then all right. You have until nine o'clock, Alex," the President said carefully.

"The pilot requests that I tell him exactly where you wish to go," Irwin Mann said to the FBI agent, "so that he may file a flight plan for the closest airport. I had another thought, Mr. President, while I was phoning to see if the airplane was available. Former Director Greenwell has no official status, but if Agent Neumann's theory proves to be accurate, perhaps he will be redeemed from some of the issues which prompted his resignation. Should he not be included in this...confrontation?"

The President opened his mouth and was about to say that Dwight Greenwell did not belong on any official government endeavor. Then the logic of Irwin Mann's suggestion struck him full force, and he smiled. If Alex Neumann planned to go to Missouri so that he could shoot this Henry Bowman character before the clock ran out, Greenwell's presence would be a deterrent. If things went wrong anyway, Greenwell could also serve as a scapegoat.

"I think that is an excellent idea, Mr. Mann. Lawrence, perhaps you could have one of your people get word to Dwight Greenwell and see if he would be interested in accompanying Alex to Missouri." Alex Neumann opened his mouth to protest, but thought the better of it and turned to Irwin Mann.

"How soon can we go?"

"We can leave now, if you are ready. Do you need to make any calls first? There is a telephone on the airplane."

"That will be fine. Shall we?" Neumann asked as he stood up. It was obvious that he hoped Dwight Greenwell might not make it in time if he and Irwin Mann hurried.

***

"My fellow Americans, the events of the past months have been tearing our country apart. I am not going to mince words. America has fallen into a civil war. There is no other term which more accurately defines the misery in which we have become mired. Citizens are engaged in the systematic assassination of elected officials and the murder of federal agents. Every day, more people in our government are killed. Almost six hundred have died in a space of less than one month, and with each new death, our country moves closer to a violent revolution from which there may be no retreat.

"A close friend of mine keeps a framed quote on his wall. It says 'Those who refuse to remember history are destined to repeat it.' As terrible as our current situation is, we must not forget our history, for history has shown us that here in America, things have been much worse. More than a century ago, the United States was wracked by a civil war that claimed the lives of six hundred thousand Americans, at a time when our citizens numbered less than thirty million. If the civil war we face today continues and claims the lives of the same fraction of our population as a whole, we will suffer five million dead.

"That is what happened once. It must not happen again. We must remember our history, not repeat it. The Civil War that began in 1861 was initiated by people who were willing to fight to preserve their culture. Slavery was a fundamental tenet of that culture, and the nation as a whole could not countenance the preservation of slavery in a country founded on the principle of freedom. One out of every ten of our country's adult males died in the Civil War, and even more were wounded. That was what it cost America to reconcile this issue of freedom.

"The conflict we face today is once again based on culture, and once again, the central issue is freedom. This time, however, it is the so-called rebels who are championing freedom, and the government that is chilling the people's rights. When the United States government suspects a citizen has failed to pay a five dollar federal tax and then spends more manpower and more money spying on that citizen than it spent on surveillance before the invasion of Haiti, there is something wrong. When government tax agents carry guns and wear black ski masks to hide their faces, the evil has become institutionalized. And when those government agents shoot nursing mothers and burn women and children alive over $200 tax matters, then you have a government that is out of control.

"In 1995, we took a belated look at what our government had become, but what we saw was too painful to acknowledge. We fell into arguing partisan politics instead of facing up to the fact that our government is out of control. We must now face the truth and stare it in the eye: America was on the brink of descending into the horror of totalitarian government. Many saw this, but one man acted. When he did, thousands of others followed. America owes Wilson Blair a debt of gratitude for forcing this issue of freedom into the open when he did. The cost in lives has been a tragedy for every person who lost a loved one, but it is tiny compared to what it could have become. Freedom is never without its price, and history has shown us that those who are unwilling to pay that price ultimately lose everything. We must never forget the man who, like our Founding Fathers, was willing to risk his life for freedom, and who first gave the call to arms. Even more importantly, we must never forget the countless others who rallied behind that call. These men and women stood foursquare behind our Constitution, even when those in power were bound to ignore it. It is our country's great fortune that these men and women are still standing firm.

"When General Lee surrendered in April of 1865 at Appomattox Court House, the Civil War ended. Freedom had triumphed over slavery. With that triumph, the states of the former Confederacy were welcomed back into the Union. General Lee climbed onto his horse, Traveler, and rode home. And when Lee rode home, he did so as a free man. Lincoln's soldiers did not disarm him first. Lee went back to Richmond with both his saber and his pistol on his belt.

"The same was true of every soldier who had fought for the Confederacy. These men had killed Union soldiers in their fight to preserve a slave-owning culture. Yet after they surrendered, Lincoln did not disarm these men and prohibit them from owning guns. Lincoln welcomed them back as full citizens of the United States of America, with the same rights as the victors. He granted these men an amnesty for everything that had happened before Lee's surrender.

"If Abraham Lincoln did that for Americans who fought the federal government to preserve a culture of slavery, I can do no less for Americans who have been fighting the federal government to preserve a culture of freedom.

"I have spoken at length with the people who have been leading this fight, and together we have negotiated an agreement to end the hostilities. Wilson Blair has agreed to join with me and call for an end to the war he and thousands of others have been waging in the fight for freedom. Effective immediately, I am granting an amnesty. The amnesty applies to all crimes committed against federal employees and elected officials at every level of government from July tenth of this year to the present moment. All suspects now in custody for any crime committed against any government employee or elected official during this time period will be released, all charges dropped, and all such investigations closed. Furthermore, I am issuing a Presidential pardon to all individuals involved.

"I am also granting a Presidential pardon to all persons currently serving time for or who have been convicted of violations of the National Firearms Act of 1934, the Gun Control Act of 1968, the McClure-Volkmer Act of 1986, the firearms and magazine provisions of the Crime Law of 1994, and all other federal, state, and local anti-gun laws, including any and all anti-concealed carry laws. I will continue to issue pardons for any future convictions under these statutes until such statutes are repealed by the federal, state, and local legislatures.

"The issue has been resolved. Now the fighting must end. In 1865, both Union and Confederate soldiers who ignored the termination of hostilities and continued to fight after the war was over were committing murder. From this moment on, any further attacks on elected officials or government employees will once again be treated as murder or attempted murder. I say again: the fighting is over, and freedom has been restored. Good night and God bless you." The President put down his papers.

"Well, Harry, that's what I agreed to, with my own spin put on it. What do you think?" Harrison Potter had a tiny, lopsided smile on his face. He glanced at his watch.

"Seven minutes, fifteen seconds, more or less," he reported. "That's a good length."

"I know the length is all right, Harry. What about the content?"

"I thought it was inspired, Mr. President." The younger man brightened visibly.

"What about saying we owe Blair our gratitude? You don't think I'm digging my own grave with that?" the President asked.

"Is it true? That's the real question, isn't it, Mr. President?" Potter asked. "Will the country really be better off now, or not? If it's true, then history will look favorably on your words, regardless of what the newspapers say tomorrow morning. Reagan took a lot of heat for calling the Soviet Union an 'Evil Empire', but he was telling the truth: Socialism was evil. History rewarded his candor, Mr. President. Freedom won out." Potter ran his hand through his thinning white hair, then continued.

"Is what you've agreed to do a good thing, or would America be better off if it were disarmed? Would we thrive with more police power, more 'clipper chips', more prohibitions on cash, more incarceration without bond, more regulations, and more severe penalties for noncompliance? Only time will tell, Mr. President.

"But if you believe, as I do, that where we will be tomorrow is a great improvement over where we were three months ago, then you must acknowledge the debt we owe to Blair and Jones and the thousands of others who followed their lead. You must."

The President nodded in agreement. Later, he would reflect on the fact that it was the first time in their long friendship that Harrison Potter had ever told him he had to do something.

***

"Are your guests all right back there?" the pilot asked, briefly touching the yarmulke on his head. "I believe there are sodas in the cabinet, if they wish for some refreshment."

"They're fine," Irwin Mann assured him. The old man was crouched down in the space behind the pilot's seat and empty copilot's seat. He looked very nervous. "Ah...can you change your flight plan while we are in the air? Tell...the controllers that you wish to land somewhere else? Is that a problem?" The pilot laughed at the question.

"No problem at all. Pilots do it all the time."

"I, uh, guess I'll go back to my seat now," Irwin Mann said.

"If you're anxious about flying, these may help," the pilot said, pulling a pair of earplugs from his breast pocket. "Keep your seatbelt on also."

"Thank you," Mann said as he took the plugs and pressed them in his ears. Then he stepped back and slid into the forwardmost port-side seat on the eight-passenger aircraft.

The pilot checked his instruments and made sure the engine temperatures and power settings were what he wanted The twin-engined jet was flying at Flight Level 35 on a bearing of 262 degrees. They were 90 nautical miles west of Philadelphia, and the ride was glass smooth. When he was convinced that everything was as it should be, the pilot checked his trim settings, engaged the autopilot, and slid two of the yellow foam plugs into his own ears. Then he unfastened his lap belt and swung his legs over the side of the seat.

As the man slid out of the pilot's seat and half-stood in the cramped aisle behind the cockpit, he drew a 5"-barreled Smith & Wesson .44 Magnum from an inside-the-pants sharkskin holster worn over his right kidney. The gun had been made in 1959, one of a special order of two hundred 5"-barreled guns made for the H.H. Harris Hardware Company of Chicago.

Dwight Greenwell and Alex Neumann both looked up at the same time.

"Oh, my G–"

"You'll crash th–"

Both men's words were cut off by a blinding flash and a deafening muzzle blast as the gun fired. An entire case full of Hercules Bullseye pistol powder roared out the muzzle, creating a large fireball which vanished as quickly as it had appeared. Pushed ahead of the burning powder was a .429" diameter projectile which had been lathe-turned from half-inch nylon bar stock. The cylindrical plastic bullet struck Dwight Greenwell between the eyes at a velocity of over 3000 feet per second and disintegrated as it homogenized the former ATF Director's brain. Both eyeballs blew out of their sockets as the corpse collapsed in the seat.

"Don't even think about drawing on me, Agent Neumann. Just keep your hands where I can see them." Neumann sat there, absolutely stunned. His ears were ringing and his eyes were watering. Greenwell was obviously dead, and now Neumann was looking down the muzzle of the largest revolver he had ever seen in his life. The gun was steady in the pilot's two-handed grip.

A hundred different thoughts ran through Alex Neumann's brain as he stared at the man in front of him. He noticed the cheeks were different from the one picture he'd seen earlier. *Pads up under his gums* Neumann realized as his guts churned over. *And maybe a bit of nose putty. Dark makeup, too.* Then, because the issue had been discussed recently, Alex Neumann blurted out a query. It was something which, but for his agitated state, he would have considered unimportant.

"Why'd you use a 20mm instead of a regular rifle?" Neumann asked. The pilot raised one eyebrow and gave a tight smile.

"It was the last gun my dad gave me before he died. That a good enough reason?"

What if the last gun he'd given you had been a Beretta .25 auto Neumann thought giddily as he fought the hysteria that was building inside him.

"You...you were home when I called, not fifteen minutes before we got on the plane." The FBI man was forcing himself to remain rational.

"Amazing invention, call forwarding," Henry Bowman said. "Any other questions?"

***

"I still haven't heard from him," the President said, looking at his watch.

"Don't worry about things you can't control," his wife said soothingly. "Here. Sit down and I'll rub your neck. It's only 8:30. Let's get some of this tension out of you before you give your speech."

"Oh yes. This is just what I need," the President said as he closed his eyes. His wife's slender build belied a very strong set of forearm and wrist muscles that had come from her lifelong passion for gardening. He relaxed and gave himself up to her strong fingers digging into his trapezius muscles.

After ten minutes of concentrated effort, the First Lady told her husband that his neck and shoulders were as relaxed as they were going to get.

"Thanks, hon," the President said as he ran his fingers through his wife's long black hair. Then he scowled.

"Still worried about Alex Neumann?" she asked.

"No, I–" he started to say, then stopped. "Well, yes, of course I still wonder where he is," the President corrected himself, "but that's not what I was thinking of just now. Jews don't eat pork, at least Orthodox Jews don't, but do they *raise* it?"

"What on earth are you talking about?"

"It was something Irwin Mann said this morning. I had a lot on my mind and it didn't register. Now it doesn't make any sense. I'm sure I heard him correctly, though; his accent's not that heavy. It was when I asked him if he really did have business to attend to in Missouri."

"What did he say?"

"He said yes. He said he had to go feed his hogs."

About the Author

John Ross is an investment broker and financial adviser in St. Louis, Missouri. He has degrees in English and Economics from Amherst College in Amherst, Massachusetts. Mr. Ross is a certified personal protection instructor, and the author of *Self-Defense Laws and Violent Crime Rates in the United States*, which was the first published work to empirically assess the effect of concealed-carry laws on violent crime in America. He has also authored several firearms-related technical works for *Precision Shooting* magazine and *Machine Gun News*. Since the age of eight, Mr. Ross has been an avid participant in many aspects of the shooting sports. He fires upwards of 20,000 rounds of ammunition per year and is, by his own admission, a member of the gun culture.

Unintended Consequences is his first novel.